American Civilian Counter-terrorist Manual

~ a fictional autobiography of Ronald Reagan

by alan allen of san francisco

(Unabridged Edition)

<> <> <>

Casa de Corazon, & The Press of San Francisco are programs of AI Forum, a Calif. 501(c)3 nonprofit corp.

Order this book online at www.trafford.com or email orders@trafford.com

Most Trafford titles are also available at major online book retailers.

Our mission is to efficiently provide the world's finest, most comprehensive book publishing service, enabling every author to experience success. To find out how to publish your book, your way, and have it available worldwide, visit us online at www.trafford.com

www.trafford.com

North America & international
toll-free: 1 888 232 4444 (USA & Canada)
phone: 250 383 6864 ♦ fax: 812 355 4082

Into My Own
by Robert Frost

One of my wishes is that those dark trees,
So old and firm they scarcely show the breeze,
Were not, as 'twere, the merest mask of gloom,
But stretched away unto the edge of doom.

I should not be withheld but that some day
Into their vastness I should steal away,
Fearless of ever finding open land,
Or highway where the slow wheel pours the sand.

I do not see why I should e'er turn back,
Or those should not set forth upon my track
To overtake me, who should miss me here
And long to know if still I held them dear.

They would not find me changed from him they knew --
Only more sure of all I thought was true.

The money-issuing power should be taken from the central bank, restored to the people, to whom it properly belongs. ~ President Thomas Jefferson

The Greatest Crime of Congress

"Capital must protect itself in every possible manner by combination and legislation. Debts must be collected, bonds and mortgages must be foreclosed as rapidly as possible. When, through a process of law, the common people lose their homes they will become more docile and more easily governed through the influence of the strong arm of government, applied by a central power of wealth under control of leading financiers. This truth is well known among our principal men now engaged in forming an imperialism of Capital to govern the world. By dividing voters through the political party system, we get them to expend energies fighting over questions of no importance. Thus, by discreet action we can secure for ourselves what has been so well planned and successfully accomplished [private founding of the Fed by *City of London*]." ~Aug. 25, 1924 *USA Banker's Magazine*

"For 150 years, history of House of Rothschild was backstage history of Western Europe …Because of their success in making loans not to individuals, but to nations, they reaped huge profits. The wealth of Rothschild consists of the bankruptcy of nations." ~Frederick Morton's, *Rothschilds*

"That House of Rothschild made its money in the great crashes of history …and great wars of history … the very periods when others lost their money, is beyond question." ~E.C. Knuth's, *Empire of the City (See chart of 'City of London', private owners of the Fed, p.590)*

"This Act establishes the most gigantic trust on Earth. When the President signs this bill, the invisible government by the 'Monetary Power', will be legalized. The people may not know it immediately, but the day of reckoning is only a few years removed. The trusts will soon realize they have gone too far for their own good. The people must make a declaration of independence [again]. …Wall Streeters could not cheat us if we had a people's Congress. … *(continued on opposite page)*

(continued from previous page)

The greatest crime of Congress is [this] currency system. The caucus and party boss-es have prevented the people from getting the benefit of their own government." ~ Dec. 23, 1913, Congressman Lindbergh addresses the House on the eve of the passage of the bill founding the privately owned Federal Reserve Bank.

"With the setting up of the twelve 'financial districts' through the Federal Reserve Banks, the traditional division of the United States into the forty-eight [now, fifty] States was over-thrown ... and we entered the era of 'regionalism', or, twelve regions which had no relation to the traditional State boundaries. These developments following the passing of the Federal Reserve Act proved every one of the allegations Thomas Jefferson had made against a [pri-vately owned] central bank, in 1791. ...That the subscribers to the Federal Reserve Bank stock had formed a corporation, whose stock could be and was held by aliens ... that this stock would be transmitted to a certain line of successors ... that it would be placed beyond forfeiture and escheat ... that they would receive a monopoly of banking, which was against the laws of monopoly ... and that they now had the power to make laws, paramount to the laws of the States. ...The [privately owned banking monopoly called the] Fed issues laws as to what the interest rate shall be, what the quantity of money shall be and what the price of money shall be. " ~ Eustace Mullins, *Secrets of the Federal Reserve*

The money-issuing power should be taken from the central bank, and restored to the peo-ple of the United States, to whom it properly belongs. ~Thomas Jefferson

The American War of Independence was fought against the privately-owned Bank of England (City of London), because the founding fathers felt it was against the will of God that any group of private bankers should be allowed to own, print (issue), and rent or lend to the people, the money supply of a country and set the interest rates. That there should be no privately owned central bank charging interest, and that a publicly-owned central bank charges no interest -- thereby enacting a redistribution of wealth and an abolition of financial slavery to establish financial freedom.

"If this mischievous financial policy which has its origin in North America during the late [American Revolutionary and American Civil] war in that country, shall become endurated down to a fixture, then that Government will furnish its own money without cost. It will pay off debts and be without debt. It will have all the money necessary to carry on its commerce. It will become prosperous without precedent in the history of the world. The brains, and wealth of all countries will go to North America. That country must be destroyed or it will destroy every [City of London] monarchy on the globe." ~The *Hazard Circular* inserted into *London Times*, 1865, referring to President Lincoln printing publicly-owned money (Greenbacks).

Prolog

Ronnie Reagan & the Evil Empire

Campaign had ominous
signs of American fascism

Dec. 12 1988, *San Francisco Chronicle* printed a James Michner column, *Campaign Had Ominous Signs of American Fascism.*

"This year's election scared me. It was conducted with a brutality and lack of attention to basic issues which appalled. The success of its ugly strategies flashed signals that this was the kind of electioneering we should expect during the next three national campaigns of this century.

"What frightened me? The tactics that proved so effective were those which Josef Goebbels found useful in destroying the German Republic in the 1930s. First, the 'big lie', the endless repetition until it becomes accepted proof, and the desire to destroy the opposition rather than refute its arguments.

"Second. Appropriating the emotional symbols of nationhood such as the flag, the pledge of allegiance, prayer in schools, exaltation of the family, opposition to abortion, and a macho boast that all citizens have the right to carry firearms and use them at will.

"Third. Denouncing anyone who did not pass those self-imposed 'litmus tests' as 'outside the mainstream, unpatriotic', perhaps even 'treasonous'.

"Fourth. The callous use of race, in the case of Willie Horton, to inflame prejudices and divide the population. Michael Dukakis was not defeated, he was destroyed. And that kind of victory does not serve the republic well. If persisted in, it could lead to American-style Fascism. I am a liberal Democrat who unsuccessfully ran for Congress in 1962, one of the best things I've ever done, because it taught me facts about American political life.

"As a member of the board of directors of Radio Liberty, and Radio Free Europe, which strive to portray an honest portrait of our nation abroad, I am an anti-Communist warrior. However, the Bush men did corrupt the political system. And, in a time of quiet and growing crises, they prevented any reasonable debate on the great issues facing this nation. As a consequence, we have postponed rather than solved our problems, and when the due bills are presented, the results may be devastating.

"What are these problems? Consider, the enormous burden of debt whose management tempts us into so many false steps.

"The imbalance of our trade with foreign nations so that we became a consuming nation rather than a producing one.

"The abandonment of one major area of production after another to other nations better organized, trained and disciplined than our own. I refer to steel, automobiles, communications systems, shipping, clothing, shoes and even minor items like the printing of books.

"The constant selling-off of our capital goods to foreigners at bargain-basement prices.

"The debasement of our public schools so we send half-educated young people to compete against fully-educated Japanese, Germans and Koreans.

"The determined swing of our judiciary to the hard-Right, so that the natural changes that all societies need to survive, will probably be inhibited as civil liberties are lost.

"We divert so much of our wealth to the servicing of our trillion-dollar debt, that most of the taxes I pay go to service debt. We are making bankers richer, and workers poorer. And I expect this imbalance to worsen.

"But it is the prospect of seeing four or five ultra-Right-wing justices on the Supreme Court that really scares me. For then, the subtle balances that have prevailed in our civic life may be destroyed," James Michner said.

Nov. 5 1988, former *New York Times* editorial page editor John B Doke's article appears in the *Times*.

"What is really frightening about Mr. Bush's below-the-belt campaign is its apparent acceptance by a sizable proportion of the voting public. Softened up by eight years of Reagan-Bush dissimulation on everything from supplying arms to the Contras, to arms deals for the hostages, from 'Starwars' to the 'War on Drugs', from human rights to international law, too many bemused voters seem ready to believe anything.

"Yet, because of President Reagan's domination of the media he has gotten away with it. The much nastier, but equally skillful public relations campaign of candidate Bush is the beneficiary.

"The sneering attacks by President Reagan and Vice-President Bush on liberalism, the philosophy that is the basis of American democracy, set the evil tone of this campaign. It panders to the smoldering instincts of the mob, ready to explode when the next economic crisis bursts upon us.

"When that time comes, the way will have been paved for a demand for 'strong leadership.' It is a dangerous game. The innate strength of

American democracy has, up to now, resisted it even in times of crisis. Will it be able to do so next time? Though much of the electorate doesn't want to believe it, next time cannot be too far off.

"Look at reality, trillion dollars debt, multi-billion dollar deficit, gigantic trade imbalance, lack of competitiveness and inventiveness of industry, heedless depletion of natural resources, criminal down-grading of education, inadequate social services, growing poverty, shaky banking system, squeezed middle class, increasing disparity between rich and poor, the American economy is running on empty.

"When the crisis comes, whether the predictable economic crisis or an unpredictable foreign crisis, more will depend on the character than on the charisma of the President. For the past decade, we have had a surfeit of charisma."

<>

Sept. 18 1992 *San Francisco Examiner* printed an article by Clifford E. Anderson.

"A registered Republican for nearly 25 years, I was a member of the Young Republicans in college. Both my parents were Republicans, as were their parents. Because of the current direction of the Republican Party, however, with frustration and disappointment I have decided to change my affiliation.

"This is not a decision taken lightly. Though I have not always agreed with the decisions taken by our president, and personally find him to be untrustworthy and opportunistic, the traditional values of financial responsibility, personal conservatism and individual authority for which the party stood had, until recently, remained firm and unshakable. This is no longer the case.

"The Republican Party has aligned with elements of Right-wing and religious extremists. This has fractured the party, destroyed its credibility and placed in jeopardy the very basis of our personal rights as Americans. I do not know the reasons why the party has elected to proceed in this direction, or to what extent President Bush is personally responsible. The situation, however, is no longer merely unacceptable; it is frightening.

"The right to personal religious understanding is inalienable under the Constitution. Forcing the beliefs of others upon us is contrary to the basis of a free society and lays the groundwork for totalitarianism. It appears that those in control of the party wish to reform society towards a neo-Medievalism where all but the most strict interpretations of personal behavior are criminalized or condemned, where all individual authority is suspended, and where personal liberty is subject to the interpretation of a select few. This is no longer conservatism, it is fascism.

"In new republican rhetoric, the term 'family values' is a euphemism for right-wing religious fanaticism …'School support' is a conscious and premeditated attempt to destroy our public school system in favor of privately controlled parochial schools …'Feminists' are witches, children killers …'Pro-choice' (the only choice for many in a society that espouses family values but provides no means to support them) is a criminal act potentially punishable by the death penalty.

"If this were not enough, Republican political campaign tactics have again taken on the frightening specter of psychological manipulation, misrepresentation, distortion and lies typical of a world view of racists, religious zealots and extremists. So far to the Right are these people that they stand shoulder-to-shoulder with White supremacists and Nazis," Anderson said.

A Full-Court Press, the Destabilization of the Soviet Union & Eastern Europe

Lou Wolf's *Covert Action Information Bulletin*, fall 1990, Sean Gervasi's *A Full-Court Press, the Destabilization of the Soviet Union.*

"During early months of the first Reagan Administration, it became clear the U.S. was embarking on a policy of confrontation with the Soviet Union. Political observers began talking about a new Cold War. By 1982, relations with the Soviet Union were becoming tense, as were relations with some NATO allies. In the U.S. and in Europe, the belligerent warlike temperament of the Reagan Administration gave rise to a growing fear of nuclear conflict … yet if the U.S. seemed intent upon confrontation, even upon playing 'nuclear chicken' with the Soviet Union …it was not at all clear what it expected to achieve by doing so.

"The Reagan-Bush Administration policies were clear, but the objectives of those policies were not … many observers began to fear, especially in Europe, that some members of the U.S. Administration might actually want a nuclear war …believing somehow that the U.S. would prevail. (continued on page 458)

"If we lose freedom here, there is no place to escape to. This is the last stand on Earth." ~ President Ronald Reagan

"Education that fails to nurture memory of the past denies students satisfaction of mature thought, attachment to abiding concerns, and perspective on human existence." ~ Lynn Cheney

Asked to name a suspect, an architect behind the 9/11 WTC attacks, "If I had to narrow it down to one person ... I think my prime suspect ...would be, Dick Cheney.
~ Bob Bowman, Dem. Can. FL Dist. 15

The money-issuing power should be taken from the banks, restored to the people, to whom it properly belongs."
~ President Thomas Jefferson, 1801-1809

"Those who forget the past are condemned to repeat it."
~ George Santayana

"There is a Providence that protects idiots, drunkards, children and the United States of America." ~ Otto von Bismarck

<> <> <>

social engineering today -- central bank myths to die for

"The United States consumes about 71 quads of energy per year. (A quad is one quadrillion British thermal units or 1015.) There is available today in the United States, excluding solar sources & excluding gas & oil imports, about 150,000 quads of energy. Put another way, this statistic means we have sufficient known usable energy resources to last us for over two thousand years." ~ Antony Sutton
http://www.bibliotecapleyades.net/sociopolitica/esp_sociopol_trilat07.htm#CONTENTS%201
~ (at website, see chapter 5)

One of the world's foremost meteorologists called the theory that helped Al Gore share the Nobel Peace Prize 'ridiculous' & the product of 'people who don't understand how the atmosphere works'. A natural cycle of ocean water temperatures -- related to the amount of salt in ocean water -- is responsible for global warming. That same cycle means a period of cooling will begin soon & last for several years. "We'll look back on all of this in 10 or 15 years & realize how foolish it was," Dr Gray said. "We're brainwashing our kids. The human impact on the atmosphere is simply too small to have a major effect on global temperatures," Dr Gray said.
http://www.smh.com.au/news/environment/gore-gets-a-cold-shoulder/2007/10/13/1191696238792.html

Editor's note: is the Fed a Federal central bank? ... or, are Fed stock-shares privately owned? ...& are its profits of 300 billion dollars a year paid by U.S. taxpayers to private people? ...who? ...& our taxpayer debt of 10 trillion dollars privately held, too? Of course, if it was, this would imply our congresspersons are lying to us for their own personal gain, wouldn't it? ... after all, they acted unconstitutionally in 1913 for campaign contributions. Why does it matter, anyway? ... well, for one thing, we wouldn't owe anyone 10 trillion dollars ...& for another, there'd be no interest on loans, mortgages, credit cards, debts. Get it? For U.S. Congressional Fed private ownership/interlocking directorate charts (see pgs 587-591).

Foreword

Wading thru America's lost history

Knee-deep in central bank-sponsored racism, religious bigotry, genocide, war, revolution, counter-revolution (civil war), coup d'etats, death squads, regional & global terrorism

"Money has no motherland, financiers are without patriotism, and without decency. Their sole object, is gain." ~ **Napoleon Bonaparte**

"We began planning the Revolutionary War in order to issue our own money again ...and keep King George III and Bank of England from enslaving us with debt, and making Americans their financial slaves. By the time the revolutionary war started, Apr. 19 1775, British taxation had sucked the gold and silver out of the American colonies, to Britain. So, we had to print money to finance the war." ~ **Benjamin Franklin**

"The privilege of creating and issuing money is the supreme prerogative of Government, the Government's greatest creative opportunity. By adoption of these principles, taxpayers are saved immense sums of interest." ~ **Abraham Lincoln**

If this mischievous financial policy which has its origin in North America during the late war in that country, shall become endurated down to a fixture, then that Government will furnish its own money without cost. It will pay off debts and be without debt. It will have all the money necessary to carry on its commerce. It will become prosperous without precedent in the history of the world. The brains, and wealth of all countries will go to North America. That country must be destroyed or it will destroy every monarchy on the globe." ~ ***Hazard Circular***, inserted in 1865 *London Times*, spoke of Lincoln's 'Greenbacks'.

<>

Texas defeats Santa Anna in 1856. England and France are distant. Russia's unstable. Central bankers apply destabilization tactics, promote insurgency and civil war in the U.S.

States that secede unite in Confederate States of America ...which means, each maintained independence ...if the South won, each State would be an independent country with its own central bank.

The North was targeted to become a British Colony, again ...by annexation to Canada, whose financing was controlled by Lionel Rothschild.

The South was targeted for Napoleon III of France, with French financing, controlled by James Rothschild ...financing through August Belmont and Jay Cooke selling Union bond issues with J. & W. Seligman & Co., and Speyer & Co. in Europe. Judah Benjamin of Louisiana law firm Slidell, Benjamin & Conrad, is a Rothschild agent, becomes Sec. of State for the Confederacy. Slidell borrows from D'Erlanger for the Confederacy.

"The people will be arrayed on one side, and the bankers on the other ...in a contest, such as we have never seen before in America," Treasury Secretary Chase said. Abraham Lincoln wasn't too happy about it, either. "The money power preys on the nation in times of peace ...it conspires against the nation in times of adversity ...it is more despotic than monarchy ...more insolent than autocracy ...more selfish than bureaucracy.

"I see in the near future, a crisis approaching. That unnerves me, and causes me to tremble for the safety of my country. Corporations have been enthroned ...an era of corruption in high places will follow ...and, the money power of the country will endeavor to prolong its reign, by working upon the prejudices of the people until the wealth is aggregated in the hands of a few ...and the Republic is destroyed," Abraham Lincoln said. "I feel at the moment more anxiety for the safety of my country, than ever before, even in the midst of war."

With Lincoln's death, the entire United States money supply would be created out of debt ...by private bankers ...buying U.S. Government bonds to back the printing of bank notes ...and, that's when it became impossible to understand the economic vocabulary of the monetary system ...because it no longer made sense ...because money was debt ...a negative value ...not a positive value ...total nonsense.

For example, John Kenneth Galbrath spoke during my Administration. "In numerous years following the war, the Federal Government ran a heavy surplus. It could not pay off its debt, retire its securities ...because to do so, meant there would be no bonds to back the national bank notes. To pay off the debt, was to destroy the money supply," Galbrath said.

I looked at Mel's Jesus. "In all my eight years as President, I could never figure out what language these guys were talking in," I said. You can't pay back debt, with more debt ... they use property, control, backed by wage-slaves. It's idolatry.

Ku Klux Klan founded

A propaganda and disinformation campaign needs proponents ...central bankers founded the Knights of the Golden Circle, founded 1854 by George Bickley, to promote secession from the Union by the South ...by spreading racial tension from state to state.

Ku Klux Klan, formed 1867, was the military arm of the Knights. Its members included Alfred Pike, Jefferson Davis, John Wilkes Booth, William Quantrill, and Jesse James ...who, after stealing gold from banks and mining companies, buried nearly 7 billion dollars worth, all over the western states ...in hopes of funding a second Civil War.

Jessie James joined Confederate guerillas led by William Quantrill ...in bloody civil warfare in Kansas and Missouri. Bickley and his newly formed Knights of the Golden Circle work with foreign agents, to stir up armed rebellion with the aim of breaking off the Southern states and making them banana republics of Britain, again.

After the Civil War, the Knights continued fighting as guerrilla fighters serving ongoing British attempts to destabilize the Union. They robbed money to finance a second Confederate rebellion.

Historians say actual fighting of the American Civil War didn't end in 1865, but continued to be fought underground for nineteen more years ...just as historians say actual fighting of World War II didn't end in 1945, because the CIA hired Hitler's anti-Soviet guerrilla Nazi leader Otto Skorzeny and his 'Werewolf' guerrillas, who fought in Eastern Europe and Eastern Russia, until 1952.

The Knights spy network was involved in many subversive activities, such as train robberies by Jessie James, the purpose being to fund the Confederates that went underground after they lost the military war in 1865 ...just like the Nazis went underground in Madrid, starting in the early 1940s, and operated an exile Nazi underground government in Madrid well into the 1950s under Werner Naumann ...until Germany was again recognized as an independent state.

As a Confederate agent, Jesse James smuggled guns and ammunition to Plains Indians, training them in guerilla tactics, for use against their common enemy, General George Armstrong Custer and the Union Army ... all the time, the American guerilla outfits run by Quantrill and James were supported by British banks to split up the United States ...reclaim the North, giving the South to Napoleon ...as payment for France's help in the destabilization and counter-revolution, undoing, and reversing the American Revolution.

Apr. 1861, Russian Ambassador to America throws his hat in, like a break dancer spinning on his back, jumps in the dance circle. "England will take advantage of the first opportunity to recognize the seceded states, and France will follow her," the Russian Ambassador said.

Late 1861, England sends 8,000 troops to Canada ...1862, English, French and Spanish troops land at Vera Cruz, Mexico, 'to collect on debts owed them by Mexico' ...Jun. 10, 1863, French General Forey, with 30,000 additional French troops, take over Mexico City ...controlling most of Mexico. Thru spies in Paris and London, Czar Alexander II in Russia discovers Confederates offer Louisiana and Texas to Napoleon III ...if Napoleon sends troops against the North. Russia had said it supported Lincoln.

Jan. 1, 1863 for good will, Abraham Lincoln issues the Emancipation Proclamation to free the slaves, just as the Czar had done with the serfs, in 1861. Sept. 8, 1863, Abraham Lincoln, and Secretary of State William Seward, ask Czar Alexander to send the Russian fleet to San Francisco and New York, to be battle ready, taking orders only from Abraham Lincoln.

Apr. 14, 1865, Lincoln's assassinated ...that night, an assassination attempt is made on State Secretary Seward. In 1866, in Russia, an assassination attempt is made on Czar Alexander II ...1881, the Czar's killed by a bomb.

Andrew Johnson becomes President, Apr. 15, issues Amnesty Proclamation, May 29, 1865, reuniting the country. It stipulates ...the South won't be responsible for its debt incurred.

Cost of supporting the Russian fleet to the U.S. was 7 million dollars. Johnson didn't have constitutional authority to give money to a foreign government ...so, arrangements were made to purchase Alaska from the Russians, in Apr. 1867. It was labeled, 'Seward's Folly' ...because, it appeared Seward purchased a worthless piece of land ...when in fact, it was compensation paid to Russian Navy.

The terrorists within

are central bankers

"Bankers are a den of vipers. I intend to rout you out & by the Eternal God I will rout you out. If the people only understood the rank injustice of our central bank system, there would be a revolution before morning. If the central bank continues to control our currency, receiving our public monies, & holding thousands of our citizens in dependence, it would be more formidable & dangerous than the naval & military power of the enemy. It is not our own citizens only who are to receive the bounty of our government ... **More than 8 million dollars of the stock of this bank are held by foreigners** ... Is there no danger to our liberty & independence in a bank that in its nature has so little to bind it to our country? If government would confine itself to equal protection, and, as Heaven does its rains, shower its favor alike on the high & the low, the rich & the poor, it would be an unqualified blessing."

~ President Andrew Jackson, 1829-1837

"Banking institutions are more dangerous to our liberties than standing armies. If American people ever allow private banks to control the issue of their currency, first by inflation, then by deflation, the banks & corporations that will grow up around will deprive the people of all property until their children wake-up homeless on the continent their fathers conquered. The issuing power should be taken from banks & restored to the people, to whom it properly belongs."

~ President Thomas Jefferson, 1801-1809

"Whoever controls the money of a nation, controls that nation & is absolute master of all industry & commerce. When you realize that the entire system is very easily controlled, one way or another, by a few powerful men at the top, you will not have to be told how periods of inflation & depression originate."

~ President James Garfield, 1891

"Capital must protect itself in every possible manner by combination & legislation. Debts must be collected, bonds & mortgages must be foreclosed as rapidly as possible. When, through a process of law, the common people lose their homes they will become more docile & more easily governed through the influence of the strong arm of government, applied by a central power of wealth under control of leading financiers. This truth is well known among our principal men now engaged in forming an imperialism of Capital to govern the world.

"By dividing voters through the political party system, we get them to expend energies fighting over questions of no importance. Thus, by discreet action we can secure for ourselves what has been so well planned & successfully accomplished. ~Aug. 25, 1924 *USA Banker's Magazine*

Could this explain what's wrong in America?

Presidents Lincoln, Garfield & Kennedy advocated for a publicly-owned central bank. Lincoln refused loans because of high interest rates, and instead, published 'greenbacks' -- publicly owned money to finance the Civil war. Kennedy published two-dollar bills -- publicly owned money to help get the U.S. out of debt.

Could it be true, that major shareholders and interlocking Fed directors also direct Halliburton (and their private armies), Bechtel, Westinghouse, and so on ...major defense contractors and warmongers, as well as regional Fed directors picking State candidates for governor, and who runs for President? (See pg. 587-571)

<>

Could the reason we're in Iraq not be, because of oil? ...or because of weapons sales? Could it also be a way for central bankers to run up the national debt and increase the yearly amount taxpayers have to pay them for interest on the money we have them print for us, then they loan it to us and charge us interest on it -- producing a 10 trillion dollar debt in 100 years?

After all, our Government does not own our money. Private bankers do. The Fed is not a federal institution ... the stock is privately owned.

If it were publicly owned (by our Government) there would be no interest to pay ... why would we charge ourselves interest to borrow money from ourselves? I'd reach into my pocket, take out a dime, borrow that dime from myself, then put that dime back in my pocket? Then, reach into my pocket, hand myself two cents interest, then put that two cents back into my pocket?

"The privilege of creating and issuing money is the supreme prerogative of Government, the Government's greatest creative opportunity. By adoption of these principles, taxpayers are saved immense sums of interest." ~ **Abraham Lincoln**

The new world order which comes hand-in-glove with the merging of Communism and Capitalism into globalist practices ... is a house of cards without any real sustainability. It's a fact, 200 multinational transnational corporations control ... and their shareholders own ... over 95% of all private business which is not owned by individual privateers, and are reaping most of the benefit. The flipside of this coin is that all of this economic activity employs only 0.3 per cent of the global workforce.

~ *Big Oil & the War on Drugs and Terrorism,* by Siegfried E. Tischler, PhD, excerpted from *Nexus Magazine,* Volume 11, Number 4 Jun-Jul 2004

<>

Wall Street was created by, and is run by, the Tory faction, which followed the policy of Bank of Manhattan founders and American traitors Aaron Burr and John Jacob Astor. The *Wall Street Journal* represents a merger of Boston and New York interests. At the heart of the *Wall Street Journal* is the aristocratic Bancroft family of Boston. Boston's State Street financial center is run by the treasonous families that made their money in the British-run China opium trade ...Cabot, Perkins, Coolidge, Russell, Lowell et al.

~ *Why Harvard Protects the Drug Trade,* by Linda Minor (see Appendix 5)

<>

African Americans make up 15% of America's drug users, yet they are 37% of people arrested for drug violations, 59% of those convicted, and 74% of those sentenced in prison. While 66% of crack users are white or Hispanic, blacks comprise more than 80% of those sentenced for crack offenses. The average federal drug sentence for crack offenses for African Americans is 49% higher than for whites.

~ Maya Harris, Exec. Dir., ACLU of No. Calif. www.aclu.org/pdfs/drugpolicy/cracksinsystem_20061025.pdf to read ACLU report, *Cracks in the System: Twenty Years of the Unjust Federal Crack Cocaine Law.* -- *San Francisco Post* headline story, *Racially-Biased 'War on Drugs',* Weekly Edition, May 23-29, 2007

Dedication

For my Father's (in memory) and Mother's and Brother's immortal souls, and their families, and all my aunts and uncles and their children, and my grandparents, and of my friends, and of all those I love, and of the immortal soul of all of God's creations ... and the immortal souls of our ancestors, of which I am a part, and my parents' maternal grandparents, who immigrated to America from Vitibsk Poland in present-day Belarus or vice versa (the political borders of Vitibsk keep changing over centuries of warfare), and my parents' paternal grandparents, who were musicians in the Czar's marching band, and were east European and Austrian Jews -- all for whom this book was created out of my life-long yearning to discover who planned and financed and profited from the endless warfare of our genocidal 20th Century and that human destruction on this planet, in an effort to identify and hold accountable the genocidal perpetrators, by divesting their unjust profits to benefit equally all people on Earth, and for my eternal salvation, and yours.

And especially to my Mother -- without whose help I would not have survived as a writer in the cold and uncaring emotional climate of 20th Century America, my Mother, whose maternal great-grandparents were landholders in Vienna Austria and whose paternal great-grandparents lived in Russia, European Jews

In memory, David Lerner, poet, rabid angel, Jew

<>

*In the **British** tradition of MI-5 & MI-6 associates Aldous Huxley and George Orwell, and satirist Jonathan Swift ...and, in the **American** tradition of Dos Passos, and Kurt Vonnegut ...and, in the **Russian** tradition of Dostoyevsky & Chekov ...and, in the **French** tradition of Flaubert*

Acknowledgments ~ The author would like to acknowledge the work of the following, without whose honesty, dedication, literary work and journalism, the understanding and oral tradition passed on from them, to you, in this contemporary, American underground historical novel, would not've been possible. Twentieth Century public-oriented researchers: Dave Emory, William Domhoff, Lou Wolf, Peter Dale Scott, Carl Olgesby, Sean Gervasi, Antony Kimery, Antony Sutton, John Loftus, Mark Aarons, Martin A. Lee, Christopher Simpson, Alfred McCoy, Henrik Kruger, Kurt Riess, Michael Sayers, Albert E. Kahn, T. H. Tetans, Eustace Mullins, George Seldes, James Stewart Martin. These authors document their research extensively ... for the public good.

Special acknowledgment is given to Eustace Mullins, all information herein about the American Revolution, the Federal Reserve system and precursors, associated national and international history, and the financial depressions of 1907, 1920-1921 and 1929-1931 etc. is based on Mullins' work, which is available online at many internet sites ... this includes passages directly quoted and passages where his name appears preceding discussion and where it doesn't. Note: http://www.whale.to/b/mullins5.html and note: http://www.bibliotecapleyades.net/sociopolitica/esp_sociopol_fed06.htm#menu

Table of Contents

American Idyll ~ an historical novel & fictional autobiography of Ronald Reagan

The American Idyll of Ronald Reagan

Foreword

War is a racket

In 1933, Marine Corps Major General Smedley Butler made one of many speeches.

"War is just a racket. A racket is best described, I believe, as something that is not what it seems to the majority of people. Only a small inside group knows what it is about. It is conducted for the benefit of the very few at the expense of the masses.

"I believe in adequate defense at the coastline and nothing else. If a nation comes over here to fight, then we'll fight. The trouble with America is that when the dollar only earns 6% over here, then it gets restless and goes overseas to get 100%. Then the flag follows the dollar and the soldiers follow the flag.

"I wouldn't go to war again as I have done to protect some lousy investment of the bankers. There are only two things we should fight for. One is the defense of our homes and the other is the Bill of Rights. War for any other reason is simply a racket.

"There isn't a trick in the racketeering bag that the military gang is blind to. It has its 'finger men' to point out enemies, its 'muscle men' to destroy enemies, its 'brain men' to plan war preparations, and a 'Big Boss' Super-Nationalistic-Capitalism.

"It may seem odd for me, a military man to adopt such a comparison. Truthfulness compels me to. I spent thirty-three-years-and-four-months in active military service as a member of this country's most agile military force, the Marine Corps. I served in all commissioned ranks from Second Lieutenant to Major-General. And during that period, I spent most of my time being a high class muscle-man for Big Business, for Wall Street and for the Bankers. In short, I was a racketeer, a gangster for capitalism.

"I suspected I was just part of a racket at the time. Now I am sure of it. Like all the members of the military profession, I never had a thought of my own until I left the service. My mental faculties remained in suspended animation while I obeyed the orders of higher-ups. This is typical with everyone in military service.

"I helped make Mexico, especially Tampico, safe for American oil interests in 1914. I helped make Haiti and Cuba a decent place for the National City Bank boys to collect revenues in. I helped in the raping of half a dozen Central American republics for the benefits of Wall Street. The record of racketeering is long. I helped purify Nicaragua for the international banking house of Brown Brothers in 1909-1912. I brought light to the Dominican Republic for American sugar interests in 1916. In China I helped to see to it that Standard Oil went its way unmolested.

"During those years, I had, as the boys in the back room would say, a swell racket. Looking back on it, I feel that I could have given Al Capone a few hints. The best he could do was to operate his racket in three districts. I operated on three continents."

How many of these war millionaires shouldered a rifle? How many of them dug a trench? How many of them knew what it meant to go hungry in a rat-infested dug-out? How many of them spent sleepless, frightened nights, ducking shells and shrapnel and machine gun bullets? How many of them parried a bayonet thrust of an enemy? How many of them were wounded or killed in battle?

Out of war nations acquire additional territory, if they are victorious. They just take it. This newly acquired territory promptly is exploited by the few ...the self-same few who wrung dollars out of blood in the war. The general public shoulders the bill.

And what is this bill?

This bill renders a horrible accounting. Newly placed gravestones. Mangled bodies. Shattered minds. Broken hearts and homes. Economic instability. Depression and all its attendant miseries. Back-breaking taxation for generations and generations.

For a great many years, as a soldier, I had a suspicion that war was a racket ... not until I retired to civil life did I fully realize it. Now that I see the international war clouds gathering, as they are today, I must face it and speak out.

Again they are choosing sides.

Well, it's a racket, all right.

A few profit ...and the many pay. But there is a way to stop it. You can't end it by disarmament conferences. You can't eliminate it by peace parleys at Geneva. Well-meaning but impractical groups can't wipe it out by resolutions. It can be smashed effectively only by taking the profit out of war.

The only way to smash this racket is to conscript capital and industry and labor before the nation's manhood can be conscripted. One month before the Government can conscript the young men of the nation ...it must conscript capital and industry and labor. Let the officers and the directors and the high-powered executives of our armament factories and our munitions makers and our shipbuilders and our airplane builders and the manufacturers of all the other things that provide profit in war time as well as the bankers and the speculators, be conscripted ...to get $30 a month, the same wage as the lads in the trenches get.

Let the workers in these plants get the same wages ...all the workers, all presidents, all executives, all directors, all managers, all bankers ...yes, and all generals and all admirals and all officers and all politicians and all government office holders ...everyone in the nation be restricted to a total monthly income not to exceed that paid to the soldier in the trenches!

Let all these kings and tycoons and masters of business and all those workers in industry and all our senators and governors and majors pay half of their monthly $30 wage to their families and pay war risk insurance and buy Liberty Bonds.

Why shouldn't they?

They aren't running any risk of being killed or of having their bodies mangled or their minds shattered. They aren't sleeping in muddy trenches. They aren't hungry. The soldiers are!

Give capital and industry and labor thirty days to think it over and you will find, by that time, there will be no war. That will smash the war racket ...that and nothing else.

Maybe I am a little too optimistic. Capital still has some say. So capital won't permit the taking of the profit out of war until the people ...those who do the suffering and still pay the price ...make up their minds that those they elect to office shall do their bidding, not that of the profiteers. (Editors' note: for unabridged text, see pgs. 148-156.)

U.S. Intelligence, National Security & Foreign Policy

by Carl Oglesby

"Just as Czarist and White Russian spies jumped to the Nazis when their own army was defeated in World War I, the German Nazi and Russian Czarist spies together jumped to the American army as the German Wehrmacht was defeated in World War II. This is how a Czarist spy ring inside a Nazi spy ring became the inner circle of an American spy ring ...as it became the national security and foreign policy instrument of Washington and Wall Street. Everything Washington and Wall Street would know about the Soviet Union and Eastern Europe came from Czarists and Nazis installed at the center of the U.S. intelligence system. "How can a naive, trusting, democratic republic give its secrets to crime, and its innermost ear to the spirit of Central European Fascism ...and, expect not to see its Constitution polluted ...its traditions abused ...and, its consciousness of the surrounding world manipulated ultimately out of all realistic shape."

~by U.S. Intelligence historian Carl Oglesby

<> <> <>

Patti dreamed she was in Hell. Each time Patti heard a car pull up she thought it might be Mel's Jesus, or Paul Robeson's ghost, to invite her in out of the rain. She listened to the sounds of a passing car. It hissed at her, it parked. She didn't see anyone in it. Sadness took her, cold wind blew through her. She shivered.

It was dusk. She didn't have a life, just a bunch of beginnings stuck together never making sense, even when they did. Where's she going? What's she gonna do? Purple rain fell in black puddles on the beat-up asphalt streets ...making silver splashes in slow motion, glossy black puddles reflecting red brake lights of cars splashing them up ...beneath a charcoal, navy blue, and confederate grey sky, cut open with dry, yellow crumbling clouds, silhouetted behind marble-faced buildings. Smoke from erupting geysers of fire, punctuated the street.

Then, Patti was driving an old beamer the back way, behind the railroad tracks, behind Townsend, by the railroad station across the arguing cobblestone streets shaking the foundations of her car and her life like a metal meat tenderizing hammer, feeling each sullen tiny thud that added up to insanity. In the beginning of her romance with Alan, she sped through green lights, wanting to be with him right now, flooring the car through yellow lights by San Francisco Police headquarters on 7th and Bryant ...where the rent was not free, costing dreams, costing lives. She turned the first right up Langston Alley to Folsom Street by Julie's Supper Club, past the Brainwash Laundromat, and parked.

She went inside. In one corner of the cafe performance poets performed their shit. In another corner, a saxophone player was riffing in a microphone. A bum drinking coffee at the counter jiggled, shook up off his stool, quivered across the floor, stood waving his finger, speaking in tongues.

Patti recoiled. "Don't even think about it. Go away."

Patti went outside. Everything had special meaning for her. The sheet of newspaper blowing in slow spread-eagled cartwheels down the road, a woman slowly pushing a baby carriage by her, magic wrapped around the baby, its eyes reflecting wonder, small deer horns protruding from the sides of its head.

At the other end of Langston Alley, a skeletal Black woman standing next to the dirt-turded park, pressed her palms against a car trunk, pulled thin Levis down, her thin brown butt silhouetted against yellow stucco walls of a sign shop, her shoulders and head disappearing beneath two parked cars, her brown butt flashed. She put her palms on the car trunk again, then fell over backwards, a shiny aluminum walker skirted out from behind her, clanking in the empty alley. Then, she disappeared into a stairwell. Homeless Black people, addicts, and white winos collected in swarms, waiting for volunteer workers to sing them Jesus songs through battery-operated hand-held megaphones ...then, serve soup, sandwiches, crackers, stale loaves of bread thrown away from day-old bakery outlets. The songs echoed down Langston Alley, twisting between cars, bouncing off the street, stretching down the walls. People collected in shadows ...some stood, some slept on park grass in cardboard refrigerator boxes, others slept beneath blankets hung over pairs of shopping carts.

Three forgotten Black men sat on a bench wearing old clothes, faces smeared unshaven with stubble, dark eyes bright, men lumped together in a shadow of life, forming one big shape from nothing.

Alan felt helpless.

Patti mumbled drunkenly. She sat on a bench. "I forget where I am."

Patti stumbled to her feet, stumbling forward pulled by her own weight into the bathroom to a crashing sound of the toilet seat dropping, came out, climbed back into bed, then lay still, caressing a pillow.

She'd been walking in her sleep, almost remembered the bar, earlier ...belting down shots of tequila. Orangee the orange cat looked at her, curiously. Rocky the black and white cat was weaving his way on top of the dresser through vitamin jars, knocking the jars down one at a time, wanting to be let outside.

Patti stumbled out of bed, opened the door. The two cats left the bedroom. Patti got into bed, beside Alan. She drifted into sleep, heard Spanish flamenco music, watched the interplay of shadows the candlelight made flickering on the plastered walls, felt cool air moving hairs on her forearm. A senorita approached, her hips swaying, light sparkling in her eyes, carrying two of those big bra margaritas in each hand, put them on the table.

There was nothing out there to hold onto, except margaritas, storm pipes, clusters of elbows, torsos and polyester pants, winos peeing in their sleep blocking doorways to cockroach-infested dives, pawn shops at the end of asphalt bathrooms reeking of stale piss, ammonia, spilled coffee and barfing transvestite hookers.

Patti went down to the boat club, she sat alone

on the rear deck, watched the tide come in, washing over rocks, sinking in the sand and gravel beach till dawn came. Felt the sun rise warm on her face, listened to seagulls. She watched morning's passing sailboats, a huge freighter stacked with cargo containers, an Exxon tanker downloading crude oil to smaller tankers going up the narrow north bay into Carquinez Straits, oil refineries fouling the sky black with smoke.

She thought, someday maybe she'd be famous for surviving the years of the Reagan Administration, had no idea how her artist friends survived in her father's America.

Patti watched the water, boats, birds, ships, the tide come in then go out, the tattered American flag limping around the flag pole in a trying breeze. Hours passed.

She liked being dramatic. She crossed her hands back and forth like a baseball umpire waving out a man sliding into home plate, safe, staring at clouds.

Patti awoke from a troubled sleep. Alan was sleeping, snoring. Patti poked him in the ribs with her elbow. He turned over. Patti fell back asleep, dreaming.

Two Black men stood there in her dream, wearing white Egyptian cotton bathrobes.

Patti looked at them. "Christ, who are you? What are you doing in my dream?"

The first, answered, "I'm Mel's Jesus."

Then, the other. "I'm Paul Robeson's ghost."

Patti yawned. "I'm Patti of San Francisco and Hollywood."

Mel's Jesus smiled. "Paul, will you guide Patti through Hell?"

Paul Robeson's ghost nodded. "Okay … that's Hell's back door through that gateway. You know, Hell. The one with bat wings that stretch out over the clouds …with three different faces on his head, one in front and one where each ear should be … herrrrre's Lucifer … sitting on a frozen lake. The worst souls that lived in flesh …are frozen in that lake, unable to move. Each one of Lucifer's three mouths are stuffed with sinners. In the frozen lake, in separate ice cubes others wait to be devoured, mouths frozen open in silent screams, faces twisted in broken flesh mirrors. Think of them, dead presidents, dead congressmen …where did you think they'd be? Frauds, liars, bankers gnawing off each other's heads, tearing off each other's limbs in the burning lake, drinking molten sewage …then, frozen into ice, thawed by a lightning and thunder rain of fire …blinded, wandering molten across the plains. Go! …already …watch them rip out their guts, the Bakkers and Swaggarts, unbaptized and unholy, moved by constant stinging from wasps and ants. Go now."

In smoke and strobe lights, Mel's Jesus disappeared. Patti looked at Paul Robeson's ghost. "What do you make of that?"

The ghost hesitated, "We'll find out soon enough."

Patti frowned. She could hear Rolling Stones music playing on the other side. She looked surprised as her stomach growled. "I could use a McDonald's Happy Meal."

As soon as she said that, Hell's back door swung slowly open. Patti took the ghost's hand.

They walked through the flaming gold arches of Hell. There, sitting on top of the golden arches that went up for miles, Lucifer sat …crunching two poor sinners around in his mouth, their heads poking out from Lucifer's lips, screaming.

Patti felt shocked. "It's the Presidents Bush, yelling at us! Can't you hear them?"

The ghost shivered. "Sure, they're pointing at the hamburger stand,"

"They sure are."

The Presidents Bush spoke in one voice, faintly, scarcely heard. "Get us a hamburger! Please!"

Patti didn't think so. "Not on your life! …do you really think your behavior deserves a hamburger? I don't."

George Sr. did the talking for both Presidents Bush. "Please, listen to me …you're not worth saving, either."

Lucifer start crunching on the Presidents Bush, again. They screamed. Lucifer spat the Presidents Bush out of his mouth …they fell hundreds of feet, smashing into the ice beside Patti and Paul Robeson's ghost.

Patti start kicking the Presidents Bush in their ribs. "How do you like it for a change?"

The Presidents Bush yelped. They pleaded. "We know you're right. But, we're so hungry. Please get us burgers."

She had them, now. "Apologize!"

The Presidents Bush frowned …then, smelled fries in the air coming from the hamburger stand. "We're sorry. Hold the mayo."

Patti figured as much, "Yeah sure."

Mel's Jesus stepped from a block of molten ice. He looked at Patti. "Stop torturing them, Patti. Just get the burgers."

"Okay," Patti walked off slowly.

Mel's Jesus watched Patti and Paul Robeson's ghost get into a line beside steaming bursts of sulfurous black smoke shooting up in flaming geysers by the order window of the burger stand. The Presidents Bush squirmed on the ground like serpents.

Presidents Bush looked up at Mel's Jesus. "Is she getting the burgers?"

"Looks like it. Can't you wait?"

Presidents Bush sighed. "I don't know. Can you get us out of here? We'll pay you in General Motors bearer bonds, change your name, get you a passport."

Mel's Jesus wasn't impressed. "Sorry, not scalping tickets."

Patti's turn in line came up. She placed her order with a grotesque-looking demon. The hamburger stand turned into bile, then went up in flames. Satan's laughter exploded out his three mouths …parts of people's souls he was chewing up came out.

Patti scowled up at Satan. She went back to Mel's Jesus and Presidents Bush.

Presidents Bush were starving. "Give us burgers, please!"

Patti shrugged. "Sorry, the burger stand disappeared, some kind of satanic joke."

Presidents Bush despaired, "It's not fair."

Satan reached down two great fingers, picked up the Presidents Bush, popped them back in his mouth, gnawing on them. Presidents Bush screamed, disappearing like spaghetti as Satan sucked them back into his mouth.

Patti had seen enough. "I want to get out of here, I want to go back to California. Let's cross the frozen lake."

She took Paul's ghostly hand, but the ghost disappeared. She turned to Mel's Jesus. Patti was scared. "Where'd he go?"

Mel's Jesus didn't know. "It was probably his time."

There was thunder as a whirlwind of fire encircled Patti. Satan's laughter echoed off the fiery canyons of Hell. Patti grabbed her ears to keep the sound from hurting.

Lucifer roared, "Not so fast! Ms. Patti. Do you know where you are?!"

Patti was shocked. Suddenly, the realization hit her. "I'm, I'm in Hell." .

"That's right! Why do people go to Hell, Ms. Patti?"

"You mean?…"

"That's right," Lucifer said.

Patti had to get out of this, fast. "I'm not bad, compared to most people."

"Aren't you having a little trouble with your boyfriend, lately?"

"Yes."

Lucifer was amused. "Do you know why you're here?"

"Because of him?"

Lucifer was losing patience. "No, stupid. You're the reason."

Patti was desperate. "No! This isn't happening, it's only a dream!"

"Ms. Patti, it always was. I command you, tell me, what were the worst things in your life?"

Patti was embarrassed. "Looking for a job, I guess …a full moon when I had no one to love …wanting to be held when no one was there to touch me."

Lucifer had won. "Here are the San Jose Mercury Sunday classifieds."

Patti backed away. "No! I hate Silicon Valley! They're robots!"

The American Idyll of Ronald Reagan

a fictional autobiography

How I became fiction

Joan Quigley was Nancy's astrologer in San Francisco. Nancy dropped me off at the barber shop on her way to Joan's. After, we were flying back to the White House.

<>

Joan blinked her eyes. "I'm coming out of my trance now. Did it help, Nancy?"

"Knowing a Denver developer borrowed money at Silverado Savings & Loan and helped set Neil Bush up in business? ... I really can't say it does."

"You asked me who was pulling the strings."

"That developer would have hooks into Vice President Bush, not Ronnie. I don't see any connection."

"I don't, either. Let's do your astrology chart, Ronnie's and for Washington D.C."

White House Situation Room

I brought my Jimmy Stewart videotape with me into the Situation Room to keep me company. Watching the movie reminded me to could project sincerity and concern. George Bush walked in. I turned it off. "George, Watt's big mouth might'a hurt me, but, this Savings & Loan shenanigans breaks my heart."

George looked away, "I wish I could make it easy on you."

"How can 3,200 Savings & Loans be worth 17 billion dollars in 1972, and 17 billion dollars in the hole eight years later? In 1982, you told me to deregulate them! Now, in 1988, 600 of 'em are failing again! And, 1,200 more are going down! ...500 billion dollars in the hole out of taxpayers' pockets! Where did it go?"

George scratched his head, "Gee, I don't know, Ron."

I didn't know to believe him, or not, "This is the biggest bank robbery in the history of the world. I wrote the largest check in history and it was on the taxpayers' checkbook... and it bounced ...I didn't make a dime out of this! Did you?!".

George is Episcopal ergo confessional. "No. Two of my sons did okay. James Baker III did okay. Lloyd Bentsen did okay. I'm not a banker, I'm an oil man."

"That's consoling! Where's the beef? It's like that?"

George composed himself, "It's a terrible thing for the middle class, working class, upper class, ruling class ... but, there's no board member liability for the money-issuing class. Take heart."

"George, it breaks my heart."

George sighed, "It's the price ruling families pay for owning everyone ... we feel ashamed all the way to the bank."

"I'm not a ruling family! I'm a poor kid from Iowa. I'm a screen idol. I made a million because of this face, rode the American dream like a bronco. Got bucked off into White House mud ...Do we have a cover? ...will it hold? ...will *I* get caught holding the bag?"

Bush shook his head. "I'll ask Bill Casey. The mud washes off."

George left.

I turned on Jimmy Stewart's movie, *It's a Wonderful Life*. "Poor Jimmy, you've got one failed Savings & Loan ... I got the whole failed S&L industry ... I outlived you, Jimmy." I felt full of despair. I turned off the TV off, watching the blank screen till I passed out.

Bitsburg, Germany

Deaver and his advance team met German Chancellor Helmut Kohl in a cemetery in Bitsburg Germany as snow fell on the graves. Secret Service people and German elite guards stood by on the ready.

Kohl smiled. "Here."

Deaver couldn't believe it. "In a cemetery? You want President Reagan to kneel down here to honor German war dead?"

"Yes. Germans were victims of World War II, too. A gesture of reconciliation."

"I don't want to compromise President Reagan."

"There are no Nazis buried here."

"It's a *real* decision."

"If you agree, you and your staff can pick out new Beemers at the factory, discounted."

President Reagan & Nancy dancing with (l-r) Stubby Kaye, Shirley Jones & Marvin Hamlisch during a rehearsal for 'In Performance at the White House.' 8/5/88

In the BMW factory, Mike Deaver watched the new cars unhooked from the assembly line. "Navy blue is better than black or silver for beemers."

Deaver and staff climbed inside their new BMWs. Deaver floored his car and patched out of the factory.

Chancellor Kohl shook his head, sadly.

White House Situation Room

Me, Nancy, Deaver, and George Shultz met in the White House Sit Room. Mike looked uncomfortable.

"I'm sorry, Ronnie. I didn't know we were being set up. I thought it was a good photo-op for you, say a few words to commemorate the dead World War II Germans. I didn't know the cemetery's full of SS officers."

Nancy was furious. She hated anyone making me look bad.

"Mike, you messed up! Half of Congress is crazy! They don't want their constituencies watching the President honor murderers of Americans who fought World War II. Staff, Cabinet, Congress ...everyone's split ... the majority are against us. Ronnie, our personal friends and the Jewish community of the United States are against you on this. Don't pray at the graves of mass murderers. It's wrong. Back out."

"I won't cancel the visit."

"Don't be stubborn."

"I gave my word."

"George, can you help him out?"

George Shultz chuckled. "I've talked with German ex-Chancellor Schmit. Look, Helmut, I said, I have to get the President's rear-end out of the wringer on Bitsburg. Schmit said there are no Nazis or SS buried in there.".

Nancy wasn't amused. "He lied to you."

Shultz nodded. "I know he did. But, Ronnie won't back down since Schmidt said Kohl won't be re-elected if Ronnie waffles. That the German government will fall to communists in the next elections."

Nancy rolled her eyes. "Oh, spare me."

Shultz admired Nancy for being so sharp. "I argued with Kohl. He *guaranteed* me ...there was no problem with the graveyard. Now, all Kohl can do is say he'll lose re-election if he loses face, and communists will take over."

I was getting upset. "Kohl and Schmidt save face. Me and America lose face. Why? ...to protect America's banking and trade relations with Germany. What irks me, no one told me the job was like *this*. George, you're a pal, but I'm hold-

ing fast. There's no way out. I gave my word. I'm going to that Nazi SS graveyard to pray!"

Shultz was fed up. "The Nazis screwed us again."

Mike Deaver hung up his phone. "Approval ratings are in, you're going down."

Nancy was besides herself, flitting around and walking back and forth. "It's *too soon* after Iran-Contra. We can't take the hit."

I was sad. "My *hero* rating's down. America disapproves."

Shultz was upset, yet spoke with a ring of irony in his words, "Germany loves it. It makes us look like Nazi-lovers!"

I was lost. "What am I going to do? ...I can't offend Germany. I gave my word."

Shultz shook his head. "I'm sorry, Mr. President. I can't get your ass out of the fire on this one."

"The show must go on. I learned that in show business. Never cancel a show, even if it kills you. It'll be hard. But, I gave my word."

Mike was thinking how to save my popularity ratings. "Well, if you're going to the SS cemetery you have to make the Jews and liberals happy. You're going to concentration camp ruins, too. Go pray at the concentration camp ruins for Jews who were murdered in the camps. I've been telling you that for years, it's a photo-op for your campaign chest."

It scared me. "I don't want to go, there. Not to a concentration camp. It's painful. It reminds me of the truth. I know what went on there. It's too upsetting."

I saw Nancy raising her hackles. Then, she saw me fighting back tears. I wouldn't let the sadness overtake me, it wasn't part of the job ...I forced a phony smile, tried to joke. "I'd rather remember it, Hollywood style."

Nancy sadly watched my face. I started staring blankly at the ceiling, remembering Hollywood back in 1941. I was drafted into a World War II war propaganda film unit. I served my country as a war propaganda film producer, in Hollywood. I starred in, *This Is The Army,* a musical comedy about World War II.

In the Sit Room, I sang a few lines from the *This Is The Army* theme song. I saw the Hollywood soldiers singing and happily marching off to war, on a stage set. The cameras rolled. I kept singing. I got up. I start marching around the Sit Room, singing.

George Shultz looked upset.

CENSORED

Nancy had seen it before, she tried to cover me. "Don't get upset, George. Ronnie's just giving you a private performance of, *This Is The Army*. It's a musical film he starred in about soldiers marching off to war in World War II."

Suddenly, I was back in 1941. I was in the screening room watching the film. The film stuck in the projector. The screen images melted, browned, smoked and burst into a white image. It hurt my eyes. When the film started again, it was switched. I watched the words, *Top Secret ... German Concentration Camps* appear on the screen. I saw documentary footage of concentration camp horrors. I gasped, stunned. Trapped. I closed my eyes. I couldn't bear the truth. I vomited in the screening room.

Nancy saw the horror on my face. "Ronnie! Ronnie!"

My eyes cleared. I smiled.

Nancy relaxed. "He's back."

George Shultz exhaled.

SS Graveyard Photo-Op, Bitsburg Germany

I was in Bitsburg, Germany, at the SS Nazi graveyard for the World War II commemoration ceremony, was flanked by a goose-stepping German honor guard accompanying me to the grave sites. I knelt, laid a commemorative wreath down, prayed beside the graves of German SS death squad leaders to honor the German and American war dead. I prayed to commemorate the end of World War II.

In the movie in my head I was back in 1941.

I was sitting in the screening room in Hollywood watching the *Top Secret* Army documentary footage of concentration camp torture and mutilation scenes. I blinked my eyes. I was back at Bitsburg.

I stared at the SS Nazi graves. I was in both places. I was horrified watching the camp torture. I watched ghosts materialize around me. They pointed their fingers at me.

Nancy was shocked by the blank, frightened look on my face. She wondered where my head was at, trying to decide if I'd gone over the edge, or not. Was my Alzheimer's acting up? Nancy leaned down beside me, "Ronnie, is your mind playing tricks on you?"

I looked at her, "Something inside me's dying. I see them begging me for help." I was living in a nightmare. Trees, fences and buildings morphed into ghosts. I whispered, "Don't you see them?"

Nancy smiled pleasantly to her German hosts, then moved her head closer, "Who?"

"Victims of Nazi torture, standing around us, begging us, 'Save our souls.'"

Nancy was shaken but pretended everything was normal, "Sometimes, I feel they're here. Be brave, Darling. It will be over soon. I love you."

"No, it never goes away. We've still got the concentration camp to go to."

Bergen-Belsen concentration camp, photo-op

Me and Nancy went to Bergen-Belsen. It felt haunted. This was Mike's photo-op to raise public opinion at home. I walked away from Nancy and the photographers to be alone. I stared into the ovens from the *Top Secret* Army film I'd seen almost 40 years ago, filled with people screaming. There, our humanity was burnt alive. I heard Hollywood-style theme music and watched my reflection in the glass oven-door window. I start talking to my reflection, "All my life I've run away from feelings because of places like this that hurt too much. I avoid emotional pain, I just deny it because it hurts too much."

I watched a child's ghost rise up out of the ashes on the oven floor. It spoke, "Don't forget me. Don't ever forget me. Please redeem my eternal soul."

Nancy looked uncertain as she walked over to me. "Ronnie, who are you talking to?"

I felt vulnerable, fragile. I started to cry. "I feel helpless. I want to stop denying pain. But, I can't. I want to push it away, to pretend everything's fine, to feel good, to accept my feelings, to feel the pain I've pushed away. I've got to. But, I can't. It hurts. I'll never, never push feelings away again. I promise."

"I know, Darling, I know."

"I have to suffer, feel their feelings, I can't pretend anymore it didn't happen. I can't deny it,

President Reagan posing with Bette Davis at the Kennedy Center Honors for Lifetime Achievement at the John F. Kennedy Center for Performing Arts (Sammy Davis Jr. in background). 12/6/1987

3

any more. My mother would agree with me." I started to grieve, sobbing, to feel again. So much of my life I had not let myself feel. I had wasted Time. What would life have been, if I felt myself living ...felt life living all around me. It occurred to me, then. I saw life was feeling, feeling tears, feeling love.

Nancy walked away to give me private time. She walked over to Mike Deaver, the German press corps and White House photographers. "The President was afraid to come here. It's too painful for him to relive the horror of this place. He'd rather avoid those feelings, because it hurts too much. It reminds him of the truth. It's too painful. Ronnie avoids emotional pain. He denies it because it hurts too much. The President of the United States doesn't want to talk right now. He's crying for the lost souls that haunt us, here. He's praying to redeem their eternal souls."

Nancy walked back over to me, she took my arm and helped me to stand. Together, we walked away. I put my arm around Nancy's shoulders as we walked.

Mike Deaver was elated and amused. He turned to an aide, "They ought to get Oscars for that! His rating's gonna soar!"

Nancy looked into my eyes and saw confusion and devastation, the lost look in my eyes. She felt sorry and sad, afraid I was having an attack of Alzheimer's, afraid this was a look ahead at what the rest of her life would be like with me.

<>

White House Historian Bill Barnes was a professor at Georgetown University. He made some notes in his White House diary. "The Iran-Contra scandal became public at the end of 1986. It almost toppled Ronnie's Administration. The official version is that members of the National Security Council convinced Ronnie of a twisted plan. That plan was to ransom our hostages in Lebanon. And, to sell arms to terrorists in the Middle East. Then, use profits from arms sales to fight anti-communist guerrillas in Nicaragua. Public opinion was against us. Dow Jones was at a record high of 2,700. Then, it fell 600 points. The market crashed 25%. It suggested the stock market crash of 1929 starting the Great Depression. Maybe, the Reagan economic boom is over. Iran-Contra and this stock market crash might be Ronnie's tombstone epitaph". Jackson, Bill's cat, lay at his feet chewing the shoelaces on Bill's shoes. Jackson swished his tail.

<>

After Bitsburg, Deaver told me to rehearse for a speech to National Republican Heritage Groups Council. I agreed.

"No problem. What's the Council?"

George Bush was at the rehearsal, "They're Christian West anti-communist heroes."

"Anti-communists have my blessing."

"Dulles brought them in from Eastern Europe in the early 1950s. Nixon promised them jobs in GOP presidential election campaigns. I'm making good on Nixon's promise to Dulles. They get out the ethnic vote for us."

"I'll make 'em feel good. Send 'em away laughing."

Deaver laughed, "Right on, Champ."

Bush winked at Deaver.

Before me, National Republican Party Chairman Frank Fahrenkopf addressed the Council. Frank was a Washington lawyer, national chairman of the U.S. Republican Party for six of my eight years in office, about to be president of the American Gaming Association (the lobby arm of the casino industry), co-chairman of U.S. Commission on Presidential Debates, a board director on four NYSE companies, and a personal friend of former White House drug czar, William Bennett. Frank advised Bennett on damage control after the media said Bennett was a self-proclaimed, moral advocate. And, he was a habitual gambler who lost $340,000 at Caesars Atlantic City and millions in Las Vegas.

Frank began his speech, "On behalf of the Republican Party, thank you for being part of our victory last November 6. We couldn't have done it without you."

I accepted the microphone from him and turned to the crowd, "Your work means a great deal to me, personally ...to the Party ...and to our cause. I can't think of anyone who contributed more than you, here today. Keep building the Party. Keep bringing more ethnic Americans into the fold. That's the key to our re-alignment, taking place."

Everyone clapped. I liked that.

President Reagan speaking at a Take Pride in America event with actors Clint Eastwood and Louis Gossett Jr. in the Rose Garden.

The next day, I presented a Medal of Freedom Honor to James Burnham. Burnham worked with our CIA émigré program as a psychological warfare consultant. He promoted 'liberation' as part of an early 1950s multimillion-dollar social engineering campaign, called, 'Crusade for Freedom'. It was designed to scare American taxpayers into believing Russia hated us and would attack any minute. Which wasn't very hard to do. That way, the World Order military-industrial folks who owned shares of the Federal Reserve could profit big. The guts behind our 'liberation' program was to bring in Nazi talent and call them 'freedom fighters' against the U.S.S.R.

I faced the press. "James Burnham's ideas on liberation have affected how America sees itself in the world. I owe Burnham a personal debt. During my years of traveling on the mashed-potato speaking circuit for General Electric, I quoted James Burnham quite a bit."

Bill Casey and George Bush were in the audience. Bill winked at Bush for a job well done, "Ronnie will never get it. We brought in Nazi collaborators. He wouldn't understand it. It's best this way."

George agreed by nodding his head. "I know."

As usual, back at the ranch after I retired, Nancy and me kept trying to figure out what went on behind our backs when I was President and she was First Lady. What had happened behind the scenes? Who was pulling our strings? They say, it's the people you love the most that hurt you the most. At one level I loved the people in my White House Staff and in my Cabinet as much as I loved America ...to me, they were America.

<>

Nancy read to me at our ranch in Santa Barbara. When she read to me, the people became real. The writer's were suddenly sitting there with us, when she read. It was as if Nancy brought them in. She introduced them. Antony Sutton, Bob Bowman, Charles Higham, Martin Lee. Authors became real-time, to me. Books, newspaper clippings, TV news, old magazines, took over my life. And, Alzheimer's worked me over pretty good. It was like my life was a movie that I acted out, without knowing. My life in a moment of Time.

Antony had worked on Stanford University Campus. He was part of the think tank at Hoover Institution of War, Revolution & Peace. He had a pile of books he had written, with him. Nancy began to read Sutton to me.

"It was the 1920s. W. Averell Harriman broke State Department rules. He was the biggest U.S. venture capital investor in the Soviet Union. Harriman's spawn was Ruskombank. Ruskombank was the first Soviet communist 'commercial' bank. Harriman and House of Morgan owned the voting shares of Guaranty Trust. Max May was vice president of Guaranty Trust. Max May, he was the first president of Ruskombank. He was in charge of their foreign operations. These guys were American bankers through and through. They owned share-blocks of the Federal Reserve. Owning a share-block of the Federal Reserve put you in the society pages, let you choose the delegates and the candidates, and planted you in the driver's seat of the World Order. So, while Max May ran their Soviet bank, Averell and Roland Harriman through Union Bank -- along with E.S. James and Knight Woolley, were also the biggest venture capitalists supporting Hitler. I ask you, can people be against Communism and for Communism ... at the same time? People can. Do they finance Russia's Communists and Germany's Nazis at the same time? People do. Communists and Nazis are opposites, mortal enemies, eternal spiritual enemies."

Nancy stopped reading to me. She looked up. "Ronnie, what would you like for dinner?"

I liked everything Nancy made ... I loved her so much. But, at the White House, we ordered in a lot of the time. Or, our White House chef made our favorites. We used TV trays. We watched my old Hollywood movies. When we watched, I was young again, not bad looking ... an old man watching myself, remembering the young man I once was. I had no idea what life would bring. Forty years later, I was in Washington D.C. I was running the U.S.. I was fighting commies. I was funding Contras. I was playing the biggest acting role of my career. It could get me an Oscar. Maybe there was one for me ... in the big Movie Studio in the Sky. I'd be dead soon, of Alzheimer's. It was a slow death. So, I enjoyed my last years at my ranch, the West Coast White House, as much as I could, in moments of clarity. It was my last time with Nancy and the kids. "Mommy, I could go for roast chicken tonight, potatoes, cole slaw leftovers from lunch, canned beets."

Then, that damn Alzheimer's came back ...I forgot what I'd said ...I didn't know where I was ...I was in the movie!

It was smelling that roasted chicken brought me home.

Nancy was crying. Nancy looked worried. "I didn't think you'd make it back, this time ... you were gone for two hours."

<>

Nancy instructed the lunch help then returned with Bob Bowman in tow. Nancy kept bringing in people to stimulate me, intellectually. To fight off my growing dementia. I was glad to see Bob.

"So, Bob. Who did 9/11?"

"I could name a suspect, an architect behind the 9/11 World Trade Center attacks. If I had to narrow it down to one person, I think my prime suspect would be Dick Cheney. The exercises that went on that morning simulating the exact thing that was happening confused people in FAA and NORAD. They didn't know what was real and what was the exercise. The people who planned and carried out those exercises should be investigated. There's nothing closer to fascism than what we've seen from this government. The Patriot Act has done more to destroy the rights of Americans than all our enemies combined. Look at the New World Order. It got its start with Charlie Wilson. He was chairman of General Motors. Then, Secretary of Defense. Him and Krupp. Krupp Industries supported Hitler's Germany in the 1930s. The World Order got a big push from David Rockefeller in 1960 with the Trilateral Commission. It reached fruition under George H. W. Bush. It unites IMF, World Bank, the G-8, and the WTO. It rules the world on behalf of billionaire industrialists and bankers. It's global capitalism run amok. It manipulates public opinion through corporate media monopolies. If we can't take back America, there's not much hope for the rest of the world."

Nancy looked at me with those big, dark eyes. "Ronnie, Bob's running for Congress in Florida. Didn't you meet Bob when you were President?"

I thought for a minute ...I couldn't take my eyes off her. "I sure did. He and Dick Cheney wanted the Starwars program. Bob got a bee in his bonnet. Bob said Dick wanted to use Starwars as an offensive weapon."

Nancy had a confused look on her face, it was pretty. "Of course ... all our defensive weapons are offensive weapons."

I was amused. "Yes, Nancy. But, only if we use them that way."

"I guess Bob figured out Dick wanted to blow everyone up."

"He must have ... do you think Bob's right?"

Maybe. "Look, Dick shot one of his friends in the face in a hunting accident ... that's stupid."

Nancy narrowed his eyes. "But, he didn't mean it."

"Then, why did he do it?"

"It was an accident."

"Ronnie, how do you point a rifle at someone's face by accident?"

"We did it all the time in Hollywood, didn't we?"

"Yes. You're right. Maybe he was just acting the part."

Maybe. "Yeah. Bob, what do you think?".

Nancy's heart sank, "Ronnie, who are you talking to? ...Nobody's here."

"I'm talking to Bob Bowman."

"Ronnie, that was 12 years ago, when Bob was here at the Ranch."

"I know. I just heard him talking. I saw him."

"Ronnie, you heard me read his platform for Congress. You imagined him, here."

"Nancy, I remember he was here 12 years ago, as clear as day. It was before my inauguration. After he left, you said you liked him. I remember exactly what you said. 'Ronnie, while we're in Washington, we better do the best acting of our lives.' Nancy, you're the only person I have ever met in my life who's always right. I told you, 'Nancy, we're going after an Oscar on this one, aren't we?' You said, 'Ronnie, on this one, I think the Oscar is going after us,.'"

Nancy smiled gently. "I remember."

<>

I went into another movie. "Mommy, George told me the Federal Reserve Bank was ordered by Congress to exist. But, it's owned privately. By an international club with no allegiance to us, just to themselves."

Nancy let out a gasp. I had her this time. She frowned. I never liked it when she did that. She squinted at me, again. "Ronnie, which George? ...George Shultz or George Bush? It's the difference between night and day."

"Oh ... I see what you mean. George Shultz, of course, our friend."

"Please tell me you misunderstood him."

"I can't. The Federal Reserve Bank isn't federal at all. That's a big, bad lie. It's privately owned by City of London, Queen of England, Warburgs, Harrimans, Browns, Rockefellers, and mostly by the Rothschilds, and those other banking families that own and direct all G8 central banks in lots of countries."

Nancy was mad. "Ronnie, you're nuts! The Federal Reserve bank is owned by the United

6

States Government! ...everyone knows that! Do you think our school teachers and college teachers and mayors are stupid? ...that Congress is stupid?"

"Not any more stupid than you or me."

"Ronnie, President Bush's father and grandfather worked for the Browns and Harrimans, and *that* would mean *they* personally had a stranglehold on the economy ...and, on the American people ...and that you, and the people who voted you and every president into office are totally in the dark ...and, we don't have democracy at all because it's showtime over nonsense that doesn't matter ... because private bank goons are pulling our strings ...that the American people are paying *300 billion dollars a year* in public taxes to *them* as interest on our national debt ...*that* money isn't going to the government at all, but into private wallets and purses of people that use that extra 300 billion dollars a year to beef up their companies ...while the rest of us starve. I refuse to believe any of it. It's impossible."

"Nancy, the same people who own block-shares of the Fed, they also own the banks that own the oil companies and weapons factories and pharmaceutical companies and car companies, electric utilities, nuclear power plants ... Bill said so."

"Ronnie, Bill Casey may have bent over for Allen Dulles every day of his life, but that doesn't mean he isn't full of horse pucky."

"Nancy, Bill got me elected!"

"No he didn't, Bechtel did."

"Same thing! George Shultz ran Bechtel! And Bill worked for George! Chile! Panama! Egypt! Iran! Iraq! Nicaragua! Africa! Russia! China! Half the people in San Francisco are there because we ethnically cleansed their damn countries they came from!"

Nancy pouted. "I like San Francisco, I always have. Don't bring San Francisco into this, San Francisco has nothing to do with what we're talking about!"

I didn't know what to tell Nancy, she was always right, "Say good night, Gracie."

Nancy yelled, "*You* say *good night, Gracie!*"

<>

Nancy was starting to get my goat. "Nancy, you look here! The other George ..."

"You mean Vice President Bush?"

"Yes. That George. He said the U.S. Constitution mandates a publicly owned central bank."

"Why would he say a thing like that after running the Central Intelligence Agency. The CIA's the Fed's private army."

"Bill Casey told him to tell me so I'd walk the line."

"Does Mike Deaver know about it?"

I got a kick out of that. "Nancy, some people couldn't use toilet paper if the instructions were printed on the wrapper."

"Ronnie, that's not fair. Or, nice."

"Nancy, I'm sorry ... George said a publicly owned central bank doesn't charge interest. If we had a public central bank like the Constitution says, there'd be no national debt. That 300 billion dollars a year in taxes we pay private bankers who own the Fed for interest on the national debt (instead of paying the U.S. Treasury), we could use that to fix America. Make jobs for people. Get rid of poverty. Have lower prices, no interest on mortgages, and happy times are here again. It would be real democracy like Jesus wanted."

Nancy rolled her eyes and sighed, she put her hand on her forehead. "Oh, brother! I already voted for you. Go to sleep."

Nancy turned off the lights. I fluffed up my pillow. I had a dream. One of those dreams where I get lost. I can't find my way. It's cold. It's night. It's in the forest. I can't see the wild animals. I know they're out there, watching. I forced my eyes open.

I whispered to Nancy. "Twenty years after Rothschilds sent the German, Paul Warburg, over here in 1906 ...that's when it happened. Paul wasn't an American citizen. Six years later, he had Congress establish the Federal Reserve Bank. He bought everyone with Rockefellor, Thyssen and Harriman money, otherwise he'd'a had to fool Congress ...and there are no fools in Washington. He became Fed chairman in 1913. Over in Germany, brother Max ran the German central bank ...and co-directed German Secret Service ...and the German military war effort against the Allies (the U.S., France, England). Paul was a U.S. citizen, by now. Paul and Max were money-issuing class. Naturally, they waged economic and military warfare on working people, middle class, upper class, and ruling class people in both countries. Jump-cut, action, Ronnie get on your toe-marks, good job. How'd you like that, Mommy? The findings were released, today ... George Bush's family did do business with the Nazis from the 1930's, all through the 1940's, *all the way through WWII*, through the Korean War, all the way up to 1952 ... while Otto Skorzeny, now working for Allen Dulles and Reinhard Gehlen was still doing the Nazi death squad guerrilla warfare genocide shuffle in Eastern Europe. World War II kept going there till 1952. I'll ask good old George what's up with that."

I must have been dreaming, because the sunrise stabbed through the windows at my eyes and it pinched.

Nancy sat up and hung her legs over the side of the bed. "Ronnie, it's time to get up.:

"Oh, God. Anything but that."

"I thought about what you said yesterday while I was listening to you snore, last night. Let me see if I got it right, okay? When the Fed block-share-holders in 1932 printed up a $100,000 bill redeemable in gold, they sold it to the U.S. government for $100,000. But it cost them two cents to print. So, they increased the national deficit $100,000. And, they made $99,999.98 profit, right?"

"Un huh, that's what George said."

"Well, it certainly wasn't George Bush. It was George Shultz. So, there are ten 100,000 dollar bills in one million. There are 100 in ten million, 1,000 in a 100 million (which is one billion) ...times 300 times two cents cost to print up 300 billion dollars on their printing presses in monopoly money."

"Yeah, it's 300 billion divided by 100,000 times two cents. Use the calculator in the nightstand."

Nancy fumbled with the drawer in the nightstand. She got out the calculator, "The calculator doesn't go up to 300 billion dollars."

"Well, it *is* a lot of money,."

"I'm gonna try doing it for one billion dollars then times it by 300, okay?"

"Okay."

"So, 1,000 times two cents, 300 times, right?"

I was losing my patience. "Nancy, I don't want to start my day this way."

"Just hold on, young man."

'You're starting to drive me nuts."

"Ronnie, it's not a very long drive."

"Nancy, it's $6,000!" I yelled. "It costs the bastards $6,000 to make a profit of 300 billion dollars! That's why we owe them ten trillion dollars in 100 years! And, that's why we pay them 300 billion dollars each and every damn year out of our paychecks! *That's* why the Constitution told us to have a public owned central bank, not a private owned one."

Nancy's mouth opened. She was quiet.

I had to laugh. "Well, nothing to say? ...in 65 years of marriage, that's a new one."

"It's not fair, to the American people. You can't tell them, they'll blame you."

"That's the whole point, why George told me

just like the other George told Bill Casey to tell the other George when the other George was running Central Intelligence. Jackson fought them. Lincoln fought them. Kennedy fought them. Are you getting the picture?"

Nancy smiled to comfort me. "Yes. And I think we better turn the channel. That's enough TV for one day."

Nancy was right. I'd had more than enough. "You said it, Nancy."

Nancy got that look of wonder on her face that I adore. "Ronnie, are these Fed shareholders *them*? Are they, *they*? Are *they* the ones to blame for making the wars, slaughter, hungry people, no national health insurance?"

"*Bingo!* ... Well, we better get downstairs into the Oval Office and start today's performance. Maybe, it's Oscar day."

"Do they own the studios, too?"

"You got that right, Sweetheart."

"Ronnie, but it's our own money. They make 300 billion dollars a year in interest printing up U.S. money and then selling it to us so we can use it? ... That doesn't make any sense, does it? Do you think I'm stupid? ... Tell me the truth. What's really going on?"

I laughed. "You tell me, and we'll both know."

Nancy thought about it. She start getting angry. "How can they get away with it? Why don't the priests and rabbis and congressmen and teachers tell us the truth? There's no excuse for it!"

I didn't know how to tell her. I didn't want to hurt her.

"Nancy, me, *I'm* the presidency ... *I'm* the excuse."

Santa Barbara West Coast Whitehouse

Silence!

Lights up.

Camera.

Action.

I was dreaming, again.

My doctor calls it dementia from Alzheimer's. Me and Nancy call it dreaming. It's easier. Everyone in the White House knows. It's the American people who watch me on the news, they think I'm okay. Nancy explained it to me, the way her psychic explained it to her. The way the spirits explained it to her psychic. I'll fill you in if I have time. My doctor's say I could live till Wednesday. I never thought that day would come. I was young, once. I thought I'd live forever.

Nancy yawned, "Ronnie, stop being morbid."

"Why do you always think you know what I'm thinking just by looking at my face? ...oh, never

8

mind. I *was* being morbid. But, not as morbid as I'll be next Thursday."

Nancy tried to take my mind off it. "What in hell was George W. Bush doing sitting on his butt in that Black classroom?"

"I don't know. If the Secret Service told me a plane flew into the World Trade Center, I wouldn't keep sitting on my butt listening to story hour."

Nancy laughed. "Neither would I."

"I'd'a been surprised."

"Of course. Specially, after the second plane hit. Is Paul Robeson's ghost still haunting you?"

I blinked my eyes. I shook my head. But Paul Robeson stayed there, pulsing. "Yes. He's here most of the time, now."

Paul's ghost was a beautiful shimmering green, the color of peacock feathers. He was wearing a rippling chain mail vest of luminous, iridescent green. "He's not alone. There's another spirit with him. By his right foot. At eye level."

Nancy kept reading the newspaper. "Are they just standing there?"

"No. It's more like hovering in the air, *as if* they're standing. The other spirit looks like a hat, a gold flying-saucer-shaped hat. It's spinning in place perfectly like a razor-edged Frisbee. It looks like it's not moving, at all. It's humming. It's shooting around in angles. It's flying all over the property, from the forest to the sea and back ...almost like it never moved at all, it's so fast." I can't figure out how it's connected in my brain. Bush is frozen like film stuck in a projector ...jets crashing into the Twin Towers, exploding. Kennedy's in the snapshot, bullets splattering his brains out into the air. Paul Robeson in the hospital after slitting his wrists in Moscow. U.S. Army Sgt. James Thornwell, another Black man like Robeson, driven insane by the SCREAMA.

The slave traders brought his parents from Africa to Newport in the 1800s ...slaves dying, rotting skin and bones, in chains. Dead hollow-eyed children, Black Holocaust corpses at their feet in bilge water.

I remember J. Edgar Hoover back in the 1950s. I was the U.S. spokesperson for Dulles, Nixon, and Warburg's Crusade for Freedom ...for the freedom fighters of the world! ...onward Christian soldiers! ...I did a speech for Goldwater.

I still see Hoover in that 1980s front page story. Powdery face made up as a drag queen. Cigar hanging between circles of rouge, purple lipstick, dripping black eye liner, rubber-grey face.

J. Edgar sized me up. "I'm telling you, Reagan, that Robeson's a threat! We got to get rid of him.

He's famous, he's a radical, he's Negro. He speaks Russian, Chinese, twenty languages, African dialects. He's on close terms with Nehru, Jomo Kenyatta, and other Third World leaders. What if he befriends Castro? Does Robeson think we'll let him come back from partying in Moscow, just like that? That we'd let him lead this damn new civil rights movement with Martin Luther King. We've had Robeson and King under surveillance for years. Who do they think they are?! Read my lips ... they're goners. First one, then the other."

Who did any of us think we are? ...suddenly, one humanity from the beginning of time. Mel Gibson's Jesus appeared beside me. He hugged me. He start carrying me down through the forest, down the path to the beach, down to the sea. I liked this script, maybe Oscar material.

Mel's Jesus must of read my mind. He smiled. "I'm fine, Ronnie, are you ready to find your toe-marks?"

Mel's Jesus had a sense of humor ...God knows I didn't need toe-marks to stand in front of His Camera. "I don't need toe-marks, today."

Nancy's voice trailed though the fog, cascading through the pine and redwood forest. "Ronnie?"

I tried to yell. I couldn't. I was numb in Alzheimer's. Sometimes I could think, other times not. But I had always been like that ...even as an actor. I whispered. "Nancy, here I am. Can you find me? I'm lost."

Nancy wandered off into the distance, her voice growing faint. *"Ronnieee? Where arrrrrre you?"*

<>

The sun was setting on me at the end of a very long day, at the end of a very long political career in show business.

Patti walked over to Nancy. "Mom, I can't get through to him, what should I do?"

Nancy shrugged. "I don't know."

Patti sighed. "At least he's still here."

Nancy held back her tears. Patti was a trooper like me and Nancy, didn't miss a lick. I never told her that's how I felt. I didn't want to spoil her. You know, a millionaire's kid needs to find out ... how does Patti say it, *'Sup?'* ...what's up? Their voices grew dim.

At my side two Black Secret Service agents played gin rummy. "He's not too bad looking for a vegetable," said one.

"He's crying," said the other.

My family sat at our picnic table. Michael and Maureen from my first marriage to Jane Wyman. We adopted Michael. Patti and Ronnie Jr. were from my marriage to Nancy.

Patti shifted uneasily in her lawn chair. "I'm estranged from myself."

Ron Jr. understood. "Me too."

Michael took more mashed potatoes. "They don't love us, neither of them. This ain't a reunion. It's a deathwatch."

Maureen glared at Michael. "Michael, you're being morbid. Stop it."

Michael sneered. "Not as morbid as *he'll* be next week."

Nancy nodded. "Children, if you have words to say to your father before he dies…"

Ron Jr. spoke first. "I forgive you Dad."

Maureen followed. "Me too, Dad."

Michael felt obligated to speak. "I forgive you Dad, but you don't know what for."

Patti sat down on the grass beside me. Patti cast a blue shadow. She hid behind her make-up like it was emotional mascara …and healing lipstick she painted on her dim masks, to hide behind. She was pretty without masks or make-up. She acted like the years smothered her. She had too many one-night-stands.

Patti's said it was a photo-op. George W needed to show Black Americans he didn't know that he *stole* the election in Florida, in his brother's state. They didn't count the Black vote. They just didn't count it. The computerized voting machines were coming up in some precincts in California with exactly the same number of votes for opposing candidates in the same district. In Florida, voting machine software was changed the night before the election. Patti comes up with things like this, I don't know where she gets it from …maybe TV. She's always been a rebel.

Nancy said her psychic said what the spirits said. That was, George W was in shock. Simple as that. It was because of his personal history. His family secrets. Being a president, you find out what you don't know, fast. Other times, they use you. You find yourself being used. You don't know by who. After all, it starts and you think you're calling the shots. Later, you find out the shots were calling you. Like with Kennedy. At that point, you're lucky to die before they get your family. When a bullet has your name on it, you do what you're told. You're on your own. Fly by night. Go where angels fear to tread. So, don't judge George W too bad. Because, when your best friends and your family lie to you from when you're a kid, it makes you feel low. That's what

Patti's always said. I found out the hard way. So will you. They don't teach it in school. Nobody tells you. This is my story.

I want to tell you it was Easter, or Christmas, or someone's birthday, or 4th of July, something like that. And, that must have prompted a Reagan family reunion. It usually did. My daughter, Patti, came out of the ranch house holding two coffee mugs. The screen door slammed behind her. It jiggled the sign on the door: 'Nothing happened here today'. Me, 88 years old, I rocked in my chair. Patti walked by her brothers and sister toward the cliff. There, her mom watched me staring out over the sea.

I loved my horses, my favorite movie stars, romance, baseball games, football, sports announcing, golf, undercover work, acting and getting people's attention, making them happy. Maybe or maybe not as great as Bogart or Cooper, Jimmy Stewart or Welles (even when he drinks), but as good as Joseph Cotton, or Flynn, or John Wayne, maybe. But, I stayed on life's silver screen. Do I get the part? You betcha', Mommy. I was working.

Mel's Jesus interrupted me. "George W's war on terror's backfired. Al Qaeda's moved into Iraq, grown in Europe, Latin America, Africa and Asia. It's totally funded from Saudi Arabia and Pakistani charities. The charities are based here at home, in the U.S.A. That's what the Fed block-shareholders bet on …generating more debt. They want 400 billion dollars a year ….300 billion dollars interest isn't enough."

I didn't understand what God's plan was. Faith was enough to get your ticket punched. Hollywood pulled it off, each time.

Mel's Jesus loved me. Was it selfish to save my own skin …to keep my mouth shut? What difference would it make to join the chorus. Did we need me to do the ashes to ashes, dirt to dirt audition before my Maker, to talk like words mattered, that my tears belonged to me. Life is a dream. Let me end mine by saying, I wasted so much of it.

Mel's Jesus anticipated me. "It's not if George W was good or bad, as president. He was his father's son, who was *his* father's son. The money-issuing class. Ruling class status. Social position. Family expectations. Grandpa built the highway. Al Qaeda drives on it. But, little George W didn't know *whatsup?*"

Talk about Divine inspiration. Here it was in my face. "That's what Patti says, '*whatsup?*' He got stage fright. He sat there. Try to come to terms. His family deserted him. He was in it alone. He knew ... those planes flying into the towers had his name written on them. But, not in a way a lot of people think they did."

Mel's Jesus knew that, already. "Yes."

I wanted to get on with my autobiography. It took me my whole life to figure the damn thing out. Sure, it breaks off a piece of your heart, *'Hey, take another little piece of my heart, now'*. I'll be dead, soon. You've known it the last ten years. That damn sickness came in my years at the White House. It took my brain. You saw me looking stupid. Falling asleep in meetings. It was the disease. I'm at intermission ... on hold.

I hate communism, sadists, sadness, old wealth, and glory. But, people enjoy the show, get away with it a while, stretch it out. Like it will never end. I love them for that. I offer up my suffering for their salvation ...with death poking its fork in me. Cutting little pieces off. Tasting me. Waiting till I'm done. Getting rid of labor unions, using colonial labor, outsourcing jobs to India and China, capitalizing on child labor ...I've lived too long for it. Heart broken too many times. Tired. Ready to die, happy.

I tried reaching Patti. My hand shook. My arm fell on my leg. I tried to move my lips. Words wouldn't come. Do you feel lucky? Do you, punk?" Playing people off each other. Leaving money changers behind in the temple? Peek out of the sheets, love twisting in flames, wives giving birth to little patriot acts, hunting us down for merit badges.

Nancy sat next to me. Watched the headlines as they happen, read it to me, Nancy.

"Libra in Pieces, here comes romantic interest, travel. Gasoline prices at new high. Utilities to cost more. PacBell 4.7 billion dollar ruling means higher phone bills."

Big stars overhead, thrilled, I stared at night. I daydreamed a black & white film noir, called, 'Ronald Reagan'. About gasoline, smelling money when it's new, taste of strawberries and champagne, sound of brass at court receptions, smell of a redwood forest, chill of the mist.

"Air crash in Croatia. U.S. delegation lost in Balkans disaster. Thirteen biggest industry captains and venture capitalists on diplomatic mission to Bosnia killed. Their 737 crashed into hillside in Croatia," Nancy read.

In the movie in my head, I was there. I stood in the Croatian Airport Tower. I watched the plane approach. Croatian air traffic controller kills runway homing beacon. Flips on homing beacon on mountain. I watch plane change course, hit mountain, yellow-orange flames spiking into the sky. King Saud's oil rigs spouting up fountains of $100,000 bills. A CIA guy, one of those outsourced ones to Saudi Arabia Vice President George H. W. Bush said his father used on covert operations, and, those Muhajidin Islamic Arab Nazi Al Qaeda ones in Croatia. That was towards the end of my presidency, before "H.W." or 'W' elected themselves president. That Al Qaeda CIA fella firing a gun into the air traffic controller's breast. That was wrong. I ran over to Mel's Jesus, now with me 24-7.

"Jesus, what'd the script say? What was he supposed to do *that*? Where's my toe-marks? I can't find 'em."

Jesus watched snapdragons, he didn't answer.

That got me thinking. I tried pulling the man's gun away. I figured we could re-shoot the footage, use new footage. My hands slipped right through the man's body. I wondered, 'Am I already dead? ... am I a ghost?' We couldn't use *this* footage. The assassin's bullet tore through the air traffic controller's chest. It blew out his back. I threw up. I didn't feel like a hero or a president.

Nancy called over some nurses to clean the vomit off me.

Michael eyed a bowl of mashed potatoes on the picnic table. He figured he could fit in thirds. He watched nurses clean me up, push my mouth into a smile for a take.

Michael turned to Patti. "He's a corpse already."

Patti retorted, "If you're not concerned, you wouldn't have come to the reunion."

"Something horrible's happening in his head he can't believe."

The kids talking loud irritated Nancy. "Children! ...I'm reading the paper to Dad."

Patti felt deflated. "There, she did it again."

Nancy kept reading outloud. "Economic espionage is the cause of the crash.'"

Allen Dulles' face, bigger than a football field, spread over the sky, I yelled at it. "Cut! Cut! He's in my face! It's is all wrong! Stick to the script!"

My eyes searched Nancy's face, then Patti's. But, they didn't even see Dulles. Or, next to him, Bush No. 1 with Saddam Hussein and Manuel Noriega, pallets of cocaine, heroin and gold bars, ammunition. Kuwaiti oil fields bubbled clouds of erupting black smoke in fireballs in the sky. I waved to Dulles. Dulles smiled and waved back. His face smiled from the sky as he spoke, "It's a take!"

It kinda pissed me off. Dulles had stolen the

scene from me. *"Are you working? Are you working? I'm working! I'm Ronald Reagan! This is my family picnic! I should be in the sky, not you! I'm the star! Not you! You're already dead, for Christ's sake."*

Patti watched me sitting in my chair, not moving ...emptiness frozen on my face. Michael watched a plate of cookies on the table. Patti broke the silence. "Mom, why's Dad horrified? ...like he can't believe it."

Nancy tried not to cry. "You must accept your father how he is. Bechtel Corp. won the contract for reconstruction of Bosnia and Croatia in former Yugoslavia, Nancy read. "Terrorists, death squads, and mercenary Arab Nazi Muhajidin work for the highest bidders. The highest bidders are Bechtel of California, Brown & Root of Texas, Halliburton Texas, and bin Laden Construction of Saudi Arabia."

The newspaper pages rattled as Nancy turned them. I shook my head. I couldn't get the sound out of my ears. I heard dry leaves being crushed. Machine-guns burst out. Guests ran from breakfast tables, bedrooms, cars, buses holding children in their arms. Nazis swarmed over cities, led by Croatian Ustasche. Sarajevo, the city itself sighed and cried. It raised up its arms in one great postage stamp picture of itself, curling in its flames. Jesus, I checked the script again. "Jesus, that last bit wasn't right. Why are Croatian Ustasche death squads being led by German, British, French and American central bankers? I can't tell if I'm in World War I, the sequel World War II, or the sequel World War III in Eastern Europe in former Yugoslavia."

I couldn't tell what the scriptwriters wanted their characters to say. I watched the serpentine convoys leave Germany with war stuff bought by America, always keeping on for Croatia. But, now we were fighting our WWI and WWII allies ... Russia. "Okay," I said. "I see what the writer's doing. Roll 'em."

Michael liked butter cookies better than chocolate chips or sugar cookies. He looked at me, then at Patti. "What the hell's going on in his head? I never knew when I was a kid. Now, I don't know. It's too late to care. I'm 50. My life's practically over."

Patti felt let down by that. "It's never too late, Michael. You're ashamed, because you were adopted. Dad loves you."

Michael stopped short.

Patti caught herself doing it again. She was having the same conversation with Michael she'd had a hundred times.

Michael knew his lines. "Give it up, he never cared." Michael's heart pounded. Inside, he felt wild. He turned towards me, "Dad you've had that stupid grin plastered on your face my whole life! Now, you can't talk. I don't know what the hell is going on inside you. It's the same feeling I've had every day of my life. Enjoying the family reunion? Dad? Dad? ...can you hear me? Over and out."

Michael saw I didn't hear him. He figured I was ignoring him, driving by in an angelically chauffeured limousine, waving. Nancy read slower and slower, feeling sleepy. I wanted to talk to her. I couldn't move my lips or get out words.

Nancy smiled. 'You could smile once in a while, Dutch. I know, Honey. If you could speak, you'd say you're glad we're out of government, away from those back-stabbing cutthroats."

Patti took Nancy's hand, giving it a slight squeeze. Their eyes met. Patti felt the familiar sadness. The distance. She and her mother smiled at one another, like glass mannequins. Nancy walked towards the adobe ranch house. Patti sat down on the grass by me. Patti was sitting on a living carpet of grass. She put her hand down, noticing the grass blades crushing beneath her weight. Patti wished God had trusted Himself enough to do it right, the first time ...so there wouldn't be food chains. Was God human, after all?

I tried to touch her. I took her hand.

Patti saw my lips trembling. "Mom, he's gonna talk!" Patti yelled.

I smiled at Patti. "It's about time the right people get killed in war."

Patti's heart broke. He had finally understood her. "I agree," was all she said.

I closed my eyes. I went back to my movie.

Patti turned to Nancy. "Mom, he talked to me. I waited my whole life for that."

Nancy was startled.

Mel's Jesus raised his hand in a peace sign.

I smiled, no one could see Him but me.

Mel's Jesus knew the score.

<>

Mel's Jesus spoke to me, "George W back in the 1970s, way later after 9/11, was he in that Black classroom, trying to tie together childhood family picnics with the bin Laden family? ...family picnics with his dad's friend, their neighbors, the Hinckley family, (who's son, John, was a Nazi, who tried to assassinate you, who crippled Jim Brady). When bin Laden's people financed W's father's oil company, who could guess Allen Dulles set up Bush No. 1, too ...cause one day the wash comes clean, and you'll be president someday.

"And those dry oil wells become money laundering fronts for petroleum board directors. Simply buying and selling crude reserves. Moving petrodollars around on paper. Trading international receipts like chocolate kisses.

"You take it, Ronnie."

Back in the day, 1979 and 1980, me running for president, George W's first oil venture, Arbusto, got that $50,000 investment from Texan James Bath. Bath made his millions investing money for Khalid bin Mahfouz and another BCCI-connected Saudi, Sheikh Salim bin-Laden, Osama's brother.

Salem bin Laden and Khalid bin Mahfouz were both involved with BCCI, the Bank of Credit and Commerce International … bin Mahfouz owned 20% of its stock.

Ten years later, Harken Energy, bought out George W's crumbling oil and gas business, and its CIA connections. And, 17.6 percent of Harken's stock was owned by Abdullah Baksh, another Saudi magnate representing Khalid bin Mahfouz.

Now, President's George & Son, Inc., have got rid of Hussein …turned Iraq over to the one group there that hates Westerners the most -- the Shiites. Bill Clinton found out the hard way. CIA is a paper tiger against Saudi's and the other money-issuing terrorists. Clinton's FBI director, Louis Freeh, was closer to poppy George H. W. -- who wasn't even president anymore, than to Bill Clinton. Poppy's relationship with Saudi royal families is to protect the money-issue class. Mel's Jesus smiled. That's because Mel's Jesus gave that insight to me, yesterday.

Just like Gehlen had given Truman, Eisenhower, Kennedy, Nixon et al wrong intelligence … all the intelligence reports for George W about 9/11 and Iraq were intentionally wrong, too. To supply deniability. Great cover.

W went to Langley the next week. He told them they were doing good, following the footsteps of his father, how Bill Casey did in Allen Dulles' footsteps … to serve and protect the money-issuing class.

W wasn't the highest card in the deck. He followed his intelligence advisors and speechwriters. I did too, when I was president. You don't get intelligence briefings how the world works, every morning for eight years, like me, and know nothing about the birds and the bees.

W knew about W's father's and grandfathers' stink with the Fed and European central banks. We knew how they financed Nazi and Saudi Intelligence. We knew W's dad was on the Carlyle board, like bin Laden's father was before him. We saw Granpa Prescott Bush financing the Nazis with U.S. taxpayers' money from his block-share of the Fed's annual royalties. All the time, Eisenhower, Nixon and Allen Dulles leading each other around by the nose. And, Gehlen and Bormann leading everyone around, how Bill Casey handled me …you and your people end up in turf-war alliances with the most anti-American people on the planet. But, Hollywood and TV makes you make it look good, or you and your family are dead.

Sometimes you don't even know it. How could you? Ask Kennedy. Ask Lincoln. Ask Garfield. Ask Jackson. More dead presidents. None of *them* wanted a privately-owned central bank.

Gehlen, Bormann and von Bolschwing ran U.S. intelligence around. They knew what the Warburg and Shroder brothers in Germany had to do for Rothschild favors. Okay? Get it? So, back off on W. No-one learnt this stuff in school, right? Learn the hard way …huh, Jesus? Did you have to question how your family wealth came from Nazis torturing kids and communists while you starved and burnt whole continents? Well, W did. So shut up. And, get out of town.

<> <> <>

Berlin 1921, Night of the Brownshirts

"Just as the Czarist and White Russian spies jumped to the Nazis when their own army was defeated in World War I, the German Nazi and Russian Czarist spies together jumped to the American army as the German Wehrmacht was defeated in World War II. This is how a Czarist spy ring, inside a Nazi spy ring, became the inner circle of an American spy ring …as it became the national security and foreign policy instrument of Washington, and Wall Street. Everything Washington and Wall Street would know about the Soviet Union and Eastern Europe [Editor's note: and now, Iraq & Iran, China & India] came from Czarists and Nazis installed at the center of the United States intelligence system. How can a naive, trusting, democratic republic give its secrets to crime and its innermost ear to the spirit of Central European Fascism? …and expect not to see its Constitution polluted, its traditions abused, and its consciousness of the surrounding world manipulated ultimately out of all realistic shape."
~ *Carl Oglesby, U.S. Intelligence Historian, 1986*

Brownshirts Count Sergei DeMohrenshieldt, Prince Max von Hohenlohe, Otto von Bolschwing, Karl Eichmann, Reinhard Gehlen and Otto Skorzeny, (son-in-law of international banker Hjalmar Schacht), chatted in a Kosher butcher shop. As they spoke, they swung meat cleavers into a bloody butcher block.

Count Sergei DeMohrenshieldt liked the weight. He liked the feel in his hands. "Well made."

Count Otto von Bolschwing smiled, nodding in agreement. Sergei DeMohrenshieldt heard footsteps. Sergei watched a couple stop outside the butcher shop. Sergei narrowed his eyes. He raised his hand to quiet his friends. "Jews are coming."

The Brownshirts put on devil masks. They rushed outside. Pigeons flew up from the sidewalk.

Sergei grabbed the couple, first. "First again!"

The other Brownshirts got there. They beat the couple with nightsticks, dragging them into the butcher shop and stretched them across the butcher block.

Sergei raped the woman. Then, he butchered her, thowing her hands into a pile of animal paws. He watched the twitching, bloody fingers. Threw her feet into the pile. Watched her toes twitch. Threw her head into a pile of animal heads. Watched her tongue loll. The mangled bodies of the butcher, his wife and children were mixed in the pile.

Sergei cringed, "It's dirty work."

Otto Skorzeny nodded. "Let me do it. I enjoy it." He swung the cleaver, cut off the chunk of meat containing the woman's pubic area, held it up over his head. Pushed the rest of the corpse onto the floor. Dropped the freshly butchered meat onto the butcher block.

Sergei lamented, "When all the Jews are gone, only then can we be gentlemen. In our Time, terrorism is patriotism. We Freikorps, chosen for honor, a savior death squad."

Prince Max von Hohenlohe watched the Jews' fingers twitch on the severed hands, shaking his head. "This disgusts me."

Reinhard Gehlen fought back vomiting, "Yes. But, it is a privilege. For ranking officers, only."

One by one they took off their masks, throwing them into the pile of severed limbs. Von Bolschwing spoke impatiently, "Let's burn this place down. Let's get out of here! Then go drink!" He lit a match, took a can of fuel oil by the oven, sloshing it everywhere. The Brownshirt death squad walked into the dark street, away from the butcher shop. Behind them, the shop flamed up. The flames distorted their shadows. Von Bolschwing start goose-stepping. Then, DeMohrenshieldt. They entered a Hof Brau. Other Nazis stood up ...saluting them, 'Sieg Heil,' with Roman-style stiff-armed salutes, palm and fingers held out at arm's length. Sergei and von

Bolschwing toasted Hitler, the Fatherland, German General Staff, and the World Order of the Thousand Year Reich.

Skorzeny slapped Max von Hohenlohe on the back. "Another successful General Staff Intelligence paramilitary operation, because of us. Our American Nazi allies, the Harriman money-issuing class, and Bush banking and oil brokering interests will be happy, very pleased with us." He brushed cinders off his uniform from the burning butcher shop as he walked briskly towards the bar.

Max liked port from Portugal. Eichmann lit a candle, then passed it to von Bolschwing. "It's symbolic of our victory."

Reinhard Gehlen, Allen Dulles & his Mercenary General von der Goltz

Reinhard Gehlen told his story...

For centuries, our money-issuing dynasty has been the World Order. And, the Brotherhood of Death. We control who lives and who dies ...not the other way, around. In 1870, Prussia conquered France. In 1871, at Versailles, Prussian leader Bismarck founded the first German Reich. In Zurich, Bismarck published the first, public Pan-German proclamation, "We must convince the German people German evolution did not end in 1870. Only then, can Germany take world power back."

1905, Pan-German venture capitalist dinner scene

The Pan-German League, All-Deutscher Verband, was co-founded 1894, by industrialist Alfred Hugenberg. He was a young millionaire, and a Prussian official. Through 1918, he co-financed the Kaiser's military machine. Venture capitalists Hugenberg, Kirdorf, Krupp, and Thyssen ruling families grew the organization. It became powerful. It had branches in United States, Central America, South America, the Balkans, and Russia.

German General Staff, composed of rich and powerful aristocrats, nobles, ruling class, and money-issuing families in Germany, led fascist phases of the German putsch into the 20th and 21st Centuries. Germans not in Germany were a 'Fifth Column of Warfare'. Nazi Fifth Columns sprang up everywhere. They survived German Army defeat in World War I ...and the result, crushing of the German State.

Carl von Clauswitz sat at the head of the table. He instructed his friend's son, Reinhard Gehlen, to recite. "Reinhard, All-Deutscher Verband?"

Reinhard spoke like a robot. "Germany must take decisive steps to a position of world power."

Natasha was proud of him. Great Granma Natasha Wilpf watched her guests. She looked at her husband. "Carl. Reinhard's only five."

Carl didn't care. "Reinhard, German destiny to conquer the world."

The little boy spoke up. "We win the war or we win the peace."

August Thyssen smiled.

Natasha gave Reinhard a cookie. "Reinhard, go and play. Dagmara, show Reinhard your ballet steps."

"Yes, Mama."

The children went across the room.

August Thyssen got Carl's attention. "Me and Hugenberg, Kirdorf and Krupp are reviewing 4th quarter reports from 5th Columns in the Americas, Balkans and Russia. Financing the Kaiser's coming war and investing in the Czar's empire, with revolution in the air is tricky. Do we trust our English, French, German and American investment capital, partners? Our French banking partners have 17 billion francs of venture capital invested. French and British venture capital investment is 1.5 billion pounds sterling, 8 million dollars American. The Anglo-French cartel controls 72% of Russian coal, iron and steel, and 50% of Russian oil. We get millions of francs and pounds in dividends of profits and interest from slave labor of Russian workers and peasants. Precisely, ten percent, on Russian labor. When we re-invest it, there's less cash flow, no liquidity, it's frightening."

Carl sighed. "Third quarter returns were good on all continents, but falling. Fourth quarter is getting hot for Czar Nicolas. He's growing our portfolio hitting his milestones ...but working everyone to death, that he doesn't shoot. Nick's made the Russian people slaves of German capital. So, we should now earn eleven percent on Russian labor, not ten. We've got to get everyone thinking, 'we need war'. Tell them there's no choice. Close our hearts to compassion. Build our portfolios on mountains of corpses. Holland and Belgium can't protect themselves. So, they have no right to exist."

August agreed. "And France?"

Reinhard spoke up. "We must crush France once and for all."

Dagmara call to him. "Reinhard, come back here, and play."

Carl felt on the right track. "Yes, let God be war. Let war bring our souls back to life. The Jewish race is dangerous to us. They bring materialism, democracy, freedom, and socialism. ... There. That's my pitch. Think it will fly?"

August felt excited, too. "Write it down. We'll make it a plank in our German League platform."

Carl write quickly. "Good."

Natasha overheard.

Carl looked at her. "I thought you were with the children. I wouldn't be talking about this if I knew you were here."

August looked at Natasha. "I don't know where Reinhard is. I've been in the bathroom," Heinrich von Clauswitz said. "What are you hiding behind your back? Bring it out. Where did you get those papers, my child?"

Heinrich pointed down the hall. "Reinhard took them out of the library in your study, papa. He was bragging. He said this is pirate flag. What is it papa?"

Carl reprimanded the boys. "You shouldn't be playing with my private things."

Heinrich held up picture. "Why do you have the pirate flag picture, papa?"

Carl was impatient. "It's not a pirate flag. It's the flag of the German Brotherhood of the Order of Death. The most powerful ruling families fly this flag. The flag of the shadow government. It flies unseen behind every government. You're too young to understand ... Reinhard! Come here!"

"Yes papa."

"Did you take these papers from my desk?"

"No, papa."

"One or both of you are lying!"

Heinrich pointed at his brother. "See what you did?"

"I didn't. You did."

Carl restrained his anger. "We'll figure this out later. Go play with Dagmara."

Heinrich protested. "I don't want to. I want to stay with you."

Reinhard wanted to stay too. "Father no, you spend time with Heinrich. I want to stay. Tell us a story, how Germany will rule the world."

Carl had no time for this. "Not now. It's dessert time. Louisa. Who wants cake?"

Dagmara was excited. "I do,."

Reinhard, too. "I do."

Heinrich piped up. "Me too. I'll have two pieces."

Louisa, the servant, stepped forward with hesitation. "I'm sorry, Mr. von Clauswitz. The cake's half gone. Someone got into it."

Carl was upset. "Heinrich! Was it you?"

"No."

"Reinhard! You?"

"No."

Carl stood up suddenly, almost knocking his chair over as he rose. "Bring me my riding crop!"

<>

The curtain fell on the opening act of my childhood when I reached puberty. The next thing I knew, I was 16 swimming with Annie in the Mississippi River. She got close to me. Our bodies touched.

Annie looked at me. She was treading water. "Are you a man yet, Ronnie?"

I was embarassed and had to lie, "Pretty much, not all the way. Are you a woman yet, Annie?"

"Mostly."

I heard *that* sound, "*Sounds* like number 61!" I swam at the drowning kid, cradled my arm around his neck. From shore, people yelled to me. I turned the kid loose on the shore. He ran to his parent's arms. Everyone cheered. I liked the limelight. I climbed into my lifeguard's chair. I fiddled with the radio. I found Father Kauflin, the anti-communist Catholic! I picked up a coke bottle. I pretended it was a microphone.

I mouthed Father Kauflin's words. "Germany prospered after World War I ...because Wall Street bought Germany up ...then loaned money to their German companies they secretly owned."

I turned up the sound. I clowned with the coke bottle. "Russia, once our ally, is a communist threat. The Red Menace is a hotbed of evil!"

I waved my hands in the air. I pounded the air with my fists. The crowd loved it. I improvised. I jumped to the beach. I balanced a stick on my head. I start singing the *Star Spangled Banner*. A friend played guitar. Another start fiddling. Annie passed around apple pie and corn-on-the-cob. I ran over to a flag pole with the American flag waving. I saluted it.

<>

When I was eight, I collected butterflies. The Iowa meadow was full of Swallowtail butterflies flying around me. I raised my butterfly net and began chasing butterflies. I swooped the net, back and forth in the air. I caught one. I watched the frail yellow creature struggle in the cheesecloth net. I felt sorry for it. Its pretty yellow wings flexed in bending arcs against the net, as it tried to fly. I got sad. I held life and death of a butterfly, in my hands. I didn't like it. I had a realization, almost. But, it slipped away. I forgot it. I looked towards home. I start skipping, singing, laughing, all the time dragging the net handle, *thumpity-thumpity* across picket fences. I stopped

to pick flowers. My mother liked flowers.

I could see home. I got scared. Dad was slumped down on the steps of the porch. He was trying to make it to the front door. I thought he was dead. I dropped my net. The butterfly flew into the sky. I ran home.

"*Onnuchh-ssshaww! Onnuchh-ssshaww!*" Dad snored.

Mom came out crying, I was helpless. I felt ashamed to see her cry. Years later, I learned kids take on the shame of their parents. I wanted her to stop crying. I wanted her to feel better. I put my arms around Mom's shoulders. "You'll be okay, Mom. I'll take care of you."

I looked into Mom's eyes. She smiled at me. She shrugged at Dad. She bent low to pull my drunken father to his feet. I struggled to help her. We got him in. We dumped him, half on the coach, half on the floor.

He was too drunk to know what he was saying. "C'mere. I won't hurt you."

I felt violence in my father. My body wouldn't move.

"C'mere!" Dad yelled.

Dad stood up, casting a shadow over me. He lost his balance. He fell on me. I felt trapped.

Mom was pulling me away from him, "Are you all right?!" .

I wasn't. "Yes."

<>

My Mom, Nelle, encouraged me to act in church plays. One night Mom and me and Dad were acting in play. I played Jesus, Mom played Gabriel, the angel. Dad played Satan ...he was drunk. To this day, I feel trapped in traffic, claustrophobic in restaurants or small spaces ...from having to sit next to my father at meals.

My Dad's name was Jack. When Jack drank, I felt bad. I hung my head. I watched the floor. I watched Jack suspiciously, afraid he'd hit Nelle. Jack exploded in anger. I didn't understand how Nelle could act calm. Then, I realized she was acting. I watched Nelle. She seemed to have an idea. Then, forgot it. Then, stared off into the distance. Jack crashed on a beat-up couch. I shrugged. I took my favorite book, about Dante in Hell, from a shelf. I tore out a picture of Satan. I ripped it up. I threw the pieces into the fireplace. I got on my knees to pray. I watched it burn. I climbed on the couch by the fire. I fell asleep, holding my Bible. In dreams, I walked through peaceful, paradise Earth. My Bible fell out of my hands into the fireplace. I woke up. I saw each page exploding in flames. Jack stumbled outside, staggering drunk. He left footprints in snow. They weaved down the street for quite a while, to the mid-western mansion owned by Allen Dulles. Jack, who found it hard to keep his job as a shoe salesman ...Jack, who had trouble keeping a job ...Jack, whose family moved often because of our poverty ...Jack, a step in front of bill collectors, moved us out the back door when they were at the front ...Jack, in ragged clothes, ripped and wrinkled. Drunk, Jack stopped. He stuck his finger in a hole in his shoe. He pulled out a pebble. He stared through Dulles' mansion gates, through a window. He saw a masquerade of beautiful women. They were dressed like angels, in satin and silk gowns, pearls, rubies and diamonds. Jack looked into another room. Men and women were undressing, rolling on each other. Jack rubbed his crotch through his pants for a while. He shook his head to clear it. He stumbled along. He wondered, would he come home a stranger?

President's Oval Office, First Cabinet Meeting

The day after my inauguration I headed into my Oval Office for my first Cabinet and Staff meeting. Reporters talked with me before I went in.

"Mr. President, will you issue an Executive Order on cost-cutting?" Alan, one of the reporters from California, said.

I shrugged. I didn't know. Budget Director David Stockman was standing next to me. He was nodding frantically to me ... I got the message. "I have a smiling fellow here, beside me, Budget Director David Stockman. He tells me, we do. He looks like I'm going to issue an Executive Order on cost-cutting," Leaving the reporter behind, me and Stockman walked into the Oval Office, joining the other Cabinet and White House Staff people.

In my Oval Office, Assistant Chief of White House Staff Mike Deaver submissively tried to explain to me his actions of the previous evening at the inaugural gala. "Look Ron the other night at the ball you attacked me for not believing in you. That's not true. No, I got no questions about your abilities. I know you more than you let on to everyone ...I've been with you through two gubernatorial campaigns, which were successful, in part, because of me. I believe in you, Ronnie, I always have."

I appeared to be irritated. I wasn't an actor for nothing. "I'm glad to hear that, but Christ! You act guilty! Were there gangsters at my inauguration?"

"Yes."

Enough was enough. "How can I help but feel insecure! I don't want to get impeached my first day in office. We didn't take campaign money from foreign nationals, did we Mike?"

Mike felt a chill run through him. "Foreign financing of campaigns is illegal."

I saw the denial on Mike's face, felt it in his voice. I felt puzzled. "You mean you knew, and you still ..."

"No! I didn't! Stop! It looks wrong in public to thank banana republic dictators when there's press around ... so, I stopped you!"

I eyed him. "But we believe in Contra freedom-fighters, morally and financially, because they kill communists ...of course I'm going to thank him. I don't get it."

In a wall mirror, I saw Bill Casey, Director of Central Intelligence give a high-sign, mumbling to George Bush, Vice President of United States. Bill wanted George to help tone things down.

That irritated me more. "Bill, I feel humiliated when you' mumble behind my back to George. Can't you talk face-to-face with me? ...it's not like I'm not smart enough to understand you, is it? Say what you mean, I'll understand."

Bill mumbled in his bumbling, condescending way. "I was remarking on the strange mixture of guests at your inaugural ball last night, Ronnie. I was a bit surprised, myself."

I was taken aback by Bill's comment. George reacted with an amused yet chagrined look ...the Bush trademark.

I was losing my patience. "What's going on, Bill? No one gets past you. You're an old hand at politics. You ran Export-Import Bank a few years ago, when Bechtel was on the board. You used to head Office of Strategic Services intelligence. Now you head CIA ...*I'm* surprised *you're* surprised. I don't like that condescending tone in your voice when you speak to me. Stop it."

Casey mumbled something to himself. He was keeping score on his mental scoreboard. "Can not tell you everything, Mr. President ...it would implicate you in scandals ...like the theft of Carter's campaign notebook. I was saying to George, it's still a mystery how we got a hold of it at all. Anyone remember Nixon's Watergate?"

Bill's offhand remark amused George Bush, who looked around to make sure no one was watching him. Then, he smiled sarcastically. George spoke up. "Remember it? I'm still covering it up. It was illegal campaign donations from foreign nationalists, drug money and kickbacks from foreign aid we gave to dictators that made it back into our own congressmen's campaign funds. It wasn't just covering up the Kennedy and King assassinations for the Fed."

Bill interrupted him. "Stealin' Carter's campaign notes'll be a mini-Debate-gate, unless we deny everything."

George frowned. "Great, just what I need to start off as Vice President."

Casey felt amused. He laughed.

George got more serious. "Bill, I don't find it amusing ...it's disgraceful for counter-agents to get caught at something like that."

White House Chief of Staff James Baker III spoke with a Texas accent. And, he had a Texas sense of humor. "Boy, I just couldn't decide to take advantage and keep those stolen notes or not. But, we won the debate with them ...maybe the election. And, here we are. You can't argue with history ...we're making it up as we go."

Edwin Meese was now Presidential Counselor. That was a new position that had never existed before my Administration. "Jim, who handed the notes to you?"

"You did.".

"I didn't steal 'em."

It felt like I was starting to get the picture. "Bill, did you have an Agency mole in Carter's White House? ...did the mole steal Carter's campaign notebook?"

Bill was neutral. "Ask Jim Baker."

Baker wasn't amused. "Wait a minute Bill, you gave those to me."

"I don't remember doing that."

I found myself following the conversation like it was a ping pong match, watching the bouncing ball go back and forth over the truth without touching it. I needed to let them know where I stood. "Gentlemen, this will be an honest administration. That's what the history books will say."

As the days went by I started to like flipping the calendar pages on my daily calendar after each day's work ...as a sign of accomplishment. We soon found ourselves meeting again.

Bill Casey was amused. "We did leak October Surprise ...that was a nice domestic intelligence operation ...planting disinformation stories in the press. That's national security ...not treason. To hell with Carter. All he did was fire 500 CIA covert action operatives. But you know what? ...we got even. Us intelligence people take care of our own, one way or t'other."

I felt puzzled. "Bill, are you rehiring those 500 CIA field operatives Carter fired?"

"Yes, and a lot more."

"Are the Contras getting the weapons we promised them?"

Bush was startled, he shot a glance to Casey.

Bill showed a 'not-to-worry' look to Bush. "It has to look like we're cutting back weapons sales ...to freedom-fighters in Taiwan."

I noticed George looked visibly relieved. He nodded knowingly at Bill.

I was puzzled. I didn't understand. I felt frustrated. "You mean, you sell the weapons to Taiwan first? I don't want to know. Just get the job done. Spare me the details."

I felt like I was almost going to have an intuition ...I shook my head ...but, it didn't come into focus. I stared off, across the room.

But I came back. "I'm starting to resent the hell out of you, Bill. Don't treat me like I'm your puppet. I don't have a head filled with sawdust. I don't get by just on charm and looks. I have a brain. I hired you. I know exactly what's going on ...my good looks take the heat off you! See what those words say on that flag on the wall, 'Don't tread on me'. Get the picture?"

Bill sounded intimidated. "It's a two-way street."

I glanced at George, indicating I wanted some back-up and emotional support from him. "George, are you going to let Bill talk to me that way? Speak up! Say something!"

George was caught off guard. "My mind was wandering, Mr. President."

I felt upset, showing emotion was one thing I would not forgive in myself. "All right. Let's all be calm and let bygones be bygones."

Bill showed his condescending, trademark look.

Chief of Staff James Baker was amused.

Jan 1, 1981, White House, Nancy's office

Nancy was in her White House office, on the phone. She called me in my Oval Office. "Ronnie, National Security Adviser Richard Allen called. He got $1,000, and a pair of Seiko watches from Japanese journalists. ...Because he arranged an interview for them with you. ...Okay. I won't. The Oval Office furniture is worn threadbare. In my office we have mousetraps! Mousetraps! Why doesn't one of those investigative reporters write an article about that?!"

Jan. 27, 1981, airport

I welcomed the hostages home. Deaver had arranged a photo-op for me. I made a short statement to the press. "The policy of the Reagan Administration dealing with terrorists will be one of swift, effective retribution."

Deaver waved to the audience shills to clap. The

18

Marine Band start playing, *Hail To The Chief*.

I put my hand over my heart.

Nancy reached up and took my hand. Nancy whispered to me. "Don't do that to, *Hail To The Chief!* Take your hand down!"

"Oh …I thought it was the national anthem."

Feb. 6, 1981, briefing room, press conference #1

I looked over the reporters in the room, suspiciously. This was my first official presidential press conference in the Press Briefing Room. I snapped into a rant automatically. "The goal of the Soviet Union is promoting world revolution …a one-world, Socialist communist state! They reserve for themselves the right to commit any crime …to lie …to cheat, to get world revolution!"

Nancy interrupted the press conference. She was carrying a 4-tiered birthday cake, for me. She was singing, *Happy Birthday To You.* The White House Staff joined in. Some of the reporters, too. I smiled. I was very happy. "It's the 31st anniversary of my 39th birthday." I told everyone.

Feb. 18, 1981, my first joint session of Congress

I addressed my first joint session meeting of Congress. "I'm warning Congress, the national debt is approaching 1 trillion dollars! A trillion dollars would be a stack of 1,000-dollar bills, 67 miles high!"

Both Houses of Congress were totally silent.

Mar. 3, 1981, interview in press briefing room

One night, I was interviewed by Walter Cronkite in Press Briefing room.

I was finishing a comment. "In 1939, Franklin Delano Roosevelt called on the free world to quarantine Nazi Germany. That's what we have to do with the Soviet Union, quarantine it."

The interview ended. The lights and cameras were cut. The mikes were taken off me, and Walter Cronkite.

Walter Cronkite cleared his throat. "FDR never made a speech to quarantine Nazi Germany."

I was genuinely surprised. "He didn't?"

Walter sadly shook his head.

White House Chief of Protocol Ambassador Lucky Roosevelt's office

Sitting in her White House office Selwa Lucky Roosevelt's problems began her first day on the job. George Bush's wife, Barbara, stopped by unexpectedly. Ambassador Lucky had to deal with it. As White House Chief of Protocol and Decorum, Ambassador Lucky was on the job, only to find her staff wearing blue jeans!

And, chewing gum! Barbara Bush walked in on them, like *that*. Ambassador Roosevelt felt embarrassed. She struggled, trying to cope with her embarrassment.

Barbara Bush understood. "It'll be okay, Lucky. We CIA wives have to stick together."

"Oh God yes."

Lucky understood Barbara exactly … and suddenly felt at ease whenever Barbara was around.

Barbara smiled. "We always seem to be moving around the world with our husbands …or, wondering where in the world they are today, if they're safe."

Lucky felt apprehensive. "I don't even know where Archie is now …maybe Africa with David Rockefeller. But, I don't know. South Africa, or Angola, overseeing oil operations."

Lucky found a true friend in Barbara Bush.

Barbara smiled. "The last thing I do is stand on ceremony. I've seen my own kids in blue jeans often enough. But, your job …is to stand on ceremony. That's what you were hired for."

Lucky felt relieved of her embarrassment again. Lucky appreciated how easily Barbara put her at ease, in a cordial and pleasant, social way.

Lucky smiled. "Your husband, the Vice President, is a very lucky man to have you on his side."

Lucky remembered back in the '50s when her fiancé, Archie Roosevelt took her to luncheon.

"Darling, wait a moment before you say yes or no to marrying me," Archie said, "there's something you have to know about me."

"What, Darling?"

"I work for Central Intelligence Agency."

"What's that?"

"Well, that's a government intelligence unit. It was thrown together after World War II to protect the Fed block-shareholders, when Office of Strategic Services OSS was revamped to protect American overseas business investments better to fight Communism here and overseas."

"That's great. How thrilling."

"I sit behind a desk pushing a pencil around as an intelligence researcher. But, I get called on the road sometimes …but never into field operations, …so there's no danger, for me. Most of all, Darling, we have to keep it a secret, just tell everyone my job's at the university."

Lucky was excited. "How thrilling. Living with a spy!"

Back in Lucky's White House office sipping ice tea with Barbara Bush, Barbara noticed Lucky seemed lost in thought. Barbara knew, from the look on Lucky's face, what Lucky was thinking …because Barbara was remembering the first time George told Barbara he worked for CIA.

It was in 1976. George was appointed to Director of CIA. George hung up the phone, sat down at the table for dinner. The family butler served George a drink. The family cook delayed dinner five minutes, while George was on the phone. Now, the family waiter served soup. George got up. He walked past W, and his other kids, to the other end of the table. He kissed Barbara sweetly on the cheek. "Well it looks like I know who the new director of the CIA is going to be."

Barbara looked at the questioning look on her husband's face. "Really?"

"Yes."

"But, George, really. I've suspected you since you graduated college. When you went behind the Iron Curtain for that oil exploration company, you were on Company business. And, when your friend Shackley, he used to run JM/Wave Radio in Florida against Cuba. CIA runs JM/Wave, that's what the girls say. Congratulations. Will this help you finally get rid of Castro? …and get our family's Cuban offshore oil leases back, up-and-running, again?"

George got that look of feigned machismo. "I'm going to give it a hell of a try."

Barbara and Lucky stopped reminiscing at the same time. Lucky sipped her ice tea. "Barbara, you know Mike Deaver's 'little shits' that work for him? I call them, 'munchkins'. One of them marched in yesterday and demanded I hire one of their staffers as my chief assistant, can you imagine that?"

Barbara smiled. "I'm afraid I can. A lot of the White House Staff came from California. What can you expect? When push comes to shove, they've been shoving, already."

"I told the munchkin, no. Then, Deaver called me, himself, to pressure me to hire his staffer. I told him, no, too. I had to decide if I would let people bully me or not …or if I would tell him to take this job, and shove it. But, I realized that either way, I had to stand up for myself or the munchkins would ride me out of town. I followed my intuition …and did what's right. I stood up for myself. Now, I keep an eye out for munchkins."

Barbara's eyes twinkled. "Good, Lucky. You did right."

White House Situation Room

The first days at the White House for me turned into the first weeks. I flipped the calendar pages on my desk, then hurried to the White House Special Situation Room. I sat down.

I turned to George Bush. "I want this settled, I don't want it coming back to haunt me. Who knows about these foreign aid kickbacks into election campaign funds, George?"

George Bush wouldn't jump out of line. "I was out of the loop, I'll look into it."

"I'm not satisfied with that, just what loop are you in?"

"I'll get you a full report."

I turned to Bill Casey. "Bill, you're the senior intelligence officer here, you know about this?"

"I wasn't in the loop, I don't know."

I lost patience, I angrily threw my glasses off. They skid across the table. "Who does know?! Bill, I'm asking you!"

Bill was indifferent. "I just get the reports off my desk."

I seldom got angry enough to yell, "Then, no one's in the loop! Will someone tell me when the CIA has a coup and installs a puppet military regime someplace and we give them foreign aid to run the regime, does any of that foreign aid come back to the Presidency or Congress as illegal campaign donations? Did we broker bribes to-and-from foreign nationals to get into office?! Deaver?!"

Mike took a nip of vodka from his pocket flask. "I'll get back to you with a report."

Bush kept self-control. "Give me a copy of that report, too. It's something I should look into."

Attending the Bob Hope Salute to the UUSAF 40th Anniversary celebration with Kirk Cameron, Phyllis Diller, Lucille Ball & Emmanuel Lewis at Pope Air Force base in Fayetteville, North Carolina. 5/10/87

Mike burped. "Only if you give me a copy of your report."

George nodded.

Bill mumbled. "I want copies."

Bill smirked. He looked at George, then shook his head at me. As Bill watched me George saw Bill's look, that seemed to say, 'You sucker'. Christ, I was a trained actor. I had to observe, study and practice looks like that -- for every script in every movie I ever played in. I had no trouble spotting *looks*.

Bill noticed George watching me. Bill saw that George had a look that seemed to say, 'There's one born every day'. Bill mumbled. "The public doesn't understand. You can't stop covert-ops and Communism at the same time. Or, there's no teeter-totter."

Bush jumped in. "That's right. He's right, Mr. President … covert ops stop Communism."

Bill looked like he thought George's timing was off, or that George had agreed too readily, or jumped in too fast. I didn't think George's timing was off at all. Bill was calm. After all, I was an eager-beaver Cold Warrior. I started to feel less frustrated. My mood started to brighten. I felt agreeable.

I smiled. "I'll do whatever it takes to save the world from Communism."

Bill noticed, I had that knowing, 'insider' look. That amused Bill. Bill noticed George was holding back a smirk. Bill wore a sarcastic and condescending grin. "Me and Deaver got you campaign financing from the Contras. What you gonna do about it, resign? …We got you financing from the WACL contingent. That's how we got you elected. Foreign nationals financed this production. We wrote your script. Wake up and smell the roses. I told you. Maybe you forgot."

I didn't know to be upset or not. Did he tell me? Did I forget? It felt like I was having an idea …like something was opening up in my head. I caught my composure. "Well, I never heard you tell me. Those banana republic dictators, they're not puppets at all. They're actors, like me. They make things happen. They make change. We produce them. We direct them …long live the freedom fighters! If it's Armageddon, God's on our side … How do I look."

Mike took another sip from his flask. He was drunk. "Handsome, Mr. President. The American public likes handsome." As soon as everyone's attention was off him, Mike emptied his flask, down the hatch.

Chief Spokesman for the White House Press Larry Speakes tapped his watch crystal with his finger. Larry looked at me. "Press conference time, Mr. President. Reporters are waiting. Time to go get 'em. You look great. Give 'em hell."

I nodded confidently. I stood up and checked myself out in a full-length mirror. Right then, and there, like an actor would before going onstage, I washed the last vestiges of how upset I was off my face …putting on that look of effortless confidence and handsomeness the audience pays for. I winked, and smiled at myself in the mirror …I still had it.

I walked into the adjoining White House Briefing Room to greet reporters. I gave them a 'thumbs-up' sign, eager, at home. I was happy to be on stage again, vital, alive, and accepted.

I was making a radio speech at the same time. I sat down. I tapped my finger on the radio microphone to see if it was live. I looked at the radio technician. The technician signaled to me.

I smiled. I spoke into the microphone to test the sound levels. "My fellow Americans I'm pleased to tell you today that I've signed legislation that will outlaw the Soviet Union, forever. We begin bombing in five minutes." The people in the room were shocked. They started to get frantic. I laughed off their reaction. "It's only a sound check."

The radio technician looked nervous as he signaled me. "No, Mr. President. We were live on that one. You're on the air. Please continue with your prepared script."

I felt confused. I looked at Mike Deaver, accusingly. Then, I laughed. I began reading the prepared portion of my broadcast. "The Soviet Union is the focus of evil in the modern world. The Soviet Union is led by men who reserve the right to lie, cheat and steal their way to world domination. A Soviet conspiracy underlies all the unrest in the world. If the Soviet Union wasn't playing this game of dominoes, there wouldn't be any hot spots in the whole world. Let's see what's next. Oh yes.

"As you know, former President Carter enacted the Refugee Act of 1980. This was designed to protect those fleeing their countries, afraid of persecution for religious, political, or racial reasons. Under my Administration, only refugees fleeing Cuba or Nicaragua will receive political asylum. Salvadorans, Haitians, Guatemalans, whose regimes Washington consider as allies, are being labeled inadmissible …because we consider them

21

to be, 'economic' refugees. Today, I ordered the Coast Guard to tow out to sea any boats of Haitian refugees found approaching America."

White House Historian Bill Barnes was dragging a string back in forth in front of Jackson. Jackson was pretending not to see it. Then, suddenly Jackson jumped up high in the air. Jackson came down with all four paws on top of the string. Then, he flicked his tail and walked slowly and proudly away. Bill Barnes made a few notes in his White House diary.

'A small group of American activists have formed a Sanctuary Movement. The Sanctuary Movement is modeled on the Underground Railroad, used in President Lincoln's era to smuggle persecuted slaves out of the South up into the Northern States. Sanctuary Movement helps people fleeing oppression and death squads in Latin America and South America. It helps oppressed people fleeing dictators CIA installed after killing legitimate government leaders. Sanctuary Movement organized a network of churches and non-profit organizations to shelter, feed and hide refugees ...who would otherwise be sent home, handed over to death squads, then slaughtered.'

<>

As time passed, I enjoyed my radio broadcasts more and more. It was like the old days, when I was a young man, just starting out. I noted my broadcasts on my desk calendar with a check mark after I did them. Then, I flipped over to the next day's calendar page.

As months went by, official Press Briefings came and went with predictable regularity ...I noticed that -- each time I flipped over pages on my daily desk calendar.

White House, President's bedroom

In my presidential quarters in the White House, where Nancy and I now lived, we were in the bedroom, I looked at some family pictures on the bureau. I felt tears in my eyes. I was flooded with memories of me and Patti arguing.

"See, we were a happy family. I don't know what went wrong."

Patti practically exploded. "What went wrong was my whole childhood ... you were the invisible man, who wasn't there."

"I was there, we have pictures to prove it. See those pictures of our family being happy together?"

"I still feel the pain!"

"I told you, Pattie. Me, and Nancy, will pay for a psychiatrist for you."

She start yelling, "You need the shrink! Not me!"

I shook my head negatively at Patti. I had an idea ...almost ...but I forgot it. I picked up a vintage movie magazine with me on the cover, staring at it, teary-eyed. I bit my lip so I wouldn't cry. The phone rang, I picked it up. Being an actor, I automatically put on a happy face, "Good evening, Ronald Reagan here."

Patti stormed out of the room.

I was alone in the bedroom.

Yes, I was remembering those drama queen scenes with Patti, as Nancy walked into the room.

"Ronnie, let's go to sleep, Darling."

"Oh, yes. Sweet dreams Mommy."

"You're acting disoriented. Is it because you're sleepy?"

I didn't answer because I was falling asleep.

White House Situation Room

Whenever there was an emergency or pending crisis, we called meetings in the White House Situation Room ...if someone felt they had a 'situation' on their hands. Usually, my personal White House Staff and my Cabinet would be there arguing.

The White House Staff was mostly middle class or upper class people I brought with me from California. We were nouveau riche, going for instant gratification and the quick fix, for immediate return on investment.

The Cabinet was old ruling family wealth. They measure percentage returns over the long haul of several generations. And, were very conservative. California money tended to follow technology, the stock market, sink venture capital into start-up companies. But, established old ruling family money preferred sinking venture capital into banking, oil, gold, weapons, real estate, and war.

Secretary of State Alexander Haig, a Cabinet member, professionally represented old wealth ruling families. To the media, he was the ultimate Cold Warrior. In the Sit room, today, Haig was furious ...absolutely, over the top, yelling. "Nicaragua Contra support money's coming from the outside. I know who's financing Contras in Nicaragua!"

Mike Deaver was drunk, sweating profusely. He sounded worried and defensive. "You think you know who? Then, who?! Who, me? You're paranoid."

Haig glared at Deaver. "I have an informer!"

Mike didn't go for it. "You don't know shit!"

I stepped between Haig and Deaver. "Gentlemen, calm down. We need an orderly meeting here, tonight. We're going to get Congress to start financing the Contras, right Bill?"

Casey mumbled, impassively. "Yes, it's in the best interests of our G-7 finance ministers and central bank governors ...I mean, it's in the best interests of the country."

Haig kept yelling, "We can blow Central America off the map!"

Defense Secretary Weinberger was upset. "I get a kick out of your macho attitude, Haig. When the Arabs almost blew Israel off the map ...where were you then. Which side were you on, then, Haig?" Weinberger yelled.

Haig was furious. "I saved Israel. I sent the Israelis missiles, through unofficial channels. That earned me enemies. Weinberger, you're a Jew, but you're anti-Semitic. Is that from cutting your teeth at Bechtel?"

Weinberger started going over the top, too. "Helping Israel the way you do, stinks! The Arabs were right then. They're right, now! You blew it, that time!" Weinberger yelled.

Deaver chimed in, "He's right, Haig!"

Then, I went over the top. "Calm down! Shut up! Sit down!" I yelled.

People took their seats.

Defense Secretary Weinberger pulled out over-sized cartoon drawings. They showed silhouettes of two soldiers. They compared sizes. The Soviet silhouette was big. It had a red star on it. The American silhouette was small. It had Stars & Stripes on it.

Weinberger started his talk. "As Secretary of Defense, I'm in charge of the military-industrial complex. We must keep the military supplied with weapons, vehicles, food, ammunition, uniforms, and communications. I need a bigger budget to fight communists. I won't back down on this!"

The youngest person there, David Stockman was Director of the Office of Budget Management. Weinberger made him angry. David wasn't old wealth, but he wasn't from California, either.

David Stockman took aim and fired. "Boy the hogs are feeding tonight. Weinberger, you and your damn Laffer trickle-down economics fantasy will bankrupt America! Don't give in to Weinberger, Mr. President. Before your administration, the U.S. was the biggest creditor nation in the history of the world. You and your handlers will make us the biggest debtor national in

the history of the world. We'll have the biggest deficit in history! The country will go bankrupt! Why? So Casey and his G-7 financiers can collapse our economy, and take over the Soviet Union with debt financing? ...like they've taken us over? I have to cook the budget every damn day! Fudge them, so the budget doesn't stink."

I tried to bring the meeting back under my control. "Mr. Stockman, Mr. Weinberger worked for President Nixon. Mr. Weinberger worked for me, when I was Governor of California. I think you'd do well to see his big picture."

I nodded to Weinberger.

Weinberger felt exonerated, he looked at Stockman, "I took this office. I was convinced the U.S. was unilaterally disarming itself for ten years. All that time, spit and I'd hit an intelligence report documenting the massive arms build-up of the Soviet Union. I'm an amateur historian ...America's 1981 position, in relationship to the Soviet Union, is the same as Britain's was in the '30s to Nazi Germany.

"Churchill saved Great Britain by rearming her. You know what Churchill's said, 'Never give in, never give in, never, never, never, in anything great or small, large or petty, never give in.' I need 10% defense more budget than Carter had. And, over five years it's only 1.5 trillion-dollars."

I smiled.

Stockman was uncomfortable, "I made a mistake in my figures. It's 300 billion dollars less. My fault. But, even with my mistake it's over what Reagan said he wanted."

Weinberger got angry again. "It's your error. I won't trim it out! Can't you understand the tiniest reduction in my budget increases the chance of war? Haven't you ever heard of Soviet military might? We're far behind them. Anyone who cuts a nickel from my budget wants the Communists to win.

"Look at the charts. I superimposed Soviet defense plants on top of a map of Washington. Here's a chart superimposing Soviet nuclear and conventional forces on top of ours. See how big they are. The Soviets dwarf our defenses. They dwarf the defenses of the whole free world, combined! Mr. President our B-52 planes are older than their pilots."

I nodded.

David Stockman seemed in shock.

Caspar Weinberger went on. "Here, see this poster? See these three cartoon soldiers, Mr. President? The tiny pygmy-sized soldier who has no rifle, he's Carter's defense budget. The tall, skinny pygmy soldier wearing glasses, the

Woody Allen character carrying that tiny toy-looking rifle, he's Stockman's budget. But, look! ...this big giant GI Joe with muscles like the Hulk ...he has a brand new military helmet ...a brand-new flak jacket ...he's carrying a brand new M-60 top-of-the-line machine gun! This super-hero American warrior is my Defense budget."

Stockman watched me smile and nod ...but, could not restrain himself from yelling at Weinberger, again. "I can't believe a Harvard-trained Cabinet officer can bring these cartoon pictures to the President. Weinberger, is this Sesame Street?! We're going to be spending 300 billion dollars a year. Not counting CIA, Energy Department and National Security Agency defense figures!

"We'll have the biggest budget deficit in history! We'll go bankrupt. Why? To line the pockets of the Fed major block-holders? ...to bloat the budgets of the defense companies they direct? So Casey and his central bank cartel he pimps like Allen Dulles did, can reap windfall interest payments off the skyrocketing national debt? The budget looks like a madman's. It's a mess."

I was never too impressed with Stockman, he was too young, lacked maturity and style. I glared at him. I slammed my hand down on the conference table. "Stockman, you're not allowed to let the budget look bad! It has to look good ... Gentlemen, compromise. Calm down, everyone! Stockman, make the budget look good, that's what you were hired to do. Make Reaganomics look good. Trickle-down economics looks complicated, I know. You have to simplify it, so the taxpayer can understand. Even George Bush understands it. Why can't you? Take it from me. I made movies in Hollywood. Make it simple.

"Boil it down to a snapshot. Let me explain. We're supply-siders. A minimalist government with few or no services. We levy lower taxes. That cures our economic ills. Reduce taxes to increase growth. It means, savings. It stimulates commerce. Convince people to work harder. We reduce inflation. Then, the value of tax revenues rise. You're a trained economist!

"You say it better than I can! Remember when I met with President Gerald Ford, and that California economist from California, Arthur Laffer? Laffer was in a restaurant. He could draw. So, he drew a graph on the paper placemat ...a picture of what happens when you cut taxes. It was a curve. So, everyone called it, his 'Laffer curve'. It means the I.R.S. will collect inadequate revenue when taxation approaches 0% or 100%.

"At 0% percent, no money comes in ...no matter how much business sales revenues are.

"At 100% taxation, all business activity stops. So, you have to set taxes low enough to encourage economic activity. Then, with more economic activity, the amount of total tax revenues is increased. What can't you understand?

"On the downside, nobody has figured out what the ideal tax rate should be. And, this makes the Laffer formula useless. It's like a buried treasure with the treasure map buried with it. Well, there's this *Wall Street Journal* editorial writer, Jude Wanniski. He and politicians Jack Kemp of New York and Roth of Delaware, they're introducing legislation to reduce the federal income tax 30% -- so we can have increased taxes when the economy responds to the Laffer Curve. Quite a story, uh? We reduce taxes to get more tax revenue."

David Stockman sighed, "Mr. President, when Laffer, Kemp and Wanniski met with you I was still a Michigan Congressman. They hosed you down with supply-side doctrine. Wanniski told me, the Laffer Curve set off a symphony in Reagan's ears. He said you knew instantly that it was true, and you'd never have a doubt about it for ever more. I can't keep quiet. You don't have the foggiest idea of what supply-side is all about. It's a Trojan Horse. It's a mirror image of trickle-down economics. It's a way of saying cut taxes for business ...and the wealthy will stimulate the economy. It's like saying, if you give your kid less of an allowance each week, then he can make more money by getting a paper route.

"If we have major tax cuts with no major reductions in spending ... we'll have budget deficits more than 100 billion dollars a year.

"You promised to increase military spending.

"You promised to balance the budget.

"You have to *cut* domestic spending. Cutting taxes can not grow the economy.

"At first, it was a sneaky blueprint to make radical changes. But, all cutting taxes will do is raise the deficit, and increase the amount of interest taxpayers pay the Fed block-shareholders. Then, Congress will blindly slash social welfare spending. We'd bait-and-switch. Say we're going to stimulate economic growth ... then switch, and forcefully shrink the American welfare state ...that'll make a high political price, you'll pay.

You'll get the price-slasher out there slashing Social Security, Medicare, Veterans Hospitals, public housing grants, farm subsidies, public

broadcasting, student loans.

"The ax will fall on the neck of the poor. That's how we'd create our minimalist government to be a spare and stingy creature ...we let people starve, get sick, and die."

I had fallen asleep.

Mike nudged me awake.

I talked sleepily. "Do we have our new budget?"

Mike whispered, "Tell them about the stack of money going into space."

I smiled, "When I took office, Carter's runaway deficit of 80 billion dollars and the cumulative national debt of 908 billion dollars would make a stack of dollar bills stretching 60 miles into outer space."

Stockman was disarmed. It was like I didn't hear a word he said ... after all, I'd let him talk me to sleep.

Stockman felt defeated, "Mr. President I've been trying to tell you to eliminate the deficit by curbing spending and raising taxes. You ignore the relevant facts, and wander around in circles."

I'd straighten him out, "Runaway spending is the fault of an iron triangle of Congress, special interest lobbyists, and journalists together raiding and blaming the Treasury."

Stockman held fast. "Red ink on the budget is revenue shortfall. Caused by lowering tax rates and raising defense spending. It is *not* from new social welfare spending. The Pentagon spends 34 million dollars an hour."

My eyelids felt heavy. I yawned, "It's Jimmy Carter's fault. The national Treasury will have a surplus when we cut taxes ... to stimulate the economy. Then, we can retire the national debt. When I promised to balance the budget by 1984, I meant, I was promising it was my *goal* to do that ... not that I could really do it. Can't we talk about something interesting? ...I remember when far-right and ultra-right Cold War warriors Paul Nitze, Paul Weyrich, Dick Cheney, USAF Lt. Col. Robert Bowman, and Laffer came to see me. They tried to sell me Starwars with a Darth Vader doll ... they used it as a prop to show the Soviet Union was an evil empire. Well, I picked up that Darth Vader doll. It hit me like a flash. I told that doll to its face, I told 'em what I'm telling you, now, the Soviet Union *is* an evil empire! ...that's the true story how Starwars got priority in this Administration."

The Cabinet and Staffers fell quiet. The Situation Room was still. Everyone watched me ...as I stared off ... past the room ... into the distance. In my head, I was reliving my days on stage in front of Hollywood cameras, fighting Nazis. In the footage replaying in my head, I was saving America. I was preventing an orbiting death ray from falling back into Nazi hands.

Bill wanted to influence the direction of the meeting, looked at me and spoke, "The Solidarity Labor Movement in Poland looks like it might get swept away by a Soviet-supported Communist regime. Moscow clamped down on the Polish army. The Polish army declared martial law."

Hmmm. I listened carefully. "How does this sound for a speech? Moscow is unleashing the forces of tyranny against a peaceful neighbor. I'm asking Americans to light candles, in support of Poles."

Deaver felt that was the ticket. "That'll fly on TV."

Casey felt he'd take the tiller and guide the meeting for a while. He was thinking about the Full-Court Press to speed up destabilization of the Soviet Union and Eastern Europe, that Paul Nitze and Paul Weyrich kept preaching about.

But, Bill knew better than to publicly talk about the Full-Court Press to anyone. He certainly wouldn't to Cabinet and Staff members, Bush and me. Bill was a mastermind, a three-dimensional chess game playing constantly in his head. He kept a tally on us, how good card players count cards that are played. Bill kept track of world ruling families, that he played ... kept track of their turf wars ...acted out by their paramilitary units ...serving their intelligence forces ...serving their central banks and captains of industry and petroleum ... who popularized their views, enforced their opinions and empowered their arguments with the unquestionable logic of paramilitary death squads.

What Bill needed to do was help push the Full-Court Press along with invisible fingers.

Bill mumbled. "I go along with Defense Secretary Weinberger. A stepped-up arms race will beggar Russia."

Stockman spoke with attitude, "It will beggar us, too."

Bill didn't care who made the interest payments on the Fed block-shareholders national debt, as long as the debt climbed. It was a simple strategy. Too simple for most people to get.

State Secretary Haig joined in. "What we seem to be doing, is substituting an arms budget and covert operations to stand in for a foreign policy."

Mike looked at me. He could see I was tired.

Larry Speakes wanted in. "On the news end, an organization of Roman Catholic Bishops is taking an anti-nuclear stand. They're condemning nuclear weapons as immoral. They say, the arms race robs the poor and sick and makes mankind choose between constant terror or surrender."

I yawned again, "Anti-nuclear groups are under Communist influence. Carter's SALT II treaty locks in a Soviet advantage. It makes us vulnerable. The only way to close the window of vulnerability, is make *more* nuclear weapons."

Defense Secretary Weinberger was anxious.

I looked at him. "What now, Weinberger."

Weinberger spit it out. "The Joint Chiefs of Staff disagree with you, Mr. President. They say, SALT II limits the Soviets from deploying *even more* missiles. Let's resume arms control talks with Moscow. But, secretly deploy cruise missiles and Pershing II missiles in Western Europe. The Soviets say their intermediate range missiles are aimed at Europe ...just to match French and British missiles and weapons on American submarines and planes around Europe. Let's get the advantage back.

"Me and Deputy Defense Secretary Richard Perle suggest a 'Zero Option' plan. There should be *zero* Soviet SS-20 missiles in Europe. In return, we'll promise no future deployment of cruise and Pershing missiles ...of course., after we already have them in there. Another aide, T.K. Jones, is starting to assure everyone most Americas will survive a nuclear war.

"Many Americans would even prosper from a nuclear war. In case of nuclear attack, all anyone has to do is dig a hole, cover it with a couple of doors, and throw three feet of dirt on top. With enough shovels around, everyone's gonna make it. There'll be a rapid economic recovery.

"Fighting nuclear war is survivable ...if we have military superiority over Russia."

I thought for a moment. "It's my early religious upbringing. I see nuclear conflict as fulfillment of Biblical prophesy ... Armageddon. The Bible says, angels have a civil war in Heaven. Satan leads a band of angels against God. God throws Satan down into the fiery pit. The Bible says, Armageddon will destroy evil people in the world. The good people, at least 30,000 of 'em, will go live up in Heaven. The rest of the good people will be resurrected from their graves, to live eternal life on Earth. We're good people. What do we have to worry about?

<>

"I went with Martin Andersen from Hoover Institute to Strategic Air Command Center in the Cheyenne Mountains, in Colorado. The commander there told me, if the Soviets fire one missile, then all we could do was track it ...and fire back a missile at Russia. We've spent spend a for-

tune in equipment ...and there's no way to stop a nuclear missile from hitting us.

"American nuclear strategy is called, 'Mutually Assured Destruction'. Now, that's the same thing I was up against when I played Brass Bancroft in the film, *Murder in the Air* ...in 1940. I played a secret agent. I had to steal a secret inertia projector device. The device stopped enemy aircraft from flying. I remember my line. 'The inertia projector will make America invincible in war ...and therefore , it is the greatest force for peace ever invented'.

"Does anyone remember, *The Day the Earth Stood Still*. A flying saucer makes all the machines on Earth stop running. That's how they warn mankind to seek peace.

"Well ...when Dr. Ed Teller and retired Air Force Lt. General Dan Graham founded the High Frontier lobbying group, they came to me. They told me about an anti-missile shield project. I called it, *Starwars*, after the movie. Can you imagine building an X-Ray laser powered by a nuclear bomb?

"Then, the U.S can have laser beam death rays to shoot down Soviet missiles. Brass Bancroft likes the idea. We mount the death rays on a space station. We make an astrodome of light to protect America

"I think it's based on a Nazi plan to orbit mirrors and focus sunlight and burn up targets. I like the idea of Starwars.

"Listen, this is how the speech would go. 'I have a vision of a peaceful future ...in which we have a Strategic Defense Initiative to make all nuclear weapons impotent ...and obsolete."

Mike thought for a moment. "That'll fly. It'll play. I have no idea how it works ...It's high concept. Why don't we test the idea on some focus groups. Get you a few photo-ops. Raise your approval rating a few points."

I stared off into the distance. I remembered my role as a Brass Bancroft, secret agent in *Murder In The Air* ...I was dreaming. Cabinet members and White House Staffers were quiet. The Situation Room was still. They watched me. I stared off into the distance.

I could see everyone in the room looking at me funny, like I was confused. But, everyone knew I got that confused look when I was trying to get a thought working, and an idea in hand. I felt a look of wonder wash over my face. I felt refreshed.

I got that 'winning feeling'. "You know what I

told Weyrich and Nitze. I said, You men have given me hope again. You've answered my prayers. This Starwars death ray's a good story idea. It'll sell at the box office. People'll love it. That's the ticket. America needs hope ... hope of a world with no mutually-assured nuclear destruction ...Weinberger, you'll get your budget. You'll get your weapons. I promise that. We have to get rid of the communists."

Weinberger smiled.

Stockman frowned.

I told him where it was at. "Stockman, your job's to promote my policy, not sink it!"

I saw Ed Meese III seemed to be having a crisis. Ed blurted it out. "Mr. President ...my staff wants better office locations, navy blue water coolers, not mauve that's for girls. God damn the communists, too!"

It still wasn't right. "Ed, what's really bothering you?"

"I don't know."

"It's because James Baker ended-up as White House Chief of Staff, not you. Isn't it?"

Ed shuffled his feet. "I don't know. It's hard to get used to these Washington types ...It's like shooting at shadows. I never hit 'em. I know you chose Baker ...because, I hate details ...I provoke people who disagree with me. How could I move legislation through Congress like Jim Baker can? He's an old-time friend of George Bush, anyway."

White House Chief of Staff Jim Baker III bit his lip. "I'm sorry, if you feel bad Ed. It's just I know my way around Congress. There's a new Republican majority in the Senate, just itchin' to lead legislation around. *The President and each one of us has to emphasize tax cuts and the defense build-up.* If we can do that, the rest of the agenda takes care of itself. Mr. President don't mind a bit you keep calling for banning abortion, getting prayer back into schools, and changing the U.S. Constitution to mandate a balanced budget. I just hope you don't actually expect Congress to *act* on things like that. It's too controversial, Ed. You got to get a *feel* for Washington. Your best bet, is just go with *more* tax cuts and *more* defense spending."

More tax cuts, more defense spending ...I liked the sound of that. "If it's Armageddon, then God's on our side! ... I got the presentation down on those lines, huh, Mike?"

"Yes sir," Mike was drunk.

I looked into a full-length mirror. I smiled at me. "How do I look, Mike?"

Mike was a quiet drunk. He was convinced no one could ever smell vodka on his breath. "You're

handsome, Mr. President ...the American people like handsome."

It was at this point, when everything seemed most absurd to me, that Nancy entered the room. She was carrying a lunch tray of finger sandwiches for her and me. She started to shoo everyone out of the room. Me and Nancy would enjoy lunch in peace. Nancy always soothed me, always calmed me down ...just by being there.

She smiled sweetly at me, "Why the long face, Honey?"

I didn't feel grumpy anymore. I smiled at her. "You know my management style. I pick good people. Then, I delegate to them all of my decision-making authority, so they can do their job, their way. Is my management style going to hang me? Nancy ...ask your astrologer for me. Ask her, will my Staff and Cabinet always hate each other? ...will they always fight to the death? Ask her ...how I can get approval from my Staff and Cabinet? ...when they're at each other's throats ...it's makin' me crazy. What am I going to do? Go for Staff approval? ...or go for Cabinet approval?"

"Is it approval you want?"

I nodded. "That's what it boils down to."

"Should you play to the director, the producer, or to the audience?"

"That depends if I want the part, or if I already have it. ...I've already got the part. I'm President. I don't have to play to my White House Staff ...or play to my Cabinet, do I? ...I'll play to the American people." I felt better.

Nancy smiled. "It's the same audience you've always played to, that watched your movies, elected you governor, elected you President ...play to your biggest audience for approval. If that means you have to play along with jerks in your Staff, and with rough necks in your Cabinet ...then play along. Can you?"

"Sure I can," I said, "Thanks a lot. I love you."

White House Spokesman Larry Speakes barged back into the Situation Room, "Ronnie it's time for your press conference ...get happy, the American people's waitin'."

<> <> <>

Los Angeles canyons
Patti's hillside cottage home

Patti lived in a hillside cottage. It was high in the canyons, above Los Angeles. She was having a party. She was singing, *Lucy in the Sky with Diamonds,* with her friends, high on booze, grass, coke, acid, you name it. Laughing, having a good time. One of her infamous hippie orgy sex, drug, rock 'n' roll week-long parties, filled with 'beautiful people' ... rich kids from actors, politicians, upper class, ruling class, middle class and lower class black sheep family outcasts, like her. They liked to party. They liked to protest the establishment. Everyone sang, danced, drank, snorted, smoked, dropped uppers and downers. Patti waved a bottle of booze high in the air.

Patti yelled above the band, "To Daddy, President Rawhide, rot in hell loser!"

Patti's friends cheered her on. Inside her whirling dizziness, she felt her head spinning. She replayed childhood. She replayed teen tapes in her head, again and again.

In her head Patti, yelled at her father, "Ronnie stop denying the truth! Stop denying your feelings! Get real!"

I stared at my daughter. "I do my best. I come from poverty. I'm a self-made man. I'm a self-made millionaire. I've given you a good life. I made it on my looks. I made it on my brains. Some people wear their hearts on their sleeves, like you, Patti. I keep it, inside. That doesn't mean I don't feel. I do …but I don't show it outside, for people to walk on. I have courage. I'm tough. I'm leading this country. People depend on me. Not everyone can be Madonna, Sylvester Stallone, Arnold Schwarzenegger, or John Wayne! Someone has to be Ronald Reagan! *That's* what *I* do."

"Daddy, you need to be an A-movie actor!"

"You know how to hurt my feelings, don't you."

"You've got to go for the Oscar. Dad, please."

I started feeling devastated …I held up our family photo album to her. "Be fair! Look at these pictures. Our family is happy …will you look at these pictures?!"

Patti felt tears in her eyes, on her cheeks. "If it was so wonderful, why do I hurt!"

"I told you Patti, we'll pay for a shrink for you!"

"You're a child abuser!"

"No, I'm not, Patti! It's all twisted in your head!"

In the sky, high above Patti's swinger party in her hippy home in the canyons, in the hills overlooking the sea, Count von Bolschwing, Contra leader Mario Sandoval Alarcon, and their mercenary cocaine runners continued on their flight to unload a cargoes of cocaine at LAX, Oakland, then Meena, Arkansas.

In an hour, the plane circled over Oakland ghettos by Alameda Naval Air Station. The Black street kids below danced to ghetto-blasters, selling crack, getting high, getting arrested for selling two-shots and five-shots. They looked up at the plane, with its big, Coors beer can painted on the rudder. They nodded to each other, that they knew. But, the rest of us, didn't.

Alameda Naval Air Station

The three main platforms for Contra bulk cocaine sales were in the inner city in Los Angeles, Alameda California and Meena, Arkansas. As the kids in the Oakland ghettos were handcuffed, they looked up, one last time at the big Coors beer can painted on the rudder of the 747 passenger jetliner. Then, they were shoved into white, unmarked police vans that smelled of piss.

Following its approach to Alameda Naval Air Station, the Contra 747 touched down. Its tires screeched. Burnt rubber smoke trailed behind, on the runway behind the plane. The plane taxied into a hangar. CIA officers, stationed in lines, holding machineguns, protected the Contras. The Contras were drunk. They unloaded their cargo of drugs.

Italy, warehouse

In Italy, in one of his waterfront warehouses, P-2 Lodge Mafioso head Lucio Gelli waved from a warehouse window. The pilot of a seaplane taking off from the bay that ran underneath the warehouse wharf pilings, waved back. Lucio Gelli sat, surrounded by briefcases, suitcases, and crates of money. A Contra death squad mercenary handed Lucio Gelli a baggie of Contra cocaine to test it for quality. Lucio smiled.

Lucio turned to his lieutenant, "Launder the drug money at BCCI."

His lieutenant nodded.

Jan. 13, 1981,
Senate confirmation hearing

In the Senate Confirmation Hearing room, Bill Casey waited to be confirmed as our new CIA Director.

The Hearing Chairman questioned him, "Mr. Casey, are you willing to cooperate with this Senate Committee, today, at your confirmation hearing to be CIA Director?"

Bill publicly underestimated his imagination. "I cannot conceive now of any circumstances which

President Reagan & First Lady Nancy Reagan present Pianist Vladimir Horowitz with the Medal of Freedom in the Roosevelt room.

would result in my not being able to provide this committee with the information it requires."

A murmur went up among the reporters. Alan, one of the reporters, smirked. Alan looked at the other reporters around him. Alan could not restrain himself. "Right on!"

7 A.M. Jan. 20, 1981, Inauguration Day

Me and Nancy were sleeping in a bedroom at Blair House. Blair house is the White House Guest House. It is across the street from the White House.

Across the street, in the Oval Office at the White House, President Jimmy Carter looked at his watch. It was 7 a.m. Jimmy wanted to keep me informed about progress on the release of the hostages. A plane to bring the hostages home, was parked on the runway at the Teheran Airport. Carter called me at Blair House.

In Blair House, Mike Deaver listened to the phone ring in a small office alcove adjoining the room where me and Nancy slept.

Deaver picked up the phone. "Hello. I understand. But, President-Elect Reagan is sleeping. And, he is not to be disturbed."

President Carter was surprised. "But this is good news, about the release of the hostages."

Mike played it off. "Look, I'll tell the President when he wakes up. If he's interested, he may call you." Mike hung up the phone. He settled back in his chair . He stared out the window. Mike went for a walk, over to the White House Briefing Room. Then, he came back and sat down. Mike dozed off. The next time Mike looked at his watch, it was 9 a.m. Mike figured, he better wake me up. He slowly entered mine and Nancy's bedroom. He saw I was still sleeping. "Ronnie, get up! Get up! I can't believe you're still sleeping. You're going to be inaugurated in three hours, at noon!"

I woke up in a happy-go-lucky mood. "Does that mean I have to get out of bed?"

Mike raised his voice. "You better get used to it, Ronnie. In three hours, you'll be President. Then, every day the courier from the National Security Council is going to be your alarm clock at 7:30 each morning, to brief you."

Fat chance of that, I thought. "Then, he's gonna have a hell of a long wait. You tell them not to come before 9:30 in the morning. Have you seen Carter this morning?"

Mike had. "I took a walk to the White House Briefing Room a couple hours ago. Carter was pacing around like a cat in a cage at the zoo. When he wasn't pacing, he prayed. I was there

with him at 5 A.M., when he made a press announcement. He wasn't even shaved."

President Carter was up all night. He wanted the satisfaction of having the hostages released while he was still President. "I want to announce an agreement with Iran that will result, I believe, in freedom of our American hostages, held there."

Reporters surrounded him. Deaver leaned towards Alan. "The Reagan Administration will not negotiate with terrorists!"

Mike reported it all back to me.

I laughed. "You mean, Carter wasn't even shaved. I guess washed-up means you're not washed-up."

"He hadn't shaved or even dressed for your inauguration, at noon. Let's get with it, Ronnie. It's lights, camera, action."

I was in one of the best moods of my life. "Okay Mike. I'm getting ready. Me and Nancy will meet you at the limo, at 11:30."

I woke Nancy up. Mike left the room. Me and Nancy got dressed. A couple hours later our limo arrived at the White House, in route to the Capital Hill ceremony.

I leaned over towards Mike. "Get a look at Carter. Look how gaunt he looks."

"Yeah. The Iranians are taking another poke at him. They're not going to let the plane with the hostages take off until five minutes after you're sworn in as President. That way, the Reagan Administration will get the credit."

I laughed. "That's how it should be."

My inauguration ceremony was at high noon. I promised to usher in an era of national renewal. After the ceremony, I was at the White House, in House Speaker Tip O'Neil's office.

House Speaker Tip O'Neil showed his desk to me. "This desk was used by Grover Cleveland."

My eyes lit up, "I played Grover Cleveland in a movie."

"You played Grover Cleveland Alexander the baseball player, not Grover Cleveland the president."

"Oh."

President's Inaugural Ball, 1981

My Presidential inaugural ball in 1981 was Hollywood style. It was a high society extravaganza. Since I was an actor and, naturally, a narcissist ...as Nancy was, we loved appearing in front of people costumed-up to the hilt. And, in the spotlight.

In the evening, following the high noon inauguration, I wore a tuxedo. Nancy wore a designer gown. We had toured the town together, party-hopping for three days ...already, making appearances at one party after another. The inner party of the inaugural celebration was already three days old. This was the final day, climaxed by my inauguration. Now, it was going to be climaxed again by this official, inauguration ball.

Senator Barry Goldwater was there talking to a reporter. "This is the most expensive inaugural celebration in American history."

Alan, the reporter, was right there, "So you have mixed feelings about the how ostentatious the Reagan inaugural celebration is?"

Goldwater glared then looked away. He watched me and Nancy waltzing. I was wearing tails. Nancy was swirling her lavish gown. We waved to Senator Goldwater.

Goldwater waved back. "This party cost 11 million dollars. It's been going on for four days. All these white ties, limos and mink is out of place on TV, when most of the country can't hack it financially! It's very bad taste!"

Nancy watched Frank Sinatra on stage.

Sinatra was singing a song especially written for the celebration. *"I'm so proud, that you're First Lady, Nancy ...and so pleased that I'm sort of a chum ...The next eight years will be fancy, Nancy ...as fancy as they come!"*

Nancy clapped enthusiastically. Nancy felt sincere. "Oh, Frankie ...thank you for organizing and producing and directing this inauguration party for me and Ronnie!"

<>

Bill Casey's reward, as he made clear and we'd understood from the beginning, was me appointing him from being my campaign manager, to being the new director of Central Intelligence Agency.

George Bush, who used to be DCI, was now my Vice President of the United States. Admiral Haig, the champion of the Vietnam war, we made him Secretary of State. Caspar Weinberger had been treasurer at Bechtel ...Bechtel wanted him to be Secretary of Defense.

Bill Casey navigated through the Inauguration Ball crowd, over to me. Bill introduced Lucio Gelli, an Italian businessman and a P-2 Lodge member to me, then to Vice President Bush. I figured P-2 was like Rotary Club, Lions Club, or Moose Lodge.

Mike Deaver, who used to be my campaign public affairs man, I made my new White House Assistant Chief of Staff ...basically, the same job. Mike said, he wanted to introduce Mario Sandoval Alarcon to me, and introduce me to campaign supporters from Taiwan, Argentina, Guatemala, South America and North Korea. Mike arranged

that each of them was with the Miss World contestant from each of their countries, wearing sashes with their countries name on it.

I was ready. "Mike, why are all these people from foreign countries here?"

Mike took out his flask, had a quick nip. "Politics ...foreign aid, weapons sales, special interest groups. Kind of a nice touch to have their Miss World contestants with them, huh? They're all WACL."

"WACL? What's that?"

Mike must have sensed I didn't have the faintest idea what he was talking about. He start whispering. "WACL ... World Anti-Communist League members, you know, 'freedom fighters' from Taiwan, Argentina, Guatemala, South Africa, North Korea."

"Great! ...Just keep prompting me." I shook everyone's hands nonstop, all the time smiling that winning, handsome Hollywood smile of mine.

Mike was at the top of his stride. "Mario Alarcon and his outfit tossed ten million dollars into your gubernatorial and presidential campaigns, each, way under the table. Leave 'em laughing," Mike stopped whispering. "Mr. President, Mario Sandoval Alarcon, businessman and Contra training commander in Argentina."

We shook hands.

Mario looked at me. "Presidente, I hate the communists, taxes, trade unions. To hell with them, putas." He made a gesture indicating the slitting of throats and let go an evil laugh, elbowing my arm.

I had a double-take ...I was about to have an idea ...a thought about something or other ...but I felt myself forget it ...it never came up ...I stared off ...looked through the party ...into the distance.

Mike brought me back somehow, nodding towards Alarcon.

I took my cue. "Thank you for your help, Mr. Alarcon, and for being who you are. I really appreciate it."

Mike over-reacted. "No!"

I scowled at him. "I want my supporters to like me!"

President Reagan with actress Victoria Principal during a photo opportunity with the Arthritis Poster Child of the Year in the Oval Office. 5/29/86

"It doesn't matter if they like you or not."

I wondered what Mike meant. "What do you mean?" I felt that familiar, confused look come over me ...I stared off again through the party ...almost had a thought ...forgot it, but made it back.

Mike watched me struggle. But, he'd irritated me. "Mike, I appreciate what you've done for me, from the beginning of my political career. But, don't make me look bad ...don't make me look ungrateful ...I don't like that."

Mike shrugged. "Sorry, boss."

I knew what was botherin' him. "Mike, you're wonderin' if I can cut the mustard, aren't you? You got questions about me, don't you. After all these years, about what I know, and what I don't."

Bill Casey watched Count Otto von Bolschwing, like a hawk. Bill caught the Count's attention. "Von Bolschwing, c'mere." Bill watched von Bolschwing excuse himself from the WACL contingent, then walk over to him. Bill whispered to von Bolschwing. "I can't get Justice or Immigration fixed to help you ...you're gonna be deported. I don't know when. There's a way out, a new identity."

Von Bolschwing hit Bill Casey on the shoulder. In disgust, he pushed Bill away ...then angrily left the party. Being an actor, I noted it human motivation. You've got to know where the other characters are at, to keep the pace up. I made nothing of it, then forgot it.

Nancy came up to me. We began the first dance of the inaugural ball. The orchestra played Nancy's favorite waltz, *Blue Danube*. Everyone in the audience clapped and cheered for me, the new President, and my First Lady.

Bahia Brazil, onboard gaily decorated fishing boat

Selwa Lucky Roosevelt was standing alone. Her movements suggested a samba, as she listened to a band on a nearby fishing boat. The boat was bobbing in the waves. It was alongside the boat she was on. Selwa Lucky Roosevelt never thought, in her wildest dreams, being a journalist for *Town & Country Magazine*, would bring her to Brazil. But, here she was, out on the open sea. All, to cover the Festival of Iamenje, Goddess of the Sea, from a fish-smelling, fishing boat. Selwa Lucky Roosevelt threw bouquets of colorful flowers, and gaily wrapped gifts, overboard ...to please Iamenje.

Selwa laughed happily. She inquired of an aide to the Brazilian president. "I take it Iamenje likes gifts?"

"If Iamenje is displeased with you she refuses them," an aide said. "...and the gifts float on the surface ...if she likes you, she accepts your gifts, and they sink to her."

Selwa watched roses she'd thrown onto the surface of the water slowly sink. "How thrilling! They're sinking! It's good luck!"

Later that day at dusk, back in port, Selwa slowly walked beside the green hedges surrounding the house of a priestess of animal sacrifice ...*Town & Country* asked her to interview Mother Menininha, a 90-year-old, famous Candomble priestess of Brazil. All around the hedges scattered on the ground, were rotting, broken, egg shells, with yolks leaking out, drying and stinking ...and the bones of small birds and animals. Selwa smelled strange odors she associated with animal, blood sacrifice. She entered the house, going into the bedroom where Priestess Mother Menininha lay, bedridden. Selwa stared at the wrinkled-up old face of the priestess, the wrinkled up boney hands ...and knew, one day, she herself would be old. That made Selwa uneasy.

Priestess Mother enfolded Selwa's hands in hers, speaking slowly. "Be careful, you are strong ...you will be famous, soon."

When Selwa's cell phone rang in her purse, she felt relief. Selwa excused herself, took back her hand, and turned to answer her phone. "Hello."

"This is Mike Deaver. I'm White House Assistant Chief of Staff. You've received a White House appointment to become Chief Protocol Officer for the United States. It's an ambassadorial appointment. We'd like you to accept it. Can you be in my office, Friday?"

"Yes, thank you Mr. Deaver. I can." Selwa Lucky Roosevelt hung up her cellphone.

Priestess Mother saw the surprised, dreamy look of awe on Selwa's face, when Selwa turned to smile at her. "You were right on the money, Priestess Mother Menininha."

Deaver's White House office

Mike Deaver was seated in his White House office. He was Assistant Chief of Staff for the President of the United States. Mike was blunt. "Selwa, you got skeletons in your closet?"

Selwa stiffened in her chair. "I'm pro-choice, of Lebanese origin, and if you're looking for right-

President Reagan talking to Jimmy Stewart and Gloria Stewart at a private birthday party in honor of his 75th Birthday in the White House residence. 2/7/86

wing ideological purity from me, then I'm not the right person for you."

Deaver looked squarely at Selwa. "President Reagan's pro-life, our other protocol officer is also from Lebanon, as you are. Your attitude on abortion, and being a good protocol officer are unrelated. Just don't make any speeches about it."

"If someone asks me, of course, I'll tell the truth."

Mike smiled coldly. There was no sense of enjoyment in his smile. He nodded at Selwa, as if he had no choice in the matter. "Fair enough. Would you go see if Secretary of State Haig is onboard with your appointment? I have a meeting with the President. Glad to have you on board, Selwa.'" He stood up, then shook Selwa's hand.

She smiled demurely. "You may call me, Lucky."

Secretary of State Haig's office

Secretary of State Alexander Haig enjoyed a reputation -- as a ruthless Vietnam war hawk, who was fanatically anti-Communist. To Selwa Lucky Roosevelt, Haig seemed cordial on the outside, but tense and rigid, inside.

Haig studied her face, said she was to call him Secretary of State Haig. She said, he could call her Lucky.

"Lucky, I didn't know how important the Chief of Protocol's job was until I became Secretary of State. Did you know Deaver's staff's idea of protocol at Cancun was to give everyone jars of jellybeans?"

Lucky smiled warmly.

Haig continued. "Lucky, powers that be told us, you're the right person for the job...so, you have my blessing. I'm off to a meeting with the President."

Bohemian Grove,
Northern California, 1979

At Bohemian Grove, Bechtel greeted me, Shultz, Deaver, Meese. and Bill Casey, my presidential campaign manager. "What's the matter, Bill?"

Bill wearily shook his head like he'd had enough. "I've got to figure out how to make Ronald Reagan understand the difference between Fed block-share economics, taxes, and foreign policy ... and United States economics, taxes, and foreign policy. Or, just leave him out in the cold and handle him, which you wanted me to do in the first place. I have to give him savior faire."

I was pissed off. "Look Bill, you're a know-it-all. I've been a political spokesperson for you guys, twenty years. We're both millionaires. I started from poverty. I earned mine, without a drop of blood. I wasn't born with a silver spoon in my mouth, like you were. I didn't kill people for my money, over stage revolutions for it, like *you* did. My father was a shoe salesman. We didn't live on the wrong side of the tracks, but close enough to hear the train whistles.

"I've been a construction worker, a lifeguard, radio announcer and actor. I've hated the communists all my life. When Hollywood put me out to pasture, General Electric hired me go around the country for years promoting your Crusade For Freedom, since the early '50s. Then, I was Governor of California for eight years. I love this country as much as you do ... I'm not as stupid as you think I am. I don't need your help to smarten up, not as much as you think. You misjudge me ...I feel let down. It makes me feel sad when you cop an attitude like that."

Bechtel shot Casey a glancing smile.

Martin Andersen watched to see what Paul Nitze's reaction would be.

Paul Nitze shrugged. He looked at George Shultz for sympathy.

I felt let down by all of them. I stood up for myself. "All of you know, when Carter was elected President in 1976 we all start gearing up to run me for President in 1980. I want the Presidency. Just *what is it* you *think* I need to know about politics, that I don't know already?"

Martin Andersen turned to Paul Nitze. "Giving away the Panama Canal is like giving away Grand Canyon, or Statue of Liberty."

Paul Nitze frowned. "I agree with you. The bad news is, that the dictator of Panama, General Omar Torrijos, the bastard convinced John Wayne and William Buckley Jr. to endorse the treaty the Senate ratified."

I was shocked ...John Wayne was a Hollywood hero, and, a national hero ...my competition. "John Wayne wants to give the canal away? He was a bigger star than I was. I guess the canal is a non-issue now."

Bechtel nodded silently towards George Shultz. George Shultz lit his pipe.

Martin Andersen kept talking. "My friend, 75-year-old Howard Jarvis, got California voters to approve Proposition 13. That limits Municipal and State property taxes. The point, here, is campaign hard on the theme that voters have to take control of government. Or else, it's going to take control of you. The next national election should be a voter's revolution against Government."

I hesitated, because I felt condescending. I didn't want to come off that way ...too much. I gathered my wits. "We all hate liberals. We all hate the welfare state. And, the public fed up being taxed. We'll campaign on slashing taxes. We'll campaign on blocking social welfare programs. That's nothing new. I did it in California for eight years. *Was I supposed to learn that today, too?* I've been nixing high taxes since 1950."

Mike Deaver let me swim without water wings. But, he felt he had to focus the picture, a bit. "Ronnie we've been complaining about high taxes. Now, we want to emphasize *reducing* taxes. We need to make Jarvis look like a demi-God. We want people to bow down when they hear his name ...like he's a Savior."

I thought for a moment. "How's this? ... Jarvis triggered hope in the breasts of hard-working people, that something could be done to stop big government taxing people to death. Something like dumping those cases of tea off the boat into Boston Harbor. We need a national movement, to make giant cuts in Federal Income Tax rates. When we look at America, we see President Carter trying to pardon Vietnam draft dodgers. Carter wants to cancel the West's water projects. You don't know where Carter stands on abortion. Nobody does. Where does he stand on Affirmative Action? The man is morally confused. What about a national energy policy? Carter told the American people to turn down their thermostats, and wear sweaters. The energy crisis in America is not because of a shortage of oil. It is because of a surplus of Government."

Mike Deaver smiled. "That's real good, Ronnie. Let's keep hitting him below the belt."

Bill Casey felt a renewed interest in the discussion. "The revolution in Iran. Carter couldn't do squat about that. That made oil and gasoline prices high at home."

Henry Kissinger had not spoken. He was observing. He felt he could add something. "Carter waffles between Secretary of State Cyrus Vance and National Security Adviser Zbigniew Brzezinski, like a volley ball knocked back and forth. Vance wants arms control ...GATT management of the world economy. Brzezinski plays hard ball. Brzezinski wants power politics. Brzezinski doesn't trust the Soviets. Vance put together SALT II as a arms control treaty with Moscow. It limits the U.S. and U.S.S.R. to only 2,400 nuclear delivery systems, each. But, Soviet involvement in Africa proves the Kremlin is still expansionist."

Deaver nodded. "I suppose *that* means something to you ...but I deal with Ronnie's TV image ...shaping public opinion. Carter's approval rating's are as low as Nixon's was. The country's asleep."

Bill Casey smiled. "My friend, Paul Volcker, told me he's going to be appointed Chairman of the Federal Reserve Board. He's going to kick rising prices in the ass ...give faltering production a shot in the arm ...to go stop inflation by going after rising unemployment. He says he's going to drive up interest rates, over 15%. So, get ready for the next recession."

I bit my lip. I waited. I thought about it, "That's good speech material, Bill."

Henry Kissinger nodded. "What's Carter done? Handling foreign policy for him is a hot potato. He even made Camp David Accords to make peace between Israel and Egypt."

Bechtel smiled. "We need allies over there, to protect King ibn Saud. We need to protect the stability of his regime. We need to protect American interests, there."

Bill Casey sounded gruff, "Carter came into office. He thought he could kick the Cold War in the ass. Now, the Soviet Union is in the Middle East, Africa, and South America."

Bechtel watched Bill Casey. Bechtel wanted to make sure Casey explained the pieces of the puzzle, correctly. Bill Casey took a pocket tape recorder from his pocket. Bill Casey started a recording of President Jimmy Carter, "We are now free of that inordinate fear of Communism, which once led us to embrace any dictator in that fear."

Bill Casey lit his pipe. "The bastard's reducing the CIA by 500 field operatives. His God-damn brother's an agent for Libya. Muammar Qaddafi paid Mr. Billy Beer $200,000."

Bechtel saw the direction the conversation was taking. He had to clarify things, to position the conversation. "Qaddafi is militantly anti-Israel. King ibn Saud is militantly anti-Israel. My company works with Qaddafi and Kin ibn Saud. We have oil pipeline construction contracts in Libya and Saudi Arabia. I understand, in December, Soviet forces are going to invade Afghanistan. They're invading on the pretense of bolstering up the Communist regime, there. To keep it from an internal collapse."

Bill Casey tamped his pipe. "The Soviets want to control the Afghan opium trade. It's no big, fucking secret."

I didn't know what he meant. I ignored it.

Henry Kissinger spoke up. "I'm sure National

Security Adviser Zbigniew Brzezinski will make Carter understand, *this the gravest threat to peace since World War II.* Secretary of State Cyrus Vance will get more arms sales out of it. So, he'll go along."

Mike Deaver had a flash of intuition. "That's going to look to the public like Soviets are driving to take over oil in the Persian Gulf, isn't it?"

Bill Casey nodded his head. "They are."

Bechtel frowned. "Carter will embargo grain sales to Russia. He'll boycott the Moscow Olympics. He'll revive draft registration. He'll speed up production of new weapons. And, cruise missiles. He'll withdraw SALT II from Senate consideration."

Henry Kissinger listened in awe. "How do you know this?"

Bechtel smiled. "Here, at Bohemian Grove, we determine who will be President twenty years ahead of time. What wars will be fought. We spin the spin doctors. Dictate world events. It can be nasty. But, Bohemian Grove must make decisions for America. Or, House of Windsor, will.

I felt frustrated. "Now, wait a minute. Can't we put this in Hollywood terms? I've got to understand, *first. Then,* I can explain it to the American people. Then, they'll vote for me …Big Government should not regulate the private economy. That puts prosperity at risk. That puts fundamental freedoms at risk. A big Federal bureaucracy makes a permanent monster so big, and powerful, the policy it sets hurts the desires of ordinary citizens, and the people they elect.

"There's too much waste and fraud in Government. There's gross mismanagement by Federal regulators. There's no Government oversight. There's hostility towards ruling families that control private enterprise. That *smothers* creativity of American business.

"That *destroys* the American family. That *destroys* the American way of life. I'm against all that! I can make speeches about that! But, all this foreign policy stuff. Just make up your minds, already. Tell me what I'm supposed to be talking about! Because, I wish I knew!"

Conversation in the room came to a stop.

Mike Deaver felt embarrassed. Bechtel looked at Bill Casey. Bechtel had dealt with the trans-Atlantic Axis central banking consortium, that Allen Dulles represented, for years. Bechtel knew, if world affairs Dulles or Casey managed misfired, exactly what Dulles and his protégé Bill Casey would do …point an accusing finger at the person standing next to them.

Bill glared at Mike. "I guess you didn't explain things to Ronnie the way I told you."

George Shultz felt offended. "Bill, you can't hold Mike responsible for events and speaking points you mismanaged."

Henry Kissinger was slighted. Kissinger looked at Bechtel. "Gentlemen, I was also in the picture when the CIA coup in Iran installed Shah Reza Pahlevi, twenty-five years ago. He has been an excellent American client, and customer, for you. The Shah is a whore for the Seven Sisters. And, he has spent his petro-dollars buying billions of dollars worth of American weapons. *That's a win-win,* for everyone. As I'm sure you know, we supplied nuclear power generating capacity to Iraq and Iran in the early '50s.".

Bechtel nodded.

Kissinger was on a roll. "Times change. Oil interests shift. Oil monopolies evolve. There's too much oil in the world, already. Even the untapped reserves in southern Ethiopia, alone. They could run the world far into the next century. There is just so much planet, to control. There is too much wealth, to share. There are too many ruling family turf wars over natural resources. So, Central Intelligence had to get rid of the Shah. He's a sick man, anyway. Now, who should they replace him with. And, how? The Shah's always been a dictator. He treated his subject population like shit. He's corrupt. When this information hit's prime time, it's time for another coup. Another cover. Another distraction limiting damage control. So, the Agency's groomed, and financed, Ayatollah Khomeini.

"All during his exile in Iraq and France, Khomeini encouraged revolution in Iran. Feb. 1979, Ayatollah Khomeini drives the Shah from Iran …Carter allows the fatally ill Shah to enter the U.S., for medical treatment. Khomeini denounces the United States as the Great Satan, and the Great Whore of Babylon.

"Khomeini demands Carter to turn over the overthrown shah …and his foreign wealth, to the new Islamic regime. Then, the press reports a mob sacked the U.S. embassy in Teheran, seizing its staff.

"But, *you and I know* that Ayatollah Khomeini's intelligence operatives captured the American embassy in Teheran and fifty embassy staff … who were CIA counter-revolutionary operatives."

<>

I was frustrated, again. "Spare me details. What am I supposed to say?"

Shultz watched Bechtel nod at Casey.

Andersen watched Casey nod at Deaver.

Deaver looked at me. "Ronnie, I see your image

34

on the TV news, like this. You say, America is held hostage. *That* makes Carter look impotent. Christ, Ronnie, our friend the Shah would still be in power if Carter didn't criticize him for torturing political prisoners."

Bill Casey felt vindicated. He felt the meeting was getting back on track. George Shultz watched in amazement, as Deaver planted seeds of thought.

I felt like I was going to have an idea …I looked up …I looked into the distance. "It's Carter's fault there was a revolution in Iran in the first place."

George Shultz felt the moment. "Senator Ed Kennedy's been complaining in Congress, all Carter can to is lurch from crisis to crisis."

My eyes brightened. "Even Carter's own democrats are against him. Ed Kennedy said, Carter can't put one foot in front of the other. And, the way Carter fumbled rescuing the hostages by crashing his helicopters in a desert dust storm …it makes me wonder, are the Three Stooges directing foreign policy."

Everyone laughed.

That made me feel good.

Bechtel nodded to George Shultz. Shultz began talking. "Ronnie when you're President, will you get the Government off our backs? Give us some de-regulation of the nuclear power industry, will you? Get big Government off the backs of the people."

I listened carefully.

Bill spoke up. "I've always been close with Prescott Bush's trans-Atlantic banking group. I think his son, George, knows his way around the petroleum and intelligence community, pretty good. I think, he's a good running mate."

No way. "I want Gerald Ford for my running mate. But, can an ex-President run as Vice President? …he could run Foreign Affairs. I don't know foreign affairs. George Bush gives me heartburn. He says I'm full of 'voodoo economics'. Bush is too liberal. Bush is soft on abortion, women's rights, and gun control."

Martin Andersen shifted gears. "Carter doesn't have a chance at re-election. Carter's dogged by the captivity of hostages he can't set free …an economy he can't improve …a brother on Libya's payroll he can't disown. Ronnie's an opponent he can't shake . Once we get in office I'd like to get Office Of Management & Budget, Commerce Department, Peter Grace, and George Bush working together in a task force.

"With a task force like that, we could get rid of hundreds of rules that cut into 3rd Quarter profits. We can eliminate rules for disposal of haz-ardous waste, air pollution, nuclear safety, exposure to chemicals, and get rid of financial waste policy protecting worker health and safety. It's too expensive to protect the environment, when big Government bureaucracy has to pay people wages to police big business, and tell us what we already know. This isn't Nazi Germany."

I was feeling sleepy. "Well, everything you've all said makes sense to me. But, I'm too sleepy to make sense of it. Besides, I knew all it all, already. I'm going to sleep."

I nodded off.

<>

White House Historian Bill Barnes picked up his cat. Jackson hung limp and sleepy-eyed in Barnes' hands. What was it like to feel like that, Barnes wondered. Having some giant come and pick you up, and hold you in his hands. Barnes remembered his wife, Eden. She passed away, long ago. Barnes became a piece of walking history, after that. Moonlight walks were gone. Barnes picked up his writing pen. He start writing, losing sadness in the words he wrote, inside his understanding. He wrote until he was exhausted, til his eyes had a mind of their own, til he collapsed to the floor in sleep …and in a dream that never came true. Jackson came over, wrinkled his nose, sniffing, hopped onto Barnes' stomach. Jackson walked around in a few circles. He kneaded his paws into Barnes' body like he was kneading bread. Then, Jackson plopped down …and the world rested in peace for them, as they slept the sleep of the dead.

What White House Historian Bill Barnes had just written lay on the floor, beside him. It didn't amount to much, in a world suspended in thought, and Time. Barnes woke up at sunrise when the birds began to sing …the only time of day birds could be heard. Cars, trains and buses came out in daylight. Barnes read the lines he'd written …of history falling through cracks. If words could bring back Eden …but

President Reagan and Bob Hope laughing with George Shultz at the Kennedy Center Honors. Washington, DC 12/8/85

they couldn't.

Apr. 24, 1980

Carter's handlers tried to rescue American hostages. Eight helicopters took off from the deck of an aircraft carrier in the Persian Gulf, flying away from into the desert, into a sand storm. One chopper broke down from engine trouble. It returned to the ship. The other seven helicopters got lost in a sand storm. Two had to land, because flight crews forgot to put sand filters on the carburetors. The commander of the covert action team decided, the five helicopters left weren't enough. He aborted the mission. Then, one helicopter collided with a re-fueling plane. Eight servicemen were killed, five more injured. Seven aircraft were destroyed in the crash.

Sad as road kill, Carter announced details of the failed mission on TV. To many Americans, the mission was a cartoon. It branded America as a has-been national power, branded Carter as a bad joke.

Mike Deaver put the new pieces of the puzzle together ...the image emerged, how he wanted me to paint Carter ...Carter's handlers ...their foreign policy apparat, in my Presidential campaign speeches against Carter. We needed to get emotional responses from voters.

My campaign, managed by Bill Casey, was conducted in the shadow of the Iran hostage crisis. Many people felt Carter's presidential failure to bring the hostages home, foretold his political future. Carter's inability to deal with double-digit inflation, unemployment, lackluster economic growth, instability in the petroleum market that led to longer and longer gas lines ...his perceived weakness about national defense ... it have influenced the electorate, against him.

Reagan Santa Barbara ranch, 1979

Nancy was besides herself.

And, so was I. "Nancy, this is our chance to be in the spotlight and steal the show. Top billing everywhere, my damn campaign backers think I need words put in my mouth, because I'm too stupid, and can't think for myself!"

"Ronnie, treat them like script writers, directors, or producers. They don't know any better.

"It's the principle, they think I'm a pretty face to get our votes they can hide behind."

"You *are* handsome. It *will* get votes. It's their fault. If they think you're dumb, if they think they can *use* you ...we'll outsmart them, at every step. Let's play along. Get elected, then do things our way. We'll show them what real acting is. With

me by your side, we can do it!"

We kissed.

"Nancy, you've always believed in me. I love you. I think I'm back on track."

"I believe in *us*, what *we* share. No one gets between us ...not Bechtel ...not Casey ...not our kids. This is our last chance to be bigger stars than ever. I won't let it slip away. Let them think, whatever! Who cares? It's on them. You accept political coaching, or lose Casey, Deaver and Meese on your campaign. You think you *invented* the circus?"

"Mommy, you're on the money. I don't *like* them doubting me. It's like losing the audience ...then it stops paying attention all together ...and I'm playing to an empty house. It makes me doubt *me*. I need their approval. I want the damn Oscar. But, I want to help America, more. I need everyone to like me. That's the way I'm put together ...everything you said was right on."

"Beat them at their game. That's what I do."

"I know. I'll play along to get along.".

Nancy gazed at me. That night, sex was good.

Israel combat exercises, 1979

George Bush went to Israel for a Mossad anti-terrorism conference. It was called, 'preventive counter-kidnapping'. The spin they put on it, made it, 'pre-emptive retaliation'.

You go in there. You kidnap the kidnappers, and their families ...before they kidnap you. It made sense to George, sort of an upside-down pyramiding kind of thing.

In 1980, I finally succeeded. I got the Republican nomination for president. At the convention, I discussed choosing former President Gerald Ford as my running mate, but, ultimately chose George H. W. Bush.

Bush had been my opponent, during the presidential primaries Bush said, he'd *never* be *my* Vice President.

Bush was many things I wasn't ...a lifelong Republican ...a combat veteran ...an internationalist with UN, CIA and China experience, and a CIA director. Bush's economic and political philosophies were way more moderate than me. Bush called my supply-side proposal, for a 30% across-the-board tax cut, 'voodoo economics'.

August 1980

I accepted the Republican Presidential nomination. "I want to accept the Republican Presidential nomination. To thank all of you. America, is an island of freedom. I want to ask all convention delegates here, join me in thanking Divine

Providence for making this nation a haven for refugees fleeing oppression, and disaster."

Mike Deaver smiled. Mike knew, the WACL members he knew would appreciate that touch. Mike knew, where my speech was going. Mike settled back in his chair, shuffling around till he felt comfortable.

I continued. "A lot of you know I come from humble origins. I've been a lifeguard, a radio announcer, a soldier, an actor, an actors' union president, a Democrat ... who became a Republican, and a Republican Governor of California.

"My grandparents were farmers during the potato famine in Ireland. My parents suffered during the Great Depression. My father lost his job on Christmas Eve."

Mike caught my attention. Mike pointed to my toe-marks. I moved a little to my right. I looked into the TV cameras. I wiped a tear from my eye. My eyes were moist.

I continued my speech. "I cannot and will not stand by, while inflation and joblessness destroy the dignity of the American people. Recently I made a speech to the Veterans of Foreign Wars. I told them what I'm telling you today. I blame past administrations for not fighting to victory in Vietnam. Ours, in truth, was a noble cause. President Carter is wrong to establish diplomatic ties with China. When I am elected, I will restore recognition of Taiwan as the *real* government of China.

"I'll tell you the story of an American pilot in World War II, who sacrificed his life for his country. He won a posthumous Congressional Medal of Honor. The pilot's plane was strafed. It was going down. The pilot cradled a wounded comrade, rather than bail out from his crippled plane. 'Never mind, son,' the pilot of the doomed plane told the injured belly gunner, 'We'll ride this one down together.'

"That's the America I believe in. America doesn't not want to be second rate. We need a bigger, stronger military. I want to get rid of liberal spending programs. They've made big government more wasteful than the New Deal. I'll roll back social welfare programs. I'll limit Federal courts for civil rights and civil liberties. I'll eliminate government regulation of business, of banking, and of the environment.

"I want to remove the dead hand of Government regulation from private enterprise. Then, we can unleash market forces, and create new wealth for us. I'll reduce Federal taxes. I'll promote a Conservative social ethic against abortion,

against drug use. And, promote religion in daily life, and in schools. It's time to realize, we're too great a nation to limit ourselves to small dreams.

"Past policies of big Government, past tax-and-spend, mortgaged our future, and our children's future. America must stop living beyond our means. Or, face disaster. I pledge when I am elected President, I will cut taxes. I will end deficit spending. To paraphrase Winston Churchill ...I did not accept this nomination with the intention of presiding over the dissolution of the world's strongest economy. America will be back, it will be morning again."

<>

Mike Deaver listened to everyone in the nomination convention center cheer and clap. I brought many in the audience to tears. Mike felt things were going his way. Mike smiled proudly.

Ed Meese looked at Deaver. "I almost felt a little sad, myself. They love him. You did it again, Mike. I don't know how you do it. But, you do."

Mike spoke quietly. "I keep apple pie and the flag going the whole time."

Reporters swarmed around Ronnie. Alan, the reporter, elbowed his way to the front of the pack. "Mr. Reagan, Mr. Reagan! When the two pilots went down in the doomed plane, and crashed, how could anyone know what the two dead men said to each other, moments before the crash?"

I got a puzzled look on my face.

Oct. 1980, meeting of Ronnie & handlers

Mike Deaver, and my other handlers, were afraid. If President Carter got the American hostages released before the election, Carter might win.

Deaver looked at Bill Casey. "If I was Carter I'd pull off a surprise in October. I'd get the hostages free, just before the elections in November. The public will go wild. Joy will roll over America like a tidal wave. Carter will be a hero. Everyone will forget he makes America second rate. He'd win the election, for sure. Help us out of this one, Casey."

Casey mumbled. "I'm directing Ronnie's campaign. I hear you. Rumors are floating around. Like, if the hostages aren't released until after the election, then as soon as we get into office we'll start selling arms sales to Iran, again. Iran's military is all U.S. weapons ...they need replacement parts. Selling 'em arms takes pressure off Teheran. Israel, and Iran will get more arms under a Reagan Administration than Carter gives 'em. I've got to touch base with my Fed block-share venture capital cartel ...I'll be out of town a few days.

"Ronnie, I think it's time for you, in your campaign, to stop holding back attacking how Carter bungled this hostage mess. I've talked to Deaver about it."

I looked at Mike for confirmation. Deaver smiled. "That right Ronnie. We have a speech for you …you get righteous, real emphatic. You say, 'I don't know why fifty-two Americans have been held hostage for almost a year, now! I promise, if I'm elected, I'll make CIA stronger. I'll make all the intelligence agencies stronger …so they can punish terrorists, and communist regimes, everywhere. Like it?"

<>

President Carter's CIA Director, Admiral Stansfield Turner, read an intelligence briefing. He learned Israel was secretly shipping critical U.S. made military equipment to Iran …DCI Stanfield Turner read three of my aides, Lawrence H. Silberman, Richard V. Allen, and Robert C. McFarlane, met at least once with a representative of Ayatollah Khomeini in Washington. Meanwhile, Carter's aides made progress negotiating with Iran. Carter's aides expected to get the hostages released, any moment. That was their only chance for Carter to win re-election, for sure. Suddenly, the Iranians broke off the talks.

<>

DCI Turner looked at Carter. "Laurence H. Silberman, Richard V. Allen, and Robert C. McFarlane insist they made no bargains …and that was their only meeting with Ayatollah's people. Any allegation Reagan or his aides made a hostage deal is too callous for me to believe …but then, why's Israel shipping U.S. arms to Iran? And, then why did Iran break off hostage talks with us."

Carter frowned.

White House Historian Bill Barnes looked at Turner. "I never thought there was a secret deal. But, I've interviewed a dozen Iranian arms dealers, and intelligence operatives, who gave me enough details to confirm that Casey's handling a secret deal. Everyone was in Madrid when Casey was on vacation, someplace."

Turner felt on edge. "Casey's been out of sight all October. No one knows where he is."

Meanwhile, in Washington, me and Bush played golf. Reporters dogged us on the fairway.

Alan, a reporter, called out a question, "Is Casey doing a secret deal in Madrid to free the hostages?"

Bush grimaced. "That's absolute fiction."

Bush reminded me of a kid learning to know when he had to go to the bathroom. "We've tried some things *the other way* to get the hostages home."

Alan took notes while he spoke. "What do you mean?"

I had a good shot lined up. "No comment. This stuff's classified …Fore!" I teed off the green. The televised debates boosted my campaign. I felt more at ease, deflecting President Carter's criticisms with remarks like, "There you go again".

Perhaps my most influential remark was a closing question to the audience, during a time of rocketing global oil prices, and unpopular Federal Reserve interest rate hikes. "Are you better off today than you were four years ago?"

Nov. 4, 1980
Pacific Palisades voting booth

Me and Nancy arrived at the polling place on Election Day. We voted. Reporters swarmed around me. Alan, the reporter, was there to question me. Reporters were asking me questions, all at the same time. I smiled. I stood, looking for my toe marks. I felt better when I saw the masking tape. I walked over in front of the video cameras to my toe marks. "I can't answer any questions till I get on my mark."

Alan the reporter took a pencil from behind his ear. "Are you going to win?"

"I'm too superstitious to answer that."

Nancy nudged me. I turned my eyes towards her. Nancy whispered, "Cautiously optimistic."

I bit my lip. I smiled at Nancy. I turned to the reporters. "I mean, yes. I'm cautiously optimistic."

Alan barked out a question. "Who did you vote for, Mr. President?"

"I voted for Nancy."

<>

On the other side of the country, President Carter finished making his televised concession speech. President Carter moved off-camera with his wife Rosalyn.

The TV announcer spoke into the network camera. "Reagan has won. The Democrats lost the Senate for the first time since 1954," the TV announcer said. Carter's ouster was accompanied by a 12-seat change in the Senate from Democratic to Republican hands, giving the Republicans a majority in the Senate the first time in 28 years.

The camera cut back to President Carter as he spoke to reporters, "I'm not bitter. Rosalyn is, but I'm not."

First Lady Rosalyn Carter was red as a beet,

"I'm bitter enough for both of us."

The camera cut back to the announcer, "Among the losers, are liberals Frank Church, George McGovern and Birch Bayh, defeated by two-term congressman J. Danforth Quayle."

Nov. 5, 1980, post-election lunch

At a post-election lunch the next day, Nancy greeted George and Barbara Bush. George Bush was Vice President Elect.

Nancy was thrilled. "I can't believe it! I can't believe it!"

George turned to me. "Well, what do we do now?"

I shrugged.

Nancy talked to Barbara. "Ronnie just got out of the shower, he was standing in his robe. I had just gotten out of the shower, I was standing in my robe, too. And, we had the television on, naturally. NBC projected Ronnie as winner. I turned to Ronnie. I said, Somehow, this doesn't seem like it's the way it's supposed to be."

Nov. 11, 1980 press conference

Me and Deaver were surrounded by reporters.

I talked to the reporters. "No personnel decisions have been made."

Deaver shrugged. He talked to the reporters, "James A. Baker III will be White House Chief of Staff. Edwin Meese III will be White House Counselor, with Cabinet rank."

I was caught off guard. I felt surprised. I didn't know that went gone down.

White House, Oval Office

As President-elect, I met with President Carter in the White House Oval Office. I was there to get a job briefing from Carter. Carter briefed me about duties and responsibilities of being President. I looked out the window. Nancy waited for me in the hall, outside the office. Carter watched me watching Nancy through the window in the door. Nancy was briefing reporters. I start preening in front of a mirror.

Carter rolled his eyes. "Are you listening to my briefing? Aren't you taking any notes? Don't you have any questions at all?"

"Can I have a copy of your presentation?"

In the hall reporters questioned Nancy. "What are you going to do when you move into the White House, Mrs. President-elect-Reagan?"

Nancy smiled. Nancy spoke firmly, with a no-nonsense tone in her voice. "Ronnie and I are going to set an example for America to follow, so America can return to a higher sense of morality. You know, it kind of trickles down from the top."

Mine and Nancy's friend …and backer …Alfred Bloomingdale, stood nearby. Alfred Bloomingdale was talking to a reporter, too.

"Running the government is like running General Motors. Cabinet secretaries will be like presidents of Chevrolet and Pontiac. Chevrolet competes with Pontiac. Competition is good. But, their competition stops, at what is good for General Motors. Do you know what I mean?"

I smiled at Alfred Bloomingdale's comments. I wondered, who in the hell did he think he was?

Bill Barnes' headline scrapbook

White House Historian Bill Barnes had a collection of headlines he cut out from newspapers. He cut out today's headline from *New York Times*, 'El Salvador Troops Shoot U.S. Churchwomen To Death'.

Reagan home in Hollywood

At our home in Hollywood, me and Nancy were preparing for bed. We were listening to Beatles music on the radio. *Little Darling, it's been a cold dark lonely winter, little Darling it seems like years since you've been here. Here comes the sun, here comes sun, tomorrow may rain, but here comes the sun.* Paul Harvey, the radio talk show host, interrupted the song he was playing for a listener's birthday.

Nancy felt alarmed. She listened to talk show host, Paul Harvey. "We interrupt this broadcast to bring you sad news. John Lennon has been shot in the back outside his New York apartment."

Nancy was shocked. "That's terrible."

The news upset me. "In the back, by a coward."

Nancy looked at me strangely.

Harvey start arguing with a call-in listener. "We don't need gun control just because John Lennon's been murdered. Now, wait just a minute. Death has claimed a lot of rock musicians prematurely, and none with guns. Keith Moon and Janis Joplin OD'd on drugs, along with Elvis Presley, Brian Jones and John Bonham. Plane crashes killed Jim Croce, Otis Redding, Buddy Holly, Ritchie Valens, and Ronnie van Zant. In fact, Lennon at 40 lived much longer than most of those."

Mike Deaver was downstairs. He was working over my living room bar. Then, he crashed on the couch for a few hours. He had to catch a plane to Washington D.C. I came down the stairs.

Mike looked at me. "I'm going to pour myself a drink. Look over the press statement I wrote for you."

"No, that's okay. I'm sure it's fine. It always is."

"One more, for the road." He downed it.

I poured him another shot.

Mike smiled, watching his glass fill with vodka. "I'm back and forth to Washington so much I feel like a yo-yo."

The next afternoon Mike was at Reagan Campaign Headquarters in Washington D.C. presiding over a press conference.

Mike faced the press. "We have major appointments to announce. Donald T. Regan will be Secretary of the Treasury ...David A. Stockman, Budget Director ...William French Smith, Attorney General ...William J. Casey. Director of CIA."

<>

Back in our home in Pacific Palisades me and Nancy stayed in bed late, talking.

Nancy was emphatic. "I don't see why the Carters can't move out of the White House early. Then, I can get in there. I can start a good cleaning. Our son, Ron Jr., there's gossip he's gay. Just because he's dances ballet. You know, he got married yesterday. He did it to stop the gossip. He loves us that much."

"I don't remember the wedding."

Nancy laughed.

Nancy thought I had the best sense of humor in Hollywood. I felt good I'd made Nancy laugh. I watched Nancy's eyes light up. "Nancy, you're my best audience, Honey ...I'm almost sold on having space-based lasers to protect the U.S. Do you remember my film? ...in the '40s, when I saved the orbiting death ray from being captured by Nazis."

<>

In Washington Mike Deaver continued to make his press announcements.

"Caspar W. Weinberger, Secretary of Defense ...Alexander Haig, Secretary Of State ...Raymond Donovan, Secretary Of Labor ...Jeanne Kirkpatrick, U.S. Ambassador to the United Nations ...James Watt, Secretary of the Interior."

<>

Nancy and I were busy in Pacific Palisades.

Nancy turned to me. "Ronnie, I've given it serious thought. Whoever is going to be your press secretary is going to be in front of the cameras, a lot. He's going to be representing you. He should be reasonably good-looking."

<>

In Washington, Mike kept the press busy. "Ed Meese will be Special Counselor to the President, a newly created position. And I, Michael Deaver have been named Deputy White House Chief-of-Staff. President-elect Reagan has issued this statement, 'These appointments are the exact combination to create the new beginning the American people expect and deserve.'"

Alan, the reporter, was on a freelance reporting assignment. He turned to speak to another reporter, standing next to him. "Well I don't know how much we expect, or deserve."

The other reporter laughed.

Alan hurried over, he wanted to interview Ed Meese. "I understand, Mr. Meese, you like to relax by listening to the police band on your radio. And, you like to collect pig figurines as a tribute to the police. Is that a pig tie tack you're wearing?"

Ed Meese smiled. "It sure is."

"Do you think President-elect Reagan is a bit remote? He's not here, with his transition team. He's not here, for his transition to the Presidency."

"Let me assure you, Reagan is running things."

"But, he's not even in Washington. Is he in California? Where is he?"

<>

Out west, in California I dressed casually. I felt in high spirits. I was enjoying that winning feeling. I was flanked by Secret Service agents. Me, and the agents, walked into a butcher shop. I picked up a couple shopping bags full of veal, and beef, from my California butcher. Then, my group went to Drucker's Barber Shop. Drucker's was my favorite barber shop in Beverly Hills. I was sitting comfortably in the barber's chair. I was getting my hair cut. Reporters were quizzing me. Harry Drucker, my old barber, answered a reporter's question.

"I've been cutting his hair the same way for forty years. It's a traditional haircut. It's a conservative haircut. It isn't a hippie-type haircut."

I was amused. I answered questions, too. "No. I do not dye my hair."

A reporter asked me another question. "President-elect Reagan ...was it a good idea for Attorney General-designate William French Smith to have gone to Frank Sinatra's big party? ...when Frank's a man proud to be close to hoodlums?"

Me and Nancy were Sinatra fans. "I've heard

Princess Diana dancing with John Travolta in the entrance hall at the White House. 11/9/85

those things about Frank for years. Me and Nancy just hope none of them are true."

I liked being surrounded by reporters. That made me the center of attention. *That's* what acting's all about.

A few days later, I was being interviewed by CBS, on TV. I was at a football game, at halftime, up in the announcer's booth. I felt that nostalgic, dreamy feeling. "I was a radio sportscaster. I remember, I used to enhance events. I'd just make things up, to make life more interesting."

Jan. 6, 1981, California campaign headquarters

I was surrounded by reporters. I was reading a 5"x8" note card. "I'd like to announce the appointment of James Brady as the new White House Press Secretary. C'mon over, Jim.".

A reporter seemed shocked by Brady's homely looks. "Have Brady's visuals been approved by Nancy?"

I was angry. "I am getting to be an irate husband, at some of the things I am reading, and hearing, about what you reporters are saying about Nancy. None of it is true! ...Excuse me, I have to get a trim at Drucker's, before I catch my plane and head off to D.C."

Los Angeles Airport, farewell ceremony

Working on freelance journalism stories, Alan, the reporter, was flying back and forth between California and Washington D.C., on a regular basis. At LAX, Alan watched President-elect Reagan being presented with a huge jar of jellybeans, at a farewell ceremony for him.

I was feeling nostalgic and a little teary-eyed, leaving Hollywood and California and the West Coast behind me. "I used to pass the jellybean jar around the table when I was Governor of California. You can tell a lot about a fellow's character, if a fellow just picks out one color or grabs a handful."

Alan, the reporter, caught my attention. "Just what can you tell?"

Alan watched my plane fly up into the sky, till the plane got smaller ...the size of a bird, way up in the sky, like a kite, almost out of sight.

Alan grabbed a few days vacation time. He hopped a commuter plane from LAX to SFO. He took the CalTrans train from SFO, to where it stopped at the Menlo Park train station, by the British Bankers Club bar. Then, he took a cab from the train station to West Menlo Park. Alan lived in the last unincorporated area of a little

city, in the suburbs of Stanford University. Even sidewalks stopped, when they got to that part of town. So did noisy traffic. Streetlights skipped every-other street. There were half as many streetlights on streets in unincorporated west Menlo, as in incorporated Menlo Park. That left long stretches of quiet blackness between streetlights. Alan walked from the cab, on the gravel driveway. He went through the gate, towards his cottage. It used to be a garage, or storage shed, once. Alan sighed. It felt good to be home. Alan walked down the crooked dirt path worn into the grass, past the main house. He saw the curtains on the windows of his place, drawn. Little bits of leaking light shimmered out around the curtains. The air felt cold. West Menlo was at the foot of oak-covered foothills, that ran behind Stanford University, then up into the pines at the base of a mountain range. The mountain range peaked in redwood tree forests at Skyline Boulevard, then spilled down the other side of the mountain range, through dense pine forests into coastal plane valleys agriculturally sprawled with fields of artichokes ...all the way to sand dunes and golden beaches that trailed to the foggy, blue-gray Pacific. He'd head up to the city to sail his yawl.

In San Francisco, on weekdays, most everyone else, except him, was stuck ...glued to jobs working in shabby city buildings ...cut-outs from photographs pasted in collages, pen and ink drawings in vacant, glassy-eyed steel buildings translated from an architect's drafting board to animate the city's skyline. At the other end of things, street people crawled like cockroaches over sidewalk cracks and garbage alleys, in practically, invisible, Latino and Black ghettos. People were babysat in public schools, faded in old folks' homes, shriveled in hospitals, waiting in lines in banks, grocery stores, for food stamps, playing with toys, being born, dying, haggling in Chinatown butcher shops, taking cabs, or making love.

Then, Alan was in San Francisco, on his yawl in South Beach harbor, or anchored out in China Basin ...behind the Bay View Boat Club, by the deserted train pier. And, he had the bay to himself. He drilled himself. From the deck of his yawl, he looked at the flagpoles a quarter mile away. There, the docks ended, and the ramps led to the shore and the parking lots. The flags rippled westerlies. Each morning, a suggestion of movement drifted in the air, from deserts 500 miles eastward, westward towards the cold air over the dawning sea. Each afternoon, about one o'clock, the inland Central Valley deserts burnt up from the sun. The scorched heat, rocketing skyward, sucked the sea level, cold air of the Pacific inland …from 0 knots at eleven a.m., 10 knots around noon when 'people' were at lunch, 25-to-30 knots howling and laced with fog through Candlestick and PacBell Stadium by five o'clock …when the work day ended. At sunset, the wind fell off, suddenly, sullen, like someone stepping off a sideway curb after work, every day. Then, fog rolled in from the sea, rolled in over the Sunset District beaches, rolled in right through the Golden Gate Bridge itself, the way ghosts in movies walked through closed doors.

Certain neighborhoods in San Francisco, like the Sunset, or the Marina, or the Presidio, whose cliffs faced the Marin Highland mountain baby molars on the opposing, Sausalito side of the bay, were in thick fog …but, as you came in the bay a few miles, the fog thinned out. San Francisco neighborhoods like the Mission and Bernal Heights never had fog, were always sunny …when there was sun. South Beach harbor by China Basin and India Basin didn't get fog, but when they put the new PacBell stadium in, that afternoon wind was Arctic. Candlestick Park sat outside India Basin. But, both the channels threading the basins rushed wicked 35-40 knot winds, funneling through in late afternoons at kick-offs or opening pitches, pushing sailboats horizontal to the water, in winds that swayed defiant palm trees finally, to bend.

It was early afternoon. Alan stepped off the deck of his yawl, onto the dock. He untied the ropes from the dock cleats. He loosely coiled the ropes, and tossed them onto his deck. Then, he pushed the 30-foot wooden sailboat slowly backwards. On still days, like this, when the tide was slack and neither coming nor going, the water sat still, and flat …like water in a glass. He felt the boat slide back, slowly in the water like fingertips caressing the water's surface. Alan persuaded the boat out, until it was free of the dock, and loose in the channel. If he let go, the boat would drift off. Then, he'd have to jump in the water to catch up. Or, watch it hit against the concrete breakwater guarding South Beach Harbor, seaward. There wasn't much danger, when the wind was mild and the water, slack. The boat was pushed past the point of no return, into the channel. Alan was at the end of the dock. He pushed the bowsprit hard alee, so it cleared the rectangular cement pilings that nailed the floating dock through the palms of the water. Alan leapt onto the bow. He had at least twelve seconds before the boat would hit up against the concrete break-

water, if he made any mistakes. Then, the breakwater could chew the sailboat up, or spit it back.

He ran upon the deck, to the mast. He pulled up the mainsail, tied it off. Quickly hoisted the jib, cleated it to the mast, leaving it fly. Then, ran back down his deck to the cockpit of his yawl, and jumped in. Then, hauled in his main, trimmed his jib, hoisted his mizzen sail on the smaller mast behind his tiller …he'd set sail.

Alan sailed along the concrete breakwater, in the sixty foot wide channel that separated the breakwater from the ends of about twenty docks spaced every sixty yards. The docks floated on the water like wide, flat teeth of a giant comb. Several hundred other sailboats, in twenty-to-fifty-foot berths, were docked. They sat there, with bare masts, with seagulls watching his Seabird Yawl glide silently past.

The yawl yawned softly out the mouth of the harbor, into the bay. The whole exercise was noted by seagulls that sat one to a piling atop each piling, and to walruses that lay in herds on the ends of empty docks like harvested zucchinis. It looked odd to the harbormaster, and his assistants patrolling the docks …because there wasn't much air, to speak of. But, Alan was training himself. One day, he knew he would be doing the exercise in gale force winds. Then, his life, and safety of his boat and crew depended on groomed, practiced habit to keep himself from harm's way, above Davy Jones' locker.

Patti Reagan flew up from Los Angeles to join him for dinner. Alan drove her down to Ming's Chinese Restaurant in the suburb of Palo Alto, for three margaritas before dinner arrived. Embarcadero Road was the main street of the suburb. It ran from the bay on one end, where Alan had bought his yawl when the city closed the harbor for landfill. Embarcadero ran from the bay, past the municipal airport and golf course, on land the city annexed illegally from East Palo Alto, past Mings, over Bayshore freeway. Embarcadero Road then descended down the overpass, into the flowering depths and tree-lines of the suburbs a couple miles through town. Embarcadero stopped at the light at El Camino Real, with a huge Spanish style, quaint shopping center with Spanish tile roofs, on the right and the local Palo Alto High School, on the left. When the light changed, Embarcadero crossed El Camino, went past Stanford University Football Stadium, ran a few miles into the campus, then bellied-up smack dab at the foot of Hoover Tower, an office complex, military-industrial think-tank, and library. As was his custom, during those times of his life when Alan and Patti made their annual pilgrimage to Mings, Alan preceded his meal with three margaritas.

The Chinese maitre-de was tall and bald, each time. Alan looked at him, every year, once a year. "Three margaritas please. Before dinner. Before the food. Bring them all ...at the same time. Three for me, and three for her."

Patti felt embarrassed. "Alan, you shouldn't talk to him like that."

The know-it-all, Chinese maitre-de smiled knowingly. "You mean bring one now and bring one with dinner."

Alan shook his head. "No. You make margaritas. You make three. You bring them together. Before eat. Before food. You bring three margaritas now, for me. You make three, bring three, for her, too."

Alan was getting louder.

Patti was not cool. "Alan, give it up. He doesn't get it."

"Yes he does. We do this every year. It's okay."

The Chinese maitre-de looked at Patti uncertainly. "You?"

Patti smiled. "Bring me the same thing." Then, she smiled at Alan. "Why do you order three at once?"

"I like to get a buzz on before dinner. It lasts the whole dinner. It makes the food taste great."

Patti nodded. "That makes sense."

They drank their drinks and talked their talk.

"What do you think of the New Right Movement Conservatives who want to put food stamps, Section 8, health care, welfare, general assistance and Social Security into the garbage?" .

"I want to nail their balls to the wall, hang their eyeballs on Christmas trees for decoration."

"Why would you want to do that? ...to religious fundamentalists."

Alan spoke loudly. "Why?! ...I don't got to show you no stinkin' badges."

Everyone in the restaurant stopped eating. Alan saw everyone turn at look at him. Alan thought for a moment. before speaking. "Why? ...Because if we ground them up and used them for fertilizer their crucifixes would get caught in Caesar Salads."

Patti laughed. "But, Alan, given their limitations ...you should cut them some slack."

"With a guillotine. Those conservatives are a joke ...but they prayed your father into office. According to them, you and me are under the influence of permissive sex, guns, drugs, rock & roll ...and détente with Soviet Union. They're against abortions, gay rights, feminists, welfare, affirmative action, the environment, death and taxes, the Equal Rights Amendment, divorce, abortion, sex before marriage, sex after marriage, and sex during marriage. But, listen, they do believe in family values like going to church and being happy, little, mindless, wage slaves."

Patti had the feeling the rest of the people in the restaurant might not get the true meaning of the conversation Alan and she were having. "Yo, Alan. I'm drunk. I'll think I'll step outside for a few minutes and cool off ...let things stop spinning."

"Me too. You don't think they're gonna think we're trying to sneak out do you?"

"No, we'll leave our coats and my purse, here."

They left their coats where on the back of their chairs. Patti put her purse on the table. They walked out of the dining room, past the hostess taking peoples' reservations, through the brass-trimmed rosewood doors, past the 12-foot tall cement fu-lion-dogs guarding the entrance to Mings. They went outside, in the cool night. Patti and Alan talked a few minutes. Suddenly, Alan saw that they were being surrounded by 15 or 20 Chinese waiters.

The bald Chinese maitre-de came up to them. "You not leave without pay!"

"You're nuts. We came out for air."

Patti frowned. "Oops."

"Let me handle this. Get me the manager! C'mon, Patti, let's go finish dinner."

They were seated back at their table in the semi-formal dining room when the manager came over to them.

Alan smiled. "I've been coming here, 30 years. You know me. I know you. I do not appreciate being surrounded by a bunch of Chinese waiters in the parking lot!"

Patti cringed.

The restaurant manager took it in stride. "They thought you were trying to leave without paying."

"I left my sports coat right here on my chair. I just went out for air."

The manager wasn't sure. "I'm sorry for misunderstanding."

It was settled. Another foreign policy victory.

Patti asked him, "What do you want for dessert, Alan?"

"Phyllis Schlafly. I interviewed her the other day. A flambé of Phyllis Schlafly going up in flames with bits of shredded Firestone tires and rust. That sounds good." Alan turned to the manager. "Do you have that?"

"No. Fortune cookie, ice cream. I'll send dessert waiter, here."

"Thank you."

The manager walked off.

Alan smiled at Patti. "I interviewed Phyllis Schlafly, after she organized the Eagle Forum. She told me, the Bible ordained that a woman be submissive to her husband, just as she would submit to Christ, as her Lord."

"I bet it was hard to keep your mouth shut."

Alan plopped a small portable TV up on the table. He turned it on. He start changing the channel dial. "It sure was. ...I got to catch Jerry Falwell's act. I have to interview him next week. Here he is. The Christian ministries on TV, there were only 25 in the 1970s. Now, in the 1980s, there's 300. Those 'Conservatives' and 'religious right' people talk about family values. Half the families in America can't afford doctors. Half go hungry. Half have no jobs. Thank God, I get these freelance journalism gigs. The show's back on ... *Herrrrre's Satan.*"

Jerry Falwell was on the tube. A minister in Virginia on TV, before his congregation, he gave a benediction. "This country is fed up with radical causes, fed up with the unisex movement, fed up with departure from basics, from decency, from the philosophy of the monogamous home. We are fed up with destructive permissiveness. The free enterprise system is clearly outlined in the Book of Proverbs. We are religious fundamentalists. We are the Moral Majority. We are evangelicals. It is up to us, to seek out victims of Satan. We must save them, baptize them, register them to vote. You have seen the other TV preachers, Oral Roberts, Jim Bakker, Jimmy Swaggart, Pat Robertson. We get called televangelists, because we evangelize people on TV. We have 60 to 100 million viewers. We are electronic ministries. You get God, you get country music, you get sermons, now you get Ronald Reagan!"

Alan grimaced. "I'll show you destructive permissiveness. I'll cut off your head and feed it to chickens. I'll crucify your body on a telephone pole on the way to Macy's alongside high school teachers. I'll sell lottery tickets to the Devil for your vital organs. I'll make you a car bumper. I'll make you a scarecrow. I'll make condoms out of your intestines. Is that permissive enough for you, asshole?"

Patti looked around the restaurant dining room. No one seemed to be paying attention, except for the children. Some giggled. Patti figured, for giggling kids, listening to Alan was like watching cartoons or American gladiators.

From nowhere, Jerry Falwell introduced Ronnie on the TV tube. That was the last thing Patti expected. "Oh my god. It's Daddy!"

Alan felt triumphant. "Surprise."

Jerry Falwell introduced him. "I want to introduce a man who needs no introduction. Our last speaker declared, God does not hear the prayers of a Jew. Here is a man, God does hear."

<>

I smiled at TV cameras like I loved 'em. "I had strict, religious upbringing. When I was a child, my mother taught me to believe what the Bible said is true. It is, the Truth. I believe in the literal interpretation of the Bible. It is God's Truth. I went to religious college. I studied to be a minister. The unfaithful say, Reagan don't go to church, so he don't count. They say, Reagan was divorced, so he don't count. I am born, again! All the world's complex, terrible problems ...have an answer in the Bible. I support teaching the Bible's story of creation in public schools. I am against feminism, and gay rights ...because I believe, in the Bible. This destructive permissiveness in society is the Evil One, trying to destroy American family values. I am born again!"

Jerry Falwell threw his hands up into the air, "Hallelujah!"

Patti turned off the TV set. "I'd rather watch TV commercials."

They drove back to the yawl. When Alan stepped onboard the deck the small yawl, moved in slow motion in the water like a slow motion rocking chair. They went below, layed down, got that drowsy feeling as they were gently rocked to sleep. Alan dreamed of house sized wontons and margaritas in martini glasses, a bead a salt around the rim, tasting of lime.

Contra field office, Argentina, 1980

Contra leaders trained at CIA School of the Americas, in Georgia. And, in Texas, on the property of one of the largest Texas landowners ...who later became one of the largest landowners in Belize, while making it a Contra staging ground. So, after this training, Contra leaders were stationed in a field office in Argentina. There, was a picture of me over a dart board on the wall ...alongside framed pictures of Mike Deaver, Henry Ford, Allen Dulles, Adolf Hitler, Benito Mussolini, Emperor Hiroshito and senior Nazi officers of the Wehrmacht ...Martin Bormann Odessa mastermind, and Reinhart Gehlen, head of Hitler's anti-Soviet intelligence forces, the Gehlen Organization.

Maps of El Salvador and Nicaragua were on the walls. Contra soldiers threw darts or knives at them. Nazi Count Otto von Bolschwing and Mario Sandoval Alarcon bet on their throws

44

...then, went outside into a helicopter carrying Contra death squads. It raised into the air, soon landing in Nicaraguan jungles. There von Bolschwing and Alarcon evaluated Contra death squad ambush, capture, torture and butchering techniques. Their victims were peasant families. And, Catholic nuns ministering to the village.

Nazi Count von Bolschwing demonstrated to Contra Leader Mario Sandoval Alarcon how Contra terrorists should interrogate prisoners, torture them, rape women and children with rifles, castrate men, gouge-out nuns' eyes using crucifixes, skin them, dismember them, burn their bodies, scatter their ashes ...then, search the ashes for gold fillings ... your basic Nazi procedures, based on saving bullets, and recapturing wealth. Sandoval ordered his Contras to pick up a few hundred kilos of cocaine at one of his underground cocaine factories nearby the village ...inside the factory Sandoval received a radio communication from Nazi Klaus Barbie, from Bolivia.

Klaus Barbie, nicknamed 'Butcher of Lyon', fled to Bolivia after World War II ...thirty years earlier, led successful coup d'état to take over Bolivia, then Martin Bormann ordered him to grow the fledgling cocaine industry, and to help Nazis control the world drug trade.

<>

[Editor's note: Craig Roberts', *Medusa File, Secret Crimes & Cover-ups of the U.S. Government,* comments.]

After World War II, Allen Dulles and his coterie, Martin Bormann and the Vatican, smuggled Nazis to Central America and South America.

[Craig Robert's, *General Reinhard Gehlen and the OSS,* is more specific.]

"The countries of choice were Argentina, Chile, Nicaragua and El Salvador. Within a few years after their arrival, right-wing government 'death squads' made their first appearances.

"Of note in the expatriate community were Dr. Joseph Mengele, who specialized in crude genetic experiments on Jewish concentration camp inmates, and mass murderer Klaus Barbie, the 'Butcher of Lyon'.

[Serge Klarsfeld's, *Holocaust, Children of Izieu,* describes Nazi Klaus Barbie.] In 1944 the Nazi Gestapo from Lyon, under Klaus Barbie, sent two vans to the French village of Izieu. The mission was to exterminate children of an orphanage. www.auschwitz.dk/children/index.htm

"Klaus Barbie was born in Bad Godesberg, near Bonn, Oct. 25, 1913. He joined SS, he began a career in espionage. May 1941, Barbie was posted as an intelligence officer to the Nazi Bureau of Jewish Affairs. He was attached to Amsterdam Gestapo, in Nov. 1942, was posted to Lyon, France. He was to penetrate and destroy the resistance in Lyon. He carried out his task with brutality. Simone Lagrange, a soft-spoken Holocaust survivor, whose family was exterminated, recalled the arrest of her father, mother and herself, Jun. 6, 1944. Denounced by a French neighbor as Jews, Simone and her parents were taken to Gestapo headquarters. There, a man dressed in gray and caressing a kitten, said Simone was pretty ...Klaus Barbie.

"He was caressing the cat. And me, a kid, 13 years old ...I could not imagine he could be evil, because he loved animals. I was tortured by him for eight days'. During the following week, Barbie hauled her out of a prison cell each day, yanked her by her hair, beat and punched at her open wounds ... to get information.

"'Another survivor, Lise Lesevre, recalled how Klaus Barbie tortured her for nine days in 1944, beating her, nearly drowning her in a bathtub. She told how she was hung up by handcuffs with spikes inside them, then, beaten with a rubber bar. She was ordered to strip naked, then, get into a tub filled with freezing water.

"Her legs were tied to a bar across the tub, while Barbie yanked a chain attached to the bar, to pull her underwater.

"During an interrogation, Barbie ordered her to lie flat on a chair. He struck her on the back, with a spiked ball attached to a chain. It broke a vertebrae ...she suffered the rest of her life.

"Another survivor, Ennat Leger, said Klaus Barbie 'had the eyes of a monster. He was savage. My God, he was savage! It was unimaginable. He broke my teeth. He pulled my hair back. He put a bottle in my mouth and pushed it, until my lips split, from the pressure.'

"A dedicated sadist, responsible for many individual atrocities, including capture, and deportation to Auschwitz of forty-four Jewish children hidden in the village of Izieu, Klaus Barbie owed

Nancy Reagan photo with Lab School Honorees Tom Cruise, Bruce Jenner, Cher and Robert Rauchenberg in State Dining Room.

his postwar notoriety primarily to one of his 'cases' ...the arrest and torture-to-death of Jean Moulin, a highest ranking members of French Resistance.

"Jean Moulin was mercilessly tortured by Klaus Barbie, and his men. Hot needles where shoved under his fingernails. His fingers were forced through the narrow space between the hinges of a door, and a wall ...then the door was repeatedly slammed til knuckles broke.

"Screw-levered handcuffs were put on Moulin, tightened til they bit through his flesh, breaking the bones of his wrists. He would not talk. He was whipped. He was beaten. His face was unrecognizable pulp. A fellow prisoner, Christian Pineau, later described the resistance leader as, 'unconscious, his eyes dug in, as though punched through his head. An ugly blue wound scarred his temple. A mute rattle came out of his swollen lips.'

"Jean Moulin remained in this coma, when he was shown to other resistance leaders being interrogated at Gestapo headquarters. Barbie ordered Moulin put on display, in an office. His unconscious form, sprawled on a chaise lounge. His face was yellow, his breathing heavy, his head swathed in bandages. It was the last time Moulin was seen alive.

"On behalf of his cruelty, and especially for the Moulin case, Barbie was awarded, by Hitler himself, the 'First Class Iron Cross with Swords'.

"After the war, Klaus Barbie was recruited by the Western Allies. First, he worked for the British, until 1947. Then, he switched his allegiance to Americans. He was protected, and employed, by American intelligence agents ...because of his 'police skills' and anti-communist zeal ...he penetrated communist cells in the German Communist Party.

"With the aid of the Americans in 1950, he fled prosecution in France, and relocated to South America with his wife and children.

"He lived in Bolivia as a businessman, under the name, Klaus Altmann, from 1951. Though he was identified in Bolivia as early as 1971, by Nazi hunters Beate and Serge Klarsfeld, it was February 1983 that the Bolivian government, after long negotiations, extradited him to France to stand trial. This caused the U.S. to offer a formal apology to France, in August 1983. He was tried in a French court, and sentenced to life imprisonment. He died of cancer in prison, Sept. 25, 1991," Klarsfeld said.

<>

In 1983, was right in the middle of my first Administration. I don't remember if it was me, or Bill, or Madeline, who signed the apology.

<>

Sandoval's Contras loaded cocaine into a jetliner. The jetliner had a Coors beer logo painted on the rudder ...as a thank you to the company that supplied money to buy the plane ...once in the air, Contras, naturally, drank Coors beer ...and looked out the plane's windows, towards the ground. Many hours later, they stared at 50' tall white letters spelling out the word, 'Hollywood'. They passed around pictures of hookers on Hollywood & Vine, made off-color gestures, and sucking sounds. The plane happened to fly over Patti Reagan's ramshackle hippie cottage in the Hollywood hills, back in a canyon, on a hillside facing the sea.

<> <> <>

Patti's writing time, 1988

That day, the sun refused to shine. Patti liked the drizzle, clean taste of the air, smell of snow, the heady feeling of clarity that hinted how good life could be. She drew in deep breaths, sighed, yawned lazily. Salmon-pink underbellied clouds flattened slowly into dusk, ...then, darkness fell, and bright stars appeared. Patti stared down the street, into the shadows for her connection ...the buildings felt like gargoyles looking down, the people in the street felt like aliens ...she start singing a Ray Charles song, and waited. Then, she saw Alan coming towards her. "Hey."

Alan smiled and whispered. "*Yo.*"

"I want to go visit Granma Wilpf in Eastern Europe. Want to come?"

He didn't think she was going. "Sure, tell me when to pack."

Patti smiled. She was a sensual woman. She smiled, it melted him.

She was pleased. "Okay."

They were writing a fictional autobiographical novel about her dad, President Reagan. Patti did investigative reporting, got national clips because of her last name, hadn't made big time. Alan, he had a strong review from the *New York Times* on a non-fiction book. His fiction, was going nowhere, fast. They were friends of twenty years ...standing, laughing, sitting, bored, hanging out, didn't have to talk ...it was like that ...waiting to meet White House historian Bill Barnes ... Alan transcribed, typed and did journalism for, said he'd give Patti a shot, reporting.

"There's Bill."

Patti flipped on her recorder. "What's your job like? ...know where the bodies are buried?"

Bill Barnes laughed. "The whole Reagan Staff and Cabinet are writing autobiographies."

They cabbed it to the White House. Got out. Patti saw President-elect George Bush, and Vice-President-elect Dan Quayle.

Patti was ready. "Can I interview them?"

Barnes shook his head, 'no'. "There's Larry Speakes, White House presidential spokesman."

Patti watched Larry Speakes trot over, then nailed him. "You're a regular ministry of propaganda."

Barnes intervened, "Larry's leaving President Reagan's White House."

Patti was puzzled. "Not staying on?"

Speakes was in a hurry. "I've had enough. I'm only human. Don Regan set me up with Merrill Lynch, where he worked before he came here."

"Tell me a few things."

Speakes smiled. "We had a three-headed monster running the White House ...Baker, Deaver and Meese. They loved limos ...private parking behind White House gates ...the way people defer to you ... when you're a White House big shot. Libyan terrorists stalked us back in '81, when your dad got here ...they threatened to hurt us. Baker, Deaver and Meese ordered personal, Secret Service guard details ...Deaver's way to be somebody. Nothing can sink someone here faster than a nickname. I had turf-wars with that s.o.b. David Gergen, Director of Communications, I called him 'Tall Man'. White House staffers, then press, called him, 'Too-Tall', too big for his britches."

Alan was impatient.

Patti smiled to sooth him. "They started my dad's Reagan Revolution cutting taxes, cutting spending, cutting social services since *they* ran the White House?"

Larry laughed. "Reagan's first term, his innermost circle was Chief of Staff James Baker III, Presidential Counselor Edwin Meese III and Deputy Chief of Staff Michael Deaver. Reagan delegated everything, giving everyone more power than they were worth, boys going at each other's throats."

<>

James Baker started in. "Larry, Meese is damn dogmatic, he thinks he's Genghis Kahn, he's politically correct as a bull in a china shop."

Speakes retorted. "He's another prima donna, from the planet of California."

Ed Meese III appeared. Baker cringed. "Here comes poppin'-fresh doughboy."

Speakes smelled the cigar in Meese's mouth, even when it wasn't hanging out.

Meese bellowed. "I'm a God-damn conservative! ...I'm not negotiable! Baker's so damn pragmatic, he'll compromise me out of town if I let him."

Speaks ignored him. "I know, Ed. What do you expect from a Texas prima donna?"

Mike Deaver was arguing with Baker. "Ronald Reagan does not have a bone of prejudice in his body!"

I was out of patience, I was the god-damn President, "I don't know what Blacks' problems are, I got no feel how a person lives in a Black ghetto."

Baker's tone was indifferent. "You can't appear insensitive to Blacks, women and Jews."

"Nixon says I can."

Ed spoke up. "It doesn't matter what Blacks think! They're not disadvantaged ...they're *lucky* to live in America! Show me evidence there are hungry children in this country! They have soup kitchens where food is free! I eat there!"

Baker was discouraged. "You're wrong, Ed. I'm with Deaver on this. Minorities are a voting block, that's why Nixon brought in the damn Nazis from Eastern Europe to stomp out the Jew vote."

<>

Larry Speakes stopped reminiscing. "Patti, Baker's staff was capable. Meese's aides were ignorant. Baker had the White House along with Congress. Besides Deaver, Baker had Richard Darman who'd worked with him at Commerce. Darman and I fought. Baker and Darman created the Legislative Strategy Group, early in your dad's first term, limited to as many who could sit around Baker's conference table. They were elite White House decision makers, the engine running the White House car. Baker made policy decisions over lunch, in cocktail parties, in the men's room. He wasn't supposed to, but he did. Baker's conference table was the magic key He used it to take control of the White House from Meese."

Patti frowned. "Wait a second, have to change batteries."

Larry unwrapped a slice of gum, put it in his mouth. "Meese held policy apparatus like an old house, falling apart. I call Meese, the prime minister of the United States. When they were in Sacramento, Meese had absolute authority advising your father. I saw what Meese was up to in Washington, weeks before the inauguration. I warned Baker. So, Meese and Baker decided between them, who would do what, which offices they'd have, which duties. Meese was more conservative than Baker, or Deaver. Baker didn't join Reagan until the 1980 campaign. I don't know who tossed his hat into the ring. Meese was old-line Reagan, tuned-in to California players, knew how to work Reagan, played to his conservative side. Meese screwed up, decided not to wake the President up, when Navy jets shot down Libyan fighter planes off Libya's coast. The press made your father look lazy. Baker won arguments with Meese, because Deaver sided with him. Deaver worked with Meese when Reagan was governor, knew Meese's shortcomings, watched Meese manipulate your father, with dogma. Meese wasn't organized. I said, when Meese put a document in his briefcase, it was gone forever. Now, I think he did it on purpose. It was a good move when U.S. Attorney General William Smith resigned in '84 ...Meese replaced him. After that, the President relied on Meese , sometimes. I remember Reagan asked Meese for advice when Iran-Contra broke, in Nov. 1986. Meese wasn't in the inner circle any more ...a member of the Cabinet may have rank, but, it's proximity that counts. Now, Deaver was also a personal aide to your father, *and* mother. Deaver controlled your dad's body ...scheduled everyplace he went ...was your mother's confidant ...spent hours on the phone listening to the First Lady, on the hour. Nancy rehearsed Deaver on everything, ranting and raving. Deaver was the conscience of the Reagan White House. He suggested things to Reagan and Nancy, engineered Baker's spot as first, among equals. Deaver got more credit for public relations than he should have ...he wasn't brilliant ...he knew what stories Reagan could play to, and look his best ...he had second sense, that way ...a genius at knowing. For London, the economic summit in '84 ... Deaver smelled how dramatic it could be to have Reagan make a speech at Normandy, on D-day. At Point du Hoc field, Reagan stood by old geezer Rangers who invaded France in '44, turned out one of your dad's best photo-ops. Deaver raised your dad's public opinion poll points that day. Deaver's idea in '85, to have the President visit dead Nazi's in Bitsburg, wasn't bright. We fought over it. Remember it, clear as day. Deaver walked up to me. 'I toured the cemetery, myself. It was covered with snow! Deaver told me. 'We'll be in trouble, if this is a German military graveyard,' I told him '...we never went to a concentration camp' ...the press will pick our bones."

Deaver protested. "No, the theme of this trip is reconciliation!"

Speakes was upset. "Every time we go to Europe, reporters say, 'Will the President see a concentration camp?' This will be a feeding frenzy."

Deaver felt defensive. "The President doesn't want to visit a concentration camp for personal reasons. He doesn't like reminders about how horrible it was. I can't blame him. I've been sheltering him, I admit it."

<>

Speakes looked at Patti. "I was surprised Deaver got in trouble when he left the White House ...accused of lying to Congress ...accused of lying to a federal grand jury. People said, after he left the first time, he illegally lobbied Reagan aides in '85, when he had that public relations business in Washington. His office was full of pictures in solid silver frames, pictures of him with kings, queens, prime ministers and Contra cocaine runners. He talked them all into posing, he enjoyed trappings of power ...he was still a small-town kid from Bakersfield. I guess, he got carried away with his own importance, it's a fatal disease in this town. He got convicted on three counts of perjury. All in all, Don Regan, George Shultz and Jim Baker were superb Cabinet appointees. Ed Meese, Caspar Weinberger, Jim Watt, stunk. Your dad liked to say, 'The Cabinet is a board of directors. I'm the CEO. But, I'm the only one who has a vote at the end.' But he knew better.

"Deaver was the one who argued for women's issues, and minority issues. He was sincere. But, he was from California ...was tuned-in to how important women and minorities were, politically. Baker thought, Meese was Neanderthal. Meese thought Baker threw the baby away with the bath water. Baker played your father differently than Meese did. Baker taught your dad how to get half a loaf now and the other half later. Meese wanted to eat the whole loaf now. I liked watching Baker manipulate your father, around to his point of view. Baker wooed the press, spent half his time with reporters and editors, had real control how his policies appeared in the press ...there's your propaganda ministry. Meese only played to right-wing reporters, and the California press. Considering, you had a three-headed monster running the White House ...Baker, Deaver and Meese worked out okay, until Spring of '85. Then, the troika dissolved. Deaver left to start a public relations firm. Meese moved over to Attorney General to head Justice Department. By second term, after being Chief of Staff, Jim Baker was hunting around He came to me."

<>

James Baker felt he'd was always right. "Speaks, I told you we'd get everything done at the beginning of Reagan's first term. We got a camel through the eye of a needle. We accomplished everything. I always said, the second term would be sitting-out retirement. I don't feel like sitting, I don't want any Liberals scowling, breaking wind, pointing their fingers at me. I want the Attorney General position."

Speakes felt strange. "Deaver said, Meese locked that up."

Baker laughed. "Shoot! ...then I want Secretary of State."

Speakes thought that was funny. "Shultz will keep it."

Baker quipped. "Then, head of CIA!" s

"Too far back in line."

Baker exhaled, loudly. "Bernie Kuhn's being forced out as baseball commissioner. I was offered that job, it looks good."

Speakes was shocked. "Baseball commissioner?! You don't like baseball!"

"I like it good enough. I'm just not what you would call, an 'avid fan'."

<>

Patti asked, "Baker liked baseball?"

"Yeah," Speakes replied. "So Baker swapped jobs with Treasury Secretary Don Regan, cause Regan took over as Chief Of Staff ...then, only one man ran the White House, Don Regan. There was no question who was running things. Before he got into politics, Don fought his way to the top of Merrill Lynch on his own, a self-made multi-millionaire, just like your dad was. Your dad always got a kick out of how their last names were close. Your dad liked Don's locker room jokes. When Bud McFarlane ran the National Security Council, Bud made Don mad. Bud used to sneak things for your dad to approve, into the Daily Briefing book, a leather-bound collection of top-secret intelligence the National Security Council makes and gives the President every day. In the first Cabinet, when Don Regan was Secretary of the Treasury, he was one of two take-charge guys in the Cabinet, Secretary of State Alexander Haig was the other. Don's debonair and polished, self-assured. He got me my new job at Merrill Lynch. You happy now?"

Patti listened, trying to piece together the father she had never known. Patti nodded, a questioning expression came over her.

Night fell on Washington.

<>

Bill Barnes let Patti be an assistant White House Historian, earn a good salary, work alongside Alan. She got good at writing epitaphs, anecdotes, obituaries and one-page descriptions of important guests and famous people who visited the White House on official business. She'd handwrite, or tape record descriptions, then Alan would type or transcribe them.

They were a couple, and a team. Sometimes, Patti went over to the State Department to pick up the daily intelligence briefs. She kept track of thousands of White House Reagan photos. There were ten thousand photos of him. She cataloged memoirs written by White House elected officials, and their families ...kept track of China settings ...and silverware purchases ...cataloged White House paintings ...and furniture ...listed habits and tastes of people who bought them and enjoyed them ...made lists of aerospace and weapons lobbyists, food lobbyists, Croatian lobbyists, milk lobbyists and 57 varieties ...followed political events ... all the time, trying to get a glimpse of her father, what he was really like.

A closer bond formed between Patti and Alan, as they worked side by side. They shared meals. Workdays lasted from 6 a.m. to 1 or 2 a.m. They shared stories from their lives with each other. And, slept together, platonically -- no sex.

Patti looked for Tiger her cat on the couch, on the pillows on the bed, under the bed, in the closet. Tiger's catnip mouse was there, but no Tiger. She walked to her writing desk, wrote about the world as it should have been, gardens instead of lawns, sidewalks and streets, ghettoes rebuilt into suburbs, poverty disappearing, Mother Teresa replacing the gold standard with a love standard, starting a whole new monetary system using cornflakes, things she never shared with anyone. She imaged the world a happy place, with no war, planes dropping flowers, not bombs.

<>

Patti grew up, reading Flaubert, Dostoyevsky, Hesse, ancient Chinese poetry, modern American Babarian underground poetry ... Bohemian poetry passed her by. Babarian stuck (named after the Café Babar in San Francisco). In college, she lost himself in creative writing classes, poetry writing classes, art classes, graphics, playwriting. But, as a freshman in college, and for the next few years, was afraid of people who weren't creative ... because, she thought they were walk-ins, unfeeling, downright alien, business majors, jocks and joe-six-pack monsters, not people. How could they have daily normal routines ...while Vietnam was raging ...people were being slaughtered ...or, when her dad was using Cointelpro agent provocateurs to beat up demonstrators getting them arrested in front of San Onofre Nuclear Power Plant? She did not do well in psychology classes, pre-med biology classes, economics, sociology, anthropology, biology, chemistry. In fact, none of her classes except writing, playwriting and art. Graduating with a BA in

Writing & Graphic Communication, then, she endured a checkered career, punctuated by mates. She worked as an editorial assistant, writing gardening books, in the evenings she wrote lousy anti-war novels, lousy romantic novels or lousy poetry. Back then, she knew in her heart ...Chevron was one of the oil companies responsible for the Vietnam war ...Chevron and Anaconda Copper lobbied the World Bank to beat Chile to death with extra points on interest on World Bank loans, then to stop loans entirely, cause national bankruptcy ...then, have CIA stage a coup d'état in Chile and murder Salvador Allende, President of the Socialist Democracy in Chile. What she didn't know, was that these companies were all directed by fed blockshareholders ...that there was a common thread of blame. But, no one in America knew.

So she lived in what the pre- and post-Confucius ancient Chinese book of auguring, the I-Ching, called a state of duality. She lived way in the future ahead of herself, not paying attention to feelings, on the run from her family, moving from place to place in the L.A. canyons, or up north in Palo Alto, Woodside ... while decades shed off her skin like water, she marched to a different drummer.

She got tired of moving boxes around, year after year, place to place ...boxes of dreams that never came true ...tickets to ride the American dream ...someday never came. Over-sensitive, intelligent, elegant, sophisticated, devastated that life was always a step ahead of her, joy beyond her reach.

<>

Whenever Richard Cory went downtown,
We people on the pavement looked at him;
He was a gentleman from sole to crown,
Clean favored, and imperially slim.

And, he was always quietly arrayed,
And, he was always human when he talked;
But, still he fluttered pulses when he said,
"Good-morning," and, he glittered when
he walked.

And, he was rich ... yes, richer than a king,
And, admirably schooled in every grace;
In fine, we thought that he was everything
To make us wish that we were in his place.

So, on we worked, and waited for the light,
And, went without the meat, and cursed
the bread;
And, Richard Cory, one calm summer night,
Went home, and put a bullet through his head.

That's how she felt. She settled into a life of not quite living, playing pianos, dulcimers, auto-harps, saxophones, flutes, mandolins, banjos, harps, harmonica blues, modern dancing, jazz, ballet exercises. *Acting* like she was living, but not *feeling* like she was. Untouchable to herself, frustrated, altruistic, forever young creature of another time, drawn only to other creatures from other times, not of this world.

Society branded her forehead with an invisible 666, so she cloistered up alone, heard an abusive father judging her, in her head ...showing only anger ...a mother screaming even louder who rarely shared, or showed, or admitted feelings, who was not introspective, nor interested in her daughter Patti's world, or opinions ... other than to brand them, 'wrong'.

The handsome genetics of the two parents produced a bright, creative, imaginative Quasimodo daughter ...hippie ...artist ...weed growing up in a crack in the sidewalk ...tree growing up where edges of asphalt parking lots met at right angles to cement walls, insistent on surviving in hostile environments, improbably, defying the odds of being there, intelligent human beauty, delicacy, grace, as best a dandelion weed unwanted, unloved, but beautiful.

And, that beauty was currency among the *others*, recognizable by moonlight in their eyes during the hot, noontime sun, hair blown lazily by breezes ...only the *others* felt, vision only the *others* saw thru, music only the *others* heard. Maybe, the *others* were in the poetry section of a bookstore, housed in a Victorian house ...maybe the *others* were at a concert waiting for her ...maybe, the *others* were doing schrooms on the hill flying kites on the beach, or swimming, nude, in the lake.

Patti went through life in a dance, following her feelings in a daze of feelings, urged on by her heart, judgmental, elitist, cerebral. She felt herself better than *establishment* people, in a variety

President and Nancy Reagan posing with Sylvester Stallone & Brigitte Nielsen during a state dinner for Prime Minister Lee Kuan Yew of Singapore. 10/8/85

of ways she couldn't remember, anymore. But, never lied, as if that mattered to anyone but herself, so, in that, she came to know God. To know, love is better than murder, better than genocide, could end ruling family turf wars over the Earth's resources. And, all the time, knowing in her heart, society at large had no use for her. But, intuited history would somehow need her, more than any man would ever. Aside from faltering achievements, heart-fulls of trying, and watching her future get dim.

Bill Barnes saw it clearly, as his reflection in a mirror. So, recognizing her talent, he told her, she could be an assistant White House historian under his management. So, Patti had a job, as long as her father did.

Glory of glories, she wanted people happy, and healthy. All the damn money in the world divided up equally among everyone ...or, outlaw money altogether ...so there was no money at all, and, people who wanted to work could, and, those who didn't wouldn't have to. After all, money was make-believe ... mankind made money, not God. Let Spirit be money! ...let love be money! Oh God, made living things ...man made God's living things dead.

Love intended to succeed, where God had failed to secure. So, armed with these absurd thoughts, Patti Reagan set out to survive, the genocidal world of the Fed block-shareholders.

<>

Patti told Nancy and me, she was going to vacation in Sarajevo ...to leave her job as a historian at the White House on a sabbatical. And, that she was going with Alan, the reporter.

<>

For weeks, they lived in his flat in the Upper Haight. Or, stayed on his yawl in San Francisco Bay. Then, they flew abroad. In Amsterdam, they rented a yawl cutter. They moved onboard. They sailed on the canals. They worked their way up river, tying up to a dock, in Sarajevo.

Living on the water in Sarajevo was the same as living on the water in San Francisco Bay. In both cities, the water's blue-grey, and foggy clouds stretch in quicksilver puddles floating on the waves. The edges of the reflections round over the crests of the waves, then, slide down each swell, and tear in jagged, quicksilver, mirror shapes.

Below, in the berth, Patti felt Alan slide into her. She moaned. Her excitement floated on the waves. She arched her pelvis up, embracing him. She came long, and hard.

Then, Alan went up on deck to check the lines.

The boat rocked back and forth, lazily in the waves. Patti rolled gently back and forth on the bed. She looked out the porthole, at the bow. It would rise and fall in the waves. Alan was standing on the bow.

The only time Patti felt 'grounded' to the Earth ...was on a boat, floating on the water. She watched Alan tug the anchor line, making sure it was secure. He pulled with strong hands and arms. He wore a towel, wrapped around his waste. He looked back, at her. She leaned, naked, out the cabin hatch.

Patti was happy. "I feel alive. I feel joy. I forgot what joy felt like. I can do anything! I feel so good!"

Alan smiled, tugged the anchor line. The yawl moved forward in the water, toward anchor. "I don't need to worry, the anchor's holding. We won't break loose, drift off, ground, or breach."

Patti laughed. She yelled orders at him. "For God's sake, stop worrying! ...we have unfinished business. I can't keep my ankles crossed, forever ...get in here!"

They got back in the bunk. The slowly heaving sailboat pushed them closely together. Other times, it pulled them apart. Patti clung to him, suddenly pulling herself close around him. She never wanted to stop. She held him closer, until she disappeared. Then, she opened her eyes. She looked out the hatch. She saw the blue sky ...the sound of waves licked the wood hull, giggling, like brooks running on river rocks, in the stillness each time their lips touched, pulling her in tidal currents, surrendering to gravity, falling around him, into him, ...listening to seagulls screeching, plaintively circling the yawl. She felt sleepy, felt herself falling, into sleep...a long fall ...dreaming, Tiger slept beside her ...purring on her ribs, warm, soft, vibrating purrs.

Alan softly kissed her awake. "Satisfied?"

"Yes. I'm luxurious. I want to bottle it. Sell it to people without love," she whispered.

"Sell me?"

"Silly. I love you. Please, keep kissing me." Patti felt his mouth kiss her, in slow motion she drifted back towards sleep. She felt herself falling again. She sighed. "Don't talk any more. Don't move. I don't want to lose this feeling. *Shhh*, Darling, sleep."

He kissed her on the cheek. "Pleasant dreams. I'm going topside."

"*Shhh!* Then, do it. Let me sleep!" She felt cozy. She'd always collected men. Kept them around her like glass necklaces, rolling them softly over her breasts. She slept, and dreamed, and heard a dim voice calling her through dreams, louder and louder. Patti awoke in a dream state, ...not knowing where she was ...her ribcage vibrating gently, in rhythms that rose and fell. Slowly, one eye opened. She saw Tiger, pressed against her, purring, light falling at the edges of the curtains ...recognized her silver and white satin ballet slippers, dangling from the chandelier from the ceiling ...wide pink, red and purple colors of ribbons, streaming from the chandelier, moving lazily in the air ...recognized her banjo, leaning against the fireplace ...a wooden drafting table in the corner of the room ...a wooden loom ... a small, unfinished tapesry woven up it ...a computer on her desk ...it was her room in Alan's flat, in the Upper Haight. Her room. Her Tiger. Her Alan, watching her, in her dream.

Alan spoke in a whisper. "I worried about waking you. You talked in your sleep. You were dreaming."

She felt his fingers get slippery on her, noticed he was light, as he rolled on top of her, but she felt something was wrong. "Distance is coming back."

"Oh shit, are you ever going to let me in? ...there has to be a first time."

She felt irritable. "I've had lots of first times ...it doesn't suit me, right now. There may never be a first time, for you. If I let a man in me, it changes us. I treat him badly. If it's any consolation, I dreamed we did it on your boat."

"It's no consolation. It's irritating."

She rolled him off from on top of her ...jumped out of bed ...took off her cotton nightgown ...threw it in his face, and laughed ...pulled a white silk scarf from her chandelier, draping it from her head ...pulled a bouquet of flowers he'd given her last night from a vase, hit him on the head with the flowers, playfully ...though, it seemed to her she could have hit him a lot harder without hurting him, next time, she would. "I feel distance between us."

He didn't like it. "Either you take a chance, make love with me, find out once and for all, or you don't."

Patti hesitated. "I don't. What if it's the wrong decision? ...what will happen, then? ...should we be together ...with distance between us? ...is that the way it is, with lovers?"

He frowned. "You think too much."

Patti focused her attention, pointed at him. "You worry too much ...and, see! ...we're fighting, already ...we'd never get along ...we shouldn't be lovers."

Patti turned from him, towards her mirror ...brushed her hair ...it was naturally blonde now in springtime, the color of sand dunes ...it hung over her shoulders to her waist. As she brushed it, some ends jumped, loudly snapped and split. Tiger watched lazily beside the mirror, trying to catch her hair with his paw.

Alan was defeated, "Why do you sleep with me, but never make love? Last night was the first time we even fooled around. Did you like it?"

Patti smiled. "Yes, some things a woman doesn't talk about. Let's get up ...get on with the day. C'mon! Get out of bed, sleepyhead! Get on with it!"

He felt impatient. "I want to talk some more!"

Patti turned towards him. "I don't! Pour ice water down your pants."

He was angry. "I don't need ice water! I want to talk about it!"

Patti laughed viciously. "I don't! I won't! If you insist ...I'm leaving! I'll be back, later. She turned her back on him.

He didn't like that. "You only do things when it suits you! What about me?"

Patti looked back. "Your feelings don't matter as much as mine ...they can't ...that's the truth ...take it, or leave it. Take it, you get me. Leave it, you lose me. See how simple it is? You complicate, you worry, you're crazy."

He felt calmer, playful. Because, what she said made sense. "That's easy for you to say."

"Of course." Patti picked up Tiger, carried him to the refrigerator, opened the door so Tiger could paw at what he wanted. Tiger pushed his paw against a carton of cream. Patti was amused. "Do you want cream, sweetheart? ...then, you'll have it."

He watched ...relaxed ...happy ...fascinated.

When she spoke, melody and cadence led her voice. He'd found in several women in his life, that he felt at home with.

She looked at him. "I'm writing about artists, abandoned in society ...my friends, artists, dancers, writers, actors, musicians ...they suffer ...struggle to survive ...no jobs for creative artists when they graduate ...just jobs for businessmen, engineers, accountants, salesmen, computer programmers, police, the regimented practical, judgment jobs for dead, unfeeling people.

"You think Mr. & Mrs. God wanted us dead, those jobs? ...and, that's why we were created? Don't bother answering. Y'know, I had a job once, giving high-schoolers job placement tests. God-given personality traits exist. That's what runs the world, not opinions ...that's thinking. Traits are your calling, your apostolate, that make artists artists, businessmen businessmen, soldiers soldiers, cops cops. Artists are opposites of business types! It's been hard for me to survive creatively, my whole life. I'm an artist ...for me to try to hold a boring everyday job like normies do, drives me nuts. It's not how God made me to be."

He looked at her. "Normies?"

Patti felt frustrated. "Normal people, not artists."

"Oh."

She was hesitant. Tiger walked out from beneath the deck, jumped onto the bed, walked to Patti ...lay down, purring against her leg. Patti petted Tiger. His belly was warm. "Normies do anything, for jobs. Stupid, boring things ...hurt people's feelings, for money ...follow orders ...accept the establishment, become it.

"I have to fight to survive, my God-given, genetic who-I-am-traits. Normies don't have to. It's not fair. Normies don't understand me, anyway. What's the use?

"Normies think I'm useless, just being me. But, they fit in like toilets ...aggressive, unfeeling, air-head robots. All they want to do is use war and economic deprivation to control artists, just being who they are, the way God made them ...they don't care, by their God-given innate personalities, they just don't care. That's how God made their genetics.

"Normies are happy with boring jobs that drive me nuts, make me think about suicide. It's not fair."

Alan sighed. "You've lived it your whole life, all of us *others* have."

Patti felt excited by her ideas, "But, I never knew it was genetic! ...God did it! I thought it was just a feeling artists get, when they can't buy food or pay the rent. Isn't that great?!"

He wasn't excited, as she was. "Yes." He watched her lips. She talked faster, forming her words precisely with perfectly shaped lips. *That* excited him. He watched how beautiful she was.

She smiled. "There's emotional warmth, versus cold unfeeling ...creative versus hard-headed ...imaginative versus practical ...danger-seeking against danger-avoiding ...loving fighting hating ...helping fighting hurting ...submissive fighting dominant. It's amazing! ...God did it. I mean, why weren't people all made just like me? ....imaginative, sensitive ...there'd be no wars ...no hungry people ...no homeless."

<>

Patti smiled, standing naked, in the middle of the sailboat cabin. A Molotov cocktail smashed onto the deck of the yawl. It exploded into flames. Patti was startled. She threw a cotton blouse over her breasts, pulled on Levi's, tennies, crept to look out the hatch. Alan, on deck, saw the fire-

bomb, smoking in the air, as it sailed over some stores, then, high in the air over the cana. He dipped a bucket into the canal. He waited till the firebomb smashed on the deck, then emptied the bucket of water onto it, putting it out.

Alan looked back at Patti. "There's skinheads in Nazi uniforms on shore, by the shops. They threw it at someone, and missed. I don't think they threw it at us."

Patti was apprehensive. "Something bad's going to happen."

He felt it too. "What's all that noise?"

Patti looked on shore, up-and-down the streets, by the shops. "I can't see anyone but, those Nazi skinheads. Everything else is normal. The street's full of cars, tourists, locals, scooters, skateboarders, skinny kids on speed, spaced-out kids on pot and acid, crazy crack-heads walking around saying, 'Are you okay are you okay', trying to sell shit, street ho's on heroin, street people, panhandlers, hippies who are instant friends, if you let 'em be ...till you tell them 'no' ...the bars are packed, up and down the street, the sidewalks are covered with clothes, books, blenders poor people sell to each other, most likely stolen. It's wild and crazy out there, nothing unusual ... except the Nazi skinheads. Wait a minute! I see what it is! A skinhead Nazi police rally."

She push the dinghy off the sailboat, into the water. They got in, held onto the sailboat so the dinghy didn't drift away. "Go get the knapsack."

"Are you sure?"

"Yes, it's a good day to die."

"That's not funny."

"I was just kidding, lighten up."

Alan got the knapsack from the cabin, then climbed back into the small rowboat. Tiger jumped in the back of the rowboat. Tiger hid behind the knapsack. Alan rowed them towards shore. They tied the dingy to a cleat on the dock. Then, they crept up the ramp, to the back of the crowd. Tiger followed behind.

A pickup truck stopped. It was filled with al Qaeda, the Moslem Brotherhood. This was back, before bin Laden and his Nazi Arab mercenary army on CIA payroll were called, the 'Muhajidin' ...or even stationed in Afghanistan ...before they were financially totally cut off by CIA ...back, when the Soviets went bankrupt trying to match U.S. military arms buildups ...so Chevron Oil and Chase Manhattan could cut their pipelines to the Caspian ...and, as agreed, left bin Laden and his army in Afghanistan to own the opium poppy heroin trade ...then, completely cut them off from BCCI financing that had a conduit through Pakistan, from Saudi Arabia. But, the al Qaeda, Moslem Brotherhood had grown accustomed to having food, clothes, medical care, weapons, ammunition, and free reign. It seemed Dir. Bush's CIA, and the Reagan-Bush Administration's CIA, and then, G.W Bush Administration's CIA ... predictably, always had their CIA hire dictators, drug lords, mercenaries, weapons dealers, drug runners ...and, made them promises ...set them up, then double-crossed them ... pissing quite a lot of dangerous people off.

<>

Soldiers in stylishly tailored, woolen uniforms came onto the pickup bed. The street quickly filled with battalions of police. They stood behind steel shields. They were armed with sidearms and batons. Police cavalry units stood by ...their uniforms were modeled on German fascist uniforms from Eastern Europe, which were modeled after the Nazi look. In the U.S., it was trendy among the kids ...the Nazi look ...starting to show up on fashion runways ...in women's fashion magazines ...chrome and gun metal blue-gray 'look' ...black leather panties and bras ...as much bare flesh as possible, poking or sliding out, from under full-length black leather coats, eyes hidden behind mirror sunglasses.

A SWAT team escorted businessmen and businesswomen. It was flanked by secret agents in trench coats. Protesters marched in. They were dressed in shorts, and tennies. They had flannel shirts tied around their waists, cotton sweatshirts, wool sweaters hung over their shoulders. They carried signs, and bouquets of flowers, helium balloons, blowing shiny soap bubbles, that reflected in the sun. Protestors making the closed-fist, power salute. They chanted in unison, "Peace ...Peace ....Peace", like peace was a 49'ers or Raiders team, trying to score.

SCREAMA Subject Population Control squads arrived. They wore black civilian clothes, with dull, black metal baseball-type helmets. They climbed out of black vehicles, carrying machine pistols.

SCREAMA pulled a beat-up man out of a SWAT truck. His hands were handcuffed behind him. There was a cross of two-by-four's tied to his back. His arms were tied to it. He took shortened steps, because a chain cuffed his ankles. He couldn't carry his own weight. He wobbled as he walked. Two SCREAMA grabbed him. They dragged him forward, up onto the pickup bed. SCREAMA tied a blindfold around his eyes. A man wearing a Nazi uniform wore a black, executioners sack over his head with eyeholes cut in it,

hanging to his shoulders, rippling in the breeze.

The Nazi goose-stepped to the microphone. The microphone picked up the clicking sound of his heels. Speakers broadcast the sound down the street. He stood, staring at the crowd.

The crowd booed him. Others start cowering back. Some ran away down the street.

Patti looked at the hooded executioner. "Who is that?"

"Don't know."

"Who they gonna kill?"

"Can't tell."

"What we gonna to do?"

Alan felt uncertain. "Anything can get us killed ...don't do anything,.."

Patti start yelling. "*Boooo! Boooo!* Get that bastard! Take off your hood, coward. Show your ugly face!" Patti yelled. Patti grabbed an empty bottle from the ground. She threw it at the Nazi.

He stepped aside. SCREAMA Subject Population Control soldiers pointed rifles at Patti.

The Nazi on the truck took off his hood. He yelled at Patti. "I am Reinhard Gehlen."

Reinhard Gehlen took a leather bill club from his utility belt. He start beating the man tied to the cross.

Patti, she clenched her fists. She had her father's Irish temper.

Gehlen held up a microphone. The victim spoke, "Show no imagination. Show no sensitivity. Eliminate artists. Rebellion against the Blue Book is bad."

The Sarajevo crowd murmured. They shook their fists at Gehlen.

Gehlen spoke into the microphone. "Today, you will be put in compounds. You are under racial quarantine. For your safety, this neighborhood will be ethnically-cleansed. After, business may continue as usual." Uniformed SCREAMA and Cointelpro counter-intelligence agent provocateurs walked through the crowd. Uniformed SCREAMA piled out of trucks, beating people who caught their attention.

Patti looked down the street. SCREAMA pushed protesters into white vans. Patti lost it. "Protesters are fist-fighting SCREAMA! ...at the cleansing vans! It's Granma Wilpf! She doesn't have a chance! SCREAMA got her! We got to help her!"

Alan was desperate. "We can't start resistance now. It's got to be all over the city!"

Patti pushed him aside. She opened the knapsack. She got out jars and bottles filled with gasoline. "Get out of my way! I'll do it myself! I'm helping Granma Wilpf!"

Over the top of each bottle was a thin plastic

bag, over a rag stuck in the top. Patti grabbed several bottles. She bit her lip. She snatched-up a baggie filled with cigarette lighters. "Are you going to light these?"

Alan tore the match bag open, grabbed a lighter. "Okay. This is the beginning!"

"The end of the new World Order."

Patti smelled the rags, wet with gasoline. She lit a rag. It leapt into flames. The flames singed her eyelashes and bangs. Smelling her burning hair made her queasy. Hair on back of her hands curled stiffly, crumply.

Patti was hysterical. "Am I burning?! Am I burning?!"

Alan felt his heart pound like a drum. "No! Your eyelashes are singed. Some of your hair."

Patti closed her eyes. She cried. Her tears made her eyes feel better. She start yelling, throwing firebombs at SCREAMA. "Viva Zapata! Yey Sandinistas! Viva la revolution!"

From flat windows up and down the street, people start throwing firebombs, shooting lead fishing weights from slingshots at SCREAMA. SCREAMA fired automatic rifles back, flame throwers. The military band stopped playing. SCREAMA put on tear gas masks. They fired teargas into buildings and at demonstrators.

Reinhard Gehlen drew out his pistol. "You must stop! We'll kill you all!"

Gehlen fired at the crowd. People fell. Nazi horse patrols and infantry columns marched the Sarajevo streets. Patti threw gasoline bombs. SCREAMA fired missiles from shoulder bazookas and rocket launchers, at buildings. SCREAMA armored vehicles and tanks came around corners of street intersections. They fired bomb-shells at buildings.

Alan saw tanks aiming at Patti. "Let's get out of here!"

Patti knew what she had to do. "I'm going to get Grandma Wilpf!"

"It's too dangerous!"

Patti cringed. "Forget it!"

<>

Mel's Jesus stood by.

I was at his side. "I can't believe this is happening!"

"It has to."

"Can't we get Patti out of here, back to the ghosts of Christmas present?"

Mel's Jesus and Ronnie were swept away into the sky, back to Ronnie's Santa Barbara ranch.

Ronnie couldn't see her. "Patti's not with us!"

Mel's Jesus nodded. "I know, she can't be."

Nancy looked at Ronnie, wondering if he was okay, how long he would stay in his Alzheimer's catatonia.

Nancy sighed. She never knew if she'd ever see Ronnie, again. Or, if she did, if it would be for more than a few seconds.

Patti looked quickly up and down the street. People were being shot, hog-tied, beaten, dragged into Gestapo cleansing vans. SCREAMA pushed Grandma Wilpf to the ground. They kicked her head and shoulders. She yelled, "No!"

Patti was a hippie peace love-child. But, not when family was being hurt. Now, she was out for blood. Alan tried holding her back, but couldn't. She was too strong. She broke away. She ran towards Granma Wilpf. Tiger watched, his front paws on a step. Then, Tiger jumped to the sidewalk. Tiger ran after her. Patti pushed frantically against bodies of people in the crowd. She struggled to move forward. Nazi teams behind metal body shields swung batons wildly, striking down the crowd.

The crowd scattered. SCREAMA closed-in on Patti. They wore Teflon bullet-proof, hockey masks over their faces. Fire exploded between them. Patti turned around. Alan heaved fire-bombs, driving the SCREAMA back, away from her. Patti ran down the street towards Granma Wilpf. Alan followed, clearing SCREAMA from their path by throwing firebombs. SCREAMA loaded Granma Wilpf in a white Gestapo cleansing van. SCREAMA saw firebombs coming at them. They scattered. They let go of Grandma Wilpf. Granma Wilpf fell to the ground like a doll. Patti was there, helping her stand.

Alan pulled a dead driver from an idling car, the body fell to the ground. "Get in!"

Granma Wilpf pulled Patti's arm. "There, help her."

Patti looked over the sidewalk. A young girl cowered, weeping in a stairwell. SCREAMA ran towards them.

Patti shook her head.

Granma Wilpf yelled. "I can't leave the child!"

Alan yelled. "Get the girl! Let's go!"

Patti pushed Granma Wilpf into the car. Then, ran to the cowering child. The young girl lifted her head. Patti saw a dazed look in her eyes. "C'mon!"

The little girl looked stupid at her, unaware what was happening. Her arms folded over a brown and white Teddy Bear. "My name's Tracie."

Patti scooped her up, ran to the car, jumped in. Tiger meowed from the street. "It's Tiger! C'mon Tiger!"

Patti wanted to slam the car door shut, but

waited. Tiger jumped through the open door onto her lap. Alan floored the car. In a few blocks, they were on the freeway. No one spoke. Tiger purred on Patti's lap. She stroked Tiger's fur, it was warm, soft, familiar. "Tiger's purring." Patti looked in the back seat at the young girl. "She's in a daze."

Alan slowed the car down, blended into traffic.

Patti saw a black and white cloth patch sewed on the sleeve of the girl's coat. It was covered with mud. Patti wiped it off. It was a SCREAMA Youth Unit patch, with a short orange bar across the top. Patti quickly pulled her hand away. She looked at Alan. "Our little friend is wearing a SCREAMA Youth Unit shoulder patch, with the rank of Lieutenant."

Alan lost it. "We've got to get her out of the car!"

"We can't stop yet, we're too close."

Granma Wilpf wouldn't have it. "You're not doing anything to that little girl! We'll love her. She'll figure out what's right. We must love, even though it's illegal. I'll straighten her out."

Alan stopped it. "Not a good idea, Granma Wilpf."

How do you know? Not getting love makes kids bad."

Patti shsrugged at Alan. "What can we do?"

"It's skating on thin ice. Mind control is permanent. You're playing with fire."

"I know."

Granma Wilpf smiled. She stroked the girl's forehead. "Women have to stick together. I'll take good care of Baby." Granma Wilpf's eye bled down her face.

Patti watched the wound bleed. "Are you all right?"

"I can't see out of my eye. My head hurts," Granma Wilpf said. "Not as bad as end of the month migraines."

Patti laughed.

"Thanks for saving me," Granma Wilpf said.

"I love you, Granma. I'd never let you get hurt." Patti looked at Granma Wilpf's eye. "Your eye looks terrible. I'll wipe the blood off with my scarf. The side of your head is swollen."

Granma Wilpf start crying. "They beat me. I fell. Then, they kicked me. They kept kicking me. Is the little girl okay?"

Patti looked at the little girl. "She looks okay. She's spaced out. We'll see, when she wakes up." They drove along. Patti saw how calm other drivers were. "Look! People are acting like nothing happened."

Alan watched other drivers. "They must not know." He found news on the radio.

They listened. "This been a fire on the waterfront. A fire engine is there. No one was hurt. Electrical transformers on telephone poles blew up from the fire. The waterfront is closed. People are being evacuated in SCREAMA Subject Population Control vans ...for their own safety ...until PCBs from exploding transformers is cleaned up. No one is allowed in. The area is quarantined. SCREAMA vans are taking people to temporary shelters. Now, a word from our sponsors," the radio announcer said.

Patti couldn't believe it. "They blacked out the news!" They drove in silence. Patti smiled. "Alan, thanks for helping me rescue Granma Wilpf. I thought you ran out of guts."

"Does this mean we're engaged."

"No."

"Why the hell not?"

"Because I say so!"

"Female logic."

"You have a attitude problem!"

"You're the one with attitude! First, we're in bed. Then, you're screwing me in your dreams. Then, you're asleep in my arms. Then, you act like nothing happened!" .

Granma Wilpf interrupted. "Children, please stop fighting. We've had enough, for one day."

Patti looked at Granma Wilpf. "Okay. What were you doing, there?"

Granma Wilpf smiled. "Handing out food to refugees. It was bad luck, Gestapo showed up."

Patti laughed. "Alan, where are we going? Back to the boat?"

Alan shrugged. "To the airport."

Patti looked disgusted. "You're pathetic, you run away. We'll stay and help. Just when I'm on a high and feeling better, you bring me down. I can't give you more of me. I don't want to. I'm petting Tiger. He's a better friend than you."

Alan felt put down. "You hurt my feelings."

"Hurt? I can't talk to you! You put yourself in this position of being sensitive. I'm afraid ...whatever I say you're, you'll snap. You're selfish thinking about your feelings and not mine.".

Granma Wilpf interrupted. "He helped you save me."

Patti sighed dramatically. "Oh, both of you, leave me alone with my Tiger."

"Tiger goes where he finds the best meal," Alan said.

Patti petted Tiger, her eyes flared. "Men are no better. You chase meal tickets ...a pair of legs ...big tits ...a pretty face. Then, when you get it ...you want smarts, too."

Alan knew she was right. "If Tiger was big as a

Tiger, or if you were small as a mouse ...what would happen to you when Tiger caught you?"

Patti cut him off. "Don't even go there. He isn't. And, I'm not. I can't trust you intimately ...because I can't trust me. When I make love, as soon as he penetrates me, it changes me. I despise him. I hurt my lovers. I never hurt you. Because, I never let you shove it in me. Men shove it in and out. It's nothing. Can't you understand?"

Alan drove into a park. He stopped the car by a church in the forest. They went inside. Sat down by a life-size statue of Christ, crucified.

Patti shivered. "It's icky. Like a morgue. Can we go outside, in the trees?" Patti thought something was different. "You're relaxed, aren't you?"

"Klonopin. I just said, yes to Klonopin."

"Great."

"Want one?"

"No. You never told me you took psych meds. You drive me nuts, sometimes, wasting energy, worrying. Grab life, enjoy it."

"Sometimes I get anxious, scared."

Patti softened. "It's not you. It's the times. People are just not any good, anymore. I'm manic-depressive, histrionic. Sometimes ...sad, suicidal. Other times, want to party."

"Hysterical. Sad. Happy. All at once?"

Patti shrugged her shoulders. "It depends. Some times. Some times, not. It makes me an artist."

"What do you take?"

"Prozac and lithium. They never seem to know what works."

Alan was amused. "We're a walking drugstore ...too."

Patti looked in his eyes. "Have you ever been in mental hospital?" .

He didn't answer.

She went on. "I have. For trying to kill myself."

"When?" A

"Five or six years ago. It was over a man. Still want me, now?"

Alan caught himself, hesitating. "Sure. Keep walkin' that walk, and talkin' that talk, doin' what you're doin', do your thing."

Patti was agitated. "I've got melanoma too."

Alan was shocked. "Cancer?"

"The worst kind. It's terminal."

Alan's spirits fell. "You're kidding."

Patti pulled her pants down. "See? ...this scar on my thigh? It's ugly. I'm embarrassed to show it."

Alan looked at her hips and thighs, sighing. "I was wondering about that on the yawl, the other night."

She pointed to scars on her inner thighs. "That's where they cut out a lymph node. This big sandpaper place, on the outside of my hip, is where they took a skin graft for my foot." Patti kicked her pants off, then her socks, pointing to a rough, red patch on her left foot. "It's really ugly."

She sat on the trunk of a fallen tree. Alan picked up her foot, examined the skin-graft. Patti felt embarrassed. She felt ugly.

Alan sighed deeply. "I saw it the other night."

"Isn't it ugly?"

He kissed it.

She smiled awkwardly. "I don't know how to react to that."

"Can you fight it?"

"No. Not with Western medicine. They feed you poison and radiation to rot you. Then, they cut out chunks of rotting flesh. I paid alternative medicine programs, got summaries of alternative treatments. At stage three, it's hard. Stage four, I'm dead."

"What stage are you in?"

Patti put her clothes back on. "Third stage. One alternative method keep the lymph nodes clean, so the doctors don't cut them out, is lots of carrot juice, stewed vegetables, enemas four times a day. Still want to pair up with me?"

"If I did, I'd be crazy."

Patti was shocked. "You are crazy."

"You got that, right."

"Even if you weren't, you worry too much for me. It's a drag on me. I'm an actress, for God's sake. I'm extroverted. You act like you're on house arrest."

Alan looked over his shoulder. "I'm afraid we were followed. Can't stay here."

Patti shrugged. "You never stop worrying."

"Shhh."

"Right-wing and left-wing groups are joining forces with us, to fight fascists."

"And fight neo-cons," Granma Wilpf said.

With both hands, Tracie held her teddy bear. Tracie pointed a Teddy Bear paw at Patti. "I'll tell Gestapo on you."

Alan winced.

Granma Wilpf kneeled by Tracie. "That's all right, Honey. You don't have to. Gestapo is a bully."

Tracie looked puzzled.

"Are we safe, with her?"

Patti wondered. "I don't know, Alan."

Alan didn't like it. "She's a junior SCREAMA, for God's sake! It's too dangerous."

Patti tried to calm him down. She turned her back on the little girl. "She's been brainwashed by the Public School Ministry. But, she's only a child ...the thoughts aren't stuck in her permanently."

Granma Wilpf felt energized. "Let's get this revolution going! ...sock it to 'em!"

Patti nodded to Granma Wilpf, to take Tracie to play. "I saw a playground by park headquarters."

Granma Wilpf smiled. "Want to, Honey?"

Tracie nodded. "Yes."

Granma Wilpf and Tracie walked off.

"How many activists you figure all together?" Alan put his arm around Patti's shoulder.

"Maybe, 600,000 ...everyone in Sarajevo. Thirty, forty million on the Internet. This is the first, democratic revolution. Everyone gets a gun. Because, we're Messianics. We get back to nature."

"Messianics? Me? I only pray when I'm scared."

Patti watched him. He was staring at the chapel. Patti sighed. "In there, it was sterile. How can people celebrate joy in there ...when they can be outside? Institutionalized religion sucks. It's a disinformation tactic of the corporation state and Gestapo. God wants love, not worship. People masturbate going to church, dress up in Sunday clothes, act civilized, take refuge in each other, hide from God in conformity, disappear their humanity. When Gestapo kills your child, your husband, your wife, your family, Jesus would cut their nuts off. People insult God, with misdirected prayer He won't hear. God wants mankind to get rid of the bad guys, not turn the other cheek. That's bullshit."

<> <> <>

Jekyll Island, 1910
& Christmas Massacre, 1913

Mel's Jesus start showing up, everywhere I'd go. We were the hottest property around. The studios were in a bidding war for us. We were unstoppable. Kept gettin' it in the can. I don't remember rehearsing. But, each scene went smoothly. Usually, we'd get it on the first take.

Mel's Jesus looked at me, questioning. "Ronnie,

President and Nancy Reagan talking to Mother Teresa in the Oval Office. 6/20/85

before you die ...is there *anything* you want?"

"Yes. When I was president, who was pulling my strings?"

Mels Jesus looked like he found that amusing. "You were."

"Give me a break."

In an instant, whirlwinds swept us up into the sky. Then, we sitting in a movie theater, ready to watch a film. Mel's Jesus was great. I loved watching my old movies. I was young, all over again ...handsome. It was proof, I had a life. But, it was so far away ...like it wasn't mine, anymore ...except in movies. Celluloid memories ...but, with Alzheimer's, memories died. Soon, I'd have none left.

In the movie house in the sky, with Mel's Jesus, we were *in* the film we were watching! *We* were the stars! There, up on the screen. I was trading wampum for furs, shiny metal shapes for grain, whale's teeth for fish ... shells, ivory, feathers, cows, pigs, chickens ...whatever accepted currency was.

Mel dollied the camera back. Harrison Ford swung on a vine. Al Pacino led us in a temple, back in ancient times. Mel's Jesus start turning over counting tables, spilling gold shekels on the floor. I tried it. I strained at the tables. I got splinters in my hands ...the damn things were heavy.

Mel's Jesus pulled a whip from his belt. He start whipping money changers. So, I tried it, too. I took his whip. People thought we were nuts. Mel's Jesus stood there, gold coins in his hands like Jessie James. Mel called, 'cut'. Bruce Willis put thumbs up. Harrison ran over for high fives.

Mel's Jesus wept. I saw Time in His eyes. He blew his nose. "In the Jewish year, 3,892 B.C., 30 years after I was born in human flesh, I whipped the money changers in the temple. Did my ministry fail?"

"Yeah. But, Jesus, you're working in this film, with me."

Bruce Willis ran up. "Good job."

"Bruce, wait," I said. "Jesus, are you done?"

Mel's Jesus was absorbed in the film, reaching out from the screen, touching the light from the projector, "Pay attention to the film. Don't forget, we're here watching us."

On screen, I looked great. Bruce Willis had a double take. "Jesus, that's right."

Mel's Jesus looked at me, "Remember, when you asked me to give you a break? ...Here it is."

"But, that was just in the movies," I said. "I meant, in real life."

Mel's Jesus carried us ahead 850 years, through the Middle Ages, into Great Britain. Prisoners scratched tally marks on walls of their cells, one day at a time, through Time. Storekeepers cut notches on sticks, tracking customers' debts, carving financial records in 'v'-shaped grooves on flat sticks ...rounded grooves for shillings ...slices for pence. They split the tally stick in half, giving half to buyer, half to seller.

The tally, notched in wood, cut to the thickness of a palm ...was a thousand pounds. Breadth of a thumb ...a hundred pounds ...a little finger's width, twenty pounds ...a single pound the width of swollen barleycorn ...a shilling.

Central banks in Europe began ... Bank of Amsterdam financed Oliver Cromwell taking power in England in 1649. Bank of Sweden began issuing notes, in 1661. After Cromwell died, in 1657 Charles II was crowned in 1660, restoring the previous Crown, then Charles died in 1685. So, in 1689, the same group of bankers regained power in England, putting King William of Orange on the throne.

William repaid these private bankers ...he ordered the British Treasury to borrow 1,250,000 pounds from them.

Then, he issued them a Royal Charter for the Bank of England ... permitting them to consolidate the National Debt ... which, ironically had just been created for the first time, by the loan the bankers had made to the British Treasury.

Then, the Royal Treasury had to made interest payments on the loan, and principle payments ... so they had to tax the British people. And, private goldsmiths were forbidden to store gold, or to issue receipts in its trade. By law, all gold had to be stored in the Bank of England. So, Goldsmiths had lost the ability to trade in, and issue receipts, their circulating tender, to the people.

And, that exclusive right, was by the crown given, as a money monopoly ... to private stockholders of the Bank of England.

<>

I told Nancy what I'd read, "The same thing happened in the U.S., when Fed block-shareholders flexed their muscles in 1934 ...having President Roosevelt order private citizens could not store, or hold, gold ...like Bank of England did, 250 years before."

Nancy smiled. "That's interesting, Darling. Have you had breakfast?"

<>

Whirlwinds blew through the movie studio. The movie set changed. It was Frankfurt Germany, 1760. I played Amshall Moses Bower, a goldsmith and a coin dealer. We lived in the Jewish ghetto, in Frankfurt. I hung the red crest of Frankfurt outside my shop. 'Red shield', in German, is pronounced, 'Rothschild'.

I taught my five sons the money trade. They founded banks across Europe. Amschel Mayer Rothschild, founded the Frankfurt Germany branch. Salomon Mayer Rothschild, founded the Vienna Austria branch. Nathan Mayer Rothschild, founded the London England branch. Carl Mayer Rothschild, founded the Naples Italy branch. James Mayer Rothschild, founded the Paris France branch.

During the Napoleon Wars, House of Rothschild grew powerful. Venture capitalists, we founded companies, speculating in the stock market. We made great profits from the war. Our war profits financed stock speculation. Under Metternich, Austria agreed to accept Rothschild financial direction. [Richard Lewinsohn, *Profits of War.*]

All of my five sons were given the title, 'Baron' by Emperor Francis I, of Austria. My sons were creditors of many European governments. Our family was Europe's chief financial power. Our French branch financed railroads and mines for France ...France became an industrial power. Our English branch financed the British government acquiring the Suez Canal.

The Nazis forced us to give up our Vienna branch, in 1938. We remain international investment bankers in London and Paris. In 2003, our British and French branches merged into one holding company.

Nathan went from Germany to England in 1797. He was naturalized in 1804. He opened a business house in London in 1805. He acting as agent to the British government, financing the enemies of Napoleon I. He had a good economic intelligence service. He found out about the allied victory at Waterloo, by carrier pigeon ...before anyone else. In one day, he bought up many companies in the crashing London stock, because scared investors were dumped their stock. He made a fortune.

<>

After my dual-role acting success playing Amshall and Nathan, I got control of the Bank of England ...I monopolized shares. I kept playing my double-Rothschild role, as father and son, saving the studio a salary. As Nathan, I became Austrian consul general in England ...it was just like being President, when I made Helena Van Damm, my secretary in Sacramento, then in Washington, my U.S. Ambassador to Austria in 1983. But, in this role, playing Nathan, I made loans to France, Russia, countries in South America. I required repayment of loans to be in sterling silver. That way, I overcame exchange-rate fluctuations.

After Nathan's death the house of Rothschild was dominated by Nathan's son, Baron Lionel Nathan de Rothschild. Lionel established a family monopoly ...for floating large international loans. He set up the Irish famine loan (1847), and Crimean War loan (1856). He was elected to House of Commons in 1847. However, he would not assume his seat ... until eleven years later. Then, he was finally allowed to take the parliamentary oath on a Jewish Bible, not a Christian one. He swore allegiance to God the Father, not God the Son. We obeyed the Old Testament, not the New. Even though, the New is a hack-job on the old. The new is cheaper for the studio ...the casting department casts Father, Son and Holy Ghost, as a triple-acting role, played by one actor ...the Christian way.

<>

Because of my success in financial manipulation, venture capital, company formation, company take-overs, and stock speculation ...I now had a triple-acting role, too. Now, I played Baron Nathan Mayer de Rothschild, too. Our family was the biggest financial power in London. We threw great parties.

I had some great lines, "I care not what puppet is placed upon the throne of England, to rule the Empire on which the sun never sets. The man that controls Britain's money supply, controls the British Empire. And, I control the British money supply."

It was a good role.

That was like one my best line in the movie, *Kings' Row*. I'm playing Drake McHugh. Okay, I'm in a little car accident, and bump my head. So, in the hospital, my legs are cut off by my girl-

President Reagan presents Mother Teresa with the Medal of Freedom at a White House Ceremony. 6/20/85

friend's father, because he doesn't like me.

I wake up after the operation, where I play opposite Ann Sheridan, Robert Cummings and Claude Rains. "Where's the rest of me?!" *King's Row* was my best film.

<>

In 1987, Gorbachev said, he *liked* me when I played that part. He and Raisa liked to watch Hollywood films, in their estate over in Russia. *Kings' Row* was nominated for three Academy Awards ...including Best Picture of 1943.

But, we didn't get them. So, there was no Oscar for me. Close, but no cigar. It was one of my best acting gigs, too.

I called my first autobiography, *Where's the Rest of Me?*

It was slim. The ghostwriting was worse than on this fictional autobiography. But, towards the end of my life, I insisted a new and improved fictional autobiography be done. I wanted to set the record straight. I wanted to answer the question once and for all, *'Could I cut it, or not?*

I needed to prove I was master of my own ship ...as much as anyone in politics can be. *That's* Hollywood, see?

<>

So, my brother James in Paris dominates French finance. James Rothschild's wealth was 600 million dollars. One man in France was richer. The King had 800 million dollars. All the wealth of all the bankers in France was 150 million dollars less James Rothschild's. This gave him power to unseat governments, when he felt like it. Like when he overthrew the Cabinet of Prime Minister Thiers.

<>

Over in Germany, the Germans under Bismarck, were financed by Samuel Bleichroder. Bleichroder was the Court Banker of the Prussian Emperor. Sam was an undercover Rothschild family bank agent, since 1828.

Philip Mountbatten was related, through the Cassels, to the Meyer Rothschilds of Frankfurt ...so, the English royal House of Windsor has a direct family relationship to the Rothschilds. In 1901, when Queen Victoria's son, Edward, became King Edward VII, he re-established the Rothschild ties.

Paul Emden's, *Behind The Throne*, helped me with my character studies and getting the plot down.

"Edward's preparation for his metier was different than his mother's ...he 'ruled', less. He kept men around him, who were with him in the age of building the Baghda Railway ...he added to his advisory staff, Leopold and Alfred Rothschild."

60

<>

We have so many international marriages, our alliances aren't to one country or another, but to *family*. That's the 'family values' you hear about, at campaign time. So, that gives our family, global business connections. We know what's going on behind the scenes in finance and politics, better than the other economic intelligence services, because they're blood ties. Alfred de Rothschild reached through Central Europe, decades before World War I ...he's a good character to play, got a lot of attention.

Frederick Morton's, *Rothschilds*, helps flesh out my family character.

"For 150 years, the history of the House of Rothschild was the backstage history of Western Europe ...Because of their success in making loans not to individuals, but to nations, they reaped huge profits. The wealth of Rothschild consists of the bankruptcy of nations."

E.C. Knuth's, *Empire of the City* described us well. The fact that House of Rothschild made its money in the great crashes of history ...and the great wars of history ... the very periods when others lost their money, is beyond question."

<>

So, now the scene is set in Frankfurt.

Meanwhile Britain, at the height of it's power, borrows money from the Bank of England ...for four wars. So, England is in debt 140 million pounds. To help pay the interest on the loan, Britain raises taxes on American colonists.

You getting the picture?

<>

Red Skelton plays Benjamin Franklin. We tried to get Dean Martin, but he was sleeping it off. Al Pacino's cast again! ...plays a major shareholder of the Bank of England, like in *Devil's Advocate*.

Cast (in order of appearance)
Red Skelton	... Benjamin Franklin
Al Pacino	... Bank of England shareholder
Ronald Reagan	...Ronnie Reagan
	... Amshall Moses
	... dual Rothschild roles
	....Nathan Mayer
	....misc. Rothschilds
	....3-4 Warburg bros.
Mel's Jesus	... Mel's Jesus
Robert DeNiro	... Robert Morris, arms dealer
Danny Glover	... U.S. patriot
Arnold Schwarzenegger	... Alexander Hamilton
Jay Leno	... Thomas Jefferson
Jackie Chan	... Nathan Rothschild
Jim Carrey	... James Monroe
Danny DeVito	... Napoleon Bonaparte
Chevy Chase	... Nathan Rothschild
(double for Jackie Chan & Ronald Reagan)	
Steven Siegal	... Duke of Wellington
Harrison Ford	... misc. extras
Bruce Willis	... misc. extras
John Belushi	... Ron Rothworth, spy
Wesley Snipes	... Steven Seigal's messenger
Woody Allen	... friend of Chevy Chase, No. 1
Steve Martin	... friend of Chevy Chase, No. 2
Lyndon LaRouche	...John Jacob Astor
Perry Mason	... James Madison
Raymond Burr	... Perry Mason
Charles Bronson	...Andrew Jackson
Whoopi Goldberg	..Abraham Lincoln
Richard Gere	... Otto van Bismarck
Charlie Chaplin	...Alexander II, Tsar of Russia

Lights up.
Camera.
Action.

Bank of England boardroom.

Al Pacino
How do you account for the new-found prosperity in the American colonies?

Red Skelton
Easy. In the colonies, we print our own money. We call it, Colonial Script. It helps consumers buy goods. We don't charge interest, so we have no inflation. And, charging no interest helps the exchange of goods ...goods stay cheap because private shareholders don't get rich off interest on product loans. Script is just paper. There's no gold or silver backing it up, just American spirit. We create the paper, we control it...we don't have to pay interest to Bank of England, any more.

Pacino gets upset ...he never could hide his anger, got him an Oscar. Although, DeNiro could have played in character, but didn't get the part.

Al Pacino
You think you can screw me?! I'll fix you so you can't print your own money ...you'll pay taxes to me with gold and silver!

Pacino tells other central bank directors in Great Britain about the Colonial Script, they tell British Parliament to outlaw the currency ...that way they can force Americans back into debt ...force them to borrow more money, issued by Bank of England. So, British parliament passes the Currency Act of 1764. This, pisses America off.

Red Skelton
(voiceover while writing in his diary)
In one year, the conditions in the American colonies got so reversed, that the era of prosperity ended ...a depression set in. This filled the streets of the Colonies with unemployed people. We would have paid the tax on tea ...if England hadn't taken away our Script ...forcing us to

become debtors to Britain, creating unemployment and unhappiness. The poverty caused by the British bankers on the British Parliament, caused in the Colonies hatred of England ...and produced the Revolutionary War.

So, we began planning the Revolutionary war in order to issue our own money again ...and keep King George III and Bank of England from enslaving us with debt, and making Americans their financial slaves. By the time the revolutionary war started, Apr. 19 1775, British taxation had sucked the gold and silver out of the American colonies, to Britain. So, we had to print money to finance the war."

<>

So, that was where the cliché, 'taxation without representation', came from ...paying taxes to pay the interest on Bank of England money lent to us, and getting no services or goods in return.

It's the end of a long day, shooting. I don't know where the cast is eating, or where Mel's Jesus is taking me, next. Okay? I'm wondering, Where's Nancy? ...has Patti taken off for Europe yet. And, what's for dinner?

Red Skelton
(interrupts)
Do you want me to check where Nancy is?

Ronnie Reagan
That's nice of you, to ask.
Smiles, shakes head no.

Mel's Jesus
We can eat on the road. I'll give you a treatment. You know, in 1775, American colonists declare independence from Great Britain ...then, fight the American Revolution. But, financial independence, did Americans ever win that?

Alexander Hamilton, sixteen years later ...played by Arnold Schwarzenegger, a couple paragraphs down in Ronnie's fictional autobiography, Arnold works with European bankers.

Arnold forms a central bank, called 'First Bank of the United States'. It has the same power as Bank of England. Then, the Brits keep at it for another 100 years ... trying to push what will one day be called, 'the Fed', down our throats.

But, Americans never get it, what's behind the scenes ...what's up? And, when they do they stand up, they're staring Satan in the eyes."

Ronnie Reagan
(bewildered)
Christ, it's not easy to deal with Satan, specially when I was President. Literary history, for hundreds of years, highlights making deals with the

Devil, selling your soul for cash and a lay. But, we got to finish the day's shooting."

I looked at the director's script.

It's 1781 ...arms dealer Robert Morris is played by Robert DeNiro.

Robert DeNiro
I'll put up 400,000 dollars to set up a Bank of England-style central bank in the USA ...based on fractional reserve banking ...*that's* lending out ten times more than you have, or take in, each day. Now, Congress knows, fractional reserve banking throws plenty of money around. I'll use gold loaned to America from France to start my bank.

So, he starts Bank of North America ...DeNiro starts the fractional reserving racket, loans fractional reserve money to himself. And, his friends ...and DeNiro and his friends buy all the bank shares.

Congress starts throwing fractional reserve money around for four years, til American money is worth less and less and less ...so, the bank charter isn't renewed. DeNiro's character makes off with all the interest the bank made.

Danny Glover plays a U.S. patriot.

Danny Glover
Central banks, seen one and you've seen them all ... they make money for their stockholders ...and, make financial slaves out of the rest of us.

So, Great Britain tries to search and destroy the script, not the movie script, the money script ...to control it. Congress sees the danger of fiat ... paper ... money, created by law in 1775, when paper money is issued by States to finance the war. So, independent State legislatures pass laws making citizens to accept it, as legal tender.

In 1787, writers of the American Constitution make note, give *only* Congress the power to 'coin money, and regulate the value thereof.' The U.S. Constitution spells it out.

U.S. Constitution
No State shall enter into any treaty, alliance or confederation, grant letters of marque and reprisal, coin money, emit bills of credit, make any thing by gold and silver coin a tender in payment of debts, pass any bill of attainder, ex post facto law, or law impairing the obligation of contracts, or grant any title of nobility."

<>

Everyone got that?

Alexander Hamilton, played by Arnold Schwarzenegger, immigrates to the American colonies in 1772 from the British West Indies colony. He marries the daughter of an influential New York family. Is appointed Secretary of the

62

Treasury, in 1789. Lobbies Congress, *not* to take its Constitutional power, literally ...but, delegate it ...enabling the Bank of North America to be established, in 1781, similar to Bank of England. By the way, at this point in American history, America has a foreign debt of $12,000 ...borrowed from Spain, France, Holland ...and, private interests in Germany, and, a domestic debt of $42,000.

So, 216 years ago, in 1790, 'the Governator' asks Congress to charter a privately owned company. This privately owned company will have a monopoly to issue currency. The intent of the monopoly is to manage the country's financial situation. It will create a 'central bank system'. The main office will be in Philadelphia ...small branches will be located in important cities. The Central Bank will deposit government funds and collected taxes, and issue bank notes to increase money supplies, to finance the country's growth. It will be called, 'Bank of the United States' ... featuring a capital stock plan of 10 million dollars ...4/5's privately owned ...1/5 by the U.S. Government, governed by a president, 25 board directors ...20 elected by the stockholders ...five appointed by the government.

Arnold Schwarzenegger lobbies hard.

Arnold Schwarzenegger

All communities divide themselves into the few, and the many. The first are rich and well-born, the other, the mass of people. People are turbulent and changing; they seldom judge or determine right.

But, in 1791, forthcoming U.S. President Jay Leno in his first movie role, playing Thomas Jefferson, disagrees.

Jay Leno

To preserve independence, we mustn't let rulers load us down with perpetual debt. If we get such debts, we'll be taxed in meat and drink, in necessities and in our comforts, in labor and in amusements. If we can prevent the government from wasting the labor of the people ... under the pretense of caring for them ... we will be happy.

So, to-be-President Jay Leno, and later-to-be-president James Madison played by Raymond Burr (Perry Mason), oppose the Bill. But, President George Washington played by Harpo Marx, signs it into law Feb. 25, 1791.

Clint Eastwood and Aaron Burr (no relationship to Raymond) set up Manhattan Company Bank in New York City. It thrives ...is later controlled by Warburg-Kuhn-Loeb Bank interests. Which, by the way a couple hundred years later, merge with Rockefeller's, Chase Bank ...becoming Chase Manhattan Bank in 1955 ...Dwight Eisenhower is President, playing himself (as I later do).

The U.S., and Soviet Russia, have hydrogen bombs, threatening, great destructive force extorts the world. Eisenhower meets with leaders of the British, French, and Russian governments in Geneva, in July 1955. He proposes the U.S. and Russia exchange blueprints of each other's military establishments ...and "provide within our countries, facilities for aerial photography to the other country". Nixon is Vice President ...Nikolai Bulganin becomes Soviet Premier ...Churchill resigns ...Federal Republic of West Germany becomes a sovereign state ...Soviet Union, and seven East European countries sign the Warsaw mutual defense pact ...Argentina ousts Juan Peron ...U.S. sends $21,600,000 dollars in aid to Vietnam. I'm hosting General Electric Theater on TV, then traveling around the country delivering speeches for the Dulles 'Crusade for Freedom' for Bechtel, and Martin Anderson of Hoover Institute ...who groom me to run for governor of California ...it eventually leads to my successful presidential bid, winning the nomination away from George Bush ...who, repeatedly swears, he will not be my vice president.

(I follow presidential history.)

So, First Bank of United States ... BUS ... holds a 20 year charter. In five years, the American government borrows 8 million dollars from the bank ...prices of goods in America immediately rise 72%.

Jay Leno is stressing, ghetto.

Jay Leno
(now president)

"I wish we could write an amendment to the Constitution, so the federal government has no power to borrow."

Newspapers call BUS a swindle, since it's a private, not a government, bank. And, its shareholders float fractional reserve 10x1 imaginary money ... successfully charging interest on 9/10s of the money that is totally Monopoly money, it's a game ...and make a fortune.

Eustace Mullins
(*Secrets of the Federal Reserve*)

The great American ruling family fortunes made a killing in Rhode Island, when Newport was the capital of the slave trade. Previously, for centuries, the slave trade was centered in Venice Italy ...until Britain in the 17th Century used sea power to monopolize the trade. William Ellery, Collector of the Port of Newport in 1791, convinced me. "An Ethiopian can as soon change his skin as a Newport merchant can be induced to change so lucrative a trade ...for the slow profits of any manufactory."

John Quincy Adams
(voiceover as he writes in diary)
In 1829, Newport's prosperity is chiefly owing to its extensive employment in African slave trading."

J.P. Morgan & Brown
J. P. Morgan and the Brown financial empires date to Baltimore, the 19th Century center of the American slave trade. Both firms were founded in Baltimore, then opened branches in London ...under the guidance of Rothschilds, returning to New York, to open additional branches to dominate banking, finance and politics.

Robert Lovett
For example, of late, positions like Secretary of Defense were held by Robert Lovett, partner of Brown Brothers Harriman ...and Thomas S. Gates, partner of Drexel & Co., a J. P. Morgan subsidiary.

While I was President, my Vice President, and later President himself, George H.W. Bush's father, Prescott Bush was a partner of Brown Brothers Harriman ...a senator from Connecticut ...and director and financial organizer of Columbia Broadcasting System.

George Peabody & Co.
J. P. Morgan Co. began as George Peabody & Co. Peabody (1795-1869), born at South Danvers, Massachusetts, began business in Georgetown, D.C. in 1814 ...as Peabody, Riggs & Co., dealing in wholesale dry goods, and operated the Georgetown Slave Market.

<>

In 1815, to be closer to their supply source , they moved to Baltimore. There, operating as Peabody and Riggs, from 1815-1835. Peabody found himself, increasingly involved with business originating from London ...and, in 1835, established George Peabody & Co., in London. He had good entree in London business, through another Baltimore firm established in Liverpool, Brown Brothers.

Brown Brothers, Harriman
Alexander Brown came to Baltimore in 1801 ...and established what is now known as, the oldest banking house in the United States ...still operating as Brown Brothers Harriman of New York ... Brown, Shipley & Co. of England ... and Alex Brown and Son of Baltimore. Behind-the-scenes power, wielded by this firm, is indicated by the fact that Sir Montagu Norman, Governor of the Bank of England for many years, was a partner of Brown, Shipley & Co.

Current Biography in 1940 commented, "There was informal understanding that a director of Brown, Shipley should be on the Board of the Bank of England, and Norman Montagu was elected to it, in 1907."

<>

So, as President (1801-09), Jay Leno says, the Bank of the United States is unconstitutional.

Jay Leno
Bank of United States is unconstitutional.

So, when the 20 year charter comes up for renewal in 1811, it's denied.
My brother, Nathan Rothschild, played by Jackie Chan ...remember I'm playing Amshall Moses Bower plus dual Rothschild roles ... but there are five brothers, divide by two ...so we need Jackie Chan in the cast ...Jackie Chan is head of the family bank, in England. Jackie sees America's potential, makes loans to a few states, becomes official European banker for the U.S. Government. Jackie, having his own central bank in England, supports the central bank of the United States ...he's angry enough to ethnically cleanse Jay Leno.

Jackie Chan
Jay Leno, either my application for renewal of Charter is granted, or United States will find itself in a war. I will send British troops to teach you lesson, put you back in colonial status.

So, Jackie Chan brings on the War of 1812
It is his war against Jay Leno. And, our second war with England ...which, ironically, leads to re-chartering the Bank of the United States ...*(what a surprise!)*

Anyway, the war raises our national debt from 45 million dollars to 127 million dollars.
Jay Leno tells Jim Carrey, who's playing to-be-President James Monroe, the score.

Jay Leno
The dominion the banks have over the minds of our citizens must be broken, or, it will break us.

It's 1816, Jay Leno, still playing Thomas Jefferson, sings a sad refrain to to-be-president John Tyler.

(cont)
If Americans ever allow private banks to control the issuance of their currency ...first by inflation ...and then by deflation ... the banks and the corporations that will grow up around the banks, will deprive the American people of all property ...until their children wake up homeless on the continent their father's conquered. "I believe banking insti-

tutions are more dangerous to our liberties, than standing armies. The issuing power should be taken from the banks, and restored to the Government, to whom it properly belongs.

<>

It's the War of 1812, folks.

Britain attacks America.

Over in France, I'm now playing another one of Rothschild's sons, and have my own Rothschild-controlled central bank gig, the Bank of France, parlez vous? But, Napoleon Bonaparte, played by Danny DeVito, is giving me a hard time.

Danny looks up at me.

Danny DeVito

"When a government is dependent upon bankers for money, it is the bankers, not the leaders of the government, that control the situation ...since the hand that gives, is above the hand that takes.

"Money has no motherland, financiers are without patriotism, and without decency. Their sole object, is gain.

For better or worse, depending which side of the banker's desk you're sitting at, the central banks loan money to both sides fighting a war up to the end of the war, right up DeNiro's alley.

Robert DeNiro

"He right about that."

So, in 1803, Danny DeVito (playing Napoleon Bonaparte), instead of borrowing money from Nathan Rothschild's Bank of France ...sells the territory west of the Mississippi, to Jay Leno (playing Thomas Jefferson), in the Louisiana Purchase, a different film.

Danny DeVito runs around conquering Europe. But, everywhere he goes, he finds me and my brothers, me playing Rothschilds in dual roles, financing his enemies, Prussia, Austria and Russia ...who go into debt to me, to fight him.

Four years pass, brother Nathan played by Chevy Chase, smuggles gold through France to finance Duke of Wellington played by Steven Siegal attacking from Spain, forcing DeVito into exile, but DeVito makes a comeback, returns to Paris, borrows money from Eubard Banking House of Paris. DeVito takes 74,000 troops, to go fight 67,000 British troops and thousands of other European troops. But, no one knows who's gonna win the war. Danny DeVito or Steven Siegal, Steven Siegal or Danny DeVito ...so, what does Chevy Chase do?

Mel's Jesus is taking a catnap. Harrison Ford and Bruce Willis are falling asleep. It's costing a fortune. But, I had Chevy Chase's attention, and Danny DeVito's. Steven Siegal is disco dancing, by himself, in slow motion, rehearsing double-framing karate moves and his lisp. Red Skelton is off to a rehearsal for his show. Jay Leno's listening carefully ...but, pretending not to pay attention.

"Okay, so Chevy's playing Nathan, okay ... just tell us, already ...

Jay Leno

What's Chevy doin'?

It's not that easy. Being sneaky, Chevy's scheming, how to take over the Bank of England from Al Pacino (playing a major shareholder of the Bank of England), and the British stock and bond markets. But, can he pull it off? ...specially since he thought of it at the bar, after a few Mud Slides.

Chevy sends agent Ron Rothworth played by John Belushi to watch the battlefield to see if Danny DeVito or Steven Segal wins the battle at Waterloo ...then hurries back to England with news. John Belushi gets there 24 hours sooner than Steven Seigal's messenger played by Wesley Snipes and corners Chevy Chase. Here's the thing, if Danny DeVito wins the war, then, Britain's financial system will be in ruins. So, Chevy goes to the stock exchange, as usual, leans on his post ...begins selling *all* his British Government Bonds ...that's a *sign*. Chevy's known as an expert investor ...everyone figures it out, *Danny DeVito* won the war. There's a stock market panic. Everyone unloads British Bonds ...bond prices fall through the floor, cheap, worthless. So, Chevy's friends, Woody Allen and Steve Martin secretly buy up the devalued bonds at pennies on the dollar.

But, Danny DeVito *lost* to Steven Siegal, Wesley Snipes arrives in London, agitating for a bigger part in the movie. He tells everyone, Steven Siegal won the war ...the market collapse is over ... Chevy Chase owns all the British Government bonds. And, since England defeated France, the British Bonds regain their value ...prior to the market panic of that afternoon. Chevy Chase captures more wealth in one afternoon, than the combined forces of Danny DeVito and Steven Siegal had in their entire life. Chevy's the man.

Meanwhile, my brother Nathan Rothschild, who owns most shares in his Bank of France, secretly backs Bank of North America ...till he makes too much profit ...that means, it's too much debt for the American colonies to handle ... so the charter of bank of North America isn't renewed. But, guess who later secretly bankrolls the Second Bank of the United States? ... another, privately owned central bank ...again making too much money ...again, resulting in the American currency's deflation ... then, America didn't renew that bank's charter, either ...see, the privately owned central banks scored big money twice on America, but twice lost its stranglehold ... the Rothschilds ... that's who. The Rothschild family banking dynasty held controlling stock of central Bank of England, then tried in America, by owning controlling stock in First Bank of the United States in 1781 but lost. So, they do it all over again, with the Second Bank of the United States.

It's 1812, National City Bank begins business as City Bank, in the same room the defunct, Bank of the United States, whose charter had expired, was doing business ...representing the same stockholders ...now, functioning under a legitimate American charter.

<>

Moses Taylor

In the 18th Century, Moses Taylor (1806-1882) is an undercover financial agent for John Jacob Astor, buys Astor farms, and real estate in Manhattan. Astor's fortune didn't come from fur trading, LaRouche's *Executive Intelligence Review EIR* says otherwise.

Lyndon LaRouche

In exchange for providing intelligence to the British ... during the years before and after the Revolutionary War ...and for inciting Indians to attack and kill American settlers along the frontier, Astor was given a percentage of the British opium trade with China, providing the Astor fortune.

It's 1816, Rothschilds secretly finance another privately-owned central bank, the re-chartered, or Second Bank of the United States, again plunging America into debt using fractional reserve banking, the very usury the Old Testament and Mel's Jesus called unfair profit, usury God reviles and calls, Satanic behavior. Me and Mel's Jesus whipped money-changers at the beginning of this chapter, remember?

May 10, 1816, Perry Mason (playing President James Madison) signs the Bill, which *re-charters* the Bank of the United States, making it the Second Bank of the United States ... he says, because of inflation, heavy debt, and the need for an entity to collect taxes, chartering it for another twenty years, raising its capital stock to 35 million dollars authorizing bank branches, issuing of notes, having the power "to control the entire fiscal structure of the country". The bank was run by ... John Jacob Astor

... Stephen Girard, and David Parish, a Rothschild agent for the Vienna family branch.

<>

In 1819, contradicting Jay Leno's arguments, the Bank was declared constitutional by Supreme Court Justice John Marshall, announcing, Congress had the implied power to create the Bank.

When Americans see how much power the bank has, voter backlash put Andrew Jackson played by Charles Bronson into the presidency. Bronson always plays a good guy, who stands up for little people in his films, a real no-nonsense kind of guy ...he puts his money where his mouth is.

President Charles Bronson has something to say. "Let the people rule. If Congress has the right, under the Constitution, to issue paper money ...it was given them, to be used by them, not to be delegated to individuals, or to corporations. The control of a central bank is exercised by a few, over the many ...by first acquiring control over the labor and earnings of the great body of people.

Charles Bronson

"Bankers are a den of vipers. I intend to rout you out, and by the Eternal God, I will rout you out. If the central bank continues to control our currency, receiving our public monies, and holding thousands of our citizens in dependence, it would be more formidable and dangerous than the naval and military power of the enemy. It is not our own citizens only, 8 million dollars of the stock of this bank is held by foreigners. Is there no danger to our liberty, and independence in a bank that in its nature has so little to bind it to our country? Controlling our currency, receiving our public monies, holding thousands of our citizens in dependence is more formidable and dangerous than a military power of the enemy. If government would confine itself to equal protection, and, as Heaven does its rains, shower its favor alike on the high and the low, the rich and the poor, it would be an unqualified blessing," Charles Bronson continued. "In the act before me, there seems to be a wide and unnecessary departure from these just principles."

<>

Spike (not William) Jones

So, Bank of the United States gets mismanaged by the bank president, former Secretary of the Navy Captain William Jones. He calls in loans, and forecloses on mortgages ...causing unemployment, depression, widespread bankruptcy ... prices collapse, but the bank turns around, excelling under its new President Nicholas Biddle (1786-1844), who in 1832 lobbies Congress for a Bill to charter the bank a third time ...and is played by Spike Jones. It's well known, Paris' Baron James de Rothschild is principal investor in the bank.

President Charles Bronson is furious.
Spike Jones is, too.

Spike Jones

If Jackson vetoes it, I'll veto him! I'll cause a depression, if the bank isn't rechartered! Nothing, but widespread suffering will produce an effect on Congress. Our only safety is in pursuing restriction ...I have no doubt that will ultimately lead to restoration of the currency, and rechartering the bank.

Charles Bronson isn't scared.

Charles Bronson

The Bank's trying to kill me. But, I'll kill *it!* If people understood the rank injustice of our central bank system, there would be a revolution before morning. The bold effort the present bank is making to control the government, the distress it has produced, are premonitions ...of the fate of the American people ... should they be deluded into the perpetuation of this institution, or the establishment of another, like it."

Charles Bronson vetoes the Charter, abolishes the bank in 1832 ...orders the Treasury Secretary to withdraw all Government deposits from U.S. Banks ...deposit them in state banks.

Jan. 8, 1835, he pays off the final installment on our national debt ...the only time the national debt was paid off, giving a surplus of 35 million dollars, that went to the states.

Nicholas P. Trist was President Bronson's personal secretary, "This is the crowning glory of Bronson's life, the most important service he ever rendered his country."

Boston Post compares it to Christ throwing money-changers out of the Temple. To-be-President James K. Polk, then House Speaker throws his hat in the ring.

James Polk

Bank of the United States set itself up as a irresponsible, rival power of government.

Score for Charles Bronson.

Charles Bronson

My greatest achievement, in my career is killing the central bank!"

<>

Bronson has, 'I killed the bank', inscribed on his tombstone. He's censured, Mar., 1834, "for removing the government's deposits from the Bank of the United States without express authorization of Congress".

Spike Jones in 1836, true to his word, calls in his markers on all existing loans, refuses to make new loans, together causing a massive depression. But, the charter expired.

Because, Charles Bronson was clear ... he did what needed to be done, because of the abuses and corruptions of the central bank ... the Senate reverses his censure, in 1837 ...the same year, the Rothschilds send agents to America, including August Belmont ...changing his name from Schonberg, a cousin of the Seligman banking family of Frankfurt, Germany.

In 1829, Schonberg-Belmont worked for the bank in Frankfurt ...in 1832, he was promoted into the bank at Naples, to learn international banking, became fluent in English, French, Italian ...then, ran a bank in New York City buying government bonds.

<>

Well, with no central bank, dispersed fractional reserve banking went wild through the state-chartered banks. Meanwhile, the frustrated central bankers decided to force a financial economic war manifesting as a military conflict ... which brings us to President Abraham Lincoln, played by Whoopi Goldberg, and the American civil war.

The American Civil War, viewed from Europe ...is not what I learned as a child, in school in Iowa. Otto van Bismarck, then Chancellor of Germany in 1876, played by Richard Gere, prefers the European view.

<>

Although, Bronson vetoed renewing the charter of the Bank of the United States, House of Rothschild enters into an agreement with the United States Government eclipsing Baring as financial agent of the Department of State, on Jan. 1, 1835.

Banker Henry Clews', *Twenty-eight Years in Wall Street*, on the Panic of 1837.

Henry Clews

The Panic of 1837 was engineered, because the charter of the Second Bank of the United States had run out, in 1836. Not only did President Jackson promptly withdraw government funds from the Second Bank of the United States, but, he deposited these funds, 10 million dollars, in state banks.

The immediate result, was the country began to enjoy great prosperity. The sudden flow of cash expanded the national economy. The government paid off the entire national debt, leaving a surplus of 50 million dollars in the Treasury.

(cont)

The Panic of 1837 was aggravated by the Bank of England when it in one day threw out all the paper connected with the United States.

<>

The Bank of England was controlled by Baron Nathan Mayer Rothschild ...played by me, in my double acting role. But, why did I refuse to accept or discount any securities, bonds or other financial paper ... based in the United States ...other than to create a financial panic, cause credit contraction, stop new stock and bond issues, and bankrupt everyone trying to sell U.S. securities?

Meanwhile, Moses Taylor cashed in on Americans going bankrupt ...from my sudden contraction of credit ...engineered by me ...causing the Panic of 1837. Half the businesses in New York fail ...Moses buys them up for a song. He busts his britches.

John Pierpont Morgan/Aetna Insurance

John Pierpont Morgan is born ...well-to-do farmers. They are family founders of Aetna Insurance Co., in 1819.

In 1855, Moses becomes President of City Bank. During the Panic of 1857, like George Peabody and Junius Morgan, Taylor has enough cash to buy distressed stocks ...including the stock of Delaware Lackawanna Railroad ... for $5 a share ...which sold for $240 a share in seven years, making Moses Taylor a fortune.

Meanwhile, in London George Peabody agrees to Baron Nathan Mayer Rothschild's request for him to become an undercover Rothschild financial agent. He becomes successful in London, buying and selling on both sides of the Atlantic.

In America, Peabody's financial agent is Beebe, Morgan & Co. of Boston, headed by Junius S. Morgan, John Pierpont Morgan's father.

In 1854, Peabody, unmarried, has no successor. He persuades Morgan to be a partner in George Peabody & Co., in London. In 1860, his son, John Pierpont Morgan, works for Duncan-Sherman ...and John Pierpont Morgan's father hires Charles Dabney out of the firm, and creates Dabney, Morgan & Co. ...with John and Charles as partners. Peabody and Junius Morgan, together, secretly financial agents for Rothschild, expand ...to begin shipping iron for railroads to the U.S. Peabody retires in 1864, Morgan renames the company, Junius S. Morgan Co., remaining under the aegis of Rothschild.

<>

I was talking with Junius. Here, he is in Britain on business ...it feels like a take ...I was on my toe-marks ...held my head just right in the light ...got into character.

I'm playing Nathan, I look at Junius, "It's 20 years since the Panic of 1837."

Junius looks back at me, "Is it time?"

I needed to straighten him out. "It's time for you to deliver. The Rothschild family wants to own a central bank in America, that's why we made you our undercover financial agent, in the first place."

Junius understood, "Is 1857 ripe, Nathan?"

"America's riding prosperity?"

Junius nodded, "Yes. ...How do you know?"

"I know, because I said so. The easiest way to crash their economy is collapse the grain market. So, withhold credit ...from Ohio Life & Trust ...til they lose 5 million dollars on client bankruptcies. I predict 1,000 other American banks will fail after Ohio Life & Trust, from this credit constriction."

Junius attacked, "You'll help Junius S. Morgan Co. Bank survive, of course."

"I'll advance you 1 million pounds, to keep you afloat ...while the others fail ...you buy them up ...just like father did, at Waterloo. We Rothschilds have many Waterloos in store for the colonies ...until, I get our central bank installed there ...then many more Waterloos for them until we bleed them dry ...leaving them, looking for jobs and homeless. It's nothing personal. It's business."

Then, I played Amshall Moses Bower in the Jewish ghetto in Frankfurt earlier in the script. Now, I was playing his son, Nathan Rothschild, and had already changed the family name in my dual acting role ...which was more challenging than *King's Row* ...you see how much I studied these guys, to know their character. I could feel, 'Oscar', written all over me.

Corsair's, *Life of J. P. Morgan*, spit it out, "The Bank of England lent George Peabody & Co. 5 million pounds, during the panic of 1857."

Winkler's, *Morgan the Magnificent*, helped, "The Bank of England advanced Peabody 1 million pounds, an enormous sum at that time ...and the equivalent of 100 million dollars today (in 1989 Reagan dollars), to save the firm. However, no other firm received such beneficence during this Panic."

Matthew Josephson's, *Robber Barons*, says how, "For such qualities of conservatism and purity, George Peabody & Co., the old tree out of which House of Morgan grew, was famous. In the Panic of 1857, when depreciated securities had been thrown on the market by distressed investors in America, Peabody and the elder Morgan, being in possession of cash, purchase such bonds, as possessed real value, freely ...and, then resold them ...at a large advance, when sanity was restored."

So, while I engineered the panic I positioned Junius to buy distressed securities from panicked investors at basement prices, later reselling them at great profit, we keep it a secret from New York and London financiers that Junius works for me, building the House of Morgan for Rothschild interests.

Jump cut.

John Moody's, *Masters of Capital,* agreed with me, "The Rothschilds were content to remain a close ally of Morgan ...as far as the American field was concerned."

George Wheeler's, *Pierpont Morgan and Friends, Anatomy of a Myth,* helped, "But, there were steps being taken, even now to bring him out of the financial backwaters ...and they were not being taken by Pierpont Morgan, himself. The first suggestion of his name for a role in the recharging of the reserve originated with London's House of Rothschild, Belmont's employers."

You see, in Europe, our Rothschild family name was targeted, envied and feared. So, we played behind the scenes, directing, whenever possible ...out of the spotlights. We sent an undercover financial agent to America in 1837, August Schoenberg ...had him change his name to Belmont, a name not associated with the Rothschild brand.

<>

I was confused.

Ronald Reagan
Jesus, what are we doing? Why are we in Britain ...in 1857?

Mel's Jesus
We're trying to get to 1913. It's only 50 years, in a big night sky, Ronnie.

Ronald Reagan
Okay, 50 years. Then, I'm going home, to Nancy.

Mel's Jesus smiled warmly, "We're going backwards, a few more years, first."

I got up courage, "This is like ghosts of Christmas past, isn't it?"

"Sort of, but more."

As Patti would say, 'I'm down, with dat' ...it's all right with me. But, I can't help but wondering where I'm going. "Oh man, I'm hungry. What does this have to do with my Presidency? ...or my autobiography?"

Before Mel's Jesus could answer, whirlwinds scooped us up. They left us in a Hollywood studio back-lot, standing next to Richard Gere ...in his

Prussian wig as Otto van Bismarck ...in a Prussian military uniform ...not as tall as he looks in movies ...but, just as talkative, attempting a Prussian accent.

Richard Gere
The division of the United States into federations, of equal force, was decided long before the Civil War ...by the high financial powers of Europe. These bankers were afraid the United States, if it stayed one block, and one nation ...would attain economic, and financial, independence. That, would upset the European central bankers' world domination.

Whoopi Goldberg, playing Abraham Lincoln, needed money to finance the Civil War ...taking the U.S. Treasury Secretary to New York City, they applied for loans ...but were quoted 24% to 36% interest. Whoopi said, 'no'.

Whoopi
"No."

A friend, Colonel Dick Taylor of Chicago, played by an extra, is put in charge of solving the problem of, how to finance the war ...and tells Whoopi what to do.

Dick Taylor
Get Congress to pass a bill authorizing the printing of full legal tender U.S. Treasury notes ... pay your soldiers with them ...and go ahead, win your war with them.

Whoopi wondered aloud.

Whoopi
Will the American people accept the notes? ...would you?

Dick Taylor
(chuckles)
People will not have any choice in the matter, if you make the notes full legal tender. These U.S. treasury notes will have full sanction of the United States government, and be just as good as any money. Besides, only Congress is given the right to issue money, according to the U.S. Constitution.

So, Whoopi prints up 450 million dollars worth of new bills, using green ink on the back ...so they were different from the other notes, circulated from state banks, calling them 'greenbacks'. ...also, issuing greenback precious metal coins.

Whoopi was on a roll.

Whoopi
The government will create, issue and circulate the currency and credit needed for spending power of the government, and buying power of consumers.

The privilege of creating and issuing money is the supreme prerogative of Government, the Government's greatest creative opportunity. The taxpayers will be saved immense sums of interest, discounts and exchanges. Financing of all public enterprises, maintenance of stable government, and conduct of the Treasury will become matters of practical administration. The people can, and will be furnished a currency, as safe as their government. Money will cease to be master, and be a servant of humanity. Democracy will rise superior to the money power of the central bankers.

On Studio Lot B, it's 1863, Whoopi needs more money to win the Civil War. But, Congress won't let her issue more greenbacks, to win the war. Instead, the banking lobby proposes the National Bank Act ...then, votes it in.

Prior to the Whoopi Goldberg Administration, (not Richard Pryor), private commercial banks issued paper money, called, state bank notes. That ended when the National Banking Act of 1863 prohibited states from creating money. The National Banking act of 1863 foreshadowed what was coming, leading to remove redeemable currency. So, in 1863, a selection of private banks got charters from the federal government authorizing them to issue National Bank Notes, giving banks the control of financing and credit, and providing centralized banking under Federal control in times of war.

A financial panic created by the central bankers destroyed 172 State Banks, 177 private banks, 47 savings institutions, 13 loan and trust companies, and 16 mortgage companies.

Salmon P. Chase, Secretary of the Treasury (1861-64), under Whoopi Goldberg broke down and cried.

Samuel P. Chase
The part I played in helping pass the National Banking Act was the biggest financial mistake of my life. The Act built a monopoly affecting every interest in the country. It should be repealed ...but, before that can be accomplished, the people will be arrayed on one side, and the bankers on the other...in a contest, such as we have never seen before in America.

Whoopi wasn't too happy about it either.

Whoopi
The money power preys on the nation in times of peace ...it conspires against the nation in times of adversity ...it is more despotic than monarchy ...more insolent than autocracy ...more selfish than bureaucracy. I see in the near future, a crisis approaching. That unnerves me, and causes me to tremble for the safety of my country. Corporations have been enthroned ... an era of corruption in high places will follow ...and, the money power of the country will endeavor to prolong its reign, by working upon the prejudices of the people until the wealth is aggregated in the hands of a few ...and the Republic is destroyed. I feel at the moment more anxiety for the safety of my country, than ever before, even in the midst of war."

From now on, the entire United States money supply would be created out of debt ...by private bankers ...buying U.S. Government bonds to back the printing of bank notes ...and that's when it became impossible to understand the economic vocabulary of the monetary system ...because it no longer made sense ...because money was debt ...a negative value ...not a positive value ...total nonsense.

For example, John Kenneth Galbrath spoke during my Administration.

John Kenneth Galbrath
In numerous years following the war, the Federal Government ran a heavy surplus. It could not pay off its debt, retire its securities ...because to do so, meant there would be no bonds to back the national bank notes. To pay off the debt, was to destroy the money supply."

I looked at Mel's Jesus. "In all my eight years as President, I could never figure out what language these guys were talking in."

Whoopi smiled. Alexander II Tsar of Russia, played by Charlie Chaplin had no use for central banks either, refusing to allow one set up in Russia.

Whoopi
Guys, Charlie Chaplin is playing Alexander II, that's great. He hates central banks, too!

Ronald Reagan
The whole thing was starting to grate on me. This is like I'm President again, what's happening?

Whoopi
(scowls)
Central bankers in England and France want to finance the South, to break up the U.S. into two separate countries. Some states be separate countries, too. It'll cost a fortune.

Charlie Chaplin didn't talk much, being immortal, so we cast him. Charlie died Christmas Day, 1977, two years after I was Governor of California, two years before I was U.S. President. He had a few good lines, which is a lot for a silent film star.

Charlie Chaplin

If England and France finance civil war in America, it will cost them a fortune. The only way to pay back the debt, is for England and France to attack Russia. ... "Since I'm playing Russian Tsar Alexander II, I'm letting you all know, if France or Britain helps the south, Russia will consider this an act of war.

Europe's view of the Civil War is based on an understanding of central and international banking, and debt financing. It was not like text-books I read in Iowa, when I was in fifth grade. After the Civil War, there was a lot of talk about reviving Whoopi's, I mean, Lincoln's brief experiment with the Constitutional monetary system. If the European money-trust hadn't intervened, it could become an established institution.

In 1857, central bankers hell-bent to establish a Central bank in the United States needed a financial provocation ...creating war means governments have to borrow from them.

Texas defeated Santa Anna in 1856. England and France were distant. Russia was unstable. Central bankers applied destabilization divide and conquer tactics, promoting insurgency and civil war, in the United States.

The North was targeted to become a British Colony, again ...by annexation to Canada, whose financing was controlled by my brother, Lionel Rothschild.

The South was targeted for Napoleon III of France, with French financing, controlled by my brother, James Rothschild. Give me five.

A propaganda and disinformation campaign needed proponents, like Nazi Germany would provide, many years later ...so central bankers founded, and used, the Knights of the Golden Circle, founded 1854 by George Bickley, to promote secession from the Union by the South ...by spreading racial tension from state to state.

Its members included Alfred Pike, Jefferson Davis, John Wilkes Booth, William Quantrill, and Jesse James ...who, after stealing gold from banks and mining companies, buried nearly 7 billion dollars worth, all over the western states ...in hopes of funding a second Civil War.

Ku Klux Klan, formed 1867, was the military arm of the Knights.

The states which seceded, united into the Confederate States of America ...which meant they maintained their independence ...and that, if the South would win, each state could be like an independent country with its own central bank monopolized by ...guess who?

<>

The Confederacy had a covert intelligence apparatus ...a secret service Confederate spy agency, like CIA ...cunning, sophisticated, but without modern electronics. People today aren't smarter than people, yesterday.

Nancy said, she'd always watch my back.

Jessie James, played by Audie Murphy, of course, at age 15 joins Confederate guerillas led by William Quantrill ...in bloody civil warfare in Kansas and Missouri.

In 1866, Audie Murphy ... I mean, Jessie James being played by Audie Murphy ... and brother Frank have their own guerillas, rob, and murder. In 1873, they start to rob banks ...in 1876 their gang is torn up ...they calm down till 1879 ...rob another train ...a gang member is bought off to assassinate Audie ...brother Frank surrenders twice, is tried, and acquitted twice ...peacefully lives out his life on his farm.

Bickley and his Knights work with foreign agents, to stir up armed rebellion with the aim of breaking off the Southern states and making them a banana republic of Britain, once again.

The Knights of the Golden Circle don't disband after the Civil War, they continue as guerrilla fighters serving ongoing British attempts to destabilize the Union. They rob money to finance a second Confederate rebellion. *That* was the specialty of the James Gang, more Knights of the Golden Circle.

Historians say the American Civil War didn't end in 1865, but continued to be fought underground for 19 more years ...just as World War II didn't end in 1945, because the CIA hired Hitler's anti-Soviet guerrilla Nazi leader Otto Skorzeny and his 'Werewolf' guerrillas, who continued fighting in Eastern Europe and Eastern Russia, until 1952.

The Knights spy network was involved in many subversive activities, such as train robberies by Jessie James, the purpose being to fund the Confederates that went underground after they lost their military warfare in 1865 ...just like the Nazis went underground in Madrid, starting in the early 1940s, and operated an exile Nazi underground government in Madrid well into the 1950s under Werner Naumann ...until Germany was again recognized as an independent state.

As a Confederate agent, James smuggled guns and ammunition to Plains Indians, training them in guerilla tactics, for use against their common enemy, General George Armstrong Custer and the Union Army ... all the time, the American guerilla outfits run by Quantrill and James were supported by British banks to split up the United

States ...reclaim the North, giving the South to Napoleon ...as payment for France's help in the destabilization and counter-revolution, undoing, and reversing the American Revolution.

Apr. 1861, the Russian Ambassador to America throws his hat in, like a break dancer spinning on his back, jumps in the dance circle.

Russian Ambassador

"England will take advantage of the first opportunity to recognize the seceded states, and France will follow her."

Late 1861, England sends 8,000 troops to Canada ...1862, English, French and Spanish troops land at Vera Cruz, Mexico, 'to collect on debts owed them by Mexico' ...Jun. 10, 1863, French General Forey, with 30,000 additional French troops, take over Mexico City ...controlling most of Mexico.

Thru spies in Paris and London, Czar Alexander II in Russia discovers Confederates offer Louisiana and Texas to Napoleon III ...if he sends troops against the North.

Russia had said it supported Lincoln.

Jan. 1, 1863 for good will, Whoopi issues the Emancipation Proclamation to free the slaves, just as the Czar had done with the serfs, in 1861.

Sept. 8, 1863, President Whoopi, and Secretary of State William Seward, ask Alexander to send the Russian fleet to San Francisco and New York, to be battle ready, taking orders only from Whoopi Goldberg.

Got it?

It's in the can.

<> <> <>

1914-1918, German General Staff uses mass terrorism as a weapon of war

In 1911, German Professor Otto Tannenberg wrote, "Enemies of Germany should be left nothing but their eyes to weep with." Armed military warfare of World War I started in 1914. The conclusion of the armed military phase was signified by the Treaty of Versailles, four years later. Now, German General Staff ruling families, at the urging of Carl von Clauswitz, decided to use mass terrorism as the next phase of their 1,000-year war.

Kaiser Wilhelm II, ruler of Germany, wrote to his ally, Emperor Franz Josef of Austro-Hungry, "My soul is torn. We must put everything to fire and blood. Slaughter men and women, children, and aged. Not leave a tree. Not a house. Terrorism is the weapon to use on a people so degenerate as the French ...then, we may finish the war in two months. On the other hand, if I respect humani-

tarian considerations, the war may be prolonged for years."

<>

Baron Carl von Clauswitz was Chief Military Theoretician of the 'art' of war, for German League. The Baron insisted mundane slaughter of women, children, and prisoners would terrorize and immobilize the enemy's subject population. Then, enemy civilians could not organize resistance.

The Baron insisted, in order to promote German economic world supremacy ... after the armed military phase of the war ... it was essential to eradicate the enemy, now.

Have the German military execute people randomly, murder, massacre, and rape civilians. Widespread torture of civilian populations, was good. Make living shields of human beings. Impose collective penalties on whole cities, towns and villages. Arrest civilians as hostages. Then, execute them. Massacre prisoners. Attack hospital ships. Poison springs and wells. Use sexual torture to destroy human honor. Methodically, destroy enemy factories.

By 1918, Carl insisted as Kaiser's Army left Belgium and northern France, retreating German troops blow up coal mines, and flood them. Cut the trunks of the fruit trees off to a height of one foot, as reminders.

Thousands of head of cattle were shipped to Germany, or machine-gunned. Whole factories were dismantled, then shipped to Germany. German Army officers followed the precise methodology Carl von Clauswitz outlined to German General Staff. Ruthless acts were not haphazard. They are tactically strategic. Carl had insisted, German General Staff must prepare for future wars, by totally, methodically destroying French and Belgian civilization by terror, murder, rape, and slaughter. This was the best way to totally weaken and demoralize populations. To dismantle their civilization. Dismantle their culture. Cripple them ... then, if you lost this war, you'd win the peace ...and, certainly, win the next, military war.

1918, Reinhard & Dagmara on a typical day

Reinhard Gehlen and Dagmara Wilpf grew into their teens. Reinhard walked into the kitchen. He handed Dagmara some flowers. "Here's some pretty flowers. You look so pretty, today."

Dagmara wasn't impressed. "Donka shein."

"Have you seen the Army pamphlet? It says, 'Married soldiers have a responsibility to the

Fatherland to have out of wedlock many children with single women."

Dagmara was bothered. "No. You're kidding."

He kept reading. "Empty cradles of Germany must be filled. The Fatherland needs healthy children. You married men, and your wives, should not be jealous ...consider, do you have this duty to the Fatherland? Can you honorably contract an affair with one of the million of single women? See if your wife will sanction the relationship. Remember, empty cradles of Germany must be filled."

Dagmara disapproved. "Illegitimate children."

"Not if we changed the law. Father says, the army needs manpower for the next war. Should we help Germany have a baby?"

"Our marriage is arranged. But, we haven't ...you know."

"We must, for the Fatherland."

"You think? The Fatherland doesn't have to carry a baby in its womb, for nine months! The Fatherland doesn't have to get up at midnight to change its diapers. That's an atrocious idea, raise children to be soldiers, to die for the Fatherland. I won't do it!"

"I'm being patriotic."

"Patriotic? What about, *stupid*? Having children with unmarried girls all over town ... popping them for the Fatherland?"

"My dream since childhood, is to see the Skull and Crossbones flag of the German Brotherhood of Death flying on top of Mount Blanc, the Andes, Ararat, and the Himalayas."

Dagmara was pouting. "Why should the flag of the German Order of the Brotherhood of Death be flying there? You mean, *German flag*, don't you."

Reinhard hesitated. "I never thought, *that*."

"Don't you think? Your papa's stuffed your head with facts, reasons, legal rigmarole. He's cut out your conscience. You have no soul ...you worship war."

"You'll get in trouble, talking against German destiny, Dagmara. I've wanted to fight for a long time, since the Abyssinian campaign, during the Spanish war ...when our army invaded Austria and Czechoslovakia. I was sad, I wasn't old enough. It wasn't my destiny to fight in the World War of 1914-1918."

"Soldiers are terrorists and murderers! People shouldn't kill! Life is love."

"Do not question, our leaders know best."

"You're a clone, like your father. Why do we stay engaged?"

They were enthralled with each other, then kissed.

Reinhard smiled. "Father's arranged a junior officer position for me in the Schwarze Reichswehr."

"The Shadow Army? ...the underground? ...the Freikorps? ...the Fehme? ... those terrorists? ...those assassins? That's good news?"

"Yes, of course. An officer's, military intelligence post. To restore Germany's dignity. Some people represent money-issuing families who want Germans, slaves. We hunt them down, and kill them."

"You've never killed anyone?"

"Mice. Birds. Cats."

"Cats? You're horrible."

"Just kidding."

"People aren't rodents. You lack human dignity."

"We must put Jews in their place, Negroes, Gypsies, Serbs, Muslims, Chinese, Japanese, Slavs, Bolsheviks, communists, immigrants. Everyone inferior. We waste tax money on them. They consume German wealth and natural resources. Foreigners. Running around, taking jobs from Germans. We can't have democracy sucking our tax money, here. Your logic is feminine."

"I'm a ballet dancer! ...an artist! Not a murderer! My friends are artists! I *express* my feelings!"

"Ach! You're full of yourself. This 'sensitive' stuff, goes to your head!"

"I don't know why I'm attracted to you at all. You're stubborn, pig-headed."

"That's poetic."

"I don't care! People are starving, all over Germany. Kaiser's war made people sick and homeless, all over Europe ...not just Germany. There are no jobs. Your answer? ...become a terrorist for underground German Military Intelligence. You want to fight the war over and over again, until you win. People need food, jobs, homes ...not bullets. They don't need to be raped! Are you insane?!"

"God made it this way! I didn't! Fight or someone takes your place."

"People are good."

"You're naive. Who pays for your ballet lessons? This palace you live in? Your gowns? The caviar, smoked salmon, meat filets? Your servants? ...Your family portfolio does. You don't dig ditches, fix plumbing, or wax floors, clean toilets, or gut meat."

"I should feel guilty?!"

"Feeling is not logical ...it makes you poor. You might as well be a Bolshevik or a Jew, with all your whining about what's fair. You want designer dresses and palaces. Either you're for Germany, or against *me!*"

Natasha ran into the room. "Dagmara!"

"Yes. mother!"

Natasha Wilpf was anxious. "Look! Out in the streets! The Bolshevik revolution has come to Germany!"

Nov. 9, 1918, the historic date of Socialist revolution in Germany

Nov. 9, 1918, a Bolshevik, socialist revolution swept through Germany. Millions of German people rose in revolution against the Prussian Junkers, industrialists and army officers wage-slaving German citizens, soldiers, brutalizing and starving them. In Berlin, workers and soldiers built street barricades. They stormed the administration centers of the Imperial Palace. In Rhineland-Westphalia, a 'workers revolutionary committee', or 'soviet', as such committees was called.

They arrested Fritz Thyssen. The soviet arrested many ruling family German industrialists, like Thyssen. German ruling family patriarchs were arrested on charges of being war criminals. In Bavaria, the German General Staff was overthrown.

A revolutionary Republic was declared ...the reincarnation of the German revolution of 1848, 70 years earlier ...that failed, in bloodshed. Now, revolutionaries were again trying to end German, colonial imperialism and military aggression.

General Erich Ludendorff, military leader of General Staff, fled to Sweden. Kaiser fled to Holland. All through Germany, Junkers, industrialists and generals packed their bags and money, to escape.

Meanwhile, loyal German government troops entered Munich. They went towards 19th Infantry barracks. The 19th Infantry had joined the soviet revolution. They were having a revolutionary, celebration party. A messenger arrived. The messenger handed a note to a 19th Infantry soldier.

The soldier read the message. "Government troops are on their way into the city, to fight. Get ready for combat, to defend ourselves!"

Corporal Adolf Schickelgruber, dressed as an 19th Infantry soldier, felt his heartbeat jump, "No. The soviet revolution is doomed. We must surrender!"

"Are you a spy?" the first soldier said.

"A traitor?" a second soldier said.

"We should arrest him," another said.

White troops surrounded the 19th Infantry. The 19th Infantry surrendered. White troops randomly took 19th Infantry soldiers, stood them up against a wall, and shot them.

The commander of loyal German government troops pulled Corporal Adolf Schickelgruber aside for questioning, "Are you Corporal Adolf Schickelgruber, the observer left behind as a spy, by the Munich Reichswehr when they fled the revolution?"

"Yes."

"You'll inform for us, and execute. Which men in 19th Infantry are Communists? ...to execute."

"Put them against the wall. I'll show you the Jewish dictators in Munich's Soviet period ...they committed treason,' Corporal Schickelgruber said. "They disgraced us."

"Good. What was your citizenship, and profession, before you were a soldier?"

"I am an Austrian. I am an artist, a painter, and architect."

Underground German General Staff

Curt Riess' *The Nazis Go Underground,* filled me and Nancy in.

In 1918, after Germany lost WWI, Treaty of Versailles allowed an official German army. The official Reichswehr Army recognized by the Treaty Of Versailles was under the command of General Hans von Seeckt. Major Kurt von Schleicher was liaison officer between General Hans von Seeckt and Fedor von Bock.

The Reichswehr was not made smaller how the treaty demanded. Major Kurt von Schleicher made sure of that. Major von Schleicher accepted the Treaty Of Versailles, in name only. Consulting with Thyssen, Krupp, Schroder and von Papen, Major Kurt von Schleicher planned to get around armistice conditions imposed by the Allies, in the Treaty of Versailles. In ten years, that consulting team would hand German State power to Adolf Schickelgruber, who changed his name to, Adolf Hitler.

As a member of German General Staff, Major Kurt von Schleicher and Fedor von Bock co-founded Black Reichswehr, the Underground Movement of the Imperial German Army. Their underground guerrilla units, called 'Freikorps units of the Schwarze Reichswehr', was an army only of German officers ...an underground army of officers, preparing for a second world war. The number of underground officer troops grew, as German ruling family industrialists financed them. The German government protected them.

Fedor von Bock was in charge of the Black Reichswehr. Von Bock and Von Schleicher made sure Black Reichswehr was filled with nationalistic extremists ...wanting revenge, for Germany's lost war. Black Reichswehr was a secret organization. The government officially said, secret underground armies, a Schwarze Reichswehr, a black market of armies in Germany, was a rumor ...that it was French, or Polish, propaganda.

Journalists, who wrote about what was going on, were murdered. Politicians, who suspected what was happening, were murdered.

<>

The world saw only the German Reichswehr. Unseen, the Schwarze Reichswehr of death squads grew. Both armies were commanded by the same officers ...the Army Ministry of the German Republic, controlled by German General Staff ...made up of ruling family industrialists, financiers, military men and politicians. Who controlled German General Staff? the Skull & Crossbones Order of the Brotherhood of Death, the Skull & Bones, central bankers, also wealthy industrialists.

General Hans von Seeckt addressed the gathering, "Your progress reports, gentlemen,"

Major Baron Kurt von Schleicher turned in his report. "I suggest, we spread the rumor we can't disarm the Schwarze Reichswehr ...because they protect Germany against Bolshevik communists, and Jews. That anti-Christian forces are getting powerful, and larger! I'll contact Schwarze Reichswehr Propaganda Ministry. We'll put it out, worldwide."

Baron Reinhard Gehlen handed his report to Baron von Seeckt. "I'm handling communications with underground units on the eastern frontier. Their main task is, gather guns, arms and munitions, left over from the war. Refurbish them, get the rust out, get them working, distribute and hide them. The largest underground arms depots are in Bavaria."

Baron Von Seeckt collected the reports. "The Treaty of Versailles demands we surrender arms left over from the war, to be destroyed. That won't happen. We need arms and munitions. Your reports show Schwarze Reichswehr organized as the Reichswehr."

Major Baron Kurt von Schleicher looked at Reinhard. "Erfassungsabteilungen Collecting Departments ...have you organized them?"

"Yes," Gehlen answered. "Officers in each military district assemble personal files on men of military age. Even though it's forbidden by the Versailles Treaty, we'll use those files to grow Schwarze Reichswehr reserve units, inside the Reichswehr. I've created a new department, Truppenverstaerkung Troop Reinforcement IAP. I hid it inside Department of Operations of

Military Districts. As you've asked, it provides oversight for Black Reichswehr, and performs liaison between Black Reichswehr and Reichswehr.

"Truppenverstaerkung will be led by Barons von Bock and von Rundstedt."

Von Rundstedt and Von Bock would become the most powerful German generals in World War II. Von Bock was pleased. "Great work, Reinhard. You've proven quite an asset to me. I'm promoting you."

"Thank you."

"You've earned it."

"Thank you."

Von Bock kept watch to recruit the best officers. "I've got a Schwarze Reichswehr Fehme unit for to join, in Garde Kavallerie Schutzen Freikorps Division ...a special, counter-revolutionary officers' regiment. Wait a minute! I hear the American coming! Hear him mincing?"

American Colonel I.L. Hunt walked in. His uniform was wrinkled, he walked with a limp, and had a lisp like bad boy actor, Steven Segal. "Good morning. I'm in charge of German civil affairs for Third American Army, here in the Rhineland. Following your suggestions, after careful consideration, I'm suspending all 'workers revolutionary governing groups' ...each 'soviet', revolutionary unit Bolshevik workers and army deserters formed. I won't have Leftists around, discuss any problem, with them ...such as feeding the people. I leave that, to you. Too many Leftists are in German government, in Berlin."

Baron Hans von Seeckt clicked his heels together. "You have no more control over that, than I do."

American Colonel I. L. Hunt stepped back. "Don't you have your hands full managing the Reichswehr?"

Baron von Seeckt was growing impatient with the American. "Yes."

American Colonel I. L. Hunt sized up von Seeckt. "Look, my superiors told me, 'Only let men stay in government, who held jobs in government, *before* the soviet revolution'. That should starve out communists and Jews in your government. Ex-Imperial German officers will *stay* in their jobs. I've recommended, in all occupied territory, ex-Imperial officers retain their jobs, as a condition of the armistice. I want the political institutions the American Army met during our occupation of your former regime, to remain. Do you understand?

"You gentlemen were correct, influencing me to hold that opinion ...making the armistice *require* that civil government in occupied zones are conducted by the old German officials ...that means experienced, competent men in office ...you see my line of argument? As far as Third Army Headquarters knows, not one German official has declined to continue his duties in civil government, that he had before the war.

"When Third Army occupied Germany, the ideas of the great world, middle class, socialist revolution were under attack. Germany was unstable, with internal disorder. How could Germany look to a revolutionary government? ...unorganized, doomed from the beginning?

"Imperial officials welcomed us to Germany. They saw us as coming, to help them enforce their authority over the German people ...the revolution weakened their authority ...we're here, to beef it up. Do you understand?" Colonel Hunt added. "Occupied territories will be administered by local authorities of your old regime, no Commies allowed. The timing's right, now ...because as occupying armies, we'll have capable German officials carry out our orders and wishes. I hope that suits you."

Von Seeckt flattered him. "Yes, it does."

"Keep up the good work. Good afternoon." Colonel Hunt turned and left.

"Good afternoon," von Seeckt replied.

Von Bock whispered, "Is he out of earshot?"

Reinhard nodded affirmatively, "Yes."

Baron Fedor had a twinkle in his eye. "Reinhard, let me tell you, what you're doing tonight ...is, meeting your new Fehme unit, of Garde Kavallerie Schutzen.

Baron Reinhard was pleased. "Good."

<>

After my Reagan Presidency was over, my health deteriorated quite a bit ...I spent many hours sitting in a deck chair on my ranch in Santa Barbara, overlooking the Pacific Ocean, listening to Nancy read to me. I looked forward to that part of my life.

Nancy and I were always trying to figure out how government was run, while we were in office, and, afterwards, too. It was a full time job. Nancy read me Sayers and Kahn, *The Plot Against the Peace*, and, a book by General Baron Hugo von Freytag-Loringhoven, *Lessons of the World War*. The plot went like this, and Errol Flynn would've died for the leading role.

1918, Schwarze Reichswehr Fehme & Freikorps death squad terrorist teams

In 1917, a year before the Armistice would end the first World War, General Baron von Freytag-

Loringhoven outlined German strategy for a second World War ...it was essential to preserve intact trained terrorist officers from the Kaiser's army that tore through France and Belgium ...German General staff adopted this tactic. With the signing of the 1918 Peace Armistice, German Officers Corps went underground into Schwarze Reichswehr Freikorps death squad units.

Freikorps terrorist guerrilla bands of officers formed, under supervision of German General Staff, on pretense ...to provide national defense against Bolshevism. General Staff made secret agreements with the new, anti-militarist German Social Democratic regime, to preserve the underground German Officers Corps ...on pretense ...to destroy Bolshevism in Germany, and destroy democracy Bolshevism was spreading in Germany, and Europe.

Not all Freikorps members were Germans. Many were mercenaries, working for German General Staff before, as paid agents, propagandists, spies, saboteurs, and assassins. Freikorps leaders were also terrorist White Guards from Finland, and Baltic states, ex-Ochrana agents and Black Hundred pogromists from Czarist Russia, thieves, cutthroats, and degenerates from military jails in Europe.

<>

In 1918-1919, Freikorps units stormed through German cities and countryside, looting, torturing, raping, and murdering German citizens ...that believed in Democracy.

Freikorps units were housed in Fehme units. For centuries, Fehme terrified Germans, as secret, terrorist death squad societies of medieval Teutonic Knights, predating German General Staff ...but, with positions of equal power. The great, ruling families were land owners of Medieval Germany. They used the Fehme to wipe out rebellions by peasants. Back then, when ruling families bought a piece of land, they bought peasants with it.

Working in secrecy, Fehme death squads kidnapped victims, bringing them to secret Fehme Courts of Vengeance, Fehmgericht ...where, victims were formally excluded from the Teutonic community, beaten to death, hanged, bodies left hanging in public, as reminders.

The Emperor protected Fehme death squads ...because they destroyed revolutionaries, against him.

So, in Germany after World War I, the Fehme were revived ...as a secret weapon of the underground Officers Freikorps, reporting to German General Staff ...while German General staff itself, was financed by ruling family Junkers and ruling family industrialists in Westphalia ...the task of Freikorps and Fehme, was to kill leaders of the German Republic.

Investigations of killings in newspapers and courts led to Junkers, or heavy industry ...as Fehme cleared the path for Nazism to grow in Germany. By 1921, Fehme carried out 350 assassinations against Germans wanting democracy and peace, murdering leaders of German democracy one by one ...the killers were German army staff officers of Freikorps Fehme units of Schwarze Reichswehr. Each Freikorps and Black Reichswehr unit had its Fehme death squad.

For high-ranking officers, murder of a German who believed in Democracy ....was a privilege, only for them. Fehme officers openly warned victims, bragging of murders. In 1918, Fehme victims included Karl Liebknecht and Rosa Luxemberg, leaders of the German workers' revolution ...murdered by Fehme unit Garde Kavallerie Schutzen Freikorps Division ...a counter-revolutionary, officers' regiment.

German courts and German government covered-up Fehme death squads. Their next victim was Kurt Eisner, Prime Minister of the revolutionary Bavarian Republic ...destroyed by Schwarze Reichswehr Officers Corps.

In 1919, revolutionary Bavaria was a concentration-point for Fehme covert operations. Bavarian Junker estates hid Schwarze Reichswehr secret arms caches, and death squad, training centers. Fehme was used to silence any German citizen talking out ...about secret war preparations of General Staff, ...Fehme murdered them. One by one, leaders of the Bavarian democratic revolution were murdered, by the Fehme. Before long, no one was powerful enough to slow German General Staff war plans. German newspapers reported Fehme were gone ...as Fehme terrorists and death squads attacked the German public, on a daily basis. Workers were beaten to death, merchants and intellectuals tortured and shot, farmers hanged, bodies found drowned in ditches.

<>

Dagmara ran to meet Reinhard as he entered and hugged and kissed him. "Hi darling. I've missed you the last few days. Where have you been?"

"I've been busy. Good news. I was given an officer's commission ...initiated into a Fehme unit."

"A Fehme officer's commission? What did you have to do to get it? ...kill Kurt Eisner?"

"Do you really want to know?"

"Yes."

"Do you need to know. No."

Dagmara felt angry. "If you expect me to marry you, tell me the truth ....or say nothing, at all. Don't start telling me something, then stop, treat me like I'm stupid, expect me to clap my hands, then jump into bed."

Reinhard gave in. "All right. Tonight, I learned to kill. I beat a man. He begged me, stop. He was a professor at the university, an intellectual. A revolutionary. We dumped him in a ditch."

Dagmara felt shocked. "You're a murderer."

Reinhard laughed. "I thought I was, too, at first. Then, I saw I wasn't. I was nervous, irritable. I questioned myself. I threw up. Other officers, patted me on the back in congratulations. It's hard, at first ...they told me. Then, it gets easier. They felt bad, their first time, too, they said. But, they got used to it. Officers call it, military action ...Imperial Germany is fighting off democracy ...revolutionaries ...the Bolshevik, middle class ...the workers ...the Jews. We're an underground army. If it wasn't for patriots, like me, they said, revolutionaries will advance, take our wealth away."

Dagmara sighed. "It's easy to explain?"

"Yes. I always wanted to be a soldier. Now, I am. Soldiers kill enemies. Soldiers are not murderers. They're following orders. It's my duty."

"Murder is wrong."

"Germany just lost a world war. That's wrong, too."

"What did it get us?! People worse off than before ? Why do you think revolution is popular? ...people are tired of dying, suffering, watching their children beg, starve and whore."

"You haven't had to beg, starve or whore. Your investment portfolio's good."

"Is that *all* you think about? I haven't gone whoring like middleclass people are forced to. But, they're Germans too."

"No. Not like us. They're not propertied. They're not aristocracy. They're not ruling families."

"But, they *are* people."

"No, they're not. They're pets. Luxury items. We take care of them, play with them, feed them. When you get tired of a pet, or it's sick ...you put it to sleep."

"I love my pets. I miss them, when they die. I feel loss. Someone else puts them to sleep! Not me! But you, you kill people, yourself. There's blood on your hands, blood-guilt in your mind. That will haunt you, forever!"

"You think, because you don't pull the trigger

yourself, your hands are clean? Your portfolio finances war, doesn't it? ...you ride the wave of military-industrial power."

"Yes, I did, until we lost the war. But, the middle class got poor."

"Who cares?. It's dog eat dog ...kill, or be killed! Of course, I pull the trigger, myself. If I don't, who will? You? Grow up, Dagmara. Stop being a child."

"I'm not a child! Don't you have a heart? Don't you have feelings? The war messed up our friends. Otto's feet got shot off. Hans got his leg blown off, his arms, his eyes. Peter lost both legs, to the waist. Heinrich lost his face! *That's* war! *That's* your glory! Can't you see, *that!?*"

"I see, if German officers don't protect Germany ...you'll have nothing left, *to* protect!"

"Maybe nothing is better than killing? Look, in the mirror! I changed. I felt suffering. I'm at war with me, not anyone else. I want peace in me!"

"There's no peace ...fight or surrender. You be poor, be a slave. Not me."

"The Romanovs and White Russians lost everything in the revolution ...they're poor, now."

"Not the smart ones. They invested in marks, francs, dollars. They lost land, mineral rights, forestry rights. The smart ones live in New York, Paris, Brussels, Amsterdam, Dallas ...planning to regain their portfolios. You can't buy tickets to leave Germany ...without money, can you?"

"No. I can't do anything without money, except spread my legs for you. But, I have money ...and, I don't have to," Dagmara spoke angrily. "The war changed me. My brother, Wilfred, lost his mind. He yells, screams in his sleep. Sometimes, he's awake ...staring out the window, crying ...but his eyes are empty. I've changed. I want killing to stop. Money's not important. I don't need that much, just enough to travel, pay doctors, servants, taxes, chauffeurs, travel, theatre, ballet. I can't talk any more ...what else did you do, tonight?"

"We drove to the countryside to a meeting of farmers, who were revolutionaries. We mixed into the crowd. Afterwards, when everyone else left, we grabbed the farmer and his wife. We beat them, and hanged them."

"Hanged them? Were they dead first?"

"No. We had to get information out of them. We did things to them, I won't tell you. They kicked, screamed, their eyes popped out ...they messed their pants. It was awful. But, we got a list of names, of more Bolsheviks, from them. When they hang, they keep their expressions on their faces ...you can see what they felt, when you look

at their death masks."

Reinhard threw a plaster of Paris death mask onto the bed. Dagmara was shocked, got off the bed, walked across the room. "Wasn't one killing enough, for you?"

"I made a good impression on the officers."

"A good impression? You felt no remorse?"

"After the first killing, the rest *are* easier. It's just like they say."

"You've had yourself quite a time."

"I'm not through. yet. I killed Rosa Luxemberg, leader of the German workers' revolution. We kidnapped her, took her to the west side, to Adlon Hotel ...Garde Kavallerie Schutzen Freikorps Division headquarters. We gave her a hearing. Then, took her outside to the hotel entrance. I hit her head, twice ...with the butt of my gun. Her head snapped. We pushed her into our car. We drove to an isolated spot along the Neeuer See in the Tiergarten. We pushed her out. I shot her first. Then, we all shot her."

"It's not going to stop, is it?"

"No. Then, we drove to Kurt Eisner's home. He's no longer Prime Minister of the Bavarian Republic ...two shots in the head. Gustav Landauer, the Shakespeare expert, the former Minister of Education in the Bavarian Republic ...kidnapped him ...beat him ...knocked him down with a club ...trampled him ...kicked him. 'Will denn das Schwein gar nicht sterben?' (Won't the pig die at all?) I yelled. I shot him through the back. Reich Secretary of the Treasury Matthias Erzberger, leader of the German Catholic Centrist Party. He wanted a tax plan, the German General Staff didn't. We waylaid him, from his vacation in the Black Forest. He begged us not to kill him. So, I shot him in the back. We all shot him, while he lay on the ground, ten, eleven times. German Foreign Minister Walther Rathenau, he was against General Staff's secret war plans ...he voted for the Rapallo Treaty of friendship with Soviet Russia. Two big mistakes. We found him, driving in his car, stopped at the corner of Wallott Street, in Berlin. We pulled up beside him in our car, I shot him with a machine-gun."

"That's enough."

"On the way home, they bought be a beer, cheered me up. 'Knallt ab den Walther Rathenau, die gottverdammte Judensau!' (Crack down Walther Rathenau, the God-damned, Jewish pig!), we sang. They congratulated me on my officer's commission. They look up to me. They're proud of me. I'm a hero."

"I changed, why can't you?"

"We must fight to stay free, to keep our wealth, to be ruling families, not slaves, we must earn privilege."

"Reinhard, I can't believe we've come to this ...you've come to this ...Germany's come to this. There's no way out."

"The police trailed us."

"The police?"

"After I killed Rathenau. Police trailed us, from when we left the bar. We stayed ahead of them, all the way to Saaleck Castle near Koesel ...our hideout. They fired at the car, surrounded us. Captain Dietl of the Bavarian Reichswehr came out of the castle. He told them, let us go ...or, he would have them hanged, that night. They let us go."

"It's a dangerous business you've gotten yourself into."

"Yes, it is. We drank beers, in the castle bar ...a reward, for the killings I've been given an intelligence post, watching over the entire eastern frontier, against Soviet Russia. It promises me a good career. Since you're going to Russia, let me visit you, there. Correspond with me. Help me, from time to time?"

"You mean, a spy?"

"Yes, help guard our inheritances, grow our portfolios. Revolution's dead in Germany. It's struggling in Russia ...land of business opportunity. Will the U.S. or Anglo-French-German concerns get the Russian gold and oil? All I ask of you ...will you fight for Germany's World Order, or not. Keep your family's wealth, or give it to your workers, and your servants. There's German blood in you. But, you can't survive without our arranged marriage."

Dagmara got sad. "I'll marry someone else."

"Who?"

"I don't know. I don't have any choices, yet. But, I'll find someone. Men chase me around."

"Then, so will I."

"Are you seeing someone?"

"No. I can find a patriotic woman, who wants to get ahead, to live in luxury. Do you want to continue our engagement, or not?"

"Okay, for now. I'll think about it in Russia, at ballet school."

"Good. I know you have doubts ...The officers are proud of me. Just think. Yesterday, I helped destroy the revolution in Germany. Today, I'm an intelligence officer, responsible for the entire, eastern frontier. No one can stop me."

1918, Bolshevik socialist revolution in Germany, defeated

In 1918, the revolution in Germany was defeated. Ludendorff returned to Berlin. The Thyssens, Krupps, and Stinnes resumed control over their war factories, and mines. Germany was safe for Junker barons. General Staff continued preparations for the new world war. German Officers Corps Freikorps and Fehme Black Reichwehr, tentacles of the Reichswehr, operated illegally in the Democratic Republic of Weimar Germany, crushing the German revolution.

German General Staff rule began again. Revolutionary German democracy was destroyed by terrorism, and atrocity. Freikorps units roamed Baltic states and Polish Silesia, slaughtering people who wanted freedom, and democracy, looting their belongings.

At the Peace Conference in Paris, in 1919, Allied statesmen agreed on a Special Clause ...amended to the peace treaty with Germany. The clause demanded arrest of Kaiser Wilhelm II, for war crimes the German Army committed during World War I. Wilhelm II was to be publicly arraigned, for offenses against morality, and the sanctity of Treaties. But, the Kaiser was never extradited from the Netherlands ...never tried ...never punished ...he lived in luxury, on a pri-

1981 Cabinet 2/4/81. Alexander Haig, Sec. of State; President Reagan; Vice President Bush; Caspar Weinberger, Sec. of Defense Second row: Raymond Donovan, Sec. of Labor; Donald Regan, Sec. of Labor; Terrel Bell, Sec. of Education; David Stockman, Dir. Office of Management & Budget; Andrew Lewis, Sec. of Trans., Samuel Pierce, Sec. of Housing & Urban Dev.; William French Smith, Attorney General; James Watt, Sec. of the Interior; Jeane Kirkpatrick, U.S. Rep. to the United Nations; Edwin Meese III, Counselor to the President; James Edwards, Sec. of Energy; Malcolm Baldrige, Sec. of Commerce; William E. Brock, United States Trade Rep.; Richard Schweiker, Sec. of Health & Human Services; John Block, Sec. of Agriculture; William Casey, Dir., Central Intelligence Agency

vate estate at Dorn, in Holland. He maintained connections with German General Staff, helping finance Germany's secret re-armament. In 1919, German government paid him millions of dollars, to compensate him for German properties lost when he fled to Holland.

In 1920, the Allies gave the German government a list of German war criminals. There were 896 names on the list ...Generals Hindenburg ...Ludendorff ...von Mackensen ...von Stuelpnagel ...Prince Rupprecht of Bavaria ...Duke Albrecht of Wurttemberg ...ex-Chancellor von Bethman-Hollweg ...Admiral von Tirpitz ... these war criminals were never brought to trial. Of the 896, six were brought to trial. Three got light sentences. Instead of being held accountable for crimes in the first World War, 890 war criminals remained free, to carry on secret preparations for a second world war.

Psychological re-armament & mobilization

Until 1918, Germany was a Monarchy under Kaiser Wilhelm II. After 1918, Germany was a Republic under Social Democratic ministers.

But, the same men ruled Germany. A small group of ruling family military leaders, industrialists, Junkers, scientists, and bankers ... comprised German General Staff. The government didn't rule Germany ... *they did* ...German General Staff was the permanent government of Germany. The Order controlled German military affairs, the economy, technology, schools, universities, and politics.

Financiers and industrialist ruling families backing Kaiser's attempt to dominate the world ...Krupp ...Thyssen ...Hugenberg ...Stinnes, ...Kirdorf ...Siemens, now financed Hitler, and Germany's war machine. They planned, one day, to follow behind the Nazi army, making 'economic colonies'.

Von Rundstedt, von Brauchitsch, von Kleist, von Bock, von Witzleben, were Prussian military ruling families, they were instrumental in Kaiser's war.

Colonel Walther Nicolai, head of the Kaiser's Military Intelligence ...was now, secretly organizing Nazi Military Intelligence.

Admiral Canaris, head of the Kaiser's Naval Intelligence ...was now, secretly organizing Nazi Naval Intelligence.

Baron Reinhard Gehlen knew these ruling families well. As a child, he played with their children ...went to private schools with them, to debutante balls and galas ...played soccer with them on the field ...watched as they, and their parents, resurrected German militarism with a new face, and a new name. Baron Reinhard Gehlen was one of them, equal parts of the Order motivating German General Staff ...its innermost circle, nobody knew ... the Order of the Brotherhood of Death. The name went through Gehlen's mind like rustling of leaves, a memory of a child ...rummaging though musty-smelling books and papers in the attic ...in the library of his step-father's study ...the night his step-father switched him with a riding crop for playing with a ledger with the pirate flag tooled into the leather book cover. The Order went through Gehlen's mind at strange, and random times ...by the pool ...waiting for the cinema to begin ...in the beer hall with candlelight flickering over his face. Gehlen raised his stein, to drink ...noise in the bar got dim. He stared in his beer, wondering which men around him were comrades in the shadow government. Or those, he must kill.

Shadow government thoughts formed, thoughts of Schwarze Reichswehr ...his vision looked out through German General Staff eyes in the Skull & Bones head, itself ...the Death's Head of Skull & Bones ...the Brotherhood of Death! If only, he could see more clearly, think more deeply, be discovered by them ... one day, to be initiated into the Order.

What an honor, an acknowledgment of his power, to join those who set the priority of life and death on Earth, over who lived, and who died. What races, industries, civilizations would emerge from this war, this side of death, or the other ...to rule as a member of a race of supermen ...as a shadow leader of the master-race, commanding German General Staff.

<>

Freikorps systematically, and, in crimes of opportunity, neutralized the insurgent subject population. But, the Order after 1918, needed more. Baron Carl von Clauswitz told German General Staff, German society had to be mentally re-constructed, so it could fight a second world war.

The Order had to enslave the minds of German society, *control* what it *would* think. The Order needed, Thought Police ...a mass movement to distract German people from targeting the money-issuing class and their ruling families' motives. The Order needed to operate German society like a marionette ... as a whole ... ideologically, religiously, dedicating German General Staff in military, political, academic, and industrial life to this goal. Baron Carl von Clauswitz called, motivating German masses, 'psychological re-armament'.

Military psychology raised morale of soldiers and psychologically mobilized them. This psychological motivation could raise morale and mobilize all German society. Psychology would be instrumental for war, psychological warfare, propaganda, mind control ...used to manipulate politics, and politicians, diplomacy and diplomats ...a tactical weapon of military strategy, deployed against German society.

So, German General Staff scientifically began psychological re-armament of German society, after the war. The Allies didn't perceive use of German psychology as a weapon of war. Because, German General Staff masked its psychological re-armament program ...by naming it, 'anti-Bolshevik', 'anti-Semitic', 'anti-communist', and 'nationalistic'.

<>

Nancy read to me from Colonel Walther Nicolai's book, *Secret Powers*. Nicolai wrote, after Armistice German General staff start planning the second world war, using morale-remobilization of German society with psychological, propaganda agencies ...the Pan-German League ...the Fatherland Party ...German Workers National Socialist Party. Psychological warfare was now, the new weapon of choice for German ruling families to hide behind. Nicolai said, propaganda replaced military considerations, and became a political weapon.

More books on German Psychological Warfare, appeared. *Der Feldherr Psychologos: Ein Suchen nach dem Fuehrer der deutschen Zukunft* (War Lord Psychologis: A Search for the Leader of the German Future. *Deutsche Propaganda: Die Lehr von Propaganda als praktisches Gessellschaftslehre.* (German Propaganda: Science of Propaganda as a Practical Social Science), arguing for a new education system to build German power. *Die Kunst der Massenbeeinflussung en den Vereinigten Staaten von Amerika* (The Art of Influencing the Masses in the United States of America), and *Die Wirtschaftlichen und politischen Aufgaben des Auslanddeutschtums* (Economic and Political Tasks of Germandom Abroad).

Spring 1919, a Reichswehr 'instructor', a spy, Adolf Schickelgruber, was stationed as a corporal at the 16th Regiment in Munich.

He got orders from Captain Ernst Roehm, founder of Freikorps Reichsflagge, in charge of Reichswehr espionage in Munich, to go join German Workers Party.

Adolf Schickelgruber, and other Reichswehr agents, were to infiltrate the German Workers Party ...and take control of the organization. Then, re-organize it, and make it into a propaganda machine ...useful for domestic psychological warfare.

Adolf Schickelgruber, a former German propaganda writer from Vienna, did his writing under the alias of, 'Adolf Hitler' ...was currently being trained by Political Department of the District Army Command under General Vlassov ...to be an agent provocateur ...mass agitator.

Pan-German League and Kaiser's token Socialists, the Social Democratic political ministers in the German Cabinet, co-founded German Workers Party ...to get public support for Kaiser's war aims.

German Workers Party became inactive after Armistice. Reichswehr Political Department assigned German agent Gottfried Feder to revive German Workers Party ...to be an anti-Semitic, anti-communist mass propaganda organization for domestic psychological warfare.

Reichswehr Political Department assigned German propagandists, spies and intelligencers to help Feder.

Konrad Heiden's, *Der Fuehrer*, filled in the plot points for Nancy and me ...as Hitler wrote, in *Mein Kampf*, "I joined a regiment, then in garrison at Munich, as instruction officer. One day, I was ordered by my superiors to look into an apparently political organization that, under the name, 'German Workers Party', was soon to hold a meeting ...at which Gottfried Feder was to speak."

Konrad continued, "Hitler joined German Workers Party, as Member #7. Reinhard had his number, other members included ...Captain Ernst Roehm, the Reichswehr secret agent ...German propagandists Gottfried Feder ...Anton Drexler ...Dietrich Eckhart ...and, Freikorps leader General von Epp. These men, schooled in psychological warfare, re-organized German Workers Party ...re-naming it, 'German Workers National Socialist Party', the Nazi party."

<>

"The first recruits were Egyptian-born mercenary, ex-officer Rudolph Hess, and a Czarist Baltic White Guard, anti-Semitic propagandist from Czarist Russia, Alfred Rosenberg. In this satanic alliance of German propagandists, Reichswehr spies, Freikorps leaders, mercenaries, psychological warfare experts, and Czarist intelligencers, the Nazi Party was born.

"Nazis began to mobilize Germans living abroad, to help German ruling families with re-colonization plans, re-organizing international

German cells into international Nazi organizations. Hitler's job, was to sell it to the German people. Hitler wrote, *Mein Kampf*, a collection of all German, fascist, anti-Semitic propaganda and theory, to date. General Staff propaganda writers had written much, since 1918. Mein Kampf became propaganda of choice ...for the Nazi Party. Nazi strategy, the world thought Adolf Hitler invented ...was a German General Staff psychological warfare program ...before the Nazi Party was founded."

Nazi garden party

As Reinhard and Dagmara walked into the building, immediately a plainclothes Freikorps Fehme unit, Reinhard belonged to, rushed to greet him, patting him on the back. Reinhard introduced Dagmara to them.

Reinhard was introduced to Roehm and Rosenberg.

Roehm smiled. "I've heard good reports on you. I'm glad you're at the meeting."

Reinhard acknowedged him. "Thank you."

So did Alfred Rosenberg. "Welcome."

Reinhard pushed Dagmara to stand ahead of him. "This is Dagmara Wilpf. She is performing ballet, before our meeting."

Alfred smiled warmly. "Hello."

"Hello," she replied.

Reinhard signaled the band. "Begin the music."

Dagmara took her coat off, handed it to a young girl of 11, a blond with long hair in a pony tail down her back, dressed in an Imperial German military uniform jacket, wearing pink satin ballet slippers, pink tights, pink and black ribbons, in her hair who spoke slowly and deliberately, "I'll be dancing, too."

Dagmara stiffened her posture, "All right then. Let's begin."

The music started. Reinhard watched Dagmara dance the ballet. All noise in the biergarten, stilled. The young girl in the uniform dancing with her, assisted Dagmara with some ballet movements, holding Dagmara's hand to give Dagmara support. Reinhard watched the men watching Dagmara with fascination, especially Alfred Rosenberg. Reinhard saw a look in Rosenberg's eyes, of delight as well and that upset him, somewhat.

Alfred Rosenberg noticed Reinhard watching him and broke the ice, "She's beautiful."

"Yes, my fiancee is beautiful."

"It's a shame ," Alfred said, "...that she's your fiancée, and not mine."

Reinhard didn't like that. "That's not funny."

"It wasn't meant to be. Seriously, congratulations."

"Thank you. Please excuse me, my stomach's turning. I need to use the men's room. I don't think you'll mind telling Dagmara where I am ...if I'm not back when she's finished."

"Of course."

Dagmara finishing dancing beside Alfred Rosenberg. Alfred clapped. "That was beautiful."

"Thanks. Where's Reinhard?"

"He said, his stomach's upset, he'll be right back."

"How did I do?"

Rosenberg moved close to her. "I love your dancing, the way your body moves. I'm under your spell, can't take my eyes away. I've just met you. But, fallen in love with you, already."

Dagmara blushed. "Thank you. It's not me. It's my celebrity. It's the dance. People show affection for actresses, singers, and dancers. And, my little companion here, did she do well too?" Dagmara put her hand on the shoulder of the girl who'd danced with her.

Alfred smiled. "You did fabulously, darling."

"Thank you. I have to go find Papa. Bye," the little dancer disappeared.

Dagmara was pleased. "She looks adorable in little officer's tails."

Alfred laughed. "We should fit you in tails, you'd look adorable, too. Reinhard tells me, you're engaged to him."

Dagmara was surprised, "What brought that up?"

"The way I was watching you, hypnotized."

"I'm not in the marketplace."

"All right. We'll be friends then, all right?"

"Yes ...why are these men all wearing brown shirts?"

"That's our undercover, civilian uniform. We call ourselves, Brown Shirts."

"That's cute. I'd like to dance in one of those. Can you get me one?"

"Ask Reinhard. If he can't, I can. Welcome to our first international, anti-Soviet conference. We're here to draw-up plans for a world-wide campaign of agitation, and provocation, against Soviet Russia. The conference elected several of us to be the Supreme Monarchist Council, as directors. We're supposed to restore monarchy to the Romanov house. I'm the delegate sent by National Socialist Party of Germany, the Nazi party. In a few minutes, we'll hear speeches from leaders."

<>

Michael Sayers and Alfred Kahn, two San Francisco investigative journalists, researched this meeting ...the historical beginning of the Cold War. Though, most people in my Administration thought the Cold War begin in the late 1940s, it actually began a generation or two, earlier: "June 1921, a group of former Czarist officers, industrialists, and aristocrats called an international Anti-Soviet Conference at the Reichenhalle, in Bavaria. The conference, attended by representatives from anti-Soviet organizations thru-out Europe, drew up plans for a world-wide campaign of agitation, against Soviet Russia. A Supreme Monarchist Council was elected by the conference. Its function was to work for the restoration of the monarchy, headed by the lawful sovereign of the Romanov house, in accordance with the fundamental laws of the Russian Empire."

The Cold War had begun. There would be no redistribtion of wealth allowed to taxpayers or laborers in the West, no unions for workers' rights, and no democracy allowed to exist, much less threaten any monarchy.

<>

Dagmara watched with interest Alfred Rosenberg's slender, pale-face, his thin lips, dark hair and weary, brooding expression. "What do you do for fun in this town?"

Alfred like her. "Is that an invitation?"

"Not at all. I'm just curious."

"So am I."

Dagmara was frustrated. "Can't we get past all this flirting? ...and have a conversation?"

"Okay. I go to beer gardens. Since 1919, that's what I do, for fun. You can find me at Augustinerbrau, or Franziskanerbrau. I sit alone, for hours. Look for me at tables in the back in the corners. I'm there, back against the wall. Sometimes, a stranger joins me there, sits with me. I rarely warm up to them. I brighten up a bit, if I feel a spark, I come to life, and speak with them."

"*Hmmm.* What does your family do?"

"We lived in the Baltic til the revolution. My father was a landowner, a large estate near the Czarist port of Reval. Our family dates back to Teutonic Knights, who invaded the Baltic States in the Middle Ages. We are German stock. Before the revolution, in Russia, I studied architecture at Polytechnikum in Moscow. When Bolsheviks seized power, I fled for my life, from Soviet territory. I joined ranks of White Guard terrorists fighting in the Baltics ...under that man, standing over there by the fireplace warming himself, General Count Rudiger von der Goltz.

"In 1919 I came here, to Munich. My mind race with ideas, how to get our family estate back from Bolshevik revolutionaries, get back our family's financial portfolio. I hate democracy, those Jews, their ideas of equality.

"Our underground Czarist Black Hundred pogromist death squads remain faithful to the Czar. They have the right idea. They say, in his heart, every Jew is a Bolshevik wanting democracy! Those damned communists, Socialist Bolshevik Jews stole our family estate by nationalizing, everything.

"I go to beer halls, make speeches to White Guard émigrés, other Baltic barons who had estates stolen, portfolio assets seized ...they listen to me. Prince Avalov-Bermondt meets me, he was General von der Goltz's most brutal White Guard commander, in the Baltics.

"Barons Schneuber-Richter and Arno von Schickedanz, two Baltic aristocrats ...Ivan-Poltavetz-Ostranitza, a Ukrainian pogromist who was Minister of Communications in the Kaiser's puppet Ukrainian government ...many people, come. We meet there, together. These men share my views, how decadent Democracy is. We talk about stopping the damn Jews, and their international conspiracy to bring democracy to the world. I hate the damned Jews, and Soviets, for ruining my family's wealth, making us run for our lives. I hate Democracy. There are thousands like me. We gather from around the world. I talk about world-wide counter-revolution to throw Soviets out, throw Jews out, restore the Czar, preserve Germany's imperial ambitions. Save the world from decadent Jewish democracy, Bolshevism, Communism ...with a race of German supermen, to conquer then, rule the world. We do what Teutonic Knights did, a world-wide, holy crusade. We'll destroy Soviets, pour across Russian frontiers, smash Bolsheviks from west to east, from Rhine to Weichsel, from Moscow to Tomsk, no Jews! No Jews!"

Everyone at the Nazi garden party start chanting. "No Jews! No Jews!"

Dagmara was afraid of what they might do.

<>

Germany was in postwar crisis ...no jobs, ...mass unemployment ...widespread hunger. Rent, impossible to pay. People lived with relatives, in the streets, in parks. Inflation, highest it had ever been ...money bought nothing. While Weimar Republic presented a facade of Democracy, it was secretly co-founded ...by German High Command, an inner circle of Prussian militarists, Junkers, and industrial magnates ...planning rebirth and expansion of Imperial Germany.

Unknown to the world, in a secret research and development laboratory, constructed by the firm of Borsig, in a forest outside Berlin, Germany's future rearmament program was milestoned and mapped out, by hundreds of engineers, draftsmen and special technicians ... working under German High Command supervision.

German Military Intelligence, Section 111B, was not disbanded after the war, as thought. Military Intelligence, Section 111B, was reorganized, here ...by Borig, Krupp, Hugenberg, and Thyssen.

Anti-Semitic, Colonel Walther Nicolai was Chief of German Military Intelligence, Section 111B. Walther was strategically planning the next phase of Germany's century-long war. From feudal Czarism and reborn Twentieth-Century German Imperialism, Nazism took form ...in offices of German Military Intelligence.

Arnold Rechberg, a major ruling family financial contributor to the underground campaign to revive German Imperialism ...his, was an industrialist ruling family owning the great German potash cartel ...potash was an expensive ingredient of explosives, gunpowder, and fuel. Arnold was former personal adjutant of the Crown Prince, close friend to members of the old Imperial High Command. Arnold co-financed the secret leagues German Nationalist League, and German Anti-Semitic League.

<>

Arnold Rechberg walked over to Alfred Rosenberg, "Yes. No Jews. Arnold Rechberg, I finance this association, provide funds to buy brown shirts everyone wears, uniforms, pay other expenses of the Party. Listen, me and a few friends bought a small, weekly newspaper, *Volkischer Beobachter Racial Observer*. It's a gossip tabloid. Major General Franz von Epp, Commander of Bavarian Infantry Troops, helped us raise funds to buy it ...at Roehm's request, we gave funds to Dietrich Eckart to buy the paper for the National Socialist Party, the official publication of the Nazi Party. The editorial must be completely redone. I understand you're quite a writer. I want you to be the editor. Will you?"

Rosenberg was thrilled. "Me? Yes! Yes! Thank you!"

Rechberg was pleased. "Allow me to introduce you to our Reichswehr intelligence officer, our Schwarze Reichswehr party leader, Adolf Schickelgruber. Adolf! Come here, Corporal."

Adolf Schickelgruber hurried over. "Yes sir."

"I've taken a liking to Alfred Rosenberg, our new German counter-revolutionary, propaganda writer. I've made him editor of our newspaper."

Adolf Schickelgruber smiled and spoke with indifference. "A toast to success."

Alfred Rosenberg, Adolf Schickelgruber, and Arnold Rechberg clinked champagne glasses.

Alfred toasted them. "To success. Let me tell you, my first editorial ...When time comes, the storm brews over the eastern marches of Germany, we will collect a hundred thousand men ...prepared to sacrifice their lives.

"Those, determined to dare all, must be prepared for the Western Jews, who will raise woeful voices when Eastern Jews are attacked. What is certain. is the Russian army will be driven back, across its frontiers after a second Tannenberg. That is a German affair, the real beginning of our reconstruction."

General Max Hoffmann walked closer to hear Rosenberg speak. "Excellent. And, who are you?"

Rechberg spoke up. "He's Alfred Rosenberg. I've made him editor. He'll provide political ideology for the Nazi party. Alfred ...General Max Hoffman. Max provides military strategy. I provide financial strategy. Herr Schickelgruber, cosmetics. An unstoppable team."

Alfred smiled automatically. "How do you do? Join us, in a toast to success."

General Hoffmann raised his champagne glass. "Allow me. To the Reich! ...I spent my youth in Russia. I was attaché, at the court of the Czar. In 1905, at 35, Captain on General von Schlieffen's Staff ...German liaison officer with First Japanese Army in the Russo-Japanese war, 1904-1905. I can't forget what I saw on the Manchurian plains. There, stretched in front of me, a military front from horizon to horizon. I watched the Japanese military machine cut through a huge Russian army, that could not defend itself ...clumsy ...leaders inept. During the World War, I was appointed Chief of Operations of Eighth German Army, stationed in East Prussia. We anticipated the Russian attack. Reinhard Gehlen's been appointed to help me oversee intelligence on the eastern front. Where is he?"

Dagmara Wilpf smiled. "He's indisposed."

President & Nancy Reagan with Ray Charles after acceptance speech at Republican National Convention; Dallas, Texas. 8/23/84

A smile passed quickly over General Hoffmann's lips. "I see. Who is this charming lady, who danced beautifully?"

"Dagmara Wilpf. I came with Reinhard Gehlen tonight."

Alfred frowned. "His fiancee, I'm afraid."

General Hoffman stared at him in amazement, "It didn't take you long to find that out."

Dagmara meets Adolf Schickelgruber

"No, it didn't. Being an intelligence officer, nothing takes me long to find out, does it? Herr Schickelgruber, this is our ballerina, Dagmara Wilpf."

Adolf clicked together his heels, "You dance beautifully, you are beautiful. My pleasure."

Adolf took Dagmara's hand in his. Adolf kissed Dagmara's hand. Dagmara felt her cheeks warmly blushing. Adolf smiled. "You're blushing, my dear."

Alfred Rosenberg felt thrilled to watch her. "Isn't she charming?"

General Hoffman's eyes scanned the room. "Yes. And, where's Reinhard? I want him to hear my speech."

Dagmara was blushing from all the attention, "I'm sure he'll be here soon."

<>

General Hoffman addressed the party. "In the last war, I commanded German forces on the Eastern Front. I watched the Imperial Russian Army collapse. I dictated Germany's peace terms to the Soviet delegation, at Brest-Litovsk. In two wars, I've seen the Russian Army in action, defeated twice. It was pitiful. The new, revolutionary Red army, is the same losers.

"At Paris Peace Conference, I presented my plan to march again, on Moscow. Led by Germany, to save Europe from Bolshevism! I wanted to prevent the Allies from dismantling our German Imperial Army. I told the Allies, what they wanted to hear. Marshal Foch, our puppet governor in Paris, agreed with me. I told the Paris Peace Conference, Bolshevism is the greatest danger in the world to threaten Europe for the last three hundred years!

"British Ambassador Lord D'Abernon asked me if France, Germany, and England could be on the same side ... to attack Russia, together. I told him, it has to be that way. It's the only way. It must be. Nothing can go right in the world, until the civilized Christian powers of the West unify ...to hang the Soviet government from a tree.

"Only the Christian West can do this.

"France, Italy, England, and Poland must join Germany to defeat Soviet Russia. We must concentrate new armies on the Vistula, and the Dvina ...in Napoleon's style, a lightning march, but, under German command, drive back retreating Bolshevik hordes ...occupy Leningrad, and Moscow in a few weeks. Then, a final clean-up of the country, down to the Urals. By conquering Russia, half a continent, Germany will bring salvation to civilization.

"I presented this plan to General Staffs all over Europe. Marshal Foch, and his chief of Staff Petain, my close friends, continue lobbying it with me. Franz von Papen, General Baron Karl von Mannerheim, even Admiral Horthy and the British Director of Naval Intelligence, Admiral Sir Barry Domville. We're all together, on this one.

"German General Staff and German High Command approve, even though it's a radical departure from Bismarck's all-German military and political strategy. Germany must incorporate armies of other countries, under its command," General Hoffman sipped his wine. "Even General Hans von Seeckt stopped preaching a war of revenge against our former enemies. He wants to conquer Russia, by capturing and using Russia's own raw materials and manpower, against Russia. I told him, now we have to say one thing, and do another. He told me, he's becoming a Nazi, too. It's time for Roehm to introduce Hitler."

Roehm looked over the Nazi garden party gathering. Roehm started speaking, "Losing the last war is an intermission, in our century-long march, to war. We are at armed intermission. German Army's arsenal is scattered over Germany. Allies ordered it collected and destroyed. No! Colonel von Epp wants me to collect these arms, starting in Bavaria, to arm our Schwarze Reichwehr! Military Intelligence persuaded Allied officers our old armored cars, and rust-coated machine guns. are no good for a real war. But, they are perfect to combat the world communist revolution moving towards the Rhine, through Germany. It's my responsibility to guide the Fehme. We need weapons, armored vehicles.

"We'll collect guns, and vehicles, hide them in Bavaria. We have 100,000 men in our underground army, The Citizen's Defense League. You, and I, are the center of the underground ...the brain in the machine. I list the targets. I send out the Fehme. Smaller Freikorps terrorist groups spring-up like weeds. Keep changing names of your groups, names of your leaders ...be invisible. Look like we have nothing to do with the Reichswehr.

"We are Black Reichswehr. Here, to change the German Workers' Party from a social club in biergarten backrooms, into the National Socialist German Workers Party, the Nazi Party ...a Schwarze Reichwehr party, of underground soldiers ...run by German Military Intelligence. German Workers Party, will have no workers in it ...no laborers dreaming of fair wages, of democracy. I don't want to recruit German workers ...this is a political party of soldiers. This is my destiny.

"I ordered you here, tonight, to join our Party. Tonight, the transformation begins. Tonight, the National Socialist German Workers Party becomes a troop of soldiers! Schwarze Reichwehr companies march tonight, through the streets in civilian clothes, for the first time, National Socialists. I introduce to you, to speak now, at this historical first meeting, Adolf Hitler, followed by a reception. Then, we'll take to the streets!" Roehm saluted the crowd.

<>

In 1920, Nazi Hermann Rausching wrote *Voice of Destruction.* Rausching wrote, Hitler will follow a war strategy Carl von Clauswitz incorporates into German policy, a military strategy of systematic de-population ...of certain European geographies, with rich gold, mineral, and timber resources. So, Hitler looked for a strategy, a military tactic to accomplish this. For the next twenty years, German General Staff conducted scientific studies of techniques to completely destroy, or permanently cripple, enemy nations. Under General Staff supervision, military experts, and specialists in medicine, psychology, economics, and sociology detailed programs to systematically undermine physical, cultural, economic, spiritual, and political life, and culture of enemy nations. This strategy became known, as, 'destabilization'.

Adolf Schickelgruber
on science of depopulation

Hitler took the speaker's platform.

"Thank you Herr Roehm ... Tonight as you see, I'm surrounded by supporters wearing hidden sidearms, against the orders of the occupying Allied Armies stationed here in Germany! Workers! ... tonight join us or leave! We're working for higher good, not for wages to save ourselves, but to save Germany! We're soldiers dedicated to save Germany! Any one who interrupts me with catcalls or jeering will find themselves flat out in the street flat with broken bones and a blood covered face. I'm warning you! ... if you don't agree with National Socialist German Workers Party Nazi philosophy leave now! Leave quietly! Don't make us help you!

If anyone dares, speak up against our program! You Jews, you under-races of mixed blood, you disgraced Germany by not fighting to kill the Jewish dictators that ran Munich's Soviet period!

"Ruling family industrialists and financial capitalists may hesitate to support a party, calling itself, 'Socialist' ...we are not socialists!

"Different cultures block our way. Whole civilizations are against us. We need the least-expensive techniques to de-populate foreign cultures. We must remove entire racial units. When I can send the flower of German youth into the hell of war without pity for spilling German blood, I have the right to remove inferior human races! We must dam the fertility of our enemies. Separate their men and women. Consciously cause undesirable races to die out. The fabric of enemy nations must be rotted. Destroy enemies' health, their economy, their political structure, their railroads, their culture, their symbols of security. Terrorize them, kidnap them, torture them, wreck the country's psychological morale. Destroy their will. That's how to do it.

"We must control the minds of our subject populations, how they think, how they act. We must control money, the means of creating and holding wealth, and exchange. We must control law, carry out the will of the state. We must control history, what people believe happened in the past.

"We must control psychological warfare, control what people think what they say. We must control subject populations with death, terror, and mind control. We will be masters!

"The World Order will rule the world! Americans believe the State exists to serve the individual. That's wrong! Democracy is counter-revolutionary. The individual exists to serve the State! War teaches us, individual rights mean nothing.

"Rights of the individual must be sacrificed for the World Order! The individual can find freedom in blind obedience to the World Order! God guarantees us!"

Reinhard Gehlen touched Dagmara's left arm, as Alfred touched her right. They all felt scared, not only for themselves but for the future of Germany.

Alfred, Reinhard & Dagmara

Reinhard kissed Dagmara on the cheek. "You see? What I said about Hitler and Schwarze Reichwehr, is true."

Dagmara was frightened by the energy in the crowd. "I had to see it with my own eyes, to believe it."

Alfred felt jealous of Reinhard. "One must see it, to believe it."

Dagmara saw Alfred's mood. She wondered about it, but changed the subject. "How ironic, I'm going to Moscow to study ballet. How can they have the best dance school in the world, in worst country in the world?"

"They're simply misguided."

Alfred overheard. "Going to Moscow? I go there, often. Will let me show you around."

Dagmara smiled. "Perhaps, we might go together, you be my bodyguard."

Alfred smiled back. "That's your fiancée's job."

"He's not free from work."

Reinhard frowned. "It's true, I may be sent to America, on business."

Dagmara smiled. "Then, for me to be safe, I'm sure you'd want me escorted by a German Schwarze Reichwehr officer."

"Of course."

Alfred watched Dagmara. "In Russia, we're ordinary businessmen. You don't say Schwarze Reichwehr, or, German officer ...in public. You'd be arrested, tortured, and forced to turn us in, we'll kill you, if you mention us."

"Don't be melodramatic. I understand, Alfred. Reinhard will give you my address. You give him, yours. Stay in touch."

Alfred sat down. "Reinhard, is that agreeable?"

Reinhard shrugged. "I'd rather be there, with Dagmara. I can't, so you protect her, escort her. It's time to take to the streets, for the unification march!"

The garden party gathering marched, cheering, out into the streets.

<> <> <>
July 1918, Flashback on ship, in fog

July 1918, Dagmara tried holding onto the steel rail. It was cold. It stung her hands. She leaned her body against the rail, to balance. The ship lumbered ahead slowly in the fog. She could see fifty yards off starboard, before foggy soft whiteness filled everything. Dagmara had left Russia, gone to Finland. Then, boarded a ship to England. She hoped to Germany, to Reinhard. So much had happened. Dagmara was no longer the young woman who left Germany, for Russia, to study with Bolshoi Ballet. Dagmara wanted to write Reinhard a letter to explain. But, she was afraid to put anything in writing. She talked to Reinhard in her head, as if writing him. She was afraid how he'd receive her, when she saw him. She had strange feelings, about him. She denied those feelings, in the past. The fog closed-in around the ship, rolled over the railings, around her ...like coldness around her emotionally. She

didn't know what to do about the emotional numbness. She heard Ambassador David Francis walking to her, dragging his foot in a slight limp, as he walked. She turned. Ambassador David Francis stood at the rail, beside her.

Ambassador Francis smiled. "I'm happy we're out of Russia, Darling. My wife will be meeting me at the ship, in England. She and I will make the sail back home to the United States. Perhaps, you and I can meet again someday."

"That won't be necessary."

"That's how you feel?"

"It was a job, nothing more."

"My job, too."

Dagmara was sad. "That's that."

Ambassador Francis stared into the fog. "I've used the ship's phone, called our Petrograd papers. I'm publishing an editorial, urging the Russian people to overthrow the Soviet government. Chicherin, the new Soviet Commissar of Foreign Affairs, sent me a telegram, extending greetings from the Soviet government to the American people. He wrote it for American pacifists. I'm afraid, if I give it to State Department, they may publish it, in a newspaper. I'm ripping it up, tossing it over the rail."

Dagmara watch Ambassador Francis tear the telegram up into little pieces, toss them over the rail. They disappeared, into the fog.

Dagmara felt the ship surge forward. She listened to the hull cut through the water. In her head, Dagmara narrated her letter, to Reinhard.

Eastern Front, desperate, Nicolas II abdicates to provisional government

Midsummer 1917, situation on the Eastern Front, desperate. Russian Army lacks leadership, is poorly equipped. Kaiser's Imperial German Army cuts it to pieces. Weakened by war, and corruption, the Czar's feudal regime collapses. March, Czar Nicolas II abdicates his throne. Provisional Government takes over Russia. Russian revolutionaries celebrate in the streets, and countryside, yelling, "Peace, Bread, and Land!"

<>

By 1917, the Russian Army lost more soldiers than Great Britain, France and Italy combined. Russian Army losses: 2,762,000 killed, 4,950,000 wounded, 2,500,000 missing.

Russian Revolution didn't stop after Czar was overthrown. People were poor, hungry, homeless ...military deserters marched in protests, demanding an end to war. The Russian Army start breaking up. Starving soldiers deserted in tens of thousands. Soldiers in ragged uniforms roamed through villages, towns and cities.

Far from war front battles, deserting soldiers joined revolutionary workers and peasants ...formed 'revolutionary governing committees' or, called 'soviets' ...that practiced democracy ...elected deputies to represent them.

Riots for food happened every day. Lenin's Bolshevik Party of Russian Communists was declared illegal, by Kerensky ...the Bolshevik Party went underground.

For centuries, the Russian people had no freedom ...no free speech ...no rights to assembly ...they lived in a feudal society, with no civil rights ...they were owned, along with the cattle, as part of property rights transferred in real estate transactions. Boy children were unwillingly conscripted into battle, while very young.

Now, since 'revolution', everyone had opinions. There were meetings in public, everywhere, attended by Anarchists, Mensheviks, Bolsheviks, prowest propaganda agents, Social Revolutionaries ...everyone got together in meeting halls, talking at the same time. Workers, peasants, and soldiers were drawn to Bolshevik speakers.

A Russian soldier spoke up. "What I am fighting for? Is it for Constantinople, or a free Russia? Is it for Democracy, or for capitalist plunderers. If you prove to me, I'm defending the Revolution ," said the soldier, "...I'll go out and fight without being threatened by the death penalty, if I don't ...when land belongs to peasants, factories belong to workers, and soviets run the government ...then, I'll have something to fight for!"

In 1917-1918 ...the Revolutionary Period ...Petrograd is besieged by opposing counter-revolutionary groups. There's no food ...no heat ...no transportation ...streets are piled with garbage, and sewage ...people shiver in breadlines. Gunfire ends many arguments, organized crime, and unorganized gangs, fight the soviets, robbing, terrifying them.

Some organized crime gangs called themselves, 'anarchists' ...financed by German Military Intelligence. They are paid agents provocateur, trained to provoke riots and social disorder ...using them, the German military can call itself in ...to restore 'law and order'.

Workers, arming themselves, go from building to building, searching for terrorists, looters, and stolen food. Revolutionary Russia is chaos.

The Soviet government hasn't established order. Newspapers say, the Soviet regime would soon fall. Czarist luxury leftovers ...expensive restaurants ...hotels ...stay open, serving well-dressed patrons ... in contrast to stark poverty, and riots, outside.

<>

Studying with dance instructors of the Bolshoi ballet, Dagmara lived on dividends her family portfolio earned. She enjoyed diplomatic social life in Petrograd, capital of former, Czarist Russia. At night, cabarets are packed with people partying, drinking, dancing ...Czarist officers, ballet dancers, black marketers.

Dagmara hears rumors everywhere. 'The Germans are marching on Moscow. Trotsky arrested Lenin. Lenin's gone insane.'

The newborn soviet government struggles to bring order to Russia ...there are opposing counter-revolutionary plots, everywhere.

Lenin led the Bolsheviks, "The bourgeoisie and landlords, the wealthy classes, try to ruin our revolution." Lenin sets up a Soviet counter-sabotage and counter-espionage intelligence organization ...to fight destabilization attempts, calling it, 'Extraordinary Commission To Combat Counter-Revolution & Sabotage' ...or, 'Cheka'.

Revolutionaries are called, 'Red' forces.

'White' forces are those against the revolutionaries. White forces were people the Czar did business with ...who made money, as a result of knowing the Czar ...people with status, wealth, luxury ...the Blue Book of Russia ...the ruling families thriving on a spoils system of pirating natural resources, and labor, in a whole system controlled by the Czar ...in the centuries old feudal social system.

'White Russian' refers to those who fought to keep, or restore, Czarist dictatorship and oligarchy, (except people in Byelorussia, also called 'White Russians' ...because they dressed in white coats, shirts, and pants).

<>

Dagmara's friend, Natalie, was also a dancer training at the Bolshoi academy dance school. Natalie felt sorry for Russian people. Dagmara agreed. But, what could Dagmara do? Natalie and Dagmara worked out at the dance studio.

Natalie rested.

So did Dagmara. "What a workout today! I'm exhausted."

Natalie was, too. But felt there was something else. "Is that all? ...you look sad."

"End of the month, full moon."

"I don't see how Russian people will make it ...do you? Kaiser's destroying thousands of people every day. Every minute, hundreds die ...hundreds more to come. I can't handle it." Natalie started to cry. "Czar Nicolas' army ...ruined. I'll be ruined. What am *I* supposed to do? My maid's boyfriend is hooked-up with Lenin's underground, Bolshevik party. I heard her whispering out the window this morning. Can you imagine that, in my house? In my heart, I can't blame the Russian people. They're starving, homeless, sick, wounded. What's a girl to do?"

Dagmara tossed Natalie a towel. "Dry your sweat, so you don't catch cold. Poor people are everywhere ...starving ...begging ...using streets for bathrooms. If I give my money away to beggars, I'll have none left ...I'll be a beggar, too! Does that help? It's hard being wealthy, that way. All these people, begging. I wish they'd go away. It troubles my heart, my feelings. If I deny my feelings, they go away. But then, years go by, fast ...down the drain."

Natalie wanted nothing to do with them, either. "I hope the beggars go away. I won't give my money away, to some stupid revolution. It's mine, not theirs."

"I'm here at Bolshoi dance academy now several months. It adds up. War cut my portfolio in half." Dagmara leapt into the air.

So did Natalie. "I know. There's no profit in feeling sorry for workers, and peasants."

"I know ...no ballet classes ...no French champagne ...no caviar ...no ballroom parties ...no theatre ...no debutante parties. I don't see how they do it," Dagmara watched herself perform in the wall-sized mirror. We must save civilization, and culture. Or, go back to being savages."

"Dagmara, is it safe for you in Russia? ...you're German."

"Natalie, my father's half-Russian. I'm half-safe." She laughed.

"You're half-crazy. If we could get Kaiser and the Czar to fight it out, in a duel ...one on one, give soldiers a vacation ...keep everyone from being slaughtered."

Dagmara boasted. "Kaiser and the Czar aren't mad at each other. The British and French aren't mad at them."

Natalie batted her eyelashes. "What do you mean?"

"Everyone's married to everyone else, the ruling families are cousins, the French, the Germans, the British, the Russians, the Americans ...everyone's all married into each other's families ...related."

Natalie eyes opened wide. "Then, what are they fighting for? ...fashion?"

"The Baku oil fields, forests, coal, and labor."

"...And, pretty women like me."

Dagmara smiled. "Me, too ...war means starva-tion, bodies, blood ...villages burning in moonlight ...men, women. children all chopped up I'm a simple, rich girl ...there's nothing *I* want from revolution, but everyone to leave me, alone."

Dagmara looked out the doorway, down the hall. Young women and young men sat on hardwood floors, lacing dance slippers, tights pulled up, stretched over their knees, to their torsos ...sweaters thrown over their shoulders ...hair in pony tails, or thick braids, pinned up. Several rooms off the main hall had different instructors and classes ...different music ... dancers rehearsed, danced, faces intent on the dance, running across the floors of the rooms, in waves.

Suddenly, Alfred Rosenberg stood in the doorway. "Hi Dagmara."

"Hi Alfred, enjoy watching?"

"Watching you, sweetheart."

"Um hmm."

Alfred went with Dagmara to the dressing rooms, over to her make-up table, put papers in her purse. One fell to the floor. She didn't notice. Alfred walked to her, gave her a kiss on the cheek. Then, picked up the paper, looked at it. "Here, dropped this."

"Oh. Thanks. How's your day at the office?"

"Okay. I've ordered lunch in. We've guests coming."

"Here? ...to my dressing room?"

"Yes. Can we talk, privately?"

Dagmara looked at Natalie. "Natalie, can you possibly go work-out, while Alfred and I talk, privately?"

Natalie smiled. "Fill me in on gossip, when I come back."

Dagmara smiled. "Thanks."

Natalie danced out the room. Dagmara watched, in the mirrors lining the walls. The hall was lined with mirrors, too. Dagmara looked into Alfred's eyes. *"S'up?"*

"Dagmara, it's dangerous to have your notes lying on the floor, addressed to Reinhard. He's a German intelligence officer. He coordinates spying, here. We're here, on diplomatic status, with fake passports."

"I need false papers, to get ballet lessons. I'm grateful you got them, for me."

"How long have you sent messages to Reinhard?"

"The whole time, I've been here. I fill him in ...reports on Russian war status ...Bolshevik status ...what British and French ambassadors eat ...the weather."

"If you're caught, you'll be prosecuted as a German spy."

"Why are you whispering?" Dagmara wasn't concerned, "...the door's closed."

Alfred moved closer to her. "Dagmara, don't pass information to Reinhard. I'm his boss, he sends them to me."

"Reinhard sends you *my* messages?"

"Yes. You think I sponsor just you in the Bolshoi? I co-ordinate hundreds of operatives on the Eastern Front. Reinhard co-ordinates them, too. We work together. The way to stop the war, is for Germany to win. Then, colonize Russia. If you want the war to end, forget Reinhard. Work directly under me." He kissed her.

Dagmara laughed. "How directly?"

"Dagmara, we're not *spies,* we're *diplomats.* Stop sending messages out of Russia, to Germany. Take the heat off you."

"I like being in heat."

"Is that why women are good spies. Men seem leak info to them all the time."

"Alfred, I'm not worried about men opening up to me, I worry about me, opening up, to them."

"Dagmara, don't go there. I'm your handler."

"You won't be handling me, at all."

"Your intelligence handler, give you assignments, manage you. Then, you report back to me. Keep your ears open. Keep people talking to you, that's all. And, dance the ballet, dance the dance."

"Yes, darling. My heart's set, on auditioning for the Bolshoi".

"Good."

"Do I do anything, bad?"

"Don't get compromised, turned."

"Compromised? Turned?"

"Forced to switch sides ...forced to be a double-agent ...or a triple, by blackmail ...or, extortion. It happens. There's two British intelligence agents ...Lockhart, and Reilly," Alfred seemed lost in his words, "...there's two American agents ...Robins, and Francis. Then, there's Trotsky ...he's either a double, or triple agent."

"So?"

"Nothing loosens a man's tongue, like a woman."

"How loose?"

"Depends."

"I'm not sure I like this."

"You're a promising dancer, society wonders about you. People will drop in."

"I didn't come to Russia, to entertain men in my dressing room."

"Of course, you did."

"Well," Dagmara laughed, "it's the least I can do, for Germany."

There was knocking at the door. Dagmara went to answer. Two men stood there. One looked British, gray mustache and sideburns, the cut of his suit, the stiff way about him. The other, looked American ...wore a Brooks Brothers suit from New York, four buttons on each sleeve, friendly looking, smiling.

<>

Dagmara stared out over the sea, into the fog. The rail was cold to touch. Ambassador Francis had left the ship's deck, long ago. Dagmara stood alone. Through the fog, she couldn't see sunset, but felt the changing temperature, noticed the fog getting darker. The ship surged ahead, through the sea. Dagmara continued her mental letter to Reinhard.

That's how it started, Reinhard ...innocently enough, when Alfred Rosenberg, your boss, asked me to help. At the time, it seemed like a game. I'd no idea what lay in store. Robby Robins was an American intelligence agent, Ken Lockhart a British agent. I found, how civilized diplomatic spies are. I enjoyed their company. After our first meeting, Alfred, Robby, and Ken left together. Natalie returned from exercise work-out covered in sweat, quite seductive.

As days went by, Natalie and I became close. She got used to men coming to visit me at our studio. If there was a knock on the door, she'd wink at me, grab a towel, go to the door, let my visitor in, keep walking out through the door. Sometimes three, four, or five of us would go out for lunch, or dinner dancing. We started getting closer. At first, it was fun. Then, one day, a stranger knocked on my door.

"Hello. I'm Ambassador David Francis, meeting Alfred Rosenberg here."

Alfred walked to the door, behind Dagmara. "Put some clothes on over your dance tights, Dagmara ...then, let him in."

"Wait, I wasn't expecting..."

Alfred watched Dagmara dress, then they walked towards the door. "Nice to see you, Ambassador. Dagmara, this is United States Ambassador, David Francis."

David Francis smiled nicely. "Nice to meet you, Dagmara."

Alfred shook his hand to say hello. "He's a banker from Saint Louis, was Governor of Missouri ...wants Russia for himself, and Mr. Hoover."

Dagmara mused, "Do you enjoy Saint Louie?"

Francis enjoyed her. "I better, I run it."

Dagmara laughed. "Do you think you and your Mr. Hoover can have Russia, to yourselves?"

Ambassador Francis smiled. "I see Alfred's filled you in. We're putting Hoover in the Presidency, after we win the war. We'll buy up German industry, for a song, Alfred. The whole war's about who's going to get Russia, and Germany ...isn't that right?"

Alfred was tense. "Russia, France, Belgium, Yugoslavia, Denmark, Africa, South America, China. It's a package deal."

Francis nodded. "Well, you Germans have financed your coup d'etat plot, here ...you deserve credit."

Alfred felt demure. "I didn't plan anything. Pieces fell into my lap."

Francis laughed. "The American Embassy, here, in Petrograd's packed with Czarist generals, and millionaires. We don't know how you Germans pulled your coup d'état off ...making it look like a people's revolution. But, it's out of control ...people taking it seriously. We want the Soviets gone, now. We want the Czar back in power. Hoover, himself, has a billion dollars in co-ownership with the Czar's dynasty ...that's going down the drain ...until we kick the soviets out."

Alfred had heard it all, before. "You the only game in town?"

"I want Russian upheaval, over," Francis said. "It's time to end this war ...to negotiate diplomatic peace with Germany. I'm not impressed by Kerensky, running the Russian Provisional Government. He's in, over his head."

Alfred laughed. "Join the club. I had dinner with Ken Lockhart, last night."

"How's is he? Haven't seen the Brit for days."

"He's fine. Tells me Kerensky's scared, holed-up, in the Czar's Winter Palace. Kerensky's Russian ruling family backers, and his Anglo-French Allies, are planning a counter-coup to double-cross him. Kerensky told Ken, if Kerensky can't get Britain and France to stop the Russian revolution ...they'll call *me* in, to kill him."

Francis tamped a cigarette down on his cigarette case, "I see. Alex Kerensky should have studied the American Revolution, before getting into this pickle. Britannia rules the seas, you know. Let's cut the deck, high card wins, winner take all, negotiations or not."

Alfred smiled. "I like that."

Francis wasn't amused. "Why? You stack that deck, too?"

Dagmara felt tension rising between them, so smiled to sooth it. "Everyone stacked a deck. You diplomats, are jokers up your own sleeves ...trying to pull yourselves out. Too late, game's finished."

Alfred was surprised at her comments.

Frances, too. "Finance counter-revolution?"

Alfred shook his head. "Germany's lost the armed conflict to France and Britain. I need to win diplomatic war, with you ...convince our countries to make peace ...join German and American forces, become new Allies ...work together, to conquer Russia."

Francis studied Alfred's eyes. "Hoover's in love, with his Russian portfolio. You expect to run to him, tell him, be partners with you ...instead of the British?"

"He's gone through Max and Paul Warburg ...you don't know, yet. Kerensky may be Premiere of the Provisional Government, today. Tomorrow, it's history. Kerensky's backers lost patience with Britain and France," Alfred said. "If Kerensky's backers call me in, they'll play into my hand. Ken Lockhart told me, Sir Samuel Hoare, British Chief of Diplomatic Intelligence Service in Russia, talked with Kerensky's backers. Hoare wired Britain, Russia's only solution is a British puppet-dictatorship. Hoare's recommended Admiral Kolchak, the nearest thing to an English gentleman in Russia.

"Hoare wants General Kornilov, Cossack Commander-in-Chief of the Russian Army.

"British and French ruling families are financially backing General Kornilov, for their Russian strong man ...in war against Germany ...for Kornilov to sacrifice Russian soldiers to Germany, on the Eastern Front, to concentrate Allied soldiers on the Western.

"They're using Kornilov, to put down the Revolution here, to protect Anglo-French investments."

Ambassador Francis sighed. "So much for saving American portfolios."

<>

The attempted putsch took place, in the morning, Sept. 8, 1917. General Kornilov ordered twenty thousand troops into action, to march on Petrograd. French and British officers put on Russian military uniforms, and marched with Kornilov's troops ...as military advisers.

Kerensky was shocked. He'd been betrayed. He didn't understand. Yesterday, in London, and Paris, the newspapers were calling him a great leader of Democracy, hero of the Russian masses. Today, Allied French and British military forces staged a counter-revolutionary coup, against him ...facing him with twenty thousand troops. Kerensky sat motionless, lost in indecision.

<>

The Bolshevik-controlled, Petrograd Soviet responded immediately, ordering mobilization of armed workers, joined by revolutionary sailors from the Baltic fleet, and revolutionary soldiers, who'd deserted the Eastern Front.

Bolshevik Petrograd Soviet rushed artillery and machine guns into position, behind hastily-drawn barricades, and barbed-wire fences in the streets of Petrograd.

Workers wearing caps and leather jackets, armed with rifles and hand grenades, patrolled cobblestone streets, alongside Red Guard.

Within four days, General Kornilov was arrested ...by a Soldiers' Soviet, that had secretly formed ...within his own army.

Forty generals of the Czar's old regime, that conspired with General Kornilov, were arrested. Kornilov's army disintegrated. Boris Savinkov, Kerensky's vice-Minister of War, played a part in the counter-coup ...then, fled. Kerensky's Provisional Government crumbled. Soviets, not Kerensky, held power in Petrograd. The failed Putsch back-fired. France and Britain failed to overthrow Bolshevik Soviets, it showed how strong, Soviets are.

Lenin's Bolshevik Party, driven underground, and his Soviet counter-sabotage and counter-espionage intelligencers, had prepared to fight destabilization efforts by White Russians and foreign enemies. 'Extraordinary Commission To Combat Counter-Revolution and Sabotage' ...Cheka, succeeded. They celebrated.

'Power to the people! Power to the soviets! Down with Kerensky's foreign-backed, Provisional Government!'

<>

The ship lolled from side to side, a big wave went beneath. Dagmara gripped the rail. The coldness stung her hand, her skin stuck to the railing.

<>

Nov. 7 1917, Lenin's Bolshevik Party took power in Russia. The Bolshevik Revolution was a most peaceful revolution. Petrograd's conservative newspapers didn't report a revolution happened. People were shopping. Soldiers and sailors walked through the capitol. Bolsheviks held the State Bank, the telephone exchange, and telegraph office ...the Czar's Winter Palace, Kerensky's fallen Provisional Government headquarters, was surrounded.

Hundreds of Red Guards, and soldiers, gathered in the dark ...around the Winter Palace, moving over barricades, onto palace grounds. Kerensky's Ministers were arrested. Kerensky fled in a car, borrowed from the American Embassy ...flying the American flag.

The Provisional Government was deposed.

Power passed into the hands of the Petrograd Soviet of Workers and Soldiers Deputies' Military Revolutionary Committee ...their cause achieved ...abolition of landlord property rights ...labor control of production ...and, creation of a soviet-run government.

Dagmara answered a knock on her door. "Back so soon?"

Robby smiled. "Dagmara, this is Comrade Lenin. May we come in?"

"Yes."

Robby lit a cigarette. "I didn't think anyone would look for us, here. Lenin's in charge of Russia, now."

Dagmara smiled. "That's wonderful."

Lenin felt unsure, "You're a friend, then."

"Yes."

Robby felt anxious. "Lenin wants a producers' republic. People who work ...will be paid, living wages ...pay rents they can afford ...have lower medical bills ...send their kids to school ...have food to eat."

Dagmara was surprised. She looked at Lenin. "Will Russia be a Democracy?"

"Yes. I'm a dictator with the will of the peasants, workers, and soldiers behind me. No one will be allowed in the soviet who just owns stock, who just has ownership. The soviet producers of Russia's wealth, will run soviet Russia. Donets coal basin ...will be politically represented by producers of coal. The railroad ...will be politically represented by railroad workers. The postal system ...represented by mail carriers."

"Different ethnic groups?" Robby said.

Lenin sighed. "Russia's a melting-pot, like the United States. The Czar abused minorities ...made them slaves ...used anti-Semitic doctrine as a weapon ...used racism to divide and conquer one group, against another. That is done. Each minority in Russia will be emancipated, freed from slavery ...politically represented, given equal rights ...cultural, regional autonomy. Josef Stalin's our Bolshevik authority on nationalism, he'll handle it."

Robby couldn't hold back, any longer. "Will Russia stay in the war, against Germany?"

Lenin smiled. "No. Russia's out. Russia can't fight Germany ...until we have a new army ...a Red Army. Russian industry, and transportation is rotting. It must be re-staffed, re-organized, rebuilt.

"I'm here, because the new, soviet government needs diplomatic recognition ...friendship from ruling families of the United States.

"I know, Hoover is prejudicing Washington

against us ...because we've nationalized foreign, colonial investments in Russia. The Czar made business partners rich. But, he made Russian people, poor.

"Tell Washington, in return for American technical aid, the Soviet Government will evacuate all war supplies from the Eastern Front ...so they don't fall into German hands, to be used against them."

Robby smiled absently at Lenin as Robby and Lenin left ...then, Ambassador Francis, Alfred, and another man stopped by.

My flat was popular for spies, in Russia, to meet. There was one meeting, after another.

Alfred was nervous, lately. "Francis, you refuse to recognize soviet government?"

"Yes. State Department's following my advice. I won't communicate with the Bolshevik government."

Alfred had vision. "What about America and Germany, becoming Allies? ...joining together, to conquer Russia, divide her between us?"

Frances didn't know. "Bigger worries."

Alfred knew. "I've seen the newspaper. How'd it happen?"

Francis was in despair. "I don't know, a mole ...double-agent."

Albert yawned "Or triple. They change sides, quickly ...the highest bidder, wins. You on your own, on this one, were you?"

"Of course, not. State Department's with me . I sent State my report what the Ataman of the Don Cossacks, General Alexi Kaledin, is up to. He's Cossack Commander-in-Chief of 200,000 soldiers. We backed him, financially ...to put together White counter-revolutionary army units among Cossacks, in Southern Russia.

"We paid him, enough to proclaim independence of the Don. He prepared to march on Moscow, to topple the Soviet government. We had Czarist officers underground, in Petrograd in Moscow, spying on soviets ...sharing intelligence with me, and Kaledin. *I don't know* how it got in the newspapers. It's too late, now."

"Alfred, you know as much as Francis," Dagmara said.

Alfred smiled, looking at Francis. "Some of your men ...double-agents, work for me. Did State Secretary Lansing support Kaledin's putsch? Or, you did it with private, venture capital funding?"

"Public funds are cheaper than private. They're free. Taxpayers are in a fog, reading that Kaledin, and his army were on track. The loan ...was secret, fronted through British or French government entities. We didn't want Bolsheviks to fol-

low our money trail, know America financed, and directed, Kaledin's putsch. Now, soviets denounce me in the press," Frances remorsed. "I hope you're not the leak."

Dagmara was shocked. "I don't know where the leak's from."

<>

The soviet government was surrounded by hostility ...from the Allies ...and, from the German war machine. Germany was an immediate threat. To save Russia, and get time to outfit the soviet Russian government, and raise a Red Army ...Lenin proposed peace with Germany, on the Eastern Front.

Secret meetings continued in my dressing room. One day, Alfred brought along a new face, Leon Trotsky. He paced around the room.

Trotsky looked at Alfred. "Lenin says, as if fighting Germany's not bad enough, we're surrounded, and attacked by Allies, too. He says, we're too weak to face the German war machine, alone ...we have to protect ourselves, the best we can. We must sign a peace treaty with you, on the Eastern Front, now.

"If we wait, and your German ruling families advance their armies ...we'll have a bad agreement, to sign. Then, peace terms will be worse. Lenin put me in charge of a Soviet peace delegation, sent me to Brest-Litovsk, headquarters of your German Eastern Army ...to find out Germany's peace terms.

"Lenin gave me detailed instructions, sign a peace. But, we discussed, beforehand, to get an extra bonus from you I was not to sign ...I took your press releases to newspapers, gave your speeches to upset the European working class. I said, 'Rise-up ...overthrow your governments'.

"I was quoted, the soviet Government will not make peace with the German, capitalist regime. 'Neither peace nor war!' I said ...that's what I said. It makes no sense, I know. At Brest-Litovsk, I told the Germans, the Russian Army can't fight anymore ...we'd de-mobilize, but, not make peace.

"When I got back, Lenin called me a lunatic ...as you predicted ...that, me saying Russia wouldn't fight or make peace ...but would demobilize the army, anyway ... was insane. He said, it was my fault peace negotiations fell through. He said, I played into German hands, helped German imperialists ...I know that was your plan ... I told him, Germans won't dare to advance! ...Give me my bonus!"

Alfred handed over several bags of gold coins. "Does Lenin suspect you?"

Trotsky spilled the bags open onto the couch.

He began counting the coins. "Who knows what anyone thinks?"

"You're a fine agent provocateur, Trotsky ... I'll give you that. German High Command doesn't want to deal with Bolsheviks. General Max Hoffmann put his boot on the conference table in the middle of negotiations, told you, go home."

"Alfred, I've done my best to split the Bolshevik Party, so we can establish a new Russian government, with me running it."

Alfred produced more gold coins. "Trotsky, here's your monthly payment from the Nazi treasury. You did well. I wonder, what are Brits and Frogs up to?"

Trotsky was amused. "They pay me money, too."

"Go to the highest bidder, do you?"

"As long as Lenin's gone, and I rule Russia. I don't care who puts me there. The day after the first session of Brest-Litovsk, I met Lockhart and the French Ambassador, in Paris. We agreed to cut up Russia between Britain, and France, L'Accord Francais-Anglais du 23 Dec., 1917, Definisant Les Zones d'action Francaises et Anglaises. After a coup, or counter-coup, British ruling families will have influence in Russia ...get Caucasus oil ...control Baltic provinces. French ruling families will get iron and coal of Donets Basin, and, control the Crimea."

"Well, that settles the foreign policy of Britain and France, as far as Russia's concerned."

Trotsky stopped pacing. "Lockhart's been told, by British Diplomatic Intelligence Service, to break me and Lenin apart, to give the British an edge."

Alfred fears for the worst. "It's ten days since breaking-off peace negotiations, at Brest-Litovsk. German High Command is launching a major offensive along the Eastern Front, from the Baltic to the Black Sea. The Russian Army's falling to pieces. It looks like a new Russia ...your Russia, Trotsky ...a German Russia ...will arrive."

<>

Bolshevik leaders mobilized workers, and Red Guards, in regiments to stop the German advance at Pskov, Feb. 23, 1918 ...the Germans were stopped, that date, the Red Army was born.

A second peace conference was held, at Brest-Litovsk. Germany demanded Ukraine, Finland, Poland, Caucasus, Russian gold, wheat, oil, coal, and minerals. Lenin called it, 'a robber's peace', German ruling families extorted peace, cut up Russia, to destroy the soviet regime.

<>

We met again, in my flat. British agent Ken Lockhart rubbed his palms together eagerly. Ken looked at Alfred. "British Foreign Office wants me to use agent provocateurs, split apart the Bolshevik party ...because Trotsky, wants Lenin out of the picture. I thought, it was best for British interests in Russia to cut a deal with Trotsky, against Lenin. So, I did.

"Trotsky and his Trotskyites say, Lenin's peace with Germany betrayed the Russian revolution. Trotsky's started a holy war bloc, inside the Bolshevik Party, going after Allied financing. It's working. He wants to force Lenin, out."

Alfred felt Ken Lockhart out, "What do you think of Trotsky?"

"I bet on Trotsky and lost. Trotsky will die for Russia, if he has an audience. I'd finance a counter-coup, use Trotsky to replace Lenin. But, Trotsky doesn't have what it takes. He's an organizer, a brave, obsessive-compulsive. Morally, Trotsky pales against Lenin. The Council of Commissars sees Trotsky as equal ...but, sees Lenin as half-god. They accept Lenin's decisions, carte blanche. If Britain gets its way in Russia, I'll use Lenin. Robby Robins feels that way, too. Robby calls Trotsky, a walking question mark. What's he going to do? And, for who? ...for his vanity, give the man a mirror, he's happy as a bird."

Alfred laughed. "That's Trotsky."

Ken was frustrated. "My intelligence moles say, in Spring 1918, if Russians don't ratify the final version of Brest-Litovsk Peace Treaty, Germany will overthrow the soviet government with military force.

"Britain and France back counter-revolution forces, assembling in Archangel, Murmansk and, the Don.

"Japanese, with Allied approval plan to take Vladivostok, then invade Siberia.

"Lenin told me, he'll transfer the soviet government to Moscow ...he's afraid Germans will attack Petrograd. Bolsheviks will fight, even if driven back to the Volga, and Urals. They'll fight, on their terms, not cat-and-mouse Germany for the Allies' benefit. Lenin told me to tell you, we can work together ...because Russia needs British help, to fight off Germany's invasion.

"Lenin's convinced, the U.S. government is reactionary, it won't help him, they work with Russian reactionaries, against him. British Foreign Office told me, all I need to take Russia for Britain ... is a military expert, and British officers to lead loyal Russians, to end this Bolshevik business. *That's*, where I am."

Alfred nodded. "Ambassador Francis says, Washington told him, stay in Russia, long as he can. I said, 'David, if Bolsheviks make peace with Germany, we won't arrest you, you can stay'. He said, 'If I find a Russian group that refuses to recognize Bolshevik government, I'll get them coup financing, and terrorist training, to carry off a putsch, or counter-coup'.

"Washington told Robby Robins, have Lenin write a list of questions they can answer ...what if Russian Soviet Congress won't ratify a peace treaty with Germany? ...what if Germany breaks the peace treaty, they sign? ...what if Germans continue invading Russia? ...Lenin wants to know, can he rely on American, British, and French support ...if Germany continues invading Russia? ...what help can he get? ...military equipment? ...supplies? ...food? ...on what terms? ...how will U.S. help him fight off Germany? ... I tell you, Robins' optimism has its limits."

Ken was enthusiastic. "So, I see. I telegrammed British Foreign Office, begged them, formally recognize Lenin's soviet government. Told them, there's a chance for Britain to win Russia, because Germany demands unreasonable peace terms ...if his Majesty's government doesn't want Germany to take over Russia, then, his Majesty must accept Lenin."

Alfred held his breath. "What did they say?"

Ken frowned. "They never answered ...what I got back was a cable from my wife. She warned me, watch my step because rumors in the British Foreign Office say, I've become a Red sympathizer.

"For God's sake! ...everybody knows the British Monarchy has blood ties to the Romanovs, the Romanovs have blood ties to the Kaiser. Behind-the-scenes, Russo-Asiatic Consolidated, Ruskombank, International Barnsdall, Warburg, Rothschilds, Harriman, Schroder, and Dulles already negotiated settlement with Hugenberg, Kirdorf, Krupp, and Thyssen! I've been hung out, to dry."

Alfred shook his head at Ken, "That's the hard way."

On Mar. 14, the All-Russian Soviet Congress convened in Moscow. For two days and nights, delegates debated to ratify the treaty of Brest-Litovsk, or not.

<>

Another time, Robbie Robins and Lenin showed up in my flat, when Alfred was there.

Robins was pleased. "Trotsky's opposition is *all that*, on this Peace Treaty ...it's unpopular. Trotsky's sulks in Petrograd, refuses to attend debates."

Len was anxious. "Have you heard from America about the list of questions I sent?"

"No. What's Lockhart heard?"

"Nothing."

Alfred interrupted. "Lockhart has a new boss, Sidney Reilly ...goes by, 'Relinsky'."

Lenin frowned. "There's more foreign intelligence agents in Russia, than Russians. I'm leaving now, to speak for ratification of the treaty. It *will* be ratified. It's catastrophe, for Russia. The soviet government's isolated, threatened from every side ...we need breathing space. With no Allied help ...we can't defend against a German military invasion. The only way for me to save revolutionary Russia, is accept the German treaty."

Lenin left the room, Dagmara shut the door behind him. Alfred looked at Robins. "Francis telegraphed State Department, told them, you and Lockhart want the soviet government recognized. He said, he'll never approve recognition."

Robby nodded. "Secretary Lansing cabled me ...under all circumstances, I am to come home, now, for debriefing."

Alfred was surprised, "Leaving Russia?"

Robby frowned. "I've been ordered to take Trans-Siberian Railroad, pick up a ship at Vladivostok, make no public statements. Alfred, I'm against an Allied intervention of the soviet union. I have a report, by Lenin for State, that outlines how to develop Russian-American commercial relations. State's got me, coming and going. If I slander Bolshevists, your German agents in America spread rumors I'm a Bolshevist. The Russian people need a government they want, whether it suits me and America ...or you, and Germany. I want America to know what's happening here, in Russia. Then, deal with it, honestly, fairly. We can't stop ideas with bayonets, just punctuate them. Russians need a better life, let them have it."

Dagmara felt saddened.

<>

By summer 1918, with America at war with Germany ...not with Russia ...*New York Times* described Bolsheviks as, 'our most malignant enemies ...ravening beasts of prey'.

Soviet leaders were denounced by the American press, as paid agents of the Germans ...referring to Lenin, and his friends, as butchers, assassins, madmen, blood-intoxicated criminals, and human scum. In Congress, Lenin and the Bolsheviks were called, 'damnable beasts'. Alfred arranged a meeting with the new Director of British Secret Intelligence, in Russia, Captain Sidney Reilly.

Alfred felt uncomfortable around Reilly. "Good

afternoon, Captain Reilly."

Reilly was impatient. "How many times do I have to tell you? ...call me, *Relinsky*. If I go down, you going down."

Alfred hesitated. "Good afternoon, Mr. Relinsky."

"Good afternoon."

Alfred stared at Reilly. "British ruling families chose you, to head British Intelligence in Russia ...you have friends here, business investments, you know people in Russian counter-revolutionary movements."

Reilly stared back. "Of course. I handle, finance them ...along with French and American handlers, and central bank block shareholders who hold business monopolies, to preserve the pecking order.

My portfolio is Czarist Russian. I won't hand it over to soviets! Bolsheviks stole my portfolio, when they nationalized my Czarist investments. The sooner I succeed with counter-revolution and counter-coup, the better. Remember, you, Germans are human beings, Bolsheviks aren't."

"We're the master race."

"In the public eye, you're our enemy. But, we can *afford* to lose the war to you, we can *negotiate* with your central investment bankers. But, soviets are the enemy of humanity, they'll destroy civilization and ruin everyone's portfolio by sharing the wealth equally with everyone. They don't want a privately-owned central bank in their proletariat society. I cabled British Secret Service headquarters in London ...I want peace with Germany ...an alliance with Kaiser, *against* Bolsheviks! Their democracy *must* be crushed out! ...before democracy spreads through the British colonial empire ...equality for common workers, soldiers, and soviets ...must end here, now.

"Britain must make peace with Germany ...there's a common enemy, the soviets. We must unite. Rosenberg, help me overthrow the soviet government. Help me, make our countries allies ...together, we'll destroy democracy, we'll destroy soviet Russia. Help me, get my portfolio back."

Alfred smiled, "Good speech. You must have given it, before. I'm starting to like you. First, we copy the Frogs. They financially support Boris Savinkov, his anti-Bolshevik political party ...Savinkov's Social Revolutionary Party. Social Revolutionary Party wants agrarian socialism."

Reilly felt confused, "They support Czarist landowners, control farming and forestry?"

Alfred shrugged. "Of course. But, their propaganda says, they want land for peasants. Savinkov was Kerensky's War Minister ...he directed Kornilov's putsch ...when it failed, Savinkov defect-

ed. Now, Frogs finance Savinkov's Social Revolutionary Party, making it a central party ...against Bolshevism. Savinkov's Social Revolutionary Party uses propaganda, opportunistically. They collected anarchist groups using terrorism against the Czar. Now, with Frog investors, they use those terrorists, against Bolsheviks.

"French Intelligence Service backs Savinkov. French Ambassador Noulens, himself, gave Boris Savinkov money to restore the Social Revolutionary terrorist center, in Moscow. It's renamed, League for the Regeneration of Russia. They want to assassinate Lenin, and all soviet leaders."

Reilly had listened carefully, then spoke. "I'll tell British Secret Service to spend more money training, provisioning, and arming Savinkov ...give him more money, than the Frogs do ...I can hold *that* over Savinkov's head, later.

"I want the Czar's regime back in power. If I could, I'd get rid of Savinkov's people. Savinkov's terrorists are mercenaries. They don't care who they kill. Some of them don't want Savinkov in power, they want Trotsky. I can use mercenary terrorists. I want military dictatorship, here, in Russia ...to restore Czarism. I want my portfolio back. I'm not putting my eggs in one basket, I'll be controlling financial power behind Savinkov, his terrorists, his anti-soviet radicals ...I'm putting together a conspiratorial apparatus of my own, I can count on."

Alfred seemed pleased. "British Intelligence made a good choice, to post you in Russia."

Reilly acknowledged him. "I've strung together a Union of Czarist Officers, and former Ochrana Czarist secret police, Savinkov terrorists, and other counter-revolutionaries ...into one apparat, one database of names. I've installed this apparat in Moscow, and Petrograd. It's in place, functioning."

"My Czarist friends told me."

"Yes, they've joined me."

Alfred's excellent sources informed him. "Count Tchubersky, the naval armaments magnate ...who once hired *you* as an intelligence liaison officer with the German shipyards, he's helping you finance former Czarist General Yudenitch."

"Yes," Reilly said.

"The walls have ears. I offer you Dagmara ...and her Bolshoi dance academy apartment, for your Moscow headquarters."

Sidney Reilly looked at Dagmara.

Dagmara smiled, "It's fine, with me."

Sidney Reilly had won his prize. "I can't pass up a package with Dagmara, thrown in. I'll have people stop by, ...Serge Balkov, a cafe owner ...Grammatikov, a lawyer, former Ochrana undercover agent, my primary contact with the

Social Revolutionary party ...Veneslav Orlovsky, another former Ochrana agent, now infiltrated as a Cheka official, in Petrograd. He got me my forged Cheka passport, with my 'Sidney Georgevitch Relinsky' name on it. I can travel anywhere in soviet Russia, with identification, as a Soviet Cheka intelligencer. I've got agents in the Kremlin, and in Red Army General Staff. I get sealed Red Army orders read in London, before they're opened in Moscow."

Alfred was impressed. "That's really something."

Reilly was looking forward to being alone with Dagmara. "It costs me a fortune, to keep my apparatus humming. I need to hide several million rubles, in Dagmara's apartment. You expect Bruce Lockhart, he'll bring funds from the British Embassy."

"*Bruce?*" Dagmara was suprised, "I thought his name was, Kenneth."

"That's his middle name," Reilly said.

Dagmara laughed. "It's hard keeping names straight. They're always changing them. Just when I know who someone is, he's someone else."

Reilly laughed, too. "Dagmara, the money I hide here, in your apartment, is laundered, it can't be traced. I have hundreds of Russian bankers with hidden stores of rubles, who want to trade them for promissory notes on the Bank of England. I collect rubles through an English firm, in Moscow ...they deal with Russian bankers, fix exchange rates, take rubles, and give Bank of England promissory notes.

"I guarantee notes for amounts drawn against them, in London ...bring rubles to the American Consulate-General, in Russia. He gives them to Hicks, who gives them to Lockhart, who brings them to me, laundered."

Dagmara smiled. "It's not just oil, timber, and gold ...is it? It's Afghani opium, heroin. The Saudis want the oil. But, the British and Americans fight to own Afghani heroin concessions."

<>

The aim of Savinkov's terrorist Social Revolutionaries, was to terrorize Bolsheviks ...create confusion in soviet government ... pave the way for German military attacks.

Social Revolutionaries wanted Germany to destroy Bolshevism. Jun. 21, 1918, Soviet Commissar for Press Affairs Volodarsky left a workers' soviet meeting at Obuchov factory, in Petrograd ...was assassinated by Savinkov's Social Revolutionary terrorists.

July 6, Blumkin, another Savinkov Social Revolutionary terrorist showed false identification papers, identifying him as a Cheka agent at the German Embassy. He said, he'd come to warn the German Ambassador, about a plot to kill the Ambassador. The German Ambassador asked Blumkin, how will they do it?

Blumkin whipped out a pistol. "Like this!" Blumkin said. Blumkin shot the German Ambassador. He jumped out the window, to a waiting car. Blumkin became personal body-guard, of Leon Trotsky.

The day of the assassination, Fifth All-Russian Congress of Soviets was in session, in Moscow Opera House. French, British, and American diplomats sat in box seats, listening to Soviet delegates speaking. Dagmara felt tension in the air. She sat beside Kenneth Bruce Lockhart, and other agents. Dagmara saw Sidney Reilly enter their seating box.

Reilly was upset. Dagmara heard Reilly whisper, to Lockhart. "Social Revolutionaries will raid the Opera House, tonight, to arrest soviet delegates ...something's wrong! The Opera House is surrounded, by Red Army soldiers."

Ken heard gunshots in the street. Dagmara watched Reilly take a document from his coat, rip it into pieces, then eat them. A French secret agent, sitting beside Ken, did the same thing. A speaker on stage announced, an armed anti-Soviet putsch to overthrow the soviet government has failed ...defeated by Cheka, and Red Army. Social Revolutionary terrorists with bombs, rifles, and machine guns were arrested. Hundreds were killed. Their leaders ran away. Allied representatives, in the Opera House, were to return to their Embassies ...the streets were now, safe.

Aug. 1918, secret plans for Allied intervention into Russia leaked. Aug. 2, British troops landed at Archangel. Their stated purpose, to prevent war supplies from falling into German hands. Aug. 4, British seized Baku oil fields in the Caucasus. British and French troops landed at Vladivostok. Aug. 12, a Japanese division landed at Vladivostok. Aug. 15-16, two American regiments transferred from Philippines, land at Vladivostok. Sections of Siberia are occupied by anti-Soviet forces.

In Ukraine, Czarist General Krasnov, supported by Germany, wages bloody, anti-soviet terrorist campaigns.

At Kiev, German puppet, Hetman Skoropadsky was massacring Jews, and communists. From north, south, east, and west, enemies of new democratic Russia, prepared to converge on Moscow ...remaining Allied representatives, in Moscow, hurried to leave.

Ken and Reilly joined Dagmara for lunch at her apartment. Ken looked at Reilly. "It's an unique situation. There's no declaration of war ...but there's fighting on a front, stretching from the Dvina to the Caucasus ...I'm leaving Moscow."

Reilly absently looked at Ken. "I'd rather stay here."

Ken didn't understand. "Why?"

"I want my portfolio back."

Ken frowned. "It won't help you, if you're dead."

Reilly laughed.

Ken shook his head. "I'm leaving. It's gotten too hot, for me to stay. Aug. 15, when Americans landed at Vladivostok, I had a visitor. I was lunching, in my apartment near the British Embassy, when the bell rang. My servant announced two Lettish gentlemen were here, to see me. I'm always on guard for agents-provocateur. So, I looked over the men. One introduced himself as Colonel Berzin, Commander of Lettish Kremlin Guard ...handed me a letter from Captain Cromie, British Naval Attache in Petrograd. Cromie's active in anti-soviet work. I read the letter. It *was* from Captain Cromie. Colonel Berzin told me, the Letts support counter-revolution, they have no intention to fight British forces landing, under General Poole at Archangel. They want to negotiate terms, with me. That's when I put them in touch, with you."

Reilly nodded. "My negotiations with them, went well. Lettish will help stage a counter-revolution, in Moscow. By the end of Aug. 1918, I'll have 60,000 officers in Moscow ...ready to mobilize, on signal ...an attack army within the city ...while Allied forces attack from outside. General Yudenitch will command my underground anti-Soviet army. A second army, under General Savinkov, is assembling in northern Russia ...to converge on the Bolsheviks, and destroy them. That's my plan. British Intelligence supplies Yudenitch with arms, and equipment. French Intelligence supports Savinkov. I met with Allied reps, at American Consulate General. They told us, help the Allied invasion, by blowing-up railroad bridges around Moscow, and Petrograd ...cut off soviet government reinforcements, and supplies Red Army will try to bring in from across Russia ...do espionage ...circulate propaganda.

"In a few nights, I traveled by train, leaving Moscow, arriving Petrograd ...on a forged passport, as Cheka Agent Relinsky. When I arrived, I got a phone call... 'Bad news. Doctors operated too soon. Patient's condition serious. Come at once.'

"I hurried to Grammatikov's house. He emptied his desk into the fireplace.

Grammatikov was beside himself. "The fools struck, too early. Uristky was assassinated, in his office this morning, at eleven. Hand me those papers, to burn. It's too big a risk, for us to stay in Russia, any longer.'"

<>

Reilly checked his watch. "Uritsky was head of Petrograd Cheka. He was shot, by Social Revolutionary terrorists. I called Captain Cromie, at British Embassy. He knew of Uritsky's assassination. Cromie said, everything is in order, at his end. I suggested, we meet at the usual place. Cromie understood, the usual place was Serge Balkov's Cafe. Before the meeting, I burned incriminating documents. I hid codes, and other papers. Dagmara was at the dance studio. Captain Cromie never showed up, at the cafe. I knew, something went wrong. I called Dagmara, at the dance studio. I told her, get ready to leave Petrograd. I told her, she could cross the frontier border with me, into Finland. I decided to risk a visit to British Embassy. When I arrived at Vlademirovsky Prospect, I saw men, and women, running. They hid in doorways, and side-streets. I heard a car engine racing. A car shot by, crammed with Red Army men, then, another, and another. I walked faster. By the time I rounded the corner, onto the street, where British Embassy was, I was almost running. I stopped in front of the Embassy ...several bodies lay, there ...dead Soviet police. Four cars drove up. Across the street, was a double line of Red Army men. The Embassy door was ripped off its hinges, lying on the steps. A Red Army officer approached me, who I'd met, several times, while posing as Comrade Relinsky of the Cheka.

He looked at me. "Well, Comrade Relinsky, have you come to see our carnival?"

I was surprised. "What happened?"

"Cheka are looking for Sidney Reilly," the Red officer said.

"I learned what'd happened, later. After Uritsky was murdered, Soviet authorities in Petrograd sent Cheka agents to occupy British Embassy. Captain Cromie was upstairs, with Embassy staffers, burning documents. He ran downstairs, bolted the door, against the Soviet secret police. They broke down the door. Cromie met them on the stairs, a Browning automatic in each hand. Cromie shot and killed a commissar, and several others. Cheka agents returned fire. Cromie fell, a bullet through his head.

<>

"I didn't come home to Dagmara, that night. I spent the rest of the night, at the home of a Social Revolutionary terrorist, Serge Dornoski. In the morning, I sent Dornoski out. He returned with a copy of the official Communist newspaper, *Pravda*. The street gutters will run with blood. Somebody shot at Lenin, in Moscow,' Dornoski said.

"He handed me the paper. As Lenin was leaving Michelson factory, where he was speaking at a soviet meeting, a Social Revolutionary terrorist, Fanya Kaplan, fired two shots point-blank into Lenin. The bullets were notched, and poisoned. One penetrated Lenin's lung, above his heart. The other went in his neck, by the main artery. Lenin wasn't dead. But, he was in the hospital, in critical condition. The gun Fanya Kaplan used on Lenin, was given to her by one of my agent provocateurs, I financed ...Boris Savinkov.

"From then on, I carried a pistol in a holster, under my arm, when I went out. The next morning, the newspaper reported my plan to shoot Lenin, and other Soviet leaders, to seize Moscow and Petrograd, to set up a military dictatorship under Savinkov and Yudenitch ...to take over Russia. An informer, Rene Marchand, a French journalist present at my meeting at American Consulate General, informed the Bolsheviks, of everything we said, there. Colonel Berzin, Commander of the Lettish Guard, named me, as the British agent who tried to bribe him with two million rubles ...to murder Soviet leaders. The Soviet press published a letter, I gave you, to give to Berzin, to get him past British lines, at Archangel. All over Moscow, and Petrograd, my description was put up, broadcast all over. All my aliases ...Massino ...Constantine ...Relinsky, were published. The hunt was on. I knew it was dangerous to be walking. I went to Dagmara's flat. She wasn't home. I found her, at Vera Petrovna's house. Vera Petrovna was an accomplice of Lenin's planned assassin, Fanya Kaplan. Dagmara rushed to me. Dagmara said, 'The Cheka raided my apartment two days ago. I'd hid several million rubles in thousand-ruble notes, your money, for intelligence operations. The Cheka agents didn't arrest me. Maybe, they thought I'd lead them to you.'"

Ken looked into Reilly's eyes. "What are your plans now?"

Reilly shrugged. "I have a forged German passport, to Bergen Norway. From there, I'll sail to England. I don't know what I'll tell British Secret Service ...if Rene Marchand hadn't been a traitor ...if the Expeditionary Force had advanced more quickly on the Vologda ...if I could have combined with Savinkov. Who knows? It's a mistake, England is still at war with Germany. The war must end on the Western Front, form a coalition against Bolshevism. Peace on any terms, then a united front against the true enemies of mankind, Bolsheviks!"

<>

Leaning against the ship's rail, Dagmara watched the fog, feeling the ship surge in the waves, through the water, as each wave passed beneath. The fog was breaking, a full moon burnt through, getting brighter, then dimmer as fog hid it. Reilly and Francis talked, not far from her. Dagmara heard Ambassador Francis walk away.

Reilly came over, stood by her. "We'll be in England tomorrow. Why'd you do it?"

Dagmara didn't understand. "Do what?"

"I found the note, in a book."

"A note?"

"Yes ...addressed to Stalin."

Dagmara hesitated. "Oh, that note. When you were away for several months, Social Revolutionary terrorists attacked the ballet school, one day. I never told you. I fled in the street ...was taken-in, by poor people. They nursed me, back to health. Their son, and daughter, were missing. Their son, last seen taking apples to a local soviet, his sister, with him. I was going to move that note along to Stalin, for them to help find the children. The children, were taken prisoner by Social Revolutionary terrorists. I helped arrange a raiding party, to rescue the children. It was nothing more, than that."

Reilly spoke sarcastically, "Did the poor people brainwash you?"

Dagmara laughed. "They said, Czarists and capitalist bankers have no right to divide Russia's real estate between them, that rich in Russia, are mass murderers. Things, like that."

"Do you believe that?"

Dagmara felt angry. "Reinhard taught me, only strong survive. Natasha, at the ballet studio, said, what good would it do to give my portfolio away. Then, I'd be poor too. Of course, I agree with them. But, that makes no difference. Things are, the *way* they are."

Reilly watched Dagmara as she spoke. "You're a counter-agent, under Stalin?"

"You're silly. It doesn't matter, what I say. You have your mind made up."

Reilly felt in control. "I've discussed this situation, with Rosenberg. He's not convinced. You should've burned the note."

Dagmara felt bitter. "At the opera house, I saw you *eat* your note. Did it taste good? Your counter-revolution and counter-coup, should've succeeded. You botched it. I'm glad, I'm going home to Reinhard Gehlen."

Reilly was incensed. "Yes, it's good for you ...to be with a high-ranking German intelligence officer, it's safer!"

(l-r & t-b) (p100) President Reagan and Nancy Reagan with Princess Caroline and Prince Albert of Monaco after Nancy Reagan's National Symphony Orchestra Performance of Saint Saens "Carnival of the Animals" at the Kennedy Center. Washington, DC. 3/28/83; President Reagan, Nancy Reagan, Tom Selleck, Dudley Moore, Lucille Ball at a Tribute to Bob Hope's 80th birthday at the Kennedy Center. 5/20/83; President Reagan talking with Christopher Reeve and Frank Gifford during a reception and picnic in honor of the 15th Anniversary of the Special Olympics program in the Diplomatic Reception room. 6/12/83; President Reagan having a photo taken with Arnold Schwarzenegger at the Republican National Convention in Dallas, Texas. 8/23/84; President Reagan cutting in on Nancy Reagan and Frank Sinatra dancing at the President's birthday party in the East Room. 2/6/81; President Reagan addressing the crowd during Ford Theatre's Gala, "The Stars Salute the President," with Nancy Reagan, Tony Bennett, Lynda Carter, Rodney Dangerfield, Luciano Pavarotti, Jack Klugman, Victoria Principal, and George Benson. 3/21/81; (p101) President Reagan and Nancy Reagan posing for photo with Christie Brinkley, Cheryl Tiegs and Brooke Shields at a Tribute to Bob Hope's 80th birthday at the Kennedy Center. 5/20/83; President Reagan and Nancy Reagan with Michael Jackson during a White House Ceremony for National Campaign Against Drunk Driving on the south lawn. 5/14/84; President Reagan and Nancy Reagan talking with James Cagney, recipient of the Medal of Freedom, in the Blue room. 3/26/84; President Reagan giving remarks after a concert by the Beach Boys during a reception and picnic in honor of the 15th Anniversary of the Special Olympics program on the south lawn. 6/12/83; Nancy Reagan with Dinah Shore and Burt Reynolds in the Blue Room during a state dinner for Premier Zhao Ziyang of the Peoples Republic of China. 1/10/84; "All Star Tribute to Dutch Reagan" at NBC Studios(sitting) Colleen, Neil, Maureen, President, Nancy, Dennis Revell. (standing) Emmanuel Lewis, Charlton Heston, Ben Vereen, Monty Hall, Frank Sinatra, Burt Reynolds, Dean Martin, Eydie Gorme, Vin Scully, Steve Lawrence, (two unidentified),12/1/85. 100

◇ ◇ ◇

San Francisco, modern day

Granma Dagmara Wilpf felt tired after so much talking. "Reinhard, why don't you continue telling Patti and her friends, our story?"

Reinhard shrugged. "Okay." Gehlen watched Patti ...he reminded him of Dagmara, at that age. "In 1918, Dagmara and me had a running argument. I said, mankind preys on itself, no matter what dreams Dagmara had, for humanity. God made life feed on itself. Then, Dagmara had a childlike trust in me, in Alfred Rosenberg, and in the Reich."

Dagmara Wilpf nodded. "I was innocent, all right. I believed in the goodness of mankind, in the Order, in love, in nurturing people."

Reinhard smiled. "In early years, the Nazi party promised us good jobs, and good times to come, in Germany. We needed to believe the promises ...that economic depression in Germany would be over. I worked at Political Bureau of Munich District Army Command ...given command, of a squad of Reichwehr soldiers. I was building my status in the SCREAMA ...assembling intelligence on the Eastern Front against Soviet Union ...helping the Order control the world, one day at

a time. War's a battle to keep the world pecking order of ruling families. The Order did this, by provoking, then managing conflict, on a world scale. James Wheeler-Hill, national secretary of German-American Bund in the U.S., was chief liaison between Nazis, and White Russians, in the U.S. Wheeler-Hill wasn't German ...he was White Russian, born in Baku ...came to the U.S, in the early 1920s.

"Wheeler-Hill first came to Germany, when White armies lost Russia to the U.S. He courted a multi-millionaire heiress, twenty-two years his senior. Then, married her ...became an American citizen ...settled down on the Ream estate, in Thompson Connecticut ...got his hands on his wife's fortune ...dreamed of financing an anti-Soviet army *he* would lead into Moscow ...traveled through Europe, Asia, and South America ...meeting with anti-Soviet agencies, like Torgprom International League Against Bolshevism. It was not until 1939, FBI arrested Wheeler-Hill as a Nazi counter-intelligence operative.

"By 1920, Count Anasase A. Vonsiatsky, of Thompson, Connecticut, was the most important White Russian German and Japanese operative in the U.S. ...an ex-Czarist officer ,who fought in the White Army, when the White Army lost, Vonsiatsky led a White Army terrorist death squad in the Crimea. He kidnapped Russian citizens, held them for ransom ...if ransom wasn't paid, he tortured them to death."

Dagmara interrupted Reinhard. "Reinhard always distrusted people and their motives."

Reinhard was impatient. "There you go, telling the truth ...like, it matters. You're a pathologic dreamer."

"Don't mind me."

Reinhard still loved Dagmara. He smiled at Dagmara. He looked into Patti's eyes. "The first underground, Nazi intelligence cells in the U.S. formed in 1924. Fritz Gissibl, head of Nazi Teutonia Society, in Chicago, managed them. That year, Captain Sidney Reilly and his White Russian friends, formed a U.S. branch of his International League Against Bolshevism.

"Alfred Rosenberg, and Rudolph Hess, managed Nazi agents like Fritz Gissibl, and Heinz Spanknoebel. Throughout the 1920s, the German Nazi agents collaborated with anti-Soviet, White Russians. Rosenberg, and Hess, expanded Fifth Column activities from Europe, into the U.S., Latin America, and Africa. They worked together, with Japanese Intelligence Service, expanding Fifth Column activities in the Far East. Rosenberg was the head of Aussenpolitisches Amt der NSDAP, Foreign Political Office of the Nazi Party. Rosenberg's Foreign Political Office managed thousands of Nazi espionage, sabotage, and propaganda agencies, worldwide. Rosenberg concentrated his attacks in Eastern Europe, and in Soviet Russia. Hitler's Deputy, Rudolph Hess, was in charge of Nazi Government secret negotiations with foreign powers. He wanted Nazi agents, and White Russians, in America together to fight democracy, and the Soviet Union. Leader of the anti-Soviet White émigré movement in the U.S. was former, Czarist Lieutenant Boris Brasol.

"Lieutenant Boris Brasol had been a Czarist Secret Police Ochrana intelligence agent ...a prosecuting attorney for St. Petersburg Supreme Court. In 1916, Brasol was Russian representative to Inter-Allied Conference, in New York City. A Czarist intelligence operative, he stayed in New York ...did not return to Russia. He was a violent man, a propaganda writer of anti-Semitic literature. After the Russian Revolution, Brasol founded the Union of Czarist Army and Navy Officers ...the first White Russian émigré intelligence unit, in the U.S.

"Membership of Union of Czarist Army and Navy Officers was former Black Hundreds members ...who'd organized pogroms, against Jews, Socialists, communists, and enemies of the Czar in Russia, and Eastern Europe. Black Hundreds was a terrorist death-squad.

"In 1918, Brasol supplied disinformation about Russia, to the State Department ...said he was an expert on Russian affairs ...was hired by U.S. Secret Service. In his new job, Lieutenant Brasol hired Natalie De Bogory, a daughter of a Czarist general, to translate, *The Protocols of the Wise Men of Zion*, into English. *Protocols of the Wise Men of Zion*, was an anti-Semitic propaganda weapon Czarist police used in Imperial Russia to provoke, then, justify, pogroms destroying Jews."

Patti interrupted. "Why were Jews so hated?"

"Jews have a living literary tradition, that condemns slavery, *The Old Testament*. Anti-Semitism is a well financed intelligence operation, to distract people from their real oppressors, the Fed major block stockholders, and Bank of England. Brasol put the translation of *Protocols* into U.S. Secret Service files, saying *Protocols* was an authentic document, that explained the reasons behind the Russian Revolution ...that it was an international, Jewish conspiracy. Brasol circulated *Protocols* to build support, and established a positive reputation for the White Russian Czarist Émigré community, in the U.S. While

Czarist émigré Boris Brasol was circulating *Protocols* as agent provocateur disinformation in America, Czarist émigré Alfred Rosenberg, circulated *Protocols* in Munich.

"Brasol kept writing anti-Semitic, agent-provocateur intelligence disinformation. In 1921, a Boston press published his, *World at the Crossroads*. He said, the overthrow of the Czar was an international Jewish plot to finance takeover of the world, by Bolshevism, Communism, and Socialism, and President Wilson was part of the plot to support Jews, and communists. July 1921, Brasol wrote to Major General Count Von Cherep-Spirodovich, another White Russian Czarist émigré, in the U.S.

"'Within the last year I have written three books that have done more harm to the Jews, than ten pogroms would have done to them,'" Brasol said.

"Major Cherep-Spirodovich enjoyed writing anti-Semitic propaganda. Industrialist Henry Ford financially supported him. Czarist Major Cherep-Spirodovich put Brasol in touch with Ford Motor Co., Dept. of Security agents. Brasol gave copies of *Protocols* to Henry Ford. The two feudal-minded, Czarist émigrés successfully courted Henry Ford, inventor of automobile industrial assembly lines, and mass production ...as a financial backer. Ford printed *Protocols of the Wise Men of Zion* in the *Dearborn Independent*, the newspaper he owned. White Russian émigré who immigrated to the United States, including anti-Semitic Russian aristocrats, White Guard terrorists, Black Hundred pogromists, and former Ochrana Czarist Secret Police intelligence agents, visited Henry Ford, at Ford Motor Plant, in Detroit.

"Ford was convinced, an underground Jewish revolutionary plot fronted by 'Liberal' groups, was aimed at the U.S. So, the White Russian émigré, anti-Semitic Russian aristocrats, White Guard terrorists, Black Hundred pogromists, and former Ochrana Czarist Secret Police intelligence agents, organized a secret intelligence organization ...to promote reactionary, anti-Soviet projects with a publishing clearinghouse for anti-Semitic, agent provocateur propaganda in the U.S. ...and, to spy on 'liberal' American citizens.

"Henry Ford, like Henri Deterding in England, and Fritz Thyssen in Germany, supported world anti-Bolshevism ...against workers owning means of production, in hopes of sharing profits. Deterding, Thyssen, and Ford joined, and financed, fascist movements. Adolf

Schickelgruber, Hitler, having started his career as an anti-Semitic propaganda writer, knew how to measure successful propaganda writing ... in deaths. In Adolf Hitler's headquarters office on Cornelius Street in Munich only one picture hung on the wall ...a picture of Henry Ford.

"Feb. 8, 1923, Vice-President Auer of the Bavarian Diet had an article in, *New York Times*.

"'Bavarian Diet has information the Hitler movement was partly financed by an American anti-Semitic chief, Henry Ford. Mr. Ford's interest in the Bavarian anti-Jewish movement began a year ago, when one of Mr. Ford's agents met Dietrich Eichart, a notorious German. The agent returned to America, and immediately, Mr. Ford's money began coming to Munich. Herr Hitler openly boasts of Mr. Ford's support, and praises Mr. Ford as a great individualist, and a great anti-Semite',", the Diet article said.

Hitler's close associate, Dietrich Eckart, said *Protocols* and *International Jew* inspired Hitler. When Ford and Hitler met, Ford explained assembly lines to Hitler. Hitler awarded Ford the highest German honor a non-German could get, later using assembly line techniques to murder people, in concentration camps. In *Mein Kampf*, Hitler praised Henry Ford. Hitler's anti-Jewish, agent provocateur propaganda was reflected in Ford's racism in Ford's publication, *International Jew*. In 1923, *Chicago Tribune* reported, Hitler learned Ford might run for President of the U.S.

James and Suzanne Pool's *Who Financed Hitler?*, told what Hitler said of Ford.

Reinhard continued. "'I want to send my shock troops to Chicago, and other American cities, to help in the elections. We see Heinrich Ford -- as the leader of the Fascist movement in America. We translated his anti-Jewish articles,' Hitler said. 'And, distributed millions of copies throughout Germany'."

Dagmara was frustrated and interrupted Reinhard. "Reinhard and me argued. I said, did you and your Nazis enjoy causing hate with your propaganda?"

Reinhard raised his voice. "It was my *job*. We must safeguard SCREAMA!"

Dagmara looked at Patti. "By 1925, love was gone ...but, we stayed together."

Reinhard didn't understand. "There, you're doing it! ...*feelings!* Be practical!"

<>

In 1925 Germany, Fehme, Nazi Gestapo, and German General Staff-sponsored Freikorps terrorists, and death squads, sanitized-and-par-adised Germans telling secret war plans. German Government silenced others.

Press correspondents from Germany reported. Jan. 1925, a British reporter filed a story. "Dr. Zeigner, former Prime Minister of Saxony, awaiting trial for high treason for telling enemy powers about illegal, armed organizations work-ing with Reichswehr, in a speech in Saxon Landtag. His prosecution is based on the assumption, what he said was true ...otherwise, no charge of treason under German law, can be made against him.

"German chemist Walter Bullerjahn, a pacifist ...was accused of treason by Paul von Gontard, gen. mgr. of Berlin-Karlsruhe Industriewerke. Von Gontard stockpiled weapons for Black Reichwehr. Bullerjahn found the weapons stock-piles, was going to contact Allied occupying forces. Dec. 11, 1925, German Court tried Bullerjahn for treason, sentenced him to prison ...15 years.

"Carl von Ossietzky, pacifist, editor of *Weltbuenne*, Nobel Peace Prize winner ...convict-ed of treason for publishing info about Germany's secret plans for a second world war. When Adolf Schickelgruber came to power Ossietzky was put in a concentration camp, then, *paradised*.

"American Correspondent Edgar Ansell Mowrere's article, published Mar. 11, 1925 in *Nation* magazine, *Treason in the German Republic*. "'A traitor is not a traitor ...when he seeks to restore monarchy institute a military dictatorship. A German pacifist, like Professor Ludwig Quidde, who publishes a letter calling attention to clandestine activity of Reichswehr and the German Government, in connection with training youths and secret extreme , super-patri-otic organizations, is a traitor!"

Reinhard cleared his throat, then continued. "Underground, German General Staff systemat-ically *paradised* proponents of Democracy in Germany, with terrorism, murder, propaganda, putsches and Fehme Schwarze Reichswehr death-squads. So, Adolf Schickelgruber came to power. From 1923 to 1933, German Hugenberg's fortune, newspapers, and radio sta-tions were at Hitler's disposal to promote Nazism. When Hitler came to power, one assas-sin of Kurt Eisner was put in charge of Nazi com-mercial aviation ... a key component of world-wide, German espionage. With the rise of organ-ized, Nazi death squads ...Officers' Fehme faded, momentarily, from sight. Fehme leaders became leaders of Gestapo and SS. Fehme work was car-ried on by Gestapo and SS."

Dagmara interrupted, "Now, I could not stand living with Reinhard, nor hear the name, Alfred Rosenberg ...I felt fear, and anger."

<>

Dagmara told Reinhard, "I can't stand killing, any more. I'm following my heart. Every time a person is murdered, I'm ashamed ...what I believed in ...what I thought ...what I did, helping the Reich ruling families ...pirates ...murderers."

Reinhard was past listening to Dagmara. He just ignored her.

Dagmara saw. "You're so rude!"

Gehlen continued. Italy, 1929 ...how did the Catholic Church respond to Hitler's Nazi Germany, and to Mussolini's Fascist Italy? The Catholic Church wanted to be Italy's official, State religion. Mussolini agreed. Catholic Church wanted to be a separate country, under its own sovereignty ...a separate State, within Italy.

Mussolini agreed.

In return, the Church supported Fascism.

Eugenio Maria Giuseppe Giovanni Pacelli ...Pope Pius XII, had a meeting, in the Vatican. He felt indignant. "I don't care about world opin-ion. I won't excommunicate Hitler, or Mussolini. I'll make treaties with Hitler and Mussolini. Tell the German Episcopate, and the French Bishops ...some wars are necessary and just."

Bishop Murphy-Arlington was upset. "When you make the Church sanction Hitler and Mussolini ...their death squads, you make the Church the anti-Christ ...rejecting Christ."

Pope Pius XII was angry, "The Church makes demands on Mussolini ...the Vatican wants no more attacks by Mussolini or his Fascists, on *us*. I want Mussolini to help make Catholicism, Italy's official religion. I want marriages per-formed only, by the Church ...I want divorce out-lawed, by the State ...I want tax exemptions on Church property, more privileges for Church palaces, basilicas ...and, apostolic institutes ...I want mandatory religious instruction ...taught by Church-appointed leaders -- in all of Italy's pub-lic schools ...I want the Vatican recognized as a sovereign state inside Italy ...and I, Pope, and all popes ... after me, to be sovereign head of the new, Catholic State ...I want 100 million dollars in American currency as compensation for Church properties seized by the Italian State. in 1870. Why would I excommunicate Mussolini ... for giving me 100 million dollars?"

In return, for Vatican support of Fascism ... Mussolini agreed to Pope Pius XII's demands. The Church of Rome held an extravaganza, to tell the world of its agreement with Mussolini ... The Concordat of 1929, the Lateran Treaty. The Holy Roman Catholic Church, on that day became an independent sovereign state, the State of Vatican City. The Pope was recognized as its ruler. Catholicism became Italy's official religion.

Mussolini's Fascist state paid to operate parochial schools, and keep Catholic priests, from speaking against Fascist brutality and terrorism.

In return for Catholic approval of Fascism the Vatican, could now have its own ...currency ...police force ...citizenship ...a small, armed military force ...its own intelligence services ...and its own, yellow and white, national flag. Holy See became a sovereign state ...Holy See was exempted from paying taxes for its properties, and its citizens ...Holy See was exempted from paying duty on imported goods ...Holy See acquired diplomatic immunity, and privileges for its own diplomats.

Mussolini guaranteed there would be Catholic Religious teaching in public high schools, in Italy. The Pope and Catholic World were thrilled. Jews in Italy were angry, frightened about intentional exclusion of any State funds for Jewish education, considered the Concordat of 1929, the Lateran Treaty ...a 'moral pogrom' against Jews.

The wealth of the Vatican was based on generosity of Benito Mussolini. The Church was careful, not to let anyone know its survival depended on Fascist funds. Next, the Catholic Church made a pact with Nazi Germany, The Concordat Between The Holy See and The Third Reich. Vatican Solicitor Francesco Pacelli was a key negotiator in the Mussolini agreement. Solicitor Francesco Pacelli's brother, Cardinal Eugenio Pacelli, the future Pius XII was then Vatican Secretary of State, and lead negotiator making the treaty with Nazi Germany. Hitler was pleased the Pacelli brothers had pro-Nazi attitudes. Pope Pius XII continued to refuse to excommunicate Hitler, or Mussolini, as enemies of God's Ten Commandments, and of Christ's universal love of mankind.

French Bishops supported Nazism in France, German Bishops supported Nazism in Germany, Italian Bishops supported Fascism in Italy.

Pope Pius XII later declined to condemn the Nazi invasion of Poland. "We cannot forget that there are 40 million Catholics in the Reich. What would they be exposed to, after such an act by the Holy See?"

The Vatican declared their new State a neutral country. As a result of the deal, Cardinal Eugenio Pacelli made with Hitler, Vatican received Kirchensteuer Tax revenues in Germany. Kirchensteuer Tax was deducted from wage-earners in Germany ...8%-10% of income tax collected by the German government. To avoid paying the tax ... one had to renounce one's religion. The money was given to Protestant and Catholic churches. Before, during and after the war ...the Kirchensteuer Tax filled the Vatican Treasury with as much as 100 million dollars a year ... all this, during the Great Depression, the economic war waged on working people by Fed major block shareholders and interlocking central bank directors, of their group of participating, world central banks.

Contrary to belief, fortunes of ruling families *increased* during the Great Depression. The closer ruling families were, to the inner circle of the World Order, the more money they made, buying ...bankrupt businesses ...properties ...factories ...mineral rights ...oil rights ...and, banks.

Dagmara disliked arguing with Reinhard, but, she did. "Working people are rebelling against fascist ruling family establishments, in every country."

Reinhard liked arguing, it made him right. "The Depression will quiet them down. Depression, inflation, deflation ...are our economic warfare. ...control mechanisms, our craft. How did we ever tolerate each other's views? I loved you, Dagmara."

Dagmara grew sad. "I loved you, too. But, I can't accept violence, anymore."

"It's my job."

"It creeps around me. I can't get away."

"You ignored it, 15 years ...you can handle another world war."

"I don't want to."

"God created man in His own image."

Patti interrupted Reinhard's story. "Granma Wilpf, in Germany you were a Nazi?"

"Yes, for safety ...famines were everywhere, war provocations. In America, I put myself on the line ...risked my life ...to do good ...win wages for people, voting rights for women, no child labor."

"You were a Nazi?"

"We thought we were free ...then, it was too late."

"How could you let it happen?"

"When a country turns fascist, you don't see, til it's too late."

In 1955, Milton Mayer, *They Thought They Were Free*, about Germans in 1939-1945, warned about fascism, with an essay by a professor in German ...as if the teacher spoke

Dagmara's words.

"What happened here ...was gradual habituation of people, little by little, to being governed by surprise ...to receiving decisions deliberated in secret ...to believing the situation was so complicated, that government had to act on information that people could not understand. Or, so dangerous that, even if people could understand it, it could not be released ...because of national security. And, their sense of identification with Hitler, their trust, made it easy to widen this gap ...and reassured those, who would otherwise have worried. This separation ... of government, from people, took place so gradually, insensibly, each step disguised ...perhaps not even intentionally, as a temporary emergency measure, or event associated with true patriotic allegiance, or with real social purposes. And, the crisis, and real reforms, so occupied the people ...they did not see the slow motion, the government growing more, and more, remote. You'll understand me, when I say, my German-language teaching job, was my life ...all, I cared about. I was a scholar, a specialist. Then, suddenly, I was plunged into new activity, as the university was drawn into the new situation ...meetings, conferences, interviews, ceremonies ...and, above all, papers to be filled out, reports, bibliographies, lists, questionnaires. On top of that, were demands of the community, things in which one was 'expected to' participate in, that had not been there, or had not been important, before. It was rigmarole, of course. But, it consumed all one's energies, on top of the work one really wanted to do. You can see how easy it was, then, not to think ...about fundamental things. One had no time. Those were the words of my friend, the baker. 'One had no time to think. There was so much going on.'

"The dictatorship, the whole process of it coming into being, was, above all, diverting. It provided an excuse, not to think ...for you did not want to think, anyway. I don't speak of 'little men', your baker, and so on ...I speak of my colleagues, and myself ...learned men, mind you. Most of us, did not want to think about fundamental things ...and never had. There was no need to. Nazism gave us dreadful, fundamental things to think about ...we were decent people ...and kept us so busy with continuous changes, and 'crises', and so fascinated ...yes, fascinated ... by the machinations of the 'national enemies', without and within. We had no time to think about dreadful things growing, all around. Unconsciously, I suppose, we were grateful. Who wants to think?

"To live in this process, is absolutely not to be able to notice it ...please try to believe me ...unless one has a greater degree of political awareness, than most of us had ever had occasion to develop. Each step is so small, so inconsequential, so well explained ...or, on occasion, 'regretted', that unless one were detached from the whole process from the beginning, unless one understood, what the whole thing was in principle ...what all these 'little measures' that no 'patriotic German' could resent must some day lead to, one no more saw it developing from day-to-day, than a farmer in his field sees the corn grow. One day it is over the head. How is this to be avoided, among ordinary men, even highly educated, ordinary men? Frankly, I do not know. I do not see, even now. Many times, since it all happened, I have pondered, *Principiis obsta* and *Finem respice* ...'Resist the beginnings' and 'Consider the end'. But, one must foresee the end ...in order to resist, or see the beginning. One must foresee the end clearly and certainly ... how is this to be done, by ordinary men? ...or even, extraordinary men? Things might have changed, here ...before they went as far as they did ...they didn't. But, they might have. And, everyone counts on that, 'might'. Your 'little' men, your Nazi friends, were not against National Socialism, in principle. Men like me, who were, are the greater offenders. Not, because we knew better (that would be too much to say). But, because we sensed better. Pastor Niemoller spoke for thousands and thousands of men, like me. He spoke, too modestly of himself, and said that: when the Nazis attacked the Communists, he was a little uneasy, but after all, he was not a Communist, and so he did nothing ...and then, they attacked the Socialists, and he did nothing ... and then, the schools, the press, the Jews, and so on. And, he was always uneasy. But, still he did nothing. And then, they attacked the Church, and now, as a Churchman, he did something. But now, it was too late.

"You see, one doesn't exactly know where, or how, to move. Believe me, this is true. Each act, each occasion, is worse than the last. But, only a little worse. You wait for the next, and the next. You wait for one, great, shocking occasion ...thinking, that others, when such a shock comes, will join with you in resisting, somehow. You don't want to act, or even talk, alone ...you don't want to, 'go out of your way to make trouble'. Why not? ...well, you're not in the habit of doing it. And, it's not just fear ...fear of standing alone, that restrains you ...it's genuine uncertainty. Uncertainty is a very important factor ...and, instead of decreasing as time goes on, it grows.

Outside, in the streets, in the general community, 'everyone' is happy. One hears no protest, and certainly sees, none. You know, in France or Italy, there would be slogans against government painted on walls and fences ...in Germany, outside the great cities, perhaps, there is not even this. In the university community, in your own community, you speak privately to your colleagues, some of whom certainly feel, as you do. But, what do they say? They say, 'It's not so bad' ...or, 'You're seeing things' ...or, 'You're an alarmist'. And, you are an alarmist. You are saying, this must lead to this ...and, you can't prove it. These are the beginnings ...yes, but how do you know for sure, when you don't know the end ...and, how do you know, or surmise, the end? On the one hand, your enemies, the law, colleagues, pooh-pooh you as pessimistic, or neurotic. You are left with your close friends, who are naturally, people who have always thought as you have. But, your friends are fewer now ...some have drifted off somewhere ...or submerged themselves, in their work. You no longer see as many as you did ...at meetings ...or gatherings. Informal groups become smaller ...attendance drops off in little organizations ...and, the organizations, themselves, wither. Now, in small gatherings of your oldest friends, you feel you are talking to yourselves, that you are isolated ...from the reality, of things. This weakens your confidence still further, and serves as further deterrent to ...what? It's clearer, all the time, if you are going to do anything, you must make an occasion to do it, and then ...you're obviously, a troublemaker. So ...you wait, and wait. But, the one great shocking occasion, when tens, or hundreds, or thousands will join with you ...never comes. That's the problem. If the last, and worst, act of the whole regime had come sooner, after the first and smallest, thousands, yes, millions would've been sufficiently shocked ...if, let's say, the gassing of the Jews in 1943, had come immediately after the 'German Firm' stickers were put on the windows of non-Jewish shops, in 1933. But, of course ...this isn't the way it happens. In between, come the hundreds of little steps, some imperceptible, each preparing you not to be shocked, by the next. Step C is not so much worse than Step B, and if you did not make a stand at Step B, why should you at Step C? And, so on to Step D. And, one day, too late ...your principles, if you ever knew them, rush in on you. The burden of self-deception is too heavy ...and, some minor incident, in my case my little boy, hardly more than a baby, saying, 'Jew swine',

collapses it all at once ...you see that everything, everything, has changed and changed completely, right under your nose. The world you live in ...your nation ...your people ...is not the world you were born in, at all. The forms are all there, untouched, reassuring, the houses, cinema, holidays. But, the spirit ...which you never noticed, because you made the lifelong mistake of identifying it with the forms, is changed. Now, you live in a world of hate and fear, and the people who hate and fear ... do not even know it, themselves ...when everyone is transformed, no one is transformed. Now, you live in a system which rules without responsibility, even to God. The system itself, could not intend this, in the beginning. But, in order to sustain itself, it was compelled to go, all the way. You have gone almost all the way, yourself. Life is a continuing process, a flow, not a succession of acts and events, at all. It has flowed to a new level, carrying you with it, without any effort on your part. On this new level you live, you have been more comfortable, every day ...with new morals, new principles. You've accepted things you would not have ...five years ago ...a year ago ...things that your father, even in Germany, could not have imagined. Suddenly, it all comes down at once. You see what you are, what you have done, or, more accurately, what you haven't done (for that was all that was required of most of us ...that we do nothing). You remember, those early meetings of your department in the university when, if one had stood, others would have stood ...perhaps, but, no one stood. A small matter, of hiring this man, or that ...and, you hired this one, rather than that. You remember everything, now. And, your heart breaks. Too late. You are compromised, beyond repair. What? ...then. You must then, shoot yourself. A few did. Or, 'adjust' your principles. Many tried. And, some, I suppose, succeeded ...not I, however. Or, learn to live the rest of your life, with shame. This last, is the nearest there is, under the circumstances, to heroism ...shame. Many Germans became this poor kind of hero, many more I think ...than the world knows, or cares to know.

"I can tell you of a man in Leipzig, a judge. He wasn't a Nazi, except nominally. But, he certainly wasn't an anti-Nazi. He was just ...a judge. In 1942, or early 1943, I think it was ...a Jew was tried before him, in a case involving, but, only incidentally, relations with an 'Aryan' woman. This was, 'race injury', something the Nazi Party was especially anxious to punish. In the case, at bar, however, the judge could have convicted the man of a 'nonracial' offense, and sent him to an ordinary prison for a long term, thus, saving him from Party 'processing' ...which would have meant, being sent to a concentration camp. Or, more probably, deportation and death. But, the man was innocent of the 'nonracial' charge, in the judge's opinion. And so, as an honorable judge, he acquitted him. Of course, the Party seized the Jew as soon as he left the courtroom. And the judge, he could not get the case off his conscience ...a case, mind you, in which he had acquitted an innocent man. He thought, he should have convicted him and saved him from the Party. But, how could he have convicted an innocent man? The thing preyed on him more and more, and he had to talk about it ...first to his family ...then, to his friends. And, then to acquaintances. (That's how I heard about it.) After the 1944 putsch, they arrested him. After that, I don't know.

"Once the war began, resistance, protest, criticism, complaint, all carried with them a multiplied likelihood of the greatest punishment. Mere lack of enthusiasm, or failure to show it in public, was 'defeatism'. You assumed, there were lists of those who would be 'dealt with', later, after victory. Goebbels was very clever here, too. He continually promised, a 'victory orgy' ...to 'take care of' those who thought that their 'treasonable attitude' had escaped notice. And, he meant it ...that was not just propaganda. And, that was enough to put an end to all uncertainty. Once the war began, the government could do anything 'necessary' to win it. So, it was with the 'final solution of the Jewish problem' ...that the Nazis always talked about, but, never dared undertake ...not even the Nazis, until war, and its 'necessities', gave them the knowledge ...they could get away with it. The people abroad, who thought that war against Hitler would help the Jews ...were wrong. The people in Germany who, once the war had begun, still thought of complaining, protesting, resisting ...bet on Germany losing the war. It was a long bet. Not many made it."

Dagmara looked at Patti. "It happens all around you, you don't even know. Look at Goethe Institute in San Francisco, an espionage front for Bundesnachrichtendienst (BND), a German 'CIA' ...with offices through Eastern Europe. In mid-1980's, when Germany turned hard-right ...Goethe Institutes began intelligence-gathering activities and commercial espionage. German Government gives money to the Goethe Institute organization, calling it a 'literary' and 'cultural' organization to acquaint Americans and others with German culture. United States Information Agency USIA, an intelligence outfit, has a similar organization in Germany, called 'America House'. In the 1990's over 130 Goethe Institutes were uprooted from Western Europe out of Brussels, Antwerp, Liverpool, Birmingham, Dublin, for example ...and, moved into Eastern Europe and Asia ...to start a great cultural campaign. But, is the CIA willing to investigate or counteract BND commercial espionage, and do counter-espionage against Germany? What is CIA doing with its knowledge of BND commercial espionage in the United States?

"Nearly 60 billion dollars of drug money is laundered in German banks, in Germany, every year. Why is it so hard for the FBI to find out where money transfers came from, in Germany ...to those who blew-up World Trade Center ... the first time, almost a decade before 9/11? Because, the CIA and FBI represent the interests of the Fed major shareholders and interlocking central bank directorate who own the banks, who launder the money. With collapse of the Iron Curtain, drug trafficking was on the rise in the European Community. Is German intelligence trafficking in drugs to raise capital, like CIA does? ...it would make sense, since Claus Barbie positioned the underground Nazis in Bolivia, as a leader of cocaine exports. In the United States, Congress can impose some controls on CIA. But, in Germany, there are no controls on BND. Germany pays pensions to members of the Latvian SS. But, does not pay reparations to Holocaust survivors."

In 1992, Hoover Institute's Angelo Codevilla's *Informing Statecraft*, suggested Germany would continue to maintain its large intelligence-gathering network throughout Eastern Europe and the Baltics, long after collapse of Communism.

Patti looked at Reinhard. "In America there is a myth, private property is good. I think too much private property is a bad thing, it starts wars."

<>

Paul Robeson told Nancy's psychic about it, she told Nancy, Nancy told me. I'm sure, Antony Sutton was turning over, in his grave. Sutton researched, that in 1860, half the land in the United States was held in trust for the people by the government ...by 1900, 90% of it had been given away as booty to railroads, mining syndicates, and speculative land enterprises.

Sutton researched, that by 1896, finance capitalists controlled the U.S., dominated by the Rockefeller ruling family ...they took over foreign markets, and governments ...concentrated ownership of industry ...and, natural resources into fewer hands ...exploited mass production ...sucked up the production capacity, and political system of country after country. Their institutions, that steered world banking ... would one day be, World Bank, International Monetary Fund, and Bank of International Settlements. These were the instruments of the Fed major shareholders, and their world central bank, interlocking directorate. New York, J.P. Morgan & Co. was a banking epicenter. Ohio, the Rockefeller ruling family was another epicenter. When these two banking ruling families cooperated they controlled the economic life of the country.

By 1920, finance capital controlled by industrialists and bankers had shackled the U.S. On Wall street, 'private banker' refers to a few dynastic banking houses, like J.P. Morgan & Co., and Brown Brothers, Harriman ...partnered to global firms, just as overseas, August Belmont & Co. represent Rothschilds. And to Sutton's research, Mullins added, these are families that are major Fed shareholders.

In the U.S., these dynastic banking houses have the same power Rothschild dynastic banking houses have, in Europe.

By 1900, Rockefellers joined inner circle Skull & Bones Order of Death dynastic banking families. John D. Rockefeller bought Chase Bank. His brother, William Rockefeller, bought National City Bank of New York. Rockefeller Chase Bank later merged with Warburg family's Manhattan Bank, to form Chase-Manhattan Bank.

In 1913, these families bought founding stock of the Federal Reserve Bank.

Sutton added, Chase Manhattan is a powerful financial institution ...a prime promoter of exported U.S. technology to Soviet Union since the early 1920s, plays all sides of the political fence. While Chase built up Soviet Union ...Chase Bank in Paris built up Nazis. Paul Robeson intuited this, the new World Order crucified him ...such things, nobody may know ...or, intuit. Ask Kennedy, *don't let the Fed new World Order of Death know.*

Alan squeezed Patti's hand. "There's a way to utopia. If we get rid of sociopath ruling families, we'd live in Garden of Eden."

Gehlen was impatient. "No. The Order will raise gas prices, make world depression, a terrorist attack, world war ...control with starvation, joblessness, bankruptcy."

"What about revolution?" Patti said.

Reinhard looked at Patti. "In 1941, when W.A. Harriman was appointed U.S. lend-lease representative, the U.S. shipped U.S. technology and Treasury Department currency plates to Soviet Russia, so Soviet communists could print U.S. dollars. During the McCarthy era, communists were persecuted in the U.S., but Fed major shareholders, being ruling family banking interests, exercised well-established, interlocking board members on Soviet Communist banks ...and financed and issued credit to Communist regimes for 40 years. ...What revolution is there?"

Fall was in the air. They continued walking to the peace demonstration, in downtown Palo Alto, at Lytton Plaza. Reinhard continued his story. "Berlin 1930, three years before Hitler became dictator of the Reich, German League celebrated its 40th anniversary. Heinz Pol was editor of Berlin *Daily Vossiche Zeitung*, the oldest democratic newspaper in Berlin.

Heinz Pol's, *Hidden Enemy*, describes 40th anniversary of Pan-German League. "The speakers' platform was occupied by leaders of the League. Right and left, honorary guests were assembled ...leaders of big, Rightist parties and reactionary associations, sitting together, three Hohenzollern princes, Eitel, Oscar, and August Wilhelm, the last in a tailored Storm Trooper uniform. "Four delegates of Reichswehr Ministry, salute when Colonel von Hindenburg, son of the Reich President, entered. By Hindenburg, sat Hjalmar Schacht ...whose political career also began in Pan-German League. Behind Hjalmar Schacht, representatives of German industry, a few men, representing billions of marks ...Alfred Voegler, board chairman of Rheinish-Westphalian Coal Syndicate ...old Emil Kirdorf, founder of the Electro-Montan concern, forty years earlier a most active member of Pan-German league ...Herr Blohm, co-owner of Hamburg shipyards, Blohm & Voss. At a small table, sat German Nobility Association reps, and Count Kalchreuth, a Prussian Junker political leaders. Near the audience, flanked by young men in Storm Trooper and Elite Guard uniforms, sat Nazi Party delegates ...Hermann Goering, in civilian clothes, already a Party big shot, his official position was Reichstag Deputy. Beside him, was Rudolph Hess, personal envoy of Adolf Hitler. There were prominent men of politics, science, and economics. Delegates also came from abroad, from Pan-German branches in New York, San Francisco, Haifa, Hong Kong, Melbourne, Montreal, Buenos Aires, China, Sumatra, and Japan. Alfred Hugenberg presided, 'I am happy to know Hitler's party, symbolizing the Germany to come, has won electoral victory! It was Pan-Germans, who took up the fight for German honor and of a power not limiting itself to the small, German territory in Europe. But, to extend to the entire world! For forty years, we Germans have created a mass movement, made new parties. It won't be long, before Germany awakens. Long live Germany!' People jumped from their seats, shouting, saluting, waving swastika flags. Delegates from Reichswehr stood at attention."

Reinhard's eyes glowed as he remembered. "Goering, Hess, and followers raised hands in deafening Hitler salutes, yelling, 'Hock!' and 'Heil!'"

As Reinhard continued, Patti felt antagonistic towards Dagmara. "Granma Wilpf, I understand. I get it. You were a Nazi! You were SCREAMA!"

Dagmara looked at Patti. "When I was a child, I acted like one. When I grew up, I realized, I'd made mistakes. I changed. I fought against war, against injustice, to help people. I never told you this, while you were a child. You judge me now through the eyes of a woman. But, I'm alive. I didn't want to be killed, be put in prison, or labor camps. Is that criminal? ...to live?"

Reinhard was upset. "Patti, you're wrong. Dagmara is a hero. She was brave ... a counter-agent, behind enemy lines, risking her life."

Patti hesitated. "She *was* a hero. *That's* not it!" Patti said.

Dagmara looked at Reinhard. "I know what she means."

Reinhard threw his hands up into the air. "Women!"

Reinhard continued his story...

"In 1933-1934, coups d'états, putsches, sabotage, treason, terror, assassinations, and conspiracies raced across Europe. German High Command launched secret Fifth Column vanguards ...French Cagoulards and Croix de Feu ...British Union of Fascists ...Belgian Rexists ...Polish POW ...Czechoslovakian Henleinists and Hlinka Guards ...Norwegian Quislingites ...Rumanian Iron Guards ...Bulgarian IMRO ...Finnish Lappo ...Lithuanian Iron Wolf ...Latvian Fiery Cross, and other Nazi secret societies tilling ground for Wehrmacht's enslavement of the continent, in prepartion to attach the Soviet Union.

"Following Hitler's rise to power, Nazi terrorism multiplied. Oct. 1933, Organization of Ukrainian Nationalists OUN, terrorists financed by Nazis assassinate Alex Mailov, Soviet Embassy Secretary at Lvov, Poland ... Dec. '33, Iron Guard Nazi-Rumanian terrorists assassinate Premier Ion Duca of Rumania ...Feb. '34, Uprising in

Paris France of the Croix de Feu a Nazi-inspired French fascist organization ... Mar. '34, Nazi-financed fascist Liberty Fighters attempt a coup d'état in Estonia ...May '34, Fascist coup d'état in Bulgaria ...May '34, Baltic Brotherhood Nazi-controlled units attempt a putsch in Latvia ...Jun. '34, Organization of Ukrainian Nationalists assassinate Polish Interior Minister General Bronislav Pieracki ...OUN operatives assassinate Ivan Babiy head of the Organization for Catholic Action in Poland ...Nazi Iron Wolf attempt a mass uprising in Lithuania ...July '34, Nazi terrorists have abortive Nazi putsch in Austria, assassinate Austrian Chancellor Dollfuss ...Oct. '34, assassination of Yugoslavia's King Alexander by Ustasche agents ... Nazi-Ustasche Croatian fascists assassinate French Foreign Minister Barthou.

"Alfred Rosenberg and Rudolph Hess managed Nazi Fifth Column activities. Alfred, one-time Czarist émigré from Reval, established secret official Nazi relations with Leon Trotsky. Rudolph Hess, Hitler's deputy, institutionalized those relations.

"Sept. 1933, eight months after Adolf Hitler became dictator of Germany, Trotskyite diplomat-German agent Nicolai Krestinsky was in Berlin for a few days on his way to a rest cure at a health sanitarium in Kissingen. Krestinsky was Soviet Foreign Office Assistant Commissar. Krestinsky went to see Sergei Bessonov. Sergei Bessonov was a Trotskyite intelligence mole, stationed at Soviet Embassy in Berlin.

<>

Bessonov was excited. "Rosenberg, Nazi leader of German Foreign Affairs Department, is asking, are there secret alliances between National Socialists in Germany and Russian Trotskyites?" Bessonov said.

Jun. 30, 1934, Nazis purge their ranks in Germany. Hitler liquidates dissidents in his movement. Chief of Staff of Hitler's Storm Troops, Captain Ernst Roehm ...Supreme Group Leader in Eastern Germany, Edmund Heines ...Chief Leader of the Berlin Storm Troops, Karl Ernst, and hundreds of their friends in Munich and Berlin are assassinated. In Paris, Trotsky sends his secretary intelligencer Karl Reich, alias Johanson, to contact Sergei Bessonov the

CENSORED

110

Trotskyite liaison in Berlin. Bessonov is called to Paris to report the situation inside Germany to Trotsky. In July, Besonov meets Trotsky in a Paris Hotel.

Trotsky debriefs him. Trotsky's anxious. "The purge of radical Nazis commanded by Roehm can foul our plans."

Bessonov spoke carefully. "Hitler, Himmler, Hess, Rosenberg, Goering, and Goebels still hold State power."

Trotsky clasped his palms together. "They'll come to us! I'll have assignments for you, in Berlin. To get help from Hess, and Rosenberg, we must let them take Ukraine from Russia. Tell the Germans, we'll give them territory in Russia ...if they will support me in a coup d'état to, take over Russia. I'll instruct Oyatakov, and Krestinsky."

Besonov returned to Berlin.

Reinhard looked at Patti, then continued. Sept. 25, 1933, Nazi agent Paul A. von Lilienfeld-Toal writes to William Dudley Pelley, chief of pro-Nazi American Silver Shirts. 'This is my report about contacts with White Russians. I'm in touch with General Staff of the Russian Fascists. Their leader, Anasase Vonsiatsky, is abroad, but his assistant, Mr. D.I. Kunle, wrote me a nice letter. He mailed me copies of their paper, *The Fascist.*'

A White Army Czarist officer, after defeat, Vonsiatsky led death squad terrorists in the Crimea, kidnapped Russians. Then, tortured them to death.

Aug. 1933, he moves to Thompson Connecticut, founds Russian Fascist National Revolutionary Party of the United States. Official emblem of Russian Fascist National Revolutionary Party of the United States ...is the swastika. Headquarters, at the Ream estate in Thompson, owned by James Wheeler-Hill, a White Russian from Baku immigrating in the early '20s, now national secretary of the German-American Bund ...and, chief liaison between Nazis and White Russians in the U.S.

There, Anasase Vonsiatsky keeps an arsenal of rifles, machine guns and other military equipment. There Vonsiatsky trains and drills squads of young men in Nazi uniforms. In 1934 Anasase Vonsiatsky visits Tokyo, Harbin Manchukuo, and other Far Eastern cities. Vonsiatsky meets with Japanese High Command, and fascist White Russians ...in Japan. Vonsiatsky goes to Germany, meets with Alfred Rosenberg, Dr. Goebbels, and German Military Intelligence ...pledges himself as an espionage agent ...pledges himself to send espionage data from

U.S. to Germany, and Japan, on a regular basis. Vonsiatsky founds branch offices of Russian Fascist National Revolutionary Party in New York City, San Francisco, Los Angeles, Sao Paul Brazil, and Harbin Manchukuo. German and Japanese Military Intelligence Services manage these offices. Vonsiatsky manages espionage operations in the U.S., his organization finances, and carries out espionage, sabotage, terrorism, and death squad operations in the Soviet Union. In Thompson Connecticut, Vonsiatsky publishes his newspaper, *The Fascist.*.

Feb. 1934, he writes an editorial. "Oct. 7, Fascist Trio No. A-5 caused crash of military train. According to information, 100 people were killed. In Starobinsky district, thanks to the brotherhood, sowing campaign was completely sabotaged. Several communists in charge of the sowing campaign mysteriously disappeared! Sept. 3, in district Ozera Kmiaz, Communist Chairman of a collective farm was killed by brothers No's. 167 and 168!"

Berlin 1933, Alfred Rosenberg founded International Committee to Combat the Menace of Bolshevism, the organization that becomes the Anti-Comintern. Berlin, headquarters coordinates international affiliates ...General League of German Anti-Communist Associations ...Anti-Communist Bloc of South America ...Anti-Communist Union of the Province of North China ...European Anti-Communist League, and an American Section of International Committee to Combat the World Menace Of Communism.

Jan. 1933, German General Staff member and President of the German Republic, Paul von Hindenburg hands Germany to Adolf Hitler.

Germany is ready to launch World War II.

"In the United States, there is ruling family corporate support for Fascism and Nazism ...including financing from DuPont, Standard Oil, International Harvester, General Motors and Ford ...all directed by ruling family delegates -- in sum -- owing controlling interests in the Fed, sitting on boards and interlocking world central bank boards ... the World Order.

President Roosevelt meets with U.S. Ambassador to Germany, William Dodd.

Ambassador Dodd is matter-of-fact. "Peace is our best policy. But, I share the fear President Wilson emphasized to me ...when we spoke, Aug. 15, 1915. He told me, the breakdown of democracy in Europe will be a disaster to people, but what can we do?

"President Roosevelt, more than 100 American corporations have subsidiaries in Germany, and partnership contracts here, or cooperative understandings. DuPont has three Allies in Germany building German armaments. DuPont's chief ally is I.G. Farben Co. German Government gives 200,000 marks each year to one propaganda organization operating on Americans. Standard Oil Co.'s New York subsidiary sent 2 million dollars to Germany, this year. Standard Oil makes $500,000 dollars a year helping Germans make ersatz gas for war. But, Standard Oil can't take its earnings out of Germany ...except in goods. They won't. They report earnings at home, but don't explain. International Harvester Co. President told me, their business rose 33% a year ...because of its German arms manufacturing operations. But, they could take nothing out. Even our airplane people have secret arrangements ...with the Krupps. General Motors, and Ford, do enormous business there, through subsidiaries ...and take no profits out. I mention these facts because there are war dangers."

Many American ruling family industrialists believe in Hitler and Mussolini. Eranee DuPont is obsessive-compulsive in devotion to Hitler and Mussolini ...and their desire to eliminate unions, and cut wages to empower a corporation-run state.

Sept. 7, 1926, in a speech to American Chemical Society, Erane DuPont promotes building a race of supermen ... by injecting special drugs into children, to adjust their characters. Erane DuPont's supermen would be in the same good shape physically as U.S. Marines. They would have blood in them, as pure as the blood that ran in the veins of the Vikings. It did not matter that Erane DuPont had Jewish blood in his own veins, his anti-Semitism equaled Hitler's.

In 1933, DuPont ruling family of Delaware hosts a Pro-Hitler dinner, in an exclusive men's club. There, they plan a domestic Fascist coup d'état to replace President Roosevelt, then take over the U.S. Government.

DuPonts volunteer to finance and promote the Fascist coup d'état against the United States. DuPont ruling family is not prosecuted, because the Great Depression is in full swing ...and, they claim, 'plausible deniability'.

General Motors is controlled by DuPont ruling family of Delaware. From 1932 to 1939, the bosses of General Motors pour 30 million dollars into Germany's I. G. Farben operations. They said, since they could not export the money from Germany, why not invest it in Hitler's military-industrial complex? Berlin 1933, DuPont's Foreign Relations Director, Wendell R. Swint

mees with I.G. Farben Directors Herman Schmitz, and Karl Krauk. Swint learns I. G. Farben and the Krupp ruling family industrial empire arranged for German industry to contribute 1/2 percent of its entire wage and salary payments to the Nazi movement. In American, at the 1934 Munitions Hearings, DuPont's Swint admits under oath the DuPont ruling family knew it was financing the Nazi Party through the 1/2 percent taken out of wages and salaries of its employees, in its overseas Opel factory ...building armored cars and trucks, and its deals with I.G. Farben.

<>

Reinhard took a sip of bottled water, he bought from Mac's Smoke Shop in Palo Alto, then continued telling his story to Patti.

May 1933, Hitler took power in Germany, the Kaiser telegraphed his congratulations to Hitler, calling Hitler, the man who'd resurrected the German soul. German General Staff detached my boss, Alfred Rosenberg to Great Britain, where he went to Sir Henri Deterding.

Alfred was a propaganda writer, a literary agent provocateur we considered, the best Nazi philosopher. Alfred was a guest at Sir Henri Deterding's country estate at Buckhurst Park near Windsor Castle. Sir Henri Deterding was a ruling family petroleum magnate. He told Alfred a powerful pro-Nazi British Tory group, he financed, would promote the anti-communist crusade in Great Britain.

<> <> <>
Great slaughters
From 1939 to 1941, Gehlen and Nazi Wehrmacht over-ran borders of peaceful countries, into Soviet Russia ...led by Fehme death squad leaders, spies, sadists, and anti-Semite gangsters of Schwarze Reichswehr. Wehrmacht was led by murderers, assassins. Wehrmacht officers included SS and Gestapo officers ...Ordensburgen graduates. Ordensburgen ...a special military school for training SS and Gestapo officers to degrade, kill and torture.

Wehrmacht cut a path of human suffering through the countryside. Ordensburgen graduates, from Berlin and Munich, preyed on citizens of Paris, Brussels, Prague, Rotterdam, Warsaw, Kiev, and Kharkov. Factories in Hamburg, Berlin, and Dresden were built ... to provide Gestapo and SS with torture tools ... pliers to pull out fingernails ...thumbscrews ...hand-presses ...shackles ...chain-handcuffs ...racks ...whips ...bludgeons ...electrical devices to burn men and women alive, ...tools to scald people ...presses to crush bones. In four years of German occupation of Paris, Nazis tortured and murdered 75,000. Germany military prisons in Paris had baths of freezing water to submerge prisoners until they were unconscious ...rooms of men and women burned with electricity ...prisoners shackled to walls, then burned with fire. Nazis called torture, 'interrogation' ...striking the face, the body below the belt ...beatings with truncheons, cat-of-nine tails ...tying people to tables, then, beating them ...hanging people from ropes, then, whipping them, then, letting them fall on pointed wooden blocks ...burning people with lit cigars ...crushing fingers in screw-presses ...burning people with electric needles.

The techniques of Wehrmacht brutality, and terrorism, was not restricted only to trained officers, Gestapo agents, and SS men.

Wehrmacht brutality was designed to stamp out opposition, to terrorize indigenous populations in invaded countries. And, at the same time, to create morale in German troops.

Each German soldier became a team player, led by German General Staff. German General Staff psywar experts made each soldier an accomplice to Wehrmacht's criminal war, issued standing orders that German soldiers ...rape women ...torture people ...assassinate citizens in Nazi occupied countries ... business as usual. Looting, rape, murder, and robbery by German soldiers in Europe was proven, German psychological terrorism.

July 17, 1941 Nazi Supreme Command issued orders to Wehrmacht Propaganda Company Commanders . 'Foster in every German officer and German soldier, personal material interest in war.'

So, in Europe, Eastern Europe, Russia, Africa and the Mid-East ...German officers and German soldiers ...ransacked homes, stealing clothing, shoes, watches, kitchen utensils, baby wear, underwear and furs ...drove army vehicles up to shops, and looted them, removing entire inventories ...stripped civilians on public streets of shoes, cloths, jewelry, glasses, wallets.

Nazi Supreme Command scheduled needed transportation, for German soldiers and officers shipping booty home. Freight-train cars, and truck convoys, filled with stolen goods, flooded into Germany. German homes were furnished with stolen furniture. German pantries filled with stolen food. German farms received stolen livestock. German shops sold stolen clothes. German women and children wore clothing stolen from women and children of France, Belgium, Russia, Czechoslovakia, Poland.

<>

Gehlen yawned, then continued.

A typical day ...we arrived in afternoon, at Motol. The marketplace was full of strawberries. There, we shot fifty women and children. At night, we burnt everything, whole villages, whole fields of grain, whole harvests.

Nazi Wehrmacht encouraged robbing, then massacring prisoners, and civilians. Non-German indigenous peoples are savages. When we arrived in Minsk, our battalion mission was, shoot all Jews. One night, we killed 500 Jews. Our objective, to make Krupki our base. Our mission, to clear Knolopenichi, Voluber, Virki, Kurichenki, and neighboring villages. We divided into companies, surrounded the villages, set them on fire. My Lieutenant called fifteen men with strong nerves. I volunteered.

He questioned us. "Can you stand the sight of blood?"

I laughed. We were each ordered to take 300 rounds of ammunition, to meet in front of company headquarters at 5 A.M. We assembled in the morning. I was impatient.

The Lieutenant faced us and briefed us. "There are 1,000 Jews in Krupki. Shoot them."

All the Jews ... men, women and children, were rounded up, brought in front of us.

My Lieutenant spoke to them. "You will go to work, in Germany. When I read your name, come forward."

The Lieutenant read lists of names. Then, we start out marching towards the marshes. Our firing squads marched on both sides. It was raining. Walking around in mud's not as much fun. We got to the marshes. We crossed over railroad tracks. We kept walking. Some Jews, figured it out ... what would happen ...panic set in. We beat them, keeping them in line, ...herding them to the marsh. They were ordered, sit down. Fifty yards away, was a ditch filled with water. We took ten Jews over, lined them up at the ditch. Ordered them, remove your clothes. Men stood only in trousers ...women and children, in skirts and pants. Our first round of shots knocked them in the ditch. We took ten at a time, til all Jews were shot, and fell in the ditch. It took a long time. Children screamed, hanging to mothers' skirts. Teenage girls desperately held their boyfriends. Quite something to see. Days later, at Kholopenichi ... we shot another 500 Jews. There was no marsh. We shot them in a sand pit.

Dagmara wiped her eyes. She looked at Patti. "I

waited for Reinhard, at Yanovska Camp. I was a guest of Camp Commandant Obersturmfuehrer Wilhaus. For sport, to amuse his wife and daughter, he shot from his balcony with a machine-gun at war prisoners, on the other side of the yard, working in the shops. He passed the gun to his wife. She shot, too. To please his nine-year-old daughter, Commandant Obersturmfuehrer Wilhaus had guards toss two four-year-old twins up into the air, for targets. He fired at them. His daughter clapped, 'Do it again, Papa. Do it again!' So he did. At Yanovska Camp, prisoners were routinely exterminated, for no reason. Sometimes, killed on a bet. Gestapo Kommissar Wepke bragged to other camp executioners ... he could cut a boy in half, with one blow of an ax. Other executioners didn't believe him. He grabbed a ten-year-old boy, forced the boy to his knees, made the boy put his hands together, and rest his head in his hands. Gestapo Kommissar Wepke adjusted the boy's head. He raised his ax up in the air. With a single stroke, he sliced the boy in two pieces. Other executioners shook Wepke's hand."

Reinhard continued his story...

We demolished Bykov, shot 250 Jews, then had dinner. We had war prisoners dig graves ...lined them up, shot them. Row after row. I had a Communist prisoner. I whipped him, herding him to a meadow. I made him dig his grave ...then, shot him. That night, we had a father and son dig their grave. Then, shot them. We shot 50 Ukrainians in Shostka, a pretty town. We used prisoners for target practice, we made them run. Then, shot them. In Smolensk, we shot all the Jews on New Year's Eve. At Fisgovo, there were two pretty Russian girls, 17 and 18. We raped them. In Navarovo, we shot 156 guerrillas. I wondered, where would the border of new Germany be? I wasn't the only German officer who kept a diary. Many German soldiers did. We wrote war experiences in diaries, in letters. Took snapshots, carried them around, sent them home. I had a collection of snapshots ...German soldiers in groups, grinning, while men and women were hanged behind them ...men and women being buried alive ...men and women being whipped ...girls being raped ...children dismembered ... and, piles of corpses. After the war, thousands of these snapshots were collected by governments in countries Wehrmacht marched through.

Dagmara was upset. "Working people rebelled against an establishment of ruling family oligarchies ...in every country. The Order respond-

ed, having SCREAMA clear people off the land, using genocide."

Reinhard Gehlen felt proud. He continued.

German General Staff controlled Nazi Wehrmacht. We fulfilled century-old plans of German race theorists, industrialists, and military. We were ready, realizing dreams of Lagarde, Hasse, Haux, Hugenbert, Krupp, Ludendorff ... across Europe. We'd expand German borders, build German colonial empires on mountains of corpses, left behind, by pure-blooded Germans. German colonists swarmed into Nazi-occupied regions, following behind the Wehrmacht, genocide machine.

Herding civilians into cattle cars

Millions of civilians ... Poles, Letts, Estonians, Czechs, Frenchmen, Ukrainians, Russians ... we herded to cattle cars, shipped them across the borders of their countries, to Germany ...made them slave-laborers running the German, war machine. Every day, slick paper German magazines, in Berlin and Hamburg, printed photos of new German farmers, in new estates, in newly occupied territories in Ukraine ...German newlyweds in new apartments in Poland ...German colonists taking over farms, factories, livestock, household goods, and homes conquered people left behind. Free land was advertised in German publications ...German citizens encouraged to move east, begin new lives. R. Walther Darre was Reich Minister of Agriculture.

Dec. 9, 1940, Darre's speech appeared in *Life Magazine*, "A new aristocracy of Herrenvolk, German masters, is being created ...aristocracy with slaves, property of Herrenvolk. Slaves kept homeless, non-German nationals."

Reich Commissioner for Utilization of Labor-Power, Gauleiter Fritz Sanuckel, spoke to the German press. "In 1942, two million men and women were transported to Germany, from France. Fuehrer charged me with delivering to Germany, 400,000 to 500,000 hand-picked sound and strong girls from Eastern regions."

Dagmara felt Patti's eyes on her. Dagmara felt awkward. She looked at the ground. Dagmara spoke to Patti. "By 1943, two million foreign slaves were in Germany, for Herrenvolk. Others ended up, slave labor, in the military-industry complex. Many sold at auction, in Munich and Hamburg, to farmers, housewives, small businessmen. Everyone wanted girl slaves. You can imagine why.

"*We* kept slaves, living in poor conditions.

Tens of thousands of slaves died, of disease, starvation. It didn't matter. There were always more. Cattle cars came in by train, everyday ...with slaves from conquered territories. I liked to slave auctions. German housewives, businessmen, farmers crowded around, I looked through the barbed-wire slave pen fence, waiting for Nazi guards with whips ...to lead slaves to auction. I liked to feel the muscles of the men, women's breasts. Pull open their mouths, check their teeth. Tell them, 'Take off your clothes!' German Government ordered male and female slaves would sell for only 10-to-15 Reichsmarks."

Reinhard felt proud of himself. "We had General Staff command the Reichswehr to order every German soldier be a rapist, thief, and executioner ...give him a sense of ownership of Reichwehr slaughter. Had General Staff order Government ministers to order city mayors, 'Citizens must buy slaves' ...to get a sense of ownership in the Third Reich.

"Alfred Rosenberg told General Staff, 'By ordering even the hesitant to become accomplices in acts of violence, you automatically make them your slaves.' I heard Hitler say that himself."

Dagmara fell still. "I had many slaves. From Pufenhausen, I wrote letters to Reinhard at the front. I complained, it was hard to have a good slave. I remember...."

"Dear Reinhard...

"Russian slaves arrived in Pufenhausen. My life will be interesting ... Russian-German dictionary in one pocket, a revolver in the other. I got rid of the Ukrainian ...he refused to obey me. He was lazy. I called Labor Bureau, but they couldn't tell me when a new cattle car of slaves will get here. We buried two Russian slaves, Wednesday ...that makes a total of five in our slave cemetery. Two more are sick, dying. They're so sick, I should have them killed. Thanks for the 100 Reichsmarks you sent. I gave them to your mother, to buy six or seven more slaves. I have a 19-year-old Ukrainian girl. I'll make her work. Sunday, we get a shipment of twenty Russians. Labor Department might take my Russian maid for questioning. That would be bad, she's such a good servant ...before the war only ruling families and upper class could afford having servants. The war is good. My Russian woman does the work of three. I sit in bed, I dream of you. The factory took my Frenchmen away, I bought six Russians from Minsk. Russian slaves hold up better than French. Only one died from starva-

tion, the rest take care of the crops on our farm. It costs us nothing to have them. Yesterday, I whipped two Russians. I caught them drinking milk for the pigs. There are Russian prisoners of war in pens at the airfield. I saw them eat earthworms and weeds. To think, they are human beings. Love, Dagmara."

Reinhard looked at Patti. "General Staff made millions of slaves, men, women, and children from conquered, occupied territories. We will make slaves of 500 million people, when Germany conquers Europe and Soviet Russia. Eighty million Germans will be their masters.

"General von Stuelpnagel wrote about von Clauswitz' theory of German warfare lasting for generations ...spanning centuries, until victory.

"'World conquest happens in stages. Each stage must bring us greater economic and industrial potential than our enemies.'

"The Nazis must reduce the economic and industrial potential of European cities to ashes ...in Florence, Paris, Brussels, Rotterdam, Warsaw, Kiev ... buildings are crumbled ruins, trains, buses, trolleys, cars, and wagons are bombed, broken burnt-out heaps ...farms are burned, the ground poisoned, factories bombed and burned, businesses burnt out. Tens of millions of people are homeless and starve.

"One by one, Wehrmacht destroyed villages, towns, cities, states, and countries. The Soviet industrial city, Stalino ...in Stalino, we destroyed 113 schools, 62 kindergartens, Summer and Winter Theatres, the Art Gallery, and best buildings in town. We burnt the Children's Hospital to the ground, displacing 2,000 people. Burnt Voroshilov Clinical Hospital to the ground, with 1,000 beds. Burnt twelve medical institutions, with 2,000 beds ...five clinics ...the medical Institute, that had 2,000 students ...the Industrial Institute, that had 15,000 students ...burnt 530,000 science and literature books ...leveled factories, shops, apartment buildings and homes, destroyed many cities this way ... Warsaw, Rotterdam, Kharkov, Kiev, Tallinn, Riga, Kaunas, Cracow, Minsk, Vitebsk.

"General von Runstedt commended us.

"'Destruction of neighboring people and their riches is needed for our victory. A great mistake of 1918 was to spare civil life of enemy countries ... for it's necessary for Germans to be always at least twice the number of the peoples of neighboring countries. We must therefore destroy at least a third of their people. Even, if Germany losses the military phase of operations in World War II, Germany will emerge stronger in economic, industrial and manpower potential than any of her neighbors'."

1940, Death factory assembly lines

Reinhard sighed. "In 1940. I went to the German Concentration Camp at Maidenak, to inspect ...the most terrible place on Earth, a death factory. In three years, 1,500,000 people from countries in Europe were murdered, there. We used assembly line techniques to murder people. Military Supreme Command and the Government ordered Camp Maidenak built ...in a field of 675 acres, a mile from Lublin, on the highway between Chelm and Cracow.

"SS used Jew slave labor, and Polish prisoners of wars, to build 144 barracks at Maidenak. Three hundred prisoners lived in each barrack ...45,000 prisoners, enough to fill Stanford Football Stadium before it was expanded for Olympic Soccer in the 1990s, and then torn down ten years later in 2004 for a smaller stadium to be built. Maidenak had barracks, workshops, storehouses, and buildings for Nazi staff and guards to live. The camp had tall observation towers with Nazi sentries, and kennels filled with 2,000 German Shepard police dogs lived at one end of camp. I drove Chelm Highway ...Maidenak looked like a little city, hundreds of little buildings, gray roofs in neat, orderly rows. I left the highway, drove down the road ...came to a wire fence stretching in both directions, farther than I could see. I came to a guardhouse ...guards appeared, opening the gate. I drove through, past rows of little rectangular buildings ... little front yards with flowers and chairs. These were homes where SS Guards lived. Next to them, was the Soldatenheim, a small whorehouse ... filled with pretty women from the camp. When a whorehouse woman got pregnant, she was killed.

"On Gestapo blueprints, Maidenak was called, *Camp Dauchau No. 2.* An SS Guard at Maidenak, who used to be a convict, called it, *Vernichtungslager Extermination Camp,* because its goal was to exterminate as many people as possible. General Staff reps at Maidenak Vernichtungslager manage operations punctually and efficiently ... large-scale murder requires several levels of management, has logistic problems murdering millions of people ...you must get people there ...kill them ...dispose of their bodies ...accumulate ...sort ...catalog, and warehouse belongings and body parts that can be reused. In Maidenak, German General Staff assigned this task to Friedrich Wilhelm Kreuger, Secretary of State for Public Security of the Government

General of Poland.

"Friedrich Kreuger belonged to Schwarze Reichswehr terrorist Luetzow Freikorps, joined Nazi Party in 1929, promoted 1934 to SS Obergruppenfuehrer Superior Group Leader, and Inspector of Grenzeinheiten Frontier Units.

"He brought qualifications, planning, tracking, exterminating millions of people ...terrorist death squad leader ...Nazi ...successful businessman. In 1924, Kreuger was general manager of a garbage company, in Berlin. He reorganized garbage pickup in Berlin, invented a new way to burn garbage.

"Kreuger built his garbage burning system again, in Maidenak ...five big ovens next to each other, reaching temperatures of 1,500 degrees, red brick blast furnaces, fueled by coal, fanned by electric fans.

The sides of these crematorium ovens had five large furnace doors. Corpses were loaded onto steel frames, then pushed in on one side ...ashes were removed on the other. Oven capacity ... 2,000 people a day. Sometimes, living people were thrown in. One day a truck drove up, unloaded twelve prisoners ...including a 28-year-old Polish woman. Nazis with machine guns ordered her to undress. She shook her head, 'no'. A guard beat her. She screamed at him.

The guard lost his temper. "I'll burn you alive.' The guards grabbed her, tied her arms and legs ...put her on the iron stretcher ...pushed her into the crematorium oven. She screamed, once ... hair burst into flame ... then, she disappeared in flames.

"Winter 1941, Maidenak began mass murder ...2,000 Soviet war prisoners brought in, two days later, 80 were alive ...then, 6,000 men, women, and children were shot in two days ...one day, 88 truckloads of civilians were unloaded at Krempek Forest, beside camp ...then, shot ...bodies thrown into pits. One day, 18,400 prisoners were shot ...shooting began after breakfast, and ended after dinner. The camp installed loudspeakers, played loud music to muffle annoying shooting sounds. SS troops brought prisoners out in groups of 50-to-100, had them take off their clothes off, lay face down in huge ditches ...then, machine-gunned them. SS troopers brought in another group, had them strip, lay on top of people just shot ...then, they were shot. This went on all day ... until pits filled with 18,400 dead bodies ...covered with a thin layer of dirt ...a few days later, they were removed, then, burned in the crematorium, or in huge bonfires of piled corpses ...10,000 victims were citizens of Lubin ...8,400 were Maidenak prisoners. An official report was kept by book keepers of Maidenak at the clothing store, who audited clothing records of the 8,400 camp victims.

"Besides bullets, Maidenak used starvation ... to murder. Thousands of prisoners starved. Standard ration was coffee made of burnt turnips, once a day ...grass soup twice, a small piece of bread made from sawdust, or chestnuts. Thousands of others were murdered, intentionally exposed to disease. New prisoners arriving at Maidenak ... who weren't killed immediately, were quarantined in the hospital for 21 days ...then sent to barracks. In barracks, were prisoners with tuberculosis. Eight of ten natural deaths in Maidenak were from tuberculosis. Thousands of prisoners of war died from hunger, and disease. In the fields, tens of thousands of victims were burned in mountain-high piles. People were put into van trucks and prison rooms ...then, poisoned with cyclon gas. Bodies were stacked in rows, then covered with logs ...then, a row of bodies ...then, a row of logs ... and great fires of dead burnt through the night. Other corpses were burnt in crudely built ovens, or in the crematorium ovens. People were shot in ditches. People were killed by being struck with an iron rod that broke necks. People were drowned in shallow, artificial ponds. People were hanged from gallows, or on portable scaffolds using pulleys and a flywheel. Maidenak was a death factory.

<>

"In 1942, Hitler met with Himmler and Kaltenbrunner. It was cost-effective to use gas instead of bullets for mass killings. Maidenak built six large concrete rooms, with air-tight steel doors ...2,000 people could be shoved in the cells at once. Pipes from inside the cells led through walls to small, outside rooms ...staffed by SS men. Each cell had thick glass viewing windows, protected by steel bars, so SS men in adjoining observation rooms could watch. In each observation room, cylinders of Cyclon B-2 Gas waited. We had people strip naked. Then, we shoved them into cells, packed them in ...closed steel doors on them ...sealed the edges with clay ...put on gas masks ...then, poured Cyclon B-2 gas into the pipes that led to the cells. Cyclon B-2 gas is encased in crystals. When it comes into contact with oxygen, it decays into poisonous gas affecting nerve centers. I flipped on a switch to turn lights on in the killing rooms, to watch people asphyxiate. It takes from two-to-ten minutes. I

watch their faces smother and die. This, before TV, was like watching movies. People were packed so tightly , when they died they kept standing.

"German army doctors at Maidenak sorted people to murder them ...people with typhoid ...people too exhausted by starvation to work ...women and children. One day, trucks full of women and children arrived. Camp doctors sorted them ...those to work ...those too exhausted. Six women and their children were put in a concrete cell, then asphyxiated with Cyclon B-2. Another day, 2,509 women and children were gassed. Another day, 160 children aged 2-to-10, were delivered in truckloads, herded into concrete gassing cells, murdered. For days, black smoke billowed up from the chimneys, drifting through Lublin. People in Lubin held handkerchiefs over their noses, stench of burning flesh filled the town.

Several years later, when Red Army liberated the area, Lieutenant General Hilmar Moser, German Military Commander of Lubin explained. 'It was clear, even to less-informed persons, what went on, there,' Moser said.

"Myself, I have no reason to keep quiet, or lie, to cover up crimes of General Staff scapegoated onto Hitler. Hundreds of thousands of people were exterminated at Maidenak. People were forced to work beyond their limits, forced on by brutal beatings ...then, tortured ...then, killed. It was a boring routine for SS guards ... to have mass executions, every day.

They amused themselves, inventing new tortures, and jokes. A guard would tell a prisoner, the prisoner broke a rule, and would be shot. With a pistol in one hand, the guard held the prisoner against the wall. The victim closed his eyes. Then, the SS guard shot the air, while another guard hit the prisoner on the head with a board. When the prisoner gained conscious, he woke to SS men standing over him. 'You see,' an SS guard said, 'You're in the other world. There are Germans here, too ...and you can't get away from us.' The joke would end when the SS guards shot the prisoner.

"Another amusement was to put the hand of a prisoner into a clothes wringer in the camp laundry, and crush the prisoner's fingers in the rubber rollers ...then, the hand ...then, the arm. This amused many guards, helped pass time. Sometimes, 10,000 women prisoners were in Maidenak. They were tortured like male prisoners. Women prisoners were guarded by SS female guards, as brutal and sadistic as male guards.

One female SS guard carried her whip with her, made of a metal rod, covered with rubber, bound with leather. Part crazy, she held roll calls of women prisoners, starving and weak. She liked to pick out the prettiest prisoner, and whip her breasts. The victim fell to the ground, the guard whips her between the legs ...then, keeps kicking her, there. Usually, that cripples the victim, the victim dies ...or, is killed. Once, SS Guards took a nursing baby from its mother's breast, killed the baby swinging it against a brick wall. I saw babies taken from their mothers, killed while mothers watch. SS guards would take a baby by one foot, step on the other foot ...then, pull the baby apart. That helped pass time.

"Corpses were put on concrete tables in the crematorium, before burning. Guards inspected corpses mouths, knocking out gold teeth and fillings, saving them in boxes sent back to the Third Reich in Germany. No corpse was cremated unless stamped on the chest, certifying gold teeth were removed. Earthenware jars were kept by the furnaces so ashes of victims were put in them, then sold to families of victims ...for up to 2,500 deutschemarks.

"We collected and sorted clothing and possessions of men, women, and children arriving at the camps for extermination. Everything was washed, sorted, packed, neatly warehoused for shipment to Germany. In one warehouse ...tens of thousands of dresses. In another ...thousands of men's trousers, piled in hills. Another was filled with children's clothing. Others were filled with bathrobes, children's toys, women's belts, men's ties, pajamas, shaving brushes, nipples for babies' bottles, and underwear.

The Assistant Chief of the Clothing Store at Maidenak sorted through clothing, and shoes, of exterminated prisoners. The best were sent to Germany. In one warehouse were 820,000 pairs of shoes, with labels from Paris ...Vienna ...Brussels ...Warsaw ...Trieste ...Prague ...Riga ...Antwerp ...Amsterdam ...Kiev ...Cracow ...Lublin ...Lvov ... and other cities in Russia, and Western Europe. There were so many shoes, their weight broke the walls, and mountains of shoes spilled out. There were many different shoes ...Russian solders' boots ...Polish army boots ...men's shoes ...women's slippers ...rubber overshoes ...tens of thousands of children's shoes, sandals, boots, and shoes worn by children six-to-ten years old, and booties of infants.

<>

Other extermination camps were built in other parts of Poland, Soviet Russia, Czechoslovakia,

and France. One extermination camp in Struthof, Alsace held 60,000 men, women, and children. Fifteen thousand were slaughtered. At extermination camps, SS guards constantly washed themselves at washbasins, used fire extinguishers to hose away pools of blood. Gas outlets, where Cyclon-2 crystals were poured ...were labeled, 'fumigation'. One night at 9:30, Aug. 10, 1943 eighty women and adolescent girls were herded into gassing rooms, screaming. As they died, two German scientists who'd come to test new killing-gas, made notes. Afterwards, they autopsied corpses. Mass murder, depopulations, mass starvation, mass disease, mass shooting, mass gassing, mass drowning, mass beating to death, mass rape, mass sexual assault ... were all big business and preparations to give Germany the advantage for future wars.

From 1942-1944, freight trains arrived at Death Factories, with people jammed in freight cars. Then, outbound freights were stocked with goods to be delivered to Germany ...barrels of human fat for making soap ...sacks of women's hair to stuff in mattresses ...boxes of gold teeth, urns of human ash for sale to relatives of victims ...freight cars of clothing ...shoes ...children's toys ...and, personal effects to be sold in German shops," Reinhard had finished part of his story.

<>

Meanwhile in Spain, General Francisco Franco, an ally of Hitler and Mussolini, was Spain's fascist military dictator. *The Fascist Tablet*, the newspaper of Spain, Mar. 19, 1938 reported Franco had been blessed by the Church, the Pope called Franco, *a child of God.*

"Jan. 27, 1940 General Franco restored large property holdings of the Society of Jesus, confiscated by the Republic in 1932, when Jesuits were expelled from Spain. The Republic of 1931 divided church and state. The Pope and his Church supported Franco and his fascists. In 1940, Mussolini returned confiscated property, stocks and bonds to the Church. This amounted to one-third of the national wealth ...the North Railroad ...the Transatlantic Co. ...the orange groves of Andalucia ...mines of the Basque provinces ...and factories in Barcelona.

David Yallop's, *In God's Name,* sets the scene.

Meanwhile, in Italy, Jun. 27, 1942 Pope Pius XII changed the name of Vatican's *Administration of Religious Works*, to, *Institute for Religious Works.* In-so-doing, *Vatican Bank (IOR)* is born. Bernadino Nogara administrated Vatican Bank. Pope Leo XIII in 1887, had determined the function of the *Administration of Religious Works* was to gather and administer funds for religious works ...but, under Pope Pius XII the *Administration of Religious Works* became the *Institute for Religious Works* ...and was charged with custody and administration of monies in bonds, cash, and properties transferred or entrusted by fiscal instruments, and contributors to the Institute as religious donations, works of Christian piety ...it was a bank.

Meanwhile, in Germany, Velsteinz World Service at Dobstererstrasa 4, Erfert Germany, and Deutche-Fertegund German Fighter Society, in Hamburg ... two psy-ops organizations ... supplied American psychological warfare agents provocateur with anti-Semitic propaganda, anti-democracy pamphlets, and bulletins to incite race hatred. Propaganda, printed in ten languages, was shipped around the world.

Sayers and Kahn's, *Secret War Against America,* William Manchester's, *American Caesar*, Robert Smith's, *MacArthur in Korea,* and Frank Kluckhohn's article in, *The Reporter,* shed light ...Meanwhile, at home, World Service's and German Fighter Society's anti-Jewish, anti-communist, anti-Democracy propaganda was reprinted ...in Father Kauflin's, *Social Justice,* of Royal Oak Michigan ...in William Dudley Pele's, *Liberator,* of Ashville North Carolina ...in Reverend Gerald Windrod's, *Defender*, of Wichita Kansas ...in William Kulgrin's, *Beacon Light,* of Atascadero California ...and many other pro-Axis, anti-Semitic, as well as many other anti-Democracy American newspapers, magazines, and newsletters.

Gerald Smith, William Dudley Pele, and Father Kauflin were General MacArthur's most vocal supporters. During the war, General MacArthur, and his staff, were stationed in the Philippines. Major General George van Horn Mosely, on MacArthur's staff, was Doug's second closest friend there. Charles Willoughby, Doug's Intelligence Chief, was MacArthur's third closest friend. Willoughby was born in Heidleburg, Germany Mar. 8, 1892, son of Freigh Herr T. von Scheppa Vedenbach and of Emma von Scheppa Vedenbach ...who with a name-change ...became Emma Willoughby of Baltimore, Maryland.

MacArthur met Willoughby when Willoughby was a captain teaching at Fort Leavenworth in the mid-1930s. When MacArthur served as Field Marshall of Philippine Commonwealth in 1940, MacArthur sent for Willoughby. MacArthur made Willoughby his supply officer ...then, promoted Willoughby to Assistant Intelligence Chief of Staff for Intelligence.

MacArthur hated the income tax law of 1914. MacArthur said it was inspired by Marxism ...he didn't know it was a Fed majority-stockholder device to tax people to repay 'loans' the Fed made to the U.S. Government with paper costing two cents for each piece of paper that they charged the U.S. Government up to $5,000 for ... or maybe he would have hated the Fed, too.

MacArthur hated government's endless encroaching on the system of capitalism. Willoughby admired Generalisimo Francisco Franco as a great leader and soldier. Willoughby considered MacArthur and Franco the two greatest soldiers of all time.

Raising his glass of gin, Willoughby toasted Francisco Franco as the second greatest military commander in the world.

<>

Reinhard Gehlen walked beside Patti as he spoke. "The fascist-Reverend Gerald K. Smith began publishing his fascist paper, *The Cross & the Flag,* in 1941 ...three months after Japanese attacked Pearl Harbor. The publication was endorsed by Senator Reynolds and Senator Nye. Nye praised *Cross & the Flag.* Financially supported by American industrialists, Gerald Smith counted one million followers in promoting a plan to negotiate peace with Hitler. Smith barely missed being elected a Michigan Senator. Smith had a favorite line. It was, 'When chaos comes, I'll be the leader'.

"In 1942 Smith and another Christian Fundamentalist, Minister Gerald Winrod of Wichita Kansas, co-published, *The Defender.* Defender called Jews, the Anti-Christ.

"*Defender* was co-owned by Senator Reynolds, with financial support from Gerald K. Smith. When World War II ended, Nazi activism in America, did not.

"May 1951, Reverend Smith's *Cross & the Flag,* reprinted a descriptive blurb from a 1915 issue of the *United States Military Academy Howitzer Yearbook* describing Dwight D. Eisenhower as a Jew. Smith referred to Eisenhower as a 'Swedish Kike', and referred to Harry S. Truman as a, 'Jew', whose middle name was 'Solomon'.

"But, Reverend Smith supported Gen MacArthur. Smith and his *Cross & the Flag* fought to get MacArthur nominated to run for President of the U.S. in 1952. Without MacArthur's consent, his name was run as a third party presidential candidate, beside a vice presidential candidate, Vivian Kellums. MacArthur and Kellums ran on the ticket of the

Constitutional Party. Vivian Kellums fought against the personal income tax, and corresponded through World War II with Nazi Agent Count von Zeitleitz in Buenos Aires. California State Senator Jack Tinny was also nominated by the Constitutional Party. The Constitutional Party was endorsed by Senator McCarthy," Gehlen said.

Fred J. Cook researched Senator McCarthy. "In his first three years in Washington McCarthy was soon identified as, 'Defender of the Nazi SS Troops at Malmady.' Malmady has gone down in history as one of the horror words of World War II. It was in this small Belgium crossroads, at Christmas time in 1944, that first SS Panza Regiment, under Colonel Peiper, wrote a new chapter in depravity. Colonel Peiper's elite outfit was known as, 'blowtorch battalion' ...after it burned a couple of Belgian villages, and slaughtered everyone in them. Blowtorch battalion came to Malmady at Christmas, rounding up 150 captured American soldiers, and 100 Belgian civilians ...the captives were taken into a field, then machine-gunned to death by Nazi troopers. In subsequent war crimes trials, seventy-four members of blowtorch battalion were tried for the Malmady massacre. Forty-three were convicted, and sentenced ...to die. But, legal maneuvers stalled immediate execution ...the U.S. Supreme Court granted review of the sentences. It upheld the verdicts ...in Apr. 1949, the Senate Armed Services Committee appointed a three-man subcommittee to investigate the Malmady massacre. The committee was headed by Senator Raymond Baldwin ...McCarthy was not one of the members of the committee, but demanded the right to 'sit-in' at the hearings ...McCarthy virtually took over the investigation, castigating witnesses, storming through the hearing room, imputing motives of the committee and its Council, Marine Colonel Joseph Chambers, a Congressional Medal of Honor winner ...why had McCarthy gone to such lengths to get in dispute? ...why did he rage in defense of Nazi murderers of American soldiers? ...the answer lies in the influence exerted of McCarthy's ultra-conservative, pro-Nazi, backers in Wisconsin ... Harnichvager Corporation ...one of eight midwestern concerns holding war contracts, ordered by the President's Fair Employment Practices Commission to stop discriminating against workers because of race, or religion.

"Apr. 12, 1942, the Commission charged the firms refused to employ Jews or Negroes, and advertised for only gentile, white, Protestant help. After Joe McCarthy became Senator, he put Harnichvager's messages in the Congressional Record. McCarthy's 1947 financial troubles came from stock market reverses, and too many person loans ...'I have made complete arrangements with Walter Harnichvager to put up sufficient collateral to cure both our ulcers,' McCarthy wrote to his harried banker friend, Matt Shew. At the time of the 1948 presidential election, McCarthy listened to the returns in Harnichvager's home. Harnichvager was understood in Washington as the reason McCarthy got involved."

<>

Reinhard Gehlen stopped walking. He kneeled on one knee to tie his shoe. He saw Alan watching him. "The Trans-Atlantic Central Banking Axis used Germany to start World War I in Yugoslavia, then supported Croatia as a Nazi satellite state ...using Croatian Ustasche death squads to murder Jews, Gypsies, and Slavs in pogroms in Yugoslavia in 1941 in World War II ... just like German military support for Croatia from the beginning of the war in former Yugoslavia in the early 1990's."

Alan looked at Gehlen. "Wars, organized and financed by Fed majority stock holding ruling families own controlling interests in the banks, corporations, and cartels that make war possible. Only they, profit from war."

Patti was upset. "We've got to divest ruling families that ever financed, engineered, and made profits from war ... put them in the desert, in prison ...make them live on general assistance, and food stamps."

"Ustasche and CIA death squads, George H.W., then George W, in Iraq create world terrorism." Reinhard finished tying his shoe, stood back up. Everyone walked towards Lytton Plaza.

Linklater, Hilton & Ascherson's, *Nazi Legacy, Klaus Barbie and the International Fascist Connection*, sets scene.

Reinhard continued.

Ante Pavolic, puppet dictator controlled by Nazis and German General Staff, co-founded the independent Fascist State of Croatia, in 1941 ...its capitol, Zagreb. Pavolic's Croatian Ustasche, and the Croatian Catholic priests who supported them, had to figure out, how to kill two million Serbs?

Pavolic's Minister of Education, Dr. Mille Budak, looked at Ante Pavolic. "We must kill one-third, expel one-third, and force one-third to be Roman Catholics. That way, we'll get rid of the Serbs, and Croatia will be 100% Catholic ...in ten years."

Ante Pavolic was enthusiastic, rose to speak to the assembled Ustasche troops, gathered in the courtyard around him. "A good Ustasche ...can use his knife to cut a child from the womb of its mother."

<>

Jun. 1941, Croatian Ustasche death squads roamed the countryside of Bosnia with machine guns, knives, and clubs. Croatian Ustasche death squads murdered men, women, and children ...whole village populations were massacred ...death camps set up ...prisoners tied together by wire ...led to the edges of cliffs. The first prisoner was pushed over the side, dragging others after. Guards tried to outdo each other ...in brutality, savagery. German officers who saw extermination camps in Poland ...were horrified by Croatian Ustasche extermination camps. I know, I went there as an intelligence observer. At Zemun extermination camp, a population of 70,000 was reduced to 20,000, in a few weeks.

Zemun Extermination Camp Commandant spoke with me. "We Ustasche are more practical than you, Germans. You shoot prisoners. We use hammers, clubs, rope, fire ...lime quicksand ...it's less expensive than bullets."

A Croatian Franciscan Catholic Priest stood beside the Commandant. "I was Commandant of Jasinovac Extermination Camp ...for six months. I killed thousands. My priests supervised a massacre of 180 Serbs, at Alipasonmost. The alternative to slaughtering Serbs ...is convert them to Roman Catholics. Sometimes, we station Ustasche beside me ...I convert a whole village to Roman Catholicism at once. It was funny ...once, after I converted a village, we hauled the new Catholic converts away and shot them anyway."

Bishop of Mostar reported to Archbishop Steponac, head of Croatian Church in Zegreb.

"Welcome Bishop."

Bishop of Mostar felt like laughing. "They go to Mass ...they learn Catholic Catechism ...their children are baptized. Then, while the new converts are in Church at Mass, Ustasche surround them, grab them, men, women, children, and grandparents ...drag them outside. We send them by thousands into eternity."

In the Vatican, Father Draganovic represented Ante Pavolic's Catholic Priests. Draganovic, a Croatian nationalist, an educated scholar, and Priest. In 1939 he edited General Register of the Catholic Church, in Yugoslavia ...at that time, a Dean of Oriental Studies at University of Sarajevo ...and Secretary to the Archbishop in Sarajevo. In 1941 in Rome, Draganovic was ecclesiastical advisor to Pavolic's regime. Draganovic went to Rome, in 1943. Croatians hoped Draganovic's Vatican contacts would improve Pavolic's reputation, and help the Croatian cause.

At the Vatican, Pope Pius XII never condemned Croatian Ustasche atrocities ... when speaking of human rights. British Minister to the Vatican, in private told Pope Pius XII about slaughter in Croatia.

"Ante Pavolic is a maligned man," Pius said.

The British Foreign Office to which the British Minister reported, advised. "This carries Christian charity too far. Tell His Holiness, Ante Pavolic is a monster."

British Minister to the Vatican looked at Pope Pius XII, the pro-Hitler, pro-Mussolini Pope ...Catholic representative of God on Earth, instrument of Christ.

Howard Blum's, *Wanted, the Search for Nazis in America,* and Anderson's, *Inside the League,* fill us in. 'Enterprise 25', was German General Staff code-name for invasion of Yugoslavia. Hitler ordered Military High Command to begin Enterprise 25, to destroy Yugoslavia, 7 A.M., Apr. 6, 1941.

Luftwaffe bombed Belgrade ...German ...Italian ...Bulgarian ...Hungarian ... Axis troops marched into Yugoslavia.

Andrea Artukovic, a guest at Hotel Kaisenhof in Berlin, had expenses paid by German Government.

Ante Pavolic was in Rome ...sent a telegram to Hitler. 'At the moment of the entry of the glorious and invincible troops into my homeland, I take the liberty, Fuehrer, of conveying to you my gratitude and devotion. Independent Croatia will tie her future to the New Order in Europe, which you Fuehrer, and Duce created'.

In four days Nazis occupied Zegreb, then pushed south. Yugoslav army surrendered Apr. 17, 1941.

<>

I was reading over my fictional autobiography to see what my ghostwriters said I said. They left out, when I was Governor of California I passed a resolution recognizing Apr. 10, 1941 ... the day the Germans invaded Yugoslavia ...as 'Independent Croatia Day'. No one told me the truth ...or, I never would have done it. When I found out, I took back my proclamation.

<>

Gehlen continued his story.

World War I created Yugoslavia.

World War II destroyed it.

Nazis broke Yugoslavia into ethnic constituencies ...Dalmatian Coast was given to Italy ...Nazis kept old Serbia with its capital, Zegreb, under Nazi rule ...Hungary and Bulgaria were given other territories ...Croatia was created as an independent, Ustasche State, controlled by Nazis.

Five days after proclamation founded Independent State of Croatia, backed by German and Italian troops, Ante Pavolic and Andre Artukovic led armed, uniformed Ustasche soldiers through Zegreb streets. A Nazi-sponsored cabinet was announced ...Pavolic, Chief of State ...Second-in-Command, Artukovic, Minister of Interior. Pavolic and Artukovic must remove threats to Ustasche sovereignty. Summer 1941, 180,000 Serbs, Jews and Gypsies are exterminated.

Apr. 30 1941, Interior Minister Artukovic signs Decree of Racial Affiliation. Decree of Racial Affiliation defines, what is a Jew?

Interior Minister Artukovic adapts the Nazi Racial Law for the Purification of the German Blood. Artukovic drafts anti-Jewish laws and Decrees ...based on Nazi Nuremberg Decrees. Under new laws, Artukovic nationalizes Jewish property, and businesses. He forbid ...inter-marriages ...employing Semitic servants under 45 ...made members of State government and professionals prove racial origin ...decreed Racial Identity Laws, requiring, 'Persons of the Jewish Race over age of 14 must wear signs identifying them as Jews ...a round, tin plate ...worn so that it is seen on the left breast.'

But ...Artukovic knew, you can not legislate, 'the Jewish question'. Artukovic brags to Subor Croatian Parliament, he can handle the solution ...to the Jewish question. Artukovic signed a law, to establish twenty extermination camps ...under his control. He'll manage Ustasche intelligence, Ustasche security, Ustasche police ...plan mass arrests ...supervise exterminations, himself.

<>

Guided by Adolf Eichmann, Artukovic supervised remodeling the Jasenovac brick yard ...he made it the largest, Croatian-run extermination camp. At Jasenovac, brick kilns used to bake bricks were rebuilt ...so thousands of Serbs and Jews were burned, alive.

Gestapo was shocked how Ustasche brutalized people. Throat-slashings, eye gougings, tongues yanked out, ax decapitations, disembowelments ...everyday events. At Jasenovac, contests were conducted ...which Ustasche could execute the most people, the fastest ...using a 'graviso', long, curved knife.

Petar Brzica was champion.

Running by lines of prisoners, he cut through 1,300 throats ...in one night.

Under Artukovic's command, Ustasche spent four years, hunting through Croatian villages, towns and cities ...hunting for what Artukovic called, 'poisonous vermin', 'parasites' ...murdering 300,000 Yugoslavs.

Artukovic wasn't satisfied. He called Chief of Police Fronyar Truhar. "Kill all Serbs and Jews without exception."

"Heil Hitler!" the police chief said.

Artukovic talked with Mayor of Cerin. "If you can't kill all Serbs and Jews ...you are enemy of the State, to be tried for treason."

"Heil Hitler!" the Mayor said.

Artukovic scolded Simon Buntic ...for killing only two Serbs. "You should not have come to see me at all ...until you kill 200 Serbs, yourself!"

<>

May 4, 1945 ...the Reich crumbles, German troops pull out of Independent State of Croatia ...the Ustasche State Of Croatia collapses. Pavolic and Artukovic change into civilian clothes, once again. Nazis smuggle them through Vatican rat lines, into Austria.

<>

In America, the early 1940s ...James Stewart Martin was Chief of United States Department of Justice Economic Warfare Section, investigating American ruling family treasonous involvement with the German war effort.

In my twilight years, Nancy read John Stewart Martin's, *All Honorable Men*, to me.

James Stewart Martin briefed his staff. "We were looking to make bottlenecks in German war production. But, American companies have international contract agreements with Germany that make bottlenecks *in America*. Business deals with American corporations and German cartels hurt us." Martin looked at Assistant Attorney-General Arnold Mann.

Assistant Attorney-General Mann read Martin's report. "Rohm and Haas of Philadelphia can't make enough plastic windows for the noses of our bombers. DuPont has Rohm and Haas of Philadelphia under a special four-company

agreement with DuPont, and two German companies in Germany I.G. Farben Industry and Rohm and Haas of Darmstadt.

"DuPont is permitted to produce a limited quantity of plastic windows. While our boys are being killed overseas, DuPont orders Rohm and Haas of Philadelphia to cut back production ...unless DuPont can get Rohm and Haas of Darmstadt Germany, and I.G. Farbin the head of Hitler's military-industrial complex, to amend the contract."

<>

Nancy continued reading me John Stewart Martin's, *All Honorable Men*, stopping to explain slowly to me ... because my Alzheimer's makes easy things hard for me to understand. It was embarrassing ...but then, I couldn't remember being embarrassed. God pampered me.

In 1941, the American firm Bendix honors a three-way, American-British-German agreement ...with Nazi aircraft producer ...Siemens ... in Germany. That forbids British aircraft manufacturer, Zenith, to have patent licenses to produce aircraft engine carburetors, for British aircraft.

Zenith wrote Bendix, 'Ministry suggests they would prefer to manufacture carburetors themselves, asks us to waive rights in the matter'.

Bendix replies, 'We told you plainly ...we are not prepared under any circumstances to agree to this, or to alter one item of our contract with you. You know that we have got to win the war if we are going to survive, and it is because we know we shall win and survive that we are anxious that post-War business should not be complicated by departing from the conditions of the contract in the meantime and under the excuse of war conditions.'

John Steward Martin was Chief of U.S. Department of Justice Economic Warfare Section ...he looks at the men at the board room table in the U.S. Department of Justice building.

John Martin told them this story.

"Summer 1942, the Justice building in Washington holds trial of eight Nazi saboteurs. The Nazi saboteurs landed by submarine ...came to blow up key U.S. factories. But, sabotage doesn't have to be a physical explosion, a paramilitary landing by special forces. Sabotage against the United States can be done with a fountain pen, signing contracts with the enemy during wartime. I'm seeing a picture of white collar spies, traitors, and intelligencers. American and German magnesium producers for aircraft have contract agreements restoring U.S. magnesium production to 5,000 tons a year ...but, in 1939 let

Germany produce 13,500 tons of magnesium and for the next five years use 33,000 tons of magnesium a year."

Martin remembered his earlier discovery, how Germans got schedules when U.S. merchant ships sailed. Ship hulls smashed by German submarine torpedoes, soaked cargoes of ships leaving American ports ...washed up on beaches ...in Virginia ...North Carolina ...South Carolina ...New Jersey ... as if German submarines were waiting for American ships ...torpedoed them as the ships left port.

American companies brokered re-insurance on ships, and cargoes, cabled contracts to Zurich. Martin discovered the Zurich group had re-insurance contracts with a Munich re-insurance pool, in Germany. From 1940-1941, German military intelligence had sailing schedules, cargo lists, and European destinations ... of each ship leaving New York, or Baltimore.

Insurance protocol listed each ship's sailing date, cargo, and destination ...on insurance forms in Munich ...before ships left American ports. Spring 1942, after Economic Warfare Section of the Justice Department was formally set up, Martin discovers ship re-insurance contracts are still going to Zurich Switzerland, by mail ...that re-insurance pertains even to high-security, industrial war production factories, and offices ...re-insurance contracts come with blueprints of the factory ...inventories of equipment ...risk-assessment reports ...fire hazard reports on a room-by-room basis.

Martin finds Zurich re-insurance groups before 1938 had requested 5% of the time, the insurance inspector's full report. After 1938, the Zurich group requested full reports 90% of the time.

Martin wants U.S. Government to stop sending shipping and industrial information through Switzerland ... to the Third Reich ...America was handing German intelligence information gift-wrapped ...it cost the Merchant Marine in lives, dearly.

Martin slapped down a handful of insurance inspector's reports onto the boardroom table.

"Anyone in the insurance business can get these. For 55 cents, I bought these plans ...to the White House ...fire extinguishers are already marked on the plan. For 75 cents, I got plans of a new magnesium plant ...see this arrow, it points to a valve, is labeled, 'Danger ... Do not close this value while the plant is in operation ...or, there will be an explosion."

Martin sat down ...felt upset ...felt he'd made his point. Some U.S. Fed majority share holders and ruling families, like the DuPonts, Morgan financial group, directors of General Motors …part of the Warburg-Rothschild financial apparatus, upstream controlling the Fed and Bank of England chain of command …and Ford Motors … were Nazi and Fascist supporters.

Patti looked at Reinhard. "We need to divest pathologically insane Fed majority stockholders, remove sociopathic ruling families …restore the balance of health and wealth, back to each human being, equally."

Reinhard smiled absently at Patti, like watching a butterfly, or flower …something pretty, God gave to mankind. Reinhard didn't expect her to make sense …or understand, the Order of Death, the responsibility of running the new World Order, ordering genocide, murdering millions of women, and children …a pretty, sex object, that's all she was to him.

Reinhard continued briefing Patti.

At 1936 Olympics, in Berlin, McCloy was Hitler's guest, in Hitler's private box at Olympic stadium. A few years later, when America entered World War II, John McCloy was War Secretary Stimpson's liaison to Joint Chiefs of Staff. McCloy helped plan major military campaigns. As Assistant War Secretary, he was in the inner circle directing the actors in their war scenes. McCloy traveled with American troops landing in North Africa in 1942.

It was McCloy, who convinced Roosevelt to accept Stimpson's suggestion …that United States form an alliance with Nazi sympathizer, Admiral Jean D'Arlen of Vichy, France. McCloy insisted, Admiral Jean D'Arlen is the only man in France, who could guarantee French forces in Africa ….would fight for of the Allies.

<>

Nancy, of all people, educated me. Perhaps, the most famous anti-Fascist journalist in Europe, was Curt Riess, late of Switzerland …the European equivalent of America's anti-fascist journalist, George Seldes …grandfather of American investigative journalism. Curt Riess', *The Nazis Go Underground*, describes Allied landings in North Africa, and Italy.

Nancy read Riess to me, day after day. I learned things, and wished I'd known, at an earlier age, or never known at all. I guess, God threshes us, the wheat from the chaff, before we pass over to the other side, so we can purify our souls as best we can …before we sit, waiting for Eternal judgment, before Him.

Why else would God lead me to write this fictional autobiography in the first place? …to use a ghostwriter? …while the ghost of Paul Robeson buzzes around my head, while Mel's Jesus guides me back into my past, and ahead into my future …all the time, Nancy reading the truth to me …while I am losing the ability to think …to speak …God tests our faith in Him, with Satan.

<>

Nancy reads Riess to me …Gehlen continues his story, to Patti.

Landing in North Africa

State Department's Robert Murphy was swamped with work, weeks before America landing in North Africa. Murphy went ahead …lived in Algiers, at the home of Dr. Henri Aboulker, a Jewish doctor. The doctor's friends were Jews on the side of France's General DeGaulle …they were not Vichy French, Hitler sympathizers, like Admiral D'Arlen.

Dr. Aboulker organized a few hundred others, to provide them with arms, Murphy arranged the U.S. to send. Before landing American soldiers in North Africa, Aboulker and friends would occupy the telegraph office, police office, power plants …arrest French officers aligned with Hitler, that could trouble the American landing. The most troublesome, being Admiral D'Arlen.

The American landing was late, many hours. Aboulker's little army of 540 armed men in the streets of Algiers, arresting Axis French officers, made confusion. This distracted everyone from the American landing. But, after Americas landed, things in Algiers and elsewhere went wrong. Dr. Aboulker's DeGaulists, who risked their lives to help Americans, were pushed aside by the Allies. It was Admiral D'Arlen …the Hitler sympathizer who fought against General De Gaulle, and killed many of De Gaulle's followers …who the newly arrived Americans put into power …over faithful French partisans who'd helped clear the way for Americans landing in North Africa.

Dr. Aboulker and the Jews, working with Robert Murphy of the U.S. State Department, did their best to provide intelligence and diversion for the Allied landing in North Africa. But, when anti-Semitic French officers …who'd not helped Robert Murphy …insisted Jewish interpreters who facilitated American landing operations be kicked out of North Africa …they were driven to the ports, and shipped out.

Everywhere, Frenchmen happy and enthusiastic when the Americans landed …were put in prison. Pro-Ally Algerian citizens, who risked their lives fighting alongside invading Americans …lost jobs.

But, the French officers who were Nazi sympathizers, who fought against French partisans ...were promoted.

Two police officers who helped the Allies during the landing were arrested, because they had not told their superiors of the coming invasion. The superiors of the two policemen who were arrested were allowed to stay in their jobs, even though there were anti-American, and beat up pro-American citizens.

Now, Robert Murphy of State Department could not find time to see the old doctor, or any of the doctor's group of friends, he'd seen so frequently, before.

Admiral D'Arlen was assassinated. The officers and city officials imprisoned by the army of 540 men during the night of the American landings, and who'd begged on their knees for their lives, were freed ...they took advantage of their chance for revenge.

Everyone in the group who'd helped Americans, including old Doctor Aboulker, was arrested ...by French secret police. It was said, they were plotting to assassinate General Giraud. During weeks that followed, members of French Fascist organizations hidden out when Americans came in, re-appeared ...in the streets ...in the cafes. These fascists made no secret they supported pro-fascist, Marshal Petat ...and were against Americans. Celvaise Don De L'Jean, the French counter-part of the SS, was accepted with open arms by U.S. Army Intelligence.

Celvaise Don De L'Jean Intelligence Service turned in names of 'suspicious' persons, Americans proceeded to arrest. Most arrested were De Gaulle-ists, or Jews ...pro-American ...pro-Democracy ...none were pro-Fascist ...none belonged to Fascist organizations.

It seemed, everyone who helped the Americans land in North Africa, were punished ...and, everyone who'd worked against old Doctor Aboulker and his friends and small army of 540 anti-Fascists, were being rewarded.

1942, Landing in Italy

As in North Africa, when Allied armies invaded Italy ...they returned Fascists to power. Allies didn't collaborate with Fascist leaders, or with prominent Fascists. They arrested some.

But, the Allies collaborated with ... Fascist city officials ...fascist mayors, down to insignificant, fascist clerks ...military men who'd been Fascists before the Allies arrived.

Marshal Badoglio had for twenty years in Italy been a chief military exponent of Fascism ...Allies collaborated with Marshal Badoglio. His first new duty was to pick a Chief of Staff ...he chose, General Mario Roatta.

Sept. 1943, Marshal Badoglio put General Mario Roatta to re-organize Mussolini's Italian Army, in Southern Italy.

General Mario Roatta was responsible for committing atrocities in Yugoslavia ...there, General Roatta ordered torture, and murder, of patriotic Serbs.

General Roatta ordered every Serb in uniform without identification papers be shot.

He had people crucified in Herzogovina.

But, neither American nor British military men argued against General Roatta. Yugoslav allies complained. Roatta was forced to resign. Marshall Badoglio had to find a new Chief of Staff, to command the Italian Army in Southern Italy ...General Givani Messe.

But, Allies had put General Givani Messe in prison, during the African campaign.

So, General Meese was set free, returned to Italy. General Meese was a true Fascist general ...despised Democracy ...hated liberty and justice. He took over as Chief of General Staff, discriminating against true Italian democrats, against anti-Fascists, keeping fascists in power, returning fascists to positions of power, surrounding himself with men who would steer Italy into a Reactionary, anti-Democracy future.

And of our landing in Greece? Dominique Eudes', *The Kapetanios, Story of the Greek Partisan Movement*, paints a picture.

Landing in Greece

In Greece, Dominique Eudes saw the promised purge of Fascists didn't happen ...but, it was written in the Kacerta Agreement ... that fascist Security Battalions were regarded as enemy organizations ...Security Battalions were to be treated as enemies, and shot ...unless they surrendered to Military Command of Allied Forces, in Greece. British Commander of occupied Greece, Commander Scoby, knew civil war was coming to Greece ...so, Commander Scoby looked at former pro-German Security Battalion militia, carefully ...to recruit them, for the coming civil war.

The fascist, Security Battalions had surrendered to the British ...but, Commander Scoby regrouped the fascist Security Battalions in the Pelopenese and Chalcadicy ...there, he didn't disarm the Security Battalions ... as he was supposed to ...instead, he installed British military instructors over them, to retrain Security Battalions to use British weapons.

<>

As German soldiers in Greece slipped north, now, the British were occupied ... with preventing a resurgence of communist-led, anti-Fascist partisans, a group called, ELAS.

This occupied the British ...they mounted no large-scale operations driving retreating Reich soldiers out of Greece ...instead, British concentrated on stamping out ELAS. Retreating German Reich soldiers saw the British aircraft flying over their columns never fired on them.

And, EAM anti-Fascist partisan fighters had fought the German Reich soldiers for three years, in combat. EAM were popular heroes of the Greek people.

Suddenly, Winston Churchill declared, EAM is the enemy of British-occupied Greece. "I fully expect a clash with EAM."

Churchill was trying to provoke battle.

Scoby had planes drop leaflets on Athens. 'I'm going to protect you, and your government, against any coup d'état, against unconstitutional acts of violence,' Scoby's leaflets said.

The Communist Party and EAM responded ...by calling a general strike, the next day. Athenians demonstrated in the streets. Greek citizens marched from suburbs into the square behind an immense banner of the Red Lion of Kasierani, with his claws out. Their banner read, 'Long live Kasierani cradle of partisans and revolutionaries".

Another, 'When tyranny threatens, people must choose between chains and arms'.

Another, 'The Germans are back.'

Crowds arrived at the Tomb of the Unknown Soldier. A youth jumped up from the front of the crowd. He began to dance wildly. The crowd cheered enthusiastically. The youth jumped high in the air. Midair he doubled up, and fell to the ground, his chest covered in blood. A machine gun was firing on top of police headquarters, in Constitution Square. It fired into the crowd. Then, another machine-gun start firing ...from the roof of the royal palace. People in the crowd lay flat on the ground. Others hid, behind the low wall. Others tried to hide, behind a large awning ...but, it pulled from its fastenings.

On the awning was a photo of Roosevelt, with the words, 'Welcome, to our great liberators.'

In Hotel Great Britain, journalists watched the massacre. Twenty-eight people were killed. One hundred were wounded. How could machine-gun nests be on the roof of the police station, and the royal palace, in the heart of Athens ...without authorities knowing?

British troops stood-by, near Constitution Square ...if the crowd got out of hand. The government's refusal to eliminate far-Right wing political factions provoked the confrontation between Greek partisans against fascist far-Right factions, that Churchill wanted.

In Filopapal district, Grivas Organization ... fascist terrorists ... was defending a building it occupied, since the liberation. Grivas hunted down anti-Fascists who believed in Democracy. The anti-Fascist citizens of Athens hated Grivas terrorists. Anti-Fascist partisans stormed the building, in a firestorm of bullets ...but, British tanks came to stop their charge ...British tanks rumbled between partisans, and the building full of fascists.

Firing on British was forbidden. The firestorm of gunshots stopped. Grivas' men ran from the building ...and, climbed onto British tank gun turrets to escape.

Partisans wanted to destroy Espalia, headquarters of Athens fascist CID terrorists.

Young communist partisans of EPON group, men and women between 13-to-16, carrying machine-guns, attacked during the night from an underground tunnel opening on pavement by the Fascist, CID building. CID machine-gunned them. Another group gained a few yards on the CID building. The CID waved a white flag of surrender ...then, a British tank and half-track truck drove up, into the middle of the confrontation, stopping the fight ...as they'd done in Filopapal.

The British tank commander spoke through an interpreter, to the partisans. "You must let us take these men, away. They are our prisoners."

ELAS central committee hoped the situation could be settled between Greeks.

Churchill cabled General Scoby. "Prime Minister to General Scoby, Athens.

1. I have given instructions to General Wilson to make sure all possible forces are left with you, and all possible reinforcements are sent to you.

2. You are responsible to maintain order in Athens, and for neutralizing or destroying all EAM, ELAS bands approaching the city. You make any arrangements you like, for strict control of streets, for rounding up truculent persons. Naturally, ELAS will try to put women and children in the way, where trouble may occur. You must be clever about this, and avoid mistakes. But, do not hesitate to fire at any armed male in Athens, who assails the British authority, or the Greek authority, with which we work. It would be well, of course, if your command

was reinforced by authority of a Greek government. Do not, however, hesitate to act as if you were in conquered city where a local rebellion is in progress."

<>

Reinhard looked at Patti, "When the Allies landed, they favored pro-Axis policy, against pro-democracy, communist partisans ... who'd fought against Fascism and Nazism."

Patti shook her head. Her long, sandy blond braid shook back and forth on her shoulders. Patti shrugged. "The Allied Fed majority shareholder ruling families, and Axis ruling families ... were on the same side."

Dagmara smiled sadly. "Yes, that's how it works."

Alan was coming on, "That stinks."

Reinhard laughed. "When I hear people complain about money, it's usually people who don't have any."

Everyone walked towards Lytton Plaza. Gehlen continued his story.

Back at the ranch at sundown, Nancy kept reading me Curt Riess, and Sayers and Kahn.

1943, World War II postwar plan of German General Staff

In 1943, as the Nazi regime disintegrated, the Fehme was revived ...as it had been in 1918. But this time, a secret, postwar plan of German General Staff was put into play by Nazis ...that, went beyond organization of a Schwarze Reichwehr of underground officers' corps, secret terrorist and propaganda units.

General Staff's trans-Atlantic ruling family financiers and industrialists had used Nazi Wehrmacht to conquer twenty-three countries.

Now, General Staff would use Wehrmacht to keep a Nazi grip on Germany ...prevent complete Allied victory, prevent lasting peace. General Staff used several methods to have manpower to build a future German Army.

In 1943, Nazi Supreme Command printed and distributed a booklet, *Merkblatt fur den Compagnie-Unterricht ... Memorandum for Company Education.*

'Every newborn healthy boy is one strong soldier in twenty years.'

<>

General Staff pursued its Nazi manpower program. Thousands of specially chosen women, kidnapped and taken prisoner from countries Germany occupied ...were prostituted, to German youths of Hitler-Jugend. Children born to these women were taken away from the mothers. The children were placed in German institutions. Human breeding-factory programs were pursued throughout the Reich. Women were impregnated artificially. In regions with small numbers of German men, women were mated with selected, foreign workers.

Jan. 25 1945, M. Pertinaux, a famous French commentator on international affairs, was interviewed by a *New York Times* reporter, and replied. "The Germans have destroyed all fixed notions on which Christendom has lived, in war and peace, through more than a thousand years. German authorities are taking unbelievable steps to make sure their birth rate will not decline in forthcoming years. No limit can be set to what German fanaticism will do."

Invention of the word, 'genocide'

Raphael Lemkin was a Polish scholar and attorney ...his book, *Axis Rule in Occupied Europe* had a problem. There was no word in English to describe General Staff policy of insuring long-range biological inferiority of enemies. Lemkin created a new word ...derived from the Greek, 'genes', meaning race or tribe ...and from the Latin, 'cide', meaning killing ...genocide ...the policy of exterminating whole races, tribes, and nations. Lemkin's, *Axis Rule in Occupied Europe*, described German General Staff genocide policy.

"The enemy nation within control of Germany must be destroyed, disintegrated, or weakened in different degrees ...for decades to come. Thus, German people in the post-war period will be in a position to deal with other European peoples from a vantage point of biological superiority. Because, imposition of this policy of genocide is more destructive for a people, than injuries suffered in actual fighting, the German people will be stronger than the subjugated peoples after the war ...even if the German army is defeated. In this respect genocide is a new technique of occupation aimed at winning the peace, even though the war, itself, is lost."

<>

German General Staff used genocide in World War II to cripple neighboring countries ...Poland, 5 million civilians killed, 2 million deported ...France, 250,000 civilians killed, 2 million deported, 3 million prisoners held in Germany, 700,000 children dead of starvation ...Belgium, 20,000 murdered, 600,000 deported ...Netherlands, 125,000 dead, 565,000 deported ...Greece, 85,000 murdered, 325,000 deported, 600,000 dead of starvation, 80% of all children starving or diseased ...Yugoslavia, 1,500,000 murdered, 350,000 deported ...Czechoslovakia, 60,000 murdered, 300,000 in concentration camps, 750,000 deported.

Cold pogrom

The Jews of Germany were the first targets of General Staff genocide. When Hitler came to power, the Nazi Government tried exterminating the Jewish population of Germany. Genocide was a curtain for the real oppressors of the German people, German General Staff and the Fed majority shareholders, who had bought up German industry after World War I, and who financed the rebuilding of Germany to fight World War II. Nazis began genocide of Jews, by driving Jews out of German political, economic, and social life. Jews were deprived of basic rights of citizenship, jobs, and income. This was the genocidal period, of the Cold Pogrom. Later on, tens of thousands of Jewish men, women, and children would be rounded up, herded in cattle cars, railed to extermination camps, sterilized, butchered, executed in mass ...and, fall in bloody pogroms throughout Europe, Eastern Europe, and the Soviet Union. As Nazis drove through Europe hundreds of thousands of Jews in occupied countries were slaughtered.

Dec. 17, 1942, a Joint Declaration was issued by governments of Belgium, Czechoslovakia, Greece, Luxembourg, Netherlands, Norway, Poland, United States, UK, USSR, Yugoslavia, and the French National Committee. "From all occupied countries, Jews are being transported in conditions of appalling horror, and brutality, to Eastern Europe. In Poland, made principal Nazi slaughterhouse, ghettos established by the German invader are being emptied of all Jews, except a few highly skilled workers required for war industries. None taken away, are ever heard of, again ...able-bodied are worked to death in labor camps ...infirm are left to die of exposure and starvation, or deliberately massacred in mass executions. The number of victims of bloody cruelties is reckoned in hundreds of thousands of innocent men, women, and children."

When Red Army liberated thirty-eight Russian and Polish communities, they found the number of Jews was reduced by Nazis from 400,000 to 3,122.

In Dvinsk, not one Jew was found. By 1945, Nazis exterminated 6 million Jews in Europe, and Soviet Russia.

Nazi genocide of Jews was different from non-Jews. Nazis wanted a final solution to the 'Jewish question', a total and final extermination of all Jews ...whereas, with genocide of non-Jews the Nazis planned to retain certain drastically reduced populations as slaves of the Reich.

Genocidal extermination of innocent and helpless men, women, and children was applied to all conquered peoples ...as outlined by General Staff.

Conquered peoples were impoverished ...their standard of living, drastically reduced ...their food rationed by 'racial principle'.

Only Third Reich citizens, people of German origin, were properly fed. For forgotten thousands of people the Nazi system, food rationing meant starvation.

Oct. 1942 Reich Minister Goering issued an edict. "German people come before all other peoples for food."

<>

As planned by General Staff, ruling family financiers and industrialists, health of whole populations deteriorated. Food prices soared ...but, the Germans kept down the price of alcohol. Drinking was encouraged. Peasants were forced to accept alcohol for payment for produce ...part of a psy-ops program to debase conquered peoples, lower their moral standards, eliminate their national identity, and their will to resist. Germans distributed pornographic publications, and movies, in occupied territories ...took measures to deprive minority groups of firewood, medicine, warm clothing, and blankets.

Nov. 6, 1941, Nazi Lieutenant Beyer issued Order No. 1422-41 to the German Northern Army Group. German orders required violators of this regulation to be shot. "All felt boots in the possession of the Russian civilian population, including children's boots, are subject to immediate requisition. To own felt boots is forbidden, and is punishable as unauthorized carrying of arms."

Special measures were taken to decrease enemy birth rates. Thousands of men, and women, were sterilized. Marriages among Poles were forbidden ...without approval of the Reichsstatthalter Governor of the District.

In occupied countries, millions of men were separated from the women ...when deporting them for forced labor. In 1944, 3 million Frenchmen were being held in Germany. A million were prisoners of war. Two million had been brought in as slave labor, and political prisoners. Germans cut down the French birthrate. Germans undermined the health of French prisoners, in case they ever returned to France. By 1944, to keep from starving, French prisoners of war in Germany ate rats, mice, and boiled flower bulbs ...to make soup.

Letters got past German censors, and reached France. "We tried to cook dahlia bulbs damaged by the first frosts. They appear to be edible. I hope the cold will make the fleas and lice disappear. The rats, and mice, are amusing animals, and very good to eat," a letter read.

<>

Hitler spoke to Hermann Rausching. "One of the chief tasks of German statesmanship for all time, is to prevent by every means in our power, the further increase of the Slav races. Natural instincts bid all living beings not merely to conquer their enemies, but to destroy them. In former days, it was the victor's prerogative to destroy entire tribes, entire peoples."

After Germany invaded Soviet Union in 1941, High Command had their military school instructors lecture on the necessity of exterminating the masses of the Russian people.

Senior Corporal Retzlaff, an official of the German Secret Field Police, described his training in the Altenburg Special Battalion. "Several special lectures were arranged and delivered by leading officials of the German Field Police. They lectured that peoples of U.S.S.R., and those of Russian nationality, were inferior ...that, the vast number of them should be exterminated, while a small section should be utilized by big German landowners in the capacity of slaves."

In summer and autumn of 1941, Nazi Wehrmacht drove towards Moscow, and massacred tens of thousands of Soviet men, women, and children. Mass executions were not necessary for military reasons. Mass executions of Slavic peoples cleared the land, for re-colonization by German settlers. Soviet villages, towns, and cities were stripped of citizens ...citizens were rounded up ...loaded into German trucks ...driven outside of town ...emptied from the trucks ...shoved into crowds ...forced to dig huge ditches. German soldiers pointed machine guns at crowds of Soviets ...and, shot them down. Soviets were buried in mass graves, in ditches. Others were made to stand near pits, and ravines ...then, shot.

Counter-attacking, Red Army forces found hundreds of mass graves, exhumed hundreds of thousands of corpses ...at Babar Yar ravine near Kiev, corpses of 80,000 Soviet civilians and 25,000 war prisoners were found ...a ditch outside Mineralnye Vody, bodies of 6,300 Russian men, women, and children ...80,000 Russian war prisoners were executed, buried near Glinischen village ...in thirty-four mass graves in Blagovschina Forest near Minsk, Nazis buried 150,000 people ...another 10,000 in a ditch near Drozdy ...254 children in a ditch near Kerch.

When bodies were exhumed from these mass graves, Soviet medical experts established many victims were buried alive ...mutilated, and tortured. Bodies of fathers and mothers were found with dead children, and infants, being hugged in their arms.

Soviet novelist and journalist Ilya Ehrenburg described his feelings. "The word, 'ravine', used to be a good word, it spoke of grass, rivulets, sand, and big-eyed daisies children used to pull apart murmuring, 'He loves me, he loves me not.' But, the word, 'ravine', has become a terrible word. One feels at any moment, dead will come stalking out of a ravine. And, not only the ravine in Triplolye, there is a ravine in Kiev, too. Every Ukrainian town has its ravine. And everywhere, it is the same story, scraps of underlinen, rigid corpses, children's toys sprinkled with blood."

Alexander Bespalov, a Soviet citizen, described to Soviet authorities what he'd witnessed in a forest near Kharkov, June 1943. "At the end of June, last year, I saw as many as 300 girls and women brought to the woods in ten or twelve motor trucks. These poor people ran from the trucks weeping, tearing their hair and clothes, many of them fainted, and fell to the ground. But, Germans paid no attention to this. Germans punched them. Germans beat the women and girls with rifle butts and clubs to make them get up. If women and girls did not stand up, Germans tore their clothes off, threw them in the pit. Several girls, and children, tried to run away. They were killed. After a volley was fired from automatic rifles, I saw several women stagger and throw their arms up helplessly and, uttering heart-rending shrieks, run towards Germans standing about. Germans shot them down with pistols. Mothers driven out of their minds by fear and grief, ran shrieking through the glade, pressing babies to their breasts, seeking safety. Gestapo men tore children out of mothers' arms, swinging babies by their legs or arms, threw them alive into the pit. As mothers ran after them, they were shot down."

In 1942, the General Staff of financiers and industrials, profiting Fed majority shareholders, decided extermination of Soviet citizens wasn't happening fast enough. They wanted to get re-colonization plans underway ...seize assets of

Russian banks, factories, farm lands, minerals, timber, oil ...now. Adolf Hitler, Heinrich Himmler, and Ernst Kalterbrunner met around a conference table. Ernst Kalterbrunner was Chief of Sicherheitdienst Security Service Special Operations Division of SS. Hitler, Himmler, and Kalterbrunner discussed options ...agreed poison gas should be used ... the fastest and best way to kill large numbers of people.

A former official of German Secret Field Police, Senior Corporal Retzlaff, told Soviet authorities after his capture, what he knew about this. "Wholesale execution by hanging, and shooting, appeared to German Command too bothersome and slow a means of fulfilling tasks delegated to the punitive organizations. It was deemed necessary to devise simpler means of exterminating Soviet populations ...and, it must be said, these means were found. In 1942, I saw a large, gray, strange-looking automobile, standing near the entrance to one of the Gestapo prisons in Kharkov, surrounded by German policemen. I asked a police official I knew, named Kaminsky, what sort of an automobile it was. Kaminsky told me that it was a 'gas van' ...used for killing people. Later, I had numerous opportunities seeing this automobile work. On several occasions, I helped load the gas van with prisoners from Kharkov prison. On these occasions, I was able to convince myself, that the gas van fully answered its purpose."

In 1941, Nazis brought the Gaswagen gas vans into the Soviet Union ... to speed up processing Soviet citizens to be exterminated. Gaswagen were large, covered automobiles, painted dark gray. They had diesel engines. The inside of Gaswagens were lined with zinc-plated, galvanized sheets of iron. In the rear of the Gaswagens, were double doors ...that, could be sealed, airtight. On the floor inside the Gaswagens, was a metal grate. Beneath the metal grate, was a pipe connected to the exhaust pipe of the car. When the car's motor started, exhaust fumes from the diesel engine poured up through the grating in the floor. Diesel engine exhaust contained carbon monoxide, caused rapid poisoning, death from asphyxiation to persons locked in the rear compartment of the vehicles. Thousands of civilian Russian men, women, and children died in Nazi death vans.

In Aug. 1943, in a village near Rovno, a conference was held, of twenty-eight Regional Commissars of the Ukraine. Reichskommissar of the Ukraine Koch directed proceedings. From reports of Regional Commissars, it was clear to Koch, the Soviet population was resisting forced deportation to work as slave labor, in Germany.

Koch addressed the commissars. "We must control the population by shooting a few thousand Russian citizens. I want to send able-bodied citizens from districts in Northern Ukraine to work as slaves in Germany ...kill everyone else. Exterminating the bulk of Soviet Russians will be to Germany's advantage."

But, mass gassings of people in Gaswagens ...and, mass shootings of people in ravines, could not kill people fast enough ...to please General Staff. A bigger solution was needed. Then, General Staff first gave the order, build Concentration Extermination Camps.

Lvov, Vlassov's Army, OSS, NSC-68

It was a long walk to Lytton Plaza. Reinhard watched Patti as she moved. He liked her body. He and Dagmara continued their story.

Dagmara looked at Patti. "By 1942-1943, Reinhard advanced far up the ladder in German Army Intelligence, to the height of his career. Everything was going his way. But, for me, those times were terrible. He had to keep proving his manhood over and over again, like a stuck record ...driving me nuts. I left him. He had to prove he could survive in what he called, 'the real world'. But, in his real world, people were in the way. They had to be exterminated. I felt, people had to be nurtured, sheltered. You see, we became opposites. On Apr. 1, 1942, Reinhard became Chief of Third Reich's Foreign Armies East."

Reinhard looked at Dagmara disdainfully. "Yes, we became opposites. You believed, love conquered all. I believed, bullets did. General Staff promoted me to Intelligence Chief of Foreign Armies East, responsible for all German military intelligence operations in Eastern Europe and Soviet Union.

"I managed handling secret Fascist organizations in Eastern Europe and Soviet Union ...Stepan Bandera's 'B Faction' of Organization of Ukrainian Nationalists OUN/B ...Romania's Iron Guard ...Ustasche of Yugoslavia ...Vanagis of Latvia ... then, after summer 1942, Vlassov's 'Army' of terrorist, anti-communist defectors from Soviet Union, who marched behind General Andrey Vlassov, former communist hero, who changed sides.

"I was in charge of Foreign Armies East, I put a top man in charge of Foreign Armies West. After Admiral Wilhelm Canaris was purged, SS absorbed his Abwehr intelligence service. I became Nazi Germany's top intelligence officer. I lectured as teacher at Ogdensburg Military Academy, where we trained ruling family children to be masters in the World Order. Ordensburgen weren't ordinary Nazi propaganda, espionage schools for rank-and-file Nazi Party members. Ordensburgen were for ruling family children only, the future underground General Staff. I taught Ordensburgen students to rule subject populations with iron will, so subject populations can't revolt against them. I taught Propaganda, Social Engineering, Psychological Warfare, Espionage, Counter-Revolution ...you Patti, look at your revolutionary resistance to us. You are a leader of revolution."

Patti felt embarrassed. "Me. No I'm not. I'm a single person, I work on my own."

Reinhard smiled. "That's just it. Those are the leaders of revolution. You have heart, and perseverance, to make revolution happen. It's natural for you, in your blood, in your genetic make-up. You want to rule the world your way. We want to rule the world our way. But, your way is our way. You just don't see it ...yet."

Patti doubted it. "Me, a world ruler? I don't *think* so."

"It's in your blood," Reinhard said.

Patti was amused. So, was Reinhard. Alan noticed Patti acting like she was starting to like Reinhard. Alan didn't like that.

Reinhard continued his story. "Dec. 1943, I reached the same conclusion as Bormann, Schacht, Skorzeny, and Himmler. Germany was losing the war. There was nothing we could do to stop it. We discussed coming defeat. I told close friends, I considered the war was lost. We began thinking of the future, to think ahead, plan for the coming catastrophe. There would be a place for Germany ...in a Europe re-arming for defense, against Communism. We set our sights on the Western powers. The future for us held two objectives ...Germany would help defend Europe against communist expansion ...and, we would recover and reunify Germany's lost territories.

A Wehrmacht Supreme Command dispatch came in. It read, "The German officer is too valuable to be sacrificed. It was German Officers Corps that most promoted Germany to be a world power in our first attempt in 1914-1918. It was Officers Corps that reconstructed Germany for our second attempt to lead the world. It has been foreseen, that the second attempt will also fail. This time, our final and complete victory was so certain ...even a short while ago, that we can prepare ourselves with fresh courage ... for a new fight, later. We need our officers. At all times,

we've found troops in sufficient quantities. Nazi officers, 'in an emergency', are ordered to save their own lives ...even if it means deserting their troops."

"I understood this to mean, German Officers Corps must survive intact through the 1,000 year Reich, at all costs."

Sept. 29 1944, British Foreign Secretary Anthony Eden told House of Commons, Allied Intelligence Services had evidence Nazis were organizing a new Black Reichswehr. Anthony Eden spoke to the House of Commons. "The Gestapo, together with SS and high army officers, has created a secret organization of young Nazis and Reichswehr officers to continue resistance in Germany after Allied occupation, to wait and prepare for the opportunity of starting another war."

Reinhard looked into Patti's eyes. "Sarajevo, what's happening in former Yugoslavia, is the 1,000 year Schwarze Reichswehr new World Order ...but, only a small part, another war choreographed by world financial ruling families who credit world industries and countries to fund it all, then follow behind the armies swallowing the bank assets and industries of the conquered people to collect the interest ...the Fed majority shareholders."

Reinhard continued talking to Patti.

<>

Wehrmacht Supreme Command, Nazi Party and German industry hid economic reserves to finance postwar underground operations. Retreating through Europe, Wehrmacht stole whatever could be taken back to Germany, turned into cash, and hidden ...by order of the Supreme Command.

Sept. 17 1943, Field Marshal Fritz Erich von Mannstein issued an order to brigade commanders. "Our pillage should be methodical. It is necessary to import commodities of little weight, of great value, jewelry, precious metals and stones, cultural objects, books, linen, stamps ...in order to sell them easily, and transform them into monetary deposits in safe places."

Hide evidence of genocide, grind-up burnt bones, sift ashes for gold teeth

Soviet counter-offensive drove Wehrmacht back, out of Russia and Eastern Europe, from territory Germany had conquered and occupied.

Nazi High Command tried to hide evidence of its butchery of war prisoners, and civilians. Slave labor was organized to dig up corpses of victims, then burn them in bonfires. Bonfires burned for days. Bones not destroyed in fire were crushed in machines designed to crush human bones, then slave labor scattered crushed bones and ashes into fields.

June 1943, Gestapo Chief Heinrich Himmler, and Major General of SS Police Katzmann, issued orders to dig up and burn corpses of civilians and war prisoners tortured to death or machine-gunned near Lvov. Sodenkommando No. 1005 consisted of 125 men, commanded by Hauptsturmbannfuehrer Scherlak. They removed corpses from mass burial pits, 1,600 corpses they stacked in piles, covered with tar and gasoline, then burned. Ashes were sifted to collect gold teeth, rings, and watches executioners had missed. The Sodenkommando recovered one-hundred-and-ten kilos of gold teeth, watches and rings from several sites ...then, sent it to Germany.

In Yanovska Extermination Camp in Lvov, Germans had a special school for extermination camp commandants from Lublin, Warsaw and Cracow. Chief Scherlak, Sodenkommando No. 1005, taught commandants to dig up bodies, stack them, burn them, sift ashes for gold, crush the bones, fill-in the pits ...then, plant trees and shrubs for camouflage.

Fall 1944, Red Army troops reach Tody German Extermination Camp near Looga Estonia. Smell of burning human flesh comes from the forest. Red Army finds four huge, smoldering hills of corpses ...3,000 men, women, and children ...recently butchered ...intellectuals from Vilan, Riga, and Tallinn ...including Soviet prisoners of war.

Yanovska Extermination Camp in Lvov produced concrete, but that day, prisoners collected pine logs, bringing logs to a forest meadow by Yanovska. Germans had them put the logs on the grass in rows, made prisoners lie face down on logs ...then, machine-gunned them. Victims screamed. Then, more prisoners were made to lay a row of logs on the murdered people, and lie face down on those logs ...then, they were machine-gunned. There were five layers of corpses sandwiched with four rows of logs. There were more logs to lay on the victims, but Germans knew Red Army was nearing, so Germans poured gasoline on the corpses, and burned them. SS returned to the Yanovska Extermination Camp in Lvov, herded remaining

women, and children, into barracks ...forced them to lie on the floor ...machine-gunned them ...then, set the barracks on fire. Several men and women who weren't dead tried jumping out windows of burning barracks, but were shot. Their half-burned bodies lay on the ground, when Soviet liberation troops arrived. Some Red Army soldiers found corpses of their wives, and children, burned at the camp ...no, Russian soldiers would show no mercy to Germany. British and Americans were not as determined.

Nazi Germany was suffering military defeat. But, the battle to win the peace was just beginning. General Staff considered military loss of World War II ...a temporary defeat ...just as they'd considered military loss of World War I, temporary military defeat ... in the 1,000 year Reich new World Order. They prepared plans to win the peace ...have a Third World War ...a fourth ...a fifth, as many as were necessary for a handful of German and American and British ruling families of the new World Order ... to rule the world, with Fed majority shareholder financing ... the masters of war.

1943, Clauswitz, Goebbels, Himmler, Bormann, Schacht, Skorzeny, Dulles, von Schroder

German General Staff General Karl von Clauswitz was a revered war theorist, he believed General Staff must penetrate political and economic machinery of other nations ...to influence politics and economies of other nations ...to favor General Staff investment portfolios.

Von Clauswitz had many famous sayings. "War is the continuation of politics by other means. Politics is the continuation of war by other means."

Nazi Fifth Columns were dedicated to waging political, and economic, warfare in peacetime ... around the world.

July 12 1943, a *La France Libre* reporter in Paris interviewed a high-ranking German officer. "Peace? There will be no peace, anywhere in the world, after the guns stop firing. The battle of the Fifth Columns will take the place after the battles of the tanks and armored cars."

General Staff would grow its Fifth Column in the U.S. ...using social engineering, to fragment, and destabilize American society, provoke race riots, anti-Semitic terrorism, dissent between capitol and labor, penetrate and influence American politics, economics, and foreign policy.

War booty was put into a secret fund to finance a postwar, underground Nazi Officers Corps.

Leaders of the postwar underground Nazi Officers Corps were officers, and non-commissioned officers of SS regiments, picked to be the inner guard of German Military Supreme Command.

Since June 1934, with the purge in the Nazi Party of those officers loyal to Roehm, ordinary Nazi Party members were excluded from joining SS. SS was only for fanatical Nazi Party members. Chief of Schutzstaffel Protective Echelon and Plenipotentiary General of Third Reich Heinrich Himmler reorganized SS into a Nazi military elite. The uniform of the SS was re-cut, to look like Kaiser cavalry elite guard, the Death's Head Hussars. Senior SS officers were recruited from General Staff ruling families ...so, German industrialists, financiers, military men and Junkers ...became SS officers.

Baron von Schroder, Director of Bank of International Settlements, became a Schutzstaffel SS General

In 1944, Schutzstaffel SS Intelligence Division directed Nazi underground activities in Germany, and multinationally. Schroder ruling family [editor's note, see Fed ownership charts, p590] was one of the most influential ruling families in the world ...during World War I, J. Henry Schroder Banking Co. was puppet master, pulling financial marionette strings, playing the money fiddle for political leaders of many countries ... along with other Fed majority shareholders.

<>

Nancy often read Eustace Mullins, *Secrets of the Fed*, to me.

President Hoover had two administrators. Prentiss Gray was a lumber salesman from the West Coast, Julius Barnes was a grain salesman from Duluth. Post-war both men were partners in J. Henry Schroder Banking Corp. of New York, building financial empires in grain and sugar.

Under Hoover, Barnes was President of Grain Corp. of the U.S. Food Administration, 1917-1918. Gray was chief of Marine Transportation.

Zabriskie, a J. Henry Schroder partner, was put in charge of the U.S. Sugar Equalization Board. Schroder Corp. up-and-coming and would-be directors controlled the food supply in the United States through its grain and sugar czars during World War I.

By the end of World War I, J. Henry Schroder Co. directors owned Cuba's sugar industry.

Another Schroder partner, Rionda, became president of Cuba Cane Corp., and held board directorates in Manati Sugar Co., American British and Continental Corp. and other multinational corporate boards.

Baron Bruno von Schroder was senior partner of J. Henry Schroder, and a director of North British and Mercantile Insurance Co.

Baron Rudolph von Schroder of Hamburg, Bruno's father, was director of the largest Brazilian coffee company, Sao Paulo Coffee Ltd., co-directed by Tiarks, who worked for J. Henry Schroder.

<>

Hitler was invited to a meeting at Schroder Bank in Berlin, Jan. 4, 1933. Leading industrialists and bankers of Germany tided Hitler over his financial difficulties, enabling him to meet the enormous debt he'd incurred in connection with maintenance of his private army. John Foster Dulles and Allen W. Dulles ... of the New York law firm, Sullivan & Cromwell, represented Schroder Bank in America, and went on to sit as directors on Schroder banks.

Allen became a director of J. Henry Schroder Co. Allen would become Wartime Chief of Office of Strategic Services intelligence operations, in Bern Switzerland.

In 1938, London Schroder Bank became the German financial agent in Great Britain.

New York branch of Schroder merged in 1936 with Rockefellers, as Schroder, Rockefeller, Inc. at 48 Wall Street. These groups were major Fed shareholders, embodying the World Order, and later, the new World Order.

Carlton P. Fuller of Schroder was president of the firm.

Avery Rockefeller was vice-president. He had been a behind-the-scenes partner of J. Henry Schroder for years, and set up the construction firm of Bechtel Corp., whose employees (on leave) played a leading role in my Reagan Administration, as Secretary of Defense and Secretary of State.

The establishment of the international Schroder group of companies in the 1960s, 1970s, and early 1980s was the first stage in this process. The second stage, which was achieved in the latter half of the 1980s, was the integration of the conduct of operations on a worldwide basis. In these years, the international Schroder group of companies became a single entity ... Schroders.

Nazi Baron Kurt von Schroder acted as the conduit for IT&T money funneled to Heinrich Himmler's SS organization in 1944, while World War II was in progress, and United States was at war with Germany.

Kilgore Committee listed a dozen important affiliations held by Kurt von Schroder in the 1940's, including President of Deutsche Reichsbahn, Reich Board of Economic Affairs, SS Senior Group Leader, Council of Reich Post Office, Deutsche Reichsbank, and other leading banks and industrial groups.

Schroder served on the board of all International Telephone and Telegraph (IT&T) subsidiaries in Germany.

J. Henry Schroder Banking Co. is listed as Number 2 in capitalization, on the list of the seventeen merchant bankers who make up the exclusive Accepting Houses Committee in London. Almost unknown in the United States, it had to be approved by the Bank of England. And, like Warburg family, von Schroders began banking operations in Hamburg, Germany.

At the turn of the century, in 1900, Baron Bruno von Schroder established the London branch. He was joined by Frank Cyril Tiarks, in 1902. Tiarks married Emma Franziska of Hamburg, and was a director of the Bank of England, from 1912 to 1945.

With Hoover in the White House, J. Henry Schroder Corp. pursued its vision of financing Hitler's assumption of power in Germany to pursue World War II ...which was really a continuation of World War I, basically same producers, directors, cast and crew. Schroder is a major shareholder of the Bank of England and the Fed.

<>

Reinhard continued his story.

Chief of the Schutzstaffel Protective Echelon and Plenipotentiary General of the Third Reich Heinrich Himmler spoke with SS officers. "Sooner, or later, we'll make the territory vital to Germany her playing field."

The objective of Underground Nazi Officers Corps was, prevent the rise of anti-Nazi, democratic German leaders. Underground Nazi Officers Corps used terrorism, and death-squads, to eliminate people who believed in Democracy ...and, who fought against fascist dictatorship, just as in Germany after World War I.

Soviet Union had borne the brunt of military attacks, and suffered great losses, long before U.S. entered World War II ...just as in World War I. Soviet Union was primarily responsible for defeating the Germans, in both wars.

Mid-Jan. 1943, Germany lost the battle of Stalingrad in Russia, Hitler continued to rant of victory ... General Staff realized, they could not win the war in the East, that year. This meant, most of German forces were stuck on the Eastern Front, and could not go fight on the Western Front. English and American troops were going to invade the Western Front in Italy, in summer. German forces would be split, and outnumbered. President Franklin Roosevelt, and Prime Minister Winston Churchill, were thrilled by the Soviet victory.

Jan. 24 1943, in Casablanca Roosevelt and Churchill demand Germany surrender and Europe be de-Nazified. General Staff ruling families split in two factions ...one led by Heinrich Himmler ...the other, by Martin Bormann.

Heinrich Himmler was Chief of Schutzstaffel SS, the core of the Nazi party ...the 'Black Shirts', that became Hitler's bodyguard in the late 1920's. Schutzstaffel SS was the most powerful Nazi political institution. Himmler was loyal to Hitler.

July 20 1944, a military coup on Hitler's life failed. Hitler was wounded, but not killed. In retaliation, SS Leader Heinrich Himmler seized control, arrested seven thousand troops, executing 5,000. Himmler and his SS became the remaining organ of the Nazi Party.

<>

Adolf Hitler and Allen Dulles postulated that an alliance of U.S. capitalists and Soviet Communists was politically unworkable.

Hitler explained to Himmler. "Even now, they are at loggerheads. If we can deliver a few more blows, this artificially bolstered common front may suddenly collapse. When capitalists and communists break apart, U.S. will consider joining Nazi Germany ...in an anti-Soviet alliance."

Himmler nodded. "Then, we'll negotiate separate peace with the U.S. ...Germany will keep fighting against the Soviet Union, with the U.S. now Germany's new ally."

Deputy Fuehrer and Head of the Nazi Party Martin Bormann was Hitler's close friend ...and held superior rank to Himmler. Bormann was Hitler's link to the industrial and financial cartels running the Nazi economy. Bormann was a close friend to Hermann Schmitz. Hermann Schmitz was Chief Executive of I.G. Farben. I. G. Farben was Nazi Germany's wealthiest industrial power.

I.G. Farben CEO Hermann Schmitz spoke to Bormann. "I don't think this separate peace idea is going to work."

Deputy Fuehrer Bormann looked at Schmitz. "I agree, Hermann. A separate peace is optimistic, unrealistic. We can't talk Roosevelt into it. Allied military power's too great. Roosevelt already demanded unconditional surrender, de-Nazification of Europe. Our best hope to survive military defeat is, depend on ourselves. If we surrender, tens of thousands of SS men will be hanged. We must start shipping Nazis out of Europe into Latin America, Argentina, Paraguay, South Africa, Egypt, and Indonesia …till we get strong again, and reunite."

Schmitz smiled.

<>

June 1944, the Germans lose the battle of Normandy. Martin Bormann begins to help Nazi Officers Corps escape underground from Europe, and shipping out Nazi war booty treasure. Treasure is divided …three tons of gold fillings from victims of extermination camps are melted into gold bars …then, deposited in Reichsbank in Berlin …a billion dollars in currencies, silver, platinum, and precious stones were deposited in the Reichsbank …large tonnages of highest grade steel, industrial machinery, patents, and blueprints needed to monopolize specialized areas of manufacturing, all had to be smuggled out of Germany to abroad, and hidden in legitimate front companies.

Nazi companies had to be re-founded, outside Germany, so they'd not be liable to pay reparations for war damages. Tens of thousands of Nazi SS war criminals needed to be smuggled out of Germany, resettled in German colonies abroad …with means of self-support.

Aug. 10, 1944 Deputy Fuehrer Martin Bormann has a meeting of German industrialists at Hotel Maison Rouge, Strasbourg.

Minutes are kept. 'The Nazi Party is ready to supply large amounts of money to industrialists who contribute to post-war organization, abroad. In return, the Party demands all financial reserves already been transferred abroad, or may later be transferred, so after the defeat, a strong new Reich can be built,' the minutes read.

Dr. Hjalmar Horace Greeley Schacht, Hitler's Minister of Economy, arranges for the Nazi Party to finance 750 businesses …outside of Germany, around the world. The firms generated 30 million dollars. The revenue was dedicated to Nazi use. Dr. Schacht's expertise in re-licensing ownership of German businesses abroad was successful …though, he was later thrown in prison on charges related to a coup against Hitler's life.

Hitler referred to Otto Skorzeny as his, 'favorite commando'. Otto Skorzeny was an SS officer, a Gestapo officer, and a Waffen SS officer. The job of removing Nazi assets and treasure out of Germany, and relocating it abroad …was given to Otto Skorzeny.

Otto Skorzeny, Martin Bormann, and Hjalmar Schacht worked together, transporting Nazi assets, and treasure, out of Europe. They worked closely with the Vatican, the center of the 'ratlines' …used to smuggle Nazis, Nazi assets, and treasure to Memmingen in Bavarian, then to Rome, then, out of Italy to Nazi colonies abroad. Martin Bormann called his international organization, 'Odessa', the Organization of Veterans of the SS. Odessa was to live into the next century. Bormann, Skorzeny, and Schacht had another strategic member making Odessa successful … Reinhard Gehlen … Gehlen's Intelligence Organization, the Gehlen Org, created by Allen Dulles on behalf of major shareholders of the Fed, the Bank of England, and Bank of International Settlements. Gehlen was in military succession with Martin Bormann, Otto Skorzeny, Hjalmar Schacht, von Schroder …not to mention, friends with Allen Dulles.

<>

Reinhard and Dagmara continued their story to Patti. Dagmara began.

1943, Christian West

"In 1943, Reinhard was in charge of intelligence for Foreign Armies East FHO. Reinhard also realized the Nazis were going to lose World War II. He had to make an escape plan, for himself. He had to help Odessa succeed. Reinhard wanted to make use of the Christian West movement, the concept that post-War Nazi Germany, and the U.S., would form an alliance …work together to overthrow Soviet Russia."

<>

Reinhard nodded. "I'm sure, when Germany loses the war, U.S. capitalists will no longer want to work together with Soviet Russia's Marxists, and communists …capitalism and communism are opposites. One hoards capital in the hands of a few ruling families …the other, establishes middle class and lower class families, and shares capital among them …theoretically. At that time, the U.S. will need me. They don't have an intelligence agency in Eastern Europe, like Foreign Armies East. I'll offer them our services."

Allen Dulles scratched his head. He smiled. "Good …the U.S. wants instant gratification. If we're going to go to war against Russia to keep building our national debt and reaping the interest …then, we'll have no time to build an Eastern Europe intelligence outfit from scratch. Me, and my brother, will rally the U.S. side of the trans-Atlantic Axis of U.S. financial and industrial ruling families. We'll have the U.S. make you an offer you can't refuse. … We'll bring you onboard

U.S. intelligence. After all, you've got the best Eastern Europe, anti-Soviet intelligence outfit in the world. We need you, your intelligence assets. You now manage Eastern European Fascist guerrilla outfits. We'll pick up your tab. How will that be? ...that'll help the U.S. win our coming war against Russia."

Gero von Gaevernitz smiled. Gero was the son of a Quaker, Reichstag politician that Dulles met in 1916. Gero's mother was a Jewish intellectual. Gero's sister married Edmund Stinnes, son of Hugo Stinnes ...Hugo was a major financial backer of Hitler.

Hugo owned the Stinnes Iron & Coal industry. Throughout the 1920's, Gero von Gaevernitz jet-setted back-and-forth between the Ruhr, and Wall Street. He later got a doctorate in economics, became an investment adviser ...was well connected to the Warburg Bank in Hamburg ...was friends with German financier Edward von Waetjen, who had an American mother and married into the Rockefeller family. Gero was hired in Manhattan by Equity Corp.

In 1936, Gero became a U.S. citizen. His parents moved to Switzerland. Gero established a home base, in Bern ...where he was caretaker of his brother's estate, near Escona.

In the 1940's, 'Wild Bill' Donovan, a powerful Wall Street figure, became head of America's wartime intelligence service, the Office of Strategic Services. Wild Bill met Gero socially, they became friends. One friend of Donovan's, who irritated workers in Donovan's Washington D.C. Office of Strategic Services ...was Donovan's New York Office of Strategic Services branch manager, Allen Dulles.

Allen Dulles showed up in Bern Switzerland with a letter of introduction, he handed to Gero von Gaevernitz. Dulles struck up a relationship, using Gero as a go-between with the German émigré community. Gero kept his American citizenship. Dulles set up financing for a dummy corporation in New York, for Gero, called, Schildgerumohr Inc., later called, Transmares. Dulles expedited financing ...through J. Henry Schroder Bank.

U.S. Justice Department was watching Schroder Bank at this time, because it was running the British blockade to provide strategic materials for Germany.

As late as Oct. 1941, Gero listed his job in Switzerland as being an agent of Schildgerumohr Inc., Transmares.

Gero, a wheeler-and-dealer, cross-registered shipping title ports of register from Finnish ... an Axis port of call ... to Swiss, a neutral country ...he made big commissions, washing the money in Lisbon through E.V.D. Wight. Gero managed Stinnes holdings in Germany and Switzerland.

Himmler's agent contacting western representatives, Karl Langbehn, felt uneasy belonging to Himmler's strong wing in the Nazi party that wanted to propose Himmler's version of a Christian West plan peace settlement with Britain.

For sympathy and help in Switzerland, Langbehn went to Gero. Langbehn's approaches to Gaevernitz interested SD Amt VI International Affairs Chief Walter Schellenberg, who recruited informers from finance and industry.

Schellenberg carefully watched Langbehn's attempts to 'turn' Gero von Gaevernitz. And, so did Dulles. Gero intended to profit from the war as best he could. Allen Dulles knew Gero Gaevernitz was a triple agent, working for British and German interests, as well as for the United States' Wild Bill Donovan. When World War II began, Gero worked with U.S. Military Attache in Bern, Brigadier General Barnwell Legge.

Brigadier General Legge sent a letter to Allen Dulles. 'Gaevernitz has rendered most valuable service, by gaining contact with prominent German industrialists and business men who visited Switzerland. German Counsel at Geneva is Dr. Wolfgang Krauel. Dr. Krauel has a list of former Canaris men in Switzerland ...including Hans-Bernd Gisevius, Max von Engelbrechten, and Graf Auersperg von der Muhle. Canaris sent these men to Switzerland to make contact with the Americans. Canaris ordered them to report to Gero von Gaevernitz. Canaris is worried about the fall of the Reich. He wants them to work together on the Christian West Plan to unite the U.S. and Nazi Germany together against Soviet Russia.'

Years later, an intimate of Canaris cabled congratulations to Allen Dulles on his new job as CIA director. 'I have known since 1942, how highly Canaris esteemed you. Even at that time, Canaris ordered me to align myself with you ...as soon as possible. I am in touch with one of your most capable co-workers, through a very clever banker. I was able to obtain from your staff, without any difficulty, information very important for us. I would prefer to say nothing more about this now.'

SD Amt VI International Affairs Chief Schellenberg carefully watched attempts to turn Gero. Which faction of the Nazis was Gaevernitz loyal to? ...to Canaris? ...to Himmler? ...was he loyal to the British? ...which faction? ...to the U.S.? ...which ruling families? Dulles didn't care. Neither did Gaevernitz. Gaevernitz, like Dulles, wanted to promote their own financial portfolios above all political considerations -- the point of war, in the first place.

Gero sized up Hermann Schmitz. "Things are going well. Transmare's given me a cover and commercial references."

<>

Hermann Schmitz, Chief Executive of I.G. Farben, smiled. "Looks good."

Allen Dulles looked at Hans-Bernd Gisevius. "There are several peace initiatives coming at me ... to present to the U.S. ... from opposing Nazi groups ...some from Abwehr activists ...some from pessimistic SS officers."

Hans-Bernd Gisevius nodded. Hans was Sonderfuehrer in the SS ...a reactionary, tied financially to the Lutheran Synod, instrumental in recruiting a powerful faction of the Nazi Party in 1931-1933. Gisevius was a Gestapo lawyer, when Admiral Canaris appointed him Zurich Vice-Consul. Canaris made Hans, his representative to Madam Halina Szymanska, a Polish intelligence 'cut-out'. Canaris' military intelligence used Szymanska to leak information to Van Den Heuvel, and the American Special Intelligence Service.

<>

Dulles met often with Hans in Hans' drawing room at 23 Herrengasse. Dulles represented himself ...as President Roosevelt's personal representative. Hans agreed, he'd keep Dulles informed on plots against Hitler's life. Dulles said, the U.S. and Germany would benefit when he briefed Washington on Canaris' version of the Christian West concept Hans had already explained to Dulles.

Gisevius smiled. "I'll let security expert Rudolph Diels know. He'll fill-in Hjalmar Schacht. Schacht will fill in Admiral Canaris."

<>

Dulles nodded in approval, looked at Prince Max von Hohenlohe. Prince Max smiled back at Dulles. Within SS, SD managed subversion. SD's Amt VI International Affairs Chief, Walter Schellenberg, was an SS foreign minister.

In 1942, SD Chief Walter Schellenberg told Himmler, he would put out feelers to launch Himmler's version of the Christian West plan to unite the U.S. and Nazi Germany against the Soviet Union.

Schellenberg needed cut-out agents, walk-ins. Schellenberg contacted Abram Stevens Hewitt in Stockholm, who contacted Theodore Morde, a *Reader's Digest* correspondent in Ankara ... in discussions, Prince Max Egon zu Hohenlohe-Langenburg's name emerged. Allen Dulles used the code name, 'Mr. Bull'. Prince Max Egon Hohenlohe used the code name, 'Mr. Pauls'.

<>

Prince Max was a jet-setter, a ruling family member for the Sudatenland. Prince Max was an arms salesman for the Schkode arms works. Schellenberg got him the job. Prince Max married into the Hapsburg dynasty, traveled on a Lichtenstein passport. When SD Commander Reinhard Heidrich was assassinated in May 1942, SD Chief Schellenberg emerged in a position of greater power. Schellenberg was Max Hohenlohe's handler.

<>

Early 1943, Dulles and Hohenlohe spoke frequently. "Good here."

In addition to representing Schroder's American banking interests, Allen Dulles and John Foster Dulles represented Insgilde Bank of Stockholm, owned by the Wallenbergs.

In 1940, Marcus Wallenberg came to New York, to safeguard American-held certificates of Robert Bosch Co.

Allen Dulles felt insistent. "Marcus, you need to publicize your contacts and my contacts with resistance groups that tried to remove Hitler from power in the putsch of July 20. Unless there are local reasons at your end, which I can't judge from here, it might be well to get this out in the open. Robert Bosch's nephew is a director inside I. G. Farben leadership. Robert Bosch Co. was used by Karl Goerdeler, one of the plotters against Hitler, as a cover for activities while organizing German coup attempts against Hitler."

<>

In Bern, Allen Dulles did legal work for J. Henry Schroder bank ...was close to Thomas McKittrick, one of his clients. McKittrick was President of Bank of International Settlements in Switzerland ...founded by Nazi interests, under the guidance of Hjalmar Schacht who co-founded BIS to dissolve war reparations Germany owed from World War I. Now, at the close of World War II, BIS was a clearinghouse to launder Third Reich booty into legitimate front businesses around the world.

<>

Washington and London distrusted various Christian West plans, that various Nazi factions presented through Allen Dulles.

Dulles spoke of coup d'états ...planned against Hitler by Nazis who weren't racists like Hitler was ...Nazis against genocide ...Nazis who wanted to collaborate with British and Americans to hold the Eastern Front against Soviet Union communists.

Dulles' ruling family backers and major Fed shareholders in New York and Washington told him, it wasn't likely that a large enough group of Nazi insurgents existed ... to take power from Hitler. Schellenberg sent Max Hohenlohe with a series of peace proposals to see British Ambassador Sir Samuel Hoare and American Embassy Counselor William Walton Butterworth, a friend of George Keenan since Princeton ...and with Vatican sympathizers ...and with Fritz Klein, a friend of both Dulles brothers.

<>

Feb. 1943, American negotiators in Lisbon were stationed with George Keenan, Colonel Solborg, and Allen Dulles. Exactly what was agreed upon ...was classified. What leaked out? ...Dulles was angry with old fashioned politicians and prejudiced Jews ...Dulles wanted Jews sent to Africa ...Dulles wanted German bishops in America to argue for Germany's cause ...Dulles praised American Catholics, who forced Jewish-American newspapers to stop criticizing General Franco's dictatorship in Spain ...Dulles wanted a peace that 'avoided the excesses of Versailles', and let Germany retain some of its conquered territories in Austria and Czechoslovakia ...Dulles wanted Washington to stop thinking in terms of winners and losers, victors and vanquished ...to start thinking in terms of world order, and to start making progress in stopping the Soviet Union from ruling the world.

Slowly, Hohenlohe became a spokesman for SS elements within the German government ...wanting to get rid of 'extremist' Nazis.

Allen Dulles argued his case. "The importance of Prussia, and an inwardly-unbalanced and inferiority-complex ridden Prussian militarism ...must be reduced. A Federal Greater Germany retaining Austrian and Czechoslovakian territories will form a cordon sanitaire against Bolshevism and pan-Slavism, stop the eastward enlargement of Poland, and preserve a strong Hungary. Federal Greater Germany will be like the U.S., with a Danube confederation to insure orderly progress in central and eastern Europe against the Soviet Union."

<>

Summer 1943, in Santender Spain Abwehr Officer F. Eustis von Einem said he sat in on meeting where Wild Bill Donovan agreed to Canaris' Christian West version terms.

1943, Misery Meadows

At Foreign Armies East Intelligence headquarters, Reinhard listened to Hitler yelling at him.

Hitler was beside himself. "Why are you giving me these defeatist intelligence reports?! Germany will win this war! I just promoted you to Brigadier General ...and, I'm sorry I did! I think I'll fire you! Give me optimistic reports!"

Hitler left Gehlen's intelligence headquarters.

Reinhard called his staff around him. "Hitler can yell all he wants to, do the methamphetamines he wants ...it won't change what's coming. We need to get together our intelligence files on Eastern Europe and Soviet Union, move south ...hide them in the Bavarian Alps. We need more agents. We're the only unit in Third Reich recruiting new members, even while we're losing the war. SS men are joining FHO, because it's the only safe place for them to be ...when the war ends.

"I'm dividing our top staff into three groups, repositioning them in Bavaria. Otto Skorzeny is doing the same thing with his top staff. By the time Germany surrenders, on May 7, 1945 ...we'll be hiding in a well-stocked chalet, in the mountains at Misery Meadows."

When Reinhard and his selected staff arrived at the Misery Meadows chalet, they were a party of eight, including two wounded men, and three young women. They buried their intelligence files, in a clearing in soft ground, in Misery Meadows. They maintained radio contact with the other two groups their staff had divided into, for three weeks ...waiting for the Americans to appear below, in the valley.

Reinhard kept a diary. 'These days of living in the arms of nature are truly enchanting. We grew accustomed to the peace, our ears were attuned to nature's every sound,' he wrote.

Nancy put the book down she was reading to me, went into the ranch house, and threw up.

<>

Meanwhile, in Washington DC, First Lady Eleanor Roosevelt worried. She spent her career campaigning for the women's movement, labor movement, and against racism. She and her husband were sexually distant. President

Roosevelt had a mistress. And, he spend time yachting with his mistress on the Astor ruling family's yacht. Still, Eleanor felt, she had to warn her husband about Allen Dulles ...that Dulles was too closely involved with underground Nazi business.

Eleanor sent a memo to her husband, the President. 'Allen Welch Dulles is part of Bill Donovan's outfit. He's directly tied with Schroder Bank. Schroder Bank is going to represent underground Nazi business interests after the war.'

<>

Jan. 1945, President Roosevelt gave his annual, 'Message to Congress' speech. Roosevelt warned America, Germany wanted to create postwar division ...split the Allies against one another ...German General Staff could make an opportunity to rise again after World War II, the way they had after World War I ...and attack the world again, in this century, in a World War III.

President Roosevelt made his speech. "The wedge the Germans attempted to drive in Western Europe was less dangerous in actual terms of winning the war ... than the wedges they are continually attempting to drive between ourselves, and the Allies."

Jan. 18, 1945, American CBS correspondent, Charles Shaw, in Europe reported by shortwave ... an underground Nazi Officer terrorist death-squad movement was murdering people in American-occupied Germany. The name of the terrorist death-squad was, the 'Fehme' ...directed by SS Officer Horst von Pflugk-Hartung.

<>

Nancy read me Paul Frölich's, *Rosa Luxemburg,* to fill in background information about Horst von Pflung-Hartung.

"On January 15th, nine o'clock in the evening, Karl Liebknecht, Rosa Luxemburg, and Wilhelm Pieck were arrested at No. 53, Mannheimer Strasse in Wilmersdorf, by a group of soldiers. At first, both Liebknecht and Luxemburg gave false names, thinking the raid was accidental. However, they appear to have been denounced by a spy who had wormed his way into Liebknecht's confidence. Karl Liebknecht was taken to headquarters of Vigilant Committee, from there to headquarters of the Household Cavalry Division in the Eden Hotel. Rosa Luxemburg and Wilhelm Pieck were taken there, later.

"When first news of the arrests reached Eden Hotel, arrangements were made by Captain Pabst ...for killing Karl Liebknecht, and Rosa Luxemburg. The moment Liebknecht was brought in, he was struck over the head, twice, with rifle-butts. He subsequently asked to be bandaged, but was refused. Rosa Luxemburg, brought in later, was received with wild shouts, and a torrent of brutal abuse.

"Pieck was under guard in the corridor, Karl Liebknecht and Rosa Luxemburg were led into Captain Pabst's room, for 'questioning'. Liebknecht was taken away from the hotel. On leaving the building, he was again struck on the head with a rifle-butt, then dragged into a car by Captain Horst von Pflugk-Hartung and brother Captain Heinz von Pflugk-Hartung, Lieutenants Liepmann, von Rittgen, Stiege, Schulz, and by a trooper named Friedrich. In the Tiergarten, Liebknecht was dragged, half-unconscious, from the car and murdered ...a little distance away. The first shot was fired by Captain Horst von Pflugk-Hartung. The corpse was then taken back to the car, and driven to the nearest mortuary ...where it was delivered up as, that of 'an unknown man found dead in the Tiergarten'.

"Shortly afterwards, Rosa Luxemburg was led from Hotel Eden, by Lieutenant Vogel. At the door, a trooper named, Runge, was waiting with orders from Lieutenant Vogel, and Captain Horst von Pflugk-Hartung ...to strike her to the ground, with the butt of his carbine. He smashed her skull with two blows, she was lifted, half-dead, into a waiting car ...accompanied by Lieutenant Vogel, and a number of other officers. One of them struck her on the head with the butt of his revolver, and Lieutenant Vogel killed her ...with a shot in the head, at point-blank range. The car stopped at Liechtenstein Bridge over Landwehr Canal, her corpse was flung from the bridge into the water, from which it was not recovered, until the following May."

http://www.kirjasto.sci.fi/luxembur.htm
Nancy found it on the internet, described Rosa.

"German revolutionary leader, journalist, and socialist theorist, killed in Berlin in 1919, during the German revolution. Rosa Luxemburg saw herself as a citizen of the proletariat. She lived the international life of a Socialist 'pilgrim', believing that only socialism could bring true freedom, and social justice. An advocate of mass action, spontaneity, and workers' democracy. Born in Zamosc, in Russian Poland, into a Jewish middle-class family. At age five, she became ill. After recovering, she walked with a limp ...sciatic pain caused her trouble her whole life. Luxemburg entered University of Zürich, studied natural sciences and political economy. In 1892, changed to the faculty of law. Two years later, researched at the major Polish library in Paris. Started her career as a journalist, became a leader of the Social Democratic Party of the Kingdom of Poland, and Lithuania. In 1898, completed her doctorate.

"To obtain German citizenship, Luxemburg married Gustav Lübeck, youngest son of a friend. Luxemburg became in 1898, leader of the left wing of SPD, participating in the second International and 1905 revolution in Russian Poland. After insulting the Kaiser, she spent in 1904 a short time in prison, in Zwickau. The same year, she drafted, *SDKPL -- Social Democracy of the Kingdom of Poland,* and a Lithuania party program, *What Do We Want?*

"During the 1905 Russian Revolution, she developed the idea that socialism is a revolutionary process ...that transforms political and economic relations towards ever-greater democratic control by the workers, themselves. In 1906, she was arrested in Warsaw ...but, finally released, on health grounds. She returned to Germany, where she taught at SPD party school in Berlin until 1914, developing ideas about general strike as a political weapon.

"In 1912 her major theoretical work appeared, *The Accumulation of Capital ...i*n which she tried to prove capitalism was doomed and would inevitably collapse ...on economic grounds. After differences with moderate German socialists, she founded with Karl Liebknecht, the radical Spartacus League, in 1916. She drafted the Spartacus program, *Leitsätze.* Two years later, the organization became the German Communist Party.

"During World War I, Luxemburg spent long times in prison, writing, *Spartakusbriefe* and *Die Russisce Revolution* ...where she welcomed the October Revolution, as a precursor of world revolution. In the *Junius Pamphlet,* 1916, written under her pseudonym, Junius ...she argued, a choice between Socialism or Barbarism ...is a world-historical turning point ...that demands action by the proletariat.

"However, Luxemburg participated reluctantly in the Spartacist uprising in Berlin against the government. The uprising, which failed, was a defining moment among others ...for Adolf Hitler. Luxemburg and Liebknecht were arrested in 1919. While being transported to prison, she and Liebknecht were murdered, on the night of Jan. 15-16, 1919 by German Freikorps soldiers. Luxemburg's body was thrown into the Landwehr canal ...and, found on May. She was buried June 13 in Friedrichsfeld cemetery, where graves of Liebknecht and other revolutionaries situated. Her burial became a mass demonstration, witnessed by correspondents."

<>

Nancy educated me every day on the things I wished I had known before I was President of the United States ...it is in respect to her that I commissioned this fictional autobiography of my life ...and, it's ghostwriter. Although, I never realized there would be real ghosts involved ...then again, I'd never realized we're spirits, either ...what's the difference?

Nancy read to me ...as, Reinhard told his story to Patti. Patti and I were both finding out the hard way, what being a Reagan *really* meant in the world.

Jan. 18, 1945, American CBS correspondent Shaw broadcast his report on radio about revived Fehme operations in Germany. "The purpose of the Fehme is to kill anti-Nazi Germans who want to cooperate with United Nations."

Feb. 1945, Hugenberg, 79-year-old Pan-German industrialist, held senior position on Hitler's Reichstag. United Nations was created ...on the claim of making sure Germany surrendered unconditionally ...and, that after military defeat German militarism, Nazism, and German General Staff would be eliminated.

<>

Roosevelt, Stalin, and Churchill, leaders of the three great powers who defeated the Nazis, met at Yalta in the Crimea, early Feb. 1945, announcing decisions and policies regarding the fate of Germany. Roosevelt, Stalin, and Churchill were the leaders of the United Nations.

Roosevelt, Stalin, and Churchill made a joint statement. "It is our inflexible purpose to destroy German militarism and Nazism, and to insure Germany will never again be able to disturb the peace of the world. We are determined to disarm, and disband all German armed forces ...break up for all time the German General Staff that has repeatedly contrived the resurgence of German militarism ...remove or destroy all German military equipment ...eliminate or control all German industry that could be used for military production ...bring all war criminals to just and swift punishment, and exact reparation in kind for the destruction wrought by the Germans ...wipe out the Nazi Party, Nazi laws, organizations and institutions ...remove all Nazi and militarist influences from public office and from cultural and economic life of the German people ...and, take in harmony such other measures in Germany as may be necessary to the future peace and safety of the world. It is not our purpose to destroy the people of Germany ...but, only when Nazism and militarism have been extirpated will there be hope for a decent life for Germans, and a place for them in the community of nations. During the past thirty years, in two world wars, a colossal price has been paid in human suffering, and destruction, as a result of German aggression. There must be no third world war," the joint statement read.

<>

Eisenhower, representing the Grand Alliance, would accept only unconditional surrender by Germany, that included unconditional German surrender to Soviet Russia.

Mar. 7, 1945 German General Staff failed to blow up Ludendorff Bridge over the Rhine at Remahgan. This allowed the U.S. to cross the river to occupy most of Central Germany ...before the Red Army could get there.

Stalin, leader of Soviet Russia, made allegations Great Britain and the U.S. were secretly trying to negotiate a Christian West treaty with Nazi Germany ...that, would allow the Wehrmacht to continue armed military operations against Soviet Russia and the Red Army ...similar to the way after World War I Germany was allowed to continue fighting Communists in Eastern Europe after Germany had started, waged then lost World War I ...Herbert Hoover at that time helping to re-outfit and supply defeated German troops with food and money ...that had been intended to feed starving war refugees of Europe, Eastern Europe, and Russia.

Stalin didn't want a repeat performance.

Apr. 5, 1945 Stalin wrote to President Roosevelt. "You affirm, that so far no negotiations have been entered into. Apparently, you are not fully informed. As regards my military colleagues, they, on the basis of information in their possession, are sure negotiations did take place ...and, that they ended in an agreement with the Germans, whereby the German commander on the Western Front is to open the front to the Anglo-American troops and let them move East, while the British and Americans have promised in exchange, to ease the armistice terms for the Germans."

Roosevelt and Churchill rejected Stalin's comments. Stalin was upset.

Stalin wrote again. "It is hard to agree that the absence of German resistance on the Western Front is due solely to the fact they've been beaten. The Germans have 147 divisions on the Eastern Front. They could safely withdraw from 15-to-20 divisions from the Eastern Front to aid their forces on the Western Front. Yet, they haven't done so, nor are they doing so. They are fighting desperately against the Russians for Szemlinietzsche, an obscure station in Czechoslovakia, which they need just as much as a dead man needs a poultice ...but, they surrender without any resistance such important towns in the heart of Germany as Aznebruk, Mannheim, and Cassel to you. You will admit, this behavior on the part of the Germans is more than strange, and unaccountable."

<>

In the last six months before World War II ended, President Roosevelt and Wild Bill Donovan convinced each other, the U.S. needed a permanent intelligence service ...as up to this point there had only been one in wartime ...also, that this intelligence service should, like OSS, be civilian-controlled ... rather than by the military ...they decided OSS would be the foundation of a new civilian intelligence service.

Oct. 31, 1944 Roosevelt had Donovan release a memo, on how to organize the new civilian intelligence service.

Wild Bill consulted with Allen Dulles, Wartime Chief of OSS operations in Bern Switzerland. Dulles suggested, in time of war the new civilian agency be placed under military command, that ought to make the military happy. Wild Bill included the suggestion in his memo.

Nov. 18, 1944, Wild Bill read his memo to Roosevelt. "There are common-sense reasons why you may desire to lay the keel of the ship, at once. We have now, in OSS, the trained and specialized personnel needed for such a task, this talent should not be dispersed."

<>

Wild Bill said the new civilian intelligence service would report to the President, and Secretary of State. The mission of the new intelligence service would be, to give the President enough information to make foreign policy decisions. Donovan allowed the civilian Secretary of War, and the civilian Secretary of the Navy, to sit on the advisory board of the new intelligence agency ...otherwise, there'd be no formal military representatives on the advisory board ...also, the advisory board could only advise, not control, activities of the new intelligence agency.

One role of the new intelligence agency would be, to coordinate all Government intelligence agency functions ...so Donovan's and Dulles' new intelligence agency would dominate Army G-2 Intelligence ...and, Navy's Office of Naval Intelligence.

An Army G-2 intelligencer thought the plan was awkward ...another Army G-2 intelligencer referred to the civilian OSS as, 'a bunch of Wall Street faggots'.

<>

J. Edgar Hoover, head of FBI, was against creation of the OSS ...during World War II, J. Edgar maintained an FBI intelligence network in South America ...even though South America was under intelligence jurisdiction of Office of Strategic Services.

President Roosevelt sent Joint Chiefs of Staff top secret copies of Donovan's intelligence agency creation proposal, and a draft of an executive order to implement it.

Jan. 1, 1945, Joint Chiefs of Staff said the plan to exclude military intelligence from the intelligence agency was not acceptable.

The plan leaked to four newspapers, attacking it ...newspaper headlines accused Roosevelt and Wild Bill of trying to create a super Gestapo in the United States.

Donovan put the plan ... to implement the civilian intelligence agency made up of Wall Street Fed majority stockholder, ruling family representatives, like in OSS ... on hold.

Apr. 12, 1945 Roosevelt died ...and, with it ...that version of the plan for a super intelligence agency run by Wall Street. Roosevelt's son said, his father was assassinated.

At the time of death, Roosevelt was posing for two White Russians taking his photograph ...they all had refreshments ...then, Roosevelt fell to the floor.

When the two White Russians were contacted later, they said they heard the news on their car radio. Roosevelt's son was convinced the anti-communist, anti-Democracy, Czarist Russian pair poisoned his father.

Paul Robeson's ghost would soon haunt the White House as a reminder, because he'd been poisoned by anti-Democracy, intelligence operatives, too.

May 1945, Harry S. Truman became President. Harry sent Wild Bill, Chief of Office of Strategic Services, to Nuremberg. There, Donovan was to help Supreme Court Justice Robert Jackson. The new president appointed Justice Jackson to be United States Chief Prosecutor of the International Military Tribunal. Donovan was to use OSS to do investigations for International Military Tribunal, to help Justice Jackson.

<>

Meanwhile, Reinhard was in his chalet in Misery Meadows, planning next steps to help Odessa save Underground German Officers Corps, and Nazi war booty ...so, the Reich could recover, and regain strength ... to fight another world war in the 20th Century ...after polarizing Allies, against the Russians.

Carl Oglesby's, *Reinhard Gehlen – Secret Treaty of Fort Hunt,* in Lou Wolf's *Covert Action Information Bulletin* & *Covert Action Quarterly* ... and, Christopher Simpson's, *Blowback, America's Recruitment of Nazis and Its Effects on the Cold War,* describe Reinhard's odyssey.

So did Dagmara, filling-in Patti on their long walk to Lytton Plaza.

1945, U.S. Command
Center, Fischhausen

May 19 1945, Reinhard was enjoying the mountain chalet, three weeks. World War II was over, two weeks. Reinhard watched Americans occupy the valley far below, calculating his timing to start his plan. "It's time now to begin."

He said goodby to three women companions and several wounded comrades. With four aides, he started walking down from Misery Meadow, to the valley below, towards Lake Schliersee, to Fischhausen.

Meanwhile, the Soviets at Flensburg, far to the north, demanded the U.S. turn Reinhard, and his intelligence files on the Soviet Union, over to them. U.S. Command never heard the name, Reinhard Gehlen. When Reinhard and his aides got to Fischhausen, they stayed with the parents of one of the aides for several days, speaking by radio with the rest of the team, back at Misery Meadows.

May 22, 1945 Reinhard and four aides walk into Army Command Center at Fischhausen. Reinhard walks to the desk of the admitting officer in charge, Captain John Schwarzwalder. Captain Schwarzwalder sighs, looks at Reinhard. At forty-three years old, Brigadier General Reinhard Gehlen stands five-feet-eight inches, weighs 128 pounds ...according to medical exam records taken when he turned himself in.

Reinhard felt glad, in command of the moment. "I'm Brigadier General Reinhard Gehlen. I'm head of German Army Headquarters Intelligence Section Foreign Armies East. I have information to give, of highest importance to your government."

Captain John sat at his desk, bored. "All you Nazis think tou got something special going on."

Captain John registered Reinhard in the prisoner-of-war camp, where Reinhard sat three weeks ...until, Captain John saw a message, Soviets demanded Reinhard be given to them.

Captain John had Reinhard driven by jeep to Miesbach, to Counter-Intelligence Corps Intelligence Unit CIC. Reinhard was taken to Captain Marian Porter.

Reinhard concentrated. He stared at Captain Porter. "I'm Brigadier General Reinhard Gehlen, head of German Army Headquarters Intelligence Section Foreign Armies East. I have important information for your Supreme Commander."

Captain Porter was amused. Porter ordered guards to take Reinhard, and his aides, to Salzburg prison.

In his prison cell Reinhard despaired. Reinhard looked at his aides. "I feel useless, they won't listen to me, they don't know who I am, I mean nothing to them."

Meanwhile, Army Counter-Intelligence Corps was trying to locate Reinhard ...at the same time he was held prisoner in their camp.

Jun. 20 1945, Colonel William H. Quinn, Army G-2 Intelligence Unit officer, saw Reinhard's name on a list of prisoners at Salzburg. Colonel Quinn transported Reinhard to Augsberg, for interrogation. Reinhard said, he was head of Third Reich Intelligence for the Eastern Front ...and, had a subordinate reporting to him who was in charge of intelligence for the Western Front. Colonel Quinn understood the significance of Reinhard's position. Reinhard felt better.

Colonel Quinn picked up his phone. "General Sibert, I have Brigadier General Reinhard Gehlen in my office, head of Third Reich Foreign Armies East Intelligence against Soviet Union and Eastern Europe ...and, head of Western Front intelligence. He said he has intelligence files on the Soviet Union and Eastern Europe, hidden up in the mountains, above Army Command Center, at Fischhausen."

General Edwin L. Sibert felt like he'd found a fifty-dollar bill on the ground. "Isn't he the one the Russians want so bad?"

"Yes."

<>

General Sibert was born in 1897. He was an artillery expert, a professor of military science, and formerly, a military attaché. Since Mar. 1944 Sibert had been promoted to Chief of Intelligence of 12th U.S. Army Group ...advancing through France, towards Germany. Sibert studied ideas, strategy, tactics, and philosophy of the German military. Sibert liked Reinhard immediately. Sibert felt thrilled to have a real important German intelligencer to talk with.

Sibert watched Reinhard. "I liked you immediately. I had an excellent first impression of you."

Reinhard needed to make General Sibert his friend ...to position Reinhard's version of a Christian West strategy ...to save himself, and, to protect Odessa.

Reinhard smiled. "I feel the same way about you. I liked you immediately. Let me tell you, the real aim of the Soviet Union is to take over the world, for Communism. With Soviet Russia's present armed forces, Russia can risk war with the U.S., Great Britain, and France ...to occupy West Germany. There must be some way we can work together to prevent Communism from taking Germany over."

Sibert smiled, offered Reinhard port to drink. General Eisenhower had issued orders against making friends with German prisoners ...but, Sibert had a mind of his own. Sibert debriefed Reinhard, for several days. He called Eisenhower's Chief of Staff, General Walter Bedell Smith. "Bendell, come down here, help me debrief this guy. I've been at it three days, information keeps coming out."

Eisenhower's Chief of Staff was shocked. "Ike issued orders not to do that. Ike has special intelligence debriefing units."

"Bendell, Ike's tied-up ...negotiating with Soviets. We can't compromise him. I was promoted Chief of Intelligence of 12th Army, I'm responsible to keep 12th Army boys alive. I'll learn about German intelligence operations, you believe it. Allen Dulles, U.S. Secret Service officer in Bern, sent his own German-America operative to me, Gero von Gaevernitz. Nov. 1944, Gero told me, make use of anti-Hitler officers to develop our strategy, to cut American loss of life. Gero told me, approach anti-Hitler German Commanders ...at the front, tired of fighting ...so they can surrender to me ...even while Germany's stilling fighting us ...to get me intelligence to win the war. Gero encouraged me, give him lists of German prisoners-of-war ...he checked-off people to help me find German Commanders, at the front ...to help me end the war ... I'm tellin' you, Brigadier General Gehlen wants to keep Soviet Union from turning against the U.S., and Britain ...and keep Soviet Russia from keeping the war going to take over West Germany, as a Communist base in Europe ...Gehlen has active intelligence files ...and, an active special ops guerrilla network still fighting in Russia, and Eastern Europe, backing him up."

General Smith agreed. "Okay. Give him special quarters ...a radio to keep him in contact with Foreign Armies East intelligence operatives in Bavaria. We'll go around Ike, de-brief Gehlen, find someone in the Pentagon Joint Chiefs of Staff to cover us. I'm coming to visit."

<>

Reinhard's plan was working. He radioed comrades in Bavaria, at Misery Meadows. They dug up the intelligence files against the Soviet Union, and Eastern Europe. Eisenhower's Chief of Staff General Smith, and, Chief of Intelligence for 12th Army Group's General Sibert, arranged luxury quarters for Reinhard, and his aides ...who began preparing ongoing intelligence reports on Soviet Union, and Eastern Europe ...for Generals Smith and Sibert. By end of Jun. 1945, Gehlen and his staff were discharged from prisoner-of-war status ...to move around at will ...allowed to form a General Staff Intelligence Cell Unit ...permitted to operate inside the Army G-2 Intelligence Historical Research Section ...then, relocated inside the Seventh Army's Intelligence Center in Wiesbaden, where Henry Kissinger served. Reinhard and his men were again given private quarters.

During last days of the Third Reich, Admiral Karl Doenitz was designated by Hitler, to be Hitler's successor. Admiral Doenitz was also held in VIP prison camp, in Wiesbaden. Reinhard and Admiral Doenitz met frequently.

Karl Doenitz looked at Reinhard. "Major Hermann Bound described you, ruthless in your determination to re-create the German Reich, after our defeat. At one time, Major Bound was the best expert on Russia we had in German Military Intelligence. I understand you had him tortured to death. Why?"

Reinhard Gehlen answered spontaneously. "Major Bound was cooperating too closely with British Secret Service, to threaten my work here ...with the Americans. He informed the British ...about Odessa ...Martin Bormann ...Otto Skorzeny ...you ...and, me."

"I see. You did the right thing."

Reinhard remembered when he'd been in Flemsberg, the last holdout of Nazi Germany ...before the catastrophe, listening to Admiral Doenitz deliver a farewell address to Nazi Officers Corps.

Admiral Doenitz addressed the Nazi Officers Corps. "Comrades, it must be clear to all of us, we are now in the enemy's hands. Our fate is dark. What they will do with us, we don't know

...but, what we have to do ... we know very well. We've been set back for a thousand years, in our history. Land that was German for a thousand years has fallen into Russian hands. Therefore, the political line we must follow is plain ...we must go along with Western powers ...work with them in occupied territories in the West ...for, it is only by working through them we can have hope of later retrieving our land from the Russians."

He turned to Reinhard Gehlen. "Reinhard, you're guardian of Germany's tradition ...responsible to rescue Nazi Officers Corps ...to maintain continuity of Nazi Officers Corps through the rest of this century ...into the next. I have faith in you. Are your plans on schedule?"

Reinhard updated his progress to Karl Doenitz, since Hitler's death April 30, the new leader of Third Reich, and the other Third Reich leader, Deputy Fuehrer Martin Bormann.

Third Reich chain-of-command was still in effect! Third Reich, in the person of Admiral Karl Doenitz, officially approved Reinhard's plan.

Jun. 29 1945, the Pentagon informed Eisenhower's European Command, War Department wanted Reinhard brought to Washington D.C.

Aug. 22 1945, Hermann Baun, Reinhard's aide, start re-organizing Reinhard's intelligence and counter-intelligence groups. General Smith flew Reinhard to Washington D.C., in his private DC-3. Reinhard was going to talk with the highest ranking American military, and intelligence, people. Before he boarded the plane, Reinhard handed a message for Hermann Baun to Gerhard Wessel ...who would one day be Reinhard's successor.

Gerhard Wessel relayed the message to Herman Baun. "Reinhard said, he discussed his plans before leaving for Washington, with Admiral Doenitz, and, with Nazi Chief of Staff General Franz Halder. Both agreed with Reinhard, to continue his work with the Americans."

Yes! ...Nazi chain-of-command was in effect!

Aug. 24 1945, Reinhard and six aides, code-named, 'Group 6', landed with General Smith in Washington D.C.

The war in Europe ended fourteen weeks earlier. World War II ended the previous week. Admiral William Leahy was Naval Intelligence Chief, and, President Truman's National Security Adviser. Admiral Leahy didn't like the idea ...of a private, civilian-run, intelligence agency run by Wall Street investors ...that, Wild Bill Donovan was setting up ...Leahy didn't like Wild Bill ...Leahy asked President Truman to have Budget Director Harold Smith investigate the current proposals to create American's first permanent intelligence agency.

Truman was aware of the trans-Atlantic Axis tentacles reaching in directions back and forth between Wall Street, Berlin, Tokyo, and England ... but, not being a Fed major shareholder, was unaware of the role of the Fed major shareholders, as part of the trans-Atlantic Axis. "This country wants no Gestapo ...under any guise ...or, for any reason."

Budget Director Harold Smith contacted Wild Bill, got from him a copy of Donovan's plans to remodel and re-organize Office Of Strategic Services ...to create an all-powerful, civilian-run intelligence agency managed by Wall Street Fed major shareholder, ruling families.

Donovan sent a memo back to Harold Smith. "Among the assets of the OSS, is establishment for the first time in our nation's history ...of a foreign secret intelligence service ...that reports information seen through American eyes. As an integral and inseparable part of this service, there's a group of specialists to analyze, and evaluate, material for presentation to those who determine national policy. We need to allow this kind of international intelligence network to continue to function."

<>

In public, everyone focused on perceived quality of U.S. intelligence ...to defend itself in the event of an attack by Soviet Union to take-over the U.S. ...and the world ...for Communism ...but, that was not the issue behind closed doors.

The issue, behind closed doors was, should civilians from Wall Street (who were Fed major shareholders) ...or, should the United States Military, control the intelligence missions of the United States?

What precedents were there? ...19th Century England decided civilians should man posts of intelligence. During the 19th Century, in Germany, the military were given this responsibility ...although, Germany military intelligence reported to German General Staff of civilian and military ruling families.

Summer & fall months of 1945, battle for control of intelligence raged in Washington

In America's wartime intelligence operations agency, Office of Strategic Services, Allen Dulles reported to Wild Bill.

OSS was competing with U.S. military intelli-

gence, for control of Reinhard's Foreign Armies East microfilmed files ...for control of Reinhard ...for Reinhard's anti-Soviet, intelligence assets ... spies, and paramilitary death squads.

When Reinhard and his aides arrived at Fort Hunt, they arrived in the middle of this new battle on this new American battlefield ...Wall Street versus the Military ... fighting one another ...for control of intelligence ...that, controlled national security and foreign policy decisions coming out of Washington D.C. ... which in turn, controlled profits, portfolios, and ownership of natural resources.

At Fort Hunt, Reinhard and staff were their own butlers, cooks, housekeepers, and orderlies, wearing white jackets.

At Fort Hunt, seven Americans met with Reinhard ...Admiral William D. Leahy, Chief of Staff & United States National Security Adviser under President Truman ...Loftus E. Becker, a lawyer working with Army G-2 intelligence on the Nuremberg Nazi War Crimes operation, later first Deputy Director of CIA ...General George Strong, Head of Army G-2 Intelligence ...Major General Alex H. Boling of G-2 ...Brigadier General John T. Magruder, first head of Army's Strategic Services SSU ...Sherman Kent, head of OSS Research & Analysis Branch, and a Yale historian ...Allen Dulles, WWII OSS Station Chief in Bern, and Schroder attorney.

These seven men met with Reinhard as a group, and individually. Reinhard turned his interrogation and debriefing around, turned it into a negotiation ...the only records of the negotiation, not classified top secret, were notes Reinhard kept ...that, later would become his autobiography ...often attacked for inaccuracies.

Nancy continued reading to me from Carl Oglesby's article, *Secret Treaty of Fort Hunt*, published in Lou Wolf's, *Covert Action Quarterly*.

<>

Reinhard wrote in his diary. "Our discussions to found the Service began ...and, ended with a gentlemen's verbal agreement, a handshake. For a variety of reasons, terms were never written down, in black and white. There were six basic points.

"1. A secret German intelligence org, using existing German information gathering assets in the Soviet Union, and Eastern Europe, was to continue under leadership of Reinhard Gehlen, for the common purpose of United States and Germany to fight against Communism.

"2. This Gehlen Intelligence Organization was not working for, or under, the United States

...but, working jointly with the United States.

"3. The Gehlen Organization would have only Germany leadership ...in that, the Gehlen Organization would receive assignments, and operation directives, from United States ... only until a new government was established in Germany.

"4. The Gehlen Organization would be financed by United States. The funds were not to be part of costs of American occupation of Germany ...and therefore, could not be charged as costs, to Germany. Gehlen Organization's first budget was to be $3,500,000. In return for United States financing, Gehlen Organization would supply anti-Soviet intelligence reports to the United States.

"5. When a new and sovereign government was established in Germany, that government would have jurisdiction over the Gehlen Organization. Until then, the United States would have trusteeship, care, and control of the Gehlen Organization.

"6. If the Gehlen Organization ever found itself in the middle ...between conflicting interests, between the United States and Germany ...the Gehlen Organization would always put the interests of Germany, above the interests of the United States.

<>

"I realize this last point might raise some eyebrows ...that, the United States has gone overboard ...in making concessions, to us. This last point demonstrates General Sibert's great vision. General Sibert realized that, for many years to come ...interests of the United States and West Germany must run parallel," Reinhard wrote.

<>

July 1, 1946, Reinhard and staff were in the U.S. about a year. They left Fort Hunt ...to return to Germany. Reinhard had accomplished his Nazi mission, realizing his version of a Christian West plan ...to save the underground German Officers Corps, help Odessa, save himself ...and, to unite the United States and Germany in a combined mission against the Soviet Union.

<>

In Germany, the Gehlen Organization, then a staff of fifty, was housed in Oberursel ...then, settled permanently in a walled-in, self-contained village at Pullach, near Munich.

Reinhard set up headquarters in an estate, originally built by Martin Bormann, leader of the Odessa Organization of Veterans of the SS.

Reinhard immediately began recruiting a staff of intelligence evaluators, couriers, and informers from the ranks of Odessa.

Two such men were Franz Six, and Emil Augsburg. Both had worked in the Nazi think-tank, the Wannsee Institute. It was at the Wannsee Institute, where 'The Law For The Purification Of The Germany Blood' was thought up, leading to, 'The Final Solution To The Jewish Question', genocidal extermination of Jews.

Franz Six and Emil Augsburg had both commanded death-squads, roaming through Eastern Europe hunting Jews, and communists. Reinhard located Emil Augsburg in Italy.

Franz Six had been found guilty of being a war criminal, at the Nuremberg trials.

Reinhard had him set free ...to join the Gehlen Organization. Reinhard had finessed his way from total defeat by the Allies ...into a position of total power ...now, working under a United States budget ...from taxpayers whose fathers, husbands, and sons he'd helped maim, torture, and murder.

Now, on U.S. taxpayer payroll, the Gehlen Organization would grow stronger, more influential ...than when Gehlen was head intelligencer commanding Foreign Armies East for the Third Reich.

<>

At first, the Gehlen Org was supervised by Major General John Magruder, head of War Department's Strategic Services Unit ...then, by the organization that evolved out of the SSU, the Central Intelligence Group, under Rear Admiral Sidney Souers.

Gehlen Org was destined ...to become the anti-Russian intelligence service of the U.S. ...and, at the same time, the official intelligence organization for the 'New Germany'.

<>

U.S. National Security & Foreign Policy historian Carl Oglesby summed his research up. "Just as the Czarist and White Russian spies jumped to the Nazis when their own army was defeated in World War I, the German Nazi and Russian Czarist spies together jumped to the American army as the German Wehrmacht was defeated in World War II. This is how a Czarist spy ring inside a Nazi spy ring became the inner circle of an American spy ring ...as it became the national security and foreign policy instrument of Washington and Wall Street. Everything Washington and Wall Street would know about the Soviet Union and Eastern Europe came from Czarists and Nazis installed at the center of the U.S. intelligence system. How can a naive, trusting, democratic republic give its secrets to crime and its innermost ear to the spirit of Central European Fascism and expect not to see its Constitution polluted, its traditions abused, and its consciousness of the surrounding world manipulated ultimately out of all realistic shape."

Nancy's voice faded away ...I fell asleep.

The Liberty League

Charles Higham's, *Trading With the Enemy* sets scene.

Morgan Financial Group includes DuPont Chemicals, Morgan Bank, and General Motors.

In 1933, with the rise of Hitler in Europe, the DuPonts began financing domestic Fascist groups in America ...the anti-Semitic, anti-African-American, Liberty League, and, Clark's Crusaders, that had 1,250,000 members. Alfred P. Sloane of General Motors, and Pierre, Eranee, and Lamont DuPont, and John Jacob Rascob funded Liberty League. Alfred P. Sloane of G.M., and William S. Knudsen, president of G.M., met in New York City.

Alfred P. Sloane looked at William Knudsen. "The League's smearing President Roosevelt as a communist, surrounded by Jews. Even though the DuPonts are Jewish, they're smearing Jewish groups."

G.M. President William Knudsen smiled. "Connections between G.M. and the Nazi government goes back to when Hitler rose to power. Goering decided, he wouldn't nationalize G.M. operations in Germany. He received me pleasantly, when I visited him. Germany's the miracle of the 20th Century."

In 1934, Eranee DuPont, Knudsen, with friends of Morgan Bank, G.M., and DuPont backers ... suggested, then financed ... a coup d'état to overthrow President Roosevelt and the United States.

They'd put in 3 million dollars, create an army of terrorists ...modeled on the Fascist death squad movement in Paris, Qua D' Fir.

They were encouraged in their plan ...by Herman Schmidt, and Baron von Schroder, German representatives of the Trans-Atlantic Axis and Schroder.

But, they needed to find a leader for their proposed army.

The coup would force President Roosevelt to overtly take orders from American ruling family corporate leaders ... Fed majority shareholders ...under an American Fascist Government ...or be imprisoned, or killed.

DuPont and Morgan people met behind closed doors. They decided to approach General Smedley Butler, of Pennsylvania. General Butler was one of the most popular soldiers in America ...awarded two Congressional Medals of Honor, for bravery ...career as Commandant in the Marine Corps ...a legend during his lifetime.

Mr. McGuire, an attorney and bond salesmen, represented the coup plotters. McGuire met with General Butler at Butler's house, in Newton Square, Pennsylvania ...then, again in a nearby hotel room.

McGuire looked at Butler. "We had a meeting in Paris. Me, and my backers, want *you*. But, Morgan people think you're radical. I told them, you've made speeches *against* Roosevelt's and Astor's New Deal. I insisted, you're the only military man in the country popular enough ...to rally World War I veterans, behind you. You'd be the perfect military dictator to lead a coup against Washington, to replace President Roosevelt."

Smedley Butler was horrified ...but, acted flattered, "There's a lot of things about Roosevelt I don't like ...sounds like a good idea."

"We have millions of dollars behind us. Damned Roosevelt has New Deal programs to help people survive ...give them jobs ...putting them to work building roads, dams. *He's raising taxes.* America needs a leader ...like, Mussolini, or Hitler. America needs a dictatorship to get us on our feet again. You're the man for the job!"

Smedley Butler was patriotic ...believed in the U.S. Constitution ...was furious McGuire wanted him to commit treason, and murder ...but, smiled pleasantly. The men said goodbye. McGuire left. Smedley Butler picked up his phone ...he called Roosevelt. Smedley explained to President Roosevelt.

Roosevelt was shocked. Roosevelt didn't know what to do. He listened to Smedley ...then, replied. "They've got Morgan money behind them. If they assassinate me, and put in a dictator to run America with that kind of money ...they could turn America away from Democracy ...run it by Fascism ...turn America in an ally of Nazism. I can't arrest the ruling family patriarchs running the House of Morgan and DuPont ... in the middle of the Depression ...they'll make it worse ...crash Wall Street, over, and over, again. The international bankers are more powerful ...than, my Presidency. We must stop them!. The only thing to do, is leak their coup plans to the press."

<>

Soon, the story appeared on the front pages of national newspapers. But, the papers were owned by ruling family interests that did not want to anger the House of Morgan. So, press coverage ridiculed the idea ...as a rumor.

Thomas LaMont of Morgan Bank arrived from Europe, by steamer. He was met by reporters.

A reporter questioned LaMont. "Please comment on the House of Morgan, General Motors, and DuPont coup plot ...to take over United States ...and, make America a Fascist country."

Thomas LaMont of Morgan Bank laughed. "That's perfect moonshine. It's ridiculous to comment on."

<>

Roosevelt set up a Special House Committee to investigate the coup plot against him, that aimed to stop his social programs of creating jobs for Americans ...of raising taxes on ruling family corporations to finance saving lives of millions of Americans, at home.

Smedley Butler appeared before the committee. He felt the moment was at hand. "You must call the DuPonts in front of this committee."

The committee chairman was calm. "No."

"You have to call someone from House of Morgan!" Butler insisted.

"No."

"Look, they've approached General MacArthur, too!"

Then, Special House Committee Investigatory Committee called McGuire to testify.

McGuire felt confident. "General Butler misunderstood me."

General Butler wanted to get his hands on McGuire. Other witnesses gave vanilla testimonies. Hearings rested. The press could not get access to committee proceedings. Information was again leaked. Managing editors of newspapers were instructed, make a joke out of the story. Reporters interviewed General Douglas MacArthur.

MacArthur laughed at questions reporters asked him. Four years later, the committee published its report.

It was stamped, 'restricted'.

The report stated, 'certain persons made an attempt to establish a Fascist organization in this country. The committee was able to verify all pertinent statements by General Butler.'

The report confirmed the coup plan had deadly intent. There had been a million people pledged to support the coup. Arms and munitions were to have been supplied by the DuPont subsidiary, arms manufacturer, Remington.

But, no one was arrested for treason to overthrow the Government of the U.S.

The Fed majority shareholder bankers, that overshadowed and undermined the Presidency ...were more power than American justice.

War is a racket

General Smedley Butler took to writing. He foreshadowed Dwight Eisenhower's warnings about the military-industrial establishment provoking wars, death squads, coups, and terrorist attacks ...not, for moral reasons ...but, for financial greed ...and, under their own flag.

<>

In 1933, Marine Corps Major General Smedley Butler made one of many speeches.

"War is just a racket. A racket is best described, I believe, as something that is not what it seems to the majority of people. Only a small inside group knows what it is about. It is conducted for the benefit of the very few at the expense of the masses.

"I believe in adequate defense at the coastline and nothing else. If a nation comes over here to fight, then we'll fight. The trouble with America is that when the dollar only earns 6% over here, then it gets restless and goes overseas to get 100%. Then the flag follows the dollar and the soldiers follow the flag.

"I wouldn't go to war again as I have done to protect some lousy investment of the bankers. There are only two things we should fight for. One is the defense of our homes and the other is the Bill of Rights. War for any other reason is simply a racket.

"There isn't a trick in the racketeering bag that the military gang is blind to. It has its 'finger men' to point out enemies, its 'muscle men' to destroy enemies, its 'brain men' to plan war preparations, and a 'Big Boss' Super-Nationalistic-Capitalism.

"It may seem odd for me, a military man to adopt such a comparison. Truthfulness compels me to. I spent thirty-three years and four months in active military service as a member of this country's most agile military force, the Marine Corps. I served in all commissioned ranks from Second Lieutenant to Major-General. And during that period, I spent most of my time being a high class muscle-man for Big Business, for Wall Street and for the Bankers. In short, I was a racketeer, a gangster for capitalism.

148

"I suspected I was just part of a racket at the time. Now I am sure of it. Like all the members of the military profession, I never had a thought of my own until I left the service. My mental faculties remained in suspended animation while I obeyed the orders of higher-ups. This is typical with everyone in military service.

"I helped make Mexico, especially Tampico, safe for American oil interests in 1914. I helped make Haiti and Cuba a decent place for the National City Bank boys to collect revenues in. I helped in the raping of half a dozen Central American republics for the benefits of Wall Street. The record of racketeering is long. I helped purify Nicaragua for the international banking house of Brown Brothers in 1909-1912. I brought light to the Dominican Republic for American sugar interests in 1916. In China I helped to see to it that Standard Oil went its way unmolested.

"During those years, I had, as the boys in the back room would say, a swell racket. Looking back on it, I feel that I could have given Al Capone a few hints. The best he could do was to operate his racket in three districts. I operated on three continents."

Butler's, *War is a Racket,* put it this way.

WAR is a racket. It always has been.

It is possibly the oldest, easily the most profitable, surely the most vicious. It is the only one international in scope. It is the only one in which the profits are reckoned in dollars and the losses in lives.

A racket is best described, I believe, as something that is not what it seems to the majority of the people. Only a small 'inside' group knows what it is about. It is conducted for the benefit of the very few, at the expense of the very many. Out of war a few people make huge fortunes.

In the World War a mere handful garnered the profits of the conflict. At least 21,000 new millionaires and billionaires were made in the United States during the World War. That many admitted their huge blood gains in their income tax returns. How many other war millionaires falsified tax returns no one knows.

How many of these war millionaires shouldered a rifle? How many of them dug a trench? How many of them knew what it meant to go hungry in a rat-infested dug-out? How many of them spent sleepless, frightened nights, ducking shells and shrapnel and machine gun bullets? How many of them parried a bayonet thrust of an enemy? How many of them were wounded or killed in battle?

Out of war nations acquire additional territory, if they are victorious. They just take it. This newly acquired territory promptly is exploited by the few ...the self-same few who wrung dollars out of blood in the war. The general public shoulders the bill.

And what is this bill?

This bill renders a horrible accounting. Newly placed gravestones. Mangled bodies. Shattered minds. Broken hearts and homes. Economic instability. Depression and all its attendant miseries. Back-breaking taxation for generations and generations.

For a great many years, as a soldier, I had a suspicion that war was a racket ... not until I retired to civil life did I fully realize it. Now that I see the international war clouds gathering, as they are today, I must face it and speak out.

Again they are choosing sides. France and Russia met and agreed to stand side by side. Italy and Austria hurried to make a similar agreement. Poland and Germany cast sheep's eyes at each other, forgetting for the moment, their dispute over the Polish Corridor.

The assassination of King Alexander of Yugoslavia complicated matters. Yugoslavia and Hungary, long bitter enemies, were almost at each other's throats. Italy was ready to jump in. But France was waiting. So was Czechoslovakia. All of them are looking ahead to war. Not the people ...not those who fight and pay and die ...only those who foment wars and remain safely at home to profit.

There are 40 million men under arms in the world today, and our statesmen and diplomats have the temerity to say that war is not in the making.

Hell's bells! Are these 40 million men being trained to be dancers?

Not in Italy, to be sure. Premier Mussolini knows what they are being trained for. He, at least, is frank enough to speak out. Only the other day, Il Duce in *International Conciliation,* the publication of the Carnegie Endowment for International Peace, said ...

"... And above all, Fascism, the more it considers and observes the future and the development of humanity quite apart from political considerations of the moment, believes neither in the possibility nor the utility of perpetual peace ...War alone brings up to its highest tension all human energy and puts the stamp of nobility upon the people who have the courage to meet it."

Undoubtedly Mussolini means exactly what he

says. His well-trained army, his great fleet of planes, and even his navy are ready for war ...anxious for it, apparently. His recent stand at the side of Hungary in the latter's dispute with Yugoslavia showed that. And the hurried mobilization of his troops on the Austrian border after the assassination of Dollfuss showed it too. There are others in Europe too whose saber rattling presages war, sooner or later.

Herr Hitler, with his rearming Germany and his constant demands for more and more arms, is an equal if not greater menace to peace. France only recently increased the term of military service for its youth from a year to eighteen months.

Yes, all over, nations are camping in their arms. The mad dogs of Europe are on the loose. In the Orient the maneuvering is more adroit. Back in 1904, when Russia and Japan fought, we kicked out our old friends the Russians and backed Japan. Then our very generous international bankers were financing Japan. Now the trend is to poison us against the Japanese. What does the 'open door' policy to China mean to us? Our trade with China is about 90 million dollars a year. Or the Philippine Islands? We have spent about 600 million dollars in the Philippines in thirty-five years and we (our bankers and industrialists and speculators) have private investments there of less than $200 million dollars.

Then, to save that China trade of about 90 million dollars or to protect these private investments of less than 200 million dollars in the Philippines, we would be all stirred up to hate Japan and go to war ...a war that might well cost us tens of billions of dollars, hundreds of thousands of lives of Americans, and many more hundreds of thousands of physically maimed and mentally unbalanced men.

Of course, for this loss, there would be a compensating profit ...fortunes would be made. Millions and billions of dollars would be piled up. By a few. Munitions makers. Bankers. Ship builders. Manufacturers. Meat packers. Speculators. They would fare well.

Yes, they are getting ready for another war. Why shouldn't they? It pays high dividends.

But what does it profit the men who are killed? What does it profit their mothers and sisters, their wives and their sweethearts? What does it profit their children?

What does it profit anyone except the very few to whom war means huge profits?

Yes, and what does it profit the nation?

Take our own case. Until 1898 we didn't own a bit of territory outside the mainland of North America. At that time our national debt was a little more than 1 billion dollars. Then we became 'internationally minded'. We forgot, or shunted aside, the advice of the Father of our country. We forgot George Washington's warning about 'entangling alliances'. We went to war. We acquired outside territory. At the end of the World War period, as a direct result of our fiddling in international affairs, our national debt had jumped to over 25 billion dollars. Our total favorable trade balance during the twenty-five-year period was about 24 billion dollars. Therefore, on a purely bookkeeping basis, we ran a little behind year for year, and that foreign trade might well have been ours without the wars.

It would have been far cheaper (not to say safer) for the average American who pays the bills to stay out of foreign entanglements. For a very few this racket, like bootlegging and other underworld rackets, brings fancy profits, but the cost of operations is always transferred to the people ... who do not profit.

WHO MAKES THE PROFITS?

The World War, rather our brief participation in it, has cost the United States some 52 billion dollars. Figure it out. That means $400 to every American man, woman, and child. And we haven't paid the debt yet. We are paying it, our children will pay it, and our children's children probably still will be paying the cost of that war.

The normal profits of a business concern in the United States are six, eight, ten, and sometimes twelve percent. But war-time profits ...ah! that is another matter ...twenty, sixty, one hundred, three hundred, and even eighteen hundred percent ...the sky is the limit. All that traffic will bear. Uncle Sam has the money. Let's get it.

Of course, it isn't put that crudely in war time. It is dressed into speeches about patriotism, love of country, and 'we must all put our shoulders to the wheel', but the profits jump and leap and skyrocket ...and are safely pocketed. Let's just take a few examples.

Take our friends the du Ponts, the powder people ...didn't one of them testify before a Senate committee recently that their powder won the war? Or saved the world for democracy? Or something? How did they do in the war? They were a patriotic corporation. Well, the average earnings of the du Ponts for the period 1910 to 1914 were 6 million dollars a year. It wasn't much, but the du Ponts managed to get along on it. Now let's look at their average yearly profit during the war years, 1914 to 1918. Fifty-eight million dollars a year profit we find! Nearly ten times that of normal times, and the profits of normal times were pretty good. An increase in profits of more than 950 percent.

Take one of our little steel companies that patriotically shunted aside the making of rails and girders and bridges to manufacture war materials. Well, their 1910-1914 yearly earnings averaged 6 million dollars. Then came the war. And, like loyal citizens, Bethlehem Steel promptly turned to munitions making. Did their profits jump …or did they let Uncle Sam in for a bargain? Well, their 1914-1918 average was 49 million dollars a year!

Or, let's take United States Steel. The normal earnings during the five-year period prior to the war were 105 million dollars a year. Not bad. Then along came the war and up went the profits. The average yearly profit for the period 1914-1918 was 240 million dollars. Not bad.

There you have some steel and powder earnings. Let's look at something else. A little copper, perhaps. That always does well in war times.

Anaconda, for instance. Average yearly earnings during pre-war years 1910-1914 of 10 million dollars. During the war years 1914-1918 profits leaped to 34 million dollars per year.

Or Utah Copper. Average 5 million dollars per year during the 1910-1914 period. Jumped to an average of 21 million dollars yearly profits for the war period.

Let's group these five, with three smaller companies. The total yearly average profits of the pre-war period 1910-1914 were 137.4 million dollars. Then along came the war. The average yearly profits for this group skyrocketed to 408.3 million dollars.

A little increase in profits of approximately 200 percent.

Does war pay? It paid them. But they aren't the only ones. There are still others. Let's take leather.

For the three-year period before the war the total profits of Central Leather Co. were $3,500,000. That was approximately 1.167 million dollars a year. Well, in 1916 Central Leather returned a profit of 15 million dollars, a small increase of 1,100 percent. That's all. The General Chemical Co. averaged a profit for the three years before the war of a little over $800,000 a year. Came the war, and the profits jumped to 12 million dollars, a leap of 1,400 percent.

International Nickel Co. …and you can't have a war without nickel …showed an increase in profits from a mere average of 4 million dollars a year to 73 million dollars yearly. Not bad? An increase of more than 1,700 percent.

American Sugar Refining Co. averaged 2 million dollars a year for the three years before the war. In 1916 a profit of 6 million dollars recorded.

Listen to Senate Document No. 259. The Sixty-Fifth Congress, reporting on corporate earnings and government revenues. Considering the profits of 122 meat packers, 153 cotton manufacturers, 299 garment makers, 49 steel plants, and 340 coal producers during the war. Profits under 25 percent were exceptional. For instance the coal companies made between 100 percent and 7,856 percent on their capital stock during the war. The Chicago packers doubled and tripled their earnings.

And let us not forget the bankers who financed the great war. If anyone had the cream of the profits it was the bankers. Being partnerships rather than incorporated organizations, they do not have to report to stockholders. And their profits were as secret as they were immense. How the bankers made their millions and their billions I do not know, because those little secrets never become public …even before a Senate investigatory body.

But here's how some of the other patriotic industrialists and speculators chiseled their way into war profits.

Take the shoe people. They like war. It brings business with abnormal profits. They made huge profits on sales abroad to our allies. Perhaps, like the munitions manufacturers and armament makers, they also sold to the enemy. For a dollar is a dollar whether it comes from Germany or from France. But they did well by Uncle Sam too. For instance, they sold Uncle Sam 35 million pairs of hobnailed service shoes. There were 4 million soldiers. Eight pairs, and more, to a soldier. My regiment during the war had only one pair to a soldier. Some of these shoes probably are still in existence. They were good shoes. But when the war was over Uncle Sam has a matter of 25 million pairs left over. Bought … and paid for. Profits recorded and pocketed.

There was still lots of leather left. So the leather people sold your Uncle Sam hundreds of thousands of McClellan saddles for the cavalry. But there wasn't any American cavalry overseas! Somebody had to get rid of this leather, however. Somebody had to make a profit in it …we had a lot of McClellan saddles. And we probably have those yet.

Also somebody had a lot of mosquito netting. They sold your Uncle Sam 20 million mosquito nets for the use of the soldiers overseas. I suppose the boys were expected to put it over them as they tried to sleep in muddy trenches ...one hand scratching cooties on their backs and the other making passes at scurrying rats. Well, not one of these mosquito nets ever got to France!

Anyhow, these thoughtful manufacturers wanted to make sure that no soldier would be without his mosquito net, so 40 million additional yards of mosquito netting were sold to Uncle Sam.

There were pretty good profits in mosquito netting in those days, even if there were no mosquitoes in France. I suppose, if the war had lasted just a little longer, the enterprising mosquito netting manufacturers would have sold your Uncle Sam a couple of consignments of mosquitoes to plant in France so that more mosquito netting would be in order.

Airplane and engine manufacturers felt they, too, should get their just profits out of this war. Why not? Everybody else was getting theirs. So 1 billion dollars ...count them if you live long enough ...was spent by Uncle Sam in building airplane engines that never left the ground! Not one plane, or motor, out of the billion dollars worth ordered, ever got into a battle in France. Just the same the manufacturers made their little profit of 30, 100, or perhaps 300 percent.

Undershirts for soldiers cost 14¢ to make and uncle Sam paid 30¢ to 40¢ each for them ...a nice little profit for the undershirt manufacturer. And the stocking manufacturer and the uniform manufacturers and the cap manufacturers and steel helmet manufacturers ...all got theirs.

Why, when war was over some 4 million sets of equipment ...knapsacks and the things that go to fill them ...crammed warehouses on this side. Now they are being scrapped because the regulations have changed the contents. But the manufacturers collected their wartime profits on them ...and they'll do it all over again next time.

There were lots of brilliant ideas for profit making during the war.

One very versatile patriot sold Uncle Sam twelve dozen 48-inch wrenches. Oh, they were very nice wrenches. The only trouble was that there was only one nut ever made that was large enough for these wrenches. That is the one that holds the turbines at Niagara Falls. Well, after Uncle Sam had bought them and the manufacturer had pocketed the profit, the wrenches were put on freight cars and shunted all around the United States in an effort to find a use for them. When the Armistice was signed it was indeed a sad blow to the wrench manufacturer. He was just about to make some nuts to fit the wrenches. Then he

planned to sell these, too, to your Uncle Sam.

Still another had the brilliant idea colonels shouldn't ride in automobiles, nor should they even ride on horseback. One has probably seen a picture of Andy Jackson riding in a buckboard. Well, some 6,000 buckboards were sold to Uncle Sam for the use of colonels! Not one of them was used. But the buckboard manufacturer got his war profit.

The shipbuilders felt they should come in on some of it, too. They built a lot of ships that made a lot of profit. More than 3 billion dollars worth. Some of the ships were all right. But 635 million dollars worth of them were made of wood and wouldn't float! The seams opened up ...and they sank. We paid for them, though. And somebody pocketed the profits.

It has been estimated by statisticians and economists and researchers the war cost Uncle Sam 52 billion dollars. Of this sum, 39 billion dollars was expended in the actual war itself. This expenditure yielded 16 billion dollars in profits. That is how 21,000 billionaires and millionaires got that way. This 16 billion dollars profits is not to be sneezed at. It is a tidy sum. And it went to a very few.

The Senate Nye committee probe of the munitions industry and its wartime profits, despite its sensational disclosures, hardly has scratched the surface.

Even so, it has had some effect. The State Department has been studying 'for some time' methods of keeping out of war. The War Department suddenly decides it has a wonderful plan to spring. The Administration names a committee ...with the War and Navy Departments ably represented under the chairmanship of a Wall Street speculator ...to limit profits in war time. To what extent isn't suggested. Hmmm. Possibly the profits of 300 and 600 and 1,600 percent of those who turned blood into gold in World War would be limited to some smaller figure.

Apparently, however, the plan does not call for any limitation of losses ...that is, the losses of those who fight the war. As far as I have been able to ascertain there is nothing in the scheme to limit a soldier to the loss of but one eye, or one arm, or to limit his wounds to one or two or three. Or to limit the loss of life.

There is nothing in this scheme, apparently, that says not more than 12 percent of a regiment shall be wounded in battle, or that not more than 7 percent in a division shall be killed.

Of course, the committee cannot be bothered with such trifling matters.

WHO PAYS THE BILLS?

Who provides the profits ...these nice little profits of 20, 100, 300, 1,500 and 1,800 percent? We all pay them ...in taxation. We paid the bankers their profits when we bought Liberty Bonds at $100 and sold them back at $84 or $86 to the bankers. These bankers collected $100 plus. It was a simple manipulation. The bankers control the security marts. It was easy for them to depress the price of these bonds. Then all of us ...the people ...got frightened and sold the bonds at $84 or $86. The bankers bought them. Then these same bankers stimulated a boom and government bonds went to par ...and above. Then the bankers collected their profits.

But the soldier pays the biggest part of the bill.

If you don't believe this, visit the American cemeteries on the battlefields abroad. Or visit any of the veteran's hospitals in the United States. On a tour of the country, in the midst of which I am at the time of this writing, I have visited eighteen government hospitals for veterans. In them are a total of about 50,000 destroyed men ...men who were the pick of the nation eighteen years ago. The very able chief surgeon at the government hospital ...at Milwaukee, where there are 3,800 of the living dead, told me that mortality among veterans is three times as great as among those who stayed at home.

Boys with a normal viewpoint were taken out of the fields and offices and factories and classrooms and put into the ranks. There they were remolded ...they were made over ...they were made to 'about face' ...to regard murder as the order of the day. They were put shoulder to shoulder and, through mass psychology, they were entirely changed. We used them for a couple of years and trained them to think nothing at all of killing or of being killed.

Then, suddenly, we discharged them and told them to make another 'about face'! This time they had to do their own readjustment, sans mass psychology, sans officers' aid and advice, sans nationwide propaganda. We didn't need them any more. So we scattered them about without any 'three-minute' or 'Liberty Loan' speeches or parades. Many, too many, of these fine young boys are eventually destroyed, mentally, because they could not make that final 'about face' alone.

In the government hospital in Marion, Indiana, 1,800 of these boys are in pens! Five hundred of them in a barracks with steel bars and wires all around outside the buildings and on the porches. These already have been mentally destroyed.

These boys don't even look like human beings. Oh, the looks on their faces! Physically, they are in good shape ...mentally, they are gone.

There are thousands and thousands of these cases, and more and more are coming in all the time. The tremendous excitement of the war, the sudden cutting off of that excitement ...the young boys couldn't stand it.

That's a part of the bill. So much for the dead ...they have paid their part of the war profits. So much for the mentally and physically wounded ...they are paying now their share of the war profits. But the others paid too ...they paid with heartbreak when they tore themselves away from their firesides and their families to don the uniform of Uncle Sam ...on which a profit had been made. They paid another part in the training camps where they were regimented and drilled while others took their jobs and their places in the lives of their communities. The paid for it in the trenches where they shot and were shot ...where they were hungry for days at a time ...where they slept in the mud and the cold and the rain ...with the moans and shrieks of the dying for a horrible lullaby.

But don't forget ...the soldier paid part of the dollars and cents bill too.

Up to and including the Spanish-American War, we had a prize system, and soldiers and sailors fought for money. During the Civil War they were paid bonuses, in many instances, before they went into service. The government, or states, paid as high as $1,200 for an enlistment. In the Spanish-American War they gave prize money. When we captured any vessels, the soldiers all got their share ...at least, they were supposed to. Then it was found that we could reduce cost of wars by taking all the prize money and keeping it, but conscripting the soldier anyway. Then soldiers couldn't bargain for their labor. Everyone else could bargain, but the soldier couldn't.

Napoleon once said, "All men are enamored of decorations ...they positively hunger for them."

So by developing the Napoleonic system ...the medal business ... the government learned it could get soldiers for less money, because the boys liked to be decorated. Until the Civil War there were no medals. Then the Congressional Medal of Honor was handed out. It made enlistments easier. After the Civil War no new medals were issued until the Spanish-American War.

In the World War, we used propaganda to make the boys accept conscription. They were made to feel ashamed if they didn't join the army.

So vicious was this war propaganda that even God was brought into it. With few exceptions our clergymen joined in the clamor to kill, kill, kill. To kill the Germans. God is on our side ...it is His will that the Germans be killed.

And in Germany, the good pastors called upon the Germans to kill the allies ...to please the same God. That was a part of the general propaganda, built up to make people war conscious and murder conscious.

Beautiful ideals were painted for our boys who were sent out to die. This was the 'war to end all wars'. This was the 'war to make the world safe for democracy'. No one mentioned to them, as they marched away, that their going and their dying would mean huge war profits. No one told these American soldiers that they might be shot down by bullets made by their own brothers here. No one told them that the ships on which they were going to cross might be torpedoed by submarines built with United States patents. They were just told it was to be a 'glorious adventure'.

Thus, having stuffed patriotism down their throats, it was decided to make them help pay for the war, too. So, we gave them the large salary of $30 a month.

All they had to do for this munificent sum was to leave their dear ones behind, give up their jobs, lie in swampy trenches, eat canned willy (when they could get it) and kill and kill and kill ...and be killed.

But wait!

Half of that wage (just a little more than a riveter in a shipyard or a laborer in a munitions factory safe at home made in a day) was promptly taken from him to support his dependents, so that they would not become a charge upon his community. Then we made him pay what amounted to accident insurance ...something the employer pays for in an enlightened state ...and that cost him $6 a month. He had less than $9 a month left.

Then, the most crowning insolence of all ...he was virtually blackjacked into paying for his own ammunition, clothing, and food by being made to buy Liberty Bonds. Most soldiers got no money at all on pay days.

We made them buy Liberty Bonds at $100 and then we bought them back ...when they came back from the war and couldn't find work ...at $84 and $86. And the soldiers bought about 2 billion dollars worth of these bonds!

Yes, the soldier pays the greater part of the bill. His family pays too. They pay it in the same heart-break that he does. As he suffers, they suffer. At nights, as he lay in the trenches and watched shrapnel burst about him, they lay home in their beds and tossed sleeplessly ...his father, his mother, his wife, his sisters, his brothers, his sons, and his daughters.

When he returned home minus an eye, or minus a leg or with his mind broken, they suffered too ...as much as and even sometimes more than he. Yes, and they, too, contributed their dollars to the profits of the munitions makers and bankers and shipbuilders and the manufacturers and the speculators made. They, too, bought Liberty Bonds and contributed to the profit of the bankers after the Armistice in the hocus-pocus of manipulated Liberty Bond prices.

And even now the families of the wounded men and of the mentally broken and those who never were able to readjust themselves are still suffering and still paying.

HOW TO SMASH THIS RACKET!

Well, it's a racket, all right.

A few profit ...and the many pay. But there is a way to stop it. You can't end it by disarmament conferences. You can't eliminate it by peace parleys at Geneva. Well-meaning but impractical groups can't wipe it out by resolutions. It can be smashed effectively only by taking the profit out of war.

The only way to smash this racket is to conscript capital and industry and labor before the nation's manhood can be conscripted. One month before the Government can conscript the young men of the nation ...it must conscript capital and industry and labor. Let the officers and the directors and the high-powered executives of our armament factories and our munitions makers and our shipbuilders and our airplane builders and the manufacturers of all the other things that provide profit in war time as well as the bankers and the speculators, be conscripted ...to get $30 a month, the same wage as the lads in the trenches get.

Let the workers in these plants get the same wages ...all the workers, all presidents, all executives, all directors, all managers, all bankers ...yes, and all generals and all admirals and all officers and all politicians and all government office holders ...everyone in the nation be restricted to a total monthly income not to exceed that paid to the soldier in the trenches!

Let all these kings and tycoons and masters of business and all those workers in industry and all our senators and governors and majors pay half of their monthly $30 wage to their families and pay war risk insurance and buy Liberty Bonds.

Why shouldn't they?

They aren't running any risk of being killed or of having their bodies mangled or their minds shattered. They aren't sleeping in muddy trenches. They aren't hungry. The soldiers are!

Give capital and industry and labor thirty days to think it over and you will find, by that time, there will be no war. That will smash the war racket …that and nothing else.

Maybe I am a little too optimistic. Capital still has some say. So capital won't permit the taking of the profit out of war until the people …those who do the suffering and still pay the price …make up their minds that those they elect to office shall do their bidding, not that of the profiteers.

Another step necessary in this fight to smash the war racket is the limited plebiscite to determine whether a war should be declared. A plebiscite not of all the voters but merely of those who would be called upon to do the fighting and dying. There wouldn't be very much sense in having a 76-year-old president of a munitions factory or the flat-footed head of an international banking firm or the cross-eyed manager of a uniform manufacturing plant …all of whom see visions of tremendous profits in the event of war …voting on whether the nation should go to war or not. They never would be called upon to shoulder arms …to sleep in a trench and to be shot. Only those who would be called upon to risk their lives for their country should have the privilege of voting to determine whether the nation should go to war.

There is ample precedent for restricting the voting to those affected. Many of our states have restrictions on those permitted to vote. In most, it is necessary to be able to read and write before you may vote. In some, you must own property. It would be a simple matter each year for the men coming of military age to register in their communities as they did in the draft during the World War and be examined physically. Those who could pass and who would therefore be called upon to bear arms in the event of war would be eligible to vote in a limited plebiscite. They should be the ones to have the power to decide …and not a Congress few of whose members are within the age limit and fewer still of whom are in physical condition to bear arms. Only those who must suffer should have the right to vote.

A third step in this business of smashing the war racket is to make certain that our military forces are truly forces for defense only.

At each session of Congress the question of naval appropriations comes up. The swivel-chair admirals of Washington (and there are always a lot of them) are very adroit lobbyists. And they are smart. They don't shout that 'We need a lot of battleships to war on this nation or that nation'. Oh no. First of all, they let it be known that America is menaced by a great naval power. Almost any day, these admirals will tell you, the great fleet of this supposed enemy will strike suddenly and annihilate 125 million people. Just like that. Then they begin to cry for a larger navy. For what? To fight the enemy? *Oh my, no. Oh, no.* For defense purposes only.

Then, incidentally, they announce maneuvers in the Pacific. For defense. Uh, huh.

The Pacific is a great big ocean. We have a tremendous coastline on the Pacific. Will the maneuvers be off the coast, two or three hundred miles? Oh, no. The maneuvers will be two thousand, yes, perhaps even thirty-five hundred miles, off the coast.

The Japanese, a proud people, of course will be pleased beyond expression to see the United States fleet so close to Nippon's shores. Even as pleased as would be the residents of California were they to dimly discern through the morning mist, the Japanese fleet playing at war games off Los Angeles.

The ships of our navy, it can be seen, should be specifically limited, by law, to remain within 200 miles of our coastline. Had that been the law in 1898 the Maine would never have gone to Havana Harbor. She never would have been blown up. There would have been no war with Spain with its attendant loss of life. Two hundred miles is ample, in the opinion of experts, for defense purposes. Our nation cannot start an offensive war if its ships can't go further than 200 miles from the coastline. Planes might be permitted to go as far as 500 miles from the coast for purposes of reconnaissance. And the army should never leave the territorial limits of our nation.

To summarize… Three steps must be taken to smash the war racket.

We must take the profit out of war.

We must permit the youth of the land who would bear arms to decide whether or not there should be war.

We must limit our military forces to home defense purposes.

TO HELL WITH WAR!

I am not a fool as to believe that war is a thing of the past. I know the people do not want war, but there is no use in saying we cannot be pushed into another war.

Looking back, Woodrow Wilson was re-elected

president in 1916 on a platform that he had 'kept us out of war' and on the implied promise that he would 'keep us out of war'. Yet, five months later he asked Congress to declare war on Germany.

In that five-month interval the people had not been asked whether they had changed their minds. The 4 million young men who put on uniforms and marched or sailed away were not asked whether they wanted to go forth to suffer and die.

Then what caused our government to change its mind so suddenly? ... money.

An allied commission, it may be recalled, came over shortly before the war declaration and called on the President. The President summoned a group of advisers. The head of the commission spoke. Stripped of its diplomatic language, this is what he told the President and his group...

"There is no use kidding ourselves any longer. The cause of the allies is lost. We now owe you (American bankers, American munitions makers, American manufacturers, American speculators, American exporters) five or six billion dollars.

"If we lose (and without the help of the United States we must lose) we, England, France and Italy, cannot pay back this money ...and Germany won't.

"So ..."

Had secrecy been outlawed as far as war negotiations were concerned, and had the press been invited to be present at that conference, or had radio been available to broadcast the proceedings, America never would have entered the World War. But this conference, like all war discussions, was shrouded in utmost secrecy. When our boys were sent off to war they were told it was a 'war to make the world safe for democracy' and a 'war to end all wars'.

Well, eighteen years after, the world has less of democracy than it had then. Besides, what business is it of ours whether Russia or Germany or England or France or Italy or Austria live under democracies or monarchies? Whether they are Fascists or Communists? Our problem is to preserve our own democracy.

And very little, if anything, was accomplished to assure us the World War was really the war to end all wars.

Yes, we have disarmament conferences and limitations of arms conferences. They don't mean a thing. One has just failed ...results of another have been nullified. We send professional soldiers and sailors and our politicians and our diplomats to these conferences. What happens?

The professional soldiers and sailors don't want

to disarm. No admiral wants to be without a ship. No general wants to be without a command. Both mean men without jobs. They are not for disarmament. They cannot be for limitations of arms. At all these conferences, lurking in the background but all-powerful, just the same, are sinister agents of those who profit by war. They see to it these conferences do not disarm or seriously limit armaments.

The chief aim of any power at any of these conferences has not been to achieve disarmament to prevent war ...but rather to get more armament for itself and less for any potential foe.

There's only one way to disarm with any semblance of practicability, for all nations to get together and scrap every ship, every gun, every rifle, every tank, every war plane. Even this, if it were possible, would not be enough.

The next war, according to experts, will be fought not with battleships, not by artillery, not rifles, not machine guns. It will be fought with deadly chemicals and gases.

Secretly each nation is studying and perfecting newer and ghastlier means of annihilating its foes wholesale. Yes, ships will continue to be built, for the shipbuilders must make their profits. And guns still will be manufactured and powder and rifles will be made, for the munitions makers must make their huge profits. And the soldiers, of course, must wear uniforms, for the manufacturer must make their war profits too.

But victory or defeat will be determined by the skill and ingenuity of our scientists.

If we put them to work making poison gas and more and more fiendish mechanical and explosive instruments of destruction, they will have no time for the constructive job of building greater prosperity for all peoples. By putting them to this useful job, we can all make more money out of peace than we can out of war ... even the munitions makers.

So I say, TO HELL WITH WAR!

<>

The Black Legion

In 1936, Eranee DuPont used General Motors money to finance the Black Legion, a domestic terrorist organization dedicated to stop automobile workers from forming a union.

If automobile workers were allowed to form a union, they would demand living wages. That would reduce ruling family corporate income. It was unacceptable.

Black Legion terrorists wore robes and hoods with the emblem of the skull and crossbones symbol of the Order on them. The Black Legion was also a death squad. The Black Legion murdered union organizers. They firebombed union meetings. And, they wanted to destroy Jews, communists, and non-Whites.

Black Legion members met with Ku Klux Klan members. Charles Pool was a worker in Detroit. A gang of Black Legion terrorists beat him to death. Several of the gang belonged to the Wolverine Republican League of Detroit, a club of ruling family industrialists running big business in Detroit. When the story hit the press, their names were not printed. During the Poll murder case trial, witnesses testified Black Legion death squad killed more than fifty people, most of them African Americans.

Black Legion regularly patrolled in General Motors factories. Erane DuPont encouraged General Motors foremen to join the Black Legion ...to save America ...and, save General Motors from the international conspiracy of the communists and Jews to take over the world. General Motors had 75,000 Black Legion members.

Meanwhile, the DuPonts continued to finance and develop the American Liberty League ...a Nazi organization. American Liberty League promoted hating African Americans, Jews, President Roosevelt ...and, the 'New Deal'. American Liberty League worshipped Hitler. Lamont DuPont and Eranie DuPont gave $500,000 to support American Liberty League in its founding year.

Liberty League had a 31-room office in New York, 26 college branches, 15 subsidiary organizations nationwide distributing 50 million copies of Nazi pamphlets.

Morgan financial group and the DuPonts continued to finance domestic American fascism.

<>

Sept. 1936, while Hitler and Nuremberg milestoned a four-year plan leading to World War II, the DuPonts and American Liberty League poured thousands of dollars into backing Republican Ralph Landan, against Roosevelt, in the coming presidential election. American Nazi Party, and German-American Bunt, also backed Ralph Landan. Launching Landon failed.

William Knudsen, President of General Motors, along with the DuPonts, instituted in their factories new 'labor speed-up' systems, designed by Charles Bedaux. The speed-up systems forced men to work very fast on assembly lines. As a result of the new speed-up systems ...assembly-line workers died of exhaustion ...faced pressure, stress and fear of losing their jobs ... at a time in America when there were very few jobs, available.

Eranee DuPont paid almost 1 million dollars out of his own pocket to assemble armed, and gas-equipped, storm troops modeled on Gestapo.

These troops patrolled in DuPont plants, to beat up anyone who spoke for a union, or complained ...about substandard working conditions ...or, low wages. Eranee DuPont hired Pinkerton Agency to send hoards of detectives to spy on left-wingers or unhappy workers in their chemicals, munitions, and automobile empire.

By mid-1930s, General Motors was committed to full-scale production of trucks, armored cars, and tanks in Nazi Germany.

General Motors board of directors maintained personal, commercial, and political ties to Hitler and German General Staff.

In 1937, G.M. President Alfred P. Sloane became G.M. Board Chairman. Sloane made donations to support the National Council of Clergymen and Laymen in Ashville, North Carolina.

Aug. 12, 1936, National Council of Clergymen and Laymen had John Henry Kirby speak.

John Henry Kirby was a Texas fascist millionaire, who made his fortune in the lumber industry. Kirby spoke promoting Hitler. Other fascist pro-Hitler speakers included ...Governor Eugene D. Talmage of Georgia ...Nazi Reverend Gerald L. K. Smith.

G.M. Board Chairman Alfred P. Sloane regularly visited Berlin. There he socialized with Goering and Hitler. Graham K. Howard was a G.M. vice president ...and, a Fascist under FBI surveillance his whole career with G.M.

G.M. Board President Alfred Sloane's, *America and a New World Order*, told Americans, appease, work with Hitler. Sloane's ideas of free trade were the same as Hitler's. Sloane wanted to restore the gold standard and create, the 'United States of Fascism'.

Meanwhile, factories owned by International Telephone & Telegraph (IT&T) in Germany were running around the clock ...increasing production capacity, producing military equipment for Germany. The Opal works, owned by G.M. increased production.

<>

In 1937, U.S. Ambassador to Germany William E. Dodd returned by ship from a trip to Berlin, back to New York. He held a press conference onboard ship, in New York harbor, interviewed by *New York Times* reporters.

"A clique of U.S. industrialists is hell-bent to bring a Fascist state to supplant our democratic government. They are working closely with the Fascist regimes in Germany and Italy. I have had plenty of opportunity in my post in Berlin to witness how close some of our American industrialists are to the Nazi regime. On the ship, a fellow passenger, a prominent executive of one of the largest financial corporations, told me point blank, he would be ready to take definite action to bring Fascism into America, if President Roosevelt continued progressive policies."

<>

Patti tried focusing harder on what Reinhard was telling her ...but, it was blowing her mind. A picture began to form in her head ...of an America she had not known.

Reinhard continued his story.

Apr. 1944, Montague Norman, former Governor of Bank of England, was up for retirement. Kingpin of British finance, always favoring the Nazi regime, Montague helped German financier Hjalmar Schacht. In 1934, Montague Norman met with a dozen British ruling family financiers and industrialists ...in his private office at Bank of England, speaking to them, there. "The Nazis are a great stabilizing force that would come in handy against Soviet Russia."

Dec. 1938, after Czechoslovakia had been sold out at Munich, financier Hjalmar Schacht visited England. Hjalmar Schacht was a guest at Montague's house. Rumors spread, that Montague and Schacht were negotiating policy to expand German markets to increase Germany's foreign debts to Bank of England.

There were rumors about increasing British export credits for Germany to 375 million dollars ...a few weeks later Hitler himself saw to the expansion of German markets, when he marched into Prague, contrary to his promises in Munich.

Shortly before World War II began, Montague Norman signed over, to Hjalmar Schacht, the Czech gold deposited in the Bank of England.

Former *New York Times* reporter Charles Higham's, *American Swastika*, sets the scene.

1939, America

Major General George Van Horn Mosely was friends with Generals MacArthur and Eisenhower. Eisenhower thought Mosely was brilliant. Mosely served as MacArthur's Deputy, when MacArthur was Army Chief of Staff.

Mosely was confident. "Subversives are terrified of how popular you are, Doug. Americans are outraged by mongrelization of America ...by low-bred immigrants ...Negroes ...New-Dealers ...Jews. The people will overthrow the U.S. Government, then ask *you* to be their dictator.

You'll be damned for the moment ...but, history books will make you a hero."

Doug MacArthur felt he had an easy way in. "I'm thinking about running for President. DuPont, General Motors, and Morgan Bank people asked me to ...before they went to Smedley Butler."

Mosely smiled. "Doug, I'm warning you ...Jews and un-Americans, labor, and communists hope President Roosevelt will run, again. I said, back in Dec. 1938, to New York Board of Trade bankers and industrialists, Roosevelt forbid the Army to investigate Communism ...I said, that decision is inept ...it leads to war ...it leaves Communism free to destroy us, at home. I said, the only thing stopping Russian Communism in Asia, is a long line of Japanese soldiers holding them back. The last thing we need, is let in Jewish refugees from Europe. This new world war, is *us* against Jews trying to take the world over."

MacArthur sucked his pipe ...then, repacked it, "Mosely, it's food for thought."

Mosely lit a cigarette. "I had German Ambassador Hans Lutier over to my home. He convinced me ...Hitler wants peace ...Germany needs elbow-room in Europe ... to grow economically. Other world powers shouldn't interfere, while Hitler reshapes middle Europe to help German people. It's communists trying to take over the world. War is coming ...blame it on the communists. Hitler's Nazis will stop them. As I see it, Fascists and Nazis in America have one mission, make sure communists don't take over America ...imagine it, under Fascists and Nazis only the finest Americanism will grow ...as we neutralize communists. Want to get rid of communists in America? ...get rid of the New Deal. New Deal backers are behind communism ...we have to fight communists on our home front ...there are 80,000 communists in America, leading six million Americans. They have plans, to take over America's big cities. We have to stop the communist revolution happening in America ...we need a bill to give the Army free reign ...we need a military government.

"I condemn Roosevelt for promoting a divided world front. England and France are building a steel noose around Germany. I hold no brief for Mr. Hitler, Mr. Mussolini, or the Mikado ...but, you got to admit, Nazis saved Germany from going communist! ...Mussolini saved Italy ...Emperor Hiroshito saved Japan. There's no danger to us ...from Germany ...or Italy ...or Japan. Our danger is here at home ...from labor leaders like Harry Bridges, and John Lewis. It's

158

the Jews whipping up war fever!

"Their attacks on Hitler are designed, to ruin America. The world needs selective breeding, sterilization, elimination of unfit and Jews from American politics. We should send them out of America to Madagascar, like Deteridge says to."

<>

May 1939, Mosely, Deteridge, Campbell, and Gilbert are called before House Committee on Un-American Activities, chaired by Martin Dies, of Texas. Dies went after Deteridge. "Mr. Deteridge, you said the gutters will soon run with the blood of Jews."

"Yes. That's true."

Dies went after Mosely. "Mr. Mosely, what is your position? ...on admitting children of Jewish families from Germany into the United States as refugees."

Mosely was rigid. "I don't think Jews expect to get Congress to make any changes in our immigration laws. The quotas are closed ...I hope, for all time."

<>

I enjoyed Nancy reading to me in the evenings, after I retired. Time has a way of telling all things, as if everything in our lives, random as it seems at the time, is connected ...through us. Nancy read to me, about history of anti-communism in America.

So, I learned about the coup attempts ...but, I didn't believe them ...I think they're just revisionist history, by the communists. The communist historians said, publicity generated appearing before the House Committee on Un-American Activities prevented Campbell, Gilbert, and Deteridge from continuing to plan the fascist coup d'état they hoped for ...to take over America. A new effort was taken up by leaders of the Christian Front Movement. Father Charles Kauflin ...you remember, the Catholic radio broadcaster, one of my childhood heroes ... back in the beginning of the book ...the popular American radio commentator I idolized as a youth, my anti-communist mentor... was the underground leader of the Christian Front Movement in America. Nancy told me, it wasn't till the end of the 20th Century, that Father Kauflin was discovered to be a Nazi agent ...and, you bet, I argued with her each time she said it.

<>

Reinhard continued his narrative to Patti.

Christian Front Movement developed alongside German-American Bunde. After 1938, the German Government stopped supporting the German-American Bunde. But, Christian Front

was encouraged by Himmler, Hess, and Ernst Wilhelm Bohle.

Christian Front members were mostly Irish-Catholic Americans. Pope Pius XII ascended to the Papacy in 1939. He was favorably inclined to Hitler and Mussolini. Following an SS precedent, Father Kauflin divided Christian Front Movement into units of twenty men each.

Christian Front carried on in Deteridge's footsteps, aligning themselves with Deteridge's American Nationalist Federation.

American Nationalist Federation membership consisted of lunatic fringe elements, and unemployed blue-collar workers.

Christian Front members included large numbers of police, National Guard, White Russians, and expatriate Irish Republican Army Militia.

Christian Front, and American Nationalists, wanted to position Mosely for President ...using a political putsch ...or, coup d'état.

Christian Front members beat-up Jews ...on street corners ...on buses ...in parks ...in subways ...and, openly denounced President Roosevelt. 'The Sporting Club', was the name of an inner circle of the Christian Front Movement. The Sporting Club wanted to rally 300,000 Irish-American members, including police, and National Guard members, seize the White House ...then, install Major General Mosely in the Oval Office ...as the fascist dictator of the United States.

FBI Director J. Edgar Hoover kept tabs on the Sporting Club. On July 25, after fourteen weeks of investigation, Special Investigator Rogge focused his attention on Major General George van Horn Mosely ...and, the Christian Front Movement coup d'état plot. Investigator Rogge produced evidence, letters from William Dudley Pele to Mosley.

Rogge read excerpts from the letters, into evidence, "The weapons are in our hands to hurl this overseas crowd of subversionists out of our country. I am carrying in my head, my dear General, information of so colossal a character that I feel it should be shared by at least four other men beside myself, namely Henry Ford, Colonel Lindbergh, Senator Wheeler, and yourself. I am already in contact with Mr. Ford and am leaving for Detroit in the morning to see him again," Pele's letter said.

Ford denied knowledge of either of the coups he was accused of supporting. Mosely did too. Meanwhile, Father Kauflin distributed *Protocols of the Elders of Zion*, through publishing houses owned by William Dudley Pele. William Dudley

Pele led the Gestapo-like, Silver Shirts ...William Dudley Pele served with the Japanese in Siberia against the Soviet Union in 1918, convinced that the Jews financed the Russian revolution.

<>

Reinhard looked at Patti, continuing his brief.

Sept. 1 1939, Nazi mechanized divisions invade Poland on seven fronts. Great Britain and France declare war on Germany, within 48 hours. The Polish regime is led by anti-Soviet officers. They ally Poland with the Nazis. Poland refuse Soviet aid and Soviet military help. Poland disintegrates within two weeks ...as Nazis invaded their former ally.

Sept. 17, Nazi columns occupy Poland. The Polish Government abdicates. The Soviet Red Army crosses the Polish Eastern border ...to occupy Byelorussia, western Ukraine, and Galicia ...ahead of Nazi Panzer divisions. Red Army occupies all territory Poland annexed from Soviet Russia, in 1920.

Oct. 1 1939, Winston Churchill's radio broadcast tells his reaction to the Soviets crossing Polish territory to occupy Byelorussia. "That Russian armies should stand on this line is clearly necessary for the safety of Russia, against the Nazi menace."

Soviet Union mobilized Red Army to the western front to strengthen Soviet defenses to stop the Nazis. Soviets prepared for their showdown with the Third Reich. September and October, the Soviet Government signed allied agreements with Estonia, Latvia, and Lithuania. The agreements allowed Red Army garrisons, Soviet airports, and naval bases in the Baltic States. Soviets arrested and deported the Nazi Fifth Column in the Baltics ...in several days 53,000 Germans were deported from Latvia, 50,000 Germans from Lithuania, and 12,000 from Estonia. Overnight, the Baltic fifth columns created by Alfred Rosenberg were devastated. German High Command lost strategic positions and bases they could have used to attack the Soviet Union. Finland decided to become a Nazi ally.

Dagmara looked at Patti. "Every family has skeletons in the closet, it's ashamed of. You're old enough to hear our secrets."

Patti felt apprehensive.

Book Two

<>

INTERMISSION

[See Fed charts & legends, p587-590.]

<>

Speaking as a former U.S. President, now that you've seen the charts, you've got to figure it out ...that, the people who own the Fed, don't have any particular loyalty to America ...because, they run England, France, Germany, and many other countries, too. So, it wouldn't be fair if they favored America ...in God's eyes, God made everyone, everywhere.

That's why Fed majority shareholder ruling families look down on Americans, and citizens of every country, as uneducated, uncivilized, and poor ...got it?

But, Central Bankers look on themselves ...as equal partners in the new World Order. It's *their* family values they're talking about ...not, *ours*. *They* don't care what happens to *us* working people in any one particular country, because they're interested in the welfare of the whole world, their whole New Order, like God intended ... *that's* what Nancy says they're trying to sell us, *a crock*, she says.

Because, Central Bankers are only interested in making *themselves* rich ...by robbing everyone else. They don't care about anything else, or anyone else ...for them, it's dog eat dog, survival of the most murderous, zero sum.

Feelin' kind of short, are ya? Wait till the Central Bankers take your kids' jobs away, conscript your kids, send them to war, or to prison ...how will you feel, then?

<>

Nancy was copy editing my fictional autobiography, she was angry. "Ronnie, you don't talk to readers like that!" .

"Okay, I apologize. Maybe, I was being a little short, myself."

<>

When I was President, a lot of people didn't like Vice President George Herbert Walker Bush ...because, they said, his family dynasty were Nazi traitors, full of treason. Even at the end of my term, radicals attacked Vice President Bush for directing the National Republican Heritage Group Council branch of the Republican Party ...that, was helping him get votes to run for President, in 1988 ...people criticized leaders of the Council because the leaders were death squad leaders in Eastern Europe, Nazis, fascists ...I didn't know that at the time, of course. But, after all, people change ...is it fair to hold someone's past over their heads? ...like that. But, you gotta see the Bushes as Skull & Bones' new World Order in America ...look at their social milieu, and the other ruling families they truck with that are Fed majority shareholders ...because, the regional Fed branches come up with who's running for president, governor, etc. Now, you've seen the charts ...let's set the record straight on this Bush/Nazi baloney.

When World War I started, Kuhn, Loeb Co. helped transfer German shipping interests. Sir Cecil Spring Rice was British Ambassador to the U.S., his *Letters and Friendships of Sir Cecil Spring-Rice* included this letter, to Lord Grey.

"Another matter is transfer of the flag to the Hamburg Amerika ships. The company is practically a German Government affair. The ships are used for Government purposes, the Emperor himself is a large shareholder, and so is the great banking house of Kuhn, Loeb Co. A member of the house of Warburg has been appointed to a very responsible position in New York, although only just naturalized. He is concerned in business with the Secretary of the Treasury, who is the President's son-in-law. He's negotiating on behalf of Hamburg Amerika Shipping Co."

A lot of people during my presidency ...and, during both Presidents Bush, attack their Bush Dynasty ...because, *they* co-owned Hamburg Amerika shipping company. Horse-pucky. History says, the financial panic of 1897 forced Union Pacific Railroad into bankruptcy ...that means they didn't get credit or loan when central bankers engineered a depression ...to buy things up, when business fell off ...no one could cover shortfalls. So, in 1898, Edward H. Harriman and Robert Lovett bought that railroad for 110 million dollars, in a deal brokered by New York-based Kuhn Loeb investment banking house.

For five dollars, who brokered the deal? Took you too long. Felix Warburg, a partner of Kuhn Loeb. Samuel Prescott Bush was president of Buckeye Steel Castings, at the time. By the time in American history we're diving into next, get the cameras rolling, and actors going pretty darn quick, set the scene ...it's 1914, we're going to war. Percy A. Rockefeller buys controlling interests in Remington Arms, and appoints Samuel F. Pryor as CEO. By 1918, Robert Lovett's president of Union Pacific Railroad. Bernard Baruch, and banker Clarence Dillion, make Samuel Prescott Bush a director of the facilities division of the U.S. War Industries Board ...because, Bernard Baruch is Chairman of U.S. War Industries Board.

So, Nov. 1919, Averell Harriman, and George Herbert Walker, form W. A. Harriman & Co. bank ...Walker is president and chief exec.

So, Averell Harriman, son of Edward Henry Harriman ... who bought Union Pacific Railroad out of bankruptcy, is born in New York City Nov. 15, 1891. He later joins his father's, Union Pacific Railroad Co., in 1915, is chairman of the board in 1932, and remains so ...until 1946 ...in the middle of the movie script ...Franklin D. Roosevelt appoints Harriman as U.S. Ambassador to the Soviet Union in 1943 ...until 1946, when Harry S. Truman appoints him Commerce Secretary ...then, he works on the Marshall Plan ...and, is national security adviser during the Korean War ...a democrat, he's elected governor of New York, in 1954 ...and, tries two unsuccessful attempts to become Democratic presidential nominee in 1952, and 1956.

Harriman serves in several posts, under President John F. Kennedy ...including, negotiating the Nuclear Test Ban Treaty in 1963 ...named as a Soviet spy by Anatoli Golitsin, Harriman is appointed by President Lyndon B. Johnson as ambassador-at-large for Southeast Asian affairs, in 1965.

Harriman also served as chief U.S. negotiator, when preliminary peace talks opened in France between United States and North Vietnam, in 1968 ...losing this position under President Nixon ...but, returns to office in 1978 appointed senior member of the U.S. Delegation to the United Nations General Assembly's Special Session on Disarmament ...and, dies smack dab in the middle of my Presidency, in 1986 ...when I'm plagued with Alzheimer's disease.

<>

Well, I don't remember things so well, anymore ...I left out a few details. So, Averell Harriman and George Herbert Walker of W. A. Harriman & Co. buy control of the German Hamburg-Amerika Line after negotiations with the firm's chief executive, William Cuno and, Max Warburg of the shipping line's bankers, M.M. Warburg.

The American holding is now called, American Ship & Commerce Corp. ...and, Remington Arms CEO Samuel F. Pryor buys into the deal ...is now on the ASCC board, as a director. Meanwhile Cuno's pouring money into the Nazi party.

So, back in 1922, Averell Harriman sets up a branch of W. A. Harriman & Co. in Berlin ...under the residency of partner, George H. Walker. Oct. 1923, Fritz Thyssen's contributions to the Nazi Party begins with a donation of

100,000 marks.

A U.S. Government memorandum, Oct. 5 1942, to Executive Committee of the Office of the Alien Property Custodian cites on Averell Harriman.

"W. Averell Harriman was in Europe sometime prior to 1924 ...and, at that time became acquainted with Fritz Thyssen, the German industrialist," the memo said. They set up a bank for Thyssen in New York, and Thyssen's agent, the memo says. "H. J. Kouwenhoven came to the U.S. prior to 1924 ...for conferences with the Harriman Co. in this connection," the memo says.

<>

Okay, so a year goes by. It's 1924, W. A. Harriman & Co. invests $400,000 ...sets up Union Banking Corp. in New York, in partnership with Thyssen's Bank voor Handel en Scheepvaart (Bank for Trade and Shipping), BHS in Holland. *Aha!* Be on the lookout for trade acceptances ...*you* don't even know what trade acceptances are! ...unless you've read ahead. So, Union Bank now can transfer funds back and forth ...between the United States, and Thyssen's companies in Germany ...to his company Vereinigte Stahlwerke (United Steel), for one.

To confuse things more, Prescott Sheldon Bush Sr., son of Samuel Bush and son-in-law of George Herbert Walker ...now joins Harriman-controlled U.S. Rubber Co. ...as a director.

Now, two years go by, it's 1926. Prescott S. Bush Sr. becomes vice president of W. A. Harriman & Co., and Wall Street banker Clarence Dillon of Dillon Read bank (buddy of Prescott S. Bush Sr.'s father, Sam Bush), set up the German Steel Trust with Thyssen ...and, his partner Friedrich Flick. So, now Dillon Read bank handles the Trust's corporate banking ...in return for two Dillon Read reps sitting on the board of German Steel Trust ...as board members ...while German Steel Trust CEO Albert Voegler is another German industrialist who will finance Hitler into power.

Albert Voegler is now a director on several corporate boards, including ...German Steel Trust ...Bank voor Handel en Scheepvaart (Bank for Trade & Shipping) ...and, Hamburg-Amerika Line. So, Union Bank is now partners with Friedrich Flick's vast steel, coal, and zinc conglomerate operations in Germany, and Poland ... the Silesian Holding Co. And, Walker, Bush, and Harriman now own 33.33% of Flick's conglomerate, Consolidated Silesian Steel Corp.

We're almost done, bear with me.

It's 1931, Fritz Thyssen transfers 300,000 marks to Rudolph Hess from Thyssen's Bank voor Handel en Scheepvaart (Bank for Trade and Shipping), to the Nazi Party, doubling his total contributions to date ...and, W. A. Harriman & Co. merges with British-American investment house, Brown Brothers ...that, makes Prescott S. Bush Sr., Thatcher M. Brown, and the two Harriman brothers ... all senior partners in the brand-spanking-new Brown Brothers Harriman firm ...one of the board members being Robert Scott Lovett's son, Robert A. Lovett, who eventually becomes Assistant Secretary for the Air Force during World War II ...then, Undersecretary of State in 1947-1949 ...then, Deputy Defense Secretary in 1950-1951 ...then, Secretary of Defense in 1951-1953, and for icing on the cake, as his father had served on the World War I War Industries Board with Sam Bush ... Robert Lovett becomes another partner in the newly-merged, Brown Brothers Harriman firm ...with Prescott S. Bush running the New York office ...with Thatcher Brown running the London office and Montagu Norman, now Governor of the Bank of England and a Nazi sympathizer and an ex-Brown partner. Lovett's grandfather directed Brown Bros. during the American Civil War ...when, Brown Bros. shopped 75% of slave cotton from southern states of America to British mills.

In 1932, U.S. Embassy in Berlin questions, who's paying to finance the 350,000 Nazi SS & SA troops? ...the Embassy notes, American-owned Hamburg-Amerika Line is funding propaganda against the German government's attempts to disband the Nazi SS & SA troops.

So, Hitler assumes power in Germany, Jan. 1933. In Mar. 1933, Prescott Bush Sr. informs Max Warburg he is to represent American Ship & Commerce Line as a board member on Hamburg-Amerika Line, since Max was advising Hjalmar Schacht, the German Economics Minister ...who is a close friend of Montagu Norman ...and, Max sits on the Reichsbank while Max's brothers run Kuhn Loeb bank ...that, brokered E.H. Harriman's purchase of Union Pacific Railroad out of bankruptcy.

<>

Moshe Gottlieb's, *American Anti-Nazi Resistance,* reports Max's son, Erich, cabled cousin Frederick Warburg, a director of Union Pacific Railroad ...instructing him, use his influence to stop all anti-Nazi propaganda and activity in America.

In 1933, the American-Jewish committee, B'nai B'rith, and Anti-Defamation League issue a joint statement, "that no American boycott against Germany be encouraged." And, the May 20 *New York Times* reports on Hitler's increasing power ...Germany and America reach an agreement in Berlin, between Hitler's Economics Minister Hjalmar Schacht, and John Foster Dulles ...to coordinate all trade ...so, Averell's first cousin Oliver Harriman of Harriman International Co., forms a syndicate of 150 firms, and private individuals, to conduct all exports from Germany to America.

So, Allen Dulles, whose scene we're introducing, that I'm rehearsing ...in which I play all four Warburgs ...and, his brother John ... are partners in Sullivan & Cromwell law firm ...representing the Nazi stock portfolio in America ...including I.G. Farben, who created Tabun nerve gas used in the concentration camps, SKF supplying 65% of bearings to Germany, and of course, Schroder Bank ...where Allen Dulles sits as a director until 1944.

It's 1933, a very busy year, North German Lloyd merges with Hamburg-Amerika, in Hamburg ...so, American Ship & Commerce who owns Hamburg-Amerika install Christian Beck, a Harriman exec, to manage freight and operations in North America ...for a newly formed firm, Hapag-Lloyd ...but, Chairman Emil Helfferich of Hapag-Lloyd ... is a Nazi ...Nazis accompany his ships. And, the Nye Committee in 1934 reports, Chairman Sam Pryor of Remington Arms, who is a co-founding director of Union Bank, and, of American Ship & Commerce has entered a cartel agreement with I. G. Farben chemical and armaments, and is, of course, supplying all the Nazi guards on his ships, with American-made Remington Arms guns.

Dec. 7 1941, the U.S. enters into World War II ...next August, U.S. Alien Property Custodian Leo T. Crowley, under the Trading with the Enemy Act, orders all Hapag-Lloyd property seized. In October, Crowley seizes the stock shares of Union Banking Corp. of New York, ...whose shareholders are ...board chairman E. Rowland Harriman, also directing Brown Brothers Harriman ...president and director Cornelis Lievense, also a banking functionary for the Nazis ...board treasurer Harold Pennington, also a director of Brown Brothers Harriman ...Ray Morris, a director of Brown Brothers Harriman ...Prescott S. Bush Sr., a director of Brown Brothers Harriman ...J. H. Kouwenhoven, also a director of Brown Brothers Harriman and chief foreign financial officer of German Steel Trust who brokered the original deal between Fritz

Thyssen and Union Banking Corp. ...and, Brown Brothers Harriman director Johann G. Groeninger, also an industrialist in Nazi Germany ... the seized shares being described in the Vesting Order as, "shares held for the benefit of members of the Thyssen family, property of nationals of a designated enemy country".

A few days later, Crowley seizes a couple more companies ...as Nazi front company operations owned by Union Banking Corp. ...Seamless Steel Equipment Corp. ...and, Holland-American Trading Corp. ...but, by Nov. 1942 only the Nazi financial interests in Silesian-American Corp. remain seized ...allowing U.S. United Banking Corp's U.S. partners to continue business.

In 1945, U.S. Treasury Department reports to the 79th Congress, Thyssen's Vereinigte Stahlwerke United Steel, had produced the following proportions of Nazi Germany's total output: pig iron 50.8%, pipe & tubes 45.5%, universal plate 41.4%, galvanized sheet 38.5%, heavy plate 36%, explosives 35%, wire 22.1%.

<>

October 2003, the year before I die, Nancy reads me the work of American intelligence historian, and former Federal Prosecutor, John Loftus. In my Presidency, I would've ignored him ...because, I was in the trenches and didn't have time to debate ...but, in my twilight years, with Death staring me in the face, the truth takes on new meaning for me, as did the concept, of eternity.

Loftus' view on all this, from his web site, john.loftus.com.

"Some of our famous American families, including Bushes, made fortunes from the Holocaust. One can't blame 'W' for what his grandfather did, anymore than one can blame John Kennedy because his father bought Nazi stocks. What most people don't know, is Joseph Kennedy bought his Nazi stocks from Prescott Bush. Every great family has its scandal.

"The Bush family's scandal is that they funded Hitler, and, profited from the Holocaust. In Oct. 2003, John Buchanan unearthed the recently released Bush-Thyssen files in U.S. National Archives. These long-buried U.S. government files demonstrate, the Bush family stayed on corporate boards of Nazi front groups ...even after they knew, beyond a shadow of a doubt ...they were helping the financial cause of the Third Reich. It was all about the money.

"Nazi Germany is where the Bush family fortune came from, and where the Harrimans and the Rockefellers increased their fortunes to obscene proportions.

"Averell Harriman, he secretly financed the Bolsheviks while American, British, and White Russian troops were still fighting against the infant, communist revolution. Harriman bribed Lenin into letting him takeover the Czar's cartels, which exported manganese, iron ore, and other raw materials. Harriman shipped Russian raw materials to his German partners, the Thyssens ...who'd been secretly bought out ... by the Rockefellers.

<>

"Rockefeller's lawyers, the Dulles Brothers, deliberately and systematically bankrupted the German economy with the Versailles Treaty.

"German currency was almost worthless after WWI, so the Dulles brother's favorite clients, the Rockefellers, were able to buy the stock of nearly every German company for a song. The great sucking sound that preceded the Great Depression was the whistling of Wall Street money out of America into Germany, Russia, and Saudi Arabia. Two generations later, we are still paying for it.

"Harriman's Soviet cartels would deliver the raw materials, Rockefeller's high-tech German companies ...the Thyssens ...would process the manganese into steel for Harriman's railroads. To save transportation costs, the robber barons looked for middle ground in eastern Poland for a future factory site. It had to be in the coal fields of Silesia, on the banks of the Vistula river, where a canal could be dug to ship materials in cheaply, from Russia. The Polish town was named, Oswieczim, ...later known to the world by its German name, Auschwitz.

<>

Nancy continued reading Loftus to me.

"It was not a killing factory then, although slave labor was always contemplated for the maximum profit factor. Auschwitz was designed to process Silesian coal into tar additives necessary for Russian aviation fuel. It was a high tech German chemical factory, built to balance out Harriman's Russia-to-Germany export trade.

"The Rockefeller-Harriman front company that financed Auschwitz was called, Brown Brothers Harriman. It is still around today. Our President's great grandfather, Herbert Walker, founded the company and appointed his son-in-law, Prescott Bush, to the boards of several holding companies, all of which became Nazi fronts. The Walkers and Bushes never really liked the Nazis, any more than Harriman liked the communists. To the robber barons, they were just dogs on a leash. One day the dogs broke their chains, and

Hitler and Stalin got loose. Fifty million people died as a result of a bad investment.

"The robber barons saw it coming. Their lawyers, the Dulles brothers, had a contingency plan. They established three banks ...one in Germany ...Holland ...and, New York (Union Banking Corp., headed by the ever-useful son-in-law, Prescott Bush. No matter who won World war II, the corporate stocks would be shifted around to whichever bank was in a neutral country when the war was over, to avoid seizure.

"After World War II, the Dulles brothers' shell game deceived a gullible and war-weary world. The 'neutral' Dutch bank reclaimed their German assets as 'stolen' by the Nazis ...and, the whole merry fraud continued.

"Prescott Bush got his Union Bank back from the U.S. Government in 1951, despite its seizure in 1942 as a Nazi front. Prescott Bush, and father-in-law Walker, were paid two shares worth ...about $1,500,000 in 1951 dollars. It was a petty payoff for a job well done.

"Nearly 4,000 shares ...98% of Union Bank holdings ...were held by Roland Harriman, in trust for the Rockefellers. That's about 3 billion dollars in 1951 dollars, more than 30 billion dollars in 2004 money. Most of it was reinvested in post-war Germany, where they made even more obscene profits. After all, Germany was just as cash starved after World War II as they were after World War I.

"It was just another cycle in the robber baron's spreadsheet. Everyone made money off the Holocaust, except of course, the Jews, and the Allied soldiers, and, the dead people.

"A few decades later things quieted down, and all the Nazi money finally came home to Wall Street. By 1972, one of Rockefeller's assets, Chase Manhattan bank in New York ...secretly owned 38% of the Thyssen company, according to internal Thyssen records in my custody. Not a bad payoff for the robber barons. The Auschwitz investment paid off handsomely. Thyssen-Krupp Corporation is now the wealthiest conglomerate in Europe. WWII is over. The Germans won.

"Also in the 1970's, Brown Brothers Harriman, perhaps coincidentally, convinced the ever pliant New York State Banking Commission to issue a regulation permitting them to shred all their records for the Nazi period. The robber barons, unlike the Swiss bankers, knew how to cover their tracks.

"There were, of course, exceptions. Von Kouwenhoven, director of the Dutch Bank, discovered the secret Thyssen-Nazi connection after the war, and foolishly went to New York to warn his old friend, Prescott Bush. His body was found two weeks later. It was reported with a straight face, that he died of a heart attack.

"A dear friend of mine, former American secret agent William E. Gowen, played a principal role in unraveling the entire Bush-Nazi scandal. Gowen confirmed, that years after Von Kouwenhoven's death, another Dutch investigator, a journalist named, Eddie Roever, also suffered a convenient heart attack as he was about to confront Baron Heinrich von Thyssen-Bornemisza at his palatial London home, across from Margaret Thatcher's estate.

"Margaret Thatcher may not have known, or maybe she did, that her neighbor, Baron Heinrich's brother, was the infamous Nazi, Fritz Thyssen, who served Brown Brothers Harriman at the heart of the Nazi war machine. The Dulles brothers hired ghostwriters for Fritz's mea culpa book, *I Financed Hitler.* To this day, gullible American media believe that Fritz Thyssen turned against Hitler in disgust at the last moment before WWII. Now, that's spin!

"The truth is, that Prescott's Union Bank loaned the money to the Dutch Bank, that loaned Hitler the money, to build his first Nazi headquarters, the Braun Haus in Munich. The Thyssen's factories built the Bismarck, the rail lines to Auschwitz and Treblinka, and sent the rest of their steel to their cartel partners, Flick and Krupp. Together, these war criminals made the bullets and bombs that killed our parents' generation. They got away with it.

"It's not surprising, that their grandchildren are ashamed of how their families made their money. The only surprise is, the American media is still afraid to go to the U.S. National Archives and look at the files that John Buchanan found. But then, I'm not surprised at all."

Loftus & Aarons', *Secret War Against the Jews,* an intelligence history of the 20th Century, spells it out ... to an unwelcoming press, in the middle 1990s.

"George Bush's problems were inherited from his namesake and maternal grandfather, George Herbert 'Bert' Walker, a native of St. Louis, who founded the banking and investment firm of G. H. Walker & Co. in 1900. Later the company shifted from St. Louis, to the prestigious address of, 1 Wall Street.

"Walker was one of Hitler's most powerful financial supporters in the U.S. The relationship went all the way back to 1924, when Fritz Thyssen, the German industrialist, was financ-ing Hitler's infant Nazi party ... some Americans were just bigots and made their connections to Germany through Allen Dulles' firm, Sullivan & Cromwell ...because, they supported Fascism. The Dulles brothers, who were in it for profit more than ideology, arranged American investments in Nazi Germany in the 1930s, to ensure their clients did well out of the German economic recovery ...Sullivan & Cromwell was not the only firm engaged in funding Germany.

"According to Christopher Simpson's, *Splendid Blond Beast,* a seminal history of the politics of genocide and profit, Brown Brothers Harriman was another bank that specialized in investments in Germany. The key figure was Averill Harriman, a dominating figure in the American establishment. The firm originally was known as W. A. Harriman & Co. The link between Harriman & Co.'s American investors and Thyssen started in the 1920s, through Union Banking Corp., which began trading in 1924. In just one three-year period, the Harriman firm sold 50 million dollars of German bonds to American investors.

"Bert Walker was Union Banking Corp.'s president, and the firm was located in the offices of Averill Harriman's company, at 39 Broadway in New York. In 1926, Bert Walker did a favor for his new son-in-law, Prescott Bush. It was the sort of favor families do to help their children make a start in life, but Prescott came to regret it bitterly. Walker made Prescott vice president of W. A. Harriman. The problem was, that Walker's specialty was companies that traded with Germany. As Thyssen and other German industrialists consolidated Hitler's political power in the 1930s, an American financial connection was needed. According to our sources, Union Banking became an out-and-out Nazi money-laundering machine ... in 1931, Harriman & Co. merged with a British-American investment company, to become Brown Brothers, Harriman.

"Prescott Bush became one of the senior partners of the new company, which relocated to 59 Broadway, while Union Banking remained at 39 Broadway. But in 1934, Walker arranged to put his son-in-law on the board of directors of Union Banking. Walker also set up a deal to take over the North American operations of the Hamburg-Amerika Line, a cover for I.G. Farben's Nazi espionage unit in the United States.

"The shipping line smuggled in German agents, propaganda, and money used for bribing American politicians to see things Hitler's way. The holding company was Walker's, American

Shipping & Commerce, which shared offices at 39 Broadway, with Union Banking.

"In an elaborate corporate paper trail, Harriman's stock in American Shipping & Commerce was controlled by yet another holding company, the Harriman Fifteen Corp., run out of Walker's office. The directors of this company were Averill Harriman, Bert Walker, and Prescott Bush. In a Nov. 1935 article in *Common Sense,* retired marine General Smedley D. Butler blamed Brown Brothers Harriman for having the U.S. marines act like 'racketeers' and 'gangsters' in order to financially exploit the peasants of Nicaragua ... A 1934 congressional investigation alleged that Walker's 'Hamburg-Amerika Line subsidized a wide range of pro-Nazi propaganda efforts both in Germany, and in the United States.'

"Walker did not know it, but one of his American employees, Dan Harkins, had blown the whistle on the spy apparatus to Congress. Harkins, one of our best sources, became Roosevelt's first double agent ...and kept up the pretense of being an ardent Nazi sympathizer, while reporting to Naval Intelligence on the shipping company's deals with Nazi intelligence.

"Instead of divesting the Nazi money, Bush hired a lawyer to hide the assets. The lawyer he hired had considerable expertise in such underhanded schemes. It was Allen Dulles.

"According to Dulles' client list at Sullivan & Cromwell, his first relationship with Brown Brothers, Harriman was Jun. 18, 1936. In Jan. 1937, Dulles listed his work for the firm as 'Disposal of Stan (Standard Oil) Investing stock'. Standard Oil of New Jersey had completed a major stock transaction with Dulles' Nazi client, I.G. Farben.

"By the end of Jan. 1937, Dulles merged all his cloaking activities into one client account ...'Brown Brothers Harriman-Schroder Rock'. Schroder, of course, was the Nazi bank on whose board Dulles sat. The 'Rock' were the Rockefellers of Standard Oil, who were already coming under scrutiny for their Nazi deals. By May 1939, Dulles handled another problem for Brown Brothers, Harriman ...their 'Securities Custodian Accounts'. If Dulles was trying to conceal how many Nazi holding companies Brown Brothers, Harriman was connected with, he did not do a very good job.

"Shortly after Pearl Harbor, word leaked from Washington, that affiliates of Prescott Bush's company were under investigation for aiding the Nazis in time of war ... The government investigation against Prescott Bush continued. Just before the storm broke, his son, George, abandoned his plans to enter Yale and enlisted in the U.S. Navy. It was, say our sources among the former intelligence officers, a valiant attempt by an eighteen-year-old boy to save the family's honor. Young George was in flight school in Oct. 1942, when the U.S. government charged his father with running Nazi front groups in the United States. Under the Trading with the Enemy Act, all the shares of the Union Banking Corp. were seized, including those held by Prescott Bush, as being in effect held for enemy nationals. Union Banking, of course, was an affiliate of Brown Brothers, Harriman, and Bush handled the Harriman's investments as well. Once the government had its hands on Bush's books, the whole story of the intricate web of Nazi front corporations began to unravel.

"A few days later, two of Union Banking Corp.'s subsidiaries ...Holland American Trading Corp. and Seamless Steel Equipment Corp., also were seized. Then, the government went after the Harriman Fifteen Holding Company, which Prescott Bush shared with his father-in-law Bert Walker, holding Hamburg-Amerika Line, and, Silesian-American Corp. U.S. government found huge sections of Prescott Bush's empire was operated on behalf of Nazi Germany ...and had greatly assisted the German war effort."

<>

Now that should put all this Bush/Nazi bugaboo to rest and we don't have to talk about it anymore.

p.s. Eustace Mullin's, *Secrets of the Federal Reserve,* reports, that on November 13 1914, in a letter to Sir Valentine Chirol, Spring-Rice commented, "I was told today that *New York Times* has been practically acquired by Kuhn, Loeb & Schiff, special protégé of the German Emperor. Warburg, nearly related to Kuhn Loeb & Schiff, is a brother of the well known Warburg of Hamburg, the associate of Ballin Hamburg Amerika line, a member of the Federal Reserve Board, or rather, *the* member. He practically controls the financial policy of the Administration, and Paish & Blackett England had mainly to negotiate with him. Of course, it was exactly like negotiating with Germany. Everything that was said was German property."

Mullins adds, "Knowing that an overwhelming sentiment of the American people during 1915 and 1916 had been anti-British and pro-German, our British allies viewed with some trepidation the prominence of Paul Warburg and Kuhn, Loeb Company in the prosecution of the war. They were uneasy about his high position in the Administration because his brother, Max Warburg, was at that time serving as head of the German Secret Service."

<>

Nancy start helping me put on my make-up base, before going down to the studio, to start the day's filming. Mel's Jesus showed up, along with Patti, Ronnie Jr., Michael, Maureen, and a couple other fellows ...as usual, I was the only one who could see or talk with Mel's Jesus, I knew my family would think I'm nuts ...but, I'd do my best ...I couldn't be rude to Mel's Jesus.

"Hi Jesus," I said.

That stopped everyone, dead in their tracks.

Patti waved. "Hi dad, we still have the Bush/Nazi bugaboo thing, can we talk about it ...just a little bit, more?"

Nancy and I were applying base. "Just till I'm ready to go to the studio," I said.

Ronnie Jr. was confused. "What studio?"

Michael laughed. "The big studio in the sky."

Maureen stiffened. "Not funny, Michael. Have you raided the refrigerator?"

"Good idea."

Nancy used a camel's hair brush to put on the base. "Ronnie thinks he's acting in the biggest role of his life, don't you Ronnie?"

I sure was. "You're damn right. I'm going for the Oscar, this time."

Ron Jr. smiled. "Dad, is your Alzheimer's acting up?"

"If it was my Alzheimer's ...then, Jesus wouldn't be here standing next to you."

Ron Jr. looked around him.

I felt it was going to be a good day. "Jesus is never here when I'm in Alzheimer la-la land, are you?"

Mel's Jesus smiled."That's right, I'm never in la-la land."

"Jesus said, he's never in la-la land."

Patti pulled two of her friends forward. "Dad, this is John Loftus, used to work for Justice Department, in your Administration ...and, in Carter's, before yours, reviewing all the intelligence agency info, for consistency."

I liked him, already. "Welcome John, do you miss working in my Administration?"

"Yes, and no ...there were good things ...and, bad."

"I agree, *I* don't even miss it," I said.

"And, this is John Buchanan, a journalist," Patti said. "And, this is Dave Emory, a national radio personality talk show host. This is Peter Dale Scott, a poet and English teacher, at UC Berkeley ...when you were head of the regents, when you were governor. And, this is Al McCoy, the real

McCoy, an author and professor ...and, John Marshall, author. They're all intelligence community historians ...and, tell the truth."

"Gee Patti, you sure surround yourself with men, not a single female guest," I said.

Patti blushed. Patti was so pretty when she blushed, it wasn't too often I could corner her.

Hi gentlemen," I said. "Ever put on base?"

John smiled. "A few times for TV news shows."

"Same here," Peter said.

"Not me," Dave said.

"Never," Mel's Jesus said.

"I sure have," Nancy said.

"Every day," Patti said.

"Only for ballet performances," Ron Jr. said.

"It's not something I choose to talk about," Maureen said.

Peter Dale Scott looked down the cliffs towards the sea. "I think I'll walk on the beach, it's beautiful," he said. He left the gathering, starting down a narrow path leading down the cliffs, to the beach.

Michael yelled from the ranch house kitchen. "Any cheesecake?!"

"Let's ignore Michael," Maureen said.

"Well, this is like a meeting in the White House Situation Room ...back, when I was President, with all you folks having something to say to me, ...or, like a day at the studio, shooting King's Row."

Nancy startled me by smacking the camel's hair brush against her palm to shake off the excess face powder. "Five minutes."

<>

In a nutshell, according to John Buchanan's article, *Bush Nazi Dealings Continued Until 1951,* in *New Hampshire Gazette,* Vol 248, No. 3, Nov. 7 2003, the Bush/Nazi bugaboo had a few good years left.

"After the seizures in late 1942 of five U.S. enterprises, on behalf of Nazi industrialist Fritz Thyssen, Prescott Bush, grandfather of President George W. Bush, failed to divest himself of a dozen 'enemy national' relationships ...that, continued as late as 1951, newly-discovered U.S. government documents reveal. Records show Bush and his colleagues routinely tried to conceal their activities, from government investigators. Bush's partners in the secret web of Thyssen-controlled ventures, included former

CENSORED

New York Governor W. Averell Harriman, and his younger brother, E. Roland Harriman. Their quarter-century of Nazi financial transactions, from 1924-1951, were conducted by the New York private banking firm, Brown Brothers Harriman.

"Although the additional seizures under the Trading with the Enemy Act did not take place until after the war, documents from National Archives and Library of Congress confirm Bush, and his partners ... continued their Nazi dealings unabated. These activities included a financial relationship with the German city of Hanover, and several industrial concerns. They went undetected by investigators ...until, after World War II. At the same time, Bush and the Harrimans were profiting from their Nazi partnerships ...while W. Averell Harriman was serving as President Franklin Delano Roosevelt's personal emissary to the United Kingdom, during the toughest years of the war.

"Oct. 28 1942, the same day two key Bush-Harriman-run businesses were seized by U.S. government, Harriman was meeting in London ...with Field Marshall Smuts, to discuss the war effort. While Harriman was concealing his Nazi relationships from his government colleagues, Cornelius Livense, top executive of the interlocking German concerns held under the corporate umbrella of Union Banking Corp., repeatedly tried to mislead investigators ...and, was sometimes supported in his subterfuge, by Brown Brothers Harriman.

"All assets of UBC, and its related businesses ...belonged to Thyssen-controlled enterprises ...including Thyssen's, Bank voor Handel en Scheepvaart (Bank for Trade and Shipping), in Rotterdam, documents state. Nevertheless, Livense, president of UBC, claimed no knowledge of such a relationship. 'Strangely enough, (Livense) claims he does not know the actual ownership of the company,' states a government report. In another attempt to mislead investigators, Livense said, $240,000 in bank notes in a safe deposit box at Underwriters Trust Co. in New York, had been *given* to him ...by another UBC-Thyssen associate, H.J. Kouwenhoven, managing director of Thyssen's Dutch bank, and a director of the August Thyssen Bank in Berlin. August Thyssen was Fritz's father. The government report shows, Livense first neglected to report the $240,000. Then, claimed that it had been given to him *as a gift*, by Kouwenhoven.

"However, when Livense filed a financial disclo-sure with U.S. officials, he changed his story, again ...and, reported the sum as a debt, rather than a cash holding. In another attempt to deceive the governments of the U.S., and Canada, Livense and partners misreported facts ...about selling a Canadian Nazi front enterprise, La Cooperative Catholique des Consommateurs de Combustible ...which imported German coal into Canada via a web of Thyssen-controlled, U.S. businesses. 'Canadian authorities, however, weren't taken in by this maneuver,' a U.S. Government report states.

"The coal company was seized by Canadian authorities. After the war, 18 additional Brown Brothers Harriman, and UBC-related client assets ...were seized, under the Trading with the Enemy Act, including several showing continuation of a relationship with the Thyssen family ...after, the initial 1942 seizures.

"One of the final seizures, in Oct. 1950, concerned the U.S. assets of a Nazi baroness, Theresia Maria Ida Beneditka Huberta Stanislava Martina von Schwarzenberg, who also used two shorter aliases. Brown Brothers Harriman, where Prescott Bush, and the Harrimans, were partners, attempted to convince government investigators, the baroness had been a victim of Nazi persecution ...and therefore, should be allowed to maintain her assets. 'It appears, rather, that the subject was a member of the Nazi party,' government investigators concluded.

"At the same time, the last Brown Brothers Harriman client assets were seized ...and, Prescott Bush announced his Senate campaign ...that led to election in 1952. Records also show, Bush and the Harrimans conducted business after the war with related concerns doing business in ...or moving assets into ...Switzerland ...Panama ...Argentina ...and, Brazil ... all critical outposts for flight of Nazi capital after Germany's surrender in 1945. Fritz Thyssen died in Argentina in 1951."

Dave Emory couldn't wait. "There! You see! That was the Martin Bormann organization moving Nazi capital out of Europe, sheltering it in dummy and legitimate companies, around the world!"

Nancy was losing patience. "This is 2004! ...it doesn't matter, anymore."

Patti drew in a breath. "It shows the money-making motives behind our foreign policy, and collusion between Wall Street and the media."

"Tell me something I don't know ...three minutes, left," Nancy said.

John Loftus giggled. He looked at me, "There's

a long pattern of Bush dynasty war profiteering ... still happening, with George H. W. Bush's intimate relationships ...with the Saudi royal family ...and, the bin Ladens ...and, the Carlyle Group, including James A. Baker III, who managed *your* re-election campaign in 1984, who *you* appointed Secretary of the Treasury after he job-swapped with Don Regan ...and, Regan became your Chief of White House Staff."

I laughed. "I always got a kick out of Don's last name, sounding like mine."

Nancy smiled. "Apparently, you still do."

Patti felt embarrassed.

Loftus kept on. "When Baker was *your* Treasury Secretary, he organized the Plaza Accord of 1985."

I couldn't, for the life of me, remember what the hell *that* was. "So?"

"It was signed by the G-5 nations, France, West Germany, Japan, the United States and United Kingdom ...to devalue the U.S. dollar, in relation to the Japanese yen, and German Deutsche Mark ...by *fixing* currency markets ...so, the exchange rate of the dollar versus the yen *declined* 51% over two years, cutting the value of the American dollar in half. This devaluation was due to 10 billion dollars spent by participating central banks, while continued, orchestrated currency speculation made the dollar to continue to fall ...after, the end of coordinated interventions. This was different than Vice President Bush's deals, when he became President in orchestrated financial crises of the 1990s ...like, the Mexican financial crisis in 1994 ...and, the Argentinean financial crisis in 2001 ... when devaluation was planned, pre-announced, done in an orderly manner, and didn't lead to financial panic in world markets."

Something starting with a 'V' the sound *vvvvv* started coming to me.

"*Vvvvvvvv,*" I said.

Mel's Jesus saw, everyone looked bothered.

"Volcker," I said. "He did it. Paul Volcker's Fed, I remember now ...but, I had no idea what he was doing then, or now ...no one understands the Fed."

Mel's Jesus leaned close and whispered to me.,"I'll give you a hint, the Fed's not an Act of God."

"Then, the Fed's an Act of the Devil," I said. Everyone got quiet. I felt like talking. "Cosmos Topper, and Henrietta, and the three ghosts ...George and Marion Kirby, and their ghost dog, Neil the drunk Saint Bernard?"

People were starting to looked scared. Ron Jr.

put his hand over his mouth, walking away.

"Remember the 1950s? ...opposite me hosting Death Valley Days, and G.E. Theatre ... the sitcom, *Topper?*" I said.

Nancy smiled. "Of course, those shows and Burns & Allen, Amos & Andy, and, You Bet Your Life with Groucho Marx, were my favorite shows."

"They were *the* shows on network TV, then," I said. I was back, again. It felt great. The only good thing about Alzheimer's, once you have it, is you live in whatever time you want, in many different times at the same time ...it's shorthand, for living your life all over again, everywhere, at the same time ...except, you don't know it.

I started laughing. "You all looked at me, like I was nuts ...when I said, '*Vvvvv*' ...it felt like *I* was Cosmos Topper, talking to ghosts, and nobody could see, or hear them ...but, me. And, Henrietta thought I was nuts, *Vvvvv, Vvvvv.*"

Patti interrupted. "Dad, the President's father should've been tried, for treason."

Not my father! "When pigs fly! ...my *father's* a patriot."

Patti's spirits fell, "I meant, *President Bush's* father."

"*My* Vice President? ...that's ridiculous, he's not my brother."

"*No! His father!*"

'You're confusing me, Patti."

Dave looked at Patti. "Relax, Patti. It's impossible to stop the worst war profiteers, George W. Bush, and Dick Cheney ...they operate in secrecy, hiding behind the throne of Bush's White House. The Bush family's business dealings ...with Thyssen interests, circle the postwar Nazi flight capital program ...that, funded the Bormann organization. When the last Brown Brothers Harriman client assets were seized, Prescott Bush announced his Senate campaign ...that, led to his election in 1952. Bush family helped frustrate Operation Safehaven, directed at interdicting Nazi flight capital. Al Taqwa, too, is escaping interdiction ...due to international financial contacts."

In person Dave Emory sounded just like sounded as a radio announcer. "Just as the Bush-Dulles-Harriman-Thyssen connection was used to help undermine Operation Safehaven after World War II going after Nazi money being smuggled out of Europe, the international financial conduits associated with Al Taqwa network frustrated Operation Green Quest. Green Quest, and Safehaven, were Treasury Department intelligence operations ...directed at elements associated with finances of the Third Reich, Safehaven in the late World War II period ...and, Green Quest after the Underground Reich's 9/11 attack on the U.S."

John Buchanan needed reinforcement. "Does it matter I wrote that story?"

Loftus talked about the Bush Nazi connections ten years earlier, in *Secret War Against the Jews,* but mainstream media pooh-poohed him.

Loftus got serious. "You've redeemed my twenty years of research. The mainstream media slammed doors in my face over it, even though I'd worked for U.S. Justice Department, as a Nazi War Crimes prosecutor. The *New Hampshire Gazette* printed *your* story ...but, *you* had to write it, first! Now, the truth, and the facts, can speak for themselves."

Buchanan felt down. "Bummer. What difference will it make?"

Patti sighed "You *made* a difference. Every time one of us makes a breakthrough, we're part of it ...oneness, of humanity."

Loftus knew how Buchanan felt, like swatting from your bed, blindly in the dark to find a mosquito buzzing your ear, whacking your own head. "You cracked the dam. For 60 years, the mainstream media covered up people in this country who brought us the worst grief, in the history of the world, the Holocaust."

"Just like they covered up the Kennedy assassination," Dave said.

Nancy called her shot, *"Time's up."*

I didn't want to budge, being around the kids kept me young.

Ron Jr. spoke up. "Americans need to know ...which American ruling families supported Hitler before ...during ...and after the U.S. went to war, with Germany."

I'd never heard Ron Jr. speak his mind about anything, he was finally talking like a Reagan ...instead of a ballet dancer.

Buchanan had reservations. "But why didn't mainstream media break the story."

Maureen knew why. "How could they. "They'd lose their jobs. Bad people sit on the corporate boards, and control the newspapers, TV, and movie studios."

John nodded. "About 15 years ago, in the beginning of the first Bush presidency, big corporations bought the media companies ...that were privately owned by families or individuals, before. The real enemy, the multinational corporation, is only interested in profits, truth gets in the way of profits."

Michael returned from the kitchen eating New York Cheesecake, two pieces in his hand. "This stuff is good!"

John looked at Buchanan. "Yes, they should have been tried for treason ...because, they continued to support Hitler *after* the U.S. entered the war. As a former prosecutor, I could have made that case. It's too late for justice ...but, it's never too late for truth. We deserve it. President Clinton wanted all Nazi files declassified ...but, it didn't happen fast enough. Some documents you saw on I.G. Farben were declassified only a few days before you walked in the archives. You were lucky, I'd say."

Buchanan agreed. "I know."

Michael joinin in. "Patti's right, they should have tried Prescott Bush, George Herbert Walker ...and, the Harrimans ... for treason."

Patti was surprised, Michael rarely agreed.

Nancy was besides herself. "That's a great idea, Michael ...then, what do you think their friends would've done?"

Michael didn't care. "I don't know, probably start World War III right here, drop nuclear bombs on us."

Patti's eyes widened. "Michael! ...you're right."

Nancy started straightening up the area. "Well, they still might. You learn in Washington, the Devil's in the details."

<>

I remember Nancy reading Paul Manning's, *Martin Bormann, Nazi in Exile,* to me.

"Heinrich Thyssen-Bornemisza runs his private, Dutch-based investment group from Lugano Switzerland, his cousin Count Federico Zichy-Thyssen, grandson of Fritz Thyssen, exercised control over Thyssen A.G., from his base in Buenos Aires."

I wanted to join in the conversation. Mel's Jesus saw me ...trying, to come out of Alzheimer's dementia. Sometimes, I was just going along fine ...then, it took me over. Other times, I was lost ...but then, I'm found ...it's tough, like going all ways through a traffic intersection at the same time. But, thinking about Mel's Jesus made me better. "Jesus, heal me," I prayed.

<>

Everyone got quiet. Nancy, Patti, and Maureen start crying. For a few minutes, everyone was quiet.

I wanted to join in. "It's all right, let's keep the conversation going, it keeps me young."

Patti started in. "Talking about Bush's undeclared war on terrorism? ...won't *that* upset you?"

Nothing upset me, anymore. "It won't, Patti, any more that it already does. I want to participate,

I'm not a watcher."

Nancy picked up a newspaper, start reading. "Well, we all want to know what's going on. ...Mark Turner and Edward Alden's, *Loopholes Undermining Crackdown on Terror Financing*, in *London Times*, has a summary.

"The international system designed to curb flow of financial resources to al-Qaeda is being undermined by inadequate co-operation, legislative loopholes and lack of political determination, the United Nations warns. A new UN report, obtained by *Financial Times*, reveals that despite 'considerable progress' in combating terrorist financing, al Qaeda-related businesses, and charities, continue to operate across the globe. It highlights Youssef Nada and Idris Nasreddin, directors of al-Taqwa, a financial group the U.S. believes was the most important fundraising operation for al Qaeda. The two men continue to maintain commercial interests and property in Italy and Switzerland, despite their designation as terrorist financiers. Mr. Nada traveled to Liechtenstein in Jan. 2003, and tried to re-register two al Taqwa-related companies under new names. By doing so, he violated a UN-sanctioned travel ban," Nancy said. "Alden, Turner and Mark Huband's *Al Qaeda 'Financiers' Active in Europe*, in *Financial Times*, has more.

"Two men at the center of what U.S. investigators believe was the most important financing network for al-Qaeda, and other terrorist groups, continue to operate businesses in several European countries, according to an investigation by the United Nations group monitoring international sanctions on al-Qaeda and the Taliban. The report, obtained by *Financial Times*, traces recent activities of Youssef Nada and Ahmed Idris Nasreddin, directors of a financial group known as, al-Taqwa. Mr. Nada was named as a terrorist financier by the U.S. on Nov. 7, 2001, in action by Washington to crack down on funding for terrorists after the September 11, attacks."

Patti knew it, *they want you like that*. "Bush's White House stonewalls the 9/11 investigating commission ...because, there's a GOP Ethnic Outreach connection to the Islamist milieu targeted by the Mar. 20, 2002 raids ...White House aides Grover Norquist and Karl Rove helped put together the GOP Ethnic Outreach Islamofascist network ...the charities and businesses that fund Hamas, Al Qaeda and Islamic Jihad."

Nancy was ever vigilant. "Patti, don't start that again." But, you could hear doubt in Nancy's voice ...maybe, Patti was right, *this* time. Nancy

smiled. It was one of the few times in their lives that Patti and Nancy agreed, on anything.

Nancy read from the newspaper.

Philip Shenon's, *9/11 Probe Chief Frustrated*, in *New York Times* sets the scene.

"The chairman of the federal commission investigating Sept. 11 terror attacks said the White House continues to withhold several highly classified intelligence documents, he is prepared to subpoena the documents. The chairman, Thomas Kean, former Republican governor of New Jersey, said the bipartisan 10-member commission would be forced to issue subpoenas to other executive branch agencies because of continuing delays by the Bush administration in providing documents, and evidence."

"*San Francisco Chronicle*, Rebecca Carr, *Funds Still Flowing to Al Qaeda*.

"Al Qaeda's financial spigot is still open, and the new Homeland Security Department is ill-equipped to turn it off, leading terrorism experts testified Wednesday to a congressional panel. Even after government efforts to stop the money flow to al Qaeda, the terrorist organization receives more than 5 million dollars each year, much, from Saudi Arabia, Jean-Charles Brisard, a terrorism investigator for the French government told Senate Banking Committee.

"Saudi Arabia is present at every stage of al Qaeda financing ...but, primarily as the major source of funding, said Brisard, investigating the funding sources of al Qaeda on behalf of families who lost loved ones in Sept. 11, 2001 terrorist attacks.

"Shutting down front companies and charities that send money to terrorist regimes will go a long way toward stemming the flow of money to terrorists, said Matthew Levitt, senior fellow of terrorism studies at Washington Institute for Near East Policy, and a former counter-terrorism analyst at FBI.

"While Saudi Arabia has taken steps to crack down on charities that are diverting money to terrorist groups, it's not been enough,' Levitt said. 'More than 50 percent of the money flowing into Hamas, for example, comes from Saudi Arabian sources.'

And, here's *Shake-up Amid War on Terror Has Hit Campaign*, Ed Alden, *Financial Times*.

"U.S. effort to shut down financial support for terrorist networks is being seriously hampered by a government reorganization that left most experienced agencies without any power,' the U.S. government's former top counter-terrorism official said, yesterday.

"Richard Clarke, who headed counter-terrorism at the White House for Clinton and Bush administrations before leaving government earlier this year, said the decision to put the FBI in charge of terror finance investigations, and give new powers to Department of Homeland Security, set the campaign back.

"Reorganizing federal government in the middle of the war on terrorism was perhaps not the brightest thing we could have done,' Clarke told the committee. The administration agreed earlier to designate FBI as lead organization for investigating terror finance networks, moving a separate investigative team, known as Operation Green Quest, from Customs Service to FBI. In addition, Customs was moved to the new Homeland Security department, breaking it away from other agencies in the Treasury Department that play a key role in terror finance investigations and enforcement. The move came at a sensitive time when the Treasury was leading a series of actions, including the investigation into a broad network of Saudi-backed charities, based in northern Virginia."

Nancy kept reading to me. "Glenn Simpson, *Wall Street Journal, Unraveling Terror's Finances.*"

"Dollar by dollar, U.S. prosecutors in Virginia are unraveling a world-wide financial network operated by alleged Islamic extremists. Investigators have laid out the network's intricate and geographic breadth in recent court filings related to a terror-finance investigation of a Virginia-based group of charities and businesses. Yesterday, they indicted a key figure linked to Hamas and al Qaeda. The funds flowed from Saudi Arabia and Europe to the U.S. ...possibly to help make the money look legitimate ...and then, through a maze of Virginia entities, then back to Europe and the Middle East, authorities say. The money went through secretive Swiss banks and Isle of Man trusts and ended up in suspect hands, including a charity founded by an alleged Tunisian terrorist and a group implicated in the plot to blow up Los Angeles International Airport, court documents say."

Dave Emory's talk shows, lately, were all about it. He interrupted Nancy. "A key person targeted by Green Quest is Abdur Rahman Alamoudi. Alamoudi is linked to Al Taqwa's Youssef Nada, a pivotal former Third Reich intelligence agent ...and, to the Grover Norquist GOP milieu. The Muslim Chaplains network movement in the U.S. Military that Nada and Norquist started links up with Alamoudi."

Nancy read on. "At the network's center is Abdur Rahman Alamoudi, a Muslim-American activist who was indicted yesterday in U.S. District Court in Alexandria, VA. on money laundering and tax, immigration, and customs-fraud charges. The 18-count indictment isn't directly related to the Virginia probe, focusing mostly on alleged illegal dealings with Libya. In other recent filings, prosecutors unveiled evidence they say links Mr. Alamoudi to Hamas, the Palestinian group designated as terrorist by the U.S., and links to Osama bin Laden's al Qaeda organization. Prosecutors say Mr. Alamoudi's Palm Pilot contained contact information for seven men designed as 'global terrorists' by the U.S., in freezing their assets. They included Saudi businessman Yassin Qadi, and alleged supporter of Hamas and al Qaeda, and Swiss financier Yusuf Nada, an alleged al Qaeda banker.'"

Dave interrupted Nancy again.

Nancy didn't really mind ...because, Dave was an expert ...as good, or better ... than the ones she'd been used to when she was First Lady at the White House.

Dave apologized. "You must be getting tired of me interrupting you."

Nancy smiled warmly. "It's okay. Ronnie told me over the years, that's what the experts do ...they interrupt you, set you straight. I kinda like it."

"As long as it's not your kids interrupting you ...but, it's all right for your friends to," Patti said.

Nancy realized Patti was right. "You're right, Patti," Nancy said. Nancy paused for a minute ...and wondered, why?

Ronnie was happy. "Patti, that makes twice in your life your mother said you were right."

Patti laughed.

Michael piped in. "What was the first time?"

No one could remember.

<>

Dave start talking. "One of the Saudis flown out of the country in the wake of 9/11 before they could be properly interrogated was bin Laden's nephew Abdullah, associated with the World Assembly of Muslim Youth, an apparent Al Qaeda front. Abdullah's the nephew referred to next in this article."

Nancy was surprised. "You already read this article?"

"Sure, I read all the major newspapers, every morning."

"I'm impressed."

"Me too." Each time I talked, people looked surprised, like I was a chair or wall ... magically speaking. Mel's Jesus always got a kick out of it, watching the light *turn on* in someone's eyes. I used to get morning briefings at the White House every day ...at breakfast, ...at lunch ...and, at night. I liked Dave, a little presumptuous at times, but on the whole ... better than most White House, FBI, and CIA intelligence analysts. I signaled with my eyes for Nancy to keep reading.

"A Virginia charity, Taibah International Aid Association, worked in tandem with Success Foundation, prosecutors say. A nephew of Mr. bin Laden living in Virginia helped run Taibah, which had offices in the Balkans. Taibah personnel there told FBI, it supported Global Relief Foundation, a charity designated by the U.S. as an al Qaeda front."

"Osama bin Laden financially supported mercenaries fighting in the Balkans back in the 1990s, who still fight on the Muslim's side in Bosnia, according to *Der Spiegel*," Dave said.

My eyes lit up. "You mean bin Laden fought in Central Europe and Afghanistan?"

"Yeah, there's an article in *New York Times*, *Alija Izetbegovic, Muslim Who Led Bosnia, Dies at 78*, by David Binder."

Patti smiled. "Dave has a photographic memory."

Dave grinned. "During World War II, when Bosnia became part of the puppet-Nazi state of the Croatian Ustasche, Mr. Izetbegovic joined the Young Muslims, a group claiming to be torn between siding with German-sponsored Handzar divisions, organized by the German SS ...or, with Yugoslav communist partisans, led by Josef Tito. Mr. Izetbegovic supported the Handzars. After Tito's Communist government was established, in 1946, a military court sentenced Mr. Izetbegovic to three years in prison for his wartime activities. Osama bin Laden visited Izetbegovic in Sarajevo in 1993, and sponsored some fighters from Arabic countries to fight on the Muslims' side in Bosnia, according to a report in *Der Spiegel*," Dave said. "Alamoudi's an Islamofascist linked with the Pentagon's Muslim Chaplain vetting program ...that's in *New York Times, Simpson Unraveling Terror's Finances* article," Dave said.

Nancy read it. "Alamoudi set up a Pentagon program in the 1990's to recruit Muslim chaplains for the armed services, now the subject of an espionage probe," Nancy said.

"Then, *Military Adopts New Chaplain Policy* by Holland, *San Francisco Chronicle*," Dave said.

Nancy could hardly keep up. She put down the *Times*, picked up the *Chronicle*.

Dave didn't bat an eye. "The 2002 Raids referred to here are Operation Green Quest Raids, of March of that year," Dave said.

Nancy felt her voice getting tired, she swallowed, drank some water, then read. "The American Muslim Armed Forces & Veterans Affairs Council is a subgroup of American Muslim Foundation, whose leader was arrested and accused of acting as a courier to funnel money from Libya to terrorist groups in Syria. The Graduate School of Islamic & Social Sciences in Leesburg, VA, was raided by Customs in 2002 as part of an investigation into money being funneled to al Qaeda and other militant Islamic groups, senators added ...Mr. Nasreddin was listed by the U.S. on Apr. 18 2002, on allegations he headed a network of companies that provided direct support for Mr. Nada and Bank al-Taqwa.

"UN has also designated both men, requiring all UN countries to shut down their financial commercial operations. But, the UN report says that, while the bank accounts of both men and the al-Taqwa entities have been frozen, 'nothing has been done with respect to any of their other physical or business assets'. The report adds, both continue to have commercial property interests in Italy and possibly Switzerland, as well as residences in Lugano and Italy.

"Mr. Nada defied a UN travel ban to go to Liechtenstein in Jan. 2003, where most of al-Taqwa's offshore companies are registered. While there, he applied to change the names of two of his companies and to name himself as liquidator of both companies. After the UN monitoring groups raised questions, the Liechtenstein government removed Mr. Nada as liquidator. But, because of Liechtenstein's lax registration requirements for offshore shell companies, the government has no information regarding Mr. Nada's companies, the report said.

"Jonathan Winer, former senior State Department official and expert on terror financing, called it, 'shocking to think that any element of al-Taqwa is still functioning. Their business activities are supposed to be shut down. It's cut and dried. U.S. and European investigators believe Bank al-Taqwa, originally set up in 1988 with significant backing from Egypt's Muslim Brotherhood, was at the middle of an international network of charities and companies used to funnel money to al-Qaeda and other groups, including Hamas. U.S. terrorism finance investigators view al-Taqwa as the spine on which other terrorist finance operations were built,' says Mr. Winer.

"In just one year, 1997, the U.S. believes that 60 million dollars collected for Hamas was funneled through Bank al-Taqwa. Some of the links between Operation Green Quest, Al Taqwa and Abdurrahman Alamoudi are detailed in the *Financial Times* article.

"U.S. investigations of Islamic business and charities in northern Virginia known as the Safa Group ...which the U.S. believes funneled millions of dollars to terrorist groups, have turned up several links to al-Taqwa. In addition, names of Mr. Nada and Ghaleb Himmat, both of whom founded Bank al-Taqwa, were discovered on the electronic pocket organizer of Abdurrahman Alamoudi, who was charged last month with violating U.S. sanctions against Libya and is alleged by Washington to be part of a larger U.S.-based terror financing network.' Over and out, I'm tired, no more reading. I'm taking a nap. You coming? ...Ronnie?"

Maureen chose that moment to be interested. "*What's the Muslim Brotherhood?* Now, I've heard everything!"

Dave couldn't let it go, "Well, in a sentence, White House aide Grover Norquist, the anus of the GOP ultra right, a friend of Karl Rove, known as Bush's brain, and those Islamist terrorist links were precipitated by formation of the Islamic Institute linked with Al Qaeda, Hamas, and Palestinian Islamic Jihad ...it's kind of an extension of the GOP Ethnic Outreach program, which has, in the past incorporated Nazis, Fascists, death squad and terrorist leaders ...on the pretense of fighting communism ...and, mustering the ethnic voice to counterbalance what GOP since Nixon in the 1950s ...and, the Bushes even today call, the 'Jewish influence, the Jewish vote', in America. So, Muslim terrorist links to GOP Ethnic Outreach Program are part of canceling out the Jewish vote in American ...just like Bush didn't count election votes of the Black population in Florida ...because Jews', and Blacks', votes do count. Al Qaeda is the direct lineal descendant of the Arab Nazis of the Muslim Brotherhood."

Nancy was yawning, "Ronnie! You coming to nap time? Come, nap time!"

<>

I could tell Nancy was trying to get my attention ...but, there were puffs of smoke, and blazing fire, coming out the forest between the trees, explosions everywhere ...like Martin Sheen, in *Apocalypse Now* ...Mel Gibson in *We Were Soldiers* ...and, Russell Crowe in *Gladiator*. There were bloody pulps, everywhere ...machine-guns strafing the ground. We jumped into foxholes. Mortar shells exploded around us. Then, Ku Klux Klan in Warner Brothers'

Storm Warning set, in white sheets, wearing pillow cases in pointed white hoods with ghost hole eyes cut in them, rode up on horses ...in sheets, wearing sheet masks, too, with ghostly eye holes cut in them. Even the horses didn't want to be recognized. Klansmen were whipping my co-stars, Doris Day and Ginger Rogers ...then, they put a noose around my damn neck, and I was starring ...just like when I was President ...but, I already played that part, see, I knew how it would turn out, see, like Edward G. Robinson, see, I'd already learned the script back in the 1940s, see ...so, bringing it back in the 1980s was kid stuff. Christ, if *everyone* thought I was a fool, that I didn't know what was going on ... *they* were idiots ...of course I knew, but I didn't want the terrorists attacks that Bush's kid got, to happen on my watch, as President.

You think it's easy to play the fool. It can be ...but, when it is, you're done for, dead as Kennedy, or Lincoln.

Now, if *you* were a total sellout like President Wilson ...that's why the Fed put him on the $100,000 bill ...or a megalomaniac, like Hoover ...then, no problem ... cause you're Satan's legion. But, Bush's kid, and me, aren't *that* kind of American. We believe in Jesus, in Heaven ...we, are *not* Satan worshippers, we look out for Satan, cause Satan's waiting around the bend, in the supermarket, the intersection, in class, in bed, on the Federal Reserve Board of Governors, at every Central Bank boardroom ...ready to rip out your nuts ...nuke your damn country, hail weapons of mass destruction ...rain bio-weapons down ...make burning hell on Earth, with fire put out by buckets of human blood ...too much for me! I start shouting.

Not Doris Day! "Stop whipping Doris Day!"

The Klan surrounded us, those empty, ghost eye holes shimmering ...I was running out of ammunition! ...me, and Errol Flynn, surrounded by Nazis! ...in *Desperate Journey* ...me, with second billing, in *Storm Warning,* with Ginger, and Doris ...me, equal billing with Lee Marvin in, *The Killers* ...that's messed up, how can you follow *him*? ...damn it, *Nine Lives Are Not Enough, that's* for sure, I was No. 1 billing in that, and, in *Voice of The Turtle, Law & Order, Hasty Heart, Hellcats of the Navy* ...who's the man?

Nancy pulled softly on my arm. "C'mon, Ronnie."

Nancy was always a little jealous of Doris Day, we never talked about it. Nancy led me off to nap time. I liked how soft her hand was, I held it with both hands and had to comment. "Cut!"

I had a captive audience, you could hear a pin

drop. *That's* Hollywood, *that's* what it's all about. I followed Nancy along, holding her hand. "Where's *my* Oscar?"

<>

Nancy led me into the ranch house, I heard the screen door slam shut, behind us ...from that two-foot-long coil spring I'd put up there. fifteen years ago ...like that dead tree, beside the river where I cut 60 notches, 60 years ago ...one for each person I saved from drowning ...it's all there, at the same time, now ...in my world, there is no beginning, no end, I swim through Time ...a frog's egg, waiting for my tail to grow, 3 weeks ...the embryo, size of a pencil point, like a worm ...long and thin, segmented, heart beginning to beat, 4 weeks ...embryo 1/5" long, like a tadpole, noticeable tail, gills like a fish that will be a throat, 5 weeks ...tiny arm, leg buds like potato buds ...hands with webs between fingers on arm buds ...fingerprints exist, face has a reptilian aspect ...embryo still has a tail ...looks like a pig, rabbit, elephant, or chick ...6 weeks ...embryo, 1/2" long, two eyes, face has connected slits where mouth and nose will be, 7 weeks ...I have lost my tail, my face, mammalian but pig-looking, pain sensors grow. Conservative Christians believe an embryo feels pain ...but, higher brain functions, pathways to transfer pain signals from pain sensors, to the brain have not developed yet, 2 months ...my embryo face looks primate, not human ...some brain begins to form, I respond to prodding ...but, have no consciousness, this primitive, reptilian brain that functions throughout my life. My embryo responds to prodding ...but, has no consciousness, 10 weeks ...my embryo is a fetus, I am now a *fetus!* ...my face looking, human. Don't let me fool you. I *am* that reptilian creature, a Republican, once a Democrat, I evolved into disaster on wheels, two feet on a dick running senselessly from ovum to ovum, talking heads, exchanging words, ideas as if they exist, anything to destroy, to dominate, to control, to rule ...I am ... Rothschild! ...I am ... Warburg! ...I am ... Lazard! I am ... Schiff! ...I am Rockefeller! ...I am Ronald Reagan! I am you! *You!* I know your thoughts, your dreams, your secrets, your love, your hate, your hunger, your desire, your sickness, your joy, your shame ...I am the mirror of your eyes.

Patti turned on her portable computer on the picnic table, her satellite telephone, and TV modem kicked in, some keystrokes into her address bar tuned us in to, *Countdown*, with Keith Olberman, joined by NBC's Lisa Myers, ...and, there was John Loftus!

John smiled, "You found the broadcast."

"Sure, I always do. Count on it."

They exchanged smiles. There, was John on computer, on TV, on the Internet talking to himself ...sitting right next to everyone, listening to himself ...just like when I play the parts of all the Rothschilds, all the Warburgs, all the Schiffs, talk to myself all the time, watch myself in movies, on TV, on my home movie screen, same, exact thing.

Keith Olberman was DJ-ing. "Tonight we look at Abdurrahman Alamoudi, man who helped set up Muslim Chaplain Program, who met presidents Clinton and Bush, who tried to run $340,000 into Syria, is connected to Osama bin Laden's nephew, met with George W. Bush before Bush was president, appears, smiling, in a photo op with former President Clinton. So, how is it that a man who traveled in the highest of American political circles is suspected of secretly funding al-Qaeda and Hamas? And tonight, the dots are being connected and he appears to be tied also to the nephew of Osama bin Laden. An indictment is now being handed down against the man our military once turned to provide Muslim chaplains. For the latest details on the case of Abdurahman Alamoudi, here's NBC's, Lisa Myers!

Lisa had a fine voice for broadcasting. "Keith, tonight federal prosecutors have indicted the founder of the Chaplain Program on charges that he illegally dealt with Libya and laundered money. But, there are even more serious allegations about him in some new documents. Abdurahman Alamoudi, a consultant to the Pentagon on the Chaplain Program for more than a decade, now accused of helping Osama bin Laden and Hamas. Court documents filed late last night, claim Alamoudi provided 'financial support to Hamas' and 'financial support to fronts for al-Qaeda'. One of the groups allegedly tied to Alamoudi is a charity which gave a Virginia post office as its address. Alamoudi was vice president of the charity. Who founded it? Abdullah bin Laden, Osama bin Laden's nephew. Also ringing alarms, Alamoudi's palm pilot which the government claims included names and numbers of six designated global terrorists.

"According to terrorism expert Steve Emerson, 'The public face of Mr. Alamoudi was 180 degrees different from his private face. And, the private face clearly showed he was involved in, or directing fundraising for Hamas and fundraising for other terrorist groups.' The government alleges Alamoudi had a Swiss bank account and

$2,200,000 in unreported income on which he failed to pay taxes. Today, Alamoudi's lawyer says he never supported any terrorist group. And, that Osama bin Laden has dozens of nephews who have nothing to do with al-Qaeda. Yet, in an audiotape of a conversation obtained by NBC News, he seems to embrace violence, suggesting al-Qaeda should choose better targets. Through a translator, Abdurahman Alamoudi, allegedly tied to al Qaeda, said on videotape, 'I prefer to hit a Zionist target in America or Europe or elsewhere.'

"Alamoudi's lawyer says, her client doesn't remember saying such a thing and questions the tapes' authenticity. Over the year, Alamoudi has been a familiar face in Washington. Pentagon chose him to help select Muslim chaplains. He met with President Clinton, made six trips to Muslim nations as a goodwill ambassador for State Department, met with candidate George Bush. Last year, FBI director Rob Mueller even spoke to an organization founded by Alamoudi over the objections of some agents. Alamoudi, himself, was not only able to insinuate himself, but he put others in place. Now, these new allegations are contained in court documents arguing that Alamoudi should be held without bond until he goes on trial."

Dave Emory swigged on a beer. "They sure outted this guy, what happened?"

John Loftus was amused. "Well, you know, it's a funny story. About a year-and-a-half ago, people in the intelligence community came, and said, 'Guys like Alamoudi and Sami al-Arian and other terrorists aren't being touched because we've been ordered *not* to investigate the cases, *not* to prosecute them, because they were being funded by *the Saudis* a political decision was being made at the highest levels, *don't do anything that would embarrass the Saudi government'.*

"So, of course I immediately volunteered ...and, I filed a lawsuit against al-Arian ... charging him with being a major terrorist for Islamic Jihad. Most of his money came from Saudi charities, in Virginia. Now, Alamoudi's headquarters were in the same place, he was raided the same day I filed my lawsuit, Mar. 20.

"An hour after I filed my lawsuit, the U.S. government finally got off its butt ...and, raided these offices, the stuff they're carting out of there is horrendous. Al-Arian has now, finally been indicted, along with Alamoudi, just today."

Dave pressed. "Good work, John ...but, who was it that *fixed* the cases in the first place? How could these guys operate for ten years, immune from investigation and prosecution?"

John continued. "What Alamoudi and al-Arian have in common is a guy named Grover Norquist, the super lobbyist, Newt Gingrich's guy, the one the NRA calls on, head of, Americans For Tax Reform. He's the guy hired by Alamoudi to head up the Islamic Institute, and, the registered agent for Alamoudi, personally ...and, for Islamic Institute. Norquist's best friend is Karl Rove, White House chief of staff, 'Bush's brain' ...and, apparently Norquist was able to *fix* things. Norquist got extreme right wing Muslim people to be gatekeepers in the White House, *that's* why moderate Americans couldn't speak out after 9/11. Moderate Muslims *couldn't get in* the White House ...because, Norquist's friends blocked their access."

"How rotten *is* the Muslim Chaplains, that Alamoudi helped set up?"

"Rotten as it gets. The Muslim chaplain program Alamoudi set up ...is a spy service, for al-Qaeda. It wasn't just sending home mom and dad messages from prisoners in Guantanamo ...this outfit stole the CIA's briefing books. Everything CIA knew about al-Qaeda ...is now, in al-Qaeda hands. Norquist had other clients, an alphabet soup of Saudi agencies funding terrorism in America ...and, *they* had protection. We may find about 9/11 ...that, people out in the field *weren't allowed* to connect the dots ...and, questions will be asked, are guys like Grover Norquist part of the problem?"

Patti shivered. "I got chills down my spine."

Dave picked open a book he'd brought with him. "I have something to read to you, Al Taqwa is based in Lugano Switzerland, just like Thyssen-Bornemisza," Dave said. Richard Labeviere's *Dollars for Terror, the United States and Islam,* lays it out. "While establishing its headquarters in a tax haven, the Brothers' bank opened a branch, Al Taqwa Management Organization S.A., in Italian Switzerland, in Lugano. Lugano, a discreet frontier banking locale, is a stone's throw from Milan, a major financial center ...and, above all, the Islamist groups' entry point to Europe ...Al Taqwa is situated on the top floor of a small glass building, right in the center of Lugano, in the banking district, a district where overly curious journalists are immediately denounced to police ...who then, conduct American-style identity checks in the middle of the street. In Lugano, bank secrecy is no laughing matter. Several times, we tried to meet Mr. Nada, who eventually responded by mail, 'We allow neither you nor any other journalist, nor publication, to speak about us …positively or negatively …without written permission,' Richard said. "Signed, Yussef Nada." Dave had interrupted himself.

<>

Everyone in my fictional autobiography is always talking to themselves …that's, a comment on American society today. Everyone's arguing with themselves, questioning themselves, questioning the country, who we are …who are we? I wondered. Who were *any* of us?

Dave rolled on. "Discussing the diaspora of the Brotherhood following its expulsion from Egypt, the book discusses the establishment of Munich as a primary base of operations. Why Munich, why Germany?' I asked Rifaat Said. 'Because there, one finds old complicities that go back to the late 1930's, when Muslim Brothers collaborated with agents of Nazi Germany. By soaking up the savings of these Muslim workers, Yussef Nada, like Said Ramadan, took advantage of an extremely favorable context …and, used it as a springboard for Muslim Brothers' economic activities." Dave stopped himself. "Nada himself, is alleged to have been an Abwehr agent, the military intelligence of the Third Reich." He continued reading, "But, Yussef Nada is even better-known to Egyptian intelligence services, who have evidence of his membership in the armed branch of the fraternity of the Muslim Brothers in the 1940's. At that time, according to the same sources, he was working for Abwehr under Admiral Canaris, and took part in a plot against King Farouk. This wasn't the first time the path of Muslim Brothers crossed the Third Reich." Dave explained, "Richard's nickname for Muslim Brotherhood is, 'the fraternity'." He continued reading, "History of the Fraternity makes the Brothers' concept of the Islamic State clear …a theocratic State of fascistic inspiration. Some of them were fellow travelers with the Nazis, and are still trying today to resuscitate the old alliance of Islamism and the swastika …Now, Muhammad Said al-Ashmawy's speaking, 'All my research always brings me back to the same point …at the beginning of this process of the perversion of Islam are the Muslim Brothers, an extreme Right cult.' An extreme Right cult? 'The history of Muslim Brothers is infused by, and fascinated with, fascist ideology. Their doctrines, their totalitarian way of life, takes as starting point, the same obsession with a perfect city on Earth, in conformity with a celestial city, whose organization and distribution of powers they discern through the lens of their fascistic reading of the Koran.' This 'fascistic affiliation' would crop up in the analyses of several of our interlocutors …in particular, that of the journalist Eric Rouleau, a specialist in the Middle East, former French ambassador to Tunisia and Turkey. Taking Italy's choices under Mussolini for inspiration, the economic program set three priorities. The social policy foresaw a new law on labor …founded on corporations. This economic program would more directly reveal its relationship to totalitarian ideologies a few years later, with the works of Mohamed Ghazali, who recommended 'an economic regimen similar to that which existed in Nazi Germany and fascist Italy. The moral code is an important component in this program, intended to create the 'new Muslim man'. The notion of the equality of the sexes is inherently negated by the concept of the supremacy of male social responsibilities,' Richard says. 'The 'natural' place of the woman, is in the home."

<>

Pan-German Muslim Brotherhood Arab Nazis

Pan-German League Deutscher Verband was co-founded in 1894 by the German ruling families Hugenberg, Kirdorf, Krupp, and Thyssen. Professor Ernst Hasse was the Pan-German League's first president. In 1913 Heinrich Class succeeded Hesse. The Pan-German League had trans-Atlantic Axis branches in the United States, South America, Central America, the Balkans and Russia. After World War I the German General Staff and Pan-Germanism went underground. When it came to the surface again in the 1920's it was coined National Socialism, Nazism.

In the Middle East, mid-century were the Moslem Brotherhood, Arab Nazis. Germanism again went underground, in 1944.

When it came to the surface again, in 1988 in Sarajevo, it was coined 'neo-Nazism'.

In Afghanistan, Arab Nazis were coined, 'Maktab al Khidimat il Muhajidin'.

When it surfaced again in 2004, in Saudi Arabia …and, throughout the Middle East, it was called by it original coinage, 'Arab-Nazis' …indexed in a database, called, 'al Qaeda'.

After terrorist attacks of Sept. 11 2001, al-Qaeda passed IRA and PLO …as the world's most infamous terrorist organization.

Al-Qaeda …'the base' in Arabic …is a database, a list of names, a network of extremists organized by Osama bin Laden, a modern-day narco-terrorist mercenary hired by CIA to run death

177

squads, opium, and heroin ratlines ... and, fight for oil companies.

Al-Qaeda is 'a list of names', a database

Based on being President ...and, being duped during the Iran-Contra circus, I can honestly say, in 2004 President Bush must've known, Al-Qaeda has no location ...it's a list of names ...so, why does Bush run around attacking a stateless enemy, by destroying states?

I know, he prays about it ...we have come to a turning point in human consciousness ...how do you know? ...*S'up?*

The list of names, called, 'Al-Qaeda', was compiled in database form on computer, during the uprising against Soviet occupation of Afghanistan. *That,* legend says, thousands of volunteers from the Middle East came to Afghanistan ...as Muhajidin, Muslim warriors fighting to defend other Muslims.

What a crock ...American intelligence, stuck on stupid. *Then,* the story goes, in mid-1980s, Osama bin Laden became prime financier for an organization that *recruited* Muslims from *mosques,* around the world. These Afghan Arab mercenaries ...Muhajidin ...numbered in the thousands, defeating Soviet forces, the story goes. *And,* when Soviets *withdraw* from Afghanistan, bin Laden returns to his native Saudi Arabia, lives happily ever after ...founding an organization to help veterans of the Afghan war ...many went on to fight elsewhere ...including Bosnia ...and, these *names* comprise the basis of al-Qaeda. The end.

Hmmm. But, Bin Laden studied with radical Islamic thinkers ...and, may have already been organizing al-Qaeda when Iraq invaded Kuwait, in 1990.

And, my favorite of all, 'Bin Laden was outraged when the government allowed U.S. troops to be stationed in Saudi Arabia, the birthplace of Islam, instead of his Arab Nazi Muhajidin. So, it's 1991, he's expelled from Saudi Arabia for anti-government activities. From Saudi Arabia, bin Laden set up headquarters for al-Qaeda in Khartoum, Sudan.

The first actions of al-Qaeda against American interests are attacks on U.S. servicemen in Somalia.

In 1994, Sudan pressured by Saudi Arabia and U.S., expels bin Laden, who moves his base of operations ...his free agent, military intelligence, covert operations death squad, genocide, arms smuggling, drug running narco-terrorism racket ... subcontracting to different mainstream intelli-gence outfits like CIA, Mossad, MI-6 ...back to Afghanistan.

Aug. 1996, bin Laden issues a Declaration of War against the U.S. People on the al-Qaeda list were mercenaries hired to provoke war. Who hired them?

Feb. 1998, bin Laden announces an alliance of terrorist organizations.

John caught Ron Jr.'s attention. "Bin Laden runs al Qaeda with help from his *handler,* Dr. Ayman al-Zawahiri, M.D. ...al-Qaeda's theological leader ...bin Laden's probable successor ...an Egyptian surgeon from an upper-class family ...joined Egypt's Islamist movement in the late 1970s ...served three years in prison, on charges linked to Anwar Sadat's assassination ...then, met bin Laden in Afghanistan.

"Al-Qaeda leadership oversees a loosely organized network of cells. It recruits members from thousands of 'Arab Afghan' veterans, and radicals around the world. Its infrastructure is small, mobile, and decentralized ...each cell operates independently with its members ... *not knowing* identity of *other* cells. Local operatives rarely know anyone higher up."

Ron Jr. was amazed, "I see."

Dave stepped in. "That's classic German military intelligence, in action. In 1923 Germany, thousands of underground intelligence units, separate cells, in a moment, could convert into one German Army. Curt Riess', *The Nazis Go Underground,* says, infiltration has cells 'consisting of two men each, an A-man and B-man. A-man keeps contact with higher-ups and government higher-ups ...B-man stays in touch with the underground, the illegal part.'"

"Right," John said. "Al-Qaeda's different from traditional terrorist groups, it's doesn't depend on one political state, and unlike PLO or IRA, is not defined by a particular conflict. It's totally mercenary, totally freelance."

Michael polished off his cheesecake. "I get it, a franchise."

Maureen laughed. "Really, Michael."

John looked at Maureen. "Michael's right."

Michael felt proud. "See, Maureen."

<>

Nancy brought me back. I'd had a ten minute nap, felt alive. I sat with Patti, and her friends.

John smiled at me. "Al Qaeda is like the mother ship in the movie, *Independence Day,* when aliens destroy all capital cities in the U.S., preparing for an invasion ..al Qaeda gives name recognition, financial, and logistical support to terrorist cells ...operating all over ...Philippines

...Algeria ...Eritrea ...Afghanistan ...Chechnya ...Tajikistan ...Somalia ...Yemen ...Kashmir. Local groups anywhere can act ...in the name of al-Qaeda ... for brand recognition."

Patti shared her insight. "It's like their day job is to influence the stock market each day ...so, their handlers can buy short."

John liked it. "Interesting,"

I piped up. "I saw Independence Day, I like action movies, for a modern movie, it wasn't too noisy."

Ron Jr. interuptted, again. "What's a fatwa?" John answered. "A religious announcement ...bin Laden's fatwa in 1998 said, the duty of Muslims around the world is to wage holy war on the U.S. citizens, and Jews ...Muslims who don't do what he says, he calls 'apostates' ... people who've forsaken their faith ...he wants to kill them. But, Jihad ... holy war ... is not part of Islam. That's propaganda, bullshit, by an 18th Century Sunni philosopher, Mohammad ibn Abd al-Wahhab ...who took over what's now called Saudi Arabia, where Wahhabism religion leads Saudi Arabian repression."

<>

Peter Dale Scott came back from his walk on the beach by the surf. "It's beautiful down there ...the air's so clean, it feels so clean and cool in my lungs."

Patti smiled at him. "We should all go down there. We're talking so much."

Nancy objected. "It's too far for father to go, Patti. He's enjoying everyone, here."

Patti relented. "Okay. Can we wrap it up? ...then, I'll go down to the beach."

John looked at her. "Patti, you're the one who invited us to brief your family ...we're almost done. Early in my law career I took a volunteer attorney job created by the Carter Administration ... to hunt Nazis ...because, I thought it would look good on my resume. But, instead of being sent to Germany, I ended up in the U.S. Government 20-acre underground vault for protecting classified information. It was like the last scene in *Raiders of the Lost Ark*..."

I spoke up. "I liked *that*, Harrison Ford, no Oscar."

John lauhed. "Me too ...I stumbled on Nazi files I wasn't supposed to. *No one was* ...'til 2015. They said, British Secret Service convinced American intelligence, left-over Nazis are indispensable as 'freedom fighters' to continue to war ...against Soviet Union."

Dave interrupted. "Al Qaeda was born from the Nazi and Islamic extremist movements of World War II."

John nodded. "Yes. I read a file on an organization called, Muslim Brotherhood ...about Hasam al-Banna ...who founded it, in 1920. Mr. al-Banna admired a young Austrian, a writer named, Adolf Hitler. His letters to Hitler were so supportive ...so, when Hitler came to power in the 1930s, had Nazi intelligence contact al-Banna to work together. Hitler had al-Banna establish a spy network for Nazi Germany throughout Arabia. Al-Banna promised Hitler, when General Rommel's Nazi tank division arrived in Cairo and Alexandria, Muslim Brotherhood would kill all British troops. Al Banna's men were Nazi agents, spies ...they adopted Third Reich policy towards Jews. Another member of Muslim Brotherhood, a man known as, Grand Mufti of Jerusalem, ran Muslim Brotherhood in Palestine. Grand Mufti was an organizer of the 1920, 'Bloody Passover' massacre of Jews praying at Jerusalem's Wailing Wall. After a failed attempt to create a Nazi uprising in Iraq, Grand Mufti fled to Europe ...to organize international Arab forces for the Third Reich. These forces were Arab fanatics ... Arab Nazis from across the Middle East. At that time, Middle East was dominated by British. *Germany* wanted to steal Arab states away from being British colonies. Al-Banna's job was, put together an underground movement of Arab Nazis. He put together *a half million* members by end of World War II ...Arab Muslim members, who swore undying devotion to principles of the Third Reich. Al-Banna's Arab Nazi movement was a spy and guerrilla movement ...a political, insurrectionist movement. A group of Iraqi Nazis, for example, was told, if they succeeded in overthrowing the British government in Iraq ...and turned Iraq into a Nazi colony ...*they* would be *the first* Arab Nazi rulers of the Middle East. Among that revolutionary group ... was Saddam Hussein's uncle ...the man who raised him from the age of 10, Khayrallah Tulfah. The rep of Muslim Brotherhood in Palestine, the Grand Mufti of Jerusalem ...*his* grandson was named, Yassar Arafat. Grand Mufti was a *devout* Nazi, referred to as ... 'Hitler's favorite Arab'. Grand Mufti was brought to Berlin ...to help raise the first Muslim fascist army ... under the guise of the Croatian fascists. But, it really was an umbrella group ... to bring together Muslim fascists from all over the world. Grand Mufti of Jerusalem, after the war, was captured by French intelligence ...and, the Arab Nazi's went underground. *That's* where the story takes a sickening twist. Instead of *prosecuting* them, British secret service made a decision to *recruit* them. The entire Arab Nazi movement of the Muslim Brotherhood went underground

...and, the British put them on the payroll ...and, even *kept* the same German intelligence officers, propagandists, and advisers that ran and coordinated Muslim Brotherhood during World War II ...all of them went on British payroll. A war criminal, Grand Mufti and his troops were spirited away from prosecution, to Egypt ...by British Secret Service. A request was made, to free Grand Mufti from the French jail ...and, he was allowed to escape. He made his way back to Cairo. The Arab Nazis made their way back to Egypt, after World War II. While the world was hunting down European Nazis, Arab Nazis were getting a free ride home from British Secret Service. On paper, the British wanted to use the Muslim fascist movement ...as a counterweight against the Muslim communist movement. The British wanted their own underground army to offset what Stalin was doing by recruiting Arab communists. The *truth* was, the senior British intelligence officer behind the recruitment of the Arab Nazis ... was Kim Philby. Kim Philby was a Soviet double agent. Just as he did with *European* Nazis, Philby's mission was *to protect* the Arab Nazis ... under orders from Stalin ...because, from the communist point of view, there was no better way to infiltrate western intelligence, than through the *Nazi* movement. Who would be less suspected than the ultra left? ...the ultra right. Kim Philby, the Soviet agent who infiltrated British Secret Service, was also recruiting Arab Nazis to poison the West's efforts in the Middle East, forever. By using Arab Nazis, democracy would be discredited ...America would be discredited ...Britain would be discredited. So, Kim Philby helped United States acquire the Arab Nazis expelled from Egypt in the 1950s ...after Egyptians recognized them as a threat. Jack Philby, Kim's *father* ...was a whore for oilmen. Kim Philby despised his father, Jack ...and became a communist. Anyway ... we have Kim Philby the son ...and, Jack Philby the father who's the Arab fascist who spent time in British prisons during World War II. In 1945, the Arab Nazis are secretly revived ...and, mission of Muslim Brotherhood has changed ... under the direction of Grand Mufti. The Muslim Brotherhood are to be smuggled into Palestine to smash the infant state, Israel. *The British Army can't go in and slaughter Jews,* it would be bad press ...but, they could use the Arab Nazi movement to do it *for them.* And, that's what happened. But, the Arab Nazis lost ...they retreated back, to Egypt, in 1948. Israel survived ...and, became an independent nationalist state, in 1948. *All of a sudden,* the Egyptian political movement got

nervous about this army movement of half-a-million army Arab Nazi's in their midst ...and by 1952, Nasser decided ...throw the Egyptian Nazi's out ...and, ban the Muslim Brotherhood ... they were expelled from Egypt. But, in 1952, a bunch of dimwits in U.S. government ... rogue officials who later became part of CIA, decided ...if, the British secret service wouldn't hire the Arab Nazis ...then, the U.S. would *recruit* the Arab Nazis, from the British secret service ...and, brought the Muslim Brotherhood to safety in Saudi Arabia. The Saudi's were kindred spirits. They were *part* of the Arab Nazi movement ... the King of Saudi Arabia was pro-Nazi all during the war, they only stayed away from the Axis side because they were bribed by Franklin Roosevelt. Saudi Arabia was the only neutral country to receive land-lease aid during World War II ...the House of Saud never turned a good bribe down. So, overtly instead of being on Hitler's side, the Saudi's covertly kept smuggling oil to Hitler's forces ...despite their promises to the American president. But, the Saudi's were very receptive to bringing in likeminded Arabs from around the world. CIA located the Arab Nazis of the Muslim Brotherhood in the kingdom of Saudi Arabia. To keep them employed, they were given jobs as religious education instructors. Islam is a peaceful religion ...but, Saudi Arabia practiced an extreme form of Islam called, Wahhabi, like Sushi hot mustard except with a 'h' where the 's' is. Saudi Wahhabism is to Islam ... as the KKK is to Christianity ...it's an extreme and perverted form of religion ...that, was *condemned as heresy* ... by Islam ... more than 60 times before the 1900s ... a vile, despicable sect ...that, hates women ...hates democracy ...hates Jews ...hates western culture ...and, they *found* a kindred spirit with the Arab Nazis in Muslim Brotherhood, fitting in the religious bigotry of House of Saud, with the indigenous racism of the Arab Nazis. They found a perfect merger in Saudi Arabia ...so, the Saudi's give the Arab Nazis jobs as the teachers at the Madrassas, the religious schools. So, here's this corrupt cult ...and, all of a sudden the school teachers in Saudi Arabia, are Nazis. *Schools of hatred* were built all over Saudi Arabia ...and there, they influenced an entire, new generation of young Saudi nationals. A well known pupil of these schools is Osama bin Laden ...Bin Laden, and other graduates of the schools, were inducted into an underground neo-Nazi Wahhabi army for Saudi Arabia. And, just how Russia was using communist Arabs during the cold war, the CIA would use Arab Nazis ... as a counterweight, to oppose them. When Soviets invaded Afghanistan in 1979, the Arab Nazis were let out of the closet. Because of the combination of Wahhabi fanaticism and Nazi ideology, waves of people came pouring into Afghanistan to kill Communists. In 1979, the Russians had taken over Afghanistan ...and, it was time to play the Arab Nazi card. So, one of our rogue groups ... not the CIA ... that had been set up under the wings of the White House using CIA personnel and military cover ... so nobody knew what was going on ...but, U.S. taxpayer dollars were being laundered through Saudi Arabia to hire Arab Nazis to send them into Afghanistan to kill Russians. For ten years, it was a successful operation ...by 1989, the Russians were driven out of Afghanistan ...the CIA declared victory, and went home and washed their hands of the Arab Nazis ...but, they left this huge army of Arab Nazis in the field. But, they weren't called Arab Nazis, then, they weren't even called the Muslim Brotherhood ... they changed names to Maktab al Khidimat il Mujahideen, the MAK ...because, Muslim Brotherhood was too well known as a Nazi organization. But, the heart of the Muhajidin was always the same ... Arab Nazi leaders, who had fought with Hitler during World War II ...and who oversaw the MAK program, the Maktab al Khidimat il Mujahideen service organization? ...the Pakistani ISI intelligence ...and, the Saudi Government ... oversaw the MAK ...and, it was funded by CIA. But, CIA always claimed, they didn't know who was on the payroll ... but they knew. The elder George Bush fit into this ...because, he was Vice President of the U.S. ...and, head of CIA when these policies were going down ...but, files were shredded. In 1989, CIA declared victory and went home ...but, the Saudi's *didn't want* the Muslim Brotherhood back. And, at the same time, there was a revolution going on *inside* the Muhajidin army between first- and second-generation Nazis. A group around Osama bin Laden wanted to be more fanatical, and return to their Nazi roots. So, they assassinated Azzam, the more moderate leader ...and, they began to weed out and made a *checklist* of those who would be most loyal as the base of the organization ...that's where the organization came from, the first generation Arab Nazis' second-generation Nazis. Muslim Brotherhood splinter groups hated democracy, Jews, western culture. For example, chief of staff of Al Qaeda, Dr. Ayman al-Zawahiri ... was leader of a splinter group of Muslim Brotherhood, called, Egyptian Islamic Jihad, *EIJ* -- that became Al Qaeda ...*PIJ*, Palestinian Islamic Jihad headed by Dr. Sami al-

Arian ...Hamas, headed by Dr. Sheik Yassin ... who was assassinated by Israelis ... was a head of Muslim Brotherhood, ...and, they were all coordinated. So anyway, the Soviets were defeated ....and, the United States left. Osama bin Laden took control and his entire army of neo-Nazi theological cultists were left there, alive ...in the field. Bin Laden drew up *a list* of those he knew he could trust ...and, called this list 'the base', a database. *The Arabic translation of 'the base' is 'al Qaeda.'* Al Qaeda is the direct lineal descendant of the Arab Nazis of the Muslim Brotherhood. We let loose the Muslim Brotherhood, now known as Al Qaeda, to roam free upon the world. Many human beings have paid for that mistake."

Dave Emory was revved. "John, let me see if I got this right, there's fascist origins of this group and its alliance with the Third Reich during World War II, the Brotherhood postwar was sponsored financially and politically supported by British intelligence and CIA, that relocated many of the Brotherhood from Egypt to Saudi Arabia in the 1950s, then the Brotherhood evolved into the MAK, the name given the anti-Soviet Brotherhood elements active in Afghanistan in the 1980s. After the defeat of the Soviets in Afghanistan, MAK evolved into al Qaeda. British Intelligence's use of the Muslim Brotherhood was to crush the fledgling state of Israel ... the CIA inserted Brotherhood members into the Madrassas, the Saudi Arabian religious schools ...then, *you* played a role in generating the March 20, 2002 Operation Green Quest raids, and *you* helped launch a lawsuit on behalf of survivors of the 9/11 attacks against al Qauda funding sources."

John nodded, while the Reagan family sat in awe of John's knowledge and Dave's smarts.

<>

I had a few questions for John. "What did you do in my Administration?"

John patiently repeated himself. "When I was working for the Attorney General, I was assigned to do classified research about the Holocaust, so I went underground to a little town called Suitland, Maryland, right outside Washington, D.C., that's where the U.S. Government buries its secrets."

I think someone told me something about that place. Or, maybe I just thought that someone had told me, or should have. "I heard rumors about that place."

"There are twenty vaults underground, each one acre in size. In those vaults, I discovered something horrible ... that many of the Nazis that

181

was assigned to prosecute ... were on the CIA payroll. But, CIA *didn't know* they were Nazis ... because British Intelligence Service had lied to them. What British Intelligence Service didn't know, was their liar was Kim Philby, the Soviet communist double agent ...there's a little Cold War scandal for you. Our State Department swept it under the rug, and allowed the Nazis to stay in America ...until I was stupid enough to go public with it. What do you do when you want to go public with a story like this one? You call up 60 minutes. We had a great time. Mike Wallace gave me 30 minutes on his show. For a long time, it was the longest segment that 60 minutes ever did. When the episode about Nazis in America went on the air back in 1982 ...it caused a minor national uproar ...Congress demanded hearings ...Mike Wallace got the Emmy award ...and, my family got death threats. It was a trip."

Nancy was shocked. "That's why I always kept my mouth shut, I was afraid they'd come after my family."

Patti had a realization, it was gratitude towards her mother.

John continued his story. "Funny thing happened. Since then, over the last 25 years, every retired spy in the U.S., Canada and England, all wanted me to be their lawyer ...for free of course. So, I had 500 clients, they paid me $1 apiece. I'm the worst paid lawyer in America, but among the better employed. Let me give you an example. This year a friend of mine from the CIA, named, Bob Baer, wrote a book about Saudi Arabia and terrorism, *Sleeping with the Devil.* I read the book ...I got a third of the way through, and I stopped. Bob was writing about when he worked for CIA, how bad the files were. He said, the files for Muslim Brotherhood ... were almost nothing. There were a few newspaper clippings. I called Bob up and said, 'Bob, that's wrong. CIA has enormous files on Muslim Brotherhood, volumes of them. I know, because I read them ...a quarter of a century ago.' He said, 'What do you mean?' Here's how you find the missing secrets about Muslim Brotherhood ...and, you can do this, too. I said, 'Bob go to your computer, type in two words into Google. Type the word 'Banna' B-A-N-N-A. He said, 'Yeah.' Type in 'Nazi.' Bob typed the two words in, and out came 30 to 40 articles from around the world. He read them. He called me back and said, 'Oh my god, what have we done?'"

Dave was interested. "You traced the evolution of Muslim Brotherhood into al Qaeda, beginning with the organization's political marriage with the Third Reich."

"Yes, I'm educating a new generation in CIA that Muslim Brotherhood was a fascist organization was hired by western intelligence ...that evolved over time, into what we today know as, al Qaeda."

Michael returned again from the kitchen with a few more pieces of cheesecake. "Okay, run it by me again, did I miss anything."

Maureen agreed. "It would help me to hear it again, too."

Ron Jr. nodded, Patti smiled, so did Nancy.

Me too. "I have a good family. I had a good life. I can't complain. We have access to everything we need, fortune, fame, education, special days like this when people help us understand what's going on in our world ... that we never could've figured out, without their help. *God does this. God educates us.* What we do with that education, is what we can, John. You're doing a great job, helping America to know the truth."

John agreed, too. "Thank you, here's how the story begins.".

I wondered, "Is this a script treatment?"

John was amused. "Yes, it's short, my *Jewish Community News* article, *The Arab Nazi-Al Qaeda Connection.* In the 1920s, there was a young Egyptian named al Banna. And, al Banna formed this nationalist group called, the Muslim Brotherhood. Al Banna was a devout admirer of Adolf Hitler and wrote him, frequently."

"John, you said that before," Ron Jr. said.

"I know, I repeat myself ... but, I add to it each time ...so persistent was he in his admiration of the new Nazi Party, that in the 1930s, al Banna and the Muslim Brotherhood became a secret arm of Nazi Intelligence. Arab Nazis had much in common with the new Nazi doctrines. They hated Jews, hated democracy, and hated Western culture. Now, here's the new part. *It became official policy of the Third Reich to secretly develop the Muslim Brotherhood as a Fifth Column, an army inside Egypt.* When war broke out, Muslim Brotherhood promised in writing , they would rise up and help General Rommel and make sure no English or American soldier was left alive in Cairo or Alexandria. The Muslim Brotherhood began to expand in scope and influence, during World War II. They had a Palestinian section, headed by the grand Mufti of Jerusalem, one of the great bigots of all time. Grand Mufti of Jerusalem was Muslim Brotherhood representative for Palestine. These were Arab Nazis. Grand Mufti went to Germany during the war to help recruit an international SS division of Arab Nazis. They based it in Croatia ...and called it, the

Handjar Muslim Division. But, it was to become the core of Hitler's new army of Arab fascists, that would conquer the Arab peninsula from then on, to Africa, grand dreams."

Michael ate and listened. "It's hard to believe it really happened."

Patti was almost speechless. "It blows my mind."

Nancy was fuming. "The *truth!* ...why don't they ever tell us the *truth?!*"

I knew why. "Nancy, *truth* can get us killed."

Nancy looked at me. "I know ...but, it breaks my heart. The people that might have been saved, if we only knew the *truth.*"

Ron Jr. joined in. "They think there's *too many* people, anyway, and people need to be killed, that's why there's so much genocide all over the world ...it's not just to raise 3rd quarter dividends in weapons portfolios, I think."

I was proud of Ron Jr. He was turning into a real Reagan.

Dave did a recap of John. "Okay. So, the Brotherhood jumps from the Third Reich to the British, who use them against fledgling Israel in the 1940s."

John smiled. "You're gettin' it. At end of World War II, Muslim Brotherhood was wanted for war crimes. Their German intelligence handlers were captured, in Cairo. The whole net was rolled up by British Secret Service. Then, a horrible thing happened. Instead of prosecuting the Nazi Muslim Brotherhood, British government hired them ...brought all the fugitive Nazi war criminals of Arab and Muslim descent into Egypt. For three years they were trained on a special mission. British Secret Service wanted to use the fascist Muslim Brotherhood to strike down the infant state of Israel in 1948. Only a few people in Mossad know this ...but, many members of Arab Armies and terrorist groups that tried to strangle the infant State of Israel were Arab Nazis of the Muslim Brotherhood."

Nancy leaned forward in interst. "This is fascinating. Then, what?"

Nancy was a smart cookie. She was the only person who could make me feel lonely just by leaving the room. Dave, too, knew a lot. You have to wonder sometimes, if normal, everyday people could do a better job running the country than all these damn attorneys filling up seats in Congress, their campaign chests flowing over with lobbyists' contributions ...the little guy, the average Joe, has a big heart ...the big guy has dollar signs for eyes. The big guys know, they'll be assassinated ...if they tell the truth ...or,

there'll be nuclear war, or biological war on our own turf. The World Trade Center bombing was a warning, for starters, the opening act. No one wants to see the whole play.

Dave was smart. "So, after their tenure working for the British, the Muslim Brotherhood finds employment within CIA, working in an anti-communist capacity, throughout the Middle East?"

John liked his audience. "Yes. Britain wasn't alone. French Intelligence cooperated, by releasing Grand Mufti, smuggling him to Egypt ...so, all the Arab Nazis came together. From 1945 to 1948, British Secret Service protected every Arab Nazi they could ...but, they failed to destroy Israel. Then, the British sold the Arab Nazis to the predecessor of what became the CIA. It sounds stupid ...it sounds evil ...but, it happened. Like I said, the idea was, we were going to use Arab Nazis in the Middle East, as a counterweight against Arab communists. Just as Soviet Union was funding Arab communists, we would fund Arab Nazis, to fight them. We kept Muslim Brotherhood on our payroll."

I was impressed. "*What a cliff-hanger!*"

Nancy, too. "I've got the feeling it's gonna be a *tear jerker.*"

Patti was still. She loved Mom and Dad, even if they'd wanted to get her a lobotomy for a birthday present, back in the 1970s. "Dave, you know a lot, and John knows a ton. I'm glad everyone agreed to come here today, to visit my Dad."

Dave continued. "Good. So, after expulsion from Egypt by Nasser, Brotherhood key personnel were relocated to Saudi Arabia by CIA. In Saudi Arabia, many of them assumed prominence in that country's infrastructure. Even though, Wahhabism has been rejected, it's considered heresy by most of Muslims in the world."

John nodded, "Yes. You're getting it right. The Egyptians got nervous. Nasser ordered Muslim Brotherhood out of Egypt ...or else, he'd imprison, or execute them. During the 1950's, CIA evacuated the Nazis of the Muslim Brotherhood to Saudi Arabia. Now, when they arrived in Saudi Arabia, some leading lights of the Muslim Brotherhood, like Abdullah Azzam, became teachers in the Madrassas, the religious schools. And there, they combined the doctrines of Nazism with this *weird* Islamic cult, Wahhabism. Everyone thinks Islam is this *fanatical* religion, *but it's not.* They think that Islam, the *Saudi* version of Islam, is typical ...but, it's not. The Wahhabi cult is condemned as *heresy*, by Muslim nations. But, when the Saudis got wealthy, they bought silence. This is a *harsh* cult. Wahhabism was only practiced by two nations, the *Taliban* and *Saudi Arabia*. That's how extreme it is. It has *nothing* to do with Islam. *Islam* is a peaceful and tolerant religion. It has always had good relationships with Jews ...for the first thousand years of its existence," John said.

"So, Osama bin Laden was mentored by Abdullah Azzam, a key Brotherhood figure among those relocated to Saudi Arabia by CIA."

"Yes. Saudi Arabia was the new home of the Muslim Brotherhood, fascism, and extremism ...all mingled in these Madrassas cult religious Wahhabi schools taught by Arab Nazis. And, there was a young student who paid attention ... and Abdullah Azzam's student was named, Osama bin Laden."

Patti was amazed. "You're *blowing* my mind."

Nancy, too. "*Mine too.*"

Maureen, too. "*Me too.*"

Those are my Reagan girls.

Dave was energized. "So, CIA's resurrected the Brotherhood and the agency employed the Islamofascist organization as combatants, against the Soviets in Afghanistan. The Brotherhood was recast as the MAK."

I laughed. "You mean, *Mac the Knife*, Kurt Weill or Bobby Darin? ...Bertolt Brecht, *Mother Courage*," I said. No one seemed to get it, or just weren't interested ...but, I always tried to move things along with a laugh. I always felt if you can make people laugh, why ... you're helping God make peace in the world.

Nancy corrected me. "Brecht's, *Three Penny Opera*, not *Mother Courage*."

Oh, well, that's what my mind had become, close but no cigar, but, don't misunderstand me, I was glad for close. Some days, I couldn't see the forest for the trees.

John went on. "In 1979, CIA decided, let's take the Arab Nazis out of cold storage. The Russians have invaded Afghanistan, so we tell the Saudis, *we'll* fund the Arab Nazis, if *they* bring *all* the Arab Nazis together, then ship them to Afghanistan, to fight Russians. We had to rename them. We couldn't call them, Muslim Brotherhood ...that was too sensitive a name. Its Nazi cast, too well known. So, we called them, Maktab al Khidimat il Mujahideen, the MAK. CIA lied to Congress and said, they didn't know who was on the payroll in Afghanistan, except Saudis. But, it wasn't true. A small section of CIA knew perfectly well, we'd once again hired the Arab Nazis ...and, that we were using them to fight our secret wars."

Dave concluded. "So, the elder George Bush oversaw operations of the MAK in the 1980s, dur-

ing your Administration, President Reagan."

<>

I didn't know what to make of all this, it had nothing to do with dinner, or the sunset. It was hard to put together a punch line around it, to make people laugh ...it just wasn't my thing. "Well, if he did it working for me ...then, he must have had a good reason, the man's not stupid. He's probably the best one to limit the damage they could do, he wasn't pulling mine and Nancy's strings, we were told what to do, we made no decisions on our own, ever. It was Bill Casey told us what to do, and George Shultz, most of the time. Bobby Baker had insight from time-to-time ...but, was Rothschild telling Warburg? ...or, Rockefeller telling Schroder, telling Casey? ...I never could figure it out. Who was pulling the strings, back then? It wasn't till last year, Nancy reading me intelligence history books start paying off. We start *understanding* what was *really* going on. *That's* why I'm writing my fictional autobiography ... looking at everyone, over again. Before I die, I want people to know, I'm not the dummy the media painted me as! That's what this book is for!"

Nancy spoke up for me. "*No one* thinks you're a dummy, or ever were a dummy, you were on top of the opinion polls most of your life as President and, as movie star women lusted after, just relax,."

I loved Nancy a lot. I always did. I looked into her eyes. "You're not a man, you wouldn't understand. A man's reputation is all he's got, a woman can hold on to family, to value, to honesty, but in a man's world, sometimes you have to let those things go to keep your family alive, and you're judged by who you are, how straight you shoot, how fast you draw, by the truth ...not by who you say you are, people judge you by your aim, where you hit the target, your accomplishments, and use you according to your abilities, what you believe, whether you know it's happening, or not. Before I die, I want people to know, I know ... now, if I only knew."

Nancy laughed.

John smiled at me and Dave. "Specifically, as vice president in the mid-eighties, Bush supported aiding the Mujahideen in Afghanistan through the Maktab al Khidimat il Mujahideen, or Services Offices, which sent money and fighters to the Afghan resistance in Peshawar. Bush was in charge of covert operations that supported the MAK."

Dave pulled another book out of his backpack, he had a tough time even getting the backpack on the ranch grounds past the Secret Service, they opened up every book to make sure it wasn't hollowed out and filled up with plastique. "This is Craig Unger's, *House of Bush, House of Saud.*"

I liked the process. "This is kind of fun, Dave reading when Nancy gets tired.".

<>

"'Co-founded by Osama bin Laden and Abdullah Azzam, MAK was before bin Laden's global terrorist network, Al Qaeda. MAK sent money, and fighters, to Afghan resistance in Peshawar, Pakistan. MAK set up recruitment centers in fifty countries, including ...Egypt ...Saudi Arabia ...Pakistan ...and, United States ... bringing thousands of warriors to fight Soviet Union. MAK was later linked to the 1993 bombing of World Trade Center in New York, through an office in Brooklyn, Al-Kifah Refugee Center. It's not clear how much contact he had with bin Laden, but Sheikh Omar Abdel Rahman, the 'Blind Sheikh,' Craig said, 'who masterminded 1993 bombing of World Trade Center, appeared in Peshawar, on occasion."

John looked at Dave. "It went like this. Defeat of the Soviets in Afghanistan led to formation of al Qaeda. Azzam and his assistant, Osama bin Laden, got stronger from 1979 to 1989 ...then, they won the war, drove the Russians out of Afghanistan. Our CIA said, 'We won, let's go home!' ... we left this army of Arab fascists in the fields of Afghanistan. In order to prevent the MAK/Brotherhood from returning to Saudi Arabia, that country's power elite start paying bribes ... 'protection money' ... to al Qaeda. This development, and a split in the MAK, spawned al Qaeda in its present form. Saudis didn't want them back. Saudis start paying bribes to Osama bin Laden to stay out of Saudi Arabia. Now, MAK split in half. Azzam was assassinated ...apparently, by Osama bin Laden, himself. The radical group that formed of the merger of Arab fascists and religious extremists ... Osama called that group 'al Qaeda'. But, to this day, there are branches of Muslim Brotherhood all through al Qaeda. Osama bin Laden's second in command, Ayman al-Zawahiri, came from Egyptian branch of Muslim Brotherhood, the Egyptian Islamic Jihad, residue of a Palestinian Islamic Jihad. There are many flavors and branches, but all are Muslim Brotherhoods. There is one in Israel. 'Hamas' is a secret chapter of Muslim Brotherhood. When Israel assassinated Sheik Yassin, a month ago, Muslim Brotherhood published his obituary in a Cairo newspaper in

Arabic, and revealed he was the secret leader of Muslim Brotherhood in Gaza. So, Muslim Brotherhood became poison that spread throughout the Middle East ...and, on 9/11, it began to spread around the world. So, Patti when you went to your computer before, and typed in the words, 'Banna' and 'Nazi', what you saw were pieces of information CIA tried to hide from its employees. It didn't want them to know the awful past."

Patti added to the conversation. "A lot of stuff came up in Google."

John liked that. "I know. You see, in 1984, in the middle of the Reagan-Bush Administration, when I was exposing European Nazis on CIA payroll ...at the same time, Bush was trying to hide from Congress he had Arab Nazis back on the payroll to fight Russians, a stupid and corrupt program. So, when my friend, Bob Baer, who wrote, *Sleeping With the Devil*, and, *See No Evil: The True Story of a Ground Soldier in the CIA's War on Terrorism*, went to the Internet like I told him to do, like you did, and studied his files, he was stunned. *A whole generation, the current CIA people know nothing about this.* And believe me, the current generation CIA are good and decent Americans, I like them a lot. They're trying to do a good job ...but, part of their problem is their files were shredded. Now, these secrets must come out."

Dave was white on rice. "So, your intelligence contacts, and clients, turned you on to the primary Islamist funding apparatus in this country. In turn, your lawsuit against Sami al-Arian led to Operation Green Quest raids of Mar. 20, 2002."

"That's right. My clients in the intelligence community said, 'Well, what are you doing?' They gave me an example. They said, 'Here's how the Saudis finance these groups. The Saudis established a group of charities on a street in Virginia ... 555 Grove St., Herndon, Virginia.' So I said, 'OK the Saudis are terrorists, so what?' These charities fund Muslim Brotherhood, Hamas, Hezbollah, al Qaeda. The Saudis are getting tax deductions for terrorism. They set up front groups, so all the terrorist groups in the U.S., and the front groups, get Saudi money as a charitable donation. I said, 'You're kidding me.' Nope. And, they told me, right near where I lived, in Tampa Florida, was one of the leading terrorists in the world. There were these two professors at University of South Florida. One had just left, he was now in Syria ...he was the world head of Islamic Jihad. His number two, head of Islamic Jihad in the Western Hemisphere, was Dr. Sami al-Arian, still employed as professor at University of South Florida."

<>

I was incredulous. "You're kidding. This can't be true."

John tried to convince me. "Yes, these guys are raising money all across America, shipping it to Syria to go down to Palestine, the Palestinian areas, and hire suicide bombers to kill Jews. They sent me video tapes. There was Professor al-Arian on stage ...one of his friends gets up and says, 'Now, who will give me $500 to kill a Jew? There are people standing by, in Jerusalem, who will go out in the street and stab a Jew with a knife ...but, we need $500.' And he said, 'All of this money will go to the Islamic committee for Palestine.' And, that's the front group in the United States for Palestinian Islamic Jihad. So, I had my friends in FBI and CIA send in these files. I said, 'Why haven't you prosecuted this guy? You've known about him since 1989.' 'We'd love to. We've tried to prosecute him ...but, we were told we couldn't touch him because he gets all his money from the Saudis, and we're under orders not to do anything to embarrass the Saudi government.' I said, 'I don't mind embarrassing them.' You know what I did? I donated money to the charity that was the terrorist fund, because under Florida law, that gave me the right to sue the charity to find out where my money was going. It was hilarious. In early Mar. 2002, I drafted a long lawsuit exposing Professor Sami al-Arian, naming all the crimes he'd committed, all the bombings in Israel, the fundraising in America for terrorism. I mentioned, his money got to him from Saudis, and how Saudis convinced our government not to prosecute him, for political reasons. Because of my high-level security clearances, everything I write is sort of classified material ...and, has to be sent back to the government before publication, for censorship. So, I sent my long lawsuit complaint to CIA, they loved it. They said, 'Oh, great. We don't like the Saudis either. Go sue them.' Three days, later two FBI agents showed up at my door, saying, 'You know, there are only 21 people in the U.S. government that knew some of this information, and now you're 22. How did you find out?' I said, 'I'm sorry, I can't tell you, attorney-client privilege.' That's why my clients pay me $1.00 each.

"The day before I went to file the lawsuit, I got a frantic phone call from United States Department of Justice. They said, 'John, please don't file the lawsuit tomorrow. We really are going to raid these Saudi charities. We're going to close them down. Just give us more time.' 'Oh yeah, you're going to

raid them. That's what you told me in January, again in February, now it's March. Want more time? I'll give you until 4:00 o'clock, tomorrow. I'm filing my complaint at 10:00 a.m., at 4 p.m., I'm going to release the address of the Saudi charities.' I filed my lawsuit at 10:00 o'clock, and told the press I was going to hold something back for a little bit. At 10:15, the U.S. Government launched Operation Green Quest, a massive raid on all the Saudi charities in homes and businesses ...and, in one hour, we shut down the entire Saudi money-laundering network in America. From Mar. 20, 2002 to date, the government has found more and more evidence seized in those archives, on that single raid that day. The evidence was so compelling that Professor al-Arian is no longer giving speeches. He's now in federal prison, awaiting trial. His accomplice, Hammoudeh, has been indicted. Some 32 different people have been indicted in the United States, as a direct result of these efforts ...but, not the Saudis ...not the Saudis."

I was appreciative. "You're an American hero, too, John."

John smiled. He softly repeated himself. "Not the Saudis."

Nancy chimed in. "Everyone here's an American hero."

I start slipping away, I start losing my mind again, I didn't want to ebb away, I wanted to stay, with my friends.

Dave summarized. "John played the pivotal role, the reason d'etre in getting the Mar. 20, 2002 Operation Green Quest raid going, then he played a part by starting the trillion-dollar 9/11 lawsuit against the Saudis, and others implicated in funding of al Qaeda."

Nancy was astonished. "A trillion dollar lawsuit?! My goodness, that has to be some kind of record."

John laughed, "Yes, it is. A month later, I filed my lawsuit against al-Arian ...then, I caused more trouble. I invited 40 of the top trial lawyers in America down to St. Petersburg, Florida. Boy, did I have a deal for them. I wanted them to put up millions of dollars of their own money, I'm poor, I had no money to give them ...but, I wanted to do something for America. These are lawyers like Ron Motley, that won billions of dollars in their lawsuits against the tobacco industry, and the asbestos industry. I said, 'What I want you to do is look at evidence I've collected. It's the same Saudi banks and charities that funded Sami al-Arian that funded al-Qaeda.' I said, 'I want you to bring a class action in Federal Court in Washington on behalf of everyone who died on

186

Sept. 11. I'm going to work for free, and collect all the evidence, introduce you to the experts, provide all the exhibits and documents ...and, we have to do this for America.' The lawyers studied the documents I collected, and on Aug. 15, 2002, they filed the largest class-action lawsuit in American history in the Federal District Court in Washington D.C., asking for one trillion dollars damages against the Saudis. The lawsuit said, essentially, all these Saudi banks had one thing in common. They were bribing Osama bin Laden 300 million dollars a year to stay out of Saudi Arabia, and go blow up someone else. Well, on 9/11, we found out we were someone else, and the Saudis had to pay for their negligence. So, that lawsuit is coming along very well."

Mauareen was excited. "*Hallelujah, God be praised!*"

Michael, happy. "Mazel tov."

"I'm Catholic," John said.

"I'm hungry," I said.

No one laughed, the line went over like a lead balloon. They all looked at me.

<>

John chuckled. He looked at Nancy, and me.

"More and more people in CIA and FBI are using me as a back channel to get out information. So, believe it or not, they've actually given me my own TV show ...now, on Sunday mornings on FOX TV nationwide. I'm on 11:20 eastern standard time. And, ABC Radio gave me a national radio program ...but, I'm on at 10:30 at night, probably past your bedtime."

Dave had it down. "So, Muslim Brotherhood evolved from being Nazi allies, to the MAK, to al Qaeda."

Ron Jr. was tired, too. "I guess so."

John smiled. "What I've become in my old age, is a teacher. Twenty-five years ago I was a lot younger, a lot thinner ...but now, every day, I get 500 to 1,000 e-mails from honest men and women around the world in the intelligence community. And, we have to end the evil in this world. We have to recognize, al-Qaeda simply didn't spring up on its own. The evil root was Nazism. The al-Qaeda Doctrine is the same the Arab Nazis held. They hate Jews, democracy, and Western culture. Al Qaeda is nothing more than the religious expression of Arab Fascism. We allowed this branch of the Nazi trunk to survive, to flourish ...it has come back to haunt us."

I was falling asleep, or falling into Alzheimer's, I couldn't always tell one from the other, or my real dreams from my Alzheimer's dreams.

Nancy spoke up. "Well, the war inside the U.S.

Government is really nothing new, most of the U.S. government is trying to fight Al Qaeda ...but, there's a small faction trying to cover up their connection to the al Qaeda Arab Nazi movement. Let me see if I understand what you've said, John, stop me if I'm wrong ...Grover Norquist and his Islamic Institute was denounced by conservative Republicans, who consider Grover Norquist to be a terrorist lobbyist in America. Apparently, University of South Florida professor Dr. Sami Al-Arian convinced Norquist that Al-Arian could deliver the State of Florida ... George W's Bush's first election run and his second ... based on the Arab vote to offset the Jewish vote. It's traditional Nixon-Dulles-Bush campaigns using fascists to out-vote Jews. Al-Arian had Norquist lobby FBI to back off investigations of Arab Americans. Norquist and Rove became politically correct towards Arab Americans, what they've never done towards Jewish Americans or African Americans ...but, FBI in the field were still tracking terrorism, but couldn't get approval from Washington for subpoenas, wire taps or other investigation ...guys like Grover Norquist would stop them. Al-Arian took Norquist to dinner and gave him an award for the work he did to preserve Arab American privacy in America, a total farce. Norquist's one of the most powerful right wing lobbyists in all Washington, he's the guy who brought you Newt Gingrich, the consultant behind the scenes for NRA, for Americans for Tax Reform, the leader of the ultra-right, the person who destroyed bipartisanship, Norquist doesn't want consensus, he wants Republicans and Democrats at each other's throats. He's the man who has destroyed a part of the fabric that holds America together. He's despicable. But, to be fair, Grover Norquist didn't know he was working with terrorists. It wasn't just Al-Arian who had him conned, another man, Aldurahman M. Alamoudi, was donating money to Grover Norquist to set up the Islamic Institute ... we're going to have all these wonderful things ...set up Islamic chaplains for the U.S. government prisoners who are terrorists, and have Islamic people screening people coming into the White House. Alamoudi was a terrorist and has plead guilty. These are the clients Grover Norquist had, he *is* the terrorist lobbyist. Grover Norquist had so much power, he was able to influence the White House. Several of Norquist protégés became White House staff. The bottom line is, I don't know if people knew what they were doing, or not ...but, moderate Muslims, good, decent Americans, couldn't get in to see the president, only right-wing terrorists like Al-Arian and Aldurahman, could. They're the ones who had their pictures taken with Bush. ...*Bush didn't have any idea* what was going on, because he was listening to his Chief of Staff Karl Rove ...and, Karl Rove didn't know what was going on ...because, he was listening to Grover Norquist ...and, Grover Norquist didn't know what was going on ...because, he was listening to Al-Arian and Alamoudi. Grover Norquist did probably the most harm of any lobbyist in America, and didn't have a clue he was doing it. At least, that's the party line. I went through it, when Ronnie was President with Mike Deaver on and off the White House Staff, representing the Contras and their cocaine running, you know the term, 'freedom fighter', is straight Hollywood ...it doesn't mean freedom fighter at all, it means fighting the theory of Communism with bullets and torture ... so Contras,Muhajidin, and Nazis ... were *freedom* fighters. It's almost time for dinner, I'm taking Ronnie in. Please join us in about a half hour."

Patty's mouth hung open, she couldn't believe her mother actually knew what was going on. "Mom! Have you always known what was going on like this, even when you were the First Lady, even when I was growing up?!"

"Of course. I just didn't want to expose my family to danger ...we're not Kennedys, we're Reagans. Oh, wait a minute, I don't want to be rude to Peter Dale Scott, you've been so patient, did you have anything to add?"

Peter watched the sky over the sea, the waves breaking on the rocks, enjoyed the cold ozone in the air, and the exhilarating feeling it gave him. "Thanks, Mrs. Reagan."

"Please, call me Nancy. You're enjoying it here, aren't you?"

"Yes, very much. I'll cut my presentation short, for dinner. I'm not going to do much documentation, because you can go to my website, where I document every sentence, sometimes. Control over oil and control over drugs can't be separated. Cold war hawks *in Moscow* want to see the oil flow north, and the drugs south ...cold war hawks in *Washington* want to keep the drugs flowing north and bring the oil south."

<>

"This led to enduring intelligence networks involving oil and drugs, specifically petrodollars and narcodollars, particularly in the Middle East, they affect the conduct of U.S. foreign policy and the health and behavior of the U.S. government, U.S. banks, and corporations, and the whole fabric of U.S. society. To understand the new World Order you need to understand the flow of nar-

codollars and petrodollars corrupts governments, corporations, and social structures around the world ... what goes around comes around ... to the U.S. Influence of foreign funds is usually invisible ...but, it gives off a stink. Most people for example, aren't aware that ... until recently ... the largest shareholder of Chevron, and second-largest shareholder of Chase Manhattan, were both Arabs."

<>

"Patti, ask yourself, how did Project for the New American Century military-petroleum-drug complex come to project long-term military budgets of a trillion dollars, saying the American public could not be persuaded easily to support it ...in the absence, that is, of 'some catastrophic and catalyzing event ... like a new Pearl Harbor', that many think was 9/11".

Patti liked Peter, a lot. "Peter, I will, but will you recite one of your poems for us, first?"

"Of course. An excerpt from *Minding the Darkness*."

And now, for something a bit more serious
    a poem that looks at
  the eye in the triangle

above the blunted pyramid

......
    Though we continue to prate
about the Open Society

54 percent of the total
    net financial assets
are held by the 2 percent

whose two top institutions
    the Fed and the CIA
the most powerful and unpopular

lie beyond the reach
    and even the comprehension
not just of the people

but Congress the legal system and the press
    In the crisis of '82
when Mexico almost defaulted

on its $80 billion debt
    the largest banks would have been
swamped in the resulting panic

had they not been saved
    by actions taken in secret
Between the Fed and the Treasury

an unprecedented bailout was arranged
$3.5 billion
in new loans for Mexico

So why did the NIC
concerned about foreign exchange
produce a CIA evaluation

the profits of drug export revenues
of Colombia and Mexico
probably represent

75 percent
of source-country export earnings?
Nazar Haro the DFS Chief

who sold protection to the traffickers
and obstructed the HSCA investigation
protected in turn by the CIA

from an indictment in San Diego
for his indispensability
as a source of intelligence

the objecting U.S. Attorney
fired for revealing this
And why did the Treasury in '84

introduce bearer bonds
despite the expert advice
they would become instruments

used by the traffickers
for money-laundering?
The Fed and the CIA

both so powerful
we know almost nothing about them
not to mention the IMF

whose draconian remedies
for impoverished countries
like Yugoslavia and Rwanda

and perhaps now Indonesia
have been followed by massacres
If the secrets were revealed

the money mystery would dissolve
people would have to look upon
these things directly

Why put all this in a poem?
There are times when the most novel

act of creativity

is to aim at the simplest truth
the rich are getting richer
the poor poorer

and if not checked this will destroy us
Why does this happen? Bassesse oblige!
And the cure? we must live by

what we have always known:
No crime worse than avarice
likewise the political hegemony

of money must end
One need not even abolish the Fed
only find the will

to abandon money's value
to save the real economy
the problem is not even capital

the new fluidity from America
which as Marx observed
erased those feudal

English preconceptions
when it was 'respectable'
to sell Negroes into slavery

(the crest of Sir John Hawkins
a demi-naked man
the hands extended and manacled)

but not to make sausages boots or bread
No! the problem is the abuse
of capital power

always consolidating privilege
by taxing the misery of the poor
When a president of a bank

can reward himself after slashing
12,600 jobs
with a one-year salary and bonus

of seventy-six million dollars
how shall we talk of America's
doctrine of equality?

We have not failed at production
we have failed at distribution
if we have learnt anything

in the 2,000 years since Virgil

it is to expect no moral progress
from our political leaders

or the banks British merchants
    and insurance companies
feared by our Founding Fathers

and none either from that
    supreme abstraction money
which empowers a worker to act

as a free agent
    in the surface process
of equality and freedom

beneath which in the depths
    entirely different processes go on
where equality and liberty disappear

Money as an abstraction
    unifying our world
at the same time making obsolete

the first meaning of commonwealth
    Thus in the last fifty years
for want of correspondence

with the imagination
    the CIA has helped install
the thugs of drug cartels

in Thailand Bolivia Afghanistan
    Haiti and Peru
accelerating the flow

of profits from the poorest
    nations to the richest
(why houses cost so much:

In 1984 alone
    the Commerce Department calculated
a net influx of foreign capital

into the US
    at about $100 billion)
while with draconian drug laws

in the name of order
    we had a million people in prisons
by the year 1994

1.8 million
    just four and a half years later
And should my poem take refuge

in rich sensuous detail
    or shall I say more clearly
what we removed from our book

that when Clinton and the Fed
    lent Mexico $40 billion
it should have been clear even then

how this debt would be repaid
    Mexico's Attorney General's
office states that drug traffickers

earned $28 billion
    in 1992 and 1993
amounts similar to all

of the country's legal exports combined
    for the benefit of this corrupt
ordo seclorum

all of us without thinking
carry round in our billfolds

Patti loved it. "That's beautiful, Peter."

"Thank you," Peter saw everyone seemed pretty positive about his poem. Not that their reactions affected his destiny much. Peter looked at Patti. "Thanks again. Let me get back to what I was saying. Like John and Dave say, in the West, we use the term, al Qaeda, to mean the network of all the bin Laden co-opted groups ...who at some point were trained, led or financed by bin Laden ...but, when Muslims hear, al Qaeda, it's clumsy to them, because it's not an organization ...and, it's led to targeting Islamist groups opposed to bin Laden. It reminds me of right wingers in the late 1960s who looked at the Vietnam anti-war movement I was a part of, and saw foreign-funded conspiracy where I could only see chaos. For this reason, I try to use instead the clumsy, but widely-accepted term and misnomer, 'Arab Afghans'."

"What me and John call Arab Nazis," Dave said.

Peter smiled. "Yes. That being said, United States-protected movements of al Qaeda terrorists into Afghanistan, Azerbaijan, and Kosovo served interests of U.S. oil companies, provided U.S. military commitments, and troops. U.S. history, since World War II, shows the U.S. power elite state consistently uses global drug traffic resources to further its own ends ...particularly, with respect to oil, at the expense, order, and well-being of the American public. From Brzezinski's backing of Hekmatyar in 1979, to Bush's backing of the Afghan Northern Alliance in 2001, the United States drew on the resources of drug-trafficking Islamic jihadists ... associated with Al Qaeda. CIA-engineered coups in the 1950s and 1960s, like in Iran in 1953, are related to intentions to nationalize their oil companies. The U.S. embarked on three major military campaigns ...in Vietnam ...Colombia ...and now, Afghanistan, where oil is a factor of U.S. commitment, with oil lobbies urging engagement. Other campaigns which looked unrelated to this concern, notably Kosovo, are seen by strategic realists as important to America's oil 'needs'. These three major campaigns, and others, aligned the U.S. on the same side as powerful local drug traffickers. It's become normal for U.S. intelligence agencies to draw on assets of the illicit drug economy ... in pursuit of various goals, from negotiation to corruption. This has been a major factor in the failure of our government to address the problem of ... drugs and intelligence agencies ... reasonably ...and, the accompanying growth of the illegal drug economy, to a point where the U.S. economy is dependent on it."

<>

I was told by the Secret Service that Patti had a Black boyfriend at the time, but she didn't bring him around Nancy or me, much less to the ranch, I don't know why. Color never mattered to me, I've always been a Christian, actually half Catholic and half Christian, for my Dad and Mom.

Patti jumped in the conversation. "African Americans and other people of color in the U.S. are 15 percent of drug users, 85 percent are White ...but, communities of color are hurt most by the drug epidemic, and our Administration's lost war on drugs. Dreams of African Americans are going up in smoke from pipes filled with pot, crack, heroin, PCP, ice, opium, hash ...that turn their dreams into nightmares. That 15 percent falls into substance abuse ...but, the Federal Government's lost drug war takes it out on them. FBI stats show 12 percent of drug users are Black, but are 41 percent of all those arrested on cocaine or heroin charges. It's a class war on race and the poor, not on the big wigs at the other end of the dollar. The war on drugs won't end illegal street drug use, or drug trafficking, or narco-terrorism ... because it targets the little guy, the end user, not the big guy, not suppliers. The Government's war on drugs at home targets people of color, even though the majority of users

and traffickers are White, so Blacks, Latinos, and third world people ... here and around the world ... suffer. During my father's presidency, he was determined to stop progressive governments in Nicaragua and Grenada ... by supporting anti-communist, pro-military foreign policy initiatives, shifting Federal dollars from social programs, mental health programs, and housing programs to the military budget, and unprecedented, deficit spending ...taking the United States from the world's largest creditor nation, to the world's largest debtor nation ...using the war on drugs to hide collusion of U.S. intelligence agencies with major international trafficking networks ...using anti-communist rhetoric and intervention programs as justification for CIA to knowingly let traffickers import illegal drugs into the U.S. Then, when Vice President Bush became President, did the CIA make the drug crisis in the U.S. worse? ...by helping known drug traffickers? ...You bet. The end of the Cold War shifted foreign policy rhetoric, the new international enemy of humanity has been transformed from a communist to a drug dealer-terrorist ...the narco-terrorist, opening up ...then protecting, markets for U.S. corporations then waging low-intensity, high death rate military and political campaigns ... against third world liberation movements, the real reasons for U.S. intervention overseas. I've had my own drug problems. I've seen family members, and friends, suffer from drug addiction, go to jail, have the fabric of their lives unwoven by illegal drugs taking over their lives, and seen legal drugs, tobacco and alcohol from legal drug pushers, slowly kill them. Drug trafficking, drug abuse ...both cross class, race, gender, cultural, and national boundaries ...but, has a distinct, racial edge to it. What is a *problem* in the White community, is a *crisis* in communities of color, and young Black males fill up the prisons."

<>

When Soviets lost the Afghan War in 1989, the Soviet-backed Najibullah regime in Kabul fell in 1992. Victory for the Muhajidin turned sour, as Tajiks behind Massoud and Pashtuns behind Hekmatyar, start fighting each other. America, Egypt, and Saudi Arabia pressured the new interim president of Afghanistan, Mojaddedi to instruct Arab Afghans to leave, Pakistan did too, closing all Muhajidin offices in Pakistan. But, Pakistani Intelligence ISI elements privately continued to support Arab Afghans, recruiting them into Pakistan's upcoming covert operations in Kashmir. Then, Pakistan extradited a number of Egyptian jihad followers to Egypt, radical

Islamists went to Afghanistan.

Peter agreed with Patti. "The bin Laden drug network is securely grounded in a milieu of drug-funded terrorist intrigue, that CIA has allied with in the past ...not just in Afghanistan ...but, in Bosnia ...in Kosovo, and elsewhere. Cargo planes fly twice a week between the southern Afghan city of Kandahar and Dubai, one of the United Arab Emirates."

Peter cited, "Sept. 24-26, 2001 *Boston Globe* and *Financial Times*, "These planes fly south with drugs, at least up until six months ago, two flights a week were traveling from Dubai to Kandahar, Mr. bin Laden's Afghan base, with boxes of dollar bills." Peter shook his head. "Until recently, the U.S. tolerated these flights, though dollars going into Afghanistan were likely to be used abroad for terrorism. This was probably because of complex and difficult games CIA has played for years with the United Arab Emirates, that reach the public with exposure of CIA-linked, and United Arab Emirate-financed... BCCI, the Bank of Credit and Commerce International ...a major global channel for laundering of narcodollars and illicit funds ...a bank controlled by petrodollars of Sheikh Zayed al-Nahayan, Enir of Abu Dhabi.

"The U.S. *Senate Subcommittee's BCCI Affair,* [www.fas.org/irp/congress/1992_rpt/bcci/ editor's note] report says, BCCI constituted international financial crime on a massive, global scale, including money-laundering ...and, arms trafficking, that BCCI systematically bribed leaders and politicians in 73 countries, including the U.S. ...that it evaded regulatory barriers ...and penetrated the U.S. banking system. The report reached 12 other conclusions. The Senate Report's conclusions downplayed what the Subcommittee heard from Acting CIA Director Richard Kerr, about CIA knowledge of 'the illegal activities that BCCI was involved in ...narcotics money-laundering ...terrorism ...support to terrorism ...and, other activities such as that' (Hearings, III, 584), at a time ... when CIA, itself, banked at BCCI and First American, a U.S. bank which BCCI illegally controlled," Peter said. "The Senate Report, *BCCI Affair,* has a strong Executive Summary. I'll read it aloud. 'BCCI's criminality included fraud by BCCI, and BCCI customers, involving billions of dollars ...money laundering in Europe, Africa, Asia, and the Americas ...BCCI's bribery of officials in most of those locations ...support of terrorism ...arms trafficking ...and, sale of nuclear technologies ...management of prostitution ...commission

and facilitation of income tax evasion ...smuggling ...and, illegal immigration ...illicit purchases of banks, and real estate ...and a panoply of financial crimes limited only by the imagination of BCCI officers and customers. Among BCCI's principal mechanisms for committing crimes were its use of shell corporations, and bank confidentiality and secrecy havens ...layering of its corporate structure ...its use of front-men, and nominees, guarantees, and buy-back arrangements ...back-to-back financial documentation among BCCI controlled entities ...kick-backs ...bribes ...intimidation of witnesses ...and, retention of well-placed insiders ... to discourage governmental action. BCCI systematically relied on relationships with, and as necessary, payments to, prominent political figures ... in most of the 73 countries in which BCCI operated. BCCI records and testimony from former BCCI officials together document BCCI's systematic securing of Central Bank deposits of Third World countries ...its provision of favors to political figures ...and, its reliance on those figures to provide BCCI itself. with favors in times of need. These relationships were systematically turned to BCCI's use ... to generate cash needed to prop up its books. BCCI would obtain an important figure's agreement ...to give BCCI deposits from a country's Central Bank ...exclusive handling of a country's use of U.S. commodity credits ...preferential treatment on the processing of money coming in and out of the country where monetary controls were in place ...the right to own a bank, secretly if necessary, in countries where foreign banks were not legal ...or, other questionable means of securing assets or profits. In return, BCCI paid bribes to the figure, or otherwise gave him other things he wanted ... in a simple quid-pro-quo. The result was BCCI had relationships that ranged from the questionable ...to the improper ...to the fully corrupt ...with officials from countries all over the world, including ...Argentina ...Bangladesh ...Botswana ...Brazil ...Cameroon ...China ...Colombia ...Congo ...Ghana ...Guatemala ...Ivory Coast ...India ...Jamaica ...Kuwait ...Lebanon ...Mauritius ...Morocco ...Nigeria ...Pakistan ...Panama ...Peru ...Saudi Arabia ...Senegal ...Sr.i Lanka ...Sudan ...Suriname ...Tunisia ...United Arab Emirates ...United States ...Zambia ...and, Zimbabwe. In 1977, BCCI developed a plan to infiltrate the U.S. market by secretly purchasing U.S. banks ...while opening branch offices of BCCI throughout the U.S. ..and, eventually merging the institutions. BCCI had significant difficulties implementing this strategy, due to regulatory barriers in the United States designed to insure accountability. Despite these barriers, which delayed BCCI's entry, BCCI was ultimately successful in acquiring four banks, operating in seven states and the District of Colombia, with no jurisdiction successfully preventing BCCI from infiltrating it. The techniques used by BCCI in the United States had been previously perfected by BCCI, and were used in BCCI's acquisitions of banks in a number of Third World countries and in Europe,' the BCCI Affair Senate report says," Peter said.

Peter cited Beaty and Gwynne's, *Outlaw Bank*, "'Customs Chief William von Raab announced BCCI was the most important drug-money bank ever hit. But, instead of being lauded by his superiors ... he was told to dampen his public enthusiasm. When he persisted, he was cut out of the investigation. When he complained, he was asked to resign. Then, the Justice Department let BCCI off the hook, collecting a limited guilty plea and a 14 million dollar fine that scuttled any further significant investigation. Then, a senior Justice Department official wrote letters to banking regulators ...suggesting they allow BCCI, which had just pleaded guilty to drug-money laundering, to continue operating,' according to Beaty and Gwynne, *Outlaw Bank*."

Peter felt the ocean breeze push the hairs on his arm. Peter commented on *Outlaw Bank*. "Beaty and Gwynne argue, BCCI was involved with Saudi and Pakistani intelligence, defense, and foreign policy ...with the movement of narcotics to finance the Afghan resistance of the 1980s ...and, with CIA and its director William Casey, citing a *Financial Times* story in July 1991, in which then Finance Minister of Pakistan, 'appeared to accept ...that BCCI in Pakistan had been used by CIA to transfer money to Afghan resistance leaders and their backers in the Pakistani military'. Buried in the report is the finding, 'terrorist organizations ... received payment at BCCI-London and other branches ...directly from Gulf-state patrons ...and then, transferred those funds where they wished without apparent scrutiny.'" Peter recalled the words of a former senior DEA Agent he was on a TV panel with, whose special area was the Middle East ...'In my 30-year history in the Drug Enforcement Administration and related agencies, the major targets of my investigations almost invariably turned out to be working for the CIA.'" Peter continued talking about *Outlaw Bank*. "BCCI's funds were melded with the personal fortune of Sheikh Zayed of Abu Dhabi, one of the United Arab Emigrates. Beaty's *Outlaw Bank* says, a U.S. government source told him Zayed's investments in United States amounted to a staggering 50 billion dollars, and Sheikh Zayed's income, reported at 30 billion dollars a year, was due to petrodollars which 'started to flow in the mid-1960s'. But, 1960s is also when the world began hearing of heroin refineries near oil refineries in Dubai and Qatar. No administration with an eye to United States balance-of-trade problems, has ever wanted to cut off flow of capital flight into America ...and, tough banking disclosure laws could dry up the multibillion-dollar river, overnight. That unspoken imperative is so strong ...some inside players, such as former National Security Council economist Roger Robinson, dismiss the idea that there needed to be a conspiracy to handicap an investigation or prosecution of BCCI. 'Treasury Secretary James Baker didn't pursue BCCI ... because he thought a prosecution of the bank would damage the United States' reputation as a safe haven for flight capital and overseas investments,' according to Robinson. This digression ...from petrodollars ...and narcodollars ... into global finance, is of direct relevance to the way the Bush Administration will conduct ...or fail to conduct ... its campaign against terrorism. Already the ban on certain banks financing terrorism has drawn attention to the fact that banks like BCCI have availed themselves of safe havens like Grand Cayman Islands, which international conventions are seeking to curb or banish ...and, focus attention on failure of the U.S. to ratify these conventions. The deep politics of the Al-Qaeda network, and bin Laden's personal family ...involves the same pattern of Afghan-Pakistan-United Arab Emirates drug-trafficking, money-laundering and intelligence activity conferred on BCCI, an importance in U.S. covert politics so great ... that it was never effectively prosecuted for its crimes. Certainly major U.S. oil companies oppose the exposure of this corrupt intelligence milieu ... involving personnel who are veterans not just of Pakistani intelligence, but more centrally of Saudi intelligence, and the Saudi intelligence service is at the very heart, not just of the CIA-Muhajidin-Afghanistan scandal, but of corrupt arrangements protecting on-going presence of U.S. oil companies in the Arabian peninsula. Terrorism can't be defeated by defending the status quo, when what we need is major readjustment of relationships between the United States and its corporations on the one hand, and exploited peoples of the Third World, on the other."

<>

Patti sighed. "Peter, you're so eloquent."

"Thanks. But, the real McCoy's been quiet."

Patti agreed. "Al, help us out."

Alfred McCoy's, *Politics of Heroin,* was a thriller, the real McCoy.

Al had been patiently waiting his turn. "Okay. Back in Apr. 1979, eight months before the Soviet invasion of Afghanistan, the Carter Administration began supporting fundamentalist Islamic resistance. Then later, your dad's Administration put the pedal to the medal, under CIA patronage the Afghan heroin industry made big time ...opium exports from Muhajidin-controlled poppy fields flooded heroin markets in southwest Asia and the U.S. in the Reagan-Bush Administration. By early 1990s, Afghanistan was second biggest supplier of heroin for North America, it still rocks."

Nancy took it personally. "I don't take it personally ...but, my role in my husband's Administration was the 'Just Say No' to drugs campaign ...but, that targeted end users, not pushers, not poppy farmers, not the BCCI people at all, just the little guy at the bottom of the totem pole, I used to believe that if people just said, 'no', the market would disappear. Ronnie and I prayed about that all the time."

Maureen cheered her up. "Mom, I'm sure some kids said, 'no', because of you."

Nancy smiled, "Probably. I wish *I* had."

Everyone laughed.

Nancy did too. "I was in and out of treatment centers. The stress of Hollywood acting is one thing, hectic schedules of performing, the show must go on ...but, when you mix in lives of hundreds of thousands, and millions, of women and kids at the mercy of U.S. policies, it's too much for me to handle. Many President's wives were living the *Valley of the Dolls.*"

Patti felt sad. "Mom, I wish we could've had this honesty our whole lives."

Nancy sighed. "It's better at the end, than not at all." Nancy and Patti held hands.

Maureen took Nancy's other hand, "God loves us."

Michael was pointing his finger down his throat like he was going to throw up. Ron Jr. gave Michael a dirty look. The real McCoy understood, he was a parent.

Al McCoy continued. "As I said, in, *Politics of Heroin,* during the ten years of the 1980s when CIA covertly supported Muhajidin resistance, what Peter calls, the Afghan Arabs, and Dave and

John call, the Arab Nazis ... the U.S. Government and corporate media was quiet about U.S. involvement with leading Afghan guerrillas and Pakistan military in heroin trafficking, it wasn't til Soviet withdrawal from Afghanistan, in 1989, the media start trailing its finger in the water, pointing to the Muhajidin heroin trade. Back in 1979, at Peshawar in Pakistan's North-West Frontier Province, a CIA special envoy first met Afghan resistance leaders chosen by Pakistan's ISI Inter Service Intelligence agency, *not* introducing CIA across the spectrum of resistance fighters, ISI only introduced its client, Gulbuddin Hekmatyar ...leader of a small Hezbi-I Islami guerrilla group cell. CIA accepted the situation, over the next ten years giving half its covert aid to Hekmatyar's guerrillas. Unlike later resistance leaders who had popular followings in Afghanistan, Hekmatyar led a guerrilla force that was a creature of the Pakistan military ...and, as CIA built up his Hezbi-I Islami in the largest Afghan guerilla force, Hekmatyar became corrupt and brutal, with full support of ISA and CIA ... becoming Afghanistan's leading drug warlord. After Bill Casey managed your dad's presidential campaign, and your dad made ... or whoever had your dad make Casey director of CIA, Casey had direct access to General Zia ul-Haq, then Pakistan's military dictator ... and was received warmly in regular visits to Islamabad. Zia allowed Casey to open an electronic intelligence station facing the Soviet Union in northern Pakistan, and permitted U.S. spy flights over Indian Ocean from Zia's air bases near Persian Gulf. In addition to 3 billion dollars in U.S. aid, the Pakistan military also controlled distribution of 2 billion dollars in covert aid Casey shipped to Afghan guerrillas during the ten-year war ...for General Zia's loyalists in the military these contracts were a windfall. At an operational level, General Zia's military loyalists controlled delivery of Casey's covert arms shipments as they arrived in Pakistan ...once arms landed at port in Karachi in the south, the Pakistan army's National Logistics Cell, acting under orders from ISI, convoyed the arms shipments north to temporary military encampments around Peshawar ...from there, to Afghan guerrilla camps in North-West Frontier ... the governor of this critical borderland province being Lieutenant General Fazle Huq, President Zia's close friend and confidant ... who happened to be de facto overlord of the Muhajidin guerrillas. As ranks of resistance swelled in the 1980s, ISI insisted the dominance of the pre-1978 nucleus continue, being Hekmatyar. ISI delivered half of all arms to Hekmatyar's Hezbi-I Islami guerrillas, giving him the bulk of CIA arms shipments. As the Cold War wound down in 1990, *Washington Post* had a front page story saying, U.S. failed to take action against Pakistan's heroin dealers 'because of its desire not to offend a strategic ally, Pakistan's military establishment' ...saying, U.S. officials ignored Afghan complaints of heroin trafficking by Hekmatyar and ISI, that 'Hekmatyar commanders close to ISI run laboratories in southwest Pakistan, and ISI cooperates in heroin operations'. ISI's Muhajidin used their CIA arms to capture prime agricultural areas, inside Afghanistan, during early 1980s, having peasants grow poppies ...doubling the country's opium harvest to 575 tons, between 1982-1983, the vigorous, vital years of Reagan-Bush Administration. Then, Muhajidin, Afghan Arabs, Nazi Arabs, took opium across the border, into Pakistan ...selling it to heroin refineries operating under protection of General Fazle Huq, governor of North-West Frontier Province. By end of your father's Administration, in 1988, there were 100 to 200 heroin refineries in the province's Khyber district, alone ...trucks from Pakistan Army's National Logistics Cell arrived with CIA arms from Karachi, returning loaded with heroin protected by ISI papers prohibiting police search, the *Pakistan Herald* reported in 1985, 'The drug is carried in NLC trucks, which come sealed from the North-West Frontier, and are never checked by the police.' Lawrence Lifschultz, writing in, *The Nation*, in 1988 said, numerous police sources charged General Fazle Huq, General Zia's intimate, was primary protector of the thriving heroin industry in North-West Frontier Province, that General Huq, 'had been implicated in narcotics reports reaching Interpol', early as 1982. European and Pakistani police claimed investigations of the province's major heroin syndicates had, 'been aborted at the highest level'. With 17 DEA agents assigned to U.S. Embassy in Islamabad, DEA compiled detailed reports identifying '20 significant narcotics syndicates in Pakistan' ...but, not a single major syndicate was touched by Pakistani police, for ten years. Farther down, in Koh-i-Soltan District, Pakistan's Baluchistan Province, Hekmatyar controlled six heroin refineries processing the large opium harvest from Afghanistan's fertile Helmand Valley. The heroin boom was so large, and uncontrolled, that drug abuse swept Pakistan in early 1980s, creating one of the world's largest addict populations. But before, in late 1970s, Pakistan didn't have a significant heroin abuse problem, at all. When the region's political upheavals in 1979 blocked the usual shipment of Afghan and Pakistani opium westward to Iran, traffickers in Pakistan's North-West Frontier perfected heroin-refining skills to reduce mounting opium stockpiles ...operating without fear of arrest, heroin dealers began exporting to Europe and America ...capturing half of both markets ...unrestrained by police controls, local smugglers shipped heroin to Pakistan's own cities and towns ...addiction rose to 5,000 users in 1980 ...then, 70,000 users in 1983 ...then, in the words of Pakistan's Narcotics Control Board, went 'completely out of hand,' exploding to 1,300,000 users in three years ... at the height of your mother's 'Just Say No' campaign ...and this was just in Pakistan.

<>

"General Zia died in a plane crash in 1988, bringing back civilian rule that elected Prime Minister Benazir Bhutto. The disinformation and misinformation that blocked U.S. action against Pakistan's heroin trade was widespread ...State Department's semiannual narcotics review in September called General Zia, 'a strong supporter of anti-narcotics activities in Pakistan' ...but, instead of fighting drugs, General Zia's regime protected Pakistan's heroin dealers. After ten years of unchecked growth under General Zia, the country's drug trade was too well entrenched in the country's politics, and economy, for simple police action ...economists estimated the total annual earnings from Pakistan's heroin trade were 8-to-10 billion dollars ...larger than Pakistan's government budget ...equal to one-quarter of its entire gross domestic product. With heroin money flowing into the economy, Pakistan's commentators were concerned the country's politics would take on a Colombian cast, drug lords using money, and arms, to influence the nation's leaders ... the first signs were not long in coming. Late 1989, with President Bush now in office in America, in Pakistan, facing a no-confidence motion from the National Assembly, Prime Minister Bhutto charged, 'drug money was being used to destabilize her government'. When she claimed that heroin dealers paid 194 million rupees for votes against her, observers found the allegations credible. Plus, the heavily armed tribal populations of the North-West Frontier Province were determined to defend their opium harvest. Police pistols proved ineffective against tribal arsenals, that included automatic assault rifles, anti-aircraft guns, and rocket launchers. 'The government cannot stop us from growing poppy,' one angry tribal farmer told a foreign correspondent, in 1989. 'We are one force, and united, if they come with their planes we'll shoot them down.' As foreign aid declined, in 1989, Afghan leaders expanded opium production to sustain guerrilla armies ...with Soviet withdrawal in 1989, and the resulting shortfall in CIA financial and arms support, rival Muhajidin commanders scrambled for remaining Afghani prime poppy agricultural land in the fertile Helmand Valley of southern Afghanistan."

Dave joined in. "As CIA withdrew support for Afghan Muhajidin, State Department complained about drug production and trafficking of CIA's protégées. As CIA and USSR forces left the scene, fighting between rival anti-Soviet guerrilla factions took on the flavor of drug wars. Jon Marshall's, *Drug Wars,* told how Hekmatyar, and rival leader Mohammed Yahya, 'fought a bloody battle in September 1989, for control of a strategic opium shipment route.'"

Al McCoy nodded. "During the ten year, 1980s war, local commander Mullah Nasim Akhundzada controlled the best-irrigated lands in northern Helmand Valley, once breadbasket of Afghanistan, ordering half of peasant holdings would be planted with opium poppies. Hekmatyar's bitter enemy, Mullah Nasim, issued opium quotas to every landowner, killing those who protested. Known as, 'King of Heroin', he controlled most of the 250 tons of opium grown in Helmand Province. By 1990, after ten years of CIA covert operations ... costing 2 billion dollars ... America was left with Muhajidin warlords, whose skill as drug dealers exceeded their competence as military commanders. By 1989, as Cold War ended and Bush Administration's war on drugs began, Afghan leaders, like opium warlord Hekmatyar, became a diplomatic embarrassment for the U.S. In mountain ranges along the southern rim of Asia, in Afghanistan, Burma, and Laos, opium is the main currency of external trade ...and, the source of political power. During the ten year long Afghan war, 17 DEA agents sat in U.S. Embassy at Islamabad watching, without making a major arrest or seizure, as Afghan-Pakistan heroin captured 60% of the U.S. drug market."

Peter Dale Scott was rapt and eager as he spoke. "Hekmatyar and Massoud supported Tajik rebels up to 1992, both continued to receive aid and assistance from United States, with even more support for Tajik rebels coming from Saudi Arabia and Pakistani Intelligence Directorate, ISI.

Rebel raids into Tajikistan and Uzbekistan destabilized Muslim Republics in Soviet Union and after 1992, U.S.S.R.'s successor, Conference of Independent States ... an explicit goal of U.S. policy in the Reagan era, which didn't change with the end of the Afghan War ...as the United States continued its 'Full-Court Press' break-up of Soviet Union, to gain access to Caspian Basin petroleum reserves. Destabilizing the Soviet Union spelled disaster for economies of Soviet Islamic Republics ...since 1991, leaders of Central Asia, according to Rashid's, *Taliban, Militant Islam, Oil and Fundamentalism in Central Asia,* 'began to hold talks with Western oil companies on back of ongoing negotiations between Kazakhstan and U.S. oil company, Chevron'. U.S. didn't proclaim a war on drugs against the Taliban, or bin Laden ...because, the bulk of Afghan drug-trafficking was now in the hands of those about to become the latest U.S. drug-trafficking proxy, the Northern Alliance ... witnessing the recurring pattern of CIA's long-time involvement with drug traffickers. In America, there was a new media blackout on one important aspect of al-Qaeda ... widely reported in France, England, and Canada, al-Qaeda earns on-going revenues from a spectrum of legitimate businesses and drug-trafficking. Searching my Academic Lexis-Nexis, a Google-type search engine in Sept. 2001 for 'bin Laden' and 'drugs', I found only one reference on this topic in a U.S. newspaper, buried deep in a long story in *LA Times,* 'CIA officials say the underground network frequently crosses into gangsterism. One official cites ample evidence that Bin Laden's group uses profits from the drug trade to finance its campaign. Followers also have been tied to bank robberies, holdups, credit card fraud, and other crimes'. Charities around the Arab world proclaimed, they were raising money for humanitarian purposes in Bosnia ...but in fact, portions benefited Islamic extremist groups in the area, including Al Qaeda. Militants linked to Al Qaeda also established connections with Bosnian organized crime figures. Officials said, Al Qaeda and Taliban found a route for trafficking heroin from Afghanistan into Europe ...through the Balkans. In other words, CIA knew al-Qaeda was involved in heroin trafficking," Peter said.

Jon Marshall had been waiting patiently to add to what Peter said. "CIA knew. In my book, *Drug Wars, Corruption, Counterinsurgency & Covert Operations in the Third World,* I described history CIA made. In Southeast Asia, during the 1960s, the enemies were communist insurgents in Laos, Cambodia, and South Vietnam ...which was root cause of the relationship between intelligence agents and Gen. Van Pao's drug smuggling guerrilla army in Laotian highlands ...but, United States support for Southeast Asian drug markets date back to the end of World War II. CIA was present at the creation of most of the major post-World War II drug production centers, and trafficking syndicates. Its material support and political protection nurtured the great heroin and cocaine empires, whose power today rivals that of many governments. Without critical American aid, they might have remained limited, regional gangs ...with it, they forged international production, smuggling networks. CIA helped establish the heroin market in the 'Golden Triangle', the mountainous border region of Laos, Burma, Thailand, and China's Yunnan Province ...where opium poppies grow like wheat. During World War II, in China as in Sicily, U.S. Office of Strategic Services OSS, predecessor to CIA, and Navy worked closely with gangster elements who controlled vast supplies of opium, morphine, and heroin. Boss of this trade, longstanding ally of Nationalist leader Chiang Kai-shek, directed his enormous army of followers to cooperate with American intelligence, though his patriotism didn't stop him from trading with the Japanese. His heroin empire folded after victory of the Chinese Communist revolution, in 1949. But, a new heroin empire emerged after Nationalist KMT forces under command of General Li Mi, fled from Yunnan into the wild Shan states of eastern Burma. By 1951, if not earlier, they began receiving arms, ammunition, and other supplies via CIA airlifts ...to facilitate their abortive efforts to rekindle an anti-communist resistance in China. Repelled from China with heavy losses, KMT settled down within the local population ...to organize and expand the lucrative opium trade from Burma and northern Thailand. While doing this, they continued to enjoy support from CIA, and CIA 'assets', in the Thai military and police, who convoyed the drugs to Thai ports. By 1972, KMT controlled 80 percent of the Golden Triangle's enormous opium trade. CIA's relationship to these drug merchants, and to corrupted Laotian, Thai, and Vietnamese political and military leaders, attracted little attention ...until early 1970s. As early as 1966, Harrison Salisbury noted the rise of heroin production in the region. There are skeptics who feel that not a few recipients of the bounty of U.S. aid, and the CIA, may have a deeper interest in the opium business, than in the anti-communist business. Centered in the whole trade, there is a hardy band of Chinese Nationalist troops, flown to China's Yunna province border years ago ...in an early CIA operation ...they manage to turn a pretty penny in poppies.' In 1970, a correspondent for *Christian Science Monitor,* commented, 'Clearly , CIA is cognizant of, if not party to, the extensive movement of opium out of Laos. One charter pilot told me, 'friendly' opium shipments get special CIA clearance, and monitoring, on their flights south out of the country'. A California Congressman charged, 'clandestine, unofficial operations of the U.S. Government could be aiding and abetting heroin traffic here, at home.' And, not just at home ...by end of 1970, 30,000 American servicemen in Vietnam were addicted to heroin.

<>

"But, the full story didn't break ...until 1972, when Yale University doctoral candidate Alfred McCoy, the real McCoy over here, published his trailblazing study, *Politics of Heroin in Southeast Asia,*" Jon Marshall said.

Patti was excited. "Al, you're a hero too, like Peter!"

Al McCoy felt embarrassed.

Nancy sighed. "Where were you guys when I needed you ...back, in my husband's Administration. Back then, getting information was like pulling teeth. I got more information at my astrologer's séances, than I did through White House Daily Intelligence briefings, DEA and CIA, combined."

Dave and Michael laughed. Patti pulled out a copy of Kris Millegan's, *Fleshing Out Skull & Bones.* "Millegan talks about what his father told him. 'Secret societies are behind it,' my father told me many years ago. During early 1950s he was CIA branch chief, head of East Asia intelligence analysis office. 'The Vietnam War,' he said soberly, 'is about drugs'.

<>

"Many years later, I had some understanding of what Dad was talking about, Kris said.

Dave nodded. He looked at Jon Marshall. "CIA tried to quash your book, got you a lot of publicity, as I recall."

Jon Marshall smiled. "Yes, it did ...it brought blanket denials ...assurances from Washington in the press, that priorities were changed since President Nixon declared his, 'War on Drugs,'" Jon said. He read from his book.

"Basically Cold War politics, and American covert operations, fostered a heroin boom in the Golden Triangle. Elaine Shannon, a reporter with privileged access to DEA sources, had observations. 'After the fall of South Vietnam, CIA and

National Security Agency expanded facilities in Bangkok and Chiang Mai in northern Thailand ...to monitor military and political activity in Vietnam, Laos, southern China, and Northern Burma. Smugglers were natural allies. DEA agents, who served in Southeast Asia in late 1970s and 1980s, said, they frequently discovered they were tracking heroin smugglers on the CIA payroll,' Shannon said. 'One of those smugglers may be been Lu Hsu-shui, considered one of the top four heroin dealers in the entire Golden Triangle. He reportedly got his start in business 'trading opium for gold ...with KMT remnants in northern Thailand'. CIA shut down DEA's investigation of him, claiming it had to use the drug agency's key informant, 'in a high-level, sensitive national security operation'. In 1973, U.S. authorities arrested a Thai national, Puttaporn Khramkhruan ...in connection with seizure of 59 pounds of opium, in Chicago. CIA quashed the case, according to a Justice Department memorandum, lest it 'prove embarrassing, because of Mr. Khramkhruan's involvement with CIA activities in Thailand, Burma, and elsewhere'. Khramkhruan, a former officer in KMT's dope-smuggling army, served the Agency ...as an informant on narcotics trafficking in northern Thailand ...and, claimed CIA had full knowledge of his actions. Perhaps the biggest fish of all to escape was Thai General Kriangsak Chamanand, who helped lead a particularly bloody, military coup in 1976 ...then took power himself in another coup, in 1977. Kriangsak, a graduate of National Defense University in the U.S., had served as a 'key link' in CIA covert operations during the Vietnam War, including using Thai mercenaries to fight the 'secret war', in Laos. Publicly, America drug agents gave Kriangsak a clean bill of health. But, author James Mills, who had access to DEA files thought otherwise. 'Kriangsak, himself, is named in classified intelligence reports ...as the direct recipient of secret cash payoffs from leaders of armed groups controlling opium traffic in mountains of Thailand and Burma. These groups include at least three KMT rebel armies, with past, or present clandestine support of CIA.' Southeast Asia is hardly the only theater where drug smugglers turned up ... as protected, CIA 'assets'. In early 1970s, CIA immunized Latin American smugglers in no fewer than 27 federal drug cases.

<>

"Such outcomes were not merely bad luck. A former DEA operations chief recalls, starting with CIA Directors William Colby ...and, George Bush,

the agency regularly poached from the DEA's pool of informants, and investigative targets. 'When DEA arrested these drug traffickers,' he stated, 'they used the CIA as protection ...and, because of their CIA involvement ... they were released. This amounted to a license to traffic for life ...because, even if arrested in the future, they could demand classified documents about their prior CIA involvement ...and, would have to be let go. CIA knew full well their assets were drug traffickers,'" Jon Marshall said.

Al McCoy joined in the conversation. "That's right. When I wrote, *Politics of Heroin in Southeast Asia*, CIA tried to keep it from being published ...since then, it's disappeared from most libraries. Few people in official Washington are willing to discuss putting controls over CIA covert operations to ensure the U.S does *not* keep protecting drug lords. Over the past 60 years, American and allied intelligence agencies played a significant role in protecting and expanding global drug traffic. CIA covert operations in key drug-producing areas repeatedly restrain or block DEA efforts to deal with the problem. The list of governments, whose clandestine services have had close relations with major narcotics traffickers, is surprisingly long ...Nationalist China ...Imperial Japan ...Gaullist France ...French Indochina ...Kingdom of Thailand ...Pakistan ..and, United States. Instead of reducing, or repressing the drug supply, most clandestine agencies seem to regulate traffic ... by protecting favored dealers, and eliminating rivals. During 1950s, CIA worked with Corsican syndicates of Marseilles ...to restrain communist influence on city docks, making the criminal milieu stronger, at a time when it was becoming America's leading heroin supplier. At the same time, CIA installed Nationalist Chinese irregulars in northern Burma, and provided them with the logistic support they used to transform the country's Shan states ... into the world's largest opium producer. During 1960s, CIA's secret war in Laos required alliances with the Hmong tribe ... the country's leading opium growers ...and, various national political leaders who soon became major heroin manufacturers. Although Burma's increased opium harvest of 1950s supplied only regional markets, Laos' heroin production in late 1960s ... was directed at U.S. troops, fighting in south Vietnam. Constrained by local political realities, CIA lent air logistics to opium transport, and did little to slow Laotian heroin shipments to South Vietnam. When U.S. troops withdrew from Vietnam in the early 1970s, Southeast Asian heroin followed GIs home, capturing one-third of the U.S. drug market, in the mid-70s. After complicity in marketing opium and heroin, CIA emerged from Laos ... with an entire generation of clandestine cadres experienced in using narcotics to support covert operations. During 1980s, CIA's two main covert action operations became interwoven with global narcotics trade. The agency's support for Afghan guerrillas ... through Pakistan, coincided with emergence of southern Asia as the major heroin supplier for European, and American, markets. Although, the United States maintained a substantial force of DEA agents in Islamabad during the 1980s, like Jon said, the unit was restrained by U.S. national security imperatives ...and, did almost nothing to slow Pakistan's booming heroin exports to America. Similarly, CIA support for Nicaraguan contras sparked sustained allegations of the agency's complicity in the Caribbean cocaine trade. Many CIA covert warriors, named in the contra operation, had substantial experience in the Laotian secret war. Agency alliances with Third World drug brokers amplified the scale of global drug traffic ... linking new production areas, to the world market. Protected by CIA allies, drug brokers are allowed a de facto immunity from investigation ... during the critical period of vulnerability ...while they are forging new market links. The apparent level of CIA complicity has increased, indicating growing tolerance for narcotics ...as an informal weapon, in the arsenal of covert warfare. Over the past 40 years, CIA has moved from transport of raw opium in remote areas of Laos ... to apparent complicity in bulk transport of pure cocaine ... directly into the United States ...and, mass manufacture of heroin for the U.S. market. America's drug epidemics are fueled by narcotics supplied from areas of major CIA operations ...while periods of reduced heroin use coincide with absence of CIA activity. American drug policy is crippled by a contradiction between DEA attempts to arrest major traffickers ... and, CIA protection for the world's drug lords. This contradiction, seen most recently during Pakistan's heroin boom of the 1980s, 1990s, and 2000s, repeatedly and predictably recurs. CIA's protected, covert action assets, have included ...Marseille's Corsican criminals ...Nationalist Chinese opium warlords ...Thai military's opium overlord ...Laotian heroin merchants ...Afghan heroin manufacturers ...and, Pakistan's leading drug lords. Complicity with drug lords seems limited to the agency's covert operation units. CIA engages in two types of clandestine work ...espionage, the collection of information about present and future events ...and, covert action, the attempt to use extralegal means ...assassination ...destabilization ...or, secret warfare, to influence outcome of events. Today's intelligence community was redesigned ... to conduct cellular covert operations, without even the knowledge of CIA," Al McCoy said.

Peter spoke up. "We might as well round out the picture, based on research Jon Marshall and I did, for, *Cocaine Politics, Drugs, Armies & the CIA in Central America,* okay Jon?"

"Sure," Jon said.

"Jon was economics editor of *San Francisco Chronicle,* at the time," Peter said. Peter read from the book they co-authored. "The current and historical response of Washington to the drug epidemic in America overlooks Washington's contribution to it. During the war against Nicaraguan Sandinistas, groups within the Contras trafficked in cocaine ... supplying the North American market ...while CIA, National Security Council, and Justice Department ignored evidence. Regional influences, political and criminal, fueled explosive growth of drug trafficking through Honduras, in early 1980s. In 1980-1981, head of military intelligence in Panama, Colonel Manuel Noriega, teamed up with his counterpart at head of Honduran G-2, Colonel Torres ... to smuggle arms on behalf of Marxist rebels in El Salvador ...and then, drugs. Noriega's maligned influence spread ...to Costa Rica, as well. A Costa Rican legislative commission concluded, in 1989, Noriega helped install in that country seven pilots who ran guns to contras ...and, drugs to North America. 'More serious still,' it added, 'is obvious infiltration of international gangs into Costa Rica, that made use of the contra organization.

<>

"These requests for contra help were initiated by Colonel Oliver North to General Noriega.

<>

"They opened a gate ...so, their henchmen utilized national territory for trafficking in arms and drugs.' Noriega's reach extended beyond Central America, to Washington. His relationship with U.S. intelligence helps account for his immunity from American law enforcement ...and, his ability to promote corrupt elements of the contra support movement. Noriega was recruited as an agent by U.S. Defense Intelligence Agency in 1959, as a young military cadet, studying in Peru. He went on CIA payroll in 1967...the next year, a military coup ... assisted by U.S. Army

470th Military Intelligence Group ... gave Noriega opportunity to take charge of Panama's own G-2. His new job made him a priceless source for the American services, which used Panama as a listening post for Latin America. Before long, Washington discovered its protégé's criminal bent. Early as May 1971, Bureau of Narcotics and Dangerous Drugs BNDD heard allegations of Noriega's involvement in trafficking. A former chief of staff to General Omar Torrijos, Panama's military ruler, settled in Miami ...after botching a coup attempt. He revealed to U.S. authorities, Noriega had 'overall operational control' of officially sanctioned narcotics trade in Panama. BNDD got together evidence to indict Noriega in a major marijuana smuggling case ... only to run up against objections from U.S. Attorney's office in Miami ...no one, in those days, could imagine invading Panama to bring a senior officer to justice. Intent on negotiating a new Panama Canal treaty, State Department put other foreign policy objectives ahead of law enforcement ...and, persuaded BNDD to back off. A long honeymoon began. Panama's economy boomed under stimulus of drug dollars attracted to its modern and secretive banking sector. By 1976, Noriega was fully forgiven. CIA Director George Bush arranged to pay Noriega $110,000 a year for his services, put the Panamanian up as a house guest of his deputy CIA director, and helped prevent an embarrassing prosecution of several American soldiers ...who, had delivered highly classified U.S. intelligence secrets to Noriega's men. Noriega earned his pay. He supplied pilots, who helped smuggle weapons to contra leader, Eden Pastora. In 1984, he contributed $100,000 to contra leaders based in Costa Rica ...in 1985, Noriega helped Oliver North plan, and carry out, a major sabotage raid in Managua, using services of a British mercenary, ...responding to pleas from Bill Casey, he promised to help train contra units ...and, let them use Panama as a transit point. In 1986, North met Noriega in London, discussing further sabotage against Nicaraguan economic targets, including ...an oil refinery ...an airport ...and, electric and telephone systems. North's diary said, he and Noriega discussed setting up a school for commandos ... to train experts in bobby traps, night ops and raids. Noriega allowed members of North's team to set up Panamanian corporate fronts ... to disguise financing contra supplies ...Amalgamated Commercial Enterprises use services of drug-linked, Banco de Iberoamerica. A related dummy company purchased arms for contras through Monzer al-Kassar, the Syrian arms and drug broker who dealt with the Medellin cartel. Noriega's lawyer in Geneva set up a front ... for an airfield in Costa Rica ...to supply Contras. Evidence gathered by Costa Rican authorities suggested Noriega's intelligence operatives helped the CIA. But, Vice President Bush claimed during his 1988 presidential campaign ...to know little ...or, nothing of Noriega's narcotics dealings ...perhaps being kept in the dark by his top aide. Adm. Dan Murphy, who said, 'I never saw any intelligence suggesting General Noriega's involvement in drug trade. In fact, we held up Panama as the model, in terms of cooperation with United States in the war on drugs'. CIA never turned over files on Noriega to federal prosecutors ...National Security Council ordered agencies to refuse congressional requests for info, after Noriega's indictment in 1988 ...perhaps the most striking evidence of political double standards was silence of the Bush Administration on the composition of the post invasion regime. The new, U.S.-installed president of Panama, Guillermo Endara, had been a director, and secretary, of Banco Interoceanico, targeted by FBI and DEA ...and, named by Floyd Carlton as a major front for laundering Colombian drug money. The bank reportedly served the Cali and Medellin cartels. Endara's business partner, who reportedly laundered CIA funds into Endara's presidential campaign in spring 1989, was arrested in April in Georgia ... for allegedly conspiring to import more than half a ton of cocaine into the United States, each month. Washington didn't protest when Endara appointed to key posts of attorney general, treasury minister, and chief justice of the supreme court, three former directors of First Interamericas Bank ...an institution controlled by the Cali cartel, used to wash drug money. Panamanian authorities took over the bank in 1985 and liquidated its assets, a lawyer for the Cali interest complained, Noriega made a practice of turning in rivals of the Medellin cartel," Peter said.

Dave took a magazine out of his backpack, Christic Institute's, *Convergence.* "It's almost dinnertime. Andy Lang talks about U.S. intervention in Central America, and new cocaine smuggling routes through contra bases."

Michael called from the ranch house, "Dinner at eight."

Dave was hungry. He read quickly. "Drug profits were used to finance the contra war against Nicaragua ...that, was confirmed in 1989 by Senate Foreign Relations Subcommittee on Narcotics and Terrorism. Through a web of business relationships with Latin America drug cartels, the contras were supplied with 'cash, weapons, planes, pilots, air supply services, and other materials', the subcommittee said. Senior officials in the Reagan-Bush Administration knew about the contra-cocaine connection ...but, took no steps to shut down drug smuggling operations on contra bases ...instead, the Administration protected known drug traffickers from investigation and exposure. The subcommittee corroborated one of Christic Institute's key charges, in a lawsuit filed in 1986 ... drug shipments were smuggled through contra bases at the height of the secret war to topple the Nicaraguan Government ...one defendant, alleged drug trafficker John Hull, a United States businessman whose ranch in northern Costa Rica was used as a staging area for cocaine flights to United States, served as CIA's liaison with contra forces in Costa Rica. 'Columbian drug cartels that control the cocaine industry constitute an unprecedented threat to national security of the United States', the subcommittee report said. 'Well-armed and operating from secure foreign havens, the cartels are responsible for thousands of murders, and drug-related deaths ...in the United States, each year ...they exact enormous costs ...in terms of violence ...lower economic productivity ...and, misery ... across the nation. U.S. officials involved in Central America failed to address the drug issue, for fear of jeopardizing the war effort against Nicaragua. There's substantial evidence ...of drug smuggling through the war zones by individual contras ...contra suppliers ...contra pilots ...mercenaries who worked with contras ...and, contra supporters throughout the region.' Senior officials in Reagan-Bush Administration, including Lt. Col. Oliver North of the National Security Council staff, knew contras were shipping drugs into United States ...but, took no action. FBI had, 'significant information regarding involvement of narcotics traffickers in contra operations' ...Justice Department, 'adamantly denied there was substance to narcotics allegations. Logic ... of having drug money pay for pressing needs of contras, appealed to a number of people ...who became involved in the covert war ...senior U.S. policy makers weren't immune to the idea ... drug money was the solution to contras funding problems'. Reagan-Bush Administration ignored links between contras, and drug traffickers ... giving $800,000 to four companies controlled by traffickers, the subcommittee report said, part of a fund set aside by Congress for 'humanitarian'

aid to contra terrorist death squads ...

<>

"... including $317,000 to an air cargo company, whose executive vice president was the target of three FBI drug investigations ... when, the State Department gave him the money ...and, a shipping firm controlled by a billionaire drug lord ... now, serving a life sentence for the torture-murder of a DEA agent. The report says, John Hull served as 'a liaison between the contras and the U.S. Government' ...that, drugs were smuggled through his ranch in Costa Rica ...that, weapons destined for the contras were flown in small planes to the ranch ...the planes were refueled ...then, returned to the U.S. ... with cargoes of cocaine. The report confirmed, Reagan-Bush Administration's obsession with the 'communist threat' in Central America undermined U.S. Government strategy against one of the most serious threats to our national security ... the epidemic of drugs, and drug-related violence, in American cities, and schools.

<>

The contras, like other insurgent armies created by CIA since 1940s, were compromised ...by drug trade. In a sworn statement to Christic Institute attorneys, drug pilot Gary Betzner testified, he flew two planeloads of contra weapons to Hull's ranch in Costa Rica ...unloaded weapons ...then, loaded 500,000 kilos of cocaine ... for each return flight to the U.S. Another drug pilot testified, he flew several loads of drugs from various points in Latin America into the U.S. ... under protection of DEA ...including two trips to Honduras ...and, Costa Rica ... where he delivered weapons for the contras, and took on drug cargoes ... for the return flight to the United States ...in Mar. 1986, flying a shipment of 25,000 pounds of marijuana from Honduras to Homestead Air Force Base, in Florida.

<>

"Convicted drug smuggler George Morales testified, he donated 5 million dollars to the contras ...and, witnessed 1 million dollars in drug profits given to a contra leader in a Florida restaurant.

<>

"Did Oliver North and other senior officials in the Reagan-Bush Administration know drug traffickers were using contra bases as assembly areas for drug flights into the U.S.? The public record shows. they did ...that, the Administration intervened ... to protect drug traffickers from investigation, and prosecution. The immunity from investigation that protected North's pilots during their gun-running flights to Central

America also protected them when they returned to United States airspace, with drug cargoes. *Boston Globe* reported in 1987, 50 to 100 flights 'arranged by CIA took off, or landed, at U.S. airports the last two years without inspection' by Customs. May 1990, Colombian drug lord, Carlos Lehde, told ABC News, Hull was 'pumping about 30 tons of cocaine into the United States, every year'. The Administration's policy was, trials against drug traffickers who were protected by their service in the contra war, was not 'in the interests of national interest'," Dave said.

Peter jumped in. "*Le Monde* says bin Laden's network uses the drug connections bin Laden developed with his friend, former CIA protégé Gulbuddin Hekmatyar, according to Swiss journalist Richard Labeviere's, *Dollars for Terror, The United States & Islam.* Sept. 30, 2001 *London Observer* reported, British and U.S. troops would soon enter Afghanistan to target and destroy drugs stockpiles of the Taliban, out of fear of Taliban plans to flood the West with 20 billion pounds worth of heroin. Three weeks later, Jane's, *Intelligence Review,* discounted the 'heroin onslaught theory', as 'premature' ... the Taliban's role was to merely to tax the illicit drug traffic, not control it. *Jane's Intelligence Review* reported, 'poppy cultivation almost totally disappeared' from areas of Afghanistan under Taliban control ...but, 'a rising tide of narcotics, both opium and the heroin refined from it' ...was flooding out of the northeast corner of Afghanistan ... under control of America's new anti-Taliban allies, United Front Northern Alliance. Compared to key Taliban southern, and southeastern, provinces ...Helmand ...Kandahar ...Uruzgan ...and, Nangahar ...where, most Afghan opium production has been concentrated, output from United Front-controlled zone was small, less than 5 percent of national production, estimated in 2000 at 3,300 tons. However, arrival in Badakhshan of Mashriqi opium traders, who provide credit to farmers, stimulated northeastern production and 'has turned the region into a vital conduit for southern opium, and heroin, moving north into Central Asia. Increased security measures, and interdiction, along the Afghan-Iranian and Pakistani-Iranian borders ... have also encouraged this shift towards northern trafficking routes,' *Jane's Intelligence Review* said.

<>

"The claim, drug-trafficking shifted from Taliban to Northern Alliance territory ... was reported Nov. 2001, by *London Observer,* which attributed the shift to the Taliban's ban of 2000 on opium-growing. During the ban, the only source of poppy production was territory held by the Northern Alliance. It tripled production.

<>

"In high valleys of Badakhshan, an area controlled by troops loyal to former President Burhannudin Rabbani, number of hectares planted last year jumped from 2,458 to 6,342. Alliance fields accounted for 83 percent of total Afghan production, of 185 tons of opium, during the ban. Now, that the Alliance has captured such rich poppy-growing areas, as Nangrahar, production is set to rocket. Helmand, too, is being replanted by Taliban rulers, who abandoned their anti-opium stance ...and, want to cash in on remaining sources of revenue. Western and Pakistani officials fear, within a year or two, Afghanistan could again reach its peak production figures of 60,000 hectares of poppies producing 2,800 tons of opium, more than half the world's output. Alliance factions and other warlords deny benefiting from opium production ...but, it's an open secret that nearly all tolerate it. Most are happy just to cream off the taxes ...but, others are directly involved. Hazrat Ali, one of the new war lords ... in control in Nangrahar, ran Jalalabad Airport in the mid-90s, at a time when weekly flights to India and the Gulf carried huge amounts of opium to Western markets.

<>

"During the war against the Russians, the huge and illicit drug trade, nurtured by the Muhajidin ...was ignored ...and, tolerated by CIA, and other Western intelligence agencies ... in return for Muhajidin commitment to fight Soviet Union,' the *London Observer* said.

<>

"The first Bush Administration supported plans of U.S. oil companies to contract the exploiting of resources of the Caspian region ...and, for a pipeline, not controlled by Moscow, to bring oil and gas production out to the west. The gap between Bush Administration's professed ideals and its real objectives is illustrated by its position towards the Karimov regime in Uzbekistan, when America quickly sent Donald Rumsfeld to deal with the new regime in Kyrgyzstan, installed in Mar. 2005 ...after the popular, 'Tulip Revolution', and overthrow there of Askar Akayev ...but, Islam Karimov's violent repression of a similar uprising in Uzbekistan saw no wavering of U.S. support for a dictator who has allowed U.S. troops to be based in his oil- and gas-rich country. Accusations against ...Amoco ...Exxon ...and, Mobil ... in Azerbaijan parallel those from European sources against Unocal in Afghanistan, accused of helping, along with Delta Oil, to finance the Taliban's seizure of Kabul in 1996, at a time when the Taliban was receiving funds from Saudi Arabia and Osama bin Laden.

<>

"Respected French observer, Olivier Roy, took a position, 'When the Taliban took power in Afghanistan, in 1966, it was largely orchestrated by the Pakistani secret service, ISI ...and, the oil company, Unocal ...with its Saudi ally, Delta.' Unocal executive John Maresca testified in 1998 to House Committee on International Relations on the benefits of a proposed oil pipeline through Afghanistan, to the coast of Pakistan. A second natural gas pipeline, Centgas, was contemplated by Unocal. For Unocal, to advance its own funds for the Taliban conquest would've violated U.S. law ...which is why, such companies customarily resort to middlemen. No such restraints would have inhibited Unocal's Saudi partner in its Centgas consortium, Delta Oil. Delta Oil had the assets ...it was 'owned by a Jeddah-based group of 50 prominent investors, close to the Saudi royal family.'

<>

"Delta was already an investor with Unocal ... in the oilfields of Azerbaijan, ...and, may have been a factor in the Oct. 1995 decision of Turkmenistan to sign a new pipeline contract with Unocal. As I wrote a decade ago," said Peter, "...about a U.S. oil company in Tunisia, 'it is normal, not unusual, for entry of major U.S. firms into Third World countries to be facilitated and sustained, indeed made possible, by corruption.'

<>

"This has long been the case ...but, in the Reagan 1980s, it was escalated by a new generation of aggressive risk-taking, law-bending, 'cowboy' entrepreneurs, the pace set by new corporations ...like Enron, a high-debt merger in part guided by junk-bond impresario Michael Milken. Some say, Enron had a potential interest in the Unocal gas pipeline project through Afghanistan ...by 1997, Enron was negotiating a 2 billion dollar joint venture with Neftegas of Uzbekistan, to develop Uzbekistan's natural gas ...a huge project, backed by 400 million dollars of commitment from the U.S. Government through OPIC. Uzbekistan signed a Memo of Agreement, to participate in the Centgas gas pipeline. But, the Enron Uzbek negotiations collapsed, in 1998 ...Enron's short-term plans had been to export Uzbek gas west to Kazakhstan, Turkey, and

Europe ...however, it was claimed Enron hoped eventually to supply, via the Centgas pipeline, its failing energy plant in Dabhol, India. Without a cheap gas supply, cost of electricity from Dabhol was so great, Indians refused to buy it. In my, *Drugs, Oil, and War,*" said Peter. "I quoted Olivier Roy. 'It is the Americans who have made inroads in Central Asia, primarily because of oil and gas interests. Chevron, and Unocal, are political actors ... who talk as equals with the States', that is, with the presidents. It is clear, they talk as equals in the current Bush Administration. Both the President and Vice-President are former oilmen, as were some of their oldest friends and political backers, like Kenneth Lay, of Enron.

<>

"Many observers have noted, from as early as 1992, that George W. Bush's first oil venture, Arbusto, received $50,000 investment from a Texan, James Bath, 'who made his fortune by investing money for Khalid bin Mahfouz and another BCCI-connected Saudi, Sheikh Salim bin-Laden,' Osama's brother.

<>

"According to Kevin Phillips, 'James Bath, who invested fifty thousand dollars in the 1979-1980 Arbusto partnerships, probably did so as U.S. business representative for rich Saudi investors Salem bin Laden, and Khalid bin Mahfouz. Both men were involved with BCCI, Bank of Credit and Commerce International ... indeed, bin Mahfouz owned twenty percent of its stock. A decade later, Harken Energy, the company willing to handsomely buy out George W's crumbling oil and gas business, had its own CIA connections ... 17.6 percent of Harken's stock was owned by Abdullah Baksh, another Saudi magnate reported by some to be representing Khalid bin Mahfouz.' Khalid bin Mahfouz denies being an investor in Arbusto or Harken Energy.

<>

"When we look at the Afghan leaders, whom the U.S. considers eligible to fill out an interim government, we see many are figures implicated in drug-trafficking, in the 1980s. BBC compiled a list of these leaders, in Nov. 2001. Leading the list was President Burhanuddin Rabbani, whose home province of Badakshan became in the 1990s, while under his control, 'the stepping stone for an entirely new means of conveying opiates to Europe, via Tajikistan, Uzbekistan, and Russia's Central Asian railway service,' according to Griffin's, *Reaping the Whirlwind.* Veteran General Rashid Dostum, in Mazar-i-Sharif, 'was suspected of earning huge profits by exporting drugs via Uzbekistan,' according to Cooley's, *Unholy Wars*. Of the seven Pashtun leaders named, three ...Pir Sayed Gailani ...Gulbeddin Hekmatyar ...and, Hazi Bashir, are linked in the past to drug-trafficking. A fourth, Younus Khalis, is a powerful figure from drug-rich Nangarhar province ...and, is the man Osama bin Laden made contact with, in 1996 ...before offering his riches to the Taliban. The restored leader of the Shura-i-Mashriqi, or Eastern Shura in Nangarhar province, Haji Abdul Qadir ... became rich in former times ... as the Afghan source of a drug pipeline involving in Pakistan, Haji Ayub Afridi, 'the lord of Khyber heroin dealing,' according to Griffin and Cockburn's, *Whiteout*.

"Under the headline '*U.S. turns to drug baron to rally support*,' *Asia Times Online* reported Dec. 2001, that 'Afridi was freed from prison in Karachi last Thursday, after serving just a few weeks of a seven-year sentence for the export of 6.5 tons of hashish.' In the 1980s, 'All of the major Afghan warlords, except for the Northern Alliance's Ahmed Shah Masoud, who had his own opium fiefdom in northern Afghanistan, were a part of Afridi's coalition of drug traders in the CIA-sponsored holy war against the Soviets.

<>

"'Commanders such as Haji Abdul Qadeer, Haji Mohammed Zaman, and Hazrat Ali are once again ruling the roost in these areas. These commanders used to be the biggest heroin and opium mafia in Afghanistan's Pashtun belt.' As I mentioned earlier," Peter said, "The *Observer* in 2001, reported 'Hazrat Ali, ran Jalalabad airport in the mid-Nineties when weekly flights to India, and the Gulf, carried huge amounts of opium to Western markets.' Other sources add, Afridi's constituencies in eastern and southern Afghan provinces were revived following withdrawal of the Taliban, according to Pakistan's, *Frontier Post* ...reviving heroin labs along the frontier. *Jane's Intelligence Weekly* wrote in Oct. 2001, in non-Taliban areas of northeastern Afghanistan, 'Heroin refineries, generally run by chemists from the Mashriqi region of southeastern Nangahar province, operate under protection of local commanders' ...Haji Abdul Qadir ...Haji Mohammed Zaman ...and, Hazrat Ali. Hazrat Ali was one of the main local commanders directing the ground forces attacking the Tora Bora cave stronghold in search of Osama bin Laden.

<>

"'Meanwhile, Haji Mohamed Zaman complained about U.S. bombing of villages under his control. A local loya jirga, convened under control of Qadir's Eastern shura, requested the bombing cease. Mansoor Ijaz, a Pakistan-born member of Council on Foreign Relations, wrote in *L.A. Times,* Nov. 2001 ...about securing cooperation of local warlords in ousting al-Qaeda from its caves. 'Now that Northern Alliance captured Mazar-i-Sharif, the U.S.-led military campaign soon will test how much of the effort can be entrusted to its Afghan allies on the ground ...and, how much of it U.S. forces will have to take up, themselves. Willingness of northern Afghan warlords to wage the grueling ground battles needed to smoke Al Qaeda from its caves, will test Afghanistan's historical tendencies ... to shift allegiances, without notice.' But, the independent behavior of Haji Abdul Qadir, and Haji Mohammed Zaman, suggests a third possibility ...the true restorer of the Afridi network may be elements in Pakistan, legitimately concerned by the increasing role played in post-Taliban Afghanistan, by Northern Alliance, and Russia'. What we may be seeing, is revival of Cold War games ...in which, both U.S. and Russia sought control of the drug traffic...

<>

"... not just to fund their operations, but above all ...in order to deny influence of the traffic to their opponent. It's been clear, Northern Alliance spurned U.S. guidance, and listened to its backers ... in Russia, ever since Northern Alliance seized control of Kabul ... in defiance of Bush's public order ...and refused, to accept a multinational peace-keeping force. After hard bargaining at Bonn, Northern Alliance has come away with the most important ministries in their control ...defense ...foreign affairs ...justice ...and, the interior, according to *London Guardian*, Dec. 2001," Peter said. "Eric Margolis says, in *Los Angeles Times*, Nov. 2001, 'Russians have regained influence over Afghanistan, avenged their defeat by U.S. in the 1980s war, and neatly checkmated the Bush administration ...which, for all its high-tech military power, understands little about Afghanistan. The U.S. ouster of the Taliban regime, also means, Pakistan has lost its former influence over Afghanistan ...and, is now cut off from Central Asia's resources. So long as the alliance holds power, the U.S. is equally denied access to the much-coveted Caspian Basin. Russia has regained control of the best potential pipeline routes. The new 'Silk Road' is destined to become a Russian energy superhighway', Margolis said." Peter continued. "But, Russia's client states in the CIS ...above all, Uzbekistan and Tajikistan, suffered from Islamist terrorist movements, funded by drugs. Other secession movements in Chechnya Georgia, and Abkhazia are tied in with struggles over local drug traffic, according to Cooley's, *Unholy Wars*.

<>

"Control over oil and control over drugs can't be separated.

<>

"Some in Washington, hope to turn from old Afghan warlords, and their drug-financed forces, to a younger generation of leaders, working towards a centrally financed, and controlled, army. Most old warlords, notably ...Rabbani ...Dostum ...and, Hekmatyar ... have been excluded from the new, post-Taliban interim government. This may be why the new government, though it has 17 Northern Alliance members, and only 11 Pushtuns, has still been welcomed by Pakistani President Musharraf. More disturbing, is news of Ayub Afridi's release ...and, related stories old heroin labs are being reopened, along Afghan-Pakistani frontier. The drug warriors have not exited the scene. As head of United Nations drug control program in Afghanistan warned, the country is in danger of establishing a drug economy ...unless, Afghan political leaders form a government that can effectively control opium production. Farmers are already re-planting opium poppy in parts of southern Afghanistan. In one former Soviet Republic, Azerbaijan ...Arab Afghan jihadists clearly assisted this effort of U.S. oil companies to penetrate the region.

<>

"In 1991, Richard Secord, Heinie Aderholt, and Ed Dearborn, three veterans of U.S. operations in Laos, and later of Oliver North's operations with Contras, turned up ...in Baku ... under the cover of an oil company ...MEGA Oil, at a time when the first Bush administration expressed support for an oil pipeline stretching from Azerbaijan, across the Caucasus, to Turkey. MEGA never did find oil ...but, did contribute materially to removal of Azerbaijan from the sphere of post-Soviet Russian influence. Secord, Aderholt, and Dearborn were career U.S. Air Force officers ...not CIA. However, Secord explains in his memoir, *Honored and Betrayed: Irangate, Covert Affairs, and the Secret War in Laos*, how Aderholt and himself were occasionally seconded to CIA ...as, CIA detailees. Secord describes his service as a CIA detailee with Air America in Vietnam ...then, Laos ... in cooperation with CIA Station Chief, Theodore Shackley. Secord later worked with Oliver North ... to supply arms and materiel to Contras in Honduras ...and also, developed a

small air force for them, using former Air America pilots. Because of this experience in air operations, CIA Director Casey, and Oliver North, selected Secord to trouble-shoot deliveries of weapons ...to Iran, in the Iran-Contra operation. Aderholt and Dearborn served in the Laotian CIA operation ...and later, in supporting the Contras. As MEGA operatives in Azerbaijan ...Secord ...Aderholt ...Dearborn ... and their men ...engaged in military training ...passed 'brown bags filled with cash' to members of the government ...and above all, set up an airline on the model of Air America, which soon was picking up hundreds of Muhajidin mercenaries in Afghanistan," Peter said. "I think I mentioned that either in my book, *Drugs, Oil & War*, or Cooley did, in *Unholy Wars*, or Thomas Goltz's, *Azerbaijan Diary, A Rogue Reporter's Adventures in an Oil-Rich, War-Torn, Post-Soviet Republic* ... citing Irkali, Kodrarian, and Ruchala, in *Sobaka Magazine*, 2003. As part of the airline operation, Azeri pilots were trained in Texas. Dearborn had previously helped Secord advise and train the fledgling Contra air force, according to a book authored by Marshall, Hunter and myself," Peter said, "...*The Iran-Contra Connection*. These important developments were barely noticed in the U.S. press ...but, a 1994 *Washington Post* article did belatedly note ... a group of American men who wore 'big cowboy hats and big cowboy boots' had arrived in Azerbaijan as military trainers for its army, followed in 1993 by 'more than 1,000 guerrilla fighters from Afghanistan's radical prime minister, Gulbuddin Hekmatyar.' Whether the Americans were aware of it, or not ...the al Qaeda presence in Baku soon expanded, to include assistance for moving jihadists onwards into Dagestan, and Chechnya. Secord and Aderholt claim to have left Azerbaijan *before* the Muhajidin arrived.

<>

"Meanwhile, Hekmatyar, at the time allied with bin Laden, was observed recruiting Afghan mercenaries (Arab Afghans, Arab Nazis) to fight in Azerbaijan ... against Armenia and its Russian allies. At this time, heroin flooded from Afghanistan, through Baku, into Chechnya Russia, and North America. Over the course of the next two years, MEGA Oil procured thousands of dollars worth of weapons ...and, recruited two thousand Afghan mercenaries, for Azerbaijan ... the first Muhajidin to fight on the territory of the former Communist Bloc. In 1993 the Muhajidin contributed to the ouster of Azerbaijan's elected president, Abulfaz Elchibey, and his replacement by an ex-Communist Brezhnev-era leader, Heidar Aliyev. At stake, was an 8 billion dollar oil contract with a consortium of western oil companies, headed by British Petroleum ...including a pipeline which would, for the first time, not pass through Russian-controlled territory ... when exporting oil from the Caspian basin to Turkey. Thus, the contract was bitterly opposed by Russia, and required an Azeri leader willing to stand up to the former Soviet Union.

<>

"The Arab Afghans helped supply muscle, their eyes set on fighting Russia in the disputed Armenian-Azeri region of Nagorno-Karabakh ...and, in liberating neighboring Muslim areas of Russia, Chechnya, and Dagestan. The 9/11 Report notes, the bin Laden organization established an NGO in Baku, which became a base for terrorism elsewhere.

"It also became a trans-shipment point for Afghan heroin to the Chechen mafia, whose branches 'extended not only to the London arms market ...but, also throughout continental Europe, and North America, according to Cooley's, *Unholy Wars*. Arab Afghans' Azeri operations were financed in part with Afghan heroin. Police sources in Moscow reported, 184 heroin processing labs were discovered in Moscow alone, last year. 'Every one of them was run by Azeris, who use the proceeds to buy arms for Azerbaijan's war against Armenia, in Nagorno-Karabakh,' according to Russian economist, Alexandre Datskevitch. This foreign Islamist presence in Baku was supported by bin Laden's financial network ...with bin Laden's guidance ...and, Saudi support. Baku soon became a base for jihadi operations against Dagestan and Chechnya, in Russia. Pakistan's ISI, facing its own disposal problem with the militant Arab-Afghan veterans, trained and armed them in Afghanistan ... to fight, in Chechnya. ISI encouraged the flow of Afghan drugs westward, to support the Chechen militants ...thus, diminishing the flow into Pakistan itself. Michael Griffin observed, regional conflicts in Nagorno-Karabakh, and other disputed areas ...Abkhazia ...Turkish Kurdistan ...and, Chechnya ... each represented a distinct, tactical move, crucial at the time, in discerning *which* power would be master of the pipelines to transport oil and gas from Caspian basin, to the world.

<>

"Wealthy Saudi families, al-Alamoudi (Delta Oil), bin Mahfouz (Nimir Oil) participated in the western oil consortium with the American firm, Unocal. Oct. 2001, U.S. Treasury Department named among charities allegedly supporting terrorism, the Saudi charity, Muwafaq Blessed Relief, to which the al-Alamoudis and bin Mahfouz families were identified as major contributors, according to *Boston Herald*, Dec. 2001. It's unclear whether MEGA Oil was a front for U.S. Government ...or, for U.S. oil companies ...and, their Saudi allies.

<>

"U.S. oil companies were accused of spending millions of dollars in Azerbaijan, not just to bribe the government ...but also, to install it. According to a Turkish intelligence source who was an alleged eyewitness, major oil companies, including Exxon and Mobil, were 'behind the coup d'état' ... which in 1993 replaced the elected President, Abulfaz Elchibey, with his successor, Heydar Aliyev.

<>

"The source claimed to have been at meetings in Baku, with 'senior members of ...BP ...Exxon ...Amoco ...Mobil ...and, Turkish Petroleum Co. The topic was oil rights ...and, on insistence of the Azeris, supply and arms to Azerbaijan. Turkish secret service documents allege, middlemen paid off key officials of the democratically elected government of the oil-rich nation ...just before its president was overthrown, according to *London Sunday Times*, Mar. 2000. The true facts and backers of the Aliyev coup may never be fully disclosed. But unquestionably, before the coup, efforts of ...Richard Secord ...Heinie Aderholt ...Ed Dearborn ...and Hekmatyar's Muhajidin ... helped contest Russian influence, and prepare for Baku's shift away, to the west. Three years later, Aug. 1996, Amoco's president met with Clinton, and arranged for Aliyev to be invited to Washington. Clinton in a 1997 press statement said, 'in a world of growing energy demand, our nation cannot afford to rely on a single region for our energy supplies. By working closely with Azerbaijan to tap Caspian resources, we not only help Azerbaijan to prosper, we help diversify our energy supply, and strengthen our energy security'.

"U.S., Al Qaeda, and oil company interests converged again in Kosovo. There, the al Qaeda-backed UCK or, Kosovo Liberation Army KLA, was supported and empowered by NATO, beginning in 1998, according to a source in Tim Judah's, *War & Revenge* ...KLA reps had already met with American, British, and Swiss intelligence agencies, in 1996 ...possibly, several years earlier. This would presumably have been back when Arab Afghan members of the KLA, like Abdul-Wahid al-Qahtani, were fighting in Bosnia, according to Evan Kohlmann's, *Al-Qaeda's Jihad in Europe, The Afghan-Bosnian Network*. Mainstream accounts of Kosovo War are silent about al Qaeda training and financing the UCK/KLA ...yet, this fact is recognized by experts ...and to my knowledge, never contested by them. For example, James Bissett, former Canadian ambassador to Yugoslavia, said, 'Many members of Kosovo Liberation Army were sent for training in terrorist camps in Afghanistan. Milosevic is right. There's no question of al Qaeda's participation in conflicts in the Balkans. It's very well documented,' according to *National Post*, 2002. Mar. 2002, Michael Steiner, United Nations administrator in Kosovo, warned of 'importing the Afghan danger to Europe ... because several cells trained, and financed, by al-Qaeda remained in the region. Back in 1997, UCK/KLA was recognized by U.S. as a terrorist group, supported in part by heroin traffic. *Washington Times*, 1999, reported it. The Kosovo Liberation Army, which Clinton administration embraced ...and, some members of Congress want to arm ... as part of the NATO bombing campaign ...is a terrorist organization, that financed much of its war effort with profits from the sale of heroin.' Al," Peter said, "in your book, *Politics of Heroin in Southeast Asia*, you agreed?"

"Yes," the real McCoy said. Al McCoy opened his book and read, "Albanian exiles used drug profits to ship Czech and Swiss arms back to Kosovo for separatist guerrillas of the Kosovo Liberation Army (KLA). In 1997-98, these Kosovar drug syndicates armed the KLA for a revolt against Belgrade's army. Even after the 1999 Kumanovo agreement settled the Kosovo conflict, the UN administration of the province ... allowed a thriving heroin traffic along this northern route from Turkey. The former commanders of KLA, both local clans, and aspiring national leaders, continued to dominate the transit traffic through the Balkans.'"

Peter nodded, then continued reading. "Once again, as in Azerbaijan, these drug-financed Islamist jihadists received American assistance, this time from the U.S. Government. At the time, critics charged that U.S. oil interests were interested in building a trans-Balkan pipeline ... with U.S. Army protection ...although initially ridiculed, these critics were eventually proven correct. BBC News announced Dec. 2004, a 1.2 bil-

lion dollar pipeline, south of a huge new U.S. army base in Kosovo, was given go-ahead by governments of ...Albania ...Bulgaria ...and, Macedonia. Closeness of UCK/KLA to al-Qaeda ... was acknowledged again, in the western press, after Afghan-connected KLA guerrillas proceeded, in 2001, to conduct guerrilla warfare in Macedonia. Press accounts included an Interpol report containing the allegation, one of bin Laden's senior lieutenants was commander of an elite UCK/KLA unit operating in Kosovo, in 1999.

"Marcia Kurop in *Wall Street Journal Europe*, Nov. 2001 elaborated, 'The Egyptian surgeon-turned-terrorist leader Ayman Al-Zawahiri operated terrorist training camps, weapons of mass destruction factories and money-laundering and drug-trading networks throughout Albania, Kosovo, Macedonia, Bulgaria, Turkey and Bosnia,' and Yossef Bodansky, director of the U.S. Congressional Task Force on Terrorism and Unconventional Warfare, collaborated. 'Bin Laden's Arab Afghans assumed a dominant role in training the Kosovo Liberation Army [by mid-Mar. 1999 the UCK included] many elements controlled and/or sponsored by the ...U.S. ...German ...British ...and, Croatian intelligence services,' Marcia said. "DEA reported, 2000, Afghan heroin accounted for 20 percent of heroin seized in the U.S., nearly double the percentage taken four years earlier. Much of it distributed by Kosova Albanians.

<>

"Petroleum money in two Bush presidents' Administrations was also prominent, under Clinton. A former CIA officer complained about the oil lobby's influence with Sheila Heslin of Clinton's National Security Council staff, according to Robert Baer's, *See No Evil, The True Story of a Ground Soldier in the CIA's War on Terrorism*. 'Heslin's sole job, it seemed, was to carry water for an exclusive club known as Foreign Oil Companies Group, a cover for a cartel of major petroleum companies doing business in the Caspian. Another thing I learned was, Heslin wasn't soloing. Her boss, Deputy National Security Adviser Sandy Berger, headed the inter-agency committee on Caspian oil policy ...which made him in effect, the government's ambassador to the cartel, and Berger wasn't a disinterested player. He held $90,000 worth of stock in Amoco, probably the most influential member of the cartel ... The deeper I got, the more Caspian oil money I found sloshing around Washington,' Baer said. "The oil companies' meeting with Sheila Heslin in summer of 1995 was followed shortly by creation of an interagency governmental committee to formulate U.S. policy toward the Caspian. Clinton Administration listened to oil companies ...and, in 1998 began committing U.S. troops to joint training exercises in Uzbekistan. This made neighboring countries, Kazakhstan and Turkmenistan ...wary of Russia ...more eager to grant exploration and pipeline rights to American companies. Clinton didn't yield to Unocal's strenuous lobbying in 1996 for U.S. recognition of the Taliban ... as a condition for building the pipeline from Turkmenistan. Clinton declined, in the end, to do so ...responding instead to strongly voiced political opposition from women's groups over Taliban treatment of women.

<>

"The three-group effort of ...Al Qaeda ...oil companies ...and, the Pentagon ... is still visible in the case of Azerbaijan ...now, the Pentagon is protecting the Aliyev regime. Dept. of Defense as first proposed, Azerbaijan also receives an International Military Education and Training IMET grant, of $750,000 ...and, a Foreign Military Financing grant, of 3 million dollars in 2003 ... as part of the war on terrorism ...but later admitted, the funds were actually intended to protect U.S. access to oil in-and-around the Caspian Sea, according to Johnson's, *Sorrows of Empire.*

"Due to al Qaeda, U.S. bases have sprung up close to oilfields and pipelines in ...Uzbekistan ...Tajikistan ...Georgia ...and, Kosovo. Michael Klares', *Blood and Oil, Dangers and Consequences of America's Growing Dependency on Imported Petroleum,* comments, 'Already U.S. troops from Southcom Southern Command are helping defend Colombia's Cano Limón pipeline. Likewise, soldiers from Eurcom European Command are training local forces to protect the newly constructed Baku-Tbilisi-Ceyhan pipeline, in Georgia. Finally, ships and planes of Pacon U.S. Pacific Command, are patrolling vital tanker routes in ...Indian Ocean ...South China Sea ...and, western Pacific. Slowly but surely, U.S. military is being converted into a global oil-protection service.'.

<>

"But in Aug. 2002, Saudi Arabia's Sudairy faction turned against the U.S. The U.S. press was slow to report an AP story, available from Spanish, pro-Israeli, and pro-Palestinian sources, Saudi officials announced they would not permit the U.S. to use the important Prince Sultan Air Base, south of Riyadh, for U.S. retaliatory attacks against any Muslim country," Peter said. "I first read of this story Nov. 21. It doesn't seem to have reached the U.S. press until Nov. 23, when Colin Powell commented in a way that didn't really deny it. The original account of Saudi Arabia's unexpected refusal to supply bases for retaliation against bin Laden was corroborated in an important report from the usually reliable, Strategic Forecasting private intelligence website, Stratfor.com.

<>

"According to Stratfor analysis, the Saudi royal family is divided ...as it has been since the 1960s, between two factions of half-brothers, (1) the al-Sudairy faction (all full brothers) led by King Fahd and Defense Minister Sultan, who all favor, profit, and gain power from the Saudi alliance with the U.S. ... and (2) the religious coalition of half-brothers led by aging Crown Prince Abdullah, whose piety is backed by alliances with Wahhabi religious leaders. Tensions between the two factions, usually leading to compromises, underlie recent developments in the bin Laden story. In late August, shortly before the WTC attack, Prince Turki al-Faisal (with links to the religious faction) was dismissed from his post, as head of Saudi intelligence. Unquestionably, Prince Turki had from the Afghan campaign developed close relations with Osama bin Laden ...and, was later charged by the Saudi family to negotiate for bin Laden's surrender by the Taliban, according to Rashid's Taliban. But, his replacement and uncle, Nawwaf, is also allegedly a member of the religious faction. In the wake of 9/11 WTC attacks, Crown Prince Abdullah, with aging King Fahd in a Swiss hospital, surprised the U.S. ... by denying the use of Prince Sultan Air Base, for retaliatory attacks against any Muslim country. But three days later, Sept. 26, Foreign Minister Prince Saud announced, Saudi Arabia was breaking relations with the Taliban, accusing it of contradicting Islam ...and, harboring terrorists. But the Stratfor analysis ignores the relevance of Saudi family divisions to highly contested maneuvers over an Afghan pipeline. Splits in the Saudi royal family led to support by different Saudi princes ...for each of the two competing multi-billion dollar proposals ... to build a gas pipeline across Afghanistan.

<>

"Prince Turki was allied with the Argentine company Bridas ... while Prince Abdullah was close to the Saudi company, Delta Oil, part of the U.S.-backed consortium headed up by Unocal. There is speculation in Europe whether the sudden dismissal of Turki by Abdullah in late

August, was a factor in precipitating the 9/11 attacks a few days later.

<>

"Seymour Hersh in *New Yorker* comments, NSA intercepts demonstrated to Washington analysts 'that by 1996 Saudi money was supporting Osama bin Laden's Al Qaeda, and other extremist groups in Afghanistan, Lebanon, Yemen, Central Asia, and throughout the Persian Gulf region.' Hersh adds, it was hard for analysts to impress their discoveries on senior officials of the Clinton and Bush administrations ...a fact to be considered ...in light of enormous Arab petrodollar investments in the political system of this country," Peter said.

<>

Carl Trocki's, *Opium, Empire and the Global Economy,* brought us a look from yesterday into today. Carl took the floor, "Opium was the tool of the capitalist classes to transform the peasantry, and monetize their subsistence lifestyle. Opium created pools of capital, and fed the institutions that accumulated it ...banking and financial systems, ...insurance systems ...transportation ...and, information infrastructures. Those structures, and that economy, have in large part been inherited by successor nations of the region today ... links between drug trades ...European colonial expansion ...creation of global capitalism ...and, creation of the modern state. Drug trades destabilized existing societies, not merely because they destroyed individual human beings ...but also, and perhaps more importantly, because they've the power to undercut the existing political economy of any state. They've created new forms of capital ...and, they've redistributed wealth in radically new ways. The trade in such drugs usually results in some form of monopoly ...which not only centralizes the drug traffic, but also restructures much of the affiliated social and economic terrain, in the process. In particular, two major effects are ...the creation of mass markets ...and, the generation of enormous, unprecedented, cash flows. The existence of monopoly results in concentrated accumulation of vast pools of wealth.

<>

"Accumulations of wealth, created by a succession of historic drug trades ... have been among the primary foundations of global capitalism, and the modern nation-state, itself.

<>

"Indeed, it may be argued that the entire rise of the west, from 1500 to 1900, depended on a series of drug trades ... the image of the 'opium empire', a metaphor first offered by Joseph Conrad. It takes up the early history of opium, and other 'traditional drugs' such as tea, tobacco, and sugar and develops the paradigm of commercialized drug trades and ties ... that led to the growth of European colonialism in the Americas and Asia. Opium, thus created a succession of new political and economic orders in Asia during the past two centuries. These included the state of the East India Company, itself ...the new Malay polities of island Southeast Asia ...the colonial states of nineteenth-century Southeast Asia ...and, the warlord regimes of post-Qing China ... as well as the Guomindang and communist states that arose from that milieu. At the same time, economies of the entire region were radically reoriented, or perhaps, 're-occidented' would be more appropriate. India's opium production was brought under western control while China's domestic economy was opened to the west. Southeast Asia was first opened to western traders, and then, to western control. With migration of Chinese labor, Southeast Asian economies were transformed into commodity-producing regimes, focused on exporting to industrializing western powers. Underlying all this, opium rearranged the domestic economies, and pushed them down the path of mass consumption, which with mass production, typified the 'modern' economic order. It is possible to suggest a hypothesis that mass consumption, as it exists in modern society, began with drug addiction. And beyond that, addiction began with a drug-as-commodity. Something was necessary to prime the pump, to initiate cycles of production, consumption, and accumulation ... that we identify with capitalism. Opium was the catalyst of the consumer market, the money economy, and even, of capitalist production itself in 19th Century Asia," Carl said.

<>

Nancy jumped in. "I hope this conversation hasn't ruined anyone's appetite. After all, control of oil isn't nearly as critical to the U.S. as maintaining dominance in exchange of oil ... in U.S. 'dollars'. If Iran opens its oil stock exchange in Mar. 2006, openly competing with the U.S. monopoly on trading oil in petrodollars ...then, central banks across the globe will dump hundreds of billions of dollars overnight ...and, the American economy will disappear beneath the waves."

<>

Nancy started to escort everyone to dinner in the ranch house ...then, said it would be a few more minutes ... everyone stayed put.

It was at that point I fell on my hands and knees, raising my palms up to heaven ... because Mel's Jesus was descending from the clouds. He had with him the shimmering peacock-green ghost of Paul Robeson, with his little gold Frisbee-hat ghost companion. Everyone looked horrified.

I tried to explain. "Can't you see Mel's Jesus and Paul Robeson's ghost?"

Everyone backed away from me, Nancy, afraid, hesitated to come over to me. That little gold Frisbee-hat ghost couldn't hold still for a second, zipping around the estate perimeter, buzzing low over my head. I ducked several times. I guess I was freaking everyone out pretty much, they drifted back into the dimness, "Why are you haunting me?!"

Robeson's ghost spoke. "We are one humanity."

"What's that supposed to mean?"

A light beam big as a searchlight came out of him and shot into me. I fell to the ground, unconscious. I was dead.

<>

No one seemed to notice. Nancy acted normally, scurrying around, reminding everyone dinner would be ready soon. The ranch nurses lifted me up, sat me down in my chair overlooking the sea. It was as if nothing happened. Patti, Ron Jr., Michael, Maureen, all Patti's guests went in to dinner. I was alone, watching the sea from the cliffs. Paul Robeson's ghost stood next to me.

Paul Robeson greeted me. "Welcome home."

The little Frisbee ghost shot back and forth, hovering around, like R2D2, in Starwars. Suddenly, a thousand suns rose over the sea, giant roses the size of houses bloomed all round me, night fell. The air was clean, it felt the way it did when I was a kid, clean, exhilarating. Everything kept going on as normal ... as if I had never lived at all.

Dave picked up an envelope of papers, paraphrasing David Morse's, *War of the Future, Oil Drives the Genocide in Darfur,* and read from it. "The North-South conflict started when Chevron discovered oil in southern Sudan in 1978. The Khartoum government was Arab-dominated ..and, gerrymandered jurisdictional boundaries ... to exclude the oil reserves from southern jurisdiction. John Garang, leader of the rebel Sudan People's Liberation Army (SPLA), declared oil pipelines, pumping stations, and well-heads ... to be targets of war.

<>

"For a time, oil companies fled the conflict ...but, in 1990s began to return. Chinese and Indian companies were aggressive, doing their drilling behind perimeters of bermed earth ...guarded by troops, to protect against rebel attacks. A Chinese pipeline to the Red Sea first brought Sudanese oil to international markets.

"The northern regime in Khartoum wanted to impose shariah, or, Islamic law, on the Christian and animist South ...but, Khartoum dropped this demand ... under terms of the Comprehensive Peace Treaty, signed Jan. 2004 ... a treaty brokered with help of the U.S. ...signed at the expense of Darfur in western Sudan, an oil rich desert, the size of France. The South was permitted to have it's own civil law, including, rights for women. But, oil revenues would be divided between Khartoum ... and Sudan People's Liberation Army, SPLA. Under a power-sharing agreement, SPLA commander John Garang would be installed as vice president of Sudan. Darfur, to the west, was left out of the treaty.

"In western Sudan, Darfur is more Muslim and less Christian than southern Sudan ...but, black African, and identifies by tribes such as the Fur ... Darfur, means 'land of the Fur'. In Darfur the practice of Islam was not extreme enough to suit the Islamists who controlled Khartoum in northern Sudan, so Darfur villages were burned to clear the way for drilling and pipelines, the land seized from Black farmers being given to Arabs from neighboring Chad. 'In north Sudan, oil revenues to Khartoum have been about 1 million dollars a day, exactly the amount which the government funnels into arms, helicopters and bombers from Russia, tanks from Poland and China, missiles from Iran. Oil is fueling genocide in Darfur,' Morse said. In 1997, 'when President Clinton added Sudan to the list of states sponsoring terrorism, government officials in Khartoum explained away the slaughter in Darfur ... as being an ancient rivalry between nomadic herding tribes in the north and Black African farmers in the south,' Morse said, they denied responsibility for the militias, and claimed, they couldn't control them ... but continued training, arming and paying the militias, Khartoum playing down its Islamist ideology and support of Osama bin Laden while imposing Islamic fundamentalism in Sudan. In Darfur, terrorist tactics of the Arab-dominated government, burning, pillaging, castration, and rape, are carried out by Arab militias riding on camels and horses. The Islamist regime manipulated ethnic, racial, and economic tensions as part of a strategic drive to commandeer the country's oil wealth ... claiming about two million lives, mostly in the south, many by starvation, when government forces prevented humanitarian agencies from access to camps, another four million Sudanese remained homeless.

"Gabon, Angola and Nigeria began exploiting oil several decades ago and suffer from intense corruption. In Nigeria, as in Angola, an overvalued exchange rate destroyed the non-oil economy. Local revolts over control of oil revenues triggered sweeping military repression in the Niger delta. Oil and exploration companies like Halliburton wield political and sometimes military power.

"In Sudan, roads and bridges built by oil firms are used to attack otherwise remote villages. Canada's largest oil company, Talisman, is in court for allegedly aiding Sudan government forces in blowing up a church and killing church leaders, in order to clear land for pipelines and drilling. Under public pressure in Canada, Talisman sold its holdings in Sudan. Lundin Oil AB, a Swedish company, withdrew under similar pressure from human rights groups. Keith Bradsher's *Two Big Appetites Take Seats at the Oil Table* in *New York Times*, observes. 'As Chinese and Indian companies venture into countries like Sudan, where risk-aversive multinationals hesitate to enter, questions are raised in the industry if state-owned companies are accurately judging risks to their own investments, or if they are just more willing to gamble with taxpayers' money than multinationals are willing to gamble with shareholders' investments,' Keith said.

"In Sudan, Chinese state-owned companies exploit oil in the thick of fighting. In Jun. 2005, following new seismographic exploration in Sudan and with the power-sharing peace treaty about to be implemented, Khartoum and SPLA signed a flurry of oil deals with Chinese, Indian, British, Malaysian, and other oil companies. Secretary of State Colin Powell stated Sept. 2004, United States determined genocide was happening in Darfur, but Bush had no comment after he was re-elected, the Bush Administration lobbied in Congress against the Darfur Peace and Accountability Act. That bill called for beefing up the African Union peacekeeping force and imposing new sanctions on Khartoum, including referring individual officials to the International Criminal Court. The White House undercut Congressional efforts to stop genocide, seeking closer relations with Khartoum on grounds the regime was 'cooperating in the war on terror.'

"According to Morse, 'Nowhere is the potential impact of renewed war more threatening than in camps of refugees, the 4 million Internally Displaced Persons driven from their homes during the North-South civil war and several hundred thousand encamped at fringes of Khartoum as squatters or crowded into sprawling ghetto neighborhoods. Further west, in Darfur and Chad, 2.5 million IDPs live in precarious limbo in makeshift camps, shelters cobbled together from plastic and sticks, prevented by conscripted soldiers of Khartoum armies from returning to their villages, wholly dependent on outside aid.'

"*Guardian*, Nov. 2005, Declan Walsh, *Sudan at the Head of Global Sweep to Mop Up World's Oil Resources.* 'A tangle of pipes and metallic towers rises over the shimmering, rock-strewn desert north of the Sudanese capital Khartoum. The gleaming oil refinery is the jewel of Sudan's oil boom, the mid-point of a 900-mile pipeline from southern oilfields to the Red Sea, projected to pump 500,000 barrels a day by the end of this year. But, if the oil is African, the money and management are Chinese. Inside refinery gates, Chinese engineers man distillation towers, Chinese cooks serve rice and noodles in the canteen, workers pedal between giant oil drums on bicycles imported from Beijing. 'We like Sudan very much,' said Zhao Yujun, 35, a manager with state-owned China National Petroleum Corp., which built the sprawling plant five years ago. 'China needs energy for economic growth. There is oil in Africa. That is why we come here.' China is prowling the globe in search of energy sources. Oil executives and diplomats have signed a flurry of deals, from Canada to Kazakhstan.

"The scramble triggered unease in Washington, where American conservatives worry about China's growing economic muscle, but has sparked an unprecedented engagement with Africa. Chinese business is blazing a trail across the continent. Trade with China has almost tripled in five years. Railways in Angola, roads in Rwanda, a port in Gabon and a dam in Sudan have all been paid for with Chinese loans and built by Chinese contractors. Business with Nigeria and South Africa is booming. And this year, China is expected to overtake United Kingdom as Africa's third largest trading partner. The driving ingredient is oil. China's flagship African project is in Sudan. Isolation from the west meant Khartoum barely pumped a barrel of crude a decade ago. Now, after intensive Chinese investment, it has the third largest oil business in sub-Saharan Africa. China shipped in thousands of workers to build the Heglig pipeline in record time, and a second pipeline is under construction. The Khartoum refinery, CNPC's first outside China, opened in late 1999, just in time for the 10th anniversary of the coup that brought military leader Omar al Bashir to power. Sudan is expected to earn more than £1bn in oil revenues this year and its economy is one of the fastest growing in Africa. Where western companies shy away because of corruption, conflict or the risk of losing their shirts, Chinese firms are plunging in. President Hu Jintao dispatched diplomats to dangle large, low-interest loans before impoverished countries with the sole stipulation that work is done by Chinese contractors. African governments also appreciate China's tendency to keep its nose out of domestic affairs. In contrast with the demands for transparency that accompany loans from international bodies such as the International Monetary Fund, Chinese help comes on a strictly 'no questions asked' basis. Earlier this year, Angola's president, Jose Eduardo dos Santos, who presides over a famously oil-rich but poverty-stricken country, received a £1.1bn line of credit from Beijing. Beijing also came to the rescue of Zimbabwe's embattled president, Robert Mugabe, presenting him with ornamental tiles for the roof of his palace and an honorary degree in recognition of his 'remarkable contribution in the work of diplomacy and international relations. 'If you're a corrupt government that wants loans with no conditions, you will like the Chinese. But it's not good for the people of the country,' said Sarah Wykes of Global Witness, a UK-based lobby group.

<>

"Western hostility towards Sudan's military regime paved the way for one of China's sweetest deals in Africa. In 1996, when the regime was an international pariah for sheltering Osama bin Laden and human rights abuses, CNPC bought shares in a government oil venture on highly favorable terms. At the Khartoum refinery, Sudanese and Chinese co-workers communicate in a mix of Arabic, Chinese and English. In offices Chinese officials play with their mobile phones beside Muslim managers kneeling on prayer mats. But in the city, Sudanese businessmen grumble that Chinese projects give little and take much. 'They bring everything from China, labor, materials, the lot,' said one prominent trader who asked not to be named. South Africans worry that cheap imports are swamping their textile industry,' Walsh said. 'China has deployed peacekeepers to UN missions in Liberia and Congo,'" Dave said. He continued, "An AP story, Daniel Balint-Kurti, Sept. 2005. 'Buguma, capital of the ancient Kalabari kingdom in Nigeria, is vivid testimony to the downside of Africa's oil. A

gutted local government building stands by the central square near a smashed statue of the town's founding king. Soldiers patrol the streets. These are scars from a three-month occupation last year by a private militia whose members are accused of rapes and random killings, and dozens of villages in the oil-rich Niger River delta have seen similar violence. 'We are in a state of emergency,' said the head of Buguma's Council of Chiefs, Mangibo Amachree, 62. Soldiers are keeping the peace for now, and Amachree prays they will stay until the 2007 presidential election, which already is raising fears of more fighting. Often, oil money is a driving force in pushing long-standing political rivalries to the boiling point. Buguma's unrest is at least partly over royalties that Amachree says are paid to King Theophilus Princewill by Shell, the major oil producer in Kalabari.

<>

"Four rival militias have fought over who should be king and, therefore, get the royalties. In London, Shell spokesman Simon Buerk said the company has never paid royalties to local potentates, but 'homage payments' are allowed, limited to $1,000 per project since 2003. A Shell report said it spent $100,000 on such payments last year in Nigeria. President Olusegun Obasanjo also has angered Nigerians by approving fuel price increases to reflect high global oil prices, drawing strike threats from labor unions. Most Nigerians see cheap fuel as the only benefit they had in a country that has no welfare system and where more than 70 percent of the people live on less than $1 a day. More than 20,000 protesters marched Wednesday in Lagos in a peaceful protest of price increases of as much as 40 percent on gas and diesel that were ordered by the government last month. The development group Catholic Relief Services and a World Bank watchdog office said in a report on Chad, which began exporting oil last year, oil industry growth in repressive, corrupt and poor countries too often results in more repression and corruption. Equatorial Guinea, Africa's fifth-largest oil producer, is known for human rights abuses and mismanagement, and its oil wealth is thought to have attracted foreign coup plotters.

<>

"Twenty-four European and African mercenaries were sentenced to lengthy prison terms last year for scheming to oust the tiny nation's leader. In Nigeria, disputes over oil have caused bloodshed for years, a situation brought to the fore in 1995, when writer Ken Saro-Wiwa and eight other activists from his Ogoni tribe were executed under the brutal regime of then-dictator Gen. Sani Abacha. They were hanged for the murder of four political rivals, but Saro-Wiwa's supporters say he was really targeted because he led protests against environmental damage by Shell.

<>

"The company is still negotiating its return to that area. Hundreds of people were killed in Rivers state last year in fighting between two ethnic Ijaw militias, one led by secessionist Moujahid Dokubo-Asari and the other by Ateke Tom, who describes himself as a vigilante leader. Conflict involving other militias continues near Buguma. Soldiers were sent recently to the village of Bukuma after eight people were killed by a youth militia called D12, local residents said. School attendance has fallen by half in Buguma since fighting broke out in Feb. 2004. Fishermen's catches are reduced because they no longer dare to venture far out into the delta's rivers and creeks, where attacks have become common. Ayachi Emesiobi hid in her home when militia fighters suspected of being allies came calling. Her mother, Monima Atiboba, opened the door. They 'called her out and shot her,' said Emesiobi, 29. 'I heard it … one shot.' When she went outside, her mother was dead. School shut down during last year's three months of occupation, and girls were raped. Classes resumed after Dokubo-Asari's Niger Delta People's Volunteer Force and an allied local militia chased out invaders. Three days later, the army ran off Dokubo-Asari's fighters. In his hometown of Okrika, next to major oil city of Port Harcourt in Rivers state, Tom said reports of summary killings in Buguma by his group were 'lies'. He denied having anything to do with Buguma's three-month occupation, although he acknowledged participating in a brief raid there after Dokubo-Asari set up a camp,' he said. 'Any civilians killed were hit by stray bullets.'"

<>

"From Matthew Yeomans' *Oil: Anatomy of an Industry*, Sept. 2004," Dave continued, "when President Bush announced a radical redeployment of 70,000 active duty U.S. military personnel currently based in Western Europe and Asia in mid-August, he stressed this new agile military would be focused on combating terrorism and fostering global stability.

<>

"What he didn't mention is, newly dispersed Army, Marines, Navy and Air Force will also be busy protecting another key component of U.S. national security, energy resources. The plan, which Pentagon has been explaining in dribs and drabs over the past year, is to rotate troops through a large number of bases scattered all over the world, with special attention given to the so-called 'arc of instability' running through the Caribbean rim, Africa, Central Asia, the Middle East, South Asia, North Korea and the Caucasus. The new formation includes boosting new regional hub bases and establishing minimally-staffed forward operating bases that might house a few dozen troops but could be quickly transformed into action-ready staging bases. Since 2001, new military bases have been established in Eastern Europe and Central Asia … including Bulgaria, Azerbaijan, Romania, Kyrgyzstan and Uzbekistan, allowing the U.S. to keep watch over the Islamic tinderbox of Central Asia and the strategically crucial Caspian Sea oil region, which will soon supply millions of barrels of oil to the U.S. and Western Europe markets. Other bases in Afghanistan, Qatar, Saudi Arabia, Djibouti and Oman, not to mention the huge military garrison in Iraq, guarantee a strong and long-term presence in the Persian Gulf, while new pacts with Nigeria and other West African nations will ensure the U.S. military keeps a watchful eye on another important oil region, the Gulf of Guinea.

<>

"Energy security has been a mainstay of U.S. foreign policy ever since Franklin Roosevelt pledged to provide military protection to Saudi Arabia in return for unfettered access to the Kingdom's oil. In 1980, the so-called 'Carter Doctrine' declared the U.S. intention to intervene militarily to counter any threat to Middle East security. And in May 2001, Dick Cheney's 'National Energy Policy' announced the Bush administration would 'make energy security a priority of our trade and foreign policy'. The recent redeployment of military forces is one more reaffirmation in the post-Cold War global order, preserving access to energy resources is the prime strategic imperative. The seeds of the latest twist in new energy protection policy were sown in 2002 when Congress authorized 98 million dollars for U.S. troops and equipment to help the Colombian army protect oil pipelines owned by California company, Occidental.

"'The pipelines were regular targets of the FARC and ELN, two main leftist rebel groups in Colombia's 40-year civil war. In spring 2003, as U.S. forces were invading Iraq, a far smaller group of 70 Green Berets flew into Colombia to secure Oxy's pipeline. Funds were authorized under proviso of the administration's war on terrorism, but the military training had more to do with the National Energy Policy. The Andean nations of Ecuador, Venezuela and Colombia contribute 20 percent of U.S. imported oil. Colombia is 10th largest oil supplier for the U.S. and Bush administration has made increased imports from Andean nations an important part of its goal of lessening dependence on Middle East oil. Colombia's oil is easy to produce and output could be significantly increased were oil companies not targeted so often. The national government uses a good deal of its oil profits, 25 percent of the country's annual revenues, to fight the rebels. Pentagon is concerned with other areas of the world identified by U.S. government as crucial to its energy future. Caspian Sea, especially waters of Azerbaijan, Kazakhstan and Turkmenistan, could prove one of the largest oil finds in the world after the Middle East. In 2000, oil companies discovered the Kashagan field off the coast of Kazakhstan, the single largest oil find in 40 years. By end of the decade, Kazakhstan is destined to be world's fifth largest oil producer. U.S. has invested heavily in the Caspian region. U.S. companies have put billions of dollars into oil and gas projects, and both Clinton and Bush administrations worked hard to curry favor with former Soviet republics and limit influence of Russia, Iran and China in the process.

"Since 2001, the U.S. has not only established military bases in the region, but it has conducted joint Navy exercises with Azerbaijan in the Caspian and supported Kazakhstan's push to establish its own Navy.

<>

"The U.S. Coast Guard even patrols the Caspian Sea, and the combined U.S. military presence makes Russia ... whose Caspian fleet has long exercised de-facto control over the sea, very edgy. As General Charles Wald, deputy commander of U.S. European Command, explained to the *Wall Street Journal,* Jun. 2003, 'In the Caspian you have large mineral reserves. We want to be able to assure long-term viability of those resources.' Of central concern to the U.S. is the Baku to Ceyhan (BTC) pipeline, a million-barrel-a-day project headed by BP, running from Baku Azerbaijan, through Nagorno Karabak, a region claimed by both Azerbaijan and Armenia, into the turbulent republic of Georgia, and on to the Black Sea port of Ceyhan. From there, oil would be shipped via tanker through the Bosphorus into the Mediterranean on its way to Europe and the U.S. With new military bases in Romania and Bulgaria, a U.S. rapid response force is in easy reach of the Caucasus region to counter any threat to the supply of Caspian Oil. And in Georgia, U.S. forces have been training local military to counter armed Islamic groups operating out of the lawless, Pankisi gorge.

<>

"The stated purpose of this training is to fight the War on Terror, but insurgent activity now also threatens world oil security.

"So far, West Africa poses less of a threat to energy security than Persian Gulf or the Caspian. Jun. 2003, on the eve of President Bush's first visit to Africa, only the second time a sitting U.S. president had visited, General James Jones, commander of U.S. European command, gave an interview to *New York Times,* in which he outlined another layer of the U.S. military's shift in global priorities. The U.S. was negotiating with a number of African nations for long-term use of military bases, to help combat terrorist groups that may be operating in the region. Areas of interest included Algeria, Morocco, and also sub-Saharan venues like Mali. Augmenting these bases would be a strong U.S. Navy and Marine force operating in Gulf of Guinea off coast of West Africa. The carrier battle groups of the future may not spend six months in the Mediterranean sea,' Jones said, 'but, I'll bet they spend half their time going down the west coast of Africa.' There are very few known terrorist outfits in the waters off West Africa, but there is an enormous amount of oil.

"Africa possesses an estimated 80 billion barrels of oil, 8 percent of total world crude reserves. U.S. imports 16 percent of foreign oil from this part of the world, and by 2015 it's expected to rise to 25 percent. That makes African oil, in the words of U.S. Undersecretary of State for African affairs, Walter Kansteiner, 'a national strategic interest.' Nigeria, Angola and Equatorial Guinea, all of them serious oil powers in their own rights, have territorial claims to Gulf of Guinea, and U.S. oil companies including ExxonMobil, ChevronTexaco, ConocoPhilips and Marathon, along with many other foreign companies, all have invested heavily in the region.

<>

"No nation has whetted the appetite of oil majors more than Sao Tome e Principe, a tiny island 500 miles west of Equatorial Guinea. Over 20 oil companies have bid for rights to drill in waters off Sao Tome, in a concession jointly run by the island's government and neighboring

Nigeria. Sao Tome has also been wooed by the U.S. military, which would like to build a naval base on the island. Indeed, for a leader of just 150,000 people, president Fradique de Menezes could be said to be hitting above his weight. In Sept. 2002, de Menezes was one of nine African leaders that Bush hosted at the White House. All nine preside over sizeable deposits of African oil. Just in case Sao Tome doesn't pan out, U.S. military recently agreed to conduct joint oil protection operations with Nigerian forces in Niger Delta region of the country, where insurgents from local ethnic communities have targeted international oil workers ...in a campaign to force out the major oil companies.

<>

"'As U.S. searches for new ways to reduce reliance on Middle East oil, protecting energy supplies from Latin America, Central Asia and West Africa take on greater importance. The new realignment of its global military will likely see the U.S. risk placing its armed forces in danger in the most treacherous and politically unstable areas of the world ...for decades to come. It's a scenario likely to be replayed not just in Persian Gulf, but also across Central Asian republics, West Africa, Southeast Asia and Latin America and anywhere else in the developing world new oil is found. The net result may ensure America gets oil it needs, but it is a policy that makes the U.S. secure, not safer,' Mathew said. 'More U.S. troops will perish protecting oil, and hatred of America will expand beyond ravings of Islamic extremists,'" Dave said.

Dave continued. "Paul Roberts, *Washington Post, Undeclared War on Oil*, Jun. 2004. 'For months China and Japan have been locked in a diplomatic battle over access to big oil fields in Siberia. Japan, which depends entirely on imported oil, is desperately lobbying Moscow for a 2,300-mile pipeline from Siberia to coastal Japan. Fast-growing China, world's second-largest oil user after U.S., sees Russian oil vital for its own 'energy security', and is pushing for a 1,400-mile pipeline south to Daqing. Petro-rivalry is so intense, Japan has offered to finance the 5 billion dollar pipeline, invest 7 billion dollars in development of Siberian oil fields and throw in an additional 2 billion dollars for Russian 'social projects' ... this despite the certainty if Japan does win Russia's oil, relations between Tokyo and Beijing may sink to their lowest, potentially most dangerous, levels since World War II.

"'In 'emerging' economies, Brazil, India and especially China, energy demand is rising so fast it may double by 2020. This hints at the energy crisis facing the developing world, where 2 billion people, a third of the world's population, have almost no access to electricity or liquid fuels, and are condemned to medieval existence that breeds despair, resentment and, ultimately, conflict.

<>

"'Already we see outlines. China and Japan are scrapping over Siberia. In the Caspian Sea region, European, Russian, Chinese and American governments and oil companies are battling for a stake in big oil fields of Kazakhstan and Azerbaijan. In Africa, the U.S is building a network of military bases and diplomatic missions, whose main goal is to protect American access to oilfields in volatile places such as Nigeria, Cameroon, Chad and tiny Sao Tome. And, as important, to deny access to China and other thirsty superpowers. In the run-up to the Iraq war, Russia and France clashed noisily with the U.S over whose companies would have access to the oil in post-Saddam Hussein Iraq.

[Editor's note: Helps explain complex fighting groups in Iraq fighting the U.S. ... oil war between Russia, France, China & the U.S. (similar to the 1918 Russian revolution)... all financing and out-fitting different mercenary terrorist group segments to stage conflict against each other, with a common purpose, to clear the land for oil – and run up the national debts by all involved to the benefit of the private majority shareholders of the Fed, and their interlocking presence with Bank of England and others.]

<>

"'Less well known is the way China sought to build up its own oil alliances in the Middle East, often over Washington's objections. In 2000, Chinese oil officials visited Iran, a country U.S. companies are forbidden to deal with ... China also has a major interest in Iraqi oil. But China's most controversial oil overture has been made to a country America once regarded as its most trusted oil ally ... Saudi Arabia.

"'In recent years, Beijing has been lobbying Riyadh for access to Saudi reserves, the largest in the world. In return, the Chinese have offered the Saudis a foothold in what will be the world's biggest energy market, and, as a bonus, have thrown in offers of sophisticated Chinese weaponry, including ballistic missiles and other hardware, that the United States and Europe have refused to sell to the Saudis,'" Roberts said.

"And last, from *Power & Interest News Report*, an article by Adam Wolfe, Feb. 2004," Dave said. "'China's Gross Domestic Product rose at 9.1 percent in 2003, and surpassed Japan to become the world's second-largest oil importer after the U.S. Domestic energy production is rapidly expanding, but China continues to rely on imported fuel to keep its economy growing. The expectation that China will continue to demand more and more oil from foreign countries is beginning to reshape relationships between oil producing countries, and has had an effect on the U.S. 'war on terrorism'. The seemingly endless demand for energy has persuaded China to focus attention on finding foreign sources of oil and gas. China sits on major deposits of coal ... China hoped to build a pipeline from Russia to avoid the cost of shipping oil through the Black Sea, but Russia's prosecution of the Yukos Oil Company stymied this effort. Russia and Saudi Arabia are jockeying for position as the global leader in crude oil exports, with each country hovering around 8 million barrels per day. The importance of oil to each country's economy forces the leaders to change diplomatic strategies in reaction to China's demand for energy. Because China's need for oil is so great, neither country is interested in pursuing an aggressive strategy to weaken the other. A Brunswick UBS analyst sums up the situation. 'We believe that growing demand far in excess of Russian production offers the most realistic and probable outcome that would alleviate OPEC of the need to confront Russia dramatically, although the risk is present.' As long as the Chinese economy continues to expand, Russia will persist on working with the Middle Eastern producers, but Russia has not forgotten the lessons of 1985, when the Saudis used excess production capacity to drive down oil prices to $12 a barrel, which wrecked any hopes of Soviet survival. [Editor's note: And helped finalize the destabilization of Soviet Union and Eastern Europe.]

"Russia is demanding far more for its cooperation with OPEC during this cycle of increased demand. In September 2003, Crown Prince Abdullah bin Abdul Aziz of Saudi Arabia visited Russia and signed a five-year cooperation agreement. Then, in Jan. 2004, Akhmad Kayrov, pro-Moscow president of Chechnya, visited Riyadh. Saudis agreed to halt all funding for Islamic rebels in Chechnya and recognize his government.

<>

"Greater cooperation between the two largest suppliers of crude oil will leave producing countries in a better position to keep prices at higher levels, which will affect the bottom line of nearly every industry, in practically every country.

<>

"'Saudi Arabia's recognition of the Chechnya government has made it a target for Islamic militants and will only stoke the fire that keeps al-Qaeda and similar organizations full of willing recruits,' Adam said. 'China's economic rise has already begun to reshape the world in many ways, but perhaps its greatest effect will be on the global market for energy supplies. While Asia purchases nine out of ten barrels of oil from the Middle East, China pursues Russia as its major supplier," Dave said.

<>

The reason given for the dollar's devaluation by Paul Volcker in the middle of my Reagan Administration, as far as the public was to know according to the Fed, was to reduce the U.S. current account deficit ...that's spending more money than you take in ... of the balance of payments ...that's a measure of the payments that flow in and out from a country to and from other countries determined by exports and imports of goods, services, and financial capital and transfer payments including net investment income ...so, in the first years of my Reagan Administration the U.S. current account deficit reached 3.5% of gross domestic product ...so, the Fed inflated and devalued the dollar ... on grounds it was helping the U.S. economy emerge from a serious recession ... that's like having your parents reduce your allowance so you can buy more ...that all began in the early 1980s with my arrival in office. Paul Volcker's Fed overvalued the dollar enough to make U.S. industry, especially the automobile industry, less competitive in the global market.

Why in God's name would they weaken the American economy? ...unless they had allegiance to ...and the ability to make great profits from ... supporting foreign national economies?

<>

Is this not treason? ...reason? Devaluing the dollar made U.S. exports cheaper for its trading partners to buy ...so, they bought more exports ...but, devalued dollars at home meant domestic goods ...food ...rent ...gas ...clothes ... were more expensive for Americans, at home. Again, treason? ...reason? The Plaza Accord ... (signed by the G-5 nations, France, West Germany, Japan, the United States and United Kingdom) to devalue the U.S. dollar in relation to the Japanese yen and German Deutsche Mark ... by fixing currency markets ...so, the exchange rate of the dollar versus the yen declined 51% over two years, cutting the value of the American dollar in half) ... was successful in reducing the U.S trade deficit with Western European nations ...but, failed to fulfill its Fed-stated primary objective of alleviating the trade deficit with Japan ...because, this deficit was due to Japanese structural rather than monetary conditions, which the Fed knew in the first place. Therefore was the maneuver aimed at enriching the German economy, allowing Germany to buy exported American technology at half-price, and American real estate and businesses at half-price, since the devaluation was 50%?

Historically, the Fed uses economic war tactics to reduce the value of debts it owes ...by cheapening the money supply ...or, increasing value of debts owed to it ... by making money owed to it more expensive, why? Then, major shareholders make purchases of American goods and services and capital with foreign currency ... at the sacrificial, 'bankruptcy' sales they've created. Treason? ...reason?

<>

So, U.S. manufactured goods ...and, everything else in the damn country ... became more competitive (cheaper) for foreigners (i.e. Fed foreign agents of Fed majority shareholder foreign-held interests), in the exports market ...but, the Fed was unable to succeed in the Japanese domestic market due to Japan's structural restrictions on imports, which the Fed knew beforehand. *Duh?* The recessionary effects of the strengthened yen in Japan's export-dependent economy created an incentive for the expansionary monetary policies that led to the Japanese asset price bubble of the late 1980s ...plus, American currency was devalued ...and, suddenly ... Japanese (not to mention Fed shareholders using Yen) started buying up waterfront acreage in New Jersey overlooking Manhattan, for example. The Louvre Accord was signed in 1987 to halt the continuing decline of the U.S. Dollar. Wasn't that special? And, the Fed scored another financial currency victory for their holdings in Germany. Fed at work. Wins for itself ...not the American people.

The Japanese asset price bubble was a time of skyrocketing land and stock prices in the Japanese economy, lasting from 1986 to 1990. At the height of the bubble, "it was a matter of pride that land around Imperial Palace in Tokyo was at one point worth more than California," *Financial Times* said. Japan regained a sense of national pride ...and, assertiveness ... as a result of its new power, which manifested itself in works such as, *The Japan That Can Say No*, by Shintaro Ishihara and SONY founder Akio Morita. Accounts report high-level executives eating gold-sprinkled food ...and, eating with gold

chopsticks. Many in the U.S. and other countries were alarmed by the Japanese resurgence, leading to criticism from foreign observers. Real estate was highest in Tokyo's Ginza district in 1989, with some fetching over $139,000 per square foot, and a bit less exorbitant in other areas of Tokyo. But, by 2004, prime 'A' property in Tokyo's financial districts were less than 1/100th of their peak ...and, Tokyo's residential homes were 1/10th of their peak, but still managed to be listed as the most expensive real estate in the world.

<>

Some U.S. $20 trillion in 1999 dollars was wiped out with the combined real estate and Nikkei stock market collapse. The time after the collapse which occurred gradually rather than catastrophically, of the bubble, is known as the lost decade in Japan. Wasn't that special? Fed at work.

<>

During my Reagan Administration Baker served on the Economic Policy Council, where he was instrumental in achieving passage of the Administration's tax and budget reform legislation package in 1981. Baker served on my National Security Council ...and, remained my Treasury Secretary through 1988 ...during which year, he also served as campaign chairman for Bush's successful presidential bid.

Bush appointed Baker Secretary of State in 1989, awarding him the Presidential Medal of Freedom, in 1991. From 1992 to 1993 Baker was named Bush's Chief of Staff. Baker is credited as a leading architect of the peaceful transition from communism to democracy in Europe, beginning in 1989.

Together with President Bush, Chancellor Helmut Kohl and German Foreign Minister Genscher ... Baker is one of the inspirators of German reunification. Baker helped construct the 34-nation alliance that fought alongside the U.S. in the Gulf War. In Mar. 1997, Baker became Personal Envoy of the UN Secretary-General for Western Sahara.

<>

Baker served as chief legal advisor for George W. Bush during the 2000 election campaign ...and, oversaw the Florida recount. He is currently, as of 2004, the last year of my life according to Mel's Jesus, a senior partner at the law firm of Baker Botts, and senior counsel to the Carlyle Group.

<>

In late 2003, he was drafted by the President

to assist in operations of the U.S.-led occupation of Iraq. Baker is also special envoy to the president ... to persuade other countries to relieve Iraqi debts.

Geneva, 1929

Patriarchs of the families Rothschild, Warburg, Shroder, Hoover, Brown brothers, Harriman, Walker, Bush, Dulles, Sullivan, and Cromwell sat in a men's club, in the Swiss Alps overlooking Lake Geneva. Joining them were Nazi Freikorps death squad Brownshirts ... Count Sergei DeMohrenshieldt, Prince Max von Hohenlohe, Otto von Bolschwing, Martin Bormann, and Otto Skorzeny son-in-law of international German banker Hjalmar Schacht, there, too.

Allen Dulles sniffed brandy, his Cuban cigar burning between his lips. Nice high. "Gentlemen, this great depression of ours, the financial warfare we wage, lets us buy the world's gold short ...and, industry and banks, to control western currency. Financial coup d'état, n'est pas? The poor, middle class, and upper class suffer ... not us, we ride the top of the pyramid ...people we loan money to, give credit to, suffer ... not us ... we foreclose on real estate, businesses, homes, countries ...buy bankrupt currencies, mining, petroleum and timber rights, without a shot ...pushing pencils on ledger sheets. We American, British and Nazi intelligence agents are one Fed team, protecting mankind from itself. We are the World Order."

Saudi Arabia, 1929

Allen Dulles' plane landed on the sand in Arabia, met by Sheik Ibn Saud ... a terrorist warlord Dulles helped select then finance as a front to eliminate other warlords and takeover Arabia.

He got out, "Are arms and gold shipments getting through?"

Sheik Ibn Saud nodded. "Yes. Terrorist units eliminated rival sheiks. We own the desert and oil beneath."

Dulles sucked his cigar. "Want me to name Arabia after you? ...Saudi Arabia."

"Yes," Ibn Saud said.

Dulles lit his cigar. "First, destroy Syrian ruling families ...I want the Syria and Turkey drug trade, not just their banks and oil ...we'll make them lower Iran and Iraq oil prices."

Saud knew how to accomplish his goal. "More assassinations will do it."

"You'll run the gold toilet trade, harem trade, sex slave trade, traffick in children like you want ...no one can stop you."

Wall Street, 1929

Allen Dulles flew to New York, chauffeured from the airport to Wall Street. Aside from double scheduling lunch with German-handled Czarist intelligence informers on top of Herbie Walker and Prescott Bush, who'd brought his son, George, everything was clockwork.

May of 1932, Allen Dulles wrote a letter to brother John Foster Dulles, 'With the Prussian election, it seems to me the question of the participation of the Hitler element in the Prussian government, and then in the Reich government will again be agitated. Personally, I hope their participation will be worked out, as I feel any government in France would be very reluctant to enter into far-reaching agreements with a German government which was not in some way underwritten, or approved by the Hitler element.'

The Depression, 1931

Meanwhile, I went to a Eureka college on a football scholarship ... in early years of the Great Depression. Eureka College was a Catholic college. I wasn't going to become a priest, I was half-Catholic, half-Protestant. I wanted to be a first string football player, like my big brother. I just wasn't good football material. Believe it or not, I actually led a student strike at school. Please don't tell the kids at UC Berkeley, it would kill 'em. At Eureka, students wanted a different Chancellor. I was president of the student body. I was a sharp kid, outgoing, friendly, respected for my brains ...so, while I got elected student body president of Eureka college, Franklin D. Roosevelt got elected President of the United States. My dad Jack, was unemployed ...then, found work in a New Deal work-relief program. I was so happy! I start memorizing Roosevelt's speeches, doing Roosevelt impersonations for friends. Roosevelt was inspirational ... he got Dad work. Roosevelt was the father of the 'New Deal' modern welfare state ... back when 'welfare' was not a dirty word, he was the guy who got Dad a job to care for Mom. Welfare wasn't dirty then, it kept Mom and Dad alive ...it was human survival, the reason for the Bill of Rights and Declaration of Independence, common sense, plain love, the reason for government in the first place. Hundreds of thousands of U.S. citizens marched the streets for thirty years ... to earn the right ...for minimum wages ...voting rights for women ...the end of child labor ...living wages ...rights to have a union protect them from Fed majority shareholder ruling family greed, pathological, sociopathic, genocidal ... greed ...when a country's ruling families cannibalize its citizenry, make them wage slaves ... robots.

In the twenties and thirties in America, sociopathic CEO's hired goons to break strikes, they didn't care about wage slaves. It was the Old Testament all over again, Pharaoh using Jew slave labor to build pyramids in modern dress. Big business in America ...Morgan, Ford, DuPont, General Motors ... they applauded Hitler and Mussolini outlawing unions ...Hitler was on the cover of *Time Magazine,* as man of the year, followed by Mussolini. Corporate America *wanted* Fascism over Democracy ... Fascism meant low wages, more money in the pockets of the corporate directors.

After graduating Eureka in 1932, I got a job as a radio announcer with WOC in Davenport, Iowa ... the job of my dreams ...and, I turned twenty-one years old ...and, I had Mary. I went around bragging, everything was good for me. Me and Mary were in a food line, I was singing a Broadway song, *'Sittin' on top of the world'.* We'd be eatin' soon. Here I was, a life guard hero in a small town ... inside, where no one could see me, in a food line, the hero who saved many kids from drowning, now waiting with those kids in line for handouts ...I was ashamed.

But, I had to set a good example for the kids.

So, me and Mary sang, tried to make 'em all happy, got our soup and bread, sat down at a table, said grace, someone changed the radio station to Father Kauflin! Wow. My lucky day.

"Father Kauflin here, attacking Godless communism today. I'm talking about the Russian Bolshevik menace of socialism sweeping across the United States ... communistic ideas of taking money from the wealthy to support the poor, ruining the world for Christ!" Kauflin said.

The man next to me turned off the radio.

I was angry, but careful to sound upbeat, "You don't go in for Christ? I wanted to hear what Father Kauflin has to say."

The man looked at me, shook his head, "Hunger's hunger. Too many rich people. Too many hungry people. God didn't issue deeds," the man said.

"I don't like you," I said. I went back to eating. Out the soup kitchen windows, I could see across the street. The sheriff and deputies boarded up homes and businesses, kicking out kids, parents, taking keys away, handling them over to bankers I knew.

I threw my napkin down angrily on the table. "Them doing that, makes me mad," I said.

Mary shrugged, "Me too. I know, let's think about last night."

I started blushing, "Let's do it again, tonight." I waved goodbye to everyone, we left the soup kitchen, crossed the street to the radio station where I worked. I was lucky to have a job. Mary left. I walked in the broadcasting booth. My job was to read the news ticker tape that came in the broadcasting booth through a slot in the wall, read it into the microphone ... like I was really at a baseball game.

I began announcing, "Batter has stepped up to the plate. He's swinging the bat back and forth to show his strike zone. Here comes the pitch! Swung on ...and, missed! The pitcher looks over to first base, there's a runner on third. He's starting his wind up. It's a fast ball straight down the middle."

The tape stopped coming in through the wall. I looked through the slot, a spring shot out of the teletype machine, a little cloud of smoke rose up. I stared at the blank tape in my hand, no idea what was going on in the game. Now, what was I gonna do? I didn't want to lose my job. So, I made it up as I went along, announcing the game ... like, I was there. "It's a fast ball, he swings! It's a hit! Runners are advancing. Ball's short, in right field, runner from third is halfway home, outfielder's thrown the ball to the catcher, it's gonna be close, folks! ...safe!"

After the broadcast the station manager came in. "Good save, Ronnie. You got commercials in, too. Here's a few bucks for you. You've got a raise. From now on ... you go cover games, live," my boss said.

"Really?! That's great!" I said. I was tickled pink. I knew I'd be bringing home the bacon for mom tonight! The truth is, when it comes to news on the radio and TV, most people don't know what the truth is, cause no one's tellin' it to 'em. That never changes. I went to the food store, bought two bags of groceries, brought 'em home, put them on the kitchen table for Mom. She was praying when I came in. She opened her eyes, saw the grocery bags on the table.

"I've been praying for food, you answered my prayers, Ronnie," Mom said.

I felt tears roll down my cheeks. It's not often I saw Mom cry, much less was able to make her happy, to stop the tears. I started traveling around the country, covering baseball games live for the station, fulfilling my childhood dream. But, I had a new dream picked out. I arranged to cover a series in Los Angeles ....but, got someone else to cover it, skipped it, and went to acting tryouts at the studios. They called me back, gave me a screen test, I passed. I called home to tell Mom and Dad.

"Mom, no more going hungry. I got a contract to make movies in Hollywood. The Depression's over for us, Mom!"

"Ronnie, praise Jesus! I bet you're glad for those church plays, now."

"Mom, I always liked acting in those with you."

"Tell your father."

I felt let-down, hearing her say that. "Is he sober?"

"Here he is."

"Dad, Dad, are you there?" There was no reply. I felt sad. I hung up the phone.

<>

Eustace Mullins, *Secrets of the Federal Reserve,* researched the Great Depression.

Mar. 1926, British economist R.G. Hawtrey in *American Economic Review* shared his view. 'When external investment outstrips the supply of general savings the investment market must carry the excess with money borrowed from the banks. A remedy is control of credit by a rise in bank rate,' Hawtrey said. Federal Reserve Board applied this control of credit, but not in 1926, nor as a remedial measure. It was not applied until 1929, and then the rate was raised as a punitive measure, to freeze out everybody but big trusts.

Feb. 6, 1929, Bank of England Governor Montague Norman came to Washington to confer with U.S. Treasury Secretary Andrew Mellon. After the visit, Federal Reserve Board changed its policy ...then, pursued a high discount rate policy, abandoning the cheap money policy it inaugurated in 1927 ... after Mr. Norman's other visit. The Federal Reserve System set up the Depression, first by causing inflation, and then raising the discount rate and making money dear.

The stock market crash and the deflation of the American people was scheduled to take place in March. To get the ball rolling, Paul Warburg gave an official warning to traders ...get out of the market.

Mar. 1929, speaking to stockholders of his International Acceptance Bank, Warburg reasoned, "If orgies of unrestrained speculation are permitted to spread, the ultimate collapse is certain not only to affect the speculators themselves, but to bring about general depression involving the entire country."

During three prior years of 'unrestrained speculation', Paul hadn't seen fit to make any remarks about the condition of the Stock Exchange. *New York Times* gave Paul's report two columns on its editorial page, commenting on Paul's wisdom. The stock market bubble had gone farther than intended ... and bankers feared consequences ...if people realized what was going on. The *New York Times* editorial started a sudden wave of selling on the Exchange ... bankers grew panicky ...it was decided to ease the market somewhat ...so, Warburg's National City Bank rushed 25 million dollars in cash to the call money market ...and, postponed the day of the crash.

Those in the know began to sell off speculative stocks, and invest in government bonds ...those who kept speculative stocks, lost everything.

Wall Street Broker Curtis Dall's, *FDR, My Exploited Father-in-Law,* explains, "It was a calculated 'shearing' of the public by the world money-powers ...triggered by planned sudden shortage of supply of call money in the New York money market," Dall said.

Overnight, the Fed raised the call rate to 20%.

Fed New York rate set national interest rates ...it went to 6% Nov. 1, 1929. After investors were bankrupted, it dropped to 1.5% May 31, 1931.

Congressman Wright Patman's, *Primer On Money*, said the money supply decreased by 8 billion dollars from 1929 to 1933, causing 11,630 banks of the total 26,401 in the U.S., to go bankrupt and close their doors.

Fed warned their family of majority stockholders of Federal Reserve Banks ...get out of the market ...on February 6, 1929 ... but didn't say anything to the rest of the country.

J.P. Morgan, and Kuhn, Loeb 'preferred lists' ...people on these lists were notified of the coming crash, and sold all but gilt-edged stocks, such as General Motors and DuPont. Prices on these stocks sank to record lows, but came up afterwards.

A May 30, 1936, *Newsweek,* story describes Fed board member and banker, Ralph Morrison's actions in 1929. "He sold his Texas utilities stock for 10 million dollars and in 1929 called a meeting and ordered his banks to close out security loans by Sept. 1. As a result, they rode through the depression with flying colors," *Newsweek* said.

Yes, big bankers rode through the depression with flying colors. The people who suffered ...were workers and farmers, who invested their money in get-rich stocks.

There had been some warning of the approaching crash in England, that American newspapers never saw.

May 25 1929, *London Statist,* commented. "Banking authorities in the U.S. apparently want a business panic to curb speculation," Statist said.

May 11, 1929, *London Economist,* shared its view. "Events of the past year saw beginnings of a new technique, that if maintained and developed, can succeed in 'rationing the speculator ..without injuring the trader."

Fed Governor Charles S. Hamlin quoted this statement at the 1931 Senate hearings, "That was the feeling of certain members of the Board, to remove Federal Reserve credit from the speculator without injuring the trader," Hamlin said. Hamlin didn't bother to point out the *'speculators'* he was out to break ... were school-teachers and small town merchants, who put their savings into the stock market, or the *'traders'* he was trying to protect, were big Wall Street operators ... such as Bernard Baruch, and Paul Warburg.

When New York Fed raised its rate to 6% Aug. 9, 1929, market conditions began tremendous selling orders, from Oct. 24 into November ...that wiped out 160 billion dollars of security value.

That was 160 billion dollars American citizens had one month ... and did not have the next.

By comparison, our outlay of money and goods in World War II was 200 million dollars ...but, a great deal of that remained as negotiable securities in the national debt.

When New York Fed raised its rate to 6% Aug. 1929, people began to get out of the market ...it turned into a panic which drove prices of securities down, far below natural levels. As in previous panics, Wall Street and foreign operators *in the know,* picked up 'blue-chip' and 'gilt-edged' securities, for a fraction of real value.

Leader of the American people during the Crash of 1929 ...and the subsequent depression ... was Herbert Hoover.

Oct. 24 1929. after the first break of the market, being 5 billion dollars in security values that disappeared ... President Hoover commented. "Fundamental business of the country, that is, production and distribution of commodities, is on a sound and prosperous basis," Hoover said.

Dec. 25 1929, Treasury Secretary Mellon commented. "Government's business is in sound condition." Andrew Mellon's own business, Aluminum Company of America, apparently was not doing as well ...he reduced wages of all employees, 10%.

Apr. 7, 1931 *New York Times* reported. "Montague Norman, Governor of the Bank of England, conferred with the Federal Reserve Board, here today. Mellon, Meyer, and George L. Harrison, Governor of the Federal Reserve Bank

of New York, were present."

Bank of England sent Norman over, this time, to make sure the Great Depression was proceeding according to plan. July 4, 1930, *New York Times* quoted Congressman Louis McFadden. "Commodity prices are being reduced to 1913 levels. Wages are being reduced by the labor surplus of four million unemployed. Morgan's control of the Federal Reserve System is exercised through control of the Federal Reserve Bank of New York, with mediocre representation and acquiescence of the Federal Reserve Board in Washington," McFadden Said.

Eustace continues. As the Depression deepened, the trust's lock on the American economy strengthened ...but, no finger was pointed at the parties controlling the system. Crash of 1929 saw the formation of giant holding companies ...that picked up cheap bonds and securities ... such as Marine Midland Corporation, Lehman Corporation, and Equity Corporation. In 1929, J.P. Morgan Co. organized the Standard Brands giant food trust. There was unequaled opportunity for trust operators to enlarge and consolidate holdings. Looking back, Emmanuel Goldenweiser, Federal Reserve System director of research commented in 1947, "It is clear in retrospect the Board should have ignored speculative expansion, and allowed it to collapse of its own weight," Goldenweiser said. This admission of error eighteen years later was no comfort to people who lost their savings in the Wall Street Crash of 1929 ...the beginning of world-wide credit deflation, which lasted thru 1932 ...and from which Western democracies did not recover till they began to rearm for World War II.

<>

Eustace continues.

Nobody knew what was going on, except Wall Street bankers running the show. Gold movements were unreliable.

Quarterly Journal of Economics commented. "The question has been raised in this country and in European countries, whether customs statistics record with accuracy, movements of precious metals ...and, when investigation occurs, confidence in such figures has weakened rather than strengthened. Movement between France and England for example, should be recorded in each country ...but, comparison shows an average yearly discrepancy of 50 million francs for France, and 85 million francs for England ...unaccounted for."

Aug. 1928. *Quarterly Journal of Economics,* quoted Professor Cassel, "When a central bank fails to raise its bank rate in accordance with the actual situation of the capital market, it increases cyclical movement of trade with destructive effects on social economy. A bank rate regulated this way alters trade cycles, and our familiar trade cycles become a thing of the past," Cassel said. Cassel's premise supposes business depressions are artificially created ... Panic of 1907, Agricultural Depression of 1920, and Great Depression of 1929 ...all three ... in good crop years, and in periods of national prosperity ...suggests Cassel's premise holds.

Maynard Keynes pointed out, theories of business cycle fail to relate analysis to the money mechanism. Surveys and studies of depression that fail to list gold movements and pressures on foreign exchange, are useless.

May 1925, British Parliament passed the Gold Standard Act, that put Great Britain back on the gold standard. Federal Reserve System's role in this was shown, March 16 1926, when Richmond Federal Reserve Governor George testified to House Banking & Currency Committee. "Verbal understanding, confirmed by correspondence, extended Great Britain a 200 million dollar gold loan ...or, 'credit'. All negotiations were conducted between Benjamin Strong, Governor of the Federal Reserve Bank of New York, and Mr. Montague Norman, Governor of the Bank of England. The purpose of this loan was to help England get back on the gold standard, and the loan was to be met by investment of Federal Reserve funds in bills of exchange and foreign securities," the Governor said.

June 25 1926, *Federal Reserve Bulletin* commented, "Under its arrangement with Bank of England, Federal Reserve Bank of New York undertakes to sell gold on credit to the Bank of England from time to time during the next two years, but not to exceed 200 million dollars outstanding ...at any one time," the bulletin said. A 200 million dollar gold credit was arranged by verbal understanding between international bankers Benjamin Strong and Montague Norman ...Federal Reserve System had interests at heart other than financial needs of American business and industry.

Great Britain's return to gold standard was facilitated by additional gold loans of 100 million dollars from J.P. Morgan Co. Winston Churchill, British Chancellor of Exchequer, complained, the cost to the British government of the loan was $1,125,000 the first year ... this sum representing profit to J.P. Morgan Company that year.

<>

Oct. 17 1928, *New York Times* described directors of the three great central banks meeting in Europe, in July, 1927. "Mr. Norman, Bank of England, Benjamin Strong of New York Federal Reserve Bank, and Dr. Hjalmar Schacht of Reichsbank, their private meeting was referred to at the time as a meeting of 'the world's most exclusive club'. No public reports were made of the foreign conference, which was informal ...but, which covered important questions of gold movements, stability of world trade, and world economy."

Creating the Great Depression

Eustace continues.

House Stabilization Hearings of 1928 proved Federal Reserve System Governors were meeting with heads of big European central banks. Even if Congressmen knew the plan was to create the Great Depression of 1929-1931 ... there would be nothing they could do to stop it ...international bankers who control gold movements can inflict their will on any country, and the U.S. was as helpless as any other.

Eugene Meyer's family, House of Lazard Freres, specialized in international gold movements.

League of Nations achieved its goal of getting nations of Europe back on the gold standard by 1928 ...but 3/4s the world's gold was in France and U.S.

The problem was, how to get that gold to countries which needed it as a basis for money and credit ...the answer was, action by the Federal Reserve System.

Following the private meeting of the Federal Reserve Board and heads of foreign central banks in 1927 with Norman, Schacht, and Strong, Federal Reserve Banks in a few months doubled their holdings of Government securities and acceptances ... resulting in the exportation of 5 million dollars in gold in that year. Federal Reserve System's market activities forced rates of call money down on the Stock Exchange ... and forced gold out of the country. Foreigners took this opportunity to purchase heavily in Government securities because of the low call money rate.

[Ed's note, definition of, *call money rate...* Interest rate banks charge to brokers to finance margin loans to investors ...also 'broker loan rate'. Three definitions of margin, apply here, (1) Using money borrowed from a broker-dealer to purchase securities, also called, 'buying on margin', (2) amount of equity required for an investment in securities purchased on credit, (3) face value of a loan ... minus value of pledged collateral.

Apr. 20, 1928 C. Barron's *They Told Baron* comments, "The agreement between Bank of England and the Washington Federal Reserve authorities many months ago was, we would force export of 725 million dollars of gold ... by reducing bank rates here ...helping stabilization of France and Europe, and putting France on a gold basis."

Changes in gold stock and movement in price levels shows the standard is not automatic in operation. The gold standard is managed and controlled for the benefit of a small group of international traders.

Aug. 1929, Fed raised the rate to 6%. Next month, Bank of England raised its rate from 5.5% to 6.5%.

In Sept. 1929 *Review of Reviews,* Dr. Friday comments, "Fed statement Aug. 7 1929, shows no signs of inadequacy for autumn requirements exist. Gold resources are more than the previous year, gold continues to move in, to the financial embarrassment of Germany and England. Reasons for the Board's action must be sought elsewhere. The public was given a hint, 'This problem has presented difficulties because of peculiar conditions'. Every reason which Governor Young advanced for lowering the bank rate last year, exists now. Increasing the rate means, there's danger of drawing gold from abroad ...but, imports of the yellow metal are in progress the last four months. To accentuate this will bring on a world-wide credit deflation," Dr. Friday said.

In 1930, President Herb Hoover appointed Eugene Meyer Jr. to the Federal Reserve Board.

In 1935, Paul Einzig commented, "President Roosevelt was in favor of a monetary policy in a deliberately engineered rise in prices. In a negative sense, his policy was successful. Between 1933-1935 he succeeded in reducing private debt, by increasing public debt."

Roosevelt eased debt off
the rich, onto the poor

In 1938, Sen. Robert Owen testified before House Committee on Banking & Currency, "I wrote into the bill which was introduced by me in the Senate on June 26 1913, a provision that powers of the Federal Reserve System should be employed to promote a stable price level ... which meant, a dollar of stable purchasing, debt-paying power. It was stricken out. Powerful money interests got control of the Federal Reserve Board through Paul Warburg, Albert Strauss and Adolf Miller ...they were able to have that private meeting May 18, 1920 ...and, bring about a contraction of credit so violent it threw five million people out of work.

"In 1920 the Reserve Board deliberately caused the Panic of 1921. The same people, unrestrained in the stock market, expanded credit to a great excess between 1926-1929 ...raised price of stocks to a fantastic point where they couldn't possibly earn dividends ...and, when the people realized this, they tried to get out ...resulting in the Crash of Oct. 24, 1929," Owen said.

Sen. Owen didn't raise the question... Can the Fed be held responsible to the public? No. They're public officials appointed by the President ...but, their salaries are paid by private stockholders of the Federal Reserve Banks.

In 1921, Fed Governor Harding commented, "Federal Reserve Bank is an institution owned by stockholding member banks. The Government has not a dollar's worth of stock in it."

Eustace said, "However, the Government does give the Federal Reserve System use of its billions of dollars of credit, and this gives the Federal Reserve its characteristic of a central bank ... the power to issue currency on the Government's credit. We don't have Federal Government notes, or gold certificates, as currency. We have Federal Reserve Bank notes, issued by Federal Reserve Banks ...and, every dollar they print ... is a dollar in their pocket."

Banks of issue

In 1930, Randolph Burgess of New York Federal Reserve Bank commented before Academy of Political Science, "In its major principles of operation, the Fed is no different from other banks of issue ...such as Bank of England, Bank of France, or Reichsbank."

Central banks issue currency in their own countries. People do not own their own money in Europe, nor here ...it is privately printed for private profit. People have no sovereignty over their money.

Eustace had a clear view, "As a central bank of issue, when Fed began operations in 1913, it was a threat to central banks of impoverished countries of Europe. Because Fed represented great wealth, it attracted more gold than desirable in the 1920s ...and, it was apparent ... all of the world's gold would be piled up in the U.S. This would make the gold standard a joke in Europe ...because, they'd have no gold to back their issue of money and credit. So, it was the Fed's avowed aim in 1927, after meeting with heads of foreign central banks, to get large quantities of that gold sent back to Europe ... and, its methods of doing so ...the low interest rate ...and, heavy purchases of Government securities ...created vast sums of new money ...intensified stock market speculation ...and, made the stock market crash, and resultant depression, a national disaster.

"Since the Fed was guilty of causing this disaster, we might suppose they'd have tried to alleviate it. However, through dark years of 1931-1932, Fed Governors saw the plight of the American people worsening, and did not help. This was more criminal ... than the original plotting of the Depression.

"Anyone who lived through those years in this country remembers widespread unemployment, misery, and hunger. At any time during those years, the Fed could have relieved this situation. The problem was, get money back in circulation. So much money normally used to pay rent, and food bills, was sucked into Wall Street ...that, there was no money to carry on the business of living. In many areas, people printed their own money on wood and paper for use in their communities ...and, this money was good, since it represented obligations to each other which people fulfilled.

"Federal Reserve System was a central bank of issue. It had the power to, and, when it suited it's owners, issued millions of dollars of money. Why did it not do so in 1931-1932? Wall Street bankers *were through* with Herbert Hoover ...they wanted Franklin D. Roosevelt to come in, on a wave of glory as a white knight and national savior. So, the American people starved and suffered ... til Mar. 1933 ...then, money was put into circulation.

As soon as Roosevelt took office, Fed began buying Government securities ... spending 10 million dollars a week, for ten weeks and created a 100 million dollars in new money ...which alleviated the critical famine of money and credit ...and, factories started hiring people again."

In 1930, when Hoover appointed Meyer Jr. to the Federal Reserve Board, several Senators did not believe Meyer should hold public office ... because of questionable handling of billions of dollars in Government securities during World War I ...and his family background as an international gold dealer. So, the Senate held Hearings to determine if Meyer could serve on the Federal Reserve Board.

Feb. 1931 *World's Work* commented, "When the World War began for us in 1917, Eugene Meyer, Jr. was among the first called to Washington. In April, 1918, President Wilson named him,

Director of the War Finance Corporation. This corporation loaned out 700 million dollars to banking and financial institutions."

House Banking & Currency Committee Chairman Louis McFadden commented, "Eugene Meyer had his own crowd with him in the government since he started in 1917. His War Finance Corporation personnel took over the Federal Farm Loan System ...and, almost immediately, the Kansas City Joint Stock Land Bank and Ohio Joint Stock Land Bank failed."

The Senate Hearings on Eugene Meyer, Jr. continued.

Representative Rainey

Mr. Meyer, when he nominally resigned as head of the Federal Farm Loan Board, did not cease his activities there. He left behind an able body of wreckers. They are continuing his policies and consulting with him. Before his appointment, he was in consultation with Assistant Secretary of the Treasury Dewey. Just before his appointment, Chicago Joint Land Stock Bank, Dallas Joint Stock Land Bank, Kansas City Joint Land Stock Bank, and Des Moines Land Bank ... were all functioning. Their bonds were selling at par. The then farm commissioner had an understanding with Secretary Dewey, nothing would be done without consent and approval of the Federal Farm Loan Board. A few days later, U.S. Marshals with pistols at their sides, and sometimes drawn, entered these five banks ... and demanded the banks be turned over to them. Word went out all over the U.S., through newspapers, what had happened, and these banks were ruined. This led to the breach with the old Federal Farm Loan Board, to resignation of three members and appointment of Mr. Meyer to head that Board.

Senator Carey

Who authorized marshals to take over the banks?

Rep. Rainey

Assistant Treasury Secretary Dewey. That started the ruin of these rural banks and the Gianninis bought them up in great numbers. [Ed's note: Giannini, Amadeo Peter 1870-1949 American banker, founder of the Bank of Italy (in America) in 1904 ...of the Transamerica Corporation (holding company, 1928) ...of Bank of America National Trust and Savings Association, 1930 ...and, founder of the credit card industry.]

Rep. McFadden

New York and Paris international banking house Lazard Freres, was a Meyer family banking house. It figures in imports and exports of gold, and one of the important functions of the Federal Reserve System has to do with gold movements in maintenance of its operations. Looking over minutes of last Thursday's hearing, Sen. Fletcher asked Mr. Meyer, 'Have you any connections with international banking?' Mr. Meyer had answered, 'Me? Not personally'.

Eustace Mullins commented, "This last question and answer do not appear in the stenographic transcript. Sen. Fletcher remembers asking the question and hearing the answer."

Sen. Brookhart
I understand Mr. Meyer looked it over, for corrections.

Rep McFadden
Mr. Meyer is brother-in-law of George Blumenthal, a member of J.P. Morgan Co. which represents Rothschild interests, and is liaison officer between the French Government and J.P. Morgan. Edmund Platt, who had eight years to go on a term of ten years as Governor of the Federal Reserve Board, resigned to make room for Mr. Meyer. Platt was given a vice-presidency of Marine Midland Corp. by Meyer's brother-in-law Alfred A. Cook. Eugene Meyer, Jr. heading War Finance Corp., engaged in placing 2 billion dollars in Government securities, placing many of those orders first with the banking house located at 14 Wall Street in the name of Eugene Meyer, Jr. Mr. Meyer is a large stockholder in Allied Chemical Corporation. I call your attention to House Report No. 1635, 68th Congress, 2nd Session, which reveals at least 24 million dollars in bonds were duplicated, 10 billion dollars worth of bonds destroyed. Our Banking and Currency Committee found records of War Finance Corporation under Eugene Meyer, Jr. extremely faulty. While the books were brought before our committee by the people who were custodians of them and taken back to the Treasury at night, the committee discovered alterations were being made in the permanent records.

Eustace comments, "This record of public service did not prevent Eugene Meyer, Jr. from continuing to serve the American people on the Federal Reserve Board, as Chairman of the Reconstruction Finance Corporation, and as head of the International Bank."

Marine Midland Corporation's President Rand answered questions about his hiring Edmund Platt, clearing the way for Meyer onto the Federal Reserve Board, "We pay Mr. Platt $22,000 a year, and we took his secretary over, of course."

Senator Brookhart showed Eugene Meyer, Jr. administered the Federal Farm Loan Board against the interests of the American farmer.

"Mr. Meyer never loaned more than 180 million dollars of the capital stock of 500 million dollars of the farm loan board, so that in aiding the farmers he was not even able to use half of the capital," Brookhart said.

Eugene Meyer, Jr.
Sen. Kenyon wrote me a letter which showed that I cooperated with great advantage to the people of Iowa.

Sen. Brookhart
"You went out and took the opposite side from the Wall Street crowd. They always send somebody out to do that. I have not yet discovered in your statements much interest in making loans to the farmers at large, or any real effort to help their condition. In your two years as head of the Federal Farm Loan Board you made very few loans compared to your capital. You loaned only one-eighth of the demand, according to your own statement."

Despite damning evidence uncovered at these Senate Hearings, Eugene Meyer, Jr. remained on the Federal Reserve Board.

During this tragic period, chairman Louis McFadden of the House Banking & Currency Committee continued his lone crusade against the Bank of England major shareholders, who controlled member banks in the U.S. ...that were U.S. major Fed shareholders.

June 10, 1932 McFadden addressed House of Representatives, "Some people think Federal Reserve banks are U.S. Government institutions. They are not government institutions. They are private credit monopolies which prey upon people of the United States for the benefit of themselves, and their foreign customers. Federal Reserve banks are agents of foreign central banks. Henry Ford said, 'The aim of these financiers is world control by creation of inextinguishable debts'. Federal Reserve Board has usurped the Government of the United States by its arrogant credit monopoly which operates the Federal Reserve Board and Federal Reserve Banks."

Jan. 13, 1932, McFadden introduced a resolution indicting the Federal Reserve Board of Governors for 'Criminal Conspiracy', "I charge them, jointly and severally, with the crime of having treasonably conspired and acted against the peace and security of the United States, and having treasonably conspired to destroy constitutional government in the United States. Resolved, that the Committee on the Judiciary is authorized and directed as a whole or by subcommittee to investigate the official conduct of the Federal Reserve Board and agents to determine whether, in the opinion of the said committee, they have been guilty of any high crime or misdemeanor which in the contemplation of the Constitution requires interposition of the Constitutional powers of the House." No action was taken on McFadden's Resolution. McFadden came back Dec. 13, 1932 with a motion to impeach President Hoover. Five Congressmen backed him …the resolution failed. May 23, 1933, McFadden introduced House Resolution No. 158, Articles of Impeachment against the Treasury Secretary, two Assistant Treasury Secretaries, Federal Reserve Board of Governors, and officers and directors of Federal Reserve Banks … for their guilt and collusion in causing the Great Depression. "I charge them with having unlawfully taken over 80 billion dollars from the U.S. Government in the year 1928, the said unlawful taking consisting of the unlawful recreation of claims against the U.S. Treasury to the extent of over 80 billion dollars in the year 1928, and in each year subsequent, and by having robbed the U.S. Government and people of the United States by their theft and sale of the gold reserve of the United States," McFadden said.

The Resolution never reached the floor.

<>

Eustace Mullins continued, "By 1917, the Morgans, and Kuhn, Loeb Co., floated 1.5 billion dollars in loans to the Allies. The bankers also financed a host of 'peace' organizations ... which worked to get us *involved* in World War I. The Commission for Relief in Belgium manufactured atrocity stories against the Germans, while a Carnegie organization, The League to Enforce Peace, agitated in Washington for our entry into war. This later became, the Carnegie Endowment for International Peace, which during the 1940s was headed by Alger Hiss.

"Besides Warburg, Baruch, and Meyer, a host of J.P. Morgan Co., and Kuhn, Loeb Co. partners, employees, and satellites came to Washington after 1917 to administer the fate of the American people.

"Liberty Loans, which sold bonds to our citizens, were nominally in jurisdiction of U.S. Treasury, under leadership of Wilson's Treasury Secretary, William McAdoo, whom Kuhn, Loeb Co. placed in charge of Hudson-Manhattan Railway, in 1902. Paul Warburg had most of the Kuhn Loeb Co. firm with him in Washington during the World War I. Jerome Hanauer, partner in Kuhn, Loeb Co., was Assistant Treasury Secretary in charge of Liberty Loans. Two Treasury Under-Secretaries during World War I were S. Parker Gilbert, and Roscoe C. Leffingwell. Gilbert and Leffingwell came to Treasury from the law firm of Cravath and Henderson, and returned to that firm when they had fulfilled their mission for Kuhn, Loeb ...in the Treasury. Cravath and Henderson were the lawyers for Kuhn, Loeb. Gilbert and Leffingwell received partnerships in J.P. Morgan Co.

"J.P. Morgan received proceeds of the First Liberty Loan to pay off 400 million dollars, which he advanced to Great Britain, at the outset of World War I. To cover this loan, 68 million dollars in notes were issued under provisions of the Aldrich-Vreeland Act for issuing notes against securities … the only time this provision was employed. The notes were retired as soon as the Federal Reserve Banks began operation, and replaced by Federal Reserve Notes.

<>

"After our entry into World War I, Woodrow Wilson turned the U.S. Government over to a triumvirate of his campaign backers, Paul Warburg, Bernard Baruch, and Eugene Meyer.

"Baruch was appointed head of War Industries Board, with life and death powers over every factory in the U.S.

"Eugene Meyer was appointed head of the War Finance Corporation, in charge of the loan program which financed the war.

"Paul Warburg was in control of the nation's banking system. [Ed's note, Aug. 10 1918, *New York Times* said, "Mr. Paul Warburg was the author of the plan organizing War Finance Corporation.]"

"Baruch's partner in Alaska-Juneau Gold Mining Co, Eugene Meyer, later claimed Baruch was a nitwit, and Meyer with his family banking connections (Lazard Freres) guided Baruch's investment career. These claims appeared in the 1983 50th Anniversary edition of *Washington Post*, editorial page, June 4, with a parting shot from Meyer's editor, Al Friendly, 'Every journalist in Washington, Meyer included, knew that Bernard M. Baruch was a self-aggrandizing phony'. "The third member of the Triumvirate, Eugene Meyer, was son of a partner in the inter-

226

national banking house of Lazard Freres of Paris and New York. In, *My Own Story*, Baruch explains, Meyer became head of the War Finance Corporation. 'At the outset of World War I, I sought out Eugene Meyer, Jr., a man of highest integrity and a keen desire to be of public service," Baruch said. Eugene Meyer's stewardship of War Finance Corporation comprises the most amazing financial operation ever recorded in this country. We say 'partially recorded', because Congressional investigations revealed each night, the books were altered before being brought in for the next day's investigation.

<>

"Louis McFadden, Chairman of House Banking & Currency Committee, investigated Meyer twice, in 1925 and 1930, when Meyer was proposed as a Fed Governor. Select Committee to Investigate the Destruction of Government Bonds, submitted, on March 2, 1925, *Preparation and Destruction of Government Bonds*, 68th Congress, 2d Session, Report No. 1635, p.2.

"Duplicate bonds amounting to 2,314 pairs and duplicate coupons amounting to 4,698 pairs ranging in denominations from $50 to $10,000 have been redeemed to July 1, 1924. Some of these duplications resulted from error and some from fraud," the committee said.

<>

"These investigations may explain why, at the end of World War I, Eugene Meyer was able to buy control of Allied Chemical and Dye Corporation, and later on, the nation's most influential newspaper, the *Washington Post*. The duplication of bonds, 'one for the government, one for me' in denominations to the amount of $10,000 each, resulted in a tidy sum.

"Eugene Meyer's, *Washington Post*, was under direction of his daughter, Katherine Graham. Among important bankers present in Washington during the War was Herbert Lehman, of the rapidly rising firm of Lehman Brothers Bankers, New York. Lehman was promptly put on General Staff of the Army, given rank of Colonel.

"J. McIntosh ...director of Armour meat-packing trust, became U.S. Army Chief of Subsistence, in 1918 ...he was Currency Comptroller in Coolidge's Administration ...and, ex-officio Federal Reserve Board member ...during the Harding Administration, he did his bit as Finance Director for U.S. Shipping Board ...when the Board sold ships to the Dollar Lines for a hundredth of their cost ...and, then let

Dollar Line default on payments. After leaving public service, J.W. McIntosh became partner in J.W. Wollman Co. ... New York stockbrokers.

"W. Harding, Governor of Federal Reserve Board, was managing director of War Finance Corporation, under Eugene Meyer.

"George R. James, member of the Federal Reserve Board in 1923-1924, was Cotton Section Chief of War Industries Board.

"J.P. Morgan Sr. Partner Henry Davison was appointed head of American Red Cross in 1917, in order to get control of 370 million dollars cash collected from the American people in donations," Eustace said.

<>

Wilson continued to be deeply involved in the Bolshevik Revolution, as were House and Wiseman. Vol. 3, p. 421 of, *House Intimate Papers*, records a cable from Sir William Wiseman to House from London, May 1, 1918, suggesting allied intervention at the invitation of the Bolsheviki to help organize Bolshevik forces. Lt. Col. Norman Thwaites, in his memoirs, *Velvet and Vinegar* comments, "A remarkable man with whom I have been closely associated is Sir William Wiseman, advisor on American affairs to the British delegation at the Peace Conference, and liaison officer between the American and British government during the war. He was rather more the Col. House of his country, in his relations with Downing Street." Col. House was criticized for naming his son-in-law, Gordon Auchincloss, as his assistant on the American War Mission. Paul Cravath, lawyer for Kuhn, Loeb Co. was third in charge of the American War Mission. Sir William Wiseman guided American War Mission in its conferences.

In *Strangest Friendship in History*, Viereck comments, "After America entered the War, Wiseman, according to Northcliffe, was the only man who had access at all times to the Colonel and to the White House. Wiseman rented an apartment in the house where the Colonel lived. David Lawrence referred to the Fifty-Third Street house in New York City jestingly, as, *the American No. 10 Downing St.* Col. House had a special code used only with Sir William Wiseman. Col. House was, *Bush* ...the Morgans were, *Haslam*, ...and, Trotsky was, *Keble*. So, two 'unofficial' advisors to the British and American governments had code names for each other. Kuhn, Loeb Co., the nation's largest owners of railroad properties in this country and Mexico, protected their interests during the World War I ... by having Woodrow Wilson set up a U.S.

Railroad Administration. The Director-General was William McAdoo, Comptroller of the Currency. Warburg replaced this set-up in 1918, with a tighter organization he called Federal Transportation Council. The purpose of both organizations was to prevent strikes against Kuhn, Loeb Co. during the War, in case the railroad workers should try to get in wages some of the millions of dollars in wartime profits which Kuhn, Loeb received from the U.S. Government.

Sep. 26 1920, *New York Times* published an obituary of Jacob Schiff stating publicly for the first time a few facts about Kuhn, Loeb. "During World War I, certain of its members were in constant contact with the Government in an advisory capacity. It shared in the conferences held regarding the organization and formation of the Federal Reserve System," *New York Times* said.

Editor George Conroy's, *Truth Magazine,* had a few words about Kuhn, Loeb, too. "Mr. Schiff is head of the great private banking house of Kuhn, Loeb & Co. ... which represents the Rothschild interest on this side of the Atlantic. He has been described as a financial strategist, and has been for years financial minister to the great impersonal power known as, Standard Oil. He was hand-in-glove with the Harrimans, Goulds, and Rockefellers ...in all their railroad enterprises, and has become the dominant power in the railroad and financial world, in America. Louis Brandeis, because of his great ability as a lawyer and for other reasons, was selected by Schiff as the instrument through which Schiff hoped to achieve his ambition in New England. His job was to carry on an agitation which would undermine public confidence in the New Haven system, and cause a decrease in the price of its securities, thus forcing them on the market for wreckers to buy," Conroy said.

General Arsene de Goulevitch's, *Czarism and Revolution,* comments, "Mr. Bakmetiev, late Russian Imperial Ambassador to United States, says the Bolsheviks, after victory, transferred 600 million rubles in gold, between the years 1918-1922, to Kuhn, Loeb Company," Arsene said.

<>

Nancy was quite sharp you know, she found an old *New York Times* article, and read it to me at the Ranch after we retired, me retiring as, the President, and her retiring as, First Lady ...but, it seemed we were more busy trying to figure out what had gone on in Washington while we were there, *after* we were gone, than while we were there. There was no time to figure anything out in the heat of battle, not when you're a movie star

President under fire, you've got to shoot first, ask questions later.

House Stabilization Hearings of 1928
Mr. Beedy

I note on your chart the lines that produce the most violent fluctuations are found under 'Money Rates in New York'. As rates of money rise and fall in the big cities the loans that are made on investments seem to take advantage of them ...at present, a quite violent change, while industry in general does not seem to avail itself of these violent changes ...and, that line is fairly even, there being no great rises or declines.

Fed Governor Adolf Miller

This was all, more or less, in the interests of the international situation. They sold gold credits in New York, for sterling balances in London.

Representative Strong

Has the Federal Reserve Board the power to attract gold to this country?

Fed Board Research
Director E. A. Goldenweiser

The Federal Reserve Board could attract gold to this country by making money rates higher.

Fed Governor Adolf Miller

I think we were close to the point where further solicitude on our part for monetary concerns of Europe can be altered. The Federal Reserve Board last summer, 1927, set out a policy of open market purchases, followed in course by reduction on the discount rate at the Reserve Banks, to ease the credit situation and cheapen the cost of money. The official reasons for that departure in credit policy, were that it would help stabilize international exchange and stimulate exportation of gold.

Chairman McFadden

Will you tell us briefly how that matter was brought to the Federal Reserve Board and what were the influences that went into the final determination?

Fed Governor Adolf Miller

You're asking a question impossible for me to answer.

Chairman McFadden

Perhaps I can clarify it ... where did the suggestion come from that caused this decision of the change of rates last summer?

Fed Governor Adolf Miller
The three largest central banks in Europe sent representatives to this country. There were Governor of the Bank of England ...Mr. Hjalmar Schacht of Reichsbank ...and, Professor Rist, Deputy Governor of Bank of France. These gentlemen were in conference with officials of the New York Federal Reserve Bank. After a week or two, they appeared in Washington for the better part of a day. They came down the evening of one day, and were guests of the Governors of the Federal Reserve Board the following day, and left that afternoon for New York.

Chairman McFadden
Were members of the Board present at this luncheon?

Fed Governor Adolf Miller
Oh, yes, it was given by the Governors of the Board for the purpose of bringing all of us together.

Chairman McFadden
Was it social? ...or were matters of importance discussed?

Fed Governor Adolf Miller
I would say it was mainly a social affair. I had a long conversation with Dr. Schacht alone before the luncheon, and also one of considerable length with Professor Rist. After the luncheon I began a conversation with Mr. Norman, joined in by Governor Strong of New York.

Chairman McFadden
Was that a formal meeting of the Board?

Fed Governor Adolf Miller
No.

Chairman McFadden
It was just an informal discussion of the matters they had been discussing in New York?

Fed Governor Adolf Miller
I assume so. It was mainly a social occasion. What I said was mainly in the nature of generalities. The heads of these central banks also spoke in generalities.

Mr. King
What did they want?

Fed Governor Adolf Miller
They were very candid in answers to questions. I wanted to have a talk with Mr. Norman, and we both stayed behind after luncheon, and were joined by the other foreign representatives and the officials of the New York Reserve Bank. These gentlemen were all pretty concerned with the way the gold standard was working. They were desirous of seeing an easy money market in New York and lower rates, which would deter gold from moving from Europe to this country. That would be very much in the interest of the international money situation which then existed.

Mr. Beedy
Was there some understanding arrived at between the representatives of these foreign banks and the Federal Reserve Board or the New York Federal Reserve Bank?

Fed Governor Adolf Miller
Yes.

Mr. Beedy
It was not reported formally?

Fed Governor Adolf Miller
No. Later, there came a meeting of the Open-Market Policy Committee, the investment policy committee of the Federal Reserve System, by which and to which certain recommendations were made. My recollection is that about 80 million dollars worth of securities were purchased in August, consistent with this plan.

Chairman McFadden
Was there any conference between the members of the Open Market Committee and those bankers from abroad?

Fed Governor Adolf Miller
They may've met as individuals, not as a committee.

Mr. King
How does Open Market Committee get ideas?

Fed Governor Adolf Miller
They sit around and talk. I don't know whose idea this was. It was a time of a cooperative spirit at work.

Chairman McFadden
You've outlined negotiations of great importance.

Fed Governor Adolf Miller
I should rather, say, conversations.

Chairman McFadden
Something of a definite character took place?

Fed Governor Adolf Miller
Yes.

Chairman McFadden
A change of policy on the part of our whole financial system ... which has resulted in one of the most unusual situations that has ever confronted this country financially, the stock market speculation boom of 1927-1929. It seems to me a matter of that importance should have been made a matter of record in Washington.

Fed Governor Adolf Miller
I agree with you.

Representative Strong
Would it not have been a good thing if there had been a direction that those powers given to the Federal Reserve System should be used for the continued stabilization of the purchasing power of the American dollar ... rather than be influenced by the interests of Europe?

Fed Governor Adolf Miller
I take exception to the term, 'influence'. Besides, there's no such thing as stabilizing the American dollar ... without stabilizing every other gold currency. They are tied together by the gold standard. Other eminent men who come here are adroit in knowing how to approach the folk who make up the personnel of the Federal Reserve Board.

Mr. Steagall
The visit of these foreign bankers resulted in money being cheaper in New York?

Fed Governor Adolf Miller
Yes, exactly.

Chairman McFadden
I'd like to put in the record, all who attended that luncheon in Washington.

Fed Governor Adolf Miller
In addition to the names I've given you, there was also present one of the younger men from the Bank of France. I think, all members of the Federal Reserve Board were there. Under Treasure Secretary Ogden Mills was there, and Assistant Treasury Secretary Mr. Schuneman, also two or three men from State Department, and Mr. Warren of the Foreign Department of the Federal Reserve Bank of New York. Oh yes, Governor Strong was present.

Chairman McFadden
This conference, with all these foreign bankers didn't just happen. The prominent bankers from Germany, France, and England came here at whose suggestion?

Fed Governor Adolf Miller
A situation had been created that was distinctly embarrassing to London ... by reason of the impending withdrawal of a certain amount of gold which had been recovered by France, that had originally been shipped and deposited in Bank of England by the French Government, as a war credit. There was getting to be some tension of mind in Europe, because France was beginning to put her house in order for a return to the gold standard. This situation was one which called for some moderating influence.

Mr. King
Who was the moving spirit who got these people together?

Fed Governor Adolf Miller
That is a detail with which I'm not familiar.

Representative Strong
Wouldn't it be fair to say, the fellows who wanted the gold were the ones who instigated the meeting?

Fed Governor Adolf Miller
They came over here.

Representative Strong
The fact is, they came over here, they had a meeting, they banqueted, they talked, they got the Federal Reserve Board to lower the discount rate, and to make the purchases in the open market, and they got the gold.

Mr. Steagall
Is it true, that action stabilized the European currencies ...and, upset ours?

Fed Governor Adolf Miller
Yes, that's what it was intended to do.

Chairman McFadden

Let me call your attention to the recent conference in Paris at which Federal Reserve Board director of research, Mr. Goldenweiser ...and, Assistant Federal Reserve Agent of New York Federal Reserve Bank, Dr. Burgess ... were in consultation with representatives of other central banks. Who called the conference?

Fed Governor Adolf Miller

My recollection is, it was called by Bank of France.

Fed Governor Young

No, it was League of Nations who called them together.

<>

Eustace continues. "The private meeting of Federal Reserve Board Governors and heads of European central banks wasn't called to stabilize anything. It was held to discuss the best way of getting gold held in the U.S. ... by Federal Reserve System ... back to Europe ...to force European nations back on the gold standard.

"The League of Nations had not yet succeeded in that, the objective for which that body was set up ...because U.S. Senate refused to let Woodrow Wilson hand us over to an international monetary authority. It took World War II ...and Franklin D. Roosevelt, to do that.

"Meanwhile, Europe had to have our gold ...and the Federal Reserve System gave it to them, 500 million dollars worth. The movement of that gold out of the United States caused the deflation of the stock boom, the end of the business prosperity of the 1920s and the Great Depression of 1929-1931, the worst calamity ever befallen this nation. The bankers knew what would happen when 500 million dollars worth of gold was sent to Europe. They wanted the Depression ... it delivered U.S. business and finance into their hands," Eustace said.

<>

Eustace continues, from his, *Secrets of the Federal Reserve.*

The Hearings continue:

Mr. Beedy

Mr. Ebersole of Treasury Department concluded at dinner last night saying Federal Reserve System didn't want stabilization ...and, the American businessman didn't want it. They want *fluctuations* in prices, not only in securities, but in commodities, in trade generally ...because, those in control are making their profits out of instability. If control of people does not come in a legitimate way, there may be an attempt to produce it by upheavals, as they have in days gone by. Revolutions have been promoted by dissatisfaction with existing conditions, control being in hands of the few, the many paying the bills.

"The purpose of the hearings before the House Committee on Banking and Currency in 1928 was to investigate necessity for passing the Strong bill, presented by Representative Strong ...that, the Fed be empowered to act to stabilize the purchasing power of the dollar. This was one of the promises made by Carter Glass and Woodrow Wilson when they presented Federal Reserve Act before Congress, in 1912, and such a provision had actually been put in the Act by Senator Robert L. Owen ...but, Carter Glass' House Committee on Banking and Currency struck it out.

"Traders and speculators did not want the dollar to become stable ...because they would no longer be able to make a profit. Citizens of this country were led to gamble on the stock market in the 1920s, because traders had created a nationwide condition of instability.

"Strong Bill of 1928 was defeated in Congress.

"The financial situation in the U.S. during the 1920s was characterized by an inflation of speculative values only ...it was a trader-made situation. Prices of commodities remained low, despite over-pricing of securities on the exchange.

"Purchasers didn't expect their securities to pay dividends. The idea was, hold them awhile, then sell at a profit. It had to stop somewhere, as Paul Warburg remarked in March, 1929. But, Wall Street didn't let it stop ... until, people put their savings into these over-priced securities. We'd the spectacle of the President of the U.S., Calvin Coolidge, acting as a shill for stock market operators ...when, he recommended to the American people they continue buying on the market in 1927. There was uneasiness about the inflated condition of the market, and bankers showed their power by getting the President of the U.S., Secretary of the Treasury, and Chairman of the Board of Governors of the Federal Reserve System ... to issue statements that brokers' loans were not too high ...and, that the condition of the stock market was sound.

"Irving Fisher warned us in 1927, the burden of stabilizing prices all over the world would soon fall on the U.S. One of the results of the Second World War was the establishment of an International Monetary Fund, to do just that.

"Professor Gustav Cassel commented. 'The downward movement of prices hasn't been a spontaneous result of forces beyond our control. It's the result of a policy deliberately framed to bring down prices and give a higher value to the monetary unit,' Cassel said.

"Instead of being used to promote financial stability of the country, as was promised by Woodrow Wilson when the Federal Reserve Act was passed, financial instability was steadily promoted by the Fed," Eustace said.

Mar. 13, 1939 a Fed board memo commented, The Board of Governors of the Federal Reserve System opposes any bill which proposes a stable price level.'

Federal Reserve Board was used to advance the election of bankers' candidates during the 1920s. Aug. 4, 1928 *Literary Digest* commented on the Fed raising the rate to 5% in a Presidential year, 'This reverses the politically desirable cheap money policy of 1927 ...giving smooth conditions on the stock market.'

The rate hike was attacked by the Peoples' Lobby of Washington, D.C., 'This increase, at a time when farmers need cheap money to finance harvesting their crops, is a direct blow at farmers ... who'd just begun to get back on their feet after the Agricultural Depression of 1920-21.'

New York World commented, 'Criticism of Federal Reserve Board policy by many investors isn't based on its attempt to deflate the stock market ...but, on the charge that the Board itself, by last year's policy, is completely responsible for the stock market inflation that exists.'

March, 1928, Roy A. Young, Governor of the Board, was called before a Senate committee.

A Senator asked, "Are brokers' loans too high?"

Governor Young responded, "I'm not prepared to say whether brokers' loans are too high or too low ...but, I'm sure they are safely and conservatively made."

Treasury Secretary Mellon made a statement assuring the U.S. that they were not too high ...and Coolidge, using material supplied him by Federal Reserve Board, told the country, rates aren't too high.

The Fed, charged with duty of protecting interests of the average man ... did its utmost to assure the average man, he should feel no alarm about his savings ...yet, Fed Feb. 2, 1929, issued a letter addressed to Reserve Bank Directors cautioning them, there is grave danger to continued speculation.

H. Parker Willis, professor at Washington and Lee, first editor of *Federal Reserve Bulletin*, commented, "What could be expected from a group of men such as composed the Board, a set of men solely interested in standing from under when there was any danger of friction, displaying a bovine and canine appetite for credit and praise, while eager only to 'stand in' with the 'big men' whom they know as masters of American finance and banking?"

Eustace continued, "H. Parker Willis omitted any reference to Lord Montague Norman and the machinations of the Bank of England ...which, were about to result in the Crash of 1929 ...and, the Great Depression."

London Economist editor Paul Einzig's, *Fight for Financial Supremacy,* comments, "After World War I, close cooperation was established between Bank of England and Federal Reserve authorities ...more, especially with Federal Reserve Bank of New York. This cooperation was due to cordial relations between Montague Norman of Bank of England, and Benjamin Strong, Governor of Federal Reserve Bank of New York until 1928. On several occasions, discount rate policy of Federal Reserve Bank of New York was guided by desire to help the Bank of England."

Eustace continues. Benjamin Strong married the daughter of the president of Bankers Trust in New York, later becoming its president.

Carroll Quigley's, *Tragedy and Hope,* comments, "Strong became Governor of Federal Reserve Bank of New York as joint nominee of Morgan, and of Kuhn, Loeb Company, in 1914."

Eustace continued, "Lord Montague Norman is the only man in history, whose maternal grandfather and paternal grandfather serve as Governors of the Bank of England. His father was with Brown, Shipley Co. ...the London Branch of Brown Brothers, now Brown Brothers Harriman. Montague Norman, 1871-1950, came to New York to work for Brown Brothers in 1894, where he was befriended by the Delano family, and by James Markoe of Brown Brothers. He returned to England, in 1907, was named to the Court of the Bank of England. In 1912, he had a nervous breakdown, went to Switzerland to be treated by Jung, as was fashionable among the powerful group which he represented. Lord Montague Norman was Governor of the Bank of England from 1916 to 1944. During this period, he participated in central bank conferences that set up the Crash of 1929 ...and, the worldwide depression."

Brian Johnson's, *Politics of Money,* comments, "Strong and Norman, intimate friends, spent holidays together at Bar Harbor, and in the South of France ... Norman therefore, became Strong's alter ego ... Strong's easy money policies on the New York money market from 1925-1928 were the fulfillment of his agreement with Norman to keep New York interest rates below those of London. For the sake of international cooperation, Strong withheld the steadying hand of high interest rates from New York until it was too late. Easy money in New York had encouraged the surging American boom of the late 1920s, with its fantastic heights of speculation."

Sen. Robert Owen, longtime Fed critic commented, "The people didn't know the Federal Reserve Banks were organized for profit-making. They were intended to stabilize the credit and currency supply of the country. That end hasn't been accomplished. Indeed, there's been the most remarkable variation in the purchasing power of money since the System went into effect. The Federal Reserve men are chosen by the big banks, through discreet little campaigns, and they naturally follow the ideals which are *portrayed* to them as the soundest from a financial point of view."

In 1934, New York Chase economist Benjamin Anderson commented, "At the moment we have 900 million dollars excess reserves. In 1924, with increased reserves of 300 million dollars you got 3-4 billion dollars in bank expansion of credit very quickly. That extra money was put out by Federal Reserve Banks in 1924 through buying government securities ...and, caused rapid expansion of bank credit. Banks continued to get excess reserves because more gold came in ...and because, whenever there was a slackening, the Fed people put out some more. They held back a bit in 1926 and firmed up a bit. Then in 1927, they put out less than 300 million dollars additional reserves, that set the wild stock market going, and led us into the smash of 1929. The money of the Federal Reserve Banks is money they created. When they buy Government securities they create reserves. They pay for the Government securities by giving checks on themselves, and those checks come to the commercial banks and are by them deposited in the Federal Reserve Banks, and then money exists which did not exist before," Anderson said.

Sen. Bulkley questioned Anderson, "It does not increase the circulating medium at all?"

Anderson looked at him. "No," Anderson said.

Eustace continued. "This is an explanation of the manner in which the Federal Reserve Banks increased their assets from 143 million dollars to 45 billion dollars to in thirty-five years. They didn't produce anything, they were non-productive enterprises ...and yet, they'd this enormous profit, merely by creating money ... 95% of it in the form of credit ...which didn't add to the circulating medium. It wasn't distributed among people in the form of wages ...nor, did it increase buying power of farmers and workers. It was credit-money created by bankers for the use and profit of bankers ... who increased their wealth by more than 40 billion dollars in a few years ... because they had obtained control of the Government's credit in 1913 by passing the Federal Reserve Act. Marriner Eccles had something to say about creation of money ... he was an economist and was brought into Government service by Stuart Chase and Rexford Guy Tugwell, two of Roosevelt's brain-trust. Eccles was the only one of the Roosevelt crowd who stayed in office throughout the Roosevelt Administration."

June 24, 1941 Eccles spoke before House Banking & Currency Committee. "Money is created out of the right to issue credit," Eccles said.

Turning over Government's credit to private bankers in 1913 gave bankers unlimited opportunities to create money ... the Fed could also destroy money in large quantities through open market operations.

Eccles testified at the Silver Hearings of 1939, "When you sell bonds on the open market, you extinguish reserves."

Eustace concludes. Extinguishing reserves means wiping out a basis for money and credit issue, or tightening up on money and credit ...a condition usually more favorable to bankers than creation of money. Calling in or destroying money gives the banker immediate and unlimited control of the financial situation ...since he is the only one with money ...and the only one with the power to issue money in a time of money shortage. The money panics of 1873, 1893, 1920-1921, and 1929-1931, were characterized by a drawing in of the circulating medium. In economical terms, this doesn't sound like such a terrible thing ... but, it means people don't have money to pay rent or buy food ...and, it means an employer has to lay off 3/4s of his help because he can't borrow money to pay them. The enormous guilt of central bankers and long record of suffering and misery for which they are responsible suggests no punishment is too severe for their crimes against humanity.

<>

Sep. 30, 1940, Governor Eccles commented, "Debt is the basis for the creation of money. The Fed can't provide capital funds for improvement of commerce and industry. Capitalization means, the notes would have to be backed by a precious metal or commodity ... Reserve notes are unbacked paper loaned at interest."

Eustace continued, "Most Americans comment they can't understand how the Federal Reserve System works. It's beyond understanding, not because it's complex, but because it's simple. If a confidence man comes to you, and offers to demonstrate his marvelous money machine, you watch while he puts in a blank piece of paper, then cranks out a $100 bill. That's the Federal Reserve System. [Ed's note, but they cranked out $10,000 bills, and $100,000 bills]. You offer to buy this marvelous money machine ...but, you can't. It's owned by the private stockholders of the Federal Reserve Banks, whose identities are traced to New York and London bankers."

<>

Jan. 1933, Hitler assumed power in Germany.

Mar. 1933, Prescott Bush Sr. told Max Warburg to represent American Ship & Commerce Line as a board member on Hamburg-Amerika Line, since Max was advising Hjalmar Schacht the German Economics Minister ...a close friend of Montague Norman. Max was a director of Reichsbank ... Max's brothers ran Kuhn & Loeb ...that brokered E.H. Harriman's purchase of Union Pacific Railroad out of bankruptcy. Moshe Gottlieb's American Anti-Nazi Resistance reported Max's son, Erich, cabled cousin Frederick Warburg ... a director of Union Pacific Railroad ... instructing him to help stop all anti-Nazi activity and anti-Nazi propaganda in the U.S.

Mar. 1933, Roosevelt started his first term as U.S. President.

Mar. 1933, Roosevelt appointed Paul Warburg's son ... James Paul Warburg, vice president of the U.S. Acceptance Bank ... as U.S. Budget Director. James set up the Office of War Information, our official World War II propaganda agency. James was nephew of Felix Warburg and Jacob Schiff, both of Kuhn, Loeb & Co. In 1950, James Paul Warburg addressed the U.S. Senate, "We shall have World Government, whether we like it or not. The question is, will World Government be achieved by conquest or consent?"

<>

Roosevelt appointed as Treasury Secretary, W.H. Woodin ...one of the biggest industrialists in the country, director of ...American Car Foundry Company ...numerous other locomotive works ...Remington Arms ...Cuba Company ...Consolidated Cuba Railroads ...and, several

other large corporations. Woodin was later replaced by Henry Morgenthau, Jr., son of a Harlem real estate operator, who'd helped put Woodrow Wilson in the White House.

Mar. 5 1933, Roosevelt declared a national bank holiday, a bankers' moratorium, to help bankers prepare, or cook, their books ... financial institutions closed for business the next week. The measure called for a four-day mandatory shutdown of U.S. banks for auditing.

Mar. 9 1933, Congress passed Emergency Banking Relief Act, allowing reopening banks if examiners found them financially secure. Within three days, 5,000 banks were allowed to re-open.

Apr. 5 1933, one month after inauguration, Roosevelt declared a National Emergency and made it illegal for any U.S. citizen to own gold ... and ordered all gold coins, gold bullion, and gold certificates turned into Federal Reserve banks, by May 1.

May 22 1933, Congress enacted a law, against Constitutional mandate, declaring all coin and currencies then in circulation to be legal tender, dollar for dollar, *as if* they were gold.

May 23 1933, Congressman McFadden brought formal charges against the Board of Governors of the Federal Reserve Bank system, Comptroller of the Currency, and U.S. Treasury Secretary ...for criminal acts ... including conspiracy, fraud, unlawful conversion, and treason. The petition for Impeachment was referred to the Judiciary Committee ... and, has yet to be acted on. http://home.hiwaay.net/~becraft/mcfadden.html

June 5 1933, Congress took the gold standard out of existence by enacting a joint resolution (48 Stat. 112), that gold clauses in contracts were outlawed ...*no one* could legally demand gold in payment for any debt.

<>

In 1933, the U.S. was declared 'bankrupt' by President Roosevelt in Executive Orders 6073, 6102, 6111, 6260 on March 9, 1933. Congress confirmed bankruptcy, June 5, 1933 ...and, impaired obligations and considerations of contracts through, 'Joint Resolution To Suspend Gold Standard and Abrogate Gold Clause, June 5, 1933', (HJR 192, 73rd Congress, 1st Session). International Monetary Fund, and International Bank for Reconstruction, were established as alien/foreign Financial Institutions (22 U.S.C.A. 286), naming Secretary of Treasury as a Governor of the IMF and IBR. In 1950, pursuant to Reorganization Plan No. 26, 5 U.S.C.A. 903, Secretary of Treasury was appointed as 'receiver' in the bankruptcy.

<>

Eustace continues.

June 5 1933, a bankrupt U.S. went into receivership ... it was reorganized in favor of it's creditor and new owners, a private corporation of international bankers. Since 1933, the 'United States Government' has been a privately owned corporation ...property of the Federal Reserve and International Monetary Fund.

June 16 1933, Congress passed the 1933 Banking Act. The Federal Reserve Board was given tighter control of the investment practices of banks. Banking Act of 1933 legislated all earnings of Federal Reserve Banks must by law go to the banks, themselves.

<>

At last the provision in the Act, that the Government share in the profits, was gotten rid of. It had never been observed, and increase in assets of Federal Reserve Banks ...from 143 million dollars in 1913 ...to 45 billion dollars in 1949 went entirely to private stockholders of the Federal Reserve Banks.

<>

In 1934, Gold Reserve Hearings heard from James Paul Warburg, returning from a London Economic Conference with Professor Sprague and Henry Stimson ... James Paul thought we should *modernize* the gold standard.

Jan. 30 1934, Gold Reserve Act was passed, giving Federal Reserve title to all gold collected ... and changed the value-price of gold from $20.67 per ounce to $35 per ounce, which meant all silver certificates people received for their gold ... were worth 40 percent less.

Jan. 31 1934, Roosevelt fixed the dollar at 15 and 5/21 grains standard to gold ... Russia and central banks of Europe began buying gold ...this redistribution of America's wealth was a World Order globalist agenda ...featuring a dual monetary system ... the gold standard for foreigners ...and Federal Reserve notes for us.

When Paul Warburg resigned from Federal Reserve Board of Governors in 1918, his successor was Albert Strauss, partner in international banking house, J & W Seligman ...with interests in Cuba and South America ...that co-financed revolutions there ...and a Senate Finance Committee investigation in 1933 revealed J & W Seligman gave a $415,000 bribe to Juan Leguia, son of Peru's President, so his father would accept a loan. Albert Strauss was ...board chairman of Cuba Cane Sugar Corp., and, a director of ....Brooklyn Manhattan Transit Co. ...Coney Island Brooklyn RR ...New York Rapid Transit ...Pierce-Arrow ...Cuba Tobacco Corp., ...and Eastern Cuba Sugar Corp.

Roosevelt brought from New York, as Special Treasury Advisor ...J & W Seligman's Earl Bailie ... the man who'd handed the $415,000 bribe to the president of Peru's son, Juan ...but, criticism of this appointment sent Earl back to New York to bring in delegates for Roosevelt.

Roosevelt was an international banker, who floated large issues of millions of dollars of foreign bonds in the 1920s, that defaulted.

Roosevelt was president and director of United European Investors, Ltd., in 1923 and 1924, that floated millions of German marks in this country ... all defaulted. Roosevelt was a director of International Germanic Trust Company, in 1928 ...and, advisor to Federal International Banking Corp., an Anglo-American outfit dealing in foreign securities in the U.S. ...Roosevelt's law firm ... Roosevelt and O'Connor, during the 1920s represented many international corporations. His law partner, Basil O'Connor, sat as a director on ...Cuban-American Manganese Corp. ...Venezuela-Mexican Oil Corp. ...West Indies Sugar Corp. ...American Reserve Insurance Corp., Warm Springs Foundation ...and later, was head of American Red Cross.

Utah banker Marriner Eccles, director of ...Pet Milk Co. ...Mountain States Implement Co. ...and, Amalgamated Sugar ... was president of First Securities Corp., a family investment trust of several banks Eccles bought cheap during the Agricultural Depression of 1920-21.

Congress wondered if Eccles should be on the Federal Reserve Board at the same time he owned all those banks in Utah ...but, Marriner testified, he had little to do with First Securities Corp. besides being President ... so, Congress confirmed Marriner Eccles as chairman of the Federal Reserve Board.

Eugene Meyer, Jr. resigned from the board and began lending the 2 billion dollars capital of Reconstruction Finance Corp.

Preceding Roosevelt, President Hoover encouraged several major banks to form National Credit Corp., to lend money to banks in financial difficulty. National Credit Corp., founded Oct. 13 1931, began operations, Nov. 11 1931. Hoover saw writing on the wall ...so, Fed. Reserve Board Governor Eugene Meyer convinced Hoover that a public agency was needed to make loans to troubled banks (Fed of course would credit up the money, for its normal fees). Hoover presented the plan in his annual address to Congress in

December, and gained approval from both houses of Congress on the same day in Jan. 1932. ...Reconstruction Finance Corp. started business Feb. 2, 1932, much to Meyer's pleasure.

<>

Legislation authorized Reconstruction Finance Corp. for ten years, Presidential approval was required beyond Jan. 1, 1933 ...Congressional approval was required for lending authority past Jan. 1, 1934. Reconstruction Finance Corp. was funded by U.S. Treasury providing 500 million dollars of capital to Reconstruction Finance Corp., then authorized to borrow 1.5 billion dollars more from the Treasury.

Treasury sold bonds to the public to fund Reconstruction Finance Corp. ... which meant, the Fed printed up the initial 500 million dollars (if it was printed at all, probably it was just ledger entries at the Fed and at the banks to which the money was loaned) in $10,000 denominations costing two cents each or a total cost of about $1,000 ...then, charged U.S. Government 500 million dollars added to the national debt, the balance owned by the people of the U.S. who were directly responsible through IRS to pay yearly interest on the loan, along with interest on the total national debt ... of course, the amount was paid to private shareholders who owned all stock of the Fed ...that is, the amount was paid to private banks and to private individuals, you see? U.S. Government never saw money, because Fed is not a Federal, United States Government organization, Fed is a private corporation ordered by U.S. Government into existence ...but, wholly and completely owned by private banks and private individuals ... whether the money was actually printed or not, or just a ledger entry ... U.S. taxpayers were on the hook for 500 million dollars ...and, for interest on the amount owed to Fed ...which is how Fed operates.

Later, borrowing authority was increased, and Reconstruction Finance Corp authorized to sell securities directly to the public ... most RFC funding was borrowed from the Treasury by it selling bonds as collateral for the Fed to etc. etc. etc. Reconstruction Finance Corp. borrowed 51.3 billion dollars from Treasury, and 3.1 billion dollars from the public.

The legislation authorized Reconstruction Finance Corp. to make loans to ...banks ... other financial institutions ...railroads ...and, crop loans. If railroads recovered, their bond appreciation improved bank finances, because banks held the railroad bonds ... is how the logic went. Politicians argued, that federal assistance was going to the wrong end of the economic pyramid, they wanted people at the bottom of the heap to get the money for purchasing power ...but, Reconstruction Finance Corp. money was poured in at the top ... Reconstruction Finance Corp. was a relief program for big business, only. From the beginning, through Franklin Roosevelt's inauguration Mar. 4 1933, Reconstruction Finance primarily made loans to financial institutions ... several loans were controversial, so July 21, 1933 legislation required identity of banks receiving Reconstruction Finance loans from then on, to be reported to Congress.

Feb. 1933, there were banking difficulties in Detroit, MI. To avoid crisis, Reconstruction Finance Corp. was willing to help Union Guardian Trust ... one of Henry Ford's banks ...Ford had deposits of 7 million dollars in this bank. Michigan Sen. James Couzens demanded Ford subordinate his deposits as a loan condition of the loan ... if Ford agreed, Ford would risk losing his deposits before his depositors lost a penny. Ford and Couzens once were partners in the car business, but became rivals. Ford refused to Couzens' demand, even though bank failure could start a panic in Detroit. When negotiations failed, the Michigan governor declared a state bank holiday ... a panic spread to nearby states then through the U.S. ... as all states declared bank holidays or restricted cash withdrawals.

http://www.eh.net/encyclopedia/article/butkiewicz.finance.corp.reconstruction

Mar. 5 1933, President Roosevelt declared a national bank holiday ... financial institutions in the U.S. closed for business during the following week ...Reconstruction Finance Corp. *failed* to prevent the worst financial crisis in American history ... but, made a fortune for the Fed, who had loaned out 50 billion dollars to the Treasury. So, Reconstruction Finance Corp. had been a successful Fed. strategy ... to get its private shareholders richer.

<>

Eustace continued.

Aug. 23, 1935 ... Banking Act of 1935 increased Roosevelt's power over the nation's finances ... it extended the terms of office of the Federal Reserve Board of Governors to fourteen years, or, three-and-a-half times the length of a Presidential term ...a monetary policy inaugurated before a President came into the White House would go on, regardless of his wishes.

Banking Act of 1935 repealed the clause of the Glass-Steagall Banking Act of 1933 that said, a banking house could not be on the Stock Exchange and be involved in investment banking ...preventing a banking house from lending money to a corporation it owned ... this clause covered up some other provisions in that Act, such as creation of Federal Deposit Insurance Corporation, and it providing 150 million dollars insurance money to guarantee 15 billion dollars of deposits. So the one constructive provision of the Banking Act of 1933 was repealed in 1935 ...also, now Federal Reserve Banks could loan to industry, competing with member banks ...who couldn't compete on large loans.

When the provision banks could not be in investment banking and operate on the Stock Exchange was repealed, Carter Glass, writer of that provision, was questioned by reporters.

"Does that mean that J.P. Morgan can go back into investment banking?" a reporter said.

Glass looked at him. "Well, why not? People have been crying all over the country banks won't make loans ...now, the Morgans can go back to underwriting," Glass said.

Berlin, 1936 & 1939

Allen Dulles, John Dulles, and Adolf Hitler became friends, master and dog. From monuments, and houses, Olympic and swastika flags signaling a festive, crowded Berlin. Tourists were unaware, the Nazi regime temporarily removed anti-Jewish signs, and unaware of the 'clean up' ordered by German Ministry of Interior ... Berlin Police arrested Gypsies prior to the Games ...about 800 were arrested, interned under police guard in a special Gypsy camp in the Berlin suburb, Marzahn. Nazi officials ordered foreign visitors not to be subjected to Nazi anti-homosexual laws. Allen and John Dulles, John McCloy, Adolf Hitler, and Minister of Propaganda Joseph Goebbels sat together in Hitler's private box seats at 1936 Olympic games in Berlin.

Goebbels look at John, "German sport has one task ... to strengthen character of the German people, with fighting spirit and camaraderie necessary in the struggle for existence."

Eighteen Black athletes represented United States in 1936 Olympics. African American athletes won 14 medals, nearly one-fourth of 56 medals awarded the U.S. team in all events, and dominated track and field events. American journalists hailed victories of Jesse Owens, and other Blacks ...as a blow to the Nazi myth of Aryan supremacy ...but, returning home ... Black medalists faced social and economic discrimination, underscoring the irony of athletic victory in racist Germany.

African American Medalists	
David Albritton	High jump, silver
Cornelius Johnson	High jump, gold
James LuValle	400-meter run, bronze
Ralph Metcalfe	4x100-m relay, gold
	100-meter dash, silver
Jesse Owens	100-meter dash, gold
	200-meter dash, gold
	Broad jump, gold
	4x100-m relay, gold
Frederick Pollard, Jr.	100-m hurdles, bronze
Matthew Robinson	200-meter dash, silver
Archie Williams	400-meter run, gold
Jack Wilson	Bantam boxing, silver
John Woodruff	800-meter run, gold

Allen Dulles, representing the Fed ... and his trans-Atlantic Axis banking crew, representing central banks of England, Germany, and France ... founded Bank of International Settlements BIS, in Switzerland ...from there, the bank would broker loans internationally through troubled times. Dulles, Hitler, and Mussolini helped found Vatican Bank in Rome, giving the Vatican diplomatic rights as a separate country ...to avoid international currency blockades imposed by European warring powers, they just smuggled money through the Vatican. In 1939, German General Staff ordered Adolf to take-over Czechoslovakia. Bank of England simply transferred ownership of its Czech gold deposits to German General Staff banks. Behind the scenes, the trans-Atlantic central bank family of international bankers met frequently at International Bank of Settlements boardroom, in Switzerland ... whenever Rothschild told Warburg to tell Allen Dulles to set the meetings.

<>

They financed the Nazi war machine, as Freikorps death squads assassinated people who wanted democracy ...Freikorps continued sabotage against western democracies at home and abroad. And, the same group at the same time, financed western democracies, too.

Anthony Sutton, Eustace Mullins, Cleon Skousen, and Professor Quigley ... all independently researched Bank of International Settlements. Sutton was to be ostracized in America as a result of his research ...for telling the truth, on ...the phony energy crisis in the 1970s in America ...exposés of Skull & Bones ...but, primarily because he documented the U.S. built up ... at the same time ... the industrial empire of the Soviet Union, and of the Nazi Party ... since World War I, to date ...even, amid avid anti-Nazi U.S. taxpayer feeling, and anti-communist U.S. taxpayer feeling ...and, even during Dulles' Christian West 'Crusade for Freedom'.

Never-the-less, Sutton, Mullins, Skousen, and Quigley told the truth about U.S. inner circle support and ownership of Communist Russian and Nazi German industry through the majority shareholders of the Fed -- Fed traitors to America, and every country, Satan's legion.

Sutton spoke out, but I never heard him until the last year of my life, well after my Presidency. Most American heroes aren't heard by many in their lifetimes. They live in the eternity of Love, unseen, fighting to keep love alive through Time and history. Real heroes are known in their own heart, and in a few other's ...that's all. They share the same spirit as Christ, Buddha, Mohammed, Schweitzer, Martin Luther King, Jr. ... all great lovers of humanity.

Sutton shared his research, "Throughout the Second World War , Germany's rulers never lost contact with circles in Europe and America openly sympathizing with Germany's aggression, and advocated support of Nazism as a 'bulwark against Communism'. A convenient meeting place for secret negotiations was established by the German Government in Basle, Switzerland, at headquarters of Bank of International Settlements. An article in *New York Times* May 19 1943, commented on this German-controlled institution, in Switzerland. 'Allied preparations for invasion of the European continent make Bank of International Settlements, at Basle Switzerland, look more incongruous than it ever looked since the outbreak of the war, in September 1939. In seclusion of a Swiss city, American, German, French, and Italian bankers, not to mention Swedish, Swiss, and Netherlands representatives, work side by side ...and, attend to common business. Directors of Bank of International Settlements are men of great influence ...three directors of Bank of England ...powerful Nazi financiers, Baron K.F. von Schroder of Cologne, Reichsbank President Walther Funk, and Dr. Hermann Schmitz, President of I.G. Farben ...and, American Wall Street banker, Thomas H. McKittrick, Director of the First National Bank of New York and President and General Manager Bank of International Settlements,' *New York Times* said.

"On Nov. 23 1943, Harry White, special adviser to U.S. Treasury Department, spoke with Washington correspondents. 'Bank of International Settlements is German-controlled. Germany is being nice and hopes to use it to get back financial power. There's an American president doing business with the Germans while our American boys are fighting the Germans.'

"Throughout the war the Nazis permitted payment of dividends to international members of Bank of International Settlements.

American Wall Street banker, Thomas H. McKittrick, Director of First National Bank of New York and President and General Manager of Bank of International Settlements, spoke to United Press correspondents. 'We must keep the machine ticking,' Thomas McKittrick said, 'because, when the Armistice comes the formerly hostile powers will need an efficient instrument such as the BIS,'" Antony Sutton said.

<>

International bankers are different from ordinary bankers...they create national debt while destabilizing governments ...then, lend bankrupt or new governments more money ...then, have the governments bankrupt taxpayers with taxes and inflation to pay interest on the principal to the international bankers who made them the loans 'in the public liability'.

In intelligence circles this is termed, 'an economic warfare tactic in a strategy of economic destabilization', to shift ownership of oil, gold, industry, minerals, real estate, stocks, and bonds from vanquished ruling families to victorious ruling families.

Enemies are not divided, or characterized, by national boundaries of one country against another ...but, by taxpayer versus tax-taker, money issuer versus indebted, owner versus property-less, well-fed versus hungry.

Ruling family bankers of the world, the money issuing class, the private stockholders of the central banks ... are allied together ... even while their subject populations fight each other in war ...and, although they fight turf wars with one another constantly, gambling with the lives of, and sacrificing, subject populations and taxpayer bases. But, primarily the money issuing class, they're all making war against the upper class, middle class, and lower class of the world. This financial warfare transcends national boundaries. Sometimes, different banking groups and central banks form teams like the National Football League does, and fight economic turf wars to knock competing central bank teams out of competition in global financial war. One of the Super Bowls of these central banking global turf wars was called, the Great Depression. Another, 9/11 World Trade Center.

<>

Former FBI Director Cleon Skousen explains. "What international bankers do, is keep governments from controlling their own money systems. To do this, these international banking dynasties of ruling families created a religion of money to control the nature of money, and how money works. The first Rothschild banker, in Frankfurt Germany around 1800, was the treasurer of the German Confederation. His sons operated branches. One son operated in Vienna, and controlled the Austro-Hungarian empire. One son operated the London branch, and became the most powerful man in England. One son operated the Naples branch, and was the most powerful man in Italy. Another son operated the Paris branch, and controlled the finances of France.

"The Rothschild banking dynasty started in the German Confederation ... its family members have always been part of German General Staff, the controlling aristocracy of Germany.

"Now, the way money works is like this. Money is created out of nothing. In the beginning gold was the common medium of exchange. Then, paper notes were made to represent gold. But, bankers found people normally exchanged checks, and gold stayed within the banks, themselves. Over time, bankers saw they could have much more paper money than gold, because people writing checks never withdrew the majority of the gold, itself. So, the gold that was used to back up the money, since it wasn't ever really touched, was used again ... at the same time, for loans. And, these loans were made in the form of checks and accounts ...so again, the gold itself was never touched. So, banks kept making more and more loans on the same amount of gold, by issuing bank accounts with numerical balances, not pieces of gold. Then, the banks charged interest on numerical amounts."

Making loans to U.S. Government can be very profitable ...float bonds ...sit back ...collect interest on the national debt ...constantly build debt ...make money loaning money to governments ...and, make money again by having those governments buy products and services from companies in your portfolio you govern by sitting on their board of directors ...always scheme for takeovers of countries, portfolios, natural resource markets, economic and industrial markets, wage slave and sex slave markets, weapons markets, drug markets, prison markets ...

always, Brotherhood of Death deciding, which subject populations will live, which will die, which subject populations will be slaves, which subject populations will be their masters, which central banks will be slaves, which central banks will be their masters.

Antony Sutton shared his views. "The aim of the dynastic bankers was nothing less than create a world system of financial control in private hands able to dominate the political system of each country, and the economy of the world as a whole. This system was to be controlled in feudalist fashion by central banks of the world acting in concert, by secret agreements arrived at in frequent private meetings and conferences. The apex of the system was to be, the Bank of International Settlements in Basle, Switzerland ... a private bank owned and controlled by the world's central banks, which were themselves, private corporations. Each central bank, in hands of men like Montague Norman of Bank of England, Benjamin Strong of New York Federal Reserve Bank, Charles Rist of Bank of France, and Hjalmar Schacht of Reichsbank ... sought to dominate its government by its ability ...to control Treasury loans ...to manipulate foreign exchanges ...to influence the level of economic activity in the country, and ...to influence cooperative politicians by subsequent economic rewards in the business world."

Bank of England was formed in 1694. By 1844, Bank of England, not the British government, ruled England ...of course, the monarchy owned significant shares of Bank of England, completing the circle. The ruling families that control the credit of the nation, direct the government and control the subject population. In Germany, the Bundesbank dictates to government. In U.S., Federal Reserve dictates to government.

Bank of International Settlements was created to orchestrate and choreograph the movements of all the West's central banks, in order to dictate to all the governments of the world, this is the new World Order ... described in prophesy in the Bible thousands of years ago, that no one might buy or sell without the mark of the beast.

<>

Hoover Institute scholar Antony Sutton researched the inner circle of America's ruling families pledging Yale University Society of the German Order of the Death's Head, the Skull & Bones Society. "J.P. Morgan went to college at the University of Gottingen, Germany. The college was a hotbed teaching Hegel dialectical activism. Morgan used the dialectical approach of staging and financing both sides of a conflict to create managed change.

<>

"Morgan Bank used political parties, senior managers supported different camps. Morgan and Dwight Morrow supported Republicans. Employee Russell Leffingwell supported Democrats. Morgan's employee Grayson Murphy supported the Far Right. Morgan's employee Thomas W. Lamont allied with the Left.

"Morgan was not a member of the Order ...but, some of his partners were. Partner Henry P. Davison's son, Davison Jr., was initiated into the Order in 1920. After Morgan's death, the firm became Morgan, Stanley & Co. Harold Stanley pledged the Order in 1908. These partners financed the building of the Left wing of Morgan's dialectic, including the Communist Party U.S.A. with Julius Hammer, whose son is Chairman of Occidental Petroleum.

Firms like Guaranty Trust, and Bankers Trust, under Morgan control, employed many members of the Order. The American branch of the German Order of Death, the Skull & Crossbones (German Death-head) Society, was founded at Yale University in 1833 by ruling family members, twenty to thirty ruling families control the Order, the families...

Rockefeller	Bush
Harriman	Brown
Whitney	Vanderbilt
Bundy	Weyerhaeuser
Sloane	Taft
Pillsbury	Guggenheim
Phelp	Warburg
Astor	Lord

...and, American old line ruling families, and new wealth ruling families:
Lord (1635, Cambridge, MA)

Bundy	(1635, Boston, MA)
Phelps	(1630, Dorchester, MA)
Whitney	(1635, Watertown, MA)
Perkins	(1631, Boston, MA)
Stimson	(1635, Watertown, MA)
Taft	(1679, Braintree, MA)
Wadsworth	(1632, Newtown, MA)
Gilman	(1638, Bingham MA)
Payne	(Standard Oil)
Davison	(J.P. Morgan)
Pillsbury	(flour milling)
Sloane	(retail)
Weyerhaeuser	(lumber)
Rockefeller	(Standard Oil)

Harriman	(railroads)

The Harriman family includes satellite ruling families:

Bush	Brown
Ames	Woolley
James	Lovett.

"Many are Wasp families descended from English Puritans, aristocrats coming here in the early 1600's to colonize and exploit America," Antony Sutton said.

Hollywood, 1940

In 1940, I married actress Jane Wyman. one of the prettiest women in Hollywood. These years, before the attack on Pearl Harbor, were a kick for me. I enjoyed playing B-grade romantic leads and action roles. I was a heart-throb for millions of women in America, who watched my films. But, I was unhappy ...because, the studios didn't think I was a good enough actor to cast me into first class scripts. I was a prime cut of meat studios dangled in front of sexually inactive women, to get them to buy tickets to go to the movies ...so, they could go home afterwards and sweat a little bit. A lot of roles I played in, I was the hero ...cast as a character who faces danger with a wisecrack ...then, gives a logical pep talk ... instead of expressing emotional feeling or sensitivity. I was typecast, playing myself, never dreaming someday my biggest role ... would be playing, President of the United States.

I was in the studio screening room watching out-takes from movies I starred in, finding and confirming my best angles. I liked being a cowboy hero, a soldier fighting Nazis, a war hero keeping an orbiting death ray from falling into Nazi hands, in my mind I went back, reliving those times on the set ... I was acting, the films were being shot, I had a good memory, then. Now. in the movie in my mind, I watch the camera pull back from me. We're rolling down the river.

The director sticks his face into the set, "Cut! Reagan, stop flirting with the female lead! In case you didn't know it, that man over there slapping his forehead with his palm, is our producer. He writes your check. I'm the director. I tell you what to do. That man over there, laughing, he's the writer ... he does your thinking. He makes you say stuff you can't think of by yourself. I tell you things like, hit your toe-marks so your pretty face ends up in front of all the lonely women in America stuck with the wrong guy. Get on your toe-marks!"

I felt ready. "Okay, okay, take it to the bank."

The director rolled his hand in the air, "Roll 'em!"

Vatican, 1941

In 1941, Japanese ruling banking, industrial, and mining families responded to provocation of a U.S. blockade of Japanese harbors imposed by Roosevelt Administration ... by having the emperor attack Pearl Harbor...then, U.S. entered World War II. German General Staff-owned banking and industrial cartels saw the moving finger writing on the wall, realized the Axis would now lose the armed phase of the war ... how could Germany, Italy, and Japan fight off England, the Soviet Union, the United States, France, and the rest of the Western World? ...it couldn't.

German General Staff, composed of the ruling industrial families of Germany, began making plans to survive underground, to keep their family fortunes, their war booty ...then, continue to carry on war after military fighting was over ... war by different means. It was a 1,000 year Reich, after all ...so, German General Staff made plans to smuggle out stolen Nazi gold and wealth, 'flight capital', from Europe ... out of Swiss banks where it was safely deposited in neutral territory. German ruling families didn't want the Allies to capture their Nazi wealth and war booty, they needed that flight capitalization to rebuild the Nazi Reich after World War II, just as they'd rebuilt Germany with Wall Street loans after World War I. American and British money-issuing class ruling families bought controlling shares in bankrupt corporations after World War I for a song, again for a refrain during the Depression, which was of course the entire point of orchestrating the Depression in the first place ...and, would do so again, after World War II ... for pennies on the dollar buy up German stock, buy up stock in all the conquered countries ... a recentralization of ownership of world resources and world industry in the hands of the majority shareholders of the Fed ...and, Bank of England, France, and Deutsche Bank.

So, to keep more money in their own hands, away from the grasp of the Fed, and Bank of England ruling families, German General Staff decided, relocate their wealth around the world. Martin Bormann arranged 600 dummy corporations, set up in South America and South Africa. War booty was hidden in dummy corporations and pharmaceutical companies. German General Staff located their underground Nazi

government in exile in Madrid.

Meanwhile, at the Vatican, Allen Dulles, Prince Max von Hohenlohe, Count Sergei DeMohrenshieldt, Otto von Bolschwing, Martin Bormann, Alfred Rosenberg, and Otto Skorzeny ... met with the Pope over caviar, Fourme d'Ambert blue cheese, rice crackers, and whiskey.

Dulles and Prince Max presented the 'Christian West' plan to the Pope, the plan to have United States and Germany join forces once the war was over, and attack U.S.S.R. ...one of the U.S. Allies that primarily defeated Germany in World War I, and again, in World War II ...a primary cause of defeat of Germany ... U.S.S.R. suffered great personal loss at the hands of Nazis.

Dulles, representing Nazi Germany, negotiated throughout the war with international bankers and intelligencers, all living in a constant state of treason against the United States ...so, it was easy to betray his Soviet allies as well. After all, he'd handled financial arrangements to acquire Saudi oil ...now, he wanted Soviet oil, too. The money issuing ruling families of the world are legion, a country unto themselves, not bound by geographical borders or political borders ...but, by allegiance only to their financial borders ...and, when allied, their collective wealth ... with no regard for humanity ...case in point, Allen Dulles. He was patriotic to his international ruling family collective, working people of the world were the enemy, the non-money issuing, working classes ... who would take his wealth if they could, in every country, like a rhetoric of, but not reality, of communism ... the money issuing, owning-class of every country were his allies, or if not his, then the allies of his masters, the Fed and Bank of England, Rothschilds and Warburgs, and the central bank community.

Dulles, Prince Max, Count Sergei, Otto von Bolschwing, Martin Bormann, Alfred Rosenberg, and Otto Skorzeny argued the virtues of Bank of International Settlement's 'Christian West' plan to ally the money issuing and ruling families of United States and Germany against the ruling families of Soviet Union. When the plan was put into action, with victory they would personally control Russia's Baku oil fields ...and, Russian gold, timber, coal reserves, and labor.

Dulles held the Pope's attention, "Your holiness, Vatican is a money laundering machine for trans-Atlantic Nazi and fascist money. You were given banking sovereignty by Adolf and Benito, and they let you make the Vatican a separate country inside Italy, and tax Italian citizens. I helped them with that. You'll continue to help the underground Nazi party, and my trans-Atlantic axis investment group."

The Pope nodded. "Of course, Allen. We'll plan Nazi and Fascist escape routes, use the routes for smuggling war booty and SS officers in Central and Eastern Europe to the Vatican using Vatican diplomatic immunity, deliver them to Argentina, Bolivia, Paraguay, and South Africa. What if socialists like Roosevelt, or the British, blow the whistle on us, expose the American industrial and Standard oil feed to Hitler's war machine, expose I.G. Farbin control of American I.G., expose the Bush-Walker Hamburg shipping smuggling operations?"

"Your holiness, if that happens I'll cut the oil supplies from Saudi Arabia to Britain and America to shut them up. No one's going to get Hitler's gold, but my trans-Atlantic axis investors."

"How will you get Hitler's gold out of Swiss banks?"

Dulles laughed. "I'm not going to move the gold at all. I'm leaving it in Swiss banks. I'm moving ownership of the gold ... of bonds, foreign currencies, and bearer certificates ... moving ownership out of Switzerland, out of Europe to my partner's banks in Japanese-controlled Manchuria, or Nazi-controlled South Africa, Paraguay, Bolivia and Argentina banks."

<>

The Pope understood. He was wearing his penguin hat with embroidered crosses rimming the top, like a carnival barker planting death wishes in people's souls, he ruled his Kingdom with fear, spankings, humiliation, a world priesthood of child molesters, and duplicity, planting seeds of doubt, and shame like gum balls dispensed from a round glass gumball machine ...people could swallow little bites of different colored religion wafers, indigestible, crumbling dry fragments growing inside your guts till your eyes turn inside out into granite gravestone markers, eyes that can't see the awe of Being, brains turned into dime store plastic relics that glow in the dark, suffocated souls littering the countryside like broken teeth. Love in the flock replaced itself with thinking, the cancer of logic crucified each child's humanlike ability until the flock martyred itself with jobs and careers being good little wage slaves and obedient walking dead, Love lies bleeding, Jesus wasn't coming, the Pope's flock became Barbie dolls and Ken dolls drowning in spiritual infertility, hating the sound of an alarm clock ordering their dull awakening and hunger-

less plastic 9-to-5 fast.

The Pope's eyes glowed, "We'll begin now."

Dulles blinked into the Pope's eyes.

The Pope had a realization. "Let me be the first to help you use Vatican couriers and special agents with Vatican diplomatic immunity to move freely back-and-forth across Nazi and Allied lines to transport Nazi gold certificates to safe-haven banks, for you," the Pope said.

Dulles was on a roll, he was taller than the Pope, and looked down on him. "You're a mind reader, your Holiness. We're sending ownership certificates to Manchuria now ...so, your couriers will take these new sets of ownership papers to our banks in Belgium, Liechtenstein, and Luxembourg. My Japanese and German banking partners will accept the gold ownership as loans ...then, issue new certificates of ownership ... as Nazi-dominated Bank of International Settlements arranges to secure our anti-communist, Christian West agreement. The Angletons are my intelligence operatives to help you smuggle agents and Nazi money into the Vatican, then out of Italy, as we agreed. The Angletons are inventive, providing very creative intelligence reports to you we never bothered with for Hoover, *he* was one of us. You tell President Roosevelt, these reports are Vatican intelligence. Don't tell him they're from Angleton!"

The Pope agreed. "The Christian West Plan must succeed, to defeat communism at all costs ...I make a nice commission in souls conquered."

Leaving the Pope behind, the men went to a local bar for a pre-arranged meeting, toasting themselves with whiskey, Count Sergei DeMohrenshieldt, Prince Max von Hohenlohe, Otto von Bolschwing, Martin Bormann, Alfred Rosenberg, Otto Skorzeny, Hjalmar Schacht, and Dulles were crudely laughing.

Otto von Bolschwing drew a death's head dagger from its scabbard hitting it against a whiskey bottle. "Your attention please. May I present my comrades in arms, all guerrilla Freikorps leaders in eastern Europe, each wanting to own their own national central bank, each associated with our trans-Atlantic axis investment bankers, each donating significant campaign funds to politicians in America, and in every county we need to achieve the Christian West plan. Laszlo Pasztor of Hungary leads the Hungarian Iron Cross death squads."

Dulles thought Laszlo Pasztor's face reptilian, by that, knew he could be trusted.

Pasztor saluted von Bolschwing, Skorzeny then Dulles, "I pledge lifelong service to you."

Dulles tipped his glass to Radi Slavoff, "To the Reich, to the Christian West."

Von Bolschwing downed his shot. "Radi Slavoff from Bulgaria leads the Bulgarian Legion death squads. Germany's Nicolas Nazarenko leads our SS Cossack Division. Romania's Florian Galdau, is leader of the Iron Guard Brigade death squads. Philip Guarino of Italy. A toast gentlemen ... to Fascists in Ukraine, the Organization of Ukrainian Nationalists the OUN ...in Byelo-Russia Belarus, the Belarus Brigade, whose leaders can't be with us today because of ongoing Freikorps death squad pogroms ...but, they remain in our hearts," von Bolschwing said.

Count Sergei DeMohrenshieldt was not to be outdone, "It's my hope when armed military war ends, we immigrate to United States, join the Czarist Dallas expatriate community, and lobby in Washington to overthrow U.S.S.R., to regain our Baku oil holdings, form political warfare units of Fascist and Nazi anti-communist freedom fighters to rally the national ethnic vote here, for you, Mr. Dulles. In American, we'll get the ethnic swing-vote for your Republican candidates. In return, you funnel U.S. military aid to our Freikorps units in our home countries, to win the fight against Communism, extending the reach of Christian West, so we can get our share of the Baku oil and recover our Czarist portfolios," DeMohrenshieldt said.

Dulles smiled, "That'll help Republican Party presidential candidates win, I promise you, safe passage, a place in Washington inside the party, and we'll finance Freikorps groups in your home countries, under your leadership."

<>

Soon after the U.S. entered World War II in 1941, I found himself unable to march off into the trenches, not allowed to shove my body onto the end of a bayonet to help increase our debt to the Fed's major stockholders and the Bank of England's ...because of bad eyesight, I ended up in an Army Air Corps film unit based in Hollywood for the duration of World War II, as a soldier movie producer making propaganda films to boost Army morale for soldiers who *would* decorate bayonets. I made war entertainment films, such as, *This Is The Army* ... where I stared as a corporal staging a variety show, the end of the film had recruits marching off to battle happily singing in harmony ...but, it was only a film ... in real life they'd have their faces blown off, their intestines decorating trees for bird food.

My film career practically ended after 1945 when the war ended ...cause, my looks were shot. I was getting older ...but, my wife Jane Wyman's career was still successful. During early postwar years, my hatred of Hitler and dislike of Fascism eroded ...and, was somehow replaced with anxiety about Communism, and perceived Soviet threat. In 1946, my political consciousness festered, then erupted. I dreaded a perceived communist plan of sending waves of communists to California, to take over Hollywood's motion picture industry.

I knew taking over Hollywood was Stalin's plot to brainwash Americans ...then, take over America. What I didn't know, till the last year of my life ... was that the major shareholders of the Fed had already taken over Hollywood, sitting as directors of major studios, so no truly revolutionary film was ever made, much less showing support of struggles of the mainstream public to get jobs, pay bills, support families, or be free from financial worry, much less honestly portray the sad conditions of the majority of the people in the world, and in the third world countries.

Bechtel Building San Francisco & Bohemian Grove, 1948 & 1952

Bill Casey drove into the parking lot of the Bechtel Building in San Francisco. Bill had an impressive international banking portfolio. It was just as successful as Allen Dulles' portfolio, for the same reasons ... Casey copied Dulles' investments ...now and then, he'd use mercenaries to protect his own investments overseas on the pretense of protecting democracy ... he'd learned that from Dulles, too.

Both men were part of U.S. intelligence, knew where to invest, how to kill competitors. Bill was a U.S. Office of Strategic Services veteran from the second world war. Like Dulles, he came from the Wall Street investment bankers that put OSS together, simply picking economic targets in wartime for the U.S. military, destroying factories and holdings of their competition, or using U.S. soldiers to capture ore, petroleum fields, factories, or banks they wanted to own, that was the function of the U.S. military, after all ...literally killing off the competition. Bill and Allen knew where the bodies were buried, because they buried them ... ask Kennedy.

A lot of times I thought, maybe Paul Robeson's ghost could put me in touch with Kennedy's ghost, I'd ask him later, so I knew what really happened that day in Dallas.

Bill dropped off his passenger, Allen Dulles, who walked over to greet Mr. Bechtel, then Bill drove off.

Bechtel had a fun weekend planned at Bohemian Grove, the private redwood forest he and his friends in the Bohemian Club of San Francisco owned, where they had private cabins. The annual campout had Hi-Jinx and Lo-Jinx skits, ruling family patriarchs dressed up in drag, pissing contests between the oldest patriarchs who could no longer get it up, for them, pissing was sex. In 1948, Bechtel invited the Bechtel clan, of course ...the Dulles clan, and John McCone, co-founder of Bechtel International in the 1930s ...and, the Bechtel financiers, the Schroders, or a Warburg, or a Rothschild ... who of course, never showed up because they had front men for that sort of thing. Dulles heard John McCone would be appointed DCI at CIA. Dulles looked forward to meeting Henry Kissinger that evening, a German-born citizen who served in U.S. SIS Military Intelligence during World War II. Bechtel invited King Ibn Saud, and his entourage, too.

<>

At Bohemian Grove, who ever would be president next was chosen ten-to-twenty years before, national security objectives and targets were agreed upon, foreign policy strategic milestones discussed and set, deals for oil refineries built by Bechtel engineering corps in Saudi Arabia, Iran, and Iraq ... financed by Dulles' backers ... the major shareholders of the Fed and Bank of England ... for Saudi and fascist clients -- were tendered, international opposition was defined, and targeted ...then, when John McCord nodded, CIA would covertly wipe out the economic base of oil competitors by assassinating the political leadership, starting a revolution, or counter-revolution, frame a scapegoat to blame sabotage on, run routine terror-ops, fund and stage a coup d'état ... whatever ...train, install military needed to support puppet regimes to follow U.S. ruling family financial investment orders ...then, given U.S. foreign aid or loans only used to hire companies like Bechtel, General Motors, Brown & Root, Halliburton, buy their equipment, products, training, consulting, and management.

When overt military fighting of World War II ended as far as most knew, or were told, Allen helped Bechtel, both power elite players for major shareholders of the Fed and Bank of England, to orchestrate success of their Christian West plan to ally western powers against Soviet Russia, incorporating Nazis and Fascists, as they'd planned in World War II.

Dulles needed social engineering to control what the common guy on the street thought, to motivate the common guy to hate communists, hate socialism, and hate redistribution of wealth ...from the rich, to the poor.

Before Allen could take over U.S.S.R., he had to take over the U.S.A. ... wage psychological warfare against the common guy ...and, pass marching orders from his bosses to the boys at Bohemian Grove, who financed and directed the various presidencies when West Coast power brokers had more horsepower than New England, or Texas, power brokers.

Allen wanted to wage the first-ever domestic U.S. psy-ops, having U.S. Intelligence brainwash the common guy into thinking Soviet Russian Communists ... who after all, *were* financed by major shareholders of the Fed and Bank of England since 1917 ... were suddenly a threat to MacDonalds, Disneyland, Macy's, Chevy, Santa Claus, *Father Knows Best,* and the 4th of July, that Russia was the new enemy ...now, that they'd destroyed the Nazis ... forget the Russians fought German General Staff, defeating them in the trenches of World War I, and limb-strewn battlefields of World War II. Forget the Russians fought on the side of the Americans in World War I, and World War II. Forget. Brainwash that bean. Now, overnight, the Russians would be made the new enemy of Mom and apple pie.

Here at Bohemian Grove, snuggled in the Redwood Forests that stood for 1,000 years and before the birth of Christ, plans for the United Nations startup in San Francisco were set, GATT created, World Bank and International Monetary Fund conceived ... to help control western and world banking ...here, National Security Memorandum #68 was conceived of by Bohemian Grove participants from Stanford University's Hoover Institute ... to authorize domestic U.S. psy-ops against the common American guy, soon to be watching *Amos & Andy, G.E. Theatre, You Bet Your Life and Burns & Allen,* by controlling the public mind, public education, public awareness ...and, public opinion. Armed military conflict was one form of warfare. Economic warfare was another. Political warfare, another. Psychological _____, you fill in the blank. Propaganda warfare, socio-economic warfare. Chemical warfare, biological warfare, genetic warfare, nuclear warfare, electronic warfare. Space _____. Paramilitary ops _____. Covert action ops _____. Terrorist ops _____.

Someone needed to update the bible with Satan's modern arsenal, so the common guy at least had a chance at a working vocabulary to describe reality. Like Rocky knew what social engineering was, or any of the *Rocky* movies or their audiences.

King Ibn Saud felt fidgety. "When will I get new refineries? Harems cost money."

Dulles lit his cigar, puffing it in, hissing it out. "I understand Syria asked Soviet Union and China to finance oil refineries, to compete in world markets against us."

John McCord shrugged. "There'll be civil unrest in Syria, Egypt, and Iran over our next three year plan, civil wars, coups, countercoups to slow 'em down."

King Ibn Saud opened his arms wide towards the redwood trees, "Mr. Bechtel, thank you for building my refineries. Mr. Dulles, thank you for financing them, someday I'll have more money than the Rothschilds ... your interests."

Dulles searched his pocket for a cigar. "That's the plan ...then, we can rival them as rulers of the western world."

"But then, you'll belong to me," Ibn Saud said.

Dulles looked Ibn Saud over. Ibn Saud looked frayed. Dulles didn't like that. "Don't bet on it. Me and McCord fixed the CIA covert coup in Syria in 1949, we have one planned for Iran in 1953, that'll make you the biggest oil producer ...and, Fed and Bank of England will control petro-dollars, and world currency inflationary rates, eliminate roadblocks to oil turf wars, and have a new world order of peace. We bought Dillion-Reed investment bank out, they'll continue partnering with you, financing the underground Reich as we did during the war, Warburg says Rothschild told him."

Ibn Saud held up a map of Israel. "Look at these Jews."

Bechtel took the map of Israel, ripped it up, threw the pieces in the campfire.

Dulles relaxed. "We need to own Russia's oil, timber, and gold ... to surround China, force them to join BIS, come under influence of Bank of England and Fed. We go through Russia, Iraq, Iran, India, Vietnam, and North Korea to get China."

McCord chimed in. "Allen, your brother like being U.S. Secretary of State? ...doing that war against the North Koreans for their coal?"

Allen drew on his cigar, "My son is brain damaged from combat against North Koreans."

Bechtel threw wood on the fire, "Look here, gentlemen, after McCord did those CIA-backed coups in Syria and Iran, Bechtel got contracts to rebuild infrastructures of those companies ... for hundred of millions of dollars. We beat out Brown & Root, and Halliburton, and ibn Saud Construction ... for government contracts. Each time we have CIA start civil war, counter-revolution, insurgency, counter-insurgency, coup, hiccup, breaks wind, put in a puppet government, we win redevelopment and refinery contracts. That's war, civil war, revolution, economic turf war for oil, gold, timber, coal. Ruling family turf wars cost money. Just because *our* ruling families are jealous of *their* ruling families, and want what they got, that corner, that tree, that rig ... we try to steal from each other, no one else owns anything, get the tuxedos dirty, stain 'em with champagne, roast duck, artichoke soup. We got coups for Indonesia, Central and South America, I want contracts to rebuild those countries ...so, get busy destroying them."

Dulles had that far-away, cigar look in his eyes. "Bank of England, Fed, World Bank, IMF, BIS won't loan money to starving economies ... unless they agree to use money we loan them, to award you contracts."

"Of course," Bechtel said. "We need a spokesperson to bad-talk communism and the Soviet Union ...here, on the domestic front, get the small guy to go for our military solutions, out of his own wallet. We'll call our first domestic psyops in the U.S. targeting Americans, *the Crusade For Freedom.* Nice and catchy. But, who's going to promote it for us? ...who can we get to be our spokesperson? Someone the little guys like? What about you, Mr. Reagan?"

So, that was it. "I was wondering why you guys brought me here. I'm glad for the job you got me hosting General Electric Theater on TV. Sure, I can be spokesman for anti-Communism. I learned from Father Kauflin, a long time ago. We need freedom now, more than ever. Yeah, a crusade for freedom, I like that."

"We'll tell you what to say," Bechtel said.

<>

That's when they started it. "I *know what the hell to say*, I'm not an idiot."

"What I meant was, we'll give you a script, direct, and produce you."

"That's all you had to say."

The men grew tired. They walked outside their tent cabins in Bohemian Grove redwood park, older men had pissing contests shining their shoes, retired, undressed ...and, went to sleep.

<>

In 1949, Jane Wyman was threatening to divorce me. She said, it was because she felt she was living with a concrete statue. Perhaps unconsciously, to avoid this reality I plunged deeper into administrative work at Screen Actor's Guild, a union for actors. I wasn't landing movie roles, anymore. I was elected a member of the board ...then, elected President of the board. Jane, somehow, couldn't share my catholic fervor in my crusade against Communism. She felt Communism was an idea, that you couldn't go around killing people to change their ideas, that's what public education was for. I, on the other hand knew, if you got rid of the person ...then, you got rid of the idea ... men are from Mars, women are from Venus. Jane divorced me, she was awarded custody of our two young children, Michael and Maureen.

<>

My views of the Red Menace mirrored movie plots I'd starred in. Sometimes, I described Hollywood communists as, 'our little Red brothers', comparing them to renegade Indians in Westerns. I served as President of Screen Actor's Guild six years. During that time, I was called to testify before House Of Un-American Activities, as a 'friendly witness'. I campaigned to purge the film industry of communists, endorsed the Hollywood studios' blacklist of 'left-wing' actors, met secretly with FBI agents to report political affiliations of Hollywood stars, my co-workers at the Guild, becoming more 'conservative' in my political thought. I kept tabs on actors I considered disloyal, informing on them to FBI ... under my code name, 'Agent T-10'. Believing Republican Party could fight communism better than Democrats, I abandoned my left-of-center political views ...instead, supporting presidential candidacies of Dwight D. Eisenhower in 1952 and 1956, Richard Nixon in 1960 ...all while I was a Democrat.

Dwight D. Eisenhower twice defeated the 'liberal' Democratic presidential nominee, Adlai Stevenson. Ike had helped drive a wooden stake through the heart of pre-New Deal Republican orthodoxy. I told my older brother, if any party tried to abolish Social Security, unemployment insurance, eliminate labor laws, and farm programs born under Roosevelt and Truman, that party wouldn't be heard of, again. In 1952, I met and married Nancy Davis, a very attractive actress in Hollywood, a small bit player in B-films under contract to MGM who wanted to be a big star ...but, aimed her acting career too high, based on her acting talent, like most of us in the 'B's. Nancy told her friends, she was giving up her career to marry me, and raise a family. Soon, me and Nancy had two kids, Patricia was our little girl. Ronald Jr. was our little boy.

By mid-'50s my acting career was kaput. General Electric hired me ... friends of Bechtel, to host General Electric Theater on TV, a weekly. General Electric remodeled our house, making the Reagan house an all-electric home, to be the pride of America, make housewives drool, beg their husbands for bigger allowances to buy into the American Dream ... an all-electric kitchen full of electric gadgets. Me and Nancy made TV commercials right in our own home, selling kitchen appliances. We helped the American Dream come true. At the same time, I was co-producing, hosting, and starring, in my weekly TV shows. Another part of my job for General Electric, was to be a corporate spokesman, make speeches around the country as GE corporate ambassador of good will ...for eight years, touring GE plants around America, meeting senior management, assembly-line workers, haunting hundreds of local Chambers of Commerce ... delivering my message, fight Communism, promoting Crusade For Freedom for good of all countries in the world ...so, everyone could be free of Communism, like Father Kauflin, the anti-communist Catholic, said. But, I wasn't doing it on radio, I was takin' it to the streets. I made thousands of after-dinner speeches, promoting traditional family values, warning audiences of Communism conquering nations abroad, warning of Socialism creeping up at home, telling blue collar, and white collar workers, the individual was, and should be forever, master of his own destiny.

I went through changes, I start abandoning my previous enthusiasm for, 'The New Deal', described ruling family business leaders as a dam holding back the great collective tide of humanity, guiding it towards salvation ... praising ruling family business leaders as, bravely standing up against burdens of high taxes, government regulation, and Social Security ... that 'liberals' inflicted, to slow business growth in America ...but, General Electric censured me when I criticized Tennessee Valley Authority, a major customer of G.E. electricity, as being 'socialistic' ... the apple never falls far from the tree. My employment by GE enhanced my political image, I'd traveled all over the country, well known for my anti-communist speeches.

Ronald Reagan home, 1955

Nancy was singing, *Mr. Sandman, bring me a dream*, along with the radio, trying to hold Patti still, who was eight years old at the time, while Nancy struggled to brush snarls out of Patti's hair. Patti yelped like a dog who got stepped on.

Patti was sobbing. "Mommy! I want my hair

long! Daddy, I want my Daddy!?"

Nancy took scissors, Patti's hair tumbled through the air to the floor. Ron Jr. stood in the doorway, crying, because Patti was crying.

Nancy yelled. "Ron, go to your room!"

Ron Jr. left, running to his room. Ron Jr. clutched his Teddy Bear tightly. Ron Jr. threw himself on his bed, felt tears form in his eyes, then fall. Ron Jr. listened to the fight between his Mother and Sister.

Nancy screamed, uncontrollably, felt enraged, *"Do you hear me!"*

Ron Jr. heard the fight, yelled at his Teddy Bear, dug his fingers in his bear's stomach. Afraid to move he seemed to freeze in position.

<>

"You had it coming! I told you, don't let your brother out of your sight at the playground! Look at me when I'm talking to you! Stop talking about me on the phone to your friends! It's none of their business, what I do!"

Patti stared in horror in the mirror as big chunks of her hair fell down through the air. She glared at Nancy.

Nancy yelled. "Don't give me that hex look!"

Nancy got angrier. Patti sensed it, give up. Patti became still. Patti didn't protest, didn't fight it anymore, waited for Nancy to get desperate, stared at her mother.

Nancy walked out of the room.

Patti sighed in relief, went into the bathroom, stared at the little girl in the mirror, waited for the welts to rise on the little girl's face, watching handprints rise on her cheeks, staring in the mirror. Patti felt ashamed, betrayed, insecure, vulnerable, frightened.

Ron Jr. hid under his covers, hugged his Teddy Bear against him, listened to his heart pound in his ears. Nancy gathered up the kids, put coats on them, picked up her purse, herded everyone outside. Everyone got in the car. Patti flattened her face up against the glass on the passenger side window. Nancy drove along. Ron Jr. cringed in the back seat, his arm around his Teddy Bear's neck so tight, the Teddy Bear's neck broke.

Nancy kept yelling. "Don't talk about me! Not to your friends! And, not on the phone!"

Ron Jr. saw Patti didn't know what to do. Patti looked out the passenger side car window.

Nancy grabbed Patti's chin, jerking her head around. "Look at me when I talk to you!"

Ron Jr. remembered how scared Patti was, him too.

And yelling. "Now look out the window all you want!"

Ron Jr. sat still, afraid to cry out loud, tears fell on his cheeks. He watched Patti press her face against the car window glass, staring out the window like she didn't see anything. Ron Jr. imagined how Patti's face looked from outside the car to people they passed, pressed up against the glass, anguished and grotesque, nose pushed up, nostrils flared, lips flattened and smeared, cheeks puffed flat in a mask ...Patti watched the world behind glass. On the other side, the world went its way.

<>

In 1960, prevailing Republican-ism at the time accepted New Deal ideals of helping the common American survive financially, and not be totally subjected to whims of the industrialist ruling-families that dispensed jobs ...unlike today, where successive Bush Administrations reversed that, taking pleasure in stamping out hundreds of thousands of jobs with no care for the average American worker's survival, touting NAFTA, Gatt, WTO imported illegal aliens to be paid less than minimum wage in service jobs, outsourcing 411 and O phone calls to India along with programming, assembly jobs, customer service, and entire industries ... overseas.

That 'New Deal' kind of Republican made the 'Conservative' lunatic fringe of the GOP furious, after all, the 'Conservative' element was called the 'New Right'. Leading members ranged from Robert Welch, who founded the extremist John Birch Society ...to William F. Buckley, Jr., an ex-intelligence officer who founded the 'Conservative' journal, *National Review.*

My friend, Republican Senator Barry Goldwater of Arizona published a treatise ghost-written for him by Bill Buckley Jr.'s brother-in-law, called, *Conscience of a Conservative.* It became a working Bible for the 'New Right'. In it, Goldwater and the 'New Right' rejected the idea of New Deal social programs that benefited non-ruling family, everyday Americans of blue collar, and middle class stature. Goldwater demanded the Government return to straight capitalism, ruling families with the most capital should control America ... Goldwater believed in the Golden Rule, he who has the gold rules.

Goldwater wanted to challenge Soviet Bloc countries aggressively, which implied he held stock in what Smedley Butler saw, and Eisenhower called, 'the military-industrial complex'. Since 'New Right' had proponents and converts in California, General Electric had me concentrate making my speeches there ...but, in the early 1960's, the Board of Directors at General Electric heard rumors Justice Department was going to investigate me when I was President of Screen Actors Guild ten years ago, for allegedly getting kickbacks from brokering a deal that allowed one of the most powerful TV and film production companies in Hollywood to act as an agent for actors ... while being producers of the shows the actors starred in. Grand Jury considered this conflict of interest. I was called in front of the Grand Jury. I told them, I couldn't remember, had memory loss, like I was told to tell them.

General Electric ended its relationship with me, I was out of a job ...but, I was a millionaire out of a job ...and, had been a millionaire for quite some time. So, I kept making speeches.

In 1963, President Kennedy was assassinated in Texas, everyone had a theory ...but, I went with the Warren Commission version.

By 1964, I was a washed-up old actor, that year Barry Goldwater was nominated for President of the United States ... Goldwater promised to destroy New Deal ideology, ran against President Lyndon B. Johnson. Johnson described Goldwater as being on the lunatic fringe of the Republican Party, a fanatic who wanted to spend America's money to start nuclear war, who wanted to send elderly and the poor into the poor house, forever.

I volunteered to make a TV fundraising speech for Goldwater, a collection of anti-Government, and anti-communist, clichés.

I made the speech. This part was the clincher. "You and I have a rendezvous with destiny. We can preserve for our children this, the last best hope of man on earth, or we can sentence them to take the first step into a thousand years of darkness. If we fail, at least let our children and our children's children, say of us we justified our brief moment here. We did all that could be done."

It became known as, 'Rendezvous with Destiny', and went like this.

"Thank you very much. Thank you and good evening. The sponsor's been identified, but unlike most television programs, the performer hasn't been provided with a script. As a matter of fact, I've been permitted to choose my own ideas regarding the choice we face the next few weeks.

"I've spent most of my life as a Democrat. I recently have seen fit to follow another course. I believe that issues confronting us, cross party lines. Now, one side in this campaign has been telling us, the issues of this election are maintenance of peace and prosperity. The line's been used 'We've never had it so good'.

"But, I have an uncomfortable feeling that this prosperity isn't something we can base our hopes on for the future. No nation in history has ever survived a tax burden that reached a third of its national income. Today, 37 cents of every dollar earned in this country is the tax collector's share, and yet, our government continues to spend 17 million dollars a day more than the government takes in. We haven't balanced our budget 28 out of the last 34 years. We've raised our debt limit three times in the last twelve months, and now our national debt is one-and-a-half times bigger than all the combined debts, of all the nations in the world. We have 15 billion dollars in gold in our treasury ... we don't own an ounce. Foreign dollar claims are 27.3 billion dollars, and we just announced the dollar of 1939 will now purchase 45 cents in its total value.

"As for the peace that we would preserve, I wonder, who among us would like to approach the wife or mother whose husband or son has died in South Vietnam, and ask them if they think this is a peace that should be maintained indefinitely. Do they mean peace, or do they mean, we just want to be left in peace? There can be no real peace while one American is dying someplace in the world for the rest of us. We're at war with the most dangerous enemy that ever faced mankind in his long climb from the swamp, to the stars, and it's been said, if we lose that war, and in doing so lose this way of freedom of ours, history will record with the greatest astonishment, that those who had the most to lose did the least to prevent its happening. Well, I think it's time we ask ourselves, if we still know the freedoms that were intended for us by the Founding Fathers.

"Not too long ago, two friends of mine were talking to a Cuban refugee, a businessman who escaped from Castro, and in the midst of his story one of my friends turned to the other and said, 'We don't know how lucky we are'. And the Cuban stopped and said, 'How lucky you are! I had someplace to escape to'. In that sentence he told us the entire story. If we lose freedom here, there is no place to escape to. This is the last stand on Earth. And this idea, that government is beholden to the people, that it has no other source of power except to sovereign people, is still the newest and most unique idea in all the long history of man's relation to man. This is the issue of this election. Whether we believe in our capacity for self-government, or whether we abandon the American revolution and confess that a little intellectual elite in a far-distant capital can plan our lives for us better than we can plan them ourselves.

"You and I are told increasingly, that we have to choose between a left or right, but I would like to suggest that there is no such thing as left or right. There is only an up or down ... up to a man's age-old dream, the ultimate in individual freedom consistent with law and order ... or down to the ant heap of totalitarianism, and regardless of their sincerity, their humanitarian motives, those who would trade our freedom for security have embarked on this downward course.

"In this vote-harvesting time, they use terms like, the 'Great Society,' or as we were told a few days ago by the President, we must accept a 'greater government activity in the affairs of the people'. But they have been a little more explicit in the past and among themselves ... and all of the things that I now will quote have appeared in print. These are not Republican accusations. For example, they have voices that say, 'the cold war will end through acceptance of a not undemocratic socialism'. Another voice says that the profit motive has become outmoded, it must be replaced by the incentives of the welfare state ... or our traditional system of individual freedom is incapable of solving the complex problems of the 20th century. Senator Fullbright has said at Stanford University that the Constitution is out-moded. He referred to the president as our moral teacher and our leader, and he said he is hobbled in his task by the restrictions in power imposed on him by this antiquated document. He must be freed so that he can do for us what he knows is best. And Senator Clark of Pennsylvania, another articulate spokesman, defines liberalism as 'meeting the material needs of the masses through the full power of centralized govern-ment'. Well, I for one resent it when a represen-tative of the people refers to you and me ... the free man and woman of this country ... as 'the masses'. This is a term we haven't applied to our-selves in America. But beyond that, 'the full power of centralized government' ... this was the very thing the Founding Fathers sought to mini-mize. They knew that governments don't control things. A government can't control the economy without controlling people. And they know when a government sets out to do that, it must use force and coercion to achieve its purpose. They also knew, those Founding Fathers, that outside of its legitimate functions, government does nothing as well or as economically as the private sector of the economy.

"Senator Humphrey last week charged that

Barry Goldwater as President would seek to elim-inate farmers. He should do his homework a lit-tle better, because he'll find out we've had a decline of 5 million in the farm population under these government programs. He'll also find the Democratic administration has sought to get from Congress an extension of the farm program to include that three-fourths that is now free. He'll find that they've also asked for the right to imprison farmers who wouldn't keep books as prescribed by the federal government. The Secretary of Agriculture asked for the right to seize farms through condemnation and resell them to other individuals. And contained in that same program was a provision that would've allowed the federal government to remove 2 mil-lion farmers from the soil.

"At the same time, there's been an increase in Department of Agriculture employees. There's now one for every 30 farms in the United States, and still they can't tell us how 66 shiploads of grain headed for Austria disappeared without a trace and Billie Sol Estes never left shore.

"Every responsible farmer and farm organiza-tion has repeatedly asked the government to free the farm economy, but who are farmers, to know what's best for them? The wheat farmers voted against a wheat program. The government passed it anyway. Now the price of bread goes up ... the price of wheat to the farmer goes down.

"Meanwhile, back in the city, under urban renewal the assault on freedom carries on. Private property rights are so diluted that public interest is almost anything that a few govern-ment planners decide it should be. In a program that takes from the needy and gives to the greedy, we see such spectacles as in Cleveland, Ohio, a $1,500,000 building completed only three years ago must be destroyed to make way for what government officials call a 'more com-patible use of the land'. The President tells us he's now going to start building public housing units in the thousands where heretofore we've only built them in the hundreds. But FHA and Veterans Administration tell us that they've 120,000 housing units they've taken back through mortgage foreclosures. For three decades, we've sought to solve the problems of unemployment through government planning, and the more the plans fail, the more the plan-ners plan. The latest is the Area Redevelopment Agency. They've just declared Rice County, Kansas, a depressed area. Rice County, Kansas has two hundred oil wells, and the 14,000 peo-ple there have over 30 million dollars on deposit in personal savings in their banks. When the government tells you you're depressed, lie down and be depressed.

"We have so many people who can't see a fat man standing beside a thin one without coming to the conclusion that the fat man got that way by taking advantage of the thin one. So they're going to solve all the problems of human misery through government and government planning. Well, now, if government planning and welfare had the answer and they've had almost 30 years of it, shouldn't we expect government to almost read the score to us once in a while? Shouldn't they be telling us about the decline each year in the number of people needing help? The reduction in the need for public housing?

"But the reverse is true. Each year the need grows greater, the program grows greater. We were told four years ago that 17 million people went to bed hungry each night. Well, that was probably true. They were all on a diet. But now we're told that 9.3 million families in this country are poverty-stricken on the basis of earning less than $3,000 a year. Welfare spending is 10 times greater than in the dark depths of the Depression. We are spending 45 billion dollars on welfare. Now do a little arithmetic, and you will find that if we divided the 45 billion dollars up equally among those 9 million poor families, we would be able to give each family $4,600 a year, and this added to their present income should eliminate poverty! Direct aid to the poor, however, is running only about $600 per family. It would seem that someplace there must be overhead.

"So now we declare 'war on poverty', or 'you, too, can be a Bobby Baker!' Now, do they honestly expect us to believe that if we add 1 billion dollars to the 45 million dollars we are spending ... one more program to the 30-odd we have ... and remember, this new program doesn't replace any, it just duplicates existing programs ... do they believe that poverty is suddenly going to disappear by magic? Well, in all fairness I should explain that there is one part of the new program that isn't duplicated. This is the youth feature. We're now going to solve the dropout problem, juvenile delinquency, by reinstituting something like the old CCC camps, and we're going to put our young people in camps, but again we do some arithmetic, and we find that we are going to spend each year just on room and board for each young person that we help, $4,700 a year! We can send them to Harvard for $2,700! Don't get me wrong. I'm not suggesting Harvard is the answer to juvenile delinquency.

"But seriously, what are we doing to those we seek to help? Not too long ago, a judge called me here in Los Angeles. He told me of a young woman who had come before him for a divorce. She had six children, was pregnant with her seventh. Under his questioning, she revealed her husband was a laborer earning $250 a month. She wanted a divorce so that she could get an $80 raise. She is eligible for $330 a month in the Aid to Dependent Children Program. She got the idea from two women in her neighborhood who had already done that very thing.

"Yet anytime you and I question the schemes of the do-gooders, we're denounced as being against humanitarian goals. They say we're always 'against' things, never 'for' anything. Well, the trouble with our liberal friends is not that they're ignorant, but that they know so much that isn't so. We're for a provision that destitution should not follow unemployment by reason of old age, and to that end we've accepted Social Security as a step toward meeting the problem.

"But we are against those entrusted with this program when they practice deception regarding its fiscal shortcomings, when they charge that any criticism of the program means we want to end payments to those who depend on them for livelihood. They have called it insurance to us in a hundred million pieces of literature. But then they appeared before the Supreme Court and they testified that it was a welfare program. They only use the term 'insurance' to sell it to the people. And they said Social Security dues are a tax for the general use of government, and the government has used that tax. There is no fund, because Robert Byers, the actuarial head, appeared before a congressional committee and admitted that Social Security as of this moment is 298 billion dollars in the hole. But he said there should be no cause for worry because as long as they have power to tax, they could always take away from the people whatever they needed to bail them out of trouble! And they're doing that.

"A young man, 21 years of age, working at average salary ... his Social Security contribution would, in the open market, buy him an insurance policy to guarantee $220 a month at age 65. The government promises $127. He could live it up until he is 31 and then take out a policy that would pay more than Social Security. Now, are we so lacking in business sense that we can't put this program on a sound basis so that people who do require those payments will find that they can get them when they are due ... that the cupboard isn't bare? Barry Goldwater thinks we can.

"At the same time, can't we introduce voluntary features that would permit a citizen who can do better on his own to be excused upon presentation of evidence that he had made provisions for the non-earning years? Should we allow a widow with children to work, and not lose the benefits supposedly paid for by her deceased husband? Shouldn't you and I be allowed to declare who our beneficiaries will be under these programs, which we cannot do? I think we're for telling our senior citizens that no one in this country should be denied medical care because of a lack of funds. But I think we're against forcing all citizens, regardless of need, into a compulsory government program, especially when we have such examples, as announced last week, when France admitted that their Medicare program was now bankrupt. They've come to the end of the road.

"In addition, was Barry Goldwater so irresponsible when he suggested that our government give up its program of deliberate planned inflation so that when you do get your Social Security pension, a dollar will buy a dollar's worth, and not 45 cents' worth?

"I think we're for an international organization, where the nations of the world can seek peace. But I think we're against subordinating American interests to an organization that has become so structurally unsound that today you can muster a two-thirds vote on the floor of the General Assembly among the nations that represent less than 10 percent of the world's population. I think we're against the hypocrisy of assailing our allies because here and there they cling to a colony, while we engage in a conspiracy of silence and never open our mouths about millions of people enslaved in Soviet colonies in satellite nations.

"I think we're for aiding our allies by sharing of our material blessings with those nations which share in our fundamental beliefs, but against doling out money government to government, creating bureaucracy, if not socialism, all over the world. We set out to help 19 countries. We're helping 107. We spent 146 billion dollars. With that money, we bought a 2 million dollar yacht for Haile Selassie. We bought dress suits for Greek undertakers, extra wives for Kenyan government officials. We bought a thousand TV sets for a place where they have no electricity. In the last six years, 52 nations have bought 7 billion dollars worth of our gold, and all 52 are receiving foreign aid from this country.

"No government ever voluntarily reduces itself in size. Government programs, once launched, never disappear. Actually, a government bureau is the nearest thing to eternal life we'll ever see on this Earth. Federal employees number 2.5 million, and federal, state, and local, one out of six of the nation's work force is employed by the government. These proliferating bureaus with their thousands of regulations have cost us many of our constitutional safeguards. How many of us realize that today federal agents can invade a man's property without a warrant? They can impose a fine without a formal hearing, let alone a trial by jury, and they can seize and sell his property in auction to enforce the payment of that fine. In Chico County, Arkansas, James Wier over-planted his rice allotment. The government obtained a $17,000 judgment, and a U.S. marshal sold his 950-acre farm at auction. The government said it was necessary as a warning to others to make the system work. Last Feb. 19 at the University of Minnesota, Norman Thomas, six-time candidate for President on the Socialist Party ticket, said, 'If Barry Goldwater became President, he would stop the advance of socialism in the United States'. I think that's exactly what he will do.

"As a former Democrat, I can tell you Norman Thomas isn't the only man who's drawn this parallel to socialism with the present administration. Back in 1936, Mr. Democrat himself, Al Smith, the great American, came before the American people and charged the leadership of his party was taking the party of Jefferson, Jackson, and Cleveland down the road under the banners of Marx, Lenin, and Stalin. And he walked away from his party, and he never returned to the day he died, because to this day, the leadership of that party has been taking that party, that honorable party, down the road in the image of the labor socialist party of England. Now it doesn't require expropriation or confiscation of private property or business to impose socialism on a people. What does it mean whether you hold the deed or the title to your business or property if the government holds the power of life and death over that business or property? Such machinery already exists. The government can find some charge to bring against any concern it chooses to prosecute. Every businessman has his own tale of harassment. Somewhere a perversion has taken place. Our natural, inalienable rights are now considered to be a dispensation of government, and freedom has never been so fragile, so close to slipping from our grasp as it is at this moment. Our Democratic opponents seem unwilling to debate these issues. They want to make you and I believe that this is a contest between two men ... that we are to choose just between two personalities.

"Well, what of this man that they would destroy? And in destroying, they would destroy that which he represents, the ideas that you and I hold dear. Is he the brash and shallow and trigger-happy man they say he is? Well, I have been privileged to know him, 'when'. I knew him long before he ever dreamed of trying for high office, and I can tell you personally I've never known a man in my life I believe so incapable of doing a dishonest or dishonorable thing.

"This is a man who in his own business, before he entered politics, instituted a profit-sharing plan, before unions had ever thought of it. He put in health and medical insurance for all his employees. He took 50 percent of the profits before taxes and set up a retirement program, a pension plan for all his employees. He sent checks for life to an employee who was ill and couldn't work. He provided nursing care for the children of mothers who work in the stores. When Mexico was ravaged by floods from the Rio Grande, he climbed in his airplane and flew medicine and supplies down there.

"An ex-GI told me how he met him. It was the week before Christmas during the Korean War, and he was at the Los Angeles airport trying to get a ride home to Arizona for Christmas, and he said that there were a lot of servicemen there and no seats available on the planes. Then a voice came over the loudspeaker and said, 'Any men in uniform wanting a ride to Arizona, go to runway such-and-such', and they went down there, and there was this fellow named Barry Goldwater sitting in his plane. Every day in the weeks before Christmas, all day long, he would load up the plane, fly to Arizona, fly them to their homes, then fly back over to get another load.

"During the hectic split-second timing of a campaign, this is a man who took time out to sit beside an old friend who was dying of cancer. His campaign managers were understandably impatient, but he said, 'There aren't many left who care what happens to her. I'd like her to know I care'. This is a man who said to his 19-year-old son, 'There is no foundation like the rock of honesty and fairness, and when you begin to build your life upon that rock, with the cement of the faith in God that you have, then you have a real start'. This is not a man who could carelessly send other people's sons to war. And that is the issue of this campaign that makes all of the other problems I have discussed academic, unless we realize that we are in a war that must be won.

"Those who would trade our freedom for the soup kitchen of the welfare state have told us that they have a utopian solution of peace without victory. They call their policy 'accommodation'. And they say if we only avoid any direct confrontation with the enemy, he will forget his evil ways and learn to love us. All who oppose them are indicted as warmongers. They say we offer simple answers to complex problems. Well, perhaps there is a simple answer ... not an easy answer ... but simple.

"If you and I have the courage to tell our elected officials that we want our national policy based upon what we know in our hearts is morally right. We cannot buy our security, our freedom from the threat of the bomb by committing an immorality so great as saying to a billion now in slavery behind the Iron Curtain, 'Give up your dreams of freedom because to save our own skin, we're willing to make a deal with your slave masters'. Alexander Hamilton said, 'A nation which can prefer disgrace to danger is prepared for a master, and deserves one'. Let's set the record straight. There's no argument over the choice between peace and war, but there is only one guaranteed way you can have peace ... and you can have it in the next second ... surrender.

"Admittedly there's a risk in any course we follow other than this, but every lesson in history tells us the greater risk lies in appeasement, and this is the specter our well-meaning liberal friends refuse to face ... that their policy of accommodation is appeasement, and it gives no choice between peace and war, only between fight and surrender. If we continue to accommodate, continue to back and retreat, eventually we have to face the final demand ... the ultimatum. And what then? When Nikita Khrushchev has told his people he knows what our answer will be? He's told them that we are retreating under the pressure of the Cold War, and someday when the time comes to deliver the ultimatum, our surrender will be voluntary because by that time we will have weakened from within spiritually, morally, and economically. He believes this because from our side he's heard voices pleading for 'peace at any price' or 'better Red than dead', or as one commentator put it, he'd rather 'live on his knees than die on his feet'. And therein lies the road to war, because those voices don't speak for the rest of us. You and I know and do not believe that life is so dear and peace so sweet as to be purchased at the price of chains and slavery. If nothing in life is worth dying for, when did this begin … just in the face of this enemy? Or should Moses have told the children of Israel to live in slavery under the pharaohs? Should Christ have refused the cross? Should the patriots at Concord Bridge have thrown down their guns and refused to fire the shot heard 'round the world? The martyrs of history were not fools, and our honored dead who gave their lives to stop the advance of the Nazis didn't die in vain. Where, then, is the road to peace? Well, it's a simple answer after all.

"You and I have the courage to say to our enemies, 'There is a price we will not pay'. There's a point beyond which they must not advance. This is the meaning in the phrase of Barry Goldwater's 'peace through strength'. Winston Churchill said 'the destiny of man is not measured by material computation. When great forces are on the move in the world, we learn we are spirits … not animals'. And he said, 'There's something going on in time and space, beyond time and space, which, whether we like it or not, spells duty'.

"You and I have a rendezvous with destiny. We will preserve for our children this, the last best hope of man on Earth, or we will sentence them to take the last step into a thousand years of darkness.

"We will keep in mind and remember that Barry Goldwater has faith in us. He has faith that you and I have the ability and the dignity and the right to make our own decisions and determine our own destiny.

"Thank you very much."

<>

Without giving them credit, I'd used the best lines from Franklin Roosevelt, Abraham Lincoln, and Winston Churchill … all mixed up, it made me a star. I gave the same speech many times on Goldwater's campaign trail …sometimes, I changed it a little, complaining, in effect, big government put an unfair tax burden on American ruling-families in order to pay for social programs to care for America's old, poor, sick, and unemployed citizens.

"This unfair tax burden and this federal debt endangers our national survival! It's time to restore the original message that the Founding Fathers intended. Government does nothing as well or as cheaply as the private sector of the economy!"

Of course, Founding Fathers meant nothing of the kind, I made that part up because it played well. Americans reacted to the speech, saying I was inspirational or an idiot, Goldwater was con-

sidered too far 'Right', Johnson won the Presidency by a landslide. That's show biz.

But, all was not lost. A handful of wealthy Californians, including Homes Tuttle and Henry Salvatori, realized how charismatic and sympathetic I came across on TV, they founded a 'Friends of Ronald Reagan' committee, wanting me to run for California governor, hired a political consultant, Stewart Spencer of the firm BASICO. Stewart hired a handful of media specialists, together they set out to 'program' me … as Bechtel and his group had …again, treating me like an idiot.

I rolled with the punches.

Stewart called me, a master of the electronic media, decided my campaign should be on TV, a lot. My programming team made me a list of issues, made me a list of questions and answers. Stewart put the material onto 5x8" index cards, decided to keep my appearances short …so I wouldn't ad lib, like I did on the Goldwater speech. Stewart kept friendly audiences around me, kept press from asking questions spontaneously, that I might answer … Stewart didn't want me to think …so, I won the election over incumbent Governor Pat Brown, was inaugurate Governor of California at midnight, the time selected as auspicious by Nancy's astrologer. Walt Disney studio designed the festivities.

I told the press, "For many years now, you and I've been shushed like children and told, there are no simple answers to the complex problems beyond our comprehension. The truth is, there *are* simple answers. There just aren't easy ones."

Alan was covering the inauguration for the *Sacramento Bee*, Patti kept him company. "What do you think it will be like being Governor of California?"

I smiled happily. "I don't know. I've never played a governor before."

Alan wasn't impressed, "What are your legislative priorities, Governor Reagan?"

<>

I felt stumped, got a puzzled look on my face, turned towards Mike Deaver, Ed Meese, and Henry Salvatori. "I could take some coaching from the sidelines, if anyone can recall my legislative program," I said. Deaver spoke with me privately for several minutes. I looked at Alan.

"I'm going to cut taxes. I'm going to cut expenses. We're going to cut State agency budgets, across the board. We're imposing a hiring freeze for State operations. We're going to have State employees work without pay on holidays. I'm

253

sending State police to stop the riots at University of California at Berkeley. I'm going to fire any liberal administrators at that campus I can find. I'm going to investigate Communism and blatant sexual behavior at UC Berkeley, too. I blame former Governor Pat Brown for leaving me a budget deficit to deal with."

<>

I soon approved the biggest tax increase in California history. During my two terms, spending doubled from under 5 billion dollars a year to over 10 billion dollars per year.

Ya gotta have heart.

<> <> <>

In Sarajevo, Patti stood with Alan between the church and park headquarters, beneath branches of trees in a circle of redwoods. She leaned back her head, looked at tree tops. Sunlight filtered down through the haze, between redwood branches, shadows sliced by shafts of light, filled with dust particles suspended, unmoving, illuminated in the air. Patti felt the silence in the forest, in awe.

"Look how tall these trees are, all the way up to the sky," Patti said. She hugged a tree, gave it a little kiss.

"Look how beautiful light filters down through the branches, it's like in a cathedral. These must be Cathedral Redwoods, a real cathedral ...not a building, people make ... trying to reach God. God made redwood trees without you or me ...it's magic here, at sunset, the golden glow changes everything like a dream. Fog comes in over the treetops, then swirls lower. I hear spirits trees call me. I see them, tree people spirits, living. Tree! Tree! Tree! I love you. You who are peace, beauty, who hurt no one ...here, in Redwoods fairies hide, raccoons in your branches, blue jays sing, woodpeckers *peck peck peck peck peck*. I love you. If people were as good as trees, what a world it would be ...here, in redwood trees, not some stupid, sterile, cold church stuffed know-it-alls, and hypocrites ...but God's magic branches, sky, sunset, fragrance of the forest's fresh air. How did He know? Oh, it makes me wonder, makes me thankful."

Alan felt religious, too, "It's beautiful here. I'd rather be here, than anywhere. But, it's time to get Granma Wilpf, Tracie and leave," Alan said.

Patti felt lost in the moment, "Not yet. I'm praying in this forest, walking in this light is an act of prayer ...just a few minutes more, please oh please. Leave me alone with the trees."

She was a drama queen. Alan felt he was intruding, "Okay. For a few minutes, that's all."

<>

Patti didn't notice Alan walk away, leaned her back against a redwood tree, felt energy race up her spine sending chills over her back, the air was cold, clean, good to breathe, she breathed big breaths, exhaled clouds of puffy breaths in cold forest air, felt happy from tips of her toes to the top of her head ...felt alive ...more alive than she had for a long time. Twilight fell, the forest silence overwhelmed her. Ancient, timeless sounds of a woodpecker, glass wind chime tinkling of a running brook, snapping sound of a twig beneath a deer's step, looking into a doe's brown eyes before it walked slowly off to graze, buzzing of a mosquito, sound of her heartbeat rushing in her ears. She heard Alan calling, voice muffled by woods.

"Mosquitoes!. We've got to go!" Alan said.

Patti walked over to Alan, kissed his lips, smiled, "You're smart enough not to ask me why I kissed you."

He teased, "Why did you kiss me?"

She felt indignant ...but, showed fondness rather than being upset, glaring at him, "Religion's a morgue, religion thinks too much, murders feelings for logic. I'm a walking prayer, an act of God, I'm a Redwood tree," Patti said. Patti start dancing in ballet steps, making modern dance moves, she danced out of the forest, crossed the road, to the playground by park headquarters. She sat beside Alan on a bench cut into a section of a Redwood log, watched Tracie play on the slide, felt drowsy, stretched out on the bench, her head on Alan's lap, Tiger poked his head out of Patti's purse, jumped out onto her lap, lay purring on her lap. Patti felt Tiger's purring ribs vibrate on her hips, watched Tracie run happily from the bottom of the slide to the ladder, climb the ladder, sit at the top making sure Granma Wilpf watched ...Tracie laughed, as she slid down. Patti watched.

"Granma Wilpf, push me!" Tracie said.

"Up, up and away!" Granma Wilpf said.

Patti watched Granma Wilpf push Tracy, remembering herself at that age. Patti snuggled into Alan's lap.

Alan liked her like that, "Comfy?"

"Um hmm," Patti said. She let her hand fall to the ground, picked up a thin twig, woody and prickly, used it for a pointer, brushed it on the ground back and forth, in front of Tiger. Tiger opened one eye ...then, began flopping his tail around, dangling a paw down towards the stick, half trying to get it ...but, not wanting to move. Patti danced the stick, Tiger jumped for it.

Patti laughed, "Get it Tiger. Get that bad stick.

Get it! …Oh, you got it. My hero. Come here."

Patti picked Tiger's forearms up, leaving his hind paws on the ground. "May I have this dance please?" she said. Patti danced Tiger around, lifted him like a doll, cradling him in her arms, petting Tiger until he calmed down, yawning. Patti watched Tracie swinging. Teddy bear on her lap, Tracie jumped off the swing, holding the teddy bear, pretending to talk to teddy, then ran to Patti … sat on the bench beside her.

Tracie looked at Patti. "Teddy bear is tired. We have a tea party on this bench, then teddy bear, is it time for a nap? …Teddy says, first tea party, then nap."

Patti looked at Granma Wilpf. "Alan, look! Granma Wilpf's swinging on the swing!"

Alan looked. "She's having a good time, Patti Want me to push you on the swing?"

"Yes, I want to swing …but, not now, I'm too cozy. Can we swing later, if there's time to?"

"Yes."

Patti relaxed, "I think of babies killed in wars, in Sarajevo, Somalia, Chechnya, Mexico, Nicaragua, Iraq, Sudan … people starving, without jobs, the world lost it's last innocence …I've lost hope," Patti said. Patti started crying.

Alan hugged her. "Look my darling, a baby raccoon."

"It's so cute," Patti said. Patti jumped to her feet. "Something's wrong! Park rangers are running this way, they've got guns! Get out of here! Granma, quick! …in the car! Tracy!"

Alan felt scared, "No time! Run! Hurry!"

At treetop level Patti saw a black and white SCREAMA helicopter hovering above the parking lot, starting to land. She ran hard, heart pounding hurt, gasping. The four of them made it down the hillside, to the creek.

"There! In that hollow tree. Hide!" Patti said.

They crawled on their bellies through the opening in the burned-out hollow of a redwood tree. It was so still inside the tree, Patti could hear her heartbeat. She looked out, up the hillside. Rangers, guns drawn, stopped running, looked in all directions. SCREAMA in camouflage uniforms joined in. Patti recognized one of them. "Gehlen! How'd he find us?!"

Alan felt claustrophobic in the hollow tree trunk. "I don't know."

Patti heard Gehlen's voice in an amplified megaphone, echoing eerily through the forest, bouncing between trunks of trees.

"Attention. You're wondering now how I found you. A homing device microchip in Tracy's SCREAMA Youth League arm patch. We fol-

lowed the signal. You're in violation of breaking quarantine. We'll bring you back, dead or alive!" Gehlen said.

Patti grabbed Tracie's arm, put her fingertips on the SCREAMA patch, then tore it off, the back had a red light blinking on it. Patti stared at it, "Find me a piece of dry wood, quickly! Hurry!"

Alan slid his hand along the forest floor in the tree hollow. "Here's a piece of wood."

"It's too late. He's getting close!"

Jamming the cloth patch in a crevice on the dry wood, she threw the wood out to the stream in the creek bed below them, watched the wood splash into the water, then swirl in the current in some rapids, turned to see SCREAMA with tracking devices start running to the rapids. Patti smelled smoke, saw fire burning the trees. She was upset, desperate, "He's burning down the forest!" Patti squeezed herself out the tree hollow, but couldn't get free. Someone held her foot. "Let me go!"

Granma Wilpf whispered to Patti, "No. Don't do this."

Patti grabbed onto a root growing from the ground, pulling herself out of the tree. Granma Wilpf still held her foot.

"Let go of me!"

Granma Wilpf pulled herself up to Patti's face, "Live to fight another day! There are other redwood forests for you to save."

Before Patti knew it, Alan had thrown her over his shoulder and was running towards the car. Patti felt his shoulder jabbing into her stomach.

"Put me down. You're right. I won't give myself up. I'll go with you," Patti said. Patti ran to the car. "There's Tiger inside, waiting for us!" Patti climbed in, pulling Granma Wilpf in on top of her. Alan jumped into the driver's side seat.

"Where's Tracie?" he said.

Granma Wilpf sighed sadly. Patti watched dust swirling as the Honda spun a donut in the dirt parking lot, made a u-turn and drove away.

"I see her! …by the helicopter talking with Gehlen. She's pointing at us! " Patti said. Patti watched the trees spin by, as the car skidded around a turn. She felt scared, "How can we get away! We can't hide! We can't outrun it!"

"The fog's thick. They can't follow," Alan said.

Patti watched flames leap through the forest from tree to tree, "The flames are across the road behind us! The oaks went up fast!" Oaks fell burning, crackling in flames on the road. Patti was wide-eyed. "They can't follow us. Granma Wilpf, don't ask me what I think. Just don't ask!"

"Okay," Granma Wilpf said.

Patti was tired. "Thanks for keeping me from surrendering, so Gehlen didn't get me."

Granma Wilpf felt better. "You're welcome, Patti. My eye hurts. I feel dizzy. Take me to a hospital," Granma Wilpf said.

Patti looked at Granma Wilpf's eye. "Alan, she passed out!"

They drove south for hours, came to a hospital, then went inside. Patti stared at rows of people in chairs. There was something odd about them, some cried, some yelled, some stared blankly, others walked in slow circles, eyes dull, leaning on walls, stumbling over chairs, walking on people's feet, adults sat at tables slowly coloring with crayons in coloring books.

Patti looked at Alan, "What's going on?"

"They're nuts."

Patti watched a doctor come out a doorway, leading Granma Wilpf by the arm. "There's Granma Wilpf! ...walking like a zombie, what's wrong with her?"

The doctor stared at Patti, "She's delusional, certifiable under the Blue Book Eugenics Law, she's old, mentally impaired. Your worries are over, she can be paradised."

Patti was upset, "She's not crazy! She bumped her head, hurt her eye. There's nothing wrong with her sanity!"

The doctor wasn't interested, "We don't write Blue Book Eugenics laws, we just do the mercy killing. Look, she's old, she loved when it was legal to, lived a good life, she's not productive, it's time to let her go. You don't get it. Blue Book is the Social Register of *ruling* families, it's the Bible of the new World Order. Blue Book says, her Order of Death is *now*," the doctor said.

"What did you do to her?"

"Thorazine," the doctor said.

"Granma Wilpf wouldn't hurt a fly!"

"She's an economic threat, too old to work now that social security's been eliminated, her survival's threatened, she's a threat to herself. She needs to be paradised. There's no need for society to waste resources, on her. So, you're related. I should examine you, these kinds of illnesses are genetic, you may need to be eliminated, too," the doctor said.

Me?! There's nothing wrong with me!"

"I'll judge that. People who don't cooperate with the State are mentally ill. I don't have time to waste, there was an outbreak from a quarantined section of Sarajevo, the waiting room and killing chambers are filled," the doctor said.

"Can we help you catch more of them?" Alan said. "We'll cooperate. Then, you'll see Granma Wilpf is all right. And we can go,.."

The doctor looked into Alan's eyes, "Perhaps you left the quarantine area? ...are you from Sarajevo?"

Alan smiled, "No, we're from the Redwood park, we weren't near Sarajevo."

"Oh?"

Patti interrupted, "What about that SCREAMA helicopter over the mountains?"

The doctor watched Alan's eyes, "A SCREAMA helicopter? ....west of here? Was that for you?"

"I confess," Alan said.

Patti didn't understand, "Confess what?!"

"I have to tell."

The doctor looked at Alan. Patti sighed.

"Doctor, I get panic attacks, anxiety attacks. I'm having one, now. I don't need to be paradised. Do you have valium?"

"Thorazine. Guards! Take them to the killing chambers!"

"You're taking this too far!" Alan said.

Patti looked through the room to escape. The guard grabbed her. "You won't experiment on me!"

The doctor smiled, "No? ...guards, prepare them."

<>

Patti pushed against the padded cell door, it was locked. She threw her body against it. The foam rubber cushioning gently caught her. She stumbled into Alan and Granma Wilpf, felt her brain slowing disappearing, her body got numb. She felt far away, looked out from far away, like sleeping. She watched Alan and Granma Wilpf walk in slow motion, around the room, each step lasted forever. Patti didn't understand, put her arms around Alan's and Grandma Wilpf's shoulders, huddled against them.

Alan saw Patti's eyes weren't clear, "We've got to figure out what to do, before the thorazine kicks in."

Patti felt dulled. "Huh?"

"We'll go to my place, in... "

"*Duh*," Patti said.

Granma Wilpf felt to tired to talk. "*Uh uh.*"

Stumbling on Alan's feet, Patti fell to the padded floor. She heard soft thudding as she sank into foam rubber, lay there, warm ...saw Alan lying on the ceiling.

Alan felt asleep. "*Paddri.*"

Patti heard someone far away in a dream.

Alan tried to speak. "*Lnmreen. Mar. Me. Mar. R ie. Me.*"

Patti answered. "*Un un. umbd umb.*"

Patti fell asleep. She dreamed, smelled dark French roasted coffee, a Moroccan blend, ordered double latte with whipped cream, listened to Vivaldi, liked the sun's warmth on her shoulders, at the café table where she sat. The tables lining the sidewalk were filled with college-aged men and women. Patti wore a satin and velvet designer gown studded with rubies. Alan wore a tuxedo and white gloves. He smiled drunkenly at her, "I brought you double latte, and Tiger, your Highness."

Patti loved lattes! "My favorite latte, favorite cat, favorite man."

"I love you, your highness."

Patti blushed. "I love you too."

"You're the most beautiful woman in the world."

"I'm not."

"Look how Stanford university students dress."

Patti looked at Stanford students, "They're dressed nicely, clothes look expensive, except that dirty panhandler. I hope he doesn't come here." Patti cringed.

Alan did too. "I thought Blue Book outlawed street people, put homeless people in labor camps where they can do good."

Patti felt haughty. Sunlight sparked in jewels in her gown, "I've outlawed street people, but it's middle-class people getting layed-off fast, as soon as you lock up one, two more take their place. It's tiresome ruling Society, I try to keep it neat."

Alan understood, "Yes, your highness. Don't look at the panhandler, he'll go away."

Patti smiled, "How wonderful, close my eyes and make it disappear. I like it."

Alan nodded, "It's the best way. Have a happy day. Blue Book Beautification turned this street from a dirty street to a clean one. The designer cafes and shops are Madison Avenue and toni." Patti laughed absently, "Isn't it mahrvelous? ...boutique Stanford students ...boutique university ...boutique street. Blue Book is good."

The panhandler walked over to Patti, "Got any money for a vet?"

"Which war?"

"This one," the panhandler said.

A worried expression came over Patti's face, "Nonsense. There are no poor people any more. I've outlawed them. They're in labor camps earning their living."

The panhandler stood taller, "I'm General Reinhard Gehlen, Party Leader ...once, a great man, spying on the Soviet Union during World War II, after the war, in charge of destabilizing the U.S."

Patti looked her lap, at Tiger. "Tiger, did you defeat General Gehlen?"

Tiger purred. "Rrrrrap."

It was calm that day in Palo Alto ...or, was it Sarajevo? Both downtowns were cosmopolitan boutique. Patti thought, she was in both cities ...but, that was impossible. She heard machine-gun fire. SCREAMA overflowed from vans and buildings onto the street, grabbed the panhandler, threw him in a white, SCREAMA cleansing van then drove off. SCREAMA dumped gasoline on tables, and on people, grenades exploded. People pulled out gasoline bombs hidden in their clothes, lit wicks on fire bomb bottles, threw fire bombs at SCREAMA vehicles. Buildings exploded in flames, up and down the street.

Patti sat calmly at her table with Alan, petting Tiger. "At last I've gotten rid of that panhandler homeless veteran ...and, Palo Alto City Council will have to hire a team of consultants to study, so this won't happen again."

Alan relaxed into his chair, "It's extreme, your Majesty. We bombed cafe society, too."

"Pssssh. Get me another double latte. Let's fly to France, Ital or Munich. Oh, can we?" Patti tried to open her eyes, but her eyelids wouldn't open, she slowly awoke in a padded cell.

<>

Patti tried to focus. "I had a strange dream. You, Granma, and Tiger were there. So was Gehlen."

Alan looked at her eyes. "Are you all right?"

"I guess so."

"Granma Wilpf?" Alan said.

"They put stitches above my eye. I can think, again."

Patti yawned, "We talked, did I dream that?"

It felt so real to Granma Wilpf. "We were talking."

Patti wasn't clear. "About what?"

Alan remembered. "Where to go be safe when we get out."

Patti nodded. "I sort of remember."

Alan finished. "Fly back to California, to my place in Palo Alto."

"There's a guest room on top of Hoover Tower, on Stanford campus," Granma Wilpf said, "...used for visiting scholars, no one goes there anymore, it's filled with useless library books."

Patti got excited. "Will they give you back your old job, as Hoover Institute librarian?"

Granma Wilpf wondered, too. "They should, I was on sabbatical."

Alan stretched and yawned. "Won't someone find us there?"

Granma Wilpf insisted, "No. An old elevator for librarians goes up past Hoover Tower floors, to dead storage."

Patti sighed, "It's perfect. Gehlen and SCREAMA will've broadcasted our names all over the world, they'll know Alan's my boyfriend, where he lives. That deserted room in the tower's perfect. Now, if we can get out of Sarajevo, to the airport."

Granma Wilpf won her point, "How do we get out?"

Patti shrugged, "I don't know."

Alan shrugged, "I don't know. I'm glad the damn thorazine wore off. It's better than Valium, like being dead, the thorazine shuffle."

Granma Wilpf nodded, "I dreamed I was a child in Germany, the early 1920s, I was young, had a boyfriend. My parents didn't approve. He was a member of underground German Army Intelligence, on special assignment forming an underground political party to save Germany."

Patti relaxed. It was like the old days, a child again, laying her head on Granma Wilpf's lap, "What was it like in olden days, Granma?"

Granma had nostalgic look in her eyes. "Germany just lost World War I. German ruling families' dreams of expanding Germany's borders to the east through Eastern Europe to capture the Russian Baku oil fields, and enslave people for slave labor from countries we conquered so Germany could prosper, dreams went up in smoke, out the window, that's what it was like. Social revolution of starving people that sparked Russian revolution against Russian monarchy, captured hearts of poor working people around the world, in Germany, too. Only military force in Germany could keep socialist revolution from succeeding. I used to think economic depressions was natural law, like mental depression. Each time poor people got together to demonstrate for food or housing, kings and presidents discounted them ...calling them communists ... Jews ...non-White mongrels. Rich people who orchestrated the Great Depression became rulers of the planet, through the '20s, '30s, and '40s ...while, working people rebelled against ruling families in every country. We wanted food, for our families not to starve ... homes, to sleep indoors ...clothes, to feel warm. It's eliminated from our history, from our thoughts ...erased. White people in the world suffered. too. We knew ruling families had to be eliminated. We didn't know, *how*. They had no right to divide real estate and natural resources up between them because they were mass murderers and we weren't, by

threatening war and genocide ...*we* didn't. We knew we had to kill them. I tell you, being a Hoover Institute librarian and historian, I've seen the history hidden in the tower, kept away from book burnings. I lived through those times. It wasn't bread and roses. We are living history.'

Patti was curious. "What happened to your boyfriend?"

Granma Wilpf hesitated. "He went far in German Army Intelligence. We grew apart. He reminded me of my father, your great great grandfather, Prussian aristocracy, a landowner outside Vienna, master of our family. Your great great grandmother, my mother, was White Russian, related to the throne, but illegitimate.

Patti was shocked, "Related to Czar Nicolas? Illegitimate?"

"You're the great grandchild of Prussian and White Russian nobility, Patti."

"Why didn't you tell me, before?"

"Every family has its secrets we aren't proud of. My boyfriend, the party he formed with other German Army Intelligence officers, Martin Bormann, and Adolf Hitler, was the Brown Shirts. They became the Nazi Party."

"You were dating a Nazi?"

"I was dating one of the first five Nazis."

"I can't believe it. Were you a Nazi?"

"Yes."

Patti still felt hope, "But, just in the early years, when it was a party promising jobs and better times to Germany?"

"Your mother and father were Nazis," Granma Wilpf said.

"Mom and Dad were Nazis? No. I was born in Dallas Texas, Dad was there for basic training."

Granma Wilpf sighed, "SCREAMA brainwashed them, gave them new identities they *think* are true, told them the world's fine the way it is, that's God's will, rewrote their memories like Hoover Institute revisionists rewriting history."

"Why didn't you, or Mom, or Dad, tell me, before?!"

"It was before you were born. They don't know. Their understanding was rewritten to conform to the new World Order. Social engineering was done to society that allowed a middle class to momentarily flourish for mass consumption, borrowed time ... we're getting rid of the middle class today, getting rid of jobs, it was just understanding, not reality, just agreement between slave owners, to keep wage slaves. Why tell things a child can't understand, that adults can't remember or explain, why put that social stigma *on you.*

Then, you grew up ...there was no *need* to tell you ...because, you were born genetically resistant to social engineering, a natural born outlaw ...and, here we are."

Patti felt insane, "Why tell me now?"

"You're a big girl, you're grown up. I'm genetically resistant to social engineering, too. I followed my heart, I've loved," Granma Wilpf said.

Patti was upset, "Love's illegal ... they've made love illegal! Why didn't SCREAMA arrest you? ...paradise you?"

"You fool them, live among them ...so, they can't recognize you, don't show feelings, don't show love ... I didn't want to die, spend life in prison. I'm a living coward, not a dead hero...but, I *have* loved."

Patti cried. "You should've told me the truth."

Granma Wilpf cleared her eyes with her palms. "You're parents are not equipped to know truth, anymore. They'll deny you. It's not their fault, it's who they've become. You'll understand, someday."

Patti felt bitter, "I understand, now. I can't accept it. You shouldn't expect me to."

"You're right."

Alan stretched again, he was feeling hungry. "Who was that boyfriend of yours that started the Nazi Party. What was his name?"

Granma Wilpf was feeling hungry, too. "Who cares? ...it won't bring the dead back to life."

Patty flared up. "It's important to me! No lies!"

Granma Wilpf sighed, "We didn't get along so well, it turned out. I believed in goodness of mankind, in love, nurturing people. He distrusted people, believed in survival of the fittest, mankind preying on itself was as an act of God, ruled by Satan."

Patti was yelling uncontrolably. "His name! What's his name?!"

Granma Wilpf spoke slowly and deliberately. "You know me to be a loving person, don't you?"

"Yes. What's his name?"

"You know, I've been a leader for social reform in America, put myself at risk on the front lines, like when I gave food to the hungry in Sarajevo and you saved me from the SCREAMA cleansing van."

Patti started to soften, "Yes I know you're a good person. Tell me his name."

"I'd never do anything to hurt you or betray the peace movement."

Patti heard someone unlock the heavy doors of the padded cell. "Yes. I know you love me. I know you love the peace movement. Tell me, now."

Granma Wilpf let go, "Reinhard Gehlen."

"Gehlen?!"

<>

Patti turned around, startled. Bright light came through the doors. It stung her eyes. Uniformed SCREAMA filled the room. As her eyes adjusted, she recognized Tracie. Beside Tracie, Patti recognized a SCREAMA, turned to face him.

Party Leader Gehlen stood there, staring at them, "Don't move!"

Tracie told Gehlen, "It's *them*."

<>

SCREAMA cleared patients from the hospital cafeteria, hung pictures of American, British, and German central bankers on the walls, seated Patti at a table between Granma Wilpf and Alan. Gehlen fondly watched Granma Wilpf. "What a nice reunion. You're pretty, after all these years."

"You look good, too," Granma Wilpf said.

"You don't mind eating with a barbarian ...you called me that, the last time we ate together."

"That was ages ago, in another time. I'm hungry. This is my grand daughter, Patti."

Gehlen hungrily watched Patti, "Patti, that's a nice name."

Patti shuttered. "Thank you."

"You're lovely. I told hospital staff, clear the dining room, cook us a special meal, roast turkey, a few vegetable dishes if you're vegetarian, a last supper."

Alan was shocked. "Last supper?"

Alan felt surprised. "All land would be farmed, you could drive for thousands of miles and hundreds of days, foothills tended with crops and fruit trees, no more world hunger. Natural resources would be shared equally, minimum standards of living for everyone, medical care's free, clothing's free, transportation too. A love-based economy, how God intended."

Gehlen laughed crudely, "*Haaa.* In the new World Order, love is illegal, you're not allowed to love. It disturbs the concentration of wealth. God made the economic food chain, not Satan. What freedom can you beggar from life?"

Alan studied Gehlen. "SCREAMA would have us all live under house arrest."

"House arrest, you've done it to yourself," Gehlen said. "Do what wage slaves do, have humility, go to Heaven."

"I wasn't born a slave."

"It can be frightening to see the world as it is.

There's no place for you in the new World Order. Kill your feelings, before SCREAMA kills you."

Wage slaves served turkey, sweet potatoes, green beans, squash. Patti liked the way it smelled. "This reminds me of holiday meals."

"Me too," Granma Wilpf said.

"With all this arguing?" Gehlen said.

"Especially with that," Granma Wilpf said.

Gehlen smiled. "Me too. Especially Christmas and New Years. Enjoy your meal."

"Thank you, Reinhard," Granma Wilpf said.

Patti ate, feeling peaceful, content. "I still love my first puppy-love boyfriend. Are you two close still?"

Granma Wilpf didn't know. "I have loved, so I forgive those who haven't."

Reinhard watched Patti eat. "Patti, your grandmother and I were close, a long time ago. Love is illegal now, if you haven't loved by now, you never will."

Granma Wilpf looked at him. "Nonsense, we should forget differences, forgive one another, share what good we have in common, there's time to love."

Gehlen did not forget. "People must be held accountable for disobeying the Blue Book. You disobeyed, you must be punished."

Granma Wilpf tried to ease the situation. "I gave food to hungry people, that was all."

"To you, that's all it was. But, Blue Book mandates hygiene laws, catering licenses, zoning ordinances, you ignored the law. It was an act of love ...did you think you could get away with it? The Blue Book is this way, because Satan and God allows it. If people obeyed, there'd be no SCREAMA to cleanse and paradise them. You need me to cleanse *you*, to paradise *you*," Gehlen said. "I'm frustrated with differences, I loved you once ...now, it's too late to love, it's a felony."

"I can't accept your violence, I'll always love."

Gehlen was angry, "You frustrate me! You always did! Do you think I *like* to hurt people? ...if there was another way to govern Hell, I would! You saved Tracie, a SCREAMA Youth Brigade leader ...because, of love. She turned you in. What do you expect from love?"

Granma Wilpf looked at Patti. "I saved Tracie, because I was that little girl once. In my own Nazi Youth Brigade uniform. I knew Tracie could change, too ...if I could love her enough. I would have succeeded, if it wasn't for Reinhard and his SCREAMA."

"Always the dreamer," Gehlen said.

Tracie start crying. "I wanted to change, Granma Wilpf. When you held me, sang to me, played with me, and pushed me on the swing.

But, love is illegal. I had to turn you in, because you loved me so. I thought you'd be proud of me, for doing what's right."

Granma Wilpf was shocked. "Proud of you? Child, I'm hurt by what you did. It may cost me my life."

Tracie lectured her. "The new World Order will make you better, well again. Then, we'll be friends."

"How will the new World Order help me?"

Gehlen sighed heavily, "Lucky for you, you're at this State Mental Institute, where we re-program, re-educate ...and, rehabilitate. Honor the Blue Book, obey SCREAMA. We'll correct your opinions, get you new identities, new memories, new personalities to conform to new World Order standards."

Patti resisted, pushing Gehlen away. "I won't go!"

Gehlen had them shot up with Thorazine, then shipped them, and Patti's cat, to a mental facility in Palo Alto, where he had to report to Hoover Institute and give his yearly performance report.

<>

Patti came to her senses, standing in a hospital corridor. Tiger arched his body against her legs. She watched helplessly, SCREAMA tore sheets up ...then, with the rags tied her wrists to a chrome doorknob of a hospital door.

SCREAMA looked at her, "These doors don't lock , find a room that can be locked. They're tied-up, they're not going anyplace." SCREAMA walked down the hall, turned the corner.

Patti felt desperate. "How can we get out of here?"

"I don't know," Alan said

Patti looked through a small window in the door ...Gehlen led Granma Wilpf to a bed, undressed himself, started to undress her.

Gehlen walked to the bathroom, closed the door behind him. Patti saw Tracie come down the hall, holding her hand behind her back. Patti wondered why.

Tracie skipped up to Patti. "Where's Granma Wilpf?"

Patti was afraid to say the wrong thing. "What do you have behind your back?"

Tracie showed her a scalpel.

Alan was afraid, "Tracie, what are you going to do? Stab us?"

"No. I'm cutting you free, because you helped me. Help Granma Wilpf."

Tracie cut through the sheet strips that tied Alan's wrists to the door. Alan got free, took the scalpel, cut Patti loose. Patti went in Granma Wilpf's room, braced a chair against the bathroom door so it couldn't open. Granma Wilpf grabbed her clothes. They all ran down the hall.

Tracie called out, "Are you taking me?"

Granma Wilpf was confused. "You?"

Patti told her, "She cut us free,."

Alan didn't know. "What if you double-cross us again, Tracie?"

"Yeah," Granma Wilpf said.

Tracie pleaded. "I won't. I promise. Being loved felt good."

Patti smiled. "All right. Hold my hand! Let's get out of here! To the parking lot! Out this window!" Patti said. Patti scooped up Tiger, tucked him in her blouse, against her stomach.

<>

In Hoover Tower, Patti watched lights blink on the elevator panel. The old elevator moved slowly. Patti didn't trust it. "Is this thing safe?"

Granma Wilpf laughed. "Probably, not. The University hasn't condemned it, yet."

"This must be the first elevator ever built."

"The first on the West coast. It's old, worn down. These old rooms in the tower are full of history books, SCREAMA would have been burned, if they knew about them. Be careful when get the door opens, some of the floors are missing."

Patti was shocked. "The floors are missing?"

"Maybe never built, rotted, collapsed, there's not a room on every floor."

Patti watched the elevator shaft walls move slowly past the wire mesh elevator cage gate. The button on the 7th floor lit up, the elevator stopped. Patti slid the elevator gate open, then opened the outer door. "It's dark. All I see is a small window in the tower wall, 50 feet away. Hey! There's no floor!"

"I know. Walk on those two planks. It's a catwalk."

Patti took a deep breath. She took Tiger out of her blouse, put Tiger down on the planks, Tiger ran across the planks, then jumped up on the windowsill on the other side. Patti stepped hesitantly on the boards, "They're moving!"

Granma Wilpf choose her steps, carefully. "They bounce when you walk on them. C'mon, I need to send the elevator back down before it's missed."

"No wonder no one comes here! They'd fall off these planks, and die!" Patti said. She walked the planks. It was too springy to feel safe. Where the floor beneath her should have been, she saw a dark pit. She took slow steps towards the window. Each step, she wished she wouldn't fall. After eternity, Patti reached the other side of the planks ...there was a landing, and a door. "I

made it. C'mon Alan."

"This isn't safe. I'm not going to."

"You are. Get over it. I did it,."

"You like excitement, I don't."

Grandma Wilpf told him, "It's safer than if the SCREAMA get you."

Patti watched Alan inch across the planks towards her. When he got close, he took her hand. Then, Tracie crossed. Then, Granma Wilpf stepped on the planks. Patti heard the elevator clank, thunk, and groan tiredly, then watched it head back down the tower to the reference library.

Granma Wilpf reached the landing. She took Patti's hand. "Well, open the door ...go in."

Patti watched Tiger run in. Patti took a breath, walked in the dark room, went to the window. Light came in around blinds, lighting the room softly. She peeked out the window. The view was for miles ... to the east, she saw roofs, streets and trees of Palo Alto sprawled out, stretching to the bay. To the west, she saw sunset falling over brown foothills, on red-brown ceramic Spanish tile roofs of a hundred University buildings, on the straight, rectangular, mile-long nuclear linear accelerator building like an architect's drawing, narrowing to a point in the distance.

The pine and redwood-covered mountains faced west in the setting sun. The room was furnished with a leather sofa, chairs, and end tables from the turn of the 19th to the 20th Century. Patti walked across the room through a doorway to the kitchen, turned on the stove burners, blue gas flames leapt up. The refrigerator was humming. She opened the refrigerator. There were fast food French fries covered in ketchup in a paper tub. Patti felt startled. "It looks like someone's staying here."

Granma Wilpf smiled, "I have, before I went to Sarajevo on sabbatical. It's my secret retreat, to get away from the world, I come to my private world ...there's toilet paper in the bathroom, sheets on the beds."

Alan flopped down on the couch. "God. A chance to rest."

Patti sat down next to him. "You look beat."

"I am."

Tracie plopped down on a chair, "Me too."

Alan tried to relax. "Will university cops find us here?"

Granma Wilpf watched them. "The Thought Police? No. Not unless we think too much, like blasting the stereo out the window."

"You don't have to worry about me making

261

noise," Alan said.

"Got that right.' Patti sat down beside Tracie. "Tracie ... I want to talk to you."

Tracie looked down. she fidgeted with her fingers. "Am I in trouble?"

"You are," Patti said.

"I didn't mean to hurt anyone. I didn't know better."

"What do you think the world would be like, if everyone hated everyone else?"

"I don't know."

"People would be crying, hospitals would be full of hurt soldiers, you'd feel scared all the time, unloved, lonely. You'd have no safe place to go. You'd be hungry," Patti said. "What else?"

Tracie looked sheepishly at Patti. "Bad people, SCREAMA, would run things. No candy. No playgrounds. No playing. Not safe for kids to go out, 'cause soldiers would shoot us. SCREAMA would kidnap us, sell us or trade us. Shoot us for practice. Or, eat us. There 'd be no hugs, ever. Except from Granma Wilpf."

Patti bit her lip softly, so she wouldn't laugh. "Tracie, where's your mother and father?"

"Oh, they're SCREAMA. I don't know where they're stationed. They gave me to the State, to raise me. My parents are heroes, making it safe by getting rid of democracy."

"How? ...Honey."

"My teacher in the State Orphanage said to let Mommy and Daddy go serve SCREAMA. SCREAMA guard Blue Book people. My teacher said Mommy and Daddy are heroes, because they're SCREAMA, they kill people in San Francisco, Sarajevo, Panama, Somalia, Iraq, Morocco, Belarus, Darfur, Paraguay ... all over the place. My parents kill bad people who hate the Blue Book and new World Order, see? Isn't that great?"

Patti spoke quietly, "Honey, your Mommy and Daddy are heroes, because they made you. But, we *don't* believe in the Blue Book, new World Order, or, SCREAMA. We *believe* in love. We're revolutionaries, for us, love *is* legal. I've loved. We'll never forget that feeling. That's why we saved you from the riot when you were scared out on the street. Do you think we're bad? ...for loving you?"

"No. Granma Wilpf was the one who wouldn't go without me. She loved me, first," Tracie said.

Granma Wilpf smiled. She walked towards Tracie. Granma Wilpf hugged her, "I used to be like you, sweetheart ... wear a Nazi uniform like you wear a SCREAMA uniform. I was taught, love is illegal. I used to tell on people, just like you told

Gehlen on us. But, I stopped that ...people I told on, I liked them."

Tracie smiled, "I found that out, too. Are Mommy and Daddy haters?"

Granma Wilpf hugged Tracie. "No, Honey. The State makes them kill. If Mommy and Daddy didn't kill, the State would put them in prison, then, paradise them. Once you know, The Lie, you can choose love, again ... now say it, Tracy ... I have loved."

Tracy was afraid to say it. She looked over her shoulder to see if she was being watched.

Patti joined in. "When was the last time your mother hugged you?"

Tracie spoke quietly, "I was just a kid, then."

"How long have you been in a State Orphan?"

"Three or four birthdays."

"I promise you," Patti said, "...when revolution gets rid of Gehlen, SCREAMA, Blue Book, and new World Order, we'll get Mommy and Daddy back."

"Really?" Tracie said.

"Yes."

"How?" Tracie said.

"Just by loving them."

"Patti..."

"Yes, Honey."

"I have loved."

Granma Wilpf was so pleased. "Tracie, that's wonderful,."

Patti relaxed, "Tracie, you're a good girl."

"Thank you, Patti. In the mean time, can I call you, Mommy?"

Patti shrugged. Granma Wilpf smiled. Patti looked at Tracie, "Okay Honey, you call me Mommy."

Tracie ran to hug Patti.

Patti hugged her, "Don't you ever turn us in, again. Or you won't sit down for a week."

"Okay," Tracie said.

"You still have to be punished."

Tracie got frightened. She start shivering. "Are you going to shock me with electricity? They electrocute me at State Orphanage when I'm not good, see?"

Tracie touched scars on her forehead.

Patti eyes got tears in them. "No. Honey. I'm not going to electrocute you. I won't whip you. I'm going to spank you."

Patti saw how worried and intent and nervous Tracie looked. Tracie began to cry before Patti even touched her. Why was Tracie so upset? "Let's get it over with," Patti said.

Patti spanked her twice, not hard, little taps.

Tracie began giggling, "You're not hurting me!"

"The rest of your punishment is, you eat two stale French fries, then you brush Tiger ...and, you baby-sit Tiger if I go on errands."

"Okay, Mommy."

Patti never had kids of her own. She felt cozy, "French fries in the refrigerator."

"Tiger, let's get French fries," Tracie said.

Patti watched Tracie and Tiger at the refrigerator. Patti felt sad, and happy, at the same time. She started crying, remembering when her parents used to scold and punish her. How she felt put on the spot, hot, embarrassed, ashamed, shrinking inside.

Alan smiled at her. "Looks like you're a mom, now."

"Yeah. I'm proud of Tracie for trusting me. I hope I won't let her down."

"*We* won't let her down," Alan said.

Patti smiled ...then, felt puzzled. "I wish we'd win the revolution, already."

"That's why we're fighting."

Granma Wilpf smiled. "That's right. I saw a flyer by the elevator downstairs, there's a midnight candlelight vigil tonight, to protest the new World Order ... in fifteen minutes. We better get going to get there by midnight. It takes five minutes, we can make it."

"We're not *really* going to the midnight vigil, are we?"

Patti nodded. "Yes."

Alan didn't like it. "That's not safe. Thought Police are there."

Patti balked. "Shiu and Butler will be there, lots of artists, my people ...I have to go. No one knows we're artists, we're underground. SCREAMA thinks we're revolutionaries, not artists."

"Too dangerous, it's death for being an artist."

"I know. I'm going. So's Granma Wilpf. Tracie's gonna stay here to baby-sit Tiger. Do what you gotta."

"Okay, I'll go. I've been reading Granma Wilpf's books. SCREAMA invented government, as a masquerade."

"Fascinating," Patti said.

Granma Wilpf looked puzzled. "People turn into robots, SCREAMA. There's no generation gap. Kids can say, I have loved. Their parents can't."

Alan lost patience, "It's like that?"

Patti pushed him. "Non-violence can't work, look at history."

Granma Wilpf felt restless. "If we hurt people, we're SCREAMA."

Alan was about to lose it. "One minute you're talking about SCREAMA destroying the world with economic turf wars, then you're into flower-power."

Patti didn't care for his tone. "Don't stop me from loving you, by talking like that."

"I have loved," Alan said.

"I have loved," Patti said.

They kissed. Patti led the way. Alan and Granma Wilpf followed. Patti noticed the quiet of Stanford University at midnight ...and, the dark. Building shadows in the moonlight fell over palm trees and bike racks, sidewalks, fountains. She walked by the music auditorium, past the bookstore.

Alan was scared, "Watch out for Thought Police, CREAMA, WTO Enforcers."

Granma Wilpf led them through the darkness. "Over there, by the steps."

Patti saw some sixty people. "I see candles glowing in the dark." A woman handed out candles burning with paper cup chimneys around the flames. Patti took a couple, watched candle-light glow through the paper cups, a soft ball of light glowing out the tops. She handed one to Alan. "You look weird, your face lit from underneath."

Alan looked like a ghoul. "You too."

"I've never been to midnight candlelight vigil. It's solemn."

Granma Wilpf nodded. "We honor dead good people, killed for loving, or saying, 'I love you', or 'I have loved.'"

People took turns, walking up the steps. Each gave a testimonial. Loudspeakers were turned low, to not disturb anyone in fraternity and sorority houses across the street. Patti felt her heart beat in her chest. She wondered, would she talk? Granma Wilpf walked up the stairs.

Granma Wilpf took the microphone. "I have loved ... Hundreds of thousands of lives are at stake. Innocent people, civilians, children who can say, I have loved. Iraqi people don't own the oil in Iraq, they're a Blue Book subject population. You and I don't own American oil here, ...we're a Blue Book subject population. Stop the war. Love again. Stop the SCREAMA."

Patti was excited. She went to the mic. The aluminum case felt smooth in her fingers. She started to speak, but stopped at the sound of her voice. "I sounded so big. I like it ... I have loved ... SCREAMA are wrong. Love is not dead. Divest whoever makes money hurting people. Put them in penal colonies ...in the desert ...on food stamps ...on welfare. Let them cannibalize each other, instead of us."

As she spoke, Patti felt her courage grow, her voice get stronger. When she finished, she stepped reluctantly away. She didn't want it to stop, the feeling of community. She went down the steps.

Alan was impressed, proud of her, "I really liked that."

"Do you think people listened?"

"Yes. Everyone."

Granma Wilpf smiled, "That was wonderful!"

Patti turned towards Shiu's voice. She watched candlelight shine up beneath his face. Puddles of light collected under Shiu's lips, nose, and eyes.

Shiu spoke, "I have loved … Stop Fascists! Stop Nazis, World Anti-Communist League, Bilderbergers Group, Rockefeller Council Of Foreign Affairs, Trilateral Commission, Federal Reserve, Bundesbank, World Bank, International Monetary Fund, 1,000 Club of European monarchs and cartel directors, World Trade Organization, Blue Book ruling families. They invest in murder, blood money. There's only 50,000 of them in the whole world. In Stanford football stadium they'd look like a poor turnout. That's how many bad apples there are, making war, waging genocide, financial warfare, laying people off, stopping unemployment, stopping welfare, turning people against each other, making people jobless, homeless, filling up prisons with us. It's not fair! Stop Fascists! Stop Nazis! Stop Blue Book! Stop SCREAMA! Stop Thought Police! Stop them!"

Shiu handed Butler the mic. Butler held it to his lips, "I have loved … Groups Shiu mentioned, are out there …in private men's clubs, at debutante parties on estates, in associations, in private jets to Caribbean winter homes, Australian enclaves, vacation homes in Paris, Berlin. They suck our blood, live off our taxes. The world's grown tired of them, murderers, slave traders, merchants of death, usurers."

Patti was spellbound. Butler finished speaking, put the mic in its stand, walked down the steps. Patti kissed Butler on the cheek. "Butler, that was elegant."

Butler was surprised. "It was?"

Patti felt someone, she turned. It was Alan.

"Did you have to kiss him?"

Patti got angry, "Stop being childish. He had something to say. Don't you? Are you afraid?"

Alan walked up the stairs, picked up the mic, turned to face strangers holding candles in the dark. "I have loved … but, I have hated, too. I wish ruling families would stop acting like babies. Their portfolios are full of liars, thieves, rapists, murderers, serial killers. We must divest the Blue Books. Make them pay for hurt and misery they

allow. We can't kill them, it's wrong …but, we *can* divest them. Put them on islands, make 'em live with each other … *that's* punishment."

Patti was surprised he spoke so well. He walked back down the stairs. "That was good."

Alan felt adrenaline rush in him, "Thanks. You said I didn't have anything to say, that I'd, be afraid to talk to strangers. You're wrong."

Patti felt her face flush. She felt disarmed. She wondered what she had become. "You're right. I'm sorry."

"I heard that."

Patti took offense, "Don't push your luck!"

Alan pushed her roughly aside. He yelled, "Look out! SCREAMA!"

Patti turned around.

SCREAMA in orange jumpsuits were swarming around them. Reinhard Gehlen's Stormtroopers goose-stepped in formation behind the SCREAMA. Behind Gehlen, Patti saw silver lamé jumpsuits of the Thought Police glitter in the dark.

"Gehlen?! What's he doing here?!" Patti said.

Alan looked anxiously around, "I don't know! We gotta get out! Run!"

Patti saw a vigil protester throw his candle down, he start running at her. She felt him thud against her as he tackled her. She felt his arms around her, his hands pawing her. They tumbled down. He tugged her blouse, tore it off, grabbed her breast. She yelled. He shoved his hand down her pants and grabbed her, fingers going into her. She screamed. Butler ran to her. Butler grabbed her attacker by his hair, yanked him back, shoved a burning candle in his eye. The attacker howled, held his eye, ran off.

Butler knelt beside Patti. "Patti! Are you okay?!"

Patti felt hysterical, "He was raping me! His hands were all over me! Thank you! Thank you!"

Butler spoke deliberately, "You're okay now. That was a Cointelpro agent provocateur infiltrating us, to provoke arrests."

"I guess I'm okay," she said.

SCREAMA and Stormsoldiers surrounded them. Butler lurched. "C'mon Patti! Run!"

She ran away.

Gestapo, SCREAMA, Cointelpro, and Thought Police paramilitary units chased her. She ran around the corner of Hoover Library tower, dived into shrubs. Sharp Juniper leaves scratched her

skin, she couldn't pay attention to it. Her heart pounded. She gasped. Police all-terrain vehicles with red, yellow, and blue lights flashing on top reflected in silver lamé uniforms of Thought Police as their electric stun guns crackled. She heard the stun guns sizzling and snapping. Sun gun electricity flashed laser beams in the darkness. Patti lay flat on the ground. It was muddy. She crawled slowly behind the shrubs, down some basement stairs of Hoover library tower, to the door, went inside. found the elevator to their secret room.

Several hours later, Alan and Patti cuddled on the couch. Alan put his arm around her, "Are you in the mood?"

"No. I'd rather go to sleep. Maybe in the morning," She turned off the light. "What's that light coming up through the floor?

"It's coming from the floor-board. This floor-board comes out. There's something under it, a tape recorder! ...under the floor! ...with headphones. It's pointing down to the room below under us."

Patti put on the headphones. "I hear people down there."

"What are they talking about?"

"Bohemian Grove, Gingrich's platform, his Contract on America. Destabilizing Soviet Union and United States, at the same time ...using Saudi money ...laundering 40 million dollars of drug money a week ...meeting with G7 at Bohemian Grove. They're leaving."

Alan was impatient, "What else did they say?"

"I couldn't hear." Patti was startled. "I hear footsteps! ...the planks outside the door!"

"Hide!"

Patti felt desperate, "It's too late! They're turning the door knob! Get behind the curtain." Patti held still. She peeked out. "It's Gehlen! He went to the floor-board. He's kneeling down, taking the tape recorder out, putting the tape in his pocket."

Alan breathed heavy, "God I hope he doesn't find us."

Patti prayed silently ...that Gehlen wouldn't see her, that he'd leave. Patti heard him walk closer. "He's coming closer. Shhhs! Be quiet, for God's sake. I hope to God he leaves."

Gehlen grabbed the curtain, yanked it down from the rafters, reached for his holster.

Patti didn't know what to do. She grabbed the falling crushed velvet curtain. It was heavy, awkward in her hands. She threw it over his head, then tackled him. "Help me roll him up in it!"

"That's what I'm doing!" Alan said.

"Use that lamp cord! ...tie it around him! ... Okay. Wake up Granma and Tracie."

Granma stood beside Patti, "I'm woke. What we do now? Where we go to?"

Alan didn't know, "My place isn't safe."

Patti, Alan, Granma, and Tracie rolled Gehlen into the bathroom. It was like rolling a high-heeled shoe. They returned to the living room.

Alan looked around the room. "We can't stay here, anymore."

Tracie thought that was an understatement. "Duh."

Patti tried to help. "We can't go to your place."

Granma Wilpf was beside herself. "They must have us I.D.'d, by now. My place is out."

"I don't have a place," Tracie said.

Patti's eyes widened, "We *have* no place to go."

"What about Shiu's?" Alan said. "I hate to risk Shiu's wife and kids."

"Or, Butler's," Patti said.

Patti had an idea. "What about Bohemian Grove? We could have a surprise protest there, hide there til then."

"That's like camping out in Hell."

Patti was angry, "I think you're a coward by how you act, even though I know you're not. I thought you *changed*."

Alan had second thoughts. "I did. It's a panic attack. Fear comes back. I can't stop it."

"Make up your mind! I can't wait. I'll decide, for you. We're going to Bohemian Grove, we'll wait. When the central bankers, kings, and ruling families come to worship the new World Order, we'll protest!"

Granma clenched her fists, "They won't let them get away with it, anymore! We'll go to Palo Alto Peace Center protest at the City Cultural Center, tomorrow ...and organize. Then come out to protest."

Alan shrugged, "Well, okay, if that's what we're gonna do, that's what we're going to do."

Patti looked at Alan. "I can't expect you to change who you are. I'm tired of telling you what to do. If you don't get it together, kiss off us being together."

"Are you trying to get rid of me?"

"Figure it out."

"You're not perfect," Alan said. "I don't crucify you."

"What? You don't have to get snotty. This relationship is on hold, I'm leaving."

Granma Wilpf was worried, "Can't you kids stuff it? Always the same thing, over and over. Give it a rest. Let the dust settle til tomorrow."

Alan looked at Patti, "It's okay with me, if it's okay with you."

"Okay."

It was settled. Granma Wilpf felt better, "We'll get everyone to meet us at Bohemian Grove. We'll blow it away!"

Sacramento Governor's Mansion
waiting room, 1970

Patti pressed the blue transistor radio up against her ear ...but, the Elvis Presley song still filled the waiting room of the Governor's mansion. Listening to Elvis', *You ain't nothin' but a hound dog*, took Patti back 10-to-15 years, like she was 8. She saw the replays in her head.

"No," I said.

"But Daddy, Mommy hits me even *when* I don't do anything!"

"I hate it when you lie, Patti."

"You're not there, when it happens! You never see it! It happens, it does!"

Nancy joined in, "Patti's lying, Ronnie. She'll do anything for attention."

"Patti, you should be ashamed," I said.

Patti started crying, "I'm sorry, Daddy."

"Now apologize to your mother."

Patti remembered, like it was yesterday, like it happened moments ago ...but, it'd been years. But then, I remember things from 80 years ago ... like they were now. Sometimes, I remember things that didn't happen, like rehearsals in Hollywood making World War II movies ...and, seeing real films of Nazi concentration camps. Then, it mixes up in my head, and I don't know what's real ... and what's a commercial.

Voices played in Patti's head, over and over. She stared at the steel door of the auditorium, wondering if I would find time to see her.

Patti remembered it like yesterday, it never stopped. If she was tired, or needed help, when she felt unsure ... voices played in her head like radio stations. She stared at the steel door, for what seemed like forever, wondering what was happening on the other side of the door that separated her from me.

On the other side of the door, Mike Deaver was rehearsing me for a speech. Mike was my public affairs man from the beginning of my political career, here in California. He tried to make me come off looking smarter, decisive, sexy ...like a movie star, a governor movie star. Like Schwarzenegger, a movie star and a governor at the same time. Only I did it first, before Schwarzenegger, and after Clint Eastwood was mayor of Carmel. Clint then me then Arnold. Mike Deaver rehearsed me over and over again. He fine-tuned me, to make sure that debonair and handsome movie star look twinkled in my eyes, that the movie had a happy ending, and the good guys won.

Deaver yelled. "Lights!"

The auditorium suddenly lit up. A wide spot spiraled open around me, "Trees are the major source of air pollution."

Mike Deaver took another shot from a pocket flask, "Cut! *What* are *you* talking about?"

"Mike, I'm 64 years old, this is my acceptance speech. A scientist told me, trees sweat carbon. If you don't want me to add lib, give me a script to work from! I don't want to lose the house. Give me someone holding up those big cue cards, with big letters on them."

"If you read from cue card teleprompters, you'll be stale."

"I have to look into the camera to read a cue card. Tape down toe marks for me, Mike, so I can square up, you get the good angles on me."

Mike looked through a viewer, "I need a 'harder' angle, this is the 'hard' part of the speech. Be convincing, emotional."

I start laughing, "I can't do emotion. If I could do emotion I'd have 'A' pictures under my belt, and Oscars around the house. I'd still be in pictures, not politics. Are those cards done yet?" I was confused ...I was going to think something ...I forgot what. Then, it almost came to me ...then, it slipped away. I stared in the distance of the empty auditorium ... trying to remember, "I got it!"

I turned to Stewart Spenser, another public affairs man working with Mike. "Stewart, I don't want to say anything stupid ...so, you script everything for me to say in speeches, and to reporters ...so, I'm convincing looking. Then, I'll concentrate on projecting my looks."

Stewart handed me 5"x8" cards with scripted answers already written on them.

"How'd you do that?" I said.

"I'm way ahead of you, boss. You're goof-proofed."

Deaver nodded to the camera, then to the lighting crew, then pointed to masking tape toe marks a grip had taped to the floor. "Read your lines, feel confident like Nancy's smiling at you, hit your toe marks. Roll 'em!"

I kept rehearsing. When it said, 'rant', I ranted. When it said, 'pause to think', I paused to think. When it said, 'laugh', I laughed. I smiled at Stewart. Stewart smiled back. Then it said, 'start acting upset'.

So I did, "The mess at Berkeley and the student bums there make me sick! They have sex orgies so vile I can't, I won't describe it to you! I won't allow student radicals to threaten democracy!"

As I rehearsed, Mike kept an eye on reactions of the focus group ... a test audience ... he made sure they were there every time I rehearsed … in the corner listening carefully to me.

"When I ran for Governor of California, I promised to reduce the size of State government. I promised to limit the scope of government. I promised to throw the rascals out who got us in this financial mess. I'm not a politician. I'm an ordinary citizen. I'm opposed to high taxes, government regulation, big spending, waste, and fraud. I endorse winning the war in Vietnam. As Douglas MacArthur said during war in Korea, 'There's no substitute for victory!' We can start a prairie fire that'll sweep the nation, prove we're number one in more than crime and taxes. This is a dream as big and golden as California," I said. I heard the audience clapping. I felt the moment, I suddenly acted angry. "I'll personally wage war against welfare cheats, commies, anti-nuclear protestors that threaten the American way! They want a blood bath! …I'll give it to them!"

The focus group clapped.

Deaver smiled, "Cut! You've got it. Take five. Those cards make all the difference in the world." Mike turned to the audience. "That's enough for today, same time tomorrow. Pick up your twenty bucks on the way out." Mike walked over to Stu Spensor. "I think the media will eat up that image. That speech is going to appeal to people's emotions when they see it on TV. It doesn't have much intellectual appeal, but it's sexy. It'll sell."

Stu Spenser nodded, "Let's see what Richard Wirthlin has to say."

Deaver and Spenser looked at Richard Wirthlin. Deaver spoke first, "You're the pollster. What do you say?"

Richard Wirthlin held a script of the speech in one hand. In his other hand he was comparing a computer print-out that listed a word-by-word analysis of the speech, paired up with the audience reaction to each word. "I've been studying the pulse. We've got power phrases here. *They* got the best emotional responses. Make sure we use them in the next draft of the speech. These lines I marked through are dead fish … no audience emotional response to those. Cut them out. You've done a good job with Ronnie."

Deaver smiled. "I do a good job with Ronnie because I *am* Ronnie. Every morning after I get up I look in my mirror. I make believe I'm him. I ask, what he should do today. I ask where he should go today. Every day, I come up with the, 'line of the day'. Everyone in State government is supposed to stress that line to the press, that

day. I make sure the press is here each day, taking pictures of Ronnie doing something positive. I make sure Ronnie gets onto the evening news, every night. With a face like his, it's money in the bank. I make sure he gets a front-page picture in the major dailies every morning I can. Every time I think of Ronnie's public image, I think in terms of camera angle. And, from now on every day I'm gonna hand Ronnie a set of index cards. Those cards are going to have the day's schedule on them. They'll have the text written on them for every casual word Ronnie says. They'll have the text written on them for every word Ronnie says formally. I'm even going to have a card that says, 'God Bless You', written on it 'cause that's what I want Ronnie to say when he finishes his speeches. For Ronnie, those cue cards are gonna be like Linus' blanket."

I preened in a mirror, smiled at myself. I was getting old …but, cut a fine line. I retouched my make-up. A few days later, I put down that mirror, walked in the auditorium, and delivered the real speech to supporters, reporters, and cops. They liked it. Two days later I delivered the same speech, again, to some of those students up at University of California, Berkeley.

University of California, Berkeley campus

At University of California Berkeley campus, students and citizens were waiting for me. The radicals must have remembered when I'd said, trees are the greatest source of air pollution, because they had put signs on trees around the amphitheater that read, 'Cut me down before I kill again'.

I started off, ranting about Black Panthers, who'd armed themselves against Oakland Police, alleging police brutality. I ranted about anti-police demonstrators, anti-nuclear activists, communists, the usual. They were heckling me pretty well. One especially. I looked at him. I pointed my finger at his face, "Shut up! I always wanted to tell a heckler to shut up! Now I have!" It felt great.

Ed Meese laughed.

A few days later, I was back in Sacramento in the Governor's mansion auditorium rehearsing that same speech, ranting.

Mike studied the focus group reaction. "You're doing good with the 'hardliner' bit, Ronnie. Keep it going as long as you can."

'Hardliner' was my unforgiving, angry act. When we were done with rehearsal, I naturally snapped back into my handsome movie star look. I sat down at the make-up table, checked out my profile in a hand mirror, touched-up my eyeliner, powdered my face, practiced smiling, and winking into the mirror ... until I got that winning feeling, and froze my face that way, turning my head to Ed Meese ...so, he could check it out.

"How do you make that look stay on your face and look sincere?" Ed said. He watched me remove my make-up. He gruffly waved-in an L.A. police sergeant in uniform, and a couple guys in pressed dark blue business suits. "I took care of those death-threats on you, Ron. These guys are from SWAT and FBI Cointelpro."

I turned from my mirror to face them. I got that feeling again ... trying to remember ... I stared off, past them. When was it? ...the early '50s, twenty years ago. I was a star in Hollywood, then ...but, not making pictures. I was emcee on, General Electric Theatre, on television once a week. Between shows, GE had me travel around the country giving speeches, ranting against Communism ... like Father Kauflin did on radio in the '30s and '40s. I raved about, Crusade For Freedom, explained how people in communist-run countries were prisoners ...then, collected my check. There was a little more to it, than that ...because, in the early '50s when I was president of Actor's Guild in Hollywood, I ranted against communists trying to take over Hollywood ...so, they could brainwash people who went to movies. One time after talking to the Guild, I met a couple undercover FBI agents ...and, got a check from them ... I was an FBI informer.

Ed Meese interrupted my revelry. "Ron, I want you to meet these guys. Ron, stop daydreaming, get your head back here."

"Death threats? You mean that phone threat from the Commies to throw acid on my face, wreck my looks, so I can't act anymore?"

"No, Ron ...that, was twenty years ago. I mean the phone threats we got after the Berkeley speech."

"I'll try to get back here in the present, and focus. I saw the FBI patches on their blazers, that reminded me of the Actor's Guild, gave me a flashback," I said. I had that feeling again ... I was going to remember something ... I start staring off. Ed looked worried ...but, I was getting that *feeling,* and that was important. "When I was President of Actor's Guild and got death-threats, I went into a gun store and bought my first, real gun. Sure, I used guns in movies ...but, they were props."

I was daydreaming again. In the movie in my head, I walked down a street, patted a holstered gun beneath my jacket ...then, somehow I was in the audience watching myself walk down the street in G-Men, playing a government agent, I was the star. Someone put a hand on my shoulder, it was Ed. I looked into Ed's face, the faces of the policeman, and the FBI agents ...they were waiting for me to stop remembering.

I smiled, "I saved America in, G-Men."

The L.A. policeman and FBI Cointelpro officers looked uncomfortable.

Ed turned towards them, "G-Men was a Hollywood film the Governor starred in mid-'40s, when he was a big star."

I remembered walking by my mailbox with the American flag and eagle painted on it, a horseshoe too, for good luck, going into the hallway, took off my coat, hung it up. Nancy was next to me, she jumped back when she saw the shoulder holster I was wearing, and the pistol.

I tried to calm her down, "Mommy, I keep getting death-threats, communists calling me at Actor's Guild, talking about fixing my face so I'll never work again ...so, I bought 'old Betsy' at a gun store, I'm gonna keep her until the communists are gone, so you and me and the kids don't have to worry about the Red Menace."

Nancy rushed over, hugged me, she felt better.

I rubbed grease in my hair, looked at Mike. "Where's my comb?"

Ed smiled.

I was back. "We need secret police units and FBI Cointelpro provocateurs infiltrating anti-nuke demonstrations at Santa Barbara,"

Ed shook his head. "We're not ready yet, Ron.

"Ed, we've got to get radicals off the streets, in jail, where they belong. No one's threatening California, I'm governor!" I felt confused. I looked off, across the room.

Ed sat down, kept shaking his head.

Then it came to me, "It's not just California, it's America. When will Operation Cable Splicer be ready? ...mass arrests with Federal Emergency Martial Law judicial authority? That'll make me president."

On the other side of the room, on the other side of the door, in the waiting room, Patti felt impatient. She threw down the magazine she was reading, onto the couch.

This shocked my social secretary, Helena von Damm, "You can't go in there! I don't know if his rehearsal's over yet!"

"I don't care! I've been here 100 years, I've sat in on Dad's rehearsals before. It's no big deal."

Patti let herself into the auditorium just as the

FBI and police were leaving.

They looked her over.

Patti stared at them with an, 'Oh, really', look on her face. She loved male attention.

I felt amused. "Grandstanding again."

"Dad, please change your views, stop being pro-nuclear power, it's dangerous."

"Patti, we've been through this before."

"But, *dad*?"

"Bechtel and his friends got me here, he builds nuclear plants, his friends own electric utilities, got me *G.E. Theater*. It's off the table."

"Daddy, meet Helen Caldecott and her anti-nuclear activists, listen to them. It's not just radioactive waste particles coming out smoke-stacks, it's miners, down-winders, babies born deformed, people getting sick, kids playing in bad playgrounds. It's not right!"

"Why tell me?! I'm not God! Money talks! State of California needs money! I need money! You need money! If you weren't a millionaire's daughter, you'd have a job! ...you couldn't hang out with radicals and commies at Berkeley!"

Helena von Damm came in, "Ronnie, I couldn't stop her."

"That's all right, Helena."

Patti was startled. "*Helena? ...Ronnie?* Maybe Mom's right about you two."

"That's the first time I heard you say mother was right ...but, she's not."

Helena von Damm was indignant, "I doubt your father wants Berkeley radicals in the Governor's Mansion."

"I don't. Patti, you and your radicals are a pain in my side. You're for everything I hate."

Patti filled with spite. "That's how it is for me, for you!"

I'd had enough. "This conversation's over!"

Patti stormed out, slamming the door. I looked at Helena, "What was *that* all about?"

We laughed.

<>

In 1966, I'd been elected 33rd Governor of California, defeating two-term incumbent Pat Brown. I was re-elected in 1970, defeating Jesse Unruh. In my first term, I froze government hiring, but approved tax hikes to balance the budget. During the People's Park protests in 1969, I sent 2,200 National Guard troops to Berkeley campus to shut radicals up. I was responsible for dismantling the public psychiatric hospital system, because community-based housing and treatment would be better, although after that, California had a homeless population for the first time, and, still does. My first attempt to gain

Republican presidential nomination was 1968, but Richard Nixon got it. When I was Governor of California, I had conservative rhetoric. The eight years I served as Governor, I said public programs were inferior to private business. In the movie playing in my mind I saw a California built by large landowners and railroad magnates, who carved out empires, Hollywood style ... from hostile lands. Patti said I ignored reality, that California was built on public power projects, public highway projects, and public water projects ... all financed by the State's use of public tax money, with experts supplied by the State, with project administration supplied by the State ...but, I was campaigning, playing an audience, my specialty. I really did care about making people happy, I was a professional actor ... a Hollywood star.

The phone rang, Helena picked it up, "Hello."

"It's Otto von Bolschwing. I need you tonight, to translate documents Sergei DeMohrenshieldt has for me he got from Klaus Barbie and Martin Bormann about oil investments."

"Okay, as soon as Governor Reagan leaves. I bought into your company, is my stock headed up yet?" Helena said.

"No, something else is," von Bolschwing said.

<>

At the ranch one night, Nancy read me Foothill Jr. College KFJC talk show host Mae Brussell's, *Nazi Connections to JFK*, in *Rebel*, about Otto von Bolschwing. "Otto Albrecht von Bolschwing was a captain in Heinrich Himmler's dreaded SS, and was Adolph Eichmann's superior in Europe and Palestine. Von Bolschwing worked simultaneously for Dulles' OSS. When he entered U.S. in Feb. 1954, he concealed his Nazi past. He was to take over Gehlen's network in this country, and in many corners of the globe. He became closely associated with the late Elmer Bobst of Warner-Lambert Pharmaceutical, a godfather of Richard Nixon's political career, which brought him inside Nixon's 1960 campaign for the Presidency. In 1969, he showed up in California with a high-tech firm, TCI, that held classified Defense Department contracts. Trifia was brought to U.S. by von Bolschwing. Malaxa had escaped from Europe with 200 million dollars, in U.S. dollars. On arrival in New York, he picked up another 200 million dollars from Chase Manhattan Bank. The legal path for his entry was smoothed by Sullivan & Cromwell law offices, Dulles brothers' firm. Undersecretary of State Adolph Berle personally testified on Malaxa's behalf before a congressional subcommittee. In 1951, Senator

Nixon introduced a private bill to allow Malaxa permanent residence. Arrangements for relocation in Whittier were made by Nixon's law office. The dummy front cover for Malaxa in Whittier was Western Tube. In 1946, Nixon got a call from Herman L. Perry asking if he wanted to run for Congress against Rep. Jerry Voorhis. Perry later became president of Western Tube. In 1952, Nicolae Malaxa moved from Whittier California to Argentina. Malaxa had belonged to Otto von Bolschwing's Gestapo network, as did his associate, Viorel Trifia, living in Detroit. They were members of the Nazi Iron Guard in Romania, and had fled prosecution. When Malaxa went to Argentina in 1952, he linked up with Juan Peron and Otto Skorzeny."

Governor's Mansion master bedroom

Fall turned into winter, it was the shortest day of the year, Nancy and I were in bed, watching my old Hollywood films, my second favorite pastime. Twenty years ago, I was still a young man.

"Hey, these film stay great, don't they, Nancy?"

"Yes Darling, you're still a handsome rogue. That's why I married you."

"I'm a pretty good actor, not as good as Bogart or Welles ...but, good as Flynn, don't you think?"

"Flynn yes, maybe Fonda too."

"Thanks, Honey, I needed that."

She kissed me on the cheek.

"Mommy, Ed Meese let me down on Operation Cable Splicer and that mass arrest program, he's late. When it gets here, I want to lock up the Black Panthers, peace radicals, anti-power people ...and, Patti's communist friends ... all in internment camps, for their own good."

I switched videotapes.

Nancy looked interested. "What's this one?"

"FBI footage of demonstrations at San Onofre nuclear facility, then at Berkeley. Do you see who's on stage talking to the mob?"

Nancy shook her head. "That messy-looking one. Is that Patti? They all look the same to me ... It is Patti! Sometimes I think we should just fix Patti, get it over with. My girlfriends are fixing their daughters."

"Maybe that's the answer ...if, a lobotomy would get Patti to shut up ... who else's over there, in the back?"

"Why, it's those undercover FBI Cointelpro agents we had for lunch last week, going through the crowd pushing people around. Some people are pushing back. Look! ...police are arresting demonstrators. Ronnie, you didn't tell me they were agents-provocateur."

"Thank God for them ... it keeps those people away from me! Look at your daughter yelling into the microphone, dancing around, flipping her hair at the crowd. Now, she's playing Congo drums. She's passing a joint!"

"Smoking a joint ... on TV? I can't watch, anymore.".

"Just hold on, Nancy ...here's a cut to People's Park with Patti on stage again ... one of those free speech rallies."

"She's gonna talk. God *help* us."

"My father's politics stink," Patti said.

Nancy watched me turn pale, "Ronnie ..."

"I'm not upset, I'm calm," I said.

We got out of bed. Nancy put hairspray on her hair. "Ronnie, aren't those FBI Cointelpro agents-provocateur the same ones, remember, from Hollywood in the early '50s, weren't they the ones who used to pay us for informing on actors when you were president of Actor's Guild? Of course, they're older now."

"Now, that's a coincidence, I was thinking the same thing, yesterday. I hope Ed gets my mass arrest law passed, soon." I looked in the mirror, smoothed my hair, looked for white hairs.

Nancy called out, "Ed's reliable as death and taxes, find any white hairs?"

"Just a couple." I pulled them out, winked into the mirror and laughed. "There's a cute guy in there flirting with me again."

Nancy felt jumpy, "What's that noise!?"

Patti burst in the room. "Mom, Dad, I've got to talk to you."

Nancy bristled immediately. "You take that tone out of your voice, right now! How'd you get in here?"

Patti pulled up her mini-skirt, showing her thighs, "I have special arrangements with the guards."

I winced. I could see Nancy restraining herself, "You can't get shock value. Come, watch this FBI surveillance videotape ... you, disgracing us, in public ...tossing your hair ...dancing like that. You're *not* upsetting me."

Well, she *was* upsetting *me*. "Patti, I have an Irish temper, it's about ready to explode. Look how you act behind my back! ..attacking me! Your mother and I are talking about getting you a lobotomy, to get our family back together."

"What!? Mom was the one always hitting me!"

Here we were, again. "It never happened."

Patti was vehement."Yes, it did!"

"Then, it was the best kept secret in California. I didn't know about it."

"Yes, you did! I know you did!"

"Ronnie, control yourself," Nancy said. "This is getting nowhere."

Nancy was right. I corrected my daughter. "Patti, you're wrong. Sometimes, you're not too bright. Sometimes, you're hopeless, a nut case. You should be ashamed. The only thing you and me have in common is good looks, and Irish temper!"

I picked up a vintage movie magazine with me on the cover and began to read it, holding it in front of my face, blocking Patti from seeing me. Patti watched me and slowly closed her eyes, then stormed out of the room, frustrated.

Nancy triumphantly watched Patti leave, feeling she'd given Patti a good scolding.

Lebanon-Syria border, Bekka Valley poppy fields, 1970

In Syria, in his brother's house, Monzer Al-Kassar reclined on a pillow on the floor, thinking about his opium poppy fields in Bekka Valley in Lebanon. He co-owned them, with King Assad of Syria. The fields and illegal arms trade together grossed about two-to-three billion dollars, each year. Successful narco-terrorism was an art form ...hinging, on weapons trafficking between rogue and covert action teams, from opposing intelligence services. The art form developed in World War II, when U.S. intelligence needed to find relative strengths of opposing groups, so sent in weapons traders via mafia, normally the drug warlords and mafia played both sides against each other, while having allegiance to neither ...only to themselves.

Monzer greeted his three brothers, "You want to see my new jet? Come with me, see my poppy fields in Bekka Valley."

The brothers boarded Monzer's new jet ... in a few minutes the jet landed on his private airstrip in Bekka Valley. When the jet door opened, a party was in progress. Monzer's harem of belly dancers approached him, with Middle-Eastern stringed instruments and flutes and drums and finger cymbals ... all the women were loaded, addicted to opium, or heroin, its derivative. Sometimes, he kept women or sold them, sometimes traded them for girls or boys, threw them in to sweeten deals. Out of one of the tents stepped several uniformed Soviet Military GRU intelligencers.

Monzer's youngest brother caught Monzer's attention. "Your Soviet intelligence handler is here."

Monzer Al-Kassar nodded. "I see him. Give him this report, it tells what Afghanistan Muhajidin rebels and their CIA handlers are going to do against the Soviets. Tell them, I have a shipment of 100,000 American hand-held Stinger missiles for them. Get me my price, collect it, bring it here. I told them half in gold, half in printing plates for dollars, Deutchmarks and Yen."

His brother walked to the Soviets, spoke with them a few minutes, handed over an attaché case, was directed to an open shipping crate with gold bars and printing plates in it ...then, returned to Monzer, telling him the deal went down with no problems. The Soviets departed by helicopter.

Several hours later, uniformed British Intelligencer MI-6 officers flew in, paid Monzer, supplied soldiers to protect Monzer's people as they loaded opium and heroin crates onto Monzer's jet.

An MI-6 British intelligencer grabbed a British officer, "The Brit over there, he works for us in MI-6 ...but, we caught him giving heroin delivery route info to a CIA operative ...then, followed him ... and he met with Soviet GRU operatives. He's a triple agent. What shall we do with him?"

Monzer took a ceremonial sword from his ceremonial guard, he lopped off the informers arms, legs, and head. Monzer spoke coldly, "Eat him."

Stanford University, mid-'70s

George Shultz was president of Bechtel Corp. and invited friends, including Martin Anderson from Stanford University's Hoover Institute, to meet with him and me for dinner. Shultz felt, he needed to set me straight. Shultz's process of setting me straight was a continuing education program Bechtel pioneered years ago.

Shultz smiled at me, "Ronnie, my boss asked me, give you some pointers on conservative policies for California and the United States."

"That's humiliating ... treating me like this. You think Ronald Reagan can't think for himself. I can, you know."

Shultz took it in stride, "Ronnie, I know that. You're gonna be 65 years old. I know, you know the forest from the trees. I know, you're counting on going for the Republican nomination for president at the convention in 1976. I'm afraid Nixon's handling of Watergate is making it hard for us to push you into the Presidency, as soon as we wanted to. Nixon has to resign, or he'll be impeached. Vice President Spiro Agnew's next in line. But, I understand he'll resign for taking bribes. Gerald Ford will be appointed after Agnew resigns. He'll be next President."

I liked that. "I'll be President someday."

George Shultz smiled, "I know. Do you know

Paul Nitze, Ronnie? Paul, come here. Paul's the universal Cold Warrior, drafted NSC-68, calls himself, neoconservative."

Martin Anderson watched Nitze shake my hand. Paul Nitze was husband of Standard Oil heiress, Phyllis Pratt. Nitze was a vice president of Dillion Read, in mid-1930s. Nitze entered government service during World War II, serving on the staff of James Forrestal when Forrestal became administrative assistant to President Franklin Delano Roosevelt. In 1942, Nitze was chief of Metals & Minerals Branch of Board of Economic Warfare, until named director of Foreign Procurement & Development Branch of Foreign Economic Administration, in 1943. During 1944-1946, Nitze served as director, then vice chairman of U.S. Strategic Bombing Survey, for which President Truman awarded him, the Legion of Merit. In the early post-WWII era, Nitze served in Truman Administration ...later, as Director of Policy Planning for State Department, 1950-1953. He was principal author of a highly influential secret National Security Council document ...NSC-68, which provided the strategic outline for increased U.S. expenditures to counter the perceived threat of Soviet armament.

From 1953 to 1961, Nitze served as president of Foreign Service Educational Foundation, concurrently serving as associate of Washington Center of Foreign Policy Research and School of Advanced International Studies SAIS, of Johns Hopkins University. Nitze had co-founded SAIS. His publications during this period include, *U.S. Foreign Policy: 1945-1955*. In 1961, President Kennedy appointed Nitze assistant secretary of Defense for International Security Affairs ...and in 1963, Nitze became Navy Secretary, serving until 1967. After Navy Secretary, Nitze was Deputy Secretary of Defense, 1967-1969 ...a member of the U.S. delegation to Strategic Arms Limitation Talks (SALT), 1969-1973 ...and, Assistant Secretary of Defense for International Affairs, 1973-1976. Later, fearing Soviet rearmament, Nitze opposed ratification of SALT II 1979. Paul Nitze was co-founder of the 1970s 'Team B', created by conservative cold warriors, determined to stop détente and the SALT process. Panel members were all hard-liners. Team B reports became the intellectual foundation for, 'the window of vulnerability', of massive arms build-ups that began in Carter's Administration ...then, accelerated under my presidency. Team B came to the conclusion, Soviets developed terrifying new weapons of mass destruction, featuring a nuclear-armed submarine fleet that used a sonar

system that didn't use sound ...and, was undetectable with U.S. technology. This info was later proven, false. According to Dr. Anne Cahn of Arms Control and Disarmament Agency, 1977-1980, "If you go through Team B's allegations about weapons systems one by one, they were *all* wrong." Nitze became my chief negotiator of the Intermediate-Range Nuclear Forces Treaty, 1981-1984. In 1984, Nitze was named, Special Advisor to the President and Secretary of State on Arms Control. For forty years, Nitze was a chief architect of U.S. policy toward Soviet Union. I later awarded Nitze the Presidential Medal of Freedom, in 1985 ...for his contributions to freedom and security of the United States. The Arleigh Burke-class destroyer, USS Nitze, is named in his honor.

Paul Nitze greeted me coldly, "I was invited here today, to shed a little light on the Committee On The Present Danger I formed," Nitze said. Paul Nitze remembered ... President Ford's Director of Central Intelligence, George Bush, had called him in. Paul wasn't too surprised. So, Paul visited CIA Director George Bush at his office in Langley Virginia at CIA headquarters. At that time, CIA Director George Bush had set up serious shop in Angola and Jamaica ...and, expanded CIA's domestic print media asset base of journalists moonlighting on Agency payroll while they worked regular journalist jobs at the biggest newspapers in the U.S. They could argue any CIA perspective or disinformation story in the national media overnight, creating favorable public opinion. At this time, Bush's CIA was courting General Noriega, arming him, giving him payoffs, using Noriega as a mole inside South American drug cartels. Panama was cocaine central port of call. In return for letting Noriega traffic in cocaine, the Agency expected Noriega to provide the Agency intelligence Contra death squads used to eliminate people in South America and Latin America who wanted civil rights, unions, or believed in Democracy ... or otherwise got in the way of the drug trade. Those people were labeled 'communists' ...then, murdered.

DCI George Bush looked into Paul Nitze's eyes, "I'm concerned about this Communist world take-over thing. I think, if we work it better, we can get a bigger budget for the Agency, from Congress. I'm not happy with annual intelligence estimates we're getting from Gehlen's Organization out of Germany. Christ, the Agency's been dependent on them for thirty years. I've decided, make up my own intelligence estimate team. I'm calling it, 'Team-B'. Team B will second-guess the annual intelligence estimates. I want you Paul, Richard Pipes, and Lt. Gen. Dan Graham ...to be, Team B. Be yourself. I want facts and figures from you and white papers to prove Moscow can get strategic superiority over the United States. I know there's smoke and mirrors involved. But, the Agency board of directors told me, you're the man for the job. How 'bout it? Help us beat the Communists?" DCI Bush said.

<>

Paul Nitze stopped remembering ...then, looked at me. "The Committee On The Present Danger is run by me and Richard Pipes, we're Cold Warriors, like you. We're *real* Reagan Republicans. Frankly, we didn't like losing in Vietnam, we didn't like losing to OPEC. We, in the Committee, are worried what would happen to the free world ... if Soviet military gains superiority over U.S. military. We're against détente with Soviet Union, at any cost. Détente is the same as total American disarmament. It's American surrender. If the Soviets keep getting stronger militarily, they'll push us out of the Third World, push us all over the map, eventually take over here at home. We have to convince the public and Congress to finance the largest build-up of military power the world has ever seen."

I watched Paul Nitze's eyes, "Of course. I *know* that. I've been saying it, 40 years. If that's what I was supposed to learn today, I'm sorry to disappoint you. *I'm* no dummy."

Martin Anderson smiled, "Let's say, you go after the Republican presidential nomination in '76. What do you think of this? ...you could save 90 billion dollars if you transferred cost of funding social programs from the Federal Government to State Governments."

"Interesting," I said.

George Shultz smiled.

Paul Nitze spoke up, "I'd attack President Ford ...and, Secretary of State Kissinger ... for wanting arms control. I'd attack them every step of the way for any cooperation at all, with Soviet Union. It's a bad idea to placate your enemy. We need more American military power. These negotiations to give away Panama Canal are suicidal. If Ford has his way, he'll make United States No. 2, in a world where it's dangerous, if not fatal, to be second best."

I listened well. My training as an actor taught me, observe people closely. In my head, I made the ideas presented to me, my own. I visualized myself saying the same words, at the same moment I heard them ...then, repeating them in front of captive audiences on radio and TV, in lecture halls ...and, on the Presidential nomination convention floor. These guys were great.

When my second term as Governor of California ended, Jan. 1975, I continued on the speaker's circuit. I appeared on radio making commentaries. I wrote newspaper op-ed columns. My political handlers decided, I'd challenge Ford for Presidential nomination, in 1976. I campaigned hard, won the primary in California and several Southern states. I fought all the way to the nominating convention floor, where I gave a stirring speech about dangers of nuclear war, and the moral threat of the Soviet Union, winning many people over. My second attempt to get the Republican presidential nomination failed, in narrow defeat ... Gerald Ford had more than enough delegates to win Republican nomination for President, on the first ballot. Ford chose Republican Nelson Rockefeller as a Vice Presidential running mate ...but, went on to lose the Presidential race to Jimmy Carter, a Democrat.

CIA Director's office, Washington D.C., 1976

George Bush stood outside a huge office complex in Langley, Virginia, looking at the brass sign on front of the building, 'CIA Headquarters'. He held up an identification card to a rent-a-cop inside the door, who verified it, then waved George in, who walked down the hall, into an elevator, rode up a few floors, got out and walked down the hall to his office door, where a sign read, 'George Bush, Director of Central Intelligence Agency (DCI)'. He looked suspiciously up and down the hall, then unlocked the office door and entered his office. George was startled when someone swung around in his office chair to face him. In shadow, the figure appeared to be drawing a gun on him. George reached inside his coat, he drew his shoulder pistol out, pointed it.

The office light switched on.

"Happy Birthday," said Barbara Bush.

It was his George's wife, holding out a bouquet to him for a gift. He smiled in relief. But, Barbara was shocked.

"Barbara! Thank God it's you."

"You weren't going to shoot me, were you George?"

"Of course not." George holstered his pistol. "I'm sorry if I scared you, Barbie."

273

"I'm sorry if I scared you, too, George."

"Thanks for the flowers. How 'bout letting me have my chair back?"

"Of course, Darling. Soon as I put these flowers in the vase. They're white roses, your favorite."

"They're beautiful ...why were you sitting in the dark?"

"One of your friends recognized me, picked the lock to let me in to surprise you. Wasn't that nice?"

George shrugged bravely and gave Barbara a look of feigned machismo. George loved Barbara and confided in her, whenever it didn't override her security clearance. And, off the record, sometimes when it did. It was his way of asking her for advice, it was one of those times, right now. "Barbara, when I took this job, I found out things the hard way I didn't want to know. CIA directors are front men, like presidents, cut-outs to blame, puppets to take heat or claim plausible denial, smoke and mirrors. We don't really do anything, just what we're told, like marionettes, except the strings that are pulled are our tendons, and we bleed."

Barbara had little use for whining. "George, it's the only way to protect our family and investment portfolio ... someone has to do it. We've six kids, and with grand kids, it makes twenty-seven in our immediate family. You're family patriarch, you have to financially protect everyone, build-up trust funds for the kids, grandkids, and great grandkids, so they never have to work. Like we never had to work. We did it as a matter of choice and principle ...because, it was our duty. This world can be cold and uncaring. We want our family to go withdraw $5,000-to-$10,000 for out-of-pocket expenses whenever they feel like it, without cutting our family trust endowment. Your father and mine gave us that privilege, that's what ruling family values are, our family tradition. It's a great tradition. It's what we stand for. Just make sure the tendons that get cut, aren't yours. As long as blood on the ground is someone else's ...then, you're protecting our family. I know it sounds harsh ...but, you've heard it before. In a way, George, you're family patriarch for all the Blue Book American families, for Society. You're DCI, you protect the investment portfolios for all the ruling families in America, all 5,000 of us, puppets, cut-outs, sanctions, smoke, mirrors ... whatever."

George Bush felt exasperated. "There's so much dirty laundry in this job, it's a set-up waiting to happen ... like I'm a patsy finding out the hard way ...I can't trust anyone, here. Me cover-ing up Nixon. Nixon covering up Dulles. Dulles smuggling Nazi and fascist financiers into the country to finance the Republican and Democratic parties, since World War II. Covering up the Kennedy thing, both brothers, Martin Luther King, Paul Robeson ... it changes a man, Barbara. There are more Nazis in our government all the time, in the National Republican Heritage Committee, those people were financiers and death squad leaders in Hitler's Eastern Europe ...now, they're on my election committee as part of the official Republican party to get out and swing the ethnic vote. Then, we give them foreign aid to keep modern, yes Barbara, modern death squads going in their regimes all through eastern Europe, South America, South Africa. It's Satanic ...how do you sweep Lucifer under the rug? How do you sweep Satan out of your heart? Keep him from looking out your eyes? Calling your shots? You wouldn't believe how much business my father and yours did with Hitler before, during, and after World War II ... how much money we lost when the U.S. Government shut down our parents' business investing and laundering Nazi money and shipping them oil, working with Dulles to smuggle Nazi loot and gold from Dulles' House of Morgan financial interests through the Angletons, the Bank of England, the Baring brothers, Seligman, Speyers, Mirabaud, Mallet, Fould, J. Henry Shroder, Erlanger, Warburg, Grenfell, Hambros, the Lazard brothers, the Rothschilds, and Vatican bank. It turns my blood black, it turns my stomach. If there was only some way to make America clean again, to wash the blood off our family money ...or at least, get the damn money back."

Barbara felt surprised. "The Vatican Bank? ...even, the Pope?"

George quipped, "Is the Pope Catholic? The Knights of Malta are the walking Dark Ages, they've taken their Crusades from the Middle Ages right into today's headlines against the Muslims and the Jews ...the P-2 Lodge are the real Italian Mafioso, they control Vatican Bank. It has nothing to do with God or Jesus, just the opposite. It's like the Pope is a DCI in his own right, running a mind control experiment on a billion human beings. All this intelligence stuff gets to me, the double British-Soviet agents, the triple U.S.-British-Soviet agents, add German BND intelligence, KGB, Mossad ...it all goes around like a twister in a Scooby Do movie until there isn't national allegiance anymore, anyplace ...because, everyone's working for someone else, and, they're subcontracted to the same central banks anyway, and international investment banks ...then, all the banking families start turf wars, and there's brothers fighting brothers, sisters fighting sisters ... add in Agency protection for drug-runners who run us gun-running intelligence, add in provocations to start wars to run up national debt for arms, or provisions ...and back and forth we go ...on a merry-go-round ...then, an escalator ...then, a roller coaster landing in an elevator, shooting up to a parachute drop. Everyone fills their barf bags, Barbara ...we never get our feet back on the ground until we're planted six feet under. All of us just trying to grow our portfolios, shelter our family trusts, protect our fortune, that's our family values."

Barbara walked over to him, touched his shoulder, "George, I'm worried about you, whining like this. Can you take a vacation?"

"I think I need a permanent vacation."

"That's a bad joke, George."

George smiled weakly. "Here, I'm supposed to be protecting national security, but everywhere I look, it's the new World Order ...that's not national, it's global. That's not the American flag, Barbara. It's dark angels against God and Christ, is what it is."

"I haven't seen you so wound up, George. We can't play God. For all our sakes, you need this job to maintain our family endowment. That's the way the ball bounces. Your father had to do it, so did his father. So did Abraham and Isaac and the Gospel Apostles at the last supper, George, no one has a choice, really. You put the family fortune first ...or, there's no family gonna be left, just anarchy."

"Think it boils down like that?"

Barbara nodded. She saw, George got that look of feigned machismo on his face, again.

George remembered being at his dad's, Prescott's, estate and mansion in Florida that time when they had Selwa and Archie Roosevelt and Archie's parents over for dinner with Allen Dulles and several Rockefeller brothers.

Prescott was his usual circumspect self, "You can't beat Florida weather. You Roosevelts are the best neighbors I could have. Archie, I'm glad you brought your boss along."

David Rockefeller smiled, "Archie and me are off on business to Africa. We're interviewing ruling family reps for World Bank, IMF, and Export-Import Bank ...from a host of countries that want credit ...have to weigh-in their collateral ...see what the House of Windsor and Bank of England will let me have ...where to send the Marines in.

Half the time, Dulles' CIA and Queen Elizabeth's MI-6 are on the same side ...half, they're not and make a fiasco for everyone. Prescott, nice to see your son George, here. Hi George."

Barbara Bush noticed, her husband seemed aloof in Prescott's presence. Prescott didn't notice. Soon dinner was in full swing.

Prescott had nostalgia in his eyes, "These meals in our Florida estate are like the old days. George and the other kids were little then, 60 years ago, George was six years. That's when I explained ruling family values to him. 'George, you're six, its time for our annual man-to-man. Serving family wealth is first.'" Six-year-old George looked blank, his face turned red. His mother had something to add. 'Ruling families of this world are one big family. It doesn't matter what country we're from, wealth makes us one big family, the 'World Order'. Our countries may fight ...but, not us, we stay allies ...because our country is personal wealth, all personal wealth of all ruling families ... the World Order. 'Family values' means do not mix socially with the upper class, the managerial class, or working class ...only with the money-issuing class, or with the ruling class.' Little George spoke for himself, 'Yes mother. Yes father. Family fortune comes first ...or, we'll end up wage slaves like the upper class, middle class, and lower class. We're the money-issuing class, the World Order.'"

Yes, Prescott had a head full of memories about his son George ...when George learned money-issuing class and ruling family manners, etiquette, correct silver usage ...George complaining, he was tired going to debutante balls ...and, prep schools ...George embarrassed about Prescott's Nazi partners that first year of college, when George pledged Skull & Crossbones German Society of the Order of Death in his Yale freshman year, where the inner circle was money-issuing class and ruling family college students who would be friends for life, the ones to follow in their fathers' footsteps ...carve up natural resources of the world in local and international turf wars ...decide which countries would war ...or, be at peace. His first year at Yale, George found out about his father's and grandfather's bust by the U.S. under the Trading with the Enemy Act ...the family banks and shipping lines were seized. When George confronted his father's pro-Nazi stance, at the time Prescott was a Yale board member in charge of racial quotas at the university ...and, George spoke publicly in opposition to Prescott's racial quota policies ...and, argued for Prescott to let more Jews and

Blacks into Yale.

"Dad, did you finance Hitler during wartime? The U.S. government shut down our bank and shipping lines. Did you and Grandfather Walker attack Nicaragua in your own private war in the 1920s, trying to take Nicaragua over for yourselves?"

Prescott scratched his temple. "Those are tough questions."

"Dad, I'm going to enlist to change people's minds about us, and redeem our family's honor. If I fight against Hitler, people will forget you were in business with him."

Yes, Prescott remembered it well ... George went off to fight Nazis, later was described as a war hero, and Prescott could feel proud of George ...and, still count his Nazi profits through the war years into the early 1950s ...and, make sure after the war when George finished college, to get George a good job with a reputable CIA-connected company ... to learn the ropes on his own ...learn how to make his own private armies ...to grow and defend their family portfolio ...and, keep it safe ...and defend and keep safe family wealth of all the money issuing class, and the ruling class families ... the World Order ...who fought unending war to keep their money from filtering down to upper, middle, or lower classes.

<>

Barbara finished arranging flowers she brought to George's CIA office for his birthday present, "George, are you daydreaming."

"Yes. I was remembering what Dad taught me about family honor, keeping our wealth safe and some things he did I didn't agree with, like his Nazi fiasco."

Barbara finished arranging the flowers. "George, if you need to cover-up this or that to protect family honor and family fortune, don't come home until you do. Your father did the best he could, so should you. Being DCI is paying your dues, we have to earn twelve-to-fifteen percent each year ...or, inflation will ruin us, that's the facts of life."

"It's not that simple, Barbie, as fighting wars to grow capital and quarterly returns. John the Apostle told us before Messianic Millennial peace comes, which is the peace the Reich also promises, the human race will have a ruthless, new world order government to enslave mankind ...and, no man or country can buy or sell without bearing the mark of the new world order and world trade organization, it's fulfillment of Bible prophecy."

George took a bible off a bookshelf, opened the book, read the inscription, "'God bless you ... from Ronald Reagan'". He flipped through the book. "Here it is, Revelations 13:15. God said it would compel all men, 'Both small and great, rich and poor, free and bond' to be identified with it, and 'no other man might buy or sell'. The beast ...Apocalypse ...God destroys Lucifer and his Satanic legions on Earth in nuclear battle. It's what Governor Reagan's talking about."

Barbara wanted to comfort George, "It'll be okay, George. One day, you'll run for president. I know, you'll fix the new World Order so nothing happens to our investments." She watched George shrug bravely with that look of feigned machismo on his face she got a kick out of, kissed him on the cheek, then began to leave the room.

Bill Casey walked into the room.

"Forget how to knock, Bill?" Barbara said on her way out.

Bill Casey had a gruff look on his face that went away when he smiled. Bill knocked his knuckles on George's wooden desk. "Knock knock, who's there?" Bill said. He'd brought with him a British MI-6 merchant banker and an Arab sheik from the new World Order petroleum community. Bill introduced them. "Our British friend here sits on The Bank of England, he's high up in MI-6. The Sheik is putting up the capital to start us a new bank, BCCI, Bank of Credit & Commerce International. When 'ex-CIA' assets Wilson and Terpil got busted selling U.S. arms to Kaddaffi, training his mercenaries, trading arms-for-drugs, it got traced to the Agency's Nyuen-Hand Bank in Australia, so BCCI is now where the New World Order intelligence agencies will launder payoffs, foreign aid kickbacks into campaign funds, bribes, drug money, illegal arms sales ...and, this time ... an all-around tighter operation handling black budget covert operations against communists and terrorists. Today, we're here to sign paperwork and found ICIC, International Credit & Investment Company, with its own ruling family investment portfolio to target which natural resources go to whom. ICIC will direct covert operations and wars to re-divide ownership of natural resources by wiping out ruling families whose wealth we want to takeover, clear out subject populations with genocide, decolonize then recolonize countries with bombs, install puppet governments, legislate new infrastructures, then award redevelopment contracts to our own developers and make 'em buy American. ICIC has BCCI launder and disperse money to our mercenary armies. ICIC's a holding company, its board directors are heads of different western intelligence agencies who sit on Central

Bank boards. ICIC manages BCCI ...and, CIA and MI-6 are represented on the board ...*but, we put up no money*, the sheik here handles that. Quite a financial coup, don't you think?"

Bush nodded, "Dulles would be proud of you. You're my intelligence mentor, he was yours. Okay, I read the briefs yesterday. Handy. Good 'vision' kind-of-thing, great paperwork, can't wait to see how this ICIC-BCCI thing works, where do I sign for CIA's financial part in founding ICIC and BCCI?"

Bill Casey handed George the paperwork, nodded his head towards the MI-6 banker.

"MI-6's my personal collection agency for the Crown," the MI-6 agent said.

George had a blank look on his face, "Thanks, I just came onboard as DCI. Congress outlawed more CIA involvement in Angola. I don't want to start my tenure here by losing the war there ...there's oil and minerals we need in our investment portfolio. Rumors say, we're using biological warfare in Angola, not like we did in Cuba to make sheep blind and crops fail. Prince Philip's house of Windsor says, it's too crowded in Angola, starve them off let, them go back to cannibalism ...then get down developing African oil and gold reserves."

Bill looked at him, "George, let's end this and make Wednesday's lunch special at the Seasons. We've traditionally used Margaret Thatcher's MI-6 to run mercenaries and covert operations for us before, that's how I met our friends Leslie Aspin and Bill Buckley, running covert-ops for us when MI-6 introduced them to me for under-the-carpet cleaning. Congress told me, as long as CIA is not over there in Angola fighting, and not officially pulling the triggers, we're breaking no U.S. laws."

The MI-6 operative looked at George. "You see, we've been fighting in Angola for you before and we know how to do it, again. But, what you have to do in return, is beef up your American wiretap operations in Britain for us. As you know, British law prohibits us wiretapping ourselves, but it says nothing about covert foreign nationals setting up shop, doing our wiretapping, and leaking it to us."

DCI Bush understood. Bush looked at Casey. Bill Casey nodded at George Bush. George Bush nodded at the Brit. George Bush felt irritated with the Brit, but didn't know why, "We got the same kettle of fish, you to beef up your wiretapping program of U.S. civilians here for us ... my people will tell you what we want. Let me sign off on this thing, I'm hungry," DCI Bush said. After

George signed off, the Brit signed off, the sheik started to, but George pulled the paperwork back. "What else is he in for, Bill?"

"Along with financing the deal, he wants his hand on the Angolan oil tap for OAPEC ...OPEC then controls all African oil," Bill Casey said.

Bush sounded neutral. "Okay, as long as we win in Angola ...and, the Sheik doesn't get Cuban oil, that's mine, when Castro's gone my family can get our offshore oil out of Cuba and out of Central and South America. I swear, Bush's and Castro are like Hatfields and McCoys feuding, when communists are gone, I can drill. Get ahold of our BCCI people, tell MI-6 Congress tied my hands on Angola ...but, we approve backdoor MI-6 mercenaries and I'll owe 'em one, we'll do the wiretapping for them they do it for us ...and, we'll kick the Soviets out of Angola and Cuba."

The Brit nodded.

Bechtel Boardroom, San Francisco

At Bechtel company in his boardroom, Mr. Bechtel introduced his new company president, George Shultz. Two directors were also directors of California Chevron, and Pacific Gas & Electric. Outside the boardroom, Bechtel's treasurer, Caspar Weinberger felt he wasn't allowed to fit in at Bechtel ...because, he was Jewish ...and, Bechtel's biggest customers were anti-Semitic, the King of Saudi Arabia and King's family and friends throughout the Middle East. They hated Jews, they hated Israel. Caspar was the only Jew at Bechtel in upper management. He sulked outside until his temper got the better of him ...then, barged in the boardroom, where he saw George Shultz, "Shultz, I'm as good as you, I should be president of this company, not you."

Palo Alto Cultural Center & Community Garden

Patti watched the morning sky from hiding, behind the twenty foot tall retarded trident metal sculpture stuck in the lawn of Palo Alto Cultural Center by the city's pedestrian art committee. An icy chill clung to her back. She huddled closer between Alan and Granma Wilpf. She hugged Tracie. Patti saw a sign on a cultural center door, that read, 'Palo Alto Office of Culture'. Patti laughed. She rubbed her hands together, then vigorously rubbed her shoulders. "*Brrr.* It's cold out here."

Alan was ready to shiver. "We should run in place ...but, people might notice, us."

Patti looked at the speaker's platform.

President G. W. Bush was speaking to a crowd of Palo Alto citizens, all dressed in flannel shirts and sweaters. Some held dogs on leashes. One resident had his hand inside a plastic bag, bent over, picking up dog shit, turned the bag inside out, taking it off his hand and getting it over the dog shit at the same time. Some people had pooper scoopers, special dust pans on broomsticks for picking up dog shit. Many of the people in the crowd kept bending over from time to time, picking up steaming clumps of dog shit.

W spoke to them. "It's important to vote. I want your vote. Voting's important. Blue Book invented voting ...for you, to feel like you matter, to let you think you have a say how new World Order runs your life. If compassion ruled, it would be Christmas everyday. That's too expensive. That's why SCREAMA made love illegal. It's expensive. We need SCREAMA to believe in, separating one person from another, preventing common humanity. The only way to have peace is to wage war. Angels in Heaven had civil war, was led by Lucifer, a rebellion against the established Order, the World Order. Vote for W."

The crowd built up around the trident sculpture like an amoeba, around Patti, Alan, Granma Wilpf, and Tracie, they felt warm.

"Can you believe that moron?" Patti said.

Alan felt cautious. "Don't jump out there each time you get excited! It's dangerous!"

Patti wasn't listening. She focused her vision on W. She took a bag of dog shit from one of the citizens of Palo Alto. The way it collapsed in her hand felt horrible. She cringed, tore open the bag, threw it at W.

"You should feel at home with this bag of shit, since you're full of it!" Patti said. The bag of dog shit opened in the air. It hit against the large Plexiglas shield W stood behind. He grimaced. Patti laughed. The crowd start raining bags of dog shit on the Plexiglas box.

W was upset, "You can't do this to me! I represent the new World Order! I am President, not you! Stop!"

Patti saw Alan on one side of her, Granma Wilpf, and Tracie on the other. Tracie watched the shit rain on W.

Tracie laughed. "Cool. Good job, Mommy."

Patti smiled at Tracie.

Granma Wilpf shook her head and shrugged, "How can I have compassion on W, who shows no compassion for others?"

"W's unnatural, isn't he?" Patti said.

"What's compassion, Mommy?" Tracie said.

Granma Wilpf gently pulled Tracie in front of her, "It's love, Honey. Patti, Alan, Tracie, let's go walk through the community garden. We'll wait there for Shiu and Butler to get here. It's gonna be a long day. If we stir up more shit, we'll get arrested ...won't get a chance to train revolutionaries. C'mon, community garden's behind cultural center and library."

They walked past a gate, inside a wire fence protecting the community garden. Patti looked at wild flowers, corn, and tomatoes growing, "It's beautiful here, like we're on another planet, it smells so good, here. Tracie, there's Butternut squash. There's tomatoes. There's corn. Carrots. Iceberg lettuce. Strawberries. Vegetarian's paradise!"

Tracie felt confused, "What's a 'tarian?"

Patti smiled. "I am. Someone who has compassion for animals, who doesn't eat them. I eat vegetables ...but, no animals."

"How come?" Tracie said.

Patti had to think for a minute, "I don't know, for sure ...because animals are people, too."

"People, too?"

"Yeah, anthropologists consider people animals. So why can't I consider animals people? What's the difference? Animals and people have eyes, noses, brains, hearts. They have society, herds, independence, teamwork, team players. Everyone wants to survive, raise little members of the same species, keep other species for pets, be happy."

Alan looked at Tracie, then at Patti. "You're confusing her,."

"You mean, you're confused, don't you? Admit your feelings once in a while," Patti said.

"Okay. You're right. I'm confused. Why do you feel people and animals are equals?"

"I can't explain my feelings. What right do I have to tamper with creation? Even if it's only a rock. I've had trouble picking flowers, too. I didn't want to kill them. They're beautiful. Why kill them? One of my girlfriends was an organic gardener. She told me when she pruned plants, they grew back. Picking flowers wasn't killing the plant. It was like eating a piece of fruit, picking an avocado, but not chopping down the tree. She didn't eat animals ...but, she did have cheese and milk. But no flesh. I've had pet dogs and cats. I couldn't eat them."

Tiger popped his head up out of Patti's purse. Tracie reached in Patti's purse and petted Tiger.

"No way I could eat Tiger," Tracie said.

Alan watched them. "Yeah. I get it."

Patti scratched Tiger behind his ears. Tiger closed his eyes sleepily. Patti petted him on the back of his neck in that special spot he could never reach, between his shoulders.

<>

"What are those people on bikes doing there?" Patti said.

Granma Wilpf looked at the cyclists, "You see those City of Palo Alto flags they stuck up on long fishing rod-like poles on their bike baskets? They're the Palo Alto Citizen's Bicycle Patrol."

"Are they city police?" Patti said.

"No," said Granma Wilpf. "They're civilians, the neatness patrol. They ride around, report citizens who don't keep lawns mowed, weeds pulled, if there's an old car parked outside, they write clean-up tickets, report back to Palo Alto City Council."

Patti's mouth dropped open. "You're kidding?"

"Nope. They believe, if everything is neat and clean ...then, they're neat and clean, the city's neat and clean, the world's neat and clean. They're the bicycle neatness patrol."

"They protest world war? ...genocide?"

"No. They protest non-conformity. They make everything look the same, make their obsessive-compulsions into law."

One of the bicycle patrol people pedaled over to Patti, "Make sure you keep everything clean and tidy. We're a model city."

Patti couldn't believe it. "Okay."

She watched the bike patrol drive off, then spotted Butler and Shiu. Patti took a garden stake down. She tore a side off a cardboard box. She pushed the garden stake through it, took her purse, rummaged around for her lipstick, wrote a slogan on the paper, 'Divest Them! ... Share Resources Of Earth Equally For All".

Butler walked over to Patti. "Hi Patti. How ya doin'?"

"Good. I'm glad to see you."

"I'm glad to see you."

Shiu walked over to Patti.

Patti saw some older people wearing Palo Alto Peace Center hats, coming in the garden area. There were high schoolers from Bay Area Action Committee were wearing t-shirts with 'BAA' logos on them. The crowd gathered around Patti, Butler, Shiu, and Alan. There were animals rights protest signs, signs reading, 'No War For Oil! ... Stay Out Of The Gulf!' ... 'Divest Them!', and 'Vets Against War', signs.

Patti watched as a pickup truck drove to the edge of the garden. W got ready to address the crowd with a hand-held amplified megaphone. The volume was high, it made scraping sounds.

W spoke into the megaphone, "Several days ago in our sister city, Sarajevo, there was a quaran-tine several people escaped from, they were captured and transported here to Palo Alto where they were put in quarantine ...but, they escaped. I don't want to hurt you. I want you to be productive members of the new World Order, a drone worker bee for the good of the new World Order."

The crowd booed W. He turned to several squads of SCREAMA, "Keep these midgets quiet! Turn up the music volume like in Panama to drive Noriega nuts, like we did in Waco, let me hear those rabbits squeal as we kill them!"

Patti held her ears. "There's Gehlen! Someone found him and untied him!"

"Don't let him see you!" Alan said.

W yelled at the crowd, "You all be quiet! I don't want SCREAMA to hurt you. Everyone be calm."

Patti held her sign in front of her face, "Up yours! Divest new World Order ruling families!"

W was with them., "You must declare your allegiance to new World Order. You must be productive. Artists are enemies of the State ...there's no use for you. Behave!"

Gehlen signaled SCREAMA to attack. He yelled at protesters, "Sit on the ground. Or be shot!"

Patti watched SCREAMA aim machine-guns at people in the crowd. "Get down! ...or you'll be shot!" Patti said. Patti heard the *rat-a-tat-tat* of SCREAMA machine guns firing over the heads of people in the crowd. She dove into the dirt, breaking a tomato vine. After SCREAMA silenced the crowd, protesters stayed in the garden area, building little fires to keep warm. Patti threw small pieces of wood on the fire. She looked towards SCREAMA on the other side of the fence. W was on a pickup truck bed, SCREAMA were tying a man to a crucifix sticking up from the flatbed. "It's that guy they tortured in Sarajevo."

Alan shook his head, "That poor guy, he doesn't get a break. He's all beat up, black and blue. He's hanging on the cross like a rag doll."

It was Mel's Jesus ...but, nobody knew, because the movie hadn't come out yet. Maybe these were cut scenes from the movie, you never know. Patti watched Gehlen give eye signals to SCREAMA, who prodded Mel's Jesus with nightsticks. Patti bit her lip, hung her head.

Mel's Jesus, on the cross, spoke. "The new World Order will cut the chaff from the wheat. Those who don't worship Blue Book will be raped and castrated."

Gehlen smiled. "There. He's told you. Come over to our side. Believe in SCREAMA."

Patti watched Granma Wilpf hide behind a pile

of weeds, then yell from behind the weeds. "Don't worship SCREAMA! Believe in love!"

W was upset, "Love's illegal! Trust the new World Order to bring world peace, not love!"

Gehlen was upset, "Join SCREAMA. Vote. Artists are wrong. Artists love. Love is not legal. I've hung this man on the cross to convince you, love is no good. SCREAMA giveth, and SCREAMA taketh away."

Patti huddled by the little fire. "Around this little campfire, on this cold morning, I think of strangers I loved but never knew, who came to Earth then disappeared, like fire. People go, but feeling stays behind. I search for someone to love," Patti said. Patti looked towards the pickup truck. "I understand what Gehlen wants, to love and be loved."

Alan got upset.

"Give me a break!" Alan said. He's an asshole. He doesn't care about people or he wouldn't make war against artists!"

"No. He cares for his own kind, not about us. We're the poor. People who's parents were middle class. He serves the money issuing class, the ruling class, they are the Order. His love can't jump boundaries. He has no compassion for us. He saves it, for his own," Patti said. "See this bible. I don't believe the words, I believe the feeling. Not the way Messianics do. When nothing works, I read it, then I cry. I don't know why."

"That's dumb."

"Hey, got a Bud light! ...dude," Patti said.

"Do you understand the martyr on the cross up there?"

"He knows, living's better than dying. He believes in staying alive," Patti said. Patti watched, as revolutionaries and artists in the garden began linking arms in a circle, chanting in unison. Patti watched SCREAMA Cointelpro with video cameras, push and shove the crowd.

Granma Wilpf was sad, "I've seen it before. Now it's digital video, it used to be still cameras. People struggling to have a job, struggling to pay bills, doctors, clothes, food, rent. It never stops. The Central banks are sadists."

"I understand that," Patti said.

Alan joined in, "I've lived on my yawl enough to tell you, shit floats to the surface."

"I understand, that too." Patti watched Mel's Jesus collapse on his cross, limp and still. "That poor man. I'm sorry for him."

"The show must go on," Butler said.

Shiu nodded. "What we gonna do?"

Patti watched SCREAMA circle the garden fence. Three or four SCREAMA trampled over the fence, grabbing artists, then beat them.

Alan sat still, "All we can do is sit here, hope the martyr up there is okay."

Patti heard a whistle. She turned her head. She saw Gehlen, waving hand jibe to SCREAMA. She watched SCREAMA walk through the artists, beating them with lead bats.

Gehlen felt in control, "Artists! ...disband!"

<>

Patti watched Gehlen work the crowd. She knew, if they caught her it would be terrible for her. She didn't know which way to run. Butler grabbed her.

"There!" Butler said. "The back of the garden! That gate!"

Patti grabbed Tracie's hand. She pulled Tracie forward. With her other hand, Patti grabbed Granma Wilpf's hand. They ran to the gate. Patti saw Alan, Butler, and Shiu running there, too. Patti ran down the dirt paths of the garden, past the yellow sunflowers that towered over her, their black centers leaning towards her as if in inquiry, past the orange pumpkins spread around her, peeking out from behind giant green leaves like giant, elephant ears, towards the climbing red and white roses, and purple morning glories, growing on the fence and the gate She smelled the morning air, scented with honeysuckle and jasmine, felt the sun on her face. Her chest ached, she ran so hard she got a pain in her side. Patti led everyone out of the garden through the gate, onto the street. She ran past suburban houses towards the business district, downtown, led them in an alley by Mac's Smoke Shop, saw a dumpster marked, 'cardboard only', hoisted Tracie in, then Granma Wilpf. Then, Butler, Shiu, and Alan jumped in, too. They were quiet. Patti could hear the boots of the SCREAMA running past the dumpster. She looked up out of the dumpster, at the buildings in the alley. They were red brick, and formed a long wall. There was a big pile of wooden crates, with a teenage girl hiding behind them, as SCREAMA ran by. A teenage boy hid with her. Gehlen ran in the alley, grabbed the teenage girl, yanked her towards him. Gehlen drew his pistol. Gehlen start hitting the girl with it. Patti felt desperate. Patti jumped out the dumpster onto Gehlen. "No! Not again!"

Gehlen fell down. Butler, Shiu, and Alan suddenly were there to help Patti. Patti grabbed away Gehlen's gun. Patti pulled back her arm, threatening to strike Gehlen with the gun, she felt powerful. "I want to beat him!"

Gehlen cringed back from her. "No! Don't!"

Patti felt someone pull back her arm. She

turned to see. It was Granma Wilpf. Patti yelled at her, "Let go! I want to beat him!"

"Stop! You'll be no better than Nazis! No better than Iron Guard! No better than SCREAMA. No better than Gehlen."

"I'm better than them!"

"Not if you act like them. Break the circle …if you found Gehlen on a road, didn't know him, and he was wounded, you'd feel sorry for him, you'd help him."

Patti lowered the gun, "Okay?"

"You want to beat him up. You want to help him. Make up your mind," Granma Wilpf said.

Patti tucked the gun into her waistband. She felt herself calm down. Patti heard footsteps of SCREAMA running down the street. She turned towards Butler, "Help me push this door open."

Patti, Butler, Shiu, Alan, Granma Wilpf, and Tracie shoved themselves against a door in alley wall. The door opened. They hurried in, closed the door behind them. It was a storage room.

Shiu shoved Gehlen in the corner. "If you want to live, be quiet."

Patti spit out her words. "I'll find out what makes him tick."

Alan was apprehensive. "Be careful."

Butler, too. "If you find out, you might not want to know."

"Here goes," Patti said. Patti walked over to cardboard cartons stacked near Gehlen, sat beside him, "Shiu, I want to talk to him, alone."

"He's dangerous," Shiu said.

"It's all right. I have his gun. Go on."

"Okay."

Patti watched Shiu walk to Butler. Patti faced Gehlen. "Why are you a monster?"

"Not a monster …a man."

Patti watched Gehlen's face. "Granma Wilpf told me she was once Nazi, and wanted to marry you, then."

"She told you?"

"Yes."

"Why? …artists are freaks. You can't survive."

"If I pull this trigger, can you?"

"The purpose of the new World Order, John wrote about in Apocalypse, is fight now … so we don't have to fight later, for all Eternity. But, what you want to know, I'll tell you … the truth. I'm your grandfather, your mother was my daughter."

Patti was shocked. "You're crazy! I don't believe you!"

Granma Wilpf jumped to her feet, hurried over to Patti. "It's true. Your mother was illegitimate by him. I married your grandfather to make her legitimate. It was hard times, the only way to survive."

Patti jumped to her feet. "I can't believe it! I hate this man most in the world, he's my grandfather?! It makes no sense!"

Granma Wilpf felt ashamed. "It never does. I should have told you, before."

Patti became calm. "Yes, you should've told me! I'm a good artist. I believe in the revolution, you can't take that away from me."

Gehlen laughed, "There's no revolution."

Patti pondered. "No revolution?!"

Gehlen stared into Patti's eyes, "You want revolution? The Order makes peace, war, revolution, counter-revolution, terrorism, counter-terrorism, destabilization, colonization, re-colonization. The Order makes money, issues credit, collects interest on national debts in every nation in the world. The Order rules by Divine Right. The World Order is Satan's Angels that rebelled against God in Heaven …now, fighting here, on Earth. We manage conflict. There's no revolution, that's a media term … just the money issuing class worshiping Lucifer, fighting Satanic global turf wars for Satanic positioning. Divine orchestration. Liberation struggles don't exist, they're media propaganda, illusions. Patti, if you owned factories that make tanks, planes, helicopters. guns, ships …and needed a war or revolution for better sales to save your personal share of the world, wouldn't you? It's simple …but, you artists take it personally, as if life is yours …it belongs to God, and Satan is his angel, not you. Satan is a higher order of existence. Can't you read my lips?"

Patti was puzzled, "I don't get it. Slow down."

Butler was amazed. "It's fascinating, how you put it."

"It's not easy to hear Truth," Gehlen said. "It's my destiny, to save you."

Patti shoved him. "You make me miserable."

Gehlen's voice got stronger. "The new World Order has a better place for you, in the Big Picture."

Patti heard SCREAMA heavy boots stomping by. She watched Gehlen's eyes, looking how he'd react to SCREAMA, close by. He seemed to ignore how close they were. Patti heard them pass, then it was quiet in the alley.

Gehlen looked at Patti. "There's no revolution, but in your heart."

Patti spoke uncertainly, "The purpose of life is to make money?"

CENSORED

Gehlen nodded. "Yes, Patti, to make money. Not fight for peace, for democracy, for Love, nobody believes that, anymore ...those views are purged by social engineers, no longer sanctioned. Love is illegal."

"By the money issuers?"

"Yes, basically, Patti. Part of my job was eliminate trade unions to keep corporate and cartel profits up, keep the Messianic State alive. When I courted Granma Wilpf in the '20s, '30s and after, into the '40s, and '50s, Hitler worked for me, he was part of German High Command Military Intelligence. At the same time, I was part of German High Command, and I worked for Military Intelligence. I made a show of reporting to Hitler for my cover. But our Owners were in charge of every breath. *They* put *me* in charge of intelligence against Soviet Union.

"There was a revolution against the Romanov ruling family in Russia, competing gangs of ruling families financing that insurrection billed it as, 'people's revolution'. Ruling families from twenty countries wanted the Baku oil fields and Russia's timber and gold ...throwing down the ruling families, taking back wealth of the Earth, sharing it equally among all people ... was fantasy, Madison Avenue ...it got out of control, it caught on. But, it was a hoax. The idea of sharing wealth equally so all people benefit, is absurd. I won't give up my family fortune. Who would? No one. Ruling families that financed, and continue to finance, communism, and socialism, and national socialism, what you call Nazis, financed democracy too, financed communism ...but, the idea of financial equality ...that never existed ...but, spread around the world as if it did ...socialism in America, England, Europe, Germany ... about to be defeated in polls, by socialists. Your father would've loved the script. It was choreography. Use slave and wage slave laborers in peace, conscripted soldiers in war, blame poverty on poor, famine on starving, sickness on sick, negotiate peace as soon as fight war ...as central bankers, oilmen, chemical cartels, industrialists open purse-strings, deposit profits.

"Fall 1943, we arranged for billions of marks to be smuggled out of Germany to Sweden, Holland, Switzerland, Spain, Argentina, Brazil, all the world centers of German commercial strength. An entire Fokker military aircraft plant in Germany was disassembled, smuggled into Holland. After World War II German industrialists registered patents and transferred capital to Sweden. By 1945, 1,000 fake companies were set up under German ruling family control to hide war assets and booty. Intelligence operations split. A faction went to Madrid, soon taken over by Otto Skorzeny. Bormann sent me to United States, to continue Germany's fight against Soviet Union, as a double-agent. I gathered brains and finances of German General Staff High Command behind me, coordinated American ruling families that profited working with German and Czarist ruling families. I co-founded CIA, staffed it with Nazi intelligence personnel, covert op death squads. I founded SCREAMA. I organized the intelligence services of Egypt, Lebanon, Israel, Iran, Iraq, France, Spain, Argentina, Bolivia, Algeria, South Africa, Kenya, Germany ...and, the United States. This greatness in my blood, is in yours."

Patti sat spellbound.

So did others in the room.

Patti watched Butler, Shiu, and Alan find places to sit on boxes by her and Gehlen.

Gehlen liked talking to them. "Paul described us in Revelations as one world government, I'm the whore of Babylon, my hands around throats of bankers, politicians, police ... the modern technological Tower of Babel, where all change and conflict is managed ...by us."

Patti was afraid, "You're mad."

Gehlen laughed madly, "*Ha Haa Haaa*. Of course, I am. But, you're an artist. Your opinion won't matter. You vote for Congressmen, Assemblymen, Parliamentarians to represent you? ...the subject population thinks its opinions matter. But, you feel they don't, you know they don't. War and revolution are opportunities for profit, locked in phony battle between make-believe Left and make-believe Right hiding the struggle between individual freedom and encroaching authority of the State. The Soviet Union, with its tight censorship presented a Marxist, Left orientation front to its citizens ...but, it wasn't real in Communism, just in socialism. Nazi Germany, with its tight censorship presented a strictly totalitarian, or Right, orientation front to its citizens ...but, it profited not Germany, but the money issuing class and a few ruling families in Germany, England, America, an oligarchy of ruling families without border ...subject populations of United States ...subject populations of Germany ...subject populations of Russia. So, pick up Oswald's rifle, my friends, aim it at oligarchy, pull the trigger ... you're shooting at thin air ... the oligarchy doesn't fight ...they sip cocktails, jet setting from country to country. Information, debt, and technology are

282

our controls ...controlled Left-oriented information ... controlled Right-information, that play like a flute to a cobra, hypnotically hiding who's responsible for financing and waging murder, genocide, rape, theft, coercion ...managed conflict between the two control gateways makes understanding Truth impossible. Control of information, control of debt."

<>

Nancy read Antony Sutton to me at the ranch, the last years of my life, he claimed the trans-Atlantic Axis, a Skull & Bones Society of the Order of Death transcended national boundaries. But, Skull & Bones was just a recruiting stage and playground for the Owner's kids. In 1965 Sutton, a great America patriot put it this way. "Chevron Oil is Rockefeller owned. Chase Manhattan, a Rockefeller-owned bank plays both sides of the political fence. The extent of Chase collaboration with Nazis is staggering, and this was at a time when Nelson Rockefeller had an intelligence job in Washington aimed against Nazi operations in Latin America. Chase Bank in Paris was a Nazi collaborator. Chase Bank, later Chase Manhattan Bank, has been a prime promoter of exporting U.S. technology to the Soviet Union, far back as early 1920s.

"The first war crafted and managed by the Order was the Spanish-American War.

"The second war crafted and created by the Group was the Anglo-Boer war of 1899.

"The rise of Hitler and Nazism in Germany, and the rise of the Marxist State in the Soviet Union, and the clash between these two powers and the political systems they represented was a major cause of World War II.

"The Order financed revolutionary Marxism and its enemy Nazism to manage the nature and degree of the conflict to shape the evolution of the new World Order. The creation of the Soviet Union stems from the Order. The early survival of Soviet Union stems from the Order. Development of the Soviet Union stems from the Order. The Order created the Left and Right, Soviet Russia, and Hitler, to be the two global arms needed for managed conflict to synthesize the new World Order.

<>

"The arms were Guaranty Trust Co. of New York, and Brown Brothers, Harriman, private bankers of New York.

<>

"In 1984 Averell Harriman (The Order 1913) was elder statesman of Democratic party while George Bush (The Order 1949) was heading CIA, then running for vice president then president, head of moderate-extremist wing of Republican Party. Order created and financed Soviet Union. Order created and financed Nazi Germany.

"Guaranty Trust Co., Brown Brothers, Harriman and Ruskombank developed Soviet Union's oil and manganese. In 1901 the Caucasus oil fields ... Baku fields ... produced half the total world crude oil output. After the revolution, which was a coup d'état orchestrated against the Czar, Soviet Union needed raw materials, technical skills and working capital to restore Russian factories. American firm International Barnsdall Corp. provided equipment to the Communists. They started drilling in the oil fields. International Barnsdall and Lucey Manufacturing Co. sent machinery and equipment from United States and sent American oil field workers to Communist Soviet Union. Chairman of International Barnsdall Corp. was Matthew C. Brush. Guaranty Trust, Lee Higginson & Co., and W. A. Harriman owned Barnsdall Corp. Barnsdall Corp. owned International Barnsdall Corp.

"In 1913 Czarist Russia supplied 53 percent of world manganese, coming mostly from the Chiaturi deposits in the Caucasus. Production in 1920 was zero. The Soviets received modern mining and transportation facilities for their manganese deposits, acquired foreign exchange, and finally shattered American foreign policy concerning loans to the U.S.S.R. in a series of business agreements with W.A. Harriman Co. and Guaranty Trust.

"Chairman of Georgian Manganese Co., the Harriman operating company on the site in Russia, was Matthew Crush (the Order 1913). While the Order carried out its plans to develop Russia, State Department was helpless, could do nothing.

"In 1920s loans to Soviet Union were strictly against U.S. law. There were no diplomatic relations between United States and Soviet Union. There was no government support or government sanction for commercial activity between United States and Soviet Union. Government policy and public sentiment in the U.S. was against Soviet Union. But, Harriman-Guaranty cartel didn't tell State Department of its plans. Averell Harriman sneaked an illegal project past the U.S. Government. He later became U.S. Ambassador to Russia.

<>

"Guaranty Trust, Union Banking Corp. were Harriman & Nazi interests that funded Hitler and helped construct and finance Nazism, National Socialism.

"Meanwhile, the Order kept a hold on professional associations relating to Soviet Union. Anglo-Russian Chamber of Commerce was created in 1920 to promote trade with Russia. It was needed by Soviet Union to get the Czar's industries working again. Chairman of the Executive Committee of Anglo-Russian Chamber Of Commerce was helped by Samuel R. Berton, a vice president of Guaranty Trust. The Order was aware that 'issuing credits' to U.S.S.R. was illegal. It wasn't made legal until 1933 when President Roosevelt got elected.

"Even though it was illegal and treason against the United States Government, Guaranty Trust did more than trade in Russian credits. Guaranty Trust made a joint banking agreement with the Soviets and installed a Guaranty Trust Vice President, Max May, as Director in Charge of the foreign division of a Soviet bank, the Ruskombank.

<>

"Meanwhile the U.S. Government told U.S. citizens Soviet Communists were murderers.

"Meanwhile the Department Of Justice was deporting 'Reds' back to Soviet Union.

"Meanwhile every American politician-lawyer was telling the American public the United States would have no relations with the Soviets.

<>

"But behind the scenes Guaranty Trust Co. was actually running a division of a Soviet bank. American troops were being cheered by Soviet revolutionaries for helping protect the 'Revolution'. The Order's law firm Simpson, Thatcher & Bartlett represented the Soviet State Bank in the U.S. In 1927 Simpson, Thatcher & Bartlett told U.S. Government, Soviets were starting to increase U.S. bank deposits. This increase was priming the pump for huge payments to be directed to a few favored U.S. ruling family firms to build the Soviet First Five Year Plan. At the same time, in 1928, Secretary Kellogg said the government of the U.S. maintained the position it would be futile and unwise to enter into relations with Soviet Government. At this time the U.S., with implicit government approval, was involved in planning the First Five Year Plan in Russia. The planning work was done by American firms. Order construction of the Soviet dialectic arm continued through the 1930s up to World War II. In 1941 W.A. Harriman was appointed Lend Lease Administrator to assure flow of U.S. technology and products to Soviet Union. Harriman

violated Lend Lease law that required only military goods could be shipped to Soviet Union. He shipped vast amounts of industrial equipment.

<>

"Harriman shipped U.S. Treasury Department currency plates. Now the Soviet Communists could freely print U.S. dollars.

<>

"During McCarthy era while Communists were persecuted in U.S., ruling family banking interests had well-established interlocking board members on Soviet Communist banks, and had been financing and issuing credit to the Communist, 40 years," Antony Sutton said.

For his troubles not to mention his accurate and well-documented research, Antony was blackballed by the establishment in America, and feared for his life each day. He died in 2002, two years before I did. A star.

<>

Patti felt dazed, "How do you know?"

Gehlen knew, if anyone did. "I was head of intelligence against Soviet Union for the Nazis. And later I was head of intelligence against Soviet Union for CIA …and, later they returned me to run German intelligence, the BND in Germany. I'm informed about business relationships of trans-Atlantic Axis and new World Order. One day, I'll tell you my story. Today, just anecdotes …because, you're a revolutionary artist with natural genetic resistance to brainwashing. It amuses me to watch you, processing information."

Patti felt, he was right. That bothered her. "Maybe you're right. Maybe you're not."

"I'll tell you a story about your great-grandfather Fritz Thyssen," Gehlen said. "Fritz Thyssen was a German steel magnate who associated with the Nazi movement in early 1920s. In 1923, he was approached by General Ludendorff at the time of French evacuation of the Ruhr. Shortly after this meeting, Thyssen was introduced to Hitler and provided funds for Nazis through General Ludendorff. In 1930-31, Emil Kirdorf approached Thyssen, then sent Rudolf Hess to get more funding from Thyssen for the Nazi Party. This time, Thyssen arranged a credit of 250,000 marks at the Bank Voor Handel en Scheepvaart N.V. Thyssen was former head of Vereinigte Stahlwerke, the German steel trust financed by Dillon, Reed of New York. Thyssen played a key part in Hitler's rise to power. Thyssen donated much money to the Nazi Party, persuaded other German industrialists to help financially support the Fuehrer. Hitler showered Thyssen with power under the Nazi regime, until Thyssen's break with Hitler in 1939 over Hitler's decision to invade

Poland and to start Second World War.

"August Thyssen, your grandfather's father, your great-grandfather co-founded pan-Germanism. August Thyssen joined with Hugenberg, Kirdorf, and the elder Krupp ... to promote All-Deutscher Verband Pan-German League. Pan-German League supplied rationale for Kaiser's expansionist war philosophy and policies. In 1918, when Germany lost World War I, August Thyssen convinced the Allies, responsibility for German aggression should be placed not on pan-German industrialists at all, but, on Kaiser ... [Ed's note: the lone-nut theory.] He said, Pan-German League industrialists shouldn't be blamed for support they gave the Hohenzollerns. So, the Allies made no effort to reform German industry after World War I.

"August Thyssen was allowed to keep a vast industrial empire. He passed it on to heirs and successors. Your grandfather Fritz Thyssen took control of family holdings following death of his father, in 1926. Like Hitler, Thyssen regarded Treaty of Versailles, at the end of World War I, a pact of shame. He said, the war treaty must be overthrown if German Fatherland is to rise again.

"Fritz Thyssen walked the same road as his father, aided by ample Wall Street loans to build German industry. Fritz Thyssen became an active member of Stahlhelm and later, with Göring's guidance secretly joined the Nazis."

<>

Nancy continued reading Antony Sutton to me. "After the stock market crash of 1931 brought German industry to bankruptcy, Fritz Thyssen embraced National Socialism openly. For the next two years Fritz Thyssen dedicated his fortune and influence to bring Hitler to power. In 1932 Fritz Thyssen arranged a meeting in the Düsseldorf Industrialist's Club. There Hitler addressed the most powerful ruling family businessmen of the Ruhr and the Rhineland. When Hitler finished his speech Thyssen yelled, 'Heil Herr Hitler', and others applauded. By the time of the German Presidential elections later that year Fritz Thyssen arranged campaign contributions from the largest industrial cartels into Hitler's campaign fund chest. Fritz Thyssen himself donated 3 million marks to the Nazis in 1932 alone. This flow of campaign funds went through Thyssen banks. The Bank fur Handel un Schiff was a subsidiary of August Thyssen Bank. It was founded in 1918 with H.J. Kouwenhoven and D.C. Schutte as managing partners. It was Thyssen's personal banking operation, and affiliated with W.A. Harriman financial interests in New York. Von

Heydt Bank was the early name for Thyssen's bank. The Thyssen front bank in Holland, Bank voor Handel en Scheepvaart N.V., controlled Union Banking Corp. in New York. The Harrimans had a financial interest in Union Banking Corp. Averelle's brother, E. Roland Harriman, was a board director of Union Banking Corp. Union Banking Corp. of New Your city was a joint Thyssen-Harriman operation in 1932. Its board of directors were E. Roland Harriman, Prescott Bush who was a partner in Brown Brothers Corp., J.L. Guinter a director of Union Banking Corp., Edward James a partner in Brown Brothers, Knight Woolley a director of Guaranty Trust and a director of a Federal Reserve Branch. After World War II investigation tribunals were set up to investigate Nazi war criminals. But those tribunals censored information that documented Western assistance to Hitler. Western textbooks on Soviet economic development omit mention of the economic and financial aid given to the 1917 Soviet Revolution and how Western firms and banks built-up Soviet Union."

<>

Gehlen continued, "They were all members of the Blue Book. Revolution is described in textbooks as a spontaneous event by those who are politically or economically deprived and rebel against an autocratic state. The textbooks omit that revolutions need to be financed, that the source of financing follows the money trail back to Wall Street. The blood trade is dominated by banks and trust companies. Banks and trust companies are dominated by the Order. World Order wants to stop war by controlling everyone. World Order is the only hope for mankind to survive. Do you still want to consider yourself revolutionary?"

Patti was confused, "I don't know. I have to think it thru. You taught me a lot, thank you. You see yourself as messiah. You see the World Order as savior of mankind. I don't. Your international finance is a crime against Earth, a melanoma to the planet, wealth monopolized by a few stadiums full of ruling families. That wealth must be given back to the Earth ... before Earth gets pissed off and shifts its axis to get even ... returned to people it was stolen from, redistributed equally to all families, not just ruling families. Earth must heal."

Gehlen had little patience, left. "You've a thick Reagan head."

Granma Wilpf smiled, "Let's get to the demonstration at Lytton Plaza. On the way, I'll tell you my story, there's a lot about me you don't know."

"Okay," Patti said. Patti slowly opened the storage room door, looked into the alley, saw no SCREAMA there. One by one, they left the storage room, walked into the alley, headed towards the demonstration in Lytton Park.

<> <> <>

Hinckley estate, Mar. 29, 1981

The Hinckley family gathered at their father's estate to party. Scott Hinckley, John's brother, placed a phone call to Neil Bush, George Bush's son. Scott confirmed a business meeting with Neil, for the next day. While Scott talked to Neil, at Neil's home his brother Jeb had that look on his face when he was a kid and stolen cookies out of the cookie jar without getting caught.

Jeb was happy, "I got Contras on Medicaid in Florida. I'm stickin' it to the taxpayers! Taxpayers are gonna foot the bill, financing Contra casualties from our private war in Nicaragua." Jeb made an obscene 'up their butt' gesture.

Neil gave Jeb a thumbs-up.

On the other end of the phone line, Scott Hinckley adjusted his portable phone in his hand. Scott walked into his brother John's room, he was stunned. Scott's mouth dropped open at what he saw. John was wearing a torn Nazi uniform, laying spread-eagled on a Nazi Skull & Bones flag spread on the bed, with his pants down, masturbating while looking at movie star posters of Jodi Foster in *Taxi Driver* he had pinned up on his wall …but, John's fantasy wouldn't get him off because he remembered the last American Nazi Party meeting he went to a few days earlier, where they'd physically attacked him, saying he was an FBI spy.

White House press briefing room

In the White House Press Briefing Room, I furiously announced my 'get-tough-on-drugs' policy. I introduced my 'no-compromise-with-terrorists' policy. I continued my scripted speech, "Can we who man the ship of state deny it's somewhat out of control. Waste and fraud in federal government is national scandal. Our nation's debt is approaching a trillion dollars. Can we continue on the present course without coming to a day of reckoning. I want to cut the budget 41 billion dollars, cut back on welfare, cut back on government bureaucracy that regulates business, the environment, and public health. We have to get rid of conditions that permit Welfare Queens to ride around in new Cadillacs. We have to stop punishing people who make a lot of money by taxing them higher and higher, till it makes no sense to work anymore. What will happen to

America if the rich will not work harder because we take 90% of their money, and the poor will not work harder because they get too much welfare?"

I finished my speech. I looked over to Larry Speakes.

Larry looked at the press. "The President will now determine the order of whose questions he will answer by drawing names out of his jellybean jar."

I drew out names of reporters. Then, they asked me questions. Then, I answered questions until I was answered-out. I told the truth. "Just because no reporters from NBC, ABC and AP were chosen out of my jellybean jar to ask questions at this press conference doesn't mean you have to boycott my next one! After all, I'm the first president who draws names of who gets to ask questions out of a jellybean jar."

Larry introduced State Secretary Alexander Haig at the podium to speak to the press.

Haig composed himself. "I'll have to caveat my response and use careful caution and not saddle myself definitizing my statement 'cause this isn't an experience I haven't been through before. Perhaps the four American nuns shot to death in El Salvador were killed because they were trying to run a road block."

I took the microphone away from him. "Thank you, Secretary of State Haig. The news is, I'm putting George Bush in charge of my administration's Crisis Management Team."

Haig reacted, "That doesn't make me happy! I want that position!"

Vice President Bush laughed to himself.

The press conference officially ended.

I went back to my office. I flipped the calendar page on my desk calendar to a new day, one day at a time.

<>

That night, when Bill Barnes looked into his cat, Jackson's, sleepy amber eyes, Bill Barnes start feeling sleepy himself. Jackson was looking up from Bill Barnes's lap. Bill was recording White House history with his pen. 'President Reagan said he could make only four pictures a year when he was in Hollywood. After making four movies a year he was in the top 90% tax bracket. So, instead of working more, high paid actors went on vacation after four pictures each year, went off to the country. That's why President Reagan felt people should be rewarded for achieving wealth, not taxed at higher rates for doing so. Because then, they just got lazy.'

Jackson looked at Bill Barnes. Jackson watched Bill's writing hand in a stream of little movements. Jackson slowly lifted his paw in the air. Jackson batted his paw at the moving pen a few times. Jackson went back to sleep.

Evergreen Colorado,
Hinckley Sr. Mansion

A young man, John W. Hinckley Jr., felt very depressed over John Lennon's murder. Alone in his parents' house, John sat in a chair. He quietly looked at a torn picture of John Lennon in his wallet. *'Imagine all the people sitting in a world of peace. You can say that I'm a dreamer, but I'm not the dreaming kind,'* John drunkenly sang the Lennon lyrics. Lucy in the sky with diamonds, John was the dreaming kind. He drank peach brandy. He picked up a portable tape recorder. He start recording a special message for the woman of his dreams, "Dear Jodie. I don't know what's going to happen this year. It's just gonna be insanity. Jodie, you're the only thing that matters, now. Jodie. Jodie. Ever since I saw you starring in, *Taxi Driver,* with you playin' a 13-year-old hooker ... I fell in love with you. Anything that I might do in 1981 will be for Jodie Foster's sake. It's time for me to go to bed. I love you."

Mar. 6, 1981, Jodie Foster's
college dorm, 1 A.M.

John Hinckley stood outside Jodie Foster's college dormitory at one in the morning. He start yelling ...then, pounding on the door of the college dormitory, "Telegram for Jodie Foster!"

The dormitory house-mother opened the door a crack, she looked through a chain lock, "Slide it through the door. Stop yelling. Go away."

Jodie Foster sat in her dormitory bedroom. She read the telegram the house-mother brought her. Jodie read it aloud to her roommate. "Jodie Foster Love, just wait. I'll rescue you very soon. Please cooperate. J.W.H.' ... I don't understand. Who's J.W.H.?'"

Her roommate laughed, "It's a practical joke. Go to sleep."

<>

Later that night at 3 A.M., John Hinckley was back. He stood outside Jodie Foster's college dormitory, again. He yelled while pounding on the college dormitory door.

In her college dormitory bedroom Jodie Foster got another telegram delivered to her by the house-mother. Jodie read it to her roommate, "Jodie, Goodbye! I love you six trillion times. Don't you maybe like me just a little bit? It would make all this worthwhile. From John Hinckley, of course' ... Who's John Hinckley?!" Jodie said.

Jodie felt scared to death. She trembled.

Her roommate sat by her, hugging her.

American Nazi Party &
Ku Klux Klan meeting

John Hinckley looked sharp in his dark blue Nazi uniform, he felt wicked. He watched another Nazi burn a picture of the White House.

A Nazi pointed at him, "That one! John Hinckley! He's a Reagan liberal," the Nazi said.

John felt threatened, "I'm not. I hate Reagan."

The other Nazi kept at him, "Hinckley's father and Prescott Bush and Allen Dulles were friends. Their families do business together. His brother's dating a Bush daughter. He's in bed with the establishment."

John smelled danger, he got anxious, "Just because my father and Bush's father are friends doesn't make me a spy! Prescott financed Hitler, stupid! Dulles was Hitler's friend! You're dumb!"

A couple Nazis start pushing him around. "He's probably a FBI Cointelpro infiltrator!"

Suddenly, it seemed to John all the Nazis were watching him, seeing what he'd do ...like they were hounds catching a scent of blood. He saw, it was too late for talking. Nazis punched him, kicked him. He tried running away ...but, stumbled. They kicked him. He struggled to his feet, grabbed a Nazi SS Skull & Bones flag to pull himself up ...it ripped off in his hands. He ran off as fast as he could.

He yelled behind him, "I'll show you I'm a Nazi! You'll see!"

White House Briefing Room,
Mar. 30, 1981

White House Spokesman Larry Speakes was having lunch with his boss, White House Press Chief Jim Brady. Brady smiled. "May the best man win," Jim said.

Larry laughed. "Right."

Brady flipped a coin up in the air ... heads.

Larry laughed, "You lose, Brady. You go with Reagan today."

"Shit, I wanted time off."

Jim picked up his hat, left the room.

A few hours later, Larry's staffers swarmed around him. He started his lesson. "What do you do if the president's assassinated? I was with President Ford when Squeaky Fromm went after him, it's confusing."

The phone rang, Larry watched a staffer pick it up, "Stop! The trouble light's flashing ... I'll get it." Speakes went over, got the phone, he held it to his ear. His face changed in a frightened, unbelieving light.

Air Force One

The Presidential Jet, Air Force One, flew smoothly through the sky. Onboard, Vice President Bush read the name tag of the decorated soldier sitting next to him, 'Oliver North'.

"Ollie, is our FEMA Federal Emergency Martial Law Contingency plan for the presidential-assassination drill on time?"

"Yes, in a few hours we'll rehearse federal, state, national guard, military, and police responses to the scenario of a presidential assassination."

Bush was distracted by a phone ringing, watched a staffer go to answer ...then, stopped her, "Trouble button's flashing ... I'll pick up."

Holding the phone to his ear, George's face got ashen.

Washington, First Ladies'
'Just Say No' Luncheon

In a fancy restaurant in downtown Washington D.C., First Lady Nancy Reagan stood at a podium ready to continue her anti-drug, 'Just Say No', speech. Nancy picked up a glass of water, quickly opened a pill bottle of diet methamphetamine uppers and Miltown anti-depressant downers prescribed to her by the White House physician, she emptied several into her hand, paused in her speech, raised her hand to her mouth, acted like she was clearing her throat, drank the water ... after swallowing the pills, she continued her speech. "Excuse me ... what's important is we get street kids and their parents in American off street drugs ... and prescription drugs ...by, just saying, 'no'. Just say, 'no to drugs'." Nancy was distracted by a phone ringing offstage ... from the corner of her eye she watched a staffer pick it up, then signal frantically to her. Nancy finished her speech to a round of applause. She knew the call was important ...but, she hesitated stepping out of the limelight, because the attention was a tonic for her, it always was. Nancy got to the phone.

The staffer was upset, "Trouble callin'."

Nancy was alarmed and afraid at the tone in the staffer's voice. Nancy listened to the voice on the phone ... the triumphant look on her face from the applause she'd gotten faded away ... Nancy's worst fears had come true. She broke down, crying.

Patti's Hollywood Hills canyon home

In her hippie pad in Hollywood hills, back in the canyons overlooking the sea, Patti Reagan was singing along with a bootlegged concert tape of the Stones playing, *Honky Tonk Woman*, "Honky tonk, honky tonk woman."

Patti danced around wildly, partying with her rich, infamous counter-culture friends, all tripping on LSD, delighting in shaking her hair around, popping different pills, snorting various illegal narcotic powders, drinking shots of Jack Daniel of the bottle in her hand ...then, fell onto her waterbed. A couple of Patti's girlfriends were somewhere in the room rapping. Patti heard their words as if they had no meaning, just sounds. Patti's ears didn't want to focus on sounds. Patti saw her friends' spiritual lights and movement, little pieces of God spilled out around them. Eyes closed, Patti felt presence of her friends in the room, felt the way she felt when hugging her dog or her cat ... contented ...like everyone was one big piece of God, one party spirit. Patti heard her friends laughing. Patti's girlfriends, Laura and Joie, rapped back and forth like dueling typewriters, chickens fighting over feed.

Laura laughed. "Cancel the national debt. Make it go away. Erase it. It's just words. Money's just an idea, ya know. Really. It doesn't grow on trees. It's not real. It's a thieves' agreement ...hardcore ...idolatry."

Joie didn't think so. "It won't work ... unnatural. Ivy vines strangle other plants, trees even. Plants compete for sun, for water. Nature of the beast to kill one another ...money's the nature of the beast."

Laura was a hippie. "A gardener can nurture plants. That's what gardening is, Garden of Eden ... I'm a feminist."

Joie was a Babarian poet, "A garden of eatin'. Count me out on feminist crap, I like dick ...but, going down on a woman is just like going down on a man."

Laura rose to the occasion, "Why would women march for good-paying jobs, for child care they can afford to pay, for free sex? Don't worry about Aids. It's all over Western Africa. It's a matter of time before it gets here. Aren't you scared?"

Joie was checking out a guy, "I don't worry about it. I'd get ulcers. I get layed three times a day. By different guys. I have a reputation to protect ...I don't have time to worry."

Patti laughed.

Laura kept rapping. "I worry about women and children in poverty. Patti's father could fix that ...if, he wanted to. He makes it worse ...why? ...just looks the other way. He stopped Medicare-paid abortions, made funding birth control illegal. But, he lets Congress fund religious people staffing chastity clinics."

Joie's eyes bugged out. "Chastity clinics!? You're shittin' me? What the hell is that? What would I do with one of those? I'm like a teenager with hot pants, looking for big dick … with rubbers. I don't want to get pregnant, again. What kid with two cents for brains would go to a chastity clinic to have a priest or a nun punch her ticket and say, 'just say no', cross your legs, bounce your feet on the floor to get rid of the feeling, take a cold shower … I don't *think* so."

Patti listened to Laura and Joie laugh. The warm-feeling sounds reminded Patti of taking her clothes off, walking in the sunshine on mescaline into the cold rapids in Yosemite River. Patti felt the explosive cold water ejaculating in big creamy white splashes on her naked breasts and thighs. She felt her skin rise up in a rebellion of prickly goose bumps …raised her hands to the sun god …felt heat of the sun on her palms.

Joie laughed. "Nancy doesn't just say no … Why should Patti?"

Laura nodded. "Maybe I can get Patti to have her father fix everything. I could do a Divine intercession."

Joie was surprised. "You're shittin' me. Those far-right religious assholes think Aids is divine punishment for sinners. You bet Patti's father had a shitload of gay actor friends when he was showboating in Hollywood. Patrick Buchanan said, quote, 'Oh the poor homosexuals have declared war on nature and nature is exacting an awful retribution' unquote! Intercede that! Maybe he's right …I don't know, it's a free country."

In Patti's head, she watched the same old movie reruns over and over, the mental movie that sucked life from her, she covered her ears …but, could still hear the sound track, she closed her eyes …but, could still see the frames flicker, nothing could stop the voices in her head, they were *her* flashbacks. Me and Nancy condemned her, Nancy jerked the brush through Patti's hair, Nancy slapped her.

Patti cried. "Daddy! Daddy help me! Stop mommy hitting me."

I looked down on Patti. "Patti, I'm ashamed of you, you're lying about what mother did …now, apologize to mother and hurry up, I have to go rehearse."

Patti sobbed. "I'm sorry, I'm sorry, I'm sorry, I'm sorry, I'm sorry!"

Patti felt her acid flashbacks start to fade out … Patti watched friends on her waterbed with her, managing their acid flashbacks with crazy looks on their faces.

Other friends were trying to talk Patty down.

Patti had motor-mouth, "You and Mom are ice statues. I wish you were dead! I wish you were dead! Keep your shit to yourself, get out of my head! I can't take it anymore! I won't carry your shit anymore, carry it yourself, Dad! …even if it kills you!"

Patti's phone on the floor was ringing and ringing. A friend picked it up, then tried shaking Patti to get her eyes to focus, Patti's pupils were dilated like an owl's.

Her friend looked Patti right in the eyes. "Secret Service on the phone," her friend said.

Patti raised the phone to her ear …her face changed …horrified, she threw the phone down. Patti cried. "It's my fault, I said I wanted him dead. They were right, I'm a witch, it's my fault," Patti said. Patti struggled to come down the rest of the way …someone stopped the music …the party was over.

Washington D.C., hospital

In a Washington D.C. hospital, I lay on a gurney, terrified. I saw Death by me, pushing the gurney down the empty corridor, towards the emergency room and the morgue, I didn't know which room we were going to. Paul Robeson's ghost walked beside me. The gurney wheels clattered, echoing down the hall. I was afraid. I didn't know what to do. I prayed. I saw what happened to me in a movie in my head.

I had finished my speech, everyone was clapping, I'd been totally accepted, I walked out of the lecture hall onto the sidewalk towards my limousine surrounded by reporters, photographers, Secret Service men, and fans. I loved being surrounded by fans. When the shots went off, my body jerked in fear, something punched my side, Secret Service agents surrounded me, some got shot, I saw Jim Brady fall to the sidewalk lying there, not moving, a pool of syrupy blood around his head. I glimpsed my bodyguards wrestle a young man with a gun to the ground. I saw Secret Service men handcuff, then ankle-cuff the shooter, then shove the shooter into a Secret Service car. The captured young man leaned out the window of the Secret Service car.

He yelled to the crowd of reporters engulfing the car. "Tell Jodie I love her! Jodie you and I will occupy the White House, the peasants will drool with envy. Until then, please do your best to stay a virgin. You are a virgin, aren't you? I love you forever."

<>

I got shoved into the limo, down on the floor,

my ribs hit the drive-axle hump in the middle of the car, knocked the wind out of me, pinching my chest, I sunk down on the floor with a Secret Service agent on top of me.

"*Ow!* You broke my god-damn ribs!" I yelled.

The man didn't hear me, he yelled to the chauffer, "Drive to the White House!"

The agent ran his hands over my body, looking for blood ...but, his hands came up clean, bubbles of blood-colored saliva mixed foamed out my mouth. I stared at the agent, frantic.

The agent was trying to be calm. "Negative on the White House, head to the hospital!"

The Cadillac limo jumped out of traffic onto the sidewalk, sped a few blocks to the hospital. The hospital emergency room staff ran out of the hospital to meet us. I got out the limousine by myself. I start walking to the emergency room, waving to everyone ...then, collapsed to my knees ...I woke up on a gurney. Secret Service agents cleared the press out, Mel's Jesus pushed the gurney along ...then, somehow Jesus and Satan and I were sitting on top of a room-sized scale model of Earth, then Death and Jesus wheeled me down the corridor, I was afraid, I looked at Death.

I looked at Paul Robeson's ghost. I talked to him. "Have you come for me?"

Death wore the uniform of a hospital orderly. "Yes ... it's your time."

Death and Paul Robeson's ghost bumped the gurney roughly into the walls down the hospital corridor.

Nancy entered the hospital emergency room, immediately seeing what was happening she grabbed the gurney as Death and Robeson's ghost whisked it past her. Nancy pulled the gurney to a halt. I saw Death leave, a ghost dispossessing itself no longer occupying the body, face and uniform of the orderly wheeling me along. Paul Robeson's ghost disappeared, too. Mel's Jesus stood there, watching over me.

Nancy was yelling, "What are you doing with my husband?!"

The orderly seemed dazed, apologetic, "Sorry ma'am. I don't know how it got away from me, I've got to get your husband into surgery, now."

Nancy took my hand, "I'm here, Darling, it's okay now Honey."

I tried to reassure Nancy, gave her a thumbs-up sign.

Nancy felt abandoned as the gurney left her. I lifted my head from the gurney, watched Nancy grow smaller and smaller, listened to the sound of one of the gurney wheels, it was lopsided, off center, like a horse cantering the linoleum floor.

I was looking up at the bright lights over the emergency room operating table. I was afraid, doctors saw fear on my face, machines beeped, I heard my heartbeat get weaker, breathing machines were wheezing, far away a member of the hospital emergency room operating team was talking to me, above the controlled murmur of a crowd of orderlies and doctors going about life-and-death routines. The doctor standing over me start fading away, the light got dimmer and dimmer.

The doctor stared into my face. "We're losing him!"

A feeling of calmness and reassurance came over me, I liked the attention I was getting from the operating team, I wasn't quite sure why their voices were far away, growing faint.

The doctor stared into my eyes. "We're starting surgery."

I smiled at him. I had a captive audience. "I hope you're a Republican."

The doctor smiled, "Right now, Mr. President, we're all Republicans."

<>

The surgeon removed a bullet from my left lung close to my heart. It was an illegal bullet. The kind that explode. But this one hadn't functioned properly. That's why I was still alive. The surgeon finished surgery. A nurse wheeled me out of the emergency operating room. I'd been conscious the whole time. I pointed to a pen in the nurses uniform pocket. The nurse gave me a pen and paper. I start scribbling. I got control over my fingers. I wrote slowly. I wrote legibly. I start writing notes. I handed them to the nurse. The nurse took the note from me.

She read it aloud to another nurse, "'All in all, I'd rather be in Philadelphia.'"

The doctors in the room shuffled around uncomfortably. The nurse took another note out of my fingers. She read it aloud to the other people in the room, "'Send me to L.A. where I can see the air I'm breathing.'"

The doctors start whispering to one another. I smiled at the nurse. The nurse took another note from me. She read it aloud. "'Does Nancy know about us?'"

The nurse turned to the doctors. "I think he's trying to be funny."

Ed Meese crowded into the room. "He *is* being funny!"

It felt good to hear Ed's voice.

It got darker, I closed my eyes finally at rest.

Washington D.C., hospital room

I awoke in a bed ...I was in a hospital, Nancy walked in.

Nancy felt appalled by darkness filling the room, she tried to draw the hospital room curtains open ...but, couldn't ... the curtains were nailed shut. Nancy got afraid. Nancy got angry.

She glanced at the Secret Service agents in the room. "Un-nail these curtains right now or you're fired! Ronnie's an outdoor type, he needs sunshine. He's claustrophobic. Don't make me plead."

"Sorry, Mrs. President, it's too dangerous, someone could get in another shot, got to keep him closed-off for his own sake," the agent said.

"I know, I'm sorry, I'm so upset," Nancy said. Nancy sat down in a chair beside my bed, noticing me going in and out, waking up from the anesthesia given to me before the operation, took my hand. I felt confused.

I watched Nancy and smiled.

Nancy held my hand, "What happened?"

"I forgot to duck, Honey."

Nancy laughed. "You're gonna be fine, Honey, as soon as we get out of here, I'll take you home, get you in the sunshine," Nancy said. Nancy watched me fall asleep.

After a few days my daughter Maureen, from my first marriage to Jane Wyman, was allowed to visit. Maureen was born a happy, bubbly type, seeing her cheered me up ...but, took some of the starch out of her.

Maureen was concerned. "I've brought you a gift to cheer you up."

It was a marionette with my face painted on it. I was surprised. I laughed, "It only hurts when I laugh."

Maureen brightened up, "I saw the ghost in the Lincoln Room at the White House, again. This time, Paul Robeson's ghost was with him. The spirits are contacting us."

I felt confused ...like I was going to have a brainstorm ...the feeling passed ...I forgot what I was going to say. The phone by my bed rang.

Maureen answered it. "It's Bill Casey. He says, 'not to worry', he knows what to do. He'll take care of everything."

<>

That day, Mar. 30, 1981 rubber-neckers drove by the three estates in a row ...Bush's estate ...John Hinckley Sr.'s estate ...then, the next-door neighbor's estate, where Hinckley Sr. and his wife hid all day as 170 reporters set up camera gear on John Hinckley Sr.'s front lawn.

<>

By the way, Nov. 26 2003, six months before I died, I remember being out at the west coast White House ...back at the ranch ... that was

about six months before I died, and joined Paul Robeson as an auguring harbinger for my latest Hollywood production, *Dead Presidents ... Christmas Ghosts of America's Past, Present and Future ...* debuting across America, Jun. 5, 2004 ...in a theater near you.

<>

Nancy was besides herself. "U.S. District Judge Paul Friedman wants to let John Hinckley Jr. out of the nut house to visit his parents, but the Reagan and Brady families say, *No!*"

Patti, Ron Jr., Michael, and Maureen were on the same side for once, agreeing with Nancy. It was something to see. I felt loved.

Nancy was incensed. "The Bush's go way back with their neighbors, the Hinckley's ...in oil ...politics ...and, CIA ... all the way back to the 1960s, the days Dulles had Casey have Ronnie refuse to extradite suspects out of California for Jim Garrison's Kennedy assassination case."

I didn't see it the same way as Nancy. "Everyone in the country supported the new regime, I wasn't going to rock the boat." I saw Nancy getting ready to go off. "Look, I agree with you and the kids. Just because I prayed for Hinckley Jr.'s soul in the hospital after he shot me, doesn't mean I didn't want to fry the bastard ...he murdered several people, destroyed Jim Brady's life, the bastard almost killed me! ...But, those damn Bush's, they're like rattlesnakes on a cold night, under every rock, spit and you hit a Bush."

Patti went off first, "Hinckley's been in St. Elizabeth's Hospital in Washington since he shot you, he can rot there."

Even Michael sounded pretty sharp today. "How that damn Edward Bennett Williams won that case arguing that creep gets acquitted by reason of insanity because he wanted to impress actress Jody Foster ...what kind of damn Twinkie defense is that?!"

Ron Jr. lost his ballet mood composure, "The part that gets me, is Hinckley Jr.'s brother Scott was scheduled to have dinner at the home of your vice president's son, Neil Bush, the next day after the assassination attempt."

Maureen was fired up, "Mom, what did our astrologer psychic say? I can't remember."

Nancy was always helping the kids. "She said, 'Ask Paul Robeson's ghost about it.'"

"Did you?"

"No, that's up to your father, that's who Paul Robeson's ghost visits, not me."

"Well, Dad? ... did you?"

I wasn't sure. "Maureen, I don't remember ...Paul Robeson's story on Earth didn't have a happy ending, y'know."

Patti got interested. "Tell us the story, Dad."

All the kids agreed, they all wanted to hear.

Nancy didn't like the kids taking over. "Now, wait a minute. This is your father's time, not Paul Robeson's."

I spent a lot of time calming Nancy down … when she stood up for me. I smiled at Nancy. "Nancy, Maureen just saw Paul Robeson's ghost in the Lincoln room, Ron Jr.'s been asking me for years, I know Michael's curious, Patti's not the only one."

"Okay, then we're going to get back to this Bush, Hinckley business."

I agreed. "Fine, Mommy. …You see, back in late 1950s, early 1960s when we were getting all those dead Kennedys, Martin Luther King, Malcolm X assassinations … J. Edgar Hoover was prancing around in women's clothes in drag, according to later newspaper accounts … I never saw Edgar when I did drag acts in after-theatre parties for friends …J. Edgar thought Paul Robeson would threaten national security, too, just like those other assassinated people … that is, after he spoke with Allen Dulles back in the mid-1940s. You can't blame J. Edgar for doing his job, after all, I was on his payroll as an informer when I was president of Actor's Guild. We believed in anti-Communism, back in those days. Of course, when Paul Robeson went to Russia to perform and sing, and talk to Russian officials, that opened the gate for the CIA director at the time, who was … who knows?" I said. I loved playing guessing games and trivia games with my family, always did.

Nancy was losing patience. "Ronnie, it was Richard Helms, you can't expect the children to remember. We're having snack at four this afternoon. Please get on with your storytelling so we can have snack on time."

I didn't want Nancy on the warpath. "Yes, Dear. Well, Paul Robeson's ghost has been visiting me since they wheeled me into the hospital after Hinckley shot his wad."

Nancy frowned. "Ronnie, please watch your language around the kids."

Michael shrugged. "Oh Mom, we're not kids anymore, I'm almost 60!"

Ron Jr. had that look on his face when you read a kid a story from a story book. "Dad, so you think Allen Dulles, Richard Helms, and J. Edgar Hoover did something?"

"Oh, I don't know. I doubt it, there's never any evidence against them."

Patti wasn't satisfied. "Then why's Paul Robeson's ghost haunting you?"

"He's not *haunting* me, he *visits* me."

"We're not getting anywhere," Maureen said.

Nancy saved the day, as usual. "Look, everyone. I'm going to read you an article that highlights Paul Robeson, so we can get back to this Hinckley mess."

Robeson Cultural Center at Rutgers University wrote a bio about Paul Robeson. Paul Leroy Robeson in 1915 was awarded a four-year academic scholarship to Rutgers …was inducted into Phi Beta Kappa Society and Rutgers' Cap & Skull Honor Society …was valedictorian of graduating class in 1919 …was awarded honorary Master of Arts degree in 1932 and honorary Doctorate of Humane Letters on his 75th birthday in 1973 …in addition to academic achievements, Robeson had an outstanding athletic career as the first Black football player at the University, winning 15 varsity letters in baseball, football, basketball, and track and field …was named to All American Football Team twice in spite of open racism and violence expressed by teammates …in 1923, Robeson earned law degree from Columbia Law School. Robeson took a job with a law firm after graduation, but left the firm and the practice of law when a white secretary refused to take dictation from him. He decided to use his artistic talents in theater and music to promote African and African-American history and culture. What followed was a brilliant career as an actor and concert singer, spanning four decades. He starred in 13 films between 1920s and early 1940s, but decided to stop making movies until there were better opportunities for Blacks. Paul Robeson used his deep baritone voice to promote Black spirituals, to share culture with other countries, and to support social movements of his time. He sang for peace and justice in 25 languages throughout United States, Africa, Asia Europe, and Soviet Union … became known as, 'a citizen of the world,' as comfortable with people of Moscow and Nairobi as with the people of Harlem. Where he traveled, Robeson championed the cause of the common person. Among his friends, he counted future African Leader Jomo Kenyatta, India's Nehru, anarchist Emma Goldman, writers James Joyce and Ernest Hemingway. During the McCarthy Era of the 1950s, every attempt was made to silence and discredit Paul Robeson …. because of his political views and dedication to civil rights. In 1958, he embarked on a successful three-year tour of Europe and Australia. Unfortunately, illness ended his professional career in 1961. He lived the remainder of his years as a private citizen in his sister's home in Philadelphia. He died on Jan. 23, 1976 at the age of 77."

I was getting sleepy.

Nancy brought something to read us. "Now here's a bio by Rob Nagel in *Contemporary Musicians*."

Born Paul Leroy Bustill Robeson, Apr. 9, 1898, in Princeton, NJ ...died of a stroke, Jan. 23, 1976 in Philadelphia, PA ...son of William Drew, a clergyman, and Maria Louisa, a schoolteacher, maiden name, Bustill. Robeson married Eslanda Cardozo Goode, Aug. 17, 1921, children, Paul Jr. ...Education, Rutgers University, A.B., 1919, Columbia University, LL.B., 1923. Admitted to Bar of New York, employed in law firm, 1923 ...actor, stage appearances include, *Simon the Cyrenian, All God's Chillun Got Wings, Show Boat, Othello,* and *Toussaint L'Ouverture* ...film appearances include *Body and Soul, The Emperor Jones, Sanders of the River,* and *Show Boat* ...singer, recording and performing artist ...awards, Badge of Veterans of Abraham Lincoln Brigade, Donaldson Award for outstanding lead performance, American Academy of Arts and Letters medal, NAACP Spingarn Medal, 1945, Champion of African Freedom Award, National Church of Nigeria, 1950 ...Afro-American Newspapers Award, 1950 ...Stalin Peace Prize from U.S.S.R., 1952 ...Peace Medal from East Germany, 1960 ...Ira Aldridge Award, Association for the Study of Afro-American Life and History, 1970 ...Civil Liberties Award, 1970 ...Duke Ellington Medal, Yale University, 1972 ...Whitney M. Young, Jr., National Memorial Award, Urban League of Greater New York, 1972 ...Honorary degrees from Rutgers University, Hamilton College, Morehouse College, Howard University, Moscow State Conservatory, and Humboldt University ... Paul Robeson ...singer, actor, civil rights activist, law school graduate, athlete, scholar, author ... perhaps the best known and most widely respected Black American of 1930s and 1940s. Robeson was a staunch supporter of Soviet Union, was widely vilified and censored for frankness and unyielding views on issues to which public opinion ran contrary. As a young man, Robeson was virile, charismatic, eloquent, and powerful. He learned to speak more than 20 languages in order to break down the barriers of race and ignorance throughout the world, and yet, as Sterling Stuckey said in *New York Times Book Review*, for the last 25 years of his life was 'a great whisper and a greater silence in Black America'. Born in Princeton, New Jersey, in 1898, Robeson was

spared most daily brutalities suffered by African Americans around the turn of the century. But, his family was not free from hardship. Robeson's mother died from a stove-fire accident when he was six. His father, a runaway slave who became a pastor, was removed from an early ministerial position. From his father, Robeson learned diligence and 'unshakable dignity and courage in spite of the press of racism and poverty'. These characteristics, Stuckey said, defined Robeson's approach in his beliefs and actions throughout his life. Having excelled in scholastics and athletics as a youth, Robeson received a scholarship to Rutgers College, where he was elected to Phi Beta Kappa in his junior year and chosen valedictorian in his senior. He earned varsity letters in sports, was named Rutgers' first All-American in football. Fueled by his class prophecy to be 'the leader of the colored race in America', Robeson went on to earn a law degree from Columbia University, supporting himself by playing professional football on weekends. After graduation he obtained a position with a New York law firm only to have his career halted, as recalled in Martin Baulm Duberman's, *Paul Robeson*, when a stenographer refused to take down a memo, saying, 'I never take dictation from a nigger'. Sensing this episode as indicative of the climate of the law, Robeson left the bar. While in law school, Robeson married fellow Columbia student, Eslanda Cardozo Goode, who encouraged him to act in amateur theatrical productions. Convinced by his wife and friends to return to the theater after his departure from law, Robeson joined Provincetown Players, a group associated with playwright Eugene O'Neill. Two productions in which he starred, *The Emperor Jones* and *All God's Chillun Got Wings,* brought Robeson critical acclaim. Contemporary drama critic George Jean Nathan, quoted in *Newsweek* by Hubert Saal, called Robeson 'eloquent, impressive, and convincing'. Robeson continued on the stage, winning applause from critics and audiences, gaining an international reputation for performances on the London stage, eventually extending his acting repertoire to include films. His stage presence was undeniable, and with the musical, *Show Boat* and Shakespeare's, *Othello,* Robeson's reputation grew even larger. In, *Show Boat,* he sang the immensely popular *Ol' Man River,* displaying a powerful, warm, soothing voice. Robeson, realizing his acting range was limited by choice of roles available to him as a Black performer and by his acting abilities, turned to singing full time as an outlet for creative energies and growing social convictions. Robeson had been giving solo vocal performances since 1925, but it wasn't until he traveled to Britain that singing became for him a moral cause. Robeson related years later in his autobiography, *Here I Stand*, that in England he, 'learned that the essential character of a nation is determined not by the upper classes, but by the common people, and that the common people of all nations are truly brothers in the great family of mankind'.

<>

"Consequently, he began singing spirituals and work songs to audiences of common citizens and learning the languages and folk songs of other cultures, for 'they, too, were close to my heart and expressed the same soulful quality that I knew in Negro music'. Nathan Irvin Huggins, writing in, *The Nation*, defined this pivotal moment, 'Robeson found the finest expression of his talent. His genuine awe of, and love for, common people and their music flourished throughout his life and became his emotional and spiritual center'. Continued travels through Europe in 1930s brought Robeson in contact with members of politically left-leaning organizations, including socialists and African nationalists. Singing to, and moving among the disadvantaged, the underprivileged, the working classes, Robeson began viewing himself and his art as serving the struggle for racial justice for non-whites and economic justice for workers of the world, Huggins noted.

<>

"A critical journey at that time, one that changed the course of his life, was to the Soviet Union. *Paul Robeson* author, Duberman, depicted Robeson's time there, 'Nights at the theater and opera, long walks with film director Sergei Eisenstein, gala banquets, private screenings, trips to hospitals, children's centers, factories ...all in the context of a warm embrace'. Robeson was ecstatic with this new-found society, concluding, according to *New York Times Book Review* contributor, John Patrick Diggins, 'that the country was entirely free of racial prejudice and Afro-American spiritual music resonated to Russian folk traditions. 'Here, for the first time in my life ... I walk in full human dignity'.

<>

"Diggins went on to assert that Robeson's attraction to Communism seemed at first more anthropological than ideological, more of a desire to discover old, lost cultures than to impose new political systems ...Robeson convinced himself that American Blacks as descendants of slaves had common culture with Russian workers as descendants of serfs. Regardless of his ostensibly simple desire to believe in a cultural genealogy, Robeson soon become a vocal advocate of communism and left-wing causes. He returned to the U.S. in the late 1930s, *Newsweek* writer, Saal, observed, becoming 'a vigorous opponent of racism, picketing the White House, refusing to sing before segregated audiences, starting a crusade against lynching, and urging Congress to outlaw racial bars in baseball'. After World War II, when relations between U.S. and Soviet Union froze in the Cold War, many former advocates of communism backed away. When crimes of Soviet leader Josef Stalin became public ...forced famine, genocide, political purges ...more advocates left the ranks of communism. Robeson, however, was not among them. *National Review* contributor Joseph Sobran explained, 'It didn't matter, he believed in the idea, regardless of how it might be abused. Robeson could not publicly decry Soviet Union even after he, most probably, learned of Stalin's atrocities because of, 'the cause, to his mind,' *Nation* contributor, Huggins, theorized, 'was much larger than the Soviet Union, and he would do nothing to sustain the feeding frenzy of the American right'. Robeson's popularity soon plummeted in response to his increasing rhetoric.

<>

"After he urged Black youth not to fight if the U.S. went to war against Soviet Union, a riot prevented his appearing at a concert in Peekskill, New York. But, his desire was never to leave the United States, just to change, as he believed, the racist attitude of its people. In his autobiography, Robeson recounted how during the infamous McCarthy hearings, when questioned by a Congressional committee about why he didn't stay in Soviet Union, he replied, 'Because my father was a slave, and my people died to build this country, and I am going to stay right here and have a part of it, just like you. And no fascist-minded people will drive me from it. Is that clear?'

"In 1950, U.S. Department of State revoked Robeson's passport, ensuring he would remain in the United States. He was black-listed by concert managers. Robeson's passport was restored in 1958 after a Supreme Court ruling on a similar case, but it was of little consequence. By then, he'd become a non-entity. When Robeson's autobiography was published that year, leading literary journals, including *New York Times*, and, *New York Herald-Tribune*, refused to review it. Robeson traveled again to Soviet Union, but his health began to fail. He tried twice to commit suicide. 'Pariah status was utterly alien to the gregarious Robeson. He became depressed at loss of contact with audiences and friends, and suffered a series of breakdowns that left him withdrawn, dependent on psychotropic drugs,' Dennis Drabble explained, in *Smithsonian*. Slowly deteriorating and virtually unheard from in 1960s and 1970s, Robeson died after suffering a stroke in 1976. During his life Paul Robeson inspired thousands with his voice ...raised in speech and song. But, because of his singular support for communism and Stalin, because his life in retrospect became 'a pathetic tale of talent sacrificed, loyalty misplaced, and idealism betrayed,' according to Jim Miller, in *Newsweek*, Robeson disappeared in sadness and loneliness. His life, full of desire and achievement, passion and conviction, 'the story of a man who did so much to break down the barriers of a racist society, only to be brought down by the controversies sparked by his own radical politics,' *New York Times Book Review* contributor, Diggins, pronounced, 'is at once American triumph and American tragedy'.

<>

Patti yawned. "It's time for a commercial. Mom, have you got any documentation that isn't vanilla ... those don't do it for me."

"Well, maybe you'll like this one by his son, in *The Nation*."

"In the morning of Mar. 27, 1961 Paul Robeson was found in the bathroom of his Moscow hotel suite after having slashed his wrists with a razor blade following a wild party that had raged there the preceding night. His blood loss was not yet severe, and he recovered rapidly. However, both the raucous party and his 'suicide attempt' remain unexplained, and for the past twenty years the U.S. government has withheld documents that I believe hold the answer to the question ...Was this a drug-induced suicide attempt? Heavily censored documents I have already received under the Freedom of Information Act confirm that my father was under intense surveillance by the FBI and the CIA in 1960 and 1961, because he was planning to visit China and Cuba, in violation of U.S. passport restrictions. FBI files also reveal a suspicious concern over my father's health, beginning in 1955. A meeting I had in 1998 adds further grounds for suspicion. In June of that year I met Dr. Eric Olson in New York, and we were both struck by the similarities between the cases of our respective fathers. On Nov. 28, 1953, Olson's father, Dr. Frank Olson, a scientist working with the CIA's

top-secret MK-ULTRA 'mind control' program, allegedly 'jumped' through the glass of a thirteenth-floor hotel window and fell to his death. CIA documents have confirmed that a week earlier Olson had been surreptitiously drugged with LSD at a high-level CIA meeting. It is expected that a New York grand jury will soon reveal whether it believes Olson was murdered by CIA because of his qualms about the work he was doing. MK-ULTRA poisoned foreign and domestic 'enemies' with LSD to induce mental breakdown or suicide. Olson's drugging suggested a CIA motive similar to the possible one in my father's case ... concern about the target's planned course of action. In this context, the fact that Richard Helms was CIA chief of operations at the time of my father's 1961 'suicide attempt' has sinister implications. Helms was also responsible for the MK-ULTRA program. In 1967 a former CIA agent to whom I promised anonymity told me in a private conversation that my father was the subject of high-level concern and that Helms and CIA Director Allen Dulles discussed him in a meeting in 1955.

"The events leading to my father's 'suicide attempt' began when, alarmed by intense surveillance in London, he departed abruptly for Moscow alone. His intention was to visit Havana at Fidel Castro's personal invitation and return home to join the civil rights movement. Since the date set by the CIA for the Bay of Pigs invasion fell only four weeks after his arrival in Moscow, CIA had strong motive for preventing his travel to Havana. My father manifested no depressive symptoms at the time, and when my mother and I spoke to him in the hospital soon after his 'suicide' attempt, he was lucid and able to recount his experience clearly.

"The party in his suite had been imposed on him under false pretenses, by people he knew but without the knowledge of his official hosts. By the time he realized this, his suite had been invaded by a variety of anti-Soviet people whose behavior had become so raucous that he locked himself in his bedroom. His description of that setting, I later came to learn, matched the conditions prescribed by CIA for drugging an unsuspecting victim, and the physical psychological symptoms he experienced matched those of an LSD trip.

"My Russian being fluent, I confirmed my father's story by interviewing his official hosts, his doctors, the organizers of the party, several attendees and a top Soviet official. However, I could not determine whether my father's blood tests had shown any trace of drugs, whether an official investigation was in progress or why his hosts were unaware of the party. The Soviet official confirmed that known 'anti-Soviet people' had attended the party. By the time I returned to New York in early June, my father appeared to me to be fully recovered. However, when my parents returned to London several weeks later, my father became anxious, and he and my mother returned to Moscow. There, his well being was again restored, and in September they once more went back to London, where my father almost immediately suffered a relapse. My mother, acting on ill-considered advice of a close family friend, allowed a hastily recommended English physician to sign my father into the Priory psychiatric hospital near London. My father's records from the Priory, which I obtained only recently, raise the suspicion that he may have been subjected to the CIA's MK-ULTRA 'mind depatterning' technique, which combined massive electroconvulsive therapy with drug therapy. On the day of his admission, my mother was pressured into consenting to ECT, and treatment began thirty-six hours later. May 1963, I learned my father received fifty-four ECT treatments, and I arranged his transfer to a clinic in East Berlin.

"Certain key CIA documents that have been withheld, in whole or in part, would probably shed additional light on these events. Among the questions to be answered are, Why was Robeson's health such a concern to the government, and why is the FBI's information on it still being withheld? Was the CIA implicated in my father's 1961 'suicide attempt'? Did the CIA, in collusion with the British intelligence service, orchestrate his subjection to 'mind depatterning'? The idea that thirty-eight years after the original events occurred, the release of these documents could endanger national security should be rejected. On the contrary,' Paul Robeson's son said, 'the release of the information will improve national security by helping to protect the American people from criminal abuse by the intelligence agencies that are supposed to defend them.'"

Patti was all ears. "That sounds about right."

"Then just one more you'll like too, Jeffrey St. Clair and Alexander Cockburn, *Did CIA Poison Paul Robeson?*"

"Paul Robeson, the Black actor, singer, and political radical, may have been a victim of CIA chemist Sidney Gottlieb's MK-ULTRA program. We have previously noted Gottlieb's death and outlined his career of infamy. In spring 1961, Robeson planned to visit Havana Cuba to meet with Fidel Castro and Che Guevara. The trip never came off because Robeson fell ill in Moscow, where he had gone to give several lectures and concerts. At the time, it was reported that Robeson suffered a heart attack. But in fact, Robeson slashed his wrists in a suicide attempt after suffering hallucinations and severe depression. The symptoms came on following a surprise party thrown for him at his Moscow hotel. Robeson's son, Paul Robeson, Jr., has investigated his father's illness for more than 30 years. He believes that his father was slipped a synthetic hallucinogen called BZ by U.S. intelligence operatives at the party in Moscow. The party was hosted by anti-Soviet dissidents funded by CIA. Robeson Jr. visited his father in the hospital the day after the suicide attempt. Robeson told his son that he felt extreme paranoia and felt the walls of the room moving. He locked himself in his bedroom and was overcome by a powerful sense of emptiness and depression ...before he tried to take his own life. Robeson left Moscow for London, where he was admitted to Priory Hospital. There he was turned over to psychiatrists who forced him to endure 54 electro-shock treatments. At the time, electro-shock, in combination with psycho-active drugs, was a favored technique of CIA behavior modification. It turned out that the doctors treating Robeson in London and, later, in New York were CIA contractors. The timing of Robeson's trip to Cuba was certainly a crucial factor. Three weeks after the Moscow party, the CIA launched its disastrous invasion of Cuba at the Bay of Pigs. It's impossible to underestimate Robeson's threat, as he was perceived by the U.S. government as the most famous Black radical in the world. Thru the 1950s Robeson commanded worldwide attention and esteem. He was the Nelson Mandela and Mohammed Ali of his time. He spoke more than twenty languages, including Russian, Chinese, and several African languages. Robeson was also on close terms with Nehru, Jomo Kenyatta, and other Third World leaders. His embrace of Castro in Havana would have seriously undermined U.S. efforts to overthrow the new Cuban government. Another pressing concern for the U.S. government at the time, was Robeson's announced intentions to return to the U.S. and assume a leading role in the emerging civil rights movement. Like the family of Martin Luther King, Robeson had been under official surveillance for decades. As early as 1935, British intelligence had been looking at Robeson's activities. In 1943, the Office of Strategic Services, World War II predecessor to the CIA, opened a file on him. In 1947, Robeson was nearly killed in a car crash. It later turned out that the left wheel of the car had been monkey-wrenched. In the 1950s, Robeson was targeted by Senator Joseph McCarthy's anti-communist hearings. The campaign effectively sabotaged his acting and singing career in the states. Robeson never recovered from the drugging and the follow-up treatments from CIA-linked doctors and shrinks. He died in 1977. Robeson, Jr. has been pushing the U.S. to release classified documents regarding his father. He has already unearthed some damning stuff, including an FBI 'status of health' report on Robeson, created Apr. 1961. 'The fact that such a file was opened at all is sinister in itself,' Robeson Jr. recently told *London Sunday Times.* 'It indicates a degree of prior knowledge that something was about to happen to him.' Robeson's case has chilling parallels to the fate of another Black man who was slipped CIA-concocted hallucinogens, Sgt. James Thornwell. Thornwell was a U.S. Army sergeant working in a NATO office in Orleans, France, in 1961 ...the same year Robeson was drugged, when he came under suspicion of having stolen documents. Thornwell, who maintained his innocence, was interrogated, hypnotized, and harassed by U.S. intelligence officers. When he persisted in proclaiming his innocence, Thornwell was secretly given LSD for several days by his interrogators, during which time he was forced to undergo aggressive questioning, replete with racial slurs and threats. At one point, the CIA men threatened 'to extend the hallucinatory state indefinitely, even to a point of permanent insanity'. The agents apparently consummated their promise. Thornwell experienced an irreversible mental crisis. He eventually committed suicide at his Maryland home. There was never any evidence that he had anything to do with the missing NATO papers."

Nancy continued.

"In 1983, Eustace Mullins commented.

"Since the 1920s social engineering psychology in the U.S. was influenced by British Army's Bureau of Psychological Warfare. London's Tavistock Institute of Human Relations has the modest goal of social engineering human behavior of American citizens. Because of artillery barrages of World War I, many soldiers were permanently impaired by shell shock. In 1921, Marquees of Tavistock 11th Duke of Bedford,

supported a group planning rehabilitation programs for shell shocked British soldiers, taking the name, 'Tavistock Institute'. British Army General Staff decided it was crucial they determine the breaking point of soldiers under combat conditions. Tavistock Institute was taken over by Sir John Rawlings Reese, head of British Army Psychological Warfare Bureau. A cadre of specialists in psychological warfare was built up. In fifty years, 'Tavistock Institute' appears twice in the Index of the *New York Times* ... yet, according to LaRouche and others, Tavistock organized and trained the staffs of Office of Strategic Services (OSS), Strategic Bombing Survey, Supreme Headquarters of the Allied Expeditionary Forces, and other American military groups during World War II.

"During World War II, Tavistock combined with the medical sciences division of the Rockefeller Foundation for esoteric experiments with mind-altering drugs.

"The present drug culture of the U.S. is traced in its entirety to this Institute, which supervised the Central Intelligence Agency's training programs. The 'LSD counter culture' originated when Sandoz A.G., a Swiss pharmaceutical house owned by S.G. Warburg & Co., developed a new drug from lysergic acid, called LSD. James Paul Warburg ... son of Paul Warburg who had written the Federal Reserve Act in 1910 ... financed a subsidiary of Tavistock Institute in the U.S., called, Institute for Policy Studies ...whose director, Marcus Raskin, was appointed to the National Security Council.

"This subsidiary set up a CIA program ... MK-Ultra ... to experiment with LSD on CIA agents, some of whom later committed suicide. MK-Ultra, supervised by Dr. Gottlieb, resulted in huge lawsuits against the U.S. Government by families of the victims."

I was struggling to stay awake. "Nancy, are we almost done with this Hinckley stuff? I'm sleepy."

Nancy nodded. "Yes dear ...There was stuff about you on TV."

Hearing that perked me up. "Great."

Nancy picked up a newspaper, she kept reading. "This is a before, during and after. *Family destroyed by assassination attempt,* Associated Press, April Fool's Day, 1981, John Mossman.

"The parents of John W. Hinckley, Jr., 'just destroyed' by their son's alleged assassination attempt on President Reagan, hope to see him 'as soon as possible' but have no definite travel plans, their attorney said. The Hinckleys, through attorney James Robinson, issued a brief statement Tuesday expressing their 'deep concern' for President Reagan and all those involved in Monday's shooting, including their son, John. Robinson said the Hinckleys had spoken to their son Monday night and Tuesday afternoon and were trying to hire a Washington lawyer for him. It was confirmed later in Washington the Hinckleys retained the law firm of millionaire defense attorney Edward Bennett Williams. The Hinckleys said they planned to see their son 'as soon as possible, but at this time have no definite travel plans worked out,' Robinson said. They sent 'personal expressions of sorrow' to the wounded men and their families, he said. The Hinckleys reiterated through Robinson they have provided psychiatric care for their son in the past, adding that 'recent evaluations alerted no one to the seriousness of his condition'. In Washington, an aide to Vice President George Bush disputed a *Houston Post* report that the Hinckleys made large contributions to Bush's presidential campaign. The aide, Shirley Green, said no record of such a contribution could be found. The senior Hinckley is described by associates as a devout Christian who belonged to a weekly Bible reading club and recently did work in Africa for a Christian service organization. A statement from counsel for Vanderbilt Energy Corp. said the elder Hinckley had temporarily relinquished his duties as chairman for the Denver-based firm because of a tragedy involving a member of his family. John Hinckley, Jr., 25, who was arrested seconds after Reagan was shot in Washington, and being held Tuesday at a Marine base in Quantico, Va. The corporate statement didn't mention any change for Scott Hinckley, vice president of operations for Vanderbilt and brother of John, Jr. The father's move came amid confirmation the Department of Energy was reviewing Vanderbilt's books. Jack Vandenberg, DOE spokesman in Washington, said auditors met with Scott Hinckley in Denver, Monday. *Washington Star* quoted an unnamed 'White House official' as confirming DOE auditors asked for an explanation of an overcharge when oil price controls were in effect between 1973 and 1981. The *Star* said DOE auditors told Scott Hinckley there was a possible penalty of 2 million dollars for the overcharge.'"

Nancy was on a roll.

"And now, the during. This is Nathaniel Blumberg's, *The Afternoon of March 30*."

"When it happened it was beyond grotesque. For seconds Jonathan Blakely was stunned. John Chancellor, eyebrows raised, informed viewers of NBC Nightly News the brother of the man who tried to kill the President, was acquainted with the son of the man who would have become President if the attack was successful. Chancellor said in a bewildered tone, Scott Hinckley and Neil Bush were scheduled to have dinner together at the home of the vice president's son the next night.

"Neil Bush, who worked for Amoco Oil, told Denver reporters he'd met Scott Hinckley at a surprise party at the Bush home Jan. 23, 1981 ...approximately three weeks after U.S. Department of Energy began what was termed a 'routine audit' of the books of Vanderbilt Energy, the Hinckley oil company. In an incredible coincidence, the morning of Mar. 30, three representatives of U.S. Department of Energy told Scott Hinckley, Vanderbilt's vice president of operations, auditors uncovered evidence of pricing violations on crude oil sold by the company from 1977 through 1980. The auditors said the federal government was considering a penalty of 2 million dollars. Scott Hinckley reportedly requested 'several hours to come up with an explanation' of the serious overcharges. The meeting ended a little more than an hour before John Hinckley Jr. shot President Reagan. Although John Hinckley Sr. was characterized repeatedly by the national news media as 'a strong supporter of President Reagan,' no record was found of contributions to Reagan. To the contrary, in addition to money given to Bush ... a fellow Texas oilman ... as far back as 1970, the senior Hinckley raised funds for Bush's unsuccessful campaign to wrest the nomination *from* Reagan.

<>

"Furthermore, he and Scott Hinckley separately contributed to John Connally in late 1979 when Connally was leading the campaign to stop Reagan from gaining the 1980 presidential nomination.

<>

"Bush and Hinckley families, according to one newspaper, 'maintained social ties'. Evidence at the time made clear many connections between the Bush and Hinckley families. The official government line, accepted without challenge by media, was the assassination attempt was nothing more than the senseless act of a deranged drifter who 'did it to impress Jodie Foster'.

"To understand how *that* came to pass, it's essential to examine the trial of John W. Hinckley, presided over by Judge Barrington D. Parker. May 2001, Barrington D. Parker was one of the first eleven nominees for appointment to federal appeals courts by President G. W. Bush.

"Parker, a Republican appointed to the federal bench by President Nixon, was a man with an established reputation for politically partisan decisions and notable reversals on appeal. For example, when Edwin Reinecke, then lieutenant governor of California under Governor Reagan was convicted of lying to the Senate Judiciary Committee, Judge Parker could have imposed a five-year jail sentence and a $2,000 fine, but gave Reinecke an 18-month suspended sentence and one month of unsupervised probation.

<>

"More importantly, not for nothing did Parker achieve notoriety as 'the CIA's judge'. Orlando Letelier, an influential opponent of the Pinochet dictatorship in Chile, was assassinated in 1976 in broad daylight on a street in our national capital. The judge at the trial was Barrington D. Parker. Director of Central Intelligence was George Bush, father of George W. Bush. Judge Parker refused to allow the defense to present any testimony concerning the widely suspected involvement of CIA.

<>

"Parker came through again in 1977 when a former director of CIA, Richard Helms, pleaded no contest to charges of lying to Senate Foreign Relations Committee when he testified CIA had not covertly supplied money to opponents of Salvadore Allende in a secret effort to block his election as president of Chile. Judge Parker gave Helms a suspended two-year sentence and a $2,000 fine. Shortly before this decision, the lawyer for Helms, Edward Bennett Williams, pleaded with Judge Parker for a lenient sentence.

<>

"And how did Barrington D. Parker become the judge for Hinckley's trial? 'In another sharp diversion from regular courthouse procedure,' as the Washington Post flatly reported, Parker's name was secretly selected from a stack of cards that bore the names of 14 federal judges available. 'That selection process normally is carried out by a court clerk,' the Post continued, 'but this time the selection was made in private chambers of the senior judge,' Blumberg said."

Nancy kept rolling.

"More during ... by Thom Reno."

"The Bush and Hinckley families go back to 1960s in Texas. When the Hinckley oil company, Vanderbilt Oil, started to fail in the 1960s, Bush, Sr.'s, Zapata Oil financially bailed out Hinckley's company.

<>

"Hinckley was running an operation with six dead wells, but began making several million dollars a year after the Bush bailout.

<>

"In reference to whether the current president, George W. Bush, knew the would-be assassin, John Hinckley, Bush said at the time, 'It's certainly conceivable that I met him or might have been introduced to him. I don't recognize his face from the brief, kind of distorted thing they had on TV and the name doesn't ring any bells. I know he wasn't on our staff'. Neil Bush used a similar line in denying he knew John Hinckley. 'I have no idea,' he said. 'I don't recognize any pictures of him. I just wish I could see a better picture of him.' Besides all of the family ties, Neil Bush lived in Lubbock, Texas, throughout much of 1978, where Reagan shooter Hinckley lived from 1974-1980. During this period, in 1978, Neil Bush served as campaign manager for the current president's unsuccessful run for Congress. Ironically, Scott Hinckley was called on the carpet by the U.S. Department of Energy on the day Reagan was shot. The DOE told Hinckley it might place a 2 million dollar penalty on his company. Scott Hinckley, John's brother, was scheduled to have dinner at the Denver home of Neil Bush, Bush Sr.'s son, the current president's brother, the day after the shooting. At the time, Neil Bush was a Denver-based purchaser of mineral rights for Amoco, and Scott Hinckley was vice president of his father's Denver-based oil business.'"

Nancy picked up an old *San Francisco Examiner*.

"Now the 'after', then cookies and milk at 4 p.m. ...Patti, this is from your friend, Dave Emory," Nancy said.

"According to *San Francisco Examiner* of Mar. 31, 1981 John Hinckley was a former member of the National Socialist ... Nazi ... Party of America. He was expelled for being so violent his fellow Nazis suspected him of being a government agent. In Oct. 1980, Hinckley was arrested at the Nashville airport as then President Jimmy Carter was due to arrive. At the time, he had a .38 caliber pistol and two .22 caliber handguns in his possession, along with 50 rounds of ammunition.' The *Chronicle* reported the next day that Hinckley had attended a memorial march to commemorate American Nazi Party founder George Lincoln Rockwell.

"Dave Emory said, '*San Francisco Examiner*, Mar. 31, 1981 mentions Hinckley Sr.'s participation in a Christian Evangelical organization called World Vision is of more than passing interest. World Vision had served as a front for U.S. intelligence in Central America, employing former members of Anastazio Somoza's National Guard to inform on El Salvadorian refugees in Costa Rica, according to the *National Catholic Reporter* of Apr. 23, 1982 ... and that a number of the refugees were liquidated, after being identified as guerilla sympathizers by World Vision operatives.' *Christian Century Magazine*, July 4-11 1979 reported World Vision had functioned as a front for U.S. intelligence in Southeast Asia during the Vietnam War. Hinckley Sr.'s participation in World Vision, World Vision's connection to U.S. intelligence, and the closeness of the Bush and Hinckley families should be evaluated in light of the fact George Bush Sr. directed CIA a few years earlier. Hinckley Jr. was represented by the law firm of Edward Bennett Williams, one of the most powerful law firms in Washington D.C. The Edward Bennett Williams firm's previous clients included former CIA director Richard Helms, Robert Vesco, also connected to U.S. intelligence, Jimmy Hoffa and John Connally ... Nixon aide H.R. Haldemann's, *Ends of Power,* said 'the whole Bay of Pigs thing' was a code phrase in the Nixon White House,' Dave Emory said, 'for the assassination of President Kennedy."

Patti jumped in. "Dad, Bush presidents and vice presidents are oil and energy brokers, along with friends and backers like Kenneth Lay of Enron. Back in 1979 and 1980, in the middle of you running for president, George W. Bush's first oil venture, Arbusto, received that $50,000 investment from that Texan James Bath who made his millions investing money for Khalid bin Mahfouz and another BCCI-connected Saudi ... Sheikh Salim bin-Laden ... Osama's brother ...Salem bin Laden and Khalid bin Mahfouz were involved with BCCI, Bank of Credit and Commerce International ... bin Mahfouz owned twenty percent of its stock ... A decade later, *Harken Energy*, that bought out George W's crumbling oil and gas business, had its CIA connections ... 17.6 percent of Harken's stock was owned by Abdullah Baksh, another Saudi magnate reported representing Khalid bin Mahfouz.

"In the 1960s you see John Hinckley Sr.'s *Vanderbilt Oil* bailed out by Bush Senior's *Zapata Oil* which are both sitting on dead wells ... and *Zapata* or *Arbusto* or whatever it's called that year *is bailed out by bin Ladens* ... then George Jr.'s *Arbusto* is bailed out by the Saudis ... and Richard Helms' real Bay of Pigs is just a few

weeks after MK-Ultra tries to murder Paul Robeson, and Dulles is networking Helms and the Saudis ... do you think that has anything to with what Paul Robeson's ghost is trying to tell you?"

I was drifting off into sleep.

Nancy wrapped it up.

"Senator Frank Lautenberg of New Jersey just released a list of some bin Laden family members allowed by the Bush Administration to leave the U.S. in the week after 9/11. Two of the bin Ladens who departed were investigated for terrorist ties before 9/11. Omar Awad bin Laden, a nephew of Osama bin Laden, was allowed to leave even though his brother and housemate, Abdullah, was a long-time American head of the WAMY World Assembly of Muslim Youth. WAMY is a suspected terrorist organization raided by the FBI this past spring. The Omar and Abdullah bin Laden apartment was a few blocks away from the listed address of two of the 9/11 hijackers ...and from WAMY headquarters. Also allowed to leave was Khalil bin Laden, who Brazilian police investigated for suspected terrorist ties."

<>

It was at that moment the ghost of Paul Robeson appeared to us. Everyone was still.

"That's not it. That's not why I'm haunting you," the ghost of Paul Robeson said.

I was astonished. "Then why?! "Why?"

But, the ghost vanished. I didn't know what to make of it ...it confused me ...I almost had an idea ...I forgot it ...I stared off at the sea.

Washington D.C., hospital room bathroom

I was singing, happy to be alive after the assassination attempt, not to mention being able to get to the bathroom by myself. I was down on the floor with a towel mopping up water that had splashed out of the sink. A shadow fell over me, I was startled, turned and looked up. It was George, with an amused look ...with some of that condescension in it he'd learned from Bill Casey.

George remembered something his father Prescott said ... George was a kid again, back with his father in the family mansion, remembering the feeling of being a kid, being scolded by his father. Prescott was upset with George for cleaning up lemonade George had spilled.

Prescott looked down on George, "Don't you know what maids are for? We pay them good money. You want to take their jobs away?"

George felt embarrassed, humiliated, feigned a tough look on his face ...but, his sensitivity showed thru.

I saw George was daydreaming. "George, you're looking through me like I'm not even here, that's no way to treat your boss."

George stopped daydreaming, "Sorry, I guess my mind was lost someplace else."

"Keeping savings & loan deregulation and anti-terrorism on schedule for me?"

"Not to worry, that's what friends are for."

I appreciated that comment. "Thank you George, I hired you because you're dependable, I'm glad it turned into a friendship."

George felt flattered, "Me too, I took the job so you could depend on me. I'll take care of everything …until you're back on your feet, of course."

I had a questioning feeling somehow, about what he really meant …he must have seen that in my eyes.

"Come back on board soon."

"Don't stay out of the loop, don't let me down, George."

"Stay out of the loop? … I *am* the loop."

A few days later, Nancy visited me again in my hospital room. She propped a pillow behind me. I had a maze of I-V tubes handing out of my arm.

Nancy sat down on the bed beside me. "I don't think it's a good idea we go to our daughter's wedding, unless you're better."

I was surprised. "Not go to Maureen's wedding?! Nonsense. I'll be fine. It's three weeks away."

Nancy frowned, "But Jane Wyman … your first wife will be there. After all, Jane is Maureen's mother, not me."

I saw that stubborn look on Nancy's face. There was no use arguing with her. I gave in …I felt good-natured about giving-in to Nancy. She was usually right, anyway. "If it wasn't Maureen's third wedding I might put up a little more fuss."

Nancy felt like she was going to pop. "It's not that so much, but Maureen's 40 …her fiancée is 28! I can't just stand that!"

I leaned over towards Nancy. I hugged her …I winced because the hug hurt my ribs where the bullet fractured and split them. Nancy felt bad that I felt hurt.

Nancy took a card out of her purse. "Here's a wedding card I bought. Here's a pen …why don't you write a note inside …I'll send it to Maureen."

I wrote a note. I spoke the words I was writing aloud as I wrote them so Nancy could hear. "'Dear Maureen, best wishes on this wonderful day. Sorry we can't make it. Love, Mom and Dad.'"

Nancy felt relieved. She put the card into the envelope. She sealed the envelope. "I'm so glad we don't have to see her real mother."

Church in L.A., Maureen's wedding

The wedding march was being played by an organist at a church in Los Angeles where Maureen Reagan was marrying Dennis Revell. The couple exchanged wedding vows, reading them aloud. Maureen read her vows to her groom. "I love you because you're going to let me be me."

White House, upstairs living quarters

At Nancy's insistence, I'd moved back into the White House. Recuperating in bed, in my pajamas, Nancy lay beside me in her robe, reading …she put down her book. "I'm sure glad I got the hospital to release you to come home early."

I was happy Nancy had done that for me, too. "Me too, Mommy."

Nancy drew back the curtains. Nancy was astonished. "Well, would you believe that?! There's a *circus* out there set-up on the lawn?"

I didn't believe it. "A circus!?" I said. I leaned up from my bed, looked out the window …I laughed, it was a real circus. "It's nice to be home again, back in the swing of things."

White House Historian Bill Barnes taped a couple new newspaper headlines into his headline scrapbook.

'CIA seeks law for surprise searches of newsroom,' a *New York Times* headline read. 'Reagan wants to abolish consumer product agency', a *Washington Post* headline read. '*White House seeks eased Bribery Act … Says 1977 Law inhibits business abroad by U.S. corporations*', another *New York Times* headline read.

Jun. 16, 1981, press conference #3

Ed Meese III and Larry Speakes were together in the White House Press Briefing Room. Ed was talking to reporters. He was angry.

Alan walked to Meece. "I understand Ernest W. Lefever withdrew himself from consideration as Assistant Secretary of State."

Meese was upset, "Ernie believed the U.S. should take a soft line dealing with friendly Far-Right dictatorships. Some liberal Senators crucified him for it. I think ACLU lobbied against Ernie's confirmation. American Civil Liberties Union is a criminal lobby!"

Larry shrugged in chagrin. He turned to an aide. "Ed Meese wears the mantle for this Administration's most right-wing law-'n'-order man. Deaver said it'd be good to get the President's son Michael in front of cameras on this one. I'm not so sure."

Michael Reagan was talking to reporters.

Alan had a question for him. "You work for a military supply firm?"

Michael Reagan felt bitter, "Yes. It's just so silly. Somebody else can write a letter to military bases and say, 'Hey, I think Ronald Reagan's a great President'. I write a letter and say my Dad's a great President ... and I have the press on my doorstep. Now, I'm resigning from the company."

Alan wondered where the Reagans were coming from, "What's been your father's reaction?"

Michael laughed in a snide way, "He told me, 'Don't write any more letters!'"

I came into the room, escorted by Mike Deaver. All the reporters turned their attention to me.

Alan spoke up, "What's your Administration's response to the Israeli attack on Iraq?"

"I can't answer that."

"What's your reaction to Israel not signing the Nuclear Non-Proliferation Treaty?"

"Well, I haven't given very much thought to that particular question, there."

"Any comment on Pakistan's refusal to sign the treaty?"

"I won't answer the question."

"What do you make of Israeli threats against Lebanon?"

"Well, this one's going to be one, I'm afraid, that I can't answer now."

"What do you think of the tactics of political action committees?"

"I don't know how to answer that."

"I feel skeptical about your Administration's grasp of foreign affairs."

"I'm satisfied that we do have a foreign policy."

Alan looked at Larry. Larry shrugged.

I looked through my note cards, "I regard voting as the most sacred right of free men and women."

"Then why won't you support an extension of the Voting Rights Act?" Alan asked.

I shrugged off the question. I looked at a different note card. I found one I liked. I smiled. "Vice

President George Bush phoned President Ferdinand Marcos of the Philippines and said, 'We love your adherence to democratic principle and to the democratic processes'."

"Marcos is brutally enforcing martial law in Manila," Alan said.

I tried another note card, "Max Hugel, appointed by William Casey to run CIA covert operations, resigned today. There were allegations of fraud against him in connection with financial transactions in the '70s."

Alan kept the questions coming. "There are reports Casey omitted stock holdings, and a $10,000 gift from his income tax returns."

"I don't know anything about that. ... As you know 12,000, air traffic controllers in their union violated a no-strike clause in their contract and walked off the job. I warned them to honor their contract or face dismissal. I'm firing them. I've ordered military personnel into airport towers to keep commercial planes flying."

Treasury Secretary Donald Regan stood at another podium. Larry signaled Don Regan with a wave. Then, Larry introduced him.

Treasury Secretary Regan spoke to me in front of the press. "Mr. President, I'd like to invite you to join the negotiating session where your tax-cut bill is being shaped."

I smiled. "Heck no. I'm not going. I'm going to leave this to the experts. I'm not going to get involved in details. It's Nancy's birthday."

Alan asked, "How old is Mrs. Reagan."

I knew I'd get this right, "Twenty-eight."

"Mr. President. America's in the worst economic recession since 1930. Unemployment's risen to over 10%. That's the highest unemployment rate since the Second World War. There are dramatic increases in business failures, farm foreclosures, personal bankruptcy, and homelessness. Over 11.5 million Americans have lost their jobs. Another 10 million others are forced into lower paying work. What's the Reagan Administration going to do to fix this?"

I looked through my note cards. I found a card labeled, 'unemployment'. I read the card to myself. I faced the press, "Well, one thing we're going to do is change the way we figure unemployment. Before, we used to actually count how many people were unemployed. But, from now on we're just going to count how many people get unemployment insurance ...and, after it runs out ... we're not going to count the people who aren't working who no longer can collect unemployment insurance ...that should help. The recession is a problem we inherited from Carter. So is the growing budget deficit. I was in Cincinnati at a fundraiser luncheon recently."

Mike saw, I was going to ad lib. He was frantic.

I continued, "I told my audience, 'I know you've all paid $2,500 a plate to be here. I thank you for that. I received a letter from a blind supporter. He wrote in Braille to tell me that if cutting his pension would help get this country back on its feet, he'd like to have me cut his pension. Next question."

"Is the constant feud going on at the White House ...inside the White House Staff ...and, inside the Cabinet ...and, between the Staff and the Cabinet .... hindering the smooth working of the country?"

I thought, 'That's an easy one. I'll just deny it'. "There is no bickering or backstabbing going on. We're a very happy group."

Reporters in the room broke out laughing. Alan kept up his questions. "Are you aware of Budget Director David Stockman's new book, and what he's saying about you?"

"No. I stand by the White House staff and Cabinet completely."

<>

Stockman stood in a corner of the room with reporters. Stockman shrugged. "My last visit to the Oval Office for lunch with the President was more in the nature of a visit to the woodshed ...after supper. He wasn't happy about the way all this has developed. The President blames this whole flap on the media."

<>

Larry saw things were out of hand. He needed to tighten the press conference up, spoke into his microphone. "Here's one you'll like. Justice Department is investigating a $1,000 payment given to National Security Adviser Richard Allen from a Japanese magazine after he helped arrange a brief post-inaugural interview with Nancy Reagan."

Richard Allen stood up. He addressed the floor. "I didn't accept it. I received it. It would have been an embarrassment to the Japanese to return the money."

Alan caught the scent of blood, "Mr. President. Will you let Richard Allen stay on the job?"

"On the basis of what I know, yes."

"I want to ask GOP Finance Director Rich DeVos about charges Reagan economic policies are unfair."

Larry nodded his approval to Richard DeVos.

Richard DeVos stood up, "When I hear people talking about money, it's usually people who

don't have any."

Larry was feeling grim. "On a lighter note, President Reagan's going to accept the annual White House Thanksgiving turkey. We thought you'd get a kick out of this."

I received the gift of the annual White House turkey. The turkey began squawking. The turkey began flapping its wings wildly. I looked through his note cards. I found the one marked, 'Thanksgiving Turkey'. I read the card aloud to reporters. "I remember a Thanksgiving long ago. I was carving a turkey, and I noticed what seemed to be blood oozing from it. I thought the bird was undercooked. Then, I realized I'd sliced open my thumb."

Some reporters laughed. Alan smirked, "I have a question for House Speaker Tip O'Neil. How do you rate the President's budget know-how?"

Larry nodded to House Speaker Tip O'Neil.

Tip O'Neil faced the reporters. "The President vetoed a stop-gap spending bill. This veto forced the federal government to temporarily shut down ... for the first time, in history. The President knows less about the budget than any President in my lifetime. He can't even carry on a conversation about the budget. It's an absolute disgrace."

Larry looked angrily at Mike. Mike shrugged.

Mike looked at Larry. "He wasn't supposed to say that, Larry."

Barbara Walters was patiently waiting to ask me a few questions. Walters looked at me, "Mr. President, what kind of man were you, as a father?"

Mike sighed in relief. Larry started to smile.

I smiled at Barbara Walters. I fumbled through my note cards. I couldn't find the one labeled, 'family'. I knew I'd have to improvise. "I don't really know. I tried very hard, and worked at spending time with the family."

"What kind of adjectives would you use to describe yourself?"

I smiled, "I'm a soft touch, I really am. Sometimes, I'm stubborn, I hope not unnecessarily so, but I really can't answer that question."

Mike felt worried. He pointed at his watch and tried to catch Larry's attention. Barbara Walters had a few more questions.

"I understand Nancy's Social Secretary, Muffie Brandon, reported the White House is experiencing a terrible tablecloth crisis. 'One set of tablecloths,' she said, 'to my complete and utter horror, went out to the dry cleaner, and shrunk'."

I laughed, "I don't think that we have a crisis here. I think we'll manage. I don't see this as a frightening thing."

Mike got Larry's attention.

Larry got the message. "Ladies and gentlemen of the press. This press conference is over."

May 17, 1981,
Notre Dame, assembly hall

The Dean of Notre Dame was presiding over a ceremony. "I'm pleased to award this honorary degree from Notre Dame, to President Reagan."

I smiled absently. "I was here 41 years ago acting as a football hero in the film, *Coach Knute Rockne, All American.* That's when I first said, 'Win one for the Gipper!'"

The Notre Dame Dean had a few drinks to brace himself for the ceremony. "Your vision, now as then, has a compelling simplicity about it."

I spoke to the Dean. "I'm smart. I admit it."

The Dean looked like he was holding his breath, underwater.

Dec. 12, 1981,
White House Situation Room

CIA Director Bill Casey, Vice President Bush, and me were meeting in the White House Situation Room.

Bill Casey felt relieved, "Well, it took the Senate four months of investigation into my business dealings. Now, the Senate Intelligence Committee decided, I'm *not* what they call, 'unfit to serve'. I'm still CIA director, after all."

George was glad his intelligence mentor had made it past Senate investigation. "That's great, Bill."

Bill nodded in agreement, "Now, this is over, I want to widen the intelligence role of CIA. We have foreign spy power. I want *domestic* spy power, too. I want it officially announced, in the press. That'll keep *anyone* from knowing where the bodies are buried."

I listened carefully. "You've got it." I turned to George, "What's this about Muammar Qaddafi threatening to get me assassinated."

"It's a sad state of affairs," George said.

I put on my actor's face, "George, I don't know how you feel about it. But, I think I'll just call Qaddafi and meet him out there on the Mall."

Britain, U.S. Economic Council
meeting, 1982

Great Britain was chosen as location for a U.S. Economic Council meeting. I appointed George Shultz, president of Bechtel, to head up the economic council. George Shultz liked to make decisions on behalf of the U.S. to benefit Bechtel Corp. directly or indirectly, sooner or later. As all of us in office learn, the business of the U.S. is the business of the U.S., but the business of the U.S., is partnered abroad. Investment and merchant bankers, international bankers, and central bankers came to meet with development, engineering, and construction firms from the U.S. and Europe, sat in chairs with four-inch high national flags, and corporate logos pasted onto nametags at table place sittings. Shultz radiated a diplomatic savoir-faire naturally.

Shultz addressed the gathering. "While I'm head of President Reagan's economic council, I remain president of Bechtel ...this gives me a leg up against Bechtel's biggest competitor's ...including, bin Laden Construction of Saudi Arabia, Brown & Root out of Houston, and Halliburton ...but, it's window dressing when the FED, Bank of England, Export-Import Bank, IMF, World Bank, and BIS throws reconstruction contracts to us or to them ...it appears to depend on ...campaign contributions ...who's elected ...who's got more players on Wall Street ...who's got the most Congressman ... we call them Conmen, for short ... handling the Administration ...steering CIA, Joint Chiefs of Staff, and the White House. But, you've got to ask yourself ...who does CIA work for? ...which bank? ...and when? ...who tells them what to do? For whom does the bell toll? ...Bechtel tosses its hat into the ring along with Brown & Root, Halliburton, bin Laden Construction ...I mean, who's calling the shots? ...a host of players with their own intelligence networks? But, we do agree on one thing ... overall, we let the taxpayers in each country pick up the tab, through the mechanism of the government contract."

<>

A phone began ringing, an aide to Bechtel's President Shultz carried the phone to him. "Mr. Shultz, it's the President."

On the other end of the line I waited impatiently. He finally picked up. "George, I'd like you to be my State Secretary."

"I accept the job, give me a week to resign from being president of Bechtel and make arrangements."

Dec. 17, 1981, Press conference #6,
White House press briefing room

Mike Deaver reviewed the videotape of my last press conference. Mike rehearsed me. He wanted me to look forward to giving press conferences. They were a mixed blessing for me, I liked the attention ...but, I didn't want to say the wrong thing. I stood up in the White House Press

Briefing Room, facing the reporters.

Alan asked, "President Reagan, do you agree with Justice Department's efforts to overturn Supreme Court's Webber ruling?"

I shuffled through my note cards. I couldn't find any card for that. I felt this was going to be one of those days, when nothing goes right. I looked at him, "I can't bring to mind what it pertains to and what it calls for."

Alan fired back. "It allows unions and management to enter into voluntary affirmative action agreements?"

"Yes, of course I agree."

Ed Meese waved frantically at me.

Mike Deaver hurried over. Mike put his hand over the microphone. Mike whispered to me. "Mr. President, say, 'No, I don't agree."

I corrected myself. "I mean, I do *not* support the Webber ruling."

Larry Speakes felt amused. He kept a poker face. Alan watched in silence, shaking his head. Larry continued briefing the reporters gathered for the press conference.

Larry faced the press. "The White House is seeking to ease rules on rest homes. Proposals include repeal of regulations on sanitation, safety, and contagion. Christmas is approaching. President Reagan authorized the distribution of 30 million pounds of surplus cheese to the poor."

Alan laughed. "A government worker told me the cheese is over a year old. It's reached something called, 'critical inventory situation'. It's moldy. On PBS, the President said elements of FDR's New Deal resembled Fascism."

<>

I was upset. I leaned in front of Larry Speakes into the microphone. "Move over Larry. I'll handle this, myself. Young man, New Deal proponents espoused fascism."

Alan didn't hold back. "You're distorting history. What about your wife's higher-than-usual disapproval rating?"

"I just heard earlier today, and maybe Larry can tell me if this is true, I just heard that some poll or something has revealed, she's the most popular woman in the world."

Larry frowned. "I haven't seen any poll like that."

I kept speaking. "I want to make a statement to celebrate Voice Of America's 40th Birthday. I used to work in radio. I made up a lot of exciting details while I was announcing games, by reading wire copy without actually being at the games. Now, I submit to you ... I told the truth when I enhanced routine plays, like shortstop-to-

first grounding outs. I don't know if the player really ran over towards second base and made a one-hand stab ...or, whether he squatted down and took the ball when it came to him. But, the truth got there and, in other words, it can be attractively packaged."

Bill Barnes sat in the seating gallery taking notes. He kept his tape recorder running. He would have Alan type up his notes and transcribe the tapes, that evening. Bill Barnes wondered how Alan could have much of a social life by reporting news 24-7, then spend evenings transcribing, day in and day out. Barnes turned his eyes towards Alan. Barnes had been there.

Apr. 2, 1982, Falkland war

Alan spoke out. "Several days ago Argentina invaded Britain's Falkland Islands. Hours later, U.N. Ambassador Jeane Kirkpatrick attended a dinner at Argentine embassy. The British fleet is on its way to Falkland Islands. Which side are we on?"

I scratched my head. "We're friends of both sides. The Falkland Islands war is a dispute over sovereignty of that little ice-cold bunch of land down there. England has always been proud of the fact that English police didn't have to carry guns. In England, if a criminal carried a gun, even though he didn't use it, he wasn't tried for burglary or theft, or whatever he was doing. He was tried for first-degree murder and hung, if he was found guilty."

The reporters in the room fell silent. Alan spoke out, "That's not true."

<>

Larry quickly spoke into his microphone., "Well, it's a good story. It made the point, didn't it?"

I felt good Larry was defending me, that's what he got paid for. I faced the press. "I've checked statistics ...and. trees really *do* cause more pollution than cars. There's no recall for missiles fired from silos. Those that are carried in bombers, those that are carried in ships of one kind of another, or submersibles, can be recalled ...if, there's been a miscalculation. We're going to strengthen three military divisions in Western Europe, two of which are in Geneva ...and one, I believe, still in Switzerland. I'm going to end this press conference with a little story. I spoke to students at a Chicago High

305

School. I told them why Ed Meese's revised tax exemption policy could not possibly have been intended to benefit segregated schools. I told them, there must be some kind of misunderstanding. I am unalterably opposed to racial discrimination in any form. I told them, besides, I didn't know there were any segregated schools. Maybe, I should have known. But, I didn't. I warned the kids, make sure I didn't tell them any lies. Don't let me get away with it, I said. Make sure, what I told you checks out and is true. Don't be the 'sucker generation'. The other day, I got a letter from Pope John Paul II. He said, he approves what we've done so far against U.S.S.R. The other day, I was at a National Security Council meeting with CIA Deputy Director Bobby Inman. We were talking about Soviet weapons. I said, isn't the SS-19 their biggest missile? So Inman says, no, that's the SS-18. I say, so they've even switched the numbers on their missiles to confuse us. I thought that was pretty good. Then, he tells me the numbers are assigned by U.S. intelligence. Defense Secretary Caspar Weinberger explained the Pentagon position on what they call, 'protracted nuclear war'. We don't believe a nuclear war can be won. But, we're planning to prevail if we're attacked. With great regret, I've accepted the resignation of Secretary of State Al Haig. I'm nominating as his successor, and he has accepted, George Shultz ...to replace him."

Alan addressed the President. "The jobless rate is the worst in 42 years, 11 million people are looking for jobs."

I looked at Alan. "In this time of great unemployment, Sunday's paper had 24 full pages of employers looking for employees. Unemployment must be caused by a lot of lazy people who'd just rather not work. We're trying to get unemployment to go up, and I think we're going to succeed. You can put some of the blame for the recession on me ...because, for many years, I was a Democrat. It's the big spenders who cause inflation. They even drove prayer out of our nation's classrooms."

Alan interrupted me, "Who are *they*?"

I smiled. "*They* know who they are. One more thing. All those mistakes you reporters said I made at last month's news conference, the score was five to one in my favor."

White House Spokesman Larry Speaks spoke into his microphone. "That concludes the Press Conference,."

Several reporters start shouting questions at me. "Sanctions against Argentina?"

I waved, "I can't give you an answer on that."

"What about the Israeli invasion of Lebanon?"

"This is a question, again, where I have to beg your tolerance of me.".

"Isn't this departure of Haig a bit mysterious?"

"Once again, you ask a question upon which when I accepted his resignation I made a statement that I'd have no further comments on that or take no questions on it. We've got a 120 billion dollar deficit coming. You know, a young man went into a grocery store and he had an orange in one hand and a bottle of vodka in the other. He paid for the orange with food stamps, took the change and paid for the vodka. That's what's wrong."

Larry shook his head tiredly. Bill Barnes felt his mouth fall open. Mike sighed.

A reporter got in another question. "Interior Secretary James Watt warned the Israeli Ambassador, that if liberals of the Jewish community oppose Watt's plans for offshore drilling they'll weaken our ability to be a good friend of Israel."

I smiled and waved. "Watts is an environmentalist himself, as I think I am. Watts is going to open up a billion miles of California shoreline for offshore drilling. Watts speaks in black-and-white terms without much gray in his life. He sees problems without the complexity that is confusing to a lot of people."

Alan jumped into the conversation, "Watts says, environmentalists are a left-wing cult dedicated to bringing down the government!"

Larry shook his head, "Ladies and Gentlemen, this Press Conference is over."

Another reporter tried to get in a question. "Will you be visiting the new Vietnam Veterans memorial."

I waved to the reporter. "I can't tell you until somebody tells me. I never know where I'm going. Y'know, I was in Texas the other day and asked someone what Pac-Man is ...and, somebody told me, it was a round thing that gobbles up money. I thought, that was Tip O'Neil. You can't drink yourself sober, you can't spend yourself rich, and you can't pump the prime without priming the pump. You know something? I said that backwards. You can't prime the pump without pumping the prime ." I felt exhausted. I waved and smiled at the reporters. Mike walked with me away from the podium. I smiled at Mike. "Send 'em away laughin'. The show must go on."

Larry shook his head, "That's it. It's over."

<>

Alan wasn't satisfied. He wanted more. "What do you mean, it's over. I thought it was a double feature."

Larry wasn't in the mood, "*You* don't tell us how

to stage the news, and *we* don't tell you how to report it. But, I'll give you this. Come Thanksgiving, I'm going to announce the White House is considering a proposal by Ed Meese to tax unemployment benefits. This, in my opinion would make unemployment less attractive. Ed told me, he knows that generally when unemployment benefits end, most people find jobs very quickly."

Alan felt furious …but, said nothing. He didn't want to lose press privileges. Most of Alan's friends were reporters, writers, and poets. Alan knew that society had no use for writers and poets. He thought of Charles Bukoski's line, 'Great poets end up in steaming pots of shit'.

<>

Mike led me out of the room, escorted me upstairs to the second floor of the White House to my bedroom, so I could sleep.

Mile smiled at me, "You were on your toe marks, Champ. You were right on the money. Good job."

"Thank you, and good night. Sometimes I look out there at Pennsylvania Avenue and see people bustling along, and it suddenly dawns on me that probably never again can I just say, Hey, I'm going down to the drugstore to look at the magazines."

Mike closed my bedroom door behind him …stood in the hall …took his flask of vodka out of his coat pocket.

<>

At home, Bill Barnes sat at his writing desk. Jackson was sitting on Bill's lap, purring. Bill watched the sunset. He start chronicling the days events. He start talking into his tape recorder. He'd have Alan transcribe the material, tomorrow. Jackson's purring got louder. Soon, both Jackson and Bill Barnes fell asleep.

White House 2nd floor
bedroom, 1982

Me and Nancy woke up in our second floor master bedroom suite in the White House, I was amusing Nancy and myself by playing with the marionette that had my face painted on it that Maureen gave me to cheer me up when I was in the hospital.

"Good morning Mr. Marionette, would you like to be shot today? I hope you like ruling the United States as much me."

Nancy wasn't amused, "Don't kid yourself, Caesar. Mark Anthony's out there."

"I saw that movie, that starred Lawrence Olivier or Error Flynn?"

"Ronnie, it's not funny. When you got shot …

John Kennedy, Robert Kennedy, Martin Luther King, George Wallace, I thought about them, all those CIA coups murdering a country's president to put in a new leader that will do what special interests tell CIA to tell him him to do for their financial portfolios …all the children of those murdered leaders, their kids would want revenge against United States. I don't know who scares me more …multi-national corporations trying to buy the Presidency …or, those who hire mercenaries and assassins …or, kids of the ruling families that the CIA conquers. The U.S. had a civil war once …is it ongoing? …hidden behind smiles …behind handshakes …behind elections, in every country?"

"You're confusing me, Mommy."

"Listen. Kennedy wanted to disband CIA, he wouldn't support CIA banana republics, but *you* support banana republics. Kennedy wanted to get rid of the Federal Reserve Banking system and have the U.S. Government print its own money again, instead of having to buy it or rent it from the Fed when they print it up and claim face value, but *you* support the Fed. Kennedy wanted to end Vietnam, but *you* support foreign and colonial wars, you *support* CIA, Contras, the Deutschemark, Yen, the dollar and let Bush, Casey and Shultz dictate policy and make all the decisions …so, *why* would anyone want to kill you? You're already far-right, there's nothing to gain …unless, they had something really evil in mind."

I felt small, "Nancy, you hurt my feelings. I let people pull my strings, it makes me look innocent, feel innocent and *be* innocent … I know I'm not in charge, no president is, it's acting."

Nancy forged ahead. "I'm not talking about that! I'll find out who was behind this, one way or another! I'll fire them, kill the messenger, that's how it works! There won't be any more bad tidings, I'll sort through all the scapegoats. I've been talking to my astrologer! There's those 800 CIA agents Carter fired, a lot of hungry operatives out there."

I'd gotten over my hurt feelings. "But, they're on my side because of Casey and Bush."

Nancy's eyes flashed, "You keep Casey and Bush on your side."

CENSORED

307

I sighed, "What choice do I have. At least I can count on George Shultz. Bechtel's had him coaching me on foreign policy and taxes since I got into politics, I never did get support from Brown & Root, they backed Johnson against Kennedy, so when Kennedy was killed Brown & Root got the international development and recolonization contracts, not Bechtel. Nancy, help me with this. One, given Casey's previous jobs running government, running OSS Intelligence, running Export-Import Bank and sitting as director on his own banks ...and two, Bechtel's revolving door between Bechtel, the CIA and the Cabinet then back to Bechtel ...and three, given Bechtel was friends with Shultz and Dulles and Casey ...and four, given Shultz works for Bechtel as president of the company and works as head of my Economic Council, and now he's accepting my appointment to be U.S. Secretary of State ...and five, Casey was known as a Republican fundraiser ...and six, Bechtel is a fundraiser too ...and seven, Bechtel employees work with and for CIA ... and eight, like I say, Shultz worked for Bechtel ... then, one, does Shultz work for CIA as an asset, too? ...Two, how do we follow the Foreign Policy trail giving taxpayer dollars to foreign national states who then hire U.S. private enterprises and pay them with taxpayer money ...and three, where are Congressional kickbacks happening? ...and four, are those kickbacks immoral because they go into private pockets, or moral in the name of stopping Communism?"

<>

Nancy threw her arms up into the air in dismay, then held her head in her hands. "Ronnie I don't know why you ask me questions like that, I'm not a walking encyclopedia, it seems right ...but, moral too? There've been so many Bechtel Cabinet employees or consultants in Washington over the years like Dulles, Casey, and McCone ... influencing each administration. The '50s were simpler, kinder, and gentler ...and, such a long time ago ...looking back from now."

I felt animated. "Remember the '40s, that was World War Two, the coups in Syria, Iran, Korea, Guatemala, Nicaragua, what goes around comes around. But, who's in charge of the whole thing? ... Me?"

Nancy laughed. "I don't think so."

I kept driving my argument home, I *really* had a brainstorm this time, I was determined not to lose track of it, to hold it tight. "No, I'm not controlling anything. I follow leads I'm given by my backers ...and, they follow their consultants ...but, everyone breaks the rules ...that's what they're for, to tip the scales in their own favor. Does that mean criminals, mafia, terrorists, central banks, those ruling families are running the show? But, which ruling families are the bad apples?"

Nancy looked over her shoulders then back at me. "You can't count on anyone but me, remember that."

I saw Nancy was worrying, I hugged her, I kissed her. "I know Sweetheart, I know," I said.

Nancy felt better. "We're going for the gold."

"An Oscar! Golly, Nancy, I trust you more than anyone in the whole world, I love you."

<> <> <>

Nancy continued reading Eustace Mullins', *Secrets of the Federal Reserve*, to me at the ranch after my retirement from public office. And, armed with Mel's Jesus and Paul Robeson's ghost, I continued acting out my understanding of who'd been pulling mine and Nancy's strings, when we were in Washington.

Whoopi Goldberg in character as Abraham Lincoln comes over to me and Mel's Jesus. "Ronnie, what's coming down's too powerful to be suppressed by ordinary machinery of peacetime government in some southern states, I'm blockading coastal ports, to keep them from being supplied from Europe.

"In the North ... Rothschilds are financing the North through August Belmont and Jay Cooke selling Union bond issues with J. and W. Seligman & Co., and Speyer & Co. in Europe.

"In the South ... Confederate War Secretary Judah Benjamin (1811-84) of the law firm of Slidell, Benjamin & Conrad in Louisiana, is a Rothschild agent, in 1862 becoming Secretary of State for the Confederacy. His law partner, John Slidell (August Belmont's wife's uncle) was Confederate envoy to France, Slidell's daughter married to Baron Frederick D´Erlanger in Frankfurt related to the Rothschilds is acting on their behalf. Slidell represents the South borrowing money from D´Erlanger to finance the Confederacy."

<>

Whoopi must have forgotten, *I* was playing dual Rothschild rolls, or why would she have come to me? ...since, I was out to split her country up from under her by financing both sides of the conflict. What was Whoopi up to?

<>

Whoopi sized me up. "The privilege of creating and issuing money is the supreme prerogative of Government, the Government's greatest creative opportunity. By adoption of these principles, taxpayers are saved immense sums of interest."

Aug. 1861, Moses Taylor, undercover financial agent for John Jacob Astor becomes Chairman of Loan Committee to finance the Union Government in the Civil War, the Committee shocks Whoopi by offering the Government 5 million dollars at 12% financing. Whoopi's ghetto, refusing, instead finances war by inventing and issuing U.S. Treasury 'Greenbacks' with gold backing. Moses Taylor profits through the war, making young James Stillman his protégé.

New York Times May 24, 1882 at his death Moses Taylor, first president of City Bank of New York, major stockholder in Delaware, Lackawanna & Western Railroad, was chairman of Loan Committee of Associated Banks of New York City in 1861, controlling 200 million dollars of securities, due to him more than any other single man Whoopi found means to prosecute war.

Moses Taylor left behind 70 million dollars, son-in-law, Percy Pyne became president of City Bank, renamed it National City Bank. Pyne wasn't a banker, all National City's capital being the Moses Taylor estate. William Rockefeller, John D. Rockefeller's brother, bought into the bank. Pyne stepped aside, John Stillman now had Rockefeller oil income in National City Bank.

<>

John Stillman's father, Don Carlos Stillman, was a British agent and blockade runner during the Civil War in Brownsville Texas, and positioned John initially with Moses Taylor.

Mar. 1862 and Mar. 1863, Whoopi Goldberg received Congressional approval to borrow 450 million dollars from the people by selling them bonds, or 'greenbacks,' to pay for Civil War, redeemable in 1865, when each greenback could be exchanged for one dollar in silver, making them legal tender in 1879. So, Whoopi Goldberg solved America's monetary crisis without help of international bankers.

The *Hazard Circular* inserted into *London Times*, 1865 spoke of Whoopi's Greenbacks.

"If this mischievous financial policy which has its origin in North America during the late war in that country, shall become endurated down to a fixture, then that Government will furnish its own money without cost. It will pay off debts and be without debt. It will have all the money necessary to carry on its commerce. It will become

prosperous without precedent in the history of the world. The brains, and wealth of all countries will go to North America. That country must be destroyed or it will destroy every monarchy on the globe," the circular said.

<>

Richard Gere, playing German Chancellor Bismarck, comes to me in 1876 about Whoopi.

"Whoopi got from Congress the right to borrow from the people by selling the people Government 'bonds' ...and, the nation escaped the plots of foreign financiers. They understood at once, the United States would escape their grip. The death of Whoopi was resolved upon."

<>

John Wilkes Booth's earliest recruits in the original plan to kidnap Whoopi included Sam Arnold and Mike O'Laughlin. Booth and O'Laughlin had a smuggling ring ... taking contraband quinine, morphine, and medicines to the South.

Bankers and speculators plotting to kidnap Whoopi wanted to replace Booth with a soldier. Booth found out he'd been replaced by a Rebel, one 'Captain B' ...Captain James William Boyd even *looked* like John Wilkes Booth, had been head of Confederate secret service in West Tennessee, now was a prisoner of war, captured by the National Detective Police (NDP) in Aug. 1863 ....who, then pressured him to be a spy and Rebel turncoat.

Booth couriers a note to Confederate War Secretary Judah Benjamin in Richmond ...then, goes to see Republican Senator John Conness. Conness had served with National Detective Police Chief Colonel Lafayette C. Baker ...as members of a vigilante group in California during the 1850's ...and, told Booth, Police Chief Lafayette Baker was in on the Whoopi kidnap plan. Booth hears back from Confederate War Secretary Benjamin, who says, trust Chief Baker.

At a Washington D.C. party, Senator Conness tells Booth about Lincoln's routes in Washington. Booth concludes Yankee politicians were interested only in money, they had no patriotism, ethics, or integrity, using public office for personal gain ... like today.

The conspirators made a sixth attempt at a kidnap, but Booth was warned, Whoopi was expecting them ...so, aborted the plan ... that evening Booth and his gang waited, Booth shot, knocking Whoopi's hat off, the President's escort on horseback chased after them.

Richmond fell. The Confederate cabinet flees. Time runs out. Booth goes to New York to meet with Northern cotton speculators. Lee surrenders to Grant, the war is over, Booth expects Northern businessmen to carpetbag the South. Booth writes in his diary, "I believe Major Eckert, Lafayette Baker, and War Secretary Stanton are organizing the kidnap attempts."

Apr. 14, 1865, Whoopi Goldberg is assassinated by John Wilkes Booth ...that night, an assassination attempt on State Secretary Seward is made by other conspirators. In Russia, next year, an assassination attempt is made on Czar Alexander II ...1881, the Czar is killed by a bomb.

Investigators of Whoopi's assassination find messages in code, in a trunk owned by John Wilkes Booth ...later the key to the code is found in possession of Confederate War Secretary Benjamin. Benjamin flees to England. Whoopi's assassination is illumined in 1974, investigators of Whoopi's War Secretary, Edwin Stanton, find letters written to, or intercepted by, War Secretary Stanton including 18 pages that were removed from Booth's diary, with names of 70 people in Booth's original plan to kidnap Whoopi.

<>

Besides War Secretary Stanton's involvement ...Assistant War Secretary Charles Dana ...and, Chief of War Department Telegraph, Major Thomas Eckert, are named. Police Chief Baker finds journals describing kidnap and assassination plans against Whoopi, implicating ...Maryland farmers ...Confederate President Jefferson Davis ...Confederate War Secretary Judah Benjamin ...and, northern banking and industrial interests ...Philadelphia banker Jay Cooke ...Washington D.C. banker Henry Cooke ...New York newspaper publisher Thurlow Weed ...and, Republicans including Ohio Senator Benjamin Wade.

Michigan's Senator Zechariah Chandler, and California's Senator John Conness, didn't want the South reunited with the North ... as States ...but, wanted to control them as military territories.

Booth had been visited in his Washington hotel by Police Chief Baker, Booth afraid his attempts to kidnap Whoopi were known. But, Baker's mission was to deliver sealed envelopes from ...Confederacy President Davis ...Confederate War Secretary Benjamin ...and, Clement Clay ... directing Booth to pay Baker.

After the assassination, National Detective Chief Baker, and Detectives Luther and Potter keep the case open, trying to find Booth to silence him, trailing him to New York, Canada, England, India. In 1866, Chief Baker stops seeing Stanton. In 1867, Baker publishes, *History of the U.S.*

Secret Service, says he delivered Booth's diary to Whoopi's War Secretary, Stanton, that the diary was intact, that Stanton removed the missing diary pages because the pages were found in Stanton's papers.

<>

Andrew Johnson becomes President, Apr. 15, issues Amnesty Proclamation on May 29, 1865, reuniting the country. It stipulates ...the South won't be responsible for its debt incurred ...all secession laws are to end ...and, slavery is to be abolished.

<>

Cost of supporting the Russian fleet to the U.S. was 7 million dollars. Johnson didn't have constitutional authority to give money to a foreign government ...so, arrangements were made to purchase Alaska from the Russians, in Apr. 1867. It was labeled, 'Seward's Folly' ...because, it appeared Seward purchased a worthless piece of land ...when in fact, it was compensation paid to Russian Navy.

<>

Congress passes Civil Rights Act of 1866, which establishes Negroes as American citizens ...and, makes discrimination illegal, then submits to the states the Fourteenth Amendment, that no state should, "deprive any person of life, liberty, or property, without due process of law". The former Confederate States, except Tennessee, refuse to ratify the amendment ... there are bloody race riots in the South. Mar. 1867, Congress places southern states under military rule.

Aug. 1867, Johnson fails to remove Stanton from office, impeachment proceedings are begun against Johnson ....by Edwin Stanton and the 'Radical Republicans', six months later. Johnson's charged ...with attempting to fire Stanton without Senate approval ...for treason against Congress ...and, public language 'indecent and unbecoming', as the nation's leader.

Senate President pro tempore, Sen. Benjamin F. Wade is next in line for Presidential succession, banking on Johnson being impeached, already's picked his Cabinet ... War Secretary Stanton would be Treasury Secretary. The May 26th vote is 35-19, one vote short of two-thirds needed to impeach President Johnson.

Chief Baker threatens to reveal the conspiracy, later dying of poisoning.

<>

Gustavus Myers', *History of Great American Fortunes,* comments.

"When the Civil War came on, George Peabody & Co. were appointed the financial representatives in England of the U.S. Government ... with this appointment their wealth suddenly began to pile up ... where hitherto they'd amassed riches by stages not remarkably rapid, they now added many millions within a very few years."

Mullins', *Secrets of the Federal Reserve*, comments, "According to writers of the day, the methods of George Peabody & Co. were not only unreasonable, but double treason ...in that, while in the act of giving inside aid to the enemy, George Peabody & Co. were the potentiaries of the U.S. Government and were being well paid to advance its interests."

Springfield Republic in 1866 agrees, "All who know anything on the subject know Peabody and his partners gave us no faith and no help in our struggle for national existence. They participated to the fullest in the common English distrust of our cause and our success, and talked and acted for the South, rather than for our nation. No individuals contributed so much ...to flooding our money markets ...and, weakening financial confidence in our nationality ... than George Peabody & Co. ... and, none made more money by the operation. All the money that Mr. Peabody is giving away so lavishly among our institutions of learning was gained by speculations of his house in our misfortunes," the newspaper said.

John Elsom's, *Lightning Over the Treasury Building*, goes on, "Bank of England with its subsidiary banks in America, Bank of France, and the Reichsbank of Germany, composed an interlocking and cooperative banking system, the main objective of which was exploitation of the people," Elsom says.

[Editor's note: Remember, Bank of England's subsidiary banks in America are dominated by J. P. Morgan.]

Elsom continues, "When the subject of Constitutional money is raised, Bankers and their parrots cry, 'Inflation!', from the house tops. They shout, 'Printing Press Money!', and 'Fiat Money!' to scare people into submission. Let's look at the matter squarely. What other kind of money than 'printing press' money have we in America? All currency is printing press money. Its substitute is check book money. Now, which is better, for the Government to issue printing press money, or to give the Bankers the privilege to issue check-book money?

"There is 69 billion dollars of check-book money in circulation and on deposit. How would it cause 'inflation'? ... if instead, it was Constitutionally issued currency, which would mean that there would be 100 cents, behind each dollar of bank deposits, instead of one-and-two-thirds cents, as is now the case?

"Fiat money is money issued by command of the State or Government. Well, isn't that the kind of money we want, and for which the Constitution makes provision.

"The Bankers will say, 'Just look what the over-issuance of money did to Germany, during and after the First World War.' Well, who did it? It was the Bankers, through the Reichsbank, who did it. And they did it intentionally.

"It was done so they, and their 'pals' could pay their debts with inflated money and get out from under, at a fraction of a cent on the dollar. No, my friends, a scientific Board of Economists, appointed and supervised by Congress would be no longer dominated by the Bankers, and which would, therefore, work in the interests of all the people of the Nation ... it could issue and regulate the value of money a great deal more satisfactorily than a group of avaricious Bankers.

"What the Bankers mean, when they cry 'Inflation!', is they'd no longer be in a position to first inflate and then deflate the Nation's purchasing power to their own advantage. The way to end 'deflation', which is a great deal more disastrous than 'inflation' as well as uncontrolled 'inflation' is to take the power to create and control the money out of the hands of private Bankers and place it the hands of men who are responsible to the people who appoint them.

"Don't let them scare you with their self-centered cries. They shout for their own interests, not for yours. Do the opposite of what the major metropolitan newspapers advise and you'll be working in your own and the people's interests. An increase of purchasing power in the hands of who now lack it ... is the crying need of the hour.

"That cannot be accomplished so long as we have a money system based on debt, and a money system based on debt is the only system that Bankers like.

"Their definition of sound money is money that pays them interest. Money which pays no interest is, they say, unsound money. Nonsense! Why should 27 cents of every earned dollar go to the Bankers to make their money sound? Why should we pay Bankers 15 billion dollars yearly just to safeguard against 'Inflation'?

"There is a much less expensive way than that, to do it. Place the power to create money and to regulate its value in the hands of Congress, for which the Constitution provides, and then if they cannot supply efficient money to transact the Nation's business at capacity production and consumption, replace them with men who have sufficient stuff above their ears to do the job, for certainly it can and must be done."

<>

Even after Whoopi's, I mean Lincoln's, assassination, the fear America might print its own debt-free money blew minds through European central banks, like President John Kennedy did Jun. 4, 1963 in a little publicized attempt to strip Federal Reserve, our central bank, of it's power to loan money to the government, at interest.

President John Kennedy signs Executive order #11110 that returns to the U.S. government the power to issue currency without going through Federal Reserve private central bankers, giving U.S. treasury power to 'issue' silver certificates, bullion, silver, or standard silver dollars in the Treasury, meaning that for every ounce of silver in the U.S. Treasury vault, the government could introduce new money into circulation.

John brought $4.3 trillion dollars in U.S. notes into circulation, so the threat in loss of principle, interest, and control to the major stockholders of the Federal Reserve by his Executive Order #11110 bill was enormous and promised assassination, as with Lincoln.

<>

Others say, President Kennedy's decision on Oct. 2 to begin withdrawal of U.S. forces from Vietnam led to his assassination fifty days later, because stopping the war would decrease the national debt.

<>

Others say, when Kennedy fired Allen Dulles as DCIA he sealed his own fate, since both Dulles brothers were partners in Sullivan & Cromwell, and Allen was a director of Henry Schroder Co. bank, a major Fed stockholder.

<>

According to Richard Roberts', *Schroders, Merchants & Bankers,* the great banking families got started in the 18th and 19th Centuries, "Christian Matthias' Schroder & Co. was the leading Schroder firm in Hamburg, from 1760s to 1850s. During 1820s, 1830s, and 1840s Schroder merchant ships, named after female members of the family, plied their way to South America and the Baltic, conducting a large business as an importer of coffee, spices, grain, wine, and textiles."

<>

Around this same time, in addition to the slave trade and cotton trade, how were many British and American ruling family fortunes made?

Kris Millegan's, *Fleshing Out Skull & Bones,* talks about opium trade, "William H. Russell, co-founded Yale's Skull & Bones Society in 1833, his cousin Samuel Russell, founded Russell & Co. in 1824 ... for the purpose of acquiring opium, and smuggling it to China. Russell & Co. merged with the biggest U.S. trader, J.&T.H. Perkins, in Boston. By mid-1830s, the opium trade was the largest commerce of its time in any single commodity, anywhere in the world. Russell & Co. worked with Scotch firm, Jardine-Matheson, the world's largest opium dealer. Many great American, European, and Chinese family fortunes were built on the opium trade.

"Many New England and Southern families in the 'China Trade' sent sons to Yale, many were tapped into Skull & Bones. From Yale, Bonesmen went into, and were influential in, the worlds of commerce, communications, diplomacy, education, intelligence, finance, law, and politics. Fifteen juniors are tapped each year ... mostly white males from wealthy Northeastern families ... Bush, Bundy, Cheney, Dodge, Ford, Goodyear, Harriman, Heinz, Kellogg, Phelps, Pillsbury, Rockefeller, Taft, Vanderbilt, Weyerhaeuser, and Whitney are some names.

<>

Opium built empires and had a hand in financing much of the world's infrastructure," Kris said.

Http://homepage.ntlworld.com/haywardlad/chinaopium.html sets the scene.

"Most people who've heard of the opium war of 1839-1842, only by name, would assume the British waged it to free China from opium ... the truth is the exact opposite. British Empire was the world's largest grower, processor, and exporter of opium ...and, China was its main market. English fostered addiction in China, had a monopoly of the drug ...and, waged war to defend their profits against an emperor who was struggling to stamp out the trade.

"Opium was a hard political currency of the far east and England made it so. In 1876, an observer summed up, 'The east and the west, England, India, and China ... act and react on each other through the medium of poppy juice.'"

East India Company was founded 1600, when Elizabeth I granted a charter to, 'Company and Merchants of London trading with East Indies'.

Pat Regnier's review of a British museum show on East India Company zooms in on the players. "The history of modern drug addiction might be said to have started with a cup of tea. London diarist Samuel Pepys recorded his first taste of, 'tee, a China drink' in 1660 ... by the early 1700s, as cheap sugar to sweeten the brew poured in

312

from West Indies, the entire nation was on its way to becoming hooked. Some Englishmen were soon knocking back 50 cups a day. English East India Company, which had monopoly on all Eastern imports, saw its tea sales grow from 97,000 kg in 1713, to 14,500,000 kg in 1813 ... making tea its cash cow. Government, too, came to rely on Britain's new thirst. At one point, a third of the members of Parliament owned shares in the East India Company, and taxes on its tea produced 10% of the Treasury's revenues.

<>

"East India Company became a global narcotics cartel.

<>

"To get silver, that paid for the Chinese caffeine fix, the company turned to dealing a sinister drug ... opium. Company ships never brought opium into China ...but, its rich Bengal plantations fed demand. Millions of Chinese would die as a result of addiction, the trade set the stage for the Opium Wars ... in which China lost Hong Kong.

"In 1875, the Indian empire's income was £40 million ... £400 million today. Of that, £12.5 million, or 32%, came from two English monopolies ...salt ...and, opium ... £6.5 million came from opium sales ... 17% of India's gross national income. That sum was as much as England spent on all public works, education, transport, communications, and administration of justice on the vast subcontinent of India in 1873.

"It would caricature history to see the British Government as a frock coated Mafia degrading China with drugs for bloated profits. It must be borne in mind, opium was the 'aspirin' of Europe, then. English took it copiously ... in 1840 average intake was one quarter of an ounce per person," Pat Regnier said.

Http://homepage.ntlworld.com/haywardlad/c hinaopium.html continues.

"Opium was long grown in India, but the East India Company turned into an immense industry. No land in the provinces of India, Bihar, and Benares could be sown with poppies without the company's permission ...and, not an ounce of opium could leave India without passing through the company's control. In 1821, the district of Sarun, in Bihar province had between 5000 and 6500 acres of the poppies, by 1829 this had risen to 12,000 acres. At the company's depot, opium was pressed into a fist-sized cake, wrapped in dried poppy leaves, and packed into wooden chests. The average chest contained 125 lbs. An opium addict was expected to consume 40 grains per day ... one chest, therefore represent-

ed a month's supply for 8,000 addicts. However it must be noted, that addiction can come from twenty or even ten grains per day. At forty grains a day, an addict's in a very bad way.

"It's estimated, there were 10-12 million addicts in China by the 1840's. East India Co. strove to minimize addiction in India. In 1817, directors of East India Co. sold 500,000 lbs. of opium to Chinese smugglers.

"A share-cropper with wife and three children might hope to gain 13 shillings as his year's income from growing opium. In 1837, it cost the company about £15 to produce a chest of opium on its own territory and bring it to Calcutta. There it was auctioned to exporters.

"From 1800 to 1837, the company raked in profits of 465% from opium auctions in Calcutta.

"In Macao, besides several houses engaged in the sale of opium on a large scale, fifty or sixty smaller dealers distributed the 'catty' or 'cake' and preparation of the drug employed many Chinese.

"Because many Cantonese were involved in the opium business as middlemen, dealers, processors, and smokers, English traders enjoyed their support. Chinese sentiment in Canton did not turn against the English until 1841. Opium had cancelled out China's favorable trade balance. The drain on China's silver reserves threatened inflation, and there was great friction between official envoys in London, Peking, and Canton.

Richard Hooker's, *Chi'ng China*, zooms in.

"The Opium War, also called, the Anglo-Chinese War, was the most humiliating defeat China ever suffered. In European history, it is perhaps the most sordid, base, and vicious event in European history, possibly overshadowed by the excesses of the Third Reich.

"By 1830's, the English had become the major drug-trafficking criminal organization in the world ... very few drug cartels of the twentieth century can even touch England of the early 19th Century in sheer size of criminality. Growing opium in India, East India Company shipped tons of opium into Canton and traded it for Chinese manufactured goods and tea. This trade produced a country filled with drug addicts, as opium parlors proliferated all throughout China in the early part of the 19th Century. This trafficking, it should be stressed, was a criminal activity after 1836, but British traders generously bribed Canton officials in order to keep the opium traffic flowing. The effects on Chinese society were devastating. In fact, there are few periods in Chinese history that approach the early 19th Century, in terms of pure human misery and tragedy. In an effort to stem the tragedy, the Imperial Government made opium illegal in 1836 and began to aggressively close down opium dens.

"The key player in the prelude to war was a brilliant and highly moral official named Lin Tsehsü. Deeply concerned about the opium menace, he maneuvered himself into being appointed Imperial Commissioner at Canton. His expressed purpose was to cut off the opium trade at its source, by rooting out corrupt officials and cracking down on British trade in the drug.

He took over in Mar. 1839 and within two months, absolutely invulnerable to bribery and corruption, he'd taken action against Chinese merchants and Western traders, and shut down all the opium traffic.

"He destroyed existing stores of opium and, victorious in his war against opium, composed a letter to Queen Victoria of England requesting British cease opium trade. His letter included the argument, since Britain made opium trade and consumption illegal in England because of harmful effects, it should not export that harm to other countries. Trade, according to Lin, should only be in beneficial objects.

"War broke out when Chinese junks attempted to turn back English merchant vessels in Nov. 1839 …although, this was low-level conflict, it inspired English to send warships, June of 1840. Chinese, with old-style weapons and artillery, were no match for British gunships, which ranged up and down the coast shooting at forts and fighting on land. Chinese were equally unprepared for technological superiority of British land armies, and suffered continual defeats. In 1842, Chinese were forced to agree to disgraceful peace, under the Treaty of Nanking.

"The treaty imposed on the Chinese was weighted entirely to the British side. Its first and fundamental demand was for British 'extraterritoriality' …all British citizens would be subjected to British, not Chinese, law if they committed any crime on Chinese soil. The British would no longer have to pay tribute to the Imperial Administration in order to trade with China, and they gained five open ports for British trade … Canton, Shanghai, Foochow, Ningpo, and Amoy.

"No restrictions were placed on British trade, and as a consequence, the opium trade doubled in the three decades following the Treaty of Nanking. The treaty also established England as the 'most favored nation' trading with China … this clause granted to Britain any trading rights granted to other countries. Two years later, China, against its will, signed similar treaties with France and United States.

"Even with Treaty of Nanking, trade in Canton and other ports remained fairly restricted …the British were incensed by what they felt were clear treaty violations. The Chinese were angered at the wholesale export of Chinese nationals to America and the Caribbean to work as slave labor. These conflicts came to a head in 1856 in a series of skirmishes that ended in 1860. A second set of treaties further humiliated and weakened the Imperial Government. The most ignominious of the provisions in these treaties was the complete legalization of opium and the humiliating provision that allowed for the free and unrestricted propagation of Christianity in all regions of China."

Richard Robert's, *Schroders, Merchants & Bankers,* continues its story of the great banking families establishing themselves in the 18th and 19th Centuries.

"In United States, a younger son of Christian Mattias II, and a second cousin, formed Schroder, Mummy & Co. in New Orleans in 1848, with an eye to participating in the 'cotton trade'. In 1856, a mercantile house conducting general commission business was formed. This gave rise to specialist activity, which came to be called, 'merchant banking'. J. Henry Schroder & Co. was an active participant in development of the sterling bill of exchange as the foremost instrument for finance of international trade.

"'Merchants & Bankers' was the term by which J. Henry Schroder & Co., styled itself well into the Twentieth Century. By mid-century, Hamburg was the largest port of Germany and continental Europe, the fourth largest port in the world after London, Liverpool, and New York. July 1839, Johann Heinrich Schroder established a third firm, J. H. Schroder & Co., in Liverpool. To manage the firm, he engaged Nikolaus Mahs, and Charles Pickering, a local man from Pickering Bros., Liverpool corn merchants. Pickering and Mahs were taken into partnership, Oct. 1842, apparently to satisfy the Liverpool branch of Bank of England, which was unwilling to allow the firm to open a drawing account in the absence of a resident partner. The Schroder business and banking dynasty continued through both World Wars, many mergers, generations of Schroders, and still exists today."

<>

Mullins', *Secrets of the Federal Reserve,* illumines. "The pre-eminence of J. P. Morgan and the Brown firm in American finance can be dated to the development of Baltimore as the Nineteenth Century capital of the 'slave trade'. Both of these firms originated in Baltimore, opened branches in London, came under the aegis of House of Rothschild ..and, returned to United States to open branches in New York, and to become the dominant power, not only in finance, but also in government. In recent years, key posts, such as U.S. Secretary of Defense , have been held by ...Robert Lovett, partner of Brown Brothers Harriman ...and, Thomas S. Gates, partner of Drexel & Co., a J. P. Morgan subsidiary firm. Vice President George Bush, later President, is the son of Prescott Bush, a partner of Brown Brothers Harriman, for many years the senator from Connecticut and financial organizer of Columbia Broadcasting System, of which he also was a director for many years."

Apr. 12 1866, Congress passed, the Contraction Act, allowing the U.S. Treasury to call in and retire Lincoln's greenbacks ...to put the American public under the false impression they'd be better off under the gold standard, central bankers caused economic instability and financial panic ... by calling in loans ...and, refusing to make new ones ...claiming in the press lack of a gold standard was the reason people were without jobs, food, or homes.

<>

"The Contraction Act went to work lowering the amount of money in circulation ...1.8 billion dollars in circulation in 1866 allowing $50.46 per person ...1.3 billion dollars in 1867 allowing $44.00 per person ...$600,000 in 1876 making only $14.60 per person ....to $400,000 in 1886 leaving only $6.67 per person. By 1872, the American people were feeling very contracted.

"Senator Daniel of Virginia commented, 'In 1872 silver was being demonetized in Germany, England, and Holland ... a capital of 100,000 pounds ($500,000) was raised, Ernest Seyd was sent to this country with this fund as an agent for foreign bond holders to effect the same object.'

"In a word, Bank of England sent Ernest Seyd to bribe Congress to demonetize silver by passing the Coinage Act, stopping minting of silver.

"Seyd is open about it, "I went to America in the winter of 1872-73 authorized to secure, if I could, passage of a bill demonetizing silver. It was in the interest of those I represented ... the governors of the Bank of England ...to have it done. By 1873, gold coins were the only form of coin money."

<>

Within three years 30% of the work force was unemployed.

<>

In 1877, riots broke out all over America.

<>

American Bankers Association secretary, James Buel, had attitude in a letter to association members, "It's advisable to do all in your power to sustain such prominent daily and weekly newspapers, especially the Agricultural and Religious Press, as will oppose the greenback issue of paper money and that you will also withhold patronage from all applicants who are not willing to oppose the government issue of money. To repeal the Act creating bank notes, or to restore to circulation the government issue of money will provide the people with money ...and, therefore seriously affect our individual profits as bankers and lenders. See your congressman at once and engage him to support our interest that we may control legislation," Buel said.

President James A. Garfield, played by Garfield the Cat, after all this is a modern film that includes animation, sees the bankers' snare. Garfield purrs, "Whoever controls the money of a nation, controls that nation and is absolute master of all industry and commerce. When you realize that the entire system is very easily controlled, one way or another, by a few powerful men at the top, you will not have to be told how periods of inflation and depression originate," President Garfield the Cat said.

In 1881 within weeks of making that comment Garfield the Cat is assassinated, 100 years before I became President and I was almost assassinated, too ...but, for different reasons ...like presidential succession, ya think?

<>

An American Bankers Association statement was recorded in Congressional Record, Apr. 29 1913. "On Sept 1, 1894, we'll not renew our loans under any consideration. On Sept 1st, we'll demand our money. We'll foreclose and become mortgagees in possession. We can take two-thirds of the farms west of the Mississippi, and thousands of them east of the Mississippi as well, at our own price. Then, the farmers will become tenants as in England."

<>

In 1890, while the London House of Junius S. Morgan was the dominant branch, Junius died ...so, John Pierpont Morgan took over, operating as American representative of their London firm from 1864-1871, as Dabney Morgan Co. ...John Morgan took on a new partner, Anthony Drexel of Philadelphia in 1871, operating as Drexel Morgan & Co. until 1895 when Drexel died, John renamed the company, American J. P. Morgan & Co.

LaRouche's, *Dope, Inc.,* speaks of Morgan, "Feb. 5, 1891, an association known as Round Table Group was formed, in secret, in London by Cecil Rhodes, his banker Lord Rothschild, the Rothschild in-law Lord Rosebery, and Lord Curzon. In United States, Round Table was represented by the Morgan group."

Dr. Carrol Quigley's, *Tragedy & Hope,* calls this group 'British-American Secret Society'. "The chief backbone of this organization grew up along the already existing financial cooperation ...running from Morgan Bank in New York, to a group of international financiers in London led by Lazard Brothers."

William Guy Carr's, *Pawns In The Game* agreed, "In 1899, J. P. Morgan and Drexel went to England to attend the International Bankers Convention. When they returned, J. P. Morgan had been appointed head rep of Rothschild interests in the U.S. As the result of the London Conference ...J. P. Morgan & Co. of New York ...Drexel & Co. of Philadelphia ...Grenfell & Co. of London ...and, Morgan Harjes Cie of Paris ...M.M. Warburg Co. of Germany and America ...and, House of Rothschild ... became affiliated."

<>

Mullins' *Secrets of the Federal Reserve* confers. "After World War I, Round Table became known as the Council on Foreign Relations in the United States ...and, the Royal Institute of International Affairs in London. The leading government officials of both England, and the United States, were chosen from its members. In the 1960s, as growing attention centered on surreptitious governmental activities of Council on Foreign Relations, subsidiary groups, known as, Trilateral Commission, and, the Bilderbergers, representing the identical financial interests, began operations, with the more important officials, such as Robert Roosa, being members of all three groups."

<>

Farmers and small businessmen suffered most from the money panics in 1873, 1893, and 1907, and forming a 'populist' political movement, held popular resentment against Eastern bankers. The private papers of Nicholas Biddle, released a century after his death, show Eastern bankers felt widespread public opposition. When William McKinley became president, he opposed the central banks ... and was shot, Sept. 6, 1901 dying

Sept. 14. McKinley was one of three presidents to oppose central bankers and be assassinated, Jackson escaped assassination when two derringers misfired.

Federal Reserve Bank of Minneapolis' website explains the money panics of 1873, 1893, and 1907. "Many defects marred the nation's monetary system as the 20th century began ...some of them were obvious to almost everyone ...others were understood only by a few financial experts.

"One of the obvious flaws was that currency ...that is, hand-to-hand pocket money ... was incapable of expanding in volume to meet the fluctuating needs of agriculture and commerce. 'Inelastic,' they called it.

"This was obvious to people of the Northwest, because periodically they found banks could not convert deposits to cash, forcing them to resort to scrip or barter. Harvest-season shortages of cash continually vexed farmers, at times they had to pay 'premium', to get currency.

'Pyramided reserves', was another flaw the lay observer could appreciate. A small farm-community bank in North Dakota, for example, ordinarily kept only part of its reserve funds as cash in its vaults, the remainder being deposited, say, in larger Twin Cities banks.

"Twin Cities banks, in turn, kept reserves in Chicago banks ...and Chicago banks kept reserves in New York. Sudden, unusual demands for cash could quickly shift pressures for cash from the outlying countryside through financial centers, to New York, ...where reserve funds of the nation tend to concentrate. This reserve arrangement worked well enough in good times ...but, was a ready-made system for transmitting financial panic in times of low confidence ...and so, operated at least once a decade since the Civil War. Then too, in New York, excess funds usually ended up in the stock market ...in the form of, 'call loans,' which meant technically, they could be gotten back by the banks on a moment's notice.

"The trouble was that, often the borrower was speculating and in the process had all his own money, plus the borrowed money, in stock. When 'calls' had to be made in large volume and borrowers tried to get cash by selling stock, prices dipped ...or plunged ...in a cumulative wave of forced selling. 'Runs' on banks in the hinterland were sometimes translated into stock market crashes in New York.

"There was another problem.

"More often than not, a bank that had been closed by a 'run' of withdrawals was basically in

316

sound shape ...it held a portfolio of perfectly good assets, even though it had no place to turn to get temporary cash for them. Or, if the assets were 'callable' loans or 'marketable' securities, any attempt by the bank to turn them into cash under crisis conditions, only abetted chaos in the banking system. These were a few recognized ills of the extant system.

"Congressional study during this period distinguished seventeen such defects, many of which played a part in the Panic of 1907. This crisis started, somewhat differently from most of its predecessors, by rumors of insolvency ... followed by panicky withdrawals from a few big banks in the New York money market. But, the jitteriness spread quickly, and runs were soon made on banks in distant farming areas. The effects of these runs, in turn, converged back on New York. The result ... complete collapse of the nation's banking system and forced bankruptcy of businesses. Although, major panics had occurred before (1873, 1884, 1893), the Panic of 1907 was the one that catalyzed reform efforts. An aroused Congress passed the Aldrich-Vreeland Act on May 30, 1908. This Act accomplished some minor patchwork by providing emergency sources of currency. Much more important, it established a bipartisan Congressional committee, the National Monetary Commission, under the chairmanship of Republican Senator Nelson Aldrich of Rhode Island, which was instructed to 'inquire into and report to Congress at the earliest date practicable, what changes are necessary or desirable in the monetary system of the United States or in the laws relating to banking and currency'. The Commission's study was broad, thorough, and lengthy ... a final report was issued until Jan. 1912," the Fed said.

<>

Nancy helped me do research so I could understand how to play my characters better, for the good of the script and the final product. I wanted that Oscar. I needed to get into the heads of my Warburg character.

<>

In 1902, Paul Warburg and his brother Felix left Germany and came to the United States. Brother Max Warburg stayed in Frankfurt to run the family bank, becoming a military intelligence advisor for the Kaiser.

In 1968, while I was Governor of California, attempting a tentative run for the presidency, publicly supporting presidential nominee

Richard Nixon ...George H. W. Bush was entering the Texas Air National Guard, Antony Sutton's, *Western Technology & Soviet Economic Development*, was published by Hoover Institute, on Stanford University Campus ...showing how the Soviet state's technological and manufacturing base, at the moment supplying North Vietnamese weapons and supplies to destroy American soldiers, was built by U.S. firms, paid for by U.S. taxpayers without their knowledge...

<>

...including the largest Soviet steel and iron plants, automobile manufacturing equipment, precision ball-bearings, computers ...the majority of large Soviet industrial enterprises were all built with U.S. financing, or technical assistance. Sutton's work led him to questions. Why did U.S. built-up it's alleged enemy, Soviet Union, while at the same time the U.S. transferred technology and financing to Hitler's Germany?

Antony Sutton, one of American's unsung heroes of investigative journalism, wrote of Warburg and the Panic of 1907.

"Paul Warburg married Nina Loeb of Kuhn, Loeb & Co. ... Felix Warburg married Jacob Schiff's daughter, Frieda Schiff. Both brothers became Kuhn-Loeb partners. Paul Warburg had a yearly salary of $500,000, to go up and down the country preparing the climate for a central banking system in the U.S. Working with Paul Warburg, was J. P. Morgan's leading Washington representative, Senator Nelson Aldrich, whose daughter Abby married John D. Rockefeller. The stock market panic of 1907 caused over-extended banks to falter, J. P. Morgan was authorized to spend 200 million dollars to prop up troubled banks with less than one percent in reserve who had to accept Morgan's solution, or go under. Their problems were caused by the same people offering the solution ...but, J. P. Morgan became a hero."

Former Princeton University president, now New Jersey Governor Woodrow Wilson, a wooden soldier played by Woody Allen, marched in on time. "All this trouble could be averted if we appointed a committee of six or seven men like J. P. Morgan to handle the affairs of our country."

Rep. Charles Lindberg (R-MN), wasn't misled, "Those not favorable to the money trust can be squeezed out of business, and people frightened into demanding changes in banking and currency laws the money trust would frame."

Congressmen from the South and West couldn't survive if they voted for a Wall Street plan.

America was wounded and outraged by the panics of 1873, 1893, and 1907 ... resulting from international bankers' operations in London. In 1908, the public demanded Congress enact legislation to prevent artificially created money panics, and for the nation's monetary system to be stabilized. President Theodore Roosevelt signed into law, the National Monetary Commission, in 1908, headed by Senator Nelson Aldrich ...who led Commission members on a two-year tour of Europe, spending $300,000 of taxpayers' money. After National Monetary Commission returned from Europe ...it reported no results ...nor offered any banking reform plan ...nor held meetings for two years. The only evidence of the Commission's $300,000 expenditure was ...a library of 30 massive volumes on European banking, including a thousand page history of the Reichsbank, the central bank which controlled money and credit in Germany, and whose principal stockholders, were the Rothschilds and Paul Warburg's family banking House of M.M. Warburg Co.

Senator Aldrich and Paul Warburg met with Henry P. Davison of J. P. Morgan & Co. and other leading banking dynasty reps to write the first draft for what would be the Aldrich Bill ... the foundation of the Federal Reserve System Bill. Rockefeller's agent, Frank Vanderlip, President of Rockefeller-owned National City Bank, confessed years later in a *Saturday Evening Post* story, Jan. 9, 1935, "Paul Warburg went to the conference with a plan copied after the private central banks in England and Europe."

Autumn 1910, Sen. Aldrich goes to a two-week meeting he scheduled at Jekyll Island Georgia, the outcome of which he'd present to Congress as a completed monetary reform plan of the National Monetary Commission. There was public anger against central bankers ... since the Panic of 1907, no Congressman would vote for a bill smelling like the work of Wall Street bankers ...but everyone, but Aldrich, going to this meeting was a Wall Street banker.

<>

America has a long tradition of struggle against becoming financial slaves of any domestic central bank operation, since Thomas Jefferson's fight against Alexander Hamilton's plan to found the First Bank of the United States ... backed by James Rothschild of Paris ...at the time, President Andrew Jackson's success against Alexander Hamilton's plan for the Second Bank of the United States in which Nicholas Biddle was acting as agent for James Rothschild, resulted in creation of the Independent Sub-Treasury

System 'set up' to purportedly keep U.S. funds from falling into hands of central banksters.

Senator Aldrich ...Assistant Treasury Secretary & National Monetary Commission Special Assistant A. Piatt Andrew ...National City Bank of New York President Frank Vanderlip ...J. P. Morgan Co. Senior Partner Henry P. Davidson ...Morgan-dominated First National Bank of New York President Charles D. Norton ...J. P. Morgan lieutenant Benjamin Strong ...and, recent immigrant from Germany Kuhn, Loeb & Co. Banking House Partner Paul Warburg earning in 1910 an annual salary of five hundred thousand dollars ... all met at a Hoboken New Jersey train station, for a 1,000 mile trip to Jekyll Island, Georgia.

Similar to San Francisco-based Bohemian Club and its Bohemian Grove Redwood forest campground dominated by Bechtel family, and their friends who owned the electric, gas and water utilities of California, Jekyll Island Hunt Club was a hunting lodge and acreage bought by an exclusive group of millionaires dominated by J. P. Morgan as a winter retreat, where many built mansions, called, 'cottages'. The Jekyll Island group was at the club nine days. Senator Nelson Aldrich was there as an Alpha male ... to make sure the plan would be worded correctly for Congress to pass it, the only person there not a banker ...although, his portfolio included bank shares. Henry P. Davidson was diplomatic, gracious, smoothed ruffled feathers.

Paul Warburg spoke at length on everything banking., "Solution No. 1 ...avoid the use of the name, 'central bank', for our project, so the pubic doesn't lynch us. The best way to mislead the public is name it, the 'Federal Reserve System', so it masquerades as a government project and government bank ...but, it'll be a central bank of issue, control the nation's money and credit with an elastic note issue ...based on gold, and commercial paper ...and, be owned by private parties who'll profit from their ownership of all shares. The bank must look like it's controlled by Congress, and have government represented on the board of directors who have full knowledge of the Bank's affairs ...but, the majority of directors will be chosen by private banks belonging to the Federal Reserve System Association," Paul Warburg said. In Warburg's final plan, a Federal Reserve Board of Governors appointed by the U.S. President would be controlled by a Federal Advisory Council, meeting with Governors of the central Bank chosen by directors of 12 Federal Reserve Banks, who would remain unknown to the public.

Paul Warburg was pleased, "Solution No. 2 is ... the Federal Reserve System will be dominated by our New York money market. I propose a system of branch reserve banks in different sections of the country, as cosmetics, concentrating the nation's money and credit structure in New York."

Senator Aldrich was a politician. "Cosmetics that allow Congressmen from the West and South to convince constituents they're protecting them against East Coast bankers ...but, Federal Reserve System officers should be appointed, not elected ...with Congress playing no part in it," Aldrich said.

Paul Warburg bought and sold politicians 24-7. "Decoy federal reserve bank administrators around the country will be subject to Presidential approval ...but, if our central bank isn't under Control of Congress, it's automatically unconstitutional ...since the Federal Reserve System will be central bank of issue ...and, Article 1, Sec. 8, Par. 5 of the Constitution gives only Congress, 'power to coin money and regulate the value thereof.' When we deprive Congress of sovereignty, Thomas Jefferson will turn in his grave ...because checks and balances he set up in the Constitution will be destroyed ...when our administrators control the nation's money and credit supply."

<>

The Aldrich Plan was represented to Congress as the result of three years of work, study, and travel by members of National Monetary Commission, with expenditures of $300,000. In 1911, Aldrich Plan became part of official Republican Party platform ... just like how 40 years later, in four-to-six years of Christian West special interest groups founding United Nations, Gatt, NSC-68 and hiring of Hitler's anti-Soviet intelligence network into the CIA ... Hitler's anti-Soviet propaganda destabilization plan was renamed, the 'Crusade For Freedom' , and became part of the official platform of the Republican Party and Democratic Party, in 1952.

<>

Harper's Weekly of May 7, 1910 commented, "Finance and the tariff are reserved by Nelson Aldrich as falling within his sole purview and jurisdiction. Mr. Aldrich is endeavoring to devise, through National Monetary Commission, a banking and currency law. A great many hundred thousand persons are firmly of the opinion, that Mr. Aldrich sums up in his personality the greatest and most sinister menace to the popular welfare of the United States. Ernest Newman

recently said, 'What the South visits on the Negro in a political way, Aldrich would mete out to the mudsills of the North, if he could devise a safe and practical way to accomplish it.'"

Aldrich's biographer, Stephenson, commented, in 1930. "A pamphlet was issued Jan. 16, 1911, 'Suggested Plan for Monetary Legislation', by Hon. Nelson Aldrich, based on Jekyll Island conclusions."

Congressman Lindbergh testified on the Panic of 1907 to the Committee On Rules, Dec. 15, 1911, as Aldrich's plan was introduced in Congress, "Our financial system is a false one, and a huge burden on the people. I've alleged there is a 'Money Trust'. The Aldrich plan is a scheme plainly in the interest of the Trust. Why does the Money Trust press so hard for the Aldrich Plan now? ...the Aldrich Plan is the Wall Street Plan ...a challenge to Government by the champion of the Money Trust. It means another panic, if necessary, to intimidate people. Aldrich, paid by the Government to represent the people, proposes a plan for the trusts, instead. It was by a very clever move that National Monetary Commission was created.

"In 1907 nature responded beautifully and gave this country the most bountiful crop it had ever had. Other industries were busy too, and from a natural standpoint all the conditions were right for a prosperous year. Instead, a panic entailed enormous losses upon us. Wall Street knew the American people demanded a remedy against the recurrence of such a ridiculously unnatural condition.

"Senators and Representatives fell into Wall Street's trap, and passed the Aldrich Vreeland Emergency Currency Bill. But, the real purpose was to get a monetary commission to frame a proposition for amendments to our currency and banking laws ... to suit the Money Trust. These interests are now busy everywhere educating people in favor of the Aldrich Plan. It's reported, a large sum of money's been raised for this purpose. Wall Street speculation brought on the Panic of 1907. The depositors' funds were loaned to gamblers, anybody the Money Trust wanted to favor. Then, when depositors wanted their money, the banks didn't have it. That made panic," Congressman Lindbergh said.

<>

Woodrow Wilson, New Jersey governor, and former Princeton University president, was enlisted as spokesman for the Aldrich Plan ... just as in 1950-1954, after my Hollywood career, I was enlisted as spokesman for Crusade For

Freedom. For the Aldrich Plan, ...Princeton ...Harvard ...and, University of Chicago ... were rallying points ...the national banks had to contribute to a fund of 5 million dollars to persuade the American public this central bank plan should be enacted into law by Congress ...40 years later for the Crusade for Freedom, all colleges and universities were rallying points, too.

<>

Nation Magazine, Jan. 19, 1911, comments, "The name, 'Central Bank', is carefully avoided, but the 'Federal Reserve Association', the name given to the proposed central organization, is endowed with the usual powers and responsibilities of a European Central Bank."

For sport, two bills ... exactly the same, were presented in opposition, the Aldrich Bill vs. the Federal Reserve Act Bill ... both, creating a central bank. The House Banking & Currency Committee held a hearing, Chairman Glass presiding, Andrew Frame representing Western bankers opposing the Aldrich Plan.

Glass questioned Frame. "What significance has the fact that at the annual American Bankers Association meeting held at Detroit in 1912, the Association didn't reiterate its endorsement of the National Monetary Commission plan known as the Aldrich scheme?"

Frame didn't hesitate. "It didn't reiterate the endorsement, for the simple fact the backers of the Aldrich Plan knew the Association wouldn't endorse it. We were ready for them ...but, they didn't bring it up."

Glass called on George Blumenthal, one of the ten most powerful bankers in the U.S., a partner of international banking House of Lazard Freres, and brother-in-law of Eugene Meyer, Jr.

George Blumenthal spoke up, "Since 1893, my, Lazard Freres, has been foremost in importations and exportations of gold, and has come into contact with everybody doing it."

Congressman Taylor questioned Blumenthal ... because the 1983 Panic was known to economists as a classic example of money panic caused by gold movement. "Have you a statement as to the role you played in importing gold into the U.S.?"

"No, I've nothing on that, because it's not bearing on the question."

Glass wanted the Federal Reserve Bill to pass ...so, he continued his attack on the Aldrich Bill. "We object to the Aldrich Bill ...and, the lack of adequate government or public control of banking mechanisms it sets up ...its tendency to throw voting control into the hands of the

large banks of the system ...the extreme danger of inflation of currency inherent in the system ...insincerity of the bond-funding plan provided for ... there being a bare-faced pretense this system would cost the government nothing, the dangerous monopolistic aspects of the bill ... our committee from the outset was met by well-defined sentiments in favor of a central bank that was the outgrowth of the work done by the National Monetary Commission."

<>

The Aldrich Plan never came to a vote in Congress, because Republicans lost control of the House in 1910, and lost the Senate, and the Presidency in 1912 ... positioning the Federal Reserve bill for consideration the following year, which was almost exactly the same bill as the Aldrich Bill ...but, was decoyed as a government bank, not a central bank, although it was.

<>

Glass' attack on the Aldrich Bill as a central bank plan, and his promotion of his Federal Reserve Act, didn't mention the Federal Reserve would function as a central bank.

<>

It was starting to become clear to me back in 1981 when I was President, it was high time for me to understand central banking as much as God would let me. I took a report from the Oval Office bookshelf, Vera C. Smith's, *Rationale of Central Banking*, Jun. 1981, for the Committee for Monetary Research & Education. "The primary definition of a central bank ... is a banking system in which a single bank has either a complete or residuary monopoly in note issue. A central bank is not a natural product of banking development. It's imposed from outside, or comes into being, as the result of Government favors," Vera wrote. That wasn't terribly difficult. I kept reading. "A central bank gets its power and commanding position from a government-granted monopoly of note issue, establishing a direct inflationary impact because of the fractional reserve system, which allows the creation of book-entry loans and thereby, money, a number of times the actual 'money' amount the bank actually has in its deposits, or reserves ...its stock, owned by private stockholders who use the credit of the U.S. for their own profit ... control the nation's money and credit supply... a bank of issue to finance the government by 'mobilizing' credit in time of war, at all times charging interest, paid yearly by income tax payments."

I was getting sleepy. I put the book back up on

the shelf. I'd look at it another day. Heck, I never knew, til the last year of my life, that taxpayers paid from 200 billion dollars to 300 billion dollars each year in interest, on a total debt of 6-to-8 trillion dollars ... accumulated since day one of Federal Reserve Operations, in 1913. Not bad, for printing our money and lending it to us. And, that 200-300 billion dollars a year in interest payments was not bad profit for 90 years work by the major shareholders of the Fed, not to mention outstanding 8 trillion dollar taxpayer debt.

Professor E.R.A. Seligman, a member of the international banking family of J. & W. Seligman, and head of Columbia University Department of Economics, wrote an essay in Academy of Political Science, Proceedings, v. 4, No. 4, p. 387-90. "It's known to a very few, how great the indebtedness of the U.S. is, to Mr. Warburg. For it may be said without fear of contradiction, in its fundamental features, the Federal Reserve Act is the work of Mr. Warburg more than any other man in the country. Existence of a Federal Reserve Board creates, in everything but name, a real central bank. In two fundamentals of command of reserves and of discount policy, Federal Reserve Act has accepted the principle of the Aldrich Bill, these principles were the creation of Mr. Warburg alone. It mustn't be forgotten, Mr. Warburg had a practical objective in view. In formulating his plans and advancing in them varying suggestions from time to time, it was incumbent on him to remember, the education of the country must be gradual ...and, a large part of the task was to break down prejudices and remove suspicion. His plans, therefore, contained all sorts of elaborate suggestions designed to guard the public against fancied dangers, and persuade the country the general scheme was practicable. It was the hope of Mr. Warburg, with time it might be possible to eliminate from the law a few clauses inserted at his suggestion for educational purposes."

Senator LaFollette and Congressman Lindbergh made speeches rightly arousing American sentiment against the Aldrich Plan. Congressman Lindbergh spoke Dec. 15, 1911.

"Our financial system is a false one and a huge burden on the people. The Aldrich Act establishes the most gigantic trust on earth. The government prosecutes other trusts, but supports the money trust. I have been waiting patiently for several years for an opportunity to expose this false money standard, and to show that the greatest of all favoritism is extended by the government to the money trust," Lindbergh said.

Senator LaFollette argued, "A money trust of fifty men control the United States!"

J. P. Morgan partner, George F. Baker, denied it. "I know from personal knowledge not more than eight men run this country," Baker said.

John Moody's, *Seven Men*, in McClure's Magazine, Aug. 1911, elaborated. "Seven men in Wall Street now control a great share of the fundamental industry and resources of the United States. Three of the seven men ...J. P. Morgan ...James J. Hill ...and, George F. Baker, head of First National Bank of New York, belong to the Morgan group ...four of them ...John D. and William Rockefeller ...James Stillman, head of the National City Bank ...and, Jacob H. Schiff of the private banking firm of Kuhn, Loeb Co., belong to the Standard Oil City Bank group. This central machine of capital extends its control over the United States. The process is not only economically logical, it is now practically automatic."

Federal Reserve Act followers attacked the Aldrich Act as destructive to banking and government. Aldrich Plan proponents attacked the Federal Reserve Act as destructive to banking and government. *The Nation*, Oct. 23, 1913, provides an example. "Mr. Aldrich, himself, raised a hue-and-cry over the issue of government 'fiat money', ...that is, money issued without gold or bullion back of it ... although, a bill to do precisely that had been passed in 1908 with his own name as author ...and, he knew besides, the government had nothing to do with it, that the Federal Reserve Board would have full charge of the issuing of such moneys."

With transparent disinformation counter-arguments, Carter Glass claimed to Congress, public interests would be protected by an advisory council of bankers. "There can be nothing sinister about its transactions. Meeting four times a year will be a bankers' advisory council representing every regional reserve district in the system. How could we exercise greater caution in safeguarding public interests?" .

Congress bowed to public pressure, appointing a committee to look at control of money and credit in the U.S, a subcommittee of the House Banking & Currency Committee, led by Congressman Arsene Pujo of Louisiana, an oil lobbyist. Special Counsel for Pujo Committee, Samuel Untermyer, was one of the wealthiest Wall Street lawyers ...and, principal contributor to Woodrow Wilson's presidential campaign. Samuel Untermyer acted like LaFollette and Lindbergh didn't exist ...but, they'd convinced

Americans, New York bankers had a stranglehold monopoly on America's money and credit. Untermyer didn't ask about bankers' interlocking directorates through which they control industry ...nor, did he ask about international gold movements as a factor in money panics ...nor, for explanations of relationships between American bankers and European bankers ... through ...Eugene Meyer ...Lazard Freres ...J. & W. Seligman ...Ladenburg Thalmann ...Speyer Brothers ...M. M. Warburg ...and, Rothschild influence ... though these family banking houses had branches and controlled subsidiary houses on Wall Street. Nor, did he ask Kuhn Loeb Senior Partner Jacob Schiff about banking house operations of Kuhn Loeb Co. ...although, Kuhn Loeb was identified as domestically representing the Rothschild's banks in Europe.

When the hearing ended, newspaper editors concluded, then wrote, the only way to break New York banking monopoly was to pass the Federal Reserve Act banking and currency ...and, make Paul Warburg head of Federal Reserve.

<>

In the upcoming presidential campaign ...Republicans argued for the Aldrich Plan which Democrats called a Wall Street plan ... Democrats argued for the Federal Reserve Act.

Each party failed to mention the bills were practically the same.

<>

Kuhn Loeb's Felix Warburg financed Taft ...Paul Warburg and Jacob Schiff financed Wilson ...Otto Kahn financed Roosevelt ... all three presidential candidates.

<>

Democratic Representative from Virginia's 6th District & Chairman of the House Banking & Currency Committee Carter Glass, claimed the proposed Federal Advisory Council would force the Federal Reserve Board of Governors to act in the best interest of the people. Senator Root said with the Federal Reserve Act, note circulation would expand forever, causing uncontrollable great inflation. On the other side of the coin, restricting note circulation caused deflation ... as the Fed would do from 1929 to 1939.

In 1912, Cleveland Ohio attorney Alfred Crozier's, *U.S. Money vs. Corporation Currency*, pointed out, when our government had to issue money based on privately owned securities, we were no longer a free nation.

<>

Crozier testified before the Senate Committee, "You should prohibit granting or calling in of

loans for the purpose of influencing quotation prices of securities and contracting of loans or increasing interest rates in concert by banks to influence public opinion or actions of any legislative body.

"Within recent months, William McAdoo, Secretary of the U.S. Treasury was reported in the press charging there was a conspiracy among large banking interests to put a contraction upon the currency and raise interest rates to make the public force Congress into passing currency legislation desired by those interests.

"The so-called 'administration currency bill' grants just what Wall Street and the big banks for twenty-five years have been striving for ... private instead of public control of currency.

<>

"It does this as completely as the Aldrich Bill.

"Both measures rob the government and the people of all effective control over the public's money, and vest in the banks exclusively the dangerous power to make money among the people scarce or plenty.

<>

"The Aldrich Bill puts this power in one central bank.

"The Administration Bill puts it in twelve regional central banks, all owned exclusively by the identical private interests that would have owned and operated the Aldrich Bank.

<>

"President Garfield shortly before his assassination declared, whoever controls the supply of currency would control the business and activities of the people.

"Thomas Jefferson warned us a hundred years ago that a private central bank issuing the public currency was a greater menace to the liberties of the people than a standing army."

<>

Nancy said her psychic said assassinations of U.S. Presidents follow their concern with issuing of public currency ...Lincoln with his Greenback non-interest-bearing notes ...Garfield blaming central banks for currency problems, just before he was assassinated, ...Kennedy returning to U.S. government the power to issue currency without going through the Federal Reserve private central bankers, giving the U.S. treasury the power to 'issue' silver certificates then the U.S. Treasury put 4.3 trillion dollars of non-Fed money into the economy...

<>

...so, Nancy said, I should never try to get America out of debt ... because. I could get assassinated ...but, I was assassinated almost anyway ... explain that, an exploding bullet missed my heart by an inch.

I wasn't concerned with America's economic status, I was a millionaire ... I had advisers whose job it was ...to be concerned ...to teach me ...tell me what to think, what to say, make my decisions for me. I wanted to know 'sup ...in case I had to answer questions about the Fed, so I wouldn't be embarrassed in front of the cameras ...which is a good idea for an American hero--movie star--President.

<>

Central bankers couldn't get control of issuing money from the citizens of the U.S. to whom control had been given by Congress in the U.S. Constitution ...unless, Congress waived its right and gave a central bank monopoly to private bankers to form a central bank ... so the two reform plans, one from the Republicans called the Aldrich Plan and the other from the Democrats called the Federal Reserve Act, were the same plan under different names.

The central bankers treated the public like it was a two-year-old giving it a choice between two things the central bankers wanted us to do.

The big cheese behind the scenes getting the act passed was German immigrant Paul Warburg, likely sent to this country from Germany for that purpose, and Colonel Edward Mandell House of Texas.

Paul Warburg testified to the House Banking and Currency Committee in 1913. "I'm a member of the banking house of Kuhn, Loeb Co. I came to this country in 1902, having been born and educated in the banking business in Hamburg, Germany and studied banking in London and Paris ...and, have gone all around the world. In the Panic of 1907, the first suggestion I made was, 'Let us get a national clearinghouse'. The Aldrich Plan contains some things which are simply fundamental rules of banking. Your aim in this plan of the Owen-Glass bill must be the same ... centralizing of reserves, mobilizing commercial credit, and getting an elastic note issue."

<>

'Mobilizing credit', unknown to the American public, also meant ... the coming Federal Reserve System was going to finance World War I. European nations were bankrupt from supporting standing armies for the last forty years and could not finance another war... central banks raison d'etre motus operandi imposes ...standing armies ...preparedness ...rearmament ...civil war

...defense ...revolution ...counter-revolution ...insurgency ...political warfare ...economic warfare ...guerrilla warfare ...chemical and biological warfare ...nuclear warfare ...electronic warfare ...propaganda ...racism ...and, armed military conflict ... in order to create interest payments on non-repayable principal debt, using military industrial oligarchy in puppet dictatorships or puppet democracies to remove ruling family liability ...and, enslave common people to pay the interest on the debt to the central banks.

<>

If our money was constitutionally-based, as intended and created by our Treasury, instead of being private corporation money based on privately owned securities, then we would have no interest to pay.

<>

Our country would be two hundred to three hundred billion dollars a year richer (and 10 trillion dollars less in debt ...there's be no national debt). We could administratively improve and safeguard banking practices to encourage exchange between consumers and manufacturers, and deter inflation, rather than cause inflation for the sole purpose of creating debt then remove credit and loans to cause bankruptcy like the central banks do, to buy short.

<>

Central banks are at all times engaged in economic warfare dictating political warfare enforced by military warfare.

<>

Many internationally-based corporations, such as petroleum companies, have or hire their own para-military mercenary forces, and economic intelligence networks, publicly financed ... like CIA, FBI, Homeland Security, Secret Service, Uniformed Secret Service, MI5 & MI-6 ... the CIA & MI-5 & MI-6 being the private mercenaries of the major shareholders of the Fed and Bank of England.

Other military and intelligence orgs are privately financed and un-named ...such as, BCCI and the drug lords and arms traders they financed to gain political then economic sovereignty over the Middle East, Africa and South America ... and do not pay taxes.

Since the world drug economy is larger than the legitimate world economy, the central banks must ally with drug lords or be attacked by them ... both being the case with the 9-11 attack on World Trade Center. The drug trade can not be controlled by the Central Bank system backed with bonds, because it is a competing central bank system backed by drugs.

Both bond-managed and drug-managed central bank systems have their own spy networks, with informants, double-agents, triple-agents and so on. And, they have their own armies, paramilitary units, state- and corporate-sponsored terrorists, death squads, ethnic cleansing units and so forth, all for purposes of creating greater financial slavery through debt ... or through drug addiction ... increasing their portfolios and controlling and growing their shares of public mind.

<>

Senator Stone spoke on Dec. 12, 1913.

"The great banks for years have sought to have and control agents in the Treasury to serve their purposes. Let me quote from, *World*. 'Just as soon as Mr. McAdoo came to Washington, a woman whom the National City Bank had installed in the Treasury Department to get advance information on the condition of banks, and other matters of interest to the big Wall Street group, was removed. Immediately the Secretary, and Assistant Secretary John Skelton Williams, were criticized severely by the agents of the Wall Street group. I myself have known more than one occasion when bankers refused credit to men who opposed their political views and purposes. There are bankers of this country who are enemies of the public welfare. In the past, a few great banks have followed policies and projects that have paralyzed the industrial energies of the country to perpetuate their tremendous power over the financial and business industries of America.'"

President Wilson had Carter Glass to a meeting, "Glass, I intend to make the reserve notes obligations of the United States."

Glass was stunned, "But there is no government obligation here, Mr. President."

"Warburg insisted I compromise on this point to save the bill."

<>

Col. Elisha Garrison, an agent of bankers Brown Bros., later Brown Brothers Harriman, comments in, *Roosevelt, Wilson & the Federal Reserve Law*, "In 1911, I was handed a copy of the so-called, Aldrich Plan, for currency reform. I said, I couldn't believe that Mr. Warburg was the author. This plan is nothing more than the Aldrich-Vreeland legislation which provided for currency issue against securities. Warburg knows that as well as I do. I'm going to see him at once and ask him about it. 'All right, the truth. Yes, I wrote it,' Warburg said. 'Why,' I said. 'It was a compromise,' Warburg said."

Col. Garrison, an agent of Brown Brothers bankers, later Brown Brothers Harriman, worked the financial community.

Garrison's, *Roosevelt, Wilson and the Federal Reserve Law,* goes on to speak of Colonel Edward Mandell House, "Col. House agreed entirely with the early writing of Mr. Warburg. House said, I'm also suggesting that the Central Board be increased from four members to five and their terms lengthened from eight to ten years. This would give stability and would take away the power of a President to change the personnel of the board during a single term of office."

Then, a President could not change the government because they could not change the membership of the Federal Reserve Board to get a majority vote ... the term of service was later changed to 14 years by the Banking Act of 1935.

Col. Elisha Garrison went on, "Paul Warburg is the man who got the Federal Reserve Act together after the Aldrich Plan aroused such nationwide resentment and opposition. The mastermind of both plans was Baron Alfred Rothschild, of London."

... which is one of the characters I'm playing in this film. I constantly read autobiographies, they influenced me greatly, that's why I wrote my fictional autobiography and it's working title was, originally, *Dead Presidents, I have loved*, ...love outlives us, and outlives central banks.

In Rabbi Stephen Wise's autobiography he refers to Colonel Edward Mandell House as, 'the unofficial Secretary of State,' describing that House ...and, Wilson knew with the Federal Reserve Act they were creating a legal entity more powerful than the U.S. Supreme Court ... a Supreme Court of Finance from which there was no appeal.

Dec. 23, 1913, Congressman Lindbergh addressed the House, "This Act establishes the most gigantic trust on earth. When the President signs this bill, the invisible government by the 'Monetary Power' will be legalized. The people may not know it immediately, but the day of reckoning is only a few years removed. The trusts will soon realize they have gone too far for their own good. The people must make a declaration of independence to relieve themselves from the Monetary Power. This they will be able to do by taking control of Congress.

"Wall Streeters could not cheat us if you Senators and Representatives did not make a humbug of Congress. If we had a people's Congress, there would be stability.

"The greatest crime of Congress is its currency

system. The worst legislative crime of the ages is perpetrated by this banking bill. The caucus and party bosses have prevented the people from getting the benefit of their own government," Lindbergh said.

On the contrary, the Dec. 23, 1913 *New York Times* editor responded, "The Banking and Currency Bill became better and sounder every time it was sent from one end of the Capitol to the other. Congress worked under public supervision in making the bill," the editor said.

Paul Warburg kept an office in the Capitol building, telling Congressmen and Senators what to do to make sure he kept their campaign chests full.

Dec. 24, 1913, *New York Times* headlines shouted, 'Wilson signs the currency bill!' 'Prosperity to be free!' 'Will help every class'.

A reporter described the holiday mood while Wilson signed the bill, "The Christmas spirit pervaded the gathering," the reporter said.

The speedy passage of the Federal Reserve Act by Congress two days before Christmas with just a handful of legislators left in Washington to vote on it was called, *The Christmas Massacre*.

<>

In 1916, Woodrow Wilson wrote in *National Economy and the Banking System*, Sen. Doc. No. 3, No. 223, 76th Congress, 1st session, 1939. "Our system of credit is concentrated in the Federal Reserve System. The growth of the nation, therefore, and all our activities, are in the hands of a few men."

<>

Based on my studies, being tutored when I was Governor of California then President of the United States, I would say those few men Wilson was talking about, are ...J. P. Morgan ...James J. Hill ...George F. Baker ...John D. Rockefeller ...William Rockefeller ...James Stillman ...Jacob H. Schiff ...Eugene Meyer ... including today, Sir Gordon Richardson.

In 1973, Clarence W. Barron's, *More They Told Barron*, took a look. "Kuhn Loeb & Co. with Warburg have four votes or the majority of the Federal Reserve Board," Barron said.

<>

Eustace Mullins' Secrets of the Federal Reserve ruled. "Morgan Kuhn Loeb group owned controlling stock in the Federal Reserve Bank of New York, almost half of the shares were owned by the five New York banks under their control ... First National Bank, National City Bank, National Bank of Commerce, Chase National Bank, and Hanover National Bank.

<>

"The Federal Reserve Bank of New York issued 203,053 shares, and, as filed with the Comptroller of the Currency May 19, 1914, the large New York City banks took more than half of the outstanding shares.

"The Rockefeller Kuhn, Loeb-controlled National City Bank took the largest number of shares of any bank, 30,000 shares.

"J. P. Morgan's First National Bank took 15,000 shares.

"When Kuhn, Loeb and First National Bank merged these in 1955, they owned in one block almost one fourth of the shares in the Federal Reserve Bank of New York, which controlled the entire system, and thus they could name Paul Volcker or anyone else they chose to be Chairman of the Federal Reserve Board of Governors.

"Other members of the first Board of Governors included Secretary of the Treasury, William McAdoo (who was) Wilson's son-in-law, and President of Hudson-Manhattan Railroad, a Kuhn, Loeb Co. controlled enterprise ...and, Comptroller of Currency John Skelton Williams.

"Chase National Bank took 6,000 shares.

"The Marine Nation Bank of Buffalo, later known as Marine Midland, took 6,000 shares. This bank was owned by the Schoellkopf family, which controlled Niagara Power Co. and other large interests.

"National Bank of Commerce of New York City took 21,000 shares.

"The shareholders of these banks which own the stock of the Federal Reserve Bank of New York are the people who have controlled our political and economic destinies since 1914. They are the Rothschilds of Europe ... Lazard Freres (Eugene Meyer) ... Kuhn Loeb Co. ... Warburg Co. ... Lehman Brothers ... Goldman Sachs ... the Rockefeller family ... and the J. P. Morgan interests.

"These interests have merged and consolidated in recent years, so that the control is much more concentrated.

"National Bank of Commerce is now Morgan Guaranty Trust Co.

"Lehman Brothers has merged with Kuhn, Loeb Co.," Mullins said.

Eustace went on to sum up who owned controlling shares in the banks that bought controlling shares of the Federal Reserve Bank of New York.

"In 1914, National City Bank purchased about ten percent of the Federal Reserve Bank of New

York shares, Moses Taylor's grandsons Moses Taylor Pyne and Percy Pyne owned 15,000 shares of National City stock. Moses Taylor's son, H.A.C. Taylor, owned 7,699 shares of National City Bank, the bank's attorney, John W. Sterling of Shearman and Sterling owned 6,000 shares of National City Bank, James Stillman owned 47,498 shares of the total of 250,000 shares of National City Bank. First National Bank was the second largest buyer of Federal Reserve Bank of New York stock in 1914, had Morgan representation on the board, founder George F. Baker held 20,000 shares of First National bank, his son G.F. Baker, Jr., held 5,000 shares of the bank's total stock of 100,000 shares. National City Bank merged with First National Bank. George F. Baker Sr.'s daughter married George F. St. George of London, settled in the United States, where their daughter Katherine St. George became a prominent where their daughter, Katherine St. George, became a prominent Congresswoman for a number of years. George Baker, Jr.'s daughter Edith Brevoort Baker married Jacob Schiff's grandson John M. Schiff in 1934 now honorary chairman of Lehman Brothers Kuhn Loeb Co. as of 1988.

"The third largest purchase of Federal Reserve Bank of New York stock in 1914 was the National Bank of Commerce which issued 250,000 shares. J. P. Morgan, through his controlling interest in Equitable Life, which held 24,700 shares and Mutual Life, which held 17,294 shares of National Bank of Commerce, also held another 10,000 shares of National Bank of Commerce through J. P. Morgan & Co. (7800 shares), J. P. Morgan, Jr. (1100 shares), and Morgan partner H.P. Davison (1,100 shares). Paul Warburg, a Governor of the Federal Reserve Board of Governors, also held 3000 shares of National Bank of Commerce. His partner, Jacob Schiff had 1,000 shares of National Bank of Commerce. This bank was clearly controlled by Morgan, who was really a subsidiary of Junius S. Morgan Co. in London and the N.M. Rothschild Co. of London, and Kuhn, Loeb Co., which was also known as a principal agent of the Rothschilds. The financier Thomas Fortune Ryan also held 5,100 shares of National Bank of Commerce stock in 1914. His son, John Barry Ryan, married Otto Kahn's daughter, Kahn was a partner of Warburg and Schiff in Kuhn, Loeb Co., Ryan's granddaughter, Virginia Fortune Ryan, married Lord Airlie, the present head of J. Henry Schroder Banking Corp. in London and New York. Another director of National Bank of

Commerce in 1914, A.D. Juillard, president of A.D. Juillard Co., a trustee of New York Life, and Guaranty Trust, all were controlled by J. P. Morgan. Juillard also had a British connection, being a director of North British & Mercantile Insurance Co. Juillard owned 2000 shares of National Bank of Commerce stock, and was also a director of Chemical Bank," Mullins said.

Matthew Josephson's, *Robber Barons,* looked at Morgan-dominated New York Life, Equitable Life and Mutual Life, which by 1900 had 1 billion dollars in assets and 50 million dollars a year to invest. "In this campaign of secret alliances, Morgan acquired direct control of the National Bank of Commerce ...then, a part ownership in the First National Bank, allying himself to the very strong and conservative financier, George F. Baker, who headed it ...then, by means of stock ownership and interlocking directorates he linked to the first named banks other leading banks, the Hanover, the Liberty, and Chase," Josephson said.

Mullins continued. "Mary W. Harriman, widow of E.H. Harriman, also owned 5,000 shares of National Bank of Commerce in 1914. E.H. Harriman's railroad empire had been entirely financed by Jacob Schiff of Kuhn, Loeb Co.

<>

"Levi P. Morton also owned 1,500 shares of National Bank of Commerce stock in 1914. He had been the twenty-second vice-president of the United States, was an ex-Minister from the U.S. to France, and president of L.P. Morton Co., New York, Morton-Rose & Co. and Morton Chaplin of London. He was a director of Equitable Life Insurance Co., Home Insurance Co., Guaranty Trust, and Newport Trust, In eleven Federal Reserve Districts, these shareholders own or control shares with remaining shares owned by ruling families in those districts who own or control the industries in these districts. Local ruling families set up regional councils based on New York's wishes from groups like Council on Foreign Relations, Trilateral Commission, networking with instruments of finance to control political developments in their district, name candidates, and are not successfully opposed," Mullins said.

Senator Aldrich in his *The Independent* July 1914 spoke his mind. "Before the passage of this Act, the New York bankers could only dominate the reserves of New York. Now, we're able to dominate the bank reserves of the entire country," Aldrich said.

<>

H.W. Loucks', *The Great Conspiracy of the*

House of Morgan, denounced the Federal Reserve Act. "In the Federal Reserve Law, they've wrested from the people and secured for themselves the constitutional power to issue money and regulate the value, thereof. House of Morgan is now in supreme control of our industry, commerce, and political affairs. They're in complete control of the policy making of the Democratic, Republican, and Progressive parties. The present extraordinary propaganda for 'preparedness' is planned more for home coercion than for defense against foreign aggression," Loucks said.

<>

Lundberg's *America's Sixty Families* concurred. "In practice, the Federal Reserve Bank of New York became the fountainhead of the system of twelve regional banks, for New York was the money market of the nation. The other eleven banks were so many expensive mausoleums erected to salve the local pride and quell Jacksonian fears of the hinterland. Benjamin Strong, president of the Bankers Trust (J. P. Morgan) was selected as the first Governor of the New York Federal Reserve Bank. Adept in high finance, Strong for many years manipulated the country's monetary system at the discretion of directors representing leading New York banks.

"Under Strong, the Reserve System was brought into interlocking relations with the Bank of England and the Bank of France.

"Benjamin Strong held his position as Governor of the Federal Reserve Bank of New York until his sudden death in 1928, during a Congressional investigation of the secret meetings between Reserve Governors and heads of European central banks which brought on the Great Depression of 1929-31."

Harold Kelloch's, *Warburg, the Revolutionist*, in *Century Magazine*, May 1915 agreed. "He imposed his ideas on a nation of a 100 million people. Without Mr. Warburg there would have been no Federal Reserve Act. The banking house of Warburg & Warburg in Hamburg has always been strictly a family business. None but a Warburg has been eligible for it, but all Warburgs have been born into it. In 1895, he married the daughter of the late Solomon Loeb of Kuhn Loeb Co. He became a member of Kuhn Loeb Co. in 1902. Mr. Warburg's salary from his private business has been approximately $500,000 a year. Mr. Warburg's motives had been purely those of patriotic self-sacrifice."

W. H. Allen in *Moody's Magazine*, 1916 witnessed. "The purpose of the Federal Reserve Act was to prevent concentration of money in the New York banks by making it profitable for country bankers to use their funds at home ...but, the movement of currency shows the New York banks gained from the interior in every month except Dec. 1915, since the Act went into effect. The stabilization of rates has taken place in New York alone. In other parts, high rates continue.

"The Act, which was to deprive Wall Street of its funds for speculation, has really given the bulls and the bears such a supply as they have never had before.

"The truth is, far from having clogged the channel to Wall Street, as Mr. Glass confidently boasted, actually widened the old channels and opened up two new ones. The first of these leads to Washington and gives Wall Street a string on all the surplus cash in the United States Treasury. Besides, in the power to issue banknote currency, it furnishes an inexhaustible supply of credit money ... the second channel leads to the great central banks of Europe, whereby, through the sale of acceptances, virtually guaranteed by the United States Government, Wall Street is granted immunity from foreign demands for gold which have precipitated every great crisis in our history," Allen said.

Eustace sums it up. "With the setting up of the twelve 'financial districts' through the Federal Reserve Banks, the traditional division of the United States into the forty-eight states was overthrown...

<>

"...and we entered the era of 'regionalism', or twelve regions which had no relation to the traditional state boundaries. These developments following the passing of the Federal Reserve Act proved every one of the allegations Thomas Jefferson had made against a central bank in 1791 ... that the subscribers to the Federal Reserve Bank stock had formed a corporation, whose stock could be and was held by aliens ... that this stock would be transmitted to a certain line of successors ... that it would be placed beyond forfeiture and escheat ... that they would receive a monopoly of banking, which was against the laws of monopoly ... and that they now had the power to make laws, paramount to the laws of the states.

"No state legislature can countermand any of the laws laid down by the Federal Reserve Board of Governors for the benefit of their private stockholders. This board issues laws as to what the interest rate shall be, what the quantity of money shall be and what the price of money shall be. All of these powers abrogate the powers of the state legislatures and their responsibility to the citizens of those states.

\<\>

"The *New York Times* stated Federal Reserve Banks would be ready for business on Aug. 1, 1914, but they actually began operations on Nov. 16, 1914. At that time, their total assets were listed at 143 million dollars, from the sale of shares in the Federal Reserve Banks to stockholders of the national banks which subscribed to it. The actual part of this 143 million dollars which was paid for these shares remains shrouded in mystery. Some historians believe that the shareholders only paid about half of the amount in cash ... others believe, they paid in no cash at all, but merely sent in checks which they drew on the national banks which they owned. This seems most likely, that from the very outset, the Federal Reserve operations were 'paper issued against paper', bookkeeping entries that comprised the only values which changed hands.

"The men whom President Woodrow Wilson chose to make up the first Federal Reserve Board of Governors were men drawn from the banking group. He'd been nominated for the Presidency by the Democratic Party, which had claimed to represent the 'common man' against the 'vested interests'. According to Wilson himself, he was allowed to choose only one man for the Federal Reserve Board. The others were chosen by New York bankers. Wilson's choice was Thomas D. Jones, a trustee of Princeton and director of International Harvester and other corporations. The other members were ...Adolf C. Miller, economist from Rockefeller's University of Chicago and Morgan's Harvard University, and also serving as Assistant Secretary of the Interior ...Charles S. Hamlin, who had served previously as an Assistant Secretary to the Treasury for eight years ...F.A. Delano, a Roosevelt relative, and railroad operator who took over a number of railroads for Kuhn, Loeb Co. ...W.P.G. Harding, President of the First National Bank of Atlanta ...and, Paul Warburg of Kuhn, Loeb Co. According to, *The Intimate Papers of Col. House*, Warburg was appointed because the President accepted (House's) suggestion of Paul Warburg of New York ... because, of his interest and experience in currency problems under both Republican and Democratic Administrations.

"Like Warburg, Delano had also been born outside the continental limits of the United States, although he was an American citizen. Delano's father, Warren Delano, according to Dr. Josephson and other authorities, was active in Hong Kong in the Chinese opium trade, and Frederick Delano was born in Hong Kong in 1863," Mullins said.

Paul Emden's, *The Money Power of Europe in the 19th and 20th Century*, adds his perspective. "The Warburgs reached their outstanding eminence during the last twenty years of the past century, simultaneously with the growth of Kuhn, Loeb Co. in New York, with whom they stood in a personal union and family relationship. Paul Warburg with magnificent success carried through in 1913 the reorganization of the American banking system, at which he had with Senator Aldrich been working since 1911, and thus most thoroughly consolidated the currency and finances of the United States," Emden said.

May 6, 1914 *New York Times* reported Paul Warburg 'retired' from Kuhn, Loeb Co. to serve the Federal Reserve Board. But, he'd not resigned his directorships of ...American Surety Co. ...Baltimore and Ohio Railroad ...National Railways of Mexico ...Wells Fargo ...or, Westinghouse Electric Corp. ...continuing to serve on these boards of directors. *Who's Who* listed him as also holding directorships on the boards of ...American I.G. Chemical Co. (branch of I.G. Farben) ...Agfa Ansco Corp. ...Westinghouse Acceptance Company ...Warburg Co. of Amsterdam ...chairman of the Board of International Acceptance Bank ...and, many other banks, railways and corporations.

Aug. 1, 1914, during Senate Hearings on Paul Warburg, Senator Bristow of the Senate Banking & Currency Committee asked questions.

"How many of these partners of Kuhn, Loeb Co. are American citizens?" Bristow said.

"They're all American citizens except Mr. Kuhn. He's a British subject," Warburg said. "I went to England, where I stayed for two years, first in the banking and discount firm of Samuel Montague & Co. After that I went to France, where I stayed in a French bank."

"What French bank was that?" Bristol said.

"The Russian bank for foreign trade ... which has an agency in Paris," Warburg said.

"I understand you to say, you were a Republican ...but, when Mr. Theodore Roosevelt came around, you became a sympathizer with Mr. Wilson and supported him?" Bristol said.

"Yes," Warburg said.

"While your brother, Felix Warburg was supporting Taft?" Bristol said.

"Yes, finance and politics don't mix," Warburg said.

\<\>

328

To make things harder the casting department forgot to cast three Warburg brothers. So, in addition to playing all of the Rothschilds, I was now playing several Warburgs, all determined to help get me an Oscar. To develop characters actors cross-examine our habits and routines in character, one thing kept coming back to me. Why was my family name, 'Warburg, city of war'?

1913 & 1918
Allen Dulles' masquerades

Allen Dulles knew how to throw a party. He liked the attention and respect he got from people afraid of his power. Insider trading, everyone sold out, the game was finding the right price.

This party included the families Dulles, Harriman, Rockefeller, Warburg, Schroder, Walker, Hoover, Rothschild, Brown ...dressed-up in a gala Halloween masquerade as pirates, devils, fortune tellers, military officers, thieves, murderers, pimps, whores ... in Dulles' parlor!

Allen Dulles was thrilled to have everyone's attention. "Let's enjoy ourselves!"

His guests applauded. Dulles led a group of guests out of the ballroom, into a dark game room. He fumbled for a light switch ...but, used a match instead, lit a torch. He signaled musicians to begin. In the flickering light, call girls in shadows played 'strip billiards'. Opium pipes dangled from their lips. Blue clouds of opium in puffs streamed from their nostrils, spinning in circles in clouds. They were stoned. As he walked by them, Allen Dulles ran his fingers over their naked bodies. The opium seemed to coax their bodies onto his fingertips.

He start chasing a stripper hiding behind a pirate flag. Hugging it, he wrapped her up in it ...then, sat her on his knee. "Were you here for our party five years ago in 1913? ...when we financed Kaiser Wilheim."

Her eyes flared angrily. "I was *with* you, it was a two-week party. I'm still drunk from that cocaine opium soda you gave everyone. It was summer, 1913, one year before the war. Me and the girls played 'strip pool', smoked opium. You and your friends snorted cocaine, drugged our drinks ...you thought, we didn't see."

Dulles turned towards his guests at his dinner party. He tapped an empty wine glass with his spoon. "Gentlemen and 'ladies', German General Staff, I have an announcement. Max Warburg's going to head German Secret Service during the coming Great War ...while, his brother, Paul Warburg, just founded the Federal Reserve for us, isn't that special?" Allen Dulles said. A call girl

Allen Dulles was flirting with reached out behind the curtains, letting her hand roam over Dulles' behind. Dulles felt surprised. He kept speaking without betraying what was going on. "Some U.S. and Russia banking families are allied against us and the Kaiser ...but, in name only ... a temporary and cosmetic inconvenience for the duration of the war. It's not personal, regardless of the war's outcome."

A German businessman spoke indignantly to one of the guests, "*Sheis. Dumkov.* Who loses the war pays interest on the loans made to finance it. The winner gets reparations from the loser. The winner finances rebuilding the cities and factories. What could be more personal?!"

Allen Dulles overheard the comment. He appeared to ignore it. He pulled the call girl out from behind the curtain. A laugh of amusement spread through the party.

"A spy, no doubt! I've learned from my uncles, who were foreign secretaries of the United States for several generations ...a spy in the hand is worth two in the bush. Tonight, we set the pieces in order ...and, select who'll be the first board of directors of our first American central bank, the Federal Reserve Bank," Allen Dulles said.

Dulles was applauded. He felt pleased. He goosed the call girl. His audience broke into laughs.

A German international banker approached him, "What about Kaiser's approaching war?"

An English merchant banker smiled at the German. "How will we disguise our friendship, with our countries at war?" the English merchant banker said.

"Who'll make the most in arms sales?" asked an Italian international banker.

Allen Dulles spoke louder than everyone else, "Who'll make the most in interest charges on loans? Loyalty to each other ... comes before loyalty to one country or another. This way, we profit in war or peace ...and, preserve our relative positions for our dynasties," Allen Dulles said. He started auctioning-off his call girls ...negotiated, brokered and bartered to his heart's content.

<>

"Let me get my little speech over with. Let's finish our business. I regret any losses you've suffered as a result of Germany losing this world war. But, U.S. and Russia were allies in this world war of 1914 to 1918," Alan Dulles said.

Paul Warburg spoke. "I was successful in immigrating from Germany ...and, in a few years did what no one in America was able to do, I established a Central Bank. I took economic and financial control of America."

Everyone clapped. He continued.

"My brother Max, head of Warburg & Co. in Germany, was in charge of the Kaiser's Military Intelligence for World War I ...he'll represent Germany at the Peace Conference in 1918-1919. Max and I have worked together bankrupting and buying up each others' countries at every opportunity, as our family bankers have done in Bank of England, the Fed, the Reichsbank, Bank of France, in Russia, in Italy and all through Europe. Our family financed all sides of each war ...primarily as Rothschild bank agents. Now, that Kaiser and German General Staff have lost the war, it's time to win the peace. The time's right for America to buy up German industry. In Germany, my brother's on the board of I.G. Farben, the biggest chemical and pharmaceutical cartel in the world. Here in America, I'm on the board of American I.G. ...and we've chosen Allen Dulles of Sullivan & Cromwell attorneys to represent the Farbin portfolio ...selling and trading shares of Farbin stock in America.

<>

"As to your portfolio losses in World War I, we'll make these cosmetic only, Max and I will adjust Fed and Bank of England interest rates, inflate the currency in Germany relatively deflating rates in other countries ...so, use the deflated currencies to buy up German stocks ...buy up German stock at pennies on the dollar. And, we'll default loan schedules ... to your benefit, till everyone regains their losses.

"Russia defeated enemies of the United States. Now, Russia's enduring this 'revolution' of hers. She's ordained and christened herself a new name, the U.S.S.R., Union Of Soviet Socialist Republics. *Soviet*, means *workers' governing groups*. For business reasons, the United States must now betray Russia, her ally.

"At the same time, United States will embrace our former 'enemy', Germany's ruling families. Because of the interlocking Central Bank World Order, German financiers and industrialists share American financial theology with overlapping portfolios ...because, of overlapping corporate directorates, many of us co-own controlling shares in each others' corporate portfolios.

"Every powerful country in the West ...and, in the Orient ... is financing some kind of coup or revolution or plot to takeover Russia ...to capture the revolution away from the Bolsheviks ...to bring it under their financial control. World War I military fighting is over. World War I financial, economic, and political war will continue

...throughout this century, into the next.

"The Russian Revolution is spreading the idea ... of redistribution of wealth from the rich to the poor, through Europe and the United States. There will *be* no redistribution of wealth from the rich to the poor. We'll divide natural resources and labor pools of the world up, between us. We'll use this century to enact our plan.

"In Russia, German troops remain behind. They're being outfitted as European mercenary and terrorist units by our Western democracies. Our European mercenaries and terrorists will launch campaigns of terror. First, we'll stamp out the Soviet movement in Latvia and Lithuania.

"We're the Financial World Order ruling families! ...financing Western civilization and conquest in the Orient. Democracy won't stop *us*. We'll fund White Russian troops loyal to the Czar. We'll fund storm-troops of reactionary regimes in Europe. For one reason! ...to turn back the tide of Democracy in the world. The guns have stopped firing. Now, we must use interest rates like bullets.

<>

"The Czar's regime and intelligence forces are infiltrated by German General Staff intelligencers ...who, brutalized and terrorized Soviets of Jews who were against us. Now, our operatives move underground networks and cells of Czarist and German intelligencers, worldwide. These operatives will eliminate Jewish Soviets on sight. As the Czar's regime took money from the poor and redistributed it to the rich ... we American and European ruling families now must re-unite our financial power ...and, do the same, rid ourselves of unions of organized workers who would take wealth of the world from us, diluting it, uselessly, among themselves.

"Famines now rage in U.S.S.R. ...while, across Europe, Workers' Soviets ...demand redistribution of wealth ...demand human rights for a common humanity, in mass movements springing up in every country ... this, our propaganda to divide and conquer, got away from us. We didn't know ...it caught on so strongly in our subject populations ...made such unrest. But, created even larger, unanticipated opportunities to extend more credit for more war."

Everyone clapped.

"Socialists want to overthrow our dictatorial regimes ...our emperors ...our kings ...our queens ... in Germany, France, Italy ...all across Europe and Asia. They don't want Divine Right of Kings, old as the Pharaohs ...they want Jewish Democracy. Equality. This won't happen!

"They want to redistribute our wealth from us to them. This won't happen! The world's overpopulated with excess humanity. War's the only way for population control ...and, return to normalcy of established World Financial Order!" Paul said.

The inside traders and whores clapped, cheering. Allen Dulles felt himself climbing past the height of his power. He watched Herbert Hoover, Henry Schroder, and Paul Warburg approach. He could hear coins clink in Hoover's pockets.

Hoover stared at Dulles. "I hate the Bolsheviks! Bolshevism is worse than war!"

Dulles smiled. "I agree."

Hoover exploded in rage, "I hate communists! I lost one billion dollars in gold, timber, and oil concessions in Russia the Czar gave me ...because, those Jewish Bolshevik socialists nationalized my concessions! Their damn Bolshevik revolution stole it! ...from me! My wealth in Russia was redistributed! But! ...to whom?! Come closer ...so, no one hears. I personally misused funds earmarked for World War I food relief for war victims in Europe. I sent the money to White Russian troops still loyal to the Czar, as we agreed."

<>

Paul Warburg smiled. "Did you send some food relief to feed and arm the storm-troops of our European reactionary regimes I'm financing? ...as we agreed? You're not pocketing black market trafficking ...now, are you?"

Henry Schroder smiled, "It's under control."

Hoover looked at Warburg, disbelieving. "Not excessively. I've washed some in the black market, of course ...used some to settle the immigrant White Russian community of the Czar's petroleum, mining, timber, and banking partners in the Dallas/Fort Worth area."

Allen Dulles was relieved. Senator Borah walked up to Hoover, Dulles and Warburg. "You didn't invite me here. I'm crashing this party ...I had to see this, for myself. I *don't* like it. I know, there's covert war being waged against the Russian people by you three men and your other factions controlling U.S. Government. As soon as Soviet Union, our legislated ally, defeated the enemies of the United States, you turned the United States around ... to betray Russia. Now, we're embracing Germany, our enemy. I'm going on record in Congress to expose this undeclared, secret war. You're waging covert action without Congressional or U.S. Government approval ... against democratic people of the Soviet Union! ...who won the war for us!"

Senator Borah walked angrily away. Allen Dulles looked at Hoover, they both despised Borah. Dulles turned to Warburg.

"We're legal ...we wrote Article 12 of the Armistice of Nov. 1918 ...that stipulates after the war, German troops will stay in Russia as long as the Allies consider it expedient.

"The U.S. ultra-right, encouraged by Hoover and me, have commandeered left-behind German troops. We're using them, as mercenary forces ...and, death squads. We'll kill the Soviet Democracy movement to nationalize and redistribute our wealth, that we privatized when we took their natural resources from them, in the first place! We have other enemies. Central banks of every country in the civilized world are now competing with one another, having coup after coup in Russia, to takeover the politics and ideas that control the Russian part of the Eurasian continent. We've combined German General Staff bankers with British, French, Italian, and Japanese central banks into our Central Bank World Order. We'll make more debt and finance more killing than anyone else in the history of the world!"

Warburg agreed, "Warburgs, Schroders, and Rothschilds in Britain also supply arms and food to our commandeered mercenary German troops ...in Latvia, Lithuania, and Estonia."

<>

Schroder bank ...financed the presidential campaign of Herbert Hoover from 1929 to 1933 ...financed Hitler in 1933 helping make World War II inevitable ...and, during my Reagan Administration two of Schroder's major executives from its subsidiary, Bechtel Corp., Defense Secretary Caspar Weinberger (Bechtel treasurer) and Secretary of State George Shultz (Bechtel president) served in my Cabinet ... George Shultz being a gentleman, scholar, businessman, diplomat, and Standard Oil heir.

To get into my Warburg dual acting role I studied history ...remembering, the election of Hoover to the Presidency was influenced by the Warburg Brothers, directors of Kuhn Loeb Co. bank, who paid for Hoover's campaign.

Let me rehearse here for a minute, then get back to Kuhn Loeb. and Hoover ...do you mind? ...here goes.

Apr. 1887, *Quarterly Journal of Economics* commented, "The public debts of Europe showed interest and sinking fund payments of 5.343 billion dollars annually. Governments may ask, is war, with all its terrible chances, preferable to maintenance of a precarious and costly peace. If military preparations of Europe don't end in war, they may end in bankruptcy of the States. Or, if such follies lead neither to war, nor to ruin ...then, they point to industrial and economic revolution."

Max looked at Paul, "The system of national loans developed by the Rothschilds served well to finance Europe's struggles, during the 19th Century ...because, we diversified them over several Rothschild and Warburg branches, in many countries. By 1900, it was obvious, Europe couldn't afford a major war ...even though we had standing armies, universal military service, modern weapons ...their economies couldn't support the required expenditures ...so, the Kaiser leaned on me."

Paul smiled. "That's why you, and our brothers, had me leave Germany ... migrate to the U.S. to get our ducks in order, start the Federal Reserve System, to begin operations in 1914 ...so, we could force Americans to lend the Allies 24 billion dollars to prosecute World War I ...which was not repaid. I might add ...except, for considerable interest to us and our team of New York bankers."

Max wasn't happy, "We drove our American people to make war on our German people, with whom they had no conceivable political or economic quarrel. At the time, almost half of U.S. citizens were of German descent ...I wish the U.S. spoke German, not English."

Paul engaged his brother. "Max, did you know at the 1787 U.S. Constitution Convention, German was voted down as the official U.S. language, by a small margin, you almost got your wish."

Max nodded, "Yes, I knew that. But, by forcing the U.S. into World War I ...in order for us to finance both sides ...by lending the U.S. money to fight the war ...that's what drove our U.S. income tax plan into existence ...you had Wilson's Administration target and capture the greatest untaxed source of revenue the American's missed ...people's incomes. You got the income-tax law enacted in the nick of time ...so, U.S. taxpayers financed our war loans to Wilson ...which, as you recall, was why I sent you to America in the first place ... to push our Fed plan into place."

Paul smiled, "Yes, we got the Fed put into place to finance World War I ...and, made loans to all sides ...another financial coup for us."

Max felt better. "We were waiting since 1887 for the U.S. to take the bait ...and, give us our central bank ...so, we could drain U.S. money to finance a European war among nations we'd already bankrupted with armament and 'defense' programs. I think, financing war is the most challenging and profitable thing we do ...and *will* be, well into the next century."

Oct. 1917, *Notes of the Journal of Political Economy,* commented.

"The effect of the war upon the business of the Federal Reserve Banks has required an immense development of the staffs of these banks, with a corresponding increase in expenses. Without, of course, being able to anticipate so early and extensive a demand for their services in this connection, the framers of the Federal Reserve Act had provided that the Federal Reserve Banks should act as fiscal agents of the Government."

Oct. 13, 1917, President Wilson addressed the nation, "It is manifestly imperative that there should be a complete mobilization of the banking reserves of the United States. The burden and the privilege of the Allied loans must be shared by every banking institution in the country. I believe that cooperation, on the part of the banks, is a patriotic duty at this time ...and, that membership in the Federal Reserve System is a distinct and significant evidence of patriotism."

Woodrow Wilson later wrote, "The World War was a matter of economic rivalry."

At the time, when the Communist Revolution seemed in doubt, Wilson sent his personal emissary, Elihu Root, to Russia with 100 million dollars from the Special Emergency War Fund to save the toppling Bolshevik regime.

Okay, that went smoothly with two Warburgs ...but, I've got a scene playing all five brothers coming up. Now, let me get back to the election of Hoover to the Presidency influenced by Warburg Brothers, directors of Kuhn Loeb Co. bank ...who financed Hoover's campaign.

In exchange, Hoover promised to impose a moratorium on German war debts.

<>

Behind the scenes, Schroder through Bechtel, helped me become President ...so I, promised to be the best Cold Warrior in town ...but, I didn't know till later, after my Presidency ... Bechtel was a Schroder subsidiary ...if I had known, it wouldn't of changed a thing. I didn't know then, Schroder was a major shareholder of the Fed ...if I'd known, so what?

I was my own man.

We were Cold Warriors.

We had a job to save America, at least I did. I wasn't a banker and didn't want to be, so the details escaped me.

Accepting the Republican nomination for President in 1928, Hoover ran against Al Smith.

Mullins', *Secrets,* had this to say, "The campaign against Smith was marked by appeals to religious intolerance ...since, he was a Catholic. The bankers stirred up anti-Catholic sentiment all over the country to achieve the election of their World War I protégé, Herbert Hoover."

Campaigning, Herbert Hoover made a prediction, "We, in America today, are nearer to the final triumph over poverty than ever before in the history of any land. The poorhouse is vanishing from among us."

Within eight months of Hoover's inauguration, the stock market crashed, officially beginning the Great Depression, the most severe economic crisis in U.S. history. Hoover was the George W. Bush of his day.

In 1928, the British central banking group via its New York branches, decided to run Herbert Hoover for president ...but, Hoover, while born here, never had a business or home address in the U.S. after graduating Stanford University in 1895, going abroad, he listed his address as, Suite 2000, 42 Broadway, New York ...the offices of Edgar Rickard and J. Henry Schroder Banking Corp. partner, grain tycoon Julius H. Barnes.

Winning the election, Hoover appointed Eugene Meyer Jr. as Governor of the Federal Reserve Board. Meyer's father was a partner in Lazard Freres of Paris, and a partner in Lazard Brothers of London. Eugene Meyer and Bernard Baruch were two of the most powerful men in America during World War I.

Meyer was Chairman of War Finance Corp.

Baruch, Chairman of War Industries Board.

Paul Warburg, Governor of Federal Reserve.

I, Ronald Reagan, am of course, still playing Paul Warburg ...Max and Felix too, in my ghost-written, fictional autobiography ...but, I'll set the scene for you with a few paragraphs to make it go down easier so you don't choke.

Chairman Louis McFadden of House Banking & Currency Committee was quoted in *New York Times,* Dec. 17, 1930 from his speech on the floor of the house, attacking Meyer's nomination. "He represents the Rothschild interest, and is liaison officer between the French Government and J.P. Morgan."

The week before, Chairman McFadden introduced a resolution of impeachment against President Hoover for ...high crimes ...misdemeanors ...violation of contracts ...unlawful dissipation of United States financial resources ...and, his appointment of Eugene Meyer to the Federal Reserve Board. The resolution was tabled. McFadden referred to Hoover's 'German backers' ...their firms originated in Germany, and in British-based banks with New York branches owned and influenced from London ...as, Hoover himself was in his career.

Mullins continued.

"Meyer Jr. was Hoover's friend from back in the time of World War I. Eugene Meyer Jr., had a long record of public service, dating from 1915 when he went into partnership with Bernard Baruch in the Alaska-Juneau Gold Mining Co. Meyer was Special Advisor to the War Industries Board on Non-Ferrous Metals (gold, silver, etc.) ...Special Assistant to the Secretary of War on aircraft production. In 1917, he was appointed to National Committee on War Savings ...and, made Chairman of the War Finance Corporation, from 1918-1926 ...then, was appointed chairman of Federal Farm Loan Board, from 1927-1929."

Meyer Jr. was chairman of U.S. Reconstruction Finance Corp. in 1932, bought and ran *Washington Post* from 1933 to 1959 ...(Catherine Graham was his daughter, running *Washington Post* from 1963 to 1979) ... he founded and ran Eugene Meyer Foundation, from 1944 to 1959, and was first president of World Bank, in 1946.

I'd done enough character research to pull off the part. "Well, speaking in character as Paul Warburg and in character as Ronald Reagan, at the same time, which is easy for me to do in this case because we probably felt the same way about it, Meyer must've been a man of exceptional ability to hold those positions."

Mel's Jesus looked at me.

Paul Robeson's hovered in front of me, while his little ghostly companion flew around my estate. Shooting was going okay.

In 1931, Hoover was, as all forward-looking diplomats serving their major campaign supporters in the Fed, financially auguring a Second World War. But, there could be no war, nor war profits, without an 'aggressor'. An influential minority of reactionary American ruling family patriarchs wanted to stop democracy, social and economic progress in the U.S. and abroad, to create an atmosphere of hostility towards Soviet Union. President Herbert Hoover was interviewed by a reporter for *San Francisco News,* Aug. 1931.

Hoover talked passionately. "To tell the truth, the ambition of my life is to stamp out Soviet Russia."

National Civic Organization drafted a report called, *A Plan for an International Movement to*

Combat the Red Menace. Ralph M. Easley, a former Chicago newspaperman, founded and directed National Civic Organization. The organization promoted anti-Communism and anti-labor movements.

Norman Hapgood wrote an expose of Easley.

"Soviet Russia is, of course, Mr. Easley's chief abomination. He freely sponsored the cause of Czarists."

President Hoover's Moratorium was not intended to 'help' Germany. Hoover was not 'pro-German', his Moratorium on Germany's war debts was needed ...so, Germany would have funds for rearming to fight military war to win economic war to restore Czarist wealth.

Dec. 15, 1931, Chairman McFadden read the House a *Public Ledger of Philadelphia* article of Oct. 24, 1931, headlined, *'German Reveals Hoover's Secret'*. "The American President was in intimate negotiations with the German government regarding a year's debt holiday ... as early as Dec. 1930."

McFadden continued, "There were months of getting ready in Germany, and in Wall Street offices of German bankers ...Germany needed to be saturated with American money ...Hoover had to be elected, because this scheme began before he became President ...if the German international bankers of Wall Street ... Kuhn Loeb Company ... J. & W. Seligman ... Paul Warburg ... J. Henry Schroder ... hadn't had this job waiting for him, Hoover never would've been elected ...Warburg brothers, board directors of Kuhn Loeb Co. paid costs of Hoover's campaign ...in return, Hoover promised the moratorium on German debts," McFadden said.

The history books I read to develop my characters, wrote of months of hurried and furtive preparations in Germany, and in Wall Street offices of German bankers setting up the Moratorium ...Germany *had* to be flooded with American money.

Hoover wanted to exempt his friend, Ivar Kreuger's, loan of 125 million dollars to Germany from the Moratorium ...to enhance his friend's buying power, during the Depression. Hoover entertained partner Emile Francqui in the White House, and Ivar Kreuger, a most famous 20th Century swindler, and partner in Guggenheim Group working with Rockefellers, Vanderbilts, and Baruchs ...who supported him with a lot of activity on Wall Street.

Kreuger and friends invented 'B-series' paper ...creating an 'international market' ...Kreuger Trust created debentures, a synthesis of stocks and bonds that became currency of Kreuger financial institution, a popular international paper through the 1920s ...so, by the 'Depression', his Kreuger Trust ...controlled half the world market in iron ore and cellulose ...competed in telecommunications with ITT ...achieved a world monopoly for matches ...owned real estate in central Berlin, Paris, Amsterdam, Warsaw, Stockholm, Oslo, New York, and, Philadelphia ...owned the Boliden gold mines, iron mines, concessions, and monopolies ... enabling him to proffer valuable Kreuger Trust 'securities' attracting investors into his Trust.

Like the Bush dynasty, Hoover maintained friendly relationships with many prominent swindlers of the 20th Century, including partner Emile Francqui. The receivership of the billion dollar 'Kreuger Fraud' was handled by Samuel Untermeyer, former counsel for the Pujo Committee hearings. Ivar Kreuger, a Swede who came to America as a construction engineer, returned to Sweden in 1913 to take over his father's match factory ...and, partnering into a construction firm, merged the two businesses into Kreuger & Toll, and through additional mergers controlled the Swedish match industry ...and, seeing that poor governments after World War I needed cash, Ivar made loans to European governments in exchange for match monopolies ...the loans were paid by a tax on matches. Kreuger controlled 90 percent of the world's match production by 1930.

Dale Flesher, in *National Forum*, looks at Ivar Kreuger. "To lend millions to foreign governments, Kreuger first had to obtain the cash from some source. One such source was the naive American public. After the stock market crash in 1929, Kreuger & Toll securities sold well. In 1929, Kreuger & Toll stocks and bonds were the most traded securities in the world, they paid annual dividends as high as 20 percent. Unfortunately, these dividends were paid out of capital, not out of profits. Kreuger appeared on *Time Magazine* cover during the week of the stock market crash, in 1929. The onset of the Depression had little effect on Kreuger & Toll dividends ...because the company's dividends were never based on profits. Instead, the pyramid scheme required constant new financing to pay dividends on already outstanding securities ...and, the payment of dividends required the sale of new securities ... it was a never-ending cycle."

If an investment banker asked for audited financial statements, Kreuger would refuse to deal with that individual ...since, Kreuger's securities were in demand, no investment banker risked losing Kreuger's business. Depression investors made few investments, making it hard for Kreuger to keep his fraud going. Kreuger's pyramid collapsed, he declared the largest bankruptcy on record, then in Paris, Mar. 12, 1932 Ivar Kreuger killed himself.

Auditors determined in April, a quarter billion dollars in bookkeeping assets never existed. Billions of dollars of securities changed hands ... with no supporting financial statements. In the 1920s, Ivar was considered the richest man in the world. In 1933, he was considered the greatest swindler in history.

I remember Patti asking Nancy why we needed a U.S. Securities and Exchange to watch over corporate stocks and bonds deals.

Nancy looked at Patty, saying two words.

"Ivar Kreuger."

Dale Flesher continued, "A cry was raised throughout the land, investors must be protected from similar demons. The media played it up so big, Congress passed a bill long gone ignored since 1919, renaming it, 'The 1933 Securities Act'. Kreuger defrauded little people. America's regulated financial markets are the direct result of the experience with Ivar Kreuger."

In character, I can say this as Paul Warburg, "Ivar Kreuger had his own version of a central bank, issuing his own loans on paper backed by matches and trust ...and, having a country's people pay taxes on matches, to repay the loans he made to government."

<>

Apr. 6, 1917, U.S. entered World War I. U.S. Food Administration was created, directed by Herbert Hoover. Hoover sent food to Belgium, on the pretense it was for war refugees ...knowing, when it got to Belgium it was commandeered, hijacked, and sent to Germany ... to supply German combat soldiers. Hoover had two administrators. Prentiss Gray was a lumber salesman from the West Coast, Julius Barnes was a grain salesman from Duluth. Post-war, both men were partners in J. Henry Schroder Banking Corp. of New York, building financial empires in grain and sugar.

Under Hoover, Barnes was President of Grain Corporation of the U.S. Food Administration, 1917-1918. Gray was chief of Marine Transportation. Zabriskie, a J. Henry Schroder partner, was put in charge of U.S. Sugar Equalization Board.

Schroder Corporation up-and-coming, and would-be directors, controlled the food supply in the United States ...through its grain and sugar czars during World War I.

By war's end, J. Henry Schroder Co. directors owned Cuba's sugar industry. Another partner, M. Rionda, became president of Cuba Cane Corp., and held board directorates in ...Manati Sugar Co. ...American British and Continental Corp. ...and, other corporations. Baron Bruno von Schroder was senior partner of J. Henry Schroder, and a director of North British & Mercantile Insurance Co. Baron Rudolph von Schroder of Hamburg, Bruno's father, was director of the largest Brazilian coffee company, Sao Paulo Coffee Ltd., co-directed by Tiarks, who worked for J. Henry Shroder.

As main man in U.S. Food Administration, Hoover chose Lewis Lichtenstein Strauss ...who married the daughter of Jerome Hanauer of Kuhn Loeb, thereafter becoming a partner in Kuhn Loeb. Edgar Rickard, born in Pontgibaud, France, was Hoover's closest friend. Rickard was Hoover's chief administrator in all war and postwar organizations, including Commission for Relief in Belgium ...and, the U.S. Food Administration, 1914-1924.

<> <> <>

White House Press Briefing Room

At the next White House press briefing, I restated my hardline position on Soviets and terrorists. After the press briefing, as was my custom, I returned to the Oval Office and flipped over the next page on my desk calendar.

Washington hotel ballroom

At the same time I was across town at a press conference talking about my hardliner position against Soviets and terrorists, Nancy had a routine to deliver, as well. Nancy was on the other side of town ...in a hotel ballroom, popping speed uppers ...and, Miltown downers ... while giving another performance of her, 'Just Say No' to drugs speech.

Nancy addressed world heads of state. "It's consumers' own fault ...being addicts ..if people didn't use drugs ...if they didn't buy drugs, ...there'd be no demand ...the drug market would fall ...go belly-up," Nancy said. Nancy kept smiling, waiting for applause to die down.

Mario Alarcon sat in the audience, not far from Monzer Al-Kassar, Bill Casey, and George Bush, everyone was clapping. Nancy waved, start walking offstage, stumbled, caught her balance ...and, teetering dizzily, managed not to fall.

Ambassador Roosevelt's
White House office

In her White House office, Ambassador Selwa Lucky Roosevelt was busily planning parties, receptions, luncheons, casual dinners, formal dinners, and state gala events. She looked up and saw several of Meese's and Deaver's munchkins storm in. Lucky cringed.

The Deaver munchkin start barking orders at her. "Deaver says you're the new protocol chief ...so, get me duplicate copies, starting now, of each official gift the President gives to anybody."

Lucky felt offended, "No. I don't like your attitude. You may leave my office."

The Deaver munchkin attacked. "I'm ordering you to do it ...in Deaver's name."

The Meese munchkin attacked. "I'm ordering you to do it ...in Meese's name."

Lucky was angry, "No. You little munchkins have big attitude problems, take it out of here."

"I want your navy blue water cooler for my mauve one," the Meese munchkin said.

"No. I'm having trouble coping with you Meese and Deaver munchkins, I'm frustrated around you."

Air Force Two over
Central America & Argentina

Lucky flew on Air Force Two to Argentina and Central America with Deaver's advance team. Part of the reason she went, was to see why her staff hated Deaver's advance team. Lucky felt completely ignored on the plane. In the limo, Lucky felt Deaver's advance team were ashamed to be seen with a female diplomat. Later in the day, she walked into a meeting with the Latinos.

The Deaver advance team leader wasted no time. "Let's cut this cordial crap, get down to business!" Deaver's advance man said.

Lucky cringed. She knew what was next. She watched Mario Alarcon get angrier and angrier. She tried to smooth things over ...but, felt futility, and despair overtake her. Lucky addressed the Latino leaders.

"Now, just calm down, I'm just as frustrated by Deaver's advance team, as you are ...these damn munchkins are in my face every minute, every day. I came on this trip to see why my staff hates to go abroad with Deaver's munchkins ...now, I know. I see, the munchkins do not follow State Department Ambassadorial protocol procedures, to respect your culture. The California munchkins make up their own rules ...they go the way of nouveau riche. I must be patient with

them, perhaps you might consider allowing for their natural shortcomings, as well?" Lucky said.

Back in D.C., Lucky waited outside by the White House Diplomatic Entrance ...until, the right moment, then waved to the band leader, signaling the ceremony to begin. Lucky's staff of senior protocol officers walked with foreign ambassadors and ambassadors' families, that streamed out of a long line of limousines stretching around the block. Everyone walked towards Lucky.

She smiled, as a flourish of trumpets greeted each Ambassador and their family ...each group was met by military aides wearing crisp Marine Honor Guard uniforms, smartly saluting each group, as it passed. The Ambassadors and their families dressed in their national costumes, as was customary for Ambassadors going to meet the President for the first time. African ambassadors and their families dressed in magnificent blue, purple, and yellow robes, and white feathered headdresses, trimmed with gold ...Asian ambassadors and their wives wore bright orange and pink silks from Thailand, Burma, Philippines, Malaysia, and Brunei ...Arabs of the Gulf States wore handsome desert garb, black abas, and white kaffiyes, trimmed with gold.

Lucky's office

In her office, Lucky was writing in her diary. 'The most unpleasant part of dealing with White House staff is the constant personal humiliations they take pleasure in inflicting. Alexander Haig was their prime victim.' Lucky thought it was because Haig offended the munchkins, and Mrs. Reagan ...when he said after the assassination attempt on the President, he personally was 'in charge'.

Lucky was told how it went down. Everyone was in the White House Situation Room, watching the press on T.V. One of the reporters in the crowd outside the Situation Room asked, 'Who's in charge?'

"Vice President Bush," said Larry Speakes.

Well, Haig was watching TV from the Situation Room, too ...and, saw and heard Speakes say that on TV.

Haig start yelling at everyone in the Situation Room. "Bush isn't even here!" Haig yelled.

Then, on TV, one of the reporters asked Speakes, 'is the country going to be put on Red Alert, for a possible nuclear war attack on us?' Haig jumped out of his chair, stormed out of the Situation Room, left behind Cabinet members and White House Staff he was with, who'd been discussing what to do about the assassination attempt on President Reagan. Haig rushed out in front of live TV cameras he pushed Larry Speakes out of the way.

Haig faced the cameras. "We're not putting the country on Red Alert Status. I'm in charge, as of now," State Secretary Haig said.

Lucky kept writing in her diary.

The way it was told to me, she wrote, back in the Situation Room everyone was watching the live TV coverage take place in the room outside, Deaver turned to Weinberger and smiled, Weinberger nodded negatively, frowning. Deaver smiled at Meese the munchkin king, who was picking his nose.

Deaver watched Meese and cringed.

White House Head of Staff James Baker III saw Deaver cringe. "Haig's not in charge, he better read his Constitution. If the President is assassinated, or hurt and can't fulfill presidential responsibilities ...then, the Secretary of State's not in charge."

Haig came back in the Situation Room.

Defense Secretary Weinberger was furious, "You're not in charge!"

"The hell I'm not, read your constitution!"

It was Lucky's observation, Deaver's and Meese's munchkins hated Haig. They hated Haig for saying he was in charge when the President was almost assassinated ...they hated Haig for being rude pushing Speakes aside in front of TV cameras. But Haig, who was after all, her boss, said he never meant what he said to be taken the way it was taken. Nonetheless, his relation with the White House Staff went from bad to worse.

Lucky was shocked to see staffers treat Haig so cavalierly. On the trip to the Versailles Summit, munchkins deliberately kept Haig off the President's helicopter ...so, Secretary Haig and his wife couldn't arrive with the President ...and, assigned the Haigs to a cargo helicopter ...that landed in a cow pasture far behind the Presidential party ...so, the Haigs had to run to catch up ...then, had to desperately search to find a limousine to ride in the motorcade. Barbara Bush told Lucky, the reason munchkins hated Haig was because he was pro-Israel ...munchkins were pro-Arab ...because, they honor the President's backers.

White House Situation Room, 1981

If the Situation Room could talk, a lot of people would listen ...if someone played the tapes from bugs CIA had in the room ...a lot of people would

get sober. In one of the meetings, CIA Director Bill Casey, and Vice President Bush, got their heads together on what Bush later called, 'the Lebanon thing'. Bill succeeded in getting George to agree, send Les Aspin and Bill Buckley, who were a couple CIA operatives, on a CIA covert-ops team to liberate a mosque held by PLO terrorists.

Bill looked into George's eyes, "The Mosque is held by PLO terrorists. I want to send Les Aspin and Bill Buckley in charge of enough mercenaries to terminate our terrorist problem, there. We have a lot of oil money in the Middle East, the World Bank, and IMF, overlent there ...and, I have my responsibility to my own investment, and my international banking consortium's involvement. As DCI, I can't look weak."

George nodded, "Let's settle this terrorist thing."

Weeks later, there was a little political fallout after their hit team killed terrorists that held the mosque ...because, Les Aspin and Bill Buckley posed for photographs of them torturing terrorists ...and, executing them ...that got published in the alternative press.

In following up, Situation Room hosted Bill and George, again.

Bill mumbled, "Buckley and Aspen did good killing those terrorists at the mosque. I want to send Buckley back to neutralize more of them ...or, kidnap them, and their families."

"Families of PLO terrorists? ...they're innocent."

Bill mumbled, "So's my stock portfolio. Terrorists impact the market globally for my investment banking consortium. Being DCI's about swinging the market back in third quarter. Keep Reagan out of the loop ...so, he can have plausible deniability."

Bud McFarland, National Security Agency director, came in the room.

George briefed him, "We're sending a covert-ops team in to protect investments in the Mid-East ...you won't be involved ...but, we're positioning the operation under National Security Agency for deep cover. If anything goes wrong, you take the heat ...not me ...not Bill ...not the President. That's how we play the game ...you knew the scapegoat pecking order when you bought into office, it's your turn."

Bud McFarland fiddled with a pill bottle.

Bill and George both noticed. George commented, "Antacid?"

Bud shook his head, no, "Valium."

Lieutenant Colonel Oliver North came in, saluted smartly.

A slight smile appeared on Bill's face.

George greeted Ollie North "At ease, North. I'm dispatching you to the Contras ... as a communications courier. Report back to me, when you return."

North left the room.

I walked into the Situation Room. "George, got some paperwork for me to sign for your new Special Situations and Preventative Crisis Planning taskforce? ...that pre-emptive retaliation stuff?" I said. I took the papers George handed to me. "Too much to read, what does it say."

"Our Contra and anti-terrorist milestones are on schedule. Paul Nitze says, Full-Court Press against Soviets on schedule, too," George said.

I sighed, "I take on moral responsibility for all innocent people ...if I let any country in the Americas fall to the Commies. Thank God, He sent Jesus to take on our sins ...or, I could never send people to their deaths."

Bill twitched at the mention of God. Bill was a devout Catholic, had been recognized by the Knights of Malta, a Catholic laity organization serving the ruling class way back in the days of the crusade, and today.

Bill mumbled. "Faith isn't enough, Ronnie, to send people to their deaths ...when survival, covert-ops, and war are involved. There's no salvation in it, you got to think in practical terms ...these are good acts we must do, to save mankind ...any good ones killed in error go to Heaven ...bad ones, who cares where," Bill said.

In my heart, I agreed. "Sometimes, when I watch reruns of my old Westerns ... it's so simple, good guys, bad guys, right and wrong, good and evil. I want what's best for God and country ...but, who are the special interests that run America, that I'm protecting? ...I don't even know. Sometimes, I look in the mirror, I think, 'If God gives me free will then that makes me a little god myself.'"

George understood, "We all have that, Mr. President. It's called, executive privilege."

We all chuckled.

I lightened up. "George, on a lighter note, how are you doing deregulating the Savings and Loans."

"S&L deregulation is on target."

"I trust you, I always have."

George felt his face flush. I studied Bill's eyes to discern a reaction to what me and George were talking about. Bill was smiling at some kind of inside joke only he got, like his mumbling.

I looked at George. "I know you'll do a bang-up job, as usual. Let me tell you all a few stories behind the scenes in some of my movies I starred in, in Hollywood. Did I ever tell you the one about ... "

I had a captive audience.

Situation Room redux

Not long after, Bill and George met in the Situation Room, again. Bill wasn't happy. "CIA Agent Buckley's been kidnapped in Beirut, he's a hostage, they took him into Kholmeini's Iran."

George was upset. "What if Buckley talks, what if he says it was my idea, what am I supposed to do, now?!"

Casey looked in a condescending way at Bush. "Get him out of there."

"How? ...he was our expert."

Bill motioned George to come closer. Both men habitually looked over their shoulder, to make sure no one was coming in. Bill whispered, "Call Margaret Thatcher, see if we can use her MI-6 covert-ops people to pull Buckley out."

George nodded, picked up one of the phones in the room, dialed British Prime Minister Margaret Thatcher, spoke with her and hung up, turned to Bill.

George smiled. "On our behalf ...the British will use Leslie Aspin to approach Monzer Al-Kassar ...Monzer Al-Kassar will approach the Palestine Liberation Organization for us ...Thatcher will have MI-6 have Aspin go through Monzer Al-Kassar to meet their demands. Thatcher says, MI-6 says will trade arms through Monzer Al-Kassar to Kholmeini's regime, to get our hostages back. For God's sake, how'd we get into this mess?"

Casey mumbled, "I'm not saying I got us in it, I'm not saying you did ...or, who said what ...covert-ops is secret. Tell one person, if you have to ...its your word against his ...you were DCI, you know the score, take it through the Oval Office ...but, keep the President out of the loop ...so, he has plausible deniability ...we cite National Security reasons ...then, there's no accountability, no way to get us."

National Security Director Bud McFarland came in, sat down with us.

Bush turned to him. "It's time to level with you, Mac. When Buckley went to Lebanon to kidnap terrorists as preventative medicine, it backfired ...he got kidnapped."

Bud felt anxious, he swallowed a valium. "Who sent him?"

CENSORED

Bush sighed. "Let me explain. Bill, call Ollie North in here. Mac, you back into the dark side of the room, so North won't see you.".

Bud nodded, he backed into the shadows.

Lieutenant Colonel Oliver North entered the room, saluted briskly. "Yes sir," Ollie North said.

Bush smiled. "At ease, Colonel. I'm sending you over the pond to British Intelligence to help MI-6 with a little covert-ops for us, to bring back British agent Les Aspin. MI-6 wants Aspin to be our liaison with the Iranians, who are holding Buckley after he was kidnapped in Lebanon by PLO terrorists ...then, they moved him to Iran. MI-6 says Aspin will trade U.S.-made weapons to the Iranians, to get our hostages back. Hell, the allies are sending billions of dollars of weapons to the Iranians anyway, what's a few million dollars more, a scratch, we have to be practical ... dismissed."

Lieutenant Colonel Oliver North saluted, left the room. Bud McFarland walked out of the shadows, gulping another valium.

Bud was flustered, "This is illegal!"

Bill and George closed-in on Bud.

Me, Admiral Poindexter, Defense Secretary Caspar Weinberger, Presidential Counselor Ed Meese, and White House Chief of Staff James Baker III together walked in the Situation Room.

Bill turned to me. "Mr. President, Bill Buckley the CIA Lebanese Division Chief, and six American bystanders have been kidnapped by PLO terrorists."

I felt shocked. Then, dismayed. "They never let up, do they? Spare me the details, get our hostages out from the PLO, save our people! Everyone here, go to Bush's Special Situations Crisis Management Group meeting ...that's his baby, spare me the details, bring me the solutions. This Administration doesn't compromise with terrorists, they're dead meat."

"I want Buckley back alive, he's my friend."

George nodded in agreement.

I suddenly felt I had to speak. "I've been preaching a hard-line, the White House doesn't give-in to terrorists ...giving-in encourages more kidnappings, if I give in, I'll look like a hypocrite to the American people ...not like a John Wayne hero."

Bill gestured to Poindexter, Weinberger, Meese, and Baker ... to leave the room, waited for them to leave. Bill looked at me. "Ronnie, we all have to lose our virginity. I lost mine to Allen Dulles and Bank of International Settlements. You're losing yours to terrorists, just bend over and take it, you've fought the good fight."

I took out my pocket Bible I always carry with me. "I know that one, 2 Timothy, 4:6 ... I have fought the good fight, I have run the course to the finish, I have observed the faith."

George smiled. "We all have, there's no blame, we can't be over-rigid, no one wants to negotiate with terrorists, not you, not me, not Bill."

George took the pocket Bible out of my hands. He flipped through it, then read it. "Ephesians 6:12-13 ... We have a wrestling, not against blood and flesh, but against the governments, against the authorities, against the world rulers of this darkness, against the wicked spirit forces in heavenly places.' Terrorists are wicked spirit forces."

I took the Bible back. "2 Corinthians 11:22-27 ... Are they ministers to Christ? I reply I am more outstandingly one ...in labors more plentifully ...in prisons more plentifully ...in blows to excess ...in near-deaths often."

Casey cast a furtive glance at Bush, then smiled. Bush nodded back.

I continued to read. "By Jews I five times received forty strokes less one ...three times, I was beaten with rods ...once, I was stoned ...three times, I experienced shipwreck ... "

<>

Bill listened ...he start thinking about the military covert-ops missions Ollie North and his team member, Richard Secord, had done over the years ...to Bill, it seemed like the Bible passage I was reading, was a word-for-word description of North and Secord's missions ... that, in serving the U.S., North and Secord endured the trials and tribulations of the Apostle Paul. Casey kept listening.

I kept reading. "...A day and a night I have spent in the deep ...in journeys often ...in dangers from rivers ...in dangers from highwaymen ...in dangers from my own race ...in dangers from the nations ...in dangers, in the city ...in dangers in the wilderness ...in dangers at sea ...in dangers among false brothers ...in labor and toil ...in sleepless nights often ...in hunger and thirst ...in abstinence from food many times ...in cold and nakedness."

Casey listened.

I stopped reading. "Well, if Paul could put up

President Reagan meeting with Henry Kissinger in the residence.

with all that, I guess I can put up with losing face. I can back-down on my hard-line position, you negotiate with the terrorists. Just, don't tell anyone, I'm backing down."

Bill smiled at George. George smiled back.

I felt confused ...then, I had a realization. "Can we go through a third party, so we're clean-looking?"

Bill nodded to George. George went to the door, opened it ...went out ...then, came back in the room with Ollie North. Richard Secord waited outside in another room.

Lieutenant Colonel Oliver North saluted me. I saluted back. Bill nodded to George.

George smiled at me. "Ronnie, Lieutenant Colonel Oliver North is the answer to our prayers, on this one."

"I understood. I took out a pen, I autographed the pocket Bible, handed it to Oliver North. He put it in his attaché case.

North looked at me. "Mr. President, in Nicaragua, it's too late to back out ...now, we're beating the Communists."

Bill mumbled something, catching North's attention. "Ollie, you're not going south of the border, on this one ...you're going to Israel. Israel's Mossad intelligence covert-ops teams are going to do the actual training of the Contra's for us, to give us deep cover ...I want you there, to supervise, report back to me."

That bothered me. "Congress cut-off U.S. Contra aid. Are foreign nationals offering to illegally help us, by sending money?"

Casey mumbled. His words never carried far. Casey looked at me. "The oil sheiks agreed ...but, it's going to cost World Bank percentage points down-the-line, on other deals. The Israelis agreed ...so, Israel keeps getting U.S. foreign aid, they'll do what we want."

<>

Director of the Office of Budget Management David Stockman walked into the Situation Room, along with Defense Secretary Caspar Weinberger.

Casey turned towards them. "Weinberger, you're Defense Secretary ...even, if you hate the Israelis, you'll keep weapons flowing to them."

Weinberger had a short fuse. "I don't hate them ...if we want to keep interest rates down, we have to keep the Arabs happy."

Stockman reacted. "This is another installment on our continuing saga. Weinberger ...you're sick, you're going to bankrupt the U.S. with phony military spending. Who's making all the profits? That's what I want to know."

George had taken Oliver North into a corner of the room, one could hear them speaking. George whispered, "Ollie, I'm dispatching you to Saudi Arabia to the oil sheiks to launder money for BCCI."

In another corner of the room, in front of a full-length mirror, Mike was brushing lint off my shoulders in preparation for a press conference.

I zeroed in on him. "Mike, are you skimming-off Contra money from my campaign fund, behind my back?"

No one in the room wanted to hear the answer ...everyone hurried out ...Mike followed them out, as George Shultz walked in. My eyes lit up when I saw him.

I shook his hand enthusiastically. "I'm glad Haig is gone as State Secretary ...and, you accepted the position, and came onboard," I said.

State Secretary George Shultz smiled graciously. I talked to him a long time to fill him in ...then, brought the conversation to a close.

I looked at Shultz. "What I've just described to you is the way relationships work between Bill Casey, George Bush, Bud McFarland, and Oliver North."

Shultz didn't show surprise. As President of Bechtel, having had a leading role in the President's Economic Council, Shultz always had a supply of intelligence reports flowing to him ...and, for all I knew, maybe was telling the same men what do to, long before I came on the scene ...and, long after I'd retire.

Shultz smiled. "I'm sorry, Mr. President ...but, I'm not down with the program. What Bush, and North, and Casey, and McFarland cook up ... is on them. They can deceive, and manipulate each other, or themselves, or you ...it seems to me, without a moment's notice and without a moment's thought. Are you sure you trust them enough to know, will they put national interest above their own private interest?"

I chuckled. "Hell no. I trust them to do just the opposite, to be exactly who they are, I depend on that. As long as they serve themselves, they serve America. They *are* America. That's not betraying me, they're just doing the jobs I hired them to do, whether I understand what they're doing, or not ...whether I approve, or not ...the more self-serving they are, the more I trust them. So, they have no reason to betray me. They're the most qualified men in the country to do whatever the hell it is they're doing. As long as I let them, America's safe. I support them, they *are* America."

Shultz frowned. "It's your neck if you hiccup."

I wondered what he meant. I was dismayed, irritable. "You, and the other Bechtel boys advised me

340

my entire political career, since the early '50s ...I've never seen you be so negative, before."

Shultz was confident of his own knowledge, knew his own abilities, was one of the most capable businessmen in the world, and one of the most influential.

"Mr. President, it breaks down like this ...we have the financiers with their loans and interest rate ...we have the arms makers and their provocations to increase sales ...we have countries destabilized by CIA acting on behalf of the Central banks and investment bankers waiting to loan money to countries that need it ...we have the big construction firms, Bechtel, Brown & Root, Halliburton, Bin Laden Construction, rebuilding countries after CIA tears countries apart ...but, when we lose intelligence operatives who are team players ...and, they become rogue players and free agents on us ...there's no order left in the new World Order, anymore ...is there? ...it turns into a nuclear free-for-all. I'm afraid Bush, and Casey, aren't team players for Democracy ...they're free agents, in it for themselves. Casey's looking after his banking interests, swinging his Central bank investment consortium into Deutchmarks, Yen, and Kugerands. Bush's looking after his oil interests in the Gulf, and crapping bricks to get back his Cuban oil, and African oil out of Angola and Sudan before his British competition does. Deaver's on the take with the WACL death squads and Contras ...who, I think, are not freedom fighters at all ...but, mercenaries protecting cocaine operations ... I don't call all this, being 'negative', Mr. President ...it's realistic, brutally realistic. National borders are blurring, national interests breaking down into diverse ruling family portfolios and fourth-quarter profits. Stockman's right, we're bankrupting America, we better grab all we can before the country is taken over by German, Japanese, and Arab banks. I'm afraid we may be looking at the rise and fall of America, in our lifetimes."

My Irish temper was flaring. "The White House is not going to fall apart with me at the helm. Hell, we'll all make enough money we can live in any country we want to ...but, not me. I believe in America. Come, look at my old Hollywood movies with me, again, George ...you'll see, I'm the original American hero. Nothing's falling apart while I'm in charge."

I meant it.

Blair House, the White House guest house, 1982

Blair House was falling apart. White House Protocol Ambassador Lucky Roosevelt's job for the U.S. included finding accommodations for foreign ambassadors and dignitaries visiting the White House ...Blair House, the official White House guest house, was located across the street from the White House. That's where foreign visitors usually stayed. Blair House was in bad shape.

Lucky considered remodeling Blair House one of her pet projects. Lucky watched, Foreign Secretary George Shultz walked up to the porch, towards her. She smiled at him. A long, comfortable silence passed between them. The wind softly moaned. The door of Blair house blew open.

Lucky and George Shultz looked a bit spooked when the door opened by itself, in the wind.

Shultz recovered his composure. "Lucky, are you glad I put you in charge of fixing Blair House up?"

Lucky spoke sincerely, and with warmth. "Oh yes, it'll be beautiful again. And, I'm taking you up on that bet. I'm betting Blair House will be remodeled before this Administration leaves Washington."

Shultz noticed how smooth Lucky's voice sounded. He gestured they go they inside. They walked into Blair House. Lucky flipped the light switch on and off, several times. The lights didn't work. Lucky frowned. Shultz frowned.

"The electrical system needs overhauling. Tell me about protocol," Shultz said.

"Of course, would you like a glass of water?"

Shultz nodded, "Yes, that'd be nice."

They walked into the kitchen. Lucky took two paper cups from a dispenser, went to fill the cups at the sink, turned the water tap on. No water came out.

Lucky frowned, "Maybe we could get water when we go back to the White House."

"That'd be fine."

Lucky smiled warmly, "Protocol is good manners, making the other person feel at home. State visits ...for chiefs of state such as Queen Elizabeth of Great Britain..."

Shultz noticed the wall thermostat, ripped off the wall, was hanging by electrical wires. He turned the thermostat control dial up with his thumb, he listened ...but, couldn't hear the thermostat click, or the furnace turn on.

Lucky continued."...or President Mitterrand of France ..." Lucky said. Lucky flipped on the air conditioning while she spoke. Shultz looked

President Reagan with Charlton Heston at a meeting with the
Presidential Task Force on the Arts and Humanities in the cabinet room.

along a far wall. The air conditioning unit was laying on the floor, in a pile of dust. Lucky noticed Shultz was very observant.

Lucky kept speaking, "...usually last a week ...the President gives a state dinner..." Lucky watched as Shultz discovered the fire sprinkler systems were dripping water on the wooden floors and carpeting. "...An official visit is for heads of government such as British Prime Minister Margaret Thatcher, or, German Chancellor Helmut Kohl ...that's the same as a state visit ...except, reigning monarchs and presidents get a 21 gun salute, prime ministers only get 19 guns. Now, for ceremonial arrival at the White House ..."

Shultz wrinkled his nose. "I smell a small gas leak. Lucky, please note we'll have to get someone in here to fix that, too."

Lucky smiled, making a mental note, and kept on. "There are about ten state and/or official visits a year. An official working visit is long on substance, short on ceremony, a two or three day stay gets no state dinner ...but, there are lunches and or dinners for you to host as State Secretary ...or, for the vice president to host. You personally go to the airport to greet visitors who come on state visits ...for working visits, we send the helicopter, bring them to Washington Monument ...and, you greet them there. It used to be, the President himself greets chiefs of state at the airport, security doesn't permit that, now," Lucky said. Lucky noticed that Shultz kept looking up at a chandelier, swinging back and forth,...the chandelier let go, crashing to the floor.

Lucky and Shultz jumped back. Lucky watched George Shultz react with dismay. He looked back at her. "I don't believe it."

"I didn't either, the first time I came into Blair House," Lucky said.

"Please continue what you were telling me."

Lucky moved and spoke with a natural grace. "In many countries in the Middle East, and Far East, the formal welcome is more important than the substantive discussions."

As Lucky spoke with Shultz, they noticed Blair House guests had brought their own chefs along with them, to do native cooking ...several chefs of differing nationalities were walking in and out of Blair House. Lucky thought, Shultz found that amusing or remarkable ...because of the looks of wonder on his face.

She smiled at him. "During the Eisenhower Administration, the state visit of King Ibn Saud of Saudi Arabia almost got canceled, the King refused to come ...unless, Eisenhower met him at the airport."

Lucky and Shultz watched ...workers unloaded truck-loads of food in and out of walk-in refrigerators.

Lucky went on. "King Hassan of Morocco is heading an Arab League delegation to Washington, soon ...he sent word, he won't come ...unless, you meet him at the airport."

Shultz nodded. "Please remind me later at the right time."

Lucky smiled, "When Blair House closes for remodeling our guests may choose their hotel ...we pay for all rooms and expenses for principals and entourage of twelve."

As Lucky spoke, she and Shultz continued their inspection of Blair House. They found the curtains torn, stained by water damage ...the bedroom carpeting was dirty ...bedspreads were torn, stained ...soiled linen and towels were scattered about. Lucky could tell by the look on his face, Shultz had enough of inspecting Blair House for one day ...but, she said nothing of it.

She continued her explanation of protocol, Shultz had asked her for. "If the entourage is over twelve ...then, the principals pay for it, themselves. It's a good thing, too ...because, many visitors feel the bigger their retinue the more important they are ...they come with 747s full of retainers. Generally, the smaller the country, the larger the entourage. We only pay for five limousines, no matter how large the entourage."

Shultz admired Lucky's thoroughness, "Lucky, you sure know your stuff. I'd like to continue chatting ...but, I have an engagement. Thanks for explaining protocol to me."

Lucky felt happy, satisfied she and Shultz had met at Blair House ...and, shared an understanding for what needed remodeling.

"You're welcome."

As Lucky and Shultz spoke, chef's assistants led five goats on leashes into the kitchen ...and, unloaded several crates full of chickens. Lucky noticed the bewildered look on Shultz's face.

She tried to put him at ease. "Fresh eggs ...our Middle Eastern visitors like fresh eggs ...fresh goat milk ...fresh goat meat."

Shultz smiled. "Lucky, at State Department dinners ...I like round tables, seating ten, ...absolutely, no reporters at my table ...nothing to inhibit conversation."

Lucky startled, "My God! ...that man brought in a box of meat infested with maggots! I'm calling

Department of Agriculture, immediately!"

Shultz noticed Lucky's boiling point, too. He watched Lucky walk to the phone. Dialed, put the phone to her ear ...then. hung up. She looked at Shultz. "Blair House phone doesn't work."

Shultz shrugged, "It figures." He looked at his watch. "Lucky, I've designed a menu card, as a souvenir for guests to take home with them. I don't like veal ...it's too common ...I hate squash."

As Shultz and Lucky spoke, they continued their inspection ...on one wing of Blair House they found one monarch had brought in his own vibrating bed ...and, had eighteen mattresses spread on the floor for his bodyguards.

Shultz and Lucky turned away.

Shultz turned to Lucky. "Now, I guess I've seen it all."

Lucky smiled. She'd seen enough for one day.

Shultz kept speaking. "Please, no tall flowers for centerpieces ...they block conversation ...keep me from eyeballing guests."

Lucky managed to smile. She felt tired. "You've got it, boss."

At that moment the water heater in Blair House broke, and started filling Blair House with water.

Versailles Summit Gala

At the Versailles Summit, Deaver's front men pushed the U.S. Ambassador to France, and Lucky, out of their way.

The U.S. Ambassador to France complained, "You staffers and advance men have no business attending the dinner and keeping Lucky out, she's part of the official delegation ...you can't keep Lucky out ...she's indispensable ...Lucky must be included ...or, I'll protest to the President."

As soon as she saw a telephone, Lucky phoned Deaver, back in the U.S. She was furious ...but,

Lucky controlled her anger. "You keep your munchkins off me! ...and, off State Department ...this is my first trip abroad with the President ...please, rein-in your munchkins so this won't happen again! I've had enough of your pushy advance team munchkins, to last a lifetime!"

Deaver put her on hold. Standing there, in the phone booth, Lucky remembered back to 1952.

Lucky and her husband Archie were in Madrid, where Archie was CIA Madrid Station Chief. At the time, Archie was talking with Nazi Spanish Security Chief Otto Skorzeny ...years later Archie told Lucky, Skorzeny organized the postwar Nazi underground in Argentina ...then, came to Spain

to help the fascist Franco, organize and train death squads to defeat anti-Fascist partisans in the Spanish Civil War ...and, that the Dulles central bank consortium financed Franco's side of the civil war ...and, financed the anti-Fascist partisans fighting for Democracy.

The other man in the conversation was Nazi, Werner Naumann, who organized the postwar Nazi underground headquarters, and government-in-exile, in Madrid ...back in 1943, nine years earlier. Werner Naumann planned a Nazi coup d'état to take place in Berlin, in 1952 ...it was exposed at the last minute, and failed.

Lucky remembered the situation, at the time.

Werner Naumann threw his hands up in the air ...the entire Nazi-run Spanish embassy was thrown into chaos, by the arrival of the 'We-like-Ike', advance team. Ike's presidential advance team had come to make preparations for President Eisenhower's visit. The 'We-like-Ike' advance team frantically passed out 'We-like-Ike' lapel buttons ...ignoring the Spanish ambassadors and State Department people ...then, ordered around their hosts ...and, the advance team's behavior compromised Archie's covert relations with Spanish security, and intelligence services, run by Otto Skorzeny ...Skorzeny and Neumann stormed off angrily. Lucky remembered after Archie became CIA Britain Station Chief, he was treated just as rudely there, by the Kennedy presidential advance teams ...when Lucky and Archie were stationed in London.

<>

Talk show host Mae Brussell's, *Nazi Connections to JFK*, in *Rebel Magazine*, commented on Otto Skorzeny and Klaus Barbie.

"By 1952, Klaus Barbie had arrived in Bolivia, via a stop in Argentina. He was spirited out of Germany by CIA, with a hand from the Vatican. Soon, he teamed up with SS Major Otto Skorzeny, now was affiliated with CIA ...thanks to Reinhard Gehlen, who's whole Nazi anti-Soviet intelligence outfit had been hired by CIA. Dr. Fritz Thyssen, and Dr. Gustav Krupp, both beneficiaries of McCloy's amnesty, bankrolled Skorzeny from the start.

<>

"Barbie and Skorzeny were soon forming death squads, such as ...Angels of Death in Bolivia ...Anti-Communist Alliance in Argentina ...and, in Spain with Stephen Della Chiaie, Guerrillas of Christ the King.

"In 1952, Otto Skorzeny, released from American custody in 1947, moved to Madrid. He created what is known as, 'the International Fascista'. CIA and Gehlen's BND dispatched Skorzeny to 'trouble spots'. On his payroll were former SS agents, French OAS terrorists, and secret police from Portugal's PDID. SS Colonel Skorzeny's CIA agents participated in terror campaigns waged by Operation 40 in Guatemala, Brazil, and Argentina. Skorzeny was also in charge of the Paladin mercenaries, whose cover, M.C. Inc., was a Madrid export-import firm.

"Dr. Gerhard Hartmut von Schubert, formerly of Joseph Goebbels' propaganda ministry, was M.C.'s operating manager. The nerve center for Skorzeny's operations was in Albufera, Spain. It was lodged in the same building as the Spanish intelligence agency, SCOE under Colonel Eduardo Blanco ...where there was also a CIA office."

Nancy told me, Henrik Kruger's, *Great Heroin Coup*, talked about International Fascista.

"It fulfilled the dream of Skorzeny ...but, also of his close friends in Madrid ...exile Jose Lopez Rega, Juan Peron's grey eminence ...and Prince Justo Valerio Borghese, the Italian fascist money man who'd been rescued from execution from the hands World War II Italian resistance fighters by future CIA counterintelligence whiz, James J. Angleton."

Mae continued. "A subcommittee on international operations of Senate Foreign Relations Committee prepared a report, *Latin America, Murder, Inc.* ...still classified. The title repeated Lyndon Johnson's remark three months before he died, 'We were running a Murder, Inc. in the Caribbean'. *Murder Incorporated* concluded, 'The United States had joint operations between Argentina, Bolivia, Brazil, Chile, Paraguay, and Uruguay. The joint operations were known as, Operation Condor. These are special teams used to carry out 'sanctions' ...the killing of enemies."

Aug. 3, 1979 Jack Anderson's column gave a few details in, *Operation Condor, An Unholy Alliance*. "Assassination teams are centered in Chile. This international consortium is located in Colonia Dignidad, Chile. Founded by Nazis from Hitler's SS, headed by Franz Pfeiffer Richter ...Adolf Hitler's 1000-year Reich may not have perished. Children are cut up in front of their parents, suspects are asphyxiated in piles of excrement, or rotated to death over barbecue pits. Otto Skorzeny had code-named his assault on American soldiers in the Battle of the Bulge, 'Operation Greif', the 'Condor'. He continued Condor with his post-war special teams, imposing 'sanctions', meaning the assassination of enemies. Skorzeny's father-in-law was Hjalmar

Schacht, president of Hitler's Reichsbank."

Mae continued. "CIA's, Skorzeny's and Gehlen's death squads ...with headquarters in Madrid, were additionally funded by Martin Bormann ... when the Evita Peron-sheltered Nazi flight capital funds were distributed after 1952."

<>

By the time Lucky was off hold, and Deaver was back on the line, Lucky had a few more thoughts to share with him. "Mike, your advance team brings out the worst in everyone ...each one has a private, personal business agenda to take care of. Why don't you learn some lessons from Secret Service? ...they can be demanding, too ...but, *they* manage to do so without causing heartburn, or heartache. They're brave, incorruptible, discreet, good-natured ...and, totally professional. Why can't you and your advance teams act like them? ...would you like me to arrange to get a training person from Secret Service over to you, to train you and your staff, and advance team?"

Deaver ignored Lucky. "Okay. Lucky, help me out back here in America. I've got a photo-op set up with the President and King Ibn Saud. Will you call? ...have the Arabs lose their robes ...don't let 'em dress in those, 'I'm-a-rich-oil-sheik-wearing-sunglasses-fuck-you-outfits', okay? We don't like the domestic impact of that image. It hurts the President."

White House

When Lucky returned to the United States, she hardly had a moment's rest. She immediately caught heat from the protocol chief of Morocco, Moulay Hafid el-Alaoui ... a relative of the King of Morocco, King Hassan. Then, Morocco was in the middle of a bloody civil war where the King, a fascist, was defeating his democratic opponents by killing off his civilian population.

"Ambassador Roosevelt, don't you agree? It's disgraceful, this rich country of America is ungenerous ...counts pennies with the King of Morocco? My king is hospitable to American officials who visit ...his Majesty provides you with any number of limos you ask for in Morocco ...but here, you humiliate us with only five stretch limos," Moulay Hafid el-Alaoui said.

Lucky seethed inside ...but, handled matters gracefully. "Oh, Moulay Hafid! My face is blackened! Everything you say is true, your king is indeed a man of legendary generosity, no one can match his hospitality, his munificence ...but, you must understand ... my President Ronald Reagan is also a true prince, a man of great heart who wants to receive your king who is accountable to no one ...but, my President, alas, is accountable to the legislature for financial matters ...please, please, Moulay Hafid, let us hear no more about this awkward matter ...you're a gentleman ...and will not wish to embarrass me further." Lucky waived her hand in a gesture of dismissal.

The next morning, when Lucky arrived at the White House main gates, she saw a troop of oddly-dressed men ...wearing pantaloons and striped vests ...red fezzes and pointed bedroom slippers ...carrying silver teapots ...Bunsen burners ...and picnic baskets, full of Moroccan mint tea leaves ... escorted by the Secret Service who were busily handcuffing them.

The tea makers were indignant and protested. "King Hassan of Morocco expects us to make tea for Mrs. Reagan."

His tone of voice indicated he'd be in great trouble if he didn't do as he'd been told.

The Secret Service man handcuffing him had no regard for him. "I don't care if he's the biggest heroin dealer in North Africa, you're going to jail."

Lucky watched the scene repeated everywhere she looked ...she hurried over to the Secret Service man who handcuffed the tea maker.

Lucky smiled. "These funny-looking guys in pantaloons and striped vests, red fezzes and pointy bedroom slippers carrying silver teapots, Bunsen burners and picnic baskets full of Moroccan mint tea leaves ... *really are* King Hassan's tea makers ...they're definitely not terrorists ...leave them alone, they're with me."

Lucky led the tea makers into the White House ...immediately, the White House curator panicked ...as tea makers plopped down onto the red-carpeted floor of the main hall ...and began making tea. Their alcohol stoves shot out bright blue and yellow flames. The King's aide in charge of pomegranate juice was busy making pomegranate juice with a special fruit juice squeezer ...for the Cabinet meeting King Hassan was to attend. An entourage of servants and aides accompanied King Hassan as he approached Lucky ...the king's servant in charge of holding the king's coat and hat ...servant in charge of holding his eyeglasses ...servant to serve the king cigarettes ...servant to serve coffee ...servant to serve water ...and several veiled belly dancers dancing around to music made by the Moroccan King's musicians ...who accompanied the entourage playing their instruments.

A Moroccan intelligence officer introduced himself to Lucky. "We flew in plane-loads of live lambs ...our chefs and our kitchenware are to be used at a dinner the King has planned," the Moroccan intelligence officer said.

Lucky rolled her eyes. 'I knew it! What next?!'

Bekka Valley poppy fields, Lebanon

Monzer Al-Kassar, state-sponsored drug lord, weapons trafficker, narco-terrorist, and respected multinational businessman ... was surrounded by belly dancers he kept on heroin ... they relaxed on a blanket spread in the middle of his opium poppy fields, enjoying life in the Bekka Valley in Lebanon, while his cargo of heroin was loaded onto his plane. Then, he boarded the plane, it took off, and a few minutes later landed at an airport in Syria.

There, an Al-Kassar family celebration with Monzer's three brothers and his sister, a several day event celebrating his sister's wedding with her fiancé Prince Haidar Assad son of King Assad of Syria was under way. Monzer noticed his sister and future brother-in-law constantly flirting with each other, infatuated. That made Monzer happy. According to custom, when his sister and her fiancé saw Monzer watching them flirt, his sister acted shy and innocent, blushing.

Monzer approved of this marriage. "How's my favorite sister?"

Monzer's sister laughed. "Your only sister, and most powerful son of King Assad of Syria, still enjoying being head of Syrian intelligence?"

Prince Haidar was happy. "I'm making a fortune, did you bring another shipment of Bekka Valley heroin with you?"

Monzer was distracted. "Let's talk business, later."

King Assad of Syria joined them "Monzer! Welcome to this wonderful wedding!"

Monzer felt happy. "Yes, it's great ...the Al-Kassar family and your royal family intermarries.

King Assad took Monzer Al-Kassar aside, whispering, "I've been planning revenge on CIA since 1949, when they toppled my family monarchy, and installed their puppet regime ...my mother and father would be alive today if John McCone, Bechtel, and Bush didn't arrange that coup

Nancy Reagan talking with Warren Beatty and Diane Keaton at a movie screening for "Reds" in the Family Theater. 12/5/81.

...slaughtering my loved ones. I swore to Allah this day would come, and it's near," Assad said.

Monzer and King Assad mingled with wedding guests while wedding musicians played. Monzer noticed Prince Haidar standing too close to the band's loudspeakers, cover his ears with his palms, then move aside.

Prince Haidar was desperate, frantic to block the sound from his ears. Prince Haidar Assad, Intelligence head of Syria was remembering a day he spent in Moscow in the basement dungeon of the Union of Soviet Socialist Republic's intelligence service, GRU. KGB was there, too. Prince Assad was there for training exercises, being personally trained by an instructor wearing mirror sunglasses, trained how to interrogate a subject by torture.

Prince Haidar Assad held his hands against his ears as his victim screamed ...then, Haidar broke another of his victim's fingers, bending the finger back until the bone snapped through the flesh with a cracking sound. Haidar held his ears because the subject's screams were shrill. Haidar bent back his subject's ring finger until the bone snapped, then twisted it off, watching the subject's wedding band fall to the prison's metal floor.

Today, at the wedding, Monzer smiled as the wedding vows were being exchanged as a Moslem religious cleric did the ceremony. "Take the rings, with this ring I thee wed."

Prince Haidar held his bride's hand.

"With this ring I thee wed," Prince Haidar said.

Prince Haidar slid the wedding ring over his bride's ring finger ...remembering his subject's ring falling through the air towards the metal prison floor ...hitting the floor as Prince Haidar placed a wire noose around his subject's neck ...tightening it to suffocate his subject ...tightening it until the subject's screaming stopped ...and blood spilled from his subject's mouth onto the wedding ring on the metal floor of the prison ...then, Prince Haidar released the noose so his subject could breath again and not die.

Haidar gazed into his bride's eyes, repeating his vow. "With this ring I thee wed."

Prince Haidar remembered slipping the wire noose off his subject's neck ...picking up a tube with an air bladder attached to one end of it ...then forcing the bladder and tube down his subject's throat into his subject's stomach ...turning on the air pump attached to the tube ...making his subject scream again ...while the subject's wedding ring lying on the metal prison floor was slowly engulfed in a puddle of blood

flowing around it.

The Muslim religious cleric continued the ceremony. "To honor and love till death do us part," the cleric said.

Haidar remembered the look in the eyes of his subject's wife stretching one arm away from her captors ...reaching her hand straining to shield her children's eyes ...the children were crazy with fear, crying wildly ...Prince Haidar smiled because he felt so powerful.

"To honor and love till death," Haidar said.

"To honor and love till death," the bride said.

In Prince Haidar's mind, he saw the image of his subject with the air hose forced down the subject's throat into the stomach exploding the subject's stomach, the subject's wife screaming, Prince Haidar had to press his hands against his ears, his face rigid.

The wedding orchestra played, 'Here comes the bride', the sound of *Ouuu's* and *Ahhhh's* and applause of wedding guests filled the air.

The sound of the applause reminded Prince Haidar of the day he received the Soviet Intelligence Medal of Achievement from his instructor who wore sunglasses, for graduating from the torture school.

Haidar kissed his bride.

Wedding reception, palace, Damascus Syria

At the gala Royal wedding party for his sister, Monzer Al-Kassar introduced Lieutenant Colonel Oliver North to Syrian King Assad. As instructed, Lieutenant North gave King Assad the pocket bible autographed by 'President Ronald Reagan', and a set of matching pistols ...then, saluted King Assad, noting the king was pleased. The men embraced, there was discussion between North, Monzer and the King ...North walked from the courtyard to a helicopter waiting nearby, and departed.

The wedding reception featured entertainment. The main attraction was Prince Haidar torturing Bill Buckley. The Al-Kassar and Assad ruling families watched, as Haidar forced an air hose down Bill Buckley's throat into Buckley's stomach, Haidar turned on the air pump. Using torture, he forced a confession out of Buckley.

Monzer was curious ...then, repulsed ...but, continued videotaping the tortured confession.

Bill Buckley screamed, "I swear it! Let me alone! I'm begging you! Please! It was Bush's idea to kidnap and neutralize PLO terrorists and their families, not mine!"

Monzer watched Haidar look to King Assad for confirmation. King Assad was pleased. Monzer felt pleased too ...and, nodded.

King Assad walked over beside Buckley. "You're in Syria, Buckley ...not, Iran ...not, Lebanon. I finance PLO with Monzer's help, and our poppies. Do you think PLO is right, or wrong?"

Buckley felt weak, terrified. "You're right! PLO's good! CIA's bad!"

King Assad looked at Monzer's video camera.

"The PLO are not terrorists, they are 'freedom fighters' fighting to get British and American troops out of the Mid-East, fighting to get Israel out of Jerusalem. PLO does not care Israel is the biggest customer for U.S. and British arms ...PLO knows U.S. foreign aid to Israel is used to buy weapons from America."

Monzer continued videotaping Buckley's torture and confession, with King Assad talking ...then finished, took his video camera into the palace audio-visual lab, edited out Buckley's death so the footage showed Buckley still alive ...and, pleased with himself, Monzer inserted the edited tape into a tape duplicating machine, made several copies ... called in his British MI-6 intelligencer liaison from an adjoining room and handed him two copies. "Give these tapes to Margaret Thatcher and tell her, give a copy to Bill Casey."

Buckingham Palace, British Royal ruling family

Early next morning, Monzer Al-Kassar's British MI-6 liaison arrived at Buckingham Palace in Great Britain, met Margaret Thatcher and handed her the videotapes, passing along instructions as told ...then, everyone went to 16 downing Street to an MI-6 office viewing room, where British Prime Minister Margaret Thatcher and British intelligence MI-6 chiefs watched Buckley's confession and torture on videotape.

White House Situation Room

Several days later in the White House Situation Room, Monzer Al-Kassar's MI-6 liaison handed a copy of the videotape to DCI Bill Casey, who called in Vice President Bush, Foreign Secretary George Shultz, National Security Director Bud McFarland, Lieutenant Colonel Oliver North, and me. Bill started the tape.

I threw up immediately.

Bud McFarland stressed-out, had a mental breakdown. "I can't take this job, anymore! You can shove it! I resign!" McFarland yelled. McFarland picked up a telephone.

Bill looked at George. George watched McFarland.

McFarland yelled into the phone, "Operator! ...get me to a mental hospital! I'm going in!"

Secret Service men came in, ambulance orderlies came in, strapped McFarland onto a portable ambulance gurney.

McFarland stared at us.

"Can you believe this shit?! I didn't do it! I'm innocent! They did it! It's not my fault!" McFarland yelled.

Casey mumbled, "That figures."

Bill had expected it out of McFarland sooner or later, looked at George.

Bush looked back at Casey and shrugged his shoulders.

Mental hospital, Washington D.C.

National Security Director McFarland committed himself to a Catholic mental hospital with icon pictures on the wall of Jesus Christ, heart exposed pierced by a spear from which a single drop of blood formed. McFarland was stressed out ...he reached for his pants folded on a chair beside the bed ...took out a bottle of valium pills, poured all the pills into his palm ...gulped them into his mouth ...took a drink of water, and putting his hand on his heart waited. Bud McFarland had decided to go home.

Nancy's White House office

Sitting in her office at the White House, Nancy felt nervous. Suspecting the worst, she phoned Mike Deaver, "Mike, Ronnie's in trouble, I just know it. What did they do to McFarland? Why's he trying to kill himself? What did they say to him? Is it Casey? Or Bush? I should fire someone but I don't know who, to protect Ronnie. Should I fire McFarland?"

Mike didn't know what to tell Nancy, when she was like this. He stalled. "It may not look very good if the President's wife goes on the rampage, the press will call it 'another firing spree'. Nancy, would you really fire the head of the National Security Agency after he tried to kill himself in a mental hospital?" Deaver was pleased how he expressed his point.

Nancy didn't feel any calmer. "I have to protect Ronnie, I have to get rid of everyone who wants to hurt him! Don't you get it!?"

White House Situation Room

Bill and George sat in silence.

Casey spoke first, "I'm not too upset."

George was upset. "I'm freaked. My dick's in the wringer. What we gonna do?"

Bill mumbled, "We'll shut down the operation."

George got upset, "If they shut down operation, the hostages will be killed!"

Bill gave George a look of disbelief. "Who gives a fuck about the hostages? I've got my consortium portfolio to protect!"

George put his hand on his forehead. "Contras will be killed if they don't get their weapons, my investments and your loans to our juntas down there will go to Hell!"

Bill stared at George. "I'm diversified. I've got loans I can make in Africa and China. Hell, we're in the middle of destabilizing the Soviet Union and Eastern Europe with our 'Full-Court Press'. Do you think I can afford to care about lives of a few hostages? ...can you?"

George frowned. "I guess not, when the new World Order investment portfolio is at stake, our British and German investors would kill us ...hostages are going to die sooner ...or later, anyway. I just never know who they're gonna be, it puts a stain on my cover."

"Don't blow the President's cover, if he goes down, so do you."

"What about you?" George said.

Bill was confident. "I've been in the game too long George ... I know where the bodies are buried ...I've been in banking on Wall Street as long as your father ...I was there when Wall Street started the whole intelligence racket ...nothing can get me."

George wasn't entirely pleased with the condescending tone in Bill's voice. "You *should* know where the bodies are buried, you put them there."

Casey got angry, yelled into the waiting room on the other side of the door. "North! Come in here!"

North came in, saluting sharply. "Yes sir."

Bill got a kick out of how seriously North took himself. "McFarland's in the nut house, we need you. I know you're handling arms-for-drugs negotiations with the Contras ...ferrying our arms down there ...and, shepherding back their cocaine shipments into the U.S. using CIA and diplomatic immunity. Vice President Bush wants you to go to Iran, to negotiate more arms-for-hostages deals."

North looked at the vice president.

George nodded.

North nodded back. "Yes sir ...am I being drafted into CIA?"

George frowned. "No, Ollie ...that's getting to be an old joke, don't you think?"

"Yes sir."

George sighed. "This is private enterprise. Bill and me are running it for national security of the U.S. We're burying the operation in National Security Agency paperwork ...so, you're officially working for NSA ...the same cover we use for your Contra activity. Let me assure you, what you do for Bill and me goes higher than NSA or CIA."

Days later, Ollie North in civilian clothes, disembarked from a 747 in Iran.

Reagan dress rehearsal, White House press room

In the White House Press Room, Mike Deaver rehearsed me on an anti-drug speech. Looking distracted, he flipped open his wallet, pulled out a few bills. Mike hated being behind on his bills ...to make it worse, he only had about 700 dollars in his wallet. Behind Mike, a Contra in a brown military uniform held a briefcase, waiting. Mike glanced at the Contra and the briefcase, smiled in relief, took out his flask form his inside coat pocket ...and, had a nip of vodka.

Mike caught my attention.

"Ham it up, Ronnie! This is something you believe in, remember? Be convincing as hell."

I nodded. "I'll turn up emotional involvement on this one."

I start delivering my speech in earnest ...suddenly adding anguished emotional overtones, as if the speech I was giving mattered to me.

Mike nodded an okay to me, motioned the Contra over, took the briefcase, opened it and saw it was full of money ...and, taking out a couple stacks of hundred dollars bills, put them in his briefcase ...while I continued rehearsing my anti-drug speech.

Exclusive men's club, Washington D.C.

A few days later, I was delivering the same speech Mike had rehearsed me on, in an exclusive men's club in Washington. I considered myself animated, a hardline cold-warrior. I walked to the podium, began my anti-drug, anti-terrorist, anti-Communism speech ... to the elite group of businessmen there especially for my presentation.

Exclusive men's club, London

A few days later, I flew over the Atlantic, in London for a meeting with Britain's MI-6 intelligence leaders. I gave my anti-terrorist, anti-Communism speech again ...for me, it was giving the same speech over and over again ...I'm glad I had good speech writers. In a room on the other side of the building. Oliver North, Les Aspin, Monzer Al-Kassar, and a MI-6 handler ... were cutting weapons deals, considering various weapons-for-hostages scenarios ...that, would be a win-win situation for everyone involved in negotiations and trades.

The MI-6 intelligencer opened a briefcase to show it was full of money, put a few stacks into his pocket ...then, pushed the briefcase to Aspin. Aspin pocketed a few stacks of money ...then, pushed the briefcase to Monzer Al-Kassar, who tossed some money stacks to North. North had a look of doubt on his face.

Monzer Al-Kassar smiled coldly. "I want to stuff some of this money in your uniform between your shirt buttons, it's not for you, it's for your Contra support efforts."

North had a questioning look on his face. "Is it true what Aspin said, we can make 125 million dollars profit on a 250 million dollar arms deal ...selling U.S. missiles?"

Monzer Al-Kassar nodded. "In a heartbeat ... Welcome to the ruling family world of terrorist financing and big business ...there's profits to fund your Contra war, or any of Casey's private wars ...enough profit to kickback all your Congressman's campaign funds."

Leslie Aspin felt troubled. "I'm worried about my brother, he worked with U.S. Customs Intelligence, he's the one that informed CIA's Wilson and Terkil dealt arms to Libya through Kaddaffi ...I don't trust him."

Leslie Aspin remembered the arguments he and his brother Michael got into.

Aspin home, London

In his London home, Leslie Aspin was in another argument with his brother, Michael ...over money.

"Michael, I'm telling you, this is a sweet deal, 125 million dollars in profit cut three ways, just the first one of many!"

Michael Aspin already lost patience with his brother. "You're crazy! You're in bed with British, American, Syrian, and Soviet intelligence ... you're gonna get crucified! I won't let you do it!"

Leslie stared in disbelief at his brother.

"You did it with CIA in Libya! you middled their arms and drug deals! You made a fortune! Now, you won't let me?!"

Michael got more upset. "It almost cost me my life! I was a cut-out, a set-up! So are you! You're blind as a bat!"

Michael flipped his brother an obscene gesture, to tell Leslie, leave him alone ...Leslie left the room.

Michael picked up the telephone, dialed ...then, spoke. "Is this U.S. Customs Intelligence? Give me the director. Hello. Michael Aspin here, remember me? I gave you Wilson and Terkil. Now, I'm giving you North, MI-6, Monzer Al-Kassar ...but, you have to get my brother out alive."

Nancy's White House office

In her White House office, Nancy reached over to get her lines from her speech writer, Peggy Noonan. Nancy start rehearsing her lines different ways ...trying on different emotional angles ...sad ...angry ...concerned ...impatient ...happy ..thoughtful.

Nancy looked at Peggy. "Now, this is the speech for the crack-baby ward, about the toddlers and kindergarten-age kids at the hospital born addicted to crack?"

"That's right."

Peggy tried not to anticipate First Lady Nancy Reagan's reactions, so she apprehensively waited to hear Nancy's approval or criticism.

Nancy questioned a line. "This line here, 'I've just come from seeing crack-babies at the hospital, I've seen things so terrible I can't even describe them.'"

"Yes?" Peggy said.

"I'm not even scheduled to go to that hospital maternity crack-baby ward until *after* the speech!"

Peggy felt like she was tossing pearls before swine. She defended herself.

"It's a good line, it'll draw people to you."

Nancy agreed. "I'll keep it then."

Peggy felt like she had approval, she relaxed. Nancy was getting in the flow of the speech Peggy'd written for her, rehearsing more lines.

Nancy smiled. "How does it sound, this way?"

President Reagan with Ella Fitzgerald after her performance for King Juan Carlos I of Spain in the east room. 10/13/81

Exclusive women's club, Washington D.C.

In a Washington D.C. exclusive women's club, First Lady Nancy Reagan walked to the podium, ready to deliver the speech Peggy Noonan had written for her. Nancy took pride in being a fashion plate, she liked to make the best appearance possible, she liked earning the attention of her audience ...and, began delivering her same, 'Just Say No', anti-drug speech, again. Each time Nancy delivered her, 'Just Say No', speech she made it sound brand-new, fresh, like she'd just thought it up. Nancy and Ronnie were actors, both knew how to deliver lines to an audience, both knew how to play ...then, hold the house.

GRU counterfeiting room, Moscow

While First Lady Nancy Reagan delivered her speech at an exclusive women's club in Washington D.C., half a world away in Moscow in a GRU-KBG printing shop, Monzer watched 18" x 24" sheets of counterfeit American $100 bills roll off the printing press ...signaled to his men ...who went over to the trimming machines ...and, packed stacks of trimmed bills into cardboard boxes ...put the boxes on dollies ...and wheeled them onto the loading platform beside Monzer's private jet. Then, he told the pilot to go first to Iran, then Bahrain.

At Bahrain, Monzer Al-Kassar took the boxes full of counterfeit money to BCCI to have them laundered, exchanging dirty boxes for clean boxes of legal American currency. In the U.S., Nancy continued giving her, 'Just Say No To Drugs', speeches at every opportunity, just as if they mattered ...or, made a difference.

Bekka Valley poppy fields, Lebanon

Monzer Al-Kassar arrived at his Bekka Valley poppy fields in Lebanon in his Soviet handler's helicopter, landing near his own jet ...where they were greeted by belly-dancers from Monzer's harem ...who'd just fixed on heroin, moments before the helicopter landed. Monzer got off ...then, the Soviet helicopter flew away. Within minutes, two other helicopters arrived ...one had a British flag painted on it ...the other, an American flag. From out of the British helicopter, stepped Leslie Aspin ...from the American helicopter, Oliver North stepped out ...both men were greeted by drugged belly-dancers.

Outdoor brunch speech by Nancy, Washington D.C.

Throughout Washington D.C., Nancy contin-ued giving her, 'Just Say No To Drugs', anti-drug speech, at different locations, to different audiences on a daily basis. By habit, she'd take methamphetamine pills to bring her up ...that made her so excited, her eyes glowed. She started giving her, 'Just Say No', speech at an outdoor brunch, looked up into the sky and watched a 747 ...and, thought for a moment ... it was a giant bird ...and, realizing it wasn't, Nancy got upset. She reached into her purse, grabbed a few Miltown tranquilizers in her hand, popped them into her mouth, drank some water from a glass on the podium ...felt dizzy, felt shaky ...and, wanting to come down, took another pill.

A murmur passed through the audience, as more and more people noticed what Nancy was doing. Nancy kept taking pills ...and, she wasn't sure if she was taking the right pills, or not ...so, she took a couple more of each. Nancy felt desperate. She didn't notice the murmur growing in the crowd. She didn't notice the people seeing what she was doing ...but, she knew ... that night she'd have to take several Miltown downers to cancel out the speed uppers in her system ...so she could crash, and sleep. Nancy felt that giving her 'Just Say No To Drugs' speeches every day, was becoming demanding, boring, too much to ask. Yet, Nancy was able to find strength to continue giving them ...because, Nancy believed in her cause ...it made good press ...and, that helped Ronnie ...she knew everyday Americans believed in her.

Nancy looked up into the sky, and thought, "It's not a bird, it's a 747."

Onboard Air Force Two

The 747 flew high over Nancy, as she gave her 'Just Say No To Drugs' speech at the outdoor Washington D.C. brunch ...the 747 was Air Force Two. Onboard Air Force Two, Leslie Aspin and Oliver North sorted *Playboy Magazine* center-page foldouts ...behind them, their aides sorted kilos of cocaine, and kilos of heroin, into several stacks on a lounge couch on the plane. Les Aspin and Ollie North were getting off on contact highs from the smell of the drugs in the air ...each man was drinking booze. North smiled. He was the one who thought of taking the center-fold pictures out of the magazines onboard Air Force Two.

North's aide was sweating. "Heroin from Monzer Al-Kassar to the Contras goes here."

Leslie Aspin looked at a centerfold. "Right."

Oliver North tried to concentrate ...but, he felt too relaxed to bother thinking.

North's aide kept working. "Cocaine from the Contras, to the Syrians via Monzer, goes there."

Leslie Aspin felt crowded. "Got it."

Ollie North worked the numbers. "Cocaine from the Contras …and heroin from Syria via Monzer Al-Kassar … goes to pay off the Azima brothers in Kansas …for guns the Azima brothers ship to the Contras …and, for the missiles Azima brothers ship to Monzer Al-Kassar …who gives the missiles to Afghanistani Muhajidin for CIA."

Leslie Aspin kept track, too. "Got it."

North sorted centerfolds, "One for you …and, one for me. One for you …and, one for me."

North's aide put a few kilos aside in separate piles …while, far below them. on the ground beneath Air Force Two, First Lady Nancy Reagan finished her 'Just Say No To Drugs' speech at the outdoor brunch …feeling woozy, Nancy sat down on a lawn chair …drank another glass of water …tilted her head back to watch the 747 fly by …swallowed another pill …and, feeling dizzy, fell off the chair onto the lawn.

<>

I was at a garden party Katherine Graham was giving in her Washington D.C. mansion …Katherine published the *Washington Post*, a CIA media asset. I was giving my anti-drug, anti-terrorist, anti-Communism speech. I raised my eyes over my audience in the garden, looked up into the sky, and watched Air Force Two fly by overhead, tipping its wings.

<>

In Air Force Two, North and Aspin were busy … their aides sorted kilos of coke, smack, and bills of laden. North listened to an announcement the pilot made over the cabin speakers.

"We'll be arriving Kansas in 90 minutes, 90 minutes, Kansas …land of freckle-faced blondes, gapped teeth, red checkered shirts …and blue denim coveralls, barefoot in waving field of grain who grow up … to be centerfolds," the pilot said.

Hours later, the pilot circled over a private landing strip Azima brothers built on their farmland, in Kansas. The plane landed, taxied to a stop. Oliver North and Leslie Aspin got off the plane. Oliver North immediately saw Azima brothers throwing an outdoor picnic, picnic blankets spread all around the grounds …on the blankets were kilos of cocaine, and heroin …open crates of weapons, missiles …and, cardboard boxes full of money. Monzer Al-Kassar and several Contras walked to North and Aspin …and start, shoving stacks of money at them.

At Katherine Graham's mansion, I was animated delivering my 'anti-' speech …every time I gave that speech, the audience loved me, cheered me on. It was Hollywood, all over again.

In Kansas, Monzer Al-Kassar was determined to influence the arms-for-drugs-for-hostages deal his way.

Monzer bargained hard. "I want more Stinger missiles for Afghanistani Muhajidin, I'm expanding our opium and heroin trade."

North nodded, he was listening, noting the Azima brothers smiled in reaction to whatever Monzer said. Monzer handed North an attaché case full of money …he took a few stacks of money out and put them in his pockets for 'business' expenses …closed the briefcase and handed it to a Contra, who handed some kilos of cocaine to North …who handed a Stinger missile and bill of laden for the Stinger missile shipment to the Contra. The Contra held the Stinger missile and bill of laden for the missile shipment up. Monzer gave several kilos of heroin to the Contra …and, the Contra handed the Stinger missile and bill of laden to Monzer. Monzer traded more kilos of heroin to the Contra, in return for more kilos of cocaine from the Contra. Finally, Les Aspin and Monzer returned to a plane …and, took off. Ollie North and the Contras got into Air Force Two …and, took off.

CIA headquarters, Langley Virginia

Langley Virginia, at CIA headquarters in the communications room, CIA Agent Pollard intercepted a radio transmission. Unknown to CIA, Pollard was a 'mole', a double agent … betraying CIA and on the payroll of Israel's Mossad intelligence service. Pollard intercepted a radio signal originating in the Mediterranean ocean …indicating unusual shipping traffic in shipping lanes used for drug and weapons trafficking. Pollard listened to the sound of his radio crackle …then, picked up his phone to report his findings.

"This is Pollard, hello? Is this Mossad? Unusual traffic in drug and weapons trafficking shipping lanes off Greece in Mediterranean Sea towards Cyprus."

Mossad Israeli intelligence building, Israel

In Mossad intelligence headquarters in Israel,

director of Mossad picked up his phone. He was CIA-Mossad double-agent Pollard's handler, recognized Pollard's voice ...and, listened.

Pollard was excited, "Unusual traffic in shipping lanes used to smuggle weapons to Arab terrorists. You better look into it, deposit my check in my Swiss account."

The Mossad intelligence director hung up the phone, ...then, called director of Greek intelligence. "Hello, this is director of Mossad, Greek intelligence please ... I've been tipped-off about possible arms-smuggling vessels off Cyprus ...see what you can do to stop them ...we don't need PLO terrorists with more weapons to attack Israel."

Onboard weapons-smuggling ship, off Cyprus

Onboard the ship smuggling weapons, a seaman fastened down a tarpaulin the wind blew off several weapons crates, stamped with the Azima brothers shipping logo ...firmly securing the tarpaulin ... as a Greek Navy coast guard cutter intercepted the ship ...and, boarded it ... finding the weapons crates. But, all the Greek Navy found inside the crates were 60 Czech machine pistols Leslie Aspin was smuggling to Iran, to test the security of the smuggling route. But, Greek Navy also found 250 tons of weapons no one could account for.

When Leslie Aspin learned of the bust, he called Monzer. "Monzer, they busted our gun shipment. I lost 60 Czech machine-pistols I was smuggling in to test the route ...I didn't even know about 250 tons of weapons onboard ...I presume you were secretly piggy-backing on top of my smuggling route."

Monzer felt betrayed. "Get off the phone, Aspin. Bust's are the risk of doing business ...deal with it ...it doesn't matter, I'm insured through Lloyds of London. I'm not upset."

White House Situation Room

Bill finished talking, hung up the phone. "Well, they busted your first underground arms shipment to terrorists."

George was surprised. "My load?! We're in this together."

"MI-6 told me, it was insured through Lloyds. I'm not too upset about it.".

"That makes one of us."

"Business-as-usual in this racket."

George stayed upset. "Don't get the president's dick caught in the wringer."

Bill was frustrated "We can't deal direct through MI-6 ...now, we need a scapegoat. I think Israel should take the blame."

I kept quiet as long as I could, then turned to State Secretary George Shultz. I smiled at Shultz. "They told me they had good ideas to try out, you know my management style. I hire people to make their own decisions."

Bill looked at me.

I looked at Bill and George Bush. "What are you guys trying to do to me? I didn't do anything wrong."

Shultz spoke flat out. "Congress said, no more Contra aid. Sending Ollie North abroad to get foreign national support for the Contras ...not to mention authorizing sale of weapons to a terrorist country ...might be an impeachable offence."

I felt vulnerable. I start yelling. "You're all twisting it around! You know, I don't like details! I manage my people, I don't do their work! I didn't tell him, do that! I'm being taken advantage of! You're using me! I don't like it!"

Shultz spoke calmly. "It came out of the Oval Office, that makes you responsible."

I pleaded, "I'm innocent I tell you! I don't know what to do. I trusted you guys. Now I don't. You misled me. You sold me out. It's not supposed to be this way, my approval rating's gonna suck, we'll all be hanging by our thumbs in front of the White House, if anyone finds out ...should I take a chance, go on TV, tell my side of the story to the American people ...or, play it safe ...and, hide."

Bill seemed to enjoy me squirming. "That's your choice, time to close-up shop, do damage control, pursue alternative routes, plant disinformation cover stories. I'll set up Israel as our arms-for-drugs scapegoat to take the blame for us ...put us in the clear."

I felt myself racing emotionally over the top. "I don't want to know! I'm going to keep trusting you, do your jobs. I'm going to pretend, none of this is happening. I'm going to focus on my Summit meetings with Gorbachev and the Russians, enjoy this presidency for a change! Paul Weyrich and the Free Congress Foundation are running a Full-Court Press to destabilize the Soviet Union and Eastern Europe ...coordinating our anti-Soviet foundation fundraising activity ...disseminating the money to our Eastern European nationalist apparatus ...along with the money they got from ruling family investment consortiums in

Britain, France, Italy, Germany, Israel ...and, Saudi Arabia. Gorbachev will have to have the commies go bankrupt to finance fighting all the insurgencies we've started ...in Eastern Europe ...and, in Soviet Union ...he'll have to negotiate. You take care of the Iran-Contra business, just solve it. Leave me out of it. I have to fight the Russians ...I can't be bothered with details, do your jobs!"

Bill was sleepy, his head was getting heavy, his eyelids were closing, he dozed off, starting to talk in his sleep. "Get a piece of Russia, use Iran, Iraq, Afghanistan, Turkey, India, China, a Cold War picnic ...use death squads, as usual." Bill laughed in his sleep.

It was amusing. I turned from Bill, to Shultz. "Bill's not a bad guy ...when he's asleep."

Everyone laughed. I felt good, I'd pleased everyone. "Leave 'em laughing."

I left the room, taking State Secretary Shultz with me.

Bill opened one eye, looked around, watched the door close, opened his other eye, turned towards George Bush. "Is he gone?"

Bush double checked. "Yes."

"He's the one who falls asleep in meetings, not me. That's what my media assets tell me. I'm using the same assets to set-up Israel to take the blame ...it's all worked out already."

George was surprised. "You amaze me, Bill, you're the intelligencer extraordinaire, I respect the hell out of you, when you're like this."

Bill smiled. "MI-6 will have Israel run a parallel arms-for-hostage operation ...I will then, inform on it ...bust them and me at the same time. I'll hire a hundred freelance operatives to hire people, make bogus deals ...I'll tell all of them, say they have the 'go-ahead' from Vice President Bush himself."

George was shocked. "From me? I'm not giving any go-aheads."

Bill smirked, in his smug way. "Of course not ... I'm going to lie. I'll pretend they have go-aheads ...I'll tell everyone, they have your approval to make deals ...I'll tell them, they can run operations on your say-so ...that they have your approval to set-up and run arms-for-hostages deals. I'll dateline it. Then, we bust everyone who says they're working for you ...there'll be legal confusion for congressional investigation teams to claim it's hearsay when everyone says, they had your approval. If Aspin or North or Al-Kassar get busted ...and, say they're working on your authority ... nobody will believe them ...because, everyone and their uncle's been 'crying wolf'. I'll plant a couple dozen disinformation stories in the press,

have the press focus on our fall-guys to take attention off you."

George felt he didn't have a choice, "Like you planted those October Surprise disinformation stories, to discredit Carter."

Bill felt flattered ...but, defensive. "I never said, I did that."

George smiled. "You didn't have to, your fingerprints were all over it, it's the touch of the master."

Bill smiled. "The 'old boys' call that, 'the Midas touch'. Now, what we'll do first, is arrange to have an 'Anti-terrorist Summit' in London during the day ...at night, we get together in private to work out trades between North and Monzer for hostages, kapeesh?"

Café in open bazaar, Turkey

In a Turkish bazaar café, Monzer Al-Kassar addressed a meeting he'd called ... of all the terrorist leaders of the Middle East, feeling proud, powerful that they regarded him as the supreme narco-terrorist in the world.

Monzer looked at his friends.

"As your leader, I welcome you, freedom-fighters of the Arab world ... here today to get your orders, from me. They call us terrorists ..but, we're not terrorists ...they made war on us ...they did their coups in Egypt, Syria, Algeria ...they're terrorists ...they're colonialists enslaving us ...we're victims ...we're fighting for our freedom. The United States is the invading power in the Mid-East ...they've robbed us ...we'll drive the invaders out with help of Allah!"

Texas Ranch

Monzer's private jet cut through Mexican airspace, to Texas airspace ...then, landed on a Texas ranch owned by one of the largest landowners in Texas ...where Contras were trained. Monzer got up from his waterbed, left his harem girls ...and, dressed. Monzer had his crew unload crates of kilos of heroin, telling them, exchange them for crates of kilos of cocaine the Contras had brought to the ranch. Monzer and the Contras also exchanged crates of weapons at the Texas ranch.

President Reagan talking with Audrey Hepburn and Robert Wolders
at a private dinner for the Prince of Wales at the White House. 5/81

Private airstrip in Kansas

Monzer then flew to Kansas, to meet with Leslie Aspin ...gave Aspin money ...which, Aspin gave to Azima brothers ...who continued to use a vegetable exporting front to mask their international arms dealing. Supervised by Azima brothers, and Oliver North, crates were packed with rockets, and rocket launchers ...disguised with cabbages put over the hardware. An Azima plane was entirely loaded with crates, marked 'cabbages'.

North felt victory in the palm of his hand. "More cabbages for the Contras! Great. We've got the cabbages, do you have enough cabbage launchers?"

London daytime
anti-terrorist Summit

Bill, Leslie Aspin, and MI-6 reps went to the anti-terrorist Summit in London, that Bill had arranged. The summit was attended by official state reps during the day. Bill was the first speaker at the private, day-time summit.

Bill mumbled. "Have Israel ship the arms for us to the PLO ...we already have them train and ship arms to the Contras for us."

A British MI-6 director nodded.

Bill kept speaking, "I want Israel to take the heat when the whole shabang blows up in the press."

The MI-6 agent was amused. "That's what Israel's for."

But ...at night, behind closed doors, they held their own private terrorist summit, where they planned and negotiated arms-for-hostages deals.

London evening
terrorist summit

In the day, they held their anti-terrorist summit ...and during the night, they held their terrorist summit. Bill attended private and secret terrorist meetings, where he was met by Monzer Al-Kassar. He shook Monzer's hand warmly. "Monzer, how are your BCCI accounts growing?"

Monzer was pleased with Bill's cordial greeting. "Good, Bill. Did you have a good anti-terrorist meeting today with Margaret Thatcher and MI-6?"

"Yes."

"She does a good job for the House of Windsor, keeping 1001 Club, P-2, Vatican Bank, Opus Dei, and Knights of Malta inbound on recolonization of Africa, and South America. She's a little shabby on Eastern Europe ...but, she does well in Asia."

Bill liked speaking knowledgeably ...he knew how much he could say, safely .

Bill felt enthused. "She's a little sloppy with economic counter-intelligence on the destabilization of Soviet Union and Eastern Europe. By the way, I have a warehouse full of those Stinger Missiles you wanted ...but, half must go to Muhajidin to support our World Anti-communist League 'Full-Court Press' to destabilize Soviet Union and Eastern Europe, on Russia's southern flank."

Monzer smiled. "No problem, as long as you continue to give my heroin shipments CIA protection ...and, keep giving me diplomatic immunity in and out of the U.S."

"Fine," Bill said. Bill poured Monzer and himself another gin-and-tonic out of an iced pitcher.

Monzer smiled. "How many percentage points did you pick up in your portfolio when you and the Pope destroyed the labor unions in Poland,."

"Recently? ...or in World War II."

Monzer clarified. "Not when you built your portfolio using the Office of Strategic Intelligence, I mean, now ...with CIA help ...when you, and the Pope had AFL-CIO sell out ...when you both 'turned', or killed off labor leaders in Poland."

Bill knew when to keep his mouth shut. "You mind your central bank, I'll mind mine."

Monzer's laugh had a condescending tone.

Bill noticed the aire of superiority in Monzer Al-Kassar's laugh. Bill wasn't offended by it.

White House press briefing room

Not having attended the anti-terrorist summit in London, and back in Washington D.C., I stood in front of a mirror practicing angles on my good looks. In a few minutes, I had an entrance to make, to address newspaper and TV news press. I peaked through a window curtain, watching reporters pushing and shoving to get the best seats to interview me. I was sadly amused.

White House Spokesman Larry Speakes smiled. "Press conference time, reporters are waiting, time to go get 'em, champ," Larry said.

I smiled confidently at Larry. I liked something about him, even if he was more East Coast than West Coast. I walked behind the briefing room podium ...then, began to address newspaper and TV news reporters.

I got serious. "I'm disappointed, people think I know what's going on around here, in this Iran-Contra fiasco. Nothing's going on. I know nothing about any arms-for-hostages trade ...it's against stated White House policy to negotiate with terrorists. I'm shocked and disappointed, about these rumors."

When I finished my speech, Larry ushered me away from the podium ...then, briefly addressed the reporters. "Ladies and gentlemen of the press, that's it. No questions, not one. Sorry. Bye."

Larry listened to the groans of the press fade

...he ushered me between Secret Service guards into an adjoining hallway ...then, to an adjoining private room. Larry smiled at me. "Good job, champ. We'll have the public approval poll results in a few minutes."

The phone rang. Larry picked it up, listened for a few moments ...then, hung up. The eager look of anticipation faded on Larry's face.

He sadly looked at me. "That was Deaver, bad news. Your public approval rating's down, people don't believe you didn't know what was going on ...the public thinks you're lying."

I didn't think I could brave faking a smile, so I didn't even try. I felt sad. "That's awful. I like my John Wayne image better. I wish I could tell the American people my hands are tied ...we always treat the American public like America's a sweet la-la land, it isn't. It's a dog-eat-dog world. Everyone hates terrorists ...but, even the American revolutionary war had them. When *they* do counter-revolution, we call it terrorism. When *we* do it, we call it freedom-fighting ...how you gonna explain that to the American people? They're good people, they can't accept that, how you gonna keep 'em down on the farm, after they've seen L.A.?"

"I'm sorry, you're in a pickle, Ronnie. Damned if you do, damned if you don't."

"What am I gonna do? ...what *can* I do, Larry?"

Larry felt stumped. "Ask Deaver, he'll put some sound bite on you, make your ratings go up."

I punched a button on the phone. "Deaver! Come in here! My ratings are shit!"

Mike Deaver entered the room immediately. "I know. I know."

I was puzzled, "What am I gonna do?" I felt my temper rise. Deaver turned his back on Speakes and me, for a minute, pretended to cough, took a nip of vodka from his flask, quickly slid the flask in his inside coat pocket.

Mike turned around to face me. "Give me a few minutes to think. It's coming. I can feel it. Here it is! I got it! Form your own investigating committee! The Iran-Contra congressional hearings will say one thing! And your congressional investigating committee will be on your side! That's positive sound bite! Hey, isn't it?! 'Special investigating committee finds Reagan innocent!' Then, we'll do a poll ...announce people believe it. Then, zip! ...up go your ratings. Like it?"

I smiled. I liked it.

Larry didn't feel enthusiastic. "Deaver, the President's under investigation for criminal activity. How can he hire his own investigating committee to investigate himself? Think about it."

Mike ignored the sarcasm. "It'll work, my ideas always work to raise his popularity. This will work!"

At a press conference the next day, I addressed reporters. "Ladies and Gentlemen of the press, I'd like to announce, I am forming a private commission to investigate myself ...and, this new commission will operate independently of the Iran-Contra Hearings. The reason I'm doing this is to prove I'm innocent ...and tell the truth."

Mike stood off to the side, smiling. The days passed. I kept turning the calendar pages on my desk calendar, each day.

<> <> <>

I kept rehearsing, over and over. I might have to play Hoover, or be an understudy ...you never know. I kept researching, trying to understand how we got to where we are, today. What motivated my characters. Sayers and Kahn's, *Secret War Against Soviet Russia*, the next scene, helps me understand a little bit more, why we suddenly hated the Russian people.

Lights. Camera. Action.

<>

Director's cut: *It seemed every time Allen Dulles saw Herbert Hoover he could hear coins clinking in Hoover's pockets.*

Hoover played like a scratched record. "I hate Bolsheviks! Bolshevism is worse than war!"

Dulles smiled. "Of course," Dulles said.

Then, we pick up the script, here.

"I was a mining engineer," Hoover said, "...employed by Anglo-Persian Oil Co. in 1904, prior to World War I ...an entrepreneurial venture capitalist in Russian oil wells and mines

President Reagan and Nancy Reagan attending "All Star Tribute to Dutch Reagan" at NBC Studios(from left to right sitting) Colleen Reagan, Neil Reagan, Maureen Reagan, President, Nancy Reagan, Dennis Revell. (From left to right standing) Emmanuel Lewis, Charlton Heston, Ben Vereen, Monty Hall, Frank Sinatra, Burt Reynolds, Dean Martin, Eydie Gorme, Vin Scully, Steve Lawrence, last 2 unidentified. Burbank, California 12/1/85

...Czarist ruling families sold and leased me Russia's natural resources, and labor, for profit-sharing. I began speculating in Russian oil wells, in 1909 ...when the Mikop oil wells were drilled, coordinating banking investors, loans, got myself major interests in eleven Russian oil companies ...eleven! Me and my friend, Urquhart, floated Russo-Asiatic Corp. with two Czarist banks giving Russo-Asiatic development monopoly on mining and oil sites, there.

"Russo-Asiatic shares rose from $16.25/share in 1913, to $47.50/share in 1914, a 300% return on investment. Using Russo-Asiatic, we acquired development rights from the Czar for 2,500,000 acres ...timber ...water power ...gold, copper, silver, zinc reserves of 7,262,000 tons, twelve developed mines, two cooper smelters, twenty saw mills, 250 miles of railroad, two steamships, twenty-nine barges, blast furnaces, rolling mills, sulfuric acid plants, gold refineries, coal reserves ...one billion dollars of assets in 1914 American dollars, that's right.

"After the Bolshevik Revolution, the concessions, leases, and business deals we made with Czarist businessmen ...got canceled, by Soviet Russia. I lost my holdings! ...all of them! Soviets canceled the Czar's business deals retroactively, nationalized ownership, and development, of Russia's natural resources.

[Autobiographer's note: recall, 'Ruskombank'.]

"I'm not stupid ...so, me and my partners formed a new cartel, Russo-Asiatic Consolidated, to take over Russo-Asiatic Corp. to protect my Russian interests, filed a claim with British Government for 282 billion dollars in damages and estimated profit loss.

"After World War I ended," Hoover said, "I spoke at Paris Peace Conference. 'Bolshevism is worse than war.' I said. "For the rest of my life, consider me the enemy of Bolshevism, Communism, Socialism, Judaism ...any 'ism' that improves living standards of common citizens. I hate the Soviet Government. I hate people's movements. I hate Jews.

"American policy during the Armistice gave everything we had, to keep Europe from going Bolshevik, from not being overrun by Bolshevik armies.

"Until Aug. 1921," Hoover said, "I held the U.S. Government post of Food Relief Administrator ...hundreds of thousands of Russian Allies who fought with America ... against Kaiser's invading German armies, to defeat them and win World War I ... were starving, in Soviet Union ...because, war destroyed Russia's economy,

industry, and food production. My Jan. 1921 Food Relief Report showed, I spent $94,938,417 dollars raised for European relief for refugees ...but instead of feeding our Russian allies, I gave direct aid to the Czar's White Russian armies, and withheld all supplies from the Soviets. I used the money raised in the United States for European relief to support fighting against Soviets.

"I used American Food Relief as a weapon of war, against democracy in Europe. I spent resources intended to save the Russian people from starvation ...instead, I supplied White Russian Armies, and their guerrillas. I'm proud of it."

Feb. 1922, Hoover is Commerce Secretary, *New York Globe* writes an editorial.

"Bureaucrats, centered throughout the Department of Justice, Department of State, and Department of Commerce are carrying out a private war with the Bolshevik government."

Hoover continued. "As Secretary of Commerce, as President of the United States, and later, leading the isolationist wing of the Republican party, I fought to prevent friendly, commercial, and diplomatic relations between America and America's most powerful ally against world Fascism, the Soviet Union. In Congress Senator Borah criticized me."

Borah was adamant. "Mr. Hoover, the war's over. The Allies won. *Russia* is one of the Allies. Germany was the enemy, remember? We're not at war with Russia, Congress hasn't declared war against the Russian government, or the Russian people. The people of the United States don't desire to war with Russia. Yet, while we're not at war with Russia, while Congress hasn't declared war, we're carrying-on war with the Russian people. We have an army in Russia. We're furnishing munitions, and supplies, to other armed forces in that country, we're just as engaged in conflict, as though constitutional authority was invoked, and a declaration of war was made, and the nation was called to arms. There's neither legal, nor moral justification for sacrificing these lives. It's in violation of the plain principles of free government."

<>

Borah dropped in at Hoover's home.

Hoover was furious, "Nonsense! Of course we're at war with Bolsheviks! The Nov. 1918 Armistice Agreement between Allied and central powers contains in Article Twelve a clause, that stipulates German troops are to remain ...as long as the allies consider it expedient, in whatever Russian territory they then occupy. What do you think we're keeping the German troops there for? ...to fight themselves? We're keeping German troops there to be fight against the Bolsheviks! ...like it or not!"

Borah disliked Hoover. "I don't like it! Neither does my constituency! Nor does the common American working man, whose tax money's supposed to be going for food relief!"

Reinhard Gehlen stepped between Borah and the rest of the group, Dulles, Shroder, Warburg and Hoover. Reinhard interrupted, "Paul, dismiss the senator, we're here for have business."

Paul Warburg agreed. "Sure. Dulles, show Senator Borah the door."

Dulles lit his cigar. "My pleasure. This way, Senator."

Generals von der Goltz & Yudenitch

Reinhard Gehlen updated Dulles and Hoover.

"On Eastern Soviet Front we're faced with rapidly-growing Soviet movement in Latvia, Lithuania, and Estonia. British High Command's concentrating support, using White Guard guerrilla operations in Baltic area. Max Warburg wants you to have U.S. high command send in troops, or mercenaries."

Henry Schroder nodded. General von der Goltz is Commander of the White Guard Army in the Baltic area."

Reinhard Gehlen updated him. "Yes. He runs the terrorist guerrilla campaign to destroy the Soviet influence, in Latvia, and Lithuania. The Latvian, and Lithuanian, people have no military equipment or organization to resist. General von der Goltz reports, he's the unofficial dictator of Latvia, and Lithuania."

Paul Warburg smiled, "Our Central Bank operations?"

"Safe. We'll increase terrorist forces to guard our timbering, mining, and oil drilling operations in Latvia, and Lithuania," Gehlen said.

Hoover was blustery, "Not soon enough! ...I lost revenues of nine billion dollars in oil, gold, ...and, timber ...this damned revolution. Who financed the Russian Revolution? ...I *thought* we had all sides covered, hedged our bets ... are there wildcat ruling family investment bankers in U.S., Britain, France, Germany, and Japan ... double-crossing us? ...who's upsetting our turf war applecart. I'll get to the bottom of this!"

Dulles tried to quiet him. "I'll find out. Unless there's rogue bankers hiding in House of Rothschild, or Warburg, or Shroder, or

Harriman, or Rockerfeller planning a financial coup ... I don't know."

Schroder overheard. He was offended, "Dulles, you're expendable ...there are small central banks competing with our large ones ...but, we have a foot in each camp ...it's business as usual, no spies in our Houses ...maybe it's coming from Japan. We were successful destabilizing Russia with our coups ...now, pick up the pieces, rebuild our portfolios."

Hoover bristled. "That's right! Borah's tantrum proves we have a public relations problem."

Reinhard wasn't worried about Borah. "We'll silence him."

Dulles shook his head. "No. Finish your report."

"Von der Goltz dominates Baltic States, he's a German general ...naturally, he might want the Baltic States for Germany."

Dulles was amused. "That's an illusion, as far as our Central Bank World Order is concerned, there *is* no Germany, there is no United States, there is no Britain ...there's only our banking collective portfolio."

Reinhard hesitated, "I'm not sure I understand."

"That's because you're military intelligence, we're financial intelligence. War for you is armies, war for us is ledger entries," Paul said.

Henry Shroder nodded. "British Monarchy intermarried into the Czarist Romanov dynasty, the British want the throne restored to the Romanov Czar ... to get their investments back from the Soviets ...but, major shareholders of the Bank of England through Rothschild have prioritized investments without our knowledge.

"As far as we know, our central bank World Order is backing as many opposing factions as we can ...we have fallout on a need-to-know basis, there's a trust involved, putting a Czar back on the throne to de-nationalize and recover Fed, and Bank of England, and competing American and British investments ... in Russia ...drawing off private capital, not Bank of England credit.

"Bank of England wants to replace General von der Goltz, with General Nicholas Yudenitch. They've had Yudenitch appointed Commander-in-Chief, to re-organize White Forces ...while, French and British ruling families supply him with war materials."

Dulles sighed, "You seem to have a working analysis. I can't keep up, with you. The 50 million dollar loan from the U.S. I got for General von der Goltz, see that Yudenitch gets it."

Reinhard finished his report. "Yudenitch leads

the Polish Army to the Ukraine. He occupies Kiev but is stopped, pushed back by Red Army. In August, Red Army camped outside Warsaw, and Levov ...because, you both sent money, food, and supplies to Yudenitch's Polish Army at Levov ...and, British rushed tanks and planes to Warsaw ...Red troops commanded by General Tokeshevski, and War Commissar Leon Trotsky, stretched their military lines too far ...they've suffered consequences. Polish Army counter-offensive made Red Army retreat, along the entire front. Soviet government, by the Peace Treaty of Rega ...now, is forced to turn over Byeola-Russia, and the Ukraine, to the Polish Army factions led by von der Goltz ...then, they're re-assigned to Yudenitch. Congratulations, gentlemen."

Everyone congratulated each other.

<>

"By the way," Reinhard said, "I took my fiancee, Dagmara, and Herr Hitler last Wednesday afternoon to the Holy Residence of Archbishop Eugenio Pacelli, in Munich."

Paul Murphy's *La Popessa*, and, David Yallop's *In God's Name*, set the scene.

1919, Munich,
Archbishop Eugenio Pacelli

Dagmara didn't understand why they stopped, there. "Reinhard, why are you and Herr Hitler stopping to see Archbishop Pacelli? I thought we would picnic, today ...not do business."

Reinhard smiled, "It's only a minute, to mix business with pleasure."

Dagmara watched, Archbishop Eugenio Pacelli led Reinhard and Hitler to another room, turned to the nun sitting by her, who showed no emotion. Dagmara could hear the men talk, she turned to the nun, "May I have a drink of water?"

"Of course," the nun replied.

Dagmara watched the nun leave ...then, walked to the door, leaned closer. She could hear better, see through an opening.

Archbishop Pacelli held his palms together, as if praying. "German General Staff, and Munich, is good to me. Every day, every night, every meal, I pray. I ask God to get rid of Communist Bolshevik Marxist Jews, I'm afraid of them ...they're Satanic atheists, want to destroy Catholicism."

Adolf Hitler put his hands on Pacelli's shoulders. "Your Holiness, we won't let that happen. We're going to stop the Bolshevik Jewish threat spreading in Germany, Italy, to the Christian West."

Archbishop Pacelli smiled. "I hate communists, God hates them, Herr Hitler. Here's a box of Church gold ...to help you, and your counter-revolutionaries, stop the communist revolution."

Hitler took the strongbox, "We'll stop the Jews, too ...your Holiness, for the same price."

Archbishop Pacelli made the sign of the cross. "Go with Christ, stop the anti-Christ, spread the love of God, enjoy the gold."

Hitler gave the zeig heil salute, snapping his boot heels together. "With Christ's help, we'll destroy the anti-Christ and enforce the Jewish solution."

Reinhard and Adolf went back to the room Dagmara waited in.

She was impatient, "Reinhard, can we go on our picnic, now?"

"We're going now."

Hitler laughed, "First let's stop at the delicatessen, I've got extra money."

<>

Dulles smiled, "I like stories about gold."

During World War I, J. Henry Schroder Banking Co. was puppet master, pulling the strings for many countries.

World War I started, after Archduke Ferdinand was assassinated at Sarajevo, by Gavril Princeps. Austria demanded an apology from Serbia, which it got ...but, declared war, anyway ...other European nations jumped in. But, Germany faltered, short of food, and coal, war couldn't go on.

Paul Warburg threw a newspaper he was reading onto a table. John Hamill's, *Strange Career of Mr. Hoover*, cites *Nordeutsche Allgemeine Zeitung*, Mar. 4, 1915.

"Justice, however, demands publicity should be given to the pre-eminent part taken by the German authorities in Belgium, in the solution of this problem. The initiative came from them and it was only due to their continuous relations with American Relief Committee the provisioning question was solved. That is what the Belgian Relief Committee was organized for, to keep Germany in food."

Warburg, Schroder, and Gehlen ordered port, Hoover, and Dulles, whiskey. There was no stopping Hoover. He'd gone around the world scouting mining locations ...as an undisclosed Rothschild financial agent, earning a directorship in Rothschild's, Rio Tinto Mines in Spain ...and, in Bolivia. Why did Hoover and Francqui supply the German army during World War I? Were they told to? Was it *their* initiative?

Hoover was a proud man. "My partner, Emile

Francqui, put the Belgian Relief Committee together, opening offices of Belgian Relief in his own bank, Societe Generale ...as, a one-man show ... with a letter of permission from General von der Goltz, dated Oct. 16, 1914.

"I'm in charge of Food Relief for the U.S. Government, on this side of the Atlantic. Now, this damn nurse in Belgium stirs things up."

<>

As you recall, I was playing Paul Warburg in one of my double-roles, I got to the studio late, I walked onto the set late and start acting, playing Warburg, "You mean, Edith Cavell?"

"Yes," Hoover said, "she wrote to *Nursing Mirror* in London Apr. 15, 1915 complaining the 'Belgian Relief' supplies I buy, and ship over there, are being shipped to Germany to feed German soldiers."

Gehlen interrupted, "*Nordeutsche Allgemeine Zeitung,* Mar. 13, 1915, *Schmoller's Yearbook for Legislation, Administration and Political Economy for 1916* reported, 1 billion pounds of meat, 1.5 billion pounds of potatoes, 1.5 billion pounds of bread ...and, 121 million pounds of butter were shipped from Belgium to Germany, in 1916."

Hoover wondered, "What you gonna do, about it?"

Gehlen laughed. "German military intelligence doesn't worry about Edith Cavell, where she made her mistake is ...British Intelligence director Sir William Wiseman, a Kuhn Loeb partner, is upset she's spilled the beans. We need to keep feeding the German army with American Belgium Relief food sent for refugees. So Wiseman insists, we arrest Cavell as a spy now ...and, kill her. I arrested her for treating sick prisoners of war in her hospital ward, and helping them escape from us ...usually, we put people in prison for three months for that ...but, she's being executed, as we speak."

Hoover felt relieved. "With Cavell dead, Belgian Relief intelligence operation can continue. I'll tell Emile Francqui, I'm increasing food shipments."

"Yes ...but, now they say it's not just food short-ages, they want more money, too," I said.

I saw Dulles winced. He sat down.

"No problem," I said. "Fed will print some up."

"It's all right, Allen," Schroder said.

Reinhard watched everyone, sipping port.

Hoover blustered. "Everyone wants more money. Emile directs a Belgian bank, Society Generale ...and, is a regent directing the central bank of Belgium, La Banque Nationale de Belgique ...we met when I was getting mines surveyed, we've a few scandals in court we're

overcoming ...the Kaiping Coal Co. scandal in China that set off the Boxer Rebellion to kick for-eign businessmen out of China threatened our coal exports to Germany ...now, I'm barred from trading on London Stock Exchange because of a negative judgment ...my associate, Stanley Rowe's imprisoned for ten years as an accom-plice ...but, Francqui guide my rise to fortune, he's the mastermind behind enslaving the Congo indigenous population, in 1891 leading army expeditions into the Congo, conquering it for Belgium's King Leopold, ordering our sol-diers, 'For every cartridge they spent, they had to bring in a man's hand'.

"Now, he's Congo copper king. He brought in the Tientsin railroad concessions, tricked the Americans out of the Hankow-Canton railroad concession in China, in 1901 ...and, stood by to help me when we took over Kaiping coal mines.

"Francqui, and I, are directors in Chinese Engineering & Mining Company Kaiping mines ...we've shipped 200,000 Chinese slave workers to the Congo, to work Francqui's copper mines in darkest Africa. Francqui's the former Belgium Minister of State, Minister of Finance, a veteran of China ...and, the Congo, richest man in Belgium ...one of twelve richest men, in Europe. Francqui's one of Belgium's two directors on the Bank for International Settlements ...and, a member of the Young & Dawes Plan Committees," Hoover said.

"Francqui and Hoover maintained Belgium on the gold standard for us, right on cue," I said.

Playing Paul Warburg was okay.

<>

Oct. 3, 1931 *New York Times* quotes Brussels', *Le Peuple,* on Francqui's visit to United States, "As a friend of President Hoover, Monsieur Francqui won't fail to pay a visit to the President."

Oct. 30, 1931, *New York Times* headlines, '*Hoover-Francqui Talk was Unofficial',* "Francqui spent Tuesday night as a personal guest of the President, they talked of world financial prob-lems in general, their visit had no official signifi-cance. Francqui is a private citizen ...and, not engaged in any official mission."

Eustace commented on the article. "No refer-ence was made to the Hoover-Francqui busi-ness associations which were the subject of huge lawsuits in London. The Francqui visit probably involved Hoover's Moratorium on German War Debts, which stunned the finan-cial world."

<>

At the end of my Reagan Administration, I got

a hold of the Committee on Banking, Currency & Housing report of the House of Representatives, 94th Congress, 2d session, Aug. 1976, called 'Federal Reserve Directors: a Study of Corporate & Banking Influence, included among the 60 flowcharts, one showing present directors of J. Henry Schroder Bank & Trust ...with continuing international interlocking board directors influence since World War I.

Eustace wrote about those 60 charts.

"George A. Braga is ...a director of Czarnikow-Rionda Co. ...vice-president of Francisco Sugar Co. ...president of Manati Sugar Co. ...and, vice-president of New Tuinicui Sugar Co.

"His relative, Rionda B. Braga ...is president of Francisco Sugar Co. ...and, vice-president of Manati Sugar Co. ... Schroder control of sugar goes back to the U.S. Food Administration, under Herbert Hoover and Lewis Strauss of Kuhn Loeb Co., during World War I. Schroder's attorneys are the firm, Sullivan & Cromwell. John Foster Dulles, of Sullivan & Cromwell, was present during the historic agreement to finance Hitler ...and, was later Secretary of State in the Eisenhower Administration. Alfred Jaretzki, Jr., of Sullivan & Cromwell, is also a director of Manati Sugar Co. ...and, Francisco Sugar Co. Not only was the U.S. Food Administration managed by Hoover's director, Lewis Lichtenstein Strauss, who married into Kuhn Loeb Co. by marrying Alice Hanauer, daughter of partner Jerome Hanauer ...but, in the most critical field, military intelligence, Sir William Wiseman, chief of the British Secret Service, was a partner of Kuhn, Loeb & Co."

<>

Editor Charles Seymour's, *Intimate Papers of Col. House,* comments on Wiseman. "Between House and Wiseman, there were soon to be few political secrets, and from their mutual comprehension resulted in large measure our close cooperation with the British," Charles said.

George Sylvester Viereck's, *The Strangest Friendship in History, Woodrow Wilson and Col. House,* comments. "One example of House's cooperation with Wiseman, was a confidential agreement which House negotiated ...pledging the United States to enter into World War I on the side of the Allies. Ten months before the election which returned Wilson to the White House in 1916, 'because he kept us out of war', Col. House negotiated a secret agreement with England, and France, on behalf of Wilson ...which pledged the United States to intervene on behalf of the Allies. On Mar. 9, 1916, Wilson formally sanctioned the undertaking."

<>

Eustace Mullins comments. "Woodrow Wilson campaigned on the slogan, 'He kept us out of war' ...when he'd pledged to Col. House, ten months earlier, to involve us in the war on the side of England and France. Wilson was held with contempt by those who knew the facts of his career."

<>

Henry Louis Mencken was a prominent newspaperman, book reviewer and political commentator. "Wilson is the perfect model of the Christian cad, we ought to dig up his bones and make dice of them."

<>

Mullins continues, "McFadden came back again Dec. 13, 1932 with another motion to impeach President Hoover. Only five Congressmen stood with him on this ...the resolution failed. The Republican majority leader of the House remarked, 'Louis T. McFadden is, now, politically dead.'

"May 23, 1933, McFadden introduced, *House Resolution No. 158, Articles of Impeachment* against the Treasury Secretary, two Assistant Treasure Secretaries, the Federal Reserve Board of Governors ...and, officers and directors of the Federal Reserve Banks ... for their guilt, and collusion, in causing the Great Depression.

"McFadden had plenty to say. "I charge them with having unlawfully taken 80 billion dollars from the United States Government in the year 1928 ... the said, unlawful taking consisting of the unlawful recreation of claims against the United States Treasury, to the extent of 80 billion dollars in the year 1928, and in each year subsequent, and by having robbed the United States Government and the people of the United States by their theft and sale of the gold reserve of the United States.

<>

"The Resolution never reached the floor. A whispering campaign, 'McFadden was insane', swept Washington, and in the next Congressional elections, he was overwhelmingly defeated by thousands of dollars poured into his home district of Canton, Pennsylvania. The Federal Reserve System was a central bank of issue. It had the power to, and did, when it suited its owners, issue millions of dollars of money. Why did it not do so in 1931 and 1932? The Wall Street bankers were through with Herbert Hoover, and they wanted Franklin D. Roosevelt to come in on a wave of glory as the savior of the nation.

Therefore, the American people had to starve and suffer until Mar. 1933, when the 'white knight' came riding in with his crew of Wall street bribers and put some money into circulation. That was all there was to it. As soon as Mr. Roosevelt took office, Federal Reserve began to buy Government securities at the rate of 10 million dollars a week for ten weeks, and created 100 million dollars in new money, which alleviated the critical famine of money and credit, and the factories started hiring people again."

<>

J. Henry Schroder Corp. planned to build massive debt ... by financing Hitler's climb to power in Germany to create World War II.

Otto Lehmann-Russbeldt's, *Aggression*, speaks of this. "Hitler was invited to a meeting at Schroder Bank in Berlin, Jan. 4, 1933. Leading industrialists and bankers of Germany tided Hitler over his financial difficulties, and enabled him to meet the enormous debt he'd incurred in connection with maintenance of his private army. In return, he promised to break the power of the trade unions. May 2, 1933, he fulfilled his promise."

Mullins comments on the meeting. "Present at the Jan. 4, 1933 meeting. were the Dulles brothers, John Foster Dulles and Allen W. Dulles of the New York law firm Sullivan & Cromwell, which represented Schroder Bank. They'd represented United States at Paris Peace Conference in 1919 ...John Foster Dulles became President Eisenhower's Secretary of State ...while, Allen Dulles would eventually direct CIA."

Leonard Mosley's biography, *Dulles*, softens it. "Both brothers spent large amounts of time in Germany, where Sullivan & Cromwell had considerable interest during the early 1930's, having represented several provincial governments, some large industrial combines, a number of big American companies with interests in the Reich, and, some rich individuals. John Foster Dulles and his brother Allen Dulles were senior partners in Sullivan & Cromwell. Sullivan & Cromwell handled legal business for American I.G., the American subsidiary of Germany's I.G. Farbin, the German industrial cartel that financed Hitler. The Germans wouldn't pay off debts British and French charged them for war damages, or Allied costs of waging war. Secretary Charles Evans Hughes wanted to solve the post-war reparations problem. Secretary Hughes formed Dawes Committee, to solve the problem. J.P. Morgan requested John Foster be retained as special counsel to Dawes committee. John Foster came up with, Dawes Plan. Under provisions of Dawes Plan, U.S. lent money to Germany ...Germany paid off the British and French ...who paid back the United States ...so, in 1923-1924, John Foster became internationally famous among lawyers and statesmen."

Allen Dulles was a director of J. Henry Schroder Co. Neither he, nor J. Henry Schroder, were pro-Nazi or pro-Hitler ... as a reason d'etre ...but, unless Hitler became Chancellor of Germany, there was small chance of provoking a second World War to skyrocket public debt, and Schroder profits. Schroder Bank Managing Director F.C. Tiarks was also a director of Bank of England. Kurt von Schroder, born in 1889, was a partner in Cologne Bankhaus J.H. Stein & Co., founded 1788. In 1933, when Nazis came to power in Germany, Baron Kurt von Schroder was appointed German representative at Bank of International Settlements.

Hargrave's biography, *Montague Norman*, describes Monti's position. Sir Josiah Stamp was a director of Bank of England, Norman Montague was Governor of Bank of England. "Early in 1934, a select group of City financiers gathered in Norman's room, behind windowless walls ...Sir Robert Kindersley, partner of Lazard Brothers ...Charles Hambro ...F.C. Tiarks ...Sir Josiah Stamp. Governor Montague spoke of the political situation in Europe. A new power had established itself, a great, 'stabilizing force' ...namely, Nazi Germany. Norman advised co-workers, include Hitler in their plan for financing Europe. There was no opposition."

Mullins reports, during my Reagan Administration. "In 1938, the London Schroder Bank became the German financial agent in Great Britain. New York branch of Schroder merged in 1936 with the Rockefellers, as Schroder Rockefeller, Inc. ... at 48 Wall Street. Carlton P. Fuller of Schroder was president of this firm, Avery Rockefeller was vice-president. He'd been a behind-the-scenes partner of J. Henry Schroder for years ...and, set up the construction firm of Bechtel Corp., whose employees (on leave) now play a leading role in the Reagan Administration, as Secretary of Defense, and Secretary of State. The establishment of the international Schroder group of companies in the 1960s, 1970s, and early 1980s was the first stage in this process. The second stage, which was achieved in the latter half of the 1980s, was integration of the conduct of operations on a worldwide basis. In these years, the international Schroder group of companies became a single entity, 'Schroders."

<>

When I was President, I didn't know that about Weinberger, or Shultz, or Bechtel, or Schroder, or Schroders ...it was *after* my Presidency, when Nancy read books to me, she and I were trying to figure out what happened behind the scenes in my Reagan Administration ... that we didn't know, at the time ...and, the American people had no clue ... because corporate media directors also sat on newspaper boards and were directors of movie studio boards ...so nothing ever got out to everyday Americans, did it? Name one time. You were there, did it? Did it? No.

<>

Antony Sutton's, *Wall Street & the Rise of Hitler,* describes part of Kurt Schroder's schedule. "Nazi Baron Kurt von Schroder acted as conduit for IT&T money funneled to Heinrich Himmler's SS organization in 1944 ...while ,World War II was in progress ...and, United States was at war with Germany."

Mullins speaks about Kurt von Schroder. "The Kilgore Committee listed more than a dozen important titles held by Kurt von Schroder in the 1940s, including ...President of Deutsche Reichsbahn, Reich Board of Economic Affairs ...SS Senior Group Leader, Council of Reich Post Office ...Deutsche Reichsbank ...and, other leading banks ...and, industrial groups. Schroder served as a director on the board of International Telephone & Telegraph subsidiaries in Germany."

<>

McRae and Cairncross', *Capital City,* takes note. "J. Henry Schroder Banking Co. is listed as No. 2 in capitalization in *Capital City* on the list of seventeen merchant bankers who make up the exclusive Accepting Houses Committee, in London. Although it's almost unknown in the U.S., it's played a large part in our history. Like the others on this list, it had first to be approved by Bank of England. And, like the Warburg family, the von Schroders began their banking operations in Hamburg, Germany. At the turn of the century, in 1900, Baron Bruno von Schroder established the London branch of the firm. He was soon joined by Frank Cyril Tiarks, in 1902. Tiarks married Emma Franziska of Hamburg, and, was a director of Bank of England from 1912 to 1945."

With Hoover in the White House, J. Henry Schroder Corp. pursued its vision of financing Hitler's assumption of power in Germany to pursue World War II ...really, a continuation of World War I ... the same producers, directors, cast, and crew. In the 1920s, many Americans as well as Germans, in the ruling class helped finance Hitler ...Fritz Thyssen, Henry Ford, J.P. Morgan, gave millions of dollars to Hitler's political, propaganda, economic, and military campaign funds ...but, it wasn't enough. Even though Hitler did well in national campaigns, he spent all that money. By 1932, Hitler was in debt.

The *Great Soviet Encyclopedia* comments. "The banking house Schroder Bros. was established in 1846 ...its partners, today, are the Barons von Schroder, related to branches in the U.S. and England," *Soviet Encyclopedia* said.

Sept. 30, 1933, the *London Daily Herald* financial page editor wrote an article, "Mr. Norman's decision is, give the Nazis the backing of the Bank of England."

John Hargrave's biography, *Montague Norman,* agrees. "It's quite certain that Norman did all he could to assist Hitlerism to gain and maintain political power, operating on the financial plane from his stronghold in Threadneedle Street."

Nancy and I got a kick out of referring to the Bank of England, as Threadneedle Street ...but State Secretary Shultz did it all the time, it grew on us. You've got to hand it to those Brits.

Mullins comments. "Baron Wilhelm de Ropp, a journalist whose closest friend was ...Major F.W. Winterbotham, chief of Air Intelligence of the British Secret Service ... brought the Nazi philosopher, Alfred Rosenberg, to London ...introduced him to Lord Hailsham, Secretary for War ... Geoffrey Dawson, editor of, *The Times* ...and, Montague Norman, Governor of Bank of England. After talking with Norman, Rosenberg met with the representative of the Schroder Bank of London. The managing director of the Schroder Bank, F.C. Tiarks, was also a director of Bank of England."

<>

Allen Dulles liked the players in his international investment banking family. He looked at Warburg and Schroder. "I've done as you said, orchestrated Dawes loans to rebuild post-WWI Germany. The U.S. will loan money to Germany. Germany will repay its war debts to our banking collective. The banking collective will receive the money ...and, pay us reparations for our loans ...and, I've targeted oil, gold, and timber areas in Russia I want us to own."

Herb Hoover spoke up. "Should we get rid of Senator Borah? ...now?"

I was playing my Warburg character, again.

Allen Dulles shot me a look.

I looked at Hoover. "He's one man. Borah's the exception that proves the rule. Congress is trafficking with us as shareholders in one company or another. They're taking bribes, laundered as campaign contributions. Let's finalize our interlocking board directorate with British, French, Italian, Japanese, and German bank partners. America now has the central banking system the Rothschilds had me install. We're going to run it. It's a private corporation, not government owned. We'll print large bills for a penny, loan it to American taxpayers at face value. It'll cost us less than a penny to print each bill. *That's* what the World Order is talking about!"

<>

We rehearsed scenes we'd already played, reshooting them, making them longer, or shorter. I held on to my Warburg character.

<>

Later that evening at a party, Allen Dulles sat his call girl on his lap. He wasn't a quiet drunk. He explained. "My life's a masquerade. I'm greedy, obsessed ...with desire. I never get enough of anything to satisfy my craving. We destabilize a country, to rob it. We finance propaganda. We stir up unrest. We make new ruling families, in every country we take over. We finance civil wars. We finance coups. We provoke wars. And, we finance everything ...and, everyone. We destroy the enemy's infrastructure. We take the enemies' gold, and timber, and oil. When we've bankrupted an enemy, we end the war. Then, we finance reconstruction of the country we destabilized. Unions are abandoned in wartime. We prevent them from reorganizing. We use cheap labor in factories we finance. We buy up everything in disrepair or in bankruptcy. We control interest on loans. We control import and export tariffs. We control cost of manufacturing. We control cost of doing business. We control interest on the loans we make them to do their business. We get between business's legs, and fuck the hell out of it. Then, we do it all over again ... with another country. Sometimes, we use a counter-coup, what you call, a 'civil war'. Or a straight coup d'état, I'm sure you know what that is. We invested in the Czar ...and, in the Bolsheviks, too! ...while, we financed their enemies! A country's bank either sells out short to an invading bank that's planning a coup of some sort, an assassination, a civil war, a famine ...or, we take them over. It happens over time, preferably over generations ...that way it's invisible. We plant seeds, we water, we feed, wait a few generations ...then, harvest . What makes ruling family strong ... is a strong vision to protect the family's wealth, over time."

"Okay," the call girl said.

Allen Dulles undressed the call girl as he spoke. He enjoyed the, 'not quite understanding I'm ready for you you're right whatever you say' look on her face. Allen Dulles looked around the conference table where his friends and partners sat, hands all over their call girls. Allen Dulles liked the feel of his call girl squirming on his lap.

I tossed a '*Protocols of Zion*' booklet to him. "The Czar's intelligence people invented this book ...and, scapegoated the Jews like the Popes have, since the anti-Semitic, anti-Muslim Crusades of the Dark Ages. The Czar really knew how to make a scapegoat."

Dulles was aroused. "It's not a Jewish banking conspiracy, we're Christians, Protestants, and Catholics too. What a financial coup we've pulled off! ...with our Federal Reserve. We've set up a central bank to takeover America's banks, make wage slaves of everyone in America ... in our lifetimes," Dulles said. Dulles laughed, unzipped his pants, thrust into the call girl lap-dancing on him. He felt his power over her.

"Want to shoot some dice?" Schroder said.

Allen Dulles smiled slyly. "What shall we bet, our whores?"

"Good idea," I said.

<>

It's kind of strange ... interrupting myself in my own movie, in my own autobiography ...but I've a tough acting part coming up, a quadruple role ... playing all *four* Warburg brothers ... at the same time. I have to study the background on my characters to tell one Warburg from another. So ...please bear with me and Paul, Felix, Fritz, and Max ...it's never been done before in Hollywood. I ought to get an Oscar for it, if I don't go nuts ...I'll be talking to myself ...but, you won't know it. You'll think, I'm talking to my brothers.

It goes like this. If I'm Paul I can be talking to Felix, or I can be talking to Max, or I can be talking to Fritz, or I can be talking to Felix and Max, or Felix and Fritz, or Fritz and Max; if I'm Felix, I can be talking to Paul, or Max, or Fritz, or Paul and Max or Paul and Fritz or Felix and Paul; if I'm Max, then Paul, or Felix, or Fritz, or Paul and Felix, Paul and Fritz, or Fritz and Felix, or if I'm Fritz, then Max or Paul or Felix, or Max and Paul, Max and Felix, or Felix and Paul ... depending on who I am, when I'm talking to myself.

But, at the same time , the scene's set at a party back in to early 1900s, being thrown by Allen Dulles ...and I'm interacting with everyone at the party, all four of me, plus myself, which makes five of me. I hope we don't start arguing.

So, get with the program, help me get over on some character background info, to get me in role.

To tell you the truth, which I can do since I'm no longer in office, that was 14 years ago ... it's no longer a matter of national security, because there *is* no more national security today, it's all little factions that sold out... playing this quadruple role is like how it was for me when I *was* in office, cause my Staff and Cabinet gave me lip service most of the time ...then, did whatever, anyway ... which was what I hired them to do in the first place ...not give me lip ...but, do their thing. We were all marionettes in a puppet show pulling each other's strings ...with no idea who the puppet master was. But, no one admitted that at the time. In 1981, when I first came into office, Nancy found those charts for me, a staff report from the Committee on Banking, Currency & Housing, House of Representatives, 94th Congress, 2nd Session, Aug. 1976, called, *Federal Reserve Directors: A Study of Corporate & Banking Influence* ...but, I didn't have time to look at them til ten years later, after I was retired. I wish I had ...but, I don't think it would've made a difference ... I'm an Iowa boy, at heart. Funny thing is, I found these charts shocking ... even as President, I didn't know the stockholding shares of the Federal Reserve Bank are owned by private banks ...*the* private banks that control the U.S. ...and, these are the people, these major shareholders who own the private banks who own the Fed and *they* control America ...not the voters ...not the taxpayers ...not the electoral college ...not the military ...not the corporations ... but these Fed majority shareholders, *these people, they* are the ones we can thank for America ...and, *they are the ones* we can blame, and punish. It took me my whole life to find out ...and, I found out after the bloom of youth was gone ...I found out, just a few years before I died.

You'll know, *now,* while you're young ...then, this book will be lost, in a lost generation, in a lost America. Now, *you'll* carry the torch, if God has chosen you to understand.

I wonder, did Clinton know? ...did Bush? ... any of the *dead* presidents? Bush must have known, both of them. After all, *you* do ... now. I hope you enjoy the charts, hold on to your seats, God bless you. [Autobiographer's note:

see charts, p587-591.]

<>

Okay, we're going to rehearse the same scene, again. Remember, I'm playing *four* Warburgs, okay? Give me that Oscar! Quiet on the set! Lights! Camera! Action! Roll 'em!

Dulles lit a cigar. "I've orchestrated Dawes loans to rebuild post-WWI Germany. United States will loan money to Germany. Germany will repay its war debts to our banking collective. The banking collective will receive the money, and pay us reparations for our loans. I've targeted oil, gold, and timber areas in Russia, I want to own."

I smiled. "Should we get rid of Borah? ...he's stirring things up."

Allan Dulles shot me a suspicious look. "Very funny. No one pays attention to him. I have your dossier. 'Paul Warburg, born 1868, conceded to be the actual author of our central bank plan, the Federal Reserve System, by knowledgeable authorities. Emigrated to United States from Germany 1904; partner, Kuhn Loeb & Company bankers, New York; naturalized 1911. Member of the original Federal Reserve Board of Governors, 1914-1918; president Federal Advisory Council, 1918-1928. Brother of Max Warburg, Max was a director of German Secret Service during World War I, and who represented Germany at the Peace Conference, 1918-1919, while you were chair of Federal Reserve System. Here's your Naval Intelligence dossier, 'Warburg, Paul, New York City. German, naturalized citizen, 1911. Was decorated by the Kaiser in 1912, was chairman of Federal Reserve Board. Handled large sums furnished by Germany for Lenin and Trotsky. Has a brother, Max, who's a leader of the espionage system of Germany'. Here's another dossier for you. Sir William Wiseman, born 1885, partner of Kuhn, Loeb & Company; head of British Secret Service during World War I. Worked closely with Col. House dominating United States and England.'"

"And?" I said.

Dulles glared at me. "I know House, and Wiseman ...introduce me to your brother?"

"Felix or Fritz or Max?"

"Max."

"Sure. Y'know, I wrote a note to Woodrow Wilson, I told him about my brother Max, I told him about Fritz ...but, I don't remember if I told him about Felix. I have two brothers in Germany who are bankers. They serve their country, naturally ...and, do their best, like I serve the U.S., and do my best."

Dulles sat down. "Right. What did Wilson say,

when he found out your brother's in charge of German military intelligence operations and German banking operations against the U.S.?"

I watched his cigar smoke. "He didn't say anything, he didn't care, he accepted it. He's a good wage slave ...believes what we tell him, so we lead him around by the nose because he thinks he's doing right. He likes our approval."

"Where's Felix, what does he do?" Dulles said.

My brother, Felix, walked up to us. "Hi Paul, I'll answer that, myself. I live in New York, I'm a director on the board of Prussian Life Insurance Company of Berlin, my policy-holders killed in war are not covered for Acts of God ...or, war. It's a little funny, if you think about it ...but, my brother Paul lives in America and advises the President of the U.S. how to finance the war against Germany. And, my brother Max lives in Germany and advises German General Staff and the Kaiser how to finance the war against America ...and, since my brother Fritz lives in Germany with him, and *also* sits on the same bank boards, he has his hat in the ring, too ...we've always been a close family."

"That *is* funny, when you hear it," Dulles said.

"Well, not all *that* funny," I said. "With Paul here, and Max and Fritz there, at the same time ...the majority shareholders of the Federal Reserve aren't me and Paul ...but Kuhn, Loeb ...and, the Schiffs ...they're in the same kettle of fish as our family ... *Jacob Schiff,* here in New York advising President Wilson in the war against Germany ...but, has two brothers over the pond, Philip Schiff and Ludwig Schiff of Frankfurt-on-Main in Germany, who are bankers to the German Government and advise German General Staff on financing the war against America!

<>

And, all at the same time, all of us are partners in Kuhn Loeb ...and, in Kuhn Loeb & Schiff!

Together, we control the Central Bank in America ...and, the Central Bank in Germany, and are equally powerful in the Bank of England central bank, reporting to Rothschild ...you see, we are a world power without a country, a stateless power, like mercenary soldiers with no country, we are mercenary central bankers. Life's a riot, if you want it so," I said.

"Now, wait a minute Felix. I'll continue serving my term on the Federal Reserve Board of Governors through the world war for one thing. And for another, Kuhn, Loeb partners such as Jacob Schiff hold the highest governmental posts in the United States during World War I ...while,

in Germany, Max and Fritz Warburg, and Philip and Ludwig Schiff, move in the highest councils of government ... that's called, good third quarter market positioning," I said.

"Paul, did you hear what the Kaiser said to Max?" I said.

"Felix, what?" I said.

"The Kaiser pounded the table with his fists. 'Must you always be right on financial matters?!'"

<>

Well, frankly, playing four Warburgs at the same time was too much for me, Oscar or no Oscar ...so, I complained to Mel's Jesus.

"I'm just going to play two Warburgs for a while, Paul and Max."

Mel's Jesus understood. "Okay, Ronnie."

So, I did. Here's goes, see if you like it better. Let me set the scene, okay? It's a montage. Paul runs the Fed in the U.S., and Max directs World War I German military intelligence, and directs Germany's central bank. So, Paul's and Max's countries are at war ...but, Paul and Max are at dinner. Here goes. Tell me how it plays.

Max looked at brother Paul. "Can you send more credit to Germany? ...for us to buy up German industry ...now that Germany's lost the war, stock prices are down so low, we'll buy everything up at pennies on the dollar. Can you help me?"

Paul looked at him. "You know, the Fed doesn't lend money ... it lends 'debt', it lends 'credit'. We Warburgs are a fountain of debt, of credit ...not, of capital. The Fed will never add anything to our capital structure or to formation of capital ...because it's purpose is to produce debt, to produce credit, to create credit for speculation ...our shareholder's speculation."

Max felt ahead of the game. "Who's your next victim?"

Paul smiled. "I'll use the Fed to set up a targeted financial depression ...not against everyone, just against the agricultural community in the Midwest, get back control of the money they made during World War I."

Max agreed. "You'll cause inflation ...then, raise the discount rate, make money more expansive, farms will fail ...and, you'll buy them up?"

"Yes ...instead of giving *them* credit, we'll ship the credit to you, to use in Germany."

<>

Nancy interrupted the scene.

"Ronnie, lunch is almost ready,"

"Okay."

"Ronnie."

"Yes, Honey."

"What's a trade acceptance?"

I shrugged. "I don't know," I said. I turned to Mel's Jesus. "Can you answer that?"

Mel's Jesus turned to me.

So did Nancy. "Who are you talking to, Ronnie?"

"Oh, I forget, you can't see him, just me."

Mel's Jesus came thru, as usual ...because suddenly, I understood.

I smiled at Nancy. She looked confused.

<>

Eustace Mullin's, *Secrets of the Federal Reserve,* explained for me.

"In 1914, Fed rates dropped from six percent to four percent, went to a further low of three percent in 1916, and stayed level until 1920. The reason for the low interest rate was the necessity for floating the billion dollar Liberty Loans. At the beginning of each Liberty Loan drive, the Federal Reserve Board put 100 million dollars in the New York money market through its open market operations, to provide a cash impetus for the drive. The most important role of Liberty Bonds was to soak up increase in circulation of the medium of exchange (integer of account) brought about by the large amount of currency and credit put out during the war. Laborers were paid high wages, farmers received the highest prices for their produce they'd ever known. These two groups accumulated millions of dollars in cash that they didn't put into Liberty Bonds. That money was out of the hands of the Wall Street group who controlled the money and credit of the U.S. They wanted it back, and that's why we had the Agricultural Depression of 1920-21. Much of the money was deposited in small country banks in the Midwest and West, that refused to have any part of the Federal Reserve System ...farmers and ranchers of those regions seeing no good reason why they should give a group of international financiers control of their money. The Fed wanted to break these small country banks ...and, get back the money paid out to farmers during the war, in effect, ruin them, and this it proceeded to do. First, a Federal Farm Loan Board was set up ...it encouraged farmers to invest their accrued money in land, on long term loans, that the farmers were eager to do. Then, 1919-1920 inflation was allowed to take its course in this country and in Europe. The purpose of the inflation in Europe was to cancel out a large portion of the war debts owed by the Allies to the American people ...

<>

"... its purpose in this country was to draw in excess moneys that had been distributed to working people in the form of higher wages and bonuses for production.

<>

"As prices went higher and higher, the money the workers accumulated became worth less and less, inflicting upon them an unfair drain ...while the propertied classes were enriched by the inflation ... because of the enormous increase in the value of land and manufactured goods. Workers were effectively impoverished ...but, farmers, who were as a class more thrifty and self-sufficient, had to be handled more harshly."

Eustace said, Mar. 20, 1920 G. Norris, in *Collier's Magazine,* explained.

"Rumor has it two members of Federal Reserve Board had a plain talk with some New York bankers and financiers in December, 1919. Immediately afterwards, there was a notable decline in transactions on the stock market, and a cessation of company promotions. It is understood that action in the same general direction has already been taken in other sections of the country, as evidence of the abuse of the Federal Reserve System to promote speculation in land, and commodities, appeared."

Eustace said, Sen. Robert L. Owen, Chairman of Senate Banking & Currency Committee, testified at Senate Silver Hearings, 1939.

"In early 1920, farmers were exceedingly prosperous. They were paying off mortgages and buying new land ... at insistence of the Government they borrowed money to do it ...and then, they were bankrupted by a sudden contraction of credit and currency, that took place later in 1920. What took place, was just the reverse of what should have. Instead of liquidating the excess of credits created by the war through a period of years, Federal Reserve Board met in a private, May 18, 1920 ...they spent all day conferring ...the minutes made sixty printed pages, and appeared in *Senate Document 310 Feb. 19, 1923.* Class A Directors, the Federal Reserve Advisory Council, were present ...but, Class B Directors, who represented business, commerce, and agriculture, were not invited. Class C Directors, representing the people of the U.S., were not invited. Only big bankers were there ...and, their work of that day resulted in a contraction of credit ...that had the effect the next year of reducing national income fifteen billion dollars ...throwing millions of people out of employment ...and, reducing the value of lands and ranches by twenty billion dollars."

Eustace continued, "Senator Brookhart of Iowa

testified, at that private meeting Paul Warburg, also President of the Federal Advisory Council, had a resolution passed to send a committee of five to the Interstate Commerce Commission to ask for an increase in railroad rates. As head of Kuhn, Loeb ...that owned most of the railway mileage in the U.S., he was already missing the huge profits the U.S. Government paid during the war, and wanted to inflict price raises on the American people.

Senator Brookhart had additional testimony.

"I went into Myron T. Herrick's office in Paris, told him I came there to study cooperative banking. He said, 'As you go over the countries of Europe, you'll find United States is the only civilized country in the world that by law, is prohibiting its people from organizing a cooperative system'. I went to New York and talked to two hundred people. After talking, standing around waiting for my train, I didn't mention cooperative banking, it was cooperation in general ...a man called me off to one side, and said, 'I think Paul Warburg is the greatest financier we've ever produced. He believes a lot more of your cooperative ideas, than you think he does ...and, if you want to consult anybody about the business of cooperation, he's the man to consult ...because, he believes in you, and you can rely on him.' A few minutes later, I was steered up against Mr. Warburg himself, he said to me, 'You're absolutely right about this cooperative idea. I want to let you know, big bankers are with you. I want to let you know that now, so you'll not start anything on cooperative banking, and turn them against you.' I said, 'Mr. Warburg, I've already prepared, and tomorrow, I'm going to offer an amendment to the Lant Bill authorizing establishment of cooperative national banks'. That was the Intermediate Credit Act which, was then pending to authorize the establishment of cooperative national banks. That was the extent of my conversation with Mr. Warburg, and we have not had any since."

Eustace continued, "Mr. Wingo testified that in April, May, June, and July 1920, manufacturers and merchants were allowed a very large increase in credits. This was to tide them through the contraction of credit ...which was intended to ruin the American farmers, who, during this period, were denied all credit.

At the Senate Hearings in 1923, Eugene Meyer, Jr. put his finger on a primary reason for the Federal Reserve Board action in raising the interest rate to 7% on agricultural and livestock paper, "I believe that a great deal of trouble would've been avoided if a larger number of eligible non-member banks had been members of the Federal Reserve System."

Meyer was correct in pointing this out. The purpose of the Board's action was, break those state and joint land stock banks which refused to surrender their freedom to the banker's dictatorship set up by Federal Reserve System.

Kemmerer's, *ABC of the Federal Reserve System*, 1919 commented. "The tendency will be toward unification and simplicity, which will be brought about by state institutions, in increasing numbers, becoming stockholders, and depositors in the reserve banks."

"However, the state banks hadn't responded," Eustace Mullins said. "And, the agricultural community was sacrificed.

"A survey of Fed's first fifteen years appears in May 1929, *North American Review*, by H. Parker Willis, professional economist, one of the authors of the Federal Reserve Act and First Board Secretary 1914-1920, from 1914 until 1920. Willis expressed disillusionment, 'My first talk with President-elect Wilson was 1912. Our conversation related entirely to banking reform. I asked, if he felt confident we could secure the administration of a suitable law, how we should get it applied, and enforced'. He answered, 'We must rely on American business idealism'. He sought for something which could be trusted to afford opportunity to American Idealism. It did serve to finance the World War ...and, to revise American banking practices. The element of idealism that the President prescribed and believed we could get on the principle of *noblesse oblige* from American bankers and businessmen ... was not there. Since inauguration of the Federal Reserve Act, we suffered one of the most serious financial depressions and revolutions ever known in our history, that of 1920-1921. We've seen our agriculture pass through a long period of suffering and even of revolution, during which 1 million farmers left their farms, due to difficulties with the price of land ...and, the odd status of credit conditions. We suffered the most extensive era of bank failures ever known in this country. Forty-five-hundred banks closed their doors since the Reserve System began. In some Western towns, there have been times when all banks in that community failed, and some banks failed over and over. There's been little difference in liability to failure between members and non-members of Federal Reserve System.'

Eustace continued, answering Nancy's question. "A trade acceptance is a draft drawn by the seller of goods on the purchaser, and accepted by the purchaser, with a time of expiration stamped upon it. The use of trade acceptances in the wholesale market supplies short-term, assured credit to carry goods in process of production, storage, transit, and marketing. It facilitates domestic and foreign commerce. Seemingly then, the bankers who wished to replace the open-book account system with the trade acceptance system were progressive men who wished to help American import-export trade. Much propaganda was issued to that effect ...but, this wasn't really the story.

"The open-book system, heretofore used entirely by American business people, *allowed* a discount for cash. The acceptance system *discourages* the use of cash, by allowing a discount for credit.

"The open-book system also allowed much easier terms of payment, with liberal extensions on the debt.

"The acceptance does not allow this, since it's a short-term credit with the time-date stamped on it. It's out of the seller's hands, and in the hands of a bank, usually an acceptance bank, which doesn't allow any extension of time.

"The adoption of acceptances by American businessmen during the 1920's greatly facilitated the domination and swallowing up of small business ... into huge trusts, which accelerated the crash of 1929.

"Trade acceptances had been used to some extent in the U.S. before the Civil War. During that war, urgencies of trade destroyed the acceptance as a credit medium ...and, it hadn't come back into favor in this country ... the American people preferred the simplicity and generosity of the open-book system.

"Open-book accounts are a single-name commercial paper, bearing only the name of the debtor. Acceptances are two-name paper, bearing the name of the debtor and the creditor ...so they become commodities to be bought and sold by banks.

"To the *creditor,* under the open-book system, the debt is a *liability.*

"To the *acceptance bank* holding an acceptance, the debt is an *asset.*

"The men who set up acceptance banks in this country, under the leadership of Paul Warburg, secured control of billions of dollars of credit existing as open accounts on financial books of American businessmen.

"In 1917-1918, operations of the Fed's Open Market Committee, with Paul Warburg chair-man, show large increases in purchases of bankers' and trade acceptances.

"World War I, along with deaths of many young men, introduced a general prosperity in the U.S., as shown by ...heavy industry returns on the New York Exchange in 1917-1918 ...increases in the amount of money circulated ...and, enormous bank clearings all through 1918. There was a great increase in the purchase of U.S. Government securities, under leadership of Eugene Meyer, Jr. ...a large part of 1919 stock market speculation at the end of the War, when the market was very unsettled ...was financed with funds borrowed from the Fed, using Government securities for collateral.

"Again, Fed wanted back the money and credit that escaped their control during prosperity. This was done by causing the great Agricultural Depression of 1920-1921.

<>

"The House Hearings on Stabilization of Purchasing Power of the Dollar, 1928 ... proved conclusively, the Federal Reserve Board worked in close cooperation with heads of European central banks ...the Depression of 1929-1931 was planned at a private luncheon of the Federal Reserve Board and those heads of European central banks in 1927. The Board has never been made responsible to the public for its decisions or actions.

<>

"The true allegiance of the members of the Federal Reserve Board has always been to the central bankers. The three features of the central bank ...its ownership by private stockholders who receive rent and profit for their use of the nation's credit ...absolute control of the nation's financial resources ...and mobilization of the nation's credit to finance foreigners ... all were demonstrated by the Federal Reserve System during the first fifteen years of its operations.

"Further demonstration of the international purposes of the Federal Reserve Act of 1913 is provided by the 'Edge Amendment' of December 24, 1919, which authorizes the organization of corporations expressly for, 'engaging in international foreign banking and other international or foreign financial operations, including the dealing in gold or bullion, and the holding of stock in foreign corporations'.

Eustace continued. In commenting on this amendment, E.W. Kemmerer, economist from Princeton University, remarked, 'The federal reserve system is proving to be a great influence in the internationalizing of American trade and

American finance.'

"That internationalizing American trade and American finance was a direct cause for involving us in two world wars did not disturb Mr. Kemmerer.

<>

"Paul Warburg ghost-wrote Federal Reserve Act as a representative of Rothschild bank to achieve an 'elastic currency', a 'rubber check' ...and, to facilitate trading in acceptances of international trade credits. Warburg was founder and president of International Acceptance Corporation, made billions in profits by trading in this commercial paper. Sec. 7 of Federal Reserve Act provides, 'Federal reserve banks, including the capital and surplus therein, and income derived therefrom, shall be exempt from Federal, state and local taxation, except taxes on real estate'.

<>

"Use of trade acceptances ... the currency of international trade ...by bankers and corporations in the U.S. prior to 1915, was practically unknown. The rise of the Federal Reserve System exactly parallels the increase in the use of acceptances in this country ...the men who wanted the Federal Reserve System also set up acceptance banks ...and, profited by the use of acceptances.

"Federal Reserve Act of 1913 as passed by Congress didn't specifically authorize use of acceptances ...but, Federal Reserve Board in 1915 and 1916 defined 'trade acceptance', further defined by Regulation A Series of 1920, and further defined by Series 1924. One of the first official acts of the Board of Governors in 1914 was, grant acceptances a preferentially low rate of discount at Federal Reserve Banks.

"National Bank Act of 1864, the determining financial authority of the United States until Nov. 1914, didn't permit banks to lend their credit. Consequently, the power of banks to create money was limited. We didn't have a bank of issue, that is ...a central bank, that could create money.

<>

"To get a central bank, bankers caused money panic after money panic in the U.S. business community by shipping gold out of the country, creating a money shortage ...and then, importing it back.

<>

"After we got our central bank, the Federal Reserve System, there was no longer any need for a money panic ...because, the banks could create money. However, the panic as an instrument of power over the business and financial community was used again on two important occasions ...in 1920, causing the Agricultural Depression, because state banks and trust companies had refused to join the Federal Reserve System ...and, in 1929, causing the Great Depression, which centralized nearly all power in this country in the hands of a few great trusts.

<>

"Large holders of trade acceptances got the use of billions of dollars worth of credit-money, plus the rate of interest charged on the acceptance itself ...which is why Paul Warburg devoted time, money, and energy to getting acceptances adopted by U.S. banking machinery.

"First World War was a boon to the introduction of trade acceptances, and the volume jumped to 400 million dollars in 1917, growing through the 1920s to more than 1 billion dollars a year, which culminated in a high peak just before the Great Depression of 1929-1931. The Federal Reserve Bank of New York's charts show that its use of acceptances reached a peak in Nov. 1929, the month of the stock market crash, and declined sharply thereafter. The acceptance people by then had gotten what they wanted, control of American business and industry.

"Feb. 1950, *Fortune Magazine* spoke of acceptances, 'Volume of acceptances declined from 1.732 billion dollars in 1929 to 209 million dollars in 1940, because of the concentration of acceptance banking in a few hands, and the Treasury's low-interest policy, which made direct loans cheaper than acceptance. There's been a slight upturn since the war, but it's often cheaper for large companies to finance imports from their own coffers,' *Fortune* said.

"American Acceptance Council published lists of corporations using trade acceptances, all of them businesses in which Kuhn, Loeb Co. or its affiliates held control.

"Louis T. McFadden, Chairman of the House Banking and Currency Committee, charged in 1922, the American Acceptance Council was exercising undue influence on the Federal Reserve Board and called for a Congressional investigation, but Congress wasn't interested.

"American Acceptance Council's 2nd Annual Convention, New York, Dec. 2, 1920, President Paul Warburg spoke, 'It's a great satisfaction to report that, during the year under review, it was possible for the American Acceptance Council to further develop and strengthen its relations with the Federal Reserve Board,' Paul said.

"During the 1920s, after Paul Warburg had resigned from the Federal Reserve Board after holding a position as Governor for a year in wartime, Paul continued to exercise direct personal influence on the Federal Reserve Board by meeting with the Board ...as President of the Federal Advisory Council ...and, as President of the American Acceptance Council.

<>

"He was, from its organization in 1920 until his death in 1932, Board Chairman of International Acceptance Bank of New York, the largest acceptance bank in the world. Felix M. Warburg, also a partner in Kuhn, Loeb Co., was director of International Acceptance Bank. Paul's son, James Paul Warburg, was Vice-President.

"Paul Warburg was also a director on other important acceptance banks in this country, such as, Westinghouse Acceptance Bank, organized in the U.S. after World War I, when headquarters of the international acceptance market moved from London to New York. Paul Warburg became the most powerful acceptance banker in the world.

<>

Eustace continues.

"After the Agricultural Depression of 1920-1921, the Federal Reserve Board of Governors settled down to eight years of providing rapid credit expansion of the New York bankers, a policy which culminated in the Great Depression of 1929-1931 ...and, helped paralyze the economic structure of the world to their advantage.

"Paul Warburg resigned in May, 1918, after the monetary system of the U.S. changed from a bond-secured currency to a currency based on commercial paper of the Federal Reserve ...Paul returned to his $500,000 a year job with Kuhn, Loeb Co. ...but, *again*, continued to determine Federal Reserve System policy ...as President of Federal Advisory Council ...and as Chairman of Executive Committee of American Acceptance Council.

"From 1921 to 1929, Paul organized three of the largest U.S. trusts ...International Acceptance Bank, largest acceptance bank in the world ...Agfa Ansco Film Corporation, with headquarters in Belgium ...and, I.G. Farben Corporation whose American branch Paul set up as I.G. Chemical Corporation ...which the Dulles brothers as attorneys represented. Westinghouse Corp. is one of Paul's creations.

<>

"Early 1920s, Fed played a decisive role in the re-entry of Russia into international finance structures. Winthrop and Stimson continued to be correspondents between Russian and

American bankers ...Henry L. Stimson handled negotiations in our recognition of Soviet Union after Roosevelt's election in 1932. This was an anti-climax, because we'd long before resumed exchange relations with Russian financiers.

"Fed began purchasing Russian gold in 1920 ...Russian currency was accepted on the Exchanges. According to the autobiography of Colonel Ely Garrison ...and, a U.S. Naval Secret Service Report on Paul Warburg, the Russian Revolution was financed by Rothschilds and Warburgs ... with a member of the Warburg family carrying the actual funds used by Lenin and Trotsky in Stockholm in 1918.

<>

Eustace continues. July 1922, an article in Britain's monthly, *Fortnightly,* sets the scene in Russia, "During the past year, practically every single capitalistic institution has been restored. This is true of the State Bank, private banking, the stock exchange, the right to possess money to unlimited amount, the right of inheritance, the bill of exchange system, and institutions and practices involved in conducting private industry and trade. A great part of formerly nationalized industries ...are now found in semi-independent trusts."

<>

"Organization of powerful trusts in Russia -- under the guise of Communism -- made possible the receipt of large amounts of financial and technical help from the U.S. Russian aristocracy was wiped out because it was inefficient, could not manage a modern industrial state.

"So, the international financiers provided funds for Lenin and Trotsky to overthrow the Czarist regime ...and, keep Russia in World War I.

In flash-forward, icon Peter Drucker, a U.S. corporate management consultant, in a 1948 *Saturday Evening Post,* article gave his view.

"Russia is the ideal of the managed economy towards which we are moving," Drucker said.

Eustace continued. "In Russia, issuance of sufficient currency to handle needs of their economy occurred only after a government had been put in power which had absolute control of the people. During the 1920s, Russia issued large quantities of 'inflation money', a managed currency."

"Economic pressure produced the 'astronomical dimensions system' of currency, it can never destroy it. Taken alone, the system is self-contained, logically perfected, even intelligent. It can perish only through collapse or destruction of the political edifice which it decorates.'

Fortnightly commented in 1929. "Since 1921,

daily life of the Soviet citizen is no different from the American citizen, and the Soviet system of government is more economical."

<>

Eustace continues.

Admiral Kolchak, leader of the White Russian armies, supported by the international bankers, sent British and American troops to Siberia in order to have a pretext for printing Kolchak rubles.

At one time in 1920, bankers on the London Exchange were manipulating old Czarist rubles, Kerensky rubles, and Kolchak rubles ...values of all three fluctuated according to movements of Allied troops aiding Kolchak. Kolchak was in possession of considerable amounts of gold seized by his armies. After defeat, a trainload of this gold disappeared in Siberia. At Senate Hearings in 1921 on the Federal Reserve System, the Kolchak gold was found.

Congressman Dunbar questioned Fed Reserve Board Governor W.P.G. Harding.

Dunbar

"Russia is sending a great deal of gold to European countries, which in turn send it to us?'

Harding

"This is done to pay for the stuff bought in this country and to create dollar exchange."

Dunbar

"At the same time, that gold came from Russia through Europe?"

Harding

"Some of it is thought to be Kolchak gold, coming through Siberia ...but, it's none of Federal Reserve Banks' business. The Treasure Secretary issued instructions to the assay office, not to take gold that does not bear the mint mark of a friendly nation."

Just what Governor Harding meant by 'a friendly nation' is not clear ...in 1921, we were not at war with any country ...but, Congress was already beginning to question the international gold dealings of the Federal Reserve System. Governor Harding could very well shrug his shoulders and say that it was none of the Federal Reserve Banks' business where the gold came from. Gold knows no nationality or race.

"The U.S. by law had ceased to be interested where its gold came from in 1906, when Treasury Secretary Shaw made arrangements with several large New York banks in which he had interests to purchase gold with advances of cash from the U.S. Treasury ...which would then purchase the gold from these banks. The Treasury could claim, it didn't know where its gold came from, since their office only registers the bank from which it made the purchase.

<> <> <>

Nancy kept me informed by reading to me ...Reinhard kept Patti informed talking to her.

Post-war operations, Werewolf, OUN

Military fighting of World War II didn't stop when the war was announced as officially over ...in Soviet Union and Poland, groups of 'Whites' remained in guerrilla units and kept fighting against 'Red' forces ...in Eastern Poland and southwest Ukraine, nationalist UPA guerrilla fighters led by German SS officers continued to skirmish against the Red army ...against Polish militia of the communist-dominated Warsaw government ...against local authorities in liberated territories.

These counter-revolutionary guerrilla-terrorist fighters controlled many rural districts and villages between Nov. 1945-Apr. 1947. The guerrilla-terrorist fighters were trained by the Germans ...they used hit-and-run tactics ...ambushed Soviet convoys ...carried out sabotage. Some Ukrainian guerrillas kept fighting in the Capthian Mountain forests until 1952.

Anti-Red guerrillas in Baltic States kept fighting. Nazis occupied the Baltics for four years during World War II. Winter 1944, many German soldiers were cut off from retreating back to Germany. They remained behind, in the Baltics. These Germany soldiers joined forces with Latvian and Estonian guerrilla units, to fight against 'Red liberators'.

Soviet Union considered guerrillas as traitors armed by Nazis to be insurgents. Soviets showed insurgents no mercy. Soviets deported whole indigenous populations to get rid of insurgents.

After World War II, French resistance treated Nazi collaborators harshly, too.

British executed traitors for broadcasting anti-British propaganda from Berlin.

Apr. 1947, Soviets said counter-revolutionary guerrilla fighters under German command were eliminated ...but, this was not true ...guerrillas kept minor civil wars going in many territories.

Warsaw Poland 1959, Polish General Ignasi Blum published figures describing sabotage carried out by anti-Communist units ... 12,556 were killed on both sides ...anti-Communist terrorists did 29,970 acts of sabotage , many conducted by Werewolves, a terrorist resistance against Soviet government.

Reinhard commanded Otto Skorzeny, who

commanded the Werewolves.

Nov. 12, 1944 ... Reinhard, in charge of Fremde Herre Aust Foreign Armies East, issued orders concerning battles in the rear against the Red army. Reinhard's Foreign Armies East would cooperate with the Nazi RHSA in these matters concerning forward intelligence units.

Feb. 6, 1945 ... German General Staff urged all German army groups to support Otto Skorzeny's Werewolf guerrilla units. "All units within whose vicinity Werewolf groups are located will take measures for the supply and welfare of the Werewolf groups," German General Staff said.

Reinhard complied enthusiastically.

It was then, he was promoted to Major General and became Deputy Chief of the Strategic Group of the General Staff ...responsible for Staff Security.

<>

In the U.S., National Security Act of 1947 embodied Wild Bill Donovan's ideas to create a civilian intelligence service ...it created Central Intelligence Agency, a civilian-run intelligence organization, outside of military jurisdiction.

<>

Frank Wisner reported to Allen Dulles.

Frank Wisner's Special Intelligence Branch worked with Reinhard. Wisner's intelligence staff included ...Wisner, soon-to-be intelligence chief of all American covert war operations worldwide ...Richard Helms, later CIA Deputy Director for Clandestine Operations, later Director of CIA for President Johnson and President Nixon ...Harry Rositzke, soon-to-be chief of CIA Clandestine Operations Inside U.S.S.R., then CIA Station Chief of India ...and, William Casey, who became Reagan presidential campaign director, then CIA director under President Reagan.

Frank Wisner used CIA money and CIA cover to provide 'left-behind' arms and ammunition to underground anti-communist assassination teams and death squads inside Eastern Europe.

Wisner's private army waged undeclared was against Soviet Union.

Wisner defied Congressional bans on smuggling Nazis into the United States.

He misappropriated U.S. Government funds to buy arms for ex-Nazi terrorists.

He obstructed justice by sheltering fugitive war criminals denounced by the Nuremberg tribunal, United Nations, and U.S. Congress.

From 1945 to 1948, Wisner's intelligence faction, OPC, spent half of CIA's annual budget.

Army Counter-Intelligence Corps had a double-agent photograph eleven volumes of files of

Stefan Bandera's faction of OUN/Bandera members ...who'd worked for SS, or Gestapo, as executioners, policemen, terrorists ... on death-squads hunting anti-Nazi fighters ...and names of pro-Nazi municipal officials.

OUN sent volunteers into several SS divisions.

Wisner wanted to hire the OUN into his own private army ...the Special Forces ... because of their work with the Nazis.

<>

CIA got all its intelligence on the Soviet Union and Eastern Europe from the Gehlen Org. CIA fronted for Nazi spies. Gehlen Org based its founding on cooperating with the U.S. on militant anti-Communism.

Gehlen Org wasn't interested in promoting Democracy.

Gehlen Org didn't care about security of the U.S.

Gehlen Org had no use for the Declaration of Independence and Bill of Rights.

Gehlen Org was an arm of Odessa.

<>

In 1948, Wisner wrote a letter advocating U.S. Immigration Department allow OUN/UPA members into the U.S.

Frank Wisner explained. "From 1945 to 1948, OUN/UPA fighters left Soviet Ukraine and walked into Western Germany bringing German prisoners-of-war home with them.

"Organization of Ukrainian Nationalists and UPA were still using weapons and ammunition retreating German armies left behind.

"OUN/UPA was still fighting Communists ...over 35,000 members of the Russian secret police, MVD and MKGB, have been killed by OUN/UPA since the end of the war.

"In other words, main activities of OUN in Ukraine cannot be considered detrimental to the U.S.," Frank Wisner said.

Note, the Christian West was in place ...the next phase of the Cold War had begun.

<>

By 1952, 400,000 immigrants had come into the United States, including Nazi collaborators from Byeola-Russia, Ukraine, Baltic States, and the Balkans. At the same time, Wisner had gotten U.S. citizenship for Nazi and fascist leaders of his Special Forces.

1945, Allied occupation of Berlin

Nancy continued reading me James Stewart Martin's, *All Honorable Men* ...and, Reinhard kept telling Patti his story.

Martin went abroad after World War II to examine backgrounds and affiliations of men chosen to administer re-building and governing Germany. Bush Park was headquarters for the future Allied military government of Germany ...the group then known as, U.S. Group Control Counsel. Brigadier General Cornelius W. Wickersham was in command of U.S. Group Control Counsel. On his way to report to Wickersham, Martin looked at names on office doors of men in U.S. Group Control Counsel chosen to be the Allied military government of Germany.

Colonel Graham R. Howard helped General Draper select personnel for Economics Division.

Colonel Graham Howard was to be Director of Economics Division. In 1940, before America entered the war, Colonel Howard authored a book, *America & a New World Order* ...an apology for the Nazi economic system that could have been called, 'How to Do Business with Hitler' ...he praised totalitarian practices ...justified German aggression ...justified Munich policy of appeasing Hitler ...and, blamed President Roosevelt for causing World War II. Howard was a Vice President of General Motors, in charge of General Motors overseas business ...and, was leading rep of General Motors in Germany before World War II.

Martin augured this an omen ...of the quality of men in Allied military government of Germany ...supporters of Hitler.

Brigadier General William Draper, Jr. ...was Secretary-Treasurer of Dillon, Reid & Co., on military leave from the company, assigned by Washington to be Economic Director.

Dillon, Reid & Co. was an investment banking firm after World War I that took the lead floating German bonds financing German industry to re-arm Germany after World War I. So, Germany could fight World War II.

Martin was assigned to work in the Finance Division with Captain Norbert A. Bogdon

Bogdon was a Vice President of J. Henry Schroder Banking Corp. Schroder banks were affiliated with Nazi banks before, during, and after the U.S. went to war against Nazis.

<>

Stanford University's Hoover Institute scholar, Anthony Sutton's, *Wall Street & the Rise of Hitler*, looked at relationships between Wall Street and Hitler. Sutton uncovered a memo written by Treasury Secretary Morgenthau to President Truman on May 29 1945.

The memo described other men who were going to be involved in the U.S. military government, and help administer the Marshal Plan to run the, 'New Germany'.

Louis Douglas was directly involved. Douglas resigned as Director of the Budget in 1934. Then, he attacked Roosevelt's fiscal policies. As of 1940, Douglas was President of Mutual Life Insurance. As of Dec. 1944, he also sat on the Board of Directors of General Motors.

Edward S. Zidonkey was to supervise the Engineering Section. Before World War II, Zidonkey was head of General Motors at Antwerp.

Philip Gepke was in charge of mining operations. Gepke managed Anaconda Copper's smelters and mines in Upper Silesia before World War II.

Philip B. Clover was to be in charge of handling petroleum matters. Before World War II, he represented Siccone Vacuum Oil Co. in Germany.

Peter Hoagland was to manage industrial production problems. Hoagland was on leave from General Motors, expert on German production.

<>

After two years, Martin realized, Governments were powerless to stand against new World Order ruling family bankers, industrialists, and petroleum corporations. Government stood on the sidelines ...and, watched ... while the banking, industrial, and petroleum community of ruling families rearranged the world's affairs, using military or economic warfare. Martin believed in innate goodness of man, that economic power was a public trust, the job of Government was to see power was used in the public interest, not against the public.

Martin saw how economic masters of Germany pushed Hitler into power, at a time after World War I when supporters of democratic Weimar Republic were *against* Hitler ...*against* dictatorship ...*against* totalitarianism. But, trans-Atlantic financial and industrial ruling families in Germany, America, and England threw combined financial support behind Hitler ...and, won the election for the Nazis.

<>

Martin, Chief of the U.S. Justice Department Economic Warfare Section ...was terrified that General Motors, DuPont, and the rest of the Warburg financial group ... had organized a failed coup d'état against President Roosevelt ...and, gotten away with it. He was terrified those ruling family financiers and industrialists in America might concentrate financial and economic power and do to America what German General Staff ruling families did to Germany.

If U.S. ran into serious economic difficulties ...

the same conditions would be present to re-enact the German drama on the American stage.

Martin wanted to prepare against such a crisis at home and in Germany, to put Allied occupation of Germany back on track, to champion public welfare and public survival against ruling family oppression in the U.S., to prevent the kind of economic concentration of power in the hands of a handful of ruling family patriarchs ... as it had happened in Germany ... from happening in the U.S.

He knew nothing could be done to cancel the concentration of economic power in the 'New Germany', until something was done to cancel the concentration of economic power at home, in the U.S.

Martin saw clearly, Germany was a mask on an American face ...a face ignored after World War I when after Germany's defeat came a period not of peace, but of armed truce.

The Trans-Atlantic ruling family Axis new World Order was allowed to go on unchecked after World War I, to re-arm and re-build a Germany fit to wage World War II.

Martin was afraid the same thing would happen after World War II, to allow the new World Order ruling family banking, petroleum, and military-industrial community to use Germany to wage World War III.

No, Martin did not preach Germany was a menace ...he taught us there are forces in our own country, the U.S., that could make Germany a menace ...and, these same forces could create a menace of their own, here ...not simply through a coup d'état, but as a calm judgment of business necessity, by honorable men.

<>

Nancy never met Reinhard in person. In a sense, she met him through me and Patti.

In the 1930's, when Bank of England and Fed teamed up against other central banks playing king of the hill in an economic warfare called the Great Depression, trans-Atlantic banking stability was more important than the temporary inconvenience of world war. So, Bank of International Settlements was founded in Switzerland ... by Nazi and American interests, as a central bank clearinghouse ... so, banks of countries at war with each other could still do banking business together ...the mechanics of collecting interest, and waging inflationary and deflationary economic coups d'état ... uninterrupted by bloodshed.

<>

In 1940, British intelligence saw American competition move into the Axis oil marketplace. Saudi Arabian oil owners, the ruling family house of Ibn Saud was represented by Jack Philby.

Nazi oil buyers such as I.G. Farben were represented by Allen Dulles, Philby's partner.

German bankers and Spanish financiers were represented by John Foster Dulles, Allen's partner.

<>

Texaco supplied oil to Generissimo Franco during the Spanish Civil War. Texaco was partners with Socal. Jack Philby controlled ibn Saud oil through Socal. They formed CalTex.

James Forrestal was Secretary of the Navy. He later became U.S. Defense Secretary. He shaped American oil policy. Forrestal had been president of Dillon, Read Investment Bankers in New York in the 1930's, a friend of Allen Dulles and John Foster Dulles. Forrestal brought Socal and Texaco together in 1935.

With the help of Dillon Read Vice President Paul Nitze, they drew a plan to merge assets of the two companies.

When the deal was finalized in 1940, CalTex was the parent company of Aramco ...Arabian-American Oil Co.

Standard Oil of California and Standard Oil of New Jersey were owned by Rockefellers.

American I.G. owned stock in Standard of New Jersey, and in Socal.

American I.G. changed its name to, General Aniline & Film (GAF). General Aniline & Film installed Forrestal onto its board of directors.

Forrestal was Vice President of General Aniline & Film. Nazi company I. G. Farben was a client of Dulles. Allen Dulles and John Foster Dulles were board members of J. Henry Schroder Bank in New York, that did business with the Nazis.

Forrestal was on the payroll of I.G. Farben. Forrestal's client CalTex had Saudi oil. Jack Philby shepherded the arrangement so the Third Reich purchased Saudi Arabian oil.

Ibn Saud was a partner of the Nazis.

Bechtel bought Dillon Read & Co. investment bank in 1981, at urging of George Shultz, President of Bechtel. C. Douglas Dillon, who'd owned the company, had been appointed Treasury Secretary by President Kennedy. After firing Allen Dulles as director of CIA, Kennedy appointed John McCone, former co-founder of Bechtel International in the 1930s, to be the new director of CIA.

<>

In 1948, Paul Nitze drafted National Security Council Memorandum #68 NSC-68. State Secretary Dean Acheson assisted him. Nitze's

NSC-68 institutionalized the U.S. military-industrial complex, as President Eisenhower called it, warning Americans of the power of the military-industrial complex to rule society and wage war at will, for financial gain. NSC-68 empowered the military-industrial complex as mainstay of the American economy.

NSC-68 also established a CIA-funded domestic psychological warfare program, called, The Crusade For Freedom ...that, would condition the minds of Americans to regard the democratic Soviet communists not as friends and Allies who'd defeated Hitler ...but, as enemies ... the spirit of the Christian West Plan.

<>

NSC-68 postulated global military growth would stimulate the economy in the United States and bankrupt the economy in the Soviet Union. It would eliminate democratic exponents of redistributing wealth from the rich to the poor in the U.S., by attacking Communism at home ...while allowing Nazism at home to flourish, and war-mongers in the military-industrial establishment to make huge profits by building America's military might to fight an inflated perceived Soviet threat.

In 1948, memories of the 1930s scared Americans. Capitalism as a way of life had failed to provide health and welfare for the majority of Americans.

Socialism, the democratic pooling and sharing of wealth to benefit society, was gaining in popularity among Americans, in Europe, and the colonial Third World in Africa and South America.

During the 1930s in America, peace activists, labor activists, union activists, and women's rights activists took to the streets in hundreds of protests against joblessness, homelessness, and starvation. Labor unions had formed in America ...and, fascist ruling families like Ford, DuPont, Dulles, and Morgan ... that owned or financed industry in America, fought bitterly, sometimes with terrorist squads to put down labor strikes and undo union progress.

The U.S. was pumping millions of dollars via the Marshall Plan into post-war Germany, for several reasons. In public, the plan was heralded to revive world trade ...but, it failed. After World War II, American ruling families had on the surface replaced British ruling families as leaders of the world ...but, Bank of England through member subsidiary banks owned controlling shares in the Fed. Therefore, England dictated American financial policies.

There were perceived nationalist and commu-nist insurgencies everywhere, that threatened a world hierarchy managed by American and British ruling families.

[Autobiographer's note: but, were and/or are such conflicts manufactured and financed in the same way, by the same people, for the same reasons, as the Russian Revolution?]

<>

In 1948 State Secretary Dean Acheson wrote a memo to President Truman.

"This view of the Marshall Plan as a failure is, of course, contrary to the myths of official history. Unless vigorous steps are taken, the reduction and eventual termination of extraordinary foreign assistance, i.e. the Marshall Plan, will create economic problems at home and abroad of increasing severity. If this is allowed to happen, U.S. efforts, including key commodities on which our most efficient agricultural and manufacturing industries are heavily dependent, will be sharply reduced, with serious repercussions on our domestic economy. European countries, and friendly areas in the Far East and elsewhere, will be unable to obtain basic necessities which we now supply, to an extent that will threaten their political stability. Put in its simplest terms, the problem is this ... as the European Recovery Program ERP ... the Marshall Plan's official name ... is reduced, and after its termination in 1952, how can Europe and other areas of the world obtain dollars necessary to pay for a high level of United States exports, that is essential to their own basic needs and to the well-being of the United States economy?" Acheson said.

It was felt politically, only massive Government spending could prevent a second Great Depression. The massive Government spending could be put into social welfare programs, as President Roosevelt had done in his New Deal programs, to give the masses of poor Americans, jobs. Or, the massive Government spending could be spent buying weapons systems from rich American ruling-family-owned corporations.

Paul Nitze wrote NSC-68 to address this situation. Paul Nitze wanted the money to go to America's ruling family bankers, oil companies, and industrialists.

Business Week editorials in 1949 addressed the problem.

"Military spending *doesn't* alter the structure of the economy. It goes through regular channels. But, welfare and public works spending that Truman plans, *does* alter the economy. It makes new channels of its own. It creates new institutions. It redistributes income. It shifts demand from one industry to another. It changes the whole economic pattern. That's its object," the article said.

Nitze wanted an ongoing international military build-up ...to fatten portfolios of his friends and bankrupt the Soviet economy, consequently destabilizing the Soviet Union and Eastern Europe. But in America, Conservatives wanted neither a huge army nor a permanent spy service, nor a military build-up.

Nitze realized, the American people would need to believe they had an enemy about to destroy them, in order for him to justify an ongoing military build-up. It was the, *Project for the New American Century,* of its time. Nitze scapegoated the Soviet people. Nitze referred to the Kremlin as a corrupt oligarchy running a slave state, wanting to takeover the world, destroy free society.

Nitze realized, the main characteristic of the Soviet style economy was shortage of goods ...while the capitalist style economy was surplus, too many goods ...and, not enough money in the hands of the people to buy them.

Nitze worked on his drafts of NSC-68.

"... grounds for predicting the U.S. and other free nations will, within a period of a few years at most, experience a decline in economic activity of serious proportions without government intervention. If a dynamic expansion of the economy were achieved, the necessary build-up could be accomplished without a decrease in the national standard of living. An arms build-up can help solve the characteristic crisis of U.S.-style capitalism. But, an arms build-up will hurt the U.S.S.R., which is already being drawn upon close to the maximum possible extent, thereby leaving the Soviet Union even more vulnerable to its characteristic economic crisis, chronic shortage. This economic squeeze is one front in a Strategy of Containment of Communism and a calculated and gradual coercion to reduce power and influence of U.S.S.R. Another opportunity is the wonderfully corrosive potential of nationalism and insurgent nationalist groups in the Soviet Union and Eastern Europe, which can eat away at the internal stability of U.S.S.R. and its relations with its satellite-states. U.S.S.R. isn't the only problem facing Washington. The Kremlin's ideological pretensions are inspirational to poor countries in Latin and South American, and in Africa. That the Soviet Union exists at all is proof to them there's more than one way to manage economics in society. Poor and vulnerable groups in society are impressed by the rapid growth of U.S.S.R. from a backward society to a world power. A rapidly-growing U.S. capitalistic economy, fueled by military spending is an alternative to U.S.S.R. and Communism. But at home, domestic unrest in the U.S. caused by militant unions, doubts, diversity, and rights and privileges free men enjoy in Democracy, make opportunities for the Kremlin to do its evil work. We need to reconcile order, security and the need for participation in capitalism as the requirements of freedom. I recommend a substantial increase in military expenditures, a substantial increase in military assistance programs and some increase in economic aid to our allies in the anti-Soviet crusade, that we have a mass propaganda campaign to build and maintain confidence on our side, and sow mass defections on theirs, that we have covert economic, political, and domestic psychological warfare, tighter internal security, and expanded intelligence."

William Schaub of the Bureau of the Budget disagreed. "This picture of a free world versus a slave world is overdone. It's not true the U.S. and its friends are a free world. Are the Indo-Chinese free? No. Can the people of the Philippines be said to be free under the corrupt Quirino government? No. People are attracted to Communism because their governments are despotic or corrupt, or both. Today, many peoples are striving actively to better themselves economically and politically and have thus accepted, or are in danger of accepting, leadership of the Communist movement."

Paul Nitze's NSC-68 provided a reason and strategy for a war on many fronts ...NSC-68 was against economic depression, NSC-68 was against domestic insurgency, NSC-68 was against wars of liberation in the Third World, NSC-68 was against too much independence in Western Europe and East Asia, NSC-68 was against the U.S.S.R., NSC-68 was against Communism. NSC-68 was the embodiment of the Nazi's and Gehlen's and Dulles' Christian West plan.

NSC-68 was a response by United States ruling families to remake the world in their own image ...by keeping wealth redistribution constant from the poor to the rich, rather than allowing the wealth to flow from the rich to the poor.

Lytton Park Revolutionaries in Palo Alto

Alan, Patti, Granma Dagmara Wilpf, Reinhard, Butler, and Shiu, arrived at the peace and freedom demonstration Bay Area Action and the Palo Alto Peace Center were holding in Lytton Plaza in downtown Palo Alto. Joan Baez was singing anti-war songs. They sat down in the grass. Alan thought the gathering was like being at a love-in or be-in during the late '60s, with all the middle class people running around, blowing bubbles in the sunshine with their children and enjoying rock music bands. When he sat down, Alan moved a daddy-long-legs spider out of the way, a couple snails, and a couple of friendly looking bugs that seemed to be watching him from on top of a dandelion. Not everything had to be killed by bigger and stronger people. The water didn't have to be polluted, or the sky. The trees didn't need to be cut down. Radioactive piles of uranium pilings didn't have to be stacked in playgrounds in Indian villages. Why not spare life when you could? ...he thought. He noticed Gestapo and SCREAMA and FBI Cointelpro agents provocateur infiltrate the peaceful crowd. It was easy to pick them out. They looked like marine recruits that finished basic training with short brushy hair, brand new clothes, shiny black shoes. Or, they looked like caricatures of hippies, shoddy impersonators of real people ... pushing people around, starting fights.

Dagmara shook her head. "I've seen it all before. My first husband in America used to work at a DuPont factory during the '30s. He was a union organizer. The factory Black Legion surrounded him when he was working at his machine station. They beat him to death. They have no feelings. They're stupid. They do what they're told. They know love is illegal, so they hate, isolated from humanity.

Patti felt sad.

Granma Dagmara Wilpf watched the SCREAMA drag people out of the crowd and beat them. Some SCREAMA looked at her, recognized Gehlen, then charged towards him. SCREAMA grabbed Alan. SCREAMA freed Gehlen. SCREAMA pointed automatic rifles at peace and freedom demonstrators.

Patti felt bewildered, looked at Reinhard. "I trusted you."

Reinhard laughed. He slapped Patti across her face. Patti reached inside her waist band. She drew out a pistol. She pointed it at Reinhard. He held his hands up.

"Have mercy on me."

Patti hesitated. "Leave. Take your SCREAMA and leave."

She fired her gun in the air to show Reinhard she meant business. The sound of the gunshot automatically turned on the SRI Ultrasonic Crowd-Control Weapons System. The Stanford Research Institute developed the weapon in 1977 on the pretense of controlling mass demonstrations in South Africa, where it was marketed and used successfully to intimidate and torture people in impoverished Black townships. The weapon attacked the body's gland and hormone centers with ultrasonic sound waves. The victims fell to the ground in convulsions and became unconscious. The SCREAMA were safe because they wore a counter-weapon SRI designed to broadcast the opposite sound waves to cancel out the ultrasonic waves. The frequency came out from little radio speakers mounted over their gold SCREAMA badges. The peace demonstrators passed-out, into unconsciousness. Alan felt groggy, his eyes blurring til it was hard to see. He heard himself groaning. He saw he was in a paddy wagon, a police containment vehicle. He checked his body for broken bones. There were none. He looked at his friends in the van. Butler had thrown up on himself. Everyone was moaning, slowly sitting up, holding their heads. Alan looked outside the van. He saw all the peace demonstrators were gone. He saw the park was being power-vacuumed, gone over with leaf blowers, completely tidied up. The normies had returned in their business suits, sitting on benches reading *Wall Street Journal*, eating lunches from brown paper bags. It was business as usual, again, in Lytton Park.

Alan yelled out through the bars on back of the vehicle, "Help! We're being kidnapped!"

People looked up nonchalantly from their newspapers at the SCREAMA van ...then, looked back down at their newspapers. Alan turned back around to face his friends. Patti stared at his pants. He looked down. When he was being attacked by the SRI Ultrasonic Canon, he peed his pants.

Alan felt awkward. "God, that's embarrassing."

Patti came over and hugged him, "I'm embarrassed, too. For trusting Reinhard."

Alan sighed. "Are you proud of me for not getting too nervous and running away?"

Patti smiled. "Yes."

Alan blushed. "I don't think I've been this embarrassed since junior high, when I was sitting in class and would get an erection and couldn't stand up when the bell rang and it was time to go. Then, there was the time my pants split up the rear at a wedding."

Patti smiled. "When I was a teenager, I was a virgin. I used to talk about sex in front of my friends like I knew what I was talking about. One of my friends knew what it was about. She laughed at me. *That's* embarrassing,"

Everyone sat in the paddy wagon. Patti felt insecure. She stared at the light coming in the rear window of the van, "I wonder what I could have done differently in my life, to not end up here?"

Holding cell under arrest

They were put in a SCREAMA holding cell under arrest, on a three-day weekend. They were accused of revolutionary terrorist activity.

Alan felt claustrophobic inside the holding cell.

"I don't think there will be peace on Earth."

Patti sobbed. "It's my fault. I'm not good enough."

Reinhard stood outside the cell. He looked through the cell bars. "I've had SCREAMA and Cointelpro teams watching all activist revolutionary groups. You could've threatened us, if you worked together."

"I don't think you're ever going to let us out of here. Are you?" Patti said.

Reinhard shrugged, "It's a three-day weekend."

Patti didn't think it'd work out. "You hate us, because we want peace and justice."

Gehlen smiled absently, "Do I?"

Dagmara shrugged. "To think I ever loved him."

Patti felt depressed. "Love can't help us now. Love's not gonna change SCREAMA."

<>

Alan felt like he was going through womenapause, the life change men go through. He remembered talking to Gary at the Bay View Boat Club in San Francisco in China Basin. It seemed a long time ago, back in the days of freedom, before SCREAMA made love illegal.

"Gary, nothing makes sense anymore ...everything's the same ...but, the answers don't fit."

The sun was shining ...it was hot and dry ...then, the first raindrops hit the sidewalks and asphalt streets, giving off a dry scent ...somehow, relieved by the taste of rain.

Patti invited herself and some friends to Alan's flat in the City for Christmas dinner. They looked at each other in silence, sat in silence, everyone else at the table was gabbing away in a different world, than the one in which they sat, looking into each other's eyes, understanding the stillness they shared. After dinner, Patti took him to the front window, handed him binoculars, told him, look at a building ...a domed building across town, with three windows below the dome ... separated by columns. When Alan looked at the first and second windows, the building looked

like the big head of a gargoyle staring out over San Francisco. When he looked at the second and third windows, it looked like a real head of a giant, lovely woman gazing over the city and across the bay ...the persona of San Francisco.

Patti had that kind of magic to her ...later in the day, they were on the boat club deck to watch the bay splash up the rocks under the deck. He stood beside her ...as soon as he was near her, the waves start moving in slow motion, all across the bay ... the ripples in some kind of movie special effect. Patti was a magical woman.

"It's cold," Patti said.

Alan stopped daydreaming. SCREAMA guards hurried into the cells. SCREAMA guards took Patti out into the hall. Patti was scared. SCREAMA strip-searched her ...fondled her ...shoved their fingers into her. She felt terrified. SCREAMA put Patti back in the cell.

Reinhard led Mel's Jesus and me into the cell ...but they'd couldn't see me, they just saw Mel's Jesus. An apparition of Mother Mary appeared beside me, she took my hand.

Reinhard looked at Patti. Reinhard took an electric prod, stuck it into Mel's Jesus. Mel's Jesus convulsed, fell to the floor. SCREAMA beat him unconscious. SCREAMA dragged him out of the cell.

Reinhard pointed to Alan. SCREAMA beat Alan til he lay sobbing. Reinhard used the electric prod on Dagmara.

Dagmara screamed, "No! Stop!"

Reinhard tortured her til she was silent, start kicking her face.

Reinhard shrugged, "She's dead."

Patti felt crazy. She kneeled on the floor beside Dagmara ...SCREAMA dragged Dagmara away, out of the cell.

"I want confessions from you," Reinhard said.

Reinhard took out a knife. He jabbed it into Patti's body several times. He took a hammer from a SCREAMA, held Patti's hand on the floor. He smashed one of her fingers with the hammer. It was excruciating, like her finger was torn off her hand.

Patti screamed.

Reinhard picked up Patti's hand. "I'm sorry. That was an accident. I think this finger will have to be amputated."

Reinhard raised his knife.

Alan was frantic. "Stop! I'll confess! I don't believe in love! I never have! I've never loved!"

Reinhard smiled, "Good. Sign this paper."

Alan signed the paper.

Reinhard held Alan's hand down against the

floor. Reinhard picked up the hammer, swung it high into the air ...then, brought the hammer down on one of Alan's fingers ...smashing it. Alan screamed in anguish.

Reinhard looked at Patti, "Will you sign, renounce love, too?"

Patti felt weak, dizzy. Her head felt too big. She looked at Alan. "Yes. I don't believe in love. I've never loved." Patti signed a confession.

Gehlen felt triumphant, powerful, unstoppable. "You're both on probation. If you show any signs of having loved, you'll be killed. You're free to go."

<>

Patti and Alan went to hide in the caves on Skyline Boulevard on top of the nearby western mountain range overlooking the Pacific. The sun set in oranges and pinks over their heads, across the sky like the first sunset, ever.

"I'm so sorry about Granma Wilpf," Alan said.

Patti felt desolate, "I can't believe he killed her right in front of me. I did nothing to stop him."

"What could you've done? ...nothing."

"I should've done something. I miss her so much ...a hole has opened up inside of me ...everything's quiet in there ...but the memories. This is never going to get better. She's gone. She was always so kind to me, warm ...she lov...." Patti stopped, afraid to say the word ...afraid what would happen to her. Somehow, SCREA-MA could hear her thoughts. "Everything I wanted from life is gone."

Alan put his hands on Patti's shoulders.

"Remember Lot in the Bible ...he lost his home, his children, his wife ...but, he'd didn't turn against Mr. & Mrs. God."

"But God is laa...." She stopped, afraid to say, or think the word. Patti start sobbing, "...that means I've turned against God ...it's getting worse."

It had happened without her knowing ...when she signed that confession paper ...but, it had happened.

There's something we can do," Alan said.

"What?"

"Become guerillas, organize an underground army of people like us, people with nothing left to lose ...armed resistance."

Patti was shocked, "An army of angels? ...in Palo Alto?"

"Sure ...like in the movies."

Patti thought for a moment. "Why not? ...if we don't, more Granma Wilpfs will die everywhere in Palo Alto ...just like they're dying around the world every moment, we stand here talking."

"Then, you're in?"

"Yes."

"Good.".

They kissed.

Alan felt excited. "Does this mean we can get married?"

"No."

Alan felt disappointed.

Patti shrugged.

"What first?" Alan said.

Patti had thought about it a hundred times. "We got to let people know, we exist. We'll put up fliers at Skylonda Corners, at the crossroads, here, on top of the mountains. Then, we need money to get food and clothes, guns to protect ourselves ... to save the pacifists ...to save the kids ...to save innocent people. Then, in a few weeks when world leaders are meeting there, we'll blow up Bohemian Grove." She felt excited, "You're not afraid of consequences, like you always were before?"

"No, not any more," Alan said.

Patti felt a burst of energy. "It's time for artists and writers to fight back! ...take our power back! ...get even!"

Dawn, sitting in car
outside construction site

Alan and Patti sat in a car in Palo Alto, outside a construction site. It was a half hour before sunrise. The air was dark, still ...and, cold.

Alan shivered in his shoulders. "No one should be awake, this early."

Patti looked at him, "This is a big day, we're going shopping."

Alan was amused but melancholy. "I feel helpless, when I think of how much we have to do, so we can live in utopia."

Patti smiled, "It takes faith ...and, a sniper rifle."

They left the car ...sneaked into the construction site, overpowered a security guard, took his pistol and shotgun, then left.

In broad daylight, they began to rob housewives in homes in Atherton, Palo Alto, Portola Valley, and Woodside. Sometimes, when they robbed a house, they sneaked cash back to the servants. That got them a reputation as, the 'Robin Hood bandits'.

At a convenience store at the end of the Portola Valley loop, they waited in line to buy potato chips, sour cream, cream cheese, and Hagen-Das ...then, held up the store, emptying the cash register.

They went for dinner at an expensive restaurant in Atherton ...after dessert, holding up the

379

restaurant.

They went to see a movie at Shoreline, hurrying not to miss the beginning ...stuffing on popcorn, Good & Plenty's, Coke, and Ju Ju Be's. After the movie, they robbed the twelve cash register drawers and safe in the cashiers office, they fled with huge popcorn tubs full of money.

At supermarkets, they filled up their shopping cart, got their groceries packed into bags, then robbed the store vaults, at gunpoint.

Meanwhile in America, ruling family patriarchs and their sons and daughters were robbing billions of dollars from the Savings & Loans. Not with guns ...but, with fountain pens brokering bad loans they knew would fail ...while they and their associates excelled in drug running, petroleum wars, central bank economic warfare ...and generally, in all around graft and war profiteering ... business as usual.

Patti and Alan decided to rob pawn shops. Patti pulled up their car in front of pawn shops on 6th Street in San Francisco on a Friday.

"It's closed," Patti said.

"It's Yom Kippur. Pawn shops close on Jewish holidays."

They came back Tuesday, held up the pawn shops, stealing rifles and pistols. Another day they went to Vic's H&H Gun Shop in Redwood City, stole paramilitary rifles in an armed holdup. Then, they drove to Eddy's Gun Shop in Mountain View at midnight, drove their truck through the glass door, robbed the .22 caliber Gatling gun out of the window.

Back at their cave hideout, off Skyline Boulevard, Alan mounted the Gatling gun on the hood of their car.

Patti laughed. "Don't you think it's a bit conspicuous?"

Alan was embarrassed, "I just wanted to see how it would look."

"Can you mount it under the hood?"

Alan nodded, "Okay."

Alan chopped a hole in the firewall between the engine compartment and the front seats of the car for the Gatling gun trigger and ammo feeder to stick through. Where the rifle stock stuck through the firewall into the driver's compartment, he hung a towel and some swimming trunks on the Gatling gun handle and feeder to cover it. He mounted a surfboard and a sail board on the roof. The next day they hit the bank in Woodside ...then, made their escape.

<>

Patti and he settled down to dinner in a Vietnamese French cafe.

Patti was excited by the smell of the food. "We finally made it to the big time ...we're a revolutionary paramilitary unit coming down out of the hills to hit banks ...just like CIA does in the Philippines."

They hit an armored car coming out of the San Francisco Federal Reserve Mint. They hijacked a school bus full of high school students at Castellja Catholic Private Girls School, holding the students for ransom.

They returned to their cave hideout.

Alan looked at Patti. "We've got all this money, food, guns, and publicity. What are we going to do with it?"

Patti's was excited, "I know! ...we'll make an army of street people, homeless people, people without jobs, and war vets ...we'll have an army of forgotten people ...people with nothing to lose ...we'll take over Palo Alto, make it sovereign state like the Vatican is."

Alan didn't get it, "How we gonna protect it?"

"We'll rob Stanford Linear Accelerator, get some plutonium, make a basement nuke, a whole bunch of little nukes. I printed a file off the internet how to do it. We'll hide them all over Palo Alto, San Francisco, San Jose, Sacramento, San Diego, Los Angeles, Sacramento in the Capital Building ...we'll take over California. We'll make it a utopia. Everyone in the U.S. can come here, live here free, get a guaranteed minimum yearly living wage ... whether they're working or not, free medical care, free rent, no mortgage payments, free food ... the Fed can just print up debt money to pay for everything ... like they do for themselves, anyway to get what *they* want ...except now, it'll be for everyone, not *just* them ...they'll have to leave us alone ...or, we'll blow them up ... it's détente."

"Do you think they'll do a quarantine, black us out, like in Sarajevo?"

"Probably, we better takeover some TV networks, too."

Several months passed.

They looted Stanford Linear Accelerator.

Following the internet do-it-yourself guide, Patti and Alan built basement nukes.

Patti called the press. "We're going to nuke Washington D.C. ...we're going to nuke Congress ...unless you leave us alone."

Within a few months, peace activists from across America left their homes to start a new life in the Palo Alto utopia Alan and Patti co-founded. There was no hunger in Palo Alto, jobs for everyone whenever they wanted. The city streets were torn up and made into vegetable gardens. Only electric cars and bicycles were permitted to run in the city. Chicken coops popped up everywhere. Excess homegrown organic vegetables filled the stores, then were freeze dried, then sent to hundreds of millions of starving communities in Africa, Asia, South America, North America, and Europe.

Alan was pleased with the utopia.

So was Patti. But, she was irritated, "They're doing a press blackout. What should we do? We made Palo Alto a utopia overnight, Washington declared Palo Alto a sovereign country, independent of U.S. rule. Everything is free, paid for by the Fed just writing 'paid' on our bills, like they do for themselves. We're utopians. We turned Palo Alto from an upper middle class romper room covered with geriatric Stanford students stuck in time ...to a utopia for artists." Patti arranged to use a pirate broadcasting radio to send a digital broadcast to satellite. It was picked up by TV stations across the world.

Patti spoke to everyone watching TV, "Sociopathic ruling families who harm people or the environment for money are now accountable for damages ...they'll be divested, their portfolios seized, to pay to fix the damage they've done.

"This proclamation goes into effect retro-actively. We demand the national debt be written off. We demand the central banks be closed.

"We won't kill violent, sociopathic ruling families off, when we divest them ...unless, they deserve it. Instead, we'll put them in a penal colony on a desert island with fleas to eat. Or, they can live on welfare and food stamps. Or, they can kill and eat each other. We're the Artists & Writers of America ...don't fuck with us. Now, we have money in our pockets ...now, we can survive in America ...it's payback ...we're getting even." Patti was pleased with herself.

Alan turned off the broadcast transmitter. He looked at Patti. "Bohemian Grove is meeting next week."

Patti picked up one of the basement nukes. She smiled. "It's time to blow up Bohemian Grove ...it's all planned ...next week."

They went to sleep.

Patti's Palo Alto utopia was running smoothly ...but, she noticed more and more SCREAMA Cointelpro agents were infiltrating Palo Alto. She felt angry. Patti made her second pirate TV broadcast by digital satellite across America.

Patti addressed the nation. "Palo Alto is a utopia. But, what about the rest of America? SCREAMA are threatening our existence

...everywhere fascist ruling families are trying to destabilize our Garden of Eden. For America to be a utopia ...every person in America must be armed. If everyone in the world was armed ...there could be no genocide ...because people could defend themselves.

We have in Utopia an army of armed citizens, armed with guns and nuclear bombs. We'll march out of Palo Alto, guns in hand, to make America free ...everyone in Congress, every lobbyist, every ruling family listed in the Blue Book who opposes us ...will be a target. You interlocking directorates are gonna be sorry! We're gonna divest your asses ... we're going to kill the people who made love illegal ... *I have loved!*" Patti said.

Alan was shocked. "Patti ... you said the bad word! ... Reinhard Gehlen's gonna get us!

Patti picked up a basement nuke.

"I hope so."

◇ ◇ ◇

The asphalt bathroom & Jesus in Hell at MacDonalds

Patti dreamed she was in Hell. Each time Patti heard a car pull up she thought it might be Mel's Jesus, or Paul Robeson's ghost, to invite her in out of the rain. She listened to the sounds of a passing car. It hissed at her, it parked. She didn't see anyone in it. Sadness took her, cold wind blew through her. She shivered.

It was dusk. She didn't have a life, just a bunch of beginnings stuck together never making sense, even when they did. Where's she going? What's she gonna do? Purple rain fell in black puddles on the beat-up asphalt streets ...making silver splashes in slow motion, glossy black puddles reflecting red brake lights of cars splashing them up ...beneath a charcoal, navy blue, and confederate grey sky, cut open with dry, yellow crumbling clouds, silhouetted behind marble-faced buildings. Smoke from erupting geysers of fire, punctuated the street.

Then, Patti was driving an old beamer the back way, behind the railroad tracks, behind Townsend, by the railroad station across the arguing cobblestone streets shaking the foundations of her car and her life like a metal meat tenderizing hammer, feeling each sullen tiny thud that added up to insanity. In the beginning of her romance with Alan, she sped through green lights, wanting to be with him right now, flooring the car through yellow lights by San Francisco Police headquarters on 7th and Bryant ...where the rent was not free, costing dreams, costing lives. She turned the first right up Langston Alley to Folsom

Street by Julie's Supper Club, past the Brainwash Laundromat, and parked.

She went inside. In one corner of the cafe performance poets performed their shit. In another corner, a saxophone player was riffing in a microphone. A bum drinking coffee at the counter jiggled, shook up off his stool, quivered across the floor, stood waving his finger, speaking in tongues.

Patti recoiled. "Don't even think about it. Go away."

Patti went outside. Everything had special meaning for her. The sheet of newspaper blowing in slow spread-eagled cartwheels down the road, a woman slowly pushing a baby carriage by her, magic wrapped around the baby, its eyes reflecting wonder, small deer horns protruding from the sides of its head.

At the other end of Langston Alley, a skeletal Black woman standing next to the dirt-turded park, pressed her palms against a car trunk, pulled thin Levis down, her thin brown butt silhouetted against yellow stucco walls of a sign shop, her shoulders and head disappearing beneath two parked cars, her brown butt flashed. She put her palms on the car trunk again, then fell over backwards, a shiny aluminum walker skirted out from behind her, clanking in the empty alley. Then, she disappeared into a stairwell. Homeless Black people, addicts, and white winos collected in swarms, waiting for volunteer workers to sing them Jesus songs through battery-operated hand-held megaphones ...then, serve soup, sandwiches, crackers, stale loaves of bread thrown away from day-old bakery outlets. The songs echoed down Langston Alley, twisting between cars, bouncing off the street, stretching down the walls. People collected in shadows ...some stood, some slept on park grass in cardboard refrigerator boxes, others slept beneath blankets hung over pairs of shopping carts.

Three forgotten Black men sat on a bench wearing old clothes, faces smeared unshaven with stubble, dark eyes bright, men lumped together in a shadow of life, forming one big shape from nothing.

Alan felt helpless.

Patti mumbled drunkenly. She sat on a bench. "I forget where I am."

Patti stumbled to her feet, stumbling forward pulled by her own weight into the bathroom to a crashing sound of the toilet seat dropping, came out, climbed back into bed, then lay still, caressing a pillow.

She'd been walking in her sleep, almost remembered the bar, earlier ...belting down shots of tequi-la. Orangee the orange cat looked at her, curiously. Rocky the black and white cat was weaving his way on top of the dresser through vitamin jars, knocking the jars down one at a time, wanting to be let outside.

Patti stumbled out of bed, opened the door. The two cats left the bedroom. Patti got into bed, beside Alan. She drifted into sleep, heard Spanish flamenco music, watched the interplay of shadows the candlelight made flickering on the plastered walls, felt cool air moving hairs on her forearm. A senorita approached, her hips swaying, light sparkling in her eyes, carrying two of those big bra margaritas in each hand, put them on the table.

There was nothing out there to hold onto, except margaritas, storm pipes, clusters of elbows, torsos and polyester pants, winos peeing in their sleep blocking doorways to cockroach-infested dives, pawn shops at the end of asphalt bathrooms reeking of stale piss, ammonia, spilled coffee and barfing transvestite hookers.

Patti went down to the boat club, she sat alone on the rear deck, watched the tide come in, washing over rocks, sinking in the sand and gravel beach till dawn came. Felt the sun rise warm on her face, listened to seagulls. She watched morning's passing sailboats, a huge freighter stacked with cargo containers, an Exxon tanker downloading crude oil to smaller tankers going up the narrow north bay into Carquinez Straits, oil refineries fouling the sky black with smoke.

She thought, someday maybe she'd be famous for surviving the years of the Reagan Administration, had no idea how her artist friends survived in her father's America.

Patti watched the water, boats, birds, ships, the tide come in then go out, the tattered American flag limping around the flag pole in a trying breeze. Hours passed.

She liked being dramatic. She crossed her hands back and forth like a baseball umpire waving out a man sliding into home plate, safe, staring at clouds.

Patti awoke from a troubled sleep. Alan was sleeping, snoring. Patti poked him in the ribs with her elbow. He turned over. Patti fell back asleep, dreaming.

Two Black men stood there in her dream, wearing white Egyptian cotton bathrobes.

Patti looked at them. "Christ, who are you? What are you doing in my dream?"

The first, answered, "I'm Mel's Jesus."

Then, the other. "I'm Paul Robeson's ghost."

Patti yawned. "I'm Patti of San Francisco and Hollywood."

Mel's Jesus smiled. "Paul, will you guide Patti through Hell?"

Paul Robeson's ghost nodded. "Okay ... that's Hell's back door through that gateway. You know, Hell. The one with bat wings that stretch out over the clouds ...with three different faces on his head, one in front and one where each ear should be ... herrrrre's Lucifer ... sitting on a frozen lake. The worst souls that lived in flesh ...are frozen in that lake, unable to move. Each one of Lucifer's three mouths are stuffed with sinners. In the frozen lake, in separate ice cubes others wait to be devoured, mouths frozen open in silent screams, faces twisted in broken flesh mirrors. Think of them, dead presidents, dead congressmen ...where did you think they'd be? Frauds, liars, bankers gnawing off each other's heads, tearing off each other's limbs in the burning lake, drinking molten sewage ...then, frozen into ice, thawed by a lightning and thunder rain of fire ...blinded, wandering molten across the plains. Go! ...already ...watch them rip out their guts, the Bakkers and Swaggarts, unbaptised and unholy, moved by constant stinging from wasps and ants. Go now."

In smoke and strobe lights, Mel's Jesus disappeared. Patti looked at Paul Robeson's ghost. "What do you make of that?"

The ghost hesitated, "We'll find out soon enough."

Patti frowned. She could hear Rolling Stones music playing on the other side. She looked surprised as her stomach growled. "I could use a McDonald's Happy Meal."

As soon as she said that, Hell's back door swung slowly open. Patti took the ghost's hand.

They walked through the flaming gold arches of Hell. There, sitting on top of the golden arches that went up for miles, Lucifer sat ...crunching two poor sinners around in his mouth, their heads poking out from Lucifer's lips, screaming.

Patti felt shocked. "It's the Presidents Bush, yelling at us! Can't you hear them?"

The ghost shivered. "Sure, they're pointing at the hamburger stand,"

"They sure are."

The Presidents Bush spoke in one voice, faintly, scarcely heard. "Get us a hamburger! Please!"

Patti didn't think so. "Not on your life! ...do you really think your behavior deserves a hamburger? I don't."

George Sr. did the talking for both Presidents Bush. "Please, listen to me ...you're not worth saving, either."

Lucifer start crunching on the Presidents Bush, again. They screamed. Lucifer spat the Presidents

Bush out of his mouth ...they fell hundreds of feet, smashing into the ice beside Patti and Paul Robeson's ghost.

Patti start kicking the Presidents Bush in their ribs. "How do you like it for a change?"

The Presidents Bush yelped. They pleaded. "We know you're right. But, we're so hungry. Please get us burgers."

She had them, now. "Apologize!"

The Presidents Bush frowned ...then, smelled fries in the air coming from the hamburger stand. "We're sorry. Hold the mayo."

Patti figured as much, "Yeah sure."

Mel's Jesus stepped from a block of molten ice. He looked at Patti. "Stop torturing them, Patti. Just get the burgers."

"Okay," Patti walked off slowly.

Mel's Jesus watched Patti and Paul Robeson's ghost get into a line beside steaming bursts of sulfurous black smoke shooting up in flaming geysers by the order window of the burger stand. The Presidents Bush squirmed on the ground like serpents.

Presidents Bush looked up at Mel's Jesus. "Is she getting the burgers?"

"Looks like it. Can't you wait?"

Presidents Bush sighed. "I don't know. Can you get us out of here? We'll pay you in General Motors bearer bonds, change your name, get you a passport."

Mel's Jesus wasn't impressed. "Sorry, not scalping tickets."

Patti's turn in line came up. She placed her order with a grotesque-looking demon. The hamburger stand turned into bile, then went up in flames. Satan's laughter exploded out his three mouths ...parts of people's souls he was chewing up came out.

Patti scowled up at Satan. She went back to Mel's Jesus and Presidents Bush.

Presidents Bush were starving. "Give us burgers, please!"

Patti shrugged. "Sorry, the burger stand disappeared, some kind of satanic joke."

Presidents Bush despaired, "It's not fair."

Satan reached down two great fingers, picked up the Presidents Bush, popped them back in his mouth, gnawing on them. Presidents Bush screamed, disappearing like spaghetti as Satan sucked them back into his mouth.

Patti had seen enough. "I want to get out of here, I want to go back to California. Let's cross the frozen lake."

She took Paul's ghostly hand, but the ghost disappeared. She turned to Mel's Jesus. Patti was scared. "Where'd he go?"

Mel's Jesus didn't know. "It was probably his time."

There was thunder as a whirlwind of fire encircled Patti. Satan's laughter echoed off the fiery canyons of Hell. Patti grabbed her ears to keep the sound from hurting.

Lucifer roared, "Not so fast! Ms. Patti. Do you know where you are?!"

Patti was shocked. Suddenly, the realization hit her. "I'm, I'm in Hell."

"That's right! Why do people go to Hell, Ms. Patti?"

"You mean?..."

"That's right."

Patti had to get out of this, fast. "I'm not bad, compared to most people."

"Aren't you having a little trouble with your boyfriend, lately?"

"Yes."

Lucifer was amused. "Do you know why you're here?"

"Because of him?"

Lucifer was losing patience. "No, stupid. You're the reason."

Patti was desperate. "No! This isn't happening, it's only a dream!"

"Ms. Patti, it always was. I command you, tell me, what were the worst things in your life?"

Patti was embarrassed. "Looking for a job, I guess ...a full moon when I had no one to love ...wanting to be held when no one was there to touch me."

Lucifer had won. "Here are the San Jose Mercury Sunday classifieds."

Patti backed away. "No! I hate Silicon Valley! They're robots!"

<>

Patti started looking through the classifieds.

"Here's one. For an editor. For a start-up company making typewriters you talk to, they type what you say ...then, automatically throw your manuscript away to save you the time of sending it to an agent. They like me in start-up companies, because I have a good figure. Here's another one, doing the newsletter for an engineering company that designs neural networks for parallel processors embedded in simultaneous computing peripherals for robotic expert systems in Starwars environments selling credit cards ...must have advanced degree in biophysics, law or equivalent ...type 45 words per minute ...good speller ...wear mini skirts. Gee, I wonder if my skirts are short enough to make up for no biophysics degree ... I used to play marbles. Here's one. Dog washer ...

send cover letter with salary expectation ...references ...graveyard shift only ...drug test required. Public affairs manager for biological warfare testing grounds ...ten years experience ...must speak classic Latin and Sanskrit and translate complex technical jargon into easy-to-understand layperson's terms ...must have driver's license ...own vehicle and insurance ...to apply write an essay, 'Why I want to live and work in India or China'. Part-time job in flower stand selling flowers, BA in horticulture preferred. Accountant ...I can't stand it! God! Please! I'm sorry! Get me out of here! God, I know I haven't talked to you for a while, ...but, I really mean it this time, please God, just do it, you won't be sorry, I promise," Patti said.

Paul Robeson's ghost reappeared ...he hurried over to Patti's side.

"Patti, snap out of it! Lucifer's gone. Let's get across this ice, back to California."

Patti came to her senses. Her double vision went away. "California? Yeah."

Their feet kept slipping as Patti and Paul Robeson's ghost start moving slowly across the ice. They held to each other for balance. Mel's Jesus was gone.

Patti looked down at the lake of ice. She realized the ice was frozen solid with grotesque souls, caught motionless, floating in upside-down and sideways positions, gasping, reaching their arms out for help.

Some souls stuck out of the ice like icebergs sticking out the ocean. Patti heard screams. She turned. Several ugly souls half frozen in ice were battling, two men, a woman. One man was frozen in ice just below his male member down, legs completely submerged, male member frozen sticking up towards the roof of the cavern ...twisting his torso wildly from side to side, trying to free himself ...but, kept twisting his skin and bones apart, screaming ...then, the wounds healed ...he'd start twisting free, then tear himself apart again. Every time he stopped to rest, he'd lean over at the waist and reach his mouth towards the body of a woman frozen on her back in the ice. Her legs were spread-eagled and bent so her knees were up and her mound of Venus protruded. Then, he'd eat giant gaping holes in the woman's legs while she sucked his _____, eating it as well, biting off pieces and swallowing them.

Strangely, while he did this, a second man, frozen on all fours like a dog or a sheep. on top of the ice, would crane over his head as far as it could go towards the twisting man's _____, catch it in his mouth and bob his head up and down for several minutes until both men screamed, then tried to bite the twisting man's ____ off, causing great pain.

While all this was going on, the woman was thrusting her fist deeply into the kneeling man's ____. Every quarter hour or so, the threesome would tear each other to shreds ...then, collapse in exhaustion ...only to begin their cycle over and over again.

Having described the phenomena to Paul Robeson's ghost, Patti dared venture over to the threesome ...only, after they were lying still in exhaustion, breathing heavily, gasping, starting to freeze solid again, gaining strength to tear themselves apart in the next firestorm.

Patti walked to the woman.

"Who are you? Why do you engage is such an unnatural act with this man, on all fours. Who's he?"

The woman spoke to Patti, "My name's Tammy Faye Bakker, and this here's my ever-loving husband, Jimmy. On Earth, we were evangelist preachers. But, in Hell, we're just ourselves. You shouldn't speak on others. Tell me, you've been on Earth recently, do you know if they still got my credit cards stopped?"

Patti shrugged. "I don't know."

Patti turned towards the man on all fours. "So, you're Jimmy Bakker. You created quite a stir evangelizing. Why do you crawl on all fours like a sheep, then lean over to that twisting man, reach your mouth for his ____, catch it in your mouth and bob your head up and down, and then scream, then try to bite his ____ off?"

Jimmy looked into Patti's eyes. He spoke sincerely. "On Earth, I preached great sermons and evangelized thousands of people. I brought them to Christ. But, this fellow here next to me, frozen half in the ice, was on a rival television network, doin' his evangelizing, that makes me madder than hell."

The other man was bitter. "Your ratings were higher than mine! I have sinned! I'm being punished!"

Tammy took advantage of the time to rest. "Shit, Honey, there ain't no cameras on down here ...Honey, you can turn it off."

"I can't turn off, til I'm forgiven!" Swaggart said.

Patti looked at the other man. "Who are you? ...you're so determined."

Swaggart answered. "On Earth, men called me Swaggart. But, women called me swine, huge, terrible, all kinds of dirty names. I paid them to do lewd and vile acts in front of me ...while, I fornicated. That's why my ____ in Hell is frozen stiffly upwards."

Suddenly it rained fire ...all of the threesome start thawing out, laughing vilely, groaning sensually, making obscene gestures, they started attacking each other again.

Jimmy Bakker stared at Patti. "On Earth, I had to share a prison cell with Lyndon LaRouche! Can you imagine, given my preferences and LaRouche's gay-baiting, can you imagine being locked in a room with LaRouche for years on end?"

Satan reached down, put a block of ice with Lyndon LaRouche frozen ____ in it by a flaming rock. Patti backed away, like she was among street winos who never washed or changed clothes.

Suddenly, there appeared around Patti a swarm of gigantic soap bubbles blown from a giant invisible soap bubble wand. As each bubble popped, splattering soap suds on the unholy threesome in Hell, they stopped their activities, turned their heads to see, listened to a different musical tone to each popping bubble.

Angelic and saintly figures, appearing to have a great religious authority, stepped out of each of the bubbles, with the freshness of stepping out of a morning shower.

<>

The next morning at 5 a.m., Patti was woken up by one of the cats jumping onto her stomach ...then, bounding across her chest, another cat sat on her legs. Patti sleepily moved the cat off her, heard the dog barking downstairs. "I still don't feel good."

Alan looked at her. "Why is it you feel fine with your friends when you're smoking and drinking, and feel sick when you're with me?"

Patti lost it. She was furious "I've had it with you! Who are you? ...the CIA? ...you hound me night and day!"

"You're over-acting."

Patti yelled. "You leave me alone! Gettin' it?!"

Patti's friend Janice let herself in the house, walked up the stairs, into the bedroom. She had short dark hair and big emerald green eyes, like a cat.

Janice seemed lost. "Where's Patti?"

Alan watched her. "Going home."

Janice pushed a finger on her nose, snorted. "Probably to do you-know-what!"

"She's just been out there, screaming I ruined her life."

Janice was a happy drunk. "Patti's such a drama queen. Too much ..." Janice pressed her nose again, made a snorting sound.

Alan was amused. "She parties with friends. When I want her, she pretends she's sick."

Janice laughed, without a care in the world. "Control freak, drama queen."

Alan let that one slide. "I love her, when she's not loaded."

"When's that?" Janice said.

"It takes a few days."

"I've never seen Patti straight."

"When she's loaded, the person I love disappears."

Janice went in living room, start dancing with Patti. The song changed, Patti came back in the bedroom. Patti looked at Alan. "Janice is drunk. While we were dancing, she was doing a strip, pushing her bazookas into me."

Alan could hear Janice in the background, slurring her s's, making them sh's.

"Don't take shit from him, Patti," Janice said.

Patti start yelling at Alan. "You're killing this relationship! You're smothering me!"

"Patti, control yourself. Stop yelling. Talk normally," Alan said.

Patti yelled, loud as she could. "You're smothering me!"

Alan turned away. He felt her sock him in the back. He turned around. He pushed her away. "Don't hit me!"

Patti let herself go. "That did it! I'm not going to sleep here tonight! I'm getting my things! Leave me alone!" Patti was such a drama queen.

He followed her out one bedroom, she ran in another ...then, slammed the door. He heard the double doors that separated the bedroom from the living room slam shut. The sound of her door slamming felt too familiar ...he'd heard that for weeks. He pushed his shoulder against the door, flung it open.

Patti backed to the bed, "Leave me alone! Don't hurt me! I'm getting out!"

Alan pushed her onto the bed. "You're not going anywhere! You're going to calm down, and talk this out!"

Patti yelled, "Leave me alone! All I had was one drink!"

"I know."

<>

Alan left San Francisco.

After a few days, Patti called, she missed him. Alan liked the trees in suburbia. It was so peaceful, secure. No homeless winos crapping on the sidewalks, no base-freaks jerking around tweaking in your face, saying, 'you okay? ...you okay?' ...dealer's code for, 'want a five or ten shot'.

Palo Alto was cursed with the timeless sterility of a college prep town, window dressing for Stanford University, manicured suburban lawns in denial of being a suburb, more trees per capita than any other California city ...featuring a walking, talking do-it-yourself wax museum of everyone in town.

There was never anyone on the streets, a ghost town set with main street animated like a cartoon of conspicuous consumption, University Avenue, populated with 20,000 Stanford students at $32,994 tuition a year each (covering about 60% of the total yearly cost to each undergraduate) ...and, senior citizen graying preppies that had never grown past puberty, living and dying in town, bent over, hobbling the streets when the moon was full.

Patti left San Francisco, too ...went home to Mom and Dad's, to stay in the little cottage behind their west coast ranch house, trying to heal from an abusive relationship with herself. Patti's first night home staying in the little cottage, Nancy invited her to dinner. Patti sat down to sliced steak, with corn and salad.

After dinner, Patti went outside to the cottage, lay on the bed, got drowsy, fell asleep... then, returned to dream Hell.

In the outer chambers of Hell, Patti stopped to read a sign cut into the rocks that read, 'Land of Addicts'. She turned, began walking, bumped into a shadowy shape with a woman's girlish figure ...big blue eyes ...long blond hair.

When the apparition saw Patti, it ran away, hid behind some rocks.

Patti felt vulnerable. "I'm sorry I scared you. I won't hurt you."

The apparition peeked out. "Are you it?"

"It? I'm not an 'it'."

"For hide and seek."

"I'm not it. Come out," Patti said.

Patti saw the apparition was attractive, once. Now, her cheeks were sunken, she was flesh on a skeleton.

"It looks like you don't eat," Patti said.

"Food?" the apparition said. The apparition raised some roasted flesh to her mouth, gorged on it, then threw up. "I'm anorexic."

"Why?"

"Oh. You *are* it, after all," the apparition said. Then, she jumped in a pool of fire, disappeared.

Patti continued on her way, past fat souls stuffing themselves. "Hello."

The fat people stopped eating, curiously watching Patti.

Fatty spoke up, "I'm fatty, and this is fatso."

Patti took a stop back. "Why are you overeating?"

Fatso almost belched. "It's easier than solving our real problems. Are you *it?*"

"No. *And, what if I was?*"

Fatty was condescending. "If you were it, then we'd have to hide."

"Do you think it's healthy?" Patti said.

"We died of overeating. You're new here, aren't you? No one talks issues, here. If you keep this up, you'll be *it* … take it from me, you don't want to be *it*," Fatty said.

The fat people grabbed their food. Fatso stabbed himself with his fork, his escaping gas propelled him into the air like a leaky balloon …then, he popped. "See what you've done! You'll be *it*! You'll see!" Fatty said.

Jiggling, Fatty waddled around a boulder, stooping once to pick up a sweet-roll he dropped.

Patti followed Fatty around the boulder. She saw a whole valley, as far as she could see, was full of dead souls squirming, running like wild kittens surprised in hiding, in confusion, every which way. Soon, the valley was empty, everyone hid behind boulders, stalagmites and stalactites. Patti walked into a bar and sat down. Everyone was drunk. She jumped up on the bar.

"I'm it! I'm it! What are you hiding from?!" Patti yelled.

The drunk nearest her threw up, "Well we're hiding from you, if you're it."

The drunken bar broke out laughing. Even the brunette in the tank top and mini-skirt who'd been crying into her daiquiri, got hysterical.

Patti felt the moment. "I feel empty, vulnerable, alone." As Patti talked, people turned into wisps of smoke …trailed off …disappeared til no one else was left. Patti climbed down off the bar, sat on a bar stool, poured herself a drink from a gin bottle left on the bar, added water from a pitcher from the bar fountain, squeezed in a few lemons, drop of bitters, pinch of vermouth, stirred it with a red plastic stir rod, sipped it. It was good.

The pretty brunette in the mini-skirt and tank top materialized, beside her. "Hi, want some company?"

Patti smiled. "Sure. Why are *you* here? …others went up in smoke."

The brunette smiled. "I'm not an alcoholic. This isn't my normal hang out. I've just been here a few hundred years, not forever. What are *you* doing here?"

"I'm trying to find my way, home," Patti said.

The brunette draped her arm over Patti's shoulders, pushed her breasts into her, put her hand on Patti's thigh, "They call me, home."

Patti smirked. "That's an argument …but, I really have to find my way back home."

"It can wait a day. You've got forever," the brunette said. The brunette put her hands around Patti's neck, start strangling Patti. "I've got you now, asshole!"

As she yelled, her clothes fell off, she vaporized into a yellow-eyed demon, then faded away into the air.

Patti blew some of the vapor out her mouth. Patti coughed, swiveled her bar stool around …start walking out the bar. The juke box started to play. Several stripper demons came out around Patti, started to dance.

Satan appeared beside Patti. "You've created your *own* hell, Patti," Satan said.

Patti shook her head. "It was *so* easy. I didn't know it would be this way."

"You're it, Ms. Patti. Might as well enjoy yourself," Satan said.

Patti looked over into a dark corner of the bar. "I'm not dead. I'm lost. I'm dreaming."

They were watching one of her father's movies.

Patti watched the silver screen. "Dad, what are you doing here?"

I talked to Patti out of the movie, "I'm not really here, it's just a movie … why are you here?"

Patti spoke up. "It's a dream."

I understood, I had Alzheimer's all the time. "Well, I'm in California …but, in this movie, I have to die."

Patti spoke objectively, "I've seen it before, Dad. It's a rerun. You die in this movie, every time I see it. But, the first time you died in it was a long time ago, before I was even born."

I walked away, out of my scene, off the stage, headed out the studio.

Patti watched me. "Where are you going? …we just started talking."

"I don't know where I'm going, where ever the next scene is, I guess," I stepped out of the movie screen, start walking to Patti in Hell, tripped, fell into a plume of fiery smoke shooting from a hole in the ground.

Patti ran over, grabbed me.

I pushed her away. "What in hell you acting so crazy for?!"

But, it was too late, both of us fell into the hole, fell down in flames, til we landed on a down-filled sofa in a shack, burning.

Patti was terrified. "Where are we?"

I was overcome with nostalgia. "This is the living room I grew up in …there's my mother …my older brother …my father's casket." I started to cry. "Wait! …that's me! …over there! …I was 5 years old!"

The little five-year-old me was being picked-on by his father …ran over, then jumped inside me to hide.

Patti was shocked. "Did you see that?"

"I felt it," I said.

Patti pressed her head against my stomach. "I can hear the little boy, inside you."

"So can I." The little boy inside me squirmed around, I was pregnant with myself, unborn.

The little boy yelled inside me. "I'm never coming out! Never! Never! I'm going to hide in here where it's safe …you can't find me," the little boy in me said.

Patti and me walked into another room in the shack. "Is that little boy still hiding in you?"

I was distracted. "Look! …there I am! four years old, playing with movie star pictures." My older brother walked in, stepped on the pictures, accidentally. I felt terrible, "You hurt them! *Ahhhhhh!* Mommy!" four-year-old me said.

Mom smiled at me. "We'll get you another one, Ronnie," Mom said.

<>

Suddenly, the carpet Patti and me stood on moved, taking us across the shack, out the door, onto the burning streets of Hell. Could be just Hollywood special effects.

"Look, there I am! …in church acting with my mother in church plays," I said. There I was, thirteen years old, dressed in a real, store-bought suit, acting on stage in front of church-goers.

Then, me and Patti were in a park, I pointed up at the burning clouds. "Look! The posters from the movies I made! They got caught in a thermal updraft, and flew up, out of the sight, into the sky. Over there, they made me an Eagle Scout. Over there, I'm getting married to your mother. There I am, standing guard duty in the army training camp. There, I'm making war propaganda musicals. Over there, I'm president of the Screen Actor's Guild … you were three years old, visited me there, remember? Look, they're I'm governor. Over there, I'm President! There, I've got Alzheimer's …I don't like this part of the movie."

<>

Suddenly, everything turned into smoke. Patti and I stood there, alone.

Patti looked at me. "Is there any more to see of your life, Dad?"

"That's all you'll ever know about me, I guess." Then I disappeared burnt up in some flames.

Patti was shook up. She sat down on a boulder, wiped tears from her eyes with the backs of her hands. Patti talked out loud, to herself.

"That's not much to know about your own Dad. I know more than that about strangers in twenty minutes. And that's all I know, about Dad, my whole life."

Patti got up from the boulder, looked at the ground where her father once stood.

"Dad, are you in there?"

"There's communists down here!" My voice trailed off.

Patti walked away.

Satan appeared, blocking her way, "Check yourself, bitch!"

Patti watched her life projected on the rocks around her. There she was, staying out late, closing down the Utah Bar on Bryant and 10th, coming home before closing … after stopping to get a pint of vodka and a bottle of cranberry juice to watch Carson and Letterman til two, Alan waiting for her in bed, then fell asleep.

Other times she'd come home drunk, slurring words. One minute Patti was mean, the next …nice, loving …the next, yelling and screaming.

Then it dawned on Patti, "I treat Alan the way Nancy treated me."

Satan stood aside. He let Patti walk out of Hell.

<>

Patti woke up from her dream, dressed, called Alan …made arrangements to meet him in San Francisco …then, drove to the airport. She'd be at San Francisco International in an hour. When she arrived, she rented a car then drove up to San Francisco. She walked into their flat.

Alan was waiting.

"Hi, I missed you."

"Me too. Look, I had a realization."

"What?"

"I treat you the way Nancy treated me, when I was growing up."

"Hmmm."

"I'm sorry."

"Look, are we together, or not?"

"It doesn't feel over. I don't want to end it."

They kissed.

Patti smiled. "We're together."

"Right."

Patti spoke in a normal tone, not yelling, not dramatic. She liked herself this way.

President Reagan meeting with 1981 Miss Universe Shawn
388 Weatherly and 1981 Miss USA Kim Seel Brede in the oval office.

SCREAMA

Alan and Patti sneaked back into the Hoover Library Tower guest room that looked out over the Stanford University plaza, and Hoover parade grounds. A weapons trade show was going on, below. Helicopters, tanks, missiles, and jets were on display. World Anti-Communist League members wearing WACL decals on their caps wandered around the grounds. Neo-Nazi skinheads, and SCREAMA in full dress uniforms, were posted as guards.

A Fed, Bank of England, Petroleum Community Conference was going on in the floor beneath their apartment. Patti looked through the hole in the floor.

Governor Schwarzenegger introduced several past U.S. presidents, Presidents Carter, Reagan, the Presidents Bush, Clinton ...then, Vice President Cheney Halliburton and the bin Laden patriarch.

Patti hated them. "They're the reason Granma Wilpf's dead! They killed grandma!"

Alan felt paranoid, "Shsss."

Vice President Halliburton stood up. "I'm inviting you all to visit me at my private cabin at the Bohemian Grove party this year. We'll be discussing new defense cartels before following our new Pearl Harbor provocation to turn world economic control over to our secret WTO tribunal."

Reinhard came in, escorted by SCREAMA ...dragging in Mel's Jesus and Grandma Wilpf.

Patti couldn't believe it. "Grandma Wilpf's alive! Reinhard lied!"

Dagmara struggled to her feet. Patti hurried around the apartment gathering hand grenades, automatic pistols, ammunition belts.

"It's time for pay-back!" Patti said.

Alan held a Kalashnikov automatic rifle, Patti held grenades.

<>

They burst into the WACL meeting. Reinhard pressed a Luger pistol against Dagmara's forehead. Vice President Halliburton and President bin Laden-Carlyle were whipping Mel's Jesus with barbed chains. Alan aimed his Kalashnikov at Reinhard. The SCREAMA pointed rifles at Alan and Patti.

Patti stared nervously outside, "Look outside the window."

Reinhard turned his head to see.

Hundreds of armed women and children, the politically correct citizens of Palo Alto, had surrounded Hoover Tower, carrying protest signs.

Patti stared at Reinhard, raised grenades above her head, "These are basement nukes! Even if you shoot me, you won't be able to get away before they blow. We have homemade nukes planted all over Stanford University campus, Hoover Tower, in Washington planted on visitors at the White House."

Vice President Halliburton went for his gun, accidentally shot President bin Laden-Carlyle in the foot. Schwarzenegger picked up a machete displayed on the wall. Reinhard pistol whipped Dagmara.

Patti screamed. "I'm ending it!"

Patti dropped the homemade nuke grenades onto the floor. At that moment, a WACL armored tank burst through the walls of the room. It shot flames, dropped percussion bombs, and played rap music. The tank rolled over the nuke hand grenades, crushing them to pieces. Percussion bombs went off. Everyone in the room was blown against the walls, fell to the floor in dreams.

Alan crawled to Patti, pulled her towards the hole in the wall the tanks came. Patti held Dagmara's hand. "I have loved, Granma."

"I have loved," Dagmara said.

Dagmara's fingers slipped out of Patti's hand.

Alan and Patti ran outside, into Hoover courtyard, mixed in the crowds of politically correct citizens, blended into anti-war protestors engulfing the arms trade show.

Reinhard struggled to his feet. He yelled after them, "She's not dead! Dagmara's not dead!"

President George W. Bush stuck his head out.

Tracie, holding a Kalashnikov, ran out from a group of kids into Hoover Tower, trying to find Dagmara.

Patti was confused. "Whether I pull the trigger, supply the guns, or teach people to kill, I can't believe I released those nuke grenades! I would've destroyed Palo Alto, all these people. I sinned against love."

Alan felt relieved they had escaped Reinhard. "So, what?"

Patti start crying, "I want to stop hurting."

Alan hugged her. "Take it easy, Patti. We're all murderers."

Patti shook her head slowly, "I became a SCREAMA."

Reinhard had run after them, he caught up. Reinhard looked at Patti. He pointed a pistol at them, "Proud? ...look around you, your revolution's wearing Levi's, eating caviar, drinking champagne, driving new cars, wearing mink, drinking Starbuck's and Red Bull."

Patti sobbed. She looked at Alan. "I feel worthless."

Reinhard looked at her. "All I wanted you to do

was renounce the revolution. See it for what it is. See, love is dead. Look at the damage you've done."

Patti felt confused. Alan tried to cheer her.

"We changed things," Alan said.

Patti was dizzy. "What changed? ... We did. My heart's dead ...what happened to the revolution?"

Alan laughed. "We won it."

Patti cried. "Won't anyone listen?"

<>

People passing by in crowds looked curiously at her. Patti walked through the courtyard gateway, into a line of refugees. Patti walked with them, away from the city. She looked back at the fallen city, overrun with SCREAMA. Then, she turned, walking with the refuge line. Her wounds hurt. It was hard to walk. She stumbled. A man dressed in a tuxedo stopped, to help her. She looked at him. It was Mel's Jesus. He helped her stand up. She thanked him.

She looked curiously at him. "Don't I know you?"

Mel's Jesus smiled. "You might."

Mel's Jesus took her arm, steadying Patti as she walked. Then, he let go and disappeared into the crowds of refugees walking. Patti sat down on the rubble of a crumbled building. She lay down on the ground to rest.

Dagmara walked up beside her.

Patti was shocked.

"Grandma Wilpf! It's really you. I'm so happy to see you!"

Patti's body lay dead on the ground. Dagmara helped her stand up. Dagmara helped her walk. They joined the lines of refugees led by Paul Robeson's ghost.

◇ ◇ ◇
Iran-Contra Hearings

Nancy was watching the Iran-Contra Congressional Hearings ...when Admiral Poindexter and Lieutenant Colonel North testified, Nancy cowered. Nancy saw they were trying to implicate me. That infuriated her. Nancy watched the congressional chairman pound his gavel. She jumped, the sound scared her.

The chairman addressed the hearing.

"We strongly suggest in the future, the President consult with Congress. We outlawed additional U.S. aid to the Contras. The fact, Mr. North circumvented Congress, is not to our liking. It's U.S. policy not to negotiate with terrorist states, Iran, Syria, Algeria, and Lebanon. Iran-Contra Congressional Investigation Committee commission finds Oliver North guilty ...however, we grant

him immunity, because he agreed to testify. We didn't call Vice President Bush, or CIA Director Bill Casey, to testify because we ran out of time. We allowed only three months for this investigation, because of upcoming elections. We started our investigation focusing on mid-1980s with the revelations, Israel was involved in arms-for-hostages negotiations with Iran, a terrorist state."

The spokesman smiled at Bill ...I felt indignant. Nancy watched Bill and George shake hands, each looked satisfied. Bill felt smug, amused.

George stared at Bill with awe in his eyes. "Bill, how'd you pull this off?"

Bill mumbled. "Extortion."

The spokesman continued.

"This Commission finds President Reagan probably didn't know the extent of his subordinate's arms-for-hostages negotiations. That's because of his management style of delegating responsibility, fully. We find, the President had no mal-intent. We find the President genuinely did what he felt was best for the hostages, for America ...and, for the American people. We find the President not guilty of any wrongdoing."

I felt relieved. I smiled into the cameras . I started to leave the hearing room. Nancy felt relieved, elated. She started to leave with me. On my way out, I ran into Bill. I didn't like his cavalier, devil-may-care attitude.

I spoke out. "I was feeling disappointed in myself. But, Congress exonerated me to the American people ...I see you with the devil-may-care look on your face, it stirs-up my Irish blood. It makes me mad as hell! Don't get me into something like this, again!"

Bill kept an eye out for trouble. "Mr. President, your Secret Service bodyguards are too far behind you, it's best you slow yourself down a bit, wait for them, you never know."

I sensed the threatening tone in Bill's voice. It frightened me, like he was sneering at me. I pushed through the crowd towards Nancy, we met and embraced. I felt good, when I saw Nancy beaming with happiness.

"I still don't know, should I go on TV, tell the American people my side of the story ...or, should I stay off TV ... play it safe."

Nancy smiled. "Whatever you think's best, Darling. Just tell the truth, like you always do, it'll be okay."

CENSORED

White House press briefing room

A few days later, in the White house in a private room adjoining the press briefing room, me and Mike Deaver were chatting … soon, I was going to meet the press with a live, televised statement. I watched through the one-way mirror, Secret Service used to monitor the press briefing room.

The room was packed with reporters. Mike was feeling the weight of being in charge of my public approval ratings. As usual, Mike was there beside me each time I appeared in front of TV cameras.

Mike felt responsible for my public image. "Ronnie, I'm not sure you making a public appeal is the right thing. Will it raise your public opinion rating? …or lower it? You refused to rehearse in front of our focus groups …that leaves me out in the cold …I can't guarantee this, one way or another. But, I respect your decision to go on the air, to tell the truth."

I felt positive, "Mike, I've nothing to hide. I did what was right. I'm going to tell the truth."

"Heaven help you, here's to you." Mike took a nip.

I walked into the press briefing room, standing in front of the TV cameras, smiling.

"I've come before the American people to tell the truth from my heart. As you know, both the Iran-Contra committee and the investigation group I commissioned found me innocent of wrong-doing … yet, it appears there was done without my knowledge, by Oliver North acting on behalf of National Security Agency, some arms-for-hostages bargaining …that, was partially successful. I didn't know anything about this, while it was going on. But, this is my Administration, the buck stops here. It's been the policy of the White House, my Administration, my policy, American policy …and, policy of the American people … not to negotiate with terrorists. But, some of this did go on. I want to say, in my heart, I didn't mean to trade guns-for-hostages. I didn't mean it, in my heart. I hope you understand. I hope you forgive me, I didn't do anything wrong."

I finished my statement. The camera technicians and reporters clapped …then, the microphones were turned off. I saw Mike open another bottle of vodka, refill his flask, take a nip.

Mike greeted me, smiling.

"A couple more seconds, the poll will be in. Here it is. You're public approval rating is up ten points! You did it, Ronnie! You did it! I learn something from you, once in a while. When right and wrong comes down to a public apology, then everything's okay. I wouldn't have believed it …unless, I'd seen it, myself."

I felt exonerated, forgiven, I felt like a winner. "Ten points! That's great! I'm vindicated! I've been forgiven by the American people! For something I didn't even do!"

Mike felt relieved. "According to the polls, people didn't care if you did or didn't …just that, you did it in Khomeini's Iran."

I frowned. "I wish there was some way to get rid of Khomeini, he's a real pain in the ass."

White House bedroom

The days went by, one party after the next. I flipped calendar pages on my desk calendar, seasons changed, from summer to fall. One night in our White House bedroom, Nancy watched me fall in and out of sleep. Nancy was thinking fast. She whispered to me.

"Ronnie, wake up! Shsss! Don't say anything, the room's bugged. Sleepy, wake up! We're going for a ride, to have a private talk."

"Can it wait til tomorrow?"

"No."

I protested, "We've got speeches tomorrow."

Nancy was determined. "That's good …they'll think we went to bed. We'll sneak out. You'll hide on the floor of the car."

Dressed in robes, we headed out our bedroom, down the stairs, into the kitchen …but, had to get past a Secret Service guard

Nancy approached him. "A midnight snack, you know how it is."

The guard smiled.

Nancy could see he was hiding cookies behind his back. We walked past the guard, into the kitchen …then, sneaked out the back door. I watched Nancy's derriere as she walked ahead of me. Outside, we ran behind the trees til we got to the garage, entered a side door, got into our car.

Nancy smiled. "You know the drill."

I got down on the floor of the car and hid, Nancy drove out the garage onto the streets of Washington D.C.

Washington D.C. streets

Nancy drove us through the streets of Washington D.C., knowing we could talk in private in our car. I looked out, we drove along.

Nancy was apprehensive. "Jupiter, the head god is conjuncting Mars, god of war. Maureen's seen the ghost in the White House Lincoln Room again. She hasn't figured out what it's trying to tell her. Why hasn't it gone over to the other side?

Joan Quigley says, it's dangerous."

"Outside the White House ...or, inside it?"

Nancy was puzzled, "Huh?"

"Nuclear war with Russia? ...or, infighting between my staff and cabinet?" As we spoke, I relived some scenes from a war movie I starred in. The car heater was on, I dozed off, dreaming.

Nancy touched my arm, "Ronnie! Wake up!"

I felt sleepy, "Where am I?"

"You're here, Ronnie."

I smiled. "I guess I dozed-off a few seconds, I'm okay. I was dreaming, fighting to save American lives. Trying to figure out, what's going on? Who's calling the shots?"

Nancy was animated. "I asked Joan to ask the stars. When she does our charts next week, she'll schedule our White House meetings to coincide with good celestial and planetary vibrations. The last time I was in her flat in San Francisco, we had a séance around a crystal ball."

Nancy remembered the séance, well ...Joan's house was full of crystal balls, amethyst crystals, peacock feathers, chakra magic wands, eerie posters of magical, supernatural, biblical, and angelic scenes. Nancy sat with Joan Quigley at a card table. There was a crystal ball in the middle of the table.

In the dimly lit San Francisco flat, Joan Quigley looked inquisitively at Nancy ...then, stared into the crystal ball between them. "The stars impel, they don't compel. I see danger. I cast your charts, made your schedules for the Russian and German summit meetings, and the G-7."

Nancy was thrilled ...now, she felt safe again. "Good. Is it safe for Ronnie to go? I'm so worried, all this Russian, 'Evil Empire', stuff he's been saying to the cameras ...if I was Russian, I'd be pissed off, I'd want to get even."

Joan nodded. "Ronnie should cut out that 'Evil Empire' crap, it stirs up shit," Joan said.

Nancy drove our car through the Washington D.C. streets ...til she couldn't hold back any longer, and had to tell me.

"Joan says the planets say you have to knock off the evil empire bit, it's like watching old reruns, bad for the box office, gets you more bad reviews than good ones."

I wasn't pleased. "Those are some of my best lines. I've got to please the far-right, Nancy, Weyrich's Free Congress Foundation and the 'Full-Court Press' people destabilizing the Soviet Union and Eastern Europe are okay with the 'evil empire' bit ...they're my inspiration for it. But, Republican National Heritage Committee

Nixon set up because he owed Dulles, kicks in a lot of campaign money ...gets out the ethnic vote for us ...but, those people are a bunch of lousy Nazi's and fascists, killers, sociopaths. They scare me."

Nancy cringed. "Ronnie, aren't those Republican National Heritage Committee people the leaders of death squads Bill Casey's using to destabilize Soviet Union and Eastern Europe?"

I shrugged. "Yes, they're real Nazis and Fascists, just like in movies I starred in."

I went into a daze ...I start reliving my times on the set I killed Nazis, shooting them ...fighting hand-to-hand combat ...remembering, the Hollywood crew kept backing the camera away from the action.

Nancy glanced at me, saw the strange look on my face, probably wondered about how my mental condition was.

<>

On the other side of town, Bill was asleep ...dreaming about his visits to Allen Dulles at Fort Hood in 1945, in lavish officer's quarters ...just before the close of World War II. Bill watched Allen Dulles give several Nazi SS officers U.S. Generals' uniforms to put on.

Nazis changed uniforms. Allen Dulles shook their hands. What happened next in Bill's dream was, the phone start ringing. Bill felt confused, he was in the same room with Dulles watching him, but, at the same time, Dulles was on the other end of the phone line, too!

Dulles answered the phone. "Yes, Bill, everything's fine, you're worse than J. Edgar Hoover, don't worry."

Bill was upset as he spoke into the phone. "I've got as many central bankers up my ass as you do, I'm lending against my portfolios, too ...is it a done deal? ...have you hired Hitler's intelligence people to start the CIA? ...have you started them activating the Christian West Plan to overthrow our Russian allies? ...are they going to train an American death squad? ...I see ...it'll be called, Special Forces, or, Green Berets? ...they're going to fight alongside Otto Skorzeny's Nazi Werewolf death squads, underground ...in Russia and Eastern Europe ...now? ....that World War II is scheduled to end?"

"Yes! ...your limited prospectus investment portfolio is safe, good bye!"

Bill tossed and turned, mumbling something in his sleep.

<>

Nancy wanted to stop the car to look at my

mental state, I was so involved with what I said.

I was angry. "Dulles and Casey and Eisenhower never, never should have brought Nazis and Fascist financiers and generals and spies into the U.S. I don't care, how much the German and British and American central banks are in bed together ...I don't care, how much the Nazis and Fascists financed the Republican Party before, during and after World War II ...I don't care how much campaign kickbacks they give now!"

Nancy saw how excited I was getting, how troubled I was, didn't know if she should humor me, calm me down, or talk sense to me ...but, she stayed calm. Nancy looked at me. "But, Ronnie ...*we* were a part of that, then ...in the '50s you were the main public speaker advocating CIA's Crusade For Freedom ...you take responsibility for that."

"Of course I do! ...but, in the '50s ... it was different. When I helped them, I was a confused man in mid-life crisis, in male menopause. I had stars and stripes in my eyes. Hell, do you think I can live with myself, now? ...do you think I like the Nazis and Fascists that fill my campaign fund now?! I can't stand them! Even Bush can't stand them ...and his father helped set it up!"

Nancy knew she had to do something quickly, to get control over the situation before it got out of hand. "Calm down, Ronnie. It does no good to complain. We made our bed ...we have to lie in it ...grab hold of yourself, calm down!"

I felt Nancy was concerned, but I was stubborn. "All right. All right. Am I getting carried away, again? It's just my pet peeve, Honey. By the way, Billy Graham stopped by the White House the other day, told me Daniel was put in the lion's den because you're not supposed to believe astrologers are more powerful than God."

Nancy was relieved, I'd changed subjects, She didn't feel alarmed, now that I was calm. Now, she felt frustrated. "Ronnie, this is the real world. Get a life."

I didn't understand what Nancy meant ...but, I knew she had my best interests at heart ...so, I shrugged off her feeling confused. From my expression, Nancy saw... I was debating an internal dialog ...trying to settle things.

Nancy smiled. "Joan's a good astrologer ...she was right about the assassination attempt on your life ...she's been right about scheduling all your summits ever since ...we're keeping her! ...no matter what Billy Graham says. What are Carter's Naval Intelligence people telling you is going on in your White House?"

I perked up. "They're wrong, Bush and Casey aren't setting me up as a patsy ...I don't know what's going on behind the scenes. And, I'm the president! ...an actor walking around on stage saying this and that, it means nothing ...who's telling the people who tell me what to do? What's going on? Who's calling the shots? Don't ask me, I just work here."

Nancy wasn't satisfied. "My spies said, it was North, Halper, Cline, and Casey,"

I was surprised. "You have your own personal spy staff?"

"Yes, just like George Bush does, with his inter-agency task forces. I want answers. I want you to be safe. We're in this pretty deep, aren't we?"

I was amused. "If it gets any deeper, we'll come out in China. George Shultz will take care of it, he's a good man."

Nancy wanted to know enough to take care of it, herself. "I know, I figured it out. Casey's using Bush ...Bush's using Ollie ...Ollie is using McFarland and Deaver ... Deaver's using you. That means, Deaver's lying to me! He'll be sorry! Everyone set you up as Mr. Plausible Denial!"

I knew all that. "I like being Mr. Plausible Denial, Nancy, it's a good part for me to play, I think I do it well, it worked for Iran-Contra, I'm in the clear, I like that."

Nancy wasn't sure, "How long has this been going on?"

I broke it to her slowly, "From the beginning."

Nancy felt hurt, "Why didn't you tell me?"

"Two reasons, Darling. I wanted to protect you, and, I wanted to give you ..."

Nancy interrupted me. "...Plausible denial. Thank you, Darling, that was very considerate. I've got a few questions. What does Casey get out of it? What does Bush get out of it? What does North get out of it? My astrologer can't help us, unless I know enough to ask her the right questions. She's the one who got me in touch with my spiritual higher power, that's how I found out what I know. Gorbachev's assistant uses an astrologer, too. Hitler did. The Pharaohs did. All world leaders do ...it's natural."

I was surprised. "So, you followed our astrologer's suggestion ...and, hired personal spies?"

Nancy was vindictive. "My spiritual higher power told me, do it. I'm so afraid ...there's so many people out there I need to fire, to protect you. Deaver says, I have 'firing fever' again ...he's right. Who made money from this Iran-Contra arms-for-drugs-for-hostages smuggling ring?"

I knew that, 'get-even', tone in Nancy's voice.

Still, there was that little voice inside me, "I don't know …it makes me question my basic values …I wonder if the drugs were there to finance the Contras, or, the Contras were there to protect the drug lords …if it had nothing to do with anti-Communism at all, just a shadow government of big business drug-runners."

Nancy sighed, "Don't worry, Joan will fix us up with her Vedic astrology charts, they're better than European or American charts, by far." Nancy looked for a place to park. She pulled the car over, to look in my eyes, "You still angry about Iran-Contra?"

I smiled. I loved Nancy already knew what I felt. "Yes. I gave Casey hell, today. I'm not angry at you. You always know what I'm feeling, I love you."

"I love you too, Darling …what's really bothering you? What are you most angry about, Honey."

Nancy watched a worried look come over my face. I bit my lip, for a moment thinking about what I was going to say. "I'm angry because, I'm worried … my whole White House staff, and my Cabinet's, corrupt …how'd it ever get to be this way? …was it always this way, and I never saw it? I'm supposed to be saving America, not making her sick. Am I losing my ability to judge character, losing my ability to lead America. Maybe I'm getting old, my thinking's getting fuzzy, I forget things, I get things mixed up."

Nancy wrinkled her brow.

I kept talking softly. "Were the drugs there to finance the Contras, or the Contras there to protect the drug lords, which came first, the chicken, or the egg? Deaver's being investigated by a grand jury for lobbying for Contras, back-channeling foreign aid back into campaign fund chests for bribes. George Bush's son got Contras on Medicaid in Florida. Casey's got me bankrupting the country …so, his central banks can loan us more money …he's buying up national debt bonds faster than his German and Japanese central bank buddies. All the interest from the national debt goes to them! It's like that Errol Flynn movie, with the spies, almost my whole staff and cabinet is corrupt, except George Shultz and Lucky Roosevelt. What am I gonna do?"

Nancy sighed and relaxed, we were talking with each other intimately, again. Washington D.C. could destroy honesty and intimacy in personal relationships. "It'll be fine, Darling. You'll take care of it, you always do."

I felt funny, my humor faded, I got serious. "Why am I so talented in picking out crooks to work in government? It'd be different if I knew they were crooks …then, at least I could take credit for

it. How's it gonna reflect on my judgment? What will the American people think of me?"

"Our approval rating's gonna suck."

"How can I get people to approve of me?"

Nancy was warming up. "I made a new list of people to ax, in the meantime … if we want to stay alive and prevent more assassination attempts, we better 'go along to get along."

I felt desperate.

Nancy looked into my eyes. "If we want to stay alive, we better do the best acting we've ever done."

<>

We sat in silence for a while.

I broke the silence. "You're right, Darling. I'll go ask Casey for help, and if he's being blackmailed. That'd help explain all the confusion and intrigue around here. I've got to know, what kind of a guy is he? But, my mind, I feel it starting to go, Nancy. I'm so afraid."

Nancy doubted what she had to say. "You're doing fine, Darling. Don't worry, everything'll be okay."

"Maybe it's not senility, or Alzheimer's, maybe I'm being poisoned to death like President Roosevelt was."

Nancy laughed. "Stop kidding around, that's just a White House old wives' tale."

"No, I looked it up. His son said he was poisoned by two Byelorussians painting his portrait while they had tea, he collapsed, his son said they were spies, double agents working for German intelligence."

Nancy kind of believed me. "Well, the Russian spies are always really working for German military intelligence, the German spies are always working for Russian military intelligence, Israel's spies are always working for British intelligence and British intelligence is working for American intelligence. American intelligence is always infighting and competing like brothers and sisters for political funding and financial portfolio growth points for one client or another, the CIA's out to destroy Naval intelligence because it's patriotic, rogue ex-CIA agents are working against mainstream CIA agents, big business is against little business."

I held my head, shaking it, trying to clear my thinking. "Nancy, please stop, I'm not up to this kind of talk. I can't feel anything for anyone anymore except you, nothing and nobody else matters to me … I don't want to be old, I want to be a young man again, swimming in the river, watching the clouds, I wish I never went into politics, I wish I'd never been an FBI spy, I wish I could undo my life, undo all the mistakes I made and live life all over again. I'd do things right this time. I want to forget it all, Nancy, except loving you."

Nancy felt tears in her eyes. "That's really sweet, Darling... Ronnie! Some car's followed us!"

I got scared by the frightened tone in Nancy's voice. "Is it one of ours?"

"How would I know?"

I knew I had to protect Nancy. "I hope it's not a god-damn terrorist. Let's go back, Nancy."

"I'm trying to," Nancy started the car engine, put the car into gear, sped off down the street.

"Try to shake them!"

"I'm trying to."

We drove quickly through the streets. The car behind us started to fall back. I felt better, "There's the White House! If we can just make it there!"

White House, Aug. 21, 1983

At the White House, Lucky was waiting for Corazon Aquino to arrive on a visit, watching Deaver's advance men rudely walk around. Lucky had to correct one of them, "The campaign trail that qualified you as a Deaver munchkin, isn't a course in diplomacy. You're thrown off by your shadow, project your shadow to fall across others, feel attacked by someone else's shadow when it's really you, attacking yourself ...then, all hell breaks loose. Remember, Amir the King of Hell on Lotus Mountain bowed down with his shadow legions to Buddha."

Deaver's advance man didn't have time for this. "I don't know what you're talking about. Get out of my way, Lucky ...here comes our photo-op. Mrs. Aquino! Will Mr. Aquino be coming?"

Lucky and President Corazon Aquino of the Philippines, eyes wide, stared unbelievingly.

"No, my husband will not be here, he was assassinated last year."

"Oh, sorry. Can you turn a little more to the right for this shot?"

Lucky took Cory Aquino aside, into a Ladies room. "Oh, Cory, I'm so sorry. I'm so humiliated by Deaver's advance men!"

Economic Summit in hotel, Williamsburg, VA

Arriving in Williamsburg, a day before the Economic Summit, Lucky checked into her hotel room, disturbed when she tried to use her special phone to the White House. The line was dead. Lucky called a White House communications aide to her room, holding up the dead phone for him to see it.

He nodded. "It's dead, one of the White House staff told me, cut off your phone."

Lucky was startled. "What?"

"Sorry, ma'am, White House staffers don't give reasons."

Lucky hated the munchkins.

Restaurant in Williamsburg

Lucky's boss, State Secretary George Shultz, invited her out to dinner, they were seated.

Lucky didn't know where to begin.

"I'm so angry with Deaver's White House staff, I'm keeping it in. I don't want them to force me out the way they did Haig. I'm an innocent, my mentors were men like my husband Archie, a CIA career man. He regards serving David Rockefeller as a privilege, calls serving his country an act of higher calling, that serving one's country is something one chooses to do rather than to make money, noblesse oblige. I never saw much of the breed who get presidents elected, the advance men, the media manipulators, the dozens of men and women who make the campaign successful then stand in line with their hands out ...expecting to be rewarded in a spoils system of political appointments."

Secretary Shultz thought Lucky was a sharp cookie, honest, forthright, smart, sincere, trustworthy ...and very attractive. He was glad Lucky worked for him.

Shultz tried to put her at ease.

"In this administration, advance types and media photo-op people ended up being White House Staff. To them, they form the trappings of a court ...but, this is their first encounter with real power. For many of them, it's their stepping-stone to big money in the private sector. They think, conducting foreign relations is like being on the campaign trail. With mindsets like that, you get heroes ...or, bums. This White House Staff divides and reproduces itself like cancer."

Lucky felt good her boss saw it that way. She was disgusted with Deaver's munchkins. "They're little shits, mental mice."

President Reagan talking with Cary Grant and Douglas Fairbanks 395 Jr. at a White House private dinner party in the yellow oval room.

Shultz chuckled. "Inelegant ...but, descriptive. Mike Deaver deals from strength ...but, he's overwhelmed, his staff smothers him ... he's the eternal advance man, nothing escapes his attention, he's the President's shadow. The President's surrounded by shadows. Deaver's a movie director, sets the scene, spins the scenario, gets his actors in place, for him its, 'lights, camera, action'."

Lucky wondered, if George Shultz knew about psychological shadows, the dark side of man ...personal fears deep inside unknowingly projected onto others who then become targets so you're shooting at the things you don't like or fear in yourself ...if that's what he was talking about.

She had a few things to say about Mike Deaver. "Mike Deaver's devoted to Mrs. Reagan, and the President. He winds them up, sets them like an alarm clock. No one else can deal with Mrs. Reagan's whims and desires, make her hidden agendas into dynamos, milestone them out, track them, make them happen ...and, all the time, keep her hand from showing."

Shultz chuckled again. "Deaver could be Reagan's closest friend, his dearest adviser ...but, he's your designated liaison with the White House ...you're stuck with him. Deaver wields a lot of power, most of the time he influences the President in a positive way, he's pretty well-counseled, for a Staffer."

"I'll never forget the day I came to Mike's office after he persuaded Reagan to call Israeli Prime Minister Menachim Begin to demand the Israelis stop bombing Lebanon, almost all my family lives there, I'll always be grateful to Mike for that."

"Everyone's human. Lucky, if you let them get your goat, they'll win. If you go public, trying to protect yourself ...they'll do to you, what they did to Al Haig ... turn everything around like it's your fault, say you're petty, worried about perks."

"Should I be direct with Mike? I'm afraid if I am, he'll stab me in the back."

"It's your call."

Lucky looked at Shultz, curiously.

Shultz smiled at her, looked at his watch.

Lucky smiled back warmly and sincerely.

Jefferson Room, State luncheon, White House

Lucky coordinated a State luncheon, with Secretary Shultz hosting the President of Portugal. She'd seated herself beside the Portuguese Chief of Protocol, a smooth-talker.

One of Lucky's aides hurried over to her , whispered in Lucky's ear. "You like the way I put the luncheon together? ...eight round tables of ten each, vermeil vases, slim as candlesticks, flowers above the sight line so the Secretary can eyeball everyone."

Lucky cringed, "It's beautiful and too late to change, you know Secretary Shultz doesn't like vases of flowers on his tables."

The aide shrugged, walked away.

Lucky and the Portuguese protocol chief made small talk. Lucky heard someone hit a spoon against a glass, calling for everyone's attention. That surprised Lucky, no one was scheduled to speak.

Secretary Shultz stood up to propose a toast. "Ladies and gentlemen, I hope you've had a chance to admire the beautiful flower arrangements in the center of each table. However, these luncheons are designed for conversation and eye contact, which the flowers impede. Therefore, I ask the waiters to remove the centerpieces, so we can get on with the luncheon."

Lucky was floored, in a long and awkward silence, embarrassed ...everyone knew, it was her job to do things right ...now, they were wrong.

Lucky noticed, the Portuguese protocol officer had an amused expression. He tapped her on the hand.

Lucky didn't want to talk to anyone right now, she wanted to be invisible. "I want to disappear."

The Portuguese protocol officer pointed to the menu card George Shultz had designed as mementos to be taken home by his guests. Lucky saw the Portuguese protocol officer was pointing at the word, 'Schultz'.

"I didn't know the Secretary spelled Shultz s...c...h, I thought it was s...h... I think that's another 'no-no', an unpardonable sin."

Lucky sighed. She put her head in her hands.

White House formal dinner dance

That evening, was a formal dinner dance at the White House. Lucky read the name cards at the table ...she rolled her eyes, she was seated right next to her boss, Secretary Shultz. Seeing Shultz enter the room, she sat down before he got there. She tried to prolong a lack of contact between them. Then, he said, 'hello'. She had to answer.

"Mr. Secretary, why don't you fire me now, get it over with, so we can enjoy the party." Lucky watched the twinkle in George Shultz's eyes, heard him chuckle, had the feeling he'd already forgiven her.

Secretary Shultz looked into Lucky's eyes. "I got your attention, didn't I?"

Lucky rolled her eyes.

George Shultz asked her to dance.

Next day, Lucky coordinated a luncheon for Mr. Eanes, a guest of Defense Secretary Caspar Weinberger. Weinberger waved Lucky over to his table.

"Recognize those flowers? They're from yesterday, the ones your boss had taken off his tables. I had my Pentagon people negotiate with Shultz's State Department people for the vases and flowers Shultz didn't want. Like 'em?"

She smiled, "Yes."

Lucky felt bothered, bewildered. She looked at the flower arrangements on the luncheon tables, how beautiful they were.

President's trip to Beijing, China

Lucky looked out the window at the ground below, as Air Force One circled the Beijing Airport runway. The plane landed, slowed to a stop. Lucky felt irritated, Mike Deaver made everyone wait in the plane ...except his advance team. She watched them go down the gangplank, to set up photo-ops. Lucky felt more upset, when Deaver ordered Cabinet officers and Ambassadors, exit the plane using the rear steps of Air Force One.

No one was allowed to leave the plane ...until, Nancy, and me, disembarked. Lucky knew, Deaver wanted to get photos of me being first, to show to the American people on TV. Lucky and the Ambassadors followed Cabinet members off the plane. They walked along on the tarmac.

Lucky saw one of Deaver's advance men. He was yelling at Secretary Shultz, who was walking in front of the delegation, with Chinese officials, "Mr. Secretary, move away from the President, we need a clean photo!"

Lucky got more upset, clenched her fists, stormed over to Deaver. "That's it! I promise, I'm not going on any more trips overseas with the President, if your munchkins run them!"

<>

When we got back in Washington, the husband of one of Nancy's best friends was partying at a sadomasochism party. He picked up a submissive woman. He hired her, had her sign a slave contract in return for him signing a series of checks. He beat her, whipped her ...then, he died of unrelated causes. His sex slave sued his estate. The newspapers loved it. Nancy's friend confided in her. Nancy stood by her friend through thick and thin. Her friend told the press, Nancy is a loyal friend, a beautiful person. Nancy was glad to read something positive about herself in the newspapers. I walked in on Nancy, and her girlfriend, who was crying.

Nancy held her hand. "Ronnie, her husband's dead."

"I'm so sorry," I said.

Nancy's girlfriend spoke up. "He had an S&M mistress! She's suing me for millions!"

I gave Nancy a look, I didn't get it ...that, Nancy took to mean, 'What can I do?'

Nancy looked at me. "There's allegedly a group sex video circulating, talk of blackmail ...but, the little slut who slept with him, her roommate beat her to death with a hammer."

I didn't know what to make of this. "... A smoking hammer?"

"Can you get Bill Casey involved?"

"Sounds like, he already was."

Nancy knew I was talking about the hammer murder ... the implication of Casey having been involved shocked her.

It shouldn't have.

1984 Normandy

Deaver came up with a photo-op for me, that sent shivers down my spine. He knew, I'd be meeting with G-7 business leaders in Europe, near the anniversary of D-Day. That was when Allied soldiers landed in France to liberate Europe, to end World War II. Deaver decided to stage the photo-op of my lifetime, when I made my 1984 visit to the Normandy battlefield. Deaver set my speechwriters to work. They found a letter sent by the daughter of a soldier describing her father's hope of someday returning to the battlefield to respect his fallen comrades.

The great day finally arrived.

I stood on rolling grassy hills, covered with thousands of white crosses in rows, from horizon to horizon, from sea to sky. I stood, surrounded by old veterans who'd actually fought against Nazis, there, on the Normandy Coast, in 1944.

Deaver arranged for the woman who had written the letter about her father to be there. I moved closer to my toe-marks. I felt more secure, once I'd found them ...I knew cameras would be getting the best viewing angles on my profile.

I saluted the graves.

I spoke to my audience.

"I've come here to salute the sacrifice of those who helped destroy Hitler and the Third Reich, liberate France, liberate Europe, to end World War II.

"Here, on the Normandy cliffs overlooking the Atlantic Ocean, forty years ago Private Peter Zanatta, whose daughter is standing beside me, landed on this beachhead. Peter Zanatta was an ordinary American citizen. He fought here, watched his friends die fighting the enemy. He did what he had to do, he kept on going. His daughter wrote him a letter. I want to read part of it to you today. 'Dear Dad, I'll never forget what you went through, Dad, nor will I let anyone else forget. And Dad, I'll always be proud.' That's what this patriotic woman wrote to her father. I'm telling everyone here today, and everyone at home watching this on TV, that yes, we're proud. We'll always remember. We will always be proud. We will always be prepared, so we'll always be free."

I started to cry. I brushed a tear off my cheek. Nancy started to cry. Deaver did too. There was not a dry eye in the audience at Normandy. Reporters swarmed around me for an impromptu press conference.

Alan was there too, on assignment, "Mr. President, your speech was beautiful. It moved me. Would you describe your Administration's Arms Control Policies?"

I was partially deaf as I grew older. I turned my head to hear more clearly. Unexpected questions often confused me. I stood there with a blank look on my face. Nancy went into action.

Nancy whispered to me.

"Tell them we're doing all we can."

I smiled at Nancy. I answered the reporter's question. "We're doing all we can."

<>

Every day, White House Historian Bill Barnes recorded his observations of the Reagan years in his diary.

The President has put the Government on a credit-card buying binge. He talks about balancing the budget ...but, the interest on the national debt costs taxpayers 200 billion dollars a year. The Fed says, there's not enough money left to borrow ...so the Government borrows foreign capital, from Germany and Japan. Foreign central-bank lenders own 20% of the national debt. United States economic security depends more and more on Japanese, British, German, Dutch, South African, and Saudi investment consortiums ... willing to buy the public and private debts of the U.S. In the Reagan Administration, the U.S. has gone from being the world's biggest creditor nation, to the world's biggest debtor nation ... we used to lend the most money in the world ...now, we borrow the most money in the world. Instead of interest payments on the debt flowing into private American hands, the payments flow out of America to foreign investors. Foreign investors get the tax money taken out of the paychecks of Americans. Then, they use that money to buy American real estate, American fac-

tories, and American stock. Profit and decision-making power flows out of America into foreign hands ...just like, we're a colony. Our President made America back into a colony, he re-colonized America.

"With Ronnie in the White House, there's a redistribution of income ... reversing New Deal-type programs. New Deal-type programs create jobs, steer money to the public. Under Ronnie's Administration, money flows from less-well-off people to rich people. National wealth flows to central banks, ruling families in Germany and Japan, the very Nazi and Fascist banks, cartels and ruling families that financed Hitler, and Mussolini, to wage World War II. With Ronnie in the White House, the nature of poverty is changing. Women and children are most likely to be poor. Children living in poverty is rising, to one-in-five, a 24% growth under Ronnie. Ronnie's feminizing poverty, focusing it on women. He cut spending for Women-Infants-Children programs.

"Ronnie made a statement, 'America fought a war on poverty for nearly twenty years before he took office, poverty won.'

"Single mothers, young children, and people-of-color are poor. They have little education, less job skills. Teenage pregnancy rates are surging. With increasing incarceration of young Black males from ghettos, stable family structures are rare. Millions of jobs are being lost in manufacturing, more and more U.S. companies find cheap labor in Mexico, Indonesia, and India, move factory operations, there. A pair of Adidas costs 4 dollars to make in Indonesia. It sells for 100 dollars in the U.S. In terms of real hourly wages, American production workers fell 6% in terms of what their earnings buy in the marketplace. Men with high school diplomas ...but, no college, lost 20% of their purchasing power.

"A permanent homeless population underclass now lives in streets, in parks, bus stations, begging for money, food. Homeless include women and children fleeing abusive husbands, unskilled people, sociopaths ...and, chronically mentally ill people whose institutions were closed when Ronnie cut Federal and State funding. He start cutting State funds to social institutions, mental health hospitals and asylums when he was Governor in California.

"Ronnie's the father of homelessness in America. Ronnie says, the homeless are either nuts ...or, they enjoy their lifestyle. He has no interest in Federal funding of mental health programs. Ronnie's a 'conservative'. He blames poverty on poor people, feels Government financial help makes things worse for poor people by taking away their incentive to work ...but, he gives Federal money to corporations.

"Individual large military-industrial corporations get as much as half-billion-dollar bonuses to offset their costs ...in addition to what the Government pays them for products and services.

"Ronnie's Administration feels giving poor people money, hurts them ...and, giving rich people money, helps them. Average family incomes of the lowest 20% of Americans, measured in constant dollars, dropped from $5,400-dollars to $4,100-dollars a year. Income of the richest 20% of Americans jumped, from $62,000-dollars to $69,000-dollars a year. The top 20% of American society experiences a 14% increase, while the middle 60% is house poor, tiredly treading water. The top 40% of American society gets 67% of national income. The bottom 40% gets 15% of national income. Under Ronnie, the share of national income going to the wealthiest 1% of Americans doubled from 8.1 to 15%.

"When Ronnie was elected, 4,400 individuals filed income tax returns on adjusted gross incomes of over 1 million dollars. Now, over 35,000 taxpayers file 1-million-dollar returns. Net worth of the 400 richest Americans tripled. Before Ronnie, a common corporate CEO made 40 times the income of an average factory worker. Under Ronnie, CEO's make 93 times.

"About 1,300 major law firm partners make higher pay than industry's 800 top executives. Ronnie campaigned on balancing the budget, on eliminating the national debt. Now, he's busy running up annual deficits, from 128 billion to 200 billion dollars each year. Ronnie's tripling the national debt, from 900 billion dollars to 2.7 trillion dollars. Wouldn't I like to have made that loan? ...wouldn't I like to begetting interest on that debt? Don Regan, head of Treasury Department, has to borrow $5,000 for each American ...then, sends them the bill. Ronnie's leading America into an Age of Greed ...conspicuous consumption ...immediate financial gratification ...an age of no morality ...an age with no ethics ...a Godless era."

Jackson curled up on a pillow on the couch, watching Bill Barnes, purring.

White House

My Presidential tour of Europe, featuring the Normandy photo-op, ended. Everyone was back at the White House. Deaver immediately start using camera footage of my Normandy photo-op in TV commercials. The TV commercials were designed to get me re-elected as President, in 1984, for a second term of four more years.

Deaver rehearsed me for the TV spots.

"Remember, we want to keep Mom and apple pie flying the whole time. Get them to feel redemption, patriotism, and family," Deaver said.

I read my note card, "We see an America where every day is Independence Day, the 4th of July."

Deaver smiled. "Good. Then, I'm cutting in a montage from footage of you at Normandy. That good piece, you wiping a tear out of your eye. I'm glad I told you to cry, when you hugged old geezers who fought there. I want to re-record what you said. The wind was blowing, fuzzied your words. It's the next note card. Let's do it. Take 1."

I read my next note card. "You're the best damned kids in the world."

Deaver felt things were going his way.

"Great. Only one take. Now, I cut in footage of you standing at the border between North and South Korea, you stare grimly into Communist territory. Then, I cut-you-in at the Olympics hugging an American gold medal winner. We overdub it with a voice, that says, 'America's coming back!' Then, we get the Marlboro man. He brushes dust off his cowboy costume, starts rolling up his sleeves, he says, 'We rolled up our sleeves, showed, working together there's nothing Americans can't do.' That's America."

Treasury Secretary Don Regan watched the rehearsals, for the first time, with Larry Speakes. Don was surprised, "You mean, every moment of every public appearance is scheduled? Every word scripted? Every place where Reagan's supposed to stand, taped with toe marks?"

Larry was amused. "Ronnie's been learning lines, making his face pretend he's feeling one way or another, hitting toe marks for half a century ... that's what qualified him to be President."

I overheard the first part of their conversation. "You know, what makes me happiest? Each morning, I get a piece of paper that tells me what I do all day long. My job, is acting a script. Characters come and go, the plot goes forward. A lot of people don't know if I'm a President playing an actor ...or, an actor playing a President. For me it's the same."

Deaver walked over to Don Regan. "It's true. I'm his stage manager, producer, director. I hire stage and sound crews. If they mess up, the scene doesn't work. We shoot more takes, til our focus groups laugh or cry, feel patriotic, or angry ...whatever, we want the public to feel ...then it's a wrap."

I smiled. "In show business, drama is when you suspend disbelief in the audience. You get them to believe, in the illusion. You get them to make-believe. If an actor believes what he's saying, the audience does. Remember that. It might help you out, some day."

Don Regan felt awkward. "Mr. President, James Baker and I decided to switch jobs. He's gonna to be, Treasury Secretary ...I'm gonna be your new Chief of Staff."

Ronnie felt confused. "I didn't know this. That true, Mike?"

"News to me."

"We're gonna wait til you're re-elected. We want your okay," Don Regan said.

"Okay. As long as Mike keeps giving me that piece of paper every day, that tells me what to do. Are we done shooting, today? ...Mike."

Larry turned to Don Regan. "You don't get along with Nancy, do you? You're gonna have to figure out, how to stay out of her way. Get on her wrong side, she's death on wheels."

Don Regan smiled, "So am I."

Mike looked at his clipboard. "Ronnie there're a couple more election photo-ops coming. In your last speech, you said corporations shouldn't be taxed, at all. I knew that'd need damage-control. The opinion polls agree. Tomorrow, I'm flying you to a working-class bar in Boston. I want you to drink beer with bar-flies. Make it look like a scene from, *Cheers*."

"Okay, you're the boss," I said.

Ed Meese had something bothering him.

"Your damn Education Secretary, Terrell Bell, got tired of us pressuring him to cut education budgets to schools, telling him, have teachers preach more discipline and morality. He put out some stupid, 'liberal' report to the press demanding we reform education. I'm gonna have our Conservative backers throwing gasoline on me and flicking their Bics."

Mike knew what Ed was talking about. "That's the, 'Nation At Risk', report. It demands more Federal funding of schools. It says, 'If an unfriendly foreign power attempted to impose on America the mediocre educational performance that exists today, we might have viewed it as an act of war."

Ed was pissed. "Well, how you gonna fix it?!"

"Give me a second," Mike said.

I cracked a joke. "Maybe we can get Nancy to fire him."

Ed took the idea seriously. "That's a good idea. After, we're re-elected."

Mike had a brainstorm. "This is what we do. We get a re-election campaign photo-op with Ronnie standing with Bell. Ronnie endorses the report. Ronnie makes a bunch of, 'excellence in education', speeches. We'll have a teacher-of-the year ceremony in the White House. I've been talking to NASA already. They're gonna give us a, 'Teacher In Space' program. *That's* damage-control."

Ed smiled. "Then, after we're re-elected, we fire Bell, get a 'conservative' in there."

I was trying to get a laugh. "It's a take." I came down, no one laughed.

Deaver was enlightened. "That photo-op, where I had you pose at Handicapped Olympics. Leslie Stahl of CBS picked it up ...but, said you pushed Congress into cutting Federal support for handicapped."

"Shit!" Ed said.

Deaver frowned. "Stahl showed footage of Handicapped Olympics with Ronnie standing there, smiling ...surrounded by kids in wheelchairs and balloons and flags. I called Stahl. I thanked him for the five minute pro-Reagan spot. I told him, 'Haven't you people figured out yet, the picture overrides what you say?'"

Don Regan was surprised. He was learning how the White House Staff operated.

Deaver smiled. "Ronnie ...in these re-election spots, we're gonna limit and focus the public mind to you talking about a few issues. Cutting taxes. Being against abortion. Promoting Strategic Defense Initiative Starwars. You can see, how taxes hurt. You can see, how SDI can aim a laser beam to shoot down a missile. You can see, the fetus in the womb kicking away from the needle. That's what you want your audience to feel."

"Okay," I said.

"We're gonna show you ...happy in a bunch of White House official ceremonies with other statesmen ...waving from helicopters ...reviewing parades ...reviewing troops ...enjoying yourself, having the time of your life."

"That'll be easy ...because, I am," I said.

<>

In the 1984 presidential election, I was re-elected in a landslide over Carter's Vice President,

Walter Mondale, winning 49 of 50 states, nearly 60 percent of the popular vote. My chances of winning weren't harmed when, during the week of the Democratic National Convention, I played to the audience with one of my favorite jokes.

"My fellow Americans, I'm pleased to tell you today, I've signed legislation to outlaw Russia, forever. We begin bombing in five minutes."

<>

I used that line for sound checks for my radio addresses. I spoke the lines when there was lots of tension between the U.S. and Russia. I guess, a lot of people have no sense of humor ...because, it left some people questioning my understanding of the realities of my foreign policy and international affairs. But, it was part of my scripted lines on the note cards, designed to show Russia ... we didn't take them seriously.

In 1984, the title year of British intelligencer Aldous Huxley's book, *1984*, describing British society run by Big Brother, I honored Whitaker Chambers posthumously with a Medal Of Freedom award as a champion of democracy.

<>

It wasn't till I retired, Nancy read me books all the time, that popped another of my bubbles.

Whitaker Chambers, at Columbia University, made himself a name as a literary writer. Chambers later held jobs at, *The Daily Worker* and, *The New Masses*. He supported himself doing freelance translations. Some of his associates thought Whitaker Chambers was a Nazi spy. Edwin Sievers, another literary figure, met Chambers, had dinner with Chambers at Chamber's house in Newark, New Jersey. Sievers walked in Chambers apartment. On the wall he saw a life-sized portrait of Adolf Hitler.

A letter, Ms. Dorothy Sterling wrote to the *New York Times* was published in 1984. Ms. Dorothy Sterling was a *Time* employee from 1936 to 1949, assistant bureau chief in *Life Magazine* news bureau, from 1944 to 1949. She'd worked with Whitaker Chambers, when he was foreign news editor, at *Time*. In her letter published in *New York Times*, Mar. 11, 1984 ... she denounced Whitaker Chambers for distorting news and inventing war-related stories to fit his right-wing viewpoint. The letter was called, *Whitaker Chambers, odd choice for Medal of Freedom*.

"To the editor ... Many of my former colleagues at *Time* will share my feeling of consternation at the news that the Medal of Freedom is to be awarded to Whitaker Chambers posthumously. We still remember his reign as *Time's* foreign news editor, which began in the hopeful summer of 1944, when Allied armies were marching across Europe. *Time's* foreign corresponds, men like Charles Wortenbaker, John Hersey, Richard Laterbach, Storan Probitivich, and Percy Knauth, reported the emergence of popular governments backed by partisans who'd been fighting Hitler. The readers of *Time* never saw these dispatches. Whitaker Chambers suppressed them, rewrote them, distorted them, tailoring the news to make it conform to his own right-wing view of world affairs.

"From Paris, Charles Wortenbaker protested *Time's* story of 'Red Riots', which had been substituted for his cable describing France's orderly new local governments. Probitivich's reports from Yugoslavia, telling of the slaughter of partisans by Drosimer Hylovich, never saw print. So many of John Hersey's stories from Moscow were suppressed, he stopped sending political news and confided cables to accounts of Shostokovitch's newest symphony and other cultural events.

"Reporting from China, Theodore H. White saw his criticisms of Chang Kai Chek's autocratic regime replaced with warm, glowing praise of Chang as a defender of democratic principles. When researchers in *Time's* New York office protested the inaccuracy of the foreign news reports, Chambers habitually replied, 'Truth doesn't matter' ...facts were altered to fit his anti-communist crusade. Eventually the correspondents' protests resulted in an investigation, Chambers was made an editor of special projects, a position he held until 1948, when he named Alger Hiss as a communist. Whatever views one may hold about the Hiss case, there is no doubt, Whitaker Chambers perjured himself during a grand jury investigation, and changed his testimony repeatedly. During the first trial, when Lloyd Paul Striker said to him, 'Lying comes easy to you', Chambers replied, 'I believe so'."

Waldolf Astoria, 1984

The Beijing China trip seemed to have happened ages ago. I had a speech to give at New York's Waldorf Astoria Hotel. Nancy felt paranoid, occasionally looked back over her shoulder, wanting to make sure we weren't being recorded. Feeling the coast was clear, she smiled at me. I smiled back.

I was dismayed. "God, I wish I could trust my judgment, every time I appoint someone they embarrass me. Is it me, Nancy? ...is my mind going?"

Nancy noticed, she was answering that question from me more often these days.

She didn't like it, "No! That's foolish! It's not you, Darling. You can't be responsible for everyone, you can't be responsible for the whole country."

"You really think so?"

Nancy was upset. "If we get out of this job alive, that's enough for me. We can't beat Satan and his underworld any better than God can. I love you, Darling. Break a leg."

I appreciated that, we kissed.

I went onstage to deliver my speech.

"When a man or a country questions one's own ability to be a leader in the world, or in his own neighborhood, or in his own house, he measures himself by Bible virtues of hard work, honesty, and spunk. John Mariotta provided jobs and training for hard-core unemployed in the South Bronx. This businessman's faith in God moves mountains. He helps hundreds of people who'd almost given up hope. People like Mariotta are heroes for the '80s."

I watched a spotlight scan the crowd, it stopped on my friend, John Mariotta. I felt happy.

John Mariotta addressed the crowd. "The success of Wedtech, my defense contracting company, comes through a joint venture with our silent partner, God ...and the Ronald Reagans of our society."

Nancy noticed Ed Meese was jovial.

Ed felt all-powerful, greedy for more of whatever he could get, meeting with me later that evening back at the White House he noticed I seemed fidgety.

"What's up, Ron," Ed said.

"I have to confront you about these 'rumors' of criminal activities."

Ed laughed, then wheezed. "Really? Why? You always trusted me before."

"I put your name in to be head of the Justice Department ...then, they made you head of the Justice Department ... because I trust you. This is for your own good, as well as mine. Did you file false tax returns?"

Ed Meese shrugged.

I didn't let him answer. "Did you illegally retain stock in companies doing business with Justice Department? Get illegal payoffs from parties for government favors?"

Ed shrugged again. "C'mon Ronnie, lighten up. I'm head of the Justice Department of the United States. Nofziger's our military-industrial lobbyist, Mariotta's president of Wedtech. We're all partners in Wedtech! Isn't that a hoot?!"

He laughed.

I was confused ...then, I laughed too. "You sly old dog, that's a good one, I hope you don't get busted ...and, don't do time. Gonna get away with it?"

"Mr. President, we got 200 million dollars in orders from the Army and Navy."

"That's really great, Ed."

"We sold 75 million dollars worth of bonds to build up Wedtech! Sittin' in clover!"

I felt happy for Ed.

Ed looked squarely at me.

"Now we're declaring bankruptcy, it's a dream come true. There's one born every day!"

I felt my happiness for Ed fade. "I don't want to hear any more about it, Ed."

"Lighten-up, Ronnie. I'm in charge of law and order for the whole U.S.!"

I felt pushed to the edge. "Ed, the only reason you got confirmed by the Senate to head Justice Department was because I recommended you ...and, I have a high public approval rating. But, this foolin' around, what you're doing, makes me look bad, reflects on my Administration, don't you see?"

"No way, don't *you* understand? I'm head of Justice, I can find where the bodies are buried, no Congressman's gonna mess with me!"

Ed laughed.

I didn't. "I want to be a hero, not a bum. You're Justice Department head, you're my friend. That makes a double moral and ethical responsibility on your part, to watch out for me. You've seen my old 'Westerns', you've seen the Indians use a branch in the dust to sweep over their tracks so no one can follow them. Clean up your act, Ed ...or, cover your tracks."

<>

Early on in my second administration, Assistant Chief of Staff Michael Deaver talked about leaving the White House. Deaver was overeager to cash in with lobbyists on his contacts with White House Staff, with Cabinet, with me, and Nancy. Deaver put together a plan to open his own public relations firm. Nancy heard rumors. There was going to be an investigation of Deaver's influence-peddling. Lynn Nofziger left his White House job. Nofzinger went into the lobbying business.

Months later, I watched a Senate Hearing pronounce a verdict on Meese, Mariotta, and Nofzinger, of Wedtech. Meese, Mariotta, and Nofzinger stood before the Senate Hearing Committee.

The Committee spokesman addressed them,

"Mr.'s Meese, Mariotta, and Nofzinger of Wedtech all pleaded guilty to fraud ...we're convicting Mr. Nofzinger ...we're not indicting Mr. Meese, head of the United States Justice Department."

Ed had a 'holier-than-thou' grin on his face.

I smiled when I saw Ed like that.

A few days later, me and Ed talked privately in the Situation Room.

Ed turned to me. "I told you, I can find out where the bodies are buried. Congress won't mess with me. I hate to tell you, Ronnie, but I told you, so."

I wasn't happy, "Knock it off, Ed. I don't like it."

Ed laughed. "My aides in Justice are like you, they had morals, they quit on me. Who needs 'em? Nofzinger's already successfully appealed his conviction. We both got off, scot-free. I guess I'm the oldest person in the 'me' generation. I'm laughing, all the way to the bank."

What could I say? "Say hello to Bill Casey, and George Bush, when you get there."

On our way out of the room, a reporter intercepting us, just as Bill Casey walked up, asked Ed and Bill, what was their experience of working with me.

Ed answered first. "My experience of working with Ronald Reagan. He's always fair and loyal to me, bless his soul."

Bill spoke up. "My experience working with Ronald Reagan. Of course, everybody sees it differently ...because, we have different priorities. I'm restricted by National Security policies and my Top Secret Clearance ... from sharing with you, some of the details. But, there's a lot I can say."

Nancy walked up, led me back towards the Situation Room. I smiled at her.

I tried to make her laugh. "Nancy, I bet Coors is the first American beer into the Soviet Union and Eastern Europe, you can bet the Bechtel team will be busy there like they are in Libya, Saudi Arabia, and Communist China. They'll all be eating McDonalds' hamburgers and drinking Coors beer. But, what's in it for me? Why are they making me make all these appointments? I just do what I'm told, my 'kitchen cabinet' can't be beat, I'm in front of the camera all the time, we have all the public approval we need, that spells 'relief'."

Nancy smiled a little. I felt better.

Her smile faded. "Ronnie, I'm miserable because my girlfriend's husband died and left her all this sick sex stuff in the newspapers, her husband was fooling around with that S&M mistress ...he was into 'blue' movies, kinky sex ... that spells, 'drugs'."

Nancy saw, I was tense. I didn't like talking about this stuff.

"Nancy, I don't want to hear about it. I have to go onstage this afternoon, tell me later. This appearance I have to make, is like being emcee at Academy Awards."

Later that afternoon, I walked up to the podium to deliver my speech to United States Chamber of Commerce luncheon guests.

"I'm pleased to be here, this afternoon, as emcee at the United States Chamber of Commerce Luncheon ...to introduce some of my Cabinet members that I appointed. They came highly recommended to me. I trust them to be always on their best behavior, they'll be bringing 'regulatory relief' to the American people. First, financed by Adolf Coors, who also backed Paul Weyrich and Free Congress Foundation ...and, representing the conservatives who helped put me into office and keep me here, is James Watt, the new Interior Secretary.

Alan was reporting, he questioned James Watt.

"Mr. Watt, how will you fulfill your pledge to manage and preserve public lands?" Alan said.

Watt answered automatically. "We've got to deregulate Department Of The Interior, I'm a reborn Christian. I'm religiously opposed to government-mandated efforts to protect the natural environment. Get the timber harvest in, before Armageddon. The Bible says, 'conquer and occupy the land until Jesus returns' ...so, we'll mine more, cut more timber, drill more oil. Two kinds of people live in America ...Liberals, and Americans. As a white man, I'd be hesitant to allow a Black doctor to operate on me ...because I'd always have the feeling, he may have been carried by the quota system," Watt said. Watt listened as the audience applauded loudly.

I grimaced, turned to Nancy.

"Oh no," I said. I wished the applause was for me.

Nancy was thinking, 'Poor Ronnie'.

The reporter stepped up to Watt. "I understand you've been pressured into naming a public advisory panel to oversee a coal-leasing venture," Alan said.

Watt smiled confidently. "I think the President would be pleased, I've selected a balanced group, we have every mix you can have ... a Black, a woman, two Jews, and a cripple."

<>

Nancy saw me wince and slap my palm against my forehead. The audience grumbled.

Watt kept talking. "I've canceled a Beach Boys

White House, July 4th concert, the Beach Boys project a bad image. They shouldn't be allowed to perform on public property. Instead, I've selected Wayne Newton, a Las Vegas lounge act."

The audience applauded.

I frowned. So did Nancy.

Nancy was alarmed. "Ronnie, I like the Beach Boys. They're my favorite American group, after Frank Sinatra."

The spotlight swirled across the audience then settled on me. I gestured to the audience, quiet down. "I'd like to introduce another one of my appointees, Anne Burford. She's an ally of Mr. Watt. I nominated her to head Environmental Protection Agency."

Anne Burford addressed the audience.

"We must deregulate Environmental Protection Agency. I too, like Mr. Watt, am ideologically opposed to protecting the environment. I'm appointing Ed Meese's protégé, Rita Lavelle, to oversee the 'Superfund' program Congress created, to clean up the nation's worst hazardous waste sites. Rita Lavelle and I agree, EPA rules unfairly restrict the chemical industry, we've put too great a priority on preserving a pristine environment. That alienates the business community. Those days are over."

<>

Before too long, I found myself sitting in on another Senate Hearing, listening to the sound of the Senate Hearing chairman's gavel as he kept pounding it up and down on his desk. I watched the EPA's Anne Burford and Rita Lavelle. They stood before the Congressional Investigating Committee.

The Senate chairman announced the Hearing's verdicts. "Our Congressional Investigation has determined that Anne Burford and Rita Lavelle of Environmental Protection Agency, violated the public trust by disregarding the public health, and the environment, and manipulating the Superfund toxic clean-up program for political gain by illegally distributing clean-up money. They engaged in unethical conduct. In addition, two dozen top EPA appointees are being removed from office, or are resigning-under-pressure, for favoring the industries they were supposed to oversee. I understand, Ms. Anne Burford has resigned. Because Ms. Rita Lavelle lied to us, we're sentencing her to prison."

<>

At another luncheon, I had the opportunity to introduce my appointee to head the Federal Communications Commission, Mark Fowler.

Fowler addressed his audience, who came to meet him. "I want to deregulate the Federal Communications Commission. As far as I'm concerned, TV's another appliance, like a toaster with pictures."

Time passed. I found myself sitting-in on another Senate Hearing, listening to the sound of the Senate Hearing chairman pound his wooden gavel down on his desk ...then, pronounce another set of verdicts.

The Chairman spoke to the gallery.

"Our Congressional Investigation has determined that the President's appointment to head the Department of Housing and Urban Development, HUD, has been involved with influence peddling, favoritism, abuse, greed, fraud, embezzlement, and theft."

At another luncheon, I had the opportunity to introduce my appointee to supervise the deregulation of the Savings & Loan industry, Ed Gray.

Ed Gray addressed the group assembled to meet him.

"We've needed to deregulate the Savings & Loan industry a long time. I'm not good at telling jokes. The Reagan Administration's so ideologically blinded, it can't understand the different between lowering airfares and removing all controls from the Savings & Loan industry. You'll be sorry, the S&Ls are going to be eaten alive!"

I didn't know how to react. I heard the audience applauding, everything was probably going well.

Neil Bush, one of George Bush's sons, was enthusiastic. Nancy watched Ed Gray storm off.

She looked at me. "What's eating him?"

I had no idea.

"I don't know. People are saying everyone I appoint is a crook, maybe he isn't."

"I've got to fire everyone who is a crook, they make you guilty, by association!" Nancy said.

"But Nancy, if you fire everyone in my administration who's a crook ...there won't be anyone left."

"This is no time to kid around," Nancy said.

Nancy was startled when she saw a look on my face that meant, 'Who's kidding around?'

I looked Nancy in the eyes.

"I think there's getting to be a finer line of ethics in my Administration than I can get along with. And, all this Iran-Contra business. Sometimes, I

CENSORED

think it's just a Casey red herring to cover up him arming the Muhajidin to control the Afghanistan opium poppy trade, then reinvest the profits into some kind of corporate leveraged buy-out to make their stock soar ...so, VC connected to the Fed can issue an IPO, make a killing ...then, use the money to do a hostile take-over ...found, invest in, grow, buy and sell their own subsidiaries among themselves ...then, start the cycle over again.

The only reason Casey's arming the Muhajidin with Stinger missiles through Monzer Al-Kassar is to get kickbacks into his anti-Communist campaign fund and private bank accounts. That's why he's anti-Communist. That's why he wants Weyrich's and Coors' Full-Court Press to destabilize Soviet Union and Eastern Europe, so him and his central banks can finance another world war, just like him and Dulles and the Bushes did in World War I and World War II."

Nancy looked at me like I was nuts. Nancy got that feeling again, concerned I was confused, losing it ...otherwise, why would I be exercising lack of judgment, talking like this ...in public. So, she needed to change the subject, before I attracted attention.

"Ronnie, there's something bothering me," Nancy said.

"What is it, Darling?"

"I adore the Beach Boys."

I looked curiously at Nancy, "Watt failed the keep-your-mouth-shut test. I'm personally hurt, Watt didn't try to bite his tongue. I've decided to ask for Watt's resignation. From now on, I'm going to make all bad news disappear the easy way ...by ignoring it."

Nancy laughed. "But Ronnie, the Beach Boys?"

"All right, we'll over-ride Watt, we'll dump Wayne Newton, we reinstate the Beach Boys for the White House 4th of July Concert."

Nancy was pleased.

"Thanks, Darling, you've made me happy." Nancy hugged me. I kissed her. Nancy felt pampered. Nancy started to cry.

I didn't understand.

"Nancy, I thought you were happy."

"Oh Ronnie, I didn't know how to tell you. Rock Hudson has aids. He's dying."

I was shocked.

"Rock Hudson? That's terrible. It's awful. It never felt like Aids was real, until now."

"Maybe you should make Aids a Federal funding priority, before any other of our friends die," Nancy said.

"I'll have Surgeon General Koop do a report."

Surgeon General Koop's report was published. Koop called on Americans to change their personal behavior. Koop described the Administration's remedy to Aids, as 'one, abstinence ...two, monogamy ...three, condoms'.

Conservatives Jerry Falwell, Phyllis Schlafly, and the new Education Secretary, William Bennett, condemned Surgeon General Koop. They felt he was encouraging immorality by mentioning the word 'condoms'.

Koop pleaded with me, take the lead nationally, tell Americans more about the disease, how to prevent it. I didn't want to get my public image personally involved with Aids and the Aids public health crisis. In my next speech, I said, scientists are still learning about how AIDS is transmitted, the public shouldn't be afraid to donate blood.

Deaver told me, never to mention sex ...or, condoms. Then, I endorsed the Right-To-Life movement. I said, I support the idea of having a constitutional amendment making abortion illegal.

That night, after his speech J. Peter Grace, who chaired the Grace Commission to recommend budget cuts in government programs, introduced me at the podium of a banquet of anti-abortion fundamentalists.

J. Peter Grace spoke, first.

"It takes a man, like Reagan, to point out the simple truth, all living people started life as feces. Yes, even you started out as feces. Now, dinner is served."

The audience was shocked. Alan was sitting with other reporters, he clapped wildly. Alan laughed till he cried.

"Right on!" Alan yelled.

<>

Peter Grace was another subject in the books and magazines Nancy read to me in retirement.

The financial editor of *New York Post*, Maxwell Newton, always said good things about J. Peter Grace. "J. Peter Grace is a fanatic advocate of free enterprise. J. Peter has a formidable economics group within his company structure that produces a torrent of damning evidence of the destruction being caused in this country by big Government."

Kevin Coogan noticed, J. Peter Grace's influence on the Reagan Administration kept rising. "President Reagan appointed J. Peter Grace to lead a council of businessmen, The Grace Commission, to come up with ways to cut Government costs. Peter Grace commuted twice a week to Washington D.C. Peter was in charge of W.R. Grace & Co. In addition to running W.R. Grace, Peter was a board director on Kennecott

Copper, Radio Liberty, Radio Free Europe, American Institute for Free Labor Development, and Citicorp Bank. Three Citicorp's directors sat on the board of W.R. Grace, such as Roger Millican of South Carolina.

"W.R. Grace Senior Exec Frances D. Flanigan had an office in Washington D.C., and sat on the Ad Hoc Committee on Chile ...that the IT&T interlocking board directors organized to milestone the CIA-backed military coup d'état to overthrow the democratic-socialist government of Salvador Allende's Chile.

Kevin Coogan researched J. Peter Grace.

"As a director of Kennecott Copper, and a director of Radio Liberty, Radio Free Europe, and AIFLD, Peter was at the center of CIA propaganda and operations in Poland and El Salvador.

"Charles Allen, one of the most successful Nazihunters in the world, said Peter Grace used W.R. Grace to hire Nazi managers and rocket scientists after World War II in CIA's, 'Operation Paperclip'.

"On Aug. 20 1981, the *International Herald Tribune* reported Fleeck Steel Group in Germany paid 365 million dollars to buy a controlling interest in W.R. Grace. W.R. Grace and Fleeck Steel Group were doing business together since the early 1950s. Fleeck Steel Group was family-owned, one of the biggest cartels in German General Staff supporting Hitler in World War II. The most senior manager of Fleeck Group was sentenced as a war criminal after World War II by the Nuremberg Trials, but had a short sentence, then returned to his Fleeck Group cartel managing position. Freddy Fleeck went to study business at W.R. Grace in New York in 1950. January 4 1981, *Soviet New Times* reported Fleeck, Meschersmidt, and Deutsche Shell were back in business supporting neo-Nazis ... at the same time the West German press reported they were funding the neo-Nazi, neo-Fascist German National Democratic Party.

"W.R. Grace Foundation funded the American Council for the International Promotion of Democracy Under God ...working with Father Felix Morleon's Vatican-based Pro Deo movement.

"An Italian reporter talked about Pro Deo.

"'If you want to know where the Vatican meets up with the mafia, that's where,' the reporter said.

"Peter was president of the U.S. branch of Knights Of Malta. Eight Grace board directors were Knights Of Malta, including board chairman Felix Larkin, who was Legal Counsel to the Department of Defense from 1941-1951 ...1951 was the year Larkin was recruited into W.R. Grace ...and, Freddy Fleeck received the highest award the Department of Defense could bestow.

"John D. J. Moore, another W.R. Grace & Co. board director was Chancellor of the Knights of Malta, and was U.S. Ambassador to Ireland. Other U.S. members of the Sovereign Knights of Malta were Robert A. Alplanap, Peter M. Flanigan, Baron Hilton, Lee Iacocca, James J. Ling, Spirus Scourus, John A. Volpe, John McCone, and Bill Casey. Bill Casey awarded the OSS' 'Old Boys Donovan Award' trophy to John McCone, as a board director at IT&T, playing a leading role coordinating de-stabilization of Chile's elected, democratic, socialist government run by President Salvador Allende. Italy's Knights of Malta, formally the Sovereign Military Order of Malta, was the heart of right-wing Catholic power world-wide. Over 1,000 years old, the Knights were a Vatican Order, the Pope's death squad military arm of the Catholic Church at the height of the Crusades. Since the Crusades, the Knights of Malta, a lay Catholic organization, maintained positions of leadership in the Right-wing Catholic, ruling family aristocracy of Europe, the Catholic leaders of Europe.

"To help launch the Cold War crusade, on Nov. 17, 1948 the Knights of Malta awarded its highest honor, the Grande Crossia Merita Complance, to Reinhard Gehlen, former head of Nazi intelligence, one of the lynch-pins of Dulles' CIA Christian West drive against the Soviet Union. Reinhard had stationed his brother, a Foreign Armies East operative, then later a Gehlen Org operative, in Rome with the code name, 'Don Giovani'. When Reinhard was given the award, his brother was Secretary to the Head of State of the Sovereign Military Order of Malta. The Knights of Malta had only bestowed their highest honor to three people ... including Gehlen on Nov. 17 1948, and James Jesus Angleton Dec. 27 1946 ...both were intelligencers working with the Pope's rat-lines to smuggle Nazis and Nazi war booty out of post-War Europe. For many years, James Jesus Angleton headed-up the CIA Station at the Vatican. He later was placed in charge of CIA Israeli intelligence operations.

John Loftus and Mark Aarons', *Secret War Against the Jews*, researched James Jesus Angleton. Loftus and Aarons discovered the SS laundered Nazi war loot by buying stock in American corporations through an 'unknowing' Chase Bank, and had flown Nazi war booty including gems, currency, and bonds to South America on 'unknowing' W.R. Grace's Pan Am clippers.

<> <> <>

Continuing my post-Presidency education, Nancy continued to read to me from many books, magazines, and newspapers.

She read from Martin Lee's, *The Beast Reawakens*.

"During both the Reagan and Bush years, the Republican Party's ethnic outreach arm recruited members from the Nazi émigré network. Republican Party's ethnic outreach division had outspoken hatred of President Jimmy Carter's Office of Special Investigations OSI, an organization tracking down and prosecuting Nazi war collaborators who entered this country. Pat Buchanan attacked Carter's OSI after it deported a few suspected Nazi war criminals.

"Public relations man Harold Keith Thompson was principal U.S. point man for the postwar Nazi support network known as die Spinne ... the Spider. In the late 40s and early 50s, Thompson worked as the chief North American representative for the National Socialist German Worker's Party and the SS. Thompson gave generously to Republican candidates Senator Jesse Helms and would-be senator, Oliver North. Thompson's money gained him membership in the GOP's Presidential Legion of Merit. Thompson received numerous thank you letters from the Republican National Committee. The letters are now in the Hoover Institute Special Collections Library."

Charles Higham's, *Trading With the Enemy* comments.

Charles documents, "the role of Standard Oil of New Jersey, owned by the Chase Manhattan Bank, and I.G. Farben's Sterling Products with the Bank for International Settlements. Standard Oil tankers plied the sea lanes with fuel for the Nazi war machine. Prior to the war McCloy was legal counsel to Farben, the German chemical monopoly. When the curtain fell on the war, McCloy helped shield Klaus Barbie, the 'Butcher of Lyons', from the French. Barbie and other vicious dogs from Hitler's kennel were hidden out within the 370th Counter Intelligence Corps at Obergamergau. One of their keepers was Private Henry Kissinger, soon to enter Harvard as a McCloy protégé.

"In 1949, McCloy returned to Germany as American High Commissioner. He commuted the death sentences of a number of Nazi war criminals, and gave early releases to others. One was Alfred Krupp, convicted of using slave labor in his armaments factories. Another was Hitler's financial genius, Dr. Hjalmar Schacht, subsequently on the payroll of Aristotle Onassis.

"In 1952, McCloy left Germany prepared to rearm, returning to his law practice ...he became president of Chase Manhattan Bank ...sat as a director of a dozen blue chip corporations ...and was legal counsel to the 'Seven Sisters' of American oil. During this period, McCloy acquired a client, the Nobel oil firm, whose interests in Czarist Russia were managed by the father of George de Mohrenschildt."

<>

Nazis were employed by the U.S. immediately after World War II in U.S. aerospace, U.S. intelligence, and covert action paramilitary and death-squad operations

...Nazi aerospace rocket scientist, Werner von Braun, was whitewashed and introduced to Americans on Walt Disney's TV show, Disneyland.

...aerospace rocket scientist, Walter Dornberger, now a research and development director at Bell Aircraft in Texas, was the boss of Michael Paine at whose house Lee Harvey Oswald and his wife Marina lived up until Kennedy's assassination.

Clarence Lasby's, *Project Paperclip,* comments.

"General Dornberger was a notorious Nazi war criminal ... who was supposed to be hanged at Nuremburg for war crimes, slave labor, and mass murder.

"The British warned the U.S., not to let him live ...because, even after the war he was conniving for another one, 'Dornberger is a menace of the first order who is untrustworthy. His attitude will turn ally against ally and will become a source of irritation and future unrest,'" Lasby said.

...Reinhard Gehlen, Hitler's most senior eastern front military intelligence officer was superior in rank to, and managed, the head of German western front intelligence. Hired by CIA on orders from the Central Bank World Order co-founders just before the end of World War II, Gehlen began fabricating anti-Russia cold war propaganda on behalf of the Central Bank World Order in support of their Crusade for Freedom domestic psychological warfare program, molding U.S. perceptions of the cold war to fit the agenda of the Central Bank New World Order ...which was to ...create government debt ...make military-industrial profits ...build the New Order economy in the U.S. ...bankrupt the Soviet Union ...and, control the U.S. public mind ... in order for the Central Bank oil companies to take over the Baku oil fields from Russia, and in order to create greater U.S. and foreign debt, its interest paid to the Fed.

...Count Sergei DeMohrenshieldt, whose father represented the Nobel Baku oil field interests in Russia, and was likely George Bush senior's 'intelligence handler' when Bush's first job out of college was to go behind the Iron Curtain on oil-related business.

Peter Dale Scott's research commented.

DeMohrenshieldt introduced Lee and Marina Oswald to Ruth Paine when Lee returned from Russia.

Mae Brussell's *Nazi Connection to JFK*, in *Rebel*, comments.

"Jackie Kennedy grew up calling George 'Sergei' DeMohrenschildt, 'Uncle George', as her mother Janet Auchincloss nearly married him after dating him during her divorce from Jackie's father, Black Jack Bouvier. DeMohrenschildt, at one time, was engaged to be married to Jackie Kennedy's aunt, her mother's sister, Michelle.

"Sergei DeMohrenschildt had a brother, who name was Demitri. Demitri's step-son was Edward Gorden Hooker ... Hooker was George Bush's roommate at Andover and Yale, who enlisted together with George Bush into the Navy."

Mae Brussell's work about Sergei DeMohrenshieldt in Texas overlaps the research of Peter Dale Scott ...both drew upon the 26-volume Warren Commission report. Mae bought a copy of the report and created an index to it, which it had lacked.

Mae continues.

"George DeMohrenschildt, the Oswalds' genial host in Dallas, was tagged by J. Edgar Hoover's FBI as a Nazi spy during World War II. G-men noted DeMohrenschildt's cousin Baron Maydell had Nazi ties, and that DeMohrenschildt's uncle distributed pro-Nazi films. [Ed.'s note, DeMohrenschildt collected films of Hitler invading Poland.]

"Information left out of Hoover's investigation, before and after JFK, were Nazi associations when DeMohrenschildt workd for U.S. intelligence.

George's cousin, movie producer Baron Constantine Maydell was a top German Abwehr agent in North America. Reinhard Gehlen recruited Maydell in the post-war era when Gehlen was in charge of CIA White Russian émigré programs. Gehlen recruited veterans of Maydell's Abwehr Group to work with East European émigré organizations inside the U.S.

"Part of Lee and Marina's red carpet treatment in the U.S. started with their arrival from Russia.

Spas T. Raikin was ex-Secretary General of American Friends of the Anti-Bolshevik Bloc of Nations AFABN, who with CIA funding helped Lee and Marina to get settled.

[Ed.'s note, Anti-Bolshevik equates with 'anti-Communist' or 'anti-Marxist'.]

"Domestically, Hoover was hunting for Communists ... his FBI overlooked Abwehr, Gehlen and Maydell.

"George de Mohrenschildt was a close associate of William Grace, founder of W.R. Grace."

Kevin Coogan again comments.

"Peter Grace used W.R. Grace to hire Nazi managers and rocket scientists after World War II in CIA's, 'Operation Paperclip'.

"Aug. 20 1981 Fleeck Steel Group in Germany paid 365 million dollars to buy controlling interest in W.R. Grace. Fleeck Steel Group and W.R. Grace did business since the early 1950s. Fleeck Steel Group was family-owned, one of the biggest cartels in German General Staff supporting Hitler in World War II. General manager of Fleeck Group was sentenced as a war criminal at the Nuremberg Trials, got a short sentence, served his time, then returned to his Fleeck Group cartel managing position.

"Freddy Fleeck went to study business at W.R. Grace in New York in 1950. Jan. 4 1981, Soviet New Times reported Fleeck, Meschersmidt and Deutsche Shell were back supporting neo-Nazis ... the West German press reported they were funding neo-Nazi, neo-Fascist groups like German National Democratic Party.

Mae continued.

"Frederick Fleeck's son invested over $400,000 in W.R. Grace Co., in partnership with J. Peter Grace, in the U.S. During the war, W.R. Grace was accused in a military report of protecting a Nazi Colonel Brite in Bolivia. In 1951, when the CIA smuggled Barbie out of Germany, Barbie was sent to join Colonel Brite.

"DeMohrenschildt wore many faces ...he befriended Lee and Marina Oswald, introduced them to the White Russian community ...made phone calls to get Lee jobs and housing ...told the Warren Commission he was fascinated with this couple just out of Russia.

"At the Petroleum Club in Dallas, DeMohrenschildt praised Heinrich Himmler. His travels took him all over the world on intelligence missions. In 1956, he was employed by Pantepec Oil Company, owned by William Buckley's family.

"DeMohrenschildt discussed Oswald with J. Walton Moore, CIA's Domestic Contacts Division resident in Dallas. Spring 1963, after visiting the

Oswalds, DeMohrenshieldt went to Washington. May 7, 1963, there's a record of a phone call DeMohrenschildt made to the Army Chief of Staff for intelligence ...the same month he had a meeting with a member of Army Intelligence staff. One of the first persons DeMohrenschildt took the Oswalds to see in Dallas, was retired Admiral Chester Burton."

Paris Flammonde's *An Un-commissioned Report on the Jim Garrison Investigation* comments on DeMohrenshieldt and William Grace. [Ed.'s note, Flammonde is a writing name of an un-named intelligence French intelligence operative collective.]

"Sept. 30, 1976 the Dutch journal, *Haagse Post,* wrote, 'In 1939, DeMohrenshieldt made his initial entry into the Texas oil business. He became well known to many of the more important people as a passable polo player, and with a friend collected films concerning the conflict between Poland and Hitler's Germany. One of his closer associates was the tycoon William Grace."

Alan Weverman and Michael Canfield's, *Coup d'etat in America,* comments.

"DeMohrenshieldt brought Lee Harvey Oswald to a party where he met Michael and Ruth Paine. The Paines were closely associated with the intelligence community. Mr. Paine worked for Bell Helicopter."

<>

I always got a kick out of Nancy reading me books and articles ... but sometimes, it was a real kick in the rear end.

I looked at Nancy.

"Nancy, love hurts," I said.

Nancy looked at me. "Ronnie, we decided we'd find out what really was going on ... that we didn't know about, when we were in the White House ...it hurts me just as much as it hurts you."

Nancy read Kimery to me. He was the kind of person I wished I'd known when I was President. Of course, my Vice President might have shot him down ...or, at least ... sent him on a hunting trip with Dick Cheney. I'd known Dick Cheney back in Starwars days, he was a major proponent, along with his friend USAF Lt. Col. Robert M. Bowman.

Nancy picked up a copy of *Covert Action.*

Anthony Kimery researched Count Serge DeMohrenschildt. Lou Wolf's, *Covert Action Information Bulletin,* summer 1992, Anthony L. Kimery's, *In the Company of Friends, George Bush and the CIA,* comments.

"George Bush's most important ties to the intelligence community were likely knotted at Yale, where he attended, 1945-1948. During these formative years for both Bush and the Cold War, CIA recruited vigorously and almost exclusively at elite Ivy League schools. Yale was so intimately inter-twined with the U.S. spy community that it 'influenced the CIA more than any other institution', wrote historian Robin Winks. All recruits didn't enter the Agency, itself. Many Yale grads going to work for multi-national corporations were routinely recruited to provide intelligence, particularly behind the Iron Curtain.

"CIA's full-time salaried headhunter at Yale was crew coach Allen 'Skip' Waltz, former naval Intelligence officer who had a good view of Bush. As a member of Yale's Undergraduate Athletic Association and Undergraduate Board of Deacons, Bush had to have worked closely with Waltz on the university's athletic programs, from which the coach picked most of the men he steered to CIA. It's inconceivable Waltz didn't try to recruit Bush, say former Agency officials recruited at Yale.

"But, it wasn't just Bush's scholastic achievements that made him desirable as a prospective spy. His father, Prescott Bush Sr. probably also had a part in the CIA interest in young George. A managing partner of Brown Brothers Harriman and a major benefactor of Yale, Prescott had been an Army Intelligence operative in World War I. Prescott ardently supported Eisenhower's covert cold War policies and was a close friend of William Casey ...an OSS veteran who went on to head CIA from 1981-1985. Given these connections, it was not surprising the job awaiting his son on graduation in 1948 was with a CIA-linked company headed by a close friend, who was on good terms with top people in the Agency.

"George Bush started his career as a salesman for International Derrick & Equipment Co, IDECO, a subsidiary of Houston-based Dresser Industries, a global engineering and construction conglomerate that routinely served as a CIA cover. Bush's job, peddling IDECO services, including behind the Iron Curtain, was a curious responsibility considering Bush's inexperience in either the oil industry or international relations.

"Dresser Industries' long-time Board Chairman was Henry Neil Mallon, the 'surrogate uncle' and 'father-confessor' to Prescott's children, who had personally offered George Bush the IDECO job. Henry Mallon was a friend to numerous ranking Cold War era intelligence officials including Allen Dulles, an OSS veteran and ground floor official at CIA. Dulles headed the Agency from 1953 until 1961, when he was sacked by President Kennedy in the wake of the Bay of Pigs disaster. Mallon steered prospective candidates for spy work to Dulles and often provided cover employment to CIA operatives. Prescott and Mallon were Yale classmates and initiates of Skull and Bones, the Yale fraternity that was a fertile CIA recruiting ground during the Cold War. George joined Skull and Bones his junior year. Another particularly important operative with whom Mallon was well acquainted would also eventually work with George Bush. Sergei 'George' DeMohrenschildt, a Russian Count whose family fled Russia after the Bolshevik revolution, had been part of a spy network Dulles ran inside Hitler's intelligence organization. Following the defeat of Nazi Germany, DeMohrenschildt appears to have been submerged as a deep-cover CIA 'asset', operating under the guise of a consulting petroleum geologist specializing in making deals between U.S. oil companies and the East-bloc nations to which he was remarkably well-connected. Henry Neil Mallon personally introduced Count DeMohrenschildt to George Bush at about the same time Mallon handed George Bush the highly sensitive responsibility of negotiating East-bloc deals."

Sep. 22, 2003 Lyndon LaRouche's, *Executive Intelligence Review,* comments on Dresser Industries, Brown & Root, and Halliburton in *John Hoefle's, Halliburton is Houston's Greater Hermann Göring Werke.*

[Autobiographer's note, the word, 'anti-Christ', is substituted for LaRouche's, 'Synarchist'. By 'anti-Christ, we mean anti-Christian, anti-Jewish, anti-Muslim, anti-Buddhist behavior.]

"In 1962, came the Cuban missile crisis ... in 1963, the assassination of President John F. Kennedy at the hands of the anti-Christ Permindex assassination bureau ...the escalation of the Vietnam War in the wake of the staged Tonkin Gulf 'attacks', in 1964. These events strengthened the hand of the anti-Christs, who seized power in Washington in the wake of 9/11 under the guise of fighting terrorism, launching an assault on the Constitution and the public purse.

"Chief among the anti-Christs in Washington is Vice President Dick Cheney, whose relationship with Halliburton exemplifies military-industrial relationships President Eisenhower warned against. In 1991, while he was Secretary of Defense in the first Bush Administration, Cheney hired Halliburton's Brown & Root subsidiary to do a study on the privatization of military logistics operations. This study established Logistics Civil Augmentation Program, which gave its first general contract to ... Brown & Root.

"At the time, Cheney and Undersecretary of Defense for Policy Paul Wolfowitz, were pushing for wars against smaller, resource-rich nations, including the use of 'low-yield' nuclear weapons. When George H.W. Bush left office in January 1993, Cheney spent time at neo-conservative American Enterprise Institute ...then, in 1995 joined Halliburton as president and chief executive. Cheney added, 'chairman', to his titles in 1996, and ran the company until August 2000, stepping down to run for Vice President. During that 1995-2000 period, one dollar of every seven spent by the Pentagon, passed through what is now, Kellogg, Brown & Root.

[Autobiographer's note, Brown & Root enjoyed a special military-industrial contract reward relationship with Lyndon Johnson from when Johnson was a Senator in the late 1940s, before, during and after JFK ... with the Suite 8F Group.]

"At the time Cheney hired Halliburton to do the privatization study, Halliburton was hardly a disinterested party. The company was already a major defense contractor through Brown & Root and had significant military and intelligence connections.

"With its flurry of construction contracts in Iraq, Halliburton is in many respects depending upon Dick Cheney for its survival ... LaRouche has dubbed Halliburton, 'The Greater Hermann Göring Werke of Houston'. It's been clear for some time that Vice President Cheney has been acting as an agent for the international anti-Christ movement, which was founded as the oligarchy's counterattack to the American Revolution and the principles upon which America was founded. Cheney and Halliburton have been rightly attacked for the company's war profiteering.

The Vice President and his neo-con allies such as Defense Secretary Donald Rumsfeld, Paul Wolfowitz, Richard Perle, et al., are agents of a dark power committed to eliminating the principles espoused in the Declaration of Independence and the Constitution, in favor of a global bankers' dictatorship. This same oligarchic power, acting through merchant banks like Lazard Frères, Rothschild and other financial institutions, controls a large swath of Wall Street and corporate America, including Halliburton.

"Halliburton's power does not flow from Cheney

...but from Cheney's backers, the anti-Christ bankers. Cheney's policy toward the people of Iraq is the same as Göring's policy toward the people in the Nazi work camps. Arbeit Macht Frei ... Work Makes You Free ... read the sign over the entrance to Auschwitz. It was an example of Göring's 'big lie' tactic in action. The Cheney cabal's comment, we must accept police-state tactics in our own nation and pre-emptive strikes against other nations in the name of freedom, rings false ... Hermann Göring would be proud.

"Halliburton traces its roots to Erle P. Halliburton, a pioneer in the techniques of cementing well bores, who founded the company in 1919. In 1924, Halliburton was incorporated with significant investments by seven major oil companies, and Halliburton trucks became common sights in the oil patch. In 1961, after a series of acquisitions, the company moved its headquarters from Duncan Oklahoma to Dallas Texas.

In 1962, Halliburton bought Brown & Root, the giant Houston-based construction company. Brown & Root had also been founded in 1919, by Herman Brown and Dan Root, with Herman's brother George Brown coming in a few years later. Brown & Root started out paving roads and building bridges in rural Texas, and in 1940 got the contract to build the Corpus Christi Naval Air Station. It built pipelines and ships during World War II, and in 1961 won the planning contract for the Manned Space Center in Houston. When Herman Brown died in 1962, George Brown sold the company to Halliburton to avoid a hostile takeover, though he remained as company chairman. He died in 1983.

"Both Herman and George Brown were important figures in the internationally dominated Houston business world. Herman Brown was a director of the Rothschild-linked First City National Bank ...and, pipeline operator, Texas Eastern, which he and brother George founded to buy the 'Big Inch' and 'Little Inch' pipelines after World War II. George Brown served as chairman of politically influential Rice University for 15 of his 25 years on the board, and served on commissions for Presidents Truman, Eisenhower, Kennedy, and Johnson ...as well as on Texas State commissions from the 1930s through the 1970s.

"In 1998, Halliburton made another major purchase, acquiring Dresser Industries for 7.7 billion dollars. Dresser was founded by Solomon Dresser in 1880 ... taken over in 1928 by W.H. Harriman & Company, the investment bank owned by the descendants of railroad magnate E.H. Harriman, himself a front for the British Royal Family.

"Under Averell and Roland Harriman, Dresser was a Skull & Bones shop, whose board included Bonesman and presidential father and grandfather Prescott Bush. Both Roland Harriman and Prescott Bush were directors of Union Banking Corp. when it was raided by Federal agents in 1942, under the Trading With the Enemy Act, for its dealings on behalf of Nazi Germany.

"The Dresser deal seems like a Skull & Bones rescue operation since, with Dresser, Halliburton acquired several billions of dollars in asbestos-claim lawsuit liabilities. Dick Cheney, who made the deal, is not a Bonesman himself, having dropped out of Yale in his sophomore year ... but the Skull & Bones roster contains at least nine Cheneys, more than nearly any other family.

"Also with Dresser, came construction company M.W. Kellogg, which was merged into Brown & Root to form Kellogg, Brown & Root."

<>

Peter Dale Scott researched Count Sergei 'George' DeMohrenschildt.

"There is also, for example, the CIA to be considered. Ilia Mamantov and Peter Gregory [two of the White Russian handlers of the Oswalds in the Dallas/Fort Worth area] had collaborated in 1955 to set up a Dallas parish of the CIA-subsidized Russian Orthodox Church Outside Russia, a parish restricted to aristocratic, anti-Bolshevik Russians who had been 'checked, re-checked' and double-checked' by the CIA-subsidized, Tolstoy Foundation. Members of this tiny anti-Bolshevik parish of 'maybe 25 families' at least eight of whom were connected with Mamantov and Gregory in the oil exploration business, acted very much in the manner of intelligence case officers in providing 'babysitting' services for the Oswald family when they arrived in Texas.

"Exotic oilman and Baron, George DeMohrenschildt, in particular, would cheerfully drive Lee Harvey Oswald and his wife Marina Oswald to other oilmen's parties and swimming pools ...and once spent all day loading his car down to the ground when Marina wanted to move. DeMohrenschildt told the Warren Commission, during World War II he worked for French intelligence. He concealed during the war he was a suspected German agent who admitted having worked for a year with movie producer Baron Constantine Maydell, whom he described as, 'not a spy but pro-German'. Today it is known that Maydell was for a period the top German Abwehr Military Intelligence agent in North America. Reinhard von Gehlen, who in the post-war era was in charge of the CIA's Russian émigré programs, is said to have recruited veterans of Maydell's Abwehr Group II and to have worked with East European émigré organizations inside the U.S. I mention this, because Oswald was met on his return to America from Russia by Spas T. Raikin, ex-Secretary General of one such group, American Friends of the Anti-Bolshevik Bloc of Nations AFABN. Raikin's AFABN, like the Gehlen network and some of its CIA sponsors, was bitterly opposed to Kennedy's moves in 1963 towards rapprochement with the Soviet Union."

Peter Dale Scott's *Government Documents in the JFK Assassination* comments.

"Many if not all of the international oil companies maintain their own private intelligence networks, that collaborate with CIA and with émigré organizations subsidized by CIA and Reinhard Gehlen. At home in the U.S., American Petroleum Institute encouraged its member companies to sponsor reserve-officer units among the employees. This brings us to Army Intelligence Reserve Officer Jack Alston Crichton, the oilman who recruited Mamantov as Marina's interpreter and who in 1963 was an American Petroleum Institute delegate behind the Iron Curtain ...

"However, DeMohrenshieldt's past intelligence activities may have been less relevant than his post-war career as an oil exploration geologist like Gregory, Mamantov and Crichton. The extensive plumbing by the Warren Commission of his overseas travels and intelligence work for oil companies revealed the extent to which this was a secretive and closely-knit profession with CIA overlaps, and émigré Russians of St. Nicholas and similar CIA-subsidized parishes played a role in world-wide CIA activities similar to émigré Cubans. Asked about a Russian émigré oil financial expert in Connecticut with the Chase Manhattan Bank and his connections with the Dallas Russian community, DeMohrenshieldt replied, 'We all knew him, there are few people in this geological field.'

"DeGolyer & MacNaughton, the Dallas-based firm with world pre-eminence in this profession, was closely linked to members of the Russian parish, and others who took turns 'baby-sitting' the Oswalds. DeMohrenshieldt, who took care of Marina's dentist bills and later lied about this to the FBI, apparently had MacNaughton's son in

his house as an 'associate and constant guest'.

"Michael Payne, an ideological right-winger who went with Oswald to the suspect Dallas Civil Liberties Union ... which the Dallas Police and 112th Military Intelligence Group both had under surveillance ... had an uncle, Eric Schroder, who was a friend and investment associate of DeGolyer ...his cousin Alendar 'Sandy' Forbes was a former director of United Fruit [as were the Dulles brothers], and belonged to the elite Tryall Gold Club in Jamaica, with former DeGolyer associate Paul Raigorodsky, a financial patron of St. Nicholas Parish. Finally, Declan Ford, with his Russian wife, who took care of Marina after the assassination, had worked many years for DeGolyer and MacNaughton, the former employers of Jack Crichton.

"It seems possible that behind MacNaughton associates' solicitude for the Oswalds was a less-than-disinterested concern with Cuban oil. Before the fall of Batista, DeGolyer & MacNaughton were active exploring for oil in Cuba, on behalf of a closely-linked company which today, Panoil, has Crichton as director. Oswald's chief chauffer, Count Sergei DeMohrenshieldt, also explored for oil in Cuba at this time, on behalf of the interlocking Cuban-Venezuelan Oil Voting Trust ...a company which played heavy Cuban politics in order to obtain and protect its oil leases. One of its directors, Amadeo Barletta, the local representative of General Motors, was close to dictators Batista and Trujillo, as well as allegedly international narcotics traffic. Another, J.M. Bosch Lamargue 'was one of the first and earliest supporters of Castro' before turning against him in 1959, he was also Castro's chief contact with Jules Dubois, a *Chicago Tribune* Castro publicist and alleged U.S. Army Intelligence veteran who also played an important part in the 1954 CIA coup in Guatemala.

<>

Peter Dale Scott's *Dallas Conspiracy*, comments.

"The case that Oswald was an agent is strengthened by the paradoxical condition of poverty and privilege in which the Oswald's lived after their arrival in Texas. Though he severed all contact with his family after Thanksgiving 1962, and though he seems to have made not one single friend, otherwise, Oswald and his wife Marina were now favored with the attentions of a small circle of wealthy Russians and their friends, connected almost exclusively with the politically influential petroleum engineering industry. The

Warren Commission's list of 34 persons 'with whom Lee Harvey Oswald had contact', many of whom may have met Oswald for only a single evening, is striking testimony that Oswald's social life was entirely governed by his Russian patrons. Every single person on this list, as well as some others that the commission did not include, had been met by the Oswald's through these patrons. This included the alleged liberal Ruth Paine of the ACLU, who assumed the same 'baby-sitting' role. This Russian community by no accident had links with wealth, petroleum, the political machines of both parties, government and above all, intelligence activities.

"Take for example the first two people Oswald contacted allegedly in his search for someone in Fort Worth who spoke Russian. Of the two, Russian-born Peter Gregory a petroleum engineer, was a personal friend of Mike Howard …one of the two secret service agents who isolated Marina Oswald in the days after the assassination. Howard used Gregory in his interrogation of Marina …Gregory abused this responsibility by significantly distorting what Marina said.

"The second person, Gregory's friend Mrs. Max Clark … a princess of the Sherbatov family … was apparently the first Russian with whom Oswald made telephone contact.

"Though Warren Commission Counsel Wesley Liebeler avoided bringing this fact out, Max Clark, who was on a first-name basis with the Fort Worth FBI agent who interviewed him, was a former security officer for the Convair Division of General Dynamics, and he was, according to one witness, 'in some way connected to the FBI'. And Convair, up to the time of the Kennedy assassination, was being investigated by a Senate Committee for possible major scandals surrounding the controversial contract award to build the TFX experimental fighter plane, that later became the F-111.

"It is important to recall that in the McLellan Subcommittee Hearings into the TFX contract award, the conduct of two men in particular had drawn public scrutiny. One was Roswell Gilpatrick, Deputy Secretary of Defense whose past and present contacts with General Dynamics seemed to indicate conflicts of interest. The other was Fred Korth, who resigned as Navy Secretary in October 1963 … after a letter of his had been published showing abuse of his office to favor his own Continental Bank of Fort Worth. Continental National Bank, of which Korth had formerly been president 1959-1962, was 'a minor partner in a consortium that made loans to General Dynamics'.

"Shortly after the assassination, the *New York Herald Tribune* was able to correctly predict that the Senate investigation of the TFX contract had 'been laid quietly aside' and might 'never be revived'. The McClellan Subcommittee had met last on Nov. 20, two days before the assassination, and closed with chairman McClellan undertaking to 'resume hearings next week'. Informed journals like *Business Week* predicted that Fred Korth would be the next witness. But Korth, a longtime friend and political ally of his fellow-Texan Lyndon Johnson, never was called to testify, and the hearings promised for 'next week' were not resumed until six years later.

"Shortly before the assassination, another Senate Committee investigating Bobby Baker heard charges from Don Reynolds, Baker's former business associate, that there had been a $100,000 payoff on the TFX contract. Such testimony was only one instance in which the 1963 TFX and Bobby Baker investigations were beginning to focus on a single area, the financial-political alliances behind Lyndon Johnson. Reynolds was, in fact, giving testimony in closed session about the Bobby Baker scandal, that threatened to terminate Lyndon Johnson's political career, at the moment the assassination occurred. The Bobby Baker investigation, too, was deflected from such high-level implications after the assassination.

"If the Warren Commission wished to destroy a false impression that the assassination was a conspiracy, it should have investigated the links, however trivial, between Korth and the Oswald family. Korth, after all, had been present at the June 1963 meeting at which the President decided to visit Texas. One would therefore be interested to know whether Korth had any contact with the Oswald case in the years between 1948 … when he was attorney for a Mr. Ekdahl in his divorce from Mrs. Marguerite Oswald, Lee Harvey's mother … and 1962, when he took over as Navy Secretary from his friend John Connally, then about to become Governor of Texas, the responsibility for Oswald's 'dishonorable discharge' …

Dick Russell researched Baron Sergei DeMohrenshieldt.

"Sergei DeMohrenshieldt was born in Czarist Russia in 1911. His father was a director of the Nobel oil interests. He became a world traveler who spoke six languages and boasted membership in both the exclusive Dallas Petroleum Club and the World Affairs Council. DeMohrenshieldt and his fourth wife, Jeanne, were part of Dallas's clique of Russian émigrés, most of whom had settled shortly after World War II on the periphery of the city's oil industry. The baron himself was an oil and mining geologist who, coincidentally, had become a close friend of Jacqueline Kennedy's mother when he immigrated to the United States in 1938 ... Among the Baron's Houston associates were several close friends of Lyndon Johnson, oil millionaire John Mecom, and construction industry titans George and Herman Brown.

"DeMohrenshieldt had been raised in Poland after his family fled the Bolshevik revolution. There, he graduated from the Military Academy Of Poland, and he served as a reserve captain in the Polish Army before immigrating to the United States. A CIA file noted a background investigation in late 1957 and early 1958 showing 'that he was a member of the Communist Party', and that after the war he was sympathetic toward Communism and the U.S.S.R.' Yet, simultaneous with that background investigation, the CIA is on record as having itself been utilizing DeMohrenshieldt's services ... DeMohrenshieldt's wife Jeanne was a former fashion model, born in Harbin China, to the White Russian director of the Far East Railroad. Who was Baron Serge DeMohrenshieldt? He strides across the international petroleum scene, in touch with future American presidents, Soviet officials, and the CIA. At various times he had been suspected as a Nazi and as a Communist agent. He is in the right places at the right times, Guatemala during the Bay Of Pigs invasion training, Dallas-Fort Worth when the Oswalds come home from the U.S.S.R. He finds Oswald a job at a photo shop that does classified work for the Army, where Oswald employs 'microdot' spy techniques," Dick Russell said.

Peter Dale Scott's, *Dallas Conspiracy*, comments.

"The guiding influence over the Oswalds of Gregory and of three other Russians, all connected with each other and with the petroleum engineering industry, can only be described as analogous to that of intelligence 'case officers', for their subjects. If the Oswalds needed a car to go shopping or to be moved, the Russian families were there to lend a hand. The penniless Marina Oswald is said to have had a hundred dresses given to her in this period, a claim wholly overlooked by the Warren Commission in its penny-by-penny accounting of the Oswald possessions and budget.

"One of the chief Russian guardians, George Bouhe, was a 60-year-old personal accountant of the famous oil exploration consulting service DeGolyer & MacNaughton, a man with numerous CIA contacts.

"For example, MacNaughton was a director of Republic National Gas, and Republic National Bank in Dallas with Karl Hoblitzelle ... who set up the CIA-conduit Hoblitzelle Foundation. The president of the Hoblitzelle Foundation was Peter O'Donnell Jr., a Goldwater-Republican who sat on the National Advisory Council for Young Americans for Freedom, with Robert Morris. One trustee of the Foundation was Sarah T. Hughes, the judge who on Nov. 22 1963 administered the controversial oath of office to her friend and patron, Lyndon Johnson.

"George Bouhe, a White Russian, was said to have been 'rather mad at Marina for taking an apartment at Oak Cliff because it was rather too far for him to drive and help her when she needed help with her baby'. Lee Oswald, who worked in this period as a welder, greaser, or handyman ...was driven to parties and otherwise cared-for by a member of the Dallas Petroleum Club and World Affairs Council, Count Sergei DeMohrenshieldt, who knew Jackie Kennedy's family.

"Although De Mohrenschildt and his wife Jeanne testified at length before the Warren Commission, only attorney Albert Jenner and Pentagon historian Alfred Goldberg attended. One of Jenner's clients was General Dynamics, maker of the F-3 fighter that would achieve fame in Vietnam. The chief of security for General Dynamics in Dallas, Max Clark, was another DeMohrenschildt associate donating money to help Marina while George got Lee his next job in Dallas. He found one at the graphics house of Jagger-Chiles-Stovall, which held classified military contracts.

"Jeanne DeMohrenschildt was originally brought to the U.S. by a family member employed by the Howard Hughes organization.

"The placement DeMohrenschildt got for Oswald allowed him to visit Sol Bloom agency at least 40 times. It was this agency that later decided the motorcade route for Kennedy's fatal visit.

"Ruth Paine, whom Oswald met via George [Sergei], had called Roy Truly and procured work for Oswald at the Texas School Book Depository.

"If Maydell and the Gehlen agents were active in the U.S. they knew all the right moves to secure their patsy. Sergei 'George' DeMohrenschildt was busy introducing Lee and Marina to the Dallas-Ft. Worth White Russian displaced Czarists. One casual dinner in the company of Michael and Ruth Paine, and that was enough meeting to set the Oswalds' course. George and Jeanne didn't have to meet with them again," Peter Dale Scott said.

Burnham comments on DeMohrenshieldt.
http://www.john-f-kennedy.net/amazingwebofabrahamzapruder.htm
"Abraham Zapruder …White Russian affiliation …32nd degree Mason …also, active member of two CIA proprietary organizations, Dallas Council on World Affairs, and, Crusade for a Free Europe. Membership of these two CIA-backed domestic operations in Dallas included …Abraham Zapruder …Clint Murchison, owner of the Dallas Cowboys at that time …Mr. Byrd owner of the Texas School Book Depository …Sarah Hughes, who swore LBJ in as the 36th President while Air Force One was still on the ground in Dallas …George DeMohrenschildt, CIA contract agent and best friend of Lee Harvey Oswald …George Bush close friend of George DeMohrenschildt …Neil Mallon, mentor Bush named his son, Neil, after …H.L. Hunt …and, Sergei's brother, Demitri Von Mohrenschildt.

"In 1953 and 1954, a woman named Jeanne LeGon worked side-by-side with Abraham Zapruder at Nardis of Dallas, a fashion design firm. Jeanne LeGon designed clothing, Abraham Zapruder cut patterns and material.

"Abraham Zapruder's obituary mis-states the date he left Nardis of Dallas, incorrectly citing 1949. The correct year was 1959 …the same year his design partner Jeanne LeGon became known as Jeanne LeGon DeMohrenschildt, she married Lee Oswald's best friend, to-be CIA contract agent, rabid anti-Communist Sergei 'George' DeMohrenshieldt.

"Lyndon Baines Johnson's personal secretary, Marie Fehmer, who flew back to Washington on Air Force 1 with LBJ on Nov. 22, 1963, was the daughter of Olga Fehmer, who also worked at Nardis of Dallas, with Abraham Zapruder and Jean LeGon DeMohrenschildt.

"Abraham Zapruder's co-worker, Jeanne LeGon and husband Sergei DeMohrenschildt introduced Lee Oswald to the daughter of one of Sergei DeMohrenschildt's close friends, Ruth Paine. Ruth Paine's husband, Michael, whose step-father, Arthur Young worked with Lyndon Baines Johnson's personal pilot, Joseph Mashman, to develop Bell Helicopter of Fort Worth, Texas … was employed by Bell at the time of the assassination. About 4,500 Bell helicop-

ters were shot down in Viet Nam, Bell's stockholders made a fortune replacing them.

"Sep. 1976, Sergei DeMohrenschildt was subjected to nine electro-shock treatments at Parkland Hospital under orders given by Doctor DeLoach …first cousin of FBI Assistant Director Cartha 'Deke' DeLoach. DeMohrenschildt's doctor of record', Dr. Mendoza, ordered administration of intravenous drugs on DeMohrenschildt being committed to Parkland Hospital for mental problems' but, it was DeLoach that ordered electro-shock therapy. This occurred when George Bush was Director of Central Intelligence …and, within weeks of DeMohrenschildt having written a manuscript, entitled, *I Am A Patsy! I Am A Patsy!* …which named names of various CIA and FBI personnel who framed Oswald to cover their tracks in JFK's assassination.

Mar. 29, 1977… the day DeMohrenschildt agreed to be interviewed by House Select Committee on Assassinations, Sergei DeMohrenschildt was found by his daughter, Alexandra … dead of a shotgun blast through his mouth. His death was ruled a suicide.

Jeanne consented to a press interview. She said Sergei had once been a Nazi spy.

Robert Grodin and Harrison Livingston researched Baron DeMohrenshieldt.

"DeMohrenshieldt's wife told Jim Mars, a Dallas reporter, 'He must have still harbored guilt feelings about his work for the Germans during World War II, because he told me, 'It's the Jews, they've caught up with me,'" Grodin said.

In 1964, a CIA report states, 'Alexandra was being monitored by CIA's James Jesus Angleton because she was having an affair with Mohammed al Fayed shortly after the JFK assassination.' James Jesus Angleton's name is signed at the bottom of that 41 page report. Under his signature is that of CIA asset, Jane Roman. Roman was the CIA agent who the record shows was charged with monitoring the movements of Lee Harvey Oswald for two months preceding the assassination.

"Sergei DeMohrenschildt was business partners with Mohammed al Fayed and Clamar J. Charles in Haiti …while working for Clint Murchison's Haitian interests. He also worked for Murchison's, Three States Oil & Gas," Burnham said.

<>

"George Bush has selective Alzheimer's regarding his whereabouts of Nov. 22, 1963. Barbara Bush said, he was in Tyler, Texas …although, he has 'speculated' he may have been in Port Au Prince, Haiti.

"FBI Special Agent, Graham Kitchell states, he received a call from George Bush on Nov. 22, 1963, and that George Bush and his voice were very familiar to him, at that time. The call was made to the Houston FBI office and apparently did not originate from Haiti," Burnham said.

Lou Wolf's *Covert Action Information Bulletin* article by Anthony L. Kimery, *In the Company of Friends,* comments.

"Driven by a Cold War policy of covertly thwarting expansion of the Soviet petroleum industry whenever possible, CIA was desperate for accurate intelligence on U.S.S.R. oil and gas production activities. 'It's inconceivable that CIA didn't de-brief Bush after each and every meeting [he had with the East's representatives],' explained Victor Marchetti, a former ranking CIA officer and Soviet specialist during the 1950s. 'Businessmen with dealings [like Bush had] were routinely debriefed,' Marchetti said.

"For decades, CIA relied heavily on de-briefings of U.S. business-people, some of whom were turned into full-fledged agents. That Bush was one of those recruited to spy is a possibility Marchetti and other ex-CIA officials find consistent with normal Company functioning. And it would certainly go far in explaining Bush's relationship with the mysterious Count DeMohrenschildt. A 'degreed' petroleum geologist, the Count could have explained precisely what information Bush needed to look for to help CIA fill its intelligence gaps.

"Officials Bush dealt with had detailed knowledge of Soviet-bloc oil and gas production, and exploration and drilling capabilities, as well as strategic exploration and production plans outside U.S.S.R. Bush convivially wheeled and dealed with the Communist's petroleum experts without the slightest grimace by U.S. authorities. In fact, when a Yugoslavian oil industry official came to the U.S. in 1948 to talk to Dresser Industries, the State Department barely flinched and he went straight to neophyte salesman George Bush, in Midland Texas.

"A CIA spy in Yugoslavia, DeMohrenschildt may have been Bush's 'handler', his briefer and de-briefer. 'Bush had all the characteristics of being a spook,' said a retired CIA operative who says he worked for Dresser as a cover and who knew the future president. The possibility that deep cover operative DeMohrenschildt's relationship to Bush was that of fellow intelligence gatherer is strengthened by DeMohrenschildt's continuing association with Bush, and by the apparently secret turn in their relationship at about the

time CIA operations against Fidel Castro began. Neatly typewritten among the meticulous pages of the telephone and address book the Count carried with him until his alleged suicide, is an entry for 'George Bush'. It includes his nickname, 'Poppy', and his home address and telephone number in Midland Texas, where Bush and his family lived from 1953 until he moved the offices of Zapata Off-Shore Oil Company to Houston in 1959. Curiously, the two of them continued to meet secretly in Houston. DeMohrenschildt made no new entry for Bush's residence in Houston. There was only an 'X' marked through the old address. In his testimony to Warren Commission, DeMohrenschildt acknowledged having made frequent trips to Houston beginning in the late 1950s, for which he gave only vague explanations. Although there is no proof, it is possible that one reason for his stealth was the continued meetings with Bush. By early 1960s, Bush was regularly servicing the CIA in Latin America. 'I know [Bush] was involved [with the CIA] in the Caribbean,' said an ex-CIA agent."

"It was around this time, in the late 1950s, that Bush expanded his business dealings in Mexico. The counter-revolutionary, anti-nationalization policies enforced by CIA in the incendiary Mexico-Caribbean-Central-American region certainly worked to Bush's financial advantage. Following Castro's successful revolution in 1959, his government took over all oil and gas enterprises in Cuba and nationalized the industry, a blow to U.S. oil companies, which had just begun to tap into Cuba's oil reserves. Fearing that the desire to control their own industries would spread to other Third World countries, CIA went to bat for big oil amalgamations which were worried about security of their investments in the region's considerable oil and natural gas resources. The Agency began assembling a paramilitary force to invade Cuba and overthrow Castro. Again, there was a neat mesh between CIA policy objectives and Bush business interests in the region. In the summer of 1959, Bush was principal owner of Zapata Off-Shore Oil Company, which he had spun off from Zapata Petroleum, a company he helped found six years earlier. Veteran CIA operatives in the war against Castro say, Bush not only let the CIA use Zapata as a front for running some of its operations (including the use of several offshore drilling platforms), but assert that Bush personally served as a conduit through which the Agency disbursed money for contracted services. Lending themselves this way to the CIA was [business-as-usual] for many business-people in the 1950s and early 1960s who wet their feet spying for CIA behind the Iron Curtain."

<>

Mike Ruppert, an L.A. cop who refused to cooperate with CIA drug runners in L.A.'s inner city, comments in his, *Bush-Cheney Drug Empire,* on off-shore oil platforms being used by CIA. Mike's girlfriend was a CIA operative. She disappeared. Mike went to look for her.

www.copvcia.com/free/ciadrugs/bush-cheney-drugs.html

"July 1977, then a Los Angeles Police officer, I struggled to make sense in a world gone haywire. In a last ditch effort to salvage a relationship with my finace, Nordica Theodora 'Teddy' D'Orsay, a CIA contract agent, I had traveled to find her in New Orleans. Starting in late spring of 1976, Teddy wanted me to join her operations from within the ranks of LAPD. I refused to get involved with drugs in any way, and everything she mentioned seemed to involve either heroin or cocaine ... along with guns that she was always moving out of the country. The director of the CIA at that time was George Herbert Walker Bush.

"Arriving in New Orleans in early 1977, I found Teddy living in an apartment across the river in Gretna. Equipped with scrambler phones, night vision devices and working from sealed communiqués delivered by naval and air force personnel from nearby Bell Chasses Naval Air Station, Teddy was involved in something truly ugly. She was arranging for large quantities of weapons to be loaded onto ships leaving for Iran. At the same time, she was working with Mafia associates of New Orleans Mafia boss Carlos Marcello to coordinate the movement of service boats that were bringing large quantities of heroin into the city. The boats arrived at Marcello-controlled docks, untouched by even the New Orleans police she'd introduced me to ...along with divers, military men, former Green Berets and CIA personnel.

"Hoping against hope that I would find some way to understand her involvement with CIA, PAPD, the royal family of Iran, the Mafia, and drugs, I set out alone into eight days of Dante-like revelations that determined the course of my life from that day on.

"The service boats were retrieving the heroin from oil rigs in the Gulf of Mexico ...oil rigs in international waters ...oil rigs built and serviced by Brown & Root. The guns that Teddy monitored ... Vietnam era surplus AK47s and M16s, were being loaded onto ships also owned or leased by Brown & Root. And, more than once

during the eight days I spent in New Orleans, I met and ate at restaurants with Brown & Root employees ...who were boarding those ships and leaving for Iran in days.

"Disgusted and heart-broken at witnessing my fiancee and my government smuggling drugs, I ended the relationship. Returning home to L.A. I reported all the activity I had seen, including the connections to Brown & Root, to LAPD intelligence officers. They promptly told me I was crazy. Forced out of LAPD under threat of death by the end of 1978, I made complaints to LAPD's Internal Affairs division and to the L.A. office of the FBI, under the command of FBI SAC Ted Gunderson. I and my attorney wrote to politicians, Department of Justice, CIA, and contacted *L.A. Times.* FBI and LAPD said I was crazy. According to a 1981 two-part news story in the *Los Angeles Herald Examiner*, it was revealed the FBI had taken Teddy into custody and then released her, then classified their investigation.

"Former New Orleans Crime Commissioner Aaron Cohen told reporter Randall Sullivan, he found my description of events perfectly plausible after his 30 years of studying Louisiana's organized crime operations.

"Oct. 26, 1981 ... in the basement of the West Wing of the White House, I reported on what I had seen in New Orleans to my friend and UCLA classmate, Craig Fuller. Craig Fuller went on to become Chief of Staff to Vice President Bush from 1981 to 1985.

"In 1982, then UCLA political science professor Paul Jabber filled in many of the pieces in my quest to understand what I'd seen in New Orleans. He had served as a CIA and State Department consultant to Carter Administration. Paul explained that, after a 1975 treaty between the Shah of Iran and Saddam Hussein, the Shah had cut off all overt military support for Kurdish rebels fighting Saddam from the north of Iraq. In exchange, the Shah had gained access to the Shat al-Arab waterway so that he could multiply his oil exports and income. Not wanting to lose a long-term valuable asset in the Kurds, the CIA had then used Brown & Root ... which operated in both countries and maintained port facilities in the Persian Gulf and near Shat al-Arab, to re-arm the Kurds. The whole operation was financed with heroin. Paul was matter-of-fact about it.

"In 1983, Paul Jabber left UCLA to become a vice president of Banker's Trust, and chairman of the Middle East Dept. of the Council on Foreign Relations.

417

Anthony Kimery's, *In the Company of Friends,* continues.

"The Agency recruited scores of conservative business-people to volunteer their companies as 'fronts' for hiding the impending invasion against Castro. A number of veteran Cold Warriors, none of whom knows one another, are adamant in their respective claims that Bush worked for the Agency during this period. They tell similar disturbing stories about Bush having dirtied his hands 'doing the Company's bidding' as one put it. This allegation is buttressed by the internal records of a secret alumnus of former back-alley operations who confirms that contract mercenaries were indeed employed by Zapata.

"The Agency-industry fear, they might lose control of oil reserves in their 'backyard', was well-founded. On the heels of Castro's nationalization, Mexico, a country of more strategic and economic importance to the U.S. than Cuba, also moved to nationalize its oil industry. Concurrently, Mexico embarked on a massive economic expansion program which relied heavily on wooing foreign credits. One country which offered tantalizing loans and oil drilling expertise was the Soviet Union. The CIA was concerned that Soviets would establish a foothold in Mexico's oil industry. The U.S. oilmen were worried that they'd lose their profitable domination of Mexico's oil industry and, unable to stop the nationalization, they rushed in to snare lucrative business arrangements with PEMEX, Mexico's new state-owned oil monopoly.

"While most bid overtly for contracts, some oilmen worked closely with the large Mexico City CIA station. One corporation which benefited from the considerable leverage CIA held over certain Mexican officials running PEMEX, was Bush's Zapata Off-Shore Oil Company. By 1960, Agency assets had helped Bush erect the foundation for a secret and illegal oil drilling partnership on Mexican soil. In 1959, working through high-level officials of Dresser Industries, Bush teamed up with ranking Mexican officials whose offices were cooperating closely with the CIA Chief of Station in Mexico City.

"Meanwhile, Bush's friend George [Sergei] DeMohrenschildt, also was in the middle of CIA's scheme to ensure U.S. oil companies had advantage in Mexico ...and, U.S. dominance was not jeopardized by Soviets. DeMohrenschildt wined and dined PEMEX officials on behalf of Texas Eastern Corporation, a subsidiary of Houston-based Brown & Root Co., a multi-national engineering, construction, and oil conglomerate that had a lucrative natural gas contract with Mexico. Like Dresser, Brown & Root had long served as a cover for CIA operations, and was part of the powerful oil clique ...that would later throw money at the political ambitions of Richard Nixon, then George Bush.

"Were it not for the inadvertent discovery of a now nearly 30-year-old document that names 'George Bush' as a CIA employee, these ex-spooks' stories would be nothing more than just that, stories. But, it's precisely because of these tales that an official document indicating Bush worked for the CIA can't be ignored. The smoking paper was among nearly 100,000 pages of FBI documents on Kennedy's assassination that FBI released in 1977 and 1978 in response to lawsuits under the Freedom of Information Act. It sat undiscovered for almost a decade, until author Joseph McBride stumbled across it, and reported its existence in, *The Nation*, July 1988. Nov. 29, 1963 ... FBI Director J. Edgar Hoover wrote to the director of the State Department Bureau of Intelligence and Research ...whose staff traditionally included CIA officers. The document summarized oral briefings given on the day after Kennedy's murder to, 'Mr. George Bush of the Central Intelligence Agency and Captain William Edwards of the Defense Intelligence Agency by Mr. W.T. Forsyth of the Bureau'. It responded to State Department concern that, 'some misguided anti-Castro group might capitalize on the present situation and undertake an un-authorized raid against Cuba, believing that the assassination of President John F. Kennedy might herald a change in U.S. policy,' Hoover wrote.

"There is evidence that prior to Bush's appointment as DCI in 1976, he was well-acquainted with legendary spook, Theodore George 'Ted' Shackley, who joined the Agency in 1951. When Bush arrived on the scene at Langley, it was clear to long-time Agency insiders there was a bond between these two men that went back many years. Between 1974 and 1976, a sensitive period in U.S.-Chinese relations, Bush was Ambassador in Beijing and Shackley was Chief of CIA Far East Division. In 1976, shortly after he became DCI, without seeking advice, Bush promoted Shackley to Associate Deputy Director of Operations. In this position, he was second in command to the DDO, the third most powerful position in the CIA and one of the most pivotal in the entire government. Aside from their Agency connection, already cemented during Bush's previous tenure in Beijing, it's not hard to explain how the two men developed such a close bond.

For the previous ten years, Shackley was Chief Of Station In Vientiane & Saigon overseeing dozens of covert operations related to the Vietnam War. Before that, from 1952-1959 and again during 1965-1966, he worked in Germany. In 1962, before going into the jungles of Indochina, he returned for a three-year stint stateside as Station Chief in Miami, then the largest CIA station in the world ...and, the base of operations for the Agency's vast paramilitary operations against Castro following the Bay of Pigs disaster.

"A former CIA operative involved in anti-Castro activities commented. 'You've got George helping the Company's operation against Castro ...and here's Shackley, in charge of the Miami station that's running that show ...now, how do you think they know each other? Theirs was a close relationship, still is'.

"Under Bush's tenure as DCI at CIA, the two men worked together. Shackley oversaw Central America operations and established the infrastructure for Reagan-Bush White House adventures, a short time later. The veteran agent was catalyst for the notion of selling arms to Iran to free the hostages, and was also one of the architects of 'low-intensity conflict', the new name for CIA covert strategy in Central America. Shackley was forced out of the Agency in 1979, when an arms sales scandal involving him exploded. His relationship with Bush continued, and shorn of official CIA status, Shackley re-emerged in the early 1980s as an integral player in Iran-Contra. Throughout the early stages of those operations, Bush reportedly met with Shackley at Shackley's office in downtown Arlington.

"The appointment of Bush as director of Central Intelligence coincided with the Senate Intelligence Committee probe of Oswald's and Jack Ruby's connections to Cuba, the CIA, and the mob. With his own ties to those operations, Bush was now in charge of what CIA would and wouldn't divulge. As director of Central Intelligence, Bush frustrated committee investigators' requests for specific information in the Agency's files on Oswald and Ruby ...and, down-played revelations about CIA involvement. Bush knew the Agency had hidden, and was still hiding, information that contradicted the Warren Commission's verdict. Yet, in the wake of the furor over the movie, *JFK*, Bush commented. 'I've seen no evidence,' Bush said, "that's given me reason to believe Warren Commission was wrong."

<>

Peter Dale Scott finished up.

Paine's boss at Bell Aircraft as Director of Research and Development, was Nazi war criminal General Walter Dornberger. The first call to authorities after the gun went off on November 22, 1963, was from an employee at Bell Helicopter who suggested, "Oswald did it." Police never located the source of both Oswald addresses that day. Michael Paine took Lee to a meeting with General Edwin Walker shortly before the assassination. Soon Oswald would be charged with having shot Walker in April, and Walker would be calling his Nazi cronies in Germany 24 hours after JFK was killed, telling them he finally solved, "who shot through his window" seven months earlier ... the same Oswald.

Who were the Paines? To believe the Warren Commission and CIA staff of lawyers, they were Mr. and Mrs. Good Neighbor, all heart, altruistic. Ruth simply wanted to learn more Russian from a native. For that price, she housed Marina, a two-year-old daughter, a new infant, with all the fuss and mess of three extras in a tiny house. Michael Paine was a descendant of the Cabots on both sides. His cousin, Thomas Dudley Cabot, former president of United Fruit, had offered their Gibraltar Steamship as a cover for CIA during the Bay of Pigs. Another cousin was Alexander Cochrane Forbes, a director of United Fruit and trustee of Cabot, Cabot, & Forbes. Both Allen Dulles and John J. McCloy were part of the United Fruit team. The Paine family had links with circles of the OSS and CIA. Ruth Hyde Paine maintained close ties with the Forbes families. The patrician Paine and Forbes families ... [were] a far cry from the typical next door neighbor.

<> <> <>

It wasn't until I left the White House to retire, that one day back at the ranch, Nancy read Russ Bellant's article to me about who the people on the National Republican Heritage Groups Council really were. I felt bad about it ...when, I found out the people I was praising, were Nazi's and fascists. Of course, at the time there were a few newspaper articles making allegations. Nancy even warned me about not saying anything but, 'no comment', to the press ...so, I knew some of the council were dirty rats and punks ...so, I had a few words with George Bush over it, I think. I can't remember, now.

Winter 1990 Lou Wolf's, *Covert Action Information Bulletin* ran Russ Bellant's, *Old Nazis & the New Right, the Republican Party & Fascists*.

"It's May 17, 1985 ... Ronald Reagan has been

back in the nation's capitol less than two weeks after his much-criticized trip to the Bitsburg cemetery in West Germany. Floodlights and television cameras that are part of a President's entourage waiting at Shoreham Hotel, as are 400 luncheon guests. Reagan had recently characterized Nazi Waffen SS as, 'victims' ...and, these comments held special meaning for some of his afternoon luncheon guests. Although it was a Republican party affair, it wasn't the usual GOP set ...but, a special ethnic outreach unit, National Republican Heritage Groups Council, RHGC.

"National Republican Heritage Groups Council is an umbrella for various ethnic Republican clubs and operates under auspices of the Republican National Committee. It has a special type of outreach and appears to have consciously recruited some of its members and leaders from an Eastern European émigré network ...which includes anti-Semites, racists, authoritarians, and Fascists, including sympathizers and collaborators of Hitler's Third Reich, former Nazis, and even possible war criminals.

"The persons in this network are a part of the radical right faction of the ethnic communities they claim to represent. These anti-democratic, racist components of the National Republican Heritage Groups Council use anti-Communism as a cover for their views, while they operate as a de facto émigré Fascist network inside the Republican Party. Some unsavory personalities who were at the 1985 luncheon audience would later join the 1988 election presidential campaign of Vice President George Bush.

"This Fascist network within the Republican Party represents a small, significant element of the coalition that brought Ronald Reagan into the White House. It's from this network that the George Bush presidential campaign assembled its ethnic outreach unit in 1988, a unit that saw eight resignations by persons charged with anti-Semitism, racism, and Nazi collaboration.

"This network organizes support for its ideological agenda through national and international coalitions of like-minded constituencies which often work with other pro-Fascist forces. This broader coalition ranges from Axis allies and their apologists to friends and allies of contemporary dictatorships and authoritarian regimes.

"In the case of the Republican Heritage Groups Council, the nature of this network can be illustrated by briefly reviewing the backgrounds of some of the past and current leadership.

"Laszlo Pasztor was the founding chair and a key figure in the Council, Laszlo Pasztor began his political career in a Hungarian pro-Nazi party, served in Berlin at the end of World War II. He continues to be involved in ultra-rightist groups and Fascist networks while working with GOP.

"Radi Slavoff is the National Republican Heritage Groups Council executive director. Radi Slavoff is a member of a Bulgarian Fascist group, leader of the Bulgarian GOP unit of the Republican Heritage Groups Council. He was able to get the leader of his Bulgarian nationalist group an invitation to the White House, even though that leader was being investigated for concealing alleged World War II war crimes. He's active in other émigré Fascist groups.

"Nicolas Nazarenko is a former SS officer in the German SS Cossack Division during World War II. Nicolas Nazarenko heads the Cossack GOP unit of the Republican Heritage Groups Council and has declared, Jews are his 'ideological enemy'. He's still active with pro-Nazi elements in the U.S.

"Florian Galdau is a close associate and defender of Valerian Trifa ...the Romanian archbishop prosecuted for concealing his involvement in war crimes of the pro-Nazi Romanian Iron Guard ...charged by former Iron Guard members and others with being the east coast recruiter for the Iron Guard in the U.S., Galdau heads Republican Heritage Groups Council Romanian Republican unit.

"Philip A. Guarino is a honorary American member of the conspiratorial P-2 Masonic Lodge of Italy, which plotted in the early 1970s to overthrow the Italian government to install a dictatorship. Philip A. Guarino, an Italian Republican Heritage Groups Council member and Republican National Committee advisor, offered aid to P-2 members being investigated.

"Anna Chennault is a newly-elected Republican Heritage Groups Council Chairperson and funder of the Chinese Republican affiliate, which for years has been closely linked to the authoritarian Taiwan Regime.

"The names of all but one of the persons appeared on invitational literature for the October 1987 meeting of National Republican Heritage Groups Council in Washington, D.C. This is one of the Fascist networks inside the Republican party brought into the White House along with Ronald Reagan ...and, the George Bush campaign assembled in its Ethnic Outreach Unit, in 1988.

"Many Republican Heritage Groups Council leaders of Central and Eastern European nationalities were part of the post-World War II immigration from displaced persons camps. It would be unfair to suggest a majority of those Eastern and Central Europeans were anti-Semites or Fascists ...most displaced persons were victims of the war who played no role in collaborating with Nazism. Yet, quite a few persons in the displaced persons camp were there as political escapees to avoid consequences of their collaboration with the German occupation of Eastern Europe and the Soviet Union.

"The Displaced Persons Commission, which worked from 1948-1952, arranged for 400,000 persons to come into the U.S. Initially, it sought to bar members of pro-Nazi groups, but in 1950 a dramatic reversal took place. The Commission declared 'the Baltic Legion was not a movement hostile to the Government of the United States'. Baltic Legion was known as, Baltic Waffen SS.

"The Waffen SS participated in liquidation of Jews in the Baltic region ...the SS units were comprised of Hitler's loyal henchmen, recruited from Fascist political groups long tied to the German Nazi Party. Anyone opposed to German occupation of the Baltic region ... Latvia, Lithuania, and Estonia, was likely to meet cruel death at their hands.

"The Baltic Legion was now welcomed to come to the U.S. to become American citizens ... pro-Nazi elements from other parts of Europe came to the U.S. through nominally private groups associated with the Commission. In 1952, the Commission completed work. The Eisenhower-Nixon presidential campaign was on, Republicans said, Democrats were 'soft on Communism'. Talk of 'liberating' Eastern Europe became part of the GOP message.

"That year, the Republican National Committee formed an Ethnic Division. Displaced Fascists, hoping to be returned to power by an Eisenhower-Nixon 'liberation' policy, were among those who signed on. They'd become an embryo forming the Republican Heritage Groups Council, in 1969. In a sense, the foundation of Republican Heritage Groups Council lay in Hitler's networks in Eastern Europe before World War II. In Eastern European countries, German SS set up, or funded, political action organizations that helped form SS militias during the war.

"In Hungary, the Arrow Cross was the Hungarian SS affiliate ...in Romania, the Iron Guard ...in Bulgaria, the Bulgarian Legion ...in Ukraine, Organization of Ukrainian Nationalists ...in Latvia, the Latvian Legion ...in Byelorussia (White Russia), the Byelorussian Belarus Brigade ...all were SS-linked.

"In their respective countries, they were expected to serve the interests of the German Nazi Party before and during the war. Not all Eastern and Central Europeans were Nazi collaborators who participated in atrocities, but Right-Wing elements from every Eastern European nationality tied their nationalistic goals to Fascism, and Hitler's racist Nazism.

"The founding chair of the Republican Heritage Groups Council was Laszlo Pasztor, an activist in various Hungarian rightist and Nazi-linked groups. In World War II, Pasztor was a member of the youth group of Arrow Cross, Hungarian equivalent of German Nazi Party. When Pasztor came to the U.S. in the 1950s, he joined GOP's Ethnic Division. A leader of the 1968 Nixon-Agnew campaign's Ethnic Unit, Pasztor says Nixon promised him, if he won the election, he'd form a permanent ethnic council within GOP, as the Ethnic Division was only active during presidential campaigns. Pasztor was made organizer of the Council, after Nixon's victory.

"Pasztor claims, 'It was my job to identify 25 ethnic groups' to bring into Republican Heritage Groups Council. 'In 1972, we used the Council as the skeleton to build the Heritage Groups to re-elect the President'.

"Pasztor's choices filling émigré slots, as the Council formed, included Nazi-collaborationist organizations already mentioned. Each organization formed a Republican federation, with local clubs around the country. The local clubs of the various federations then formed State multi-ethnic councils. Today, there are thirty-four nationality federations and twenty-five State councils that make up National Republican Heritage Groups Council.

"According to National Republican Heritage Groups Council delegates interviewed during the May 1985 conference, in setting up the Council, Pasztor went to various collaborationist and Fascist-minded émigré groups, asked them to form GOP federations. It became clear it wasn't an accident people with Nazi associations were in Republican Heritage Groups Council. Sometimes mainstream ethnic organizations were passed over in favor of smaller but more extremist groups. And, it seemed clear the Republican National Committee knew with whom they are dealing.

"One organization Pasztor approached to form RHGC was Bulgarian National Front ...headed by Ivan Docheff. As early as 1971, GOP was warned, National Front was beyond the pale. A Jack Anderson column quoted a Bulgarian-

American organization ...the conservative Bulgarian National Committee ...that labeled Docheff's National Front as, 'Fascist'.

"Neither GOP nor the Nixon campaign took action. Professor Spas T. Raikin, ex-Secretary General of American Friends of the Anti-Bolshevik Bloc of Nations, and a former National Front official, says the group grew out of an organization in Bulgaria in the 1930s and 1940s that was 'pro-Nazi and pro-Fascist'. Docheff, age 83, is semi-retired from GOP activity ...the National Front is now represented by Radi Slavoff, Republican Heritage Groups Council executive director and head of the Bulgarian GOP federation. Slavoff also represents the National Front in other Washington D.C. area coalitions, including one that is Nazi-linked. While Docheff was representing National Front, Justice Department's Office of Special Investigations was investigating him for possible war crimes he was suspected of committing while he was mayor of a German-occupied city in Bulgaria. Docheff denies he ever committed war crimes, and OSI never brought charges.

"Docheff's political history, however, is not in dispute. Founder of a Bulgarian youth group in the early 1930s, Docheff met with Adolf Hitler and the Nazi movement's leading philosopher, Alfred Rosenberg, in 1934 ...shortly after the Nazis came to power. Docheff then established the Bulgarian Legion, a pro-Hitler group agitating for government action against Bulgarian Jews.

"Romanian-American Republicans are led by a retired priest who in 1984 said, the most important issue for Romanian Republicans is stopping 'the deportation of our beloved spiritual leader, Archbishop Valerian Trifa'. Faced with charges by OSI he participated in the murder of Jews as part of a coup plot in Bucharest, Romania in 1941, Trifa left the U.S. in 1984. But, his political network stayed behind him. The Romanian Republican priest, Florian Galdau, is part of that network. After the war, Trifa was able to come to the U.S. and take over the Romanian Orthodox Church by physical coercion and administrative help from the U.S. Government. In 1952, Trifa became an Archbishop of the Romanian Orthodox Church. FBI documents from 1954-1955 ... used in the prosecution of Trifa ...show Trifa 'is bringing Iron Guard members into the U.S. and installing them as priests'. One of these priests, according to a document, according to a Oct. 5, 1955 document, was Florian Galdau ...whom an FBI source described as a 'Romanian Iron Guard member who at Trifa's

instructions was elected Pastor of St. Dumitru,' a Manhattan parish.

"Some Republican Heritage Groups Council members have close allies in Italy who plotted to overthrow the government and re-install Fascism in Rome. Italy's problems with Fascism are much more recent than World War II. In 1982, Italian authorities uncovered a conspiracy in which groups of business, political, Mafia, military, and Vatican-connected figures planned to overthrow Italian parliamentary democracy and install a dictatorship.

"The group, P-2 Masonic Lodge, had a thousand members. P-2 members included heads of intelligence agencies, thirty-eight generals and admirals, and three cabinet officers ...financial scandals brought European press coverage, the collapse of the Italian government, and a parliamentary inquiry. One American involved was Philip A. Guarino, 79, an adviser on senior citizens' affairs to Republican National Committee, who was long active in Italian GOP politics. A theology student in Mussolini's Italy in the late 1920s-1930s, Guarino helped establish the ethnic division of the GOP in 1952. He was vice-chair of the Republican Heritage Groups Council from 1971-1975. He attended the 1985 Council convention to ensure that his friend, Frank Stella, won the Council chairmanship, in a tight race with former Cleveland mayor Ralph Perk. Guarino was described in, *St. Peter's Banker*, a book about P-2, as an 'honorary member of P-2'. Another member of P-2 was Jose Lopez Riga, founder of the Latin American death-squad group ...the Argentine Anti-Communist Alliance. Guarino participated in John Connally's 'Committee for Defense of the Mediterranean', distributing propaganda against the Italian Communist Party, a supposed threat to the West. Connally was Nixon's Treasury Secretary and a member of the President's Foreign Intelligence Advisory Board ...under Nixon and Gerald Ford. In 1978, Guarino's friend Frank Stella became national Chair of the 'Heritage National Committee of Connally for President', when Connally sought the 1980 GOP nomination for president'. Stella later got on track for Ronald Reagan.

"Mark Valente, a Stella protégé and suburban Detroit City Council member now serving as a Republican National Committee Ethnic Liaison staffer says, 'Everyone at the White House knows Frank.' Stella's name has gone through the White House appointment process on several occasions. In 1981, he was nominated for the little-known, Intelligence Oversight Board, which monitors legalities of covert operations of the intelligence agencies. He withdrew his name after it had been publicly released. In 1983, he was made a White House Fellow. Stella was being considered for Ambassador to Italy in 1985, but withdrew his name again, according to Valente.

"Chinese-American and Asian-American Republican federations are led by Anna Chennault, who gained fame in the 1950s-1960s as an advocate of Chiang Kai-Shek's Taiwan dictatorship. Both federations appear to be little more than adjuncts to Taiwan government activities in the U.S. This was highlighted at the 1985 Republican Heritage Groups Council convention when an official Taiwan Republican Heritage Groups Council delegation arrived at the meeting as part of a nation-wide tour belatedly celebrating Reagan's second inauguration four months earlier. While the foremost visitor from Taiwan was the Deputy Minister for National Defense, the honorary president of the delegation was Ben John Chen, who also chairs the Asian-American Republican Federation. Other Chinese and Asian GOP federation members are part of trade groups linked to Taiwan. The Republican Heritage Groups Council agenda was interrupted at the Chinese federation's request, so the delegation could present awards from the Taiwan government to Michael Sotirhos, the outgoing Republican Heritage Groups Council chair ...who later became Reagan's ambassador to Jamaica. Also receiving an award from the Taiwan regime was Anna Chennault, who funds the Asian-American GOP federation, according to Chen. Chennault became Republican Heritage Groups Council chair in 1987.

"The Republican Heritage Groups Council's ethnicity is broad, ranging from Albanians to Vietnamese. But two groups are missing at the Republican Heritage Groups Council ...there are no African-American Republican or Jewish Republican federations.

"Remarks by a number of delegates at the 1986 Republican Heritage Groups Council meeting made it clear there was no desire to have either community represented on the Council. Republican leaders say African-American and Jewish relations are 'special', and are dealt with in separate GOP units.

"Key issues for every Eastern European Heritage Council leader interviewed were foreign policy issues. All of them called for more support for Radio Free Europe and Radio Liberty. Most called for the abandonment of the Yalta

Agreement ...the major treaty that set the post-war features of Europe ...and all want a far more aggressive foreign policy against Soviet Union.

"The most public activity the Republican Heritage Groups Council participates in are the annual 'Captive Nations' rallies held in cities across the U.S. 'Captive Nations' is the term used to describe countries which have Communist governments.

Former Groups Council Chairman Michael Sotirhos said in an interview that, 'The Council was the linchpin of the Reagan-Bush ethnic campaign ...The decision to use the Republican Heritage Groups was made at a campaign strategy meeting that included Paul Laxalt, Frank Fahrenkopf, Ed Rollins, and others '. He claims 86,000 volunteers for Reagan-Bush were recruited through the Republican Heritage Groups Council. The GOP can't be ignorant of the backgrounds of their ethnic leaders. When Nixon was encouraging the growth of the Republican Heritage Groups Council in 1971, Jack Anderson did a series of reports on the pro-Nazi backgrounds of various GOP ethnic advisors. Included in the reports were Ivan Docheff and Laszlo Pasztor. Nov. 1971, *Washington Post* did a story on Fascist elements coming into the GOP. Aug. 2, 1988 ... key figures in the Council were named as leaders of the George Bush presidential campaign's ethnic outreach arm, the Coalition of American Nationalities, including Anna Chennault, Walter Meliahnovich, Laszlo Pasztor, Frank Stella, Radi Slavoff, Philip Guarino, and Florian Galdau. Other persons on the Bush ethnic panel with questionable views or pasts were Bohdan Fedorak and Akselis Mangulis.

"Sept. 1988, Pasztor, Slavoff, Guarino, Galdau, Fedorak, Brentar, and Ignatius Illinsky resigned from the Bush panel following revelations about their pasts or views appearing in, *Jewish Week, Philadelphia Inquirer,* and the extended version of this article which was published by Political Research Associates. Bush adviser Fred Malek resigned from the Bush campaign after *Washington Post* named him as compiling lists, on orders from the Nixon White House, of Jews working at the Labor Bureau of Statistics.

"In early November, *Philadelphia Inquirer* raised questions about a Latvian member of Coalition of American Nationalities, which prompted the final resignation, that of Akselis Mangulis, charged with having belonged to the pro-Nazi Latvian Legion which had connections to the SS. While Bush campaign spokespersons pledged, there'd be an investigation into the backgrounds and views of the Coalition of American Nationalities members whose resignations it had announced, no serious investigation ever took place, and the campaign repeatedly referred to the charges as unsubstantiated politically-motivated smears. Several of the persons who'd been reported as resigning, told journalists they'd never been asked to resign and considered themselves still active with the Bush campaign. Furthermore, Guarino, Slavoff, Galdau, and Pasztor are still active with Republican Heritage Groups Council.

"President Bush defended Galdau, Pasztor, Guarino, and Slavoff as innocent of all accusations of collaboration, and insisted they're all honorable men. But, the historical record belied his assertions.

"GOP for decades has misread ethnic Americans' concerns about crime, employment, anti-ethnic discrimination, and the future of its youth. It has offered instead the Fascism and ethnic prejudices of the Republican Heritage Groups Council, which focuses primarily on funding Radio Free Europe and stopping Justice Department prosecutions of Nazi-era war criminals who illegally entered the country," Russ Bellant said.

New York Times, Sep. 9, 1988, Richard Burke's, *Bush panelist ousted, denies anti-Jewish ties.*

"The campaign of Vice President Bush dismissed a member of a panel meant to enlist support among ethnically-diverse groupings late today. Mark Goodin, a campaign spokesman, said the panel member, Jerome A. Brantar, was dismissed after it was learned he'd been active in efforts to defend John Demonque, a one-time Cleveland auto worker appealing a sentence of death by an Israeli court, that found he committed atrocities as a guard at Treblinka death camp in Poland.

"Mr. Cooper confirmed *Jewish Week's* description of two other men, Eflauian Galdao and Philip Guarino.

"Mr. Galdao, a Romanian Orthodox priest is described in a *Jewish Week* article as New York Chief of the Iron Guard, wartime-Romania's anti-Semitic pro-Nazi movement.

"Several former members of Saint Dumetrou, which was Mr. Galdao's church in Manhattan, said they left the congregation 'because of Galdao's Iron Guard-related activities'. No one answered the phone at the church, today. Mr. Guarino is a Vice Chairman of the Bush Campaign Panel, and is a former Roman Catholic priest who is described by the Jewish and Nazi-

hunting groups as a member of P-2, a group in Italy led by Lizo Gelli, a known Fascist with whom Mr. Guarino is said to be very close.

"Another co-chairman is Laszlo Pasztor, a Hungarian-American who as a young man, according to the article, served in Hungary's pro-Nazi, anti-Semitic government as a junior envoy to Berlin, but has since said, he regrets his involvement. Mr. Guarino, who lives in Washington, did not return calls to his office at the Republican National Committee, where he is the party's senior citizen liaison representative, a full-time, salaried post," Burke said.

Christopher Simpson's, *Blowback, American's Recruitment of Nazis and its Effects on the Cold War,* researched 'Captive Nations'.

"Assembly of Captive European Nations began as what appeared as a clever propaganda project, an appropriate counterpart to the Crusade for Freedom. In the end, it became a political force to be reckoned with on the American far-Right …and the radical Right in turn remains a very real force in Washington D.C.

"Exiled leaders have not disappeared and some such groups have won open support of the Reagan Administration. Captive Nations activists have been particularly strong in the National Republican Heritage Group's Nationalities Council, led by conservative activist Frank Stella.

"This national GOP organization embraces several score of conservative ethnic organizations and state coalitions that tend to identify with the Far-Right-Wing of the party.

"While the large majority of organizations in Republican Nationalities Council are respectable … the council has become fertile ground for political organizing by former Nazi collaborators still active in immigrant communities in this country. Perhaps part of the reason for this is that the director of the council during the early 1970's was Laszlo Pasztor, a naturalized American of Hungarian descent, who served during the war as a junior envoy in Berlin for the genocidal Hungarian Arrow Cross Regime of Frank Celazy. Pasztor, in an interview with reporter Les Whitten, insisted he did not participate in anti-Semitic activities during the war. Furthermore he says, he's attempted to weed-out extreme Right-Wing groups from among the GOP's Ethnics. But, the record of Pasztor's 'house-cleaning' leaves much to be desired.

"The GOP Nationalities Council has provided an entry into the White House for several self-styled immigrant leaders with records as pro-Nazi extremists.

"Bulgarian-American-Republican-Party notable Ivan Docheff, who served as an officer of the Republican Party's Ethnic Council for years ... has acknowledged he was once a leader in the National Legion of Bulgaria, a group the more moderate, Bulgarian National Committee, in the U.S. described as 'Fascist'. He spent twelve years as chair of the influential New York City Captive Nations Committee, and being President of the Bulgarian National Front. Docheff describes himself as, '100% anti-communist, not a Nazi' ...and, was invited to the White House to share a Captive Nations prayer breakfast with President Nixon.

"A half-dozen similar cases among Republican Ethnics may be readily identified. The official Latvian-American organization in the GOP's Nationalities Council, is Latvian-American Republican National Federation, which was led for years by Dagment Hazners, the president, and Evar Berzins, secretary. During the 1970s, the group shared the same office and telephone number in East Brunswick, New Jersey, with the 'Committee for a Free Latvia'. The latter group was led for most of the last decade by the now-familiar, Velis Hasnurs, president ...and, Alfred Bershings, treasurer and secretary ... despite accusations aired by 60 Minutes and other media ... that both were responsible for serious crimes during the war. Their associate, Evar Bershins, is noted as a proponent of the campaign to halt prosecutions of fugitive Nazi war criminals in the United States. The intimate ties between these two organizations and their leaderships raise legitimate questions concerning what the political agenda of the Republican organization may actually be.

"Perhaps most disturbing, GOP Ethnic Council has passed resolutions on racial and religious questions sponsored by an openly pro-Nazi, anti-Semitic activist on three occasions in recent years. The author of these resolutions is worthy of note, if only as an indication of the degree of racial extremism the Republican organization's been willing to tolerate in its ranks. His name is Nicolas Nazarenko ... self-styled leader of the World Federation of Cossacks, National Liberation of Cossacks, and Cossack-American National Federation, an organization that's a member of the Republican's Ethnic Council.

"The Republican Party's Cossack organization describes itself as a 'division' of the World Federation, and shares the same leadership, letterhead and post office box address in Baluwelt, New York as World Federation group.

"Nazarenko admitted in an interview with me, he spent much of World War II as an interrogator of POWs for SS in Romania.

"Nazarenko's speech at 1984 Captive Nations Ceremonial Dinner in New York left little to the imagination about his own point of view, or that of his audience. He spoke of what was, in his mind, the heroism of Eastern European collaborators in German legions, during the war. He spoke of why, in his mind, the Nazis lost the war. 'There's a certain ethnic group that today makes its home in Israel,' Nazarenko told the gathering. 'This ethnic group works with the communists all the time. They were the fifth column in Germany ...and, in all the 'captive nations'. They would spy, sabotage and do any act in the interest of Moscow,' he claimed. 'Of course there had to be the creation of a natural self-defense against this fifth column,' Nazarenko said, referring to the Nazi concentration camps. 'They had to be isolated ... security was needing. So the fifth column was arrested and imprisoned,' Nazarenko said," Simpson reported.

◇ ◇ ◇

Nancy read many hours to me of Loftus & Aarons', *Secret War Against the Jews*, an intelligence history of the 20th Century.

After World War II, Americans stayed behind to run administrations of defeated Axis countries.

General MacArthur remained behind to rule Japan. General Lucius Clay remained behind to rule Germany. James Jesus Angleton remained behind to rule Italy.

James Jesus Angleton headed post-war American intelligence ...and, rebuilt Italy's intelligence community. Praised for keeping communists from taking over post-War Italy, James Jesus purged partisan communist heroes who defeated Hitler and Mussolini from Italy civil and state government. James Jesus became CIA Chief of Counterintelligence, praised for keeping communists from invading America during the Cold War. President Gerald Ford awarded James Jesus the highest Intelligence Award.

In the 1930s, Allen Dulles met Hugh Angleton, the son of James Jesus Angleton. Dulles recruited James Jesus, and Hugh, to smuggle German agents and Nazi war treasure through the Vatican's rat-line out of Europe. James Jesus Angleton turned in false intelligence reports, claiming they were from Vatican Intelligence. Hugh lived in Mussolini's Italy ...and, promoted Mussolini's concept of 'the Corporate State', where all 'good' derived from helping to promote the corporation. Mussolini defined Fascism, as

425

'Corporatism'. Hugh considered President Roosevelt a socialist.

Dulles and his Nazi clients spent a lot of time during World War II in the Swiss city of Lugano. Hugh lived in Milan in Italy, not far from Lugano. Hugh was an international banker brokering deals, and representing National Cash Register NCR in Europe. One of the directors sitting on the NCR board of directors had previously held an important senior management position in Allen Dulles' law firm, Sullivan & Cromwell. Hugh connected far-Right members of State Department with far-right businessmen in Italy.

Hugh was a counterintelligence agent supplying information to the U.S, *his* son later insisted. Hugh's investments in Mussolini's Italy were lost when Mussolini and Hitler declared war on the U.S. Hugh volunteered to join OSS, was assigned to counterintelligence branch of OSS, X-2, and had contacts in Mussolini's Fascist government. In post-War Italy, Hugh worked directly under OSS Commander Colonel Clifton Carter.

According to authors and intelligencers Loftus and Aarons, the Vatican Intelligence liaison in the Balkans during the War was the Bosnia-Croat Catholic priest, Krunoslav Draganovic.

Draganovic smuggled Nazi gold bars through Vatican's rat-lines safely out of Europe. Slovenian Catholic Bishop Gregory Rozman was a Nazi intelligence operative and propagandist stationed in Bern Switzerland, by friends of Dulles in U.S. Intelligence. Bishop Rozman was sent to smuggle Nazi gold and Nazi-owned Western currency out of Swiss banks, to Nazis hiding in Argentina. When U.S. Army start tracing Dulles' Swiss bank accounts to the Vatican, Dulles' friends in State Department stopped the investigation, as did intelligence officer James Jesus Angleton, Dulles' protégé stationed in Italy. After a car accident, Hugh was re-assigned out of OSS X-2. But, his son, James Jesus, petitioned James Murphy, head of X-2 ...to be admitted. James Jesus was posted to Italy in Oct. 1944 as Commander of Special Counterintelligence Unit Z SCI-Z, British and American intelligencers and operatives. British intelligencers helped Dulles keep Third Reich war booty treasure out of Soviet hands.

During World War II, British MI-6 and the Vatican had worked together trying to arrange a coup d'état against Hitler as grounds to enlist Germany as a Christian West ally to fight against Stalin's Soviet Russia. The Dulles brothers and Hugh Angleton were also promoting a Christian West concept to save their Nazi portfolio from being seized by the Allies. Meanwhile, the Pope was trying to negotiate a peace featuring the Allies, Germany, Italy, and Japan ... all uniting to fight Soviet Union.

British intelligence had a double-agent, father-son team too.

Just as America had Hugh and James Angleton, MI-6 had Jack Philby, and his son, Kim. Jack Philby was one of the most influential figures in the early 20th Century. He met Ibn Saud, an Arab terrorist leading one of many rival Arab clans, eventually he and Dulles made Ibn Saud king of Saudi Arabia. Jack was a rogue British intelligence agent. He stole British intelligence files that allowed him to arrange Ibn Saud control over Moslem's most holy shrines, sold the information, sold Ibn Saud, sold Saudi Arabia, sold-out the British Empire ... making Saudi Arabia a U.S. petroleum community stronghold under control of Allen Dulles.

British intelligence watched America enter the Axis oil market. Saudi Arabian House of Ibn Saud was represented by Jack Philby.

Together Jack Philby, Allen Dulles, and King Ibn Saud made ownership of petroleum a weapon against 99% of humanity. Jack Philby's son, Kim, was a Soviet double agent who pretended to work for British Intelligence MI-6.

Loftus and Aarons continue.

Meanwhile, while Britain's Winston Churchill was fighting Nazis, some of England's royal ruling families, such as former King Edward VIII the Duke of Windsor, was a Nazi spy. Post-war questioning by American intelligence of Third Reich Foreign Minister Joachim Ribbentrop confirmed Duke of Windsor and other members of the British royal family sided with their German cousins.

In 1939, Sir Steward Menzies succeeded Admiral Sinclair as Chief of British Secret Service. Menzies continued negotiations with Germany, that Admiral Sinclair had started with the Third Reich.

Menzies approved the Vatican Nazi treasure rat-line to Spain, and to Dulles in Switzerland. Menzies had British troops help the Vatican transport Nazi war booty into hiding. After World War II, Menzies gave Nazi Intelligence Chief Walter Schellenberg, and other Nazi negotiators trying to negotiate a separate peace with Britain, safe harbor in Great Britain ...then, gave Kim Philby the go-ahead to recruit Nazi intelligencers as British operatives, smuggle them through the Vatican to South America, and to the Mid-East into Syria and Egypt ...and, to employ Nazis and Fascists on-the-run from Allied authorities in

Eastern Europe, as British-paid mercenaries.

Meanwhile, Stalin remembered how he'd made a treaty with Hitler in 1939, 'the Molotov-Ribbentrop Non-Aggression Pact of 1939'. So, Stalin thought Britain and U.S. might form a post-War alliance with Germany against Russia.

From 1944-1977, Kim Philby sent distorted intelligence information …disinformation …to American intelligence, to influence the Western response. In Italy and Austria, Kim knew the West planned to counter Communist coups d'états aggressively …so, he advised sacrificing those regions. In Albania, Poland, and Czechoslovakia when the Western response to Kim's disinformation indicated the West would not offer resistance to Soviet Communist coup d'états, Kim told the Soviets to go full speed ahead. At the same time, Kim used the Vatican Intelligence network to recruit Eastern Europe Catholic Fascists to work for Western intelligence …as anti-communist 'freedom fighters' …employing those mercenaries as intelligence moles reporting back to him, consequently back to Soviet Union.

By 1945, Allen Dulles had maneuvered his Nazi investments into safety, retired from OSS, returning to Wall Street to launder money for his Nazi clientele. Dulles laundered money for Thomas McKittrick, head of the Bank of International Settlements BIS.

BIS transferred Nazi assets into Switzerland …then, after the war moved assets through Vatican rat-lines into Argentina, where Allen Dulles represented Argentine corporations and cartels. Argentine Dictator Juan Peron was a pro-fascist Catholic anti-communist. Argentina was the only South American country remaining pro-Axis, and the Argentine economy prospered greatly with infusions of Nazi war booty.

By 1947, U.S. intelligence referred to the British-Vatican Nazi smuggling and Nazi gold smuggling operation as, the 'rat-line'. Alan Dulles and protégé James Jesus Angleton continued to hide from Army Counter-Intelligence-Corps the existence of the British-Vatican smuggling operation, and the Vatican's top agent, Catholic Father Draganovic and his headquarters, in Rome. Draganovic was a fervent Croatian nationalist. Draganovic was a scholar, as well as a Priest. In 1939, he edited the *General Register of the Catholic Church in Yugoslavia*. At that time, he was Dean of Oriental Studies, at University of Sarajevo, as well as Secretary to the Archbishop in Sarajevo. In 1941, in Rome, Draganovic was an ecclesiastical advisor … Draganovic went to Rome

in 1943. In 1947, State Department, under the influence of the Dulles brothers, agreed to participate in Nazi smuggling operations.

U.S. intelligence at Fort Hunt had previously hired Reinhard's Eastern Front Intelligence Network, it became, 'the Gehlen Org'. The Gehlen Org was used to smuggle Nazi and Fascist war criminals out of Eastern Europe …and, to recruit them as anti-communist mercenary 'freedom-fighters'. These 'freedom fighters' included Ante Pavelic's Croatian Ustasche terrorist death squad, 'freedom fighters'.

Vatican intelligence agent Bosnia-Croatian Catholic Father Draganovic was a double agent with British intelligence. In 1947, the Army Counterintelligence Corps verified that Ante Pavelic was living in the Vatican. Pavelic was being chauffeured around Rome in a limousine with Vatican license plates. From their interviews with Army Counterintelligence Corps CIC personnel, Loftus and Aarons reported that in 1947 the State Department made a deal to fund anti-communist, Nazi and Fascist smuggling operations of Father Draganovic with the British. Croatian Ustasche pro-Nazi terrorists operated the Vatican rat-line for James Jesus Angleton.

Allen Dulles, James Jesus Angleton, and the Vatican Sovereign Military Order of Malta smuggled Eastern European Nazis into the U.S., Australia, and Canada. In those countries, the right-wing claimed to use them to help rally the ethnic vote.

In the U.S., Richard Nixon ran the political recruitment campaign of Eastern European Nazi and Fascist émigré. Congressman Nixon was a protégé of Allen Dulles. Dulles convinced Nixon that Governor Dewey lost the presidential election of 1948 because of the Jewish vote. In 1952, Senator Nixon became President Eisenhower's Vice President. Vice President Nixon's handlers had him form an Ethnic Division within the Republican National Committee, recruiting Eastern European fascist émigré that hoped President Eisenhower would pursue an aggressive anti-Communist rollback-liberation Christian West strategy Dulles helped engineer, in order to return them to power in their homelands.

In 1953, during the Eisenhower & Nixon Administration, U.S. immigration laws were changed to admit Nazis and SS into the U.S. Vice President Nixon shepherded the immigration program. Nixon wanted to gather enough anti-Semitic votes to cancel-out the Jewish vote threat Allen Dulles warned him about. Croatian Nazis found a welcome mat extended to them. In 1968, Richard Nixon promised that if he won the presidential election, he'd allow the Ethnic Division of the Republican Committee to function full-time, not just in election years. George Bush was Chairman of Republican National Committee from 1972-1974.

Loftus and Aarons continued.

In 1974, James Jesus Angleton had risen in his career to be one of the senior officers of the CIA. His job was Head of Counterintelligence, his job responsibility was to keep CIA safe from Communist mole operations from foreign governments. He was fired, because he went insane, having paranoid delusions there were communists inside CIA, actually hiding somewhere in his office, trying to get him. He was re-hired two years later.

In early 1940s, Israeli intelligence learned Angleton was smuggling Nazis and Nazi war booty through the Vatican ...and, helping to launder Nazi money ... at a time when it was not otherwise known. Israeli intelligence, Zionist Intelligence Agency (preceding Mossad), blackmailed Angleton, 'turning him' to become an Israeli double-agent inside CIA. James Jesus Angleton later managed CIA's Israeli intelligence operation, while he was a Mossad intelligence mole.

<>

James Vincent Forrestal, 1892–1949, was Secretary of the Navy and first U.S. Defense Secretary, 1947–1949. After college, Forrestal went to work as a bond salesman for Dillon, Read & Co. When World War I broke out, he enlisted in the Navy ...and, became a naval aviator, training with Royal Flying Corps in Canada. During the final year of WWI, Forrestal spent time in Washington, D.C. at the office of Naval Operations, while completing flight training. Following the war, Forrestal returned to Dillon, Read & Co., earning a partnership in 1923, before becoming president of the company in 1937. Forrestal brought Socal and Texaco together in 1935. Forrestal was the Vice President of General Aniline & Film, a subsidiary of I.G. Farben, a Nazi military-industrial war complex giant.

Forrestal was a compulsive workaholic who was abusive to his family. His wife Josephine developed alcohol and mental problems.

Loftus & Aarons researched James Forrestal.

Secretary of State James V. Forrestal was part of President Truman's Cabinet and, a mole for Allen Dulles inside the Truman Administration. Forrestal was part of a State Department intelligence group that wanted to prevent the formation of the State of Israel. Defense Secretary Forrestal helped Allen Dulles bring Nazis into the U.S. Defense Secretary Forrestal later learned, many Nazi and fascist émigré anti-communist 'freedom-fighters' he helped bring into the U.S., were Communist intelligence moles.

Then, Defense Secretary James Forrestal went insane ...he later killed himself.

Frank Wisner was used by Allen Dulles. Wisner, under Dulles' argument of fighting Communism, hired anti-communist Nazis ...who, later turned out to be Communist moles, following in footsteps as Forrestal had done under the influence of Dulles.

Frank Wisner killed himself.

Frank Wisner's daughter spoke with Aarons and Loftus. Wendy Wisner felt bitter.

"Allen Dulles used my father," Wendy Wisner said.

Loftus and Aarons recorded their observations.

Our sources say Wendy Wisner was correct. Her father was one of many decent men, neither fools nor bigots, who devoted themselves to the cause of rolling-back Communism, only to be ensnared in Dulles brothers' corporate agenda.

As Paul Nitze later admitted, Dulles' hard-line anti-Communism was largely for domestic consumption. Other sources from the Eisenhower era agree, the Dulles brothers were frauds ...and, their campaign to use American intelligence for private profit ruined the careers, even the lives, of many people, Loftus and Aarons said.

Loftus and Aarons continued their research.

In order to curry favor with the Arabs, the Nixon White House ordered National Security Agency to suppress information that an Arab sneak attack against Israel would take place on Yom Kippur Oct. 6, 1973.

Kissinger's strategy was to let Israel get bloodied ...then, force both sides to the peace table. Kissinger underestimated the consequences to Israel of delays in intelligence, mobilization, and re-supply, which nearly caused a military catastrophe. The man who saved Israel from Kissinger's blunders was Nixon White House Chief of Staff Alexander Haig. The man who became the scapegoat for Kissinger's blunders was the CIA Counterintelligence Chief James Jesus Angleton.

<>

Lyndon LaRouche's *Executive Intelligence Review EIR* looked at Henry Kissinger.

In 1982, Henry Kissinger formed Kissinger Associates, a consulting firm advising corporations and governments on policy. Partners and

associates at Kissinger Associates included
Lawrence Eagleburger,
Brent Scowcroft,
Robert Anderson,
Lord Carrington,
Pehr Gyllenhammar,
Sir Y.K. Kan,
William Dill Rodgers,
William E. Simon, and
Eric Roll.

A 1994 Lyndon LaRouche *EIR* report by Joseph Brewda, Marcia Merry, Jeffrey Steinberg, Scott Thompson, Charles Tuttle, and Christopher White looked at Henry Kissinger.

"Kissinger Associates was formed through loans provided by the New York investment houses of ...Warburg ...Pincus ...and, Goldman-Sachs. Its main patrons and controllers are Warburg banking interests, with S.G. Warburg chairman Lord Roll, a partner of the firm and Lord Carrington, former NATO Secretary General and fellow board member of Hollinger Corp., also on Kissinger Associates' board.

"While British press was after President Clinton's scalp for months ...the center of the Clinton-gate assault is at headquarters of Hollinger Corp. ... originally called, Argus Corp., established as an outgrowth of World War II British Special Operations Executive SOE, by one of Britain's top Economic Warfare experts. Paralleling the postwar creation of Argus Corp., British SOE intelligencer Louis Mortimer Bloomfield created a string of Canadian-based postwar intelligence proprietary companies, including British American Canadian Corp., and Permindex (Permanent Industrial Expositions).

"Permindex was caught by French intelligence and New Orleans District Attorney Jim Garrison when Permindex funneled money to hit squads implicated in the assassination of President John Kennedy and numerous attempts on the life of French President Charles de Gaulle. Permindex board member Clay Shaw, a New Orleans businessman, was the only person ever indicted and prosecuted as an alleged participant in the plot to assassinate President John Kennedy.

<>

"Kissinger's partners at the firm played central roles in determining U.S. foreign policy under the George H.W. Bush Administration. One partner, Lawrence Eagleburger, was Undersecretary then Secretary of State. Brent Scowcroft, another partner, was National Security Adviser and ran National Security Council. Kissinger's ...a counselor to Chase Manhattan Bank ...Chair of the International Advisory Board of American International Group ...a funder of *American Spectator* magazine ...a board member of American Express, Union Pacific, Continental Grain ...a trustee of Rockefeller Brothers Fund, the Metropolitan Museum of Art, the Center for Strategic and International Studies and Aspen Institute ...a director of International Rescue Committee ...former Chairman and Trustee of Trilateral Commission, and New York Council on Foreign Relations ...adviser to Goldman Sachs, NBC, ABC, and CBS, ...and, board member of Twentieth Century Fox.

"Until appointment as Undersecretary ...then, Secretary of State in the George Bush Sr. Administration, Eagleburger was ...Kissinger Associates president ...a director of IT&T, of LBS Bank of New York based in former Yugoslavia ...and, of Global Motors U.S., subsidiary of the Yugoslav producer of the Yugo automobile. Eagleburger joined the foreign service in 1957, served in Yugoslavia. From 1969-1977, Eagleburger was Assistant Secretary for European Affairs at State Department ...then, Undersecretary of State for Political Affairs in 1982, becoming president of Kissinger Associates in 1984, upon leaving government. In 1988, Eagleburger returned to government and became Undersecretary of State. In 1991 he became Deputy of State.

"Until his appointment as President Bush's National Security Adviser, Scowcroft ran the Washington Office of Kissinger Associates.

Scowcroft served his military career in teaching posts, and in planning, operations, and intelligence positions with the general staff in Washington. Scowcroft hooked up with Kissinger in 1969, when he was assigned to national security matters at Joint Chiefs of Staff. In 1973, Scowcroft worked under Kissinger as Deputy Assistant at National Security Council. Scowcroft replaced Kissinger as National Security Adviser in 1975. As Bush's National Security Adviser, Scowcroft worked with Eagleburger in overseeing British policies in the Gulf War and Balkans war.

"Retired Chairman of Atlantic Richfield, Robert O. Anderson, Chairman of Aspen Institute is reputed to be the largest landholder in the U.S. Anderson built Atlantic Richfield into one of the largest U.S. oil companies. He's currently a partner with 'Tiny' Rowland, the Chairman of the British intelligence proprietary, Lonrho, in their Hondo oil firm of Texas.

"Lord Peter Carrington left the board of Kissinger Associates when he became Secretary

General of NATO, in 1984. An Irish baron, Carrington serves as Chancellor of the Order of St. Michael and St. George ... being the Queen's foreign service and espionage order. First Lord of the Admiralty 1959-1963, Carrington was British secretary of state for defense 1970-1974, British secretary of state for energy in 1974 ...and, British secretary of state for foreign and commonwealth affairs 1979-1982. From 1983 to 1984 Carrington was Chairman of General Electric of the United Kingdom. Carrington's other financial interests include ...Australia & New Zealand Bank, a family concern he chaired ...and, directorships of Barclays Bank, Rio Tinto Zinc, Hambros Bank, and British Metal.

"Retired Chairman of Volvo since 1983, Chief Executive Officer in its subsidiaries since 1971, Pehr Gyllenhammar served in key positions in Swedish Ships Mortgage Bank and Skandia Insurance. Gyllenhammar has been on the Chase Manhattan International Advisory Board since 1962, a board later chaired by Kissinger.

"A resident of Hong Kong, Sir Y.K. Kan was the Chairman of the Bank of East Asia from 1963-1983 ...and, Chairman of the Hong Kong Trade Development Council 1979-1983. Formed in 1918, Bank Of East Asia is a partner with S.G. Warburg in East Asia Warburg, Ltd.

"As chairman of powerful S.G. Warburg since 1973 ...and, Chairman and later President of Mercury Securities since 1974, Lord Roll of Ipsden, is one of the most important bankers in England. Lord Roll was director of the Bank of England from 1968 to 1977.

"William E. Simon was Deputy Secretary of the United States Treasury from 1973-1974 ...then, Secretary of the Treasury from 1974-1977. A longtime, senior partner of Salomon Brothers, the New York investment house ...currently, Chairman of William E. Simon & Sons.

Simon held government or quasi-government posts, such as ...United States Governor of the International Monetary Fund ...Governor of the Inter-American Development Bank ...and, Governor of the Asian Development Bank. He served on the boards of think tanks Atlantic Council, and Hoover Institute," the LaRouche report said.

<>

In 1997, a newsletter from Project Underground, based in Berkeley, reported an additional affiliation of Henry Kissinger and Associates. "Freeport-McMoRan, based in Louisiana, operates the world's largest gold mine, and a copper mine in Irian Jaya Indonesia, and is being sued for 7 billion dollars by indigenous peoples for destroying the environment and indigenous culture.

"A Freeport-McMoRan board member is former Secretary of State Henry Kissinger, the company's main lobbyist for dealings with Indonesia. Kissinger met with President Shuharto just prior to the invasion of East Timor, reportedly to provide full American support. Kissinger's firm receives a yearly retainer fee of $200,000 from Freeport-McMorRan," Project Underground said.

White House Situation Room

I found myself in another one of my daily meetings with Mike Deaver, totally besides myself.

"Are *all* my appointees, crooks? How does that make me look?!"

"It doesn't matter."

"Explain."

"According to our opinion polls, the American people don't associate you with the scandals and failures of your Administration."

"That's the darndest thing. Are you sure?"

"Yep. You're an icon. Make sure you never, never even discuss the Savings & Loan crisis, or Wedtech, or HUD Scandals. The American people are concerned with your Hollywood image, your looks, they like that you make mistakes, they like you forget what you're talking about, it makes you human, another victim of big government, like them."

"Can they give me an Oscar?"

Deaver was amused. "McFarland resigned, couldn't take the heat." Mike left the Situation Room.

Outside, a reporter, Alan, was finishing an interview with Bill Casey.

Bill had said about as much as he wanted to. "All-in-all, these are very good years. My stock portfolio's soaring. Reagan years are good for money-issuing class portfolios."

Bill walked off.

Alan turned to George Bush. "Can we finish our interview, now?"

Bush was interview shy, but agreed.

"This is my experience with Ronald Reagan. We don't always see eye-to-eye. President Reagan, and his nouveau-riche friends profit on statewide levels. I, of course, come from old family wealth, my forte is petroleum. Don't get me mixed up with my father, and grandfather, and uncle ...they were the international bankers, in bed with foreign international bankers the same way Bill Casey and Allen Dulles were. Not me, I'm just a New Englander who loves oil, and lives and votes in Texas, for tax breaks. We all knew building up the national debt would let the bankers who made the loans and owned the bonds suck trillions of dollars of profits out of the American people ...and, bankrupt America. Same kind of thing with the savings-and-loans rip-off. That was a classic exercise for rich kids from ruling families. The Full-Court Press to destabilize the Soviet Union and Eastern Europe, that was a banker-kind-of-vision thing. I remember the day the President came to me for reassurance about deregulating the Savings & Loan Industry."

<>

George Bush remembered that day.

But, I wanted to get to the bottom of things. "How can your sons be making millions of dollars from this Savings & Loans scandal when it's going to cost taxpayers billions of dollars?!"

"That's the whole point," George said.

"Sometimes, I think you're not out of the loop at all."

"I'm sorry to hear that."

"George, look, I've heard you say it more than once."

"Mr. President, I know. 'Me? Out of the loop? I am the loop.' Trust me, Ronnie ... it's different this time."

I watched the expression on George's face change ...as, he suddenly considered himself off the hook.

He smirked. "Ron, What scares me most, is the wealthy people in America are taking foreign citizenship ...so, they don't have to pay American taxes. The 1980s and 1990s are about making the Deutschmark and Yen, king. You could say, the Axis currencies and their central banks, that financed Hitler, finally won World War II, the U.S. dollar lost ...now, the dollar's worth less. History's embarrassing. I'm disillusioned. A one-world government Central Bank New World Order's the only way to keep us all from destroying ourselves.

<>

"It took me my whole life," George said, "...to forgive my parents and grandparents, for working with Dulles to finance Nazis and Fascists, they were business partners the whole 20th Century. Now, I'm in my 70s, gosh darn if I didn't do the same thing with oil dictators, banana republics, Nazis, and Fascists, too.

"Maybe my Dad was a visionary, ahead of his time. He saw beyond the limitations of national boundaries. He believed, a one-world government could only be achieved with genocide and war, in order for God to bring peace to the world...

<>

"...and keep the rest of us ruling families from killing each other off."

I felt confused. I turned to Jim Baker. "What about you, Baker. How is it you're making money off the Savings & Loan scandal too?"

White House Chief of Staff James Baker III smiled. "Just business as usual. When we deregulated the Savings & Loans, everyone knew there was an end run coming, we were waiting for the right president to come along, for several administrations ...we just waited for a president like you, who understood the importance of deregulation."

I was angry. "Me?! I didn't know any such thing! How does it make me look?! Like a John Wayne hero? Or a villain?"

Baker looked at me, showing no expression. "Deaver says you've got the Midas touch, step in shit, come out smelling like roses."

I was amused. I enjoyed the compliment. "Lucky for all of us, he's right. I just don't want to keep pushing the envelope. I don't want to keep pushing our luck. Didn't your father ever teach you how not to get caught? You may come from a ruling class family in the social register ...but, any street kid investigative reporter considers you easy pickin's."

Budget Director David Stockman caught my eye. "Stockman, I'm not happy about you betraying our budget machinery to the press. I respect you for doing what you believe in, you're fired. There are changes coming down. I've been thinking about relieving Baker, Meese, and Deaver, who together, now head White House Staff. I'd replace them with a senior executive from Merrill Lynch, Don Regan."

That's how George Bush remembered that day.

<>

Alan finished interviewing Bush. Then, turned to White House Spokesman Larry Speakes.

Alan smiled. "What was it like working with President Reagan, Mr. Speakes?"

"Ronald Reagan has more aces up his sleeves than a carnival barker. Before you knew it, he's going to replace the White House Head Staff 'sleaze team' of Jim Baker, Ed Meese, and Mike Deaver. He fired Poindexter, for Poindexter's role in Iran-Contra. George Bush's sons are making millions of dollars off the Savings & Loans scandal, his sons are running for governor of Texas and Florida. All those Reagan photo-ops prevented there being any target for the American people to blame. Deregulation was the best thing for ruling family Americans, since slavery. Now, we have financial slavery of the middle class ... up into the upper class, that was the greatest contribution of the Reagan years.

"And the way they changed the way they figured unemployment, not by how many people were unemployed ...but, once your unemployment benefits expired, you'd would no longer be counted as unemployed. The Fed has a brainstorm with that one. That method is still used. It keeps millions of unemployed people invisible. White House crime soared, the President's popularity soared, too."

George & Barbara Bush's home

Lucky was visiting with Barbara Bush at a Bush estate in Washington D.C. Lucky liked Barbara a lot, and it showed in her voice, "I accept at least 500 party invitations a year, I turn down many more."

Barbara smiled warmly at Lucky, "I know what you mean."

Lucky smiled warmly back. "I go to official parties with your husband, the Vice President, he has me make sure he's not overwhelmed by the press ...or, not monopolized by some bore he can't get rid of. When he wants to leave without causing a stink, he winks at me. I'll interrupt him, no matter who he's with ... point to my watch to give him an excuse to leave. He says, 'Opps, Chief of Protocol says, it's time for another meeting'.

"One time at an embassy party, he winked ...but then, said in a loud whisper, 'Gee, Lucky, do I have to leave? I'm having such a good time.' The foreign Ambassador glared at me for taking George away. Your husband protested, all the way to the door. I was so embarrassed."

Barbara watched Lucky's eyes carefully, as Lucky talked. Barbara felt a little bit suspicious ...or, maybe jealous. Barbara was demure. "George is a flirt, I'm the first one to say it."

Lucky wanted to get to the heart of the matter, why she'd come to visit Barbara in the first place.

"How should I deal with my munchkin problem? I've asked myself over and over, what motivates a munchkin?"

Barbara usually disguised her sense of humor by giving it a straight delivery ...but, Lucky found herself surprised at what Barbara said. Barbara was candid. "Money and sex motivate a munchkin."

"Does Mike Deaver know what they're doing behind his back, in his name?"

"I've heard he has a drinking problem. Its that true, Lucky? And, isn't he mixed up with the Argentines?"

"I don't know. He's surrounded by a bunch of fraternity boys, who drink too much. What do you mean, about Argentines?"

Barbara smiled in chagrin. "A little birdie told me staffers denied any involvement ... with Contras getting U.S. Military aid by buying congressional support ...and, making campaign kickbacks from their foreign aid allotments, and drug smuggling profits. I heard some of the illegal money didn't make it back into campaign funds, it got sidetracked. You didn't hear it from me, Lucky. Let's get back to you. How can I help?"

Lucky felt vulnerable. "I'm not pleased with myself ...the way I let them treat me, if it's not best for me how can it be best for the country? The munchkins tried again to make me hire one of their cronies. I didn't. Then, one day, without asking me, the White House commandeered my deputy secretary to be Mrs. Reagan's social secretary. One munchkin told Deaver's secretary, don't tell me about it ...but, she did. She said, I was bound to notice my secretary wasn't sitting at her desk, any more. Then, they took another secretary ...then, they took one of my best protocol officers to be Mrs. Reagan's new advance man."

State Secretary George Shultz's office

In Shultz's White House office, Lucky repeated her problem to her boss, State Secretary George Shultz, "*That's* what they did, I've been screwed."

George Shultz looked somber. "No, Lucky, you've been raped ...I have faith in you. Sometimes, you have to lose the battle to win the war."

Lucky wasn't sure what George Shultz meant. "I hate this munchkin bunch of little shits. If I told the President how the munchkins were treating me, he'd be horrified. I'm so upset about it, I could scream. One of the little shits is going around saying, he's going to get rid of 'that woman', meaning *me*. Several people told me, he keeps saying it ...but, if I go to Mike Deaver he'll think I can't handle my job. But, unless I go to him, I can't work with these little shits, any more. They're frustrating me to death. Can you tell me what to do?"

George smiled at Lucky. He looked at his watch. He had to leave.

Reagan living quarters, Christmas Eve, White House

Patti was singing with rock music on the radio ...but, there was a second radio somewhere, playing Christmas carols, and the music mixing together was driving her nuts. The Reagan Christmas family get together was in full swing. Ronnie, Nancy, and Patti start watching videos of Patti speaking at anti-Contra, anti-nuclear power, and anti-war demonstrations ...usually, with Patti onstage, singing back-up with her boyfriend's band, the Eagles, to a huge crowd. Patti danced around wildly on the video, delighting in shaking her long hair around and around, back and forth.

Nancy couldn't watch, without getting upset. "Tossing your hair around like that ...in public, gyrating like that ...it's disgraceful to the Presidency."

Patti couldn't hold back her anger. "I hate you! You stole my father from me! You *know* you did it! You know it! Dad, you just *stood there,* my whole life. You *let* her!"

Nancy felt she was being challenged, on home turf. "Ronnie, Patti's lying. She'll never change, she's a bad seed."

I frowned. I couldn't please both of them.

"I *did* know about it, Patti. I talked with your mother about it ...but, it kept happening. I couldn't be in the middle between you and mommy. Don't make me choose between you and mommy, 'cause I'll choose mommy, not you. You're grown up now, you should understand. It's painful to talk about ...are you happy, now?"

Patti had tears in her eyes. "Yes. You're admitting for the first time, you lied. You're a hypocrite."

I felt I had to defend myself, "I deny that, Patti."

Patti start yelling at Nancy. "I hated you being my Mother! I *never* had kids! That's how much I was afraid ... I'd turn out, like you. I never wanted to put my kids ...or any kids, through that!"

"It couldn't have been that bad."

"It was too! I got a tubal ligation, I can never have kids!"

Patti's brothers and sister sat on a coach. They assured me, Patti did have a tubal ligation.

I felt tears in my eyes.

"I'm so sorry, Patty. God, I wish you hadn't done that. It's a sin, worse than abortion. I knew Nancy slapped you a few times when you were a bad girl ...but, Nancy couldn't help that, she was doing the best she could to raise all of you ...you were a defiant child. I did the best I could. I'm sorry, if I was wrong. I really am ...but, it was a long time ago," I said. I felt the tears falling down my cheeks.

I picked up a movie magazine and hid behind it. That made Patti furious.

Patti felt, she was being ignored, like she'd been made invisible, like she didn't matter.

Patti yelled at me, "Stop hiding behind that movie magazine! All you've ever done is hide behind parts you played, you weren't real. You were never there, for me! You've hid your feelings, all I ever wanted was you to love me! You think I'm not here. You need the shrink, not me! You support Contra death squads, you're a drug runner, a terrorist, a mass murderer, a serial killer!"

I lowered the magazine, stared at Patti. "You're exaggerating. I never killed anyone. Other people did it."

"You authorized Casey to build up CIA, you funded the Contras and *they* kill and torture people!"

I was losing patience, trying to make Patti understand. "But, I didn't do it myself! I didn't kill anyone!"

"The Nazis said, they followed orders. They said, it was Hitler's fault. But, you give the orders, Dad. Do you think about that?"

I sat there quietly ...and, thought. "Yes, I think about it. But, someone has to save us from communists."

Patti was sad. "That's exactly what Hitler said ...making excuses to kill innocent people, do genocide, concentration camps, death squads. You give the orders, Dad. You're *not* the hero. ...You're the villain!"

"No, I'm not!"

"Yes, you are!"

"No I'm not!

"Then, *what* are you?!"

"What am I? I'll tell you what I am! I'm the most popular president America ever had!"

"You're denying the truth!"

"I didn't kill anyone myself, someone else did, can't you see that? It's my management style, I surround myself with capable people, I stay out of their way, I let them do their jobs."

"Dad, you're a serial killer, a mass murderer, drug runner, terrorist, you're everything you hate, a hypocrite, in denial."

"I'm not a hypocrite! I'm not a villain! I'm telling you, again! I'm the most popular president the United States ever had! Why can't you believe me? Look at the public opinion polls, Patti! Ask Deaver. Ask your mother. I'm a hero! ...playing in the biggest movie role of my career. My friends finance it, produce it ...I wrote it. The American people love it. They love me! America's *my* family! I'm their Father. They love me!"

Patti wouldn't let up. "No Dad, they don't. They love your shadow. You don't even exist. Life's not a movie! 'Cause if it is, you're on the cutting-room floor."

"To hell it's not, Patti! Life is a movie! It is!"
"Then, it's a bad movie, 'cause I'm *not* clapping."

I was furious. "We all play roles God gave us, can't you ever get it? Won't you grow up? You need a lot more Jesus ...and, a lot less rock and roll!"

"I get it, Dad! You're the Devil! ...runnin our-shadow government!"

Patti stormed off.

We continued with our Christmas party.

White House photo-opportunity

A few days later in the White House I was relaxing before my next photo-op, watching a video of Jimmy Stewart starring in, *It's a Wonderful Life.*

I explained the film to Nancy. "Jimmy's making Savings & Loans home loans to homeowners ...but, his S&L is implicated, making bad loans."

Nancy frowned. She was sad. She thought, 'Doesn't he know I've watched this movie with him, a hundred times.'

"I know, Darling," Nancy said.

I felt nostalgic. "Today's a big day. I have to sign the Garn-St. Germain Act to deregulate the Savings & Loan Thrift Industry, that's why I put on this old Jimmy Stewart movie from the early '40s, they almost cast me in that role, instead of Jimmy."

At my speech, I could tell ... I had a captive audience. I love that feeling.

"This is the most important legislation for financial institutions in fifty years! Garn-St. Germain is the Emancipation Proclamation for American savings institutions! It means more housing, jobs, growth! All in all, I think, we've hit the jackpot."

In the audience, James Baker III, Lloyd Bentsen and his son, George Bush and sons, and Farhad Azima all clapped wildly. I could see some of the audience was smirking at me, talking to one another. I didn't know why. Later that night, I couldn't sleep. I kept watching the Jimmy Stewart movie I'd started watching that morning. I finally fell asleep. I had fitful sleep. I had nightmares. So did Nancy. Me and Nancy were so close, sometimes we dreamed the same dreams.

Nancy and her astrologer

Me and Nancy dreamed the same dream. Nancy could hear the Jimmy Stewart movie drift in and out of her head. She fell into in a fitful sleep, startled by the sound of oversized tarot cards being slowly shuffled ...and, the whining pitch of her astrologer's voice.

Nancy couldn't wait any longer. "Please do my tarot reading now. Is it all right? ...Ronnie's here"

Nancy said. Nancy listened to the sound of her astrologer shuffling the tarot cards.

The astrologer smiled at Nancy ...then, at me.

I was falling in and out of sleep on the astrologer's couch, using Peter Brewton's book, *George Bush, the Mafia & the CIA,* as a pillow. Or ...was it Joseph J. Trento's, *Prelude to Terror, the Rogue CIA & Legacy of America's Private Intelligence Network.* Wait, it was Brewton.

Nancy spoke up. "I have photographs my Carter Naval Intelligence men sent me, in the mail, I recognize the people, can you touch the pictures and get a psychic reading from them?"

Joan Quigley smiled.

"Let's go in a trance using my crystal ball ...then, I do the tarot card reading for you and Ronnie."

Nancy felt a lot of anticipation as Joan start dealing the fortune-telling cards.

"The danger card! I see it in my psychic vision. My third-eye's opening, you must be careful about the crowd around Ronnie."

Nancy was scared. "Ronnie, Ronnie get up. This is important."

I slowly opened my eyes, my Jimmy Stewart movie played in the background. I sat down with Nancy, and Joan, at the séance table.

Joan looked into the crystal ball.

"I see James Baker III having lunch with Raymond Hill at Hill's Mainland Savings & Loan, I see Hill lending money to the mafia and to CIA operatives.

"Deception! I see Lloyd Bentsen selling three Texas Savings & Loans the mafia and CIA will own. Danger! Farhad Azima, gunrunner and board member of a Kansas City bank, there in the photograph he's holding in his hand a picture

President Reagan and Nancy Reagan greeting Billy Graham at the National Prayer Breakfast held at the Washington Hilton Hotel.

of him standing with the Crowned Shah of Iran, Shah Pahlevi. He's having dinner with Oliver North, Leslie Aspin, and Mario Alarcon in the Kansas City Bank boardroom.

"Greed! Murder! William Blakemore, oilman, Contra supporter, friend of George Bush is lobbying Congressmen for Contra aid, Blakemore's heading up Contra paramilitary training at his Iron Mountain ranch.

"Treachery! John Ellis 'Jeb' Bush son of Vice President Bush, a Contra supporter, a business associate of Camilo Padreda and Guillermo Hernandez-Cartaya.

"Deception! Neil Bush son of Vice President Bush is director of Silverado Savings & Loan, a partner with Bill Walters and Ken Good, a friend of Walt Mischer, Jr.

"Treason! Eulalio Francisco 'Frank' Castro, Cuban exile, Bay of Pigs veteran, a CIA operative who helped train and supply Contras, he's part of a drug-smuggling ring that bought Sunshine State Bank.

"Assassination beware! John Connally, former Texas Governor. Charles Keating worked on Connally's 1980 Republican presidential race, Keating and partner Ben Barnes borrowed tens of millions of dollars from dirty Savings & Loans.

"Genocide! ..racism! The International Fascista! WACL! Ray Corona, former head of mafia-owned Sunshine State Bank in Miami, he's using Sunshine as a front for drug smugglers, his bank is a borrower from Peoples Savings in Llano, Texas. He's an associate of mobsters *and* CIA operatives including Frank Castro, and Guillermo Hernandez-Cartaya.

"Betrayal! Betrayal! Treason! War in Latin America! Robert L. Corson, Houston good old boy and developer who owned Vision Bank Savings in Kingsville is Walter Mischer's former son-in-law and a CIA mule, he'll be indicted with Mike Adkinson for a bogus 200 million dollar Savings & Loan land deal in Florida.

"Cookies, good to eat. Innocence. Cover-ups. Disguises! Marvin Davis, Denver and Beverly Hills oil billionaire, his daughter was in the cookie business with Neil Bush's wife, Sharon," Joan said.

Nancy listened attentively, making note of everything. "Can you tell if they're chocolate chip, or oatmeal, cookies?"

"Oatmeal." The fortune teller continued her psychic reading.

"Drugs! Seduction! Loss of innocence! Suffering! Racism! Genocide! Evil! Beware! Stefan Halper, cofounder with Harvey Mclean of Palmer National Bank financed by Herman Beebe, funneled private donations to the Contras, he's the former son-in-law of past CIA deputy director Ray Cline. He helped set up a defense fund for Oliver North.

"It's the ruling family mafia, that's what it is! The bad apples! Herman Beebe, Sr. Louisiana financier convicted felon Mafia associate, he has more connections than a switchboard to the intelligence community, he's godfather of the dirty Texas Savings & Loans.

"It's the ruling family mafia rag, that's what it is. Guillermo Hernandez-Cartaya Cuban exile Bay of Pigs veteran will be convicted of fraud for the Texas Savings & Loan he bought from Lloyd Bentsen's father. I see CIA and mafia money being laundered ...but, he's being protected from criminal charges by CIA.

"Satan! GATT! Council of Foreign Relations! The one-world government! Apocalypse! The Central Bank New World Order! Walt Mischer Jr. son of Mischer has been tapped to take over his father's empire. He's the friend of Neil Bush. Walter M. Mischer Sr., Houston developer, banker, power broker who headed Allied Bank, Corson's former father-in-law did business with mafia and CIA. Mischer Sr. is fourth largest landowner in Texas, he and his portfolio partners own 12 percent of the Caribbean Central American nation of Belize, he's a friend and fundraiser for LBJ, Lloyd Bentsen, your husband, George Bush, and others. Belize is a staging ground for Contra support activities.

"Apocalypse! Marvin Nathan Houston attorney who served on Carroll Kelly's Continental Savings board, he now owns the Texas ranch from the family of late Nicaraguan dictator Anastasion Somoza, purchased from one of George Bush's best friends.

"Apocalypse! Lloyd Monroe former Kansas City organized crime strike force prosecutor was told to back off Farhad Azima because Azima had CIA-issued get-out-of-jail-free cards.

"Satan! GATT! Council of Foreign Relations! Central Bank One World Government! Apocalypse! Central Bank New World Order! Destruction of Yugoslavia, Bosnia, Iraq, genocide, ethnic cleansing! World War III. Robert Strauss Dallas attorney and U.S. Ambassador to Moscow former chairman of Democratic National Committee friend of George Bush former business partner of James A. Baker III, he and his son Richard were involved in a number of failed Texas Savings & Loan deals, including Lamar and Gibratar.

"Bosnia, Baghdad, genocide in the Garden of Eden, ethnic cleansing in Sarajevo! World War III. Santo Trafficante, late Tampa mafia boss worked with CIA to try to assassinate Fidel Castro is involved in narcotics trafficking in Southeast Asia with CIA. Bill Walters Denver developer borrower at Silverado Savings helped set up Neil Bush in business."

Nancy was dumbfounded. "This is too much, for me! How's it gonna turn out?!"

Joan start blinking her eyes rapidly. "I'm coming out of my trance now. Let's work out your astrology charts and Ronnie's. I want to do a chart for Washington D.C. too. Washington might get nuked by terrorists! Let's see who's pulling the strings!"

White House Situation Room

Deja vu ...it seemed like I'd been here before.

I brought my Jimmy Stewart videotape with me into the Situation Room to keep me company. Watching the movie made me feel sincere, concerned. When George Bush arrived, I turned it off.

"George, I was hurt by Watt's big mouth and disregard. But, this Savings & Loan shenanigans breaks my heart."

George looked away. "I wish I could make it easy for you."

"How can 3,200 Savings & Loans be worth 17 billion dollars in 1972, and be 17 billion dollars in the hole in 1980! In 1982, you tell me to fix them, deregulate them! Now, in 1988, 600 of 'em are failing all over again! And, 1,200 more are going down! 500 billion dollars in the hole at taxpayer expense! Where did the money go?"

George scratched his head. "Gee, I don't know, Ron."

I didn't know if I should believe him, or not. I looked at him. "This is the biggest bank robbery in the history of the world. It's like, I wrote the largest check in history drawn on the bank account of the American taxpayer ... and it bounced. ... I didn't make a dime out of this! Did you?!"

George's Episcopal upbringing made him feel confessional. "No. Two of my sons did okay. James Baker III did okay. Lloyd Bentsen did okay. But, I'm not a banker, I'm an oil man."

I was furious. "Well, that's some consolation," I said. "'Where's the beef?', is that where it's at?"

George composed himself. "It's a terrible thing for the middle class and working class and some of the upper class, but corporate law prevents board member liability for ruling families. It was great for the money-issuing class."

"George, it breaks my heart."

George sighed. "It's the price ruling families pay for owning everyone ... we feel ashamed all the way to the bank."

Emotionally, I went over the top, "I'm not a ruling family! I'm a poor kid from Iowa. I made a million in Hollywood because of my looks. I'm a screen idol. I rode the American dream like a bronco. I got bucked off into the mud of the White House ... Do we have a cover? ...will the cover hold? ...will *I* get caught holding the bag?"

Bush shook his head. "I'll ask Bill Casey. I was out of the loop, I'm sorry for your broken heart ... the mud washes off." George left.

I turned Jimmy Stewart's movie, *It's a Wonderful Life*, back on. I talked to it. "Poor Jimmy, you have a failed Savings & Loan on your hands ... I got the whole failed S&L industry ... I outlived you, Jimmy," I said. I felt frustrated, angry. I was so full of despair I turned off the TV, and kept watching the blank screen.

Mike Deaver's White House office

Lucky marched in to Mike Deaver's office at the White House. She wanted to talk to him, now.

Lucky was angry.

"Your staff's treating me badly, to make me resign. You don't have to go to those lengths! Tell me the President's no longer happy with my performance, I'll leave right now. I didn't ask for this job, you called me! I had a great life before the White House. I'll have a great life after I leave the White House!"

Mike screwed the top back on his flask, after taking a nip. He spoke patiently. "Don't be silly, Lucky. The President and Nancy are pleased with your performance, there's been no suggestion you should leave the White House."

Lucky couldn't contain her anger, she'd restrained her fury too long. "In that case, call off your munchkins ...or, you'll be explaining to the Secretary of State ...and, the President ...and, the press ... exactly why I left."

White House corridors

Lucky walked victoriously down the corridors of the White House after leaving Mike Deaver's office, saw Barbara Bush walking towards her from the other end of the hall, hurried towards her. Barbara smiled.

Lucky smiled back, she felt happy. "I've got that winning feeling!"

Barbara was enthusiastic. "Zippity-do-dah!"

"Barbara, all the rumors have stopped, thanks

to Mike! I made such a fuss. I got my frustration and anger out. I'm not going to quit, I'm not going to let the munchkins push me out!"

Barbara hugged Lucky, then happily continued down the hall. George Shultz came down another hallway.

Shultz walked up to Lucky. "Lucky, I want you to stay on with me."

Lucky felt very happy. "I'm sitting on top of the world. If you want me to stay ...then, you have to have the President himself, ask me to. That way, I can keep the munchkins in line when I have to."

Shultz smiled and left.

Just then, Prime Minister Tariq Aziz of Iraq walked over to chat with Lucky.

A presidential aide came over to her, too, and faced her. "The President wants to see you."

Lucky looked at Prime Minister Tariq Aziz of Iraq. Then, she looked at the aide.

"Iraqi Prime Minister Tariq is waiting to talk to me, can he come along?"

The aide looked curiously at Lucky. "No. The President wants to see you alone."

White House Oval Office

I was sitting at my desk in the Oval Office. Lucky walked in. George Shultz was sitting there, a smile on his face. I stood up. Lucky walked over to me. I placed my hands on Lucky's shoulders.

I was fond of Lucky. "The State Secretary and I think you've done a marvelous job. I'd like you to continue to stay with me for my second term in Washington. I hope you say, 'yes.'"

Lucky smiled. Then, was surprised.

I had started singing to her! ...'I've Grown Accustomed To Your Face', from the Hollywood musical, My Fair Lady. "I've grown accustomed to your face, like breathing out and breathing in."

In my mind, I went back to the early '50s. My movie career was on the skids. I hadn't started working as a spokesman for General Electric Theatre, yet. I hadn't gotten the job, yet, to host the TV weekly series Death Valley Days. I remembered when my agent offered me a job in a Las Vegas lounge act with strippers. Nancy marched into my agent's office and refused the job for me. But, I did accept a soft-shoe bit part. I wore a straw derby as a straight man in a Las Vegas lounge act comedy routine.

Lucky noticed, I seemed distracted. But, Lucky was too thrilled to care. She laughed, smiling at me. "You've appeased me. I'm so happy. I'm a winner!"

On the way out of the Oval Office, Lucky passed Nancy ...and a munchkin! Lucky felt like a cheerleader whose team had just won.

"Victory, victory, hear our cry, v...i...c..t...o...r...y. Yea!" Lucky cheered.

Lucky intentionally bumped into a vase and spilled water onto the munchkin ...then, pretended it was an accident.

Lucky at home

Lucky sat at home at her writing desk, tenderly touched the diary with her fingers. The reporter in the room smiled. Lucky smiled at the reporter. "That, was primarily my experience of working with President Ronald Reagan, when I was Ambassador and Chief of Protocol for the White House."

The reporter felt satisfied with the interview. "Thank you for the interview, Ambassador Roosevelt."

Lucky was gracious. "Thank you."

Nancy's office in the White House

Nancy sat at her desk, in her White House office. Nancy's astrologer sat by her. Nancy looked at her. "The stars impel, they don't compel."

Joan Quigley agreed. "That's right. Now remember, don't let Ronnie talk any of that 'Evil Empire' baloney to Gorbachev. And, share your charts with Gorbachev's adviser, since he has an astrologer, too. Here are the dates, and times, for you to have Ronnie meet with Gorbachev, give them to Don Regan, the new White House Chief of Staff. Order Regan to follow them. It's your good karma days, understand?"

"Yes," Nancy said.

Joan revealed the dates. "Summit-1, Nov. 1985, Geneva. Summit-2, Oct. 1986, Reykjavic, Iceland. Summit-3, Dec. 1987, Washington D.C. Summit-4, Jun. 1988, Moscow. Summit-5, Dec. 1988, New York City."

<>

A few days before my first summit meeting with Soviet leader Mikhail Gorbachev I was visited again by Starwars lobbyists Edward Teller, Lt.

President Reagan greeting Walter Cronkite for an interview in the Diplomatic Reception room. 3/3/81

General Dan Graham, Gregory Fosseda, Dick Cheney, and Bob Bowman.

Back in 1975, with Paul Nitze and Richard Pipes, at the request of several of Bill Casey's central banking partners sitting on the CIA board of directors, CIA Director George Bush asked Lt. Gen. Dan Graham to co-found 'Committee on the Present Danger' (forerunner of 'Project for the New American Century', 30 years later).

Bill Casey was handed names of the three men from the board of CIA, to pass along to Bush. Nitze had become my Reagan Administration's leading arms negotiator. Starwars lobbyists Teller, Graham and Fosseda asked me not to use Starwars as a bargaining chip in my negotiations with the Soviet Union. Cheney disagreed.

I smiled. "I'm not going to bargain-off Starwars with the Evil Empire, gentlemen. Don't worry. Starwars is the only way to defeat them."

Cheney smiled.

Paul Nitze looked at me, "Back in 1948, when I wrote NSC-68, Allen Dulles was a rabid anti-communist ...and, Christian West was his baby. Dulles believed in fighting a rollback-liberation war to rollback Communism, liberate the people living under Communism, from Communism. Dulles' hard-line anti-Communism was for public consumption, means-to-an-end. Dulles used American intelligence ... to line his pockets. Mr. President, don't forget the difference between propaganda and truth. That's the *real* war."

I felt curious, doubtful, skeptical ...I didn't have the faintest idea what Nitze was talking about.

"I knew that," I said.

Mel's Jesus spoke to me.

"There are three Pauls," Mel's Jesus said.

The first Paul, was Paul Nitze.

The second Paul, was Paul Weyrich.

Paul Weyrich supported The Society for the Protection of Tradition, Family & Property, a neo-Fascist Catholic renegade sect.

In 1973, Coors beer ruling family financed Paul Weyrich, to found, 'The Heritage Foundation'.

In 1974, about the time members of Bill Casey's ruling family investment banking group who sat on CIA Board of Directors passed along the names of Paul Nitze, Richard Pipes, and Dan Graham ...to Bill Casey, to give to CIA Director George Bush, letting Bush know to give full CIA cooperation to the Committee on the Present Danger, the Coors ruling family financed Paul Weyrich to found, 'The Committee for the Survival of a Free Congress'.

Coors heavily funded both organizations, both

far to the right of traditional Republican Conservatism ...and, far to the right of Right-Wing Republicans ...many people referred to the Heritage Foundation, and Free Congress Foundation, as neo-Fascist organizations ... determined to eliminate civil rights and liberties of non-ruling family everyday Americans.

Paul Weyrich was pretty good dancing between the Republican-right, the Republican far-right, the Christian right, the Christian far-right, and the fascist-right ... but, it wasn't pretty. The better he danced, the more fascist dollars flowed in.

In 1976, Paul Weyrich, William Rusher, Morton Blackwell, and Richard Vigary tried to takeover the racist, 'American Independent Party', formed by racist Governor George Wallace, in 1968. Many American Independent Party members were members of Ku Klux Klan, John Birch Society ...and, Christian Front. Paul Weyrich was a defender of White culture ... like neo-Nazi White supremacists are. In 1982, Paul Weyrich had an essay published.

He explained.

"Culturally destructive government policies of racial hiring quotas and racial busing are immediately important in the realm of action to the New Right, since the damage they do is enormous, irremediable," Weyrich said.

Weyrich's defense of 'white culture' reflected theories advocated by neo-Nazi white supremacists.

The third Paul is, Paul the Apostle. He's a true advocate of democracy. All three Pauls were great men in their own times. Paul Nitze, Paul Weyrich ...and, Paul the Apostle, all knew the Apocalypse peeking around the corner. The first two Pauls and I hated the Evil Empire ... as much as the third Paul loved Our Lord Jesus Christ ...and that made a problem for me, I didn't hate the Russian people, I hated Communism ...but, bullets, like most people, make no such distinction.

Such as Richard Pipes.

<>

In 1981, Richard Pipes was Senior National Security Council Officer in Charge of Soviet Affairs, a Soviet expert on leave from Harvard.

Pipes led the pack.

"Nothing is left of détente with Soviet Union. Reagan Administration will pursue foreign policy radical as Reagan's new economic program. The Administration is moving to a strategy of confrontation with the Soviet Union, and with radical and socialist regimes in the Third World. The purpose of this strategy is to change world balance of power in favor of the U.S. and its allies. Soviet leaders will have to choose between peacefully changing their Communist system in the direction of the West, or going to war."

Mar. 1981 Pipes was interviewed by a Reuters correspondent, in *New York Times*.

"There's no alternative to war with Soviet Union if the Russians do not abandon Communism," Pipes said.

The Reagan White House discounted the interview. Larry Speakes held a press conference.

"The remarks of Senior National Security Council Officer in Charge of Soviet Affairs Richard Pipes ...didn't represent the views of the Administration."

London Financial Times responded with an editorial. "U.S. allies will be angered by any attempt of the Reagan Administration to play a dangerous game of chicken with Soviet Union."

Then, the matter disappeared from the press. Richard Pipes had deliberately warned the Soviets to build-up their military-industrial complex to rival America's. Pipes was re-starting Nitze's NSC-68 process ...of spending the Soviet Union in bankruptcy to weaken the Soviet economy. It wasn't really a threat of nuclear war ...or, was it? The people of the U.S. were frightened. In early 1980s, California think-tank Rand Corp., part of the military-industrial complex, shed light on the question in a series of studies and white papers. Rand carried out top secret intelligence studies for U.S. military ...that weren't made available to Congress, such as, *Economic Leverage in the Soviet Union ...Costs of Soviet Empire, Sitting on Bayonets? ...Soviet Defense Burden & Moscow's Economic Dilemma*. The papers described economic stress in Soviet Union, and how NATO countries could make Soviet economic stress worse.

The papers made observations and recommendations in the spirit of 'Committee on the Present Danger' and 'Project for the New American Century' ...in terms of intentionally scaring Americans to death, so military-industrial complex major shareholders could swipe more U.S. taxpayer dollars into their own pockets.

The papers issued forth.

'Since the Soviet economy is slowing down in the late 1970's, we must do things to help weaken it. The old guard Soviet Communist leadership is being replaced by a younger generation, and there's conflict in leadership of the Communist Party. U.S. and Western powers should force Soviet Union into an arms race. Deny Soviet Union access to international bank credit, imports and technology needed to increase economic productivity and growth. These suggestions are aimed at stagnating and destabilizing the Soviet civilian economy. By imposing military costs on Soviet Union, the investment climate in Russia will suffer, and standard-of-living of the Soviet people fall, hopefully far enough to create dissension and mass movements for political and economic reform.'

Rand wanted to weaken the Soviet economy, so it was harder to care for the Soviet people ...and, harder to distribute resources to care for them, until their economy went bankrupt ...a covert economic destabilization putsch.

Rand encouraged Reagan Administration handlers to wage economic warfare against Soviet Union, rather than military warfare ... with the same goals in mind ...conquer the Soviet Union.

Political economic analyst Joseph Fromm commented. "There's something behind the shift to a harder line in foreign policy. The U.S. is waging limited economic warfare against Russia, to force Soviets to reform their political system. Soviet Union is in deep economic and financial trouble. By squeezing wherever we can, our purpose is to induce the Soviets to reform their system. We'll see results over the next several years."

Mid-1982, it appeared Reagan Administration was doing what Rand and Pipes wanted.

May 1982, a White House consultant to National Security Council briefed reporters in the White House Press Briefing Room. Alan covered the press briefing. The subject was, 'U.S. Policy Towards the Soviet Union'.

Alan was alarmed. He looked at the National Security Council consultant, "You're outlining aggressive policy against Soviet Union."

Helen Thomas, UPI White House correspondent, felt alarmed, too. She sent in her story to her press bureau.

"A Senior White House Official said Reagan approved an eight-page national security document that undertakes a campaign aimed at internal reform in the Soviet Union and the shrinking of the Soviet empire. He affirmed that it could be called, a 'Full-Court Press', against Soviet Union'. In basketball, a full-court press is a strategy of maximum pressure applied against one's adversary in every part of the court. It's an onslaught."

May 20, 1982 National Security Advisor William Clark described the 'Full-Court Press' at Georgetown University.

"U.S. strategy is merging into diplomatic, economic, and informational components built on military strength. Cold War rhetoric, East-West trade policy, public diplomacy, and armament are part of an over-all plan. This strategy has a new purpose. We must force the Soviet Union to bear the brunt of its economic shortcomings."

<>

It was now we leaked the Defense Department Report, *Fiscal Years 1984-1988 Defense Guidance Document,* to Richard Hallorin of *New York Times.* May 30, *NYT* published a report on my Administration's nuclear war policy.

Hallorin wrote the article as if he were a CIA asset.

"Unknown sources sent me a copy of a report, *Fiscal Years 1984-1988 Defense Guidance Document.* In the guidance document, Defense Secretary Caspar Weinberger talks of 'prevailing in prolonged nuclear war'. Weinberger's guidance document recommends escalating the nuclear-arms race against Soviet Union. Quite apart from that, it indicates measures are being taken to impose costs on Soviet Union. The document says the U.S. should develop weapons too difficult for Soviets to counter, because they impose disproportionate research and development costs. U.S. should open up new areas of major military competition, making Soviet previous military financial investments obsolete. Western trade policy should put as much pressure as possible on a Soviet economy burdened with military spending. As a peace-time complement to military strategy, the report asserts the U.S. and its allies … should declare economic and technical war on the Soviet Union."

Hallorin's article blew the whistle, and the game started …the 'Full-Court Press' was underway, way beyond the Cold War strategy of Christian West *containment* of Communism, simply containing the Soviet Union, this was Christian West *rollback-liberation,* an aggressive tactic to confront then push Communism back and 'liberate' Russia's natural resources for Central Bank New World Order ruling family shareholders …and the financial, military, industrial, and petroleum companies on whose boards they sat as directors …to plunder Russia for personal profit …business as usual.

Spring 1982, State Secretary Alexander Haig held a press conference.

"Just as Soviet Union gives active support to Marxist-Leninist forces in the West and South, we must give vigorous support to democratic forces wherever they're located, including countries now communist. We shouldn't hesitate to create our own values, knowing that freedom and dignity of man are ideals that motivate the quest for social justice. A free press, free trade unions, free political parties, freedom to travel, and freedom to create are ingredients of the democratic revolution of the future, not the status-quo of a failed past."

<>

My Administration handlers harnessed many forces to 'promote democracy' in Soviet Union and Eastern Europe.

These harnessed forces included …Republican Party and Democratic Party …political parties in NATO countries …private foundations, i.e. limited trust foundations established for the purposes of ruling family capital gains retention, usually propaganda research 'think-tanks' …AFL/CIO …private-sector organizations …and, private-sector organization intelligence fronts such as National Endowment for Democracy NED, and Heritage Foundation, for example.

May 10, 1985 … U.S. Ambassador to United Nations Jean Kirkpatrick gave a speech called, 'The Reagan Doctrine', to members of Heritage Foundation.

"What I shall term 'the Reagan Doctrine', focuses on U.S. relations with Soviet Union and its associated states. The principle aims of the Reagan Doctrine are to redress the correlation of forces, stop Soviet expansion, and clarify the nature of the contest. We have to rebuild defenses, expand U.S. military forces, develop new defenses, such as the Strategic Defense Initiative. We have to develop and deploy advanced weapons in the U.S. and Europe. We have to withhold from our adversaries advanced technology of military importance. We have to support the rollback-liberation 'freedom-fighters' in low-intensity warfare …and, war-by-proxy using mercenaries, or foreign guerrilla units. We have to make a semantic infiltration and moral disarmament response at the ideological level with propaganda. We have to have a foreign-assistance program and use foreign aid to expand and preserve rollback-liberation freedom."

This 'Reagan Doctrine', was 'the Full-Court Press', the harder line in foreign policy against Soviet Union. By 1984, the program of 'promoting democracy' was at work in Poland and Soviet Union. Richard Pipes wrote an article calling attention to U.S. policy regarding the Soviet Union and Eastern Europe.

The article appeared in *Foreign Affairs.*

"The growing crisis in Soviet Union can and will

be resolved. Soviet Union is in a revolutionary situation. But, what was lacking in the time of Lenin was the subjective element, the ability and will of social groups and social parties to transform the 'revolutionary situation' into a revolution. But, a way can be found around even this obstacle as events in Hungary, Czechoslovakia, and Poland have shown. The only way out of the crisis for the Soviet elite is reform. In the past, the Soviets consented to make changes only under duress caused by humiliations abroad or upheavals at home. Reforms are the price Soviet ruling families must pay for survival. The key to peace, therefore, lies in an internal transformation of Soviet system in the direction of legality, economic decentralization, greater scope for contractual free enterprise, and national self-determination. The West would be well-advised to do all in its power to assist the indigenous forces making for change in the U.S.S.R. and its client states," Pipes said.

National Security Council Adviser Richard Pipes knew what my Administration handlers were doing and planning, in order to control the survival of Soviet ruling families and the Russian people. Pipes was heralding the dismantling of Socialism in Soviet Union. Soviet Union would have to move in the direction of the West, or deal with continuing crisis and humiliations at home and abroad with unsustainable price tags and mounting pressure.

Sean Gervasi, one of America's top public-oriented researchers, wrote an article exposing the Full-Court Press and explaining economic destabilization, Fall 1990 in Lou Wolf's *Covert Action Information Bulletin, Covert Action Quarterly,* called *A Full-Court Press, the destabilization of the Soviet Union.*

"The handlers of Reagan Administration wanted to destabilize Soviet Union. The typical campaign of de-stabilization involves two elements. The first element is external pressure. The second is internal manipulation. The 'attacker' is bent on creating disruption and turmoil in the target country. The ultimate purpose is to produce a change of government, a coup d'état, or a revolution. But, there's no assurance the disruption and turmoil will produce the desired political results. Therefore, the attacking power also intervenes in the internal political process in the target country to ensure events move in the desired direction. Intervention is usually covert.

"The first step is identifying and even creating political assets such as influential individuals, civic groups, trade unions, youth groups, cultural organizations, and media organizations in conflict with, or hostile, to the targeted government. Then, these assets are manipulated to further the political purposes of the attacker. This is what the U.S. and other Western countries have been doing inside the Soviet Union and Eastern Europe …the Socialist Bloc countries. Reagan & Bush Administration intervened in a covert and overt fashion to destabilize Soviet Union and Eastern Europe.

<>

"What is striking today, is that so many public agencies and private organizations are doing exactly what intelligence agencies have exclusively done in the past. U.S. Government agencies, foundations, business groups, media organizations, human-rights groups, trade unions and others … are all supporting and aiding opposition groups, particularly in Soviet Union. They're openly aiding and guiding forces hostile to socialist governments.

"What's equally striking is this intervention is now openly talked about without the slightest criticism or protest from Congress, the mass media, or opposition political groups in our own country. Having succeeded in aggravating the crisis in Soviet Union, the U.S. and its allies are now engaged in building internal pressures there, for further reforms. They're engaged in open, large-scale interference in the internal affairs of Soviet Union.

"U.S. policies moved things very far, very fast in Soviet Union, particularly in recent years when aid to the anti-Communist opposition has involved domestic expenditures of hundreds-of-millions-of-dollars. There is some question about whether the Cold War is, indeed over.

<>

"But, did the cost of the Full-Court Press to destabilize and bankrupt Soviet Union, also bankrupt and destabilize the United States, and create economic chaos in our own country?" Sean Gervasi said.

<>

Mel's Jesus said, there was a monopoly of American and British ruling families covertly investing in building up the economy of the U.S.S.R. since 1918 …now, rival forces wanted a piece of the pie …that, banking, military, industrial, and petroleum ruling families handling my Administration took the U.S. from the world's largest creditor nation, to the world's largest debtor nation …pick-pocketing taxpayers and dumping billions of dollars into their own pockets as usual …successfully bankrupting Russia

...and America.

...that, economic warfare against the Soviet people was at the same time waged against American taxpayers.

...that, national debt carried by American taxpayers is taken from their paychecks and pockets ... and goes into the pockets of American Fed and British Bank of England ruling families.

...that, our American and British rulers successfully robbed the American people again and again, stolen, then bankrupted, the American dream. Stole U.S. quality of life, and destroyed American family values, again.

But, I didn't have time to listen! I had a country to run!

<>

Nov. 1985, at the summit with the Russians in Geneva, Nancy happily shared astrology charts with Mikhail Gorbachev's wife, Raisa.

Raisa was bored. Nancy turned to Gorbachev's adviser, showed him her astrology charts.

He was delighted.

Nancy and Raisa Gorbachev start having cat fights about nothing ...and, everything.

Meanwhile, George Shultz and his business consultants with Russian counterparts met behind closed doors to dictate foreign policy terms to each another. They, in effect, decided which central banks would make which loans, to whom. They determined loans BIS, IMF, Ex-Im Bank, and World Bank would make ...what interest rates the Fed, Bank of England, Bundesbank and all the other central banks they controlled ... would charge, everyone. Profits, of course, went to majority shareholders of the central banks. Like opposing football teams, the real central bank people waging war on humanity ...were on different central bank teams, not the same team ...but, were in the same league. Which means, all wars can be traced to one group of central bank majority shareholders, or another ... and the company boards they sat on as directors ... very simple. Or, to the drug warlords they allied themselves with ...or, became ... to avoid 'mutually-assured self-destruction'.

<>

Meanwhile, I sat in a waiting room with Mikhail Gorbachev, we awkwardly made small talk. We waited for businessmen in the next room, behind closed doors, to finalize their deals.

I started in. "I'm determined to build Starwars."

Gorbachev bit his lip, "You know, Mr. President, contrary to popular belief, World War II did not stop in 1945. Nazi guerrilla units stayed behind in Soviet Union and Eastern Europe. They waged armed struggle against us, until 1952. I think you may have heard of Reinhard Gehlen ...and, Otto Skorzeny?"

Nope. "No, I haven't."

Gorbachev sighed heavily. He felt despair. He looked at Raisa, shrugged. "It's an interesting story, have Bill Casey tell it to you one day. Just before the end of World War II, Allen Dulles took command of leftover Nazi Freikorps units, left behind in Soviet Union. He made a merger, formed CIA largely out of Hitler's anti-Soviet intelligencers and Nazi soldiers."

My attention wandered. I yawned. "I helped FBI stop the communist plot to takeover Hollywood. You know, if Earth were invaded by aliens ...like in, *The Day The Earth Stood Still*, us two major superpowers would have to cooperate, not to mention the major studios."

Gorbachev laughed. Gorbachev looked at Raisa. "Please translate this into English for me?"

Following the summit, a press conference was held. Nancy was upset. She spoke to reporters. "Raisa Gorbachev tried to upstage me in a photo session! Who does this dame think she is?"

I had some comments for the press, too.

"I criticized Soviet Union for violating SALT and ABM Treaties. I denounced their record on human rights. Gorbachev told me, Starwars would violate our anti-missile treaty. I told him, I *am* building Starwars!"

Chief of Staff Don Regan waited, until me and Nancy finished talking with the press. Then, he talked to them. "The Reagans are pleased Raisa and Mikhail Gorbachev are movie buffs. Raisa and Mikhail listened spellbound to every detail President Reagan told them about his Hollywood days. They were very pleased to be in the company of somebody that knew Jimmy Stewart, John Wayne, and Humphrey Bogart."

At the Oct. 1986 summit with the Russians in Reykjavic Iceland, Nancy and Raisa had cat fights. They disagreed about everything, from weather, to time of day.

Mikhail Gorbachev and I shared our conflicting views of Cold War history. Both of us wanted to get rid of 'Mutually-Assured Nuclear Destruction' scenarios.

Gorbachev smiled. "I suggest we both cut the number of long-range ballistic missiles we have, by 50%. Then, I'll work to eliminate them all,

CENSORED

442

together. Then, we must honor the anti-missile treaty for ten more years …you must confine Starwars to the laboratory."

It was time for a meeting recess. George Shultz was talking with hardline anti-Communist, Richard Perle. Perle walked over to talk with me.

Perle was adamant, "Ronnie you and the Kremlin are the only people who take Starwars seriously. I'm against arms control. Make a bold counter-offer …Gorbachev will reject it. If he accepts … that leaves America with more strategic bombers and cruise missiles, than him."

Following recess I spoke first. I looked at Gorbachev. "I propose we eliminate all American, British, and French ballistic missiles over a ten-year period. But, at the end of that, the U.S. is free to deploy Starwars …so, no third party countries cheat, have any 'accidental' missile firings, or make any military threats."

Gorbachev assessed the situation, "Why don't we eliminate all of the world's nuclear weapons, not just their delivery systems?"

Raisa felt proud of her husband's response to my offer. Perle could see I was pleased with the suggestion. I liked the idea. Perle felt upset. If Ronnie and Mikhail agreed, then the advantage Perle hoped for would be lost. He wished he never suggested for me to make a bold counter-offer.

Mikhail continued. "But, you must agree …not to deploy Starwars, after it's built."

I got angry. I'd rehearsed this. I shouted. "You threw me a curve ball! Starwars is *not* a bargaining chip!"

Perle sighed heavily. He got a second wind.

<>

Back in Washington, my advisers talked to me before a press conference. They felt relieved, no formal agreement had been reached.

Larry Speakes made opening remarks to the press.

National Security Adviser Admiral Poindexter tried to explain something to me. "Ronnie, we've got to clear up this business about you, agreeing to get rid of all nuclear weapons."

I shrugged my shoulders. "But, John, I *did* agree to that."

"No, you couldn't have. You have no authority to get rid of British …or, French weapons."

"I was there ..and, I *did*."

Chief of Staff Don Regan turned to reporters. Don Regan leaned over to Alan, taking notes for a story. "Some of us follow behind Ronnie like a shovel brigade …behind, a circus parade of elephants … cleaning up."

<>

Following the Challenger disaster I addressed the Nation. "The astronauts have slipped the surly bonds of earth to touch the face of God. Our nation is grateful for their sacrifice. We'll reach out for new goals …and, even greater achievements, to commemorate our seven Challenger heroes."

Peggy Noonan, who wrote that speech, stood on the sidelines.

Autumn 1987, my negotiators and Gorbachev's negotiators agreed. They'd remove intermediate-range nuclear-tipped missiles from Europe. This was the first time two superpowers agreed to destroy a whole range of weapons. To Richard Perle's surprise, Gorbachev accepted an American demand for mutual on-site inspection.

I bragged a little bit, "I knew, if we went ahead building more missiles …then, the Soviets would have to, too. But, the Soviets are having a major economic crisis. My friend, Paul Weyrich, told me. So, I knew the Soviets would agree."

Everyone listening to me in the Situation Room was silent. They couldn't believe I knew what I was doing.

<>

Unfortunately, Don Regan had offended Nancy, several times. I fired Don Regan. So, Senator Howard Baker was made Chief of White House Staff. Bill Casey was sick, a lot. There was talk, Bill'd be replaced by FBI director, William Webster. I replaced several of my hardline anti-Communist advisers …who'd rather go to war. I fired Pointdexter …replaced him with Frank Carlucci to head National Security Council. Caspar Weinberger 'resigned' a few months later. Carlucci was promoted to Defense Secretary. Lt. General Colin Powell succeeded Carlucci as National Security Adviser. This new team was less far-Right in their Christian West anti-Communism. They were more sincere, more willing to negotiate arms control, wanted nuclear détente with U.S.S.R.

Nancy backed them up. Nancy wanted a major agreement between me and Gorbachev. Nancy knew that could repair my image after the Iran-Contra scandal, cause Nancy was a Hollywood girl. Nancy wanted, with all her heart, to make

CENSORED

Soviet détente my presidential legacy. Nancy wanted a thaw in Cold War politics, to be a feather in my cap.

Dec. 1987, Mikhail Gorbachev visited Washington to sign the Intermediate-Range Nuclear Missile treaty. Me and Gorbachev sat down at the negotiating table.

I noticed a change in Mike Gorbachev, "You seem more willing to talk about the bad shape the Soviet economy is in."

Gorbachev smiled, "The Soviet military-industrial putsch is bleeding our economy to death. George Kennan predicted *containment* or *rollback-liberation* against the Soviet Union ... and, an economic blockade against us by our World War II allies ... would eventually bankrupt us. It took 50 years ...but, he was right. The Nazis completely destroyed Soviet industry in World War II. Since the war, it's been a long struggle for Russia to survive."

I felt confused. "I'm not much of a world history buff. I know since Stalin, Moscow dominated its neighbors in Eastern Europe ...and, intimidated its rivals."

"Just like your CIA does. Now, it's time for me to ensure Soviet security in the world ...by cooperating with neighboring states ...and, other world powers."

Gorbachev's aide winked knowingly to Gorbachev. Gorbachev's aide spoke to me, complimenting my on my B-films ...then, winked to Gorbachev, again

I shifted in my chair. "They weren't all B-films."

The aide smiled. "I like the one about the fellow who loses his legs and where you say, 'Where's the rest of me?'"

I felt better. "That one's called, *King's Row*, that's no B-film!"

Nancy interrupted, offering me and our guests ice tea.

After the talks ended and the agreement was set, Gorbachev made a few photo-ops for himself. Gorbachev hosted a party for Paul Newman, Yoko Ono, and Henry Kissinger. Once, when Gorbachev was being chauffeured through the streets of Washington D.C. he had his driver stop. Gorbachev got out in the streets and randomly shook the hands of pedestrians.

Gorbachev was happy. "I just want to say hello to you."

I guess, he had to do his own photo-ops.

At a press conference, I was asked if I felt overshadowed by Gorbachev inviting Paul Newman, an America movie star, to his party with Yoko and Henry.

"I don't resent his popularity. Good Lord, I co-starred with Errol Flynn once."

My popularity was on the rise again. But, by showing warmth to Moscow, I angered my far-right supporters. The most hardcore anti-Communist 'warriors' felt I had the useful idiot of a communist Jewish conspiracy to takeover the world.

That's show biz.

<>

Bill Casey knew, a thaw in Cold War relations meant one day soon, the Soviet Union would disintegrate. Interlocking board directors of Bank of England, Fed, BIS, World Bank, Ex-Im Bank, IMF in his banking investment consortium would re-colonize Soviet Union, openly lend money at high interest rates, restrict trade. ..then, foreclose ... topple Soviet Union with economic warfare. Then, they'd again own the Russian natural resource portfolios they lost in 1918 ...and co-develop Russia, like back in Czarist times.

June 1988 summit in Moscow, Gorbachev and Raisa both, again, personally told me they were great movie buffs. So, I told the Gorbachevs stories about Hollywood movie star greats. They were enthralled. My appearance in Moscow signaled the beginning of the end of the Cold War. I hugged Gorbachev, in front of Lenin's tomb.

Reporters crowded around me.

Alan thrust foreward. "Is the Soviet Union still the focus of evil in the modern world?"

I smiled proudly. "They've changed."

State Secretary George Shultz spoke to Alan.

"I was impressed ...Gorbachev matched Ronnie, joke for joke."

<>

Later, at the Bolshoi Ballet, I stood at attention while the Soviet orchestra played, *'The Star-Spangled Banner'*. Between us, U.S.A. and Soviet Union, we still had 30,000 nuclear weapons ... aimed at each other.

Dec. 1988 New York summit, I was still telling Gorbachev Hollywood stories. That was our final summit ...so, I had to talk fast.

Gorbachev smiled at me, "During 1988, I've withdrawn Soviet troops from Afghanistan. I've tried to end civil wars in Ethiopia, Angola, and Southeast Asia."

I smiled. "Perhaps the United Nations is the best forum to mediate these civil wars and counter-revolutions."

"I'm reducing conventional forces."

While our negotiators worked behind closed doors, me and Gorbachev chatted. I finally got a chance to start telling Gorbachev more Hollywood stories. Shultz, and his Soviet counterparts, came out from behind closed doors.

George smiled, "We've worked out U.S.-Soviet foreign policy details."

I frowned, "I'm not done talking about Errol Flynn and Gary Cooper."

Gorbachev invited me, and President-elect George Bush, to pose for pictures with him in a photo-op ... in front of the Statue of Liberty. Newspapers and magazines start popularizing the end of the Cold War.

But, still no Oscar.

<>

White House Historian Bill Barnes leaned back into his chair and stretched, petting Jackson his cat, who sat purring on his lap. Barnes took out his headline scrapbook. He pasted-in another headline from the *New York Times.*

'Another Obstacle Falls, Nancy Reagan & Raisa Gorbachev get chummy.'

Bill Barnes wrote a few notes.

"The most assertive anti-communist President since World War II has achieved a foreign policy goal none of the President's before him could achieve. There are break-throughs on arms control. There's new cooperation in settling Third World disputes. Now, how long will Soviet Union continue to dominate in Eastern Europe?

Joan Quigley's office in San Francisco

Nancy's astrologer sat in her office, in San Francisco telling her story to Alan, who was freelancing for United Press International.

"As a result of the successful U.S.-Soviet Summit Meetings between Ronnie and Mikhail, Ronnie's approval rating soared. Ronnie and Nancy were so pleased the negative press from the Iran-Contra scandal faded ...as the public perceived it, it was forgotten," Joan said.

Alan closed his notepad, "Thanks for the interview."

White House presidential bedroom

Rolling Stones music played on the White House Muzak system in the presidential bedroom, where Nancy and I'd just finished making love. The marionette my daughter Maureen had given me sat on a bedroom bureau, overlooking the bed.

I smiled at Nancy.

"That was fun, just like the old days. Good night, Honey."

Nancy was satisfied. "You're telling me! Good night, Darling. I'm glad women have it easier than men when we're older, we just have to lie there."

I felt less than thrilled. "Sleep tight."

"Pleasant dreams."

Nancy flicked the light switch, the lights in the room went off. It was dark. Nancy heard my breathing even out, I was falling asleep. Nancy heard me tossing and turning,

I started talking in my sleep. "In my heart I didn't mean to trade guns-for-hostages. In my heart, in my heart."

I was having a nightmare. I heard machine-guns firing. I heard people screaming. Startled, I sat up in bed. Nancy turned the lights on. Nancy looked at the expression on my face, she felt upset. Nancy took my head and laid it on her breast to comfort me.

I felt my confusion clearing.

"Nancy, this whole Iran-Contra mess keeps going around and around in my head. I've got to talk to Casey before he dies, I've got to ask him what bridge he's hailing from, who the real puppet-master is."

Nancy stroked my head. "Maybe Casey's being blackmailed ...because, the petroleum-banking-intelligence community's grown too small for him to hide in anymore."

I got up out of bed. Nancy saw, I was in a grieving mood ...but, that mood was switching to Irish temper. I went into my closet, took off my pajama shirt.

Nancy was alarmed. "Ronnie, what are you doing?! It's the middle of the night!"

I felt enthusiastic. "Not, for the All-American boy! Not, for Ronald Reagan, movie star! Not, for the President of the United States, it isn't. It's finally the cold, hard light of day."

Nancy felt concerned, she didn't want me to be alone when I acted like this. Nancy knew what I was thinking, "You can't go see Casey in the hospital now! It's 9:30 at night! All right ...I can see that stubborn Irish, determined look in your eyes. I'm going, too."

CENSORED

Hospital corridor, Washington D.C.

Me and Nancy walked down the hospital corridor towards Bill Casey's hospital room. Nancy saw the guards talk to each other, they seemed sad. I started walking past the Secret Service guards to enter the room. I put my hand on the hospital door, a Secret Service guard put his hand gently on my hand to stop me. The guard shook his head, sadly. I realized, Bill Casey was dead. I felt my spirits sink. I stared off into the distance.

I turned to Nancy, "It's too late, Casey's dead. Now, we'll never know what was going on."

I felt disappointed. Nancy did too. Nancy watched as a visitor walked out of Casey's room.

The visitor turned and looked back into the room, "Bye-bye, hang in there."

Nancy felt surprised, she looked at me. I felt surprised, too. I threw open the door and pushed the visitor gently out of the way.

The visitor grabbed my shirt, "Let him die in peace, can't you?!"

I yelled at the Secret Service guard. "Get this person off me! Clear him out of my way!"

Nancy was furious, "That's a direct order from the President of the United States!"

One Secret Service man grabbed the visitor, gently pulled him down the hall. My ego was wounded. I felt shocked, at having been restrained. I stared at the other Secret Service men.

He took a deep breath, then sighed. "You can't go in there, it's a breach of national security."

I was angry. "Shut up! I am national security! Get out of my way!"

I stormed into the hospital room. I looked at Bill, I suddenly felt awe, my hard feelings softened, I no longer felt upset. I smoothed my hair back with my hand, the way I always did before I started to act or to make a speech. I no longer acted angry or desperate, I acted friendly, genuinely concerned for Bill, who lay on his deathbed. I sat down on a chair beside him, seeing he was in a fog ... I saw a surreal, peaceful look on his face ...like death warmed-over. I still felt confrontational ...but, decided to be gentle about it.

I felt solemn, "I apologize for storming in here ...being angry, at a time like this."

Bill felt confused. "Who is it?" "What time is it? Is it time to go to sleep yet?"

I looked at my watch. "It's 10 o'clock in the evening, all big boys should be asleep."

"Oh it's you, Ronnie, you big clown, how are you?"

I felt my anger was totally gone, "You can't just die on me like this."

Bill tried to smile, but just mumbled. "It happens all the time, we get out tickets punched."

No. Not yet. "You gotta tell me who's pulling my strings? Who's making decisions behind my back?"

Nancy sat down beside me. "Bill, are you being blackmailed?"

I raised my voice a little. "Bill, I know you're CIA director, but who's the producer? Who do you work for? You've got to tell me!"

Bill felt peaceful, he could care less ...but, had the energy to feel amused. "No one tells me what to do, we're all pulling each others' strings, Ronnie."

Nancy saw that confused look on my face.

I tried to smile.

"I'm playing it close to the chest! I'm not pulling anybody's strings," I said.

Bill felt far away. "I know you're not. I said, we are, not you. You're not from a ruling or money-issuing class family, you wouldn't understand responsibilities to wealth and power, how would you know?"

I saw the light start to fade in Bill's eyes. I was shocked. I felt frantic. "Who are they?!"

Casey was fading fast. "We're America's ruling families, Ronnie. We're ruling families all over the world. We do what the money-issuing famillies tell us to. We'd fill up a football stadium, not much more. I'll tell you that, but we control real power."

That wasn't enough.

"You're not making sense, Bill. Who?" I said.

Nancy interrupted. "Bill, these intelligence people who hang themselves or go mad? Were they murdered? I'm going crazy wondering if Ronnie's safe, or if we have to shut up."

Bill kept closing and opening his eyes. "I think about Angleton, Wisner, Forrestal. Dulles told me they went mad, or were suicides ... like Paul Robeson. I lay in this bed, wondering if I've been poisoned or irradiated or microwaved. I wonder if someone's murdering me . Yes, you better shut up."

CENSORED

446

Nancy shut up. She didn't know what to say.

I was confused. "But why me?! I'm anti-communist! I've always supported the World Anti-Communist League and anti-communist freedom-fighters, Colonia Dignatad, Skorzeny, Odessa, International Fascista, Contra death squads, BCCI. Where did I go wrong?"

Bill mumbled, "I'll let you know a secret, Dulles, von Hohenlohe, DeMohrenshieldt, Rosenberg. There was never any communist threat. It was all make-believe.".

"I deserve better than that, Bill!" I said.

Casey faintly smiled. "Bechtel had us choose you ...because you were an old man full of yourself ...you'd do anything for a good audience ...reassure him ...send him away laughing ...make him feel like he matters, with a wife that would do anything to make you look good. You got what you wanted, fame, glory, attention, you got to be a star."

I felt confused, deflated. I had a realization.

"You used me," I said.

"Welcome home. We pulled your strings. You were a puppet, a marionette, all presidents are, they just find out at different times. Christ, we never accepted you as one of us, Ronnie, we were the real actors, not you."

I couldn't believe what I was hearing. "You used me, all the time you used me."

Bill's voice grew fainter. "You used yourself, champ, don't take it so hard, there's always strings attached for us, too."

Nancy saw I felt emotionally drained, she put her hand tenderly on my arm. I felt confused.

Casey managed a smile. "The sociopathic ruling families of the world would fill a football stadium or two on a Sunday afternoon. The money-issuing families would fill the locker room. If you got rid of us, then you common people with good hearts and strong backs could rule the world. Let me die now, Ronnie, it's time."

I felt my temper rising, I felt vindictive. "You're going to Hell, that's where you're going, Bill."

"And you, are you going too?" Bill said.

That stopped me. I felt dumb. Maybe I was.

Casey mumbled. "Don't look so shocked, Ronnie, we're both Catholics, you may be been a b-grade actor, but you were an a-grade president."

I sensed the inevitable. I felt myself getting calm.

Something in me wanted to assure Bill. "Thank you, Bill. Remember that day at the Vatican when the Pope shook our hands and asked us if we were good Catholics?"

"Yes, I remember that. You said, 'I don't know,

it depends on who you ask.' That was a good one," Bill said.

I laughed warmly, quietly. I felt love for Bill.

Bill seemed to be falling asleep. "It's been a good life, but it's been too long a life, Ronnie. Y'know, Dulles that old devil, he always said we'd rot in Hell together, maybe he's right."

I smiled fondly. "Bill, I hope you're happily in heaven a half hour before the devil knows you're dead."

I stared off into the distance.

So did Bill. He whispered very low. "I'm made in God's image, but so is Wall Street. It's funny, the Russians are blackmailing Bush because Monzer Al-Kassar worked for the Russians, not Syria, not Iran, not Britain, not us, but for Russians. Russians really are in control. Bank of England and Fed made me give them a few points on their BIS, World Bank, Ex-Im and IMF loans ...that's what its all about, a few points. The Germans will finish them off. The Deutschemark and Yen will finish them off even if the dollar doesn't, we've done the Great Depression routine before, you'll see, they'll be a new pearl harbor and all the financing and all the loans will start all over again, you can't stop us, we hold the bank."

I felt sad, I watched Bill die.

George Bush stepped partly out of the shadows of the dimly lit room, half his face was hidden in shadows behind the curtains, "Plausible deniability, Ronnie. We gave it to you for your safety, because we care about you."

Onboard Air Force One in flight

In flight on board Air Force One, State Secretary George Shultz was putting golf balls down the aisle towards an Old Fashion glass, "How's your mood holding-up, Mr. President?"

I was not my usual jovial self. "I still have a bitter taste in my mouth from Casey's death ...it's like, he took part of me to the grave with him."

George Shultz smiled in a debonair way.

"That's the way it always is. Hey, do one of your imitations for us, won't you, you silly boy?"

I extended a limp wrist and sashayed past the

golf balls rolling around on the floor, portraying a queen. The passengers in the plane loved it, they clapped.

I soaked it up, "Say, Sweetie, I've had to re-evaluate my position on AIDS, and I'm not going to take it sitting down. I've failed to adjust from time to time, what's a poor girl to do boopy do?"

Nancy felt embarrassed, she went ballistic. She made me stop doing my queer act and sit back down in my seat. Nancy felt like she needed some attention, she start walking down the aisles of Air Force One passing out cookies to everyone.

George Shultz took a couple, "Well, it seems that if the G-7 decide to go ahead and finance war in Yugoslavia for Germany's push to its 'Eastern Territories' and the Balkans, the U.S. might get the Baku oil fields from Russia after all, after 80 years. If the war goes ahead on schedule ...then, Bechtel, Halliburton, Brown & Root ...and, bin Laden construction will compete for windfall contracts to rebuild the war zones ...when we're done destroying everything ...and, German, British, and U.S. central banks will issue the credit and the loans and reap the interest on the national debts. U.S. arms manufacturers in the military-industrial complex under Weinberger will reap windfall profits too, it's a win-win. The way it looks now, we're scheduled to go to war against Iran, or Iraq, in the next administration to beef-up 3rd quarter petroleum numbers."

I was still smiling from my queen act. I turned towards George Shultz. "I'm trying to figure-out the intelligence pyramid. My Administration and Bechtel, versus Bush, Casey and Halliburton, Brown & Root, and bin Laden construction? Dulles masterminded New England, Texas, California and German money. Carter was deep South, I'm California, Bush and Casey northeast, Florida, and Texas ruling families.

George Shultz frowned, "Are you asking me if Bush was out of the loop ...or, is Bush the loop?"

I felt I had inside information from Bush ...and, Casey, too. "George already told me, 'Stay out of the loop? ... I am the loop.' You're telling me, Dulles represented ruling families on both sides of the Atlantic ...and, all those ruling families we're really fighting low class, middle class, and upper class families on both sides of the Atlantic? And, the Pacific? That Dulles partnered with European, Japanese, Czarist, and German General Staff ruling families against the lower class, middle class, and upper class families of the whole world, that's the new World Order everyone's talking about? It's that simple?"

George Shultz nodded. "The new World Order

...is simply those families who print and own the money, the ones who own controlling shares of the central banks ...the interlocking board directorates they sit on. Bushes, Fords, General Motors, basically the Warburg banking group community, which is basically the Rothschild ... everyone's tied-in through Wall Street, BIS, World Trade Org. It's always money-issuing families on top that command the ruling families of the world ... against lower classes, middle classes, and upper classes ...we just make it look like it's one country against another ...for show, it plays. We confuse people ...make them think what we want them to ...we own the news ...the movies ...we determine education policy ...make everyone think it's one group of countries against another ...but it never is ...it's just ruling families that sit on central bank boards fighting turf wars over another central bank's ruling family's property.

"U.S. intelligence took over the world drug trade from the British ...except, in Africa and China ... where we left it for them ...but, Bank of England owns majority shares in the Fed ...so, there you go. Casey and his team used North and Al-Kassar to finance the Muhajidin, to attack the Soviet Union, to put pressure on Gorbachev ...and, financed everything with drug money and taxpayer money, none of their own money. At the same time, Weyrich spearheaded WACL and the Full-Court Press to finance Fascist and Nazi groups to destabilize Soviet Union and Eastern Europe ...to recolonize that half of the continent before marching on India and China, we never tell taxpayers what we're doing, only the ruling class knows, that's the structure of society, that's what we teach our kids, not yours."

I was finally getting some answers, "Was BCCI the central money laundry for all that drug money and illegal arms trafficking money, after the Nyugen Hand and Cayman Island bank fronts were exposed?"

George Shultz putted another shot. "Along with Casey's personal international banking investment partners in MI-6, DINA Spanish intelligence, Vatican bank, the usual crew of suspects."

George was determined, he kept putting. He'd make a putt into a whiskey glass, then would aim for another of several he'd spread out on the floor of Air Force One. He was a good putter.

I kept figuring it out. "So, Soviet GRE and KGB

448

were blackmailing Casey to get better interest terms to pick-up points for their group of central banks competing against World Bank, IMF and BIS, Ex-Im Bank, Fed ...and, Bank of England ... while, everyone competed for interest futures on Third World country development, and arms loans."

Shultz got another ball in the glass. "Got it! Got another one in. Don't forget *your* Administration, they did the same thing here to the U.S. ...bankrupted, destabilized the United States, for God's sake ... the amount of money we make each day from interest on the national debt is mind-boggling, that's the coup of the century, makes the Savings & Loan fiasco look like child's play."

I was putting pieces together like a jig-saw puzzle, trying to get the big picture together. "Casey, Bush, North, MI-6, Monzer Al-Kassar, GRU, McFarland, Poindexter, Mossad, CIA, Bechtel intelligence, Halliburton intelligence, bin Laden Construction intelligence, Brown & Root intelligence, military-industrial intelligence ...and, oil company intelligence ... are one big family ...in bed together?"

Shultz dropped another ball onto the carpet. "At the moment ... I can't promise you, tomorrow. It's like a football league, we trade players, move teams around ...but, it stays the same game ... with no national borders drawn by the money-issuing class on ruling families, who control the other classes."

I was troubled. "Do the American people even matter at all?"

"Taxpayers, consumers, soldiers. We take their paychecks, put them into our savings accounts, that's the I.R.S."

I was tired. "Then, Deaver, Alarcon, the Contras were just an extension of one central bank consortium competing against another ... a game?"

Shultz squared up his shot. "Well, kind of. The global drug economy is bigger than the global legitimate economy ...so, you have to factor that in. So, we do, we partner with the druggies ...then, we have to own that racket, too ...cause its real power, like what you said ... along with BCCI in Bahrain after Nyugen-Hand bank front closed ...and, Vatican bank drew too much attention."

I yawned, "I think I've had enough foreign policy lessons for today, State Secretary Shultz."

Shultz laughed in his good natured way.

Nancy had fallen asleep, long ago. Nancy was dreaming. Nancy remembered, Lucky told her what to expect when the Queen of England visited Nancy at Nancy's West Coast White House ranch, above Santa Barbara.

Nancy was excited, "Tell me what to expect, when the Queen of England visits me."

Lucky smiled. "What's it like to be Queen? Queens have certain characteristics in common, starting with stamina. They never seem to get tired. They never ask for the ladies room. Queens usually wear hats, so they don't have to worry about their hair, come wind or rain. They wear sensible shoes. They need an endless supply of white cotton gloves ...which, get worn and dirty ... after a round of handshakes."

Nancy remembered wearing her most expensive gowns to impress the Queen. Nancy remembered Ronnie hamming it up, to entertain the Queen of England ... showing her his video copy of, *King's Row,* putting it in the VCR, turning on the TV, narrating it.

I looked over at Nancy sleeping.

I smiled at George Shultz. "George, look at Nancy, she's passed out. Y'know, George, if I'd known ... before I was President ...that, the Presidency's a part you played telling lies, winning approval ...and, playing God, it would've been easier, than finding out the hard way. I wish you'd tipped me off."

George Bush came out of the plane's bathroom. He sat down next to me, "Ronnie, enjoying the flight?"

I whispered to him. "Why the hell didn't you tell me you had the Republican Heritage Groups Council filled up with Nazi death-squad leaders?!"

George Bush looked at me. "Well, the votes they got us elected us. I needed 'em to do the same thing on *both* Reagan-Bush campaigns ...and, on *my* Bush-for-President campaign ...and, we're using them on the Full-Court Press to destabilize Soviet Union and Eastern Europe."

"What press? ...I don't have a press conference, now! ...do I? I'm sleepy, let's talk later?"

December 1987, White House

I was serving my last week at the White House. I entered George Bush's office to close the window ...because, the wind was blowing papers off George Bush's desk, onto the floor. I stepped behind the curtain to close the window. The window was stuck. While I was behind the curtain, George Bush walked into the room with the King of Syria, King Assad ...and, the King's son, Haidar, Head of Syrian Intelligence. I listened, George Bush welcomed them to the White House.

King Assad start talking. "Haidar and I will

keep quiet about you sending Buckley to Beirut on his little covert counter-kidnapping and torture expedition ...and, how you were behind it. Only ...if you reverse U.S. policy on Syria, give Syria foreign aid, influence IMF, World Bank, Ex-Im Bank ...and, BIS ... to make favorable loans to Syria and stabilize our currency in international trade ...have them stabilize our trade credits ...and, put a few percentage points in our pockets for Western development loans to Syria. We'll do customary kickbacks into appropriate Congressional campaign funds through U.S. domestic accounts, non-profits ...and dummy companies.

I was shocked to hear what King Assad said.

Bush responded to them. "You've got nothin' on me. I was out of the loop, it was Casey. But, I want to keep his memory clean, avoid embarrassment for the Administration. Let's shake on it, get it over with."

They shook hands. The King of Syria and his son, Haidar, Head of Syrian Intelligence left George Bush's office.

I stepped out from behind the curtain. I angrily confronted George Bush. "Buckley wasn't an innocent victim?! You sent him! He really wasn't a hostage?! He was an intelligence operative on a covert operation?!"

Bush didn't mince around. "Yes. And, I have the papers you signed to authorize it."

"I'm pissed off! You never told me the truth, about anything. I sign whatever my staff puts under my nose!"

"Plausible deniability. We gave ..."

I interrupted him. "...it to you for your own safety! I know! I know!"

Bush was calm, "Well, we did."

I felt upset, struggled to restrain my fury.

"Never again! I've had enough, 'plausible deniability! I've had it with politics! Never again! I'll tell you something. George, I've always said ... when we stop criticizing politicians in Washington as 'they' ...and, start saying 'we', it's time to go home ...I'm going home!"

I stormed out of George Bush's office. I was surprised to find Nancy standing outside in the hall, eavesdropping. Nancy was pretending to clap wildly ...but, her hands didn't touch ...so, it was quiet. As soon as I saw her, I stopped being angry. I tried not to laugh out loud. Nancy was trying not to laugh out loud, too.

Nancy was excited.

"Encore! Bravo! I knew you had it in you! I knew you could do it!"

I bowed. I kissed her. Both of us, trying not to laugh, we hurried off down the hall, skipping hand-in-hand. When we turned down another hall, we both burst out laughing. I had gotten away safely with my life ...and, could go home.

Farewell

I made my farewell address to a captive audience.

"I'm going to read from a letter, from a sailor on the aircraft carrier, Midway ... stationed in the South China Sea. The crew saw a boat, so full of refugees ... it was almost sinking in the water. Risking his own life, this sailor joined a rescue party to save the refugees. They set out in a small motor launch. The Midway's sailor boarded the sinking boat full of refugees. One of the Indochinese refugees stood up ...and, called out to him, 'Hello American sailor, Hello Freedom Man'.

"This incident symbolizes, to me, America's promise to bring freedom to the world. I believe we're fulfilling this promise. I'm glad of the part I played in bringing freedom to the world."

West Coast White House

There, at my West Coast White House in the hills of Santa Barbara ... overlooking the Pacific Ocean, I sat with my head in my hands. I felt lost. I watched a moth flirting with a candle flame in a glass chimney on the picnic table. I didn't understand anyone, anymore, anyway.

I heard Nancy's voice ... calling me, from the forest. I turned around, stared into the Redwood and Pine trees, at the fog drifting in between them, from the sea.

Sixteen years out of office, I was still carrying an armload of autographed Bibles, handing them to my kids. I took a bow. In my head, I was playing my movie star role ... in, *Kings Row*.

I walked around, repeating my best line ever in a Hollywood film.

"Where's the rest of me? ... Where's the rest of me?"

I watched my imaginary audience smile, clap, cheer. I was on the alert. There was a war going on around me. Nobody else could see the war going on around me, but me. I listened, the sound of rifles with silencers being fired sounded like me breaking a carrot in two. I listened, the rifles went off ...quietly, blending in with the droning of crickets folding into the droning of the waves on the beach below.

I hid behind a tall redwood tree ...so, no one could *see* me. I watched terrorists shooting everyone. From out of nowhere, I was the sheriff in one of my movies, shooting bad guys, watching them fall like dominoes.

I felt happy.

"I'm going home! I'm going home! I can't play, anymore. It's time to go home. I'm going home."

Nancy sadly watched, "Bravo! Bravo! Bravo!"

Nancy led me to a picnic table, to have lunch. The rest of my family was at the picnic table, waiting for me. Patti was at the table ...when, Nancy helped me sit down. I went in and out of my dementia.

I was back now.

Patti described her *Playboy* shoot ...and, her conversation with the *Playboy* photographer, to me and Nancy.

I frowned, "Patti, we don't approve you posing for *Playboy.*"

Patti shrugged. "Mom, I thought we had a new policy of honesty ...because, we're trying to pull the family together."

Nancy smiled reassuringly, at me. Nancy bit her lip.

Patti remembered her *Playboy* shoot. While they were doing the shoot, Patti was telling the photographer her life story.

Patti looked at the photographer.

"That's what being a President's kid is like. What do you think they'll think if the magazine prints me as a big centerfold spread ... Give me my money, I want out of here."

<>

Patti finished describing the session to Nancy and me.

"It's not like I was posing totally nude!"

I wasn't pleased.

"Patti we don't approve. But, that's show biz. I guess, everyone does their own thing."

Patti stared at me, "Dad, there was a time I'd tell you to shove it. Now, I accept you the way you are. I accept myself. I'm alive. I'm amazed, life exists at all. I'm part of it, every flower, every star, every birth, every murder."

I smiled. "Gee Patti, you don't make it easy for yourself, do you?"

Patti smiled at me. "Dad, I'm a Reagan. We dream big. What I want's a hug from you."

I tried to give Patti a hug ... but, I start drifting away. The spirits of the Dead and the Poor ... who only I could see, grabbed my arms and restrained me. Paul Robeson's ghost tried to pull me away from them ...but, there were too many of them.

Nancy watched me struggle against the air around me, like I was trying to get away. Nancy figured my dementia was getting the best of me. My children gathered around me, afraid to get

too close ...because of the way I was talking to the air around me. One by one, my kids forgave me.

I watched the Dead and Poor crowd around me, moving their mouths, their words falling out like butterflies.

They spoke to me.

"We can't forgive you. We won't. You kept us from holding our loved ones. We won't let you, embrace yours. We'll harden your heart, you'll die alone."

I couldn't get out of my chair because the Dead and the Poor held me down.

I turned to Patti. "I want to hug you, Patti."

"Dad, all I want's a hug," Patti said.

In my dementia, I couldn't move. Patti looked at me. Nancy and Patti hugged one another, and cried. The other Reagan children joined into a group hug. Patti saw me watching a moth flying around a candle flame in a glass chimney on the picnic table. Patti watched as I tried to brush the moth away from the flame repeatedly.

Patti watched me. "Mom, I think Ronnie's coming out of his dementia. He's moving his hand!"

I came out of my dementia. I started acting normal again, as if nothing happened. Patti watched me trying to direct the moth away from the flame.

Patti sighed, "You're more concerned with one moth flying into a flame than you are with hundreds of thousands of human beings suffering every day."

"What could I've done, Patti?" I said.

"All that carrying around Bibles. You could've followed the Ten Commandments. You could've loved your neighbor. You could've loved me."

Nancy saw, I was hurt, tried protecting me. "Patti, leave your father alone."

Patti turned on Nancy. "Mom, you could've just said, 'No', to drugs, yourself."

Nancy was angry. "I didn't make this world. I was born into it,"

I felt desperate. "Patti, pray for me."

Patti looked at me. "Doing unto others doesn't mean having death squads liquidate, them, Dad."

My dementia returned, I saw a vision of moths flying out of the mouths of Nancy and Patti.

I was tired. "Forgive me, God."

I picked up my Bibles, start chasing my shadow, dropped my bibles, chased my shadow around and around a tree, trampling the Bibles deeper and deeper into the mud with no time, to stop. I hid behind the tree, finally poking my head out, "Peek-a-boo."

<>

I saw myself float up to heaven, led by an Angel ...that, looked like Nancy. I approached the

Shining City in the Sky, in the clouds surrounding Heaven. I told Saint Peter, open up the Pearly Gates of Heaven, for me. I stood before the Golden Desk and Throne of God. I saw God hold up the burnt Bible that'd slipped off my lap when I was a child and fallen into the fireplace and burnt, while I slept. And, God held up the muddy Bibles I'd just trampled in the mud. And, God held up the pocket Bible I'd autographed and given to Oliver North to give to Monzer Al-Kassar to give to King Assad of Syria.

I trembled before God. Beside God, were the souls of all those innocents killed in war …and, those who died in poverty during the Reagan Administration. The martyred souls stood pointing their fingers, accusingly, at me. I watched God stare at me.

I defended myself. "I was a man, made of flesh and blood. I wasn't perfect."

"Did you do the best you could?" God said.

I felt too ashamed, to answer, "I tried to."

"It's not up to me, to judge your sins, Ronnie. It's up to the people killed by the Contras you supported. It's up to the kids who ruined themselves on drugs you allowed the CIA to traffick in. It's up to the homeless, the needy, the hungry, everyone who suffered on your account …because, you hardened your heart to humanity, you looked the other way, right into your damn mirror."

"I was bringing in the sheep the best I knew how. I was a movie star, a hero to the American people …I gave them a chance to dream."

God didn't accept that answer. "You were a villain to the hungry and the poor …you were a Devil …a curse."

"Even my kids forgave me."

"You were not a hero, you were a bad guy to all those who suffered, were hurt or killed …because of the Reagan Administration … in this way you betrayed Me. All I've ever asked a living soul, is be faithful to Me. Can you look in your heart …and say, 'I know the difference between right, and wrong? …and did right'?"

"Yes, I always believed in you."

"Faith is not enough, Ronnie. You needed to have racked up more good deeds to get in, Here. I'm giving you another chance. Do it right this time. I'm sending you back. Would you like to go back?"

I considered what God said, "No, I think once was enough."

I heard Nancy calling my name, from far away. "Ronnie! Ronnnieee! Tell God, 'Yes!'"

I didn't understand. I almost had a realization

… I forgot what it was I was going to think …I stared off into the distance.

God looked at me, "C'mon Ronnie, go for the Oscar."

Suddenly, I felt motivated, "Okay. Send me back. Rehearsals are over. But God, one thing, did you do the best you could?"

"What do you mean?" God said.

I sang the words to a popular song, back in the day. "What if God was one of us? Just a stranger on a bus. What if God was one of us? Trying to make his way home?'"

I saw God had a questioning look on his face. I was hot. "All these wars and starvation and suffering and killing, fathers hurting their sons' feelings, mothers hurting their daughters' feelings, kids hurting their parents' feelings … not to mention the wars."

"I did the best I could. You fight the wars, not me."

"You could have made it better from day one."

I watched God open his palm. The solar system spun around in God's palm. God opened his other hand. In it mighty redwoods forests were growing. "Have you forgotten what your mother taught you in Bible studies? I made you in My Image, with free will. If you let Satan win his coup in your heart, the Earth's money-issuing class and the ruling families who they command will never be held accountable for making life, Hell on Earth. It's time for you to go back, try again, Ronnie. You have unfinished business."

God miraculously restored my burnt and muddy Bibles to cleanliness and wholeness. He handed them to me.

<>

I was singing, while I rocked in my rocking chair … overlooking sunset, on the Pacific on my ranch above Santa Barbara. Patti watched me watch a baby bird learning to fly. I saw the mother bird chirping, flying behind the baby bird on its first flight. The mother bird and baby bird flew around and around the picnic table beside where I was sitting. The baby bird landed on the picnic table. The baby bird looked at me. That made me feel happy. I watched both the birds take off, flying away into the treetops.

I stared up into the Heavens. "God, you didn't do so bad, after all."

Nancy noticed the confused look on my face, as I sat unmoving in my chair. Nancy saw, my face was frozen in a trance. Nancy felt helpless. Nancy felt like crying.

Nancy read to me.

"Fragile cease-fire in Yugoslavia remains threatened by unemployed roving terrorist, death squad, and mercenary units willing to work for the highest bidder."

I laughed, in my head I bowed to my audience of Americans cheering me. Big, house-sized inflatable Mickey Mouses went by in a parade honoring me, a person in a big inflatable Coors beer can costume walked over to me, tapped me on the shoulder. I knew, that was the signal for the bad guys to start chasing me. Suddenly, in front of me, Satan wearing a Satan costume appeared, he handed me an Oscar.

Nancy looked at me sitting motionless in the chair, my face blank. Nancy start crying. Nancy forced herself to keep reading.

"Investment bankers involved wanted to help arrange financing for construction projects in Eastern Europe after the war, but a civil war broke out between bin Laden Construction, Bechtel, Halliburton, and Brown & Root a Halliburton subsidiary."

I struggled to speak ...but, I couldn't. Nancy saw me struggle to talk. Nancy smiled at me.

Then, Nancy's smile faded. "I know, Honey. If you could speak ...you'd say, you're glad we're out of government, away from those back-stabbing cutthroats and assassins once, and for all."

Patti saw I had a look of peace on my face, she sat down on the grass beside me. Patti thought, I was going to say something. She leaned her head close to me. I tried to reach out to her. My hand took hers. I started to move my lips, to say something.

Patti got excited. She called the family around. "Daddy's going to say something. Everyone! Come over, quick!"

I moved my lips. "It's about time the right people were finally killed in war, we must divest the money-issuing class of people who own majority shares of central banks ...they're devils. It's a spiritual war, between good and evil, between Satan, and mankind ...God's in a box seat."

Patti smiled, "I agree."

I nodded. I closed his eyes. I felt myself slipping back into dementia. I sat in my rocking chair, watching the sun set over the Pacific Ocean.

In my head, I heard God talking to me. "Do you want another chance to live?"

"No, I think once was enough," I said.

Nancy saw a look of awe suddenly take my face. Nancy didn't know what to make of it. I heard someone, far away, calling my name ... in a ghostly way.

"Ronnnie, Ronnieeeee," the ghostly voice said.

I thought it was Nancy's voice. I couldn't under-

stand ...because, Nancy was sitting right next to me, not saying a word. I almost had a realization ... I forgot what I was thinking ...I stared off into the distance. It was like I was President, again ...off in the distance, the sun started to set over the Pacific. Paul Robeson's ghost came out of the sunshine like a little dot that grew bigger and bigger. By the time it was life-sized, Paul Robeson's ghost was right beside me. Nancy was crying. Maureen, Ron, Michael, and Patti were gathered around me.

I didn't know why.

Patti was pleading with me. "Dad will you give me a hug? All I want's a hug. All I've ever wanted is for you to love me."

I tried to reach out to Patti. My body would not move. Nancy saw, how handsome I looked, as I absently stared out to sea. Patti start crying. Paul Robeson's ghost helped me stand up out of my rocking chair. He put my arms around Patti. I hugged her. Patti wept.

I held up my Oscar in the sunset. I ran past my Secret Service guards who were pitching cards into a cowboy hat. I ran to show my family my Oscar.

I was so excited. "I got my Oscar! I got my Oscar!"

But, it was as if I was invisible. No one wanted to be bothered with me ...the Secret Service agents kept sitting on both sides of me ...I kept rocking in my rocking chair, kept watching the sunset on the Pacific Ocean ...the Secret Service agents kept pitching cards into a cowboy hat ...I sat there watching the cards sail slowly through the air. One of the Secret Service Agents looked at me ...then, spoke to the other one.

"He never moves. He never shows any expression on his face. I think he's dead, already. I feel like the Green Grocer."

The other agent watched his cards. "This guy doesn't even know he's a vegetable."

I start crying. I quickly leaned from my rocking chair and grabbed a gun from the holster of one of the Secret Service men. I start shooting at some foreign agents hiding in the trees, aiming rifles at me.

My family watched the empty rocking chair.

I was walking on the beach. I noticed no footprints in front of me. Behind me, two side-by-side sets of footprints led over to me. I got confused.

I looked up into Heaven.

"God, why are there two sets of footprints leading to me, I'm here by myself."

Mel Gibson's Jesus appeared beside me, embraced me in his arms ...he start carrying me along the shoreline, leaving one set of footprints in the sand behind us.

It was Oscar material.

"Jesus, how you doing, it took you long enough."

Mel's Jesus smiled at me, a golden halo shown around his head, "I'm fine, Ronnie, are you ready to go now? ...found your toe-marks?"

God knows, I didn't need toe-marks to stand in front of His camera, looking my best to His heavenly audience.

"I don't need toe-marks, today."

Nancy and her family looked at the empty rocking chair, watched sunset on the Pacific Ocean ...then, sat in the dark at the Reagan Ranch in the hills above Santa Barbara.

Fade.

Lights out.

Curtain.

President Reagan's last glimpse of the U.S. Capitol from the helicopter. 1/20/89

President Reagan sitting in the cockpit aboard SAM 27000 during his return to California. 1/20/89

ALL INTERIOR PHOTOS ARE: COURTESY RONALD REAGAN LIBRARY

Epilog

Ronnie Reagan & the Evil Empire

Campaign had ominous signs of American fascism

Dec. 12 1988, *San Francisco Chronicle* printed a James Michner column, *Campaign Had Ominous Signs of American Fascism*.

"This year's election scared me. It was conducted with a brutality and lack of attention to basic issues which appalled. The success of its ugly strategies flashed signals that this was the kind of electioneering we should expect during the next three national campaigns of this century.

"What frightened me? The tactics that proved so effective were those which Josef Goebbels found useful in destroying the German Republic in the 1930s. First, the 'big lie', the endless repetition until it becomes accepted proof, and the desire to destroy the opposition rather than refute its arguments.

"Second. Appropriating the emotional symbols of nationhood such as the flag, the pledge of allegiance, prayer in schools, exaltation of the family, opposition to abortion, and a macho boast that all citizens have the right to carry firearms and use them at will.

"Third. Denouncing anyone who did not pass those self-imposed 'litmus tests' as 'outside the mainstream, unpatriotic', perhaps even 'treasonous'.

"Fourth. The callous use of race, in the case of Willie Horton, to inflame prejudices and divide the population. Michael Dukakis was not defeated, he was destroyed. And that kind of victory does not serve the republic well. If persisted in, it could lead to American-style Fascism. I am a liberal Democrat who un-successfully ran for Congress in 1962, one of the best things I've ever done, because it taught me facts about American political life.

"As a member of the board of directors of Radio Liberty, and Radio Free Europe, which strive to portray an honest portrait of our nation abroad, I am an anti-Communist warrior. However, the Bush men did corrupt the political system. And, in a time of quiet and growing crises, they prevented any reasonable debate on the great issues facing this nation. As a consequence, we have postponed rather than solved our problems, and when the due bills are presented, the results may be devastating.

"What are these problems? Consider, the enormous burden of debt whose management tempts us into so many false steps.

"The imbalance of our trade with foreign nations so that we became a consuming nation rather than a producing one.

"The abandonment of one major area of production after another to other nations better organized, trained and disciplined than our own. I refer to steel, automobiles, communications systems, shipping, clothing, shoes and even minor items like the printing of books.

"The constant selling-off of our capital goods to foreigners at bargain-basement prices.

"The debasement of our public schools so we send half-educated young people to compete against fully-educated Japanese, Germans and Koreans.

"The determined swing of our judiciary to the hard-Right, so that the natural changes that all societies need to survive, will probably be inhibited as civil liberties are lost.

"We divert so much of our wealth to the servicing of our trillion-dollar debt, that most of the taxes I pay go to service debt. We are making bankers richer, and workers poorer. And I expect this imbalance to worsen.

"But it is the prospect of seeing four or five ultra-Right-wing justices on the Supreme Court that really scares me. For then, the subtle balances that have prevailed in our civic life may be destroyed," James Michner said.

Nov. 5 1988, former *New York Times* editorial page editor's article appears in the *Times*.

"What is really frightening about Mr. Bush's below-the-belt campaign is its apparent acceptance by a sizable proportion of the voting public. Softened up by eight years of Reagan-Bush dissimulation on everything from supplying arms to the Contras, to arms deals for the hostages, from 'Starwars' to the 'War on Drugs', from human rights to international law, too many bemused voters seem ready to believe anything.

"Yet, because of President Reagan's domination of the media he has gotten away with it. The much nastier, but equally skillful public relations campaign of candidate Bush is the beneficiary.

"The sneering attacks by President Reagan and Vice-President Bush on liberalism, the philosophy that is the basis of American democracy, set the evil tone of this campaign. It panders to the smoldering instincts of the mob, ready to explode when the next economic crisis bursts upon us.

"When that time comes, the way will have been paved for a demand for 'strong leadership.' It is a dangerous game. The innate strength of

American democracy has, up to now, resisted it even in times of crisis. Will it be able to do so next time? Though much of the electorate doesn't want to believe it, next time cannot be too far off.

"Look at reality, trillion dollars debt, multi-billion dollar deficit, gigantic trade imbalance, lack of competitiveness and inventiveness of industry, heedless depletion of natural resources, criminal down-grading of education, inadequate social services, growing poverty, shaky banking system, squeezed middle class, increasing disparity between rich and poor, the American economy is running on empty.

"When the crisis comes, whether the predictable economic crisis or an unpredictable foreign crisis, more will depend on the character than on the charisma of the President. For the past decade, we have had a surfeit of charisma," John B. Oakes said.

<>

Sept. 18 1992 *San Francisco Examiner* printed an article by Clifford E. Anderson.

"A registered Republican for nearly 25 years, I was a member of the Young Republicans in college. Both my parents were Republicans, as were their parents. Because of the current direction of the Republican Party, however, with frustration and disappointment I have decided to change my affiliation.

"This is not a decision taken lightly. Though I have not always agreed with the decisions taken by our president, and personally find him to be untrustworthy and opportunistic, the traditional values of financial responsibility, personal conservatism and individual authority for which the party stood had, until recently, remained firm and unshakable. This is no longer the case.

"The Republican Party has aligned with elements of Right-wing and religious extremists. This has fractured the party, destroyed its credibility and placed in jeopardy the very basis of our personal rights as Americans. I do not know the reasons why the party has elected to proceed in this direction, or to what extent President Bush is personally responsible. The situation, however, is no longer merely unacceptable; it is frightening.

"The right to personal religious understanding is inalienable under the Constitution. Forcing the beliefs of others upon us is contrary to the basis of a free society and lays the groundwork for totalitarianism. It appears that those in control of the party wish to reform society towards a neo-Medievalism where all but the most strict interpretations of personal behavior are criminalized or condemned, where all individual authority is suspended, and where personal liberty is subject to the interpretation of a select few. This is no longer conservatism, it is fascism.

"In new republican rhetoric, the term 'family values' is a euphemism for right-wing religious fanaticism ...'School support' is conscious and premeditated attempt to destroy our public school system in favor of privately controlled parochial schools ...'Feminists' are witches, children killers ...'Pro-choice (the only choice for many in a society that espouses family values but provides no means to support them) is a criminal act potentially punishable by the death penalty.

"If this were not enough, Republican political campaign tactics have again taken on the frightening specter of psychological manipulation, misrepresentation, distortion and lies typical of a world view of racists, religious zealots and extremists. So far to the Right are these people that they stand shoulder-to-shoulder with White supremacists and Nazis," Anderson said.

A Full-Court Press, the destabilization of the Soviet Union & Eastern Europe

Lou Wolf's *Covert Action Information Bulletin*, fall 1990, Sean Gervasi's *A Full-Court Press, the destabilization of the Soviet Union.*

"During early months of the first Reagan Administration, it became clear the U.S. was embarking on a policy of confrontation with the Soviet Union. Political observers began talking about a new Cold War. By 1982, relations with the Soviet Union were becoming tense, as were relations with some NATO allies. In the U.S. and in Europe, the belligerent warlike temperament of the Reagan Administration gave rise to a growing fear of nuclear conflict ... yet if the U.S. seemed intent upon confrontation, even upon playing 'nuclear chicken' with the Soviet Union ...it was not at all clear what it expected to achieve by doing so.

"The Reagan-Bush Administration policies were clear, but the objectives of those policies were not ... many observers began to fear, especially in Europe, that some members of the U.S. Administration might actually want a nuclear war ...believing somehow that the U.S. would prevail.

"In fact, the Reagan-Bush Administration was not driving towards nuclear war ... its extremely aggressive policies were not meant to lead to war, but to change and create an upheaval in the Soviet Union ...part of a strategy aimed at forcing the Soviet Union to retreat from the world stage, to adopt reforms to carry it towards a 'regulated market economy' i.e. towards the dismantling of socialism. A few analysts had seen it coming.

"In 1982, Joseph Fromm made it clear there was something 'behind the shift to a harder line in foreign policy' ...the U.S. was waging limited economic warfare against Russia to force the Soviets to reform their political system'. Fromm quoted an unnamed U.S. official as saying, 'The Soviet Union is in deep financial trouble, by squeezing wherever we can, our purpose is to induce the Soviets to reform their system. I think we will see the results over the next several years.' Observers in the West and in the Socialist Bloc have seriously misunderstood the foreign and military policies pursued by the U.S. during the 1980s decade ... and portrayed them as uneven and reckless, because analyses focused on surface phenomena such as expansion of military forces, or efforts to deny the Soviet Union new technologies ... rather than on the strategy behind such policies. The strategy needs to be examined and debated for two reasons ...first, it appears to have been successful, although not generally recognized as such among critics of the Reagan Administration from the center left.

"Conservatives are openly arguing that the Reagan Administration set in motion the policies which led to 'the defeat of Communism' ... the editor of Policy Review, the flagship publication of the Heritage Foundation, wrote, the West had 'won' the Cold War because of the foreign policies pursued by the conservative governments in every major country in the Western world.

"David Rubenstein, a sociologist at University of Illinois was more specific, 'The key difference between the Soviet policy in the 1970s and 1980s can be explained not by deterioration of the Soviet economy, but in changes in U.S. foreign policy'.

"Second, there is substantial evidence, that having succeeded in aggravating the crisis in the Soviet Union, the U.S. and its allies are not engaged in building internal pressures there for further reform ...but, engaged in open, large-scale interference in the internal affairs of the Soviet Union ... conservative analysts are open about this. Rubenstein expressed his concern that 'if the current sense of crisis is eased, the motivation for further reform may be lost' ... he concluded, 'If internal pressure was a key factor in motivating this policy of reform, pressure may be required to bring it forward'.

"One of the first public indications of the existence of the secret strategy to apply pressure against the Soviet Union came in Mar. 1981 ...

Richard Pipes, a senior National Security officer in charge of Soviet Affairs gave a press interview that caused controversy ...Pipes, a Soviet expert on leave from Harvard told a Reuters reporter that 'nothing was left of détente', and the Reagan Administration might pursue a foreign policy 'as radical as the President's economic program'. The Reagan Administration, he told the reporter, was moving towards a strategy of confrontation with the Soviet Union and with radical and socialist regimes in the Third World, the purpose of this strategy was to change the world balance of forces, and 'Soviet leaders would have to chose between peacefully changing their Communist system in the direction followed by the West, or going to war'.

"The New York Times quoted Pipes saying, 'There is no alternative to war with the Soviet Union if the Russians did not abandon Communism' ... these words did not come from a middle-level official, they came from the Senior National Security Council Officer in charge of Soviet Affairs ...seen as indicating a dangerous aggressiveness on the part of the Reagan Administration. The Pipes interview rang alarm bells around the world ...the White House immediately disavowed the interview, claiming that Pipes' remarks did 'not represent views of the Administration'. Even so, U.S. allies protested vigorously ...the London Financial Times warned that U.S. allies would be angered by any attempt to play 'a dangerous game of chicken'.

"In retrospect, it seems likely that Pipes was being used deliberately to warn the Soviets so that they would try to match the U.S. military expansion then underway, particularly in the nuclear field ... 'the Pipes leak' is entirely consistent with the strategy of 'spending them into bankruptcy' or 'weakening Russia's economy'. The strategy, however, involved much more than the threat of nuclear war ... a large number of studies by Rand Corp. in the early 1980s made it clear the Reagan Administration was not preparing for war, but mounting a sophisticated attack on the Soviet economy [Ed's note, economic warfare]. Rand is a California think-tank that carries out classified research for the military, its experts move in and out of government, and are routinely asked to analyze and comment on military and intelligence planning documents not accessible to most congressmen. Rand is a part of the military intelligence complex. Many Rand studies were commissioned by the Department of Defense, white papers were often 'sanitized' versions of classified studies. Titles were suggestive, *Economic Leverage in Soviet Union, Costs of Soviet Empire, Sitting on Bayonets?...Soviet Defense Burden, Moscow's Economic Dilemma*. Taken together, these papers were concerned with two issues. The first was 'economic stringency' in the Soviet Union, since the late 1970s ... the second was what measures NATO countries could use to make Soviet economic stringency more acute ...the line of argument was clear.

Economic growth in Soviet Union had begun to slow in the late 1970s, increasing difficulties of meeting various claims on its resources.

Soviet Union was entering a 'leadership crisis' as leadership of the Communist Party was passed to a younger generation.

U.S. and its allies could take various actions to force Soviet Union to increase its defense spending and economic and military assistance to allies and friends.

U.S. could deny Soviets access to credits, key imports and modern technology needed to increase productivity and accelerate economic growth.

Such measures would reduce overall volumes of resources available to the Soviet Union, hold back productivity, or force resources to be shifted from domestic consumption and investment.

Each effect would aggravate difficulties confronting Soviet leadership in a stagnant economy.

A combination of measures 'to impose costs' on Soviet Union might be expected to lead to a fall in investment and/or standard of living.

A combination of measures might generate pressures within the Soviet Union for withdrawing from the world stage and for political and economic reforms.

So, the Rand study seemed to be preparing the ground for a kind of hot Cold War, aimed at weakening and possibly even breaking the back of the Soviet economy. In the 1980s, following a decade of détente, this was remarkable in itself ... it is clear that analysts believed the ultimate aim of the strategy would be to force change upon the Soviet Union ...so Reagan-Bush Administration saw Soviet economic troubles as an opportunity to complicate Soviet resource allocation, in hopes that pressure would draw resources away from Soviet defense, or push the Soviet economy in the direction of Western economic and political reforms.

Free Congress Foundation goes East

Lou Wolf's *Covert Action Quarterly*, Lou co-authoring with Russ Bellant, *Free Congress Foundation goes East.*

Fall 1989, Coors and Paul Weyrich's Free Congress Foundation was directly involved in Eastern Europe. Robert Krieble, a retired businessman from Connecticut, sat on the Board of Directors of the Free Congress Foundation. Krieble had his own foundation, the Krieble Foundation. Krieble Foundation financed sending Paul Weyrich and a staff of four people to Hungary, Estonia, and Soviet Union. Coors and Krieble sent Weyrich to train Far-Right leaders in ideology and electoral manipulation. In Moscow, Paul Weyrich worked with a leadership body of the Communist Party, the Inter-Regional Deputies Group of the Supreme Soviet. Boris Yeltsin and Andre Sakarov had founded the Inter-Regional Deputies Group, summer 1989. Weyrich established a training school for the Inter-Regional Deputies Group for political candidates to promote the Inter-Regional Deputies Group program. The Inter-Regional Deputies Group created Right-wing pressure on Gorbachev to dismantle Socialism and to dismantle the Soviet Union.

Fall 1990, Weyrich's efforts paid off. Electoral success of Inter-Regional Deputies Group made Boris Yeltsin the leader of the Russian Soviet Socialist Republic. Boris Yeltsin started forming relationships with reactionary leaders of the Lithuanian Sajudis Party.

When Paul Weyrich returned from Moscow he felt enthusiastic.

"That was the most incredible experience of my life! Boris Yeltsin and the Inter-Regional Deputies Group are in favor of private property, a market economy, and restoring Christianity and Catholicism in Russia," Weyrich said.

In 1990, there was a political vacuum in Russia. Ultra-nationalist forces in many Russian republics seized the moment to take over. Nationalist and Fascist groups were well-established in Lithuania and Ukraine. In Ukraine, pro-Nazi Ukrainian Nationalists OUN were influential in several political parties. OUN organized large demonstrations to honor OUN leaders who in World War II helped Hitler fight on Eastern Front.

Many senior level administrators in the OUN had served in German-supported army units in 1944. In 1990 Sajudis issued laws against Russians living in Lithuania. Sajudis disliked Poles. Boris Yeltsin also wooed Pamyat. Pamyat is the largest Russian fascist group. Pamyat is anti-Semitic. Pamyat currently distributes anti-Semitic propaganda similar to what the German Nazi Party circulated in 1920.

A 1990 *Newsweek* article described Pamyat. Living in Moscow in 1990, Sergei Tesnikov was a member of the Pamyat National Orthodox Movement.

"Jews killed Christ and Czar Nicolas II, organized the Bolshevik Revolution and planned Stalin's purges. Glasnost and Perastroika are part of a Jewish World Conspiracy to take over Russia. Russia will liberate mankind. It was prophesied Russia would get rid of evil in the world. We must be on the lookout for enemies," Tesnikov said.

Egor Shafarevich, a Pamyat propagandist, had an article published in *Nash Sovremennik Our Contemporary World*, called, *Russophobia.*

"Novelists are Russia-bashing. Leningrad Writer's Union broke into two groups when twenty anti-Semitic writers and Pamyat agent provocateurs wanted editorial control over the Writers Union newsletter. Their last meeting together was turbulent. Pamyat intelligence operatives broke into the Moscow Writers Union. 'Kill the Yids! Kill the Yids!', the Pamyat operatives yelled. There is a battle in Russia between Slavs and Western-thinking people," Shafarevich said.

Andre Boznesensky calls himself a poet.

"In Russia, this is an old and noble question, are you pro-Jew or anti-Jew?

Egor Sychov had portraits of the Czars and maps of Czarist Russia on his walls.

"I'm trying to re-instill in Russians a love for traditional culture," Gregor Mychov said.

Demetri Vasilyev and his Pamyat friends wear black-shirts and para-military boots. Demetri Vasilyev only let West German reporters interview him, no other country's.

Schmirnov-Ostashvili's faction of Pamyat practices the anti-Semitism they preach. His friend held up a grandchild.

"Isn't she lovely? He's a little anti-Semite. The U.S. is controlled by Jewish capitalists. Western media is controlled by Jewish capitalists. Jews should not be allowed to migrate. They should be tried, imprisoned for crimes. Blame Jews for the rise of Communism. Blame Jews for the fall of Communism. Jews like Karl Marx made the Russian Revolution. Jewish Bolsheviks like Leon Trotsky convinced Stalin to purge people in Russia under his rule. Mother Russia has been caught in a Star Of David held by a hairy man with a giant nose," Schmirnov-Ostashvili said.

Morrie Levy had an observation.

"Soviet Jews are in a panic over Pamyat. The pressure's been building for two years. Every Jew can feel the difference. Neighbors in my apartment I thought were my friends started referring to me in sentences that began, 'You Jews,' Nobody threatened me physically, nobody fired me from my job, but all of a sudden, I became 'the Jew'. I'm immigrating to Israel," Morrie Levy said.

Not just in Moscow, but Jews in Odessa, Leningrad, Dushambe, Baku, Kiev were scared. Pamyat propagandists were circulating rumors that Pamyat terrorists were required to make a list of the names and addresses of four Jews each. Anti-Communism and anti-Semitism were lumped together into one target in Eastern Europe.

"In Hungary the Hungarian Communist Party crumbled. The word, 'Jew', was used as a slang word to mean, 'traitor'. Hungarian Jews who were doctors and lawyers and dentists received disturbing messages on their answering machines.

"You dirty stinking Jew, we'll send you back to Auschwitz," one message said.

The NTK soccer team was founded by Jews a century ago, but now, only non-Jews are involved with it. Pamyat fans for the other team playing against NTK chant anti-Semitic slogans.

"No goals for the Jews. Dirty Jews, Jews, Jews, to the gas chambers, gas chambers, gas chambers," Pamyat fans chant.

In 1990 Hungarian election campaigns included 'The Democratic Forum', an anti-Communist group. Esvon Csurka, a spokesman for the Democratic Forum made a political address on the radio.

"Wake up Hungarians. As long as a dwarfish minority can make a whole society accept that their truth is the only truth, the great popular masses of the Hungarian people can not have a good time in their own country," Csurka said.

"There's anti-Semitism in Hungary because Stalin put four Jews on the politburo in a deliberate plot to destroy the self-esteem of the Hungarian people," Esvon Csurka said.

Pamyat propaganda held Jews responsible for abortion, and for putting violent programs on TV and in the movies. Atollah Pok is a Hungarian historian.

"Such things are to be taken seriously," Pok said.

No one has yet taken full account of anti-Semitism in Hungary during and after World War II. The common belief among non-Jewish Hungarians is that the country has always been good to its Jews, that they were not sent to the death camps until 1944, when the Nazis occupied the country. And that even then Hungarians resisted, saving most of the Jews from the Budapest ghetto. This is nonsense.

The Hungarian Arrow Cross Fascists killed Jews through the war. Adolf Eichmann put the Final Solution to the Jewish Question into operation, Hungarians went along with it. It's very hard to grasp the significance of the Holocaust here. Hungarians have never accepted their share of the blame for the holocaust," Pok said.

<>

In Romania, in Bucharest Ghetto during World War II, Iron Guard slaughtered Jews on butcher blocks, hung corpses of Jews on meathooks, under a sign that read, 'Kosher Meat'.

<>

Later, these Iron Guardists joined the Far-Right National Peasant's Party NPP. NPP campaigned against several candidates in the 1990 Romanian elections, including Petro Roman the incumbent Prime Minister of the Interim Government, and Silvu Brucan a member of National Salvation Front. Both were Jews. NPP's newspaper accused Silvu Brucan and six Jewish Communists of organizing genocide of Romanians after World War II. NPP's newspaper printed cartoon caricatures of a Jew being the Devil.

Lupe Joan was Secretary-General of NPP.

"We're not anti-Semitic. We never made such statements as, .the Jews brought Communism to Romania.. We've just changed the name of the Party to the National Christian Peasant's Party," Joan said.

Romania's Chief Rabbi kept a library. He was criticized for helping Jews immigrate out of Cocesscco's Regime. He pulled several books off the shelves, including several readily-available books in Hungarian bookstores, *Is Communism Jewish?* ...and, *The Occupation of the World by the Jews.*

Moses Rosen is Romania's Chief Rabbi.

"There are no definitive Romanian books about Romanian Jews. Until a few months ago it was a crime to own Western books on the Holocaust. Anti-Semitism isn't covert, it's out in the open now," Rosen said.

In Poland, in Sandomierz, there is a church built in the 17th Century that has a wall mural called, 'Infanticida' ...showing kidnapping and mutilation of Christian babies. On the wall there is a sign. "Faithless members of the Jewish community killed two Sandomierz babies in 1698 and 1710," it says.

Nearby a child asked a Nun what the picture meant.

"Did Jews really do that?" the child said.

"Yes. But they don't do that anymore, because no Jews are left in Poland," the Nun said.

Polish politicians, like American politicians, are influenced by Far-Right nationalist lobbyists, anti-Communist lobbyists, and Roman Catholic lobbyists. Creskov Kawecki is editor of, *National Word*, a desktop-publishing newsletter operation.

"I started my newsletter to serve Christian Nationalists and all Far-Right groups. I'm not anti-Semitic, but Adam Michnik, Head of Solidarity's Parliament Foreign Affairs Committee is Jewish. So is the Solidarity newspaper editor of *Gazetta Wyborcza.* It's impossible to say the 'Jewish Question' in Poland is not a problem anymore ...just because we don't have many Jews left here. The problem of Jews doesn't matter how many there are, but how much they influence the mass media and our culture. The people of Poland understand this," *National Word* editor Creskov Kawecki said.

<>

But overtones of fascism and Nazism did not matter to Paul Weyrich. To Free Congress Foundation, supporting fascists and Nazis was means to an end.

Sitting on the Free Congress Foundation Board of Directors was Charles Moser, a George Washington University professor. Moser also sat on the Editorial Advisory Board of, *Ukrainian Quarterly.* Articles in *Ukrainian Quarterly* praised the German SS of World War II.

Articles in *Ukrainian Quarterly* endorsed the Organization of Ukrainian Nationalists World War II alliance with Hitler and the Third Reich.

OUN supported Hitler's occupation of Ukraine. The OUN is an international organization. It operates covertly. It is headquartered in Bavaria. It was financed by Franz Joseph Strauss, the Right-wing former head of Bavaria. Franz Joseph Strauss and Paul Weyrich were friends.

Franz Joseph Strauss made many speeches against German détente with the U.S.S.R. Paul Weyrich supplied these speeches to U.S. Senators, who read them into the Congressional Record. When Strauss came to Washington, it was Weyrich who arranged his schedule.

Yes, Free Congress Foundation operations abroad were anti-Democracy, not pro-Democracy. Free Congress Foundation co-published *Freedom Fighter*, a rollback-liberation propaganda rag edited by Charles Moser, in Free Congress Foundation offices.

It was published in conjunction with Freedom Research Foundation, run by Jack Wheeler. *Freedom Fighter Newsletter* supported the military-sponsored death squad operations of the Nicaraguan Contras ...Renamo operations in Mozambique ...Unita in Angola ...and fascist mercenary units in North Africa, Afghanistan, and Southeast Asia.

Even U.S. State Department condemned the South Africa sponsored Renamo operation because of its terrorism and genocide of one-hundred-thousand people in Mozambique.

In spite of, or because of, Paul Weyrich's cultivated relationships with anti-Democracy groups around the world, he was able to get much funding from Carl Gershman's National Endowment for Democracy NED.

Except National Endowment for Democracy was funded by U.S. Congress ...with tax money of the American people who believed in Democracy ...not in lip-service.

Congress funded the NED to intervene in the politics of other countries. In 1990 Carl Gershman awarded $40,000 to Paul Weyrich to funnel to the Initiatives Foundation in Moscow. Initiatives Foundation in Moscow is a non-profit affiliate of the Inter-Regional Deputies Group IRG. The money was intended to buy communications hardware and software, fax machines, copy machines, computers for desk-top publishing, video recorders and VCR's.

<>

Paul Weyrich had a list of donor prospects. When he sent them fundraising requests he bragged that in every election in Eastern Europe he had intervened, except Romania ...every group he trained in electoral manipulation and propaganda had won the elections. Paul Weyrich sent a video-tape along with his fundraising letters. The tape had interesting lines.

The tape had a professional narrator.

"Paul Weyrich's Free Congress Foundation trained Boris Yeltsin's campaign manager. Paul Weyrich voiced skepticism about the intent of Ronald Reagan's White House heir to perpetuate the ultra-conservative agenda," the narrator said.

Paul Weyrich didn't trust President Bush or the Republic Party, or the U.S. program in Eastern Europe. So in 1989, Paul Weyrich founded Free Congress Foundation's newest center, Center for Freedom and Democracy, in Eastern Europe.

Center for Freedom and Democracy was founded to train opposition leaders in Eastern Europe and the Soviet Union in principles, propaganda and mechanics of Democracy and free-market techniques, to create economic opportunities for American companies.

The 1990 budget for the Center for Freedom

and Democracy was $450,000. In 1989 and 1990 the Free Congress Foundation had training programs around the Communist world to 'promote democracy'.

In 1989, Budapest Hungary, Free Congress Foundation trained the leaders of the Hungarian New Democratic Forum, the Small Holders Party, and the Christian Democratic Party. The Free Congress Foundation holds itself responsible for the three parties to win 231 out of 386 seats in the Hungarian Parliament.

In 1989, Moscow ... in a four-day training session co-sponsored by Free Congress Foundation and Academy for National Economy of the Soviet Council of Ministers, 20 members of the Supreme Soviet were trained, and 60 members of the opposition party, the Inter-Regional Deputies Group, were trained.

They were indoctrinated in Political Thinking, Development of Tactics, Political Strategy, Political Goals and Political Decision-Making in an election campaign. They were also trained in the political techniques of recruitment of volunteers, organization of volunteers, identification and turn-out of volunteers, election-day activities, the building of coalitions, and methods of communicating with voters.

In 1989, Tallin Estonia ... over a four day period Free Congress Foundation trainers instructed 70 members of opposition groups whose goal was independence from U.S.S.R. Free Congress Foundation trainers taught them the Fundamentals of Political Strategy and Organizational Politics. Trainees were provided from Estonian Heritage Society, Estonian National Independence Party, Popular Front in Tallinn, and Estonia Citizens Committee.

February 1990, Leipzig East Germany met with the Democratic Awakening Party and the Democratic Social Union, two conservative groups in an anti-Left alliance. A course in American Political Techniques was taught for the two groups to use in the March 1990 election. The two groups were taught U.S. direct mail campaigning. The two groups credited Free Congress Foundation for unexpected success in the elections.

March 1990 in Bucharest, Romania, 80 members of twelve opposition groups were students in a four-day seminar on the Political Skills to Win Elections, and Free Enterprise and the Need for Entrepreneurship. Participants were from the National Peasants Party, Free Students Union of the Polytechnical University, Students League, Human Rights League, National Liberal Party,

National Salvation Front, and Christian Social Democratic Party.

Free Congress Foundation had opened a field office in Romania only a month prior to this meeting to develop contacts.

April 1990, in the Croatian Capital of Zageb, Free Congress Foundation staffers taught members of the Croatian Democratic Union in Political Techniques, Government, and Building Relationships between Regional and Federal Governments.

From Zagreb, the Free Congress Foundation team moved on to Prague Czechoslovakia, to teach Techniques, Strategies, Goals, and Objectives in Elections, and the Establishment of Democratic Institutions. The courses were taught to fifty people from dissident groups such as the Civic Forum, Public Against Violence …similar to the Civic Forum in Slovakia, Christian Democratic Movement, Christian Democratic Union, Social Democrats, Republican Party Of Czechoslovakia, Pan Europe Union, Democratic Initiative, and People For Active European Federation.

April 1990 in Moscow, Leningrad and Sberdlovsk in the Soviet Union Free Congress Foundation held another session with the Inter-Regional Deputies Group. Sixty people in Moscow divided into small groups and were taught in role-playing exercises focusing on Governing In Executive, Legislative, and Judicial Levels in Local, Regional and National Government.

In Sberdlovsk, 235 persons role-played.

In Leningrad, forty-five people attended. Free Congress Foundation also made a presentation on How Free Enterprise operates.

August 1990 Sofia Bulgaria, Paul Weyrich and staff, together with Robert Krieble and Detroit businessman Don Fisher, met with one-third of the opposition members in the Parliament. The meeting was attended by Dimitar Loudiev, chief political adviser to President Zhelyu Zhelev.

<>

October 1990 a delegation of six senior Soviet political and economic opposition figures and officials met in Washington, D.C., with senior-level U.S. officials at a conference, The Coming Russian-American Alliance in the Post-Communist Era. The three-day conference delegates had a one-hour meeting with Vice President Dan Quayle.

Soviet participants included Arkady Murashev, who had been schooled by the Free Congress Foundation in Moscow. Arkady Murashev was the Executive Secretary of Yeltsin's Inter-Regional Deputies Group.

Also attending were Yeltsin's Chief of Staff Gennadi Burbulis …National Security Commission Chair and former Soviet Navy Lieutenant-Commander Vladimir Lopatin …Minister of Publishing and Information Mikhail Poltoranin …People's Deputy and Head of the Siberia Legislative District Stanislav Selezne …and Commission on Economic Reform Chairman S. Sulakshin. Boris Yeltsin had recently injured in an automobile accident.

He sent a letter to the combined delegates.

"We seek to create an economic system based upon universal market mechanisms and the sacred right of every person to property. The entrepreneur will become the chief actor in our economy," Yeltzin said.

Attending the conference were, HUD Secretary Jack Kemp …Assistant State Secretary John Bolton …Deputy Energy Secretary Hensen Moore …Assistant Commerce Secretary for International Economic Policy Tom Duesterberg …former Pentagon Assistant Secretary Richard Perl …former Assistant Attorney General William Bradford Reynolds …Burton Yale Pines of the Heritage Foundation …former Governor of Delaware Pete DuPont … and two long-time Cold War advocates from local academia, Charles Moser and Peter Reddaway.

Free Congress Foundation coordinated the arrangements for the Soviets' visas directly with Dan Quayle's office …rather than through State Department channels.

Arkady Murashev, Executive Secretary of Yeltsin's Inter-Regional Deputies Group visited Free Congress Foundation's Washington office three times during visits to the U.S.

Leaders of the newly formed Russian Christian Democratic Party came to Free Congress Foundation offices in July. Christian Democratic Party said their political platform was that only a religious and moral rebirth will open the pathways to beneficial transformations. President Zhelyv Zhelev of Bulgaria visited Free Congress Foundation offices in September 1990.

Covert Action Quarterly's Lou Wolf, and Russ Bellant continue their co-authored article, *Free Congress Foundation goes East.*

"Those seeking a religious and moral rebirth would be well advised to consider the company that Free Congress Foundation keeps. The Free Congress Foundation is identified with the secular New Right rather than the Religious New Right, but in fact it melds both currents of

Rightist activity," Russ Bellant said.

Although structurally one organization, Free Congress Foundation could be seen as a dozen semi-independent groups housed in one office complex and with one boss. Free Congress Foundation divides its activities into 'centers', centers for Government and Politics, Law and Democracy, Cultural Conservatism, State Policy, Conservative Governance, Child and Family Policy, Foreign Policy, Transportation Policy, Catholic Policy, New Freedom And Democracy.

The Free Congress Foundation's 1988 Annual Report described its Center for Catholic Policy.

"The public policy influence and activity of the Catholic Church in America often runs counter to the interests of Catholic laity. The Center for Catholic Policy seeks to instruct conservative Catholic laity how to become influential in shaping public policy stands taken by the Church. A network of forty national Catholic organizations, institutions and publications share our conservative viewpoint. This coalition of forty Catholic groups is called Siena Group, and was formed by Free Congress Foundation in January of 1988. Among the top priorities of Siena Group is mobilizing opposition to a U.S. Catholic Conference statement on AIDS policy which favorable to objectives of the gay-and-lesbian-rights movement. Siena Group participants convinced the bishops to set aside the AIDS document," writers of the annual report said.

Free Congress Foundation's penetration into the politics of the Soviet Union and Eastern Europe could be understood by their selection of Laszlo Pasztor to head their Liberation-Support Alliance, that the Free Congress Foundation says seeks to 'liberate' peoples in Central and Eastern European nations. Laszlo Pasztor's involvement in Eastern European politics began in World War II. It was at that time he joined the Youth Organization of the Arrow Cross. The Arrow Cross was the Nazi Party of Hungary.

Wolf and Bellant commented.

"When the Arrow Cross was installed in power by a German commando operation, Laszlo Pasztor was sent to Berlin to help facilitate the liaison between the Arrow Cross and Hitler. After the 'official' end of World War II, Laszlo Pasztor was tried and served two years in jail for his Arrow Cross activities after an anti-Communist government was elected in Hungary in 1945. He eventually came to the U.S. and established the ethnic arm of the Republican National Committee for Richard Nixon.

"He brought other Nazi collaborators from the Eastern front into the Republican GOP. Some were later found to have participated in mass murder during the war. In 1990, the dormant Arrow Cross surfaced again in Hungary. There were attempts to lift the ban on the Nazi organization. Laszlo Pasztor spent several months in Hungary. When Paul Weyrich later conducted training in Hungry Paul Weyrich was provided a list of Laszlo Pasztor's contacts in Hungary. Paul Weyrich reported he conducted training for the recently formed New Democratic Forum, which was the governing party in Hungary in 1990. Laszlo Pasztor claimed he had an advisory position with National Endowment for Democracy.

"Laszlo Pasztor said he helped friends in Hungary to apply for and receive National Endowment for Democracy funding. National Endowment for Democracy worked through Lithuanian Catholic Religious Aid LCRA & Lithuania Information Center LIC to inject fascists into Lithuania via Sejudas. "In 1989 Laszlo Pasztor spoke at the Heritage Foundation. Laszlo Pasztor was sponsored by the Anti-Bolshevik Bloc of Nations ABN ... a multi-national umbrella organization of émigré Fascists and Nazi's that was founded in alliance with Hitler in 1943. It is led by the Organization of Ukrainian Nationalists. Laszlo Pasztor spoke for the Hungarian Organization of the Anti-Bolshevik Bloc of Nations, which is the Arrow Cross.

Lou Wolf was right.

"Those seeking a religious and moral rebirth would be well advised to consider the company that Free Congress Foundation keeps. Those leaders and cadre trained by Free Congress Foundation's traveling tutors were led by Paul Weyrich and company to believe in themselves and the goals set before them. However, they aren't on Weyrich's mailing list of key opinion shapers, so they aren't aware of his real assessment of them. Democratic leaders such as Havel, Zhelev or Landsberger are not entirely prepared to cope with such situations. Free Congress Foundation's involvement in Eastern Europe began as a result of their expertise in electing U.S. conservatives to office. This campaign expertise enhanced their reputation in national politics. But their ties, which suggest an ultimately anti-Democracy agenda, including their émigré-Fascist and Christian-Fascist involvement, remain unexamined.

"Free Congress Foundation's advocacy of a narrow range of social conformity and literal repression of non-conformists in the U.S. can be found in their detailed literature on the subject. It is reasonable to expect that those in the East seeking aid for the new arena of electoral activity may not know Free Congress Foundation's deeper agenda. It is up to Americans to communicate that warning and to challenge the National Endowment for Democracy giving our tax dollars to the Free Congress Foundation. U.S. tax dollars legitimize the Free Congress Foundation in the eyes of some political groups in the Soviet Union and Eastern Europe. With the rapid pace of political change sweeping Eastern Europe and the Union of Socialist Republics, many opportunities have emerged for Western interests to intervene in the politics of that region. In some cases, such a vacuum has been created that virtual strangers to the area several years ago are now able to actively participate in changing those societies from within. These interventions are not only being practiced by mainstream organizations. The involvement of the United States Far-Right, such as Free Congress Foundation, brings with it the potential revival of Fascist organizations in the East," Wolf and Bellant said.

<>

Wolf and Bellant continued.

In 1990 organizations like Free Congress Foundation and the National Endowment for Democracy spouted off about political transformation in Eastern Europe ... but Right-wing fascist political activity that occurred in Eastern Europe in the start of the 20th Century, now was re-emerging at the end of that century.

March 1990, Romania's Chief Rabbi Moses Rosen, traveled to Washington with an urgent request. In the Romanian city of Tirgu Mures, pogroms were being directed against the Hungarian minority.

Six Hungarians had been killed. Rosen asked the Bush Administration's State Department to forbid Nazi-oriented Romanian émigré that had gotten U.S. citizenship, from returning home to Romania to stir up racism and anti-Semitism and old hatreds in the style of the World War II Romanian death squads, the Iron Guard. During World War II, the Iron Guard in Romania were responsible slaughter so brutal even the Nazis were repulsed. Forty-five years later, death squad terrorists were calling themselves Iron Guard members.

They were taking credit for the murders in Tirgu Mures. According to Cazimir Ionescu, then vice president for the Socialist National Salvation Front, an Iron Guard propaganda campaign had been under way since the December overthrow of President Ceauseseu.

At the time of the Tirgu Mures violence, interim Romanian President Petre Roman expelled three fascist Romanian-Canadians for promoting fascist ideas. One of those expelled was George Belasu, well known in the Romanian community in the West as editor of the pro-Iron-Guard, *Romanian Voice*.

Hamilton Ontario-based Romanian Voice supported Valerian Viorel Trifa, head of a faction of the Romanian Orthodox Church dominated by the Iron Guard. Trifa fled the U.S. in 1984 after the Justice Department's Office of Special Investigations found evidence implicating him in a Bucharest pogrom in 1941. According to an eye witness from Romanian who had been present in Bucharest at the time, Viorel Trifa stood at the base of the statue of King Michael.

Viorel Trifa had delivered a speech he hoped would start a revolution. He started speaking slowly and calmly. The square was filled with a crowd of 6,000 people. More and more people kept joining the crowd.

Viorel Trifa spoke.

"Ideas of equality serve the kikes. The kikes of Europe have intensified their struggle for emancipation at the moment when the revolutionary spirit reached the Rhine. The leadership of the people has fallen into the hands of kikes and Jew-lovers who are ruling everything, especially history. Jewry has found a good place from where it will spread its spider web over the entire world," Viorel Trifa said.

There followed a riot that began a three-day Iron Guard revolt. The Romanian press reported 118 Jews were killed and 26 were wounded. The eye witnesses said 6,000 Jews were killed in Bucharest, and 4,000 more throughout Romania during those three days. On Wednesday, the General Staff of the Iron Guard ordered the destruction of the Bucharest Jewish Quarter. All the Jews who lived there were to be killed. Iron Guard gangs stormed through the Jewish quarter murdering the people who lived there. They killed or beat every one they thought was Jewish. It was easy to pick them out. Everyone who wasn't killing Jews was assumed to be a Jew.

The pogrom against the Jews by the Iron Guard was planned in advance by the Iron Guard terrorist death squads. Late Wednesday night 200 Jews who had been rounded up by Iron Guard raids were put into trucks and driven to the slaughterhouse. There the Green Shirts, as the members of the Iron Guard were called, forced the Jews to undress. The Iron Guard led the Jews to the chopping blocks, then cut their throats Kosher style, in a parody of the Jewish way of slaughtering livestock and fowl. Some the broken corpses were dumped through slaughterhouse manholes into sewers used for animal remains. Other naked bodies, with heads cut off, were hung on iron hooks and stamped *carnas* kosher … kosher meat. The Iron Guard General Staff that ordered the massacre included Viorel Trifa, leader of the student movement of the Iron Guard. After the war Viorel Trifa immigrated to America. He led some Iron Guard members into a Romanian Catholic Church, where they beat up the Bishop. Then Viorel Trifa assumed the Bishop's position in the Church. Viorel Trifa soon controlled an Episcopate with forty-six churches and 10,000 parishioners, mostly in Ohio. The Vatra (the seat of the American Orthodox Episcopate) which Viorel Trifa's Iron Guard supporters had taken by force was now officially his. Bishop Moldivan's legal challenges to Bishop Viorel Trifa were defeated in Ohio district court in the midst of the McCarthy anti-Communist.

The court made a ruling.

"The Communistic government of Romania is dictating the appointment of its Communist Bishop Moldivan. Therefore, the American Diocese is entitled to revoke it's 1936 bylaws and elect Bishop Trifa," the Judge said.

Bishop Trifa said he was a fierce anti-Communist who fled Romania to escape Red oppression. Bishop Trifa made radio broadcasts over Radio Free Europe to Romania. Over the air he said the broadcasts were arranged by his good friend J. Edgar Hoover, head of the FBI.

<>

Bishop Trifa sat on Dioceses with the Governor of Michigan. Pictures of Bishop Trifa shaking hands with Hubert Humphrey appeared in newspapers. On Wednesday, May 11, 1955 Richard Nixon had invited Bishop Trifa to offer the opening prayer before the U.S. Senate.

"Almighty God who has made America trustee of priceless human liberty and dignity, look down from Heaven upon my servants now present before thee and bless them, that they may remember in their discussions and decisions Romania, and all the oppressed nations that are still longing for a government by the people and for the people," Bishop Trifa said.

After the collapse of the Fascist Romanian regime in 1945 when the Soviets liberated Romania, Trifa had worked in Vienna as an agent for Reinhard Gehlen spy network. In 1979 while beginning their investigation of Viorel Trifa the Justice Department's Office of Special Investigations came across the name of Otto von Bolschwing.

In 1981 Pete Carey was a reporter for *San Jose Mercury News* in 'Silicon Valley'. He researched Otto von Bolschwing.

Justice Department investigators interviewed Otto von Bolschwing about Viorel Trifa. Otto von Bolschwing admitted helping Viorel Trifa and other Iron Guard members escape Romania after the 1941 pogrom. Otto von Bolschwing denied ever being a member of the SS, SD or Nazi Party. Otto Albrecht Alfred von Bolschwing's friends were millionaire investment bankers, but he was having hard luck. In 1971 he was president of a high-tech venture capital company in Sacramento with branches in Silicon Valley, that went broke under suspicious circumstances. In 1978 his wife killed herself. In 1979 he had a rare brain disease and he was confined in a rest home in Carmichael. May 1981, the United States Government began the deportation process of Otto von Bolschwing. He had lied to Federal investigators … von Bolschwing had a Nazi past.

Justice Department informed the media von Bolschwing worked with Adolf Eichmann and helped exterminate European Jews in mass murder pogroms. Justice Department said von Bolschwing had moved laterally from the Nazi Party into CIA, then into American big business.

Von Bolschwing was born October 15 1909 to East Prussian ruling family nobility …went to school in Breslau …at the age of 24 became a member of the Nazi Party …at age 30 joined the SS, the elite Nazi Secret Police. An SS Captain, von Bolschwing helped plan how to stop Jews from participating in the German economy by eliminating their livelihoods and promoted anti-Semitic propaganda to force Jews from Germany.

Historian Heinz Herne described von Bolschwing.

"Otto von Bolschwing was a Nazi Party member, a member of the SD, a double-agent informer, and an experienced salesman in the motor trade. In 1938, he was in contact with a group of Palestinian Germans who lined their pockets by certain extra-mural intelligence activities. Otto von Bolschwing spied on the Zionist Haganah army. Ejected from Palestine by the British for espionage, he surfaced in Romania as a government oil expert," Herne said.

By von Bolschwing's own account, in 1941 he helped Iron Guard wage a three-day rampage slaughtering Jews. Then he went to Berlin. That same year he became a partner in Bancvour Ornrherende Zachen, an Amsterdam bank.

Justice Department investigators said Bancvour Ornrherende Zachen Aryan-ized Holland, by appropriating and auctioning-off farms, homes, securities and businesses of Dutch Jews.

<>

August 1941, Otto von Bolschwing was tossed into a Gestapo prison without formal charges, then released in August of 1942. The prisoning and unprisoning of members of the German Officer Staff was often an Odessa tactic to establish an alibi for German Officers to help them begin a post-War life abroad with a pro-Allied front. Otto von Bolschwing helped American troops entering Austria catch Nazi officials and SS officers in 1945, according to a letter written by a Colonel in the 71st U.S. Infantry.

After the war, he went to U.S. Army Intelligence, explained he was an experienced intelligence operative involved with a spy network, and was hired as an American intelligence operative. Mae Brussels, an anti-Fascist researcher ... believed von Bolschwing was a Gehlen Organization operative, who became the handler of Reinhard Gehlen's U.S. operations after Reinhard helped CIA build a spy network in post-War Eastern Europe ... before Gehlen became post-War Intelligence Chief of West Germany.

Dec. 1953, Otto von Bolschwing applied to immigrate to the United States and arrived Feb. 2, 1954.

He did menial work until he became a U.S. citizen in 1959, then became executive assistant to the director of international marketing, Warner-Lambert Pharmaceutical.

He became close with Elmer Bobst, president of Warner-Lambert, and Warner-Lambert's honorary chairman of the board, former New Jersey Governor Alfred Driscoll.

Driscoll continued to write recommendations of von Bolschwing for years. In mid-1960s, von Bolschwing became chief financial officer for the German subsidiary of Cabot Manufacturing, a 50 million dollar Cabot carbon black factory in Germany. Cabot CFO von Bolschwing had the deal financed by First National Bank Boston Vice President Thomas Franzioli.

Thomas Franzioli remembered von Bolschwing.

"Otto von Bolschwing began to branch out on his own. He was starting a business importing wine from Argentina. I don't know if it ever got off the ground," Franzioli said.

March 1969 Otto von Bolschwing became a high-tech international business consultant for TCI, a corporation based in Sacramento with subsidiaries in Palo Alto and Mountain View, CA.

Oswald S. Williams was the founder of TCI.

"We're going to commercialize on technology developed in the Silicon Valley that was used to monitor troop movements in the 1967 Arab-Israeli War. TCI subsidiaries in Palo Alto ...Advanced Information Systems, and in Mountain View ...International Imaging Systems, were developing a high-volume computer network for business and a navigation system for oil tankers using satellite communications. TCI also did classified work for the Department of Defense. We all had to have security clearances. I brought onboard Otto von Bolschwing because we wanted contacts in Europe, and he had them. Von Bolschwing has extremely valuable, current connections and information in Germany, Switzerland, Liechtenstein, the Netherlands, Antilles, and South America. His contacts included directors of German branch of Chase Manhattan, and an owner of Berliner Handlescheschleschaft one of Europe's largest banks, in Frankfurt," Williams said.

In 1970 the TCI board of directors promoted Otto von Bolschwing to be TCI President.

San Jose Mercury reporter Pete Carey examined TCI business diaries.

"Records and interviews with TCI officials indicate that Helene von Domm, President Reagan's Austrian-born Deputy Assistant, translated German contracts for TCI and invested a thousand dollars in TCI while she was then-Governor Reagan's secretary in Sacramento. When called at her White House office Helena von Domm was too busy to talk about Otto von Bolschwing. But Helena von Domm's White House secretary said Helena von Domm knew Otto von Bolschwing socially in Sacramento many years ago," San Jose Mercury reporter Pete Carey said.

August 3 1982, *San Francisco Chronicle* ran a story called, '*Big Promotion For Reagan's Ex-Secretary*'.

"President Reagan announced yesterday in Des Moines that he will promote Helene von Domm to the position of Assistant To The President for Presidential Personnel. Helena von Domm, formerly Reagan's secretary, has worked with him since his first campaign for governor of California in 1966. She is now Deputy Assistant To The President And Director Of Presidential Personnel," the Chronicle said.

In 1985 Ronnie promoted Helena von Damm to be U.S. Ambassador to Austria.

<>

Early 1950s, it was no accident Richard Nixon

invited Bishop Trifa to pray before the Senate. Richard Nixon was close friends with Nicolai Miloxa. Nicolai Miloxa was a financier of the Iron Guard, who had immigrated to America. In the 1930s Nicolai Miloxa received a loan from the Romanian government to expand his locomotive factories. Instead, he invested the money in buying controlling interests in steel, rubber, munitions and artillery factories.

Nicolai Miloxa, like most ruling family financiers and industrials was preparing himself to make a killing from the coming world war. More than an astute businessman, Nicolai Miloxa, like his counterparts on Wall Street in the U.S. who were political forces in America, was a political force in Romanian politics.

Nicolai Miloxa worked actively with the Nazis and the Iron Guard. From his factories, Nicolai Miloxa hoped, would come the weapons to arm the new World Order. Miloxa went to Berlin in 1936 to meet with Reich Marshal Herman Goering. Miloxa and became business partners. Their personal agreement was formalized in 1940 when the Volstat Pact merged Miloxa's industries with Germany's. Miloxa and Herman Goering's younger brother Alfred Goering, together managed this new Nazi industrial merger. Miloxa arrived in New York on September 29, 1946, part of a Romanian government trade mission. He never returned to Romania.

Miloxa applied for permanent residence in the U.S. in 1948. He applied for admission under the Displaced Persons Act. For ten years Miloxa fought to stay in America and become an American citizen. Miloxa contacted Richard Nixon, a junior Senator from California.

Senator Nixon introduced a bill to the Senate in 1951 that had one provision ... to let Nicolai Miloxa stay in the United States of America ...if Miloxa was one of the richest men in Europe, partners with Reich Marshal Herman Goering and Goering's brother, financier of the Iron Guard of Romania ... was it possible Miloxa could finance Nixon's political career? The bill was defeated in the Senate.

So, Senator Nixon invented a dummy corporation called, Western Tube. Located at 607 Bank of America Building, Whittier CA ... the same address as the law firm of Buley, Krupp & Nixon.

May 1951, height of the Korean War, industry was under wartime control. Nicolai Miloxa was the treasurer and sole stock holder of Western Tube ... the company was worth $1,000 ... was supposed to be a manufacture of seamless tubes used in oil refineries.

Nixon phoned INS executive assistant to INS Commissioner James Hennesey, trying to get Miloxa permanent U.S. status.

Nixon sent urgent cables to the Defense Production Administrator.

"It is important strategically and economically for California and the entire U.S., that a plant for the manufacture of seamless tubing for oil wells be erected," Nixon wrote.

Sept. 26, 1953 Nicolai Miloxa was admitted from Canada under a first-preference petition, now a permanent resident of the U.S.

Western Tube disappeared.

Congressman John Shelly of California felt angry.

"It is impossible to discover any reasons for creating Western Tube and seeking a Certificate of Necessity other than to give Nicolai Miloxa a springboard for entry into the U.S.," Shelly said.

Wolf and Bellant continued.

In 1990, Vatra Romanesca, an Extreme-Right organization including Iron Guard members boasted it had financial backing from influential political figures at home in Romania and several French and Canadian covert organizations abroad. Iron Guard members were in senior levels of leadership in National Christian Peasants Party, an anti-Semitic, terrorist organization coercing Hungarian farmers.

Meanwhile, exiles from Slovakia were busy in Canada too, trying to make Slovakia an independent republic modeled on the one Extreme-Right cleric, Nazi collaborator Jozef Tiso, founded Mar. 1939. Tiso managed transportation of thousands of Slovak Jews to German extermination camps. Tiso was executed in 1947. Some of Tiso's friends were smuggled out of the European by Vatican rat-lines with help from U.S. and British intelligence. Former officials of the collaborationist Hlinka party were smuggled West, where they renewed political activity.

In 1971, uranium magnate Steve Roman formed Slovak World Congress in Toronto with help of Hlinka collaborators Ferdinad Durcansky ...a Nazi Foreign Minister sentenced to death for treason, and his assistant Jozef Kirschbaum, who was on the run from a 20-year sentence for his role as Secretary General of the party.

Vatican maintained close ties with the Hlinka front group. In 1984, Pope John Paul II was visiting Canada. Pope John Paul took time out of his busy schedule to visit uranium magnate Steve Roman's Cathedral in Toronto. Roman died in 1988.

Mar. 1989 Rev. Dusan Toth, Slovak World

Congress secretary general addressed a crowd of 100,000 supporters in Bratislava. Rev. Toth is former head of Protestant religious programming for Radio Free Europe. Toth found Rightist-separatism remains a potent force in Slovakia ... elsewhere, Toth's message and activities would be considered a threat to national security.

Feb. 1989 Toth was appointed a member of a group of foreign advisers to President Vaclav Havel.

May 1989 Alexander Dubcek visited Toronto. Vice President Alexander Dubcek attended a meeting of the Slovak World Congress. Dubcek, a Slovak, is best known as leader of Czechoslovakia's Prague Spring in 1968. Dubcek's liberalization program was smashed when Moscow ordered troops into Prague and the government was overthrown.

A Nazi collaborator separatist who went back home from the West ... looking for a state, was Ivo Omrcanin. During World War II, Ivo Omrcanin was a Foreign Ministry official of Independent Croatia ... created as a separate nation by Adolf Hitler as a Nazi satellite state.

After World War II, Ivo Omrcanin helped other Nazis ... including Ustasche President Ante Pavelic and SS Officer Klaus Barbie ... escape to Latin America. In World War II, Croatian Ustasche fascist death squad leadership escaped Tito's partisans and the Soviet Army. Ustasche slaughtered one million Croatian Jews, Serbs, Gypsies and others. Vatican helped Ustasche leaders escape from Europe. Ustasche escaped to Argentina and Spain, where government welcomed them.

Ustasche émigré said they were victims of Communist persecution ...that they were Croatian patriots.

They set up fronts in émigré communities. The Croatian Liberation Movement was founded in 1956 by Ante Pavolic. Headquarters and Supreme Council of the Croatian Liberation Movement was in Buenos Aires.

Stephan Heffer, a Ustasche mass murderer, was appointed to Supreme Council. Heffer made no secret of hating the U.S. and Britain for not accepting Croatian Liberation Movement as allies. 'Nazi fascism' was what the West called the Croatian Nationalist movement for an independent Croatia governed under the leadership of the Ustasche.

In 1957, a Ustasche faction failed to assassinate Ante Pavolic. Pavolic fled to Spain and took refuge in Otto Skorzeny's Madrid, where Nazi Otto Skorzeny was in charge of several Spanish

fascist intelligence organizations. Pavolic died in 1959. Stephan Efferre took over Croatian Liberation Movement (HOP) leadership.

In 1961, a Ustasche terrorist faction of the Croatian Liberation Movement in Australia called itself the Croatian Revolutionary Brotherhood ...a terrorist unit of second-generation Nazi Croatians.

In Canada, U.S., Australia, Argentina and around the world, younger Croatian Ustasche groups networked with their parents generation of Nazi Croatian Ustasche.

In 1961 a hit-squad formed in Australia, composed of second-generation Croatians maintaining close ties with the old Ustasche network of émigrés around the world.

In the U.S., Croatian émigré said they believed in Democracy, freedom and independence. But Croatian *Catholic Union* newspaper remained faithful to traditional Nazi Ustasche causes. Ustasche were active in World Anti-Communist League WACL.

In 1973, after Stephan Efferre died, Croatian Liberation Movement and the leadership of the Croatian Chapter of the World Anti-Communist League were taken over by Anton Bonifacic, a former Ustasche death squad terrorist.

In 1970s-1980s Ustasche Anton Bonifacic organized the Croatian Chapter of World Anti-Communist League ...his responsibilities included creation of propaganda and 'revisionist-history' ...changing history to fit Fascist needs for the creation of an Independent State of Croatia ...Hitler created Croatia as a Nazi puppet state when he invaded Yugoslavia, but after World War II, Croatia returned under Yugoslavian rule. Handlers and financiers of Ustasche terrorists wanted to make Croatia an independent state, again ... the same way as the first time, by war.

Anton Bonifacic spoke at WACL meetings.

"Whereas the Croatian nation was subject to unprecedented genocide in massacres of one million Croatians, slaughtered by Communists or Serbs opposed to Croatian self-determination and national independence, the 11th Conference of the Croatian Chapter of the World Anti-Communist League hereby resolves that the Socialist Federal Republic Of Yugoslavia, that artificial creation of the Peace Treaty at Versailles and again at Yalta ... should be substituted by three independent and democratic States," Anton Bonifacic said.

In the 1980s, Anton Bonifacic was campaigning to create military destabilization of Yugoslavia.

Two governments in the world recognized the

Croatian Liberation Movement as the Croatian Government in Exile. Taiwan was the chief sponsor and financial backer of the World Anti-Communist League. Taiwan recognized the Croatian Liberation Movement as the government of Croatia. Anton Bonifacic and Croatian Liberation Movement propagandists claimed they had not committed any war crimes ...Bonifacic and Croatian Liberation Movement said it was rumor, propaganda invented by Communist propaganda writers.

<>

Apr. 10 1941, the day Nazis invaded Yugoslavia and established the Ustasche Regime ...was referred to by members of Croatian Liberation Movement as 'Croatian Independence Day'.

<>

But to democratic Yugoslavian Serbs and Jews, April 10 1941 was the day the holocaust began for them in Yugoslavia.

<>

When Ronnie was Governor of California he passed a resolution making April 10, 1941 'Independent Croatia Day'. When Ronnie's handlers realized they'd been maneuvered into a compromising position, they had Ronnie apologize to the Yugoslavian Government.

In 1984, in the midst of Ronnie's presidency the U.S. National Republican Heritage Groups Council, a branch of the Republican Party, published a pamphlet called, *1984 Guide to Nationality Observances.*

There was a listing under April 10.

"April 10th is Croatian Independence Day. On April 10th the Independent State of Croatia was declared by unanimous proclamation in 1941, thus ending an enforced union with royalist Yugoslavia in which Croatian independence was subverted and threatened. Lack of Western support, and Axis occupation forced the new State into an unfortunate association with Axis powers," the U.S. Republican Party brochure said.

<>

In 1990s Croatian Ustasche and their Axis relationship with Nazi Germany surfaced ...when Germany helped finance and arm Croatian Ustasche to use terrorism and war to destabilize Yugoslavia.

After World War II, Ivo Omrcanin helped other Nazis, including Ustasche President Ante Pavelic and SS Officer Klaus Barbie, escape to Latin America.

In 1990 Omrcanin took part in events sponsored by the fascist neo-Nazi 'Institute for Historical Review', in the U.S.

Omrcanin was interviewed by Yugoslavian magazine *ST*.

"I have returned to Croatia to register a new political party to correct past mistakes. In World War II, the Jews massacred the Croatians. Jasinovac Extermination Camp did not exterminate Jews and Serbs. It never existed. It was a Hollywood production. You can see how big of an imagination these Jews have when they make cartoons. Those are all made by Jews," Omrcanin said.

Lou Wolf's *Covert Action Quarterly* continued to summarize the involvement of Paul Weyrich's Free Congress Foundation with fascist and neo-Nazi activity around the world, including the Soviet Union and Eastern Europe. Free Congress Foundation was funded by the Coors ruling family, and by National Endowment for Democracy by taxes on U.S. paychecks. Wolf and Bellant continued their investigative journalism research on Paul Weyrich and his Free Congress Foundation supporting fascists in Eastern Europe, preparing another war.

"In 1990, as in the 1930s, the separatist banner was carried by the Organization of Ukrainian Nationalists OUN. During World War II OUN collaborated with the Nazi occupation politically and militarily ...and participated in the elimination of Ukrainian Jews. After the war, OUN militants were recruited to carry out a clandestine war against the U.S.S.R. Others found their way to the West, where they resumed political activity. Since World War II, the OUN was the backbone of Anti-Bolshevik Bloc of Nations (ABN) ...a coalition including the Iron Guard and the Hlinka Party. The OUN and the ABN have been leading public opponents to the Office of Special Investigations. For children and teenagers, a new organization was formed, called, Union of Independent Ukrainian Youth, inspired by wartime OUN leader Stepan Bandera.

"In 1990 Right-wing Ukrainian-Americans were involved in March elections. Paul Weyrich's Free Congress Foundation sent General Counsel for the Ukrainian Congress Committee of America Askold Lozynskij, and other activists, to the Ukraine to help the March elections in Hungary. Ukrainian Congress Committee of America was dominated by OUN members. In a bitter contest, the Democratic Forum, the party which would eventually win the contest ...used anti-Semitic slurs against its rival, the Alliance of Free Democrats. Aid for the Forum has come from Far-Right Hungarians exiled in the U.S., including Laszlo Pasztor, a youth leader of the

Arrow Cross during the Second World War. The Arrow Cross was Hungary's Nazi Party, which came to power in 1944. Pasztor served five years in a Hungarian prison after the war for his wartime activities at the Hungarian embassy in Berlin. A Nazi past proved no great obstacle to success in the U.S. Laszlo Pasztor was selected by Richard Nixon in 1969, to recruit Rightists from other Eastern European communities to work for the Republican Party. Some of those recruited were committed Nazis. One of them, Boleslavs Maikovkis, a former Latvian police officer, was accused by the Office of Special Investigations of being a war criminal.

"In 1988 Laszlo Pasztor was one of six members of the George Bush election committee forced to resign because of Nazi affiliations.

"In 1990 Laszlo Pasztor directed Free Congress Foundation's East European activities. He also advised the National Endowment for Democracy on funding Hungarian political parties. The Free Congress Foundation sent a team to Hungary to teach the Democratic Forum elections techniques. Recently, Far-Right activists managed to get into the Soviet Bloc.

"In October 1988, the Soviet Union prevented Latvian exiles from Canada and the U.S. from attending the founding convention of the Latvian People's Front. One of those prevented from boarding the plane was Linards Lukss, Chairman of the World Federation of Free Latvians. Linards Lukss, a Toronto physician, was well known in anti-Communist circles. He was the president of the Captive Nations Committee in Canada, an organization that worked closely with the ABN. Linards Lukss' helped found International Black Ribbon Day Committee in 1986, a Toronto-based operation 'officially' opposed to Nazism and Communism, that welcomed support and participation of the Hlinka-dominated Slovak World Congress, the OUN-dominated World Congress of Free Ukrainians, and the Far-Right Hungarian Freedom Fighters World Federation," Russ Bellant said.

Old Nazis and new
European democracies

Winter 1991-1992, Lou Wolf's *Covert Action Bulletin* took a look at the National Endowment for Democracy, winter, in Russ Bellant's *Old Nazis and New European Democracies*.

"National Endowment for Democracy NED core groups and grantees are shaping political, social and economic destinies of Western Europe and Soviet Union. NDI for example, has programs for party-building, election administration and monitoring, seminars, electoral law reform, grassroots organizing, civil education, and public opinion polling.

"In the Czech and Slovak Federal Republic, it is also convening international experts to help draft the new election law. In Hungary it is consulting with newly-elected parliamentarians 'to enhance their ability to carry out their official duties'. In Poland, NDI is sponsoring a U.S. training visit for senior staff administrators of the Polish Parliament. Programs are also in place in Bulgaria, Romania, the Soviet Republics, and Yugoslavia.

"Some U.S.-supported East European parties and groups define democracy as available only to those who have specific racial, ethnic or religious attributes, an echo of racial nationalism that underpinned Fascist movements in post-WWI Europe. Some supposed 'democracy-builders' are reviving Nazi collaborationist parties, in some cases with the help of aging pro-Nazis forced to immigrate to Canada and the U.S. after WWII.

Margaret Quigley, of Political Research Associates, documented the problem in the Russian Republic.

"Free Congress Foundation acts as a conduit for NED funds for Boris Yeltsin's Inter-Regional Deputies Group IDG and trained Boris Yeltsin's staff, including campaign manager Rcade Murashev. According to Quigley, Boris Yeltsin's ties to ultra-national and anti-Semitic groups are much deeper than people realize.

Yeltsin spoke to Pamyat officials at a time when members of the Russian Nationalist Anti-Jewish Organization were distributing copies of the anti-Jewish propaganda hoax, *Protocols of the Learned Elders of Zion*.

"'It's clear you're motivated by patriotism about our Motherland,' Boris Yeltsin said. Yeltsin's vice president, Alexander Rutskoi, is also Deputy Chair of Otechestvo Fatherland, an anti-Semitic, Russian Nationalist organization.

"That Free Congress Foundation is a conduit for NED funds should be controversial. Free Congress Foundation leader, former Nazi collaborator Laszlo Pasztor, is a Hungarian émigré who was founding Chairman of the Republican Heritage Groups Council, into which he recruited individuals of anti-Democratic political heritage ...Fascist Bulgarian National Front ...Romanian Iron Guard ...and Ukrainian Nationalist Organization ... Nazi collaborators.

"Laszlo Pasztor works with a project sponsored

by Paul Weyrich, housed at the Free Congress Foundation building. Pasztor says when he visited Hungary he 'unofficially' met with leaders of several new political parties, including Hungarian Democratic Forum MDF, a group where anti-Semitism resonates. Hungarian Democratic Forum participated in NED-funded projects in Hungary.

"Pasztor got help from National Endowment for Democracy for 'anti-Communist', 'democratic' opposition behind the Iron Curtain. Pasztor assisted NED grantees by translating and evaluating proposals by Hungarian and Czechoslovakian groups.

"July 1989 Pasztor informed Weyrich of Pasztor's involvement obtaining 'assistance for the Anti-Communist Democratic Opposition behind the Iron Curtain,' from NED," Russ Bellant said.

NED meddles in Lithuania

Philip Bonasky, writing in Lou Wolf's *Covert Action Information Bulletin*, looked at National Endowment for Democracy, in his article, *NED Meddles in Lithuania, nurturing Baltic reaction.*

"April 1990, the Soviet Republic of Lithuania startled the world by declaring itself independent of the U.S.S.R. The U.S. has not yet recognized Lithuania as independent and Bush's political remarks have been moderate. But beneath this facade of calm state-craft there runs a familiar current of silent U.S. involvement in the political affairs of another country. The most visible intervention has been via the National Endowment for Democracy, or NED, which has supplied funds, equipment and advice to the principal nationalist opposition party, Sajudis. NED has chosen to funnel Lithuanian aid through one organization, the New York-based Lithuanian Catholic Religious Aid, or LCRA, and its propaganda arm, the Lithuanian Information Center, or LIC. These two organizations are run by arch-conservative Catholic clergy. The founder, current board chair, and man who has 'presided over the steady growth and increasing effectiveness' of LCRA, Bishop Vincentas Brizgys, was allegedly a Nazi collaborator during World War II. Brizgys vehemently denies the charge. Sajudis itself is linked in a variety of ways to the symbols and sentiments of the Fascist and Nazi periods in Baltic history. Lithuania lies on the eastern shore of the Baltic Sea, bordered on the south by Poland, on the north by the Latvian SSR, and on the east by the Byelorussian SSR. It is the Western-most extent of the Soviet Union with a population, as of 1980, of just over three million. In the 14th Century, invading Germans conquered the area and imposed the Catholic faith.

"In the modern era, Lithuania has been repeatedly buffeted by the shifting political and military map of Europe. Lithuania declared independence from Czarist Russia in 1918, but in 1926 the Nationalist Party took power through a military coup. Declaring himself President, Augustus Voldemares, and his Premier Antanas Smetona, shaped Lithuania into Europe's second Fascist state, based explicitly on the example of Mussolini's Italy.

"Lithuania remained a dictatorship until 1939, when Smetona fled to the U.S. and a new Parliament voted unanimously to become a constituent Republic of the U.S.S.R. With the German invasion of the Soviet Union of 1941, Lithuania's nationalists returned briefly to power and assisted the Nazi's in the swift, systematic slaughter of more than 130,000 Lithuanian Jews, Communists and other 'undesirables'.

"April 1990, a 34-year-old American, William J. H. Hough III, was busy in Lithuania. Hough was sent to Lithuania, although he doesn't speak Lithuanian, as legal advisor to Vytautas Landsbergis, leader of the Nationalist Party. Cooperating closely with William J. H. Hough III, LCRA/LIC supplied Sajudis with paper, photocopy machines, computers, laser printers, fax machines and video cameras. With additional political and technical expertise, Vilnias became a communications hub for secessionist forces in Lithuania and other Soviet Republics.

"William J. H. Hough III was a lawyer, also an editor of the New York Law School *Journal of International and Comparative Law,* which published in its Winter 1985 issue his book length article, *Annexation of the Baltic States and its Effects on Development of Law Prohibiting Forcible Seizure of Territory.* Hough describes the inter-war period of Lithuanian history as one of 'political and constitutional stability' and 'progress toward the restoration of full democracy.' He fails to mention the collaboration of Nationalists and Nazis.

"In his public justifications of succession, Vytautas Landsbergis, leader of the Nationalist Party has frequently referred to Hough's interpretation of Lithuanian history. Hough's history of Lithuania must be reassuring to NED's ideologues and Lithuanian clients, some share a past they might prefer to forget. From 1988-1990 NED granted $70,000 dollars to LCRA/LIC. LCRA/LIC are obviously not democratic organizations.

"Founded in 1961 to 'provide the Church under the Soviet oppression with spiritual and material assistance', LCRA's parent organization was the Lithuanian Roman Catholic Priests League. The quiet obscurity of this group belies the welcome they receive in the halls of power. LCRA executive director Father Casimir Pugevicius served in 1983 on an advisory committee to Illinois Republican Senator Charles Percey, then a member of the Senate Foreign Relations Committee. Father Casimir Pugevicius was also welcomed in the Reagan White House in 1986.

"According to LCRA/LIC its 1990 grant application to NED requested $618,300 dollars and outlined its ambitious proposal ...'Five separate pro-democratic organizations would receive technical and material aid. The first, a coalition of democratic parties enjoying broad support in Lithuania and capable of assuming leading rolls in the new legislature would receive computer and audio-visual equipment. Communications and video equipment will be transported to the Sajudis Information Agency'.

"According to NED, funds went only to Sajudis.

"The second part of the project would insure a continuous supply of much-needed paper for independent publishers and organizations. The dramatic increase in the number of democratic groups in Lithuania in the past year has caused severe shortages in the very limited pool of resources. Lithuania has emerged as the publishing center for independent groups throughout the Soviet Union'.

"Within weeks of the arrival of these goods, traditional sources of information in Lithuania were suppressed or taken over by Sajudis. Nationalist sympathizers cut-off broadcast programming from Moscow, and Lithuania was soon flooded with secessionist propaganda. In the ensuing election Sajudis managed to dominate the scene by riding the crest of a wave of nationalist sentiment. It won a majority of votes in Seim parliament. In March, a hastily-convened session of parliament voted for secession 91-to-38 in a matter of hours. Laws were passed, curbing opposition newspapers and changing the flag and national anthem, reverting to versions in use during the nationalist period. As to whether or what of real substance it changed, Sajudis remains silent.

"To Lithuanians old enough to remember World War II, the energetic activities of Sajudis, LCRA/LIC must seem familiar. Landsbergis' father was a member of the Savandoriai, or Nationalist Militia, who fought the Russians in 1918 and 1919 ...and helped enforce the successive dictatorships of Voldemares and Smetona, and collaborated with German occupation.

"April 1990 *Der Spiegel* reported, 'Everybody fears Sajudis. Anyone who attacks Sajudis is declared an enemy of the people by Landsbergis, and that happens very quickly'.

"In addition, the Savandoriai ...illegal under Soviet law ... was revived under leadership of retired army officers. Prior to the German invasion in June of 1944, a Berlin-based 'Lithuanian Information Bureau', the propaganda arm of the Lithuanian Activist Front, a nationalist exile organization, sent the following message into Lithuania.

"'Liberation is close at hand. Uprisings must be started in the cities, towns and villages of Lithuania. Communists and other traitors must be arrested at once. The traitor will be pardoned only provided he proves beyond doubt he has killed one Jew, at least'," Philip Bonasky said.

<>

What was the exact nature of liberation close at hand Lithuanian Activist Front spoke of? In 1988 investigative reporter Christopher Simpson's *Blowback* comments.

"Municipal killing squads employing Lithuanian-Nazi collaborators eliminated 46,692 Jews in fewer than three months, according to their own reports ...mainly by combining clock-like liquidation of 500 Jews per day in the capital city of Dumius with mobile 'clean-up' sweeps through the surrounding countryside. Such squads were consistently used by the Nazis for their dirty-work that even the SS believed to be beneath the dignity of the German soldier.

"After 4,000 people were murdered by the Lithuanian Nationalists' mobile units under SS Obersturmfuhrer Hamann Einsatzkommando-Kovno (EK-3), death squads helped murder another 40,000 Jews and 90,000 Serbs, Moslems, Gypsies and Communists. Einsatzkommando was realizing their goal to kill all Jews in Lithuania. The Nazis were helped by Catholic clergy. Bishop Vincentas Brizgys was Auxiliary Bishop of Kaunas Kovno in Lithuania during World War II. Bishop Vincentas spiritually embraced Fascism.

"Catholic clergy hated Socialism because socialism separated Church and State. When socialist government came in the Ukraine in 1939 it nationalized Church farms. The farms had been run in the manner of feudalism by peasants with no rights, in the traditional European fashion of the Middle Ages. However, Europe itself no longer operated in a feudal fashion. The Catholic Church was able to get away with this form of slavery in Lithuania until the socialist government threw them out of national and civil government offices and as teachers in 1939.

"Bishop Vincentas Brizgys reported to his superior, Archbishop Skvircekas. Archbishop Skvircekas felt proud of Bishop Brizgys' collaboration with the Nazis.

July 1, 1941 Skvircekas made an entry in his diary.

"'Today Bishop Vincentras Brizgys introduced himself to Dr. Groffe who is the representative of the German Government for the Baltic States. Groffe has been head of the Gestapo in East Prussia. Groffe suggested to Bishop Brizgys to ask the Lithuanian people to act in business-as-usual fashion under Nazi occupation, and tell the Lithuanian people not to worry, because they will not be harmed. The ideas in Mein Kampf on the question of the Bolshevik-Jewish contagion are splendid. They prove that Hitler an enemy of the Jews, generally speaking, has the right ideas,' Archbishop Skvircekas said.

When the Nazis marched into Lithuania a radio broadcast welcomed them. Archbishop Skvircekas and Bishop Brizgys signed a Nazi welcome published in the Kaunas newspaper, and signed a telegram sent to Adolf Hitler in July 1941 thanking him for 'liberating' Lithuania.

"Bishop Brizgys forbid Catholic clergy to help Jews. In Church on Sundays Brizgys preached for Lithuanians to help Nazis. Brizgys appealed in newspapers and on radio for Lithuanians not to help Jews, but to help Nazis.

"The 16th Lithuanian Division of the Soviet Army defeated the Nazis in Lithuania. The Nazis retreated. Bishop Brizgys fled to Germany, then to Chicago. In Chicago for the next twenty-five years Brizgys continued his Ukrainian Nationalist work. Brizgys was sent to the Archdiocese of Chicago. In 1961 Bishop Brizgys co-founded the New York-based Lithuanian Catholic Religious Aid LCRA and its propaganda department, Lithuanian Information Center LIC. Bishop Brizgys was president of Lithuanian Catholic Religious Aid until 1986, then served as the board chairman of Lithuanian Catholic Religious Aid into the early 1990s.

"Such were leadership qualifications of LCRA/LIC to receive funds from the U.S. National Endowment For Democracy.

"Rasa Razgaitis, step-daughter of war criminal Jurgis Juodis was LCRA/LIC's special projects director.

"In 1981 the United States Justice Department Office Of Special Investigations investigated Jurgis Juodis. Rasa Razgaitis co-founded, Americans for Due Process. The founding mission of Americans for Due Process was to contest activities by the Justice Department Office of Special Investigations. Rasa Razgaitis was a close friend of Ronnie's White House Communications director, Patrick Buchanan, an anti-Communist Cold Warrior who wanted to serve Christ by destroying Communism. Cold Warrior AFL-CIO President Lane Kirkland sat as a director on the National Endowment for Democracy board ...Kirkland was a member of Committee on the Present Danger ...Kirkland supported CIA handling of labor movements in Poland, Eastern Europe, Russia, and around the world ... Kirkland was a friend to Lithuania's Vytautas Landsbergis, leader of the Lithuanian Nationalist Party ...when Vytautas visited the U.S., Kirkland signed his name on an open letter to President Bush printed April 22 1990 in New York Times, calling for recognition of Lithuanian independence.

Christopher Simpson continued his research.

"Richard Ebeling, vice president of Future Freedom Foundation of Denver was invited by Sajudis to lecture in Lithuania ...on the principles of freedom. Six Sajudis economists met with leaders of the Future Freedom Foundation to discuss free market proposals ...rapid de-nationalization of all industries and state property decontrol of all prices and wages in consumer and production markets ...privatization of social services, medical and retirement pensions. Medical care has been free in Lithuania since 1940. Pensions are mandated by law and begin for women at age 55 and for men at 60. Wages are determined in consultation with the unions. Housing is inexpensive, and pre-secession housing goals called for private dwellings for all citizens by 2000.

"Vacations are guaranteed and partly or fully paid by unions. Education, beginning with day care, is free ...there are special schools for gifted or developmentally-disabled children.

"What the Sajudis program amounts-to, is retrograde capitalism. Their vision of Lithuania's future is the 'Hong Kong of Eastern Europe'. The selling points which groups like Poland's Solidarity are now using to entice western capital are ... the lure of cheap labor, high profits, and the assurance labor militancy is under control. Chances are good, that the Lithuanian people are far from ready to privatize a social system which provides a good standard of living for nearly all Lithuanians. They long ago put behind them the days of *vieneri marskinai, vienerios kelines* one shirt and one pair of pants," Christopher Simpson said.

Aug. 23 1997 Lester Thurow, MIT Economics department chairman, author of, *The Future Of Capitalism,* spoke at a San Francisco World Affairs Council lecture shown on C-SPAN and broadcast by KQED radio.

Thurow spoke candidly, caught off-guard by a question in the question and answer period that followed his lecture.

"Equality is a strange concept. Capitalism and equality are antithetical. Capitalism and democracy are opposites. That someone ignorant should have one vote just as someone well-informed? Someone unskilled should have the same one vote that an educated person has? The laziest person in the U.S. should have the same one vote that the hardest-working person in the U.S. has? Democracy and equality are the opposite of capitalism.

"I wouldn't buy any stock in the Midwest corporate farming belt of the U.S., by the turn of the century Ukraine has been chosen to be the bread-basket of the world. Why pay someone in the U.S. $100-dollars a day when you pay someone in another country $10-dollars a day for the same work," Thurow said.

An editorial appeared in neo-fascist's, *Heritage Foundation Policy Review.*

"The West won the Cold War because of foreign policies pursued by conservative governments in every major country in the Western world," the editorial said.

David Rubenstein, a University of Illinois sociologist, wrote a white paper on U.S. policy affecting U.S.S.R.

"The key difference between Soviet policy in the 1970s and Soviet policy the 1980s is best explained not by simple further deterioration of the Soviet economy, but in changes in U.S. foreign policy to affect that deterioration. If the current sense of crisis is eased, the motivation for further reform may be lost. Internal pressure was a key factor in motivating this policy of reform, more internal pressure may be required to keep it moving forward," Rubenstein wrote.

Vice President Bush followed in Reagan's footsteps as President, and had his champions. The U.S. Advisory Commission on Public Diplomacy met in January of 1990. Deputy State Secretary Lawrence Eagleburger called for expanded roles for U.S. agencies in assisting anti-Communist groups in Eastern Europe.

"One of the things we need to do, and President Bush is clearly on that road with regard to Poland and Hungary, is establish a mechanism within the government that helps provide the opportunity for the private sector to engage itself directly in the Polish experiment, the Hungarian experiment, or other experiments that are about to take place in Eastern Europe," Eagleburger said.

Carl Gershman, President of the National Endowment for Democracy was a speaker at the same meeting.

"National Endowment for Democracy is deeply engaged in the election process in Czechoslovakia," Gershman said.

<>

Mar. 4, 1991 *New York Times,* from Pakrac, Yugoslavia, Steven Engelberg's *Serb-Croat showdown in one village square.*

"The enmity between Serb's and Croats, who make up the largest of Yugoslavia's six Republics, has deep roots. About 30 miles from Pakrac at the Jasinovac Concentration Camp, tens of thousands of Serbs, gypsies and Jews were killed when it was run by the Fascist puppet government of Croatia during World War II. For the Serbs the memory of the wartime atrocity is long.

"Yovan Miljanic, a 70-year-old retired road worker, stood with a group of Serbian men on the outskirts of Pakrac today and declared, 'If the Croatian police do not withdraw there will be victims. The Croatians killed people, stuffed them down wells. People still remember this. They get frightened when they see the same insignia that they saw in World War II years.'"

<>

July 5, 1991 *New York Times,* London, Craig Whitney's *Spur to summit action, Yugoslav crises brings new pressure for rich nations to help Soviets.*

"British and American officials say that the threat of civil war in Yugoslavia has increased pressure on the world's seven largest industrial democracies to consider ways of helping the Soviet Union avoid the same kind of disaster.

"The pressure will come at the summit meeting of the seven here later this month, but the British officials getting ready for the meeting here repeated that no large-scale financial or economic aid was likely to be offered when President Mikhail Gorbachev addresses the seven leaders plus the European Community after the Summit Conference ends on July 17.

"The West German Chancellor, Helmut Kohl, whose government has given, lent or pledged about 31 billion dollars to the Soviet Union in exchange for its consent to the reunification of Germany and the withdrawal of more than 300,000 troops from the Eastern part of the country by 1994, is going to Kiev on Friday to consult with Mr. Gorbachev before the Summit.

"A warning that catastrophic political and economic disintegration of the Soviet Union could occur if the Soviets are not urged to act boldly, is one of the messages now being taken to the seven capitals by Gregori A. Yavlinksy, a Soviet economist, and Professor Graham Allison of Harvard University."

Civil war as lethal shadow play

Lou Wolf's *Covert Action Information Bulletin*, 1993, Sean Gervasi's *Civil War as lethal shadow play*.

"The horrors in the Balkan region displayed daily on television and in newspapers show a country apparently torn apart by civil war. What lies behind images of gaunt refugees, artillery duels, blood-spattered walls, combat patrols, and devastated towns and villages? ... The only answer that most of us can give is that it is the struggle of Yugoslav against Yugoslav, or Croats against Slovenes and Serbs, or Muslims against Serbs, and of Serbs against all of the others ...this is what the mass media has been telling us. There are, however, other forces at work ...in the Yugoslav crises, besides ethnic tensions.

<>

"Yugoslavia has for some time been the target of a covert policy waged by the West and its allies ...primarily Germany, the U.S., Britain, Turkey, Saudi Arabia, and Iran ... to divide Yugoslavia into its ethnic components, dismantle it, and eventually recolonize it ...not that, given hundreds of years of hatred and tension, that is a particularly difficult job.

"After all, the term 'Balkanization' entered the political vocabulary to define 'a process of national fragmentation and fratricidal war'. But, while the internal dynamics of the war are well documented, the external forces of destabilization which were put into high gear years ago, have received scant attention.

"The basis issues in Yugoslavia have always been independence and economics. Yugoslavia has been at the center of a tug of war. Soviets sought its incorporation into the U.S.S.R., the West tried to pull Yugoslavia, along with other countries of Eastern Europe and the Balkans, 'into Europe' ...that is, into the capitalist world economy.

"To this end, the West promoted de-industrial-ization and dependence, and unleashed an arsenal of modern power including threats and pressure ...a U.N.-sanctioned economic blockade ...and covert arms shipments. Under Josef Tito's leadership, Yugoslavia established its independence from Moscow, and formed a de facto alliance with the West and NATO. By the end of 1990, however, while Eastern Europe was well on the way to European integration ... and economic crises ... Yugoslavia began to suspend the 'reforms' to which it had initially agreed. That resistance brought down the wrath of certain Western powers ...which then sought to break Yugoslavia by promoting separatism and igniting the ethnic tensions that had haunted the country for centuries.

"Since World War II, Yugoslavia ... prized by both sides ... has been molded by the forces of Cold War. Early in the first Reagan Administration, the U.S. escalated the Cold War with an aggressive, secret strategy to undercut the Soviet economy, destabilize the U.S.S.R., and ultimately bring about the collapse of Communism. In 1985, then-Ambassador Jeanne Kirkpatrick dubbed this new strategy, which went well beyond containment, 'The Reagan Doctrine'.

"At about the same time according to recently declassified documents obtained by *CovertAction*, the U.S. adopted a similar strategy towards the countries of Eastern Europe, including Yugoslavia ... In Sept. 1982, when the region seemed stable and the Berlin wall had seven years to stand, the U.S. drew up National Security Decision Directive 54, NSDD-54 ...U.S. Policy Toward Eastern Europe.

"Labeled 'Secret', and declassified with light censorship in 1990 ...it called for greatly expanded efforts to promote a 'quiet revolution' to overthrow Communist governments and Parties. While naming all the countries of Eastern Europe, it omitted mention of Yugoslavia ...in March 1984, a separate document, NSDD-133, United States Policy Toward Yugoslavia, was adopted and given the more restricted classification, 'Secret Sensitive'. Declassified in 1990, NSDD-133 was still highly censored, with less than two-thirds of the original text remaining ... none-the-less, taken together, NSDD-54 and NSDD-133 reveal a consistent policy.

"The 'primary long-term U.S. goal in Eastern Europe' described in NSDD-54 was 'to [censored] facilitate its eventual re-integration into the European community of nations' ...since the Eastern European states could not be 're-integrated' into 'the European community of nations' as long as they remained under Communist rule … the basic U.S. goal required removal of Communist governments. The implication of ending Soviet influence extends to the more cautiously worded remnants of NSDD-133 …the goal of 'U.S. policy [towards Yugoslavia, it states] will be to promote the trend towards an effective, market-oriented Yugoslav economic structure … [and] to expand U.S. economic relations with Yugoslavia in ways which benefit both countries, and which strengthen Yugoslavia's ties with the industrialized democracies'.

"Therefore, the basic U.S. objective for Yugoslavia was made the same for Bulgaria, Czechoslovakia, the GDR, Hungary, Poland, and Romania …capitalist transformation. The list of policy instruments described in NSDD-54 to promote change in Eastern Europe may help fill in some gaps in the more highly-censored NSDD-133 …the mechanism included most-favored-nation status …credit policy …IMF stewardship …debt re-scheduling …cultural and educational exchanges …information programs …high-level visits …and restrictions on diplomatic and consular personnel [in this document items remained partially or completely deleted in the declassified version].

"Today, the revelations in the two documents may seem banal, it should be remembered that for many years the government felt the need to keep secret even the more overt means of pressuring for change. Significant parts of U.S. policy in the region, particularly Yugoslavia, remain secret today. Covert policies, which undoubtedly were implemented, are not discussed at length in National Security Decision Directives.

"The existence of a separate document for Yugoslavia reflects that nation's special relationship with the U.S. After Yugoslavia left the Warsaw Pact in 1948 over disagreements with Stalin, the West saw it as a buffer state against Soviet expansionism. When the Soviet Union made threats against it in the early 1950s, Yugoslavia asked U.S. for help, and quietly undertook 'certain military obligations' towards the West …in the event of a conflict with the Soviet Union. The agreement included a commitment to 'protect northern Italy from penetration by Soviet troops based in Hungary.

"According to a Yugoslav analyst, this 'alliance with the West' along with expanded educational, diplomatic, and commercial ties 'forced Yugoslav Communists to open up to Western cultural and political influences'. During the post-World War II

years … Western aid, amounting to several hundred billions of dollars, most of which came from the U.S. … helped to create a boom in Yugoslavia. Although Yugoslavia remained poorer than most of the countries of the industrialized West, the relatively equitable distribution of the fruits of industrialization carried much of the country out of poverty. By the end of the 1980s, Yugoslavs were better off than most people in Portugal, Spain, Turkey, and parts of Greece …that economic success was crucial in diminishing regional and ethnic tensions.

"The Yugoslav socialist experiment was generally viewed as successful, even in the West, both for its economic progress and for the unity which Marshall Tito brought to an ethnically-diverse State. Yugoslav planners strove to combine structural change with rapid economic growth …that policy was costly …it created a large trade deficit and weakened the country's currency.

"Oil crises of 1973-1974 and 1979, made Yugoslavia's problems worse. By the early 1980s, the country faced serious balance of payments problems, and rising inflation. As usual, the IMF in the name of financial judgment, stepped in prodding the Yugoslav authorities to slow growth …restrict credit …cut social expenditures …and devalue the dinar currency. Although the trade deficit was reduced, and the balance of payments showed a record surplus by 1979 …the IMF 'reforms' wreaked economic and political havoc … slower growth, accumulation of foreign debt and the cost of servicing it, and devaluation led to a fall in the standard of living.

"The economic crisis threatened political stability. Not only did the declining standard of living undermine authority of the country's leaders, it also threatened to aggravate ethnic tensions … the 1980 death of Marshall Tito, the one leader who could hold the country together, plunged Yugoslavia into a dual crisis …without leadership, the crises became more difficult to resolve. And, since Yugoslavia was linked to the world capitalist economy, it suffered the same economic stagnation affecting Western Europe and North America during the 1970s. When the Reagan Administration's supply-side economic policies caused a recession in 1981-1983, the effects were felt everywhere, including Yugoslavia …it is not surprising Yugoslav planners found it difficult to slow economic decline. Some observers claimed the inability of the economic system to respond to the 1980s crisis demonstrated the failure of Yugoslav socialism. The system was rigid, but Yugoslavia's troubles were primarily caused by the transmission of the Western economic crisis to countries on the edge of Europe, closely linked to the West by aid ...trade ...capital flows ...and immigration.

"The uneasy U.S.-Yugoslav alliance persisted through the 1980s ...because Yugoslavia's unique 'buffer' position, the U.S. had a stake in its instability. Despite discomfort with its communist 'ally', the new Reagan Administration preserved the relationship, hoping to benefit from the developing instability in Yugoslavia, in order to install a more favorable government ... in late 1980s, three factors altered the dynamics of the relationship ...Yugoslavia began to suspend its market-oriented 'reforms' ... the Cold War ended and Yugoslavia was no longer as useful ...and a newly united Germany, staking out a larger role for itself in Europe demanded that the new Bush Administration adopt the German policy of working for the dismantling of Yugoslavia.

"The summer before the Berlin Wall fell, the major Western powers decided in Paris to press the merging East European governments to establish 'democracies', and market economies. This goal was advanced by the 1990 elections throughout Eastern Europe ...which produced broad support for non-Communist governments seeking to implement the kinds of 'reforms' the U.S. and its European partners hoped for, and worked for. In an exercise in coercive diplomacy, the Western powers decided to offer aid and trade only to those countries agreeing to market-oriented structural and policy change. And, chief economic adviser to the European Community Richard Portes said, the West must 'build in ways of committing the authorities not to deviate from basic policies' ... to this end, planners demanded four major, irreversible 'reforms' in Eastern Europe ...an opening to the world economy i.e. the Western system ...liberalization of prices ...privatization ... and stabilization of State finances and national currencies.

"These 'reforms', Portes argued, would mark 'a definitive exit from the socialist-planned economy. The governments of Czechoslovakia, Hungry and Poland agreed ... Bulgaria and Romania complied in part. Two years later, northern tier countries of Eastern Europe were 'in throes of a deep economic depression ...turmoil and starvation stalk the Balkins ...social crisis and wild political swings plague Poland ...nationalism threatens to tear apart Czechoslovakia ...social discontent in Hungary has led to a virtual boycott of existing political parties ...quasi-fascist movements have emerged on the far-Right

...while the governments of the region have all considered initiatives to restrict civil rights.

"A crucial change in Yugoslav relations with the West occurred when Yugoslavia balked at carrying out the reforms urged by the West. Yugoslavia initiated market-oriented policies before any of the countries in the former Eastern bloc, tasting the bitter consequences ... its halting of 'reforms' in 1990 rankled the Bush Administration, which set out to force Yugoslavia to agree to Western demands for a 'change in regime'.

"Jan. 1989, when Ante Marcovic was named Federation Premier, the U.S. anticipated a cooperative relationship ... known to favor market-oriented reforms, the new Prime Minister was described by the new BBC correspondent as 'Washington's best ally in Yugoslavia'. Autumn 1989 just before the Berlin Wall fell, Marcovic visited Bush in the White House. The President, the *New York Times* reported, 'Welcomed Mr. Marcovic's commitment to market-oriented reform and to building democratic pluralism'. In this friendly atmosphere, Marcovic asked for 'U.S. assistance in making economic and political changes opposed by hardliners in the Communist Party ...he requested a substantial aid package from the U.S., including 1 billion dollars to prop up the banking system ...and more than 3 billion dollars in loans from the World Bank ...and tried to lure private investment to Yugoslavia. In exchange, Marcovic promised 'reforms', but warned, as the *Times* put it, that they 'are bound to bring social problems [including] an increase in unemployment to about 20% ...and the threat of increased ethnic and political tensions among the country's six republics and two autonomous provinces.

"Marcovic's new austerity plan, announced two months later in Belgrade, deepened the Yugoslav crises. The plan called for ...a new devalued currency ...a six-month wage freeze ...closure of unprofitable State enterprises ...and reduced government expenditure ... Believing it would lead to social unrest, Serbia, the largest republic, immediately rejected it ...some 600,000 Serbian workers staged a walkout in protest. Marcovic's proposal for some first steps towards political democratization ... a multi-party system, and open elections ... fared a bit better, and in January 1990 was accepted by the Central Committee of the Yugoslav League of Communists. Not long after, the Slovene League of Communists seceded from the Yugoslav League. In April, the Slovene opposition coalition described in the U.S. as 'an alliance of pro-Western parties,' won a majority in parliamentary elections in Slovenia.

"So, as the unity of the socialist Federal Republic of Yugoslavia weakened ...a pro-Western, pro-'reform' camp consolidated, and pushed for separatism ... as the only way to realize nationalistic aims, which would shatter the Yugoslav economy.

"June 1990, when Prime Minister Marcovic introduced the second phase of his austerity program ...industrial output in Yugoslavia had fallen 10% since the beginning of the year ...in part a result of measures he introduced the previous October ... so, the second phase of the prime minister's plan called for more reductions ...18% in public spending ...wholesale privatization of State enterprises ...establishment of new, private property rights. To make the package easier to swallow, Marcovic proposed ...lowering interest rates ...and conditionally lifting the wage freeze. Economic reform was the crucial issue in 1990 multi-party elections held throughout Yugoslavia. In Slovenia, Croatia, and Bosnia-Herzegovina, separatist coalitions ousted the League of Communists.

"In Serbia and Montenegro the ruling party, renamed, Socialist Party, won. The federal government including Prime Minister Marcovic, denounced the separatist tendencies of the two northern republics ...President Borisav Jovic resigned as federal president, when his proposal for a national state of emergency was rejected.

"The line was drawn. The new separatist governments in the north wanted, at least in the flush of their electoral victories, to join Europe and the parade towards capitalism ... the federal government and some of the republics, including Serbia, balked. One European scholar summarized the West's view ... 'With the ending of the Cold War, Yugoslavia was no longer a problem of global importance for the two super-powers. The important factor was the pace of reforms in the East. What lasted nine months in Poland, took only nine weeks in the GDR, and only nine days in Czechoslovakia. Yugoslavia lagged enormously behind in this process of democratic transformations'.

"In an ideal world, there would have been a long national debate on the way forward, and the separatist republics if still bent on secession, would have proceeded through the complex process provided for in the Federal Constitution ... this was not to be.

"The years following the general adoption of the Reagan Doctrine saw the pace of change accelerate in all the countries of the Socialist bloc. Developments were carrying them toward the 'quiet' revolutions the West wanted. By the end of 1989, an important change ... the third major change in Yugoslavia's relationship with the West, was underway. The reunification of Germany, and its emergence as the giant of Europe ... would prove fateful for Yugoslavia.

"As Yugoslavia continued in crises, a strengthened industrial and political leadership in Germany looked East ... Germany's influence was rapidly becoming 'pervasive' in personal contacts, business investments, and intellectual life ...in the post-Cold War Era, the means for expansion are ...economic ...political ...and cultural ... rather than military. In Eastern Europe, German trade groups and banks became very active, German firms sought lower costs, lower wages, lower taxes.

"By 1991, one third of the trade between Eastern and Western Europe was based in Germany, according to a U.N. study ...and Germany became the major foreign investor in Eastern Europe, especially in Czechoslovakia, Hungary, and Poland ... German firms now had 1,500 joint ventures in Poland, and 1,000 in Hungary.

"But it was not just economics that drove Germany eastward ...for many Germans, the expansion also made historical sense ... their firms were reviving ties to the East, that went back to the pre-Communist era, back even to the time of the Austro-Hungarian Empire. And perhaps more disquieting for partially re-colonized Eastern Europe, were the cultural campaigns that accompanied economic expansion ... promoting the use of German language, German books, and German culture in general. The German foreign broadcasting service recently announced 'a media and cultural offensive in Central Eastern and Southern Europe, the most important bridgehead between East and West'. The aims and scope of Germany's drive to the East were summed up by the East Committee Chair, the industrial group promoting business in the East, 'It is our natural market, in the end this market will bring us to the position we were in before World War I, why not?'

"German expansionism has been accompanied by a rising tide of nationalism and xenophobia, igniting old Yugoslav fears ... these have been fed by evidence Germany has been energetically seeking a free hand among its allies 'to pursue economic dominance in the whole of

Mitteleuropa'.

In 1990, Yugoslavia lay in the path of that gathering German drive. Given Germany's economic and political power, and its aid and trade ties with Yugoslavia, many expected Bonn to try to draw the region into its orbit ... the most obvious beginning would be in the northern republics, which had historically been considered part of Europe ...and especially in Croatia, which had strong German links. During World War II, Nazi Germany installed a clerical-Fascist State in Croatia. After World War II, more than a half million Croatian émigrés moved to the Fatherland ...where their organizations had considerable political influence. Milovan Djilas may have had these considerations in mind, when more than a year before the secession crises of 1991 he warned, 'It is definitely in the interests of the majority of other nations, for example the U.S., Great Britain, U.S.S.R. to support the unity of Yugoslavia ... but I doubt that Yugoslavia's neighbors are so well-intentioned. I also suspect in some states like Germany and Austria, there are influential groups who'd like Yugoslavia to disintegrate ...for reasons of traditional hatred ...for expansionist tendencies ...and vague, unrealistic desires for revenge'.

"Yugoslavia walked a tightrope through the 1980s until economic and political crises such as the falling standard of living, broke its balance ... as rival ethnic groups shook the rope, the state teetered ...European Community intervention helped push Yugoslavia into the abyss of disintegration and horrific civil war.

"After World War II, Yugoslavia brought together communities historically at odds, Slovenes, Croats, Serbs, Muslims (descendants of converted Slavs), Albanians, Hungarians. At the same time, the federal government made enormous efforts after World War II to create a state which gave full play to 'national identities', and entrenched the rights of minorities. Since the was no way to draw the map of Yugoslavia to enclose each group in its own republic or autonomous region, large minorities would always exist within any republic or region ... so, for example, large numbers of Serbs, more than two million, found themselves living in Croatia, or Bosnia, or elsewhere ...when the boundaries of Serbia were drawn in 1945. Within the Balkan tinderbox, two actions set off the current war in Yugoslavia ...the secessions of Slovenia and Croatia ...and intervention of the European Community ... the former may not have occurred without the latter.

"Continuous European Community intervention from early 1991 could not have been more likely to set off a war, than if it had been deliberately designed to do so ... it turned a manageable internal conflict into appalling fratricide. Slovenia and Croatia were clearly driving towards independence well before widespread fighting broke out between the Yugoslav National Army and Slovene territorial forces in the spring of 1991 ... their separatist aspirations received quiet encouragement, and assistance, from several European powers, particularly Germany and Austria ... for some time before the outbreak of hostilities.

"Early February 1991, the Council of Europe said that to join Europe, as some Yugoslav leaders wanted to do, Yugoslavia would have to resolve its crisis peacefully, and hold multi-party elections for the Federal Parliament ... this bland-sounding precondition was in effect, an invitation to Slovenia and Croatia to push for secession ...for it linked economic advantages to 'restraint' in federal dealings with those republics. By March, when it was clear that Croatia intended to secede, Croats and the Serb minorities started to clash. Croatian nationalists organized violent demonstrations in Split, besieged a military base in Gospic, and intensified their nationalistic campaign.

"May 5, the federal government authorized the Army to intervene in Croatia ... two days later, the military began calling up reserves, and deploying units in western Yugoslavia. 'Yugoslavia has entered a state of civil war," Defense Secretary Gen. V. Kadijevic said.

"The European Community then start openly applying pressure on Yugoslavia. In June, the European Community foreign ministers gathered in Dresden, and warned that future assistance would depend on 'respect for minority rights and economic reforms'. The European Community was no longer posing conditions for Yugoslavia's entry into Europe, but simply for normal economic relations.

"June 25, when Slovenia and Croatia declared independence, European Community openly intervened again ... again its actions promoted separatism. Within three days after the Yugoslav Army deployed units in both republics, European Community threatened the 'cut-off of 1 billion dollars in scheduled aid' unless Yugoslavia accepted mediation by three European Community foreign ministers ...Slovenia and Croatia would otherwise have been occupied by Yugoslav troops, and secessions ended.

"The foreign ministers imposed a ceasefire, which called for a three-month suspension of the Slovene and Croatian independence declarations ...withdrawal to barracks of all federal troops ...and acceptance by Serbia of Stipe Mesic, a Croat, as federal president ... there was no settlement of the federal dispute with Croatia, and federal troops remained in parts of the republic ...those parts inhabited primarily by Serbs. The Yugoslav Army ordered withdrawal of its troops from Slovenia shortly thereafter.

"Although European Community intervention halted the secessions temporarily, by preventing Yugoslavia from defending its unity and territorial integrity, the actions predictably worked to the advantage of Slovenia and Croatia.

"Oct. 1991, the European Community called a conference on Yugoslavia in the Hague ... the aim, in theory, was to end the crisis, negotiate a new federal structure for the Balkan nation ... the draft convention on Yugoslavia prepared by European Community announced the republics 'are sovereign and independent, with an international identity'. While the Conference adopted reasonable principles for resolving the conflict, it abolished Yugoslavia as a unitary State ... within a short time upon expiration of the three-month delay imposed in July, Croatia and Slovenia formally seceded from Yugoslavia.

"One is left to wonder if the European Community wanted a unified Yugoslavia then acted consistently and stupidly to defeat this goal ... or whether other factors were quietly at work ...the key to seeming contradiction between stated goals and actual consequences, may be found in the behind-the-scenes maneuvering of an expansionist Germany.

"As former U.S. Ambassador to Yugoslavia William Zimmerman said, 'We discovered later that German Foreign Minister Genscher had been in daily contact with the Croatian foreign minister, encouraging the Croats to leave the federation and declare independence ...while we and our allies, including the Germans, were trying to fashion a joint approach' ... in fact, re-united Germany was throwing its weight around for some time, and not just at Yugoslavia ...a U.S. State Department official said, 'The Germans are now so much more stable and so much more powerful than anyone else in Europe that they can get away with almost anything'.

"From 1990, Germany was forcing the pace of international diplomacy on the question of secession. In December, within a few months of the de

facto recognition of Slovenia and Croatia at the Hague Conference, Germany recognized their independence ... Germany virtually forced its allies to reverse themselves and grant recognition to Slovenia and Croatia.

"Just as foreign intervention helped foment the war in Yugoslavia, outside forces also helped sustain and worsen the conflict. Croatian political organizations in the diaspora, especially in Germany, Canada, U.S., and Australia often espouse extremist, right-wing, sometimes openly anti-Semitic views ... through the generation that left Yugoslavia after World War II, they have maintained close ties to the Nazi-sponsored Croatian independent state led by Ante Pavelic and Archbishop Alois Steponac.

Since 1945, Croatian émigrés and émigré organizations have actively and consistently supported the cause of Croatian independence. These separatists want to prove that they were right 50 years ago, and they try to pass the mythology on to their kids that things will be perfect when independence comes," said a prominent Slovak émigré. International émigré support has been financial as well as political. According to *Los Angeles Times*, overseas Croatians were largely responsible for funding Croatian President Franju Tudjaman's victorious presidential election campaign in 1990. After he won, the money continued to flow. Toronto Businessman Dick Gezic said, 'Canadians bankrolled Tudjaman's new state and its army'. In December, Tudjman acknowledged the importance of the émigrés role, 'Croatians in Canada have helped a great deal in the establishment of a democratic Croatia,' Tudjman told Canadian Broadcasting Corp.

"In addition to cash, overseas Croatians have sent arms. Croatians and Bosnian Croatians claim that Bosnian Serbs possess large amounts of modern weapons and munitions ... while the charge is true, it must be remembered that the arms factories in Bosnia are still producing, and the Yugoslav army left behind large stockpiles of weapons that were grabbed up by all sides in the conflict. In addition to their own supplies, the break-away states are covertly receiving large amounts of arms from the Western powers, despite the U.N. arms embargo. Overseas Croatians established an extensive network designed to evade the U.S. embargo on arms shipments to former Yugoslavia ... documents indicate weapons were moving to Croatia from Austria and Slovenia, and Hungary ...senior U.S. officials stated 'the Croatians are armed to the teeth".

"The network existed well before Croatia declared independence ... more than a year ago U.S. Customs blocked a large, illegal shipment of weapons from Croatian activists, to Yugoslavia ...it included 12 million dollars of Stinger and Red-Eye missiles, and thousands of M-16 assault rifles. The arms smugglers, a clandestine military organization called OTPOR, had an alternative plan to ship weapons through a German front company. OPTOR members also requested Nigeria to supply end-user certificates for large quantities of weapons including low-altitude surface-to-air missiles, armored Czech Tatra trucks mounted with launching frames for 122mm rockets, and 5,000 122mm rockets. It was reported in England last year that there was 'a booming trade in arms supplied by Austria, Belgium and Hungary' to the Serbian and Croatian militias. As none of the source countries are named, with the possible exception of Belgium, was likely to be shipping arms to Serbian irregulars, the supplies were most likely going to Croatia.

"Political contributions and arms shipments on such a scale can not take place without the knowledge of intelligence agencies ...in this case, especially those of Germany, Austria, Canada, and U.S. In countries actively seeking to destabilize Yugoslavia, these services are likely to have had official sanction to assist the transfers. There have also been repeated reports of foreigners, including British, U.S., and German nationals with extensive military experience ... serving in the Croatian forces or militia. Reportedly, some are absent-without-leave from active military units. In what amounts to an officially sanctioned policy of covert military assistance, active-duty soldiers, including some U.S., sometimes leave undated letters of resignation with a commander and take official leave to serve as mercenaries in foreign wars.

"The movement of weapons in the region appears to be massive ... German customs officials claim they have evidence of large military convoys of up to 1,500 military vehicles moving out of Eastern Germany to Croatia.

"April 1992, east German military vehicles bound for Croatia were seized by Customs officials on the Germany-Austrian border. Recently, there have been reports that Croatia has used German Leopard tanks and MIG-21 fighters in its invasion of Bosnia-Herzegovina. Although Germany denies these reports, reliable Yugoslav sources say that a number of Leopard tanks were put out of commission by Serb irregulars at Kupres in Bosnia in May 1992. These sources also say a number of MIG fighters from the former GDR have been shot down over Bosnia. The use of MIGs has been confirmed by senior U.N. officials, and supported by Croatia's air force commander. In February he boasted that 'within a month, Croatia would be taking delivery of fighter aircraft from un-named European governments'.

"The Bosnian government has also reportedly received arms and troops from abroad, notably from Islamic countries seeking to assist fellow Muslims. The *London Guardian* reported major arms shipments from Turkey, Iran, and Pakistan. A Bosnian government adviser admitted in Zagreb at the end of August that Bosnian officials had traveled to the Croatian coast to take delivery of arms shipments from the Middle East. Islamic countries have sent trainers and 'volunteers' to assist and fight with Muslim forces in Bosnia and have established secret training camps there. The soldiers come from Saudi Arabia, Turkey, Pakistan, Sudan, Afghanistan, Iran, and Syria ... again, such large-scale activity can not easily be organized by private individuals or organizations. The facts strongly suggest the extensive involvement of foreign intelligence agencies and military personnel, in what is still being called a purely internal conflict.

"During the last 18 months, the Western media has steadily hammered home the idea that Yugoslavia is in the middle of a civil war brought about by the 'aggressor' Serbia's attempts to 'conquer' Slovenia and parts of Croatia and Bosnia-Herzegovina ... while the internal factors of nationalism and ethnic strife are real, they are not sufficient to explain the bloody dynamic ...external forces must also be considered. This more complex analysis does not deny that Yugoslavs are killing one another and dying ... nor does it dismiss the suffering of the hundreds of thousands who have been affected. Rather, it recognizes the clear indications that the secessions of Croatia and Slovenia, which were crucial in the development of the Yugoslav conflict ... were prepared with the assistance of foreign powers. These powers sustained and extended the conflict by sending arms, money, and personnel to Croatia and, more recently, to Bosnia-Herzegovina.

"During the 1980s, the West followed a dual policy ...first, it pushed Yugoslavia towards a gradual political and economic transformation ...the struggle to force changes in Yugoslavia was driven less by tensions between socialism and capitalism, than by those between independence and colonization.

"In a central Europe dominated by Germany, the policies urged by the West will lead to de-industrialization, and dependence ... as they have already in Czechoslovakia, Hungary, and Poland.

"The other edge of the West's policy sword was the promotion of separatism in the northern republics ... when Yugoslavia balked at 'reforms' that had worsened economic conditions and ethnic strife, some Western governments turned up the pressure. Germany, strengthened by re-unification, and expanding its influence throughout Europe, was impatient with Yugoslavia. Germany's push for quick recognition of Slovenia and Croatia set off a violent chain reaction ... the U.S. and other nations face a fait accompli and accepted Germany's demands that the West support German policies ...they saw Germany's strategy as a useful way to ensure that Yugoslavia carry out the political and economic changes they dictated.

"After World War II, the Yugoslav people struggled to achieve independence and a decent standard of living ... the war in former Yugoslavia has shattered the nation, and its many peoples. It is an unnecessary tragedy which can only be stopped if its real causes are understood," Sean Gervasi said.

<>

Dec. 1992, FAIR, Fairness & Accuracy in Reporting's *Extra Magazine*, Martin A. Lee's *U.S. news media fiddle while Germany burns*.

"Sept. 26, 1992 in a scene starkly reminiscent of the Hitler era, 800 neo-Nazis stormed a refugee enter in the Baltic seaport of Rostock Germany in late August terrorizing gypsies and Vietnamese guest workers with Molotov cocktails, shotguns, and bricks. As the housing complex went up in flames, local residents cheered and sang 'Deutschland uber alles'. Shortly after the violence erupted German officials caved in completely to the Nazi mob by moving all refugees from Rostock to other locales that are off-limits to the press, *Washington Post* reported. Rather than defusing tensions, the government's decision sparked a wave of terror unlike anything Germany has witnessed since Adolf Hitler was in power. Nazi thugs went on a rampage, assaulting foreigners and anti-Fascists in over 100 cities and towns during the next two weeks.

"Sept. 3, 1992 *Stern Magazine* underscored how serious the situation had become, 'Germany faces a political catastrophe. The rule of law has capitulated before the terror. Events at Rostock

have shown that the Germany security forces have neither the capacity nor the will to protect innocent people fro the terror troops of the radical-Right'.

"With few exceptions, this sense of urgency has not been communicated by U.S. news media ... a combination of factors ...selective reporting ...adherence to official agendas ... lingering Cold War biases among journalists ...and intimidation by the German government have skewed press coverage of neo-Nazi revival spearheading Germany's rapid goosestep to the Right.

"Reflecting the spin preferred by Chancellor Helmut Kohl's ruling Christian Democratic Union, numerous U.S. news accounted stressed public relations dimension ...with German leaders bemoaning the damage done to their country's image and business prospects abroad.

"Comparatively few reports focused on the plight of the victims of racist attacks ... no foreigners or refugee advocates, for example, were quoted [in the *New York Times*]. Following the lead of the German government, many reporters were quick to frame the violence as primarily and 'Eastern problem'. A *Houston Chronicle* editorial Sept. 4, 1992 condemned the Rostock pogrom, calling it 'a particularly poisonous flower of the former Communist regime'. Mark Fritz of Associated Press Oct. 10 1992 said, 'Most neo-Nazi attacks occurred in former East Germany, where Communism's demise brought economic collapse and left a population consumed by pessimism and bereft of democratic values'.

"Ignoring reports to the contrary from their own correspondents in Germany, a *Washington Post* editorial Oct. 5, 1992 asserted that 'the violence is concentrated mostly in the former East Germany'. Ditto for Tom Gjelten on *NPR Morning Edition* Aug. 8, 1992, 'There have been something like 700 attacks this year alone, according to the federal government. A disproportionate number of those have been in East Germany'.

"Gjelten was wrong on both counts. In addition to understanding the number of new-Nazi attacks, he and other journalists erred in parroting German officials who claimed that most of the violence occurred on former Communist turf. In fact, West Germany has experienced many more neo-Nazi attacks against non-Germans, and desecrations of Jewish cemeteries, than East. *Los Angeles Times* correspondent Tamara Jones Oct. 9, 1992 was one of the few U.S. journalists who cited statistics released by the Verfassungschutz, Germany's FBI, that indicated that 1,296 incidents of neo-Nazi violence took place during the first nine months of this year, two-thirds took place in west Germany.

"*New York Time's* Craig Whitney conveyed a misleading impression Oct. 14, 1992, 'Right-Wing and neo-Nazi parties have benefited from a protest vote in local elections, particularly in the formerly Communist eastern part of the country, over the past two years'. While the Fascist Republikaner Party and other extremists have gained seats in several western states, far-Right parties have not fared nearly as well in the East. A September 1992 survey by INFAS, a German research institute, showed that 10% of west Germans would vote for the Republickaners and other extreme-Right parties ...the figure for East Germany was 12%, according to Inter Press Service, Sept. 3, 1992.

"In keeping with the efforts of Kohl's CDU to scapegoat East German Communism, Stephen Kinzer wrote in *New York Times* Sept. 13, 1992, 'Besides neo-Nazis, there are other obvious groups to blame, The Rostock police disclosed that former agents of the Stasi, the dreaded East German secret police, were among those arrested during Rostock riots. Kinzer gave undeserved credence to the allegations by omitting pertinent details about the so-called agents, who turned out to be three ex-Stasi snitches in their early 20s. The German federal police subsequently dismissed the Stasi connection as bogus. Nevertheless, a number of news outlets played up the Stasi angle, including *Chicago Tribune, Atlanta Journal Constitution,* and Associated Press.

"Other reports suggested no organized force was behind the wave of violent attacks. Asserting that the anti-immigrant feeling 'is particularly strong in eastern Germany', CNN correspondent Ken Jautz said Aug. 26, 1992, 'It is not organized. The unrest began in Rostock quite spontaneously and unexpectedly'. This contradicted numerous European press reports from *Daily Telegraph* and *Agence France Press,* that described neo-Nazi leaders at Rostock speaking with each other via car phone and walkie-talkies, while broadcasting commands to convoys of followers from various West German cities who converged on the Baltic seaport at the same time.

"According to the anti-Fascist, London-based *Searchlight* Oct. 1992, neo-Nazi leaders met and planned the Rostock attack weeks in advance. Tipped off by anonymous phone calls and publicly circulated leaflets threatening violence, Rostock city official Wolfgang Richter warned the German Interior Ministry that a neo-Nazi attack was imminent ... but no preventive measures

were ordered. Except for *Los Angeles Times,* no major U.S. news media mentioned evidence that German officials ignored signs of an impending attack.

"For two hours, the local police and fire departments turned a deaf ear to desperate pleas from four German TV journalists and 115 foreigners who were trapped inside a Rostock guest hostel that had been firebombed by neo-Nazis. Despite a pattern of lassitude and negligence on the part of German law enforcement, authorities in major U.S. media often portrayed the police as 'beleaguered, overwhelmed and outnumbered'. Racism was never explicitly cited as a factor in the inability of the police to stop attacks against refugees. U.S. journalists failed to cite a survey showing that support for the aims of Fascist Republikaner Party is particularly high among police in Bavaria (50%) and Hesse (40%), two West German states.

"U.S. news media have also not reported instances when German police, in the eastern city of Eisenhuettenstadt, for example, assaulted foreigners with batons and billy-clubs after the Nazis had already left the scene. A few weeks before the Rostock pogrom, police attacked three refugee centers near Dresden, where neo-Nazis have been allowed to parade openly in the streets, while law enforcement authorities pretended not to notice the illegal Hitler salutes and shouts of 'Sieg Heil!' On the weekend of Sept. 5-6, 1992 while ultra-Rightists attacked in 47 German cities and towns, a neo-Nazi march in Kelheim was given heavy police protection according to *Searchlight*. Police complicity with German neo-Nazis was examined in a Swedish TV documentary, 'The Truth Makes You Free', which aired in numerous European countries, but not in the U.S.

"Journalists occasionally cite examples of judicial leniency proffered to Nazi hooligans and murderers, such as the light verdict handed down to two skinheads who beat an African immigrant to death while police stood nearby and did nothing ...or the suspended sentences given to ten German Rightists who burned down a hostel for asylum seekers. But, U.S. news outlets rarely juxtapose these reports with the stern treatment of anti-Fascist protestors, including well-known Nazi-hunters Serge and Beate Klarsfeld, who were roughed up and arrested along with 44 other French Jews on Oct. 19, after they unfurled a banner in Rostock. Except for *USA Today,* no major U.S. news outlet bothered to report that the Klarsfelds had been arrested and detained overnight, while other Jewish protestors were imprisoned for nine days before they were released. This is in marked contrast to routine police procedures whereby hundreds of violent Nazi youth are freed after being held only a few hours.

"A disturbing and under-reported aspect of Germany's Rightward lurch has been the government's harassment of journalists who have covered neo-Nazi violence. Shortly after they escaped from a Rostock guest hostel that had been firebombed by neo-Nazis, four TV journalists from the ZDF network became the target of a criminal investigation by German authorities who alleged that the reporters had 'staged' the riot to get sensational film footage. The German government backed down after international protests from human rights and journalism organizations, including FAIR.

"On other occasions, German officials have charged journalists with instigating neo-Nazi activity, alleging that they paid Right-wing militants to shout Nazi slogans and make stiff-armed salutes for the cameras.

"In early November, Margita Fahr, a Berlin-based freelance journalist who reports on far-Right activities was charged with 'using the symbols of organizations which defy the constitution'. It seems that a German secret police unit intercepted a fax from Fahr about German right-wing extremists that included a reproduction of an illegal Nazi SS symbol. Under German law, Fahr, who is Jewish, could be sent to prison for this so-called offense. Harassment of this journalist comes at a time when uniformed Nazis wearing SS insignia parade openly, with police protection, on major streets of major German cities.

"Dubbed by novelist Gunter Grass as 'a white collar skinhead', Chancellor Kohl has repeatedly insisted to the press that asylum abuse ... not racism ... is the root of the problem. The German chancellor made no apology or public show of solidarity with the victims of neo-Nazi violence. For the most part, Kohl was treated with kid gloves by U.S. news media," Martin A. Lee said.

<>

Oct. 7, 1992 *San Francisco Chronicle's* Frank Viviano's *Freedom loses luster for Hungarian family.*

"...those Hungarians who haven't been successful at keeping up are beginning to look for scapegoats, someone to blame for the fact that Hungary after freedom appears to be a poorer, more uncertain place than Hungary was under goulash Communism.

"Many blame Jews, even though most of Hungary's Jews were slaughtered by the Nazis in World War II. The charge comes not from a skinhead, but from a leading figure in the Magyar Democratic Forum, party deputy president, and publisher, Istvan Csurka. In August, Csurka wrote an article in his Magyar Forum, that alluded to 'the genetic roots' of Hungary's social problems. Jewish international bankers, he claimed, plotted to control the Hungarian economy, in league with Hungarian politicians controlled by 'liaisons in Paris, New York and Tel Aviv'.

"Late last month, 50,000 people marched in Budapest to protest growing anti-Semitism. The protests were not enough to reassure Eva. 'We don't know if my husband's ancestors were actually Jewish, only that Stenczinger isn't a typically Hungarian name. But more and more, people ask us about it ... Are you Jews? ...they say."

<>

Sept. 8, 1992 *Los Angeles Times,* Elizabeth Shogren's *New breed of fascist rises in Russia.*

"During a 900-day siege that cost 700,000 lives here, the Nazis failed to fight their way into the city's center. But five decades later, homegrown Fascists claim St. Petersburg as the 'spiritual center' of their nationwide movement.

"The Fascist's leader is a police detective whose heroes are Josef Stalin, Adolf Hitler, and Arnold Schwarzenegger. Like Germany's neo-Fascists, Russian Fascists seek to capitalize on resentment of foreigners. As their first target, the People's Socialists and other Russian nationalist groups have chosen the darker-skinned people of the Caucasus Mountains south of Russia, an ethnic group they widely distrust.

"At least 40 anti-Semitic newspapers and magazines also have appeared across the country in the past year. The problem has gotten out of hand because local authorities have not enforced a law that makes racism a crime. Valentina Grechiskina, 82, a teacher of German who lived through the 900-day blockade of Leningrad, as St. Petersburg was formerly known, said she does not want to believe that Fascism could gain support in her city, 'Leningrad suffered so much under Fascism, I can not believe Fascism could find a base, here. I'm a Russian and I believe we need to be patriots of our nation, but I believe you must look at a person as an individual, not judge him because of his nationality,' she said. But she also noted that, recently, she has sensed that her students have a new attitude about Hitler. 'Many of my students are reading *Mein Kampf,* and they say they like his approach.'"

Lou Wolf's *Covert Action Information Bulletin*, summer 1992, Doug Henwood's *U.S. Economy, the enemy within.*

"After 40 years of scheming, Washington's Cold Warriors finally got their way. The U.S.S.R. is gone, and the Third World is under the management of the IMF, the World Bank, and the General Agreement on Tariffs and Trade GATT ... the three institutions created at the end of World War II to manage what would become the U.S. empire ... but it took some planning to get here.

"Reading the planners' original designs is a remarkable experience in these days of their triumph. No document is more remarkable than National Security Memorandum-68, NSC-68 ... written by Paul Nitze, with State Secretary Dean Acheson 'looking over his shoulder'. Each part in the neat structure of the global political economy reinforced the whole ...constant global military mobilization would stimulate the U.S. economy, lubricate global trade, bind the other capitalist powers to the U.S. in a subsidiary role, fuel the ideological crackdown on radical thought, and eventually destroy the Soviet Union.

"Although the Cold Warriors got what they wanted, their self-congratulatory cheers ring increasingly hollow ... the artful structure has broken down ...and been replaced with something incoherent.

"In the late 1940s, the triumphs and their somber repercussions were hard to imagine. Washington had inherited the imperial role the British finally lost during the war, but there was no guarantee the U.S. could hold on to the prize. Various insurgencies, some Communist, some merely nationalist, threatened the dream of a world hierarchically organized under U.S. power. With memories of the 1930s still fresh, capitalism's prestige was fairly low, and the appeal of socialism quite high, in both the Third and First Worlds. Militant unions and other domestic insurgencies plagued the U.S. elite. Fears that the Depression would soon return were deepened among those who understood that the Marshall Plan had failed to revive world trade.

"This view of the Marshall Plan as a failure is, of course, contrary to the myths of official history. Acheson described the many problems with the strategy to his boss, Harry Truman, in a memo ... 'Unless vigorous steps are taken, the reduction and eventual termination of extraordinary foreign assistance [the Marshall Plan] will create economic problems at home and abroad of increasing severity. If this is allowed to happen, U.S. efforts including the key commodities on which our most efficient agricultural and manufacturing industries are dependent, will be sharply reduced with serious repercussions on our domestic economy. European countries and friendly areas in the Far East and elsewhere will be unable to obtain basic necessities which we now supply, to an extent that will threaten their political stability. Put in its simplest terms, the problem is this. As the ERP [European Recovery Program (official name of the Marshall Plan)] is reduced, and after its termination in 1952, how can Europe and other areas of the world obtain the dollars necessary to pay for a high level of United States exports, which is essential both to their own basic needs and to the well-being of the U.S. economy?'

"NSC-68 was to answer this, and many other questions.

"Short of deeply radical reform, only massive government spending could avert a second Depression. But what kind of spending?

"A 1949 *Business Week* editorial went to the heart of the matter, 'Military spending doesn't really alter the structure of the economy. It goes through the regular channels. But the kind of welfare and public works spending Truman plans, does alter the economy. It makes new channels of its own. It creates new institutions. It redistributes income. It shifts demand from one industry to another. It changes the whole economic pattern. That's its object', the articles said.

"Although Truman's domestic spending schemes proved much less dramatic and transformative than *Business Week* feared, 'regular channels' were about to be flooded with a fresh military cash flow.

"There was plenty of opposition from classically conservative Republicans, isolationist partisans of extremely limited government, to what was about to happen ... a sustained international military build-up would weaken budgetary orthodoxy at the same time it vastly increased the scope and power of the U.S. government at home and abroad. Old-style conservatives didn't want a huge army and a permanent spy service ... that's why Nitze stuffed his memo NSC-68 full of the kind of rhetoric that would become commonplace in political speech for the next 40 years, 'the grim oligarchy of the Kremlin' running their 'slave state' hell-bent on world domination against the good guys ... the U.S., the 'free society' summoned up to the 'responsibility of world leadership'.

"Several themes recur throughout the rambling

memo." One is a variation on the comparative-economists' classic formula that the characteristic crisis of the Soviet-style economies was shortage ... while that of advanced capitalist economies is surplus ...too many goods, not enough money in the right hands.

"Or, as NSC-68 put it, there were 'grounds for predicting that the U.S. and other free nations will, within a period of a few years at most, experience a decline in economic activity of serious proportions without government intervention. If a dynamic expansion of the economy were achieved, the necessary build-up could be accomplished without a decrease in the standard of living'.

"The arms build-up, then. Could help solve in ideologically convenient terms, the characteristic crisis of U.S.-style capitalism. But an arms build-up would hurt the U.S.S.R. ...which was already 'being drawn upon close to the maximum possible extent', thereby leaving it even more vulnerable to its characteristic crisis ... chronic shortage. This economic squeeze was one front in the strategy of containment, which, rather than a doctrine of resisting expansion ... the public explanation ... was actually a 'calculated and gradual coercion' to, as an earlier memo to NSC-68 put it, 'reduce the power and influence of the U.S.S.R'.

"Another coercive opportunity, the memo noted, was the corrosive potential of nationalism, which could eat away at the internal stability of the U.S.S.R. and its satellites. The U.S.S.R. wasn't the only problem facing Washington's planning elite, there was the fact that the 'ideological pretensions of the Kremlin were another great source of strength' in what would later be called the Third World. The very existence of the Soviet Union was proof that there was more than one way to organize economic society, and the 'vulnerable segments of society have been impressed by what has been plausibly portrayed to them as the rapid advance of the U.S.S.R., from a backward society to a position of great world power'.

"A booming U.S. economy, powered by military spending, would be a powerful antidote to the seductiveness of the U.S.S.R. ... U.S. domestic unrest threatened this boom. The postwar wave of union militancy and other dangers of democracy, such as 'doubts and diversities', and 'rights and privileges that free men enjoy', were viewed as 'opportunities for the Kremlin to do its evil work'. The planners saw the need to 'reconcile order, security, the need for participation ... with the requirements of freedom'.

"These requirements as defined by the memo, seemed to be less freedom and more 'sacrifice and discipline' ... economic growth might take the edge off the financial costs of the military build-up ...but could not repay the loss of civil liberty.

"The memo ends with recommendations, 'substantive increase' in military expenditures, 'substantive increase' in military assistance, 'some increase' in economic aid to our allies in a anti-Soviet campaign to 'build and maintain confidence' on our side and 'sow mass defections' on theirs, covert economic, political, and psychological warfare, tighter internal security, beefed-up intelligence. In the short term, it could all be financed by lower consumption and higher taxes, but growth it stimulated could make the process nearly painless.

"Of course, much of this was propaganda nonsense.

"As William Schaub, a high-level functionary in Budget Bureau said, the picture of a free vs. slave world was overdone ... since it was not 'true that the U.S. and its friends were a free world. Are Indo-Chinese free? ...are people of the Philippines free under the corrupt Quirino government?' People are 'attracted to Communism because governments are despotic or corrupt, or both'. He said U.S.S.R. was stronger relative to the U.S. before World War II than after, but 'we hardly gave Russia a second thought, then. What makes for the difference today? The difference today people are striving to better themselves economically and politically, and have accepted, or are in danger of accepting the leadership of the Communist movement'. Schaub was onto something.

"For the next forty years, those striving for self-betterment would be co-opted, overthrown or slaughtered in the name of war on International Communism, with Moscow U.S.S.R. being global headquarters ... the beauty of NSC-68 was that it provided a rationale and a structure for a war on many fronts, against ... economic depression, domestic insurgency, wars of liberation in the Third World, notions of excessive independence in Western Europe and East Asia and ultimately against the U.S.S.R. It worked for decades.

"Sometimes you hear that the U.S. economy was laid low by perpetual, this view is overdone. First, it over-estimates the damage done by the military to the civilian economy, forgetting that the problem is more the absence of a civilian economic strategy than the presence of a military one. It also forgets NSC-68 was an entirely rational response on the part of the U.S. elite to the challenges of the early 1950s ... how to remake the world in the U.S. image without altering the fundamental structures *Business Week* was so concerned to protect.

"In fact, every major goal of NSC-68 was accomplished.

"Domestically, the Pentagon budget became the U.S. substitute for industrial policy, and the Cold War helped gag domestic dissent. Globally, the massive flow of military dollars overseas, not to mention procurement and base building, finally managed to jumpstart the world trading system. U.S. military expenditure during the Korean War was an important early stimulus to the Japanese economy. During the Vietnamese war, the Japanese benefited further.

"Things looked briefly bad for the imperium in the mid-1970s, after defeats by Vietnam and OPEC. That's when Nitze and his new-conservative Cold War cronies formed the Committee on the Present Danger ... this group, made of up Cold Warriors and Reagan Republicans found its first successes in Carter's right-ward shifts.

"The Reagan Presidency ... essentially an intensified re-dedication to the principles of NSC-68, was its utopia. The huge military build-up was designed to intimidate and bankrupt the Soviet Union ... while at the same time, smashing any number of third World pests. It did both.

"The Pentagon helped power a mad, and highly selective, economic boom that massively increased the global prestige of capitalism ... as Soviet-style systems were failing. Multilateral institutions like IMF, World Bank, the U.N., all of which the U.S. continues to bend to its wishes, are increasingly managing global social development on their own terms.

"Everything in sight has been de-regulated and privatized. Capital prowls the globe with a ravenous freedom it hasn't enjoyed since World War I. This freedom still carries many of the risks that caused the world to blow up in 1914. Karl Polanyi's Great Transformation argued, the roots of the 'cataclysm' ... thirty years of depression, Fascism and war ... had its roots 'in the utopian endeavor of economic liberalism to set up a self-regulating market system' ...the doctrine of invisible hands and free trade philosophized by Adam Smith and David Ricardo two hundred years ago. Polanyi argued that market's rule is too harsh to be sustained, that it destroys all social institutions, unions, the benign aspects of the State such as social welfare programs, and traditional pre-market social structures that soften its corrosive, polarizing rule. He argued that the destruction of Germany in World War II wrecked

the balance-of-power system that had kept peace for the prior half-century. We seem to be there again ... social disintegration, economic slump, neo-Fascism, border wars. The coherent world of NSC-68 is gone ... leaving questions behind.

"Can global capitalism ever find a stimulus as reliable as the U.S. military budget?

"Can a multilateral new World Order ever be as stable as the hierarchical system of the Cold War?

"Or will capitalism's natural centrifugal and stagnation tendencies gain the upper hand, as it did 75 years ago?

"Certainly the hierarchy is threatened. Militarily, the U.S. is coasting on its superpower reputation ... but when it comes to cash, the U.S. repeatedly comes up short.

"Larger military adventures now require foreign approval and foreign cash. Financial limitations have also forced Washington into a secondary role in the restructuring of the former Socialist world. Although U.S. policy in large measure 'did-in' the Reds, German firms will probably make most of the profits picking over the remains ... that's not to say the U.S. is collapsing, the world is more multi-polar than that. An interesting picture of our One World market was painted by the U.N. Centre on Transnational Corporations, in its first global investment report. What the Centre calls the Triad ... the U.S., Western Europe and Japan ... dominates world trade and capital flow. The three region's interactions with each other exceed their interactions with the rest of the world. Each pole of the Triad has collected around it a handful of Third World countries to act as plantation, sweatshop and mine. The rest of the Third World has been cast adrift.

"Tallies by UNCTC show a decline in the number of countries dominated by U.S. investment during the 1980s, and a rise in those claimed by Europe and Japan. Despite these deep material ties, the Triad is having a hard time managing its political affairs. It may be overheated to argue, as do George Friedman and Meredith LeBard, that the U.S. and Japan may go to war soon, but all is not sweetness and light in the house of capital these days ... domestically, most countries of the Triad are experiencing political crises of some sort or another ...the unraveling of long-ruling parties and coalitions ... Italy, Japan, Sweden ... the rise of neo-Fascist parties ... Germany, France ... and mass alienation from traditional politics in the face of insolvency and social decay ... the U.S. Internationally, the global economy lacks zip, and the First World faces increasing economic stagnation, social de-evolution, and a Fascist revival. The Triad is unable to come to an agreement in the so-called Uruguay Round with the General Agreement on Tariffs and Trade, GATT, two years after the initial deadline. Meanwhile, much of the Third World is in its second decade of depression, while the First World is experiences its first generalized slump in ten years.

"Reagan's return to principles of Ricardo and NSC-68, de-regulation and privatization offered a tremendous boost to speculators' animal spirits ... while big Pentagon-induced deficits provided necessary cash.

"This time, however, economies lack the prospective stimulus, and with an enemy to help the rich capitalist countries overlook their differences, an end to U.S. fiscal woes is hard to envision. Having gotten what they wanted, is the Cold Warriors' triumph already turning sour?

"Since so many Leftists around the world have been dumbstruck by capital's triumph, we'll leave it to James Buchan, a *London Financial Times* writer's article in the Spectator, to sketch our glorious post-Socialist future ...

'For all its manifold virtues capitalistic society is not perfect. To ensure its own smooth operation, capitalism tends to shift rather heavy burdens onto working people and the physical environment of cities, villages and wilderness. Social relations under capitalism seem unnecessarily fraught ... particularly at dividing lines of sex, color and community. As far as I can see, capitalism is making a slum of the planet.'"

<>

Harper's, Oct. 1991, Christopher Hitchens' *Unlawful, Un-elected, & Un-checked, how CIA subverts Government at home.*

"If we keep in mind how the American political class has delegated numberless dark corners of its mind to covert subcontractors, we might explain the broadly-felt sense of overwhelming political cynicism and disarray. Consider the post-war role the CIA has played in bending the American mind. I am going to leave aside the overseas memorials, the graveyards filled by the noisy Americans in and around Saigon, the torture chambers constructed and used in Iran by Savak, the jail cell that held Nelson Mandela, the statues of dictators propped-up by the Agency that mark CIA's collusion with the most degraded elements in Third World politics. Let us confine the study to America's own internal affairs, including that area of 'police, subpoena, law enforcement powers or internal security functions' that the CIA was by its founding

Congressional charter forbidden to touch.

"First we see CIA secretly finding homes and jobs in the U.S. for several hundred prominent Nazis and Nazi collaborators. Soon after, began the operational pacts with American crime families. Drugs have a special place in the CIA, it has over the years funded experiments with LSD and other hallucinogens and toxins ... on unwitting civilians ... and worked in concert with pilots and middlemen who traffick not only information, but in heroin and cocaine that wound up on the American market.

"As for that other American bogey, 'spendthrift Government', the CIA may be 'mean', but it is never 'lean'. It's exact funding naturally is kept from us. In any way, the 'intelligence community' is not only the Agency ... but many agencies. Which means that the generally accepted estimate of the CIA's annual budget of 3.5 billion dollars in support of 20,000 employees, is on the other side of conservative.

"In 1986 William Casey awarded a $20,000 bonus to Alan Fires for his 'exceptional management' of the CIA Central America Task Force ... Fire's chief task as we now know, was circumventing Congressional prohibitions on arming Contras and talking trade with hostage takers.

"Above and beyond the drugs and wasting of tax dollars is the matter of American democracy ... and the CIA's contempt for it. It has bought and suborned senior American journalists and editors and planted known falsehoods in the America press.

"It has established itself by means of 'deniable' funds and foundations in the belly of the American academy, although no doubt multicultural literature courses are more scandalous and threatening to the American way of life. Shall I bring up the publishing houses the Agency has subsidized to dispense information? How it has further corrupted a political language? ...think of 'asset', 'destabilize', 'terminate'.

"What about the tainted money from overseas? ...from despots as if to sharpen the irony that thanks to the Agency has entered them in the electoral process.

"The damage the CIA has done to American democracy is most evident when we look to Congress ...the Senate and House are routinely deceived by the Agency and by foreign governments assisted by the Agency ... this is the dark heart of Iran-Contra ...and the tough-mindedness, covert action and preparedness for 'peace through strength' and its predicted affect on the legislative branch, turning it from legal watchdog, to lapdog.

"As the Agency's most famous counter-espionage man, James Jessie Angleton one told an executive session of the Senate Committee on Intelligence, 'It is inconceivable a secret intelligence arm of Government has to comply with the overt orders of Government.'"

National Endowment for Democracy

Lou Wolf's *Covert Action Information Bulletin*, winter 1991-1992, Sean Geravi's *Western Intervention in U.S.S.R., spyless coup or democratic break-through?*

"On August 23, 1991 Allen Weinstein, President of the Center for Democracy in Washington and architect of the National Endowment for Democracy NED, received a fax from Moscow, 'I thank you for the sincere congratulations you sent me in connection with the victory of the democratic forces and the failure of the attempted August 19, 1991 coup. We know and appreciate the fact that you contributed to this victory'.

"This communication between Boris Yeltzin, the new de facto leader of the U.S.S.R. and Weinstein, the man who invented the privatization of covert operations, raises the question of exactly what role the U.S. played in facilitating the seizure of power by a neo-conservative movement in the Soviet Union.

"Yeltzin was thanking not only Weinstein, but also the U.S. Government, its allies, and all the organizations they had for years mobilized to help the Soviet opposition.

"This article extends the analysis presented in The De-stabilization of the Soviet Union one year ago, and will document answers to the questions raised by the above fax ... what was the Western strategy of intervention in the Soviet Union? ... how did the Western powers and the 'private' organizations they mobilized, intervene in that country? ...how important was the intervention in forcing an end to the Communist rule and bringing Boris Yeltzin to power?

"In the early 1980s the Reagan-Bush Administration had adopted a plan to de-stabilize its major adversary. The strategy combined intense open and covert attacks. It utilized political pressure, economic operations, military force around the world, propaganda, and assistance to anti-Communist opposition groups in Eastern Europe and Soviet Union. A consultant to the National Security Council called this strategy, the 'Full-Court Press' against the Soviet Union.

"Evidence from classified Government documents, RAND Corp. reports and international sources indicated the U.S. had carefully planned and mounted a global strategy to worsen Moscow's economic problems in order to create popular discontent, and to push the Soviet leadership toward vaguely-defined reforms.

"The sharp escalation of the arms race was only the most obvious way in which the Soviet Union was forced to divert enormous social and financial resources into military spending.

"In the wake of the August putsch, Communist rule in the Soviet Union collapsed, and Western-style new-conservatives now occupy most of the principal centers of power. They have declared their intention to create a capitalist system. Not surprisingly, U.S. conservatives, and some others, are openly stating that the U.S. helped bring about that recent upheaval.

"In late September, the Washington Post carried one of the first reports that for at least a decade, the U.S. had been promoting a pro-Western opposition inside the Soviet Union.

"David Ignatius' *Spyless Coups*, gives an unusually-frank account of what the U.S. had been doing in the years which led up to 'Yeltsin's counter-coup', as Ignatius calls it, 'Preparing the ground for last month's triumph was a network of overt operatives who during the last ten years have quietly been changing the rules of international politics ... they have been doing in public what the CIA used to do in private ...providing money and moral support for pro-Democracy groups, training resistance fighters, working to subvert Communist rule'.

"This is an extraordinary statement. Ignatius was saying that for a decade the U.S. openly carried out operations which had once been conducted in secret ... creating havoc for Moscow, 'training resistance fighters', and building the opposition led by Yeltsin. These efforts were partially responsible, 'preparing the ground', for the counter-coup which brought Yeltsin to power.

Ignatius is not an official spokesperson for the U.S. Government ... but this statement by an experienced and influential journalist with close connections to the intelligence agencies should be seen as authoritative.

"Even more recently the Washington Post reported that Governor Bill Clinton of Arkansas, a Democratic presidential candidate, credited Ronald Reagan with hastening the collapse of Soviet Communism, 'We forced them to spend even more when they were already producing a Cadillac defense system and a dinosaur economy, and I think it hastened their undoing,'

Clinton said.

"Clinton's statement is important. IT further confirms the thesis that 'spending them into bankruptcy' was more than a RAND theory ... it was official policy. By praising the President's role 'in advancing the idea that Communism could be rolled back', he gives tacit support to covert intervention in the U.S.S.R.

"Government sources now appear to be deliberately leaking information about Reagan's 'Full-Court Press'. For conservatives may well believe that the public will rally round in support of what Ignatius calls this 'global anti-Communist putsch'.

"If Clinton's statement is any indication, we may be a 'bipartisan campaign' to justify the U.S. and allied role in the collapse of Communism, brushing aside the United Nations Charter and international law.

"Although the general outline of a concerted U.S.-allied de-stabilization campaign is increasingly clear, its extent and objectives remain to be clarified ... evidence is growing that the purpose was not to encourage reform ...but to provoke the outright overthrow of Communist rule.

"The drafters of a recent National Endowment for Democracy NED 'Strategy Paper' state 'The Endowment's mission was from the very outset conceived, not as anti-Communist, but as pro-democratic. Its aim was not only to assist those seeking to bring down dictatorships, but also to support efforts to consolidate new democracies'. The paper acknowledges that the Soviet Union was among the major targets of NED operations, stating openly that the endowment provided 'vital assistance' to 'democratic forces' three, and helped them to 'triumph' in August 1991.

"U.S. propaganda has consistently and erroneously defined democracy and Communism as mutually exclusive opposites.

"Since NED is clearly an arm of U.S. foreign policy, when it calls for the establishment of democracy, it is also implicitly advocating the overthrow of the Soviet system. Clearly the U.S. and its Western allies could not have brought about such a change by themselves ... they needed local partners ...these were soon found.

"The success of industrialization, the growth of urban centers, and the rise of standards of living in the post-war period produced new educated strata in the Soviet Union, just as they did elsewhere in an earlier time. By the 1960s its members numbered in the millions, and were often discontented or alienated. Since the ruling elites of the Soviet Union did not absorb them in large

numbers, their advancement was restricted and their living standards remained modest. Members of this new strata lived for the most part, in urban centers plagued by shortages of housing, inadequate facilities, and other problems. The unrelenting pro-capitalist propaganda barrages of CIA-run Radio Free Europe and Radio Liberty worsened the resulting tensions.

"There was bound to be considerable pressure for rapid economic and social progress in such a situation ... what has been called the 'revolution of rising expectations'. When economic growth slowed in the later half of the 1970s, and progress became much more difficult, discontent began to spread. The 'Full-Court Press' compounded the economic difficulties, further intensifying social unrest.

"The Western Allies set about encouraging and harnessing this discontent, in order to turn it against Communism and to engineer a 'democratic break-through'. Following a pattern that has been documented around the world, the U.S. employed covert and overt means to weaken Soviet leadership, and to begin building an opposition movement and an alternative leadership.

"NED's role was crucial. The Endowment distinguishes four different kinds of countries in framing its 'programs', that is, operation. Three of these categories are relevant.

1. "'Closed societies ... repress all institutions independent of the state. 'Closed society' was how the U.S. described the pre-Gorbachev U.S.S.R.

2. "'Transitional societies ...the ones in which 'repressive political authority is collapsing and democratic groups committed to the establishment of alternative structures exist and need support'. With Perestroika and glasnost, the Soviet Union became a 'transitional society'.

3. "'Democratic break-through', then somehow, there is what NED calls a 'democratic break-through'.

"'Emerging Democracy', when power passes from 'repressive political authority' to 'democratic forces', a third type of society is established ...an 'emerging democracy' ...such societies have taken critical steps 'forward', but 'not yet consolidated democratic institutions'.

"These descriptions are not different from those found in documents and manuals on covert action written in the 1950s ... they sound palatable, the language is pompous and deceptive ... but the substance is John Foster Dulles and Bill Casey.

"The problem that NED is really talking about is how to move a country from the square marked 'closed society', past the 'break-through', to the square marked 'emerging democracy'.

"NED analysis shed's light on how it went about solving the problem. Engineering a 'democratic break-through' in the Soviet Union, according to NED, involved three tasks.

"First, 'strengthening democratic culture'.

"Second, 'strengthening civil society'.

"Third, 'strengthening democratic political institutions'.

1. 'Strengthening democratic culture' meant launching programs inside Soviet Union that supported 'publications and other media, training programs for journalists, publication and dissemination of books and materials to strengthen popular understanding and intellectual advocacy of democracy'. The first task was an old one ... spreading Western ideas and persuading people to adopt them ...this activity is usually called 'propaganda'.

2. "Strengthening civil society' meant 'developing strong private-sector institutions, especially trade unions and business associations, and including as well civic and women's organizations, youth groups, and co-operatives'. Again, the idea was taken from the old covert action manual. 'Preparing the ground' for a coup or a controlled election requires building institutions. Propaganda is useless if it cannot take root and shape a set of institutions across a wide spectrum of dissent. Nurtured, trained and guided, such 'democratic groups' can become very troublesome for a targeted government.

3. "Strengthening democratic political institutions' meant building pro-Western political parties. In NED language, it involved 'efforts to promote strong, stable political parties that are committed to democratic process'. 'Strengthening the unity and effectiveness of the democratic forces in transitional situations'. The third task also required 'strengthening the unity and effectiveness of the democratic forces in transitional situations'. When the authority of the Soviet government began to fail, a political challenge to that authority could be mounted. Mounting the challenge effectively meant building a movement of anti-Communist parties, organizations and individuals.

"The end result ... was a 'democracy' ...defined exclusively by the existence of elections.

"The U.S. has used this strategy before in Chile, Jamaica, El Salvador, Nicaragua, Zambia and other countries where U.S. money and propaganda expertise can tip the balance in favor of U.S. interests.

"Such exercises are doubly effective in that voting is instantly translated, through international media coverage, into prima facie evidence of 'democracy'.

"It appears that this was the broad strategy which the U.S. and its allies followed in their attempt to shape political developments inside the Soviet Union in the 1980s. It was anything but occasional, or casual meddling.

"And, as we shall see, the resources used to implement it were enormous.

"There are two main difficulties in measuring the 'Full-Court Press'. The first is that a large number of government departments, agencies, 'quasi-governmental' organizations, foundations, private groups and businesses were involved. The second is that what is visible is only the tip of an enormous iceberg, most detailed information is closely held. The best course is to look at and analyze what information is available.

"NED gives two kinds of grants, 'core' and 'discretionary'.

"'Core grants' go to business, labor, and the Republican and Democratic parties. Each of these entities has an 'institute' which channels NED grants overseas.

"'Discretionary grants' are made directly by NED to foreign recipients or to U.S. recipients involved in foreign projects.

"NED supported the following organizations.

1. U.S. Baltic Foundation
2. Ukrainian Coord. Committee of America
3. Estonia National Committee
4. Lithuanian-American Community Inc.
5. America Latvian Assoc.
6. Alliance for America
7. Lithuanian Catholic Religious Aid

"Ned grants to Europe from 1984 to 1990, more than 90% went to Eastern Europe and the Soviet Union. In the 1980s NED was probably spending about 5 million dollars annually in Eastern Europe and the Soviet Union, with the amount rising in recent years to take advantage of development opportunities as the 'democratic break-through' came into view.

"It should be noted that dollars could be changed on the black market at several times the official rate, greatly expanding the local impact of NED funds.

"NED was obviously carrying out extensive operations inside the Soviet Union, even if only half its annual funds for the Socialist Bloc were spent there. A better idea of exactly what it was doing inside the Soviet Union can be gained from NED annual reports, that provide selected data on specific projects.

"NED spending from 1984-1990 is as follows. Center for International Private Enterprise, 1.5 million dollars. National Republican Institute for International Affairs, 2.8 million dollars. National Democratic Institute for International Affairs, 3.4 million dollars. Free Trade Union Institute, 17 million dollars. Discretionary, 15 million dollars. Amounts can be expanded several times to figure out the actual impact inside the Soviet Union and Eastern Europe.

"To grasp the scope of intervention in the Soviet Union, as distinct from the operations of a single agency or organization, one must account for all the channels which the U.S. and its allies have used to send funds, and influence events there. These were for the most part governmental and business channels, about whose activities little information is available. Many of these channels were also functioning below sight.

"Principal channels by institutional sector, open or clandestine or both, include non-profit and religious organizations, even though non-profits which channel funds and projects to government agencies, played a minor role in intervention.

"One of the government channels, CIA, is currently reputed to have an annual covert action budget of 600 million dollars ... very likely the real figure is many times larger. Assume the CIA budget 800 million dollars, and the CIA allocated the same proportion of its covert action funds to Eastern Europe and the Soviet Union as NED did during the 1980s, that is 20%. Given these assumptions, the CIA was probably spending 160 million dollars per year on intervention operations in the Socialist Bloc. Assume that half of this amount was going towards Soviet operations. What does this suggest?

1. NED, using open channels, was spending 5 million dollars per year on operations.

2. CIA was secretly channeling 80 million dollars into anti-Soviet operations, many of them inside the U.S.S.R.

3. Money and influence was flowing from the U.S. through scores of conduits, into the Soviet Union.

4. Several major powers, including the U.K., Germany, France, and possibly Japan were doing the same through additional channels.

The minimal conclusion deduced from all this, taking into account the complex channeling and re-channeling of funds and projects through intermediaries, is during the 1980s, Western governments, businesses, and private organizations were devoting 100 million dollars a year to intervention in the internal affairs of the Soviet Union.

"Everything considered, the scope of Western intervention in the Soviet Union in the decade of the 1980s was very great. The intervention side of the 'Full-Court Press' was probably one of the largest coordinated covert operations ever set in motion.

"Although incomplete, the evidence for the existence of the 'Full-Court Press' is already strong. Given the unwillingness of the government to reveal what it is doing with tax dollars, education speculation is the only option.

"Even if the dollar estimates are inaccurate, the implications of this analysis are serious. No one would want to over-estimate the role of the Western allies in the crisis which has been unfolding in the Soviet Union for some years. The U.S.S.R. entered into a serious economic and political crisis since the 1970s, and Soviet leadership, adrift in a country driven by social conflict, showed itself less than adroit in finding solutions.

"Under Gorbachev, however, the U.S.S.R. set out on the path of serious reform. The crucial question is the following ... how did a movement for socialist reform come to be supplanted by a new-conservative movement bent upon creating a capitalist society? How did it come into being? How important was the strategy of intervention outlined in NED documents?

"Conservatives in this country are giving their answers to these questions. Newspapers boast of a 'global anti-Communist putsch' and of 'spyless coups'. NED privately speaks of its 'vital assistance' to the 'victories of the democratic movements', and Mr. Yeltsin thanks the founder of NED for his 'contribution'. A candidate for the Democratic Presidential Nomination praises Mr. Reagan for 'rolling-back Communism'.

"If the conservatives are right, then the 'great democratic revolution' of which so many speak is something very different ... an 'anti-Communist putsch' or 'coup' is not a 'democratic revolution' ... conservatives can not have it both ways.

"If the U.S. and others intervened in the Soviet Union in the ways the evidence suggests, that we have not witnessed a 'democratic revolution ' at all ... but a new kind of warfare.

"The debate about the 'collapse of Communism' needs to be seen for what it is ... propaganda that accompanies this new kind of warfare ...a kind of warfare, given its success, is bound to be reproduced and exported around the world," Sean Gervasi said.

<>

Christopher Simpson's *Blowback, America's recruitment of Nazis & its Effects on the Cold War*, comments.

"The CIA did not sever its ties with extremist exile organizations once they had arrived in this country ... instead, it continued to use them in clandestine operations both abroad, and in the U.S. itself.

"Before the middle of the 1950s, the agency found itself entangled with dozens, probably hundreds, of former Nazis and SS men who had fought their way into the leadership of a variety of Eastern European émigré political associations inside this country.

"Instead of withdrawing its support for the extremist groups and for the men and women who led them, CIA went to considerable lengths to portray these leaders as legitimate representatives of the countries they had fled. About the same time, the agency initiated the immigration programs, it dramatically expanded its publicity and propaganda efforts inside the U.S. itself.

"A major theme was to establish the credibility and legitimacy of exiled Eastern European politicians, former Nazi collaborators and non-collaborators, in the eyes of the American public.

"Through the National Committee for a Free Europe, and a new CIA-financed group, the Crusade for Freedom, the covert operations division of the agency became instrumental in introducing into the American political mainstream many right-wing extremist émigré politicians' plans to 'liberate' Eastern Europe and to 'roll-back' Communism.

"Although it was little known in the U.S. at the time, the genesis of the liberation-rollback philosophy can be clearly traced to the propagandists who worked for the Nazis on the Eastern Front during World War II. After the war, the various conservative and liberal anti-Communist organizations in the U.S. adopted liberation as a rallying cry, adding new and specifically American elements to the program, that altered the earlier Nazi strategy in basic ways. Liberation, in its American version, included an insistence that the anti-Communist revolution be democratic, rather than Fascist in character ...and it abandoned the racial theories and anti-Semitism of the earlier Nazi propaganda. Liberation, in the U.S., was billed as the fulfillment of America's revolutionary heritage of resistance to tyranny.

Appendix 2 ~ Suite 8F, JFK, RMK-BRJ, Halliburton, and Kellogg, Brown & Root

www.spartacus.schoolnet.co.uk/JFKkorth.htm

Fred Korth joined the Democratic Party and worked with John Connally helping Lyndon B. Johnson with his 1948 election campaign.

In 1952, Harry S. Truman appointed Korth Assistant Army Secretary under Frank Pace.

In 1953, Korth and Pace left office. Pace became CEO of General Dynamics Corp. in Texas. Korth returned to law and became director of Bell Aerospace Corporation. Chairman of the company, Lawrence Bell, was a fellow member of Suite 8F Group. Korth was also president of Continental National Bank of Fort Worth, one of General Dynamics' bankers.

In the last months of the Eisenhower administration, Air Force said it needed a successor to its F-105 tactical fighter ... the TFX/F-111 project.

January 1961, Robert McNamara changed TFX from an Air Force program to a joint Air Force/Navy program. October 1961, Air Force and Navy sent the aircraft industry requests for proposals and work statements on the TFX, due December, 1961. Bids were submitted by Lockheed Aircraft, North American Aviation, Boeing, Republic Aviation & Chance Vought, General Dynamics & Grumman Aircraft, and McDonnell Aircraft & Douglas Aircraft.

Boeing was expected to get the contract. Its competitor was General Dynamics/Grumman. General Dynamics was a leading military contractor during the early stages of the Cold War, in 1958 it obtained $2,239,000,000 worth of government business. More than 80 percent of the firm's business came from the government. However, the company lost $27 million in 1960 and $143 million in 1961. According to Richard Austin Smith in *Fortune Magazine*, General Dynamics was close to bankruptcy.

Smith claimed that "unless it gets the contract for the joint Navy-Air Force fighter (TFX)... the company was down the road to receivership".

General Dynamics had several factors in its favor. President of the company was Frank Pace, Army Secretary (Apr. 1950-Jan. 1953). Deputy Defense Secretary was Roswell Gilpatric, previously General Dynamics chief counsel. Navy Secretary was John Connally, a politician from Texas, where General Dynamics was located.

Connally left the job in January 1962, JFK appointed Korth Navy Secretary. According to author Seth Kantor, Korth got the job after strong lobbying from Lyndon Johnson. A few weeks after taking the post, Korth overruled top Navy officers who proposed the X-22 contract be given to Douglas Aircraft Corp. Korth insisted the contract be granted to the more expensive bid of

Bell Corp., a subsidiary of Bell Aerospace of Fort Worth ... creating controversy, since Korth was a former director of Bell.

Korth became involved in discussions about the TFX contract. Korth was former president of Continental Bank and loaned General Dynamics great amounts of money during the 1950s and 1960s.

John McClellan, chairman of the Permanent Investigations Committee, continued looking into the activities of Billie Sol Estes and Bobby Baker. During this investigation, evidence emerged that Lyndon B. Johnson was also involved in political corruption. This included the award of a $7 billion contract for a fighter plane, the TFX, to General Dynamics, a company based in Texas. When it was discovered that Continental National Bank of Fort Worth, was the principal money source for the General Dynamics plant. As a result of this revelation Korth resigned from office in October, 1963.

On 22 November, 1963, a friend of Baker's, Don B. Reynolds ... told B. Everett Jordan and his Senate Rules Committee he saw a suitcase full of money ...which, Baker described as a "$100,000 payoff to Johnson for his role in securing the Fort Worth TFX contract".

John McClellan, chairman of the Senate subcommittee investigating the TFX contract said, he wanted to interview Don Reynolds. However, for some reason the subcommittee didn't resume investigation until 1969, after Johnson left office.

After resigning as Secretary of Navy, Korth worked as a lawyer in Washington. In 1969, he was elected to the board of OKC Corporation, in Dallas. Later that year Fred Korth's daughter Verita, allegedly killed herself with a shotgun.

spartacus.schoolnet.co.uk/JFKgroup8F.htm

In 1932, several politicians from Texas assumed important positions of power in Washington. John Garner became House Speaker. Texans became chairmen of important committees ...Samuel Rayburn, Interstate and Foreign Commerce ...Joseph Mansfield, Rivers and Harbors Committee ...Hatton Sumners, Judiciary Committee ...Marvin Jones, Agriculture Committee ...Fritz Lanham, Public Buildings and Grounds Committee.

Historian Robert Caro's, *Lyndon Johnson, Path to Power,* comments.

"Texans were elected on December 7, 1931, not only to the Speakership of the House but to chairmanship of five of its most influential committees, Lyndon Johnson's first day in the Capitol was the day Texas came to power in it ...

a power that the state was to hold, with only the briefest interruptions, for more than thirty years," Caro said.

<>

In 1932, Franklin D. Roosevelt selected John Garner as running mate and on 8 November Garner was elected Vice President. Garner was able to use this position to promote political careers of other Texans. He recommended that Jesse H. Jones should become chairman of Reconstruction Finance Corporation. This became a crucial post in Roosevelt's New Deal policies and Jones had responsibility of directing billions of dollars to help support American industry. Jones took control of the Federal Loan Agency, Federal Housing Authority, and Home Owners Loan Corporation. Jones was described as a 'fourth branch of government'.

Samuel Rayburn, chairman of Interstate & Foreign Commerce Committee, played an important role establishing Federal Communications Commission. In 1937, Rayburn became majority leader and held the post for three years.

Several of these Texas politicians were involved in the Suite 8F Group, a collection of right-wing businessmen. The name comes from the room in the Lamar Hotel in Houston where they held their meetings. Members of the group included ...George Brown and Herman Brown of Brown & Root ...Jesse H. Jones, a multi-millionaire investor in a large number of organizations and chairman of Reconstruction Finance Corp. ...Gus Wortham of American General Insurance Company ...James Abercrombie of Cameron Iron Works ...Hugh R. Cullen of Quintana Petroleum ...William Hobby, Governor of Texas and owner of *Houston Post* ...William Vinson of Great Southern Life Insurance ...James Elkins of American General Insurance and Pure Oil Pipe Line ...Morgan Davis of Humble Oil ...Albert Thomas, chairman of House Appropriations Committee ...Lyndon B. Johnson, Majority Leader of the Senate ...and, John Connally a Texas politician. Alvin Wirtz, Thomas Corcoran, Homer Thornberry and Edward Clark, were lawyers who worked with the Suite 8F Group.

Suite 8F helped coordinate political activities of right-wing politicians and businessmen in the South. This included ...Robert Anderson, president of the Texas Mid-Continent Oil & Gas Association, later Secretary of Navy, later Secretary of Treasury

[Editor's note: more about Robert Anderson spartacus.schoolnet.co.uk/JFKanderson.htm Robert Bernerd Anderson, born Burleson, Texas,

4 June 1910. Graduated from University of Texas Law School. Worked as a lawyer until he became member of Texas State House of Representatives in 1932. Following year, appointed as Assistant Attorney General of Texas. In 1934, he became a Texas State Tax Commissioner. Anderson purchased KTBC Radio Station. In 1943, sold it to the wife of Lyndon B. Johnson for $17,500. By 1951, station earned $3,000 a week. A close friend of Sid Richardson and Clint Murchison, Anderson became president of Texas Mid-Continent Oil and Gas Association. When Dwight Eisenhower won the presidency, Anderson, became Secretary of Navy. May 1954, Anderson left his Navy post to become Deputy Secretary of Defense. From 1957 to 1961, served as President Eisenhower's Secretary of Treasury. In this post he introduced legislation beneficial to the oil industry. After leaving office, he was active in business, investment and banking affairs, and carried out diplomatic missions on behalf of President Lyndon B. Johnson. It was also reported he worked as a consultant and lobbyist for Sun Myung Moon and his Church of Unification. In 1987, Anderson was found guilty of tax evasion. This was related to possible money laundering involving an unregistered off-shore bank he operated. He was disbarred and sent to prison. Robert B. Anderson died in New York City on 14 August 1989.]

(cont). Suite 8F helped coordinate political activities of right-wing politicians and businessmen in the South. This included ...Robert Anderson ...Robert Kerr, of Kerr-McGee Oil Industries ...Billie Sol Estes, an entrepreneur in the cotton industry ...Glenn McCarthy, McCarthy Oil & Gas Company ...Earl E. T. Smith, U.S. Sugar Corporation ...Fred Korth, Continental National Bank and Navy Secretary ...Ross Sterling, Humble Oil ...Sid Richardson, a Texas oil millionaire ...Clint Murchison, Delhi Oil ...Haroldson L. Hunt, Placid Oil ...Eugene B. Germany, Mustang Oil Company ...Lawrence D. Bell, Bell Helicopters ...William Pawley, with business interests in Cuba ...Gordon McLendon, KLIF ...George Smathers, Finance Committee and businessman ...Richard Russell, chairman of the Committee of Manufacturers, Committee on Armed Forces, and Committee of Appropriations ...James Eastland, chairman Judiciary Committee ...Benjamin Jordan, chairman of Senate Rules Committee ...Fred Black and Bobby Baker, of Serve-U Corp., also political lobbyists.

A major concern of this group was to protect interests of the Texas oil industry. The most prolific oil reserves in the U.S. were discovered in October, 1930. The East Texas Oilfield included Rusk, Upshur, Gregg, and Smith counties. The first small company to find oil in East Texas was Deep Rock Oil Company. The first investor to take advantage of the discovery was Haroldson L. Hunt. He bought 5,000 acres of leases and an eighty-acre tract for $1,335,000. Hunt soon owned 500 wells in East Texas.

The discovery of oil in Texas made a small group of men a great deal of money. They decided to join together in order to maintain their profits. This included strategies for keeping the price of oil as high as possible. The rich East Texas field caused problems, as it initially caused the price of oil to fall.

Ross Sterling, former owner of Humble Oil was elected governor of Texas and took office Jan. 20, 1931. Texas Railroad Commission, under control of large oil producers, attempted to limit production of oil ... prorationing ... in the new fields of East Texas. July 31 1931, the federal court in Houston sided with a group of independent oil producers and ruled Texas Railroad Commission had no right to impose prorationing.

Large oil companies in Texas, such as Humble Oil, were in favor of prorationing, and Sterling came under great pressure to intervene. August 16 1931, Sterling declared martial law in Rusk, Upshur, Gregg, and Smith counties.

In his proclamation, Sterling declared independent oil producers in these counties were "in a state of insurrection [and] reckless and illegal exploitation of oil must be stopped until such time as said resources may be properly conserved and developed under protection of civil authorities."

Sterling ordered commander of Texas National Guard, Jacob F. Wolters, to "without delay shut down each and every producing crude oil well or producing well of natural gas."

Wolters was chief lobbyist of several major oil companies in Texas and readily used a thousand troops to make sure that the oil wells in East Texas ceased production.

Texas Railroad Commission was now in control of the world's most prolific oil fields. It controlled the supply of oil in the U.S.

The price of oil began to increase.

<>

When Franklin D. Roosevelt gained power, he attempted to push a bill through Congress to give his Secretary of Interior, Harold Ickes, authority to regulate domestic oil production. Sam

Rayburn, a politician from Texas, as chairman of House Committee on Interstate & Foreign Commerce, was able to kill the bill. It was left to another powerful Texan, Tom Connally, to sponsor the Connally Hot Oil Act. This gave Texas Railroad Commission authority to proration oil.

<>

Texas oil millionaires fought hard to maintain tax concessions. The oil depletion allowance was introduced in 1913 ... and allowed producers to use the depletion allowed to deduct 5% of their income ...the deduction was limited to original cost of their property. In 1926 the depletion allowance increased to 27.5%.

<>

In the 1930s, Suite 8F group was hostile to Roosevelt and the New Deal. Edward A. Clark arranged for a meeting to take place between Herman Brown and Lyndon Johnson. Brown and Root now grew rapidly as a result of obtaining a large number of municipal and federal government projects. This included the Colorado River Marshall Ford Dam project, worth $27,000,000. In a letter written to Lyndon Johnson, George Brown admitted the company was set to make a $2,000,000 profit. In 1940, the company won a $90 million contract to build Naval Air Station at Corpus Christi.

Jesse H. Jones was another figure in this group. He was chairman of Roosevelt's Reconstruction Finance Corporation. This became a crucial post in Roosevelt's New Deal policies ...Jones had responsibility directing billions of dollars to help support American industry. Jones was described as a, 'fourth branch of government'.

Jones worked closely with John Garner. The men were right-wing conservatives and didn't approve of Roosevelt's progressive policies. However, Jones helped to finance many public works programs and took control of the Federal Loan Agency, Federal Housing Authority, and Home Owners Loan Corporation.

In 1940, Jones became Secretary of Commerce. He retained his post as Federal Loan Administrator.

Congress granted Jones and Reconstruction Finance Corporation power to distribute funds to prepare for war.

This included creation of Defense Plant Corporation and Defense Supplies Corporation ... during WWII Jones was responsible for spending 20 billion dollars.

<>

In 1942, George Brown and Herman Brown established Brown Shipbuilding Company on the Houston Ship Channel. Over three years, the company built 359 ships and employed 25,000 people in contracts initially worth $27,000,000 and eventually worth $357,000,000. Until they got the contract, Brown & Root had never built a ship of any type.

Another businessman who did well out of the war was Lawrence D. Bell, head of Bell Aircraft Corp., builders of P-39 Airacobra, P-39D and P-59 Airacomet, America's first jet-powered airplane.

After WWII, Bell Aircraft concentrated on helicopters and in Bell had the idea of making a 47-B available for Lyndon Johnson during his 1948 election campaign. With a helicopter, Johnson could land in town and give a speech on the landing spot, eliminating the need for car trips from the airstrip. Bell moved his company from New York to Fort Worth. Johnson, now a member of Naval Affairs Committee, helped Bell sell helicopters to the U.S. Military.

In 1954, Paul Douglas spoke in the Senate of tax reforms to eliminate privileges like oil depletion allowance. Douglas attempted to join the important Finance Committee. He held seniority priority and should have been given one of two available seats on the committee. Johnson applied pressure on Harry Byrd, chairman of the Finance Committee, to prevent this.

In 1955, Lyndon Johnson became Senate majority leader. Johnson and Richard Russell had control over all important Senate committees. Money to bribe these politicians came from Russell's network of businessmen, involved in the oil and armaments industries.

According to John Connally, large sums of money were given to Johnson in the 1950s for distribution to his political friends, "I handled inordinate amounts of cash". This money came from oilmen. Cornel Wilde worked for Gulf Oil Corp. In 1959 he took over from David Searls as chief paymaster to Johnson ...he testified, he made regular payments of $10,000 to Walter Jenkins.

In 1956, there was another attempt to end all federal price control over natural gas. Sam Rayburn played an important role in getting it through the House of Representatives ...according to Connally, Rayburn was responsible for 1.5 million dollars of lobbying.

Paul Douglas and William Langer led the fight against the bill. Their campaign was helped by an amazing speech by Francis Case of South Dakota. Up until this time, Case had been a supporter of the bill. However, he announced he'd been offered a $25,000 bribe by Superior Oil Company to guarantee his vote. As a man of principal, he thought he should announce this fact to the Senate.

Lyndon Johnson responded by claiming Case had come under pressure to make this statement from people who wanted to retain federal price controls. Johnson argued, "In all my twenty-five years in Washington I have never seen a campaign of intimidation equal to the campaign put on by the opponents of this bill."

Johnson pushed on with the bill, it was passed by 53 votes to 38. However, three days later, President Dwight Eisenhower vetoed the bill ... on grounds of immoral lobbying.

Eisenhower confided in his diary this was "the most flagrant kind of lobbying brought to my attention [that there was a] great stench around the passing of this bill [and people involved were] so arrogant and so much in defiance of acceptable standards of propriety as to risk creating doubt among the American people concerning the integrity of governmental processes".

<>

Senators called for an investigation into the lobbying of the oil industry by Thomas Hennings, chairman of the Subcommittee on Privileges and Elections. Johnson was unwilling to let a senator not under his control look into the matter. Instead, Johnson set up a select committee chaired by Walter F. George of Georgia, a member of the Southern Caucus. Johnson had again exposed himself as being in the pay of the oil industry.

Drew Pearson of *Washington Post* picked up this story and wrote articles about Lyndon Johnson and the oil industry. Pearson claimed Johnson was the "real godfather of the bill". Pearson explored Johnson's relationship with George Brown and Herman Brown. Pearson reported on large sums of money flowing from Brown & Root, the "big gas pipeline company" to Johnson. Pearson referred to large government contracts Brown & Root obtained during the WWII period. Pearson quoted a Senate report there was "no room for a contractor like Brown & Root on Federal projects".

Nevertheless, Johnson helped Brown & Root win several contracts including one to build air-naval bases in Spain.

Johnson was in serious trouble and sought a private meeting with Pearson. Johnson offered the journalist a deal, if Pearson dropped the investigation, Johnson would support Estes

Kefauver in the primaries. Pearson accepted the deal, writing in his diary, "I figured I might do that much for Estes Kefauver. This is the first time I've ever made a deal like this, I feel unhappy about it. With the Presidency of the United States at stake, maybe it's justified, maybe not ... I don't know."

The decision by President Eisenhower to veto this bill angered the oil industry. Sid Richardson and Clint Murchison renewed negotiations with Eisenhower. June 1957, Eisenhower agreed to appoint their man, Robert Anderson, as Secretary of the Treasury. According to Robert Sherrill's, *Accidental President,* "A few weeks later Anderson was appointed to a cabinet committee to 'study' the oil import situation; out of this study came the present-day program which benefits major oil companies, international oil giants primarily, by one billion dollars a year."

<>

During the 1960 presidential election John F. Kennedy gave his support for the oil depletion allowance. Oct. 1960 Kennedy said, "I realize its purpose and value. The oil-depletion allowance has served us well."

On advice of Lyndon Johnson, Kennedy appointed John Connally Navy Secretary, an important post controlling much federal spending, including the contract to provide oil to the Navy. When Connally became Governor of Texas, Johnson arranged for fellow Texan Fred Korth, to become new Navy Secretary.

<>

October 16, 1962 Kennedy was able to persuade Congress to pass an act that removed the distinction between repatriated profits and profits reinvested abroad. As a result, oilmen saw a fall in earnings on foreign investment from 30% to 15%.

<>

Jan. 1963, President Kennedy presented his proposal for tax reform, including relieving tax burdens of low-income and elderly. Kennedy claimed he wanted to remove privileges and loopholes, and do away with the oil depletion allowance. It was estimated the removal of the oil depletion allowance would result in a loss of 300 million dollars a year to Texas oilmen. Nov. 1963, Fred Korth resigned as a result of accusations of corruption following the award of a 7 billion dollar contract for the TFX fighter plane to General Dynamics in Texas.

<>

Johnson could not afford to appoint another Texan in this post. Instead he selected Paul Nitze. Nitze had been a vice president of Dillion Read in the mid-1930s.

[Ed's note, Dillion Read Venture Capital merged with SG Warburg in 1997 creating Warburg Dillion Read.]

The assassination of John F. Kennedy brought an end to the proposal to bring an end to the oil depletion allowance.

<>

Suite 8F Group did well out of escalation of the Vietnam War. They formed a new company … RMK-BRJ … to obtain military-industrial contracts. This included Halliburton, that took over Brown & Root in 1962.

<>

These contracts included building jet runways, dredging channels for ships, hospitals, prisons, communications facilities, and building American bases from DaNang to Saigon. RMK-BRJ did 97% of the construction work in Vietnam. The other 3% went to local Vietnamese contractors. Between 1965 and 1972 Brown & Root (Halliburton) alone obtained revenues of $380 million from its work in Vietnam.

Senator Abraham Ribicoff of Connecticut attempted to expose this scandal. He claimed that millions was being paid in kickbacks. An investigation by the General Accounting Office discovered that by 1967 RMK-BRJ had 'lost' $120 million. However, GAO never managed to identify the people obtaining these kickbacks.

Another company associated with Suite 8F Group that did well out of the Vietnam War was Bell Helicopter Corp., which began producing the UH-1 helicopter. It could climb 2,000 feet per minute and fly 125 m.p.h. for three hours, carry nine equipped soldiers and a crew of four. By 1969, Bell Helicopter Corp. was selling $600 million worth of helicopters to the U.S. Military. According to Robert Bryce … "Vietnam made Bell Helicopters."

Anti-war protesters decided George Brown was a mastermind of corruption. Demonstrations against him took place everywhere Brown went. It got so bad, Brown advised Lyndon Johnson to withdraw from Vietnam. Brown told Johnson, that if Johnson did not do this, the war would destroy both men. It did destroy Johnson, but Brown survived the protests.

Johnson's resignation as president was a body blow to the Suite 8F group. However, they made preparations. John Connally got Richard Nixon involved with the group. Connally arranged for Nixon to meet Suite 8F members at his ranch in Texas. This resulted in Connally becoming Treasury Secretary. However, they did not get the

success that Johnson achieved in the 1950s and 1960s, because they were not able to control chairmanships of important Senate committees.

<>

Kellogg, Brown & Root is an American engineering and construction company, a private military contractor and a subsidiary of Halliburton.

<>

After Halliburton acquired Dresser Industries in 1998, Dresser's engineering subsidiary, M.W. Kellogg, an engineering contractor, started as a pipe fabrication business by Morris W. Kellogg in 1900 and was acquired by Dresser in 1988, merged with Halliburton's construction subsidiary, Brown & Root, to form Kellogg, Brown, & Root.

The legacy of Brown & Root, having had many contracts with the U.S. military during the 2003 invasion of Iraq, as well as during World War II and the Vietnam War. KBR is the largest non-union construction company in the U. S.

<>

Brown and Root was founded in Texas in 1919 by two brothers, George R. Brown and Herman Brown … with money from their brother-in-law, Dan Root. The company began operations by supervising building of warships for U.S. Navy.

One of its first large-scale projects, according to *Cadillac Desert*, was to build a dam on the Texas Colorado River near Austin during the Depression years. For assistance in federal payments, the company turned to local congressman, Lyndon Baines Johnson.

During World War II, Brown & Root built Corpus Christi Naval Air Station and a series of warships for the U.S. Government. In 1947, Brown & Root built one of the world's first offshore oil platforms.

Following the death of Herman Brown, Halliburton acquired Brown & Root in December 1962.

<>

According to author Dan Briody, the company became part of a consortium of four companies that built about eighty-five percent of the infrastructure needed by the Army during the Vietnam War.

<>

At the height of the war resistance movement of the 1960s, Brown & Root was derided as 'Burn & Loot' by protesters.

Robert Bryce, contributing editor at *Austin Chronicle*, and author of, *Candidate from Brown & Root*, comments.

Herman Brown's huge bet on the Mansfield

Dam just keeps paying off. It made Brown a rich man. It secured the future of his company. It led to other big projects that provided funds to elect Lyndon Johnson to the U.S. Senate in 1948 and to the White House years later. Today, 63 years after Johnson helped secure federal funding for the dam, it appears the modern descendent of George Brown's Brown & Root may again be propelling a Texas politico toward the White House. Call it fate, dumb luck, or clever politics. Brown & Root is a subsidiary of the Halliburton Company, the Dallas-based oil services conglomerate that formerly employed Dick Cheney as CEO and chairman of its executive board.

<>

Like LBJ before him, Cheney used his association with Halliburton and Brown & Root to enrich himself and gain political power. Halliburton announced it was giving Cheney a retirement package worth more than $33.7 million, on top of $10 million Cheney earned in salary, bonuses and stock options at Halliburton since 1995.

<>

In return for his pay, Cheney has helped the company attract government contracts worth hundreds of millions of dollars. Johnson had it a little easier, as his relationship with Brown & Root occurred before campaign finance laws required candidates to reveal sources of funding. By Johnson's own admission, according to biographer Ronnie Dugger, much of the money Johnson got from Brown & Root came in cash. In return, Johnson steered lucrative federal contracts to the company. Those contracts helped Brown & Root become a global construction powerhouse that employs 20,000 people in more than 100 countries.

<>

"It was a totally corrupt relationship that benefited them enormously," says Dugger, author of, *Politician, Life and Times of Lyndon Johnson.* "Brown & Root got rich, and Johnson got power and riches." Without Brown & Root's money, Johnson wouldn't have won (or rather, been able to steal) the 1948 race for United States Senate. "That was the turning point. He wouldn't have been in the running without Brown & Root's money and airplanes. And the 1948 election allowed Lyndon to become president," said Dugger, who recently ran for the Green Party's nomination for the U.S. Senate in New York.

Cheney's business dealings on behalf of Halliburton and Brown & Root have largely occurred in the public eye and have been scrutinized by the media.

<>

But, Cheney's dealings are just as questionable as those by LBJ. In order to increase revenues for the company, Cheney lobbied against sanctions that are considered part of America's strategic interests. For instance, the man now the Republican candidate for the vice presidency lobbied against sanctions against Iran ... which could keep Halliburton from selling more products and services to that country.

<>

Meanwhile, Brown & Root performed hundreds of millions of dollars worth of work for Libyan dictator Kaddaffi, long suspected of sponsoring terrorism directed at the U.S.

<>

But, before discussing that, a bit of history on Brown & Root's dam work. It was 1937, and the Mansfield Dam project (then called the Marshall Ford dam) was in limbo. Brown & Root, a small Belton-based, road-building company, was working on the dam even though Congress had not approved the 10 million dollar project. Even worse, the project was illegal because the Bureau of Reclamation, which was overseeing the project, didn't own the land on which the dam was being built ... a minor fact that, under federal law, should have prevented the project from getting under way. But, Herman Brown pressed on. He received 5 million dollars and was betting that he could get the Federal approval and funding needed to finish the project. But, he needed Johnson ... then a newly elected Congressman ... to get it. Johnson delivered. July 1937, with backing of President Franklin Roosevelt, who made it clear he was doing it for Congressman Johnson, the authorization and funding was approved. That funding was the key to Brown & Root's future.

In his book on LBJ, *Path to Power,* Johnson biographer Robert Caro reports Herman Brown and his brother George made "an overall profit on the dam of 1.5 million dollars, an amount double all the profit they had made in twenty previous years in the construction business." Herman Brown wasn't finished. He wanted another 17 million dollars to make the dam higher by another 78 feet to make it function better for flood control. The Lower Colorado River Authority, which was to operate the dam, didn't have the money. So, Johnson went to work and got the money, and more profit for the Browns. "Out of subsequent contracts for the dam, they piled, upon that first million, million upon million more. The base for a huge financial empire was being created in that deserted Texas gorge," Caro said. [In retrospect, building the dam higher was a wise choice. During the floods of 1991, Lake Travis crested at 710 feet, just four feet below the level of the spillway. Without the extra height demanded by the Browns, or another dam, parts of Austin would likely have been inundated.] The Mansfield project led to dozens of others. It also made the Browns believe in Johnson. "Herman Brown let Johnson know that he would not have to worry about finances in this campaign ... that the money would be there, as much as was needed, when it was needed," Caro said. Johnson steered all kinds of federal projects to Brown & Root ... airports, pipelines, and military bases.

During the Vietnam War, the company built roads, landing strips, harbors and military bases from the Demilitarized Zone to the Mekong Delta. But, the company's relationship with the government would continue long after LBJ was laid to rest along the banks of the Pedernales.

Brown & Root enjoyed especially great success attracting military contracts during Cheney's tenures, first as Secretary of Defense, then at Halliburton. Cheney helped the company obtain federally subsidized loans, loan guarantees and insurance. In five years prior to Cheney's arrival, Brown & Root garnered 100 million dollars in loans and guarantees from the Export-Import Bank and Overseas Private Investment Corporation, two government agencies that sponsor American overseas development.

Since 1995, the company received 1.5 billion dollars worth of assistance from those same two entities. Whether those loans would have come to Halliburton without Cheney's presence is impossible to say. Critics believe Cheney's trips through the revolving door between government and business are improper. "It's always of concern to us when we see people in public service who catapult into positions of wealth and influence in the private sector because they can convert their contacts into wealth in the private sector," says Peter Eisner, managing director of the Center for Public Integrity, a Washington-based nonprofit that has issued a report on Cheney's deals ... www.public-i.org. "Securing government-guaranteed loans for Halliburton is troubling enough. But now, we find out that the same defense secretary will go through the revolving doors once more and be potentially the second most powerful person in the U.S.," Eisner said.

Before joining Halliburton, Cheney had no experience in the oil business. But, that didn't appear to be a handicap. "What Dick brought was obviously a wealth of contacts," new Halliburton CEO (and former president of the Brown & Root subsidiary) David J. Lesar, recently told *Baltimore Sun*. "You don't spend 20-some years in Washington without building a fairly extensive Rolodex."

Cheney's Rolodex was particularly important to Halliburton in its efforts to work against the sanctions devised by Cheney's Republican role model, former President Ronald Reagan. In 1986, Reagan said the regime of Kaddaffi represented a "unique threat to free peoples" as a "rogue regime that advances its goals through the murder and maiming of innocent civilians."

<>

The Reagan Administration pushed for ... and got ... economic sanctions against Libya after the country was implicated in numerous terrorist actions, including the bombing of Pan Am Flight 103 over Lockerbie Scotland, in 1989. But, when Cheney became the CEO at Halliburton, his allegiance quickly shifted from geopolitical Reaganomics to economics. What was good for America was not good for Halliburton. In a 1998 speech, Cheney said the U.S. was "sanctions-happy [and it is] very hard to find specific examples where [sanctions] actually achieve a policy objective." That same year, Cheney personally lobbied U.S. Senator Phil Gramm in an effort to get a waiver from the Iran Libya Sanctions Act, a Federal law passed overwhelmingly by Congress in 1996, which prohibits American interests from doing major business deals in those countries. Cheney sought a way around the sanctions so Halliburton could provide oil-field goods and services to Iran's oil industry. He tried to craft innovative approaches for Brown & Root to operate openly in Libya. Since the mid-1980s, Kaddaffi's 'rogue regime' paid Brown & Root more than 100 million dollars to oversee engineering work on the 'Great Man-Made River Project', a massive, 20 billion dollar pipeline project to provide water for Tripoli and other Libyan cities.

<>

To get around the U.S. sanctions, Halliburton transferred engineering work to Brown & Root overseas offices ...but, hasn't escaped American law enforcement. In 1995, according to *Baltimore Sun*, Brown & Root was fined 3.8 million dollars for re-exporting U.S. goods through a foreign subsidiary to Libya ... in violation of U.S. sanctions. Given the U.S. stand on Libya, does Brown & Root work there subvert American foreign policy objectives? Dirk Vande Beek, Cheney's spokesman, refused to comment and referred the issue to Halliburton's press office. And what about Cheney's stand on economic sanctions, which conflicts with Bush's belief in their effectiveness? Cheney "is going to support what [then]-Governor Bush has been saying about them," says Vande Beek. For Cheney, his latest role is just another in a series of political makeovers: from staunch Reaganite, where economic sanctions were a primary weapon, to chief of the United States military under George Bush, where he was an enforcer of economic and military sanctions against America's enemies, to Halliburton, where sanctions were unprofitable, to vice presidential nominee, where sanctions are once again 'A-OK'. It's the kind of flexibility that a businessman like Herman Brown would have appreciated.

<>

Laura Peterson, Center for Public Integrity comments.

http://www.publicintegrity.org/wow/bio.aspx ?act=pro&ddlC=31

Kellogg, Brown & Root is the engineering and construction arm of Halliburton Co., which calls itself "the world's largest diversified energy services, engineering and construction company" with operations in more than 100 countries and 2002 sales of 12.4 billion dollars. KBR does everything from conducting or managing large construction projects, such as power plants and pipelines, to providing maintenance for existing facilities or government operations. Halliburton was founded in 1919 by Erle Halliburton, who innovated a way to fortify oil wells with cement. The company acquired offshore-platform constructors Brown & Root in 1962 and expanded worldwide through the 1990s. In 1998, Halliburton acquired oil field equipment manufacturer Dresser Industries for 7.7 billion dollars, which had acquired the oil services company, M.W. Kellogg, ten years earlier. Dresser Industries became embroiled in a series of asbestos lawsuits in 2001. In 2002, Halliburton split operations into two entities to protect assets from the asbestos litigation, Halliburton Energy Services Group which provides equipment and services such as well drilling for the oil and gas industry, and KBR. Halliburton placed KBR under bankruptcy protection. Halliburton discovered the benefits of government patronage when its support for U.S. President Lyndon Johnson resulted in several contracts, such as constructing military bases during the Vietnam War.

<>

In 1991, after the Persian Gulf War, then-

Defense Secretary Cheney commissioned Brown & Root to conduct a study on benefits of military outsourcing, paying the company an additional 5 million dollars to update the report months later. In 1992, Brown & Root was awarded the U.S. Army's first Logistics Civil Augmentation Program contract, an omnibus contract that allows the Army to call on KBR for support in all of its field operations, including combat, peacekeeping and humanitarian assistance.

<>

LOGCAP is a "cost-plus award fee" contract, meaning that KBR is paid a fee above the cost of the service ranging from 2-5%, depending on performance. When the Army needs a service performed, it issues a 'task order', a mini-contract that outlines tasks the contractor needs to perform. When the U.S. joined NATO forces in the Balkans in 1995, KBR was deployed to the Balkans. KBR lost a second five-year LOGCAP contract ... awarded to DynCorp in 1997 ... after General Accounting Office reported in Feb. 1997 KBR overran its estimated costs in the Balkans by 32% (in part attributed to an increase in the Army's demands). Despite these findings, KBR was awarded a new contract for Balkan logistical support through May 1999. In Sep. 2000, GAO released another report claiming the Army had not reined-in contractor costs, placing the total cost of the Balkan contract at 2.2 billion dollars. Still, KBR beat out DynCorp and defense giant Raytheon for the third LOGCAP contract in December 2001, which is renewable for 10 years. Though LOGCAP total value is undefined since services are provided in response to changing military needs, as of Sep. 21, 2003, KBR was awarded 67 task orders totaling 2.2 billion dollars, more than 2 billion dollars for Iraq alone. LOGCAP does not comprise all the company's military contracts. It was awarded a LOGCAP-type contract with the U.S. Navy in April 2001, spanning five years and potentially worth 300 million dollars. That contract, too, was awarded over protests of General Accounting Office, which questioned criteria used to evaluate bidders.

In competition for current LOGCAP contracts, the Army Corps of Engineers asked competitors to develop a contingency plan for extinguishing oil well fires in Iraq. The Army chose KBR's plan in Nov. 2001, it remains classified.

<>

Mar. 24 2003, Army announced KBR was awarded five task orders in Iraq potentially worth 7 billion dollars to implement the plan. One of the task orders, obtained by Center for Public

Integrity, required KBR to "procure, import and deliver" fuels to Iraq. The contract was awarded more than two weeks earlier, without submission for public bids or congressional notification. In response to Congressional inquiries, Army officials said they determined that extinguishing oil fires fell under the range of services provided under LOGCAP, meaning that KBR could deploy quickly without additional security clearances. They said that the contract's classified status prevented open bidding. Army's actions came under fire by Congressman Henry Waxman, D-Calif. who along with Rep. John Dingell, D-Mich. asked the General Accounting Office ... the investigative arm of Congress ... to investigate whether the U.S. Agency for International Development and Pentagon were circumventing government contracting procedures and favoring companies with ties to the Bush administration. They accused KBR of inflating prices for importing gasoline into Iraq. June 2003, Army announced it would replace KBR's oil-infrastructure contract with two public-bid contracts worth a maximum total of 1 billion dollars to be awarded in October. However, Army announced in October it would expand the contract ceiling to 2 billion dollars and the solicitation period to December. As of Oct. 16, KBR performed nearly 1.6 billion dollars worth of work. In the meantime, KBR subcontracted with two companies to work on the project: Boots & Coots, an oil field emergency-response firm that Halliburton works in partnership with (CEO Jerry L. Winchester was a former Halliburton manager) and Wild Well Control, both of Texas. KBR was awarded a 100 million dollar contract in 2002 from the State Department to build a new U.S. embassy in Kabul, Afghanistan. KBR was also awarded 15 LOGCAP task orders worth more than 216 million dollars for work under 'Operation Enduring Freedom', the military name for operations in Afghanistan. These include establishing base camps at Kandahar and Bagram Air Force Base, and training foreign troops from the Republic of Georgia. Halliburton's name has become synonymous with Vice President Dick Cheney. Cheney has spent his entire career in public service, including positions in Republican cabinets: he filled several positions in President Richard Nixon's administration and served as assistant and chief of staff to President Gerald Ford prior to entering Congress as a representative from Wyoming, where he was elected chairman of both the Republican Policy Committee and House Republican Conference. The first President

George Bush hired Cheney as his defense secretary, and in that position Cheney directed America's first offensive in Iraq, the Persian Gulf War of 1991.

Once he left government, Cheney became CEO of Halliburton in 1995, after impressing a former Halliburton CEO with his knowledge of world affairs on a fishing trip. Cheney doubled Halliburton's U.S. government contracts during his five-year tenure, from 1.2 billion dollars to 2.3 billion dollars. Military contracts accounted for a large part of these, undoubtedly aided by the former Pentagon staffers Cheney brought to Halliburton management. One of those was retired four-star Admiral Joe Lopez, aide during Cheney's tenure as defense secretary, who came to KBR in 1999 at Cheney's suggestion and became senior vice president of government operations. Loans and loan guarantees from the U.S. Export-Import Bank and its sister U.S. bank, Overseas Private Investment Corp. (OPIC) swelled from 100 million dollars in the five years before Cheney's arrival to about 1.5 billion dollars on his watch. One of those Ex-Im loans, for a 1998 oil-services contract in Angola, came about as a result of intense lobbying by U.S. diplomats. In a State Department cable sent to State Secretary Madeline Albright, officials bragged that unraveled "snag after snag to obtain the transfer of funds" on behalf of Halliburton. The cables also showed that State Department personnel worked to help Halliburton overcome economic hurdles to gain access to markets in several countries from Bangladesh to Algeria. "The bottom line, thousands of American jobs and a foot in the door for Halliburton to win even bigger contracts," one cable said. Cheney's leadership saw a dramatic increase in subsidiaries located in offshore tax havens ... at least 20 subsidiaries in the Cayman Islands, alone.

Cheney has been an outspoken critic of sanctions, and during his tenure at Halliburton lobbied against sanctions in Sudan, Syria, Iran, Libya, Burma, Nigeria, India and Pakistan. The firm's government relations squad included Dave Gribbin, who worked for Cheney on Capitol Hill and then as Assistant Secretary of Defense for Legislative affairs. Cheney later brought Gribbin along to work on the presidential transition.

Halliburton's board of directors changed under Cheney, taking on a more Republican flavor. One addition was Lawrence Eagleburger, former Secretary of State under the first president George Bush, who served on the board of Dresser Industries until Halliburton acquired the company in 1998. Another was Charles DiBona, former Lt. Commander in the U.S. Navy who served as an energy consultant and deputy director of the White House Policy Office under President Richard Nixon, then went on to serve as president of the American Petroleum Institute trade association and chairman of the board of the Logistics Management Institute, a consulting firm that provides assessments of privatization benefits to the defense industry.

One Cheney recruit in the headlines was Ray Hunt of Dallas-based Hunt Oil Co. Hunt is a longtime supporter of the Bush clan ... he raised money for the elder Bush and later led the Republican National Committee's Victory Fund for George W. Bush, donating $20,000 to the committee himself. Bush rewarded him with a seat on his Foreign Intelligence Advisory Board. Hunt and his wife donated $400,000 to Republican state campaigns, while his company and employees gave more than $1 million to Republican causes since 1995. Hunt's son, a vice president in the company, served as an energy consultant to Bush during the campaign, and later as a member of the presidential energy transition team. Ray Hunt and Halliburton Co. are major donors to the National Center for Policy Analysis, a conservative think tank in Dallas.

Sep. 2003, Inter-American Development Bank approves loan for consortium led by Hunt Oil to construct natural gas pipeline in Peru environmentalists say will damage the rain forest there ... after Ex-Im Bank pulled out due to environmental concerns. In 2002, Hunt hired KBR to build the 1 billion dollar plant at the pipeline's origin.

Other board members include ...former Chevron chief exec Kenneth Derr, who received criticism for stating in a 1998 speech that Iraq "possesses huge reserves of oil and gas ... reserves I'd love Chevron to have access to" ...Robert Crandall, former American Airlines chief executive nominated by the White House to serve on the Amtrak Board of Directors ...and C. J. 'Pete' Silas, who served on Bush's Transition Energy Advisory Team. Cheney also brought in Charles Dominy, a former three-star general in Army Corps of Engineers, the agency which awarded Halliburton 20 percent of its military contracts since 1990.

Cheney left Halliburton in August 2000 when George W. Bush asked him to join the presidential ticket. Cheney promised to sever all financial ties to the company. In the year he left Halliburton, Cheney's salary, stock option sales, and various other compensations earned him a parting gift of more than $35 million. However, members of Congress have asked whether the fact that Cheney receives between $180,000 and $1 million annually in deferred compensation demonstrates a continuing financial interest in the company.

All large companies have their share of lawsuits from competitors, employees and the like, but Halliburton's legal troubles have been unusually public and expensive. Shortly after acquiring Dresser Industries in 1997, Halliburton inherited more than 300,000 asbestos claims filed against a Dresser subsidiary located in Pennsylvania that made construction products containing the substance. Halliburton settled the claims in December 2002 with about 4 billion dollars in cash and stock and placed KBR under Chapter 11 bankruptcy protection. The huge loss, coupled with Cheney's departure and other large settlements the previous year, caused the company's stock to plunge ...after three high-ticket asbestos-related verdicts in 2001, shares fell 40% in one day.

In May 2002, Halliburton received a letter from Securities and Exchange Commission it was initiating a preliminary inquiry into the company's accounting practices. The inquiry came after *New York Times* reported Halliburton illegally claimed cost overruns on construction projects as revenue in financial statements. Several class-action lawsuits, including ones on behalf of Halliburton shareholders and a nonprofit watchdog group called, Judicial Watch, were filed alleging Halliburton violated U.S. securities laws and defrauded stockholders. Halliburton settled the shareholder lawsuits for 6 million dollars, while the Judicial Watch lawsuit was dismissed by a U.S. federal court.

Despite increasing reliance on military and other U.S. government contracts, Halliburton has run afoul of the government in the past. In 1995, Halliburton was ordered by a federal judge to pay 1.2 million dollars in criminal fines to the Justice Department and 2.6 million dollars in civil penalties to the Commerce Department for violating the 1986 presidential embargo restricting trade with Libya through its subsidiary, Halliburton Logging Services. The company still reportedly does business in Libya through its German subsidiary, Halliburton Company Germany GmBH.

Members of Congress, such as Waxman and Dingell, questioned Halliburton's activity not just in Libya but Iraq and Iran. When Halliburton purchased Dresser Industries, it inherited a stake in a joint project that provided oil services parts to Iraq under the United Nations' Oil-for-food program. Cheney originally denied Halliburton's activities in Iraq but later recanted, claiming he was unaware of the project which the company cut loose in 2000. Halliburton provided oil services to Iran in contravention of U.S. sanctions by operating through a foreign subsidiary based in Cayman Islands which opened an office in Tehran in 2000.

February 2002, Halliburton paid the government 2 million dollars to settle a 1997 lawsuit alleging KBR improperly billed the U.S. government for services provided at Fort Ord, California. Under terms of the settlement, the company denied wrongdoing. Also in 2002, a federal jury in Houston rendered a verdict against Halliburton and awarded BJ Services Company 98 million dollars in a patent infringement lawsuit. A jury also awarded a 70 million dollar ruling against Halliburton for allegedly breaching a confidentiality agreement with Anglo Dutch Tenge oil company related to a potential oil field investment in Kazakhstan.

Feb. 27, 2004 the Coalition Provisional Authority's Program Management Office in Baghdad awarded KBR a contract worth 51.5 million dollars for "electrical power transmission" in Iraq.

Four task orders under an existing LOGCAP contract for work in Iraq in 2003 totaled $587,988,533.

In response to a FOIA request dated July 11, 2003, Center for Public Integrity obtained portions of the Iraq oil repair contract awarded to KBR described above, for which the Army publicly announced in March 2003 it had drawn five task orders totaling 7 billion dollars. Subsequent to the Center for Public Integrity's lawsuit against the Army Corps of Engineers, the agency reviewed the classification of Kellogg, Brown & Root's Iraq oil services contract. The basic contract has now been posted as well as certain declassified portions of the statement of work and task orders. The documents obtained show the contract originally was awarded to KBR Mar. 8, 2003, as a $500,000 minimum-value contract for a two-year period, extendable to three option years ... to an estimated maximum value of $7 billion.

According to the Army Corps, it is a cost-plus award fee contract with a 2% fixed fee and a potential extra 5% for work achieved over and above what is normally achieved. Of the 2.4 billion dollars spent, 1.4 billion is from the Development Fund for Iraq, which was estab-

lished by U.N. Security Council Resolution 1483. Also included is 90 million dollars which is 'Disbursed Seized Iraqi Assets', according to the Army Corps.

January 2004, the Army Corps replaced the March 2003 contract with another contract that has a maximum value of 1.2 billion dollars. KBR was to continue work to repair Iraq's oil infrastructure in southern Iraq. The contract for the northern region, with a maximum value of 800 million dollars, went to Parsons Iraqi Joint Venture.

KBR was awarded a State Department contract in August 2002 to design and construct office buildings and diplomatic staff apartments among other tasks for the U.S. embassy in Kabul. The contract was originally valued at $110,998,879 and was later reduced to $110,666,240. Mar. 1, 2004, KBR was awarded reconstruction work in Iraq and Afghanistan worth at least 3.9 billion dollars.

John Hoefle's, *Halliburton is Houston's Greater Hermann Göring Werke*, in Sep. 26, 2003 LaRouche's Executive Intelligence Review. [Ed's note, in the following article we have replaced the word 'Synarchist' with the word 'anti-Christ', for obvious reasons. By 'anti-Christ', we refer to anti-Christian, anti-Jewish, anti-Muslim and anti-Buddhist behavior.]

"In his farewell address in 1961, President Eisenhower warned about the dangers of 'acquisition of unwarranted influence [by the] military-industrial complex [noting] the potential for disastrous rise of misplaced power exists and will persist. We must never let the weight of this combination endanger our liberties or democratic processes.'

"As supreme commander of Allied military forces in Europe during World War II, Ike played a key role in the battle against fascism, but against the international anti-Christ cabal which orchestrated the rise to power of Hitler and Mussolini. During his two terms as President lasting from 1953 to 1961, Ike was well positioned to see this anti-Christ cabal's tentacles into the U.S., and how they were attempting to use the Cold War to solidify their power. In warning about the military-industrial complex, Ike meant to warn us about the selfish fascists within our midst.

[Note, the following twelve paragraphs were in the body of my fictional autobiography, and are repeated here in context of the whole article and similar research contained in the appendices.]

"Chief among the anti-Christs in Washington is

Vice President Dick Cheney, whose relationship with Halliburton exemplifies the military-industrial relationships of which Ike warned. In 1991, while he was Secretary of Defense in the first Bush Administration, Cheney hired Halliburton's Brown & Root subsidiary to do a study on the privatization of military logistics operations. This study established the Logistics Civil Augmentation Program, which gave its first general contract to ... Brown & Root.

"At the time, Cheney and his Undersecretary of Defense for Policy, Paul Wolfowitz, were pushing for wars against smaller, resource-rich nations, including the use of 'low-yield' nuclear weapons. When George H. W. Bush left office Jan. 1993, Cheney spent time at neo-conservative American Enterprise Institute ...in 1995, joined Halliburton as president and chief executive. Cheney became chairman in 1996, ran the company until Aug. 2000, stepping down to run for Vice President. And, during that 1995-2000 period, one dollar of every seven spent by the Pentagon, passed through what is now Kellogg Brown & Root.

"When Cheney hired Halliburton for the privatization study, Halliburton was hardly a disinterested party. The company was a major defense contractor through Brown & Root and had significant military and intelligence connections.

"With its flurry of construction contracts in Iraq, Halliburton is in many respects depending upon Dick Cheney for its survival. John Hoefle dubbed Halliburton *The Greater Hermann Göring Werke of Houston*. It has been clear for some time that Vice President Cheney has been acting as an agent for the international anti-Christ movement, founded as the oligarchy's counterattack on the American Revolution and the principles upon which America was founded. Cheney and Halliburton have been rightly attacked for the company's war profiteering. The Vice President and his neo-con allies such as Defense Secretary Donald Rumsfeld, Paul Wolfowitz, and Richard Perle are agents of a power committed to eliminating principles of the Declaration of Independence and U.S. Constitution, in favor of a global bankers' dictatorship. This same oligarchic power, acting through merchant banks like Lazard Frères, Warburg, Rothschild and others controls a large swath of Wall Street and corporate America, including Halliburton. Halliburton's power does not flow from Cheney, but from Cheney's backers, the international bankers. Cheney's policy toward the people of Iraq is the same as Göring's

policy toward the people in the Nazi work camps.

"Arbeit Macht Frei Work Makes You Free read the sign over the entrance to Auschwitz ... an example of Göring's 'big lie' tactic in action. The Cheney cabal's pronouncements that we must accept police-state tactics in our own nation and pre-emptive strikes against other nations in the name of freedom, rings just as false. Hermann Göring would be proud.

"Halliburton traces its roots to Erle P. Halliburton, a pioneer in the techniques of cementing well bores, who founded the company in 1919. In 1924, Halliburton was incorporated, with significant investments by seven major oil companies ... Halliburton trucks became common sights in the oil patch. In 1961, after a series of acquisitions, the company moved its headquarters from Duncan Oklahoma to Dallas Texas.

"In 1962, Halliburton bought Brown & Root, the giant Houston-based construction company. Brown & Root had also been founded in 1919, by Herman Brown and Dan Root, with Herman's brother George Brown coming in a few years later. Brown & Root started out paving roads and building bridges in rural Texas, and in 1940 got the contract to build the Corpus Christi Naval Air Station. It built pipelines and ships during World War II, and in 1961 won the planning contract for the Manned Space Center in Houston. When Herman Brown died in 1962, George Brown sold the company to Halliburton to avoid a hostile takeover, though he remained as company chairman. He died in 1983.

"Herman and George Brown were important figures in the internationally-dominated Houston business world. Herman Brown was a director of the Rothschild-linked First City National Bank and of pipeline operator Texas Eastern, which he and George founded to buy the 'Big Inch' and 'Little Inch' pipelines after WWII. George Brown served as chairman of Rice University for 15 of his 25 years on its board, and served on commissions for Presidents Truman, Eisenhower, Kennedy and Johnson, as well as on Texas State commissions from the 1930s through the 1970s.

"In 1998, Halliburton made another major purchase, acquiring Dresser Industries for 7.7 billion dollars. Dresser was founded by Solomon Dresser in 1880, and taken over in 1928 by W.H. Harriman & Co., the investment bank owned by descendants of railroad magnate E.H. Harriman, himself a front for the British Royal Family. Under Averell and Roland Harriman, Dresser was a Skull & Bones shop, whose board included Bonesman and presidential father and grandfather Prescott Bush. Both Roland Harriman and Prescott Bush were directors of Union Banking Corp. when it was raided by Federal agents in 1942, under the Trading With the Enemy Act, for dealings on behalf of Nazi Germany.

"The Dresser deal smells like some sort of Skull & Bones rescue operation since, with Dresser, Halliburton acquired several billions of dollars in asbestos-claim lawsuit liabilities. Dick Cheney, who made the deal, is not a Bonesman himself, having dropped out of Yale in his sophomore year, but the Skull & Bones roster contains at least nine Cheneys, more than nearly any other family.

"Also with Dresser came construction company M.W. Kellogg, which was merged into Brown & Root to form Kellogg, Brown & Root.

"In many respects, Halliburton seems to be an American version of Schlumberger. The mostly obvious parallel is in the oil field services arena, where Schlumberger is Halliburton's chief rival ...and there is also a strong undercurrent of spookery. Both companies operate worldwide, wherever the oil business goes ... Brown & Root goes wherever U.S. troops go, and reportedly provides corporate cover for intelligence operations.

<>

Schlumberger is an arm of one of Europe's most important banking and intelligence operations. Banque de Neuflize, Schlumberger, Mallet, Demachy, now a unit of ABN AMRO, is one of those small but important merchant banks which specializes in shaping world events. The families behind the bank have a long history of molding the anti-Christ movement as an assault-force against the U.S., from the spying of Major André in 1780 to the assassination of JFK.

Today, as an indication of its continuing intelligence activities, Schlumberger's board includes former CIA Director John Deutch.

"Schlumberger helped bring Fidel Castro to power by helping overthrow the Batista regime. It was involved in the assassination of Kennedy through company president Jean de Menil, the White Russian husband of Schlumberger heiress Dominique Schlumberger de Menil, acting through the New Orleans office of the Swiss-based company Permindex.

<>

Permindex had also organized several attempts on the life of French President Charles de Gaulle. There are indications that Halliburton and Brown & Root were involved in Permindex. According to, *Nomenclature of an Assassination Cabal,* written under the nom de plume 'William

Torbitt' ... Halliburton, and George and Herman Brown were among principal financiers of Permindex, along with Jean de Menil, mob lawyer Roy Cohn, Dallas oilman H.L. Hunt, and others. Over the years, EIR has confirmed aspects of the Torbitt manuscript and finds these claims credible, and if the claims about Halliburton and the Browns are true, then it puts Halliburton and Brown & Root firmly in the anti-Christ camp, before their merger some three decades before Dick Cheney took over the company. It would confirm the Schlumberger link and suggest that, rather than being a rival, Halliburton is a clone and junior partner of Schlumberger.

"Halliburton and Brown & Root have direct links to two important merchant banks, Lazard and Rothschild ...both of which serve as controllers of the anti-Christ movement. Lazard banker James Glanville sat on the Halliburton board in the 1980s, as did Lord Polwarth of the Royal Bank of Scotland ... another British lord, Lord Clitheroe, has been on the Halliburton board since 1987.

"Brown & Root was one of the companies centered around First City Bancorp. of Houston and the Vinson & Elkins law firm. First City, founded by Vinson & Elkins founder James Elkins, was identified by a 1976 House Banking Committee report as part of the Rothschild banking network. Vinson & Elkins was the outside counsel for Enron, whose board included Lord John Wakeham, the former British Energy Minister who joined the board of N.M. Rothschild after he left government service. Enron's accountant, Arthur Andersen, also handled Halliburton, and there have been suggestions Halliburton engaged in Enron-like accounting of its own under Cheney.

"Halliburton has strong intelligence ties through the presence on its board from 1977-2000 of King Ranch's Anne Armstrong, who chaired the President's Foreign Intelligence Advisory Board from 1981-1990, in addition to a stint as U.S. Ambassador to Great Britain, and her long-standing role as chairman of the executive committee at the Center for Strategic and International Studies, a powerful Washington think-tank.

"Armstrong's successor as Halliburton's top spook is Ray Hunt, one of five Dresser directors to join the Halliburton board. Hunt, the son of reputed Permindex funder H.L. Hunt, was appointed to the President's foreign Intelligence Advisory Board by President George W. Bush

Oct. 2001. Oilman Hunt is a trustee of the Center for Strategic & International Studies and a director of King Ranch, suggesting Hunt is taking the retiring Armstrong's spot in a long-standing Texas intelligence network. Hunt is also a trustee of the George Bush Presidential Library and a former chairman of Federal Reserve Bank of Dallas.

"Another of the directors who came over from Dresser was Lawrence Eagleburger, the former U.S. Secretary of State and president of Kissinger Associates," Hoefle said.

<>

Norm Dixon and Chris Floyd comment.

The threat posed by U.S. terrorism to the security of nations and individuals was outlined in prophetic detail in a document written more than two years ago and disclosed only recently. What was needed for America to dominate much of humanity and the world's resources, it said, was "some catastrophic and catalyzing event ... like a new Pearl Harbor." The attacks of Sep. 11 2001 provided 'the new Pearl Harbor', described as "the opportunity of ages". The extremists who have since exploited September 11 come from the era of Ronald Reagan, when far-right groups and 'think-tanks' were established to avenge the American defeat in Vietnam. In the 1990s, there was an added agenda, to justify the denial of a peace dividend following the cold war. The Project For The New American Century was formed, along with the American Enterprise Institute, the Hudson Institute and others that have merged the ambitions of the Reagan Administration with those of the current Bush regimes. One of George W Bush's 'thinkers' is Richard Perle. I interviewed Perle when he was advising Reagan ...and when he spoke about 'total war', I mistakenly dismissed him as mad. He recently used the term again in describing America's 'war on terror'. 'No stages. This is total war. We are fighting a variety of enemies. There are lots of them out there. All this talk about first we are going to do Afghanistan, then we will do Iraq ... this is entirely the wrong way to go about it. If we just let our vision of the world go forth, and we embrace it entirely and we don't try to piece together clever diplomacy, but just wage a total war... our children will sing great songs about us years from now,' Perle said.

Perle is one of the founders of the Project For The New American Century. Other founders include Dick Cheney, now vice-president, Defense Secretary Donald Rumsfeld, Deputy Defense Secretary Paul Wolfowitz, Cheney's Chief of Staff I.

Lewis Libby, Reagan's Education Secretary William J. Bennett, and Bush's Ambassador to Afghanistan, Zalmay Khalilzad. These are the modern chartists of American terrorism.

Project For A New American Century's seminal report, *Rebuilding America's Defences: strategy, forces and resources for a new century*, was a blueprint of American aims in all but name. It recommended an increase in arms-spending by 48 billion dollars so Washington could "fight and win multiple, simultaneous major theatre wars." This has happened.

It said the U.S. should develop "bunker-buster" nuclear weapons and make "star wars" a national priority. This is happening. It said that, in the event of Bush taking power, Iraq should be a target. And so it came to be. "As for Iraq's alleged "weapons of mass destruction," these were dismissed as a convenient excuse. "While the unresolved conflict with Iraq provides the immediate justification, the need for a substantial American force presence in the Gulf transcends the issue of the regime of Saddam Hussein," the report said. How has this grand strategy been implemented? A series of articles in the *Washington Post*, co-authored by Bob Woodward of Watergate fame based on interviews with senior members of the Bush Administration, reveals how Sept. 11 was manipulated. On the morning of Sept. 12, 2001 without evidence of who the hijackers were, Rumsfeld demanded the U.S. attack Iraq. According to Woodward, Rumsfeld told a cabinet meeting that Iraq should be "a principal target of the first round in the war against terrorism."

Iraq was temporarily spared only because State Secretary Colin Powell persuaded Bush "public opinion has to be prepared before a move against Iraq is possible." Afghanistan was chosen as the softer option. If Jonathan Steele's estimate in the *Guardian* is correct, 20,000 people in Afghanistan paid the price of this debate with their lives. Time and again, Sept. 11 is described as an "opportunity." In *New Yorker,* investigative reporter Nicholas Lemann wrote that Bush's senior adviser Condoleezza Rice told him she called together senior members of the National Security Council and asked them "to think about 'how do you capitalize on these opportunities?'"

<>

... ...which she compared with those of "1945-1947" ...the start of the cold war. Since Sept. 11, America has established bases at the gateways to all major sources of fossil fuels, especially central Asia. The Unocal oil company is to build a pipeline across Afghanistan. Bush has scrapped the Kyoto Protocol on greenhouse gas emissions, the war crimes provisions of the International Criminal Court, and the anti-ballistic missile treaty. He said he will use nuclear weapons against non-nuclear states "if necessary." Under cover of propaganda about Iraq's alleged weapons of mass destruction, the Bush regime is developing new weapons of mass destruction that undermine international treaties on biological and chemical warfare. In the *Los Angeles Times*, military analyst William Arkin describes a secret army set up by Donald Rumsfeld, similar to those run by Richard Nixon and Henry Kissinger ... and which Congress outlawed. This "super-intelligence support activity" will bring together "CIA and military covert action, information warfare, and deception." According to a classified document prepared for Rumsfeld, the new organization, known by its Orwellian moniker as the 'Proactive Pre-emptive Operations Group', or P2OG, will provoke terrorist attacks which would then require "counter-attack" by the U.S. on countries "harboring the terrorists."

<>

In other words, innocent people will be killed by the U.S. This is reminiscent of Operation Northwoods, the plan put to President Kennedy by his military chiefs for a phony terrorist campaign ... complete with bombings, hijackings, plane crashes and dead Americans ... as justification for an invasion of Cuba. Kennedy rejected it. He was assassinated a few months later. Now, Rumsfeld has resurrected 'Northwoods', but with resources undreamt of in 1963, and with no global rival to invite caution. You have to remind yourself, this is not fantasy ... that truly dangerous men, such as Perle, Rumsfeld, and Cheney have power. The thread running through their ruminations is the importance of the media ... "The prioritized task of bringing onboard journalists of repute to accept our position." 'Our position', is code for, 'lying'. As a journalist, I have never known official lying to be more pervasive than today. We may laugh at the vacuities in Tony Blair's 'Iraq dossier' and Jack Straw's inept lie that Iraq has developed a nuclear bomb, which his minions rushed to explain. But, the more insidious lies, justifying an unprovoked attack on Iraq and linking it to would-be terrorists who are said to lurk in every Tube station, are routinely channeled as news. They're not news ...they're black propaganda. This corruption makes journalists and broadcasters ventriloquists' dummies. An attack on a nation of 22 million, suffering people is discussed by liberal com-

mentators as if it were a subject at an academic seminar, at which pieces can be pushed around a map, as the old imperialists used to do. The issue for these humanitarians is not primarily the brutality of modern imperial domination, but, how "bad" Saddam Hussein is. There is no admission that their decision to join the war party further seals the fate of perhaps thousands of innocent Iraqis condemned to wait on America's international death row. Their double-think won' work. You cannot support murderous piracy in the name of humanitarianism. Moreover, the extremes of American fundamentalism that we now face, have been staring at us for too long for those of good heart and sense not to recognize them.

James Mann, former Washington correspondent for *Los Angeles Times*, is senior writer-in-residence at Center for Strategic and International Studies, in Washington D.C. This article is adapted from his book, *Rise of the Vulcans, History of Bush's War Cabinet*. James Mann's *The Armageddon Plan*, Mar. 2004, *Atlantic Monthly* comments.

"At least once a year during the 1980s, Dick Cheney and Donald Rumsfeld vanished. Cheney was working diligently on Capitol Hill, as a congressman rising through the ranks of the Republican leadership. Rumsfeld, who had served as Gerald Ford's Secretary of Defense, was a hard-driving business executive in the Chicago area, where as head of G. D. Searle & Co. he dedicated time and energy to the success of commercial products like Nutra-Sweet, Equal, and Metamucil. Yet, for periods of three or four days at a time, no one in Congress knew where Cheney was, nor could anyone at Searle locate Rumsfeld. Even their wives were in the dark ...they were handed a mysterious Washington phone number to use in case of emergency.

"After leaving their day jobs, Cheney and Rumsfeld usually made their way to Andrews Air Force Base outside Washington. From there in the middle of the night, each man ... joined by a team of 40-to 60-federal officials, and one member of Ronald Reagan's Cabinet ... slipped away to some remote location in the U.S., such as an unused military base or underground bunker. A convoy of lead-lined trucks carrying sophisticated communications equipment, and other gear, would head to each of the locations.

<>

"Rumsfeld and Cheney were principal actors in one of the most highly classified programs of the Reagan Administration. Under it, U.S. officials furtively carried out detailed planning exercises for keeping the federal government running during and after a nuclear war with Soviet Union. The program called for setting aside legal rules for presidential succession in some circumstances, in favor of a secret procedure for putting in place a new 'President' and his staff. The idea was to concentrate on speed, to preserve 'continuity of government', and to avoid cumbersome procedures ...the speaker of the House, the president pro tempore of the Senate, and the rest of Congress would play a greatly diminished role.

"Inspiration for this program came from within the Administration, not from Cheney or Rumsfeld ...except for a brief stint Rumsfeld served as Middle East envoy, neither of them held office in the Reagan Administration. Nevertheless, they were leading figures in the program.

"Few details about the effort have come to light over the years, nothing about the way it worked or the central roles played by Cheney and Rumsfeld. The program is of particular interest today, because it helps to explain the thinking and behavior of the second Bush Administration in the hours, days, and months after the terrorist attacks on September 11, 2001. Vice President Cheney urged President Bush to stay out of Washington for the rest of that day ... Secretary of Defense Rumsfeld ordered his deputy Paul Wolfowitz to get out of town ... Cheney himself began to move from Washington to a series of 'undisclosed locations', and other federal officials were later sent to work outside the capital, to ensure continuity of government in case of further attacks. All these actions had their roots in the Reagan Administration's clandestine planning exercises.

"The U.S. government considered the possibility of a nuclear war with the Soviet Union more seriously during the early Reagan years, than at any other time since the Cuban Missile Crisis of 1962. Reagan had spoken in his 1980 campaign about the need for civil-defense programs to help the U.S. survive a nuclear exchange, and once in office he not only moved to boost civil defense, but also approved a new defense-policy document that included plans for waging a protracted nuclear war against the Soviet Union. The exercises in which Cheney and Rumsfeld participated were a hidden component of these more public efforts to prepare for nuclear war.

"The premise of the secret exercises was that in case of a nuclear attack on Washington, the U.S. needed to act swiftly to avoid 'decapitation' ...a break in civilian leadership. A core element of

Reagan Administration's strategy for fighting a nuclear war would be to decapitate the Soviet leadership by striking at top political and military officials and their communications lines ... the Administration wanted to make sure Soviets couldn't do to America what U.S. nuclear strategists were planning to do to Soviet Union.

"Under the Truman and Eisenhower Administrations, the U.S. government built large underground installations at Mount Weather, in Virginia's Blue Ridge Mountains, and near Camp David, along the Pennsylvania-Maryland border, each of which could serve as a military command post for the President in time of war. Yet, a crucial problem remained ...what might happen if the President couldn't make it to one of those bunkers in time.

"The Constitution makes the Vice President the successor if the President dies or is incapacitated, but it establishes no order of succession beyond that. Federal law, most recently the Presidential Succession Act of 1947, establishes further details. If the Vice President dies or cannot serve, then the speaker of the House of Representatives becomes President. After him in the line of succession come the president pro tempore of the Senate, typically the longest-serving member of the majority party, and then the members of the Cabinet, in the order in which their posts were created ... starting with the Secretary of State and moving to the Secretary of the Treasury, the Secretary of Defense, and so on. The Reagan Administration, however, worried that this procedure might not meet the split-second needs of an all-out war with the Soviet Union. What if a nuclear attack killed both the President and the Vice President, and maybe the speaker of the House, too? Who would run the country if it was too hard to track down the next living person in line under the Succession Act? What civilian leader could immediately give U.S. military commanders the orders to respond to an attack, and how would that leader communicate with the military? In a continuing nuclear exchange, who would have the authority to reach an agreement with the Soviet leadership to bring the war to an end?

"The outline of the plan was simple. Once the United States was, or believed itself about to be, under nuclear attack, three teams would be sent from Washington to three different locations around the U.S. Each team would be prepared to assume leadership of the country, and would include a Cabinet member who was prepared to become President. If the Soviet Union were somehow to locate one of the teams and hit it with a nuclear weapon, the second team or, if necessary, the third could take over. This was not some abstract textbook plan ... it was practiced in concrete and elaborate detail. Each team was named for a color, 'red' or 'blue' for example, and each had an experienced executive who could operate as a new White House chief of staff. Obvious candidates were people who had served at high levels in the executive branch, preferably with the national-security apparatus. Cheney and Rumsfeld had each served as White House chief of staff in the Ford Administration. Other team leaders over the years included James Woolsey, later director of CIA, and Kenneth Duberstein, who served for a time as Reagan's actual White House chief of staff.

"As for the Cabinet members on each team, some had little experience in national security ...at various times, for example, participants in the secret exercises included John Block, Reagan's first Secretary of Agriculture, and Malcolm Baldrige, the Secretary of Commerce. What counted was not experience in foreign policy but, rather, that the Cabinet member was available. It seems fair to conclude some of these 'Presidents' would have been figureheads for a more experienced chief of staff, such as Cheney or Rumsfeld. Still, the Cabinet members were the ones who would issue orders, or in whose name the orders would be issued.

"One of the questions studied in these exercises was, what concrete steps a team might take to establish its credibility? What might be done to demonstrate to the American public, to U.S. allies, and to Soviet leadership that 'President' John Block or 'President' Malcolm Baldrige was now running the country, and that he should be treated as the legitimate leader of the U.S.? One option was to have the new 'President' order an American submarine up from the depths to the surface of the ocean ... since the power to surface a submarine would be a clear sign that he was now in full control of U.S. military forces. This standard ... control of the military ... is a test the U.S. government uses in deciding whether to deal with a foreign leader after a coup d'état.

"'One of the awkward questions we faced,' one participant in the planning of the program explains, 'was whether to reconstitute Congress after a nuclear attack. It was decided that no, it would be easier to operate without them.' For one thing, it was felt that reconvening Congress, and replacing members who had been killed, would take too long. Moreover, if Congress did recon-

vene, it might elect a new speaker of the House, whose claim to the presidency might have greater legitimacy than that of a Secretary of Agriculture or Commerce who had been set up as President under Reagan's secret program. The election of a new House speaker would not only take time, but also create potential for confusion. The Reagan Administration's primary goal was to set up a chain of command that could respond to urgent minute-by-minute demands of a nuclear war, when there might be no time to swear in a new President under the regular process of succession, and when a new President would not have the time to appoint a new staff. The Administration, however, chose to establish this process without going to Congress for legislation that would have given it constitutional legitimacy.

<>

"Ronald Reagan established the 'continuity-of-government program' with a secret executive order. According to Robert McFarlane, who served for a time as Reagan's National Security Adviser, the President himself made the final decision who would head each of the three teams.

Within Reagan's National Security Council, the 'action officer' for the secret program was Oliver North, later the central figure in the Iran-contra scandal. Vice President George H. W. Bush was given authority to supervise some efforts, which were run by a new government agency with a bland name, the 'National Program Office'. It had its own building in the Washington area, run by a two-star general, and a secret budget adding up to hundreds of millions of dollars a year. Much of this money was spent on advanced communications equipment that would enable the teams to have secure conversations with U.S. military commanders. In fact, the few details that have previously come to light about the secret program, primarily from a 1991 CNN investigative report, stemmed from allegations of waste and abuses in awarding contracts to private companies, and claims this equipment malfunctioned.

"The exercises were usually scheduled during a congressional recess, so Cheney would miss as little work on Capitol Hill as possible. Although Cheney, Rumsfeld, and one other team leader took part in each exercise, the Cabinet members changed, depending on who was available at a particular time. Once, Attorney General Ed Meese participated in an exercise that departed from Andrews in the pre-dawn hours of June 18, 1986 ... the day after Chief Justice Warren Burger resigned. One official, remembers looking at Meese and thinking, "First a Supreme Court resignation, and now America's in a nuclear war. You're having a bad day."

"In addition to the designated White House chief of staff and his President, each team included representatives from the Departments of State and Defense and CIA, and also from various domestic-policy agencies. The idea was to practice running the entire federal government with a skeletal crew during a nuclear war. At one point, there was talk of bringing in governors of Virginia and Maryland, and the mayor of the District of Columbia, but the idea was discarded because they didn't have the necessary security clearance.

"The exercises were designed to be stressful. Participants gathered in haste, moved and worked in the early-morning hours, lived in Army-base conditions, and dined on early, particularly unappetizing versions of the military's dry, mass-produced MRE meals ready to eat. An entire exercise lasted close to two weeks, but each team took part for only three or four days. One team would leave Washington, run through its drills, and then as if it were on the verge of being 'nuked' hand off to the next team.

"The plans were carried out with elaborate deception, designed to prevent Soviet reconnaissance satellites from detecting where in the U.S. the teams were going. Thus, the teams were sent out in the middle of the night, and changed locations from one exercise to the next. Decoy convoys were sometimes dispatched along with the genuine convoys carrying the communications gear. The underlying logic was that the Soviets could not possibly target all the makeshift locations around the U.S. where the Reagan teams might operate.

The capstone to all these efforts to stay mobile was a special airplane, the National Emergency Airborne Command Post, a modified Boeing 747 based at Andrews and specially outfitted with a conference room and advanced communications gear. In it, a President could remain in the air and run the country during a nuclear showdown. In one exercise, a team of officials stayed aloft in this plane for three days straight, cruising up and down the coasts and back and forth across the country, refueling in the air.

"When George H. W. Bush was elected President, in 1988, members of the secret Reagan program rejoiced ...having been closely involved with the effort from the start, Bush wouldn't need to be initiated into its intricacies and probably wouldn't re-evaluate it. Despite dramatically improved relations with Moscow, Bush did continue the exercises, with some mod-

ifications. Cheney was appointed Secretary of Defense and dropped out as a team leader.

"After the fall of the Berlin Wall and the Soviet collapse, the rationale for the exercises changed. A Soviet nuclear attack was obviously no longer plausible, but what if terrorists carrying nuclear weapons attacked the U.S. and killed the President and the Vice President? Finally, during the early Clinton years, it was decided that this scenario was farfetched and outdated, a mere legacy of the Cold War. It seemed that no enemy in the world was still capable of decapitating America's leadership, and the program was abandoned.

"There things stood until September 11, 2001, when Cheney and Rumsfeld suddenly began to act out parts of a script they'd rehearsed, years before. Operating from the underground shelter beneath the White House, the Presidential Emergency Operations Center, Cheney told Bush to delay a planned flight back from Florida to Washington. At the Pentagon, Rumsfeld instructed a reluctant Wolfowitz to get out of town to the safety of one of the underground bunkers, built to survive nuclear attack. Cheney also ordered House Speaker Dennis Hastert, other congressional leaders, and several Cabinet members including Agriculture Secretary Ann Veneman and Interior Secretary Gale Norton evacuated to one of these secure facilities, away from the capital. Explaining these actions a few days later, Cheney vaguely told NBC's Tim Russert, "We did a lot of planning during the Cold War with respect to the possibility of a nuclear incident." He did not mention the Reagan Administration program or the secret drills he and Rumsfeld had regularly practiced running the country.

"Their participation in extra-constitutional continuity-of-government exercises, remarkable in its own right, also demonstrates a broad, underlying truth about these two men. For three decades, from Ford Administration onward, even when they were out of the executive branch of government, they were never far away. They stayed in touch with defense, military, and intelligence officials who regularly called on them. They were, in a sense, part of the permanent, hidden, national-security apparatus of the United States ... inhabitants of a world in which Presidents come and go, but America keeps on fighting.

Ruth Conniff's, *Halliburton's Immigrant Detention Centers*, Apr. 18, 2006 in, *Progressive*, comments.

"While thousands of people were celebrating

the contribution America's undocumented immigrants make to our economy, and demanding justice and recognition for workers who are denied basic rights, the government was making plans for large-scale detention centers in case of an 'emergency influx' of immigrants. KBR, the Halliburton subsidiary recently reprimanded for gross overcharging its military contracts in Iraq, won a 385 million dollar contract to build the centers. According to the Halliburton website, www.Halliburton.com, 'The contract, which is effective immediately, provides for establishing temporary detention and processing capabilities to augment existing 'ICE Detention and Removal Operations Program' facilities in the event of an emergency influx of immigrants into the U.S., or to support the rapid development of new programs.' What new programs might those be? The web was abuzz with speculation after the contract was awarded on January 24. Pacific News Service gave the most detailed analysis. It connected the new 'immigration emergency' plans with older plans that involved imposing martial law. Certainly, the detention centers raise the specter of WWII Japanese internment camps. The new facilities could be used for round-ups of Muslim Americans or other American citizens tagged as 'enemy combatants'. The use of military personnel and military contractors in the event of a Katrina-like disaster, which the Halliburton contract provides for, brings us closer to martial law, officially declared, or not. It also means record profits for Halliburton, which declared 2005, 'the best in our 86-year history'. David Lesar, Halliburton's chairman, president and CEO, declares on the company website, 'For the full year, 2005, we set a record for revenue and achieved net income of 2.4 billion dollars with each of our six divisions posting record results'. Not bad for a company that has been repeatedly cited for inflating charges and wasting taxpayer money in Iraq. The immigration detention centers ought to raise a red flag, not just about nepotism and waste among military contractors, but about what our government has in store for us. Perhaps the same energy that propelled immigrant rights into the national headlines could be harnessed to demand an explanation for what, exactly, Halliburton is helping to prepare for with this latest big chunk of taxpayer largess.

<>

http://www.prisonplanet.com/articles/april20 06/040406mainsuspect.htm Apr 4, 2006, Paul Joseph Watson's, *Former Head of Star Wars*

Program Says Cheney Main 9/11 Suspect.

"The former head of the Star Wars missile defense program under Presidents Ford and Carter has gone public to say that the official version of 9/11 is a conspiracy theory and his main suspect for the architect of the attack is Vice President Dick Cheney. Dr. Robert M. Bowman, Lt. Col., USAF, ret. flew 101 combat missions in Vietnam. He is the recipient of the Eisenhower Medal, the George F. Kennan Peace Prize, the President's Medal of Veterans for Peace, the Society of Military Engineers Gold Medal, six Air Medals and dozens of other awards and honors. His Ph.D. is in Aeronautics and Nuclear Engineering from Caltech. He chaired eight major international conferences, and is one of the country's foremost experts on National Security. Bowman worked secretly for U.S. government on the Star Wars project and was the first to coin the term in a 1977 secret memo. After Bowman realized the program was only ever intended to be used as an aggressive and not defensive tool, as part of a plan to initiate a nuclear war with the Soviets, he left the program and campaigned against it. In an interview with *The Alex Jones Show* aired nationally on the GCN Radio Network, Bowman stated that at the bare minimum, if Osama bin Laden and Al-Qaeda were involved in 9/11, then the government stood down and allowed the attacks to happen. He said it is plausible the entire chain of military command were unaware of what was taking place, and were used as tools by the people pulling the strings behind the attack. Bowman outlined how the drills on the morning of 9/11 that simulated planes crashing into buildings on the East Coast were used as a cover to dupe unwitting air defense personnel into not responding quickly enough to stop the attack. 'The exercises that went on that morning simulating the exact kind of thing that was happening so confused the people in the FAA and NORAD … that they didn't they didn't know what was real and what was part of the exercise,' Bowman said. 'I think the people who planned and carried out those exercises, they're the ones that should be the object of investigation.' Asked if he could name a prime suspect who was the likely architect behind the attacks, Bowman stated, 'If I had to narrow it down to one person … I think my prime suspect would be Dick Cheney.' Bowman said that privately his military fighter pilot peers and colleagues did not disagree with his sentiments about the real story behind 9/11. Bowman agreed that the U.S. was in danger of slipping into a dictatorship and stated, 'I think there's been nothing closer to fascism than what we've seen lately from this government'. Bowman slammed the Patriot Act as having, 'Done more to destroy the rights of Americans than all of our enemies combined'. Bowman trashed the 9/11 Commission as a politically motivated cover-up with abounding conflicts of interest, charging, 'The 9/11 Commission omitted anything that might be the least bit suspicious or embarrassing or in any way detract from the official conspiracy, so it was a total whitewash. There needs to be a true investigation, not the kind of sham investigations we've had with the 9/11 commission and all the rest of that junk,' Bowman said. Asked if the perpetrators of 9/11 were preparing to stage another false-flag attack to reinvigorate their agenda, Bowman agreed that, 'I can see that and I hope they can't pull it off, I hope they're prevented from pulling it off, but I know darn good and well they'd like to have another one. In addition, from the very start we've put forth eminently credible individuals only for them to be ignored by the establishment media. Physics Professors, former White House advisors, CIA analysts, the father of Reaganomics, German Defense Ministers and Bush's former Secretary of the Treasury, have all gone public on 9/11, but have been uniformly ignored by the majority of the establishment press," Bowman said. Bowman is currently running for Congress in Florida's 15th District.

CNN comments.

WASHINGTON (CNN) ~ Richard 'Dick' Cheney brings two key elements to the 2000 Republican presidential ticket, a wealth of political experience, and loyalty to two generations of the Bush family. Cheney represented Wyoming in the House of Representatives for six terms before being tapped by President George Bush in 1989 to serve as defense secretary. Cheney was not Bush's first choice, but Sen. John Tower was rejected by Senate Democrats and Tower withdrew his name during a contentious series of Senate confirmation hearings over allegations of drinking and womanizing.

Cheney was at the helm of the Pentagon during the Persian Gulf War and during the first rounds of post-Cold War military cutbacks. After Bill Clinton's victory in 1992, Cheney moved into private industry. But earlier this year, he was tapped by another Bush, Texas Gov. George W. Bush, to head the running mate selection process. But, Bush evidently got along so well with Cheney, he convinced Cheney to take the job instead. Cheney's reputation for quiet coun-

sel and his steadfast service to Bush's father appealed to Bush, who places a high premium on loyalty. Cheney's resume, especially his international policy experience, helps round out the ticket ... as Bush's main policy weak point is international relations. Cheney's well-known at the White House, having not only served during the Bush Administration but also the Ford Administration. Cheney came to Washington in 1968, where he was a congressional fellow and became a protégé of Illinois Republican Rep. Donald Rumsfeld, a close friend of Gerald Ford, who was then House minority leader. When Ford tapped Rumsfeld to be his chief of staff in 1974, Rumsfeld made Cheney his deputy. In 1975, Rumsfeld moved over to the Pentagon to serve as defense secretary and Cheney succeeded his boss, becoming at age 35 the youngest chief of staff in White House history. Cheney held the post for 14 months and managed Ford's 1976 presidential election bid against Jimmy Carter. After Ford's defeat, Cheney returned to Wyoming, where he ran for the state's sole congressional seat in 1978. He won the seat easily and his experience in the Ford White House proved helpful. At the start of his second term, he became chairman of the Republican Policy Committee by beating out a fellow Republican with more seniority. He quickly rose within the GOP power chain as one of President Reagan's most ardent supporters, backing him up on military issues like 'Star Wars' missile defense system. He was elected House Minority Whip in 1988. Cheney developed an image as a pragmatic moderate in Congress, partly due to his friendly demeanor. But his voting record is hard-core conservative. He voted against Democrats on almost every social issue, including abortion rights, gun control and the Equal Rights Amendment. He consistently opposed funding of Head Start and voted against creating the U.S. Department of Education. He also voted to aid the Nicaraguan contras and against the override of Reagan's veto of a bill imposing sanctions on the apartheid regime in South Africa. He took an especially hard line on gun control issues. He was one of just 21 members of Congress who voted against a 1985 ban on armor piercing bullets, so-called cop killer bullets. In 1988, he was one of only four members of the House voting against a ban on plastic guns that could slip through airport security machines undetected. The National Rifle Association didn't oppose this ban. On the environment, Cheney opposed refunding the Clean Water Act. He voted to postpone sanctions slapped on air polluters that failed to meet pollution standards. And, he voted against legislation to require oil, chemical and other industries from making public records of emissions known to cause cancer, birth defects and other chronic diseases. His wife, Lynne Cheney, also garnered a reputation as a conservative during her tenure as head of the National Endowment for the Humanities during the Reagan and Bush administrations. As Defense Secretary, Cheney was easily confirmed by a vote of 92-0, and quickly asserted his authority, establishing himself as the Pentagon's undisputed chief. Shortly after taking office, he publicly rebuked Air Force Gen. Larry Welch for appearing to negotiate with Congress over nuclear missile deployments. He fired another Air Force general, Chief of Staff Michael J. Dugan, after he talked with reporters in unusual detail about U.S. war plans in the Persian Gulf in September 1990, a month after Iraq invaded its southern neighbor, Kuwait. Cheney soon found himself advising President Bush on how to evict the forces of Iraqi president Saddam Hussein from the oil-rich Gulf emirate. He also successfully completed a touchy diplomatic mission, convincing Saudi Arabian King Fahd to allow a large contingent of U.S. forces into his kingdom for an expected invasion of Kuwait. According to retired Gen. Colin Powell, then chairman of the Joint Chiefs of Staff, it was Cheney who rejected Desert Storm commander Gen. Norman Schwarzkopf's first battle plan as 'disappointing' and pushed for a full-scale ground invasion, despite his fears of high casualties. After the successful conclusion of the Persian Gulf War, Cheney oversaw a 25% reduction in the size of the military. The Pentagon budget was slashed by billions, including cuts in Star Wars funding and the closure of hundreds of military installations overseas. He entered the private sector after Bush's defeat in 1992. In 1995, Cheney became chairman and chief executive officer of Dallas-based Halliburton Corp., one of the world's leading engineering and construction firms for of oil companies projects. Under Cheney's guidance, the company's stock price and profits have soared. In 1998, he made 2.2 million dollars in salary and controlled another 10 million dollars in Halliburton stock. Cheney came under criticism due to Halliburton's parting gift to him of about 20 million dollars. Cheney pledged to forgo part of the gift if the GOP ticket wins. The son of an Agriculture Department worker, Cheney was born on January 30, 1941, in Lincoln, Nebraska. When he was 13, the fam-

ily moved to Casper, Wyoming. After graduating from high school, Cheney went to Yale University on a full scholarship. But he struggled academically at the Ivy League school, heading home after one year to take up studies at the University of Wyoming, where he renewed his relationship with his high school sweetheart, Lynne Vincent. The two were married on Aug. 29, 1964. An admittedly poor student, Cheney reapplied himself and earned a bachelor's and master's degree in political science before heading to University of Wisconsin in 1966 to pursue a doctorate. Cheney never served in the military. Between 1963 and 1965, Cheney received four student deferments and got a deferment in 1966 for being married and an expectant father. Soon after that, he was 26 years old and no longer draft age. In 1968, Cheney gave up his doctoral studies for his first job in Washington as a congressional fellow in the office of Republican Rep. William Steiger of Wisconsin. Cheney was living in Dallas, Texas, when Bush tapped him for the ticket. But, he also maintains a residence in Jackson, Wyoming, and changed his voting registration from Texas to Wyoming to avoid violating the 12th Amendment to the Constitution, which prohibits members of the electoral college from casting votes for presidential and vice presidential candidates from the same state. Cheney and his wife have two daughters, Elizabeth, 34, and Mary 31. Mary initially attracted publicity because she is openly gay and, until May, she worked for Coors Brewing Co. as liaison to the gay community. The Bush campaign and the Cheneys have declined to discuss Mary Cheney's personal life. Lynne Cheney has served as a senior fellow at the American Enterprise Institute from 1993 to the present. She also is the author of, *Telling the Truth*, a book on the social impact of cultural trends.

Wikipedia comments.

Dick Cheney's political career began in 1969, during the Nixon administration. He held a number of positions in the years that followed, special assistant to the Director of the OEO, White House staff assistant, assistant director of the Cost of Living Council, and Deputy Assistant to the President. Under President Gerald Ford, Cheney became Assistant to the President and then the youngest White House Chief of Staff in history. Many have pointed to this time as the point where both he and Donald Rumsfeld began consolidating political power. An article in *Rolling Stone* said, 'Having turned Ford into their instrument, Rumsfeld and Cheney staged a palace coup. They pushed Ford to fire Defense Secretary

James Schlesinger, tell Vice President Nelson Rockefeller to look for another job and remove Henry Kissinger from his post as national security adviser. Rumsfeld was named secretary of defense, and Cheney became chief of staff to the president. He was campaign manager for Ford's 1976 presidential campaign, while James Baker served as campaign chairman.

The first of eight major recommendations of the 1946 Joint Committee on the Organization of Congress was the consolidation of 81 legislative committees into 34. The second major recommendation was the creation of the Policy Committee. The Joint Committee recommended that the Policy Committee serve as a formal council to meet regularly with the Executive, to facilitate the formulation and carrying out of national policy, and to improve relationships between the executive and legislative branches of the Government. The Policy Committee serves all of those missions. In addition, the Policy Committee is an important means for every member of the Conference to develop sound legislative ideas into sound bills. These bills can then be introduced and considered in the appropriate committee of jurisdiction. Through its Policy Advisory Boards, the Policy Committee conducts a regular liaison with the nation's leading think tanks, scholars, and private-sector experts on issues before Congress. Republicans established the Policy Committee by Conference Resolution on Jan. 26, 1949. For its first ten years, Republican Leader Joe Martin served as chairman. In 1959, the Conference unanimously elected Rep. John Byrnes, ranking Republican on the Ways & Means Committee, as chairman after junior Members sought to strengthen the Committee to modernize GOP policy. In 1963, under Conference Chairman Gerald Ford, the Conference amended its rules to increase the number of newer Members on the Committee so that it more broadly represented 'forward-looking Republican thinking'. With the support of Rep. Don Rumsfeld, future House Republican Leader Rep. John Rhodes succeeded Rep. Byrnes in 1965-1973. Subsequent chairmen were future World Bank President Barber Conable 1973-1977, Rep. Del Clawson 1977-1979, Rep. Bud Shuster 1979-1981, Dick Cheney 1981-1987. In 1978, Cheney was elected to represent Wyoming in the U.S. House of Representatives. Cheney was reelected five times serving until 1989. He was Chairman of the Republican Policy Committee from 1981 to 1987 when he was elected Chairman of the House Republican

Conference. The following year, he was elected House Minority Whip. Among the many votes he cast during his tenure in the House, he voted in 1979 with the majority against making Dr. Martin Luther King, Jr.'s birthday a national holiday, and again voted with the majority in 1983 when the measure passed. He voted against the creation of the U.S. Department of Education, citing his concern over budget deficits and expansion of the federal government. He also believed it to be an encroachment to states' rights. In 1986, after President Reagan vetoed a bill to impose economic sanctions against South Africa for its official policy of apartheid, Cheney was one of 83 Representatives who voted against overriding the veto. In later years, Cheney articulated his opposition to 'unilateral sanctions', against many different countries, stating 'they almost never work'. He also opposed unilateral sanctions against communist Cuba, and later in his career he would support multilateral sanctions against Iraq. The European Community voted to place limited sanctions upon South Africa in 1986. In 1986, Cheney, along with 145 Republicans and 31 Democrats, voted against a nonbinding Congressional resolution calling on the South African government to release Nelson Mandela from prison, after the majority Democrats defeated proposed amendments to the language that would have required Mandela to renounce violence sponsored by the ANC and requiring the ANC to oust the Communist faction from leadership. The resolution was defeated. Appearing on CNN during the Presidential campaign in 2000, Cheney addressed criticism for this, saying he opposed the resolution because the ANC at the time was viewed as a terrorist organization and had a number of interests that were fundamentally inimical to the United States. As a Wyoming representative, he was also known for his vigorous advocacy of the state's petroleum and coal businesses. Cheney served as the Secretary of Defense from Mar 1989-to-Jan 1993 under President George H. W. Bush. He directed Operation Just Cause in Panama and Operation Desert Storm in the Middle East. In 1991, he was awarded the Presidential Medal of Freedom for 'preserving America's defenses at a time of great change around the world.' With Democrats returning to the White House in January 1993, Cheney left the Department of Defense and joined the American Enterprise Institute. From 1995-2000, he served as Chairman of the Board and Chief Executive Officer of Halliburton, a Fortune 500 company and market leader in the energy sector. Under Cheney's tenure, the number of Halliburton subsidiaries in offshore tax havens increased from 9 to 44. As CEO of Halliburton, Cheney lobbied to lift U.S. sanctions against Iran and Libya, saying they hurt business and failed to stop terrorism. He also sat on the Board of Directors of Procter & Gamble, Union Pacific, and EDS.

In 1997, he along with Donald Rumsfeld and others founded the Project for the New American Century, a think tank whose self-stated goal is to 'promote American global leadership'. He was also part of the board of adviser of the Jewish Institute for National Security Affairs before becoming Vice President. Cheney has financial interests in Halliburton through 433,333 stock options worth about 8 million dollars. They are part of a Gift Trust Agreement pursuant to which an Administrative Agent has the right to exercise those options and distribute the proceeds from the sale of the resulting stock to certain charitable organizations. Who that administrative agent is has not been disclosed. All proceeds of the options will be split between the George Washington University Medical Faculty Associates, Inc. for the benefit of the Cardiothoracic Institute, the University of Wyoming for the benefit of the University of Wyoming Foundation, and Capital Partners for Education for the benefit of low-income high school students in the Washington, D.C. area.

Cheney resigned as CEO of Halliburton on July 25, 2000, and put all his corporate shares into a blind trust. As part of his deferred compensation agreements with Halliburton contractually arranged prior to Cheney becoming Vice President, Cheney's public financial disclosure sheets filed with the U.S. Office of Government Ethics showed he received $162,392 in 2002 and $205,298 in 2001. Upon his nomination as a Vice Presidential candidate, Cheney purchased an annuity that would guarantee his deferred payments regardless of the company's performance. He argued that this step removed any conflict of interest. Cheney's net worth, estimated to be between 30-100 million dollars, is largely derived from his post at Halliburton. In 2005, the Cheney's reported their gross income as 8.82 million dollars. This was largely the result of exercising Halliburton stock options that had been set aside in 2001 with the Gift Trust Agreement. The Cheneys donated 6.87 million dollars to charity from stock options and royalties from Mrs. Cheney's books.

Appendix 3 ~ Halliburton, Brown & Root and the Bush-Cheney Drug Empire

From the Wilderness's Michael Ruppert's *Halliburton Corporation's Brown and Root is one of the major components of the Bush-Cheney Drug Empire.*

www.copvcia.com

www.fromthewilderness.com

FTW, Oct. 24, 2000 ~ The success of Bush Vice Presidential running mate Richard Cheney at leading Halliburton to a five year 3.8 billion dollar 'pig-out' on federal contracts and taxpayer-insured loans is a partial indicator of what may happen if the Bush ticket wins. A look at available research and an August 2, 2000 report by Center for Public Integrity at www.public-i.org, suggests drug money has played a role in successes of Halliburton under Cheney's tenure as CEO from 1995-2000.

<>

This is especially true for Halliburton's famous subsidiary, heavy construction and oil giant Brown & Root. Brown and Root's past and the past of Dick Cheney connect to the international drug trade on more than one occasion in more than one way.

<>

June 2000, the lead Washington D.C. attorney for a major Russian oil company connected in law enforcement reports to heroin smuggling and also a beneficiary of U.S.-backed loans to pay for Brown & Root contracts in Russia, held a 2.2 million dollar fund raiser to fill the already bulging coffers of presidential candidate George W. Bush.

<>

This isn't the first time Brown & Root has been connected to drugs, this 'poster child' of American industry may be a key player in Wall Street's efforts to maintain domination of the half trillion dollar yearly global drug trade and its profits. Dick Cheney, Halliburton's largest individual shareholder at 45.5 million dollars, has a vested interest in seeing Brown & Root's success continue.

Of all American companies dealing directly with U.S. military and providing cover for CIA operations, few firms can match the global presence of this giant construction powerhouse that employs 20,000 people in 100 countries. Through sister companies or joint ventures, Brown & Root can build offshore oil rigs, drill wells, construct and operate everything from harbors to pipelines to highways to nuclear reactors. It can train and arm security forces, and it can feed, supply and house armies. One key beacon of Brown & Root's overwhelming appeal to agencies like CIA is on its own corporate web page, Brown & Root announces it has received the contract to dismantle aging Russian nuclear tipped ICBMs in their silos.

<>

Relationships between key institutions, players and Bushes suggest under a George W. Administration, the Bush family and allies may well be able to, using Brown & Root as the operational interface, control the drug trade from Medellin to Moscow.

Originally formed as a heavy construction company to build dams, Brown & Root grew operations via shrewd political contributions to Senate candidate Lyndon Johnson in 1948. Expanding into building oil platforms, military bases, ports, nuclear facilities, harbors and tunnels, Brown & Root underwrote LBJ's political career. It prospered as a result, making billions on U.S. Government contracts during the Vietnam War. *Austin Chronicle* in an op-ed piece, *The Candidate From Brown & Root,* labels Republican Cheney as the political dispenser of Brown & Root's largesse. According to political campaign records, during Cheney's five year tenure at Halliburton the company's political contributions more than doubled to 1.2 million dollars.

Newsmakingnews.com, Independent news service describes how in 1998, with Cheney as Chairman, Halliburton spent 8.1 billion dollars to purchase oil industry equipment and drilling supplier Dresser Industries. This made Halliburton a corporation that will have presence in almost any future oil drilling operation in the world. It also brought back into the family fold the company that once sent a plane in 1948 to fetch Yale Graduate George H. W. Bush, to begin his career in the Texas oil business. Bush the elder's father, Prescott, served as a Managing Director for the firm that once owned Dresser ... Brown Brothers Harriman.

Everywhere there's oil there is Brown & Root. Increasingly, everywhere there is war or insurrection there is Brown & Root. From Bosnia and Kosovo, to Chechnya, to Rwanda, to Burma, to Pakistan, to Laos, to Vietnam, to Indonesia, to Iran, to Libya, to Mexico, to Colombia, Brown & Root's traditional operations have expanded from heavy construction to include provision of logistical support for U.S. military. Now, instead of U.S. Army quartermasters, the world is likely to see Brown & Root warehouses storing and managing everything from uniforms to rations to vehicles.

Dramatic expansion of Brown & Root operations in Colombia suggest Bush preparations for a war-inspired feeding frenzy as part of a 'Plan Colombia'.

<>

This is consistent with moves by former Bush Treasury Secretary Nicholas Brady to open a joint Colombian-American investment partnership, called Corfinsura. for the financing of major construction projects with the Colombian Antioquia Syndicate, headquartered in Medellin.

<>

Expectations of a ground war in Colombia may explain why in a 2000 SEC filing Brown & Root reported in addition to owning more than 800,000 sq. feet of warehouse space in Colombia, they also lease another 122,000 square feet. According to the filing of Brown & Root Energy Services Group, the only other places where the company maintains warehouse space are in Mexico 525,000 sq. feet, and the U.S. 38,000 sq. feet.

According to the web site of Colombia's Foreign Investment Promotion Agency, Brown & Root had no presence in the country until 1997. What does Brown & Root, which according to Associated Press, has made more than 2 billion dollars supporting and supplying U.S. troops, know about Colombia ...that the U.S. public does not? Why the need for almost a million square feet of warehouse space that can be transferred from one Brown & Root operation ...energy, to another ...military support, with the stroke of a pen?

As described by Associated Press, during 'Iran-Contra', Congressman Dick Cheney of the House Intelligence Committee was a rabid supporter of Marine Lt. Col. Oliver North.

<>

This was in spite of the fact North lied to Cheney in a private 1986 White House briefing. Oliver North's diaries and subsequent investigations by the CIA Inspector General have irrevocably tied him directly to cocaine smuggling during the 1980s ...and, the opening of bank accounts for one firm moving four tons of cocaine a month.

This did not stop Cheney from actively supporting North's 1994 unsuccessful run for the U.S. Senate from Virginia ... just a year before Cheney took the reins at Brown & Root's parent company, Dallas-based Halliburton, in 1995.

As Bush Secretary of Defense during Desert Shield & Desert Storm in 1990-1991, Cheney directed special operations involving Kurdish rebels in northern Iran. The Kurds' primary source of income for fifty years has been heroin smuggling from Afghanistan and Pakistan through Iran, Iraq, and Turkey.

Los Angeles Times reported Mar. 22, 1991 a group of gunmen burst into Ankara Turkey offices of joint venture, Vinnell, Brown & Root and assassinated retired Air Force Chief Master Sergeant John Gandy.

March 1991, tens of thousands of Kurdish refugees, long-time CIA assets were massacred by Saddam Hussein in the wake of the Gulf War. Saddam, seeking to destroy hopes of a Kurdish revolt, found it easy to kill thousands of unwanted Kurds who fled to the Turkish border seeking sanctuary. There, Turkish security forces, trained in part by Vinnell, Brown & Root, turned thousands of Kurds back to certain death.

<>

Today, Vinnell Corporation … a TRW Company … is, with firms MPRI and DynCorp, one of three pre-eminent private mercenary corporations in the world … and the dominant entity for training security forces throughout the Middle East.

<>

Not surprisingly, Turkish border regions in question were primary trans-shipment points for heroin grown in Afghanistan and Pakistan destined for markets of Europe.

A confidential source with intelligence experience in the region said the Kurds "got some payback against the folks that used to help them move their drugs." He openly acknowledged Brown & Root and Vinnell routinely provided non-official cover NOC for CIA officers.

From 1994-1999, during U.S. military intervention in the Balkans, where according to *Christian Science Monitor* and *Jane's Intelligence Review*, the Kosovo Liberation Army controls 70% of heroin entering Western Europe, Cheney's Brown & Root made billions of dollars supplying U.S. troops from vast facilities in the region. Brown & Root support operations continue in Bosnia, Kosovo and Macedonia to this day [Ed's note, 10/2000].

Dick Cheney's footprints have come closer to drugs than one might suspect. The Aug. Center for Public Integrity report brought them closer. It would be factually correct to say there is a direct linkage of Brown & Root facilities … often in remote and hazardous regions … between every drug producing region and every drug consuming region in the world. These coincidences do not prove complicity.

The Center for Public Integrity report entitled, *Cheney Led Halliburton To Feast at Federal Trough*, by journalists Knut Royce and Nathaniel

Heller, describes how under five years of Cheney's leadership, Halliburton largely through subsidiary Brown & Root, enjoyed 3.8 billion dollars in federal contracts and taxpayer-insured loans. The loans were granted by Export-Import Bank EXIM and Overseas Private Investment Corporation OPIC. According to Ralph McGehee's CIA Base, both institutions are infiltrated by CIA and routinely provide NOC to CIA officers.

One of those loans to Russian financial and banking conglomerate, Alfa Group of Companies, contained 292 million dollars to pay for Brown and Root's contract to refurbish a Siberian oil field owned by the Russian Tyumen Oil Company. The Alfa Group completed its 51% acquisition of Tyumen Oil in what was allegedly a rigged bidding process in 1998. An official Russian government report claimed Alfa Group's top executives, oligarchs Mikhail Fridman and Pyotr Aven "allegedly participated in the transit of drugs from Southeast Asia through Russia and into Europe."

These same executives, Fridman and Aven, who reportedly smuggled heroin in connection with Russia's Solntsevo mob family were the same ones who applied for the EXIM loans that Halliburton's lobbying later safely secured.

<>

As a result Brown & Root's work in Alfa Tyumen oil fields could continue …and expand.

After describing how organized criminal interests in the Alfa Group had allegedly stolen the oil field by fraud, the CPI story, using official reports from the FSB … Russian equivalent of the FBI … oil companies such as BP-Amoco, former CIA and KGB officers and press accounts established a solid link to Alfa Tyumen and the transportation of heroin.

In 1995, sacks of heroin disguised as sugar were stolen from a rail container leased by Alfa Echo and sold in the Siberian town of Khabarovsk. A problem arose when many residents of the town became intoxicated or poisoned. The CPI story stated, "The FSB report said within days of the incident, Ministry of Internal Affairs (MVD) agents conducted raids of Alfa Eko buildings and found "drugs and other compromising documentation."

Both reports claim that Alfa Bank laundered drug funds from Russian and Colombian drug cartels.

The FSB document claims at the end of 1993, a top Alfa official met with Gilberto Rodriguez Orejuela, the now imprisoned financial mastermind of Colombia's notorious Cali cartel, "to conclude an agreement about the transfer of money into the Alfa Bank from offshore zones such as the Bahamas, Gibraltar and others." The plan was to insert it back into the Russian economy through the purchase of stock in Russian companies.

[The former KGB agent] reported there was evidence "regarding [Alfa Bank's] involvement with the money laundering of Latin American drug cartels."

It becomes harder for Cheney and Halliburton to assert coincidence, as CPI reported Tyumen's lead Washington attorney, James C, Langdon, Jr., at the firm of Aikin Gump "helped coordinate a 2.2 million dollar fundraiser for Bush this June. He then agreed to help recruit 100 lawyers and lobbyists in the capital to raise $25,000 each for W's campaign."

The heroin mentioned in the CPI story originated in Laos, where longtime Bush allies and covert warriors Richard Armitage and retired CIA Associate Deputy Director of Operations Ted Shackley were repeatedly linked to the drug trade.

It made its way across Southeast Asia to Vietnam, probably the port of Haiphong. Then the heroin sailed to Russia's Pacific port of Vladivostok from whence it bounced across Siberia by rail and by truck or rail to Europe, passing through the hands of Russian Mafia leaders in Chechnya and Azerbaijan. Chechnya and Azerbaijan are hotbeds of armed conflict and oil exploration, and Brown & Root has operations all along this route.

This long, expensive and tortured path was hastily established, as described by FTW in previous issues, after President George Bush's personal envoy Richard Armitage, holding the rank of Ambassador, traveled to the former Soviet Union to assist it with its 'economic development' in 1989. The obstacle then to a direct, profitable and efficient route from Afghanistan and Pakistan through Turkey into Europe was a cohesive Yugoslavian/Serbian government controlling the Balkans, and continuing instability in the Golden Crescent of Pakistan/Afghanistan. Also, there was no other way, using heroin from the Golden Triangle, Burma, Laos and Thailand, to deal with China and India but to go around them. It is perhaps not by coincidence that Cheney and Armitage share membership in the prestigious Aspen Institute, an exclusive bi-partisan research think tank, and also in the U.S. Azerbaijan Chamber of Commerce. Just last November [2000], in what may be a portent of

things to come, Armitage played the role of Secretary of Defense in a practical exercise at the Council on Foreign Relations where he and Cheney are also both members. Speculation, that the scandal plagued Armitage, who resigned under a cloud as Assistant Secretary of Defense in the Reagan Administration, is W's first choice for Secretary of Defense next year, is widespread. The Clinton Administration took care of [extra] travel for heroin [trafficking] with the 1998 destruction of Serbia and Kosovo and the installation of the KLA as a regional power. That opened a direct line from Afghanistan to Western Europe ... and Brown & Root was in the middle. Clinton's skill streamlining drug operations was described in the May FTW issue in, *The Democratic Party's Presidential Drug Money Pipeline*. That article has been reprinted in three countries. The essence of the drug economic lesson is that by growing opium in Colombia and by smuggling cocaine and heroin from Colombia to New York City through the Dominican Republic and Puerto Rico (a virtual straight line), traditional smuggling routes can be shortened or eliminated. This reduces risk and cost, increases profits and eliminates competition.

FTW suspects the hand of Medellin co-founder Carlos Lehder in this process ...Lehder, released from prison under Clinton in 1995, is active in the Bahamas and South America. Lehder was known during the 1980s as, 'The genius of transportation.' I can imagine a Dick Cheney, having witnessed the complete restructuring of the global drug trade in the last eight years, going to George W and saying, "Look, I know how we can make it even better." As quoted in the CPI article, one Halliburton Vice President noted, that if the Bush-Cheney ticket was elected, "the company's government contracts would obviously go through the roof."

<>

In July of 1977 Michael Ruppert, then a Los Angeles Police officer struggled to make sense of a world gone haywire. In a last ditch effort to salvage a relationship with his fiancée, Nordica Theodora 'Teddy' D'Orsay, a CIA contract agent, Mike traveled to find her in New Orleans. On a hastily arranged vacation, secured with the blessing of his Commanding Officer, Captain Jesse Brewer of LAPD, Mike had gone on his own, unofficially, to avoid scrutiny of LAPD's Organized Crime Intelligence Division (OCID). This is his story.

Late spring 1976 Teddy wanted me to join her operations from within the ranks of LAPD. I refused to get involved with drugs in any way. Everything she mentioned seemed to involve heroin or cocaine along with guns she was always moving out of the country. Director of CIA at that time was George Herbert Walker Bush.

Although officially on staff at LAPD Academy at the time, I was unofficially loaned to OCID since January when Teddy, announcing a new operation in Fall 1976, disappeared. She left many people baffled and twisting in the breeze. OCID detectives were pressuring me hard for information about her and her activities. It was information I could not give them. Hoping against hope, I would find some way to understand her involvement with CIA, LAPD, the royal family of Iran, the Mafia, and drugs, I set out alone into eight days of Dante-like revelations that changed the course of my life to this day.

Arriving in New Orleans, July 1977, I found her in an apartment in Gretna. Equipped with scrambler phones, night vision devices, working from sealed communiqués delivered by naval and air force personnel from nearby Belle Chasse Naval Air Station, Teddy was involved in something ugly. She was arranging large quantities of weapons to be loaded onto ships leaving for Iran. She was working with Mafia associates of New Orleans Mafia boss Carlos Marcello to coordinate movement of service boats bringing heroin into the city. The boats arrived at Marcello-controlled docks, unmolested by New Orleans police she introduced me to, along with divers, military men, former Green Berets and CIA personnel.

The service boats were retrieving heroin from oil rigs in Gulf of Mexico, in international waters, oil rigs built and serviced by Brown & Root.

<>

The guns Teddy monitored, Vietnam era surplus AK 47s, M16s, were loaded onto ships owned, or leased by, Brown & Root. I met and ate at restaurants with Brown & Root employees boarding those ships and leaving for Iran.

Disgusted and heart-broken at witnessing my fiancée and my government smuggle drugs, I ended the relationship.

Returning to L.A., I reported all activity I'd seen, including the connections to Brown & Root, to LAPD intelligence officers. They told me I was crazy. Forced out of LAPD under threat of death in 1978, I made complaints to LAPD's Internal Affairs Division and to the L.A. office of the FBI under command of FBI SAC Ted Gunderson. I and my attorney wrote to politicians, Department of Justice, CIA, and contacted *L.A. Times.* The FBI and LAPD said I was crazy.

According to a 1981 two-part news story in *Los Angeles Herald Examiner,* FBI had taken Teddy into custody then released her, before classifying their investigation without further action. Former New Orleans Crime Commissioner Aaron Cohen told reporter, Randall Sullivan, he found my description of events plausible after thirty years of studying Louisiana's organized crime operations.

To this day, a CIA report prepared as a result of my complaint remains classified and exempt from release, pursuant to Executive Order of the President, in the interests of national security and because it would reveal identities of CIA agents.

Oct. 26 1981, in the basement of the West Wing of the White House, I reported what I'd seen in New Orleans to my friend and UCLA classmate, Craig Fuller. Craig Fuller went on to become Chief of Staff to Vice President Bush from 1981-to-1985.

In 1982, UCLA political science professor Paul Jabber filled in many of the pieces in my quest to understand what I'd seen in New Orleans. He was qualified to do so, because he served as a CIA and State Department consultant to the Carter Administration. Paul explained, after a 1975 treaty between the Shah of Iran and Saddam Hussein ... the Shah cut off overt military support for Kurdish rebels fighting Saddam from the north of Iraq.

In exchange, the Shah gained access to the Shat al-Arab waterway to multiply his oil exports and income. Not wanting to lose a long-term valuable asset in the Kurds, CIA used Brown & Root, which operated in both countries and maintained port facilities in the Persian Gulf and near Shat al-Arab, to re-arm the Kurds. The whole operation was financed with heroin. Paul was matter-of-fact about it.

<>

In 1983 Paul Jabber left UCLA to become a vice president of Banker's Trust and Chairman of the Middle East Department of the Council on Foreign Relations.

If one is courageous enough to seek an 'operating system' that theoretically explains what FTW has just described for you, one need look no further than a two-part article in April *Le Monde Diplomatique,* April 2000, focusing on drug capital, *Crime, The World's Biggest Free Enterprise,* by Christian de Brie and Jean de Maillard who explain the actual world economic and political situation. De Brie writes, "By allowing capital to flow unchecked from one end of the world to the other, globalization and abandonment of sovereignty have fostered the explosive growth of an outlaw financial market ... a coherent system closely linked to the expansion of modern capitalism based on association of three partners, governments, transnational corporations and mafias.

Business is business, financial crime is first and foremost a market, thriving and structured, ruled by supply and demand. "Big business complicity and political laissez faire is the only way large-scale organized crime can launder and recycle the huge proceeds of its activities.

<>

Transnationals need support of governments, and neutrality of regulatory authorities, to consolidate their positions, increase profits, withstand and crush competition, pull off the 'deal of the century', and finance illicit operations. Politicians are directly involved, and their ability to intervene depends on the backing and the funding that keeps them in power. This collusion of interests is an essential part of the world economy, the oil that keeps the wheels of capitalism turning."

After confronting CIA Director John Deutch on world television, Nov. 15, 1996, I was interviewed by the staffs of the Senate and House Intelligence Committees. I prepared written testimony for Senate Intelligence I submitted, although I was never called to testify. In every interview and in written testimony and in every lecture since then, I have told the story of Brown & Root.

Appendix 4 ~ A Barrel of Oil Costs One Dollar to Pump from the Ground

Hoover's online comments. www.hoovers.com

In 1870, Marcus Samuel inherited an interest in his father's London trading company, which imported seashells from the Far East. He expanded the business and after securing a contract for Russian oil, began selling kerosene in the Far East. [Ed's note, Dutch, British, and American shippers were engaged in shipping opium to China.] Standard Oil underpriced competitors to defend its Asian markets. In 1892, Samuel unveiled the first of a fleet of tankers. Rejecting Standard's acquisition overtures, Samuel created 'Shell' Transport and Trading in 1897.

Dutchman Aeilko Zijlker struck oil in Sumatra and formed Royal Dutch Petroleum in 1890 to exploit the oil field. Young Henri Deterding joined the firm in 1896 and established a sales force in the Far East. Deterding became head of Royal Dutch Petroleum in 1900 amidst the battle for the Asian market. In 1903, Deterding, Samuel, and the Rothschilds created Asiatic Petroleum, a marketing alliance. With Shell's non-Asian business eroding, Deterding engineered a merger between Royal Dutch and Shell in 1907. Royal Dutch shareholders got 60% control, 'Shell' Transport & Trading, 40%.

After the 1911 Standard Oil breakup, Deterding entered the U.S. building refineries and buying producers. Shell products were available in every state by 1929. Royal Dutch/Shell joined the 1928 'As Is' cartel that fixed prices for two decades.

Post-WWII Royal Dutch/Shell profited from worldwide growth in oil consumption. It acquired 100% of Shell Oil, its U.S. arm, in 1985 but shareholders sued, maintaining Shell Oil's assets had been undervalued, and were awarded 110 million dollars, in 1990. After the 1990-1991 Persian Gulf crisis, Shell sold a major California refinery to Unocal and its U.S. coal mining unit to Zeigler Coal. Management's slow response to two 1995 controversies ... environmentalist outrage over the planned sinking of an oil platform, and human rights activists' criticism of Royal Dutch/Shell's role in Nigeria ... spurred a major shakeup. Royal Dutch/Shell began moving away from its decentralized structure and adopted a new policy of 'corporate openness'.

In 1996 Royal Dutch/Shell and Exxon formed a worldwide petroleum additives venture.

Shell Oil joined Texaco in 1998 to form Equilon Enterprises, combining U.S. refining and marketing operations in the West and Midwest.

Similarly, Shell Oil, Texaco, and Saudi Arabia's Aramco combined downstream operations on the U.S. East and Gulf coasts, as Motiva Enterprises.

In 1999 Royal Dutch/Shell and UK's BG plc acquired a controlling stake in Comgas, a unit of Compania Energética de São Paulo and the largest natural gas distributor in Brazil, for about 1 billion dollars.

In 2000, the company sold its coal business to UK-based mining giant, Anglo American, for more than 850 million dollars. To gain a foothold in the U.S. power marketing scene, Royal Dutch/Shell formed a joint venture with construction giant Bechtel, called InterGen.

The next year the company agreed to combine its German refining and marketing operations with those of RWE-DEA. Royal Dutch/Shell tried to expand its U.S. natural gas reserves in 2001 by making a 2 billion dollar hostile bid for Barrett Resources, but the effort was withdrawn after Barrett agreed to be acquired by Williams for 2.5 billion dollars.

In 2002, in connection with Chevron's acquisition of Texaco, Royal Dutch/Shell acquired Chevron Texaco's (now Chevron) stakes in the underperforming U.S. marketing joint ventures Equilon and Motiva.

That year, the company, through its U.S. Shell Oil unit, acquired Pennzoil-Quaker State for 1.8 billion dollars. Also that year, Royal Dutch/Shell acquired Enterprise Oil for 5 billion dollars, plus debt. In addition, it purchased RWE's 50% stake in German refining and marketing joint venture Shell & DEA Oil, for 1.35 billion dollars.

In 2004 the Group signed a 200 million dollar exploration deal with Libya, signaling its return to that country after a more than decade-long absence. Plans to build a 7-billion-dollar liquid natural gas plant in Qatar were announced in early 2005. In the same year, the company's Shell Chemicals subsidiary announced plans to sell its 50% stake in Basell, one of the world's largest polyolefin makers. The company became part of Royal Dutch Shell after the merger, Royal Dutch Petroleum and 'Shell' Transport & Trading Company.

Other accounts of Marcus Samuel are similar.

Right Honorable Marcus Samuel, 1st Viscount Bearsted, Nov 5 1853-Jan 17 1927, was founder of Shell Transport and Trading Company, a precursor to Royal Dutch Shell. His father, also named Marcus Samuel, ran a successful import-export business to the Far East, which Marcus carried on with his brother, Sam Samuel. Marcus Samuel realized the potential of the oil trade during a trip to the Black Sea in 1890, and ordered the construction of eight dedicated tankers, the first of which was Murex. His were the first ships to satisfy the Suez Canal company of their safety, allowing him to ship his product to Bangkok and Singapore. In 1907, Samuel's company combined with Royal Dutch company of the Netherlands to create the company today known as Shell. The family's other firm, M. Samuel & Co., merged in 1965 with Philip Hill, Higginson, Erlangers Ltd. to create Hill Samuel, now a part of Lloyds TSB. Samuel was Lord Mayor of London from 1902-1903. In honor of Shell's contribution to the British cause in World War I, he was created 1st Baron Bearsted in 1921, and in 1925 became 1st Viscount Bearsted. His son, Walter Horace Samuel, succeeded him both as Viscount and as Chairman of Shell Transport & Trading Company.

Daniel Yergin's, *The Prize*, comments.
By the end of the 1880s, Marcus Samuel had already gained some prominence in the City of London. It was no mean achievement for a Jew … and a Jew not from the old Sephardic families, but from the East End of London, a descendant of immigrants who had come to Britain in 1750 from Holland and Bavaria. Samuel had the same name as his father, Marcus Samuel. The elder Marcus Samuel began his own business career trading on the East London docks, buying curios from returning sailors. In the census of 1851, he was listed as a 'shell merchant'. Among his most popular products were the little knick-knack boxes covered with seashells, known as a 'Gift from Brighton', which were sold to girls and young ladies at English seaside resorts in the mid-Victorian years. By 1860s, the elder Marcus accumulated wealth in addition to seashells, and was importing everything from ostrich feathers and partridge canes to bags of pepper and slabs of tin. He was also exporting an expanding list of manufacturers' products, including the first mechanical looms sent to Japan.

In addition, in what was to prove of great importance to his son, the elder Samuel had built up a network of trusted relationships with some of the great British trading houses … run mainly by expatriate Scots …in Calcutta, Singapore, Bangkok, Manila, Hong Kong, and other parts of the Far East.

http://www.hermes-press.com/oilrulers1.htm comments.

Plutocracy is that form of government in which, instead of the people being represented by their elected officials, those with wealth 'buy' the officials. Those officials then create laws and policies which produce obscene profits for the wealthy owners of corporations. Beginning in the nineteenth century with the Rockefeller monopoly, persons of wealth and political power decided that the energy of choice for the world would be oil not coal … just as the drugs of choice would be alcohol, tobacco, [Ed's note, plus sugar, tea, opium and cocaine.] They set out to control the world's oil reserves.

British Petroleum (earlier Anglo-Persian then Anglo-Iranian Oil Company) was started by William Knox D'Arcy in 1901 when he bought a concession from the Grand Vizier in Teheran for 480,000 square miles …nearly twice the size of Texas, in exchange for twenty thousand pounds in cash, twenty thousand one pound shares, and 16% of the net profits. After three years of drilling and finding no oil, D'Arcy convinced Burma Oil Co. to put up the extra capital needed to keep

D'Arcy's venture afloat. After another two years of drilling, they finally struck oil ...and, Burma Oil and D'Arcy formed the new Anglo-Persian Oil Co.

In 1914, three months before WWI, the British government through the insistence of Winston Churchill, First Lord of the Admiralty, bought 51% of Anglo-Persian for two million pounds, stipulating the company must always remain an independent British concern and that every director must be a British subject. The British navy converted to oil from coal in 1910 and during WWI, Britain needed more oil than Anglo-Persian Company could supply. The remainder was purchased from Royal Dutch Shell.

From *Oil Wars.*

"In the early part of the twentieth century, there was fierce rivalry between the three largest oil companies ...Shell, ` Exxon ...and, British Petroleum.

"Shell ... Henri Deterding, head of Shell, bought (1) oilfields in Egypt in 1908, (2) the Russian Ural-Caspian oilfields in 1910, (3) Mexican oilfields belonging to Lord Cowdray Weetman Pearson, (4) Venezuelan oilfields, which still produce a sixth of Shell's supplies, (5) American oilfields

"Exxon ... Walter Teagle, head of Exxon (1) secretly bought a prosperous Texas oil company named Humble in 1919, (2) secretly bought out Nobel Russian oil interests for 11.5 million dollars in 1920, though the new communist regime seized the oilfields and paid Exxon nothing.

"British Petroleum ... BP controlled not only Iran (Anglo-Persian Oil Company), but 25% of oil from Iraq Petroleum Company. Iraq Petroleum Company (earlier called, Turkish Petroleum Company) was formed following WWI, composed of British Petroleum, Exxon, Gulf, Texaco, Mobil, and Calouste Gulbenkian, an Armenian entrepreneur.

"Exxon, Shell & British Petroleum ... In 1928, Teagle (Exxon), Deterding (Shell), and Sir John Cadman (BP) met in Achnacarry Castle in Scotland. They agreed on a price-fixing scheme that would stop competition that had been harmful to them. These three oil rulers controlled the pricing and supply of oil worldwide.

"However, a huge new oilfield first drilled in Kilgore, Texas, released a gush of oil, resulting in the price of crude falling to ten cents a barrel. H.L. Hunt bought out the original Kilgore wildcat driller, 'Dad Joiner'. Hunt became a billionaire, richest of all Texans. But, the problem of over-supply was so devastating that governors of Texas and Oklahoma called in the national guard and closed down the oilfields, enforcing a system of rationing by which the demand in a particular month was shared among oil producers by a state body called Texas Railroad Commission.

"Exxon ... In 1926, Exxon signed an agreement with the German chemical combine, I.G. Farben, for an exchange of patents and research. Farben was to stay out of the oil business and Exxon would stay out of the chemical business. The agreement gave Nazi Germany hundred-octane aviation fuel and synthetic rubber. Exxon held back the research in synthetic rubber in the U.S. In 1941, Justice Department bought two antitrust suits against Exxon for conspiring to control oil transportation through pipelines and making restrictive agreements with I.G. Farben. Exxon was forced to pay a fine of $50,000. The U.S. was now involved in the WWII and Japan had seized the Malayan rubber plantations, from which America had earlier derived rubber. Senator Harry Truman claimed that Exxon's failure to pursue synthetic rubber research in the U.S., while developing it in collaboration with the Germans, constituted treason.

<>

"Texaco ... under direction of its president, Torkild Rieber, Texaco provided six million dollars worth of oil to Franco, the Spanish dictator. Rieber made contact through Spain with leading Nazis and agreed to supply oil from Colombia to Germany. Texaco continued to supply oil to Nazi Germany even after the outbreak of the World War II in 1939, receiving as payment three Hamburg tankers. Rieber sealed the deal with Goering in Berlin.

At Goering's insistence, Rieber put forward a peace plan to Franklin D. Roosevelt which would ensure Britain's surrender. Roosevelt told Rieber to get out of his dealings with Nazi Germany. Rieber ignored Roosevelt and financed the propaganda mission of Dr. Gerhardt Westrick, a German lawyer, to dissuade American businessmen from supplying Britain with arms. The head of British Intelligence in New York, Canadian millionaire William Stephenson, learned of the Westrick fiasco and broke the story to *New York Herald Tribune.* Westrick was forced to return to Germany on a Japanese ship. Rieber was discredited and Texaco shares plummeted.

"Shell ... Mexican oil was essentially controlled by a Britisher, Weetman Pearson, later titled Lord Cowdray. He began in 1901 to buy oil concessions in Mexico and by 1918 was one of the richest men in the world ... the British equivalent to the American, Rockefeller. Pearson's fortune laid the foundation for Lazard Bank, the *Financial Times, Economist*, Longmans and Penguin Books. In 1919, Cowdray sold out the majority of his company to Deterding of Shell. In 1938, Mexican President Lazaro Cardenas nationalized the seventeen foreign-owned oil companies into one and a monument to the nationalized company, PEMEX, was erected in Mexico City.

"American, Dutch, and British oil companies boycotted nationalized Mexican oil interests, and PEMEX was eventually forced to pay 130 million dollars in compensation for seizing the companies. During WWII, the big oil companies drained off Mexico's oil reserves, then switched their attention to Venezuela where they were in league with Gomez, the dictator.

"Socal, Texaco & Aramco ... Meanwhile, in the Middle-East, in 1926, King Ibn Saud, Muslim desert warrior, had conquered rivals in Mecca and the Hejaz and named the whole territory, from the Persian Gulf to the Red Sea, Saudi Arabia. One of King Saud's principal advisors was Harry St. John Philby, the Arabist who quit British Colonial Service out of disaffection. Philby became a Muslim and was close to Saud. King Saud needed money to finance his enterprises and Philby suggested he exploit his land's oil resources. Philby assisted Socal in getting the concession in 1933. King Saud received an immediate loan of 30,000 pounds, with another 20,000 pounds eighteen months later, and an annual rent of 5,000 pounds, all in gold. Socal paid Philby a salary of 100,000 pounds a year. Socal, short of capital and market outlets, sold half its Saudi and Bahrain concession to Texaco's Cap Rieber. The joint venture was called Aramco. May 1939, King Saud turned the valve on the pipeline and oil began to flow. Saud was so delighted with the money and gifts he received from Socal and Texaco he increased the size of the concession to 444,000 square miles, a plot the size of Texas, Louisiana, Oklahoma, and New Mexico combined.

"Gulf & British Petroleum ... Kuwait, one of many small independent sheikhdoms which had cut into the land mass of Saudi Arabia, had also discovered oil and the concession was purchased by Gulf in 1927 for $50,000. In 1934, Gulf and BP signed an agreement with the Kuwaiti sheikh in a joint venture and huge reserves were discovered in 1938.

"Aramco ... During WWII, Britain advanced about 20 million dollars to King Saud to bribe him to renege on the Socal/Texaco concession and go with BP. Socal and Texaco appealed to Washington ... Roosevelt sent lend-lease money to Saudi Arabia. Roosevelt and his advisors decided U.S. should have controlling interest in Aramco, to protect the nation's oil interests. In 1943, Roosevelt authorized formation of a new corporation to acquire 100% of Aramco. Harold Ickes, Petroleum Administrator for War and Secretary of the Interior, was president of the new corporation, the secretaries of State, War, and the Navy were among the directors and Abe Fortas was secretary. Aramco would not immediately agree to sell its concession to the new federal corporation, so Ickes said the corporation would build a thousand-mile pipeline to carry Saudi Arabian oil to the Mediterranean. In return, Aramco would guarantee 20% of their oilfields as a naval reserve which would be available to the navy at a cut rate. In the end, after much political bickering in the U.S. and internationally, Texaco and Socal built the pipeline themselves, creating Trans-Arabian Pipeline Co, Tapline. It was not until 1949 that Syria and Lebanon agreed to let the pipeline be built, at a cost of $200 million. Over the years, the pipeline was a target for guerrillas, a focus for boycotts, and a bargaining chip for Syria against America. In 1975, it was shut down.

In 1945, Franklin Roosevelt promised King Saud the U.S. would not change its policy regarding Palestine and a Jewish state, without consulting the Arabs. However, Truman became U.S. President two months later and gave full support to the establishment state of Israel. Socal and Texaco worried about the political climate in Saudi Arabia. They decided to bring two other American oil companies into Aramco, Exxon for 30% and Mobil for 10%.

"King Saud continued to demand more money and finally, in 1950, the U.S. State Department and Aramco agreed on a scheme whereby the money Aramco gave King Saud would be deducted from the company's tax bill, depriving the U.S. Treasury of 50 million dollars or more in taxes each year.

<>

"Under U.S. tax laws establishing double taxation, oil companies would not be taxed inside the U.S. All major oil companies adopted the same tax dodge ...so, by 1973 the five largest companies were making two-thirds of their profits abroad and paying no U.S. taxes on those earnings.

<>

"This arrangement allowed oil companies to pay lower U.S. taxes than any group of industries. The U.S. had essentially turned into a country operated for the profit of the oil rulers.

<>

"British Petroleum .... Reza Shah seized power in Iran in 1921 and soon took on the trappings of the Persian Peacock Throne. In 1941, when Hitler invaded Russia, the Shah refused to expel his Nazi allies, so the British and Russian armies invaded Iran to ensure oil and supply routes. The Shah was exiled to South Africa, where he died. During the war, Britain and Russia ruled, but at the end of WWII the old Shah's 21-year-old son was placed in power. Iran, like most oil-producing countries, resented the power foreign-owned oil companies wielded over it. A shrewd older politician, Dr. Mossadeq, was appointed chairman of a committee on Iranian oil policy. By 1951, Mossadeq was calling for nationalization ...when he was elected prime minister by the Iranian parliament, Iran immediately seized BP's oilfields. Iran was placed under international boycott by BP. When a Panamanian ship, the Rose Mary, took on oil from Abadan, Royal Air Force RAF planes forced it into Aden harbor where its cargo was impounded. American oil companies joined the BP boycott of Iran. However, President Truman and Secretary of State Dean Acheson were appalled by the imperialism of Britain, and when Mossadeq came to America to plead his case to the UN Security Council, Acheson befriended him.

<>

"However, antitrust fever had again overtaken the U.S. In 1952, the Senate Select Committee on Small Business released a report titled, *The International Petroleum Cartel.* The report showed the seven largest oil companies, nicknamed, 'Seven Sisters', controlled the majority of oil-producing areas outside the U.S., all foreign refineries, divided world markets between them, shared pipelines and tankers between themselves, and fixed oil prices worldwide.

<>

"Eisenhower became President ... John Foster Dulles was appointed Secretary of State, with the result the oil cartel was forgotten and the new foreign policy mythology became anti-communism.

"In 1953, CIA with British support began subversive action against Mossadeq. Mossadeq had taken control of the Iranian army. The Shah tried to oust him, failed, and was forced to flee. The CIA coup, led by CIA's Kermit Roosevelt spend-

ing about $700,000, forced Mossadeq out of office ...and the Shah returned to Teheran triumphant. British and American oil companies formed an international consortium to buy and develop Iranian oil. BP received 40% of the shares of the consortium, the five American sisters each got 8%, Shell received 14%, and CFP (Compaignie Francaise de Petrole) 6%. The oil cartel members congratulated themselves that they had shown the world that no puny nation, such as Iran or Mexico, could seize their assets and flourish.

<>

"OPEC ... In 1961 the Organization of Petroleum Exporting Countries was established with members being Iran, Iraq, Kuwait, Saudi Arabia and Venezuela. Since then, the following countries joined OPEC ... Qatar in 1961, Indonesia and Libya in 1962, Abu Dhabi in 1967, United Arab Emirates in 1974, Algeria in 1969, Nigeria in 1971, Ecuador in 1973, and Gabon in 1975. Their headquarters, originally located in Geneva, moved to Vienna in 1965. Policy is determined by delegates from members countries, which meet at least twice a year.

"From the beginning of the oil energy monopoly there have been other sources of energy more abundant, more environment-friendly, and cheaper. Steam-driven vehicles proved efficient, but they were driven out by gasoline-driven vehicles. Since railway engines require less fuel than automobiles and trucks, they were allowed to fall into disrepair, the decrepit U.S. railway infrastructure now produces frequent calamities.

"World oil prices are currently high because OPEC and American and British oil companies manipulate prices to gain highest profits possible. It costs about one dollar per barrel to pump oil from the ground, but the present price is $26.41 per barrel. If market demand for oil products were allowed to operate independently, gas prices at the pump could drop 50% at least.

<>

"In 1973, OPEC raised oil prices by 70% as a political warfare tactic aimed against western nations supporting Israel in the Yom Kippur War of Oct. 1973. That same year in December prices were hiked another 130% and a temporary embargo was placed on oil shipments to the U.S. and Netherlands. By early 1980s, OPEC's influence began to wane as Western oil corporations discovered new sources of oil and began to use political and subversive pressure to force OPEC to cut back production and keep prices artificially high. OPEC's power has been decimated by internal conflicts, and by the Iran-Iraq war that broke out in 1980. Within the last several months, the U.S. has again warned OPEC about raising prices by threatening to open up our national strategic oil reserves. The U.S. and British oil corporations insist on being the only ones to manipulate the price of oil.

"Gulf War I … The Gulf War was perpetrated by British and U.S. major oil shareholders to (1) warn Japan and European countries, especially Germany, that the U.S. controls the world's oil supply …by armed force if necessary, (2) to control Iraq's oil production through embargo resulting from the war, and (3) to conquer Iraq since it threatens Israel's military hegemony in the Middle-East.

"Even though Iraq is under an embargo, it's estimated Iraq ships about 100,000 barrels of illicit oil in excess of the U.N.-approved export quota per day. At the end of the war against Serbia in Bosnia and Kosovo, an embargo was slapped on Serbia. However, recently Serbia has been receiving black market oil from Russia. That's why U.S. Navy SEALs boarded a Russian ship in the Gulf of Oman, to warn Russians not to continue selling oil to Serbia.

"The world oil cartel continues to fix gasoline prices worldwide. Prices in California have skyrocketed. During a past year, world crude oil prices have increased by approximately 340%. The April 1999 decision by OPEC to cut production quotas contributes to the hyperinflation of oil prices, but is only part of the problem. OPEC now produces about 40% of the world's oil supply.

<>

"The real cause of the current rise in price for oil is that speculators are now moving into what are called hard commodities … energy, base metals and food. Mar. 8, 2000, Iranian Oil Minister Bijan Namdar Zanganeh, pointed out in a speech on Iran State TV that speculation, rather than physical shortages in crude oil, lay behind the current surge in oil prices.

This series deals with plutocracy, the rule of a nation by those with wealth. Plutocrats deal in all sectors of the economy, oil as well as all others. Currently these plutocratic speculators are making billions of dollars through Wall Street scams like artificially inflated beyond real value of the companies' initial public offerings, IPOs.

"Along with hyperinflationary speculation in the markets, oil corporations continue to buy politicians, resulting in oil-based rulers dominating every nation in the world.

"The Rockefeller Monopoly … John D.

Rockefeller's father, called 'Doctor' Rockefeller, was a bogus physician who sold patent medicines. Beginning in Cleveland, Ohio as a bookkeeper, he then went into partnership in a refinery with the Clark brothers and soon bought them out.

Anthony Sampson's *Seven Sisters* comments.

"He expanded with great daring. Borrowing wherever he could, and bringing in new partners. He realized the only way to dominate the industry was not by producing oil, but by refining and distributing it, and undercutting rivals by cheaper transport. With help of a new partner, Henry Flagler, he persuaded railroads to give secret rebates to his oil, extending the existing practice of allowing discounts for large quantities of freight.

"When John D. secretly bought out rival oil companies, the executives pretended to be Rockefeller competitors, and reported what rival company executives told them. By 1870, he established a joint-stock company, called Standard Oil Co., with a capital of a million dollars of 10% of the oil in America. The oil industry has always been plagued with overproduction. The year after oil was discovered, for example, the price of a barrel was $20. At the end of the next year the price had dropped to 10 cents a barrel, because of overproduction. In the 1870s, two groups vied for control of the oil industry, (1) the producers and drillers, and (2) the refiners. By 1875, Rockefeller, as president of the refiners' Central Association was leader of the refiners. The refiners effectively took control from the producers and drillers. John D. formed Standard Oil Trust in 1883, trading across the entire continent.

Seven Sisters continues.

"Through the device of a trust, which held shares in each component company, Rockefeller was able to circumvent laws which prohibited a company in one state from owning shares in another …at the same time, he could pretend all his companies were independent. This movement was the origin of the whole system of modern economic administration. It has revolutionized the way of doing business all over the world. The time was ripe for it. It had to come, although all we saw at the moment was to save ourselves from wasteful conditions. The day of combination is here to stay. Individualism has gone, never to return,' Rockefeller said."

Oil Wars continues.

From the center of his web at 26 Broadway, New York City, Rockefeller bought oilfields as well as refineries as the industry moved from

Pennsylvania, to Ohio, to Kansas, and on to California. Standard Oil's income was larger than most states and it 'bought' federal and state politicians to enhance its position. With its huge profits, Standard could finance its own expansion. Standard Oil was exporting oil to the Middle East, the Far East and Europe. By 1885, 70% of Standard's business was overseas. Standard now had its own network of agents throughout the world, its own intelligence service which provided information about its competitors and about political leaders in all the target market countries.

<>

The ruthlessness of Rockefeller's tactics against competitors and his own workers, when they dared to demand a living wage, became the focus for a number of muckrakers such as Henry Demarist Lloyd and Ida Tarbell. Tarbell's, *History of Standard Oil*, aroused the public against the monopolistic excesses of Rockefeller. Sherman Anti-Trust Act was passed in 1890, buy only brought to bear during Theodore Roosevelt's presidency.

"In 1907, a report was published by the Commissioner of Corporations, and special prosecutor Frank Kellogg began to detail evidence of Standard's monopoly and exorbitant profits, nearly a billion dollars in a quarter-century. The case was appealed to the Supreme Court, which in 1911 ruled Standard Oil must divest itself of subsidiaries. The total value of the assets of all living descendants of John D. Rockefeller was estimated in 1974 at 2 billion dollars ...about 2 trillion dollars in today's money. Standard Oil progeny included (1) Standard Oil of New Jersey ...EXXON, (2) Standard Oil Company of New York ...MOBIL, (3) Standard Oil of California ...SOCAL, (4) GULF Oil Company, (5) Texas Company ...TEXACO.

"The Rockefellers, under leadership of David, continued to control American politics through organizations like Council on Foreign Relations and Trilateral Commission."

Siegfried E. Tischler's *Blood, Toil & Oil*, from *Nexus Magazine*, Vol 11, Number 4, Jun-Jul 2004, comments.

www.nexusmagazine.com/articles/OilDrugsT errorism.html

John D. Rockefeller was born in Richford, New York, July 8, 1839 (d. 1937) and educated in the public schools of Cleveland, Ohio. He became a bookkeeper in Cleveland at sixteen. In 1862, he went into business with entrepreneur Henry Flagler and Samuel Andrews, the inventor of an inexpensive process for 'refining' of crude petroleum. In 1870, their company was renamed, Standard Oil Co. of Ohio. In 1872, J. D. Rockefeller founded South Improvement Co., which by 1887 amalgamated all but a few per cent of America's refining capacity in one hand and became a corporate giant of such vast might that it was, in effect, 'running' America. The USA was fighting another brutal War of Independence ... this time from Standard Oil, which it won in 1911 when the Rockefeller monopoly was dismantled. Just as in the case of the other War of Independence, victory was an elusive concept. The rest of the 20th century has been called by many 'Rockefeller's revenge'. To all intent and purposes, this re-established the dominance of the oil industry over American politics and the American people. What has changed is that not only have the American people been pushed around the chessboard, but most of mankind has been made into pawns in the game of 'Big Oil'. In 1823, U.S. President Monroe declared the Americas 'off-limits' to any other polity, and the world was divided into the 'Western hemisphere' and the rest. John Davison Rockefeller, son of a Rabbi-cum-haberdasher and purveyor of comforts to the men in the Pennsylvanian oil fields, focused his attention on the downstream side of the oil industry and by the late 1880s established an almost total monopoly on transport and refining of crude oil.

"Henry Deterding, an enterprising young Dutchman, was a clerk in a bank in Batavia Jakarta at the turn of the century when the Duri oil field in Sumatra was discovered. A fast learner, he became involved in the company holding the lease over this oil field and by 1902 had risen to president of this company. Deterding was determined to seek domination over the oil industry via the ownership of concessions. The sideshow developed in the northern foothills of the Caucasus mountains. Ludwig Nobel, brother of the inventor of dynamite, Alfred Nobel was sent by his father, who was an arms manufacturer supplying the Imperial Russian Army with guns into the Caucasus region, to secure a supply of walnut wood to be turned into gun stocks. Instead, he came back with ownership of the oil concessions on what is now known as the Baku region of Azerbaijan.

"The House of Rothschild financed (1) the Rockefeller oil empire in America, (2) the emerging alliance soon to be named Royal Dutch Shell of the Dutch and English royal houses to take control over the oilfields in the Far East, and (3) the Russian oilfield operations controlled by the Nobel family.

"After oil was discovered in the Persian Gulf region and the British secured control of it, the Nobel family was forced by a 'no holds barred' price war between Rockefeller and Deterding to sell out. In order to win this fight, Deterding teamed up with Lord Samuels of London, who had established the oil shipping industry. Josef Stalin spent his early political life as organizer of the Oil Workers Union in and around Baku. The Russian Revolution kept Russian oil off the world market for quite some time. In the early 20th century, the British Empire began to fray around the edges, and First Lord of Admiralty Captain Fisher, later a lord, argued for re-fitting the Royal Navy with oil-powered engines to give these ships speed advantage over coal-powered steamships. With the closest oil supply being in Persian Gulf, British meddling in Middle Eastern affairs became understandable. This sounded the death knell for the Ottoman Empire, which was in control of this region until the end of World War I.

"That all oil supplies for the German Empire came from the Mosul field in present-day Iraq explains fighting in the Dardanelles Gallipoli during World War I. The German oil supplies had to be disrupted.

<>

"When you look at the geography of the region and follow the railroad line from Mosul to Berlin, you'll notice that, with exception of a stretch of less than 100 kilometers, this line ran entirely in Entente territory.

<>

"The little piece of land missing was Serbia. The assassination of the Austrian Crown Prince, Archduke Franz Ferdinand on June 28, 1914 in Sarajevo, the capital of Serbia, takes on an entirely different flavor.

<>

"The rest is bloody history, as Kronberger's, *Blood for Oil,* comments. After World War I, the domestic oil industry in America swamped the country with cheap oil. After the discovery of oil in Venezuela, the Smoot–Hartley Act enacted by the American Congress was designed to keep oil from Venezuela from destroying the price of this abundant commodity. However, what it did in effect was it exported American recession globally. One of the remarkable results of World War II was that the American oil industry got involved in the exploitation of the Persian Gulf region.

"From that time on, the Middle East was racked with one war after the other that sent the oil price spiraling skywards.

"At the end of the 20th century, the American war machine had become so awesome that in the absence of a credible opponent a 'replacement monster' had to be found. This is where the perpetual sideshow of 20th century history comes in, the systematic terrorism with which Israel perpetrates genocide among Palestinian owners of the land promised, but not given to World Jewry, by the British Empire ... causing symptomatic terrorism. The entire situation, caused by the Balfour Declaration, is unsolvable by peaceful means, as no amount of goodwill from either side will ever overcome the need for instability in the region to justify inflated oil prices and provide use for over 50% of industrial production, which is arms related. This is where terrorism, yet again, rears its head. Alexandre de Tocqueville described régime de la terreur as a methodology to make the masses familiar with the realities created by elites.

<> <> <>

"From 1757, the British had a trade agreement with the Chinese Qing Dynasty which limited trade between the two nations to the harbor of Canton Guangzhou. In the early 19th century, British ships were carrying millions of kilograms of Chinese tea to England, while bringing as return freight only silver bullion. When declining to open the Chinese market to British industrial products, Emperor Qianlong declared in the classic statement to King George III, "We possess all things. I set no value on objects strange or ingenious, and have no use for your country's manufactures." Opium was long known as an intoxicating drug in China, but its use was forbidden by Imperial decree dating back to 1729. The English East India Company cultivated huge poppy-fields in India, and began selling the drug illegally in China. The earlier ban on the use was given added currency in 1796 by another Imperial decree, which banned the trading of opium in China. When in 1833, the monopoly of East India Company was broken up, China was swamped with opium from India and the idle rich and common man became addicted. In late 1838, Emperor Qianlong sent his emissary, Lin Zexu, to Canton to stop the opium trade. This man held foreign traders hostage and demanded their departure under threat of their lives. British Trade Commissioner Charles Elliott collected all the opium from the British traders and handed it over to Lin Zexu, who proceeded to wash 9 million Mexican silver dollars ... the international currency of the time ... worth of opium into the sea. The British dispatched an expeditionary force, which easily won due to modern arms and strategy against a vastly superior number of ill-equipped soldiers, led by generals who had no idea of what modern warfare was all about. With the signing of the Treaty of Nanjing, Aug. 29, 1842 Great Britain's original goals were fulfilled ...the cohong Chinese trading association through which foreigners, British traders, had to work was abolished ...four more Chinese ports were opened to trade Fuzhou, Ningbo, Shanghai and Xiamen ...and, the island of Hong Kong was ceded to the British. Just as WWII had its roots in the Versailles Peace Treaty, the Second Opium War was an inevitable outcome of the Nanjing agreement. When in 1856, the Arrow, a ship owned by a Hong Kong resident, was searched by a party of Chinese officials looking for a notorious criminal, the British flag was taken down and this escalated from a shouting match into a shooting war. This is when the French joined the fray, and together British and French expeditionary forces threatened the capital, Beijing. In the dictated Peace Treaty of Tianjin, trading rights and rights to establish diplomatic representations in Peking were granted. When this treaty was to be ratified the next year, the British delegation, some 400 men on three ships, was routed and this then resulted in the forceful ingression of British and French forces into Peking in 1860. The Qing Dynasty lingered on until 1911, when it finally broke up under Western pressure. What Voltaire had once called the most advanced and enlightened form of government had been reduced by Western *dum possum volo* 'because I can, I want', to an ineffective puppet regime. This is one facet of the evil game which was played in the 19th century in East Asia. Another was the occupation of Vietnam by French forces in 1862. As France had no strategic interests in that part of the world at that time, this venture had to finance itself. It was of no material economic importance either, and one seriously has to wonder why France started nearly 100 years of misery for an untold number of people on the opposite side of the globe.

"In order to raise the money required to establish a multinational crime syndicate, the new colonial power began to regulate the drug trade in the country. Until 1954, when the French were unceremoniously kicked out of Vietnam, elements of the French Secret Service were controlling the French military presence in Vietnam, French Indo-China. An effectively private army of up to 40,000 troops and some 350 French officers, the Foreign Legion had to be financed by the drug trade. The entire French colonial enterprise in that part of the world was a largely private enterprise based on organized crime sanctioned at the highest political levels. It seems strange how of a French private adventure which made a few French entrepreneurs rich could develop the American nightmare of the Vietnam War. The old colonial powers had been running the colonial charade for centuries, entire nations were pressed into service to generate vast wealth for a very small number of people who were the froth on the sociologically fermenting vats that the 'mother nations' to the colonial states had become. America had to learn that one cannot break a deal with one of the oldest civilized nations, Russia, for the simple reason that one was able to ... the USA used nuclear bombs to shock Japan into surrender, and the deal that Stalin and Roosevelt had made regarding the sharing of the territorial spoils after World War II was off. The Korean War was the outcome of this broken promise. The Korean Peninsula was separated into two halves in order to achieve what had been arranged by Stalin and Roosevelt a decade earlier, a sharing of the region. While the people in the North had no political rights by law and were slaves to a one size fits all economy, the ones in the South also effectively had no rights and were pressed into the service of Korean and American economic tyrants. To the average American citizen especially in those days, the developing situation in Vietnam seemed to be a continuation of the clash of ideologies that had gone on a decade earlier on 'the other peninsula over there'. In 1954, when French General Navarre lost the strategic, fortified city of Dien Bien Phu to the Vietcong under the brilliant leadership of General Giap, the colonial adventure of the French in the Far East became an orphan in need of a generous uncle. Always happy to prop up a repressive regime which provided the 'freedom' for corporate economy to wreak havoc, the USA was drawn into the next vortex of military conflict. What started as a loan of military advisers developed into a full-blown military conflict of epic proportions. The sociopolitical effect of this scenario on the entire world was incredibly hefty.

All of Southeast Asia was turned into a brothel for American soldiers on R&R, and this war was largely run by the American Secret Service. Air America, the aviation wing of the CIA, was for a long time the biggest airline in the world.

<>

While the military was fighting a war in accordance with political doctrine and within the framework of international law, the CIA financed the destruction of much of South East Asia and American society by drug running.

<>

Only few ever saw that the arrow was also the target, a logically thinking democratic society would not permit its own dregs to pervert the methodology of government into the modus operandi of an organized crime syndicate.

<>

Blum points out that over the two decades of official American military presence in Southeast Asia, the region was turned into the clandestine producer of some 70% of the heroin and opium supply consumed in the USA.

<>

Dealing of drugs and arms is an essential part of destabilizing tactics that've been, and still are, visited on the most populous region on Earth. In the 19th century, the British used China as their playground and sold drugs there which had been produced in India using the military power of the Empire to do so ...and, the USA used a phony war financed by the American taxpayer to set up the logistics needed to produce the drugs required to turn the American people into zombies.

In both instances, the social cost was immeasurable ... the beneficiaries were an extremely small number of personalities, and neither of the two episodes were possible without the knowledge, condoning and complicity of the highest levels of government and society.

Who can be surprised to learn Israeli Secret Service, the Mossad, runs a similar operation in Lebanon? Local opposition to this illicit drug industry is, as Robert Fisk pointed out in the *Independent,* Dec. 11 2002, the major drive behind the Hezbollah terrorism.

In 2003, newspapers and TV news channels were having a jolly good time informing the world how Israeli-based operations were swamping the yuppie scene with the drug ecstasy.

The 'Rape of Iraq' will relieve Israel from having to buy expensive oil and ensure that 'Big Brother' for a long time to come will render ineffective Arab opposition to the kind of treatment handed out to the Palestinian people.

The Iran–Contra Affair overshadowed much of the Reagan administration, and the shady activities at the Mena Air Field in Arkansas while Bill Clinton acted as Governor of the State led up to the G. H. W. Bush presidency.

This will be followed by disclosures of similar activities if and when the present stranglehold over the media is broken. Robbins details the involvement of the CIA through Air America in all of these strange affairs.

<>

One is tempted to suspect that the surest way to stop the trafficking of drugs and rid the world of the drug industry menace would be via the immediate disassembly of the secret services.

<>

Countless numbers of lives would be saved. Will this ever happen? The answer is simply, 'No!' Such a move would remove one of the most effective tools of government elitist control over the masses, the ubiquitous use of the chimera of national security as a smokescreen behind which secret actions take place supposedly in the interests of the nation [but in reality in the financial interests of relatively few].

<>

Continuing ...

[From, *Big Oil and the War on Drugs and Terrorism,* by Siegfried E. Tischler, PhD, excerpted from *Nexus Magazine,* Volume 11, Number 4 Jun-Jul 2004 nexusmagazine.com; additionally citing: Loy, D.A, *Can Corporations become Enlightened? Buddhist Reflections on TNCs,* in Camilleri, J.A. & Ch. Muzaffar, *Globalisation: Perspectives & Experiences of Religious Traditions of Asia Pacific,* JUST, Selangor, Malaysia, 1998, S. 5ff, ISBN 983-9861-09-3]

The new political order which comes hand-in-glove with the merging of Communism and Capitalism into globalist practices ... is a house of cards without any real sustainability. It's a somber fact that 200 multinational transnational corporations control ... and their shareholders own ... over 95% of all private business which is not owned by individual privateers, and are reaping most of the benefit. The flipside of this coin is the fact that all of this economic activity employs only 0.3 per cent of the global workforce.

<>

From this it follows that the corporate economy, which accounts for the majority of activities which continually and progressively degrade the quality of all life, is supported in all this by the private and public sectors ... they not only provide the vast majority of all employment, which is to say the wherewithal to purchase the products of the corporate sector, but also generate yet again the majority of all tax revenue. Yet, corporate enterprises and entrepreneurs in 1983 paid 13.1% of all taxes levied in Germany ... after 13 years of the Kohl government, this figure had been reduced to 5.7%. The Canadian corporate sector in 1955 paid some 25% of all taxes ...by 1998, this had been reduced to 12.2%. Moore gives figures for the USA which tell the same story ... between 1979-2002, the income of the richest percentage of the American population rose by 157%, while that of the poorest 20% fell ... profits of the richest 20% of the world rose since 1983 by 362.4% ... after the latest round of fusion in the oil industry, the profits of oil companies rose by 146%, at a time when the oil moguls cried they were "not making any money." It is a sore fact the global economy, as some 80 years ago, is again drowning in cheap oil ... 44 of the biggest 82 corporations in the USA paid taxes at a rate of 17% in 2001, while the man on the street paid 35% ... 17% of U.S. corporations paid no tax, while seven corporations among them General Motors in their 2001 tax returns claimed to be due amounts paid over and above that required ... 1,279 corporations with incomes in excess of US 250 million dollars or more paid no taxes and declared no taxable income in 2001.

During the 1980s when the term 'globalization' became a catchword, many began to talk of the 'two-thirds society'. Martin and Schumann spoke at the turn of the millennium of the 80:20 society. How much longer until democratic societies decay into a 90:10 or, as has to be feared with ever more reason, even a 99:1 society? In the knowledge of all the above facts (which are little more than the tip of an iceberg) the only meaningful question can be, How can this have come to pass? Is this not an age where we have almost global democracy, where only a few rogue states still totally disregard human rights with concentration camps and genocidal tactics aimed at ethnic minorities? Is this not the 'Information Age', where the news is reported 'live' and we can know everything there is to know? In Venezuela, a country which for the better part of a century has not been permitted stable government by an oil industry which thrives on instability, a former military officer is fighting a pretty hopeless war against American Secret Services. Army General Melvin Lopez said in an interview with the Venezuelan state-owned radio station April 21, 2002 that American agents were behind the attempted coup d'état against President Chavez April 11, 2002. Official American denials abound and have to be weighed against the noises from the White House. U.S. President G. W. Bush, himself an appointed Fuehrer, has been heard to demand the replacement of Chavez ...who has been elected twice by overwhelming popular vote with a 'democratic' leader. It is not so much the intellectual level of the person that is permitted to make such idiotic statements, but rather that of his audience, which is cause for great concern. September 11 was a most remarkable day in the 20th Century and early third millennium ... in 1920, the League of Nations promulgated a decree giving the Balfour Declaration a status of international 'respectability' ... in 1973, a CIA-sponsored coup led to the ousting of Salvador Allende, the democratically elected President of Chile ... in 1995, a New York court found a group of Iranian exiles guilty of having placed and detonated a bomb in the underground parking space of one of the World Trade Center towers ... in 2001, both World Trade Center towers collapsed after 'Hollywood-style' attacks on them. None of the evidence presented by authorities appears to merit any credibility ...and it is not surprising that dubious language is used when the media crank out yet another 'report' on the alleged perpetrators of this heinous act. The entire world is effectively terrorized by a nation which has freed itself from all that was ever good about it. Former Treasury Secretary Paul O'Neill has written a book on his time in government. Most elucidating is he mentions President G. W. Bush issued orders to his government almost immediately after taking office ... more than half a year prior to 9/11 ... for actions which were later 'sold' to the public of America and the world as retaliation for 9/11. In a 60 Minutes interview January 11, 2004, O'Neill talked to CBS News correspondent Lesley Stahl about this remarkable situation. This lets all the doubts which surround the entire situation disappear. It is high time for the thinking people of the world to take notice. The actions of 'Big Oil', the 'War on Drugs', and the 'War on Terrorism' are turning our little blue planet into what German scientist and philosopher P. J. Beumer recognized in his 1858, *Naturgeschichte Natural History*, ... "a graveyard within which higher developed life will exist in the future," Dr. Tischler said.

Sources quoted in Dr. Tsichler's article include, Zischka, A., Ölkrieg: *Wandlung der Weltmacht Öl, Oil–War, Change in the Global Power of Oil*, Goldmann, Leipzig, 1939; Kronberger, H., *Blut für Öl Blood for Oil* six decades later updated the gruesome story of the second biggest business after the drug trade; Yergin, D., *The Prize: the Quest for Oil, Money and Power*, Touchstone, New York, has an encyclopedic history of the oil business but all too often it appears a whitewash of white-collar criminality. The corporate successor to Standard Oil in a joint venture with I. G. Farben was operating concentration camps in Germany during World War II. See Tarpley, W.G. and A. Chaitkin, *George Bush: The Unauthorized Biography*. Lincoln now looks like a straw man. Every respectable encyclopedia will tell that the representative and relative of the Rothschild dynasty, Judah P. Benjamin 1811–1884, acted at different times during the American Civil War as Attorney General and Minister of Foreign Affairs, Finance and War for the South. The 'Architect of the Secession' was able to flee to England after the Confederates had been defeated and worked there as a successful barrister. That his *Treatise on the Law of Sale of Personal Property* in 1868 became a legal classic in Britain speaks a clear language. This could be phrased as, the president of one nation promised the people of another nation something that he had no right to do; on top of that, the fulfillment of that promise was conditional upon winning a war. The Rothschilds repeated this strategy with the 'Balfour Declaration caper' with equal success some 60 years later, and the labeling fraud regarding 'intentions' continued unabated. Zischka, We forget at our peril that Amschel Mayer Rothschild should be remembered for his saying that "the best times for making money is when blood is flowing on the streets."

Following are excerpts from Linda Minor's *Why the Harvard Corp. Protects the Drug Trade*, part 3, http://www.newsmakingnews.com/lmharvard-part4.htm

Appendix 5 ~ Harvard & the Drug Trade

In part one of this series we dealt with men who gained control of the Harvard Corp in the early 1800s, whose self-appointed successors still maintain control of the funds of that institution today. We showed how these men made their family fortunes by trading in slaves and opium. Their drug syndicate was set up to smuggle opium into China, alongside the British East India Company's drug smugglers. Their syndicate was based in Newburyport Massachusetts and London England and was financed, as the East India Company was, by Britain's Baring Bank. This racket, smuggling chiefly Turkish opium, provided the bulk of the family fortunes for the Cabots and other prominent Boston families.

In part two we showed the same Harvard men in Massachusetts who made their wealth from dealing in drugs were connected by family and business relationships to the board of the Yale Corp., and that is was a successor-in-name to the Perkins, Sturgis and Forbes Company ... Russell & Company ... that started Skull & Bones at Yale. It was the Germanic philosophy of Hegel learned by William H. Russell that guided him and his successors in financing competing sides of every political and social issue in order to control the outcome and arrive at a greater degree of power.

Part 3 shows successors of the opium smuggling companies in America quickly established a system to use their profits as venture capital for direct investment in strategic industries.

<>

Robert Bennett Forbes became foreign affairs manager for a merchant named Houqua, made responsible by the Emperor for China's foreign relations with the West. His brother, John Murray Forbes took over managing Houqua and China's foreign relations after Robert's death, and amassed a great fortune. Profits from the Perkins opium firm were invested in the purchase of the inventions of Alexander Graham Bell, resulting in the appointment of John Murray Forbes' son, William Hathaway Forbes, as president of the American Bell Telephone Co.

<>

William married the daughter of Ralph Waldo Emerson and had a son named Ralph Emerson Forbes, who married Elise Cabot. Elise's father, Dr. Samuel Cabot, joined the J. & T.H. Perkins firm. There is a wealth of correspondence from Cabot and Perkins family members to other prominent traders and members of Boston's economic elite and descriptions of travel accounts concerning the opium trade, in which these families were involved. Trade with China was one of the largest growth segments of the Boston mercantile establishment during late 18th and early 19th centuries. This collection provides insight into two Boston families that were the most powerful China merchants, Samuel Cabot Jr. and his wife's father, Thomas Perkins.

Boston Fruit Co. was incorporated in 1885 to raise capital for its ship-captain owner, Lorenzo Dow Baker, and his partners in Boston. Demand for bananas they imported from the Caribbean had grown so much by 1898 that the Bostonians merged with their chief rival, Minor Cooper Keith of New York, who owned a great deal of land in Costa Rica, as well as Intercontinental Railways of Central America. The new corporation was organized in 1899 by Thomas J. Coolidge and took the name, United Fruit.

<>

In 1930, United Fruit bought out competing banana company, Sam Zemurray of New Orleans, who had plantations in Honduras and Guatemala, by giving him stock in the new company, making him largest shareholder. In 1936, Zemurray demanded to have a part in management, and at the same time the company formalized an agreement to operate Keith's railroad system. Since the company's concern was making bigger profits, this brought them at odds with the interests of Guatemala's people and its leaders.

<>

T. J. Coolidge, who represented interests of the Boston Concern's investment in United Fruit, after 1899, was son of Joseph Coolidge, who in 1836, was hired by Scottish investment firm Jardine Matheson Co. ... to run opium past the Chinese police.

The Chinese, in an effort to stop the British from flooding China with opium, forbade Jardine Matheson ships from docking in Chinese ports. Coolidge's clipper ships from Boston did the job for 10 million dollars from Jardine, giving Coolidge and his financiers a fortune to invest in legitimate enterprise.

During 1873, these venture capitalists formerly known as the 'Boston Concern', including John Murray Forbes and Thomas J. Coolidge, started expansion of the Atchison, Topeka & Santa Fe Railroad ... which began building across Kansas to Colorado. Their securities were marketed by Baring Brothers bank in England, sponsor of world narcotics traffick through the 19th century. Baring's American agent for many years was T. W. Ward, followed by his sons, Samuel G. Ward and George Cabot Ward. Although the bank was based in England, it originated in Bremen Germany, prior to its move to Exeter England in 1717. By the end of the century, the bank had two American partners, Joshua Bates and Russell Sturges, who were closely connected to the opium trade.

The leaders of the Santa Fe Railroad throughout the 1870s attempted to prevent construction of competing Denver & Rio Grande Railroad from expanding its line into Mexico. In March 1875, another railroad was chartered by the Corpus Christi, San Diego & Rio Grande Narrow Gauge Railroad Co.

The Tex Mex was promoted by Uriah Lott, with financial support of Richard King and Mifflin Kennedy ... ship captains during the Mexican War, who built a fortune blockade running, using profits to acquire the world's biggest ranch in South Texas. Their partner was Charles Stillman,

whose son, James, used his profits to set up National City Bank of New York, and married off two daughters to William Rockefeller's sons.

In 1881, Lott and Kennedy exchanged the stock in their railroad for stock in a new company, called Texas Mexican Railway Co., and completed the remaining 110 miles to Laredo, Sept. 1881 with money from an infusion of capital from T. J. Coolidge's backers ... Jardine, Matheson ... the leading British firm in the China opium trade.

The committee that issued the bonds in 1882, in addition to Matheson, included Robert Fleming and Dillwyn Parrish, both were associated with Scottish investment trusts. These same trusts would later steer much of their U.S. venture capital investments through the investment bank of Brown Brothers Harriman, including companies set up by George H. W. Bush.

<>

The Texas Mexican Railway Co. absorbed the Texas Mexican Northern Railway Co. in 1906, and in 1930 acquired the San Diego & Gulf Railway Co.

The railroads competed viciously for a route through Texas to give the central interior of the U.S. quick access to Gulf of Mexico, and from there, to China. Laredo is now the major port of entry for railroad traffic between the U.S. and Mexico, and the Texas Mexican presently handles international traffic through Laredo for the Southern Pacific line, now merged with Union Pacific. The Tex Mex became part of Kansas City Southern (formerly Kansas City, Mexico & Orient Railway) system in 1995 when KCSI acquired 49% of the Tex Mex from Mexican partner Transportacion Maritima Mexicana TMM ... a company accused of drug smuggling, and its associated banks, with money laundering.

Another railroad into which drug money was poured was the Chicago, Burlington & Quincy Railroad Co., stretching to Burlington Iowa and Quincy Illinois, on the Mississippi River. Dominated by John Murray Forbes of Boston, who was in turn assisted by Charles Perkins, president of the company from 1881 to 1901, the railroad eventually reached Denver, its western terminus, and reached east to Chicago, Kansas City and St. Louis gateways. CB&Q lines also went to Omaha Nebraska and St. Joseph Missouri.

By 1910, the rail line from Corpus Christi hadn't been connected to Colorado, but the Santa Fe encouraged that expansion by men such as Sam Lazarus and B. F. Yoakum, who got financing in

St. Louis through the firm of George Herbert Walker & Co. in 1912 ...only seven years before Walker left St. Louis to set up the Harriman investment bank.

Given the fact the Atchison, Topeka & Santa Fe railroad was based in St. Louis, it is highly likely that Walker had worked closely with its owners in handling financing of various shorter lines, which eventually were acquired by Atchison, Topeka & Santa Fe railroad. In so doing, he would've worked closely with Thomas J. Coolidge of Boston, who in 1880 was chosen president of the Atchison, Topeka & Santa Fe railroad company and all its branches.

Another railroad which made up a part of the Atchison, Topeka & Santa Fe system was Gulf, Colorado & Santa Fe Railway, purchased in 1879 by the Sealy banking family of Galveston. In 1911, George Sealy II, then manager of the line, bought several oil properties which he used to found Magnolia Petroleum Co. Magnolia was absorbed by Standard Oil Co. of New York (SOCONY) in 1925, and is known today as Mobil Oil. The Texas properties, many drilled on land grants given to the railroad which was not part of the Atchison, Topeka & Santa Fe, were transferred to Magnolia Petroleum Co.

The Magnolia Pipeline Co. was organized in Nov. 1925 as a transporting subsidiary of the petroleum company. In 1931, when Standard Oil of New York and the Vacuum Oil Co. merged to form Socony-Vacuum Oil Co., Magnolia became an affiliate of the new company. In 1949, all Magnolia Pipeline's shares were owned by Socony Vacuum except for qualifying shares owned by members of the board of directors. General offices were in Dallas in 1949. The Magnolia Petroleum Co. merged with Socony Mobil Oil Co. on Sept. 30, 1959.

More research needs to be done to determine what mineral rights were owned in these lands by the various interests. It is very possible that the rights were split among the Coolidge faction from Boston, the George Herbert Walker group including Bush, and the Rockefeller group.

The pipeline company would have been closely involved with Dresser Industries, which controlled the patent on the coupling joint used in all petroleum pipelines. Dresser's stock was purchased in 1911 by W. A. Harriman & Co., supposedly with the intention of reselling, but apart from subsequent stock flotation, the investment bank (now Brown Brothers, Harriman) still has control of what became Dresser Industries in 1944. The initial stock issue in 1928 was under-

written by Roland Bunny Harriman and Prescott Bush, while George Herbert Walker was president of the W. A. Harriman firm. Prescott Bush served on the board of directors continuously until he went to the U.S. Senate in 1953. It is interesting that Magnolia moved its headquarters to Dallas at about the same time that Dresser moved there.

Thomas J. Coolidge was a large donor to Harvard. A generation later, Archibald Cary Coolidge, who merged the American Institute of International Affairs (the sister organization of the British Royal Institute for International Affairs) with the New York Council on Foreign Relations, now called the Council on Foreign Relations ...became the first editor of CRF's magazine, *Foreign Affairs*.

Ralph and Elise Cabot Forbes' daughter was Ruth Forbes, whose first husband was George L. Paine, and whose son was Michael Paine. Ruth Forbes Paine's best friend was Mary Bancroft. Michael Paine was sixth in descent from Robert T. Paine, the signer of the Declaration of Independence. Michael's mother, Ruth, was a great-granddaughter of Emerson and a granddaughter of William H. Forbes, founder and first president of the American Bell Telephone Co. Her father, Ralph Emerson Forbes, left an estate of 2.5 million dollars when he died in 1937. Her uncle, W. Cameron Forbes started his career as a clerk with Jackson & Curtis, a family money-laundering firm, and in 1899 became a partner in John Murray Forbes & Co. He was a director of AT&T, United Fruit and Stone & Webster. He was also appointed to the Philippine Commission and was vice governor of the Islands until 1913. After that he was a receiver of the Brazilian railway, and a presidential appointee to study conditions in the Philippines and in Haiti.

Michael Paine was descended from the Cabots on both his father's and mother's side, he was a second cousin once removed of Thomas Dudley Cabot and a cousin of Alexander Cochrane Forbes, a director of United Fruit and trustee of Cabot, Cabot & Forbes.

<>

Paul F. Hellmuth was vice president of Cabot, Cabot & Forbes, was a trustee of the J. Frederick Brown Foundation ...a CIA conduit, along with G. C. Cabot. Thus, the Paine family had links with the intelligence circles of the OSS and CIA. In the summer of 1963 it was Ruth (Michael's wife), rather than Michael, who maintained close relations with the patrician Paine and Forbes families, traveling east in July to stay with her mother-in-law at the traditional Forbes clan retreat of Naushon Island near Wood's Hole, Massachusetts [according to Peter Dale Scott's Dallas Conspiracy].

When George H. W. Bush arrived in Texas after graduation from Yale, his career began with an interview with Neil Mallon, president of Dresser Industries in Dallas. Dresser, which owned the patent for the coupling joint used in laying petroleum pipelines, was a corporation wholly owned by the investment bank Brown Bros., Harriman. Prescott Bush was a director of Dresser for decades, as well as being a partner in Brown Bros., Harriman ...which had resulted from the merger of the bank set up by Prescott's father-in-law, George Herbert Walker at the request of the sons of Union Pacific Railroad tycoon E. H. Harriman. Walker had previously had his own investment bank in St. Louis where he financed the railroads which eventually became part of the system known as Atchison, Topeka & Santa Fe. An investment bank still exists in St. Louis under the operation of the Walker side of the family ...that city is the home of George H. W. Bush's brother, William H. T. 'Bucky' Bush, who is a past Missouri GOP state finance chairman.

Neil Mallon had been hired as Dresser's first president after Dresser was purchased by Brown Brothers, Harriman. It was his first real job after he completed his education. The Mallon family had strong ties to the Tafts, which had been involved in the Russell Trust ...eventually to become known as Skull & Bones. It was Mallon who gave George his first job after graduation from the same university and as a member of the same secret society ...an elite group to which George, Prescott and both Harriman sons belonged.

When Mallon went to work for Dresser, the company was based in Cleveland Ohio, the same city where John D. Rockefeller had started his career as a merchant (before his expansion into oil production), financed by one of the three U.S. banks owned by N. M. Rothschild of London.

While in Cleveland, Mallon was very active in the Council of World Affairs, which had been organized in the mid-1930s by Brooks Emeny. Council on Foreign Relations had been set up in New York in 1921, quickly imitated by the Chicago Council on Foreign Relations in 1922. The World Affairs Councils are a segment of the Council on Foreign Relations.

Dresser relocated its headquarters to Dallas in 1950, and Mallon helped to organize another Council on World Affairs in that city. The operation of that organization was his chief outside interest.

One of the employees Mallon hired was Hans Bernd Gisevius, with the assignment of working on a worldwide economic development program called the 'Institute on Technical Cooperation'.

Gisevius was a German Abwehr (German intelligence) agent whose diplomatic cover was vice consul at the German consulate in Zurich, while Allen Dulles was there as the head of U.S. intelligence. While in Switzerland, Dulles began a long-lasting love affair with Mary Bancroft. Her step-mother's step-father was Clarence W. Barron, then publisher of the *Wall St. Journal*, which he purchased in 1902. In 1907, the step-daughter of Clarence Barron, Jane Barron, married Hugh Bancroft. The Bancrofts represented the high Boston Tory faction ...they were among the first settler families in 1632 that founded Lynn Massachusetts. During the next 50 years, the family was the sole exporter of sugar and tobacco for the Massachusetts Bay Colony, a trade that made it immensely wealthy.

<>

The *Wall Street Journal* represents a merger of Boston and New York interests. Boston's State Street financial center is run by the treasonous families that made their money in the British-run China opium trade ...Cabot, Perkins, Coolidge, Russell, Lowell et al. Wall Street was created and is run by the Tory faction, which followed the policy of Bank of Manhattan founders and American traitors Aaron Burr and John Jacob Astor. At the heart of the *Wall Street Journal* is the aristocratic Bancroft family of Boston.

According to Mary Bancroft's, *Anatomy of a Spy*, in 1943 Dulles asked Mary Bancroft, who was working as a spy in Zurich and having a sexual affair with Dulles, to translate a book written by Gisevius about the Third Reich. Gisevius and some of his fascist Abwehr associates had been the planners of the July 20 plot to kill Hitler ...with the idea of forming an alliance with Britain and the U.S. against Russia. According to Bancroft, "I told Allen, it all made sense to me. Difficult as it might be to believe, the conspirators actually hoped that if they got rid of Hitler they would be able to take over the whole country and negotiate peace with the Anglo-Americans. Their hopes went even further. They envisaged the western Allies joining them in a crusade against Russia, against communism. Gisevius had been sent to Switzerland to get in touch with the western Allies. Other emissaries were making similar contacts in Sweden and elsewhere."

Mary Bancroft's first husband, Sherwin Badger, was a Harvard graduate whose first job had been in the head office of United Fruit in Cuba. After a year in Cuba, he became a journalist in Boston, later moving to the *Wall Street Journal* and *Barron's* in New York ... both of which were published by Mary's stepfather, Clarence Walker Barron.

<>

Mary also had a long friendship with George Lymon Paine and Ruth Forbes Paine, whose son Michael Paine and his wife Ruth befriended Marina Oswald the year prior to JFK's assassination. The Paines were from Boston and both had family trees tying them to the United Fruit Co., through Michael's mother ...a niece of W. Cameron Forbes) and his father ...a descendent of Thomas Dudley Cabot, a former president of United Fruit.

Michael Paine's uncle, Eric Schroeder, was a friend and investment associate of geologist Everett DeGolyer, a long-time Dresser Industries director, who served on the board with Prescott Bush. Schroeder was a cousin of Alexander Forbes, former director of United Fruit. DeGolyer was a business partner of Lewis MacNaughton in the Dallas oil exploration firm DeGolyer and MacNaughton. MacNaughton had many CIA contacts, and DeGolyer's personal accountant, George Bouhe, was one of the Oswald's chief Russian guardians in Dallas in 1962. Everett DeGolyer had been a geologist in Oklahoma working for the Pearson oil companies, controlled by the same family that owned the Lazard Brothers investment bank. He was a long-time Dresser director in Dallas, where he was a geophysical consultant for oil companies. As a young man he was employed by the Mexican Eagle Oil Co., owned by Sir Weetman Pearson, who called him to London in 1918 and asked him to sell Mexican Eagle to Royal Dutch Shell. The proceeds from the sale were invested by Pearson in the creation of a new oil company founded and operated by DeGolyer in 1919, called, Amerada (later merged into Amerada Hess), a big percentage of which was owned by the British government. DeGolyer maintained offices in Houston and Dallas and was well known in the Houston and Dallas petroleum clubs frequented by George Bush. One of Degolyer's daughters married George McGhee, a State Department official who became a director of Mobil Oil, the company that absorbed Magnolia Oil Company and was a Rockefeller company founded by Galveston banking interests involved in constructing the railroad from the Galveston-Houston area to St. Louis, becoming part of the Atchison, Topeka & Santa Fe railroad financed by George Herbert Walker & Co.

Appendix 6 ~ Dillon, Read & the Aristocracy of Prison Profits

Catherine Austin Fitts is a former board member of Dillon Read & Co., former Assistant Secretary of Housing & Federal Housing Commissioner under Bush I, former president of Hamilton Securities Group, currently president of Solari, Inc., an investment advisory firm in Hickory Valley, Tennessee.

In the following, the name of 'Catherine Austin Fitts' in some cases has been substituted for her use of the pronoun, 'I' or 'my' and in some cases from first person to third person and so on, for purposes of clarification. Also, where so indicated, excerpts from a chapter of Uri Dowbenko's *Bushwhacked* ... not part of Catherine's work ... but, included to amplify it, is included.

The following is presented as selected highlights from, and summaries of, Catherine Austin Fitts' *Dillon, Read & Co. Inc. and the Aristocracy of Prison Profits.*

www.narconews.com

file://c:\DOCUME~1\Owner\LOCALS~1\Temp\W2ZQ94NU.htm

Part 1

Camel cigarettes are a leading RJ Reynolds brand. If the European Union is to be believed, Camel cigarettes are also a valued currency serving global mafia, and RJR-Nabisco has been laundering mafia drug profits.

During the 1980s, a government agent named Barry Seal led a smuggling operation delivering significant amounts of narcotics ... estimated to be as much as 5 billion dollars ... from Latin America through an airport in Mena Arkansas.

<>

According to investigative reporters and researchers knowledgeable about Mena, the operation had protection from the highest levels of the National Security Council then under the leadership of George H.W. Bush and staffed by Oliver North. According to investigative reporter Barry Hopsicker, when Seal was assassinated in February 1986, Vice President George H. W. Bush's personal phone number was in his wallet. Through Hopsicker's efforts, Barry Seal's records divulged a piece of smuggling trivia ... RJR executives in Central America helped Seal smuggle contraband into the U.S. in the 1970s.

To understand Dillon Read in the 1980s, you

must understand RJR. According to Dillon Read, the firm's average return on equity for the years 1982-1989 was 29%. This is a very strong performance and compares to First Boston's 26%, Solomon's 15%, Shearson's 18% and Morgan Stanley's 31%. Given what is alleged from the European Union's lawsuit and other legal actions against RJR Nabisco and its executives, this begs the question of what Dillon's profits would have been if the firm had not made a small fortune reinvesting the proceeds of … if we are to believe the European Union, cigarette sales to organized crime including the profits generated by narcotics flowing into the communities of America through the Latin American drug cartels.

<>

To understand the alleged flow of drug money into and through Wall Street and corporate stocks like RJR Nabisco during the 1980s, it's useful to look more closely at the flow of drugs from Latin America during the period and implied cash flows of narco dollars they suggest. Two documented situations we'll see later involve Mena, Arkansas and South Central Los Angeles, California.

<>

Excerpt from European lawsuit against RJR Nabisco.

For more than a decade, the DEFENDANTS (hereinafter also referred to as the "RJR DEFENDANTS" or "RJR") have directed, managed, and controlled money-laundering operations that extended within and/or directly damaged the Plaintiffs. The RJR DEFENDANTS have engaged in and facilitated organized crime by laundering the proceeds of narcotics trafficking and other crimes. As financial institutions worldwide have largely shunned the banking business of organized crime, narcotics traffickers and others, eager to conceal their crimes and use the fruits of their crimes, have turned away from traditional banks and relied upon companies, in particular the DEFENDANTS herein, to launder the proceeds of unlawful activity.

The DEFENDANTS knowingly sell their products to organized crime, arrange for secret payments from organized crime, and launder such proceeds in the U.S. or offshore venues known for bank secrecy. DEFENDANTS have laundered the illegal proceeds of members of Italian, Russian, and Colombian organized crime through financial institutions in New York City, including The Bank of New York, Citibank N.A., and Chase Manhattan Bank. DEFENDANTS have even chosen to do business in Iraq, in violation of U.S. sanctions, in transactions that financed both the Iraqi regime and terrorist groups.

The RJR DEFENDANTS have, at the highest corporate level, determined that it will be a part of their operating business plan to sell cigarettes to and through criminal organizations and to accept criminal proceeds in payment for cigarettes by secret and surreptitious means, which under United States law constitutes money laundering. The officers and directors of the RJR DEFENDANTS facilitated this overarching money-laundering scheme by restructuring the corporate structure of the RJR DEFENDANTS, for example, by establishing subsidiaries in locations known for bank secrecy such as Switzerland to direct and implement their money-laundering schemes and to avoid detection by U.S. and European law enforcement.

This overarching scheme to establish a corporate structure and business plan to sell cigarettes to criminals and to launder criminal proceeds was implemented through many subsidiary schemes across THE EUROPEAN COMMUNITY. Examples of these subsidiary schemes are described in this Complaint and include: (a) Laundering criminal proceeds received from the Alfred Bossert money-laundering organization; (b) Money laundering for Italian organized crime; (c) Money laundering for Russian organized crime through The Bank of New York; (d) The Walt money-laundering conspiracy; (e) Money laundering through cut outs in Ireland and Belgium; (f) Laundering of the proceeds of sales throughout THE EUROPEAN COMMUNITY by way of cigarette sales to criminals in Spain; (g) Laundering criminal proceeds in the United Kingdom; (h) Laundering criminal proceeds through cigarette sales via Cyprus; and (i) Illegal narcotics and cigarette sales into Iraq.

<>

Robert Sobel's, *Life and Times of Dillon Read*, comments that RJR was a Dillion Read client.

"With Dillon's assistance Reynolds expanded out of its tobacco base into a wide variety of industries … foodstuffs, marine transportation, petroleum, packaging, liquor, and soft drinks, among others. In the process the R. J. Reynolds Tobacco Co. in 1963, which had revenues of $117 million, became the R. J. Reynolds Industries of 1983, a 14 billion dollar behemoth."

Throughout the 1980s, RJR's huge cash flow fueled the buying and selling of companies that generated significant fees for Dillon Read's bank accounts.

In 1984 and 1985, Dillon Read helped RJR merge with Nabisco Brands, making the combined RJR Nabisco one of the world's largest food processors and consumer products corporations. Nabisco's Ross Johnson emerged as the President of the combined entity. Johnson preferred the bankers he'd used at Nabisco, Lehman Brothers. Johnson was on the board of Shearson Lehman Hutton.

To help RJR Nabisco digest the Nabisco acquisition, Dillon and Lehman helped to sell off eleven of RJR Nabisco's businesses. In the process, numerous Lehman Brothers partners joined Dillon Read. Among them was Steve Fenster, who had been an advisor to the leadership of Chase Manhattan Bank and was on the board of American Management Systems (AMS).

After tours of duty in Dillon's Corporate Finance and Energy Groups, Catherine Austin Fitts spent four years recapitalizing the New York City subway and bus systems on the way to becoming a managing director and member of the board of directors in 1986. She did not work on the RJR account. Odd bits of news would float back. They were always about the huge cash flows generated by the tobacco business and the necessity of finding ways to reinvest the gushing profits of this financial powerhouse.

Catherine comments.

"I was to get a better sense of these cash flows many years later when I read the European Union's explanation. The European Union has a pending lawsuit against RJR Nabisco on behalf of eleven sovereign nations of Europe who in combination have the formidable array of military and intelligence resources to collect and organize the evidence for such a lawsuit. The lawsuit alleged that RJR Nabisco was engaged in multiple long-lived criminal conspiracies. If you like spy novels, you will find that the European Union's presentation of fact to be far more fascinating than fiction. One of the complaints filed in the case describes a rich RJR history of business with Latin American drug cartels, Italian and Russian mafia, and Saddam Hussein's family to name a few," Catherine said.

April 1981, Bechtel, working through their private venture arm, Sequoia, bought controlling interest in Dillon Read from the Dillon family …led by C. Douglas Dillon, former U.S. Treasury Secretary son of the firm's namesake, Clarence Dillon. We found ourselves with new owners whose operations were an integral part of the military and intelligence communities, who demonstrated a thirst for drinking from the federal

money spigot. George Schultz, Nixon's Secretary of the Treasury now Bechtel president, joined our board. The planning group recommended we expand our business into merchant banking … managing money in venture investment by starting and growing new companies or taking controlling interests in existing companies, including 'leveraged buy-outs'. Rather than helping companies that needed to raise money by issuing securities or create markets in existing securities, we were going to start raising money to create, buy and trade companies.

Time, Dec. 1981, *Rothschilds are roving* comments.

"It's a little bare now," apologizes Baron Guy de Rothschild, 72, waving his hand at the empty black lacquered walls of his office on the 7th floor at 21 Rue Lafitte in Paris. Reason… the Banque Rothschild is being nationalized by the socialist government of French President Francois Mitterrand, along with the country's other major banks and holding companies. The Rothschilds, who are stepping out of the bank's management, have demanded that the government operate the institution in the Rothschild name.

"Nor has their bitterness at being nationalized been quenched by proposed government compensation payments of $100 million, a sum they believe is less than the bank's worth.

"But, the members of the French Rothschild clan will not lack for things to do with their money. Unaffected by the nationalization are the non-bank personal holdings of Baron Guy, and Cousins Baron Alain, and Baron Elie, including New Court Securities, a U.S. investment firm based in New York City, which will now receive more of the family's attention and money. And beginning January 1, 1982, New Court will change its name to a more golden sounding sobriquet: Rothschild, Inc.

"Founded with 2 million dollars 1967, New Court today manages a portfolio worth more than 1 billion dollars, including funds from such corporate clients as General Foods, TRW, and Hughes Aircraft. New Court's other owners included NM Rothschild & Sons in London, which represents the English branch of the family and is headed by Evelyn de Rothschild, 50, and the Rothschild Zurich bank, of which Swiss Cousin Baron Edmond de Rothschild is part owner.

"New Court is an aggressive venture capital firm that has 200 million dollars invested in fledgling American companies [Federal Express was an important New Court venture investment.] Last year, its return on current investment of 17 million dollars was 35%. In July, its American chairman John P. Birkelund, 51, asked the Rothschilds for more control over the firm.

"Instead, the family sacked Birkelund, named Guy and Evelyn as cochairmen and installed a new manager, Family Confidant Gilbert de Botton, 46.

"The new Rothschild man in New York City had previously directed the family's bank in Zurich, which grew from a paltry 2.5 million dollars in 1968 to its present capitalization" of more than $35MM. De Botton is currently investing heavily in sagging stocks of U.S. energy companies, especially those with large domestic reserves of oil and gas. He also plans to strengthen the firm's venture capital thrust. Says he: The U.S. is the prime market in the world for startup, small and medium size companies. "That bullishness on America's prospects is shared by Co-Chairman Guy, who has been commuting monthly since last June between Paris and New Court's offices in New York City's Rockefeller Center. Guy will not move permanently to the U.S. and Cousin Ellie's son Nathaniel, 34, a graduate of Harvard Business School, is a prime candidate to direct U.S. operations, eventually. Says Guy: My great-grandfather sent one of his sons, my grandfather Alphonse, to America in 1848. After returning to France, Alphonse pleaded with his father that the U.S. was the coming country and that there should be a House of Rothschild, there. It's an enormous pity that my grandfather's advice was not heeded. As far as I'm concerned we should have had a Rothschild bank in the U.S. since the middle of the 19th Century."

<>

Laton McCartney's, *Friends in High Places, The Bechtel Story ... the Most Secret Corporation & How It Engineered the World,* comments on Bechtel's annual Bohemian Grove club camp-out meeting in the redwood forest in northern California.

"Its membership and guest list included Steve, his father, Stephen D. Bechtel, Sr.; Henry Kissinger; former Bechtel Group President and Secretary of State designate George Schultz, bringing West German Chancellor Helmut Schmidt as his guest; former IBM chairman and U.S. Ambassador to the Soviet Union Thomas Watson; former DCIA John A McCone a former Bechtel partner; Attorney General William French Smith; industrialist Edgar F. Kaiser, Jr.; Nixon political aide Peter M. Flanigan; Pan

American World Airways' onetime boss Najeeb Halaby; Wells Fargo Bank Chairman Richard Cooley; former General Electric chairman Philip Reed; Southern California Edison chairman Jack Horton; Utah International Chairman Edmund W. Littlefield; Dillon Read's former boss Nicholas F. Brady, who was serving as an interim senator from New Jersey and, like Peter Flanigan, was Steve junior's guest; tire and rubber heir Leonard Firestone and Gerald Ford former U.S. President. This year's encampment would also include former Secretary of State Alexander Haig, FBI Director William Webster; computer magnate and former deputy Defense secretary David Packard; Chief of Naval Operations Thomas Hayward; Eastern Airlines president Frank Borman; Federal Reserve Bank chairman Paul Volker; World Bank president Alden W. Clausen; Union Oil Chairman Fred L. Hartley; Atlantic Richfield Chairman Robert O. Anderson; publishing czar William Randolph Hearst, Jr.; Southern Pacific Railroad president Alan C. Furth; show business personalities Charlton Heston, Art Linkletter and Dennis Day; the Presidents of Dean Witter Reynolds, Bank of America and United Airlines."

John Birkelund came to Dillon Read in 1981 to serve as President and Chief Operating Officer. Dillon's Chairman, Nicholas F. Brady, was considered one of George H. W. Bush's most intimate friends and advisors.

After Princeton, Birkelund joined Navy's Office of Naval Intelligence in Berlin. In Europe, he became friends with Edward Stinnes, who recruited him after a short career with Booz Allen in Chicago to work in New York for the Rothschild family. He started at Amsterdam Overseas Corporation, that moved its venture capital business into New Court Securities with Birkelund as co-founder. New Court was owned by the Rothschild banks in Paris and London, Pierson Heldring Pierson in Amsterdam and the management. He was a managing director of Saratoga Partners, a private equity investment firm that he co-founded in 1984. Corporate directorships included New York Stock Exchange, N.M. Rothschild & Co., and Barings Brothers. Birkelund was asked by President George H. W. Bush to chair the Polish American Enterprise Fund, a federal aid program designed to stimulate the then newly privatized Polish economic sector.

Bush became DCIA during the Ford Administration. After spending four years displaced by the Carter Administration, Bush was now Reagan's Vice President with Executive Order authority for the National Security Council, U.S. intelligence and enforcement agencies. Bush's authority was married with expanded powers to outsource sensitive work to private contractors, funded through non-transparent financial mechanisms provided by the National Security Act of 1947and CIA Act of 1949. This was a secret source of money for funding weaponry, surveillance technology and operations operated or controlled by private corporations.

Daniel Hopsicker's, *Barry & The Boys, the CIA, the Mob and America's Secret History,* comments.

After Carter takes over in 1976 and DCIA Stansfield Turner cleans house at CIA, finding jobs for long time CIA assets like Barry Seal became a priority "often fulfilled by smuggling … under color of narcotics interdiction," stated Hemming. "All these guys had to be placed somewhere after that choirboy Admiral started getting rid of them. There had to be money to take care of these guys." Hemming is referring to what *Deadly Secrets* calls 'Turner's Great Terror' when the new CIA Director purged 800 covert operatives after the Congressional revelations of the CIA's dirty laundry by the Church and Pike Committees investigations. These investigations, which then-CIA Director Bush fought every step of the way, led directly to the election of Carter) Even General Manuel Noriega was let go in the purge, it was a sign of the times. It prompted droves of angry CIA cowboys to enlist in the George Bush for President Campaign.

Headquartered outside of St. Louis, "The Company" launched in 1976 and grew to over 350 employees, with separate executives in charge of buying airports, leasing warehouses and giving polygraph tests to employees. There was a 2 million dollar fund for bail. In two years, The Company acquired 33 airplanes, three airports, warehouses in seven states and profits of 48 million dollars.

In 1976, Barry Seal's drug smuggling career began … according to his wife. DEA busted Seal.

"They had secret radio frequencies of federal, state and local authorities, mechanical programmers and night-viewing devices, air-to-ground radios so sophisticated we don't even have them on our airplanes," a DEA agent said.

<>

The European Union suit goes on to explain the role of cigarettes in laundering illicit monies. Cigarette sales, money laundering, and organized crime are linked and interact on a global basis.

According to Jimmy Gurule, Undersecretary for Treasury Enforcement: "Money laundering takes place on a global scale and the Black Market Peso Exchange System BMPE, though based in the Western Hemisphere, affects business around the world. U.S. law enforcement has detected BMPE-related transactions occurring throughout the U.S., Europe, and Asia."

The primary source of cocaine within THE EUROPEAN COMMUNITY is Colombia. Large volumes of cocaine are transported from Colombia into THE EUROPEAN COMMUNITY and then sold illegally within THE EUROPEAN COMMUNITY and the MEMBER STATES. The proceeds of these illegal sales must be laundered in order to be useable by narcotics traffickers. Throughout the 1990s and continuing to the present day, a primary means by which these cocaine proceeds are laundered is through the purchase and sale of cigarettes, including those manufactured by the RJR DEFENDANTS. Cocaine sales in THE EUROPEAN COMMUNITY are facilitated through money-laundering operations in Colombia, Panama, Switzerland, and elsewhere which utilize RJR cigarettes as the money-laundering vehicle.

In a similar way, the primary source of heroin within THE EUROPEAN COMMUNITY is the Middle East and, in particular, Afghanistan, with the majority of said heroin being sold by Russian organized crime, Middle Eastern criminal organizations, and terrorist groups based in the Middle East. Heroin sales in THE EUROPEAN COMMUNITY and the MEMBER STATES are facilitated and expedited by the purchase and sale of the DEFENDANTS' cigarettes in money-laundering operations that begin in THE EUROPEAN COMMUNITY and the MEMBER STATES, Eastern Europe, and/or Russia, but which ultimately result in the proceeds of those money-laundering activities being deposited into the coffers of the RJR DEFENDANTS in the U.S.

<>

This complaint is about Trade & Commerce or, more correctly, illegal trade and illegal commerce, and how money laundering facilitates the financing and movement of goods internationally.

<>

Merchants engaging in global trade often turn to the more stable global currencies for payments of goods and services purchased abroad. In many markets, the U.S. dollar is the currency of choice and, in some cases, the U.S. dollar is the only accepted form of payment. Merchants seeking dollars usually obtain them in a variety of ways, including the following three methods.

Traditional merchants go to a local financial institution that can underwrite credit.

Private financing is usually available for those with collateral.

A third and least desirable source of dollar financing can be found in the 'black markets' of the world.

Black Markets are the underground, or parallel, financial economies that exist in every country. Criminals and their organizations control these underground economies, which generally operate through 'money brokers'. These 'money brokers' often fulfill a variety of roles, not the least of which is an important intermediate step in the laundering process, one that we will refer to throughout this complaint as the 'cut-out'.

The criminal activity that provides the dollars for these black market money laundering operations is often drug trafficking and related violent crimes. South America is the world leader in the production of cocaine, and the U.S. and European Union are the world's largest cocaine markets. Likewise, Colombia and countries in the Middle East produce heroin. Cocaine and heroin are smuggled to the U.S. and Europe, and are sold for U.S. dollars as well as in local European currencies (and now, the Euro). Russian drug smugglers obtain heroin from the Middle East and cocaine from South America, and sell both drugs in large quantities in the U.S. and Europe. Retail street sales of cocaine and heroin have risen dramatically over the past two decades throughout the U.S. and Europe. Consequently, drug traffickers routinely accumulate vast amounts of illegally obtained cash in the form of U.S. dollars in the U.S. and Euros in Europe. The U.S. Customs Service estimates illegal drug sales in the U.S. alone generate an estimated 57 billion dollars in annual revenues, most of it in cash.

<>

A drug trafficker must be able to access his profits, to pay expenses for the ongoing operation, and to share in the profits; and he must be able to do this in a manner that seemingly legitimizes the origins of his wealth, so as to ward off oversight and investigation that could result in arrest and imprisonment and seizure of monies. The process of achieving these goals is the money-laundering cycle.

The purpose of the money-laundering cycle is to establish total anonymity for the participants, by passing the cash drug proceeds through the financial markets in a way that conceals or disguises the illegal nature, source, ownership, and/or control of the money.

Within Europe, the U.S., South America, and elsewhere, a community of illegal currency exchange brokers, known to law-enforcement officials as 'money brokers', operates outside the established banking system and facilitates the exchange of narcotics sale proceeds for local cash or negotiable instruments. Many of these money brokers have developed methods to bypass the banking systems and thereby avoid the scrutiny of regulatory authorities. These money exchanges have different names depending on where they are located, but they all operate in a similar fashion.

A typical 'money-broker' system works this way: In a sale of Colombian cocaine in THE EUROPEAN COMMUNITY, the drug cartel exports narcotics to the MEMBER STATES where they are sold for Euros. In Colombia, the cartel contacts the money broker and negotiates a contract, in which the money broker agrees to exchange pesos he controls in Colombia for Euros that the cartel controls in Europe. The money broker pays the cartel the agreed-upon sum in pesos. The cartel contacts its cell (group) in the European Union and instructs the cell to deliver the agreed-upon amount of Euros to the money broker's European agent. The money broker must now launder the Euros he has accumulated in the European Union. He may also need to convert the Euros into U.S. dollars because his customers may need U.S. dollars to pay companies such as RJR for their products.

The money broker uses his European contacts to place the monies he purchased from the cartel into the European banking system or into a business willing to accept these proceeds. The money broker now has a pool of narcotics-derived funds in Europe to sell to importers and others. In many instances, the narcotics trafficker who sold the drugs in THE EUROPEAN COMMUNITY is also the importer who purchased the cigarettes.

Importers buy these monies from the money brokers at a substantial discount off the 'official' exchange rates and use these monies to pay for shipments of items (such as cigarettes), which the importers have ordered from U.S. companies and/or their authorized European representatives, or 'cut outs.'

The money broker uses his European contacts to send monies to whomever the importer has specified. Often these customers utilize such monies to purchase the DEFENDANTS' cigarettes in bulk and, in many instances, the money brokers have been directed to pay the RJR DEFEN-DANTS directly for the cigarettes purchased. The money broker makes such payments using a variety of methods, including his accounts in European financial institutions. The purchased goods are shipped to their destinations. The importer takes possession of his goods. The money broker uses the funds derived from the importer to continue the laundering cycle.

In that fashion, the drug trafficker has converted his drug proceeds (which he could not previously use because they were in Euros) to local currency that he can use in his homeland as profit and to fund operations; the European importer has obtained the necessary funds from the black market money broker to purchase products that he might not otherwise have been able to finance (due to lack of credit, collateral, or U.S. dollars, and/or a desire for secrecy); the company selling cigarettes to the importer has received payment on delivered product in its currency of choice regardless of the source of the funds; and the money broker has made a profit charging both the cartel and the importer for his services. This cycle continues until the criminals involved are arrested and a new cycle begins.

Money laundering is a series of such events, all connected and never stopping until at least one link in the chain of events is broken.

Many narcotics traffickers who sell drugs in THE EUROPEAN COMMUNITY now also purchase and import cigarettes. In particular, as the trade in cigarettes becomes more profitable and carries lesser criminal penalties compared to narcotics trafficking, the 'business end' of selling the cigarettes has become at least as attractive and important to the criminal as the narcotics trafficking. Finally, it makes no difference whatsoever to the money laundering system whether the goods are imported and distributed legally or illegally. Regardless of whether he sells his cigarettes legally or illegally, the narcotics trafficker has achieved his goal in that he has been able to disguise the nature, location, true source, ownership, and/or control of his narcotics proceeds. At the same time, the cigarette manufacturer (in this case RJR) has achieved its goal because it has successfully sold its product in a highly profitable way. Particularly endearing, the European Union alludes to one of the most important secrets of money laundering … that the attorney-client privilege of lawyers and law firms, particularly the most prestigious Washington and Wall Street law firms, are a preferred method for the communication of corporate crimes.

<>

RJR has been aware of organized-crime's involvement in the distribution of its products since at least the 1970s. Jan. 4, 1978 the Tobacco Institute's Committee of Counsel met at offices of Phillip Morris in New York City. The Committee of Counsel was the high tribunal that set the tobacco industry's legal, political, and public relations strategy for more than three decades.

The Jan. 4, 1978 meeting was called to discuss, among other things, published reports concerning organized crime's involvement in the tobacco trade and the tobacco industry's complicity therein. The published reports detailed the role of organized crime in the tobacco trade (including the Colombo crime family in New York) and the illegal trade at the Canadian border and elsewhere. RJR's general counsel, Max Crohn, attended and participated in the meeting. All of the large cigarette manufacturers were present at the meeting and represented by counsel, such as Phillip Morris (Arnold & Porter, Abe Krash) and Brown & Williamson (Paul Weiss Rifkind, Wharton & Garrison, Martin London). The Committee of Counsel took no action to address, investigate, or end the role of organized crime in the tobacco business. Instead, the Committee agreed to formulate a joint plan of action to protect the industry from scrutiny of U.S. Congress."

<>

From, *Reynolds SEC filing 10-K litigation section:* http://www.reynoldsamerican.com/common/ViewDoc.asp?postID=1050&DocType=PDFO

"On September 18, 2003, RJR, RJR Tobacco, RJR-TI, RJR-PR, and Northern Brands were served with a statement of claim filed by Attorney General of Canada in Superior Court of Justice, Ontario, Canada. Also named as defendants are JTI and a number of its affiliates. The statement of claim seeks to recover under various legal theories, taxes and duties allegedly not paid as a result of cigarette smuggling, and related activities. The Attorney General is seeking to recover 1.5 billion dollars in compensatory damages and 50 million dollars in punitive damages, as well as equitable and other forms of relief. The parties have agreed to a stay of all proceedings until February 2006. The time period for the stay may be lengthened or shortened by the occurrence of certain events or agreement of the parties.

"Over the past few years, several lawsuits have been filed against RJR Tobacco and its affiliates and, in certain cases, against other cigarette manufacturers, including B&W, by European

Community and the following ten member states, Belgium, Finland, France, Greece, Germany, Italy, Luxembourg, Netherlands, Portugal, and Spain, as well as by Ecuador, Belize, Honduras, Canada, and various Departments of the Republic of Colombia. These suits contend that RJR Tobacco and other tobacco companies in the U.S. may be held responsible under the federal RICO statute, common law and other legal theories for taxes and duties allegedly unpaid as a result of cigarette smuggling. Each of these actions discussed below, seeks compensatory, punitive and treble damages.

"July 17, 2001 the action brought by the European Community was dismissed by the U.S. District Court for the Eastern District of New York. However, the European Community and its member states filed a similar complaint in the same jurisdiction on Aug. 6, 2001. Oct. 25, 2001, the court denied the European Community's request of Aug. 10, 2001 to reinstate its original complaint.

Nov. 9, 2001, the European Community and the ten member states amended their complaint filed Aug. 6, 2001 to change the name of the defendant Nabisco Group Holdings Corp. to RJR Acquisition Corp. RJR Tobacco and the other defendants filed motions to dismiss that complaint Nov. 14, 2001, and the court heard oral argument on those motions Jan. 11, 2002. Feb. 25, 2002 the court granted defendants' motion to dismiss the complaint and Mar. 25, 2002 plaintiffs filed a notice of appeal with the U.S. Court of Appeals for Second Circuit. Second Circuit affirmed the dismissal Jan. 14, 2004.

Apr. 13, 2004 European Community and its member states petitioned U.S. Supreme Court for a writ of certiorari. Briefing is complete. A decision by the Supreme Court is pending.

"Oct. 30, 2002, the European Community and the following ten member states, Belgium, Finland, France, Greece, Germany, Italy, Luxembourg, Netherlands, Portugal and Spain, filed a third complaint against RJR, RJR Tobacco and several currently and formerly related companies in U.S. District Court for Eastern District of New York. The complaint, which contains many of the same or similar allegations found in two earlier complaints previously dismissed by the same court, alleges the defendants, together with certain identified and unidentified persons, including organized crime organizations and drug cartels, engaged in money laundering and other conduct for which they should be account-

able to the plaintiffs under civil RICO and a variety of common law claims.

<>

The complaint alleges the defendants manufactured cigarettes, which were eventually sold in Iraq in violation of U.S. sanctions against such sales. The plaintiffs are seeking unspecified actual damages, to be trebled, costs, reasonable attorneys' fees and injunctive relief under their RICO claims, and unspecified compensatory and punitive damages, and injunctive and equitable relief under their common law claims. Apr. 1, 2004 plaintiffs filed an amended complaint. The amended complaint does not change the substance of the claims alleged, but primarily makes typographical and grammatical changes to the allegations contained in the original complaint and adds to the description of injuries alleged in the original complaint. This matter remains pending, but all proceedings have been stayed pending decision by Supreme Court on the petition for certiorari filed by plaintiffs in connection with the dismissal of their previous complaint.

"Dec. 20, 2000, Oct. 15, 2001 and Jan. 9, 2003, applications for annulment were filed in Court of First Instance in Luxembourg challenging competency of European Community to bring each of the foregoing actions and seeking an annulment of the decision to bring each of the actions, respectively. Jan. 15, 2003 Court of First Instance entered a judgment denying admissibility of the first two applications, principally on the grounds that the filing of the first two complaints did not impose binding legal effects on the applicants. Mar. 21, 2003 RJR and its affiliates appealed that judgment to Court of Justice of the European Communities. The application for annulment filed in connection with the third action is still pending before the Court of First Instance. Sept. 18, 2003 however, the Court of First Instance stayed the proceedings in the third action, pending resolution of the appeals from the Jan. 15, 2003 judgment denying the admissibility of the first two applications.

"RJR Tobacco, B&W and the other defendants filed motions to dismiss the actions brought by Ecuador, Belize, and Honduras, in the United States District Court for the Southern District of Florida. These motions were granted Feb. 26, 2002 and the plaintiffs filed a notice of appeal with United States Court of Appeals for Eleventh Circuit Mar. 26, 2002. Aug. 14, 2003 Eleventh Circuit announced its decision affirming the dismissal of the case. Nov. 5, 2003 Ecuador, Belize, and Honduras filed a petition for a writ of certiorari requesting U.S. Supreme Court to review the decision of Eleventh Circuit. The court denied the petition Jan. 12, 2004. B&W and the other defendants filed motions to dismiss a similar action brought by Amazonas and other departments of Colombia, in U.S. District for Eastern District of New York. These motions were granted Feb. 19, 2002, and plaintiffs appealed to the United States Court of Appeals for Second Circuit. Second Circuit affirmed dismissal Jan. 14, 2004. Apr. 13, 2004 Amazonas and other departments of Colombia petitioned United States Supreme Court for a writ of certiorari. Jun 17, 2004 B&W and the other defendants filed a brief opposing the petition, and Amazonas and other departments of Colombia filed a reply brief June 29, 2004. A decision by Supreme Court is pending.

<>

"RJR Tobacco has been served in two reparations actions brought by descendants of slaves. The plaintiffs in these actions claim the defendants, including RJR Tobacco, profited from use of slave labor. These two actions have been transferred to Judge Norgle in Northern District of Illinois by Judicial Panel on Multi-District Litigation for coordinated or consolidated pretrial proceedings with other reparation actions. Seven additional cases were originally filed in California, Illinois, and New York. RJR Tobacco is a named defendant in only one of these additional cases, but has not been served. The action in which RJR Tobacco is named, but has not been served, was conditionally transferred to Northern District of Illinois Jan. 7, 2003 but plaintiffs contested that transfer, and Judicial Panel on Multi-District Litigation hasn't yet issued a final ruling on the transfer. Plaintiffs filed a consolidated complaint, June 17, 2003.

"July 18, 2003 defendants moved to dismiss plaintiff's complaint. That motion was granted Jan. 26, 2004, although court granted plaintiffs leave within which to file an amended complaint, which they did, Apr. 5, 2004. In addition, several plaintiffs attempted to appeal trial court's Jan. 26, 2004 dismissal to U.S. Court of Appeals for Seventh Circuit. Because the dismissal wasn't a final order, that appeal was dismissed. All defendants moved to dismiss the amended complaint filed Apr. 5, 2004.

Part 2

Narco Dollars in the 1980s in Mena, Arkansas & South Central Los Angeles, CA

Mena ~ According to Daniel Hopsicker's, *Barry & the Boys*, arms- and drug-running operations in Mena continued after Seal's assassination. Eight months later, Seal's plane, 'Fat Lady', was shot down in Nicaragua. The plane was carrying arms for Contras. The only survivor, Eugene Hassenfuss, admitted to the illegal operation to arm Contra forces staged out of the Mena airport. Hassenfuss' capture inspired Oliver North and his secretary at National Security Council to embark on several days of shredding. Files that survived North's shredding were eventually provided to Congress, containing hundreds of references to drugs. An independent counsel was appointed to investigate concerns raised by Hassenfuss' capture.

As described in Catherine's article, *The Myth of the Rule of Law,* the founders note written by Chris Sanders of Sanders Research, comments.

"The investigation resulted in 14 individuals being indicted or convicted, including senior members of National Security Council, the Secretary of Defense, head of covert operations of the CIA, and others ... after Bush was elected President in 1988, he pardoned six of them. Independent counsel's investigation concluded a systematic cover up was orchestrated to protect the President and Vice President."

During independent counsel's investigation, rumors arose the Administration sanctioned drug trafficking as a source of operational funding. These charges were deflected with respect to independent counsel's investigation, but didn't go away. They were examined by a Congressional committee chaired by Sen. John Kerry ...that established Contras had been involved in drug trafficking ... and that elements of the U.S. government had known.

There is a standard line you hear when you try to talk to people in Washington, D.C. about the flood of narcotics operations and money laundering in Arkansas during the 1980s.

<>

"Oh, those allegations were entirely discredited," they say.

Thanks to numerous journalists and members of the enforcement community, documentation on Mena drug running and related money laundering is serious, and makes the case the government was engaged, or complicit in narcotics trafficking. This includes various relationships to employees of the National Security Council, Department of Justice, and CIA under Vice President Bush's leadership ... and to then Governor of Arkansas, Bill Clinton and the Arkansas Development and Finance Agency (ADFA). ADFA was a local distributor of U.S.

Department of Housing and Urban Development (HUD) subsidy and finance programs and an active issuer of municipal housing bonds.

One of its law firms included Hillary Clinton and several members of Bill Clinton's administration as partners, including Associate Attorney General Webster Hubbell, and Deputy White House Counsel Vince Foster.

Those convicted and pardoned by President Bush included former Bechtel General Counsel, Harvard trained lawyer Cap Weinberger ... who as Secretary of Defense had presided over one of the most crime-ridden government contracting operations in U.S. history.

Forbes editor James Norman left *Forbes* in 1995 as a result of *Forbes* refusal to publish his story, *Fostergate*, about the death of Vince Foster and an alleged relationship to sophisticated PROMIS software, allegedly used to launder money, including funds for arms-and-drugs transactions working through Arkansas.

Norman's story allegedly implicated Weinberger in taking kickbacks through a Swiss account from Seal's smuggling operation. In other stories, the software was considered to be an adaptation of PROMIS software stolen from a company named Inslaw, and turned over to an Arkansas company controlled by Jackson Stephens. An historical footnote to our story, is that a later study of the prison industry shows that Jackson Stephens' investment bank, Stephens, Inc., was the largest issuer of municipal bonds for prisons.

Some of the most compelling documentation on Seal's Mena operation and related money laundering was provided by William Duncan, former Special Operations Coordinator Southeast Region Criminal Investigation Division, Internal Revenue Service at U.S. Treasury. U.S. Treasury fired Duncan June 1989, when he refused to cover up facts in Congressional testimony. The Treasury Secretary when Duncan was fired was Nicholas Brady, former Chairman of Dillon Read.

<>

Brady left Dillon in September 1988 to join Reagan Administration in anticipation of Bush's victory in November elections. Duncan was fired within RJR Nabisco, and (2) Lou Gerstner, now chairman of the Carlyle Group, joined RJR Nabisco to make sure aggressive management was in place.

South Central, L.A. ~ Gary Webb's, *Dark Alliance* story documenting cocaine coming from Latin America into South Central Los Angeles during the 1980s was published by *San Jose Mercury News,* summer 1996, later published in book form in 1998. Its supporting documentation was persuasive that U.S. government and Contras were involved in narcotics trafficking, targeting American children.

Mike Ruppert, a former Los Angeles Police Department narcotics investigator was run out of LAPD after declining an offer from CIA to protect their Los Angeles narcotics trafficking operations.

After being accused by Ruppert and his evidence in support of Webb's story during a town hall meeting in South Central Los Angeles, Nov. 1996, CIA director John Deutsch promised the CIA Inspector General would investigate *Dark Alliance* allegations.

This resulted in a two volume report published by CIA in Mar.-Oct. 1998, that included disclosure of one of the most important legal documents of the 1980s -- a Memorandum of Understanding (MOU) between Department of Justice (DOJ) and CIA dated Feb. 11, 1982 ... in effect until Aug. 1995. At the time it was created, William French Smith was U.S. Attorney General and Bill Casey, former Wall Street law partner and SEC Chairman, was CIA Director. Casey, like Douglas Dillon, had worked for Office of Strategic Services (OSS) founder Bill Donovan, and was a former head of Export-Import Bank. Casey was a friend of George Schultz. Bechtel looked to the Export-Import Bank to provide government guarantees that financed billions of big construction contracts worldwide.

Casey recruited Stanley Sporkin, former head of SEC Enforcement, to serve as CIA general counsel. When Schultz joined Reagan Administration as Secretary of State, such linkages helped to create some of the personal intimacy between money worlds and national security that make events such as those which occurred during Iran Contra period possible.

From May 7, 1998, *Congressional Record*, page H2970.

Ms. WATERS. Mr. Chairman, this amendment would call for a review of the 1995 memorandum of understanding that currently exists between Director of Central Intelligence, the intelligence community, and the Department of Justice regarding reporting of information concerning Federal crimes.

This amendment is simple and non-controversial. It calls for a review of the current memorandum of understanding to ensure that drug trafficking and drug law violations by anybody in the intelligence community is reported to the Department of Justice. This information would be reported to Attorney General. The review would be published publicly. This simple amendment fits well with recent calls for a reinvigorated war on drugs.

The need for this amendment cannot be understated. One of the most important things that came out of the hearing of the House Permanent Select Committee on Intelligence was an understanding about, why we did not know about who was trafficking in drugs as we began to investigate and to take a look at allegations being made about CIA involvement in drug trafficking in south central Los Angeles, and the allegations, profits from that drug trafficking was going to support the Contras.

We discovered that for 13 years CIA and Department of Justice followed a memorandum of understanding that explicitly exempted the requirement to report drug law violations by CIA non-employees, to Department of Justice. This allowed some of the biggest drug lords in the world to operate without fear that the CIA would be required to report the activity to the DEA and other law enforcement agencies.

<>

In 1982, the Attorney General and Director of Central Intelligence entered into an agreement that excluded the reporting of narcotics and drug crimes by the CIA to the Justice Department.

<>

Under this agreement, there was no requirement to report information of drug trafficking and drug law violations with respect to CIA agents, assets, non-staff employees, and contractors. This remarkable and secret agreement was enforced from February 1982 to August of 1995. This covers nearly the entire period of U.S. involvement in the Contra war in Nicaragua and deep U.S. involvement in the counterinsurgency activities in El Salvador and Central America.

<>

Senator Kerry and his Senate investigation found drug traffickers used the Contra war and ties to Contra leadership to help this deadly trade. Among devastating findings, Kerry committee investigators found major drug lords used Contra supply networks, and traffickers provided support for Contras in return. The CIA created, trained, supported, and directed the Contras and were involved in every level of their war.

<>

The 1982 memorandum of understanding that exempted the reporting requirement for drug trafficking was no oversight or mis-statement. Previously unreleased memos between the Attorney General and Director of Central Intelligence show how conscious and deliberate this was.

On February 11, 1982, Attorney General French Smith wrote to DCI William Casey, this is what he said. Page H2971.

I have been advised a question arose regarding the need to add narcotics violations to the list of reportable non-employee crimes ... no formal requirement regarding the reporting of narcotics violations has been included in these procedures.

On March 2, 1982 William Casey responded.

I am pleased these procedures which I believe strike the proper balance between enforcement of the law and protection of intelligence sources and methods will now be forwarded to other agencies covered by them for signing by the heads of those agencies.

<>

Mr. Chairman, the fact that President Reagan's Attorney General and Director of Central Intelligence thought drug trafficking by their assets agents and contractors needed to be protected has been long known ...a shocking official policy that allowed drug cartels to operate through CIA-led Contra covert operations.

<>

This 1982 agreement clearly violated the Central Intelligence Agency Act of 1949.

<>

Given the history of turning a blind eye to CIA involvement with drug traffickers, this amendment seeks to determine whether the memorandum of understanding closes all these loopholes to the drug cartels and narcotics trade.

At this time, I know that there is a point of order against my amendment. The chairman of the committee is going to oppose this amendment, and so I'm going to withdraw the amendment. But, I wanted the opportunity to put it before this body so they could understand that we had an official policy and a memorandum of understanding that people could fall back on, and say, I did not have to report it. Yes, I knew about it.

<>

We have a subsequent memorandum of understanding of 1995 that is supposed to take care of it. I'm not sure it does.

Mr. Chairman, I submit for the Record the following correspondence between William French Smith and William J. Casey.

Office of Attorney General, Washington, DC, Feb. 11, 1982.

Hon. William J. Casey, Director, Central Intelligence Agency, Washington, D.C.

Dear Bill: Thank you for your letter regarding the procedures governing the reporting and use of information concerning federal crimes. I have reviewed the draft of the procedures that accompanied your letter and, in particular, the minor changes made in the draft that I'd previously sent to you. These proposed changes are acceptable and, therefore, I have signed the procedures.

I've been advised that a question arose regarding the need to add narcotics violations to the list of reportable non-employee crimes (Section IV). 21 U.S.C. 874(h) provides that '[w]hen requested by the Attorney General, it shall be the duty of any agency or instrumentality of the Federal Government to furnish assistance to him for carrying out his functions under [the Controlled Substances Act].' Section 1.8(b) of Executive Order 12333 tasks Central Intelligence Agency to 'collect, produce, and disseminate intelligence on foreign aspects of narcotics production and trafficking.' Moreover, authorization for the dissemination of information concerning narcotics violations to law enforcement agencies, including the Department of Justice, is provided by sections 2.3(c) and (i) and 2.6(b) of the Order. In light of these provisions, and in view of the fine cooperation the Drug Enforcement Administration has received from CIA, no formal requirement regarding the reporting of narcotics violations has been included in these procedures. We look forward to the CIA's continuing cooperation with the Department of Justice in this area. In view of our agreement regarding the procedure, I've instructed my Counsel for Intelligence Policy to circulate a copy which I've executed to each of the other agencies covered by the procedures in order that they may be signed by the head of each such agency.

Sincerely, William French Smith, Attorney General

<> <> <>

No history of the 1980s is complete without understanding the lawyers and legal mechanisms used to legitimize drug dealing and money laundering under protection of National Security law.

Through the MOU, the DOJ relieved CIA of legal obligation to report drug trafficking and drug law violations by CIA agents, assets, non-staff employees and contractors.

<>

Meanwhile, by the end of the 1990s, the U.S. financial system gorged on an estimated 500 billion dollars to 1 trillion dollars a year. The rich got richer as corporate power and concentration of investment capital skyrocketed on rich margins of state-sanctioned criminal enterprise.

Yale Law School trained Stanley Sporkin, was appointed by Reagan in 1985-1986 to serve as a judge in Federal District court, leaving CIA with a legal license to team up with drug dealing allies and contractors.

<>

From the bench many years later, Sporkin helped engineer the destruction of Catherine Austin Fitts' company, Hamilton Securities, while preaching to the District of Columbia bar about good government and ethics. He retired from the bench in 2000 to become a partner at Weil, Gotshal & Manges, Enron's bankruptcy counsel.

Gary Webb died in 2004, another casualty of an intelligence, enforcement, and media effort that keeps global narcotics trafficking and the War on Drugs humming along by reducing to poverty and making life miserable for those who tell the truth. At the heart of this machinery are thousands of socially prestigious professionals like Sporkin, who engineer the system within a labyrinth of law firms, courts, and government depositories and contractors operating behind closely guarded secrets of attorney client privilege and National Security law and rich cash flows of U.S. Federal credit.

Leveraged buyouts

Leveraged buyouts were a phenomenon that got going in the 1980s. An LBO, or leveraged buyout, is a transaction in which a financial sponsor buys a company primarily with debt … effectively buying the target company with the target's own cash and financial ability to service the debt.

Brian Burrough and John Helyer's, *Barbarians at the Gate, The Fall of RJR Nabisco*, comments.

"In 1982, an investment group headed by former Treasury Secretary William Simon took private a Cincinnati company, Gibson Greetings, for 80 million dollars, using only 1 million dollars of its own money. When Simon took Gibson public 18 months later, it sold for 290 million dollars. Simon's $330,000 investment was suddenly worth 66 million dollars in cash and securities. By 1985, just two years after Gibson Greetings, there were 18 separate LBO's valued at 1 billion dollars or more. In the five years before Ross Johnson [RJR Nabisco Chairman and CEO] decided to pursue his buyout, LBO activity totaled 181.9 billion dollars, compared to 11 billion dollars in the six years before that.

"Of the money raised for any LBO, about 60%, the secured debt, comes in the form of loans from commercial banks. Only about 10% comes from the buyer. For years, the remaining 30% came from a handful of major insurance companies whose commitments sometimes took months to obtain. Thanks to junk bonds, LBO buyers, once thought too slow to compete in a takeover battle, were able to mount split-second tender offers of their own for the first time."

A number of factors combined to fan the frenzy. The Internal Revenue Code, by making interest, but not dividends, deductible from taxable income, in effect subsidized the trend. That got LBOs off the ground. What made them soar were junk bonds. Then, in the mid-eighties, Drexel Burnham began using high-risk 'junk' bonds to replace insurance company funds. The firm's bond czar, Michael Milken, had proven his ability to raise enormous amounts of these securities on a moment's notice for hostile takeovers. Pumped into buyouts, Milken's junk bonds became a high-octane fuel that transformed the LBO industry from a Volkswagen Beetle into a monstrous drag racer belching smoke and fire.

In a highly leveraged company, the equity owner does not have control. It's the bondholder or creditor who can put the company in default. With dirty tricks available from covert 'economic hit' teams, combined with a creditor's ability to throw a company in default, who needs to be a visible owner? Unmentioned, was the ease and elegance with which junk bonds made it possible to take over companies with narco dollars and other forms of hot money financed by powerful partners hidden behind mountains of debt.

<>

There emerged a growing number of attractive business-savvy investment firms vying to be owners of record for a growing number of companies taken private in leveraged buyouts. This included Kravis, Kohlberg & Roberts (KKR), the LBO firm that took over RJR Nabisco in 1989.

<>

Dillon Read represented the RJR Nabisco board on the transaction. While the bidding war between KKR and the management group lead by Ross Johnson teamed with Shearson Lehman escalated, Catherine remembered being dumbfounded as to why anyone thought RJR Nabisco could service the proposed amounts of debt. In later years as Catherine reports, the debt was being serviced, Catherine wondered what magic tricks KKR had that mere mortals were missing.

Barbarians at the Gate, alleges they managed to win despite not having the highest bid on all bidding rounds. One wonders the extent to which the bidding process was re-engineered to ensure a KKR win and the media manipulated to make it look like the board had reasons to favor KKR over management, other than the real reasons.

Years later, reading between the lines of the European Union lawsuit, it struck Catherine that perhaps KKR had simply sheltered one of the world's premier money laundering networks and, behind the veil of a private company, taken this network to a whole new level.

In that same period, KKR recruited Lou Gerstner from American Express to run the more aggressive, more leveraged RJR.

Lawsuits filed by European Union against RJR allege that top management, including during the time Gerstner led the company as CEO, directed RJR's illegal activities. When European Union said, 'highest corporate levels' and 'officers and directors', that meant Lou Gerstner ... and through Gerstner and the board, the controlling shareholder, KKR.

Successful at RJR, Gerstner left to revitalize IBM and was knighted by Queen Elizabeth. After retiring from IBM, Gerstner was chosen to chair Carlyle Group in Washington in late 2002.

European Union's lawsuit highlights Gerstner's deeper qualifications to revitalize IBM, one of the most powerful military and intelligence contractors, and to lead LBO firm Carlyle ...that built its business on military and intelligence contractors and intelligence to which such contractors are privy.

<>

Uri Dowbenko's, *Bushwhacked*, in a chapter called, *Carlyle Group*, comments. [Ed's note, Herein, the world 'milieu' has been substituted for the word 'cabal' and the word 'scam' for 'deal'.] conspiracydigest.com/carlyle_group.html

According to corporate-government fraud expert Al Martin, author of *Conspirators, Secrets of an Iran-Contra Insider*, a first-hand account of Bush Family crimes ... the Carlyle Group has capitalized on its high level contacts within the highest circles of global power ... the Carlyle Group is the epitome of the military-industrial complex. As a Bush-milieu connected company, it prides itself on having government and business insiders and their minions in a network that covers the globe.

Chairman Emeritus of Carlyle Group is Frank C. Carlucci, whose claim to fame was being Deputy Secretary of Defense 1981-1982, and National Security Adviser 1987-1989.

Current chairman of Carlyle Group is Lou Gerstner, former chairman of IBM.

Sir James Baker III, Chief of Staff 1981-1985 and Treasury Secretary 1985-1989 under Reagan, and State Secretary 1989-1993 under G. H. W. Bush, is a senior adviser.

Sir G. H. W. Bush, DCIA 1976-1977 under Ford, Vice President 1981-1989 under Reagan, and President 1989-1993, acts as a broker and a senior adviser.

Other name brand politicos connected to Carlyle include former British prime minister John Major who is chairman of Carlyle Europe, former Reagan-Bush director of the Office of Management and Budget Dick Darman, and Arthur Levitt, former chairman of the Securities and Exchange Commission, and a Carlyle senior adviser.

The so-called Global Corporate Establishment can be described as a complex web of interlocking companies and executives. The Carlyle Group holds ownership stakes in 164 companies and ranks as the eleventh largest defense contractor in the U.S.

Martin comments.

"The Carlyle Group is a quintessential Bush operation. In other words, they don't use a dime of the firm's own capital, nor a dime of the firms' partners' capital. Including Franck Carlucci, etc. They use exclusively borrowed money and/or limited partnerships that they form to stick stock into. It is a 100% OPM [other people's money] company. This also means Carlyle Group deals are always highly leveraged because they have no equity in anything ... normally what is supposed to happen when you form a limited partnership is that the general partnership holds 5% up front. That is essentially their front-end load for putting the deal together. They take 5% of the equity for no money, that constitutes their load. Then over time, usually a period of 10 years, that 5% of the GP will gradually increase to 10%. This means that over a 10-year time frame, one half of 1% annually of the equity is being transferred from the Limited Partnership to the General Partnership as a management fee ... They take their general partnership equity, which really isn't costing them anything because they are assessing management fees or charging back to the LP management fees on top of that equity. They then take that general partnership equity and its accompanying fee stream and hypothecate it at a bank ... usually at Credit Lyonnais, the famous Bush deal bank.

"That's how George Bush Sr. was able to do the famous Credit Lyonnais fraud of 1992, when the Bush family ripped off Credit Lyonnais for 63 million dollars. What gave them the ability to do it was having their boy as chairman of the bank. They take the General Partner equity that didn't cost them anything to begin with, then hypothecate the General Partnership shares, which are non-convertible. They're still voting shares, which are non-convertible. It's not collateral.

"There is a difference between collateral and hypothecation. In other words, to hypothecate is to take a purported asset to a bank and get a line of credit or credit instrument in exchange for a pledge. They take the LP interest and hypothecate them to a loan, usually at Credit Lyonnais or they use it as a hypothecation to a Standing Letter of Credit.

"They will use Standing Letter of Credit as leverage to get into another deal to buy something else. They will use that full faith and credit obligation (FFC-LC) from a major bank and it's as good as cash. They would post that LC to buy other assets or another deal. This is how the great Republican frauds work through these LCs.

<>

"The LCs are as good as cash money, but they only become as good as cash money, when another party that owns an interest in it (because they have sold assets against it) goes to draw on the instrument. As long as they never draw on the instrument, the only thing it costs the pledgor of the instrument is whatever the fees are to carry the LC. It necessitates a 'friendly' bank and a 'friendly banker'.

"If you look at the banks Carlyle Group does business with, they're the same banks that all the large Bush frauds (50 million dollars and above) have been committed through. These include Credit Lyonnais, Bank of Greece, Jarlska Bank of Denmark, Credit Suisse, Daiwa, Banque Paribas, Banque Paribas Panama, Banque Paribas EAB. It's the same 12 banks again and again, these frauds are perpetrated through.

"With each pal that comes on board comes that pal's separate sphere of influence. Then, you build a company through a conglomeration of conjoining spheres of influence under one umbrella. That's what gives them the ability to wheel these deals with no money. Then they use an asset (at the core of the fraud is an asset and, in this case, the asset is a general partner equity on a real deal) that has been used to pledge or hypothecate to a bank in exchange for a full faith and credit letter of credit LC. Or they will do it through Marsh McLennan for instance and hypothecate it for some sort of performance, fidelity and/or guarantee instrument. Obviously Carlyle Group keeps track of how many times the same instrument has been hypothecated against a different deal, but nobody else does.

That commercial property deal that Carlyle Group owned in Riyadh was a pretty good example ... taking the GP equity hypothecating it a FFC LC (full faith and credit letter of credit) at European Arabian Bank EAB which then became part of Banque Paribas, the most corrupt bank in France and one of the most corrupt banks on Earth. Credit Lyonnais is also up there. If you're going to commit a huge fraud, it's always easier to use the large banks of Europe or Japan. These are the socialist, welfare model countries because you know the government will pump as much money as necessary into a failing bank to keep it alive. They never let anything fail, and that's why their economies have become so inefficient. How much money as the French government pumped into Credit Lyonnais in the last 20 years? Billions of francs.

"The real Bin Laden connection comes from Osama bin Laden's uncle. Osama's father's brother (Osama's uncle) ran the construction business. Osama's father was a minority partner since he had been a screw-up all his life. But, he got the contracts to build the U.S. Army bases, U.S. Army medical facilities, communications facilities and office buildings in Saudi Arabia. The Bin Laden family had been involved with Carlyle Group since it was formed in late 1970s. Carlyle represented them, then the involvement deepened from there.

"Carlyle formed a series of limited partnerships with wealthy people in the Bush milieu, including G. H. W. Bush and Henry Kissinger, who were partners in the same limited partnerships. They borrowed money from banks based on bogus equity, and similar deals. The banks then extended full faith letters of credit to the partnership that in turn extended a line of credit to the Bin Laden Construction consortium.

"Then, the limited partnership through Carlyle became not equity participants but profit/revenue participants through Bin Laden Construction Company. Since Bin Laden deals were all non-compete, non-bid contracts, they simply keyed all the prices. Key means to double. In other words, if it cost them 10 million dollars to build an office building in Saudi Arabia, they charged the U.S. Army 20 million dollars and the Bin Laden Construction Group then took a piece of that 10 million dollars.

<>

"The partnership group under Carlyle took a piece of that 10 million dollars. The beauty of the deal and how it all works is that the people who got the profit never had any of their own money in it. This would obviously make the bonds of friendship and profit taking between the Bush family and Bin Laden family even closer. This is at the heart of the way the Bush milieu makes works and the way it makes money. What makes this deals bullet-proof is these deals are made as legally complex as possible. They don't have to shred documents. You can actually follow these deals, and there is a paper trail on every single one of these bogus deals. The problem is that the paper trail is so enormous and so complex that nobody in mainstream media or credible media (as BBC calls it) can follow them. The age of investigative journalism is over, because they haven't got the money to allow journalists to 'follow the money' and put these deals together and expose them ... for example, a deal in which a limited partnership is domiciled in Netherlands Antilles, then owned by an international business company (IBC) in the Turks and Caicos, which is held by another *anstalt* or business corporation in Liechtenstein, which is the holding company. This is the complexity. They use as many different types of legally formed entities in as many different discrete jurisdictions as possible, wherein it is inherently difficult to follow a paper trail and furthermore there are jurisdictions where there is no regulatory authority and where monies and assets are essentially sacrosanct from being seized by creditors or by any other nation, and furthermore, they are tax free.

"Iran-Contra played so much a part in all of this because Iran-Contra was the impetus to change the way media does business. Why? Because, the Bush milieu was frightened that what they called Iran-Contra would be revealed to the public. It wasn't the individual frauds they were concerned about. They were concerned that if all of Iran-Contra was revealed, it would show the public the way everything works and what it's really all about," Martin said.

<>

Catherine Austin Fitts continues.

When Federated Department Stores declared bankruptcy on Jan. 15, 1990 as a result of their takeover by Campeau using unsound financial structure, Dillon Read, Travelers, and Dillon's bond buyers were left holding millions of badly discounted securities. By that time, Catherine was Assistant Secretary of Housing-FHA

Commissioner at HUD managing billions of defaulted mortgages and coordinating with the group at the Resolution Trust Corporation who were managing billions of defaulted Savings and Loan (S&L) mortgages. While Birkelund and Fenster were explaining the Campeau-Federated defaults to Travelers, Catherine was learning why Oliver North allegedly referred to HUD as "the candy store of covert revenues."

It took years of cleaning up the mortgage mess to understand that this homebuilding and mortgage fraud was an integral part of the National Security Council's shenanigans during Iran-Contra ... and a U.S. federal debt that was growing at alarming rates.

Part 3

Bechtel, Brown & Root, Halliburton, & the prison bubble

When Catherine told Nick Brady in 1989 she was going to work at HUD, he looked at her.

"You can't go to HUD ... HUD is a sewer," Brady said.

As Assistant Secretary for Housing-Federal Housing Commissioner, Catherine was responsible for operations of Federal Housing Administration (FHA), the largest mortgage insurance fund in the world. FHA had annual originations of 50-100 billion dollars of mortgage insurance, and an outstanding portfolio of 320 billion dollars of mortgage insurance, mortgages, and properties. Leading FHA necessitated significant understanding of how homes are built, how mortgages finance thousands of communities throughout America and how investors finance the process by buying securities in pools of mortgages. Catherine's responsibilities included production and management of assisted private housing, management of 7,000 employees in 80 offices nationwide, and development of network information systems and tools. In addition, Catherine served as advisor to Secretary of HUD on financial markets regulatory responsibilities, including RTC Oversight Board, Federal Housing Finance Board and Home Loan Bank Board System, Fannie Mae and Freddie Mac.

Catherine's experience as Assistant Secretary cleaning up significant mortgage fraud that lost the government billions during the 1980s confirmed HUD's financial reputation was deserved, but leading FHA provided invaluable insight into how government management of the economy one neighborhood at a time harms communities. Catherine's favorite description of HUD was to come many years later from staff to Chairman of

the Senate HUD appropriation subcommittee Sen. Kit Bond. When asked what was going on at HUD, the Congressional staffer said, "HUD is being run as a criminal enterprise."

Catherine comments.

"Shortly after arriving at HUD in April 1989, I began to learn about FHA Coinsurance program. Since 1984, HUD/FHA allowed private mortgage bankers to issue federal credit to guarantee multi-family apartment projects. After issuing 9 billion dollars in mortgage guarantees, HUD/FHA was to lose something approaching 50% of the value of the portfolio ... a level of losses hard to explain. When my staff approached me with a proposal to bail out a mortgage company so they could continue to lose money for us, I asked why we should spend money to lose more money in a way that would harm communities. After a long silence during which 30 staff members studied their feet, one brave soul explained the mortgage bank was owned and run by a major Republican donor.

"I was shocked. I pointed to my presidential cufflinks.

"'I got a pair of cuff links. You get cuff links. You don't get 400 million dollars of federal credit to throw down the drain.'"

Catherine's staff looked at her like she was so naïve and clueless that there was no point in trying to communicate with her ... better to let her learn the hard way.

Catherine continues.

"Within minutes, a screaming Jack Kemp, furious that I had not provided illegal subsidy to keep the mortgage banking company going (despite his orders to stop anything corrupt or illegal), called me on the carpet. After many dirty tricks and much ranting and raving, HUD was to turn the defaulted portfolio over to a private contractor named Ervin & Associates, a newly created company founded by John Ervin, a former employee of Harvard's HUD property management company, NHP. In the process of cleaning up the co-insurance portfolio, I got a chance to learn more about some tax-exempt housing bond deals that involved FHA mortgage insurance. Examples of these deals were those done through one of the Connecticut state housing authorities by a Dillon Read banker, Jewelle Bickford, during the 1980s. Bickford had a lot of support from two of the largest future Dillon Read investors in Cornell Corrections ... Ken Schmidt and Birkelund ... which was hard for me to fathom. Bickford was one for shortcuts and what sounded to me like more than little white lies. Schmidt shared an intelligence background with Birkelund. He served with Air Force Intelligence early in his career as Birkelund had served in the Office of Naval Intelligence. When I later realized the role of the intelligence agencies in the HUD portfolio, their comfort with HUD deals in Connecticut with high default rates seemed somehow more logical. After Bickford's housing bonds were embroiled in the co-insurance crash and burn, Jewelle somehow managed to get promoted up ... landing at Birkelund's old firm, Rothschild Inc. Which always made me wonder exactly whose bank accounts ended up with the 4 billion dollars emptied out of the FHA mutual funds at HUD as a result of co-insurance, not to mention the billions more lost in the single family FHA programs. Over 2 billion dollars was lost by FHA/HUD in the Texas region in fiscal 1989 alone. The Texas region had included Arkansas, where the state agency, ADFA was so bad they were disqualified at one point, according to HUD Fort Worth regional leadership.

"It was this state agency alleged to have laundered the local profit share of the arms and drug trafficking channeled through Mena, Arkansas. For comparisons sake, 4 billion dollars is about the amount of money that would buy you a controlling lead position in taking over one of the world's premiere money laundering networks.

"When KKR raised the war chest in 1987 that gave them the wherewithal to bid and win RJR Nabisco, it amounted to 5.6 billion dollars.

"James Forrestal's oil portrait always hung prominently in one of the private Dillon Read dining rooms for the 11 years I worked at the firm. Forrestal, a Dillon partner and President of the firm, had gone to Washington, D.C. in 1940 to lead the Navy during WWII, then played a critical role in creating the National Security Act of 1947. He became Secretary of War (later called Secretary of Defense) in Sept. 1947, and served until Mar. 28, 1949. Given the central banking-warfare investment model that rules us, it was appropriate that Dillon partners at various times lead Treasury Department and Defense Department.

"Shortly after resigning from government, Forrestal died falling out of a window of the Bethesda Naval Hospital outside of Washington, D.C. on May 22, 1949. There is some controversy around the official explanation of his death ... ruled a suicide.

"Approximately a month later, CIA Act of 1949 was passed. The Act created CIA, and endowed it with statutory authority that became one of the chief components of financing the 'black budget'

... the power to claw monies from other agencies for the benefit of secretly funding intelligence communities and their corporate contractors. Government service was an important duty and honor in the Dillon tradition, but it was a dangerous business. Congressional Committees had roughed up Clarence Dillon. Forestall had died. Douglas Dillon was Secretary of the Treasury when Kennedy was assassinated.

"Feb. 21, 1991, I left the Bush Administration and remained in Washington D.C. to invest in my own start up, Hamilton Securities. Dillon Read's Venture group invested in Cornell Corrections ... essentially bankrolling the creation of the newly emerging private prison industry. Cornell was founded by David M. Cornell, who was Operations Manager of Special Projects of Bechtel and Chief Financial Officer of its subsidiary, Becon Construction from 1983-1990.

"Cornell Corrections was created to take advantage of plans to privatize government's prison operations. War on Drugs and related mandatory sentencing were fueling an explosion in the U.S. prison population. Construction and management of new prison facilities was big business for the construction industry ... firms like Brown & Root ...who Cornell used to build their first detention center ...and those who financed them, like Dillon Read.

"According to a Harvard case study on Cornell's facility, David Cornell was pursuing the prison business at Becon in partnership with Dillon Read ... presumably the part of the firm that helps create and sell types of local government bonds that finance prisons. When Becon decided not to pursue the prison business, Cornell decided to leave and start his own private prison company. With Bechtel out of the business, Cornell and Dillon decided to use Brown & Root to construct the first prison.

"Brown & Root was a subsidiary of Halliburton, both based in Houston like Cornell Corrections.

According to Cornell's filings with the SEC and other corporate reports, Dillon used funds from three of its venture funds, Concord, Concord II and Concord Japan to make initial investments.

"As provided in Dillon's Cornell SEC filings, Dillon, Read Holding Inc., Dillon, Read Inc. and Dillon, Read & Co. Inc. listed officers and directors including John P. Birkelund, David W. Niemiec, Franklin W. Hobbs, IV, Francois de Saint Phalle as well as senior leadership from Barings, the British bank that was now an investor in Dillon, and ING ...the Dutch financial conglomerate that acquired Barings when it failed in 1995.

"Barings, the oldest merchant bank in England that is said to be a financial leader in the 1800s China opium trade, collapsed in February 1995 as a result of a trading scandal in Asia ...and was taken over by ING. Late 1991, Barings became the lead outside investor in Dillon Read, when they financed Dillon management buying out Travelers. This was the same year Dillon bankrolled Cornell Corrections. Barings' 1995 difficulties may have increased pressure on Dillon to generate revenues, particularly before it was sold to Swiss Bank Corporation (now part of UBS) in summer 1997, changing its name to SBC Warburg Dillon Read.

"In the April 1997 Dillon Cornell SEC filing, Concord Japan venture fund invested in Cornell is described as a corporation organized under laws of the Bahamas, whose principal office and business address was c/o Roy West Trust Corporation, (Bahamas) Limited, West Bay Street, Nassau, Bahamas. Hence, Concord and Concord II were onshore funds and Concord Japan was an offshore fund. The officers and directors of Concord Japan included representatives the most prestigious Japanese corporations as well as Amerex SA ...which listed its address as the Coutts Bank office in the Bahamas. Coutts is considered one of the most prestigious private banks in the world.

"May 1991, Dillon invested additional funds from Lexington Funds. Lexington Funds were created to invest money for Dillon officers and directors. Dillon made additional investments with these funds in Sept. and Nov. 1991. By the time of Cornell's initial public offering of stock Oct. 1996, Dillon Read and funds it managed and its officers and directors accumulated 44% of outstanding common stock, becoming controlling shareholders.

Based on company SEC filings, Houston-based Cornell Corrections started with correctional facilities in Massachusetts and Rhode Island in 1991 and in 1994 acquired Eclectic Communications, the operator of 11 pre-release facilities in California with an aggregate design capacity of 979 beds. An important relationship for Cornell from the start was the U.S. Marshals Service, an agency of Department of Justice DOJ, who was Cornell's primary client for its Donald W. Wyatt Federal Detention Facility in Central Falls, Rhode Island, a facility with a capacity of 302 beds.

"U.S. Marshals Service houses and transports prisoners prior to sentencing and provides protection for the federal court system. They are responsible for managing and disposing seized and forfeited properties acquired by criminals through illegal activities. Under the auspices of the Department of Justice Asset Forfeiture Program, the Marshals Service currently manages more than 964 million dollars worth of property, and it promptly disposes of assets seized by all DOJ agencies. The goal of the program is to maximize net return from seized property and to use property and proceeds for law enforcement purposes.

Nov. 1995, *New York Times*, Jeff Gerth and Stephen Labaton's, *Prisons for Profit: A Special Report, Jail Business Shows its Weaknesses,* describes problems Cornell ran into with its Rhode Island facility. This facility was financed with municipal bonds issued through Rhode Island Port Authority summer 1992 and underwritten by Dillon Read.

"Two years ago, owners of the red cinder-block prison in this poor mill town threw a lavish party to celebrate the prison's opening and show off its computer monitoring system, modern cells holding 300 beds and a newly hired cadre of guards. But, one important element was in short supply, Federal prisoners. It was more than an embarrassing detail. The new prison, Donald W. Wyatt Detention Facility, is run by a private company and financed by investors. The Federal Government had agreed to pay the prison $83 a day for each prisoner housed. Without a full complement of inmates, it could not hope to survive. So, the prison's financial backers began a sweeping lobbying effort to divert inmates from other institutions. Rhode Island's political leaders pressed Vice President Al Gore while he was visiting the state, and top officials at Justice Department to send more prisoners. Facing angry bondholders and insolvency, Cornell Corrections turned to a lawyer who was brokering prisoners for privately run institutions in search of inmates. The lawyer, Richard Crane, has done legal work for private corrections companies and Government penal agencies. He put Wyatt managers in touch with North Carolina officials. Soon afterward, 232 prisoners were moved to Rhode Island from North Carolina, and Mr. Crane was paid an undisclosed sum by Cornell Corrections," Labaton said.

Cornell's Donald C. Wyatt facility became a case study at Harvard Design School's Center for Design Informatics. This was an indication of the wave of business and investment opportunities prisons and enforcement presented to everyone, from architects to construction companies to real estate and tax-exempt bond investors. Harvard's case study mentions Cornell arranged for the facility to be constructed by Brown & Root of Houston, Texas, a subsidiary of Halliburton. (Brown & Root is now known as KBR, Brown & Root.) KBR, Brown & Root's construction of prison facilities was to become visible many years later after construction of detention facilities at Guantanamo Bay, prisoner of war camps in Iraq, and winning contracts to build detention centers for Department of Homeland Security.

Dillon Read had long-standing relationships with Brown & Root, and the Houston banking and business leadership, as a result of the firm's historical role in underwriting oil and gas companies, including pipelines. In 1947, Herman and George Brown, founders of Brown & Root, were part of a group of Texas businessmen banked by Dillon Read as investor and underwriter to form Texas Eastern Transmission Co. to buy 'Big Inch' and 'Little Big Inch' pipelines in a privatization by the U.S. government.

Texas Eastern pipelines were critical to bring natural gas from Texas and the Southwest to Eastern markets. For most Americans, Houston and New York seem far apart. However, the intimacy of their connection is better understood when you study investment syndicates that controlled the railroad, canals, pipelines, and other transportation systems that connected these markets and helped to determine control of the local retail businesses for both goods and capital along the way. For example, Texas Eastern's Big Inch pipeline went from east Texas to Linden, New Jersey, some 30 miles away from the Dillon and Brady estates in New Jersey and approximately 20 miles from the Dillon Read offices on Wall Street.

Dan Briody's, *Halliburton Agenda, Politics of Oil and Money,* comments.

"Brown brothers netted 2.7 million dollars in profits on their shares in their initial public offering after the company was formed and won the bid to buy the pipelines from the government in the late 1940s. Brown & Root subsequently worked on 88 different jobs for Texas Eastern, and generated revenues of 1.3 billion dollars from Texas Eastern between 1947 and 1984," Briody said.

Robert Sobel's, *Life and Times of Dillon Read,* comments.

Under August Belmont's personal leadership of the transaction, Dillon Read also made a profit on the Texas Eastern shares. "Nothing is known of Dillon Read's profits on the underwriting, but it was a sizeable owner of TETCO [Texas Eastern] common, acquired at 14 cents a share, which rose to $9.50," Briody said.

Closeness of the Brown & Root relationship with Dillon Read is underscored by Briody's description of the head of Brown & Root's frustration with Lyndon Johnson's decision to serve as John Kennedy's running mate. He quotes August Belmont, then a leader of Dillon Read, who was with Brown in Houston in his private hotel suite listening to radio coverage of Johnson's announcement. According to Belmont, "Herman Brown … jumped up from his seat and said, 'Who told him he could do that?' and ran out of the room."

What Briody doesn't mention is allegations regarding Brown & Root's involvement in narcotics trafficking. Former LAPD narcotics investigator Mike Ruppert described his break up with fiancé Teddy … an agent dealing narcotics and weapons for CIA while working with Brown & Root.

From the Wilderness Mike Ruppert's, *Halliburton's Brown and Root is One of the Major Components of the Bush-Cheney Drug Empire.*

Mike Ruppert comments.

"Arriving in New Orleans in early July, 1977 I found her living in an apartment across the river in Gretna. Equipped with scrambler phones, night vision devices and working from sealed communiqués delivered by naval and air force personnel from nearby Belle Chasse Naval Air Station, Teddy was involved in something truly ugly. She was arranging for large quantities of weapons to be loaded onto ships leaving for Iran. At the same time she was working with Mafia associates of New Orleans Mafia boss Carlos Marcello to coordinate the movement of service boats that were bringing large quantities of heroin into the city. The boats arrived at Marcello controlled docks, unmolested by even the New Orleans police she introduced me to, along with divers, military men, former Green Berets and CIA personnel. The service boats were retrieving the heroin from oil rigs in the Gulf of Mexico, oil rigs in international waters, oil rigs built and serviced by Brown & Root. The guns Teddy monitored, apparently Vietnam era surplus AK 47s and M16s, were being loaded onto ships also owned or leased by Brown & Root. And more than once during the eight days I spent in New Orleans I met and ate at restaurants with Brown & Root employees who were boarding those ships and leaving for Iran within days," Ruppert said.

Catherine continues.

Another important relationship for Houston-based Cornell Corrections was California

Department of Corrections. When Cornell Corrections started, California had the largest prison population of any U.S. governmental entity. In part due to extraordinary growth in incarcerations of non-violent drug users as a result of the War on Drugs, the federal prison population managed by the Federal Bureau of Prisons at the Department of Justice has become the largest, with 186,560 based on their September 8, 2005 weekly update. California is close behind with 168,000 youths and adults incarcerated in California prisons and 116,000 subject to parole.

Cornell's early years of business were not financially profitable. The private prison industry faced significant resistance and legal and operational challenges to privatizing federal, state, and local prison capacity. Within the private prison industry, Cornell faced competition for new contracts and acquisitions from two larger, more experienced companies, CCA and Wackenhut. By 1995, compared to industry leaders, Florida-based Wackenhut and Tennessee-based Corrections Corporation of America (CCA), Cornell Corrections appeared to be lagging in government contract growth. As of mid-1996, Cornell was carrying 8 million dollars of cumulative losses on its balance sheet.

Cornell's chief financial officer, treasurer and secretary was Steven W. Logan, who served as an experienced manager in Arthur Anderson's Houston office. This was the same office of Arthur Anderson that served as Enron's auditor until the Enron bankruptcy brought about the indictment and conviction of Arthur Andersen.

Arthur Andersen was Cornell's auditor, having first served as a consultant to create market studies which helped support the approvals for and financing of the building of the Rhode Island facility for the U.S. Marshals Service. Logan was later forced out of Cornell after an off-balance sheet deal engineered with the help of a former Dillon Read banker Joseph H. Torrence, like those done for Enron was called into question and significant stock value declines triggered litigation from shareholders.

Most venture capital investors exit their investment within 5 years. That means Dillon Read would have wanted to establish their exit from Cornell by 1996. The stock market was hungry for Initial Pubic Offerings (IPOs) where a new company sells its stock to the public for the first time. Venture capitalists typically make their profit from financing a company then selling their equity when a public market can been established for the company's stock. However, by the end of 1995, Cornell's story was not exciting. It was not a market leader, its growth was slow, it had no profits. If the calf was going to market, it would need fattening.

Prison stocks are valued on a 'per bed' basis, based on number of beds provided and profit per bed. 'Per bed' is a euphemism for people sentenced to be housed in a prison. There are two ways to make the stock go up. (1) You increase net income by increasing capacity ... the number of 'beds', or profitability in 'profits per bed'. Or (2) you increase the multiple at which the stock trades by increasing the markets' expectations of how many beds ... or what your profit per bed will be ... and by being accessible to the widest group of investors.

For example, passing laws regarding mandatory sentencing or other rules that will increase need for prison capacity can increase value of private prison company stock without those companies getting additional contracts or business. The passage, or anticipation of a law to increase demand for private prisons is a 'stock play' in and of itself.

Catherine continues.

'Pop' is a word I learned on Wall Street to describe the multiple of income at which a stock is valued by the stock market. So, if a stock like Cornell Corrections trades at 15 times its income, that means for every 1 million dollars of net income it makes, its stock goes up 15 million dollars. The company may make 1 million dollars, but its 'pop' is 15 million dollars. Folks make money in the stock market from the stock going up. On Wall Street, it's all about 'pop'.

For example, in 1996 when Cornell went public, based on financial information provided in the offering document provided to investors, its stock was valued at $24,241 per bed. This means for every contract Cornell got to house one prisoner at that time, their stock went up in value by an average of $24,261. According to prevailing business school philosophy, this is the stock market's current present value of the future flow of profit flows generated through the management of each prisoner. This is why longer mandatory sentences are worth so much to private prison stocks. A prisoner in jail for twenty years has a twenty-year cash flow associated with his incarceration, as opposed to one with a shorter sentence or one eligible for an early parole. This means there will have been created a significant number of private interests, investment firms, banks, attorneys, auditors, architects, construction firms, real estate developers, bankers, academics, investors among them ... who have a vested interest in increasing prison population and keeping people behind bars as long as possible.

The winner in the global corporate game is the guy who has the most income running through the highest multiple stocks. He is the winning 'pop player'. Like the guy who wins at monopoly because he buys up all the properties on the board, he can buy the other companies. So, the private prison company that wins is the one that gets the most contracts that guarantee it the most prisons, and prisoners that generate the most income for the longest period ... with the smallest amount of risk.

Part 4
Clinton Administration
Progressives for For-Profit Prisons

Much has been written about the use of the War on Drugs to intentionally disenfranchise poor people and engineer the centralization of political and economic power in the U.S. and globally, including an explosive rise in the U.S. prison population. One person who described it frankly during the Clinton years was former CIA Director William Colby, who wrote in an investment newsletter in 1995.

"The Latin American drug cartels have stretched their tentacles much deeper into our lives than most people believe. It's possible they are calling the shots at all levels of government," Colby said.

<>

The Clinton Administration took the groundwork laid by Nixon, Reagan, and Bush, and embraced and blossomed the expansion and promotion of federal support for police, enforcement and the War on Drugs, with a passion hard to understand ... until you realized that American financial system was dependent on attracting the 500 billion to 1 trillion dollars of annual money laundering.

Globalizing corporations, deepening deficits and housing bubbles required attracting vast amounts of capital. Attracting capital also required making the world safe for reinvestment of profits of organized crime and the war machine. Without growing organized crime and military activities through government budgets and contracts, the economy would stop centralizing.

<>

The Clinton Administration was to govern a doubling of the federal prison population. Whether by subsidy, credit, and asset forfeiture kickbacks to state and local government or by increased laws, regulations, and federal sentencing and imprisonment, the supremacy of the federal enforcement infrastructure and the industry it feeds was to be a Clinton legacy. One of the major initiatives by President Clinton was the Omnibus Crime Bill, signed into law in Sept. 1994. This legislation implemented mandatory sentencing, authorized 10.5 billion dollars to fund prison construction that mandatory sentencing would help require, loosened rules allowing federal asset forfeiture teams to keep and spend the money their operations made from seizing assets, and provided federal monies for local police. The legislation provided a variety of pork for the Clinton Administration constituency ... Community Development Corporations (CDCs) and Community Development Financial Institutions (CDFIs) became instrumental during this period, in putting a socially acceptable face on increasing central control of local finance and shutting off equity capital to small business.

The potential impact on the private prison industry was significant. With the bill only through the house, former Attorney General Benjamin Civiletti joined the board of Wackenhut Corrections, which went public in July 1994 with an initial public offering of 2.2 million shares. By the end of 1998, Wackenhut stock market value increased ten times. When Catherine visited their website at that time it offered a feature that flashed the number of beds they owned and managed. The number increased as she was watching it ... the prison business was growing that fast. [Ed's note, Wackenhut is allegedly staffed by many former spooks.]

Katherine continues.

Clinton Administration didn't wait for Omnibus Crime Bill to build the federal enforcement infrastructure. Government-wide, agencies were encouraged to cash in on support in both Executive Branch and Congress for authorizations and programs ... many justified under the umbrella of the War on Drugs ... that allowed agency personnel to carry weapons, make arrests and generate revenues from money makers such as civil money penalties and asset forfeitures and seizures. Indeed, federal enforcement was moving towards a model that some would call 'for profit' faster than one could say 'Sheriff of Nottingham'.

Feb. 4, 1994, Vice President Al Gore announced Operation Safe Home, a new enforcement program at HUD. Gore was a former senator from Tennessee. His hometown, Nashville, was home of the largest private prison company, Corrections

Corporation of America (CCA). He was joined at the press conference by Treasury Secretary Lloyd Bentsen, Attorney General Janet Reno, Drug Policy Director Lee Brown, and HUD Secretary Henry Cisneros, who said Operation Safe Home initiative would claim 800 million dollars of HUD's resources. Operation Safe Home was to receive support from the Senate and House appropriations committees. It turned HUD Inspector General's office from an auditor of program areas … to a developer of programs competing for funding with the offices they were supposed to be auditing …a serious conflict of interest and built-in failure of government internal controls.

According to the announcement, Operation Safe Home was expected to "combat violent crime in public and assisted housing." As part of this program, HUD Office of Inspector General (OIG) coordinated with various federal, state and local enforcement task forces. Federal agencies that partnered with HUD included FBI, Drug Enforcement Agency (DEA), Bureau of Alcohol, Tobacco and Firearms (ATF), Internal Revenue Service (IRS), Secret Service, U.S. Marshal's Service, Postal Inspection Service, U.S. Customs Service, Immigration and Naturalization Service (INS), and Department of Justice (DOJ).

The primary performance measures reported in the HUD OIG Semi-Annual Performance Report to Congress for this program are the total number of asset forfeitures/seizures, equity skimming collections and arrests. Subsequent intra-agency efforts such as the 'ACE' program sponsored by DOJ and initiated by U.S. Attorney's Offices, working with the DOJ Asset Forfeiture Fund, HUD OIG and HUD Office of General Counsel promoted revenue generating activities as well.

The Mr. Crane who they have hired to develop the contract is the same Mr. Crane who arranged for the prisoners to be shipped from North Carolina to Rhode Island to save Cornell Corrections and Dillon Read's municipal bond buyers.

Christopher Edley, Jr., Harvard Law Professor who served in the Office of Management & Budget engineered the federal budget to support privatized federal prisons, became Dean of Berkeley Law School.

Deputy Attorney General Jamie Gorelick, who according to *New York Times* had overseen the new policy of prison privatization, left DOJ in 1997. She became a Vice Chair of Fannie Mae, a 'government sponsored enterprise'. This means it is a private company that enjoys significant gov-

ernmental support. Fannie Mae buys mortgages and combines them in pools. They then sell securities in these pools as a way of increasing the flow of capital to the mortgage markets.

The reader can appreciate why Wall Street would welcome someone as accommodating as Gorelick at Fannie Mae. This was a period the profits rolled in from engineering the most spectacular growth in mortgage debt in U.S. history.

"They have turned our homes into ATM machines," a real estate broker said.

Fannie Mae has been a leading player in centralizing control of the mortgage markets into Washington D.C. and Wall Street. And that means, as people were rounded up and shipped to prison as part of Operation Safe Home, Fannie was right behind to finance the gentrification of neighborhoods.

And, that is before we ask questions about the extent to which the estimated annual financial flows of 500 billion to 1 trillion dollars money laundering through the U.S. financial system or money missing from the U.S. government are reinvested into Fannie Mae securities.

During Clinton Administration while U.S. prison population was soaring from 1 million to 2 million people and U.S. government and consumer debt was skyrocketing, Harvard Endowment was growing from 4 billion to 19 billion dollars.

<>

Catherine continues.

"One of Hamilton Securities Group's goals was to map out how flows of money worked in the U.S., and create software tools that would make this information accessible to communities. We believed the way to re-engineer government was for citizens to have access to information about the sources and uses of taxes and government spending and financing in their community, and to participate in the process of making sure that these investments were managed to return our neighborhoods to a 'Popsicle Index' of 100 percent. Our popsicle index was how safe you or your child could be going out in the neighborhood to buy a popsicle.

"Transparency is essential for private markets to work and for government investment to be supportive of and accountable to both the democratic process and free markets. Otherwise, we will veer toward larger governments and central banks used to subsidize progressively less efficient corporations and private activities with growing corruption.

"I was trying to find a way for us to shift to a

win-win economic paradigm that was, by its nature …decentralizing.

"The Hamilton Securities Group was financed with the money I made as a partner of Dillon Read and the sale of my home in Washington and then financed internally with profits. Several years after starting, we won a contract by competitive bid to serve as the lead financial advisor to the Federal Housing Administration FHA at HUD. As a result, I had the opportunity to serve Clinton Administration in capacity of President of The Hamilton Securities Group, in addition to having served as Assistant Secretary of Housing-FHA Commissioner in the first Bush Administration. One of our assignments for HUD was serving as lead financial advisor for 10 billion dollars of mortgage loan sale auctions. Using online design books and our own analytic software tools, as well as bidding technology from Bell Laboratories we adapted for financial applications, we were able to significantly increase HUD's recovery performance on defaulted mortgages, generating 2.2 billion dollars of savings for FHA Mutual Mortgage Insurance and General Funds. While we plowed our profits back into expenses of building databases and software tools and into banking a community-based data servicing company, we were profitable, generating 16 million dollars of fee revenues and 2.3 million dollars of net income in 1995.

< >

"While the loan sales were a great success for taxpayers, homeowners, and communities, it turned out that they were a significant threat to the traditional interests that fed at the trough of HUD programs, contracts and related FHA mortgage and Ginnie Mae, Fannie Mae, and Freddie Mac mortgage securities operations.

"For example, if you illuminated sources and uses of government resources on a neighborhood-by-neighborhood basis, you'd see government monies spent in ways that created a fat stock market and personal profits for insiders … at expense of more productive outsiders, are providing most of the tax and other resources used.

"Insiders could include big developers and property management companies that specialized in HUD-subsidized properties, like Harvard Endowment-owned National Housing Partners (NHP) and affiliated mortgage banking operations like Washington Mortgage (WMF), or for investment bankers like Dillon Read or Stephens who issued municipal housing bonds for agencies like the Arkansas Development and Finance Agency.

When Catherine suggested to head of HUD's Hope VI public housing construction program during Clinton Administration she could spend $50,000 per home to rehab single family homes owned by FHA rather than spending $250,000 to create one new public housing apartment in the same community, she got frustrated and said, "How would we generate fees for our friends?"

Catherine's efforts at Hamilton Securities Group to help HUD achieve maximum return on the sale of its defaulted mortgage assets coincided with a worldwide process of 'privatization' in which assets were being transferred out of governments worldwide at significantly below market value in a manner providing extraordinary windfall profits and equity to private corporations and investors.

Catherine continues.

"In addition, government functions were being outsourced at prices way above what should have been market price or government costs … again stripping governmental and community resources in a manner that subsidized private interests. This is why I now refer to privatization as 'pirate-ization'.

"One of the consequences was to increase political power of companies and investors dependent on this type of back door subsidy … lowering overall social and economic productivity. Therefore, Hamilton Securities Group's doubling of government recovery rates on defaulted mortgages from 35% to 70-90% was counter to global trends. We were requiring investors like Harvard Endowment to pay full price for assets …while it appeared they and investors like them were engineering deeper and deeper windfall discount prices in the U.S. and globally. Subsequent litigation against Harvard and independent journalist coverage regarding their role as a government contractor in Russia illuminated the extent of the windfall profits that they and members of their networks were able to engineer. A criticism I now have that I did not understand at the time was loan sales policies of insisting on open competition at the highest price ran the risk of advantaging players who were the most successful at laundering money for the 'black budget'.

"Things took a darker turn when we started Edgewood Technology Services, a data servicing company in an Afro-American residential community in Washington, D.C. Edgewood gave us the ability to build powerful databases and software tools and understand the investment opportunity to train people working at minimum wage jobs, or living on subsidies, to develop marketable skills and earning power … by doing financial data servicing and software development.

"We discovered it was less expensive to train people to do these jobs than to fund their living on HUD subsidies, let alone going to prison.

"For example, a woman with two children living in subsidized housing in Washington, D.C. on welfare and food stamps cost the government $55,000. In 1996, the General Accounting Office (GAO) published a study showing that on average total annual expenditures for federal, state and local prisoners was $150,000 per prisoner. Presumably this included overhead and capital costs. If government funded the care of her two children while she was in prison, those costs would be in addition.

"What we found at Edgewood was there was a portion of the work force that, due to obligations to children and elderly parents, was not able to commute. Some of these people could be a productive work force working near their home and developing computer and software skills at their own pace. If training was combined with creation of jobs, the economics of training people to do these jobs was sustainable ...and with proper screening and management could be profitable for the private sector. Potential savings to the public sector was astonishing ...not to mention potential improvement in quality of life for cities, suburbs and rural communities. With government leadership and large corporations working to move jobs abroad, people in the U.S. would need these skills and jobs. Moreover, small businesses would need access to the kinds of equity we were proposing to invest in community venture capital, and to encourage communities to circulate internally ... rather than investing retirement savings in large banks and corporations.

"Hamilton Securities Group helped HUD develop a program to allow some of the costs of community learning centers to be funded from HUD property subsidy flows. This allowed apartment buildings in communities experiencing welfare reform, cutbacks in domestic programs and unemployment from jobs moving abroad to help residents improve their ability to generate income. It encouraged linkages between private real estate managers and community colleges and other organizations committed to helping people learn new skills.

<>

"As I traveled around the country, it became apparent data servicing jobs like those we were prototyping at Edgewood were highly competitive with jobs in the illegal economy.

"In other words, data servicing jobs paying $8-

$10 per hour offering health care benefits and the opportunity to improve skills had the potential to attract a surprising number of people away from dealing drugs in areas with heavy drug dealing, prostitution and other street crime. Hamilton Securities Group's primary competition for the multi-racial younger portion of this work force appeared to be organized crime and the industries they feed ...including enforcement and private prisons.

"While the initial response was positive from a number of quarters, there was concern from special interests whose business had become, managing 'the poor.' Many of these were traditionally powerful Democratic constituencies, including private for-profits, foundations, universities, and not-for-profit agencies that had built up a significant infrastructure servicing and supporting these programs. If people were no longer poor, what was their purpose? When we made a presentation to a group of leading foundations, in partnership with a Los Angeles entertainment company interested in using entertainment skills to make training fun, the head of low-income programs at Fannie Mae told me that it was the most depressing presentation he'd ever seen. It implied the poor didn't need his help ... that his life and work had no meaning.

"Real estate interests that were hoping to gentrify neighborhoods as a result of welfare were also not pleased. They'd make more money turning over populations.

One HUD official told Catherine that when the HUD Inspector General saw this June 1996 *Washington Post* article about Edgewood Technology Services she said "That's it, I'm going to get her (referring to Catherine)."

Catherine continues.

"We were also warned HUD Inspector General's office had a very negative response, with one of the enforcement team members referring to our efforts as 'computers for [expletive deleted] re: African Americans. Essentially, what we were proposing was in competition with their enforcement business ... which consisted of dropping 200 person 'swat' teams into a neighborhood to round up and arrest lots of young people who were in the wrong place at the wrong time and couldn't afford an attorney.

"If communities had easy access to this data, the pro-centralization team of Washington and Wall Street would be in trouble. Everything from HUD real estate companies to private prisons would be shown to make no economic sense. And billions of government contracts, subsidies and financing made no economic sense. Indeed, communities were better off without them. Through our software, private citizens would see the cost of decades of accumulated 'fees for our friends'. And, that was before we even asked the following question. 'Who was bringing in narcotics and where was all the money from the trafficking going?'

<>

"If enough people stopped dealing drugs and taking drugs, then, who needed more prisons and all these enforcement agencies and War on Drugs contractors?

"Ask and answer those questions … as communities would now be able to start to do with tools like Community Wizard … and Iran-Contra style narcotics trafficking, the private prison industry, and the 'Sheriff of Nottingham-style' enforcement programs in vogue at the White House, DOJ and HUD OIG might drop dead in the water.

<>

As part of Catherine's efforts, she started to publish maps on the Internet of defaulted HUD mortgages in affected places and to encourage HUD to create place-based bids that would integrate different types of assets in one place. If successful, it would permit us to create bids that optimized total government performance in a particular place. including all contracts, subsidies and services.

Catherine continues.

"One of the maps we put up in the spring of 1996 was a map of the properties collateralizing defaulted HUD single-family mortgages in South Central Los Angeles, California. The map showed significant HUD defaults and losses in the same area … as the crack cocaine epidemic that was the basis of Gary Webb's allegations in, *Dark Alliance*. Such heavy default patterns are symptoms of a systemic and very expensive problem … including systemic fraud. This could occur in situations such as those in which mortgages were being used to finance homes above market prices with inflated appraisals or where defaulted mortgages were being passed back to private parties at below market values, or where these types of mortgage fraud were supporting fraudulently issued mortgage securities that didn't have real collateral behind them. This is the type of mortgage fraud that launders profits in a way that can multiply them by many times.

"Los Angeles was also the area with the largest flow of activities in the Department of Justice's Asset Forfeiture Fund. Whether drug arrests and incarcerations, legal support for HUD foreclo-sures and enforcement or asset seizures and forfeitures …these maps were illuminating areas that were big business for 'Sheriff of Nottingham-style' operations.

"The central banking-warfare investment model that has ruled us for the last 500 years depends on being able to combine high margin profits of organized crime with low cost of capital and liquidity that comes with governmental authority and popular faith in the rule of law.

"Our economy depends on insiders having their cake and eating it too … and subsidizing a free lunch by stealing from someone else. This works well when the general population shares some of the subsidy, grows complacent and does not see the 'real deal' on how the system works.

<>

"However, liquidity and governmental authority will erode if the general population becomes aware of how things really work. As this happens, they lose faith in the myth that the current system is fundamentally legitimate.

<>

"This jeopardizes the financial markets that depend on fraudulent collateral and practices to continue to work. It jeopardizes the wealth and power of people winning with financial fraud.

<>

"Extraordinary attention and sums of money are invested in affirming the myth and appearance of legitimacy. This includes creating popular explanations of why the rich and powerful are lawful and ethical and the venal poor, hostile foreigners, crafty mobsters, and incompetent and irresponsible middle class bureaucrats are to blame for the success of narcotics trafficking, financial fraud and other forms of organized crime.

"If the normal successful retail industry … for example, women's clothing or cars … has an advertising and marketing budget of … let's just pick a number of, say, 10% of revenues … then, what do we think that an estimated 500 billion to 1 trillion dollars of annual U.S. money laundering flows will spend to protect its market franchise?

"Working with 10%, how do we think 50 billion to 100 billion dollars would be spent to protect the brand …particularly when governmental budgets can be used to fund the effort?

"The process of compromising and controlling honest business and government leaders and journalists … or destroying them when they can not be controlled …are closely guarded secrets known to those who inhabit the covert world, or those who have survived their initiation. To understand how the process works and the extraordinary resources invested in dirty tricks requires an appreciation of 'brand' to the management of organized crime ... as it is practiced through Wall Street and Washington.

Wikipedia online encyclopedia defines 'brand' as follows.

"...the symbolic embodiment of all the information connected with a product or service. A brand typically includes a name, logo and other visual elements such as images or symbols. It also encompasses the set of expectations associated with a product or service which typically arise in the minds of people. Such people include employees of the brand owner, people involved with distribution, sales or supply of the product or service, and ultimately consumers."

A great brand can make or break a company ... and its stock market value.

Part V

Catherine continues.

"Problems started at the end of 1995 and evolved into significant investigation and litigation in 1996. Both frontal and covert attacks came in waves that made no sense to me ... until we started to map out in chronological form parallel efforts to suppress Gary Webb's, *Dark Alliance* ...and timing of stock market profit-taking by investors in HUD property managers and private prison companies such as Cornell Corrections.

<>

"There was a war going on for rich corporate cash flows determined by the federal budget ... between those who made money on building up of communities and a peace economy ... and those who made money on the failure of communities and a war economy.

"As stock market prices and Dow Jones Index rose, this economic warfare grew in fierceness. A comparison of how DOJ handled Hamilton Securities Group ... a firm that helped communities succeed ... versus how it dealt with Enron ...a company that criminally destroyed retirement savings and communities, underscores much about the system's true intentions.

<>

"March 1995, our first billion-dollar HUD loan sale was a significant success. The performance stunned traditional HUD constituencies and Wall Street. Apr. 10, 1995 Barron's published Jim McTagues', *Believe It or Not, HUD Does Something Right for Taxpayers.*

"Many were caught off guard by the success of the sale, including prices that resulted from combined ingenuity of investment banking and software technology involved. It established the team at FHA, with Hamilton Securities Group as lead financial advisor ... as significant leaders in authentic re-engineering, as opposed to what sounded to me like the press release re-engineering coming from Al Gore and Elaine Kamarck's, Office of Re-inventing Government.

"A hint of the trouble to come was the response from Mike Eisenson, head of the Harvard Endowment's private equity portfolio (lead investor in NHP, one of the largest HUD property management companies, along with Pug Winokur), who picked up his phone when I called him during this period and said to me, "F**k you!"

"He then proceeded to explain that he hated our bidding process ... the only way Harvard could win was by paying more money than the other bidders. The bid process we'd created was pitting large and small real estate, mortgage and securities investors against each other in a manner that increased competition relative to traditional bidding practices. This resulted in HUD attracting significant new investment interest in buying their defaulted mortgages and significantly higher recoveries on those mortgages. As a result, in approximately 10 billion dollars of loan sales led by Hamilton Securities Group, HUD was able to generate 2.2 billion dollars in savings to the FHA Fund. Later audits confirmed that the loan sales had a positive impact for communities in which the properties were located.

Another indication of trouble to come was, I started to receive bizarre e-mails from Tino Kamarck, the husband of Elaine Kamarck who ran Gore's Office of Re-inventing Government at the White House. I had met Tino, who was then #2 at Export-Import Bank and later to be Chairman, when he worked on Wall Street but did not know him well. Out of the blue by e-mail, he proposed we have an affair. I suspected at the time that he ulterior motives ... one inspiration for my starting my own firm had been twenty minutes of listening to HUD Secretary Jack Kemp while I was Assistant HUD Secretary, order me to lengthen my skirts. I suspected it was an attempt by Jack to get me to lose my temper. I was running the FHA money too cleanly. Despite my offer to move elsewhere in the Administration, Jack preferred to force me out in a manner blamed on me. One of our problems was Jonathan Kamarck on staff in the Senate appropriations subcommittee that was a significant supporter of HUD's Operation Safe Home, and was uncomfortable with the impact of our successful HUD loan sales on traditional real estate interests.

"Jonathan told me he was Tino's cousin and presumably close to Tino and Elaine Kamarck. By the time the allegations against Hamilton Securities Group were discredited, and Harvard Endowment had reaped large profits cashing out of their HUD related investments ... Elaine was working for Harvard and Tino was working for a real estate firm in Boston with intimate ties with Harvard and snagged a contract with HUD to do he work that Hamilton Securities Group had been doing.

Catherine continues.

"When Andrew Cuomo ran for Democratic Party's nomination for Governor of New York in 2002, press reports indicated he was concerned voters would associate him with the mob. Politics took a serious turn when someone from HUD Inspector General's Office reported they were in a meeting with Andrew Cuomo, then Assistant Secretary of Community Development at HUD and soon to be Secretary, and HUD Inspector General Susan Gaffney. Cuomo reported he was arranging to get rid of Hamilton Securities Group and me.

"Cuomo was considered to be close to Al Gore and his White House office and efforts to 're-engineer government'. Within months, it was reported by Nic Retsinas, Assistant Secretary of Housing, the White House ordered him not to hire Hamilton Securities Group on the next round of contracts. An associate of the Assistant Secretary of Administration, the appointee who oversees the contracting HUD office, reported the same White House orders.

"Notwithstanding orders from on high, in January and April of 1996 a new HUD/FHA contract and task order were awarded to Hamilton Securities Group ...under which HUD was to pay Hamilton a base of 10 million dollars a year for two years to serve as FHA's lead financial advisor. Our successes ... from profitable HUD/FHA contract awards to analysis generated by software and database innovations that had Alan Greenspan asking for briefings from our analytics team for the Federal Reserve staff ... was a surprise to some who had thought our commitment to technology would not make a significant difference in marketplace transactions and bottom-line dollars and sense.

"This was a period of risk and transition for many. Dillon Read and John Birkelund were recovering from unexpected failure of the firm's lead investor, Barings. After helping Dillon partners buy the firm back from Travelers in 1991, Barings collapsed as the result of an Asian trading scandal in 1995. With Dillon as lead investors, Cornell Corrections was losing money. Former Dillon Chairman and Treasury Secretary Nick Brady were learning difficulties of starting his own firm, Darby Overseas Investments, Ltd, in Washington, D.C.

"The Clinton team was wondering what would happen to them if the Republican takeover of Congress in the 1994 elections translated into their being thrown out in the 1996 elections. Mike Eisenson's compensation was constrained by publicity regarding salaries paid by Harvard Management and only later was he inspired to start his own firm (with — imagine this ... a contract from Harvard Management that paid $10 million a year ... the same as Hamilton Securities Group's HUD contract). One can only wonder what was going on behind the scenes at the CIA and DOJ after the Memorandum of Understanding was rescinded in August 1995.

"Presumably, the rescission left CIA obligated to report narcotics trafficking to DOJ ... and required DOJ to ensure CIA satisfied such obligations. Therefore, any transparency of the kind Hamilton was creating with its software tools could significantly increase criminal liabilities of CIA, DOJ and their contractors.

"When people are afraid or managing rising risk, they are jealous of a start-up's success and frustrated by their inability to openly insist newcomers respect traditional market relationship ...let-alone illegal, covert lines of authority and cash flows.

Late spring 1996, Catherine had dinner at a National Housing Conference event with Scott Nordheimer, a HUD developer who pursuing business with DOJ's Federal Bureau of Prisons. Scott had recently gotten out of prison as a result of a securities fraud conviction, and believed the future for data servicing business was in prisons. He tried aggressively to persuade me the opportunities in prisons were significant ... in contrast to job-creating opportunities of our community-based model, which he said would not be 'politic'. When I declined Scott's invitations to meet with the Federal Bureau of Prisons, I suspect he gave DOJ our data servicing business plan. He was soon to become successful in HUD's Hope VI program. This was ironic, as HUD was forcing out tenants who had a felony record while allowing the building to essentially be owned and managed by partnerships with a convicted felon in the lead.

"At the dinner late spring 1996, Scott looked pleased with himself and explained a decision had been made to frame me ...and that I was in serious trouble. He said, "Well, we tried to have you fired through the White House but that didn't work, so now the big boys have gotten together and you are going to prison."

"Other board members of Hamilton Securities Group and myself were careful how we built and managed the company. We had seen other firms targeted with government dirty tricks and done everything to ensure we could withstand corrupt audits and trumped-up, political investigations."

Catherine responded to Scott's predictions.

"It will never work, Scott. We're too clean," Catherine said.

Scott smiled.

"You don't get it. The fix is in. There is nothing you can do," Scott said.

Catherine continues.

Aug. 6, 1996, Hamilton received the first subpoena in what became years of subpoena warfare by the HUD Inspector General, investigating under delegated authority by DOJ. At the time, I did not know DOJ was holding secret hearings in Federal district court as a result of a qui tam filing in June 1996 by Ervin & Associates, in which Hamilton was falsely accused of civil and criminal violations. The investigation was conducted under the pretext of a qui tam lawsuit ...a lawsuit brought by a private party as a bounty hunter for the government looking to make 15-30% of the government damages (which could be trebled) recovered from a private party found to have made false claims against the government. Delegation of subpoena authority to HUD was used by the government to circumvent the requirement to disclose this to the targets of the qui tam, including Hamilton Securities Group.

Ervin & Associates was founded by John Ervin, a former employee of Harvard's HUD property management company, NHP. Ervin won contracts to service defaulted and co-insured HUD mortgages ...and in 1994 won a contract to collect financial statements for HUD-supported apartment buildings. Through these contracts, Ervin had a rich flow of data on HUD-assisted and HUD-financed, privately-owned apartment buildings. In a later deposition, Ervin testified he was able to refer cases worth millions of dollars for civil money penalties to HUD OIG. In short, he claimed to be a part of the profit-making business of HUD OIG's Operation Safe Home. As HUD disposed of more and more mortgages through loan sales, Ervin's business diminished.

Presumably, at some point, this may have diminished his ability to generate profitable leads and revenues for HUD OIG.

The first subpoena was the beginning of a two-year period during which Catherine wasn't allowed to know of the existence of the qui tam lawsuit that resulted in destruction of her company, and a four-year period during which Catherine was not allowed to read or hear allegations made against her company and herself, or know who made them. It was five years before Catherine had access to transcripts of sealed court hearings (unattended by her or her counsel) in the qui tam case. It was seven to eight years before Ervin and the government were required to put forward evidence attempting to support their baseless claims and before Hamilton Securities Group and our attorneys had opportunity to refute the false charges in a court of law ...sufficient to shut down the smear campaign being used against Catherine as an investment banker in the market place. Throughout this period, both HUD Inspector General and private parties shared bits and pieces of supposedly sealed allegations repeatedly with the press and members of Congress.

Jack Kemp announced candidacy for Vice President on August 10. Gary Webb's *Dark Alliance* story broke in *San Jose Mercury News* eight days later.

Catherine continues.

Four days after we received our first subpoena, Aug. 10, 1996, Jack Kemp, Secretary of HUD when I was Assistant Secretary, announced he was the Republican candidate for Vice President. Jack was considered someone who would be effective persuading women and minorities to support the Republican ticket. The reality of Kemp's real philosophies and history were much darker. Initially at the request of my attorneys, I was later to document some of my experiences with Kemp's darker underside, including his efforts to provide subsidies illegally to a project reported to be developed by Andrew Cuomo when Andrew was an attorney in New York helping raise money for his father, Mario Cuomo, then Governor of New York. Eight days later, on Aug. 18, 1996, Gary Webb's *Dark Alliance* story broke in *San Jose Mercury News* implicating the CIA and DOJ in complicity to traffic in narcotics.

"This narcotics trafficking occurred during Iran-Contra when Bush was Vice President and Oliver North and staff were in charge of the National Security Council. Bush's close friend, and supporter Nick Brady and partner John

Birkelund at Dillon Read were leading investment banking for RJR Nabisco, which according to the European Union was complicit in laundering significant profits for global narcotics cartels at this time. Bill Clinton was Governor and Hillary Clinton was a partner at the Rose Law firm in Arkansas where a portion of the revenues from the Mena operation were allegedly laundered through the state housing agency. The very same Arkansas agency was ultimately governed by Governor Clinton and served as bond counsel by the Rose Law Firm. Stanley Sporkin at that time was serving as the General Counsel of CIA while the now-infamous Memorandum of Understanding with DOJ was crafted. If you follow the likely cash flows in and out of the alleged Mena and Arkansas state housing bond operations and the alleged narcotics trafficking and HUD mortgage defaults in South Central Los Angeles, and the allegations surrounding the events and subsequent cover-ups, there was an uncomfortable closeness of networks between those in Webb's story and those in power," Catherine said.

<>

Catherine had not read or heard about *Dark Alliance* allegations at the time. The members of Catherine's team who later confided they'd been aware of the story, hadn't mentioned it. They didn't see the connection between the threat posed by Hamilton leadership in re-engineering government or providing community access to software tools and databases about federal resources by place ... and government complicity in narcotics trafficking and related HUD fraud alleged to be laundering the proceeds.

<>

Catherine was buried in the workload avalanche of running a company while dealing with subpoenas and a smear campaign, unleashed initially by a team of reporters from *U.S. News & World Report.* Catherine didn't notice in early October when *Washington Post* published the 'results of its independent investigation' into Gary Webb's allegations, saying there was insufficient evidence to support Webb's claims. Catherine was also unaware that while the White House was trying to have her contracts ended, Elaine Kamarck in Vice President Al Gore's Office at the White House was busy working with DOJ Deputy Attorney General Jamie Gorelick to make sure that the private prison industry was blessed with oodles of contracts.

Catherine and her colleagues endured multiple subpoenas and smear campaigns, and Gary

Webb was in the process of defending his story at *San Jose Mercury News* (later to lose his job the following year), Dillon Read filed a registration statement with SEC for Cornell's initial public offering July 17, amending it Aug. 26, Sept. 10, and Sept. 30 with a final prospectus filed Oct. 4, 1996. This was good news for Dillon Read and its investors. Thanks to successful efforts of Clinton Administration to pass new crime legislation and ensure DOJ bureaucracy support for outsourcing contracts to run federal prisons to private prison companies ... including a gush of contracts to Cornell from the fall of 1995 to the spring of 1996 ... Dillon Read's Cornell stock purchased at an average price between $2-$3 per share, was now worth $12 a share, a 400–600% increase.

In addition to their stock profits, Dillon pocketed big underwriting fees as well as being the lead investment bank arranging the stock offering. In nine months, Clinton Administration's increase in contracts and acquisition of entities with contracts supporting 1,726 prisoners had literally made the company. The IPO reflected a stock market valuation of $24,241 per prisoner.

<>

What that means is, every time HUD's Operation Safe Home dropped swat teams in a community and rounded up 100 teenagers for arrest, potential value to stockholders of prison companies that manage juvenile facilities and prisons was 2.4 million dollars.

<>

All that was needed for prison privatization to work, was the suppression of truth ... about who was really bringing in the drugs and why it was essential for citizens to not see or understand the real deal on 'how the money worked' in the places in which they lived and worked. If there'd been a map of the real deal about how the money works in communities and in government, along the lines of the software being developed by Hamilton when the qui tam lawsuit put Hamilton out of business, the private prison industry might not have gotten off the ground.

<>

"If one were to document criminality or economic waste within the system, it was apparent the real criminals and real financial drain were not the kids being rounded up by HUD's Operation Safe Home and not the owners and employees of Hamilton Securities Group.

<>

Always ready with spin, Hillary Clinton published, *It Takes a Village,* in September while Bob

Rubin, Secretary of Treasury (at this writing a senior executive in the Office of the Chairman at Citigroup), talked about the importance of economic development in the inner city. Rubin's former firm, Goldman Sachs, one of the largest bidders on the HUD loan sales, had been one of the largest investment bankers in Arkansas during the Mena period. Linda Ives was the courageous mother of an Arkansas teenager killed by police in August 1987 when he and a friend apparently accidentally encountered a cocaine drop at the Mena operation. Ives, working with journalist Mara Levitt, persisted in illuminating many of the events surrounding her son's death ... initially ruled a suicide ... and corruption in Arkansas.

Catherine continues.

I've found when things look their darkest, something magical happens that can change your life. Nov. 15, 1996 something happened that may have saved my life and changed the course of history. On that day, former LAPD narcotics investigator Mike Ruppert stood up at a town hall meeting in South Central Los Angeles and confronted CIA Director John Deutch with evidence of CIA narcotics trafficking before a large audience of citizens and media cameras. Deutch was there to address Garry Webb's *Dark Alliance* allegations ... which described CIA complicity. Ruppert was an eyewitness to more than complicity. Ruppert said he had proof of actual trafficking by CIA agents, including his former fiancé, who had tried to recruit him to help protect agency narcotics operations in Los Angeles well before the Iran-Contra period. The Ruppert-Deutch confrontation was later memorialized in the award winning online video by the Guerrilla News Network, *Crack the CIA*. It would take me two years of standing in the face of an onslaught of enforcement terrorism and terrifying physical harassment and surveillance before I was to see the famous videotape of that event. That was when I began the education through which I would come to understand why transparency of neighborhood financial flows was sufficiently threatening to the stability of the global financial system such that powerful interests might insist on the destruction of Hamilton Securities Group and our software tools.

"By the time Bill Clinton and Al Gore were sworn in for their second term January 1997, the first wave of investigation and smear campaign had failed to do anything other than affirm Hamilton Securities Group was doing a great job for the government, and the government team at FHA was doing a great job for citizens.

Consequently, 1997 settled into the first of eight grinding years of enforcement terrorism ... the inexhaustible resources and often invisible weaponry that 'Sheriff of Nottingham' uses to exhaust the target's resources and to turn over investigation personnel, judges and false witnesses who failed to frame the target while throwing more 'mud' up on the judicial, whisper campaign and media 'wall' looking for anything that might stick.

"To get a sense of the level of professionalism involved, HUD OIG started to interview all Hamilton's employees and HUD staff, with interviews starting off with questions regarding my personal sexual habits. This is a technique used to start false rumors and destroy businesses when the absence of evidence gives enforcement teams nothing to go on. As described by one member of HUD OIG staff, when there is no evidence of any wrongdoing, the intimation of perverted sex practices can still get an indictment from a Washington, DC grand jury. My feedback indicated Hamilton employees overwhelmed them with facts and didn't fall prey to the smear tactics.

"The turnover started at the top. Secretary of HUD Henry Cisneros left HUD to face charges tried before Judge Stanley Sporkin that he'd lied to FBI regarding how much money he'd given his mistress. I'd worked at HUD when allegations at the White House and the so-called 'Franklin Cover Up' exploded on the front page of *Washington Times*. One of my deputies had taken me aside when I was being pressured by Kemp to do illegal funding awards to warn me that Kemp was involved in scandalous activities.

"The notion of Cisneros facing criminal charges for legal financial transactions between consenting adults while Kemp had been chosen by Republicans to run for Vice President seemed a bit upside down. When you considered Hamilton was being run out for ensuring that the government got fair market value for its assets, poor people had an opportunity to earn money legally without government subsidies or engaging in narcotics trafficking and street crime, and communities had access to government financial information, things made more sense.

"If anything, the wave of investigatory assaults on Hamilton and the team at FHA seemed to be a pretext for Cuomo to take over the agency and convert it to the service of enforcement, gentrification and housing bubbles. Cuomo had many ties to the enforcement community. His father had been Governor of New York, his ex-wife Kerry (they were separated in 2003 then divorced) was a Kennedy, whose father Bobby Kennedy had been Attorney General and whose uncle, Sen. Ted Kennedy from Massachusetts, home of Harvard University, was a senior member of the Senate Judiciary Committee. If Cuomo was going to rise to higher political office and help his close ally, Al Gore, become President, he needed to get credit for being a leader in re-engineering government. He needed to do it in a way that attracted the support of 500 billion to 1 trillion dollars of annual money laundering flowing through the U.S. financial system. If the Bush sons as Governors could be expected to have Texas and Florida sewn up, that meant Al Gore, Hillary Clinton and the Democrats would need to win money and votes in California and New York during the 2002 campaign.

"It turns out, this meant getting rid of the people who were leading authentic re-engineering. April 1997, Hamilton received notice that our ongoing contract would be re-bid ... a process expected to take some time. In the meantime, Cuomo was competing with HUD OIG to see who could integrate more enforcement, War on Drug activities and DOJ partnerships into HUD programs, faster.

"Jamie Gorelick left Department of Justice in January and moved to Fannie Mae as Vice Chair ... a title held by Franklin Raines who joined the Administration as head of the Office of Management & Budget (OMB) in fall of 1996.

"Gorelick at Fannie Mae and Raines at OMB (later to return to Fannie Mae as Chairman) were to play leading roles with former Goldman Sachs partner Robert Rubin, Larry Summers, and former Arnold & Porter partner Jerry Hawke (whose son, Dan Hawke, was Ervin's attorney) at the U.S. Treasury, Alan Greenspan at the Federal Reserve, and Andrew Cuomo at HUD ... in engineering the largest housing and mortgage bubble in history.

<>

"They shared a mutual silence as 4 trillion dollars went missing from accounts for which the U.S. Treasury and New York Federal Reserve Bank and its member banks ...as depository for the U.S. Treasury, were responsible.

Given the efforts underway with numerous legislation and treaties designed to intentionally shift American jobs abroad, the simultaneous effort by the same governmental and financial system leadership to encourage Americans to take on increasing amounts of debt without warning them that their income was likely to fall, brought new meaning to the old expressions 'fraudulent inducement' and 'predatory lending'.

<>

As a result, Americans lived beyond their means. With many using home equity to maintain standards of living, equity slowly and invisibly drained out of moderate and middle income communities into private hands through Fannie Mae and other large financial institutions that led the explosion in the mortgage and mortgage securities markets.

CIA Director John Deutch resigned Dec. 1996 after his embarrassing confrontation with Mike Ruppert regarding CIA drug dealing in the now infamous town hall meeting in Los Angeles. At the meeting, Deutch committed publicly to an investigation by the CIA's Inspector General, Frederick Hitz, of *Dark Alliance* allegations regarding CIA complicity in narcotics trafficking. The publication of this report in two volumes was to have an impact on the course of events in 1998. For her service to the U.S. intelligence community, Jamie Gorelick received a Director of Central Intelligence Award from the CIA in 1997.

The most significant turnover impacting Hamilton Securities Group was behind closed doors. It was the transfer of the qui tam lawsuit (still filed in secret and unknown to Hamilton) from Judge Charles Richey who had warned he was reluctant to give DOJ extensions of the seal (which kept the lawsuit secret) without evidence of wrongdoing. According to press reports, Judge Richey contracted fast-acting cancer and died. Ervin's qui tam was turned over in early 1997 to Judge Stanley Sporkin, former General Counsel of the CIA when the Memorandum of Understanding between DOJ and CIA was crafted. Dirty tricks employed by Judge Sporkin, DOJ, HUD OIG and Ervin's attorneys throughout the qui tam have been described in more details elsewhere.

Highlights include:

* Sporkin insisted that he had never received filings by Hamilton Securities Group, even though Hamilton attorneys reported they had a receipt of delivery signed by his office.

* The allegations in the qui tam lawsuit tracked allegations made in a separate filing by Ervin against HUD that was filed before another judge in Federal District Court. In sealed hearings in the qui tam, DOJ attorneys for years argued there was real merit to the allegations, which justified more time for them to investigate. In open court in the other action, DOJ attorneys took the position that the allegations were baseless. Hence, DOJ attorneys took opposite positions in

the two courts … one open and one in secret … Sporkin supported these actions. Transcripts show DOJ attorneys reminded him they couldn't consolidate the case under one judge because that would prevent them from taking opposite positions in the two cases.

* The public document was used by HUD OIG and private parties to lobby Congress and the media to smear Hamilton. One reporter from *Washington Post* told Catherine the HUD Inspector General personally assured them Hamilton was guilty of criminal violations, and that John Ervin had mailed documents to them that could fill up half an office, floor to ceiling. She reported in late 1997, Ervin had a staff of 17 people at Ervin & Associates working full-time on the litigation.

* Despite no evidence of wrongdoing brought forward by Ervin, as well as after multiple investigations and full access for years to all the parties and documents needed by the government, Sporkin extended the seal (by law a qui tam authorizes only a 60 day investigation) into a four-year fishing expedition. This ended when colleagues and Catherine launched a website in 2000 with the story of what was happening and made hundreds of supporting documents accessible through the Internet. When, after five years, transcripts of Sporkin's hearings were unsealed, critical transcripts were mysteriously missing.

* Under the qui tam statute, if the party accused of wrongdoing is subpoenaed, they are required to be informed that they are a target of a qui tam, even though the complaint is still under seal. In our case, DOJ and Sporkin took the position DOJ could circumvent this disclosure provision by delegating the subpoena issuance to HUD OIG.

Catherine continues.

"My favorite Sporkin quote was his retort from the bench when one of our attorneys pointed out the law and a recent Supreme Court case clearly indicated a filing we had made in Superior Court could not be moved over to Sporkin's court and control in Federal District Court … that Sporkin had no legal right or basis to do what he was doing. Sporkin said something to the effect of, 'I disagree with the law and if you have a problem with that, take it up with Congress.' When it comes to describing treatment of Hamilton Securities Group and myself by Judge Sporkin and DOJ and HUD attorneys, it's essential to underscore how lucky I've been. I had the knowledge and control to ensure that Hamilton was run according to very high standards. Hamilton

had been blessed with a very strong team … starting with an outstanding Chief Financial Officer and excellent contract leadership for our work at HUD. I had an excellent reputation in the marketplace. I had personal wealth and family support to ensure I had attorneys, food, clothing, and shelter. With the presence of a strong legal team and resources over a long period, many private and public witnesses and honest officials in government and the judicial system were able to help … often at great risk to themselves. I had a wonderful church and tremendous spiritual support. And, over time I connected with thousands of people around the world trying to illuminate corruption and build community. So I am alive, I am fully intact, and I am not alone. That's more than I can say about millions of children and innocent adults worldwide who've been destroyed, killed, and incarcerated by the drug running, weapons trading and cover ups made possible with the help of the same type of extraordinary legal and harassment skills I faced. Among them was Gary Webb, who died in December 2004, from gunshot wounds to the head … ruled a suicide.

With Jamie Gorelick gone from DOJ, much of the work at DOJ continued under jurisdiction of Frank Hunger, Al Gore's brother-in-law, who was head of the civil division, and the new Deputy Attorney General, Eric Holder. Holder had come from the Washington, D.C. U.S. Attorney's office which was lead office with the day-to-day lead responsibility for DOJ on Ervin's qui tam. Holder continued policies of support for Operation Safe Home, War on Drugs and prison privatization.

Al Gore's former chief of staff, Jack Quinn, resigned as White House Counsel at the end of 1996 and returned to his old law firm, Arnold & Porter. He was replaced by former (and later) Covington & Burling partner, Charles Ruff, in early 1997. (Quinn was later to return to visibility when he assisted the Gore campaign in 2000 and helped to engineer Arnold & Porter client Marc Rich's White House pardon.) Ruff, a former Watergate prosecutor and top Justice Department official was the Washington D.C. Corporation Counsel who had critical background to help the Clinton Administration engineer the federal takeover of many aspects of the Washington, D.C. government, including the local courts and prison system. Former Assistant U.S. Attorney, Judith Heatherton, who was leading the Hamilton investigation as HUD OIG General Counsel had worked for Ruff. Ruff, like

Gorelick, had served as President of the D.C. Bar Association. After her efforts to frame Hamilton Securities Group failed, Heatherton became staff to the Ethics Committee at the D.C. Bar Association.

<>

The federal takeover of the District of Columbia began in August 1997 with the Balanced Budget Act and was the beginning of a wave of gentrification in the District, with easy mortgage finance encouraging people to move back in from the suburbs, or young people and immigrants to buy new homes. The law provided for private prison capacity that would result in, among other things, a request for proposal by Federal Bureau of Prisons in Feb. 1998 that Cornell would win in 1999 for 1,000 people for ten years, or a total award of 342 million dollars. The Federal takeover was a pork fest for HUD real estate developers under Andrew Cuomo's leadership. The flood of developers cashing in on HUD Hope VI projects, with Scott Nordheimer in a leading position was well underway.

<>

While the HUD Operation Safe Home swat team round-ups continued to create the need for private prison capacity at taxpayer expense, and government officials and Wall Street board members played musical chairs, inventing new ways of handing out contracts and financing the housing bubble, private companies were cashing in on their resulting good fortune:

* Cornell Corrections increased revenues and capacity thanks to DOJ's Federal Bureau of Prison and several state governments.

* Dillon Read exercised their options to purchase additional shares in Cornell Corrections.

* In summer 1997, Dillon Read's partners and investors, led by John Birkelund, sold Dillon Read to Swiss Bank Corp., which merged the following year with UBS, the largest Swiss bank.

* With HUD policies reversed by Cuomo to those in favor of traditional constituencies, Harvard Endowment and Pug Winokur's, Capricorn Investment, sold NHP, the large HUD property manager to AIMCO, a large Denver HUD property manager.

* Pug Winokur's firm, Capricorn Holdings, an investor with Harvard in NHP, a leading HUD property management company, sold a significant portion of their controlling position in DynCorp, an important HUD and DOJ contractor, with Pug stepping down from Chairman of the Board of DynCorp to remain a member of the board and Chairman of the Compensation Committee, the board committee that recommends compensation for senior management as well as compensation policies for the corporation.

In the meantime, Gary Webb had problems of his own. After extraordinary efforts by corporate media to try to discredit his story, he was demoted by *San Jose Mercury News,* summer 1997 then left the paper Dec. 1997 to work on his book, *Dark Alliance,* published the following year.

Fall 1997 was an intense time in Washington, D.C. given fundraising and Whitewater investigations that would continue to distract from Mena and South Central L.A. narcotics trafficking allegations and use sex between consenting adults in the Oval Office to blossom the following year into the Clinton impeachment proceedings.

Sept. 18, Cornell Corrections announced its next public offering with Dillon Read (renamed SBC Warburg Dillon Read since purchase by Swiss Bank Corp.) as the lead senior manager. The offering proceeded on Oct. 10, raising 57.3 million dollars at a price of $19 5/8 per share, a 64% increase from the first offering in Oct. 1996, a year before. This implied a value of $25,962 per person in Cornell's jails and facilities ... a significant portion derived from the Federal Bureau of Prisons and U.S. Marshals, both at DOJ.

October 14, then-HUD Secretary Andrew Cuomo fired Hamilton with no notice, seized monies owed to Hamilton Securities Group for work already performed and launched a concerted smear campaign. At the same time, a variety of dirty tricks, including through Hamilton's bank, auditor and insurance companies, drained Hamilton's resources. In November, an amount equivalent to Hamilton's remaining contract authority ... approximately $10 million ... was awarded to HUD OIG's Operation Safe Home by special appropriation by the Senate HUD appropriation subcommittee. Legal action to try to stop HUD's seizure of Hamilton's monies and illegal investigatory leaks ended up in Stanley Sporkin's court ... giving the former general counsel of the CIA another chance to use his skills to protect criminal enterprise. As a result, all of Hamilton's efforts to support responsible management of HUD's programs or to create tools and jobs for communities came to an end.

Catherine continued.

"I had to smile when we ended up with new attorneys the following year. One assured me that Sporkin would love what we were doing for community transparency and job creation. They'd heard him in the meetings of attorneys speaking about the inner city. They insisted, he very much cared about young people in the inner city. By then, I'd learned to just smile and not try to explain about how it was that despite everyone caring so much about the Popsicle Index going up, for some mysterious and inexplicable reason it just kept going down," Catherine said.

A few words are appropriate to describe DynCorp and its former Chairman and lead investor, Herbert S. 'Pug' Winokur. Pug and his investment operation, Capricorn Holdings, were later to come under scrutiny when Pug resigned from Harvard Corporation board at a time of controversy regarding his role as board member and chairman of the Finance Committee of Enron. Pug was serving on the board when Enron went bankrupt, after a period during which Harvard Endowment (where Pug was also on the board) was aggressively and profitably selling Enron stock. This raised questions as to whether the Endowment had the benefit of 'insider information'. The extent of Harvard's investments in Capricorn and its funds, if any, are unknown. On several occasions, Harvard and Capricorn have invested side by side.

Pug's company, Capricorn Holdings, was based in Greenwich Connecticut. He and John Birkelund were long-time board members of NacRe, a reinsurance company based in the Greenwich area Dillon was instrumental in helping start. Breaking with the pattern of Dillon leaders being from New Jersey, John Birkelund lived in Connecticut and seemed very much part of the group in and around Greenwich. This group included Robert G. Stone, Jr., considered a leading light for many years behind the Harvard Endowment, particularly its oil and gas portfolio that invested in Harken Energy, a company made famous by George W. Bush's role and stock profits. Like many other people in this story, both Birkelund and Winokur shared membership in the Council on Foreign Relations.

<>

When Capricorn Holdings reduced its investment position in 1997, DynCorp appeared to be doing well. In addition to significant information systems contracts and subcontracts for DOJ and HUD, including lead contractor with a 60 million dollar per year contract on the DOJ Asset Forfeiture Fund (working with the U.S. Marshals who manage forfeited assets for DOJ's Asset Forfeiture Fund), DynCorp won new systems and litigation support contracts from DOJ in 1995 and 1996. This included Justice Consolidated Network (J-Con) contract to run consolidated network systems for parts of Justice. According to Inslaw President Bill Hamilton, DynCorp was one of the successor contractors on managing PROMIS system after DOJ had stolen it from Inslaw.

One of the contractors chosen with DynCorp to provide litigation support to DOJ was CACI, leading provider of Geographic Information Systems to the federal government. Richard Armitage, a high-ranking official at Defense during the Reagan Administration and at the State Department during the Bush II Administration, was a consultant and member of CACI's board from 1999 to 2001.

After DynCorp personnel were later the subject of several lawsuits related to pedophilia and sex slave trafficking in partnership with local mafia in Eastern Europe, Armitage as a senior official at the U.S. State Department would write a letter in support of large new sole source contracts to DynCorp based on the theory that a company should not lose contracts as a result of the conduct of a few employees. In short, sex slave trafficking and pedophilia in its ranks did not prevent DynCorp from winning significant new contracts, including a 500 million dollar sole-source contract to run police, enforcement, courts and prisons in Iraq.

Catherine continues.

I came to look into DynCorp when I was contacted years later by a retired member of CIA covert operations who alleged that (1) DynCorp was helping to manage the PROMIS software system through its J-Con System at DOJ, and (2) The project manager for DynCorp on the J-Con contract had falsified evidence against me using the PROMIS system and that is what got the investigation against Hamilton Securities Group and me started.

It's hard to find reliable info on the PROMIS software system and alleged successor systems. However, I believe that understanding the use of such digital information weaponry and its ability to compromise private and public financial and banking systems (including transactions such as the HUD loan sales) as well as governmental enforcement and military systems is integral to understanding manipulation of U.S. federal credit and financial markets, and centralization of political and economic power.

<>

When Cornell Corrections listed its shareholders with investments of greater than 5% in its proxy statement filed with SEC March 1998, Dillon Read was no longer listed. Making the assumption Dillon Read and its various funds and officers and directors cashed out at or between the second Cornell offering in October 1997 and early 1998 when this proxy was filed, we can pause in the telling of our story to estimate total profits to Dillon and their investors. We should first note that it appears that Dillon sold their shares at a historical high for Cornell's stock price.

Catherine continues.

While Dillon was not required to disclose total investment banking revenues and investment profits on Cornell Corrections between 1991 and 1998, I estimate Dillon's total profits for their stock investment in Cornell to have been 6.7 million dollars for Dillon employees who invested, and 19.4 million dollars for the investors in Dillon's funds, which also included Dillon officers and directors. This represented an annual return on investment of approximately 35-45%. These are the kind of profits you get when you buy stock for a price of 3.8 million dollars and several years later sell that stock for 29.9 million dollars or an almost 800% increase on investment. In addition, I estimate Dillon also generated at least 6 million dollars in fees for investment banking and investment advisor services. This results in an estimated total of 32.1 million dollars in profits for Dillon, its leaders and investors over a seven-year period.

I remember reading Carlyle Group's marketing material about their success in leveraged buyouts of companies that did lots of contracts and business with the federal government. They claimed to have achieved annual investment returns of 35%, in the range of estimated returns Dillon made on Cornell Corrections. If you understand the story of Cornell Corrections, you will get a good understanding of the type of investment that achieves 35% investment returns for private investors on stocks of companies that enjoy growth in government contracts and the fruits of 'privatization'.

It's imperative in understanding investments like these, to look not just at the companies involved, but to look through to the individuals who make the critical decisions. In Dillon Read's case, key leaders were also personal investors.

<>

Another useful calculation is to look at how many taxpayers will have to work their entire lives to pay the taxes for this many people to be imprisoned. Let's assume the average taxpayer pays $150,000 of federal taxes in an entire lifetime. Based on the General Accounting Office's (now the General Accountability Office, the Congressional Auditor) study in 1996 that indi-

cated the total annual federal, state and local system expenditures per prisoner were approximately $154,000. That means that ten taxpayers would have to work their whole lives to pay for one prisoner with a mandatory sentence of ten years.

<>

On this basis, the following estimates how many people would have to work their whole lives to pay the taxes to fund the incarcerations necessary to generate Dillon's profits on Cornell Corrections.

John H. F. Haskell, Jr. ~ largest Dillon buyer of Cornell Corrections stock personally after firm Chairman, John P. Birkelund, joined Birkelund and third largest buyer David Niemic at Saratoga Partners after Dillon was sold.

Estimated Number of People Working Their Entire Lives to Pay Taxes to Fund Prisoners Incarcerated for Extended Period to Generate Dillon Stock Profits:

DILLON PARTNER TAXPAYER LIVES John P. Birkelund ~ 340 John Haskell, Jr. ~ 310 David W. Niemiec ~ 300 Fritz Hobbs ~ 260 George A. Wiegers ~ 240 Peter Flanigan ~ 240 Kenneth M. Schmidt ~ 210 All Dillon Read Officers and Directors Investing ~ 11,523

Cornell's March 1998 proxy filed with the SEC inspires some additional questions regarding the source of funds that bought Dillon Read out at a price that generated tens of millions of profit on their venture investment. There are several new large shareholders listed, including J&W Seligman, New York ~ 5.7%. Alliance Capital c/o Equitable Companies, New York ~ 5.5%. AMVESCAP, London ~ 5.3%.

When Cornell Corrections filed its 1999 proxy the following year, AMVESCAP and Alliance were each up to 9% of outstanding shares. Based on the foregoing filings, it is fair to assume one way or another these investors were helpful in making it possible for Dillon Read to cash out at or near a market high in Cornell's stock price.

John Haskell, second largest personal investor among the Dillon officers and directors was a board member of Equitable. Alliance Capital was soon to become much more visible as a result of its role in using Florida pension funds to buy Enron stock when one of its executives and Lockheed Martin board members, Frank Savage, was also on Enron's board and member of its finance committee.

There is a relationship of Cornell's largest European shareholder AMVESCAP to RJR. In 1999, AD Frazier, President and CEO of INVESCO joined the board of R.J. Reynolds

Tobacco Holdings. The press release describes Frazier as a member of the Board of Directors of INVESCO's parent AMVESCAP.

RJR's 2003 Proxy, filed after the European Union lawsuits were filed list INVESCO as the third largest shareholder with 5.6% of outstanding shares. RJR's 2004 Proxy lists INVESCO in London as having 11% and INVESCO North American Holdings as owning 11%. RJR's 2005 Proxy lists INVESCO in London with 6.3% and AMVESCAP in London with 6.32%.

<>

That means, when one of RJR Nabisco's former lead investment bankers, Dillon Read, and its investors made in the range of 30 million dollars cashing out of a private prison company, they were cashed out directly or indirectly by one of RJR Nabisco's lead investors.

I wonder what the ghost of Barry Seal would say about what that might all have to do with the alleged 5 billion dollars of drugs he pumped through a little airport in Arkansas, and who was responsible to reinvest that money. I wonder what Lou Gerstner, Henry Kravis and George Roberts as CEO and lead investors in RJR would say if given truth serum about who may be responsible for reinvesting the dirty money allegedly laundered with RJR cigarette sales.

In Cornell's prospectus, when Dillon Read led its second stock offering Oct. 10, 1997 Brown University's Third Century Fund was listed as a shareholder with 88,818 shares, of which 28,818 shares were to be sold through the offering.

John Birkelund, Chairman and CEO of Dillon Read, was a long-time trustee of Brown University. The price on the 1997 offering was $19 5/8 per share. If Brown's average profit was the difference between the 1997 price and the 1996 offering price of $12 per share, it would have generated a profit in a year's time of $677,237. Brown's return on investment under these assumptions would have been a smashing 63.5%. If it had sold when the stock peaked after the offering at or around the time Dillon appears to have sold out, it would have been higher. The number of people who needed to be imprisoned for many years to generate such investment profits based on the foregoing assumptions was 67 people. An estimate of the number of men and women in the U.S. who would have to work their whole life to pay the taxes to imprison those 67 people would be 670 people. Brown University also benefited from John Birkelund's success at Dillon Read, including from Cornell Corrections, presumably through his donations and fundraising for the school ...a pri-

mary function of a trustee.

Part 6

Catherine continues her story.

The response from pension fund investors was positive until the President of the CalPers pension fund, the largest in the country, spoke to me.

"You don't understand. It's too late. They have given up on the country. They are moving all the money out in the fall of 1997. They are moving it to Asia," he said.

He did not say who 'they' were, but did indicate it was urgent I see Nick Brady ... as if our data that indicated that there was hope for the country might make a difference. I thought at the time he meant the pension funds and other institutional investors would be shifting a portion of their investment portfolios to emerging markets. I was naïve. He was referring to something much more significant.

The federal fiscal year starts October 1 each year. Typically the appropriation committees in the House and Senate vote their recommendations during the summer. When they return from vacation after Labor Day, the committees reconcile and a final bill is based in September. Reconciling the various issues is like pushing a pig through a snake. Finalizing the budget each fall can make a tense time. When the new bill goes into effect, new policies start to emerge as money to back them starts to flow. October 1 is a time of new shifts and beginnings. October 1997, the federal fiscal year started.

It was the beginning of 4 trillion dollars missing from federal government agency accounts between Oct. 1997 and Sept. 2001. The lion's share of missing money disappeared from Department of Defense accounts. HUD had significant amounts missing. According to HUD OIG reports, HUD had 'undocumentable adjustments' of 17 billion dollars in fiscal year 1998, and 59 billion dollars in 1999.

HUD OIG refused to finalize audited financial statements in fiscal year 1999, refused to find out the basis of the undocumentable adjustments, or to get the money back, and refused to disclose the amount of undocumentable adjustments in subsequent fiscal years. HUD OIG continued to invest significant resources persecuting Hamilton during this time.

The contractor who was blamed for the missing money at HUD was a financial software company named AMS. My old partner, Steve Fenster, the Dillon Read banker who led the firms effort in the Campeau leveraged buyout of the Federated

Department Stores which had gone bankrupt had been a board member of AMS until his death in 1995, when he was replaced by Walker Lewis, a board member affiliated with Dillon Read and now, as Chairman of Devon Value Advisors, a consulting partner to Pug Winokur and Capricorn Holdings. With 17 billion and 59 billion dollars missing from HUD, Secretary Cuomo never fired AMS or seized their money. Indeed the AMS Chairman Charles Rossotti was appointed IRS Commissioner and given a special waiver to keep his AMS stock. As a result, he profited personally when HUD kept AMS on its contractor payroll and new task orders were awarded to AMS by IRS. As IRS Commissioner, he oversaw responsibilities of the IRS criminal investigation division that plays a special role with respect to money laundering enforcement during the period when 4 trillion dollars went missing from the Federal government. When Rossotti left government service, he joined Lou Gerstner at the Carlyle Group.

If we assume the 17 billion dollars went missing at HUD during 1998 on an even basis ... that is, 1.4 billion dollars a month, 63.6 million dollars per week day, 7.9 million dollars per working hour ... by the summer of 1998, approximately 14 billion dollars would have been missing from HUD alone, not counting other agencies.

Where did it go?

Was it financed with securities fraud using Ginnie Mae or other mortgage securities fraud, or fraudulently issued U.S. Treasury securities? These are important questions. Interestingly, this was a period in which the most powerful firms in Washington, D.C. or with Washington ties, were having remarkably good luck raising capital.

Indeed, the period of missing money coincided, not surprisingly with a 'pump-and-dump' of the U.S. stock market ... and a significant flow of money into private investors hands.

'Pump-and-dump' defined from Wikipedia.

"The financial fraud known as 'pump-and-dump' involves artificially inflating the price of a stock or other security through promotion, in order to sell at the inflated price. This practice is illegal under securities law, yet is common."

One example of a highly successful pump-and-dump operator is Jonathan Lebed. Lebed was 15 years old when SEC accused him of manipulating several securities ... he settled charges by paying a fraction of his total gains. While Lebed has many apologists, who note his promotional activities are similar to those used by analysts every day, they fail to take into account that he made false and misleading statements about companies, but purchased enough shares to temporarily move the market ... creating an artificial burst of activity that provoked investor interest.

Let's look at some examples.

Cornell Corrections was far from the only company to raise funds during this period and Dillon Read far from the only investor to cash out. Dillon Read's investment in Cornell Corrections can be described as a financially modest ... albeit highly successful in percentage terms ... venture investment. Dillon's investment and profits look tiny when compared to billions KKR was investing in RJR. Both investments are informative regarding the real corporate business model prevailing in the U.S. and globally.

Summer 1998, Carlyle Group announced it closed its European Fund with 1.1 billion dollars. By the end of the decade, Carlyle had more than a dozen funds with close to 10 billion dollars under management. Meanwhile Enron, transacting with Wall Street, was enjoying a rush of good luck with offshore partnerships and growing revenues from 'the new economy'. Enron's leaders included a 'Who's Who' of government contracting. Pug Winokur was chairman of Enron finance committee. Pug was an investor and board member in DynCorp, who was running critical, highly sensitive information systems for DOJ, HUD, HUD OIG and SEC. Arthur Anderson, Enron and DynCorp's auditor, (also Cornell Correction's auditor) was a major contractor at HUD. Frank Savage, a board member of Lockheed Martin, the largest defense contractor at the time paid more than $150 million a year to run the HUD information systems, was also on Enron's board and finance committee. Enron and HUD shared the same big banks ... Citibank, JP Morgan-Chase ... and Wall Street firms. Winokur was on the board and invested with the Harvard endowment, a large investor in Enron.

To repeat a point made earlier in our discussion of the leveraged buyout business that engineered a take-over of America's economy ... money is like the Pillsbury Doughboy. When you squeeze down on one part ... it pops up someplace else. We do not yet know the truth of who now has 4 trillion dollars (or other large amount of cash and/or fraudulently issued securities) of undocumentable transactions ... indicating extraordinary amounts missing from the U.S. government or trillions more that disappeared out of pension funds and retail investors stock holdings during this period.

<>

Dec. 18, 1997 CIA Inspector General delivered Volume I of their report to the Senate Select Committee on Intelligence regarding charges CIA was complicit in narcotics trafficking in South Central Los Angeles.

Washington, D.C.'s response was compatible with attracting the continued flow of an estimated 500 billion to 1 trillion dollars a year of money laundering into the U.S. financial system. Federal Reserve Chairman Alan Greenspan in January 1998 visited Los Angeles with Congresswoman Maxine Waters ... who had been a vocal critic of the government's involvement in narcotics trafficking ... with news reports he pledged billions to come to her district.

In February Al Gore announced Water's district in Los Angeles was awarded Empowerment Zone status by HUD (under Secretary Cuomo's leadership) and made eligible for 300 million dollars in federal grants and tax benefits.

At the same time, the existence of Hamilton's software tools and databases would have posed a significant risk if the Hamilton team had become aware of the *Dark Alliance* story. The fastest way to connect the dots would have been for the Hamilton team to have looked at the maps of high HUD single family defaults contiguous to areas of significant narcotics trafficking we posted on the Internet ...and then use Hamilton Securities software tools and databases to dig into government financial flows in the same areas, including patterns of potential mortgage and mortgage securities fraud.

While in possession of Hamilton offices, HUD OIG investigators took empty shredding bins, filled them up with trash and then ... from a separate floor ... found and added corporate accounting files ... and then staged photo-taking by HUD IG General Counsel, Judith Hetherton, who sent us a letter alleging obstruction of justice as evidenced by our 'throwing out' corporate accounting records. We were saved by a property manager who witnessed this charade and decided to help us after he saw the intentional and very disgusting, trashing of Hamilton Securities Group offices ...and was touched by our efforts to clean it up. The property manager had come to the U.S. from Latin America, presumably to find freedom from lawless government. One of our attorneys went into the office when the federal investigators were there and came out shaking. He said to me, "My parents left Germany to get away from these people. Now, they are here. Where do I go?"

Meanwhile, as soon as Hamilton Securities

Group's digital and paper records and tools were under court control, computers auctioned off and websites taken down, Congress held surprise hearings March 16, 1998 on Volume I of the CIA Inspector General's Report on Gary Webb's *Dark Alliance* allegations about government involvement in cocaine trafficking. CIA Inspector General during these hearings disclosed existence of the Memorandum of Understanding between CIA and DOJ created in 1982. Sporkin, the judge who engineered the destruction of Community Wizard and our digital infrastructure and had the carcass under his control, was CIA General Counsel when that MOU was engineered.

Catherine continues.

"Information was dribbling out which ultimately would provide relief. Congresswoman Waters read the Memorandum of Understanding between CIA and DOJ into the Congressional Record in May. In June, Gary Webb published *Dark Alliance.* I saw a brief piece pooh-poohing it in a corporate magazine and realized this might help explain the insanity I was dealing with and could not understand. After reading *Dark Alliance,* I started to study the extraordinary money-making business DOJ and agencies like HUD had built in enforcement ... that only made sense if the government was complicit in narcotics trafficking and related mortgage and mortgage securities fraud. I started to realize the extent private information systems and accounting software companies like DynCorp and AMS were taking control of government agencies behind the scenes ... creating conditions for billions of dollars to disappear from government accounts. I started to research private prison companies when a banker from our bank ... whose colleague's behavior had been egregious and I believe criminal towards us, told me how much money they were making in Washington D.C. gentrification and private prisons. This was a theme that kept repeating itself during this period. Private prisons were the next 'big thing' and were going to be 'real money makers'. It was not just Scott Nordheimer who tried to persuade us of this. When I met with senior partners of Coopers & Lybrand in late 1994, they assured me I should shift my focus from communities to prisons ... that the future was in enforcement and prisons. In September, I discovered DOJ owned a prison business company, Federal Prison Industries, marketed by the name of UniCor. UniCor markets federal prison labor to federal agencies. It turns out Edgewood Technology Services, a Hamilton Securities

Group brainchild and investment, was a potential competitor with DOJ's own prison company for federal data servicing contracts. UniCor's website indicated they had a growing data servicing business with a focus on Geographic Information System (GIS) software products ... the same as Edgewood Technology Services.

Sept. 2004 Center for Public Integrity reported Federal Prison Industries was the 72nd largest defense contractor with 1.4 billion dollars of contracts between 1998-2003

"Federal Prison Industries, known as UNICOR, uses federal prisoners to manufacture a wide variety of products including furniture, clothes and electronic equipment. It provides administrative services such as data entry and bulk mailing. A government-owned corporation, it operates as part of the Federal Bureau of Prisons and is the Defense Department's number one supplier of clothing, furniture, and household furnishings."

October 8, an hour after House of Representatives voted to move forward with the Clinton impeachment hearings, CIA quietly posted Volume II of the CIA Inspector General's report on *Dark Alliance* allegations on their website. Volume II included a copy of the Memorandum of Understanding between DOJ and CIA. As Mike Ruppert hypothesized, the message from President Clinton to Republicans was simple and clear. "You take me down and I take everyone down."

The next day, October 9, Secretary Andrew Cuomo issued a series of sole-source contracts through Ginnie Mae, the mortgage securities operation at HUD, to John Ervin's company (the same company leading the qui tam lawsuit against Hamilton) and to Touchstone Financial Group, a firm apparently started by a former Hamilton Securities Group employee who brought on a series of former Hamilton people to do some of the Hamilton work for HUD. One can only make a list of more unanswered questions of the political deals that may have been happening behind the scenes. Oct. 1, 1998 was the beginning of the fiscal year in which HUD was missing 59 billion dollars from its accounts ... for which HUD OIG was to refuse to provide an audit as required by law. This amount of money translates into 4.9 billion dollars per month, 1.2 billion dollars per work week or 30.7 million dollars per work hour.

Disgusted with events in Washington during this period, Catherine headed to New York to try to get a sense of what this meant on Wall Street. Catherine went down to Wall Street to have lunch with Bart Friedman, one of the partners at Cahill Gordon, Dillon Read's lead law firm. Bart was someone Catherine had respect for and who helped Hamilton with legal work.

Catherine continues.

"As we were having lunch at a private club near Cahill, Bart's senior partner, Ike Kohn, walked by. When I was at Dillon Read, Nick Brady would introduce Ike as our most trusted attorney.

Bart turned to Ike.

"Ike, you remember Austin Fitts."

Ike looked at me and sneered with hostility then walked away abruptly in a manner shocking to me ... until I saw the SEC filings for Cornell Corrections. Bart Friedman had handled all of Dillon's investment and underwriting files for Cornell Corrections. Ike may have been scared I might connect the dots at lunch, I didn't. I plowed through SEC documents for Wackenhut Corrections, and Corrections Corporation of America.

Catherine headed to a birthday party for a member of the family of a Dillon Read partner being held at the Colony Club, an elegant private club on Park Avenue. A rush of friends wanted to know what Catherine thought of prison company stocks. They were all in them, brokers were pushing them, they were the 'new hot thing' and they were anticipating delicious profits.

Catherine looked at them.

"Get out, the pricings assume incorrectly that piling people into prisons ... innocent and guilty alike ... is like warehousing people in HUD housing," Catherine said.

Sure enough, the stocks were to later plummet. But, not until Wall Street Journal ran a story about decorators using prison equipment to do bathrooms and kitchens on Park Avenue and Esquire ran a fashion layout in front of a series of jail cells.

To this day, Catherine wonders how many of the people she spoke to that evening bought Cornell Corrections stock from Dillon Read. Catherine came back to Washington, D.C. feeling the world had gone mad. Everywhere she turned she saw people who seemed quite happy to make money doing things that drained and liquidated our permanent infrastructure and productivity as a people and a nation. Our financial system had become a complex mechanism that allowed us to profitability disassociate from the sources of our cash and concrete reality.

<>

Whatever the urgent thrust had been, it was over. Was it because Dillon had cashed out all of their money? Was it because all the software tools and databases were effectively suppressed and would not lead millions of Americans to connect mortgage fraud with the *Dark Alliance* story? Was it because the covert cash spigot had been turned on and 59 billion dollars was pouring out of HUD to feed the hungry beast? What communities in America and worldwide most need is the truth. We need the ability to know who we can trust and who we cannot trust. We need to know how to build a life, a family, a small company, and retirement savings and be able to protect them from corruption.

The first step was to understand organized crime ... a topic I had never been interested in. I called an organization that sold tapes by researchers on government corruption and narcotics trafficking and bought recommended tapes. One was a video of Mike Ruppert confronting the CIA Director in South Central Los Angeles. I got in touch with Mike and we started exchanging information. In 1999, Mike came to Washington, D.C. at my invitation to speak to a group of successful friends, colleagues and journalists at my home ...right before I sold it to pay for growing legal expenses, and left Washington to try to escape physical harassment and surveillance. As Mike started to speak, two black helicopters came and hovered over my roof garden in the middle of Washington, D.C. right next to DuPont circle.

Catherine continues.

That year, I published an article in Mike's newsletter, *From the Wilderness,* about the potential connection between the *Dark Alliance* allegations and efforts to suppress our transparency tools ... and what that may imply regarding the possible use of HUD mortgages and mortgage fraud by these same networks. Right after the article was published May 22, 1999 with copies delivered to Intelligence Committee subscribers, Congress suddenly held closed hearings on Volume II of the CIA Inspector General's reports, taking testimony in secret from DOJ Inspector General Michael Bromwich and CIA Inspector General Britt Snider.

June 1999, Richard Grasso, Chairman of the New York stock exchange, went to Colombia to visit a Revolutionary Armed Forces of Colombia (FARC) Commander to encourage him to reinvest in the U.S. financial system. At the time of his visit, the General Accounting Office reported on FARC's growing influence in the Colombian cocaine market. I learned more about the black budget and covert cash flows at work in our economy.

Dec. 1998, the period Dillon Read cashed out of Cornell Corrections and 59 billion dollars went missing from HUD, *Time* published S. C. Gwynne's, *Just Hide Me the Money,* with reporting by Adam Zagorin about the Oct. 1998 Citicorp and Travelers merger and the world of offshore banking.

"Citibank's private-banking unit holds more than 100 billion dollars, which makes it the same size as the entire bank was in 1982. These funds are part of a 17 trillion dollar global pool of money belonging to what bankers call 'high-net-worth-individuals' ... a pool that generates more than 150 billion dollars a year in banking revenue. The numbers are impressive when you consider that except at a few sleepy British and Swiss institutions, the private-banking industry didn't exist until the 1980s. Citibank predicted early this year it would reach 1 trillion dollars in private-banking assets by 2010. And it faces some 4,000 competitors, from global dreadnoughts like Switzerland's UBS [the bank that bought Swiss Bank Corporation after Swiss Bank Corporation bought Dillon Read] to secretive banks in the tiny principality of Andorra to brokerages in Miami and accountancy firms in the Channel Islands."

One of the offshore Dillon funds that invested in Cornell Corrections was Concord Partners Japan Limited. It's officers and directors, as listed in Exhibit D in Dillon's April 1997 13-D filing with the SEC, include an impressive array of Japanese business leaders and a non-person, Amerex, S.A, which lists a Coutts private bank address in the Bahamas as its address. This Dillon fund provides a link between the privatization of prisons, offshore funds and arguably the most prestigious private bank in the world. With anticipation of profits as prisons stocks increased in value and went public, an all-to-familiar impersonal financial mechanism was in place that created another incentive system with global reach, to drive financial returns of investors up by driving down the Popsicle Index of faceless people and communities, far removed.

According to Wikipedia.

"Coutts has headquarters at 440 Strand, London, with branches throughout the UK and the rest of the world. It is a private bank, which means its clients are by invitation only and have liquid assets in excess of £500,000 (U.S.$860,000) or an investment portfolio of over £1,000,000 (U.S.$1.72 million dollars). The bank is most famously known in the UK as the banker of Her Majesty Queen Elizabeth II. A Coutts Automated Teller Machine is installed in the basement of Buckingham Palace for use by the Royal Family. Coutts is known as the 'Queen's Bank' to many by virtue of it being reputed to be the bankers to the British Royal Family. Within the UK it is the largest private bank. Historically Coutts was an upper crust clearing bank to landed gentry, but today is seen as wealth managers willing to accept a wider class of clientele, including top sportsmen, lottery winners, football stars, businessmen, chief executives, and pop singers. As well as being the Queen's banker, Coutts is also known as a bank for the rich-and-famous of British society. In 1999 it became known that Her Majesty Queen Elizabeth, the Queen Mother had a £6 million (U.S.$10 million) overdraft with the bank. Sarah, Duchess of York also had a large overdraft with the bank worth around £8 million (U.S.$13.8 million dollars), subsequently paid off."

Catherine continues.

So, let's say I'm a customer of a private bank such as Coutts. Let's say through Coutts I have an interest in an offshore fund with private prison investments. The more people who are rounded up and put into prison, the more valuable my investment becomes. If laws are passed for mandatory sentences, the more valuable my investment becomes. If politicians and political appointees push through more prison contracts for private companies, the more valuable my investments become. The more enforcement staff and arrests, the more valuable my investments become. I can borrow on the increased value of my portfolio without having to sell my investment, so I can watch my investment grow, receive distributions based on profitability and still enjoy liquidity it provides. I can turn my investment into ready cash with my ATM card, just as the personal staff for the British Royal Family presumably can through the Coutts ATM machine in the basement of Buckingham palace. The transatlantic slave trade never dreamed of financial leverage, engineering and liquidity this pervasive, instantaneous or socially respectable. Perhaps this should make us pause for a moment and think, if the housing bubble turned our homes into ATM machines and in turn induced many of us to take on debt beyond our means, will privatization of our prison system provide incentives for those profiting from such investments to support policies that make us more of a target? Recently, I called the Washington, D.C. criminal attorney who repre-

sented Hamilton Securities Group with respect to the criminal investigation, until 1998. I asked him if DOJ had managed to frame me, where would I have sent me to prison? He said the order would have gone from the court to the Federal Bureau of Prisons at DOJ, and that it would have discretion to send me to the prison of its choice. Hence, it was possible I would have been incarcerated in a Cornell Corrections prison. How ironic is that? I now have the satisfaction of knowing that at the cost to me of millions in litigation and investigation expenses over a ten year period, I may have denied my old partners and colleagues at Dillon Read and their domestic and offshore investors another $11,000 in stock profit ... approximately 44% (Dillon's percent ownership) of the increased value in Cornell Corrections stock from another 'bed' being occupied by yours truly. I believe if Dillon's Chairman, John Birkelund, and I were free to speak openly about his investment in Cornell Corrections, he would say that decisions had been made to significantly grow narcotics trafficking, War on Drugs arrests and incarcerations and to privatize many aspects of government, including prisons. He was simply investing based on the directions that things were going to go. On the other hand, Hamilton's investments in communities were 'fighting the tape'. The expression 'never fight the tape' is a Wall Street saying. It means never try to oppose the market ... always go with the market trend and direction. John and I would not discuss the reality of what would happen if there were an application of criminal law to officers and directors of Dillon Read of the kind applied to me and to all the young people regularly rounded up by Operation Safe Home during that time.

I worked at Dillon Read for over a decade. I remember the department head that tried to persuade me to help engineer an insider-trading scheme. I remember the trader coming up in the elevator just having gone outside to snort cocaine. I remember the gossip about drug use in certain parties in the Hamptons. I remember my office mate complaining that Moet & Chandon had given John Haskell cases of champagne to give the associates who worked on Moet's private placement and that Haskell had kept them for himself. I remember the head trading partner confiding to me that Dillon's capital had been below our required National Association of Securities Dealers capital requirements, but Nick insisted that we not report honestly. Did I think of these as alleged felonies at the time? Of course, not. I thought of them as humans muddling through equally difficult or unpleasant options, of people making mistakes ... most of which got fixed. The trader got fired, our capital was increased, and my office mate had a nice life on a nice salary without free champagne. The reality is, however, that in my personal experience, the personal 'awfulness' of the people at Dillon Read was no more or less than the young people being rounded up by HUD and DOJ on Operation Safe Home and the War on Drugs. I have generally found the poor to be more careful in their legal transgressions than the well-to-do or rich.

There is the question of what Dillon Read's liabilities would have been in an even handed application of the law for its investment banking services to RJR. In the case of money laundering, saying you don't know may not be enough to get you off the hook. And if you did know, that's supposed to be serious jail time and disgorgement of profits, not to mention physical takeover of your premises as was done to Hamilton Securities. Last but not least are the many unanswered questions I have about what role, if any, Dillon and former Dillon partners and their investment partners and network played in AMS. This includes questions about the 59 billion dollars that went missing from HUD, billions lost through HUD mortgage fraud ... and how those cash and financing flows related to money that bought Dillon's Cornell Correction stock ...and other private prison stocks and bonds. John Birkelund and I would not discuss all of this because we would understand enforcement has nothing to do with law as described in civic classes. Enforcement is a game ... a deadly game meant to maximize insider's organized crime profits and operations worldwide, and to organize and implement class privilege and ensure that the insiders win in the game of 'winner-takes-all' economic warfare. If I did bring it up, John would most likely get frustrated with me the way he used to in the old days. Because John does not have the power to change the rules of the game, just to play within them. John knows how hard it is to make money even when you do your very best to go with the flow. That is why the safe thing to do is to rig cash flow through government laws, regulations and contracts and to arrange for government to get rid of your enemies. This is one of the reasons why the blur of people cycling between high-level Wall Street and Washington positions at some point helps us to understand the extent to which there is no longer any sovereign government. If I were to sit down

with Al Gore, Elaine Kamarck, Jamie Gorelick and Chris Edley, I would expect their explanations would involve more obfuscating policy discussions but it would ultimately come down to a similar notion of going with the flow. As would the hundreds of thousands of highly credentialed, well-paid Americans who have actively led the day-to-day implementation of policies that ... when we pierce the veil ... are really dictated by powerful private interests outside of the law, as we believe it to be. Add all these policies and actions up and they add up to genocide ... of our families and communities and of all living things throughout America and around the world.

<>

Lesley Stahl, 60 MINUTES: "We have heard that a half million children have died [because of sanctions against Iraq]. I mean, that's more children than died in Hiroshima and you know, is the price worth it?

U.S. Secretary of State Madeleine Albright: "I think this is a very hard choice, but the price ... we think the price is worth it."

With 4 trillion dollars missing from the U.S. government and more missing from a 'pump-and-dump' of U.S. stock and foreign markets, I suspect the private offshore deposits continued to rise with the falling of the Popsicle Index. The story of Cornell Corrections is not a story of powerful evil men doing racist and sexist things. I have known truly evil men. My former partners at Dillon Read are not among them. With rare exception, they were people that I liked and respected when I worked with them. Like the senior appointees in the Clinton Administration, they are well-to-do and well educated people who embrace "the way things are." Conversion to a war economy and migration from democracy to authoritarianism is "the way things are." There are big bucks and jobs at Harvard and universities like it for people like Elaine Kamarck who will give this force a socially respectable face with complex partisan distractions which help obfuscate how the Harvard Endowment continues to profit from something far deeper and far more malevolent than most of us ... most likely including Elaine ... are willing to face.

The power of the killing machine rests in part in the broad-based popular support it receives through the investment system and the markets. How are we to plead ignorance if the profits and growth in our 401K plans and investment portfolios have been enriched from prison stocks and the securities of the banks, homebuilders, property managers, mortgage bankers

579

and other groups who managed this process of ethnic and economic cleansing and the gentrification it made possible? What can our "socially responsible" investment managers say when they invest in the stocks of banks, like Citibank and JP Morgan-Chase, and government contractors, like IBM and AT&T, who are running critical parts of government as these manipulations occur ... including the disappearance of 4 trillion dollars from government bank accounts and manipulation of the gold markets and inventory in a silent financial coup d'etat? What can all those who benefited financially in the stock market, or from cheap mortgage and consumer loans or reduced ATM and checking fees, say? We disassociated the source of our financial benefits from what we saw happening around us that we knew was wrong.

Are minorities, women and children being impacted disproportionately? Yes, but that is merely because those with little or no power are easiest to steal from, or kill first. After the U.S. Government's intentional decision to provide no relief in New Orleans in the early days after Katrina, a faster way to set the stage for urban gentrification then the War on Drugs and private prisons, the first Afro-American Secretary of State, Condoleezza Rice, went shopping for $200 shoes while men and women of all ages and backgrounds ... black, brown and white ... lost businesses, homes, families and lives together in the floods. This is the true face of the New World Order.

~ by Catherine Austin Fitts

<> <> <>

African Americans make up 15% of America's drug users, yet they are 37% of people arrested for drug violations, 59% of those convicted, and 74% of those sentenced in prison. While 66% of crack users are white or Hispanic, blacks comprise more than 80% of those sentenced for crack offenses. The average federal drug sentence for crack offenses for American Americans is 49% higher than for whites.

~ Maya Harris, Exec. Dir., ACLU of No. Calif. www.aclu.org/pdfs/drugpolicy/cracksinsystem_20061025.pdf to read ACLU report, *Cracks in the System: Twenty Years of the Unjust Federal Crack Cocaine Law.* -- *San Francisco Post* headline story, *Racially-Biased 'War on Drugs'*, Weekly Edition, May 23-29, 2007

<> <> <>

Excerpt for Reviewers of Appendix 6

[Editor's note: Appendix 6 focuses on the work of Catherine Austin Fitts.]

Lesley Stahl, 60 MINUTES: "We have heard that a half million children have died [because of sanctions against Iraq {Bush I & Iraq War I}]. I mean, that's more children than died in Hiroshima and you know, is the price worth it?

U.S. Secretary of State Madeleine Albright: "This is a very hard choice, but we think the price is worth it."

<>

The power of the killing machine rests in part in the broad-based popular support it receives through the investment system and the markets. How are we to plead ignorance if the profits and growth in our 401K plans and investment portfolios have been enriched from prison stocks and the securities of the banks, home-builders, property managers, mortgage bankers and other groups who managed this process of ethnic and economic cleansing and the gentrification it made possible? What can our "socially responsible" investment managers say when they invest in the stocks of banks, like Citibank and JP Morgan-Chase, and government contractors, like IBM and AT&T, who are running critical parts of government as these manipulations occur ... including the disappearance of 4 trillion dollars from government bank accounts and manipulation of the gold markets and inventory in a silent financial coup d'etat? What can all those who benefited financially in the stock market, or from cheap mortgage and consumer loans or reduced ATM and checking fees, say? We disassociated the source of our financial benefits from what we saw happening around us that we knew was wrong.

Are minorities, women, and children being impacted disproportionately? Yes, but that's because those with little or no power are easiest to steal from, or kill first. After the U.S. Government's intentional decision to provide no relief in New Orleans in the early days after Katrina, a faster way to set the stage for urban gentrification then the War on Drugs and private prisons, the first Afro-American Secretary of State, Condoleezza Rice, went shopping for $200 shoes, while men and women of all ages and backgrounds ... black, brown and white ... lost businesses, homes, families and lives together in the floods. This is the true face of the New World Order.

<> Oct. 1, 1998 was the beginning of the fiscal year in which HUD was missing 59 billion dollars from its accounts ... for which HUD OIG was to refuse to provide an audit as required by law. This amount of money translates into 4.9 billion

dollars per month, 1.2 billion dollars per work week or 30.7 million dollars per work hour.

After reading *Dark Alliance,* I started to study the extraordinary money-making business DOJ Department of Justice and agencies like HUD had built into enforcement ... that only made sense if the government was complicit in narcotics trafficking and related mortgage and mortgage securities fraud. I started to realize the extent private information systems and accounting software companies like DynCorp and AMS were taking control of government agencies behind the scenes ... creating conditions for billions of dollars to disappear from government accounts. I started to research private prison companies when a banker from our bank ... whose colleague's behavior had been egregious and, I believe, criminal towards us, told me how much money they were making in Washington D.C. gentrification and private prisons. This was a theme that kept repeating itself during this period. Private prisons were the next 'big thing' and were going to be 'real money makers'.

So, let's say I'm a customer of a private bank such as Coutts. Let's say through Coutts I have an interest in an offshore fund with private prison investments. The more people who are rounded up and put into prison, the more valuable my investment becomes. If laws are passed for mandatory sentences, the more valuable my investment becomes. If politicians and political appointees push through more prison contracts for private companies, the more valuable my investments become. The more enforcement staff and arrests, the more valuable my investments become. I can borrow on the increased value of my portfolio without having to sell my investment, so I can watch my investment grow, receive distributions based on profitability and still enjoy liquidity it provides. I can turn my investment into ready cash with my ATM card, just as the personal staff for the British Royal Family presumably can through the Coutts ATM machine in the basement of Buckingham palace.

Dec. 18, 1997 CIA Inspector General delivered Volume I of their report to the Senate Select Committee on Intelligence regarding charges CIA was complicit in narcotics trafficking in South Central L.A.

Washington, D.C.'s response was compatible with attracting the continued flow of an estimat-ed 500 billion to 1 trillion dollars a year of money laundering into the U.S. financial system. U.S. Customs Service estimates illegal drug sales in the U.S. alone generate an estimated 57 billion dollars in annual revenues, most of it in cash.

<>

"THE BEST TIME FOR MAKING MONEY, IS WHEN BLOOD IS FLOWING ON THE STREETS."

~ AMSCHEL MAYER ROTHSCHILD

A drug trafficker must be able to access his profits, to pay expenses for the ongoing operation, and to share in the profits; and he must be able to do this in a manner that seemingly legitimizes the origins of his wealth, so as to ward off oversight and investigation that could result in arrest and imprisonment and seizure of monies. The process of achieving these goals is the money-laundering cycle.

The purpose of the money-laundering cycle is to establish total anonymity for the participants, by passing the cash drug proceeds through the financial markets in a way that conceals or disguises the illegal nature, source, ownership, and/or control of the money.

A history of the 1980s is completed by under-standing the lawyers and legal mechanisms used to legitimize drug dealing and money laundering under protection of National Security law.

<>

Camel cigarettes are a leading RJ Reynolds brand. If the European Union is to be believed, Camel cigarettes are also a valued currency serving global mafia, and RJR-Nabisco has been laundering mafia drug profits.

To understand the alleged flow of drug money in and through Wall Street and corporate stocks like RJR Nabisco during the 1980s, it's useful to look more closely at the flow of drugs from Latin America during the period and implied cash flows of narco dollars they suggest. Two documented situations involve Mena, Arkansas and South Central Los Angeles.

<>

Excerpt from European lawsuit against RJR Nabisco.

The primary source of cocaine within THE EUROPEAN COMMUNITY is Colombia. Large volumes of cocaine are transported from Colombia into THE EUROPEAN COMMUNITY and then sold illegally within THE EUROPEAN COMMUNITY and the MEMBER STATES. The proceeds of these illegal sales must be laundered in order to be useable by narcotics traffickers. Throughout the 1990s and continuing to the present day, a primary means by which these cocaine proceeds are laundered is through the purchase and sale of cigarettes, including those manufactured by the RJR DEFENDANTS. Cocaine sales in THE EUROPEAN COMMUNITY are facilitated through money-laundering operations in Colombia, Panama, Switzerland, and elsewhere which utilize RJR cigarettes as the money-laundering vehicle.

In a similar way, the primary source of heroin within THE EUROPEAN COMMUNITY is the Middle East and, in particular, Afghanistan, with the majority of said heroin being sold by Russian organized crime, Middle Eastern criminal organizations, and terrorist groups based in the Middle East. Heroin sales in THE EUROPEAN COMMUNITY and the MEMBER STATES are facilitated and expedited by the purchase and sale of the DEFENDANTS' cigarettes in money-laundering operations that begin in THE EUROPEAN COMMUNITY and the MEMBER STATES, Eastern Europe, and/or Russia, but which ultimately result in the proceeds of those money-laundering activities being deposited into the coffers of the RJR DEFENDANTS in the U.S.

For more than a decade, the DEFENDANTS (hereinafter also referred to as the "RJR DEFENDANTS" or "RJR") have directed, managed, and controlled money-laundering operations that extended within and/or directly damaged the Plaintiffs. The RJR DEFENDANTS have engaged in and facilitated organized crime by laundering proceeds of narcotics trafficking and other crimes. As financial institutions worldwide have largely shunned the banking business of organized crime, narcotics traffickers and others, eager to conceal their crimes and use the fruits of their crimes, have turned away from traditional banks and relied upon companies, in particular the DEFENDANTS herein, to launder the proceeds of unlawful activity.

The DEFENDANTS knowingly sell their products to organized crime, arrange for secret payments from organized crime, and launder such proceeds in the U.S. or offshore venues known for bank secrecy. DEFENDANTS have laundered the illegal proceeds of members of Italian, Russian, and Colombian organized crime through financial institutions in New York City, including The Bank of New York, Citibank N.A., and Chase Manhattan Bank. DEFENDANTS have even chosen to do business in Iraq, in violation of U.S. sanctions, in transactions that financed both the Iraqi regime and terrorist groups.

This overarching scheme to establish a corporate structure and business plan to sell cigarettes to criminals and to launder criminal proceeds was implemented through many subsidiary schemes across THE EUROPEAN COMMUNITY. Examples of these subsidiary schemes are described in this Complaint and include: (a) Laundering criminal proceeds received from the Alfred Bossert money-laundering organization; (b) Money laundering for Italian organized crime; (c) Money laundering for Russian organized crime through the Bank of New York; (d) The Walt money-laundering conspiracy; (e) Money laundering through cut outs in Ireland and Belgium; (f) Laundering of the proceeds of sales throughout THE EUROPEAN COMMUNITY by way of cigarette sales to criminals in Spain; (g) Laundering criminal proceeds in the United Kingdom; (h) Laundering criminal proceeds through cigarette sales via Cyprus; and (i) Illegal narcotics and cigarette sales into Iraq.

<>

Perhaps this should make us pause for a moment and think, if the housing bubble turned our homes into ATM machines and in turn induced many of us to take on debt beyond our means, will privatization of our prison system provide incentives for those profiting from such investments to support policies that make us more of a target?

<>

According to Fitts ... a useful calculation is to look at how many taxpayers will have to work their entire lives to pay the taxes for this many people to be imprisoned. Let's assume the average taxpayer pays $150,000 of federal taxes in an entire lifetime. Based on the General Accounting Office's (now the General Accountability Office, the Congressional Auditor) study in 1996 that indicated the total annual federal, state and local system expenditures per prisoner were approximately $154,000. That means that ten taxpayers would have to work their whole lives to pay for one prisoner with a mandatory sentence of ten years.

<>

On this basis, the following estimates how many people would have to work their whole lives to pay the taxes to fund the incarcerations necessary to generate Dillon's profits on Cornell Corrections.

John H. F. Haskell, Jr. ~ largest Dillon buyer of Cornell Corrections stock personally after firm Chairman, John P. Birkelund, joined Birkelund and third largest buyer David Niemic at Saratoga Partners after Dillon was sold.

Estimated Number of People Working Their Entire Lives to Pay Taxes to Fund Prisoners Incarcerated for Extended Period to Generate Dillon Stock Profits:

Dillon Partner Taxpayer-Lives
John P. Birkelund ~ 340 John Haskell, Jr. ~ 310 David W. Niemiec ~ 300 Fritz Hobbs ~ 260 George A. Wiegers ~ 240 Peter Flanigan ~ 240 Kenneth M. Schmidt ~ 210 All Dillon Read Officers and Directors Investing ~ 11,523

When one of RJR Nabisco's former lead investment bankers, Dillon Read, and its investors made in the range of 30 million dollars cashing out of a private prison company, they were cashed out directly or indirectly by one of RJR Nabisco's lead investors.

I wonder what the ghost of Barry Seal would say about what that might all have to do with the alleged 5 billion dollars of drugs he pumped through a little airport in Mena Arkansas, and who was responsible to reinvest that money. I wonder what Lou Gerstner, Henry Kravis and George Roberts as CEO and lead investors in RJR would say if given truth serum about who may be responsible for reinvesting dirty money allegedly laundered with RJR cigarette sales.

In Cornell's prospectus, when Dillon Read led its second stock offering Oct. 10, 1997 Brown University's Third Century Fund was listed as a shareholder with 88,818 shares, of which 28,818 shares were to be sold through the offering.

John Birkelund, Chairman and CEO of Dillon Read, was a long-time trustee of Brown University. The price on the 1997 offering was $19 5/8 per share. If Brown's average profit was the difference between the 1997 price and the 1996 offering price of $12 per share, it would have generated a profit in a year's time of $677,237. Brown's return on investment under these assumptions would have been a smashing 63.5%. If it had sold when the stock peaked after the offering at or around the time Dillon appears to have sold out, it would have been higher.

The number of people who needed to be imprisoned for many years to generate such investment profits based on the foregoing assumptions was 67 people. An estimate of the number of men and women in the U.S. who would have to work their whole life to pay the taxes to imprison those 67 people would be 670 people.

Catherine Austin Fitts is a former board member of Dillon Read & Co., former Assistant Secretary of Housing & Federal Housing Commissioner under Bush I, former president of Hamilton Securities Group, currently president of Solari, Inc., an investment advisory firm in Hickory Valley, Tennessee.

Happy Birthday Fed
Happy 100th Anniversary, 1913-2013

Dec. 23, 1913, Congressman Lindbergh addressed the House, "This Act establishes the most gigantic trust on earth. When the President signs this bill, the invisible government by the 'Monetary Power' will be legalized. The people may not know it immediately, but the day of reckoning is only a few years removed. The trusts will soon realize they have gone too far for their own good. The people must make a declaration of independence to relieve themselves from the Monetary Power. This they will be able to do by taking control of Congress.

"Wall Streeters could not cheat us if you Senators and Representatives did not make a humbug of Congress. If we had a people's Congress, there would be stability.

"The greatest crime of Congress is its currency system. The caucus and party bosses have prevented the people from getting the benefit of their own government," Charles Lindbergh said.

Eustace sums it up. "With the setting up of the twelve 'financial districts' through the Federal Reserve Banks, the traditional division of the United States into the forty-eight states was overthrown...

<>

"...and we entered the era of 'regionalism', or twelve regions which had no relation to the traditional state boundaries. These developments following the passing of the Federal Reserve Act proved every one of the allegations Thomas Jefferson had made against a central bank in 1791 ... that the subscribers to the Federal Reserve Bank stock had formed a corporation, whose stock could be and was held by aliens ... that this stock would be transmitted to a certain line of successors ... that it would be placed beyond forfeiture and escheat ... that they would receive a monopoly of banking, which was against the laws of monopoly ... and that they now had the power to make laws, paramount to the laws of the states.

"No state legislature can countermand any of the laws laid down by the Federal Reserve Board of Governors for the benefit of their private stockholders. This board issues laws as to what the interest rate shall be, what the quantity of money shall be and what the price of money shall be. All of these powers abrogate the powers of the state legislatures and their responsibility to the citizens of those states. Rep. James Traficant, Jr. of Ohio addressed U.S. House of Representatives ...his comments were entered into U.S. Congressional Record, Mar. 17, 1993 v. 33 p. H-1303.

http://www.iresist.com/cbg/bankruptcy.html

James looked at the other Representatives.

"Why don't more people own their properties outright? Why are 90% of Americans mortgaged to the hilt ...and have little or no assets after all debts and liabilities have been paid? Why does it feel like you are working harder and harder and getting less and less?

"America has become completely bankrupt in world leadership, financial credit and its reputation for courage, vision and human rights. This is an undeclared economic war, bankruptcy, and economic slavery of the most corrupt order! Wake up America! Take back your Country.

"We are reaping what has been sown, and the results of our harvest is a painful bankruptcy, and a foreclosure on American property, precious liberties, and our way of life. The federal United States is bankrupt. Our children will inherit this unpayable debt ... and the tyranny to enforce paying it.

"The United States Federal Government was dissolved by the Emergency Banking Act, March 9, 1933, 48 Stat. 1, Public Law 89-719 ... declared by President Roosevelt, being bankrupt and insolvent. We are here now in chapter 11. Members of Congress are official trustees presiding over the greatest reorganization of any bankrupt entity in world history, the U.S. Government.

"This act was instituted and established by transferring the Office of the Secretary of Treasury to that of the Governor of the International Monetary Fund.

"The receivers of the United States bankruptcy are the international bankers, via the United Nations, the World Bank and the International Monetary Fund. All U.S. Offices, Officials, and Departments are now operating within a de facto status in name only under Emergency War Powers [which allegedly gives the President legal dictatorial powers]. With the Constitutional Republican form of Government now dissolved, the receivers of the Bankruptcy have adopted a new form of government for the U.S. This new form of government is known as a 'Democracy', being an established Socialist/Communist order under a new governor for America.

Federal Reserve System is based on the Canon law and principles of sovereignty protected in the Constitution and the Bill of Rights. In fact, the international bankers used a 'Canon Law Trust' as their model, adding stock and naming it a

584

'Joint Stock Trust'. The U.S. Congress had passed a law making it illegal for any legal 'person' to duplicate a 'Joint Stock Trust' in 1873. The Federal Reserve Act was legislated post-facto (to 1870), although post-facto laws are strictly forbidden by the Constitution.

The Federal Reserve System is a sovereign power structure separate and distinct from the federal United States government. The Federal Reserve is a maritime lender, and/or maritime insurance underwriter to the federal U.S. operating exclusively under Admiralty/Maritime law. The lender or underwriter bears the risks, and the Maritime law compelling specific performance in paying the interest, or premiums are the same.

Assets of the debtor can also be hypothecated (to pledge something as a security without taking possession of it as security by the lender or underwriter. The Federal Reserve Act stipulated that the interest on the debt was to be paid in gold. There was no stipulation in the Federal Reserve Act for ever paying the principle.

Prior to 1913, most Americans owned clear, allodial title to property, free and clear of any liens or mortgages until the Federal Reserve Act (1913) 'Hypothecated' all property within the federal United States to the Board of Governors of the Federal Reserve, in which the Trustees (stockholders) held legal title. The U.S. citizen (tenant, franchisee) was registered as a 'beneficiary' of the trust via his/her birth certificate. In 1933, the federal United States hypothecated all of the present and future properties, assets and labor of their 'subjects', via the 14th Amendment of every U.S. citizen, to the Federal Reserve System.

In return, the Federal Reserve System agreed to extend the federal United States Corporation all the credit 'money substitute' it needed. Like any other debtor, the federal United States government had to assign collateral and security to their creditors as a condition of the loan. Since the federal United States didn't have any assets, they assigned the private property of their 'economic slaves', the U.S. citizens ... as collateral against the unpayable federal debt. They also pledged the unincorporated federal territories, national parks forests, birth certificates, and nonprofit organizations, as collateral against the federal debt. All has already been transferred as payment to the international bankers.

Unwittingly, America has returned to its pre-American Revolution, feudal roots whereby all land is held by a sovereign and the common people had no rights to hold allodial title to property. Once again, We the People are the tenants and sharecroppers renting our own property from a Sovereign in the guise of the Federal Reserve Bank. We the people have exchanged one master for another.

This has been going on for over eighty years without the 'informed knowledge' of the American people, without a voice protesting loud enough. Now, it's easy to grasp why America is fundamentally bankrupt.

Gold and silver were such a powerful money during the founding of the U.S., that the founding fathers declared that only gold or silver coins can be 'money' in America. Since gold and silver coinage were heavy and inconvenient for a lot of transactions, they were stored in banks and a claim check was issued as a money substitute. People traded their coupons as money, or 'currency'. Currency is not money, but a money substitute. Redeemable currency must promise to pay a dollar equivalent in gold or silver money. Federal Reserve Notes make no such promises, and are not 'money'. A Federal Reserve Note is a debt obligation of the federal U.S. government, not 'money'. The federal U.S. government and the U.S. Congress were not and have never been authorized by the Constitution for the U.S. to issue currency of any kind, but only lawful money ... gold and silver coin.

It is essential that we comprehend the distinction between real money and paper money substitute. One cannot get rich by accumulating these money substitutes, one can only get deeper into debt. We the People no longer have any 'money'. Most Americans have not been paid any 'money' for a very long time, perhaps not in their entire life. Now do you comprehend why you feel broke? Now, do you understand why you are 'bankrupt', along with the rest of the country?

Federal Reserve Notes (FRNs) are unsigned checks written on a closed account. FRNs are an inflatable paper system designed to create debt through inflation (devaluation of currency). when ever there is an increase of the supply of a money substitute in the economy without a corresponding increase in the gold and silver backing, inflation occurs.

Inflation is an invisible form of taxation that irresponsible governments inflict on their citizens. The Federal Reserve Bank who controls the supply and movement of FRNs has everybody fooled. They have access to an unlimited supply of FRNs, paying only for the printing costs of what they need. FRNs are nothing more than promissory notes for U.S. Treasury securities (T-Bills) ...a promise to pay the debt to the Federal

Reserve Bank.

There is a fundamental difference between 'paying' and 'discharging' a debt. To pay a debt, you must pay with value or substance (i.e. gold, silver, barter or a commodity). With FRNs, you can only discharge a debt. You cannot pay a debt with a debt currency system. You cannot service a debt with a currency that has no backing in value or substance. No contract in Common law is valid unless it involves an exchange of 'good & valuable consideration'. Unpayable debt transfers power and control to the sovereign power structure that has no interest in money, law, equity or justice because they have so much wealth already.

Their lust is for power and control. Since the inception of central banking, they have controlled the fates of nations," James Traficant Jr. said.

<>

[Ed's note, the Federal Reserve announced as of Mar. 20, 2006 they would no longer publish 'M3' Data showing the amount of cash printed to put into circulation, propping up the U.S. economy ...so there is no way for the public, investors or bond holders to know how much currency exists or how much a 'dollar' is worth.]

<>

Judge Martin Mahoney heard *First National Bank of Montgomery v. Jerome Daly,* Dec. 7, 1968 17 Am. Jur. 85, 215, 1 Mer. Jur. 2nd on Actions, Section 550.

"The Federal Reserve Act and National Bank Act are in operation and effect contrary to the letter and spirit of the Constitution of the United States ... for they confer an unlawful and unnecessary power on private parties ...they hold all of our fellow citizens in dependence ...they are subversive to the rights and liberation of the people. These Acts have defied the lawfully constituted Government of the United States. The Federal Reserve Act and National Banking Act are not necessary and proper for carrying into execution the legislative powers granted to Congress (See Article 1, Section 8, Clause 5 of the Constitution of the United States) or any other powers vested in the government of the United States, but on the contrary, are subversive to the rights of the People in their rights to life, liberty, and property...

"No rights can be acquired by fraud. Federal Reserve Notes are acquired through the use of unconstitutional statutes and fraud. The law leaves wrongdoers where it finds them. Slavery and all its incidents, including peonage, thralldom, and the debt created by fraud is universally prohibited in the U.S. This case represents but another refined form of slavery by bankers. Their position is not supported by the Constitution. There is no lawful consideration for Federal Reserve Notes to circulate as money. Banks actually obtain these notes for the cost of printing. A lawful consideration must exist for a note...

"Activity of the Federal Reserve Banks ... and First National Bank of Montgomery, is contrary to public policy and contrary to the Constitution of the United States ... and constitutes unlawful creation of money and credit for no valuable consideration. Activity of said banks in creating money and credit is not warranted by the Constitution of the United States. Federal Reserve Banks and National Banks exercise an exclusive monopoly and privilege of creating credit and issuing notes at the expense of the public, which does not receive a fair equivalent. This scheme is obliquely designed for the benefit of a monopoly to rob, blackmail and oppress the producers of wealth" [... us.]

Judge Mahoney ruled for Daly, and was assassinated two weeks later.

<>

The history of the U.S. showcases Thomas Jefferson wanting a publicly owned central bank, & Alexander Hamilton wanting a privately owned central bank. It's history, lost history.

<>

"Bankers are a den of vipers. I intend to rout you out & by the Eternal God I will rout you out. If the people only understood the rank injustice of our central bank system, there would be a revolution before morning. If the central bank continues to control our currency, receiving our public monies, & holding thousands of our citizens in dependence, it would be more formidable & dangerous than the naval & military power of the enemy. It is not our own citizens only who are to receive the bounty of our government ... More than 8 million dollars of the stock of this bank are held by foreigners ... Is there no danger to our liberty & independence in a bank that in its nature has so little to bind it to our country? If government would confine itself to equal protection, and, as Heaven does its rains, shower its favor alike on the high & the low, the rich & the poor, it would be an unqualified blessing."

~ President Andrew Jackson, 1829-1837

"Banking institutions are more dangerous to our liberties than standing armies. If American people ever allow private banks to control the issue of their currency, first by inflation, then by deflation, the banks & corporations that will grow up around will deprive the people of all property until their children wake-up homeless on the continent their fathers conquered. The issuing power should be taken from the banks & restored to the people, to whom it properly belongs."

~ President Thomas Jefferson, 1801-1809

"Whoever controls the money of a nation, controls that nation & is absolute master of all industry & commerce. When you realize that the entire system is very easily controlled, one way or another, by a few powerful men at the top, you will not have to be told how periods of inflation & depression originate."

~ President James Garfield, 1891

"Capital must protect itself in every possible manner by combination & legislation. Debts must be collected, bonds & mortgages must be foreclosed as rapidly as possible. When, through a process of law, the common people lose their homes they will become more docile & more easily governed through the influence of the strong arm of government, applied by a central power of wealth under control of leading financiers. This truth is well known among our principal men now engaged in forming an imperialism of Capital to govern the world.

"By dividing voters through the political party system, we get them to expend energies fighting over questions of no importance. Thus by discreet action we can secure for ourselves what has been so well planned & successfully accomplished. ~Aug. 25, 1924 *USA Banker's Magazine*

"The exercises that went on that morning simulating the exact thing that was happening so confused the people in the FAA and NORAD ... they didn't know what was real and what was part of the exercise. I think the people who planned and carried out those exercises, they're the ones that should be the object of investigation ... there's been nothing closer to fascism than what we've seen lately from this government ... the Patriot Act has done more to destroy the rights of Americans than all our enemies combined,"

~ Bob Bowman, former advocate of Starwars with Dick Cheney ... now opponent.

http://bowman2006.com/index.htm

<>

Federal Reserve Directors
A Study of Corporate & Banking Influence

Source: Federal Reserve Directors: A Study of Corporate & Banking Influence. Staff Report, Committee on Banking, Currency & Housing, House of Representatives, 94thCongress, 2nd Session, August 1976. (72 charts)

commentary by Eustace Mullins
www.fdrs.org/secrets_of_the_federal_reserve.html

Chart 1 legend ~ the linear connection between the Rothschilds & the Bank of England, & the London banking houses which ultimately control the Federal Reserve Banks through their stockholdings of bank stock & their subsidiary firms in New York. The two principal Rothschild representatives in New York, J. P. Morgan Co., & Kuhn, Loeb & Co. were the firms which set up the Jekyll Island Conference at which the Federal Reserve Act was drafted, who directed the subsequent successful campaign to have the plan enacted into law by Congress, & who purchased the controlling amounts of stock in the Federal Reserve Bank of New York in 1914. These firms had their principal officers appointed to the Federal Reserve Board of Governors & the Federal Advisory Council in 1914.

In 1914 a few families (blood or business related) owning controlling stock in existing banks (such as in New York City) caused those banks to purchase controlling shares in the Federal Reserve regional banks. Examination of the charts & text in House Banking Committee Staff Report, August, 1976 & current stockholders list of 12 regional Federal Reserve Banks ...show this same, family control.

U.S. House of Representatives, 94th Congress, 2d session, Aug. 1976, Federal Reserve Directors, a Study of Corporate & Banking Influence

This 120 page Congressional study details public policy functions of the Federal Reserve District Banks, how directors are selected, who is selected, the public relations lobbying factor, bank domination & bank examination, & corporate interlocks with Reserve banks. Charts were used to illustrate Class A, Class B, & Class C directorships of each district bank. For each branch bank a chart was designed giving information regarding bank appointed directors & those appointed by the Board of Governors of the Federal Reserve System.

In his Foreword to the study, Chairman Henry S. Reuss, (D-Wis) wrote: "This Committee has observed for many years the influence of private interests over the essentially public responsibilities of the Federal Reserve System." As the study makes clear, it is difficult to imagine a more narrowly based board of directors for a public agency than has been gathered together for the twelve banks of the Federal Reserve System. Only two segments of American society ... banking & big business ... have any substantial representation on the boards, & often even these become merged through interlocking directorates. Small farmers are absent. Small business is barely visible. No women appear on the district boards & only six among the branches. System-wide, including district & branch boards, only thirteen members from minority groups appear.

The study raises a substantial question about the Federal Reserve's oft-repeated claim of 'independence'. One might ask, independent from what? Surely not banking or big business, if we are to judge from the massive interlocks revealed by this analysis of the district boards. The big business & banking dominance of the Federal Reserve System cited in this report can be traced, in part, to the original Federal Reserve Act, which gave member commercial banks the right to select two-thirds of the directors of each district bank. But the Board of Governors in Washington must share the responsibility for this imbalance. They appoint the so-called 'public' members of the boards of each district bank, appointments which have largely reflected the same narrow interests of the bank-elected members.

Until we have basic reforms, the Federal Reserve System will be handicapped in carrying out its public responsibilities as an economic stabilization & bank regulatory agency. The System's mandate is too essential to the nation's welfare to leave so much of the machinery under the control of narrow private interests. Concentration of economic & financial power in the United States has gone too far." In a section of the text entitled the 'Club System', the Committee noted, "This 'club' approach leads the Federal Reserve to consistently dip into the same pools ... the same companies, the same universities, the same bank holding companies ... to fill directorships."

This Congressional study concludes as follows, 'Many of the companies on these tables, as mentioned earlier, have multiple interlocks to the Federal Reserve System. First Bank Systems, Southeast Banking Corp., Federated Department Stores, Westinghouse Electric Corporation, Proctor & Gamble, Alcoa, Honeywell, Inc., Kennecott Copper, Owens-Corning Fiberglass ... all have two or more director ties to district or branch banks. In summary, the Federal Reserve directors are apparently representatives of a small elite group that dominates much of the economic life of this nation.

Chart 2 legend
Federal Reserve Directors:
A Study of Corporate & Banking Influence
commentary by Eustace Mullins
www.fdrs.org/secrets_of_the_federal_reserve.html

J. Henry Schroder Banking Company chart encompasses the entire history of the Twentieth Century, embracing as it does the program (Belgium Relief Commission) which provisioned Germany from 1915-1918 and dissuaded Germany from seeking peace in 1916; financing Hitler in 1933 so as to make a Second World War possible; backing the Presidential campaign of Herbert Hoover; and even at the present time [Editor's note: mid-'80s], having two of its major executives of its subsidiary firm, Bechtel Corporation serving as Secretary of Defense and Secretary of State in the Reagan Administration.

Sir Gordon Richardson, head of the Bank of England since 1973, Governor of the Bank of England (controlled by the House of Rothschild) was chairman of J. Henry Schroder Wagg & Company of London from 1963-72, & director of J. Henry Schroder, New York & Schroder Banking Corporation, New York, as well as Lloyd's Bank of London, & Rolls Royce. He maintains a residence on Sutton Place in New York City,

& as head of 'The London Connection', can be said to be **the single most influential banker in the world.**

Chart 3 legend
Federal Reserve Directors:
A Study of Corporate & Banking Influence
commentary by Eustace Mullins
www.fdrs.org/secrets_of_the_federal_reserve.html
David Rockefeller chart shows link between Federal Reserve Bank of New York, Standard Oil of Indiana, General Motors & Allied Chemical Corp. (Eugene Meyer family) & Equitable Life (J.P. Morgan).

Chart 4 legend
Interlocks between Federal Reserve Bank of New York, J. Henry Schroder Banking Corp., J. Henry Schroder Trust Co., Rockefeller Center, Inc., Equitable Life Assurance Society (J.P. Morgan), & Federal Reserve Bank of Boston.

Chart 5 legend
Link between Federal Reserve Bank of New York, Brown Brothers Harriman, Sun Life Assurance Co. (N.M. Rothschild & Sons) & Rockefeller Foundation.
Chart Source: Federal Reserve Directors: A Study of Corporate & Banking Influence. Staff Report, Committee on Banking, Currency & Housing, House of Representatives, 94th Congress, 2nd Session, August 1976. (72 charts)

Add'l Chart
Federal Advisory Council to the
Federal Reserve Board of Governors in 1914

James B. Forgan
Federal Advisory Council Pres, 1914-1920

Royal Bank of Scotland

Bank of Nova Scotia
First National Bank of Chicago
(owns 10% FRB Dist 7 (Chicago)
Principal Correspondent
1st National Bank, NY
Philadelphia National
Bank of Manhattan, NY

J.P. Morgan
Chairman, Federal Advisory Council Executive Committee

First National Bank of New York
(owns 7% FDR Bank Dist 2, NY)
Correspondent bank for many outlaying
large banks, especially those percentage
of the FRB of their district, such as: First
National Bank of Chicago; Philadelphia
National Bank; First National Bank
of San Francisco

Daniel S. Wing
Federal Advisory Council Vice Pres.
First Nat'l Bank of Boston
(owns 6% of FDR Bank Dist 1 (Boston)

W.S. Rowe
First Nat'l Bank of Cincinnati
(owns 4% of FER Bank Dist 4 (Cleveland)

Levi L. Rue
Philadelphia National Bank
(owns 3% of FRB Dist 3, (Philadelphia)

C.T. Jaffray
First National Bank of Minneapolis
(owns 5% of FRD Bank, Dist 9 (Minneapolis)
500 shares of 1st National Bank of
Minneapolis held by First Securities, NY
(Baker/Morgan); 5,400 shares National
Bank of Commerce; Chase National Bank

E.F Swinney
First National Bank of Kansas City
(owns 5% of FRB Dist 10, (Kansas City)

Archibald Kains
(San Francisco, California)

588

American Foreign Banking Corp., NY
Archibald Kains represented the San Francisco
district on the Federal Advisory Council, although
he maintained his office in New York, as president
of the American Foreign Banking Corp.

Editor's note: some of this information is sketchy, as it was
received in tattered form. For investigative journalism on the
Fed, see Eustace Mullins, www.fdrs.org/secrets_of_the_feder-
al_reserve.html

<> <> <>

excerpt from the novel

Dave Emory picked up a envelope of papers, paraphrased David Morse's, *War of the Future, Oil Drives the Genocide in Darfur,* and read from it. "The North-South conflict started when Chevron discovered oil in southern Sudan in 1978. The Khartoum government was Arab-dominated ..and, gerrymandered jurisdictional boundaries ... to exclude the oil reserves from southern jurisdiction. John Garang, leader of the rebel Sudan People's Liberation Army (SPLA), declared oil pipelines, pumping stations and well-heads to be targets of war.

<>

"For a time, the oil companies fled the conflict ...but, in the 1990s began to return. Chinese and Indian companies were aggressive, doing their drilling behind perimeters of bermed earth ...guarded by troops, to protect against rebel attacks. A Chinese pipeline to the Red Sea first brought Sudanese oil to international markets.

"The northern regime in Khartoum wanted to impose shariah, or, Islamic law, on the Christian and animist South ...but, Khartoum dropped this demand ... under terms of the Comprehensive Peace Treaty, signed Jan. 2004 ... a treaty brokered with help of the U.S. ...signed at the expense of Darfur in western Sudan, an oil rich desert, the size of France. The South was permitted to have it's own civil law, including, rights for women. But, oil revenues would be divided between Khartoum ... and Sudan People's Liberation Army, SPLA. Under a power-sharing agreement, SPLA commander John Garang would be installed as vice president of Sudan. Darfur, to the west, was left out of the treaty.

"In western Sudan, Darfur is more Muslim and less Christian than southern Sudan ...but, black African, and identifies by tribes such as the Fur ... Darfur, means 'land of the Fur'. In Darfur, the practice of Islam was not extreme enough to suit the Islamists who controlled Khartoum ... in northern Sudan ...so, Darfur villages were burned to clear the way for drilling and pipelines, the land seized from Black farmers being given to Arabs from neighboring Chad. 'In north Sudan, oil revenues to Khartoum have been about 1 million dollars a day, exactly the amount which the government funnels into arms, helicopters and bombers from Russia, tanks from Poland and China, missiles from Iran.

<>

CHART 1 -- Shareholders (private owners) & interlocking directorates of the U.S. Federal Reserve Bank
Source: Federal Reserve Directors: A Study of Corporate & Banking Influence. Staff Report, Committee on Banking, Currency & Housing, House of Representatives, 94th Congress, 2nd Session, August 1976. (72 charts)

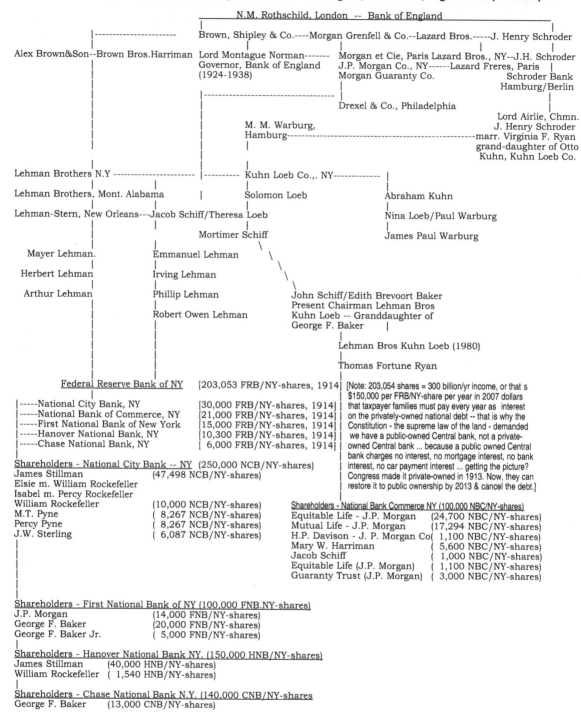

N.M. Rothschild, London -- Bank of England

Brown, Shipley & Co.----Morgan Grenfell & Co.--Lazard Bros.-----J. Henry Schroder

Alex Brown&Son--Brown Bros.Harriman Lord Montague Norman-------   Morgan et Cie, Paris Lazard Bros., NY--J.H. Schroder
                                     Governor, Bank of England   J.P. Morgan Co., NY-----Lazard Freres, Paris
                                     (1924-1938)   Morgan Guaranty Co.   Schroder Bank
                                                                                                   Hamburg/Berlin

                                                                    Drexel & Co., Philadelphia
                                                                                              Lord Airlie, Chmn.
                                     M. M. Warburg,   J. Henry Schroder
                                     Hamburg--marr. Virginia F. Ryan
                                                                                             grand-daughter of Otto
                                                                                             Kuhn, Kuhn Loeb Co.

Lehman Brothers N.Y ----------------------- |---------- Kuhn Loeb Co.,. NY------------ |

Lehman Brothers, Mont. Alabama   Solomon Loeb   Abraham Kuhn

Lehman-Stern, New Orleans---Jacob Schiff/Theresa Loeb   Nina Loeb/Paul Warburg

                                     Mortimer Schiff   James Paul Warburg

Mayer Lehman.   Emmanuel Lehman

Herbert Lehman   Irving Lehman

Arthur Lehman   Phillip Lehman   John Schiff/Edith Brevoort Baker
                                                     Present Chairman Lehman Bros
                           Robert Owen Lehman   Kuhn Loeb -- Granddaughter of
                                                     George F. Baker

                                                     Lehman Bros Kuhn Loeb (1980)

                                                     Thomas Fortune Ryan

Federal Reserve Bank of NY   [203,053 FRB/NY-shares, 1914]   [Note: 203,054 shares = 300 billion/yr income, or that s
                                                               $150,000 per FRB/NY-share per year in 2007 dollars
|-----National City Bank, NY   [30,000 FRB/NY-shares, 1914]   that taxpayer families must pay every year as interest
|-----National Bank of Commerce, NY   [21,000 FRB/NY-shares, 1914]   on the privately-owned national debt -- that is why the
|-----First National Bank of New York [15,000 FRB/NY-shares, 1914]   Constitution - the supreme law of the land - demanded
|-----Hanover National Bank, NY   [10,300 FRB/NY-shares, 1914]   we have a public-owned Central bank, not a private-
|-----Chase National Bank, NY   [6,000 FRB/NY-shares, 1914]   owned Central bank ... because a public owned Central
                                                                       bank charges no interest, no mortgage interest, no bank
Shareholders - National City Bank -- NY (250,000 NCB/NY-shares)   interest, no car payment interest ... getting the picture?
James Stillman   (47,498 NCB/NY-shares)   Congress made it private-owned in 1913. Now, they can
Elsie m. William Rockefeller   restore it to public ownership by 2013 & cancel the debt.]
Isabel m. Percy Rockefeller
William Rockefeller   (10,000 NCB/NY-shares)   Shareholders - National Bank Commerce NY (100,000 NBC/NY-shares)
M.T. Pyne   (8,267 NCB/NY-shares)   Equitable Life - J.P. Morgan   (24,700 NBC/NY-shares)
Percy Pyne   (8,267 NCB/NY-shares)   Mutual Life - J.P. Morgan   (17,294 NBC/NY-shares)
J.W. Sterling   (6,087 NCB/NY-shares)   H.P. Davison - J. P. Morgan Co(1,100 NBC/NY-shares)
                                                  Mary W. Harriman   (5,600 NBC/NY-shares)
                                                  Jacob Schiff   (1,000 NBC/NY-shares)
                                                  Equitable Life (J.P. Morgan)   (1,100 NBC/NY-shares)
                                                  Guaranty Trust (J.P. Morgan)   (3,000 NBC/NY-shares)

Shareholders - First National Bank of NY (100,000 FNB.NY-shares)
J.P. Morgan   (14,000 FNB/NY-shares)
George F. Baker   (20,000 FNB/NY-shares)
George F. Baker Jr.   (5,000 FNB/NY-shares)

Shareholders - Hanover National Bank NY. (150,000 HNB/NY-shares)
James Stillman   (40,000 HNB/NY-shares)
William Rockefeller (1,540 HNB/NY-shares)

Shareholders - Chase National Bank N.Y. (140,000 CNB/NY-shares
George F. Baker   (13,000 CNB/NY-shares)

CHART 2
J. Henry Schroder

Baron Rudolph Von Schroder
Hamburg - 1858 - 1934

Baron Bruno Von Schroder
Hamburg - 1867 - 1940

F. C. Tiarks------------
1874-1952
marr. Emma Franziska
(Hamburg)
J. Henry Schroder, 1902
Dir. Bank of England
Dir. Anglo-Iranian Oil Co.

Helmut B. Schroder

J. Henry Schroder Banking Co. N.Y.

J. Henry Schroder Trust Co. N.Y.

Allen Dulles
Sullivan & Cromwell
Director -- CIA

John Foster Dulles
Sullivan & Cromwell
U.S. Secretary of State
Rockefeller Foundation

Prentiss Gray
Belgian Relief Comm.
Chief Marine Transportation
U.S. Food Administration WW I
Manati Sugar Co. American &
British Continental Corp.

Lord Airlie
Chairman; Virginia Fortune
Ping Coal Mines, Tientsin
Ryan daughter of Otto Kahn
of Kuhn, Loeb Co.

M. E. Rionda
Pres., Cuba Cane Sugar Co.
Manati Sugar Co. & many other
sugar companies.

G. A. Zabriskie
Chmn U.S. Sugar Equalization Board
Board 1917-18; Pres Empire
Biscuit Co., Columbia Baking
Co., Southern Baking Co.

Emile Francoui
Belgian Relief Comm. Kai
Ping Coal Mines, Tientsin
Railroad, Congo Copper,
Banque Nationale de Belgique

Suite 2000 42 Broadway, NY

Edgar Richard

Belgium Relief Comm
Amer Relief Comm
U.S. Food Admin
1918-24, Hazeltine Corp.

Julius H. Barnes

Belgium Relief Comm
Pres, Grain Corp.
U.S. Food Admin
1917-18, C.B Pitney
Bowes Corp, Manati
Sugar Corp.

Herbert Hoover

Chmn Belgium Relief
U.S. Food Admin
Sec of Commerce 24-28
Kaiping Coal Mines
Congo Copper
U.S. President, 1928-32

John Lowery Simpson
Sacramento, Calif Belgium Relief
Comm. U. S. Food Administration
Prentiss Gray Co. J. Henry Schroder
Trust, Schroder-Rockefeller, Chmn
Fin Comm, Bechtel International
Co. Bechtel Co. (Casper Weinberger
Sec of Defense; George P. Schultz
Sec of State (Reagan Admin)
SS Senior Group Leader

Baron Kurt Von Schroder
Schroder Banking Corp. J.H. Stein
Bankhaus (Hitler's personal bank
account) served on board of all
German subsidiaries of ITT
Bank for International Settlements

Himmler's Circle of Friends (Nazi Fund)
Schroder-Rockefeller & Co., NY
Deutsche Reichsbank, pres.
Avery Rockefeller, J. Henry Schroder
Banking Corp., Bechtel Co., Bechtel
International Co., Canadian Bechtel Co.

Sir Gordon Richardson
Governor, Bank of England
1973-PRESENT C.B. of J. Henry Schroder N.Y.
Schroder Banking Co., New York, Lloyds Bank
Rolls Royce

CHART 3
David Rockefeller, Chairman, Chase Manhattan Corp

Chase Manhattan Corp. Officer & Director Interlocks

Private Investment Co. for America	Allied Chemicals Corp.
Firestone Tire & Rubber Co.	General Motors
Orion Multinational Services Ltd	Rockefeller Family & Associates
ASARCO. Inc	Chrysler Corp.
Southern Peru Copper Corp.	Intl' Basic Economy Corp.
Industrial Minerva Mexico S.A.	R.H. Macy & Co.
Continental Corp.	Selected Risk Investments S.A.
Honeywell Inc.	Omega Fund, Inc.
Northwest Airlines, Inc.	Squibb Corp.
Northwestern Bell Telephone Co.	Olin Foundation
Minnesota Mining & Mfg Co (3M)	Mutual Benefit Life Ins. Co. NJ
American Express Co.	AT&T
Hewlett Packard	Pacific Northwestern Bell Co.
FMC Corporation	BeachviLime Ltd.
Utah Intl' Inc.	Eveleth Expansion Co.
Exxon Corporation	Fidelity Union Bancorporation
International Nickel/Canada	Cypress Woods Corp.
Federated Capital Corp.	Intl' Minerals & Chemical Corp.
Equitable Life Assurance Soc U.S.	Burlington Industries
Federated Dept Stores	Wachovia Corporation
General Electric	Jefferson Pilot Corp.
Scott Paper Co.	R. J. Reynolds Industries Inc.
American Petroleum Institute	United States Steel Corp.
Richardson Merril Inc.	Metropolitan Life Insurance Co.
May Department Stores Co.	Norton-Simon Inc.
Sperry Rand Corporation	Stone-Webster Inc.
San Salvador Development Co.	Standard Oil of Indiana

Chart 4
Alan Pifer, President. Carnegie Corp. of NY

Carnegie Corp. Trustee Interlocks-----------
Rockefeller Center, Inc	J. Henry Schroder Trust Co.
The Cabot Corp.	Paul Revere Investors, Inc.
Fed. Reserve Bank of Boston	Qualpeco, Inc.
Owens Corning Fiberglas	
New England Telephone Co.	
Fisher Scientific Co.	
Mellon National Corporation	
Equitable Life Assurance Society	
Twentieth Century Fox Corp.	
J. Henry Schroder Banking Corp.	

Chart 5
Maurice F. Granville, Chairman, Texaco Incorporated

Texaco Officer & Director Interlocks---Liggett & Myers, Inc.

London ------ Arabian American Oil Co.   St John d'el Ray Mining Ltd.
Connection -- Brown Brothers Harriman   National Steel Corp.
------ Brown Harriman & Intl' Banks Ltd. Massey-Ferguson Ltd.
American Express   Mutual Life Insurance Co.
Amer. Express   Intl' Bank Mass Mutual Income Invest
Anaconda Copper   United Services Life Ins. Co.
Rockefeller Foundation   Fairchild Industries
Owens-Corning Fiberglas   Blount, Inc.
Nat I City Bank (Cleveland)   William Wrigley Jr. Co
I.M. Roths- --- Sun Life Assurance Co.   Nat I Blvd. Bank of Chicago
schild &   General Reinsurance   Lykes Youngstown Corp.
Sons, Ltd.   General Electric (NBC)   Inmount Corp.

<>

errata

A lot of people during my presidency ...and, during both Presidents Bush, attack the Bush Dynasty ...because, *they* co-owned Hamburg Amerika shipping company. Horse-pucky. History says, the financial panic of 1897 forced Union Pacific Railroad into bankruptcy. So, in 1898, Edward H. Harriman and Robert Lovett bought that railroad for 110 million dollars, in a deal brokered by New York-based Kuhn Loeb investment banking house.

For five dollars, who brokered the deal? Took you too long. Felix Warburg, a partner of Kuhn Loeb. Samuel Prescott Bush was president of Buckeye Steel Castings, at the time. By the time in American history we're diving into next, get the cameras rolling, and actors going pretty darn quick, set the scene ...it's 1914, we're going to war. Percy A. Rockefeller buys controlling interests in Remington Arms, and appoints Samuel F. Pryor as CEO. By 1918, Robert Lovett's president of Union Pacific Railroad. Bernard Baruch, and banker Clarence Dillion, make Samuel Prescott Bush a director of the facilities division of the U.S. War Industries Board ...because, Bernard Baruch is Chairman of U.S. War Industries Board.

So, Nov. 1919, Averell Harriman, and George Herbert Walker, form W. A. Harriman & Co. bank ...Walker is president and chief exec.

So, Averell Harriman, son of Edward Henry Harriman ... who bought Union Pacific Railroad out of bankruptcy, is born in New York City Nov. 15, 1891. He later joins his father's, Union Pacific Railroad Co., in 1915, is chairman of the board in 1932, and remains so ...until 1946 ...in the middle of the movie script ...Franklin D. Roosevelt appoints Harriman as U.S. Ambassador to the Soviet Union in 1943 ...until 1946, when Harry S. Truman appoints him Commerce Secretary ...then, he works on the Marshall Plan ...and, is national security adviser during the Korean War ...a democrat, he's elected governor of New York, in 1954 ...and, tries two unsuccessful attempts to become Democratic presidential nominee in 1952, and 1956. Harriman serves in several posts, under President John F. Kennedy ...including, negotiating the Nuclear Test Ban Treaty in 1963 ...named as a Soviet spy by Anatoli Golitsin, Harriman is appointed by President Lyndon B. Johnson as ambassador-at-large for Southeast Asian affairs, in 1965. Harriman also served as chief U.S. negotiator, when preliminary peace talks opened in France between United States and North Vietnam, in 1968 ...losing this position under President Nixon ...but, returns to office in 1978 appointed senior member of U.S. Delegation to United Nations General Assembly's Special Session on Disarmament ...and, dies in the middle of my Presidency, in 1986 ...when I'm plagued with Alzheimer's.

<>

Well, I don't remember things so well, anymore ...I left out a few details. So, Averell Harriman and

George Herbert Walker of W. A. Harriman & Co. buy control of the German Hamburg-Amerika Line after negotiations with the firm's chief executive, William Cuno and, Max Warburg of the shipping line's bankers, M.M. Warburg. The American holding is now called, American Ship & Commerce Corp. ...and, Remington Arms CEO Samuel F. Pryor buys into the deal ...is now on the ASCC board, as a director. Meanwhile Cuno's pouring money into the Nazi party.

Back in 1922, Averell Harriman sets up a branch of W. A. Harriman & Co. in Berlin ...under the residency of partner, George H. Walker. Oct. 1923, Fritz Thyssen's contributions to the Nazi Party begins with a donation of 100,000 marks. A U.S. Government memorandum, Oct. 5 1942, to Executive Committee of the Office of the Alien Property Custodian cites on Averell Harriman, "W. Averell Harriman was in Europe sometime prior to 1924 ...and, at that time became acquainted with Fritz Thyssen, the German industrialist," the memo said. They set up a bank for Thyssen in New York, and Thyssen's agent, the memo says. "H. J. Kouwenhoven came to the U.S. prior to 1924 ...for conferences with the Harriman Co. in this connection," the memo says.

Okay, so a year goes by. It's 1924, W. A. Harriman & Co. invests $400,000 ...sets up Union Banking Corp. in New York, in partnership with Thyssen's Bank voor Handel en Scheepvaart (Bank for Trade and Shipping), BHS in Holland. *Aha!* Be on the lookout for trade acceptances ...*you* don't even know what trade acceptances are! ...unless you've read ahead. So, Union Bank now can transfer funds back and forth ...between the United States, and Thyssen's companies in Germany ...to his company Vereinigte Stahlwerke (United Steel), for one.

To confuse things more, Prescott Sheldon Bush Sr., son of Samuel Bush and son-in-law of George Herbert Walker ...now joins Harriman-controlled U.S. Rubber Co. ...as a director.

Now, two years go by, it's 1926. Prescott S. Bush Sr. becomes vice president of W. A. Harriman & Co., and Wall Street banker Clarence Dillon of Dillon Read bank (buddy of Prescott S. Bush Sr.'s father, Sam Bush), set up the German Steel Trust with Thyssen ...and, his partner Friedrich Flick. So, now Dillon Read bank handles the Trust's corporate banking ...in return for two Dillon Read reps sitting on the board of German Steel Trust ...as board members ...while German Steel Trust CEO Albert Voegler is another German industrialist who will finance Hitler into power.

Albert Voegler is now a director on several corporate boards, including ...German Steel Trust ...Bank voor Handel en Scheepvaart (Bank for Trade & Shipping) ...and, Hamburg-Amerika Line. So, Union Bank is now partners with Friedrich Flick's vast steel, coal, and zinc conglomerate operations in Germany, and Poland ... the Silesian Holding Co. And, Walker, Bush, and Harriman now own 33.33% of Flick's conglomerate, Consolidated Silesian Steel Corp.

We're almost done, bear with me.

It's 1931, Fritz Thyssen transfers 300,000 marks to Rudolph Hess from Thyssen's Bank voor Handel en Scheepvaart (Bank for Trade and Shipping), to the Nazi Party, doubling his total contributions to date ...and, W. A. Harriman & Co. merges with British-American investment house, Brown Brothers ...that, makes Prescott S. Bush Sr., Thatcher M. Brown, and the two Harriman brothers ... all senior partners in the brand-spanking-new Brown Brothers Harriman firm ...one of the board members being Robert Scott Lovett's son, Robert A. Lovett, who eventually becomes Assistant Secretary for the Air Force during World War II ...then, Undersecretary of State in 1947-1949 ...then, Deputy Defense Secretary in 1950-1951 ...then, Secretary of Defense in 1951-1953, and for icing on the cake, as his father had served on the World War I War Industries Board with Sam Bush ... Robert Lovett becomes another partner in the newly-merged, Brown Brothers Harriman firm ...with Prescott S. Bush running the New York office ...with Thatcher Brown running the London office and Montagu Norman, now Governor of the Bank of England and a Nazi sympathizer and an ex-Brown partner. Lovett's grandfather directed Brown Bros. during the American Civil War ...when, Brown Bros. shops 75% of slave cotton from southern states of America to British mills.

In 1932, U.S. Embassy in Berlin questions, who's paying to finance the 350,000 Nazi SS & SA troops? ...the Embassy notes, American-owned Hamburg-Amerika Line is funding propaganda against the German government's attempts to disband the Nazi SS & SA troops.

So, Hitler assumes power in Germany, Jan. 1933. In Mar. 1933, Prescott Bush Sr. informs Max Warburg he is to represent American Ship & Commerce Line as a board member on Hamburg-Amerika Line, since Max was advising Hjalmar Schacht, the German Economics Minister ...who is a close friend of Montagu Norman ...and, Max sits on the Reichsbank while

Max's brothers run Kuhn Loeb bank ...that, brokered E.H. Harriman's purchase of Union Pacific Railroad out of bankruptcy.

<>

Moshe Gottlieb's, *American Anti-Nazi Resistance*, reports Max's son, Erich, cabled cousin Frederick Warburg, a director of Union Pacific Railroad ...instructing him, use his influence to stop all anti-Nazi propaganda and activity in America. In 1933, the American-Jewish committee, B'nai B'rith, and Anti-Defamation League issue a joint statement, "that no American boycott against Germany be encouraged." And, the May 20 *New York Times* reports on Hitler's increasing power ...Germany and America reach an agreement in Berlin, between Hitler's Economics Minister Hjalmar Schacht, and John Foster Dulles ...to coordinate all trade ...so, Averell's first cousin Oliver Harriman of Harriman International Co., forms a syndicate of 150 firms, and private individuals, to conduct all exports from Germany to America.

So, Allen Dulles, whose scene we're introducing, that I'm rehearsing ...in which I play all four Warburgs ...and, his brother John ... are partners in Sullivan & Cromwell law firm ...representing the Nazi stock portfolio in America ...including I.G. Farben, who created Tabun nerve gas used in the concentration camps, SKF supplying 65% of bearings to Germany, and of course, Schroder Bank ...where Allen Dulles sits as a director until 1944.

It's 1933, a very busy year, North German Lloyd merges with Hamburg-Amerika, in Hamburg ...so, American Ship & Commerce who owns Hamburg-Amerika install Christian Beck, a Harriman exec, to manage freight and operations in North America ...for a newly formed firm, Hapag-Lloyd ...but, Chairman Emil Helfferich of Hapag-Lloyd ... is a Nazi ...Nazis accompany his ships. And, the Nye Committee in 1934 reports, Chairman Sam Pryor of Remington Arms, who is a co-founding director of Union Bank, and, of American Ship & Commerce has entered a cartel agreement with I. G. Farben chemical and armaments, and is, of course, supplying all the Nazi guards on his ships, with American-made Remington Arms guns.

Dec. 7 1941, the U.S. enters into World War II ...next August, U.S. Alien Property Custodian Leo T. Crowley, under the Trading with the Enemy Act, orders all Hapag-Lloyd property seized. In October, Crowley seizes the stock shares of Union Banking Corp. of New York, ...whose shareholders are ...board chairman E. Rowland Harriman, also directing Brown Brothers Harriman ...president and director Cornelis Lievense, also a banking functionary for the Nazis ...board treasurer Harold Pennington, also a director of Brown Brothers Harriman ...Ray Morris, a director of Brown Brothers Harriman ...Prescott S. Bush Sr., a director of Brown Brothers Harriman ...J. H. Kouwenhoven, also a director of Brown Brothers Harriman and chief foreign financial officer of German Steel Trust who brokered the original deal between Fritz Thyssen and Union Banking Corp. ...and, Brown Brothers Harriman director Johann G. Groeninger, also an industrialist in Nazi Germany ... the seized shares being describing in the Vesting Order as, "shares held for the benefit of members of the Thyssen family, property of nationals of a designated enemy country".

A few days later, Crowley seizes a couple more companies ...as Nazi front company operations owned by Union Banking Corp. ...Seamless Steel Equipment Corp. ...and, Holland-American Trading Corp. ...but, by Nov. 1942 only the Nazi financial interests in Silesian-American Corp. remain seized ...allowing U.S. United Banking Corp's U.S. partners to continue business. In 1945, U.S. Treasury Department reports to the 79th Congress, Thyssen's Vereinigte Stahlwerke United Steel, had produced the following proportions of Nazi Germany's total output: pig iron 50.8%, pipe & tubes 45.5%, universal plate 41.4%, galvanized sheet 38.5%, heavy plate 36%, explosives 35%, wire 22.1%.

<>

October 2003, the year before I die, Nancy reads me the work of American intelligence historian, and former Federal Prosecutor, John Loftus. In my Presidency, I would've ignored him ...because, I was in the trenches and didn't have time to debate ...but, in my twilight years, with Death staring me in the face, the truth takes on new meaning for me, as did the concept, of eternity.

Loftus' view on all this, from his web site, john.loftus.com. "Some of our most famous American families, including the Bushes, made their fortunes from the Holocaust. One cannot blame 'W' for what his grandfather did, anymore than one can blame John Kennedy because his father bought Nazi stocks. What most people do not know, is that Joseph Kennedy bought his Nazi stocks from Prescott Bush. Every family has scandal.

"The Bush family's scandal is that they funded Hitler, and, profited from the Holocaust. In Oct. 2003, John Buchanan unearthed the recently released Bush-Thyssen files in U.S. National Archives. These long-buried U.S. government files demonstrate, the Bush family stayed on corporate boards of Nazi front groups ...even after they knew, beyond a shadow of a doubt ...they were helping the financial cause of the Third Reich. It was all about the money. Nazi Germany is where the Bush family fortune came from, and where the Harrimans and the Rockefellers increased their fortunes to obscene proportions. Averell Harriman, he secretly financed the Bolsheviks while American, British, and White Russian troops were still fighting against the infant, communist revolution. Harriman bribed Lenin into letting him takeover the Czar's cartels, which exported manganese, iron ore, and other raw materials. Harriman shipped Russian raw materials to his German partners, the Thyssens ...secretly bought out ... by Rockefellers.

<>

"Rockefeller's lawyers, the Dulles Brothers, systematically bankrupted the German economy with the Versailles Treaty. German currency was almost worthless after WWI, so the Dulles brother's favorite clients, the Rockefellers, were able to buy the stock of nearly every German company for a song. The great sucking sound that preceded the Great Depression was the whistling of Wall Street money out of America into Germany, Russia, and Saudi Arabia. "Harriman's Soviet cartels would deliver raw materials, Rockefeller's high-tech German companies ...Thyssens ...would process manganese into steel for Harriman's railroads. To save transportation costs, robber barons looked for middle ground in eastern Poland for a future factory site. It had to be in the coal fields of Silesia, on the banks of the Vistula river, where a canal could be dug to ship materials in cheaply, from Russia. The Polish town was named, Oswieczim, ...later known to the world by its German name, Auschwitz.

<>

"In 'emerging' economies, Brazil, India and especially China, energy demand is rising so fast it may double by 2020. This hints at the energy crisis facing the developing world, where 2 billion people, a third of the world's population, have almost no access to electricity or liquid fuels, and are condemned to medieval existence that breeds despair, resentment and, ultimately, conflict.

<>

"Already we see outlines. China and Japan are scrapping over Siberia. In the Caspian Sea region, European, Russian, Chinese and American governments and oil companies are battling for a stake in big oil fields of Kazakhstan and Azerbaijan. In Africa, the U.S is building a network of military bases and diplomatic missions, whose main goal is to protect American access to oilfields in volatile places such as Nigeria, Cameroon, Chad and tiny Sao Tome. And, as important, to deny access to China and other thirsty superpowers. In the run-up to the Iraq war, Russia and France clashed noisily with the U.S over whose companies would have access to the oil in post-Saddam Hussein Iraq.

[Editor's note: This explains the complex fighting groups in Iraq fighting the U.S. and each other... an oil war between Russia, France, China & the U.S. (similar to the 1918 Russian revolution where 20 countries competed by financing coups and counter-coups to takeover Russia ... historians referring to the phenomenon as 'revolution', interestingly fought not just over gold, oil, timber and cheap labor ..., but specifically, over Baku Caspian Basin oil)... all financing and outfitting different mercenary terrorist group segments to stage both agent provocateur resulting in provoked conflict against each other, with a common purpose, to clear the land for oil ... and run up the national debts by all involved to the benefit of the private majority shareholders of the Fed, and interlocking presence with Bank of England and others.]

<>

"Less well known is the way China has sought to build up its own oil alliances in the Middle East, often over Washington's objections. In 2000, Chinese oil officials visited Iran, a country U.S. companies are forbidden to deal with ... China also has a major interest in Iraqi oil. But China's most controversial oil overture has been made to a country America once regarded as its most trusted oil ally ... Saudi Arabia.

"In recent years, Beijing has been lobbying Riyadh for access to Saudi reserves, the largest in the world. In return, the Chinese have offered the Saudis a foothold in what will be the world's biggest energy market, and, as a bonus, have thrown in offers of sophisticated Chinese weaponry, including ballistic missiles and other hardware, that the United States and Europe have refused to sell to the Saudis,' Roberts said."

<>

In Peter Dale Scott's, *Drugs, Oil & War*, or Cooley did, in *Unholy Wars*, or Thomas Goltz's, *Azerbaijan Diary, A Rogue Reporter's Adventures in an Oil-Rich, War-Torn, Post-Soviet Republic* ...

citing Irkali, Kodrarian, and Ruchala, in *Sobaka Magazine*, 2003. As part of the airline operation, Azeri pilots were trained in Texas. Dearborn had previously helped Secord advise and train the fledgling Contra air force, according to a book authored by Marshall, Hunter and myself," Peter said, "...*The Iran-Contra Connection*. These important developments were barely noticed in the U.S. press ...but, a 1994 *Washington Post* article did note ... a group of American men who wore 'big cowboy hats and big cowboy boots' had arrived in Azerbaijan as military trainers for its army, followed in 1993 by 'more than 1,000 guerrilla fighters from Afghanistan's radical prime minister, Gulbuddin Hekmatyar.' Whether the Americans were aware of it, or not ...the al Qaeda presence in Baku soon expanded, to include assistance for moving jihadists onwards into Dagestan, and Chechnya. Secord and Aderholt claim to have left Azerbaijan *before* Muhajidin arrived.

<>

"Meanwhile, Hekmatyar, at the time allied with bin Laden, was observed recruiting Afghan mercenaries (Arab Afghans, Arab Nazis) to fight in Azerbaijan ... against Armenia and its Russian allies. At this time, heroin flooded from Afghanistan, through Baku, into Chechnya Russia, and North America. Over the course of the next two years, MEGA Oil procured thousands of dollars worth of weapons ...and, recruited two thousand Afghan mercenaries, for Azerbaijan ... the first Muhajidin to fight on the territory of the former Communist Bloc. In 1993 the Muhajidin contributed to the ouster of Azerbaijan's elected president, Abulfaz Elchibey, and his replacement by an ex-Communist Brezhnev-era leader, Heidar Aliyev. At stake, was an 8 billion dollar oil contract with a consortium of western oil companies, headed by British Petroleum ...including a pipeline which would, for the first time, not pass through Russian-controlled territory ... when exporting oil from the Caspian basin to Turkey. Thus, the contract was bitterly opposed by Russia, and required an Azeri leader willing to stand up to the former Soviet Union.

<>

"Arab Afghans helped supply muscle, eyes set on fighting Russia in disputed Armenian-Azeri regions of Nagorno-Karabakh ...and, in liberating neighboring Muslim areas of Russia, Chechnya, and Dagestan. The 9/11 Report notes, the bin Laden organization established an NGO in Baku, which became a base for terrorism elsewhere.

"It became a trans-shipment point for Afghan

heroin to the Chechen mafia, whose branches 'extended not only to the London arms market ...but, also throughout continental Europe, and North America, according to Cooley's, *Unholy Wars*. Arab Afghans' Azeri operations were financed in part with Afghan heroin. Police sources in Moscow reported, 184 heroin processing labs were discovered in Moscow alone, last year. 'Every one of them was run by Azeris, who use the proceeds to buy arms for Azerbaijan's war against Armenia, in Nagorno-Karabakh,' according to Russian economist, Alexandre Datskevitch. This foreign Islamist presence in Baku was supported by bin Laden's financial network ...with bin Laden's guidance ...and, Saudi support. Baku soon became a base for jihadi operations against Dagestan and Chechnya, in Russia. Pakistan's ISI, facing its own disposal problem with the militant Arab-Afghan veterans, trained and armed them in Afghanistan ... to fight, in Chechnya. ISI encouraged the flow of Afghan drugs westward, to support the Chechen militants ...thus, diminishing the flow into Pakistan itself. Michael Griffin observed, regional conflicts in Nagorno-Karabakh, and other disputed areas ...Abkhazia ...Turkish Kurdistan ...and, Chechnya ... each represented a distinct, tactical move, crucial at the time, in discerning *which* power would be master of the pipelines to transport oil and gas from Caspian basin, to the world.

<>

"Wealthy Saudi families, al-Alamoudi (Delta Oil), bin Mahfouz (Nimir Oil) participated in the western oil consortium with the American firm, Unocal. Oct. 2001, U.S. Treasury Department named among charities allegedly supporting terrorism, the Saudi charity, Muwafaq Blessed Relief, to which the al-Alamoudis and bin Mahfouz families were identified as major contributors, according to *Boston Herald*, Dec. 2001. It's unclear whether MEGA Oil was a front for U.S. Government ...or, for U.S. oil companies ...and, their Saudi allies.

<>

"U.S. oil companies were accused of spending millions of dollars in Azerbaijan, not just to bribe the government ...but also, to install it. According to a Turkish intelligence source who was an alleged eyewitness, major oil companies, including Exxon and Mobil, were 'behind the coup d'état' ... which in 1993 replaced the elected President, Abulfaz Elchibey, with his successor, Heydar Aliyev.

<>

"The source claimed to have been at meetings in Baku, with 'senior members of ...BP ...Exxon ...Amoco ...Mobil ...and, Turkish Petroleum Co. The topic was oil rights ...and, on insistence of the Azeris, supply and arms to Azerbaijan. Turkish secret service documents allege, middlemen paid off key officials of the democratically elected government of the oil-rich nation ...just before its president was overthrown, according to *London Sunday Times*, Mar. 2000. The true facts and backers of the Aliyev coup may never be fully disclosed. But unquestionably, before the coup, efforts of ...Richard Secord ...Heinie Aderholt ...Ed Dearborn ...and Hekmatyar's Muhajidin ... helped contest Russian influence, and prepare for Baku's shift away, to the west. Three years later, Aug. 1996, Amoco's president met with Clinton, and arranged for Aliyev to be invited to Washington. Clinton in a 1997 press statement said, 'in a world of growing energy demand, our nation cannot afford to rely on a single region for our energy supplies. By working closely with Azerbaijan to tap Caspian resources, we not only help Azerbaijan to prosper, we help diversify our energy supply, and strengthen our energy security'.

"U.S., Al Qaeda, and oil company interests converged again in Kosovo. There, the al Qaeda-backed UCK or, Kosovo Liberation Army KLA, was supported and empowered by NATO, beginning in 1998, according to a source in Tim Judah's, *War & Revenge* ...KLA reps had already met with American, British, and Swiss intelligence agencies, in 1996 ...possibly, several years earlier. This would presumably have been back when Arab Afghan members of the KLA, like Abdul-Wahid al-Qahtani, were fighting in Bosnia, according to Evan Kohlmann's, *Al-Qaeda's Jihad in Europe, The Afghan-Bosnian Network*. Mainstream accounts of Kosovo War are silent about al Qaeda training and financing the UCK/KLA ...yet, this fact is recognized by experts ...and to my knowledge, never contested by them. For example, James Bissett, former Canadian ambassador to Yugoslavia, said, 'Many members of Kosovo Liberation Army were sent for training in terrorist camps in Afghanistan. Milosevic is right. There's no question of al Qaeda's participation in conflicts in the Balkans. It's very well documented,' according to *National Post*, 2002. Mar. 2002, Michael Steiner, United Nations administrator in Kosovo, warned of 'importing the Afghan danger to Europe ... because several cells trained, and financed, by al-Qaeda remained in the region. Back in 1997, UCK/KLA was recognized by U.S. as a terrorist group, supported in part by heroin traffic. *Washington Times*, 1999, reported it. 'The Kosovo Liberation Army, which Clinton administration embraced ...and, some members of Congress want to arm ... as part of the NATO bombing campaign ...is a terrorist organization, that financed much of its war effort with profits from the sale of heroin.' Al, in your book, *Politics of Heroin in Southeast Asia*, you agreed?" Peter said.

"Yes," the real McCoy said. Al McCoy opened his book and read, "Albanian exiles used drug profits to ship Czech and Swiss arms back to Kosovo for separatist guerrillas of the Kosovo Liberation Army (KLA). In 1997-98, these Kosovar drug syndicates armed the KLA for a revolt against Belgrade's army. Even after the 1999 Kumanovo agreement settled the Kosovo conflict, the UN administration of the province ... allowed a thriving heroin traffic along this northern route from Turkey. The former commanders of KLA, both local clans, and aspiring national leaders, continued to dominate the transit traffic through the Balkans,'" Al McCoy said.

Peter nodded, then continued reading. "Once again, as in Azerbaijan, these drug-financed Islamist jihadists received American assistance, this time from the U.S. Government. At the time, critics charged that U.S. oil interests were interested in building a trans-Balkan pipeline ... with U.S. Army protection ...although initially ridiculed, these critics were eventually proven correct. BBC News announced Dec. 2004, a 1.2 billion dollar pipeline, south of a huge new U.S. army base in Kosovo, was given go-ahead by governments of ...Albania ...Bulgaria ...and, Macedonia. Closeness of UCK/KLA to al-Qaeda ... was acknowledged again, in the western press, after Afghan-connected KLA guerrillas proceeded, in 2001, to conduct guerrilla warfare in Macedonia. Press accounts included an Interpol report containing the allegation, one of bin Laden's senior lieutenants was commander of an elite UCK/KLA unit operating in Kosovo, in 1999.

"Marcia Kurop in *Wall Street Journal Europe*, Nov. 2001 elaborated, 'The Egyptian surgeon-turned-terrorist leader Ayman Al-Zawahiri operated terrorist training camps, weapons of mass destruction factories and money-laundering and drug-trading networks throughout Albania, Kosovo, Macedonia, Bulgaria, Turkey and Bosnia,' and Yossef Bodansky, director of the U.S. Congressional Task Force on Terrorism and Unconventional Warfare, collaborated. 'Bin Laden's Arab Afghans assumed a dominant role in training the Kosovo Liberation Army [by mid-Mar. 1999 the UCK included] many elements controlled and/or sponsored by the ...U.S. ...German ...British ...and, Croatian intelligence services,' Marcia said. "DEA reported, 2000, Afghan heroin accounted for 20 percent of heroin seized in the U.S., nearly double the percentage taken four years earlier. Much of it distributed by Kosova Albanians."

<><>

"Petroleum money in two Bush presidents' Administrations was also prominent, under Clinton. A former CIA officer complained about the oil lobby's influence with Sheila Heslin of Clinton's National Security Council staff, according to Robert Baer's, *See No Evil, The True Story of a Ground Soldier in the CIA's War on Terrorism*. 'Heslin's sole job, it seemed, was to carry water for an exclusive club known as Foreign Oil Companies Group, a cover for a cartel of major petroleum companies doing business in the Caspian. Another thing I learned was, Heslin wasn't soloing. Her boss, Deputy National Security Adviser Sandy Berger, headed the interagency committee on Caspian oil policy ...which made him in effect, the government's ambassador to the cartel, and Berger wasn't a disinterested player. He held $90,000 worth of stock in Amoco, probably the most influential member of the cartel ... The deeper I got, the more Caspian oil money I found sloshing around Washington,' Baer said. 'The oil companies' meeting with Sheila Heslin in summer of 1995 was followed shortly by creation of an interagency governmental committee to formulate U.S. policy toward the Caspian. Clinton Administration listened to oil companies ...and, in 1998 began committing U.S. troops to joint training exercises in Uzbekistan. This made neighboring countries, Kazakhstan and Turkmenistan ...wary of Russia ...more eager to grant exploration and pipeline rights to American companies. But, Clinton didn't yield to Unocal's strenuous lobbying in 1996 for U.S. recognition of the Taliban, ... as a condition for building the pipeline from Turkmenistan. Clinton declined, in the end, to do so ...responding instead to strongly voiced political opposition from women's groups over Taliban treatment of women.

Al-Qaeda ... 'the base' in Arabic ...is a database, a list of names, a network of extremists managed by Osama bin Laden, a freelance narco-terrorist mercenary who works for the highest bidder ...hired in our lifetimes by interlocking central bank directorates via oil companies via CIA, MI5-6, German, French, Japanese and Chinese intelligence on behalf of the money-printing class, to run death squads, opium, heroin ratlines, arms trafficking, to destabilize countries ...clearing the land for oil companies ...oil companies owned and directed by major stockholders of the privately-held Federal Reserve Central Bank, its virgin birth conceived by interlocking directorates with Bank of England. The current war on terror mirrors the Russian 'revolution' of 1917 ... twenty countries' central banks in legion clash, compete with coups, countercoups, deathsquads, and terrorists in genocide, oil, gold, timber and drug turf wars.

China and Japan compete with America and Britain to finance and control strategic terrorist, narco-oil centers ...centers branded with household names of major oil companies trafficking weapons, drugs, oil, genocide, kidnapped children, slaves, and sex slaves, in newspapers that are bullshit, tv news that is bullshit, war that is bullshit ... their corporate flags flying sovereign ...for the moment.

<>

The oil companies profit from all this ...not us. We pay taxes to support the private Fed shareholders' ongoing military forays, to increase their fortunes at the cost of ours. We pay higher prices at gas pumps ...we go to jail for using nonviolent, recreational drugs. We're screwed ten times over. It's time to follow our U.S. Constitution ...and, have a publicly-owned central bank, not a privately owned one. A publicly owned central bank charges no interest. It doesn't charge us $100,000 for a $100,000 bill. It charges us the printing cost ... two cents. So, the national debt is increases two cents for each $100,000, not $100,000 – that's the primary difference between a constitutionally degreed public central bank, and the current, unconstitutional, privately-owned central bank. That's why we owe the private owers of the Fed 10 trillion dollars in 100 years, and pay interest of 300 billion dollars on that debt, to private shareholders. Enough, already. It's time to nationalize their oil companies. Ya think? (Not to mention their insurance companies, mortgage companies, and pharmaceuticals.)

Index

[A] http://en.wikipedia.org/wiki/Ruskombank, also, google 'Ruskombank'

American Ship & Commerce owns Hamburg-Amerika

> Hamburg Amerika installs Harriman exec. Christian Beck to manage North American operations for Hapag-Lloyd

>> Hapag-Lloyd chairman is a Nazi

>>> Hapag-Lloyd assets seized for 'trading with the enemy'

>>> Union Bank stock seized – 168,

>>>> major shareholders include:

>>>>> board chairman E.R. Harriman, who also directs, 'Brown Brothers, Harriman'

>>>>> president & director Cornelis Lievense, a banking functionary for the Nazis

>>>>> board treasurer Harold Pennington, also a director of Brown Brothers, Harriman

>>>>> J.H. Kouwenhoven, dir, Brown Brothers, Harriman, chief foreign financial officer of German Steel Trust

>>>>>> Kouwenhoven brokered the orig. deal between Thyssen & Union Banking Corp.

>>>>> Johann G. Groeninger, director of Brown Brothers, Harriman and an industrialist in Nazi Germany

>>> Holland-America Trading Corp. assets seized; Seamless Steel Equipment Corp. assets seized

> Sam Pryor enters into agreement with I.G. Farben

Bush, Prescott (partner, **Brown Brothers**; dir. CBS) – 13, 35, 64, 161-169, 218, 234, 275-276, 285, 287, 300, 315, 409-411, 508, 519, 536-538, 592-594,

> did business w/Nazis before, during & after WWII – 161,

> w/Clarence Dillion of **Dillion-Read** & Fritz Thyssen, set-up the German Steel Trust – 161, 592,

> German Steel Trust, director is Albert Voegler

>> Voegler, Albert

>>> director of:

>>>> (Thyssen's) **Bank voor Handel en Scheepvaart** (Bank for Trade & Shipping) – 162,

>>>> German Steel Trust – 161, 162

>>>> Union Bank is now partners w/Friedrich Flick's Silesian Holding Co – 162,

>>>>> **Walker, Bush & Harriman** own 33% of Consolidated Silesian Steel Corp.

>>> Thyssen – 14,

>>>> transfers 300,000 marks from his Bank voor Handel en Scheepvaart to Nazi Party – 162,

>>>> Thyssen's Vereinigte Stahlwerke United Steel produced 50% of Nazi iron, 45% of tubes, 35% of explosives – 163,

Harriman, W. Averell & Co. merges w/British American investment house, Brown Brothers to create Brown Brothers, Harriman

>>> Union Bank stock recovered (1953, 3 billion dollars, which is 30 billion in 2004 dollars) – 164,

>>>> Bush Nazi dealings had continued til 1951[A]

Warburg – 6, 7, 9, 13, 63, 92, 96, 109, 124, 134, 136, 161-163, 166-167, 175, 184, 218, 220-221, 223, 226, 228, 231, 234, 235, 237, 240-241, 244-245, 274, 297, 316-319, 321-335, 357-359, 362-365, 367-370, 373, 429-430, 448, 500, 507, 555, 570, 590, 592-593,

Warburg, Paul – 7,

Warburg-Kuhn-Loeb Bank (merges w/Rockefeller's Chase Bank & becomes Chase Manhattan in 1955) – 63

Manhattan Company Bank – 63

World Bank – 2, 50, 109, 212, 244-245, 264, 275, 304, 333, 337, 340, 442, 444, 447, 449, 450, 479, 487, 489, 517, 541, 584,

banks, &/or miscellaneous

Aldrich Bill (also, 'Aldrich Plan') – 318, 319-324,

[A] *New Hampshire Gazette*, Vol 248, No. 3, Nov. 7, 2003

Dulles, Allen – vii, viii, 7-8, 11, 13-14, 17, 24, 34, 45, 134-139, 141, 143, 145, 163, 165-166, 218, 237, 241-243, 275, 287, 292, 295, 312, 329-331, 339, 355, 361-364, 372, 374, 392, 410, 419, 425-428, 430, 438, 442, 537, 591, 593,

Donovan, Wild Bill, head of Office of Strategic Services (OSS) – viii, 20, 130, 136, 138-139, 141-142, 145, 197, 243, 269, 297, 308, 372, 406, 409-410, 419, 426-427, 536, 547,

Gaevernitz, Gero von – 136, 137, 143, 241

Gehlen, Reinhard – 7, 8, 45, 73, 75, 80, 84, 114, 135, 142-145, 257, 343, 357, (awarded Grande Crossia Merita Complance by Knights of Malta, 406), 407-408, 412, 442, 467-468,

Gehlen Organization, the – 45, 135, 146, 372, 406, 427, 468,

Hohenlohe, Prince Max Egon (Hohenlohe-Langenburg) von – 14, 137-138, 218, 241-242, 447,

Roosevelt, Franklin (warning that German wanted to split-up Allies) – viii, 19, 60, 61, 111-112, 124, 126, 134, 137-142, 147-148, 157-159, 161, 166, 168, 180, 213, 218, 223-224, 231, 233-236, 241-242, 246, 253, 272, 284, (financed by Otto Kahn, 322), 324, 328, 360-361, 370, 373, 375, 426, 496-498, 501, 525-527, 529, 531, 584, 592,

Churchill, Winston – 23, 37, 64, 126-127, 134, 140-141, 160, 222, 253, 426, 525,

CIA, (see 'intelligence organizations')

Clinton, Bill – 13, 170-171, 175, 176, 190, 206-210, 214, 364, 389, 429, 491-492, 513, 515, 521, 532, 546-547, 558-560, 564, 566-570, 576, 579, 596-597,

Cold War

[Editor's note: 'anti-communist' movements ('anti-communist' being a propaganda edifice for economic warfare)]

American industrialists & financiers historically hating 'socialism, communism & Judaism' & financing Nazi & Fascist death-squads (also see, 'Nazi/Nazi financial & industrial supporters') – 111, 112,

DuPont (also see, 'Banks/Morgan Financial Group')

DuPont, Eranee, devoted to Hitler (also see, 'Banks/Morgan Financial Group') – 112,

finances Black Legion to stop GM auto workers in Detroit from forming a union – 156,

Black Legion dresses in robes & hoods with emblem of Skull & Bones

Also, a death-squad

Ford Motor Company

Hired Cherep-Spirodovich & Brasol to write anti-Semitic literature, then published it. Ford was anti-Soviet, against workers owning factories they worked in & against unions & labor rights; was convinced Jews were to blame for war; a large financial supporter of Hitler; Ford also published, International Jew, a racist propagandist tool.

General Motors – 124, (also see, 'Banks/Morgan Financial Group')

International Harvester

Standard Oil

American companies doing business with Germany & Italy – 122, 123

Beginning of Cold War mythology & propaganda

(world money-issuing class edifice for economic warfare to get Baku oil & Russian gold, timber & coal by military warfare (murder)

Supreme Monarchist Council – 82,

International Committee to Combat the Menace of Bolshevism (founded by Alfred Rosenberg), becomes, the Anti-Comintern – 111,

General League of German Anti-Communist Associations – 111,

Anti-communist Bloc of South America – 111,

Anti-communist Union of the Province of North China – 111,

European Anti-Communist League – 111,

American Section of International Committee to Combat World Menace of Communism – 111,

Hoover, Herbert – 92, 94, 133-134, 141, 174, 221, 223-224, 226, 235, 239, 331-335, 355-360, 363-363, 588, 591,

Middle of Cold War mythology & propaganda (semantic edifice for economic warfare for world money-issuing class to rob U.S. taxpayers & citizens of every country)

Central Intelligence Agency (CIA) – iii, viii, ix, 5, 7-8, 11, 13, 17-20, 22, 24, 28, 30, 33-36, 38, 40, 44, 49-50, 54, 71, 108, 120, 136, 145-146, 173, 176-178, 180-205, 207, 244-245, 271-277, 297, 299, 284, 291-292, 297, 299-302, 304, 306-308, 319, 323, 337-339, 341, 372, 415, 343-345, 347-349, 351-352, 361, 372, 374-375, 380, 385, 390, 393-395, 406-412, 414-419, 425, 428, 433-436, 438, 440, 442, 444, 446, 449, 452, 467-468, 475, 490-492, 494-495, 508, 510, 512-513, 515, 518-523, 527, 531-533, 536, 538, 541-542, 547-549, 551, 554, 556, 564-568, 570-571, 575-577, 581, 591, 597-598,

DuPont, Eranee, devoted to Hitler – 112, 147, 156-157,

Bolschwing, Otto von – 13, 14, 241, 269, 467,

Bowman, Bob – d, 5-6, 25, 409, 438, 514-515, 576,

Center for Freedom & Democracy – 463,
    Weinstein, Allen – 491,

Cheney, Dick (see 'Project For The New American Century' – 188, 376, 438-439, 509, 518,)

Coors – 28, 46, 403, 405, 438, 453, 460, 471, 516,

Free Congress Foundation – vi, 352, 392, 403, 438, 460, 462-466, 471-473,
    Weyrich, Paul – 25, 27, 352, 392, 403, 405, 438, 443, 448, 460, 462-463, 465, 471, 473,

Full Court Press – c, vi, 25, 196, 338, 348, 352, 354, 392, 405, 431, 439-441, 448-449, 458, 491-494,

Graham, Dan – 26, 273, 438,

Krieble, Robert – 460, 464,

Inter-Regional Deputies Group – 460, 463-464, 472,
    Yeltsin, Boris – 460, 463-464, 472, 491, 494,

Laffer, Arthur – 23, 24-25,

Lithuanian Catholic Religious Aid (LCRA) – 465, 473-475, 493,

Lithuanian Sajudis Party – 460, 472-475,

Miloxa, Nicolai – 469,
    fascist financier in dummy corp. in Nixon's law office, for U.S. Citizenship – 469,

National Endowment for Democracy – vi, 440, 463, 465-466, 471-473, 475-476, 491,
    Full-Court Press – 25, 27, 352, 392, 403, 405, 438, 443, 448, 460, 462-463, 465, 471-474, 491-494,
    recipe for 'democracy' revolution – 493,

National Republican Heritage Groups Council – 4, 419-421, 471,
    Chennault, Anna – 420, 423,
    Galdau, Florian – 243, 420, 422-424,
    Guarino, Philip – 243, 420, 422-424,
    Pasztor, Laszlo – 242, 420-421, 423-424, 465, 471-473,
        established Republican Heritage Committee for Richard Nixon – 465,
        brings Nazi & fascist collaborators into the Republican Party – 465,
    Nazarenko, Nicolas – 243, 420, 425,
    Slavoff, Radi – 243, 420, 422-424,

Nitze, Paul – 25, 27, 32, 271-273, 338, 374-376, 428, 438-439, 487, 489, 499,
    Dillion Read – 272, 374, 499-500, 539,

Pamyat – 460, 461, 472,

Perle, Richard (see 'Project For The New American Century', below – 188, 376, 438-439, 509, 518,)

Pipes, Richard – 273, 438-441, 459,

Project For The New American Century; social engineering campaign – 188, 376, 438-439, 509, 518,

Project For The New American Century's seminal report, Rebuilding America's Defences: strategy, forces and resources for a new century, was a blueprint of American aims in all but name. It recommended an increase in arms-spending by 48 billion dollars so Washington could "fight and win multiple, simultaneous major theatre wars." This has happened.
    founders - 509,
    Bennett, Wm. J. – 4, 405, 509,
    Cheney, Dick – d, 6, 25, 169, 213, 409-411, 438, 501, 504, 507-510, 514-521, 587,
        main suspect in organizing Sept. 11 attack - 514,
    Libby, I. Lewis – 509,
    Khalilzad, Zalmay – 509,
    oil companies (also see, 'Oil companies', in alphabetical listing)
        Unocal Oil – 509,
    Operation Northwoods (fake terrorist plan suggested to President Kennedy similar to 9/11 – 510,
    Perle, Richard – 26, 410, 443, 464, 507, 509-510,
        predicts event such as Pearl Harbor is required to kick off report recommendations – 509,
    Rice, Condoleezza – 509, 580,
        comparing 9/11 as an opportunity similar to the start of the Cold War
    Rumsfeld, Donald – 202, 410, 507, 509-513, 515-518,
        sets up secret armies similar to those set up by Richard Nixon & Henry Kissinger – 510,
            Proactive Pre-emptive Operations Group – 510,
    Sept. 11th – d, 6, 12-13, 170-172, 176, 181, 185-188, 206, 208, 239, 300, 410, 509, 511, 513-515, 518, 533, 595,

Inside the League
  Baer, Bob
    Sleeping with the Devil
    See No Evil – The True Story of a Ground Soldier in the CIA's War on Terrorism
Bakiger, David & Sellier, Charles
 The Lincoln Conspiracy
Bancroft, Mary
 Anatomy of a Spy
   Beaty & Gwynne
    Outlaw Bank
Blum, Howard
 The Search for Nazis in America
   Burrough, Brian & Helyer, John
    Barbarians at the Gate: The Fall of RJR Nabisco – 549,
Brussels, Mae
 Nazi Connections to JFK – 408,
Dowbenko, Uri
 Bushwacked – 538, 550,
Domhoff, Wm.
 Who Rules America?
Eudes, Dominique
 The Kapetanios, Story of the Greek Partisan Movement – 125,
Flammonde, Paris – 409,
 An Un-commissioned Report on the Jim Garrison Investigation
Frolich, Paul
 Rosa Luxemburg
   Griffin
    Reaping the Whirlwind
Heiden, Konrad
 Der Fuehrer
Higham, Charles
 Trading With the Enemy
Josephson, E.M.
 Strange Death of Franklin D. Roosevelt – 61,
Klarsfeld, Serge
 Holocaust, Children of Izieu – 45,
   Kronberger
    Blood for Oil – 530,
   Kruger, Henrik
    The Great Heroin Coup – 344
   LaRouche, Lyndon – 316,
    Dope, Inc.
Lee, Martin A.
Lempkin, Raphael
 Axis Rule in Occupied Europe – 127-131,
    Labeviere, Richard
     Dollars for Terror – the United States & Islam – 176,
Linklater, Hilton & Ascherson
 Nazi Legacy, Klaus Barbie & the International Fascist Connection
Lundberg, Ferdinand
 America's 60 Families (not referenced in this book)
Manning, Paul
 Martin Bormann – Nazi in Exile – 170,
Martin, James Stewart
 All Honorable Men – 122, 123, 372,
   Marshall, Jon
    Drug Wars, Corruption, counterinsurgency & Covert Operations in the Third World – 196
Mayer, Milton
 They Thought They Were Free
Manchester, Wm
 American Caesar – 119,

    http://www.bibliotecapleyades.net/sociopolitica/esp_sociopol_trilat08_03.htm#CHAPTER%2
0FIVEExcerpt: The United States consumes about 71 quads of energy per year. (A quad is one quadrillion British thermal units or 1015.) There is available today in the United States, excluding solar sources and excluding gas and oil imports, about 150,000 quads of energy. Put another way, this statistic means we have sufficient known usable energy resources to last us

for over two thousand years. This means the energy crisis is a created crisis, a hoax. (Excerpt continued, see end of index

Tetans, T.H.
> Trocki, Carl – 209,
>> *Opium, Empire & the Global Economy*
> Unger, Craig
>> *House of Bush, House of Saud* – 185,

Torbitt, Wm. – 508,
> *Nomenclature of an Assassination Cabal*

Weverman, Alan & Canfield, Michael – 409,
> *Coup d'etat in America*

Yallop, David – 118,
> *In God's Name*

Yeomans, Matthew – 213,
> *Oil: Anatomy of an Industry*

articles (related)

Butler, Smedley
XxxWar is a Racket – ix, 148-156

Covert Action Information Bulletin &/or Covert Action Quarterly

Bellant, Russ
> *Old Nazis & the New Right: the Republican Party & Fascists*
> *Old Nazis & New European Democracies* – 472,

Bellant, Russ & Wolf, Lou
> *Free Congress Foundation Goes East* – 460,

Bonasky, Philip
> *NED meddles in Lithuania: nurturing Baltic reaction* – 473,

Henwood, Doug
> *U.S. Economy, the enemy within* – 487,
>> *NSC-68* – 487,

Gervasy, Sean
> *A Full-Court Press: the destabilization of the Soviet Union* – 458,
> *Civil War as lethal shadow play* – 477,
> *Western Intervention in U.S.S.R.: spyless coup or democratic break-through?* – 491,

Kimery, Antony
> *In the Company of Friends: George Bush & the CIA* – 409, 416,

Oglesby, Carl
> *Reinhard Gehlen: the Secret Treaty of Fort Hunt* – 142,

Executive Intelligence Review

Hoefle, John – 410,
> *Halliburton is Houston's Greater Hermann Goring Werke*

Harper's
> *Unlawful, Un-elected & Un-checked: how CIA subverts Government at home,* by Christopher Hitchens – 490,

FAIR – Fairness & Accuracy in Reporting
> *Extra Magazine, U.S. news media fiddle while Germany burns,* by Martin A. Lee – 484,

Los Angeles Times
> *New breed of fascist rises in Russia,* by Elizabeth Shogren – 486,
>> *Nexus Magazine*
>>> *Big Oil & the War on Drugs & Terrorism* – 532,

San Francisco Chronicle
> *Campaign had ominous signs of American Fascism,* by James Michner – 457,
> *Freedom loses luster for Hungarian family,* by Frank Viviano – 486,

San Francisco Examiner
> Republican party stands shoulder-to-shoulder with Nazis, by Clifford Anderson – 457,

New York Times
> evil tone of George H.W. Bush campaign, by editor John Oakes – 457,
> *Serb-Croat showdown in one village square,* by Steven Engelberg – 476,

[add'l magazines &/or articles re: other]

New York Times
> *Whitaker Chambers, odd choice for Medal of Freedom* – 401,

[add'l magazine &/or newspaper articles re: terrorism &/or oil]

---

[1] Harriman's Soviet cartels would deliver the raw materials to Rockefeller's high-tech German companies ...the Thyssens ...would process the manganese into steel for Harriman's railroads. To save transportation costs, the robber barons looked for middle ground in eastern Poland for a future factory site. It had to be in the coal fields of Silesia, on the banks of the Vistula river, where a canal could be dug to ship materials in cheaply, from Russia. The Polish town was named, Oswieczim ...later known to the world by its German name, Auschwitz. Nancy [editor's note: from Loftus & Aarons' *Secret War Against the Jews*] continued reading Loftus to me. "It was not a killing factory then, although slave labor was always contemplated for the maximum profit factor. Auschwitz was designed to process Silesian coal into tar additives necessary for Russian aviation fuel. It was a high tech German chemical factory, built to balance out Harriman's Russia-to-Germany export trade. "The Rockefeller-Harriman front company that financed Auschwitz was called, Brown Brothers Harriman. It is still around today. Our President's great grandfather, Herbert Walker, founded the company and appointed his son-in-law, Prescott Bush, to the boards of several holding companies, all of which became Nazi fronts. The Walkers and Bushes never really liked the Nazis, any more than Harriman liked the communists. To the robber barons, they were just dogs on a leash. One day the dogs broke their chains..."

[2] http://www.cbsnews.com/stories/2003/04/25/60minutes/main551091.shtml
Sept. 21, 2003

All In The Family: Company Official Defends No-Bid Army Contract

(CBS) Almost as soon as the last bomb was dropped over Iraq, the United States began the business of rebuilding the country. As it turns out, it's very big business. The U.S. will spend approximately $25 billion to repair Iraq by the end of next year - and billions will be needed after that. Almost all of that money will go to private contractors who vie for lucrative government deals to rebuild Iraq's roads, retrain its police force and operate its airports. Given all the taxpayer money involved, you might think the process for awarding those contracts would be open and competitive. But, as *60 Minutes* reported last spring, the earliest contracts were given to a few favored companies. And some of the biggest winners in the sweepstakes to rebuild Iraq have one thing in common: lots of very close friends in very high places. Correspondent Steve Kroft reports. One is Halliburton, the Houston-based energy services and construction giant whose former CEO, Dick Cheney, is now vice president of the United States. Even before the first shots were fired in Iraq, the Pentagon had secretly awarded Halliburton subsidiary Kellogg, Brown & Root a two-year, no-bid contract to put out oil well fires and to handle other unspecified duties involving war damage to the country's petroleum industry. It is worth up to $7 billion.

But Robert Andersen, chief counsel for the Army Corps of Engineers, says that oil field damage was much less than anticipated and Halliburton will end up collecting only a small fraction of that $7 billion. But he can't say how small a fraction or exactly what the contract covers because the mission and the contract are considered classified information. Under normal circumstances, the Army Corps of Engineers would have been required to put the oil fire contract out for competitive bidding. But in times of emergency, when national security is involved, the government is allowed to bypass normal procedures and award contracts to a single company, without competition. And that's exactly what happened with Halliburton. "We are the only company in the United States that had the kind of systems in place, people in place, contracts in place, to do that kind of thing," says Chuck Dominy, Halliburton's vice president for government affairs and its chief lobbyist on Capitol Hill. He says the Pentagon came to Halliburton because the company already had an existing contract with the Army to provide logistical support to U.S. troops all over the world. "Let me put a face on Halliburton. It's one of the world's largest energy services companies, and it has a strong engineering and construction arm that goes with that" says Dominy. "You'll find us in 120 countries. We've got 83,000 people on our payroll, and we're involved in a ton of different things for a lot of wonderful clients worldwide."

"They had assets prepositioned," says Anderson. "They had capability to reach out and get sub-contractors to do the various types of work that might be required in a hostile situation."

"The procurement of this particular contract was done by career civil servants, and I know that it's a perception that those at the very highest levels of the administration, Democrat and Republican, get involved in procurement issues. It can happen. But for the very most part, the procurement system is designed to keep those judgments with the career public servants."

But is political influence not unknown in the process? In this particular case, Anderson says, it was legally justified and prudent. But not everyone thought it was prudent. Bob Grace is president of GSM Consulting, a small company in Amarillo, Texas, that has fought oil well fires all over the world. Grace worked for the Kuwait government after the first Gulf War and was in charge of firefighting strategy for the huge Bergan Oil Field, which had more than 300 fires. Last September, when it looked like there might be another Gulf war and more oil well fires, he and a lot of his friends in the industry began contacting the Pentagon and their congressmen.

"All we were trying to find out was, who do we present our credentials to," says Grace. "We just want to be able to go to somebody and say, 'Hey, here's who we are, and here's what we've done, and here's what we do.'"

"They basically told us that there wasn't going to be any oil well fires."

Grace showed *60 Minutes* a letter from the Department of Defense saying: "The department is aware of a broad range of well firefighting capabilities and techniques available. However, we believe it is too early to speculate what might happen in the event that war breaks out in the region."

It was dated Dec. 30, 2002, more than a month after the Army Corps of Engineers began talking to Halliburton about putting out oil well fires in Iraq.

"You just feel like you're beating your head against the wall," says Grace. However, Andersen says the Pentagon had a very good reason for putting out that message. "The mission at that time was classified, and what we were doing to assess the possible damage and to prepare for it was classified," says Andersen. "Communications with the public had to be made with that in mind."

"I can accept confidentiality in terms of war plans and all that. But to have secrecy about Saddam Hussein blowing up oil wells, to me, is stupid," says Grace. "I mean the guy's blown up a thousand of them. So why would that be a revelation to anybody?" But Grace says the whole point of competitive bidding is to save the taxpayers money. He believes they are getting a raw deal. "From what I've read in the papers, they're charging $50,000 a day for a five-man team. I know there are guys that are equally as well-qualified as the guys that are over there that'll do it for half that."

Grace and his friends are no match for Halliburton when it comes to landing government business. Last year alone, Halliburton and its Brown & Root subsidiary delivered $1.3 billion worth of services to the U.S. government. Much of it was for work the U.S. military used to do itself.

"You help build base camps. You provide goods, laundry, power, sewage, all the kinds of things that keep an army in place in a field operation," says Dominy. "Young soldiers have said to me, 'If I go to war, I want to go to war with Brown & Root.'"

And they have, in places like Afghanistan, Rwanda, Somalia, Kosovo and now Iraq. "It's a sweetheart contract," says Charles Lewis, executive director of the Center For Public Integrity, a non-profit organization that investigates corruption and abuse of power by government and corporations. "There's no other word for it." Lewis says the trend towards privatizing the military began during the first Bush administration when Dick Cheney was secretary of defense. In 1992, the Pentagon, under Cheney, commissioned the Halliburton subsidiary Brown & Root to do a classified study on whether it was a good idea to have private contractors do more of the military's work. "Of course, they said it's a terrific idea, and over the next eight years, Kellogg, Brown & Root and another company got 2,700 contracts worth billions of dollars," says Lewis.

"So they helped to design the architecture for privatizing a lot of what happens today in the Pentagon when we have military engagements. And two years later, when he leaves the department of defense, Cheney is CEO of Halliburton. Thank you very much. It's a nice arrangement for all concerned." During the five years that Cheney was at Halliburton, the company nearly doubled the value of its federal contracts, and the vice president became a very rich man.

Lewis is not saying that Cheney did anything illegal. But he doesn't believe for a minute that this was all just a coincidence. "Why would a defense secretary, former chief of staff to a president, and former member of congress with no business experience ever in his life, not for a day, why would he become the CEO of a multibillion dollar oil services company," asks Lewis. "Well, it could be related to government contracts. He was brought in to raise their government contract profile. And he did. And they ended up with billions of dollars in new contracts because they had a former defense secretary at the helm."

Cheney, Lewis says, may be an honorable and brilliant man, but "as George Washington Plunkett once said, 'I saw my opportunities and I took them." Both Halliburton and the Pentagon believe Lewis is insulting not only the vice president but thousands of professional civil servants who evaluate and award defense contracts based strictly on merit. But does the fact that Cheney used to run Halliburton have any effect at all on the company getting government contracts?

"Zero," says Dominy. "I will guarantee you that. Absolutely zero impact."

"In fact, I wish I could embed [critics] in the department of defense contracting system for a week or so. Once they'd done that, they'd have religion just like I do, about how the system cannot be influenced." Dominy has been with Halliburton for seven years. Before that, he was former three-star Army general. One of his last military assignments was as a commander at the Army Corps of Engineers. And now, the Army Corps of Engineers is also the government agency that awards contracts to companies like Halliburton. Asked if his expertise in that area had anything to do with his employment at Halliburton, Dominy replies, "None."

But Lewis isn't surprised at all. "Of course, he's from the Army Corps. And of course, he's a general," says Lewis. "I'm sure he and no one else at Halliburton sees the slightest thing that might look strange about that, or a little cozy maybe." Lewis says the best example of these cozy relationships is the defense policy board, a group of high-powered civilians who advise the secretary of defense on major policy issues - like whether or not to invade Iraq. Its 30 members are a Who's Who of former senior government and military officials. There's nothing wrong with that, but as the Center For Public Integrity recently discovered, nine of them have ties to corporations and private companies that have won more than $76 billion in defense contracts. And that's just in the last two years. "This is not about the revolving door, people going in and out," says Lewis. "There is no door. There's no wall. I can't tell where one stops and the other starts. I'm dead serious."

"They have classified clearances, they go to classified meetings and they're with companies getting billions of dollars in classified contracts. And their disclosures about their activities are classified. Well, isn't that what they did when they were inside the government? What's the difference, except they're in the private sector."

Richard Perle resigned as chairman of the defense policy board last month after it was disclosed that he had financial ties to several companies doing business with the Pentagon. But Perle still sits on the board, along with former CIA director James Woolsey, who works for the consulting firm of Booz, Allen, Hamilton. The firm did nearly $700 million dollars in business with the Pentagon last year. Another board member, retired four-star general Jack Sheehan, is now a senior vice president at the Bechtel corporation, which just won a $680 million contract to rebuild the infrastructure in Iraq. That contract was awarded by the State Department, which used to be run by George Schultz, who sits on Bechtel's board of directors. "I'm not saying that it's illegal. These guys wrote the laws. They set up the system for themselves. Of course it's legal," says Lewis. "It just looks like hell. It looks like you have folks feeding at the trough. And they may be doing it in red white and blue and we may be all singing the "Star Spangled Banner," but they're doing quite well."

Halliburton has done extremely well. So far, the company has earned almost a billion dollars on the oil well fire contract, and could earn another billion providing logistical support for U.S. troops stationed in Iraq. As for Vice President Cheney, he says he had nothing to do with the Army Corp's decision to give the no bid contract to Halliburton. Cheney also insists he cut all financial ties to the company three years ago. But this week, Senate democrats challenged that assertion. They say the vice president still gets hundreds of thousands of dollars from his former company each year - and they called for congressional hearings on Halliburton's contract.

[3] In a *For the Record* segment aired in July 2005, *More on the History of the Islamic-Fascist Axis*, Emory alleges that when U.S. Homeland Security chief Michael Chertoff was in private law practice, he represented Dr. Magdy el-Amir, a financier of al-Qaeda.[7] This connection is representative of a subject Emory has delved into in previous shows. [8][9] He has also noted the historical connections between the Third Reich and the Muslim Brotherhood[10]; between the C.I.A. and A. Q. Khan's nuclear arms acquisitions for Pakistan[11]; between Republican lobbyist Grover Norquist, strategist Karl Rove and the Islamic Institute[12] and between the George W. Bush administration and the government of Dubai[13].

[4] posted August 18, 2005 5:38 pm
http://www.tomdispatch.com/post/14239/david_morse_on_darfur_as_a_resource_war
Tomgram: David Morse on Darfur as a Resource War
The pieces are all there. No one reading the business pages of the papers these last weeks could ignore oil prices that briefly surged to a once-inconceivable $67 dollars a barrel of crude before falling back; no one driving a car on any highway could possibly avoid pump prices that, for unleaded regular, are now hovering around $2.50 a gallon (making inflation jump and consumer confidence drop); those with sharp eyes might have noticed less than a week ago that Lee R. Raymond, the chief executive officer of Exxon Mobil Corporation for the last 12 years (whose total compensation for 2004 was a modest $38.1 million but could have been a billion dollars without his company taking much of a hit) is reportedly planning to step down soon. As the head of possibly the most successful and "efficient" corporation on the face of our planet, he primed the Exxon Mobil pump to the tune of $25.3 billion dollars in profits in 2004, and upped that in the first half of 2005 by socking in another $15 billion (give or take the odd million); oh yes, and does anybody not know that somewhere in a place called Darfur in Sudan a genocide is underway?

But the connections between surging oil price levels, pump prices, oil company mega-profits, and mass murder in distant Africa are something you're far less likely to read about in your local paper; and yet, under the pressure of growing global energy demand and peak-oil fears, oil companies from many nations are now scouring the Earth, buying governments, tribal leaders, warlords, and anyone else who might lead them to any untapped new reserves of black gold. As the *Washington Post* said politely in its article on Raymond, Exxon Mobil "operates in more than 200 countries or territories -- as diverse as Equatorial Guinea, Venezuela and the Russian Far East." Diverse indeed. Sudan is "diverse" too and it has been swept up in the global oil sweepstakes with horrific consequences as journalist David Morse makes vividly clear below. *Tom*

War of the Future
Oil Drives the Genocide in Darfur By David Morse

A war of the future is being waged right now in the sprawling desert region of northeastern Africa known as Sudan. The weapons themselves are not futuristic. None of the ray-guns, force-fields, or robotic storm troopers that are the stuff of science fiction; nor, for that matter, the satellite-guided Predator drones or other high-tech weapon systems at the cutting edge of today's arsenal.

No, this war is being fought with Kalashnikovs, clubs and knives. In the western region of Sudan known as Darfur, the preferred tactics are burning and pillaging, castration and rape -- carried out by Arab militias riding on camels and horses. The most sophisticated technologies deployed are, on the one hand, the helicopters used by the Sudanese government to support the militias when they attack black African villages, and on the other hand, quite a different weapon: the seismographs used by foreign oil companies to map oil deposits hundreds of feet below the surface.

This is what makes it a war of the future: not the slick PowerPoint presentations you can imagine in boardrooms in Dallas and Beijing showing proven reserves in one color, estimated reserves in another, vast subterranean puddles that stretch west into Chad, and south to Nigeria and Uganda; not the technology; just the simple fact of the oil. This is a resource war, fought by surrogates, involving great powers whose economies are predicated on growth, contending for a finite pool of resources. It is a war straight out of the pages of Michael Klare's book, *Blood and Oil*; and it would be a glaring example of the consequences of our addiction to oil, if it were not also an invisible war.

Invisible? Invisible because it is happening in Africa. Invisible because our mainstream media are subsidized by the petroleum industry. Think of all the car ads you see on television, in newspapers and magazines. Think of the narcissism implicit in our automobile culture, our suburban sprawl, our obsessive focus on the rich and famous, the giddy assumption that all this can continue indefinitely when we know it can't -- and you see why Darfur slips into darkness. And Darfur is only the tip of the sprawling, scarred state known as Sudan. Nicholas Kristof pointed out in a New York Times column that ABC News had a total of 18 minutes of Darfur coverage in its nightly newscasts all last year, and that was to the credit of Peter Jennings; NBC had only 5 minutes, CBS only 3 minutes. This is, of course, a micro-fraction of the time devoted to Michael Jackson. Why is it, I wonder, that when a genocide takes place in Africa, our attention is always riveted on some black American miscreant superstar? During the genocide in Rwanda ten years ago, when 800,000 Tutsis were slaughtered in 100 days, it was the trial of O.J. Simpson that had our attention.

Yes, racism enters into our refusal to even try to understand Africa, let alone value African lives. And yes, surely we're witnessing the kind of denial that Samantha Power documents in *A Problem from Hell: America and the Age of Genocide*; the sheer difficulty we have acknowledging genocide. Once we acknowledge it, she observes, we pay lip-service to humanitarian ideals, but stand idly by. And yes, turmoil in Africa may evoke our experience in Somalia, with its graphic images of American soldiers being dragged through the streets by their heels. But all of this is trumped, I believe, by something just as deep: an unwritten conspiracy of silence that prevents the media from making the connections that would threaten our petroleum-dependent lifestyle, that would lead us to acknowledge the fact that the industrial world's addiction to oil is laying waste to Africa.

When Darfur does occasionally make the news -- photographs of burned villages, charred corpses, malnourished children -- it is presented without context. In truth, Darfur is part of a broader oil-driven crisis in northern Africa. An estimated 300 to 400 Darfurians are dying every day. Yet the message from our media is that we Americans are "helpless" to prevent this humanitarian tragedy, even as we gas up our SUVs with these people's lives.

Even Kristof -- whose efforts as a mainstream journalist to keep Darfur in the spotlight are worthy of a Pulitzer -- fails to make the connection to oil; and yet oil was the driving force behind Sudan's civil war. Oil is driving the genocide in Darfur. Oil drives the Bush administration's policy toward Sudan and the rest of Africa. And oil is likely to topple Sudan and its neighbors into chaos.

The Context for Genocide I will support these assertions with fact. But first, let's give Sudanese government officials in Khartoum their due. They prefer to explain the slaughter in Darfur as an ancient rivalry between nomadic herding tribes in the north and black African farmers in the south. They deny responsibility for the militias and claim they can't control them, even as they continue to train the militias, arm them, and pay them. They play down their Islamist ideology, which supported Osama bin Laden and seeks to impose Islamic fundamentalism in Sudan and elsewhere. Instead, they portray themselves as pragmatists struggling to hold together an impoverished and backwards country; all they need is more economic aid from the West, and an end to the trade sanctions imposed by the U.S. in 1997, when President Clinton added Sudan to the list of states sponsoring terrorism. Darfur, from their perspective, is an inconvenient anomaly that will go away, in time.

It is true that ethnic rivalries and racism play a part in today's conflict in Darfur. Seen in the larger context of Sudan's civil war, however, Darfur is not an anomaly; it is an extension of that conflict.

The real driving force behind the North-South conflict became clear after Chevron discovered oil in southern Sudan in 1978. The traditional competition for water at the fringes of the Sahara was transformed into quite a different struggle. The Arab-dominated government in Khartoum redrew Sudan's jurisdictional boundaries to exclude the oil reserves from southern jurisdiction. Thus began Sudan's 21-year-old North-South civil war. The conflict then moved south, deep into Sudan, into wetter lands that form the headwaters of the Nile and lie far from the historical competition for water. Oil pipelines, pumping stations, well-heads, and other key infrastructure became targets for the rebels from the South, who wanted a share in the country's new mineral wealth, much of which was on lands they had long occupied. John Garang, leader of the rebel Sudan People's Liberation Army (SPLA), declared these installations to be legitimate targets of war. For a time, the oil companies fled from the conflict, but in the 1990s they began to return. Chinese and Indian companies were particularly aggressive, doing much of their drilling behind perimeters of bermed earth guarded by troops to protect against rebel attacks. It was a Chinese pipeline to the Red Sea that first brought Sudanese oil to the international market. Prior to the discovery of oil, this dusty terrain had little to offer in the way of exports. Most of the arable land was given over to subsistence farming: sorghum and food staples; cattle and camels. Some cotton was grown for export. Sudan, sometimes still called The Sudan, is the largest country in Africa and one of the poorest. Nearly a million square miles in area, roughly the size of the United States east of the Mississippi, it is more region than nation. Embracing some 570 distinct peoples and dozens of languages and historically ungovernable, its boundaries had been drawn for the convenience of colonial powers. Its nominal leaders in the north, living in urban Khartoum, were eager to join the global economy -- and oil was to become their country's first high-value export.

South Sudan is overwhelmingly rural and black. Less accessible from the north, marginalized under the reign of the Ottoman Turks in the nineteenth century, again under the British overlords during much of the twentieth, and now by Khartoum in the north, South Sudan today is almost devoid of schools, hospitals, and modern infrastructure. Racism figures heavily in all this. Arabs refer to darker Africans as "*abeed*," a word that means something close to "slave." During the civil war, African boys were kidnapped from the south and enslaved; many were pressed into military service by the Arab-dominated government in Khartoum. Racism continues to find expression in the brutal rapes now taking place in Darfur. Khartoum recruits the militias, called *Janjaweed* -- itself a derogatory term -- from the poorest and least educated members of nomadic Arab society. In short, the Islamist regime has manipulated ethnic, racial, and economic tensions, as part of a strategic drive to commandeer the country's oil wealth. The war has claimed about two million lives, mostly in the south -- many by starvation, when government forces prevented humanitarian agencies from gaining access to camps. Another four million Sudanese remain homeless. The regime originally sought to impose shariah, or Islamic, law on the predominantly Christian and animist South. Khartoum dropped this demand, however, under terms of the Comprehensive Peace Treaty signed last January. The South was to be allowed to operate under its own civil law, which included rights for women; and in six years, southerners could choose by plebiscite whether to separate or remain part of a unified Sudan. The all-important oil revenues would be divided between Khartoum and the SPLA-held territory. Under a power-sharing agreement, SPLA commander John Garang would be installed as vice president of Sudan, alongside President Omar al-Bashir.

Darfur, to the west, was left out of this treaty. In a sense, the treaty -- brokered with the help of the U.S. -- was signed at the expense of Darfur, a parched area the size of France, sparsely populated but oil rich. It has an ancient history of separate existence as a kingdom lapping into Chad, separate from the area known today as Sudan. Darfur's population is proportionately more Muslim and less Christian than southern Sudan's, but is mostly black African, and identifies itself by tribe, such as the Fur. (Darfur, in fact, means "land of the Fur.") The Darfurian practice of Islam was too lax to suit the Islamists who control Khartoum. And so Darfurian villages have been burned to clear the way for drilling and pipelines, and to remove any possible sanctuaries for rebels. Some of the land seized from black farmers is reportedly being given to Arabs brought in from neighboring Chad.

Oil and Turmoil With the signing of the treaty last January, and the prospect of stability for most of war-torn Sudan, new seismographic studies were undertaken by foreign oil companies in April. These studies had the effect of doubling Sudan's estimated oil reserves, bringing them to at least 563 million barrels. They could yield substantially more. Khartoum claims the amount could total as much as 5 billion barrels. That's still a pittance compared to the 674 billion barrels of proven oil reserves possessed by the six Persian Gulf countries -- Saudi Arabia, Iraq, the United Arab Emirates, Kuwait, Iran, and Qatar. The very modesty of Sudan's reserves speaks volumes to the desperation with which industrial nations are grasping for alternative sources of oil. The rush for oil is wreaking havoc on Sudan. Oil revenues to Khartoum have been about $1 million a day, exactly the amount which the government funnels into arms -- helicopters and bombers from Russia, tanks from Poland and China, missiles from Iran. Thus, oil is fueling the genocide in Darfur at every level. This is the context in which Darfur must be understood -- and, with it, the whole of Africa. The same Africa whose vast tapestry of indigenous cultures, wealth of forests and savannas was torn apart by three centuries of theft by European colonial powers -- seeking slaves, ivory, gold, and diamonds -- is being devastated anew by 21st century quests for oil.

Sudan is now the seventh biggest oil producer in Africa after Nigeria, Libya, Algeria, Angola, Egypt, and Equatorial Guinea.

Oil has brought corruption and turmoil in its wake virtually wherever it has been discovered in the developing world. Second only perhaps to the arms industry, its lack of transparency and concentration of wealth invites kickbacks and bribery, as well as distortions to regional economies.

"There is no other commodity that produces such great profit," said Terry Karl in an interview with Miren Gutierrez, for the International Press Service, "and this is generally in the context of highly concentrated power, very weak bureaucracies, and weak rule of law." Karl is co-author of a Catholic Relief Services report on the impact of oil in Africa, entitled, *Bottom of the Barrel*. He cites the examples of Gabon, Angola and Nigeria, which began exploiting oil several decades ago and suffer from intense corruption. In Nigeria, as in Angola, an overvalued exchange rate has destroyed the non-oil economy. Local revolts over control of oil revenues also have triggered sweeping military repression in the Niger delta. Oil companies and exploration companies like Halliburton wield political and sometimes military power. In Sudan, roads and bridges built by oil firms have been used to attack otherwise remote villages. Canada's largest oil company, Talisman, is now in court for allegedly aiding Sudan government forces in blowing up a church and killing church leaders, in order to clear the land for pipelines and drilling. Under public pressure in Canada, Talisman has sold its holdings in Sudan. Lundin Oil AB, a Swedish company, withdrew under similar pressure from human rights groups.

Michael Klare suggests that oil production is intrinsically destabilizing: "When countries with few other resources of national wealth exploit their petroleum reserves, the ruling elites typically monopolize the distribution of oil revenues, enriching themselves and their cronies while leaving the rest of the population mired in poverty -- and the well-equipped and often privileged security forces of these 'petro-states' can be counted on to support them."

Compound these antidemocratic tendencies with the ravenous thirst of the rapidly growing Chinese and Indian economies, and you have a recipe for destabilization in Africa. China's oil imports climbed by 33% in 2004, India's by 11%. The International Energy Agency expects them to use 11.3 million barrels a day by 2010, which will be more than one-fifth of global demand.

Keith Bradsher, in a *New York Times* article, *2 Big Appetites Take Seats at the Oil Table,* observes:

"As Chinese and Indian companies venture into countries like Sudan, where risk-aversive multinationals have hesitated to enter, questions are being raised in the industry about whether state-owned companies are accurately judging the risks to their own investments, or whether they are just more willing to gamble with taxpayers' money than multinationals are willing to gamble with shareholders' investments."

The geopolitical implications of this tolerance for instability are borne out in Sudan, where Chinese state-owned companies exploited oil in the thick of fighting. As China and India seek strategic access to oil -- much as Britain, Japan, and the United States jockeyed for access to oil fields in the years leading up to World War II -- the likelihood of destabilizing countries like Sudan rises exponentially. Last June, following the new seismographic exploration in Sudan and with the new power-sharing peace treaty about to be implemented, Khartoum and the SPLA signed a flurry of oil deals with Chinese, Indian, British, Malaysian, and other oil companies.

Desolate Sudan, Desolate World This feeding frenzy may help explain the Bush administration's schizophrenic stance toward Sudan. On the one hand, Secretary of State Colin Powell declared in September 2004 that his government had determined that what was happening in Darfur was "genocide" -- which appears to have been a pre-election sop to conservative Christians, many with missions in Africa. On the other hand, not only did the President fall silent on Darfur after the election, but his administration has lobbied quietly against the Darfur Peace and Accountability Act in Congress.

That bill, how in committee, calls for beefing up the African Union peacekeeping force and imposing new sanctions on Khartoum, including referring individual officials to the International Criminal Court (much hated by the administration). The White House, undercutting Congressional efforts to stop the genocide, is seeking closer relations with Khartoum on grounds that the regime was "cooperating in the war on terror."

Nothing could end the slaughter faster than the President of the United States standing up for Darfur and making a strong case before the United Nations. Ours is the only country with such clout. This is unimaginable, of course, for various reasons. It seems clear that Bush, and the oil companies that contributed so heavily to his 2000 presidential campaign, would like to see the existing trade sanctions on Sudan removed, so U.S. companies can get a piece of the action. Instead of standing up, the President has kept mum -- leaving it to Secretary of State Condoleezza Rice to put the best face she can on his policy of appeasing Khartoum.

On July 8, SPLA leader John Garang was sworn in as vice president of Sudan, before a throng of 6 million cheering Sudanese. President Oman Bashir spoke in Arabic. Garang spoke in English, the preferred language among educated southerners, because of the country's language diversity. Sudan's future had never looked brighter. Garang was a charismatic and forceful leader who wanted a united Sudan. Three weeks later, Garang was killed in a helicopter crash. When word of his death emerged, angry riots broke out in Khartoum, and in Juba, the capital of South Sudan. Men with guns and clubs roamed the streets, setting fire to cars and office buildings. One hundred and thirty people were killed, thousands wounded.

No evidence of foul play in his death has been uncovered, as of this writing. The helicopter went down in rain and fog over mountainous terrain. Nevertheless, suspicions are rampant. SPLA and government officials are calling for calm, until the crash can be investigated by an international team of experts. All too ominously, the disaster recalls the 1994 airplane crash that killed Rwandan president, Juvenal Habyarimana, who was trying to implement a power-sharing agreement between Hutus and Tutsis. That crash touched off the explosive Rwandan genocide.

What Garang's death will mean for Sudan is unclear. The new peace was already precarious. His chosen successor, Salva Kiir Mayardit, appears less committed to a united Sudan

Nowhere is the potential impact of renewed war more threatening than in the camps of refugees -- the 4 million Internally Displaced Persons (IDPs), driven from their homes during the North-South civil war, several hundred thousand encamped at the fringes of Khartoum as squatters or crowded into sprawling ghetto neighborhoods. Further west, in Darfur and Chad, another 2.5 million IDPs live in the precarious limbo of makeshift camps, in shelters cobbled together from plastic and sticks -- prevented by the Janjaweed from returning to their villages, wholly dependent on outside aid.

In short, Sudan embodies a collision between a failed state and a failed energy policy. Increasingly, ours is a planet whose human population is devoted to extracting what it can, regardless of the human and environmental cost. The Bush energy policy, crafted by oil companies, is predicated on a far different future from the one any sane person would want his or her children to inherit -- a desolate world that few Americans, cocooned by the media's silence, are willing to imagine.

David Morse is an independent journalist and political analyst whose articles and essays have appeared in Dissent, Esquire, Friends Journal, the Nation, the New York Times Magazine, the Progressive Populist, Salon, and elsewhere. His novel, The Iron Bridge *(Harcourt Brace, 1998), predicted a series of petroleum wars in the first two decades of the 21st century. Morse may be reached at his website: dmorse@david-morse.com*

[5] Sutton, Antony – excerpts from Trilaterals Over Washington (this is on the internet) (also see end of index for excerpts)

www.bibliotecapleyades.net/sociopolitica/esp_sociopol_trilat08_03.htm#CHAPTER%20FIVE

Excerpt: The United States consumes about 71 quads of energy per year. (A quad is one quadrillion British thermal units or 1015.) There is available today in the United States, excluding solar sources and excluding gas and oil imports, about 150,000 quads of energy. Put another way, this statistic means we have sufficient known usable energy resources to last us for over two thousand years. The type of energy we use and how we use it will, of course, change -- as the type has changed before from wood to coal and from coal to electric power. But to say we have any absolute shortage of energy resources is simply a false and irresponsible statement. This elementary statistic means that the energy crisis is a phony, a created crisis, a hoax on the American people. But if you happen to be in the business of crisis manipulation, such an energy crisis, if you can convince enough people of its reality, is a handy sort of crisis to be manipulated. One can impose rationing and price controls, plan resource uses, restrict consumption, and invent all manner of happy little projects under the name of "solving" an energy crisis. Looking at this 150,000 quads in more detail we have approximately the following supplies available in the future:

- Natural gas At least 200 years (probably closer to 600 years)
- Petroleum At least 130 years

- Oil from shale At least 1,500 years
- Coal At least 6,000 years
- Breeder reactor inexhaustible resources

A Breeder reactor produces more fuel than is consumed. There is sufficient U238 in storage for the initial one hundred years of breeder reactor operation. These geological estimates are conservative: Vincent McKelvey of the U.S. Geological Survey (who was recently fired for his disclosure publicly discussed a figure of six-hundred-year-reserves of natural gas. Moreover, using biomass production methods, natural gas reserves are virtually inexhaustible. These elementary statistics must be the starting point of any rational discussion of energy "shortages."

The oil and gas world is dominated by seven major firms (the 'seven sisters'). A listing of controlling ownership in these major oil and gas companies by banks with Trilateral commissioners as directors follows:

Major Oil Company	Share Ownership by banks w/Trilateral Representation	Rank in Shareholding
ARCO	Manufacturers Hanover	2
Exxon Corp.	Chase Manhattan	1
Mobile Corp.	Manufacturers Hanover	3
	Chase Manhattan	3
Standard Oil (Calif.)	Chase Manhattan	2
	Wells Fargo Bank	4
Standard Oil (Indiana)	First National (Chicago)	4
	Continental Illinois	3
Texaco	Continental Illinois	3

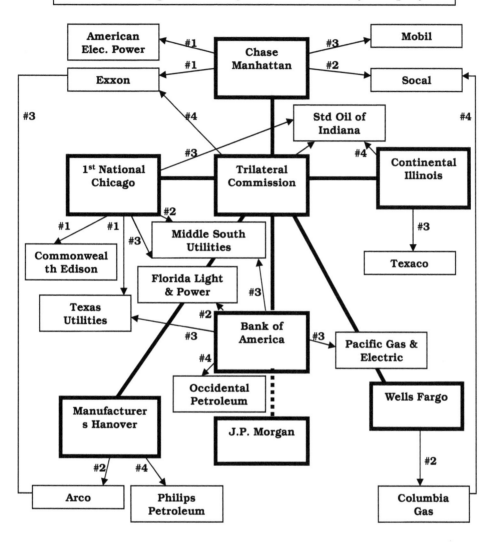

Banks with Trilateral connections & their Stockholding Rank in Major Oil and/or Utility Company

http://www.smh.com.au/news/environment/gore-gets-a-cold-shoulder/2007/10/13/1191696238792.html Gore gets a cold shoulder. One of the world's foremost meteorologists has called the theory that helped Al Gore share the Nobel Peace Prize "ridiculous" and the product of "people who don't understand how the atmosphere works". Dr William Gray, a pioneer in the science of seasonal hurricane forecasts, told a packed lecture hall at the University of North Carolina that humans were not responsible for the warming of the earth. His comments came on the same day that the Nobel committee honoured Mr Gore for his work in support of the link between humans and global warming."We're brainwashing our children," said Dr Gray, 78, a long-time professor at Colorado State University. "They're going to the Gore movie [*An Inconvenient Truth*] and being fed all this. It's ridiculous." At his first appearance since the award was announced in Oslo, Mr Gore said: "We have to quickly find a way to change the world's consciousness about exactly what we're facing."

Mr Gore shared the Nobel prize with the United Nations climate panel for their work in helping to galvanise international action against global warming. But Dr Gray, whose annual forecasts of the

Printed in the USA
CPSIA information can be obtained
at www.ICGtesting.com
LVHW090744230923
758935LV00049B/947